'By writing across the grain of his doubts about what literature can do, how much it can discover or dare pronounce the names of our world's disasters, Bolaño has proved that it can do anything'
                                                                Jonathan Lethem, *Scotsman*

'2666 held me from beginning to end – reminding me, above all, of *The Man Without Qualities* – and sent me back to read all Bolaño's other novels. You will want to experience this one' Philip Hensher, *Spectator*

'A masterpiece in its audacity . . . This novel defies summation: it is epic, tangential, nomadic, and yet a magisterial weave of differing literary genres. It is hard to believe that there will be a better book published this year'   Andreas Campomar, *Sunday Telegraph*

'Wondrous . . . 2666 is a major literary event . . . It is an important development in the novel form and an unforgettable piece of writing that will resonate for years to come'   Stephen Abell, *Daily Telegraph*

'2666 makes difficulty sexy. Or, rather, it successfully (and sexily) makes the case that art has every right to be challenging, shocking, self-referential, intellectual, intermittently insane, and to contain more corpses than a *CSI* box set. It is a novel that crackles with moral purpose'   *Prospect*

'2666 has the power to mesmerise . . . All human life is contained in these burning pages, and Natasha Wimmer deserves a medal for her fluent translation'   *Independent on Sunday*

'It's blindingly obvious you are being seduced by one of the greatest and most distinctive voices in modern fiction . . . Readers who have snacked on a writer such as Haruki Murakami will feast on Roberto Bolaño'
                                                                Sunday Times

'Bolaño's most audacious performance. 2666 offers some of the arcane allusiveness of Thomas Pynchon's work and the psychologically acute yet stylised noir of David Lynch. Edgar Allan Poe and the Marquis de Sade are also touchstones. Yet ultimately the book's most significant forebear may be *Moby-Dick*, that symphonic masterpiece'
                                                                Henry Hitchings, *Financial Times*

'A vibrant, troubling, often deeply disturbing vision of life that persuades you of its truth, so that you feel you're not just inhabiting Bolaño's world but the world as it really is, even if you wished it to be otherwise. That's what makes him a major writer'   *Irish Independent*

'2666 lingers in the unconscious like a sizzling psychotropic for days or weeks after reading. It is a novel both prodigious in scope and profound in implication, but a book ablaze with the furious passion of its own composition. As the Argentinian writer Rodrigo Fresán has observed, "What is sought and achieved here is the Total Novel, placing the author of 2666 on the same team as Cervantes, Sterne, Melville, Proust, Musil and Pynchon." Like each of these titanic forebears, Bolaño has come close to re-imagining the novel'
Richard Gwyn, *Independent* – 'Book of the Week'

'The fact that the book remains as riveting as any top-notch thriller is testament to Bolaño's astonishing virtuosity . . . 2666 achieves something extremely rare in fiction: it provides an all-encompassing view of our world'   Stephen Amidon, *Sunday Times*

'2666 is a book full of other books, and one powered by a sense of possibility and discovery . . . Goethe conceived "world literature" as a way of thinking about all books, whereas Bolaño, with his mixture of dynamism and overreach, managed to achieve it in a single novel'   *The Times*

'2666 is a masterpiece or nothing. In the States, it has been widely acclaimed as the former, perhaps even "the first great book of the twenty-first century" And I think that's not without justification'
David Sexton, *Evening Standard*, 'Book of the Week'

2666

Roberto Bolaño was born in Santiago, Chile, in 1953. He spent much of his adult life in Mexico and in Spain, where he died at the age of fifty. His novel *The Savage Detectives* was named one of the best books of 2007 by the *Washington Post* and the *New York Times Book Review*. In 2008 he won the National Book Critics Circle Award for fiction.

ALSO BY ROBERTO BOLAÑO

The Skating Rink

Nazi Literature in the Americas

Distant Star

The Savage Detectives

Amulet

By Night in Chile

Last Evenings on Earth

2666

A *novel by*
ROBERTO BOLAÑO

Translated from the Spanish
by Natasha Wimmer

PICADOR

Originally published in 2004 by Editorial Anagrama, Spain

First published in the United States 2008 by Farrar, Straus and Giroux

First published in Great Britain 2009 by Picador

First published in paperback 2009 by Picador

This edition first published by Picador 2009
an imprint of Pan Macmillan Ltd
Pan Macmillan, 20 New Wharf Road, London N1 9RR
Basingstoke and Oxford
Associated companies throughout the world
www.panmacmillan.com

ISBN 978-0-330-44743-0

Copyright © the heirs of Roberto Bolaño 2004
Translation copyright © Natasha Wimmer 2008

An excerpt from "The Part About the Crimes" first appeared in *Vice*.

"Canto nottorno di un pastore errante dell'Asia," by Giacomo Leopardi,
is quoted in Jonathan Galassi's translation.

Designed by Jonathan D. Lippincott

9 8 7 6 5 4 3 2 1

A CIP catalogue record for this book is available from
the British Library.

Printed and bound in the UK by
CPI Mackays, Chatham ME5 8TD

Visit **www.picador.com** to read more about all our books
and to buy them. You will also find features, author interviews and
news of any author events, and you can sign up for e-newsletters
so that you're always first to hear about our new releases.

For Alexandra Bolaño and Lautaro Bolaño

An oasis of horror in a desert of boredom.

—Charles Baudelaire

CONTENTS

A NOTE FROM THE AUTHOR'S HEIRS

Realizing that death might be near, Roberto left instructions for his novel 2666 to be published divided into five books corresponding to the five parts of the novel, specifying the order in which they should appear, at what intervals (one per year), and even the price to be negotiated with the publisher. With this decision, communicated days before his death by Roberto himself to Jorge Herralde, Roberto thought he was providing for his children's future.

After his death, and following the reading and study of his work and notes by Ignacio Echevarría (a friend Roberto designated as his literary executor), another consideration of a less practical nature arose: respect for the literary value of the work, which caused us, together with Jorge Herralde, to reverse Roberto's decision and publish 2666 first in full, in a single volume, as he would have done had his illness not taken the gravest course.

THE PART ABOUT THE CRITICS

The first time that Jean-Claude Pelletier read Benno von Archimboldi was Christmas 1980, in Paris, when he was nineteen years old and studying German literature. The book in question was *D'Arsonval*. The young Pelletier didn't realize at the time that the novel was part of a trilogy (made up of the English-themed *The Garden* and the Polish-themed *The Leather Mask*, together with the clearly French-themed *D'Arsonval*), but this ignorance or lapse or bibliographical lacuna, attributable only to his extreme youth, did nothing to diminish the wonder and admiration that the novel stirred in him.

From that day on (or from the early morning hours when he concluded his maiden reading) he became an enthusiastic Archimboldian and set out on a quest to find more works by the author. This was no easy task. Getting hold of books by Benno von Archimboldi in the 1980s, even in Paris, was an effort not lacking in all kinds of difficulties. Almost no reference to Archimboldi could be found in the university's German department. Pelletier's professors had never heard of him. One said he thought he recognized the name. Ten minutes later, to Pelletier's outrage (and horror), he realized that the person his professor had in mind was the Italian painter, regarding whom he soon revealed himself to be equally ignorant.

Pelletier wrote to the Hamburg publishing house that had published *D'Arsonval* and received no response. He also scoured the few German bookstores he could find in Paris. The name Archimboldi appeared in a dictionary of German literature and in a Belgian magazine devoted— whether as a joke or seriously, he never knew—to the literature of Prussia. In 1981, he made a trip to Bavaria with three friends from the German department, and there, in a little bookstore in Munich, on Voralmstrasse, he found two other books: the slim volume titled *Mitzi's Treasure*, less than one hundred pages long, and the aforementioned English novel, *The Garden*.

Reading these two novels only reinforced the opinion he'd already formed of Archimboldi. In 1983, at the age of twenty-two, he undertook the task of translating *D'Arsonval*. No one asked him to do it. At the time, there was no French publishing house interested in publishing the German author with the funny name. Essentially Pelletier set out to translate the book because he liked it, and because he enjoyed the work, although it also occurred to him that he could submit the translation, prefaced with a study of the Archimboldian oeuvre, as his thesis, and—why not?—as the foundation of his future dissertation.

He completed the final draft of the translation in 1984, and a Paris publishing house, after some inconclusive and contradictory readings, accepted it and published Archimboldi. Though the novel seemed destined from the start not to sell more than a thousand copies, the first printing of three thousand was exhausted after a couple of contradictory, positive, even effusive reviews, opening the door for second, third, and fourth printings.

By then Pelletier had read fifteen books by the German writer, translated two others, and was regarded almost universally as the preeminent authority on Benno von Archimboldi across the length and breadth of France.

•

Then Pelletier could think back on the day when he first read Archimboldi, and he saw himself, young and poor, living in a *chambre de bonne*, sharing the sink where he washed his face and brushed his teeth with fifteen other people who lived in the same dark garret, shitting in a horrible and notably unhygienic bathroom that was more like a latrine or cesspit, also shared with the fifteen residents of the garret, some of whom had already returned to the provinces, their respective university degrees in hand, or had moved to slightly more comfortable places in Paris itself, or were still there—just a few of them—vegetating or slowly dying of revulsion.

He saw himself, as we've said, ascetic and hunched over his German dictionaries in the weak light of a single bulb, thin and dogged, as if he were pure will made flesh, bone, and muscle without an ounce of fat, fanatical and bent on success. A rather ordinary picture of a student in the capital, but it worked on him like a drug, a drug that brought him to tears, a drug that (as one sentimental Dutch poet of the nineteenth century had it) opened the floodgates of emotion, as well as the floodgates of something that at first blush resembled self-pity but wasn't (what was it, then? rage? very likely), and made him turn over and over in his mind, not in words but in painful images, the period of his youthful apprenticeship, and after a perhaps pointless long night he was forced to two conclusions: first, that his life as he had lived it so far was over; second, that a brilliant career was opening up before him, and that to maintain its glow he had to persist in his determination, in sole testament to that garret. This seemed easy enough.

•

Jean-Claude Pelletier was born in 1961 and by 1986 he was already a professor of German in Paris. Piero Morini was born in 1956, in a town near Naples, and although he read Benno von Archimboldi for the first time in 1976, or four years before Pelletier, it wasn't until 1988 that he translated his first novel by the German author, *Bifurcaria Bifurcata*, which came and went almost unnoticed in Italian bookstores.

Archimboldi's situation in Italy, it must be said, was very different from his situation in France. For one thing, Morini wasn't his first translator. As it happened, the first novel by Archimboldi to fall into Morini's hands was a translation of *The Leather Mask* done by someone called Colossimo for Einaudi in 1969. In Italy, *The Leather Mask* was followed by *Rivers of Europe* in 1971, *Inheritance* in 1973, and *Railroad Perfection* in 1975; earlier, in 1964, a publishing house in Rome had put out a collection of mostly war stories, titled *The Berlin Underworld*. So it could be said that Archimboldi wasn't a complete unknown in Italy, although one could hardly claim that he was successful, or somewhat successful, or even barely successful. In point of fact, he was an utter failure, an author whose books languished on the dustiest shelves in the stores or were remaindered or forgotten in publishers' warehouses before being pulped.

Morini, of course, was undaunted by the scant interest that Archimboldi's work aroused in the Italian public, and after he translated *Bifur-*

caria Bifurcata he wrote two studies of Archimboldi for journals in Milan and Palermo, one on the role of fate in *Railroad Perfection*, and the other on the various guises of conscience and guilt in *Lethaea*, on the surface an erotic novel, and in *Bitzius*, a novel less than one hundred pages long, similar in some ways to *Mitzi's Treasure*, the book that Pelletier had found in an old Munich bookstore, and that told the story of the life of Albert Bitzius, pastor of Lützelflüh, in the canton of Bern, an author of sermons as well as a writer under the pseudonym Jeremiah Gotthelf. Both pieces were published, and Morini's eloquence or powers of seduction in presenting the figure of Archimboldi overcame all obstacles, and in 1991 a second translation by Piero Morini, this time of *Saint Thomas*, was published in Italy. By then, Morini was teaching German literature at the University of Turin, the doctors had diagnosed him with multiple sclerosis, and he had suffered the strange and spectacular accident that left him permanently wheelchair-bound.

•

Manuel Espinoza came to Archimboldi by a different route. Younger than Morini and Pelletier, Espinoza studied Spanish literature, not German literature, at least for the first two years of his university career, among other sad reasons because he dreamed of being a writer. The only German authors he was (barely) familiar with were three greats: Hölderlin, because at sixteen he thought he was fated to be a poet and he devoured every book of poetry he could find; Goethe, because in his final year of secondary school a teacher with a humorous streak recommended that he read *The Sorrows of Young Werther*, in whose hero he would find a kindred spirit; and Schiller, because he had read one of his plays. Later he would discover the work of a modern author, Jünger, with whom he became acquainted more by osmosis than anything else, since the Madrid writers he admired (and deep down hated bitterly) talked nonstop about Jünger. So it could be said that Espinoza was acquainted with just one German author, and that author was Jünger. At first he thought Jünger's work was magnificent, and since many of the writer's books were translated into Spanish, Espinoza had no trouble finding them and reading them all. He would have preferred it to be less easy. Meanwhile, many of his acquaintances weren't just Jünger devotees; some of them were the author's translators, too, which was something Espinoza cared little about, since the glory he coveted was that of the writer, not the translator.

As the months and years went by, silently and cruelly as is often the case, Espinoza suffered some misfortunes that made him change his thinking. It didn't take him long, for example, to discover that the group of Jüngerians wasn't as Jüngerian as he had thought, being instead, like all literary groups, in thrall to the changing seasons. In the fall, it's true, they were Jüngerians, but in winter they suddenly turned into Barojians and in spring into Orteganites, and in summer they would even leave the bar where they met to go out into the street and intone pastoral verse in honor of Camilo José Cela, something that the young Espinoza, who was fundamentally patriotic, would have been prepared to accept unconditionally if such displays had been embarked on in a fun-loving, carnival-esque spirit, but who could in no way take it all seriously, as did the bogus Jüngerians.

Worse was discovering what the members of the group thought about his own attempts at fiction. Their opinion was so negative that there were times—some nights, for example, when he couldn't sleep—that he began to wonder in all seriousness whether they were making a veiled attempt to get him to go away, stop bothering them, never show his face again.

And even worse was when Jünger showed up in person in Madrid and the group of Jüngerians organized a trip to El Escorial for him (a strange whim of the maestro, visiting El Escorial), and when Espinoza tried to join the excursion, in any capacity whatsoever, he was denied the honor, as if the Jüngerians deemed him unworthy of making up part of the German's *garde du corps*, or as if they feared that he, Espinoza, might embarrass them with some naïve, abstruse remark, although the official explanation given (perhaps dictated by some charitable impulse) was that he didn't speak German and everyone else who was going on the picnic with Jünger did.

•

That was the end of Espinoza's dealings with the Jüngerians. And it was the beginning of his loneliness and a steady stream (or deluge) of resolutions, often contradictory or impossible to keep. These weren't comfortable nights, much less pleasant ones, but Espinoza discovered two things that helped him mightily in the early days: he would never be a fiction writer, and, in his own way, he was brave.

He also discovered that he was bitter and full of resentment, that he oozed resentment, and that he might easily kill someone, anyone, if it would provide a respite from the loneliness and rain and cold of Madrid, but this was a discovery that he preferred to conceal. Instead he concentrated on his realization that he would never be a writer and on making everything he possibly could out of his newly unearthed bravery.

He continued at the university, studying Spanish literature, but at the same time he enrolled in the German department. He slept four or five hours a night and the rest of the time he spent at his desk. Before he finished his degree in German literature he wrote a twenty-page essay on the relationship between Werther and music, which was published in a Madrid literary magazine and a Göttingen university journal. By the time he was twenty-five he had completed both degrees. In 1990, he received his doctorate in German literature with a dissertation on Benno von Archimboldi. A Barcelona publishing house brought it out one year later. By then, Espinoza was a regular at German literature conferences and roundtables. His command of German was, if not excellent, more than passable. He also spoke English and French. Like Morini and Pelletier, he had a good job and a substantial income, and he was respected (to the extent possible) by his students as well as his colleagues. He never translated Archimboldi or any other German author.

●

Besides Archimboldi, there was one thing Morini, Pelletier, and Espinoza had in common. All three had iron wills. Actually, they had one other thing in common, but we'll get to that later.

Liz Norton, on the other hand, wasn't what one would ordinarily call a woman of great drive, which is to say that she didn't draw up long- or medium-term plans and throw herself wholeheartedly into their execution. She had none of the attributes of the ambitious. When she suffered, her pain was clearly visible, and when she was happy, the happiness she felt was contagious. She was incapable of setting herself a goal and striving steadily toward it. At least, no goal was appealing or desirable enough for her to pursue it unreservedly. Used in a personal sense, the phrase "achieve an end" seemed to her a small-minded snare. She preferred the word *life*, and, on rare occasions, *happiness*. If volition is bound to social imperatives, as William James believed, and it's therefore easier to go to war than it is to quit smoking, one could say that Liz Norton was a woman who found it easier to quit smoking than to go to war.

This was something she'd been told once when she was a student, and she loved it, although it didn't make her read William James, then or ever. For her, reading was directly linked to pleasure, not to knowledge or enigmas or constructions or verbal labyrinths, as Morini, Espinoza, and Pelletier believed it to be.

Her discovery of Archimboldi was the least traumatic of all, and the least poetic. During the three months that she lived in Berlin in 1988, when she was twenty, a German friend loaned her a novel by an author she had never heard of. The name puzzled her. How was it possible, she asked her friend, that there could be a German writer with an Italian surname, but with a *von* preceding it, indicating some kind of nobility? Her German friend had no answer. It was probably a pseudonym, he said. And to make things even stranger, he added, masculine proper names ending in vowels were uncommon in Germany. Plenty of feminine proper names ended that way. But certainly not masculine proper names. The novel was *The Blind Woman*, and she liked it, but not so much that it made her go running out to buy everything else that Benno von Archimboldi had ever written.

•

Five months later, back in England again, Liz Norton received a gift in the mail from her German friend. As one might guess, it was another novel by Archimboldi. She read it, liked it, went to her college library to look for more books by the German with the Italian name, and found two: one was the book she had already read in Berlin, and the other was *Bitzius*. Reading the latter really did make her go running out. It was raining in the quadrangle, and the quadrangular sky looked like the grimace of a robot or a god made in our own likeness. The oblique drops of rain slid down the blades of grass in the park, but it would have made no difference if they had slid up. Then the oblique (drops) turned round (drops), swallowed up by the earth underpinning the grass, and the grass and the earth seemed to talk, no, not talk, argue, their incomprehensible words like crystallized spiderwebs or the briefest crystallized vomitings, a barely audible rustling, as if instead of drinking tea that afternoon, Norton had drunk a steaming cup of peyote.

But the truth is that she had only had tea to drink and she felt overwhelmed, as if a voice were repeating a terrible prayer in her ear, the words of which blurred as she walked away from the college, and the rain wetted her gray skirt and bony knees and pretty ankles and little else, because before Liz Norton went running through the park, she hadn't forgotten to pick up her umbrella.

•

The first time Pelletier, Morini, Espinoza, and Norton saw each other was at a contemporary German literature conference held in Bremen in 1994. Pelletier and Morini had met before, during the German literature colloquiums held in Leipzig in 1989, when the GDR was in its death throes, and then they saw each other again at the German literature symposium held in Mannheim in December of the same year (a disaster, with bad hotels, bad food, and abysmal organizing). At a modern German literature forum in Zurich in 1990, Pelletier and Morini met Espinoza. Espinoza saw Pelletier again at a twentieth-century German literature congress held in Maastricht in 1991 (Pelletier delivered a paper titled "Heine and Archimboldi: Converging Paths"; Espinoza delivered a paper titled "Ernst Jünger and Benno von Archimboldi: Diverging Paths"), and it could more or less safely be said that from that moment on they not only read each other in the scholarly journals, they became friends, or they struck up something like a friendship. In 1992, Pelletier, Espinoza, and Morini ran into each other again at a German literature seminar in Augsburg. Each was presenting a paper on Archimboldi. For a few months it had been rumored that Benno von Archimboldi himself planned to attend this grand event, which would convene not only the usual Germanists but also a sizable group of German writers and poets, and yet at the crucial moment, two days before the gathering, a telegram was received from Archimboldi's Hamburg publishers tendering his apologies. In every other respect, too, the conference was a failure. In Pelletier's opinion, perhaps the only thing of interest was a lecture given by an old professor from Berlin on the work of Arno Schmidt (here we have a German proper name ending in a vowel), a judgment shared by Espinoza and, to a lesser extent, by Morini.

They spent the free time they had, which was ample, strolling the paltry (in Pelletier's opinion) sites of interest in Augsburg, a city that Espinoza also found paltry, and that Morini found only moderately paltry, but still paltry in the final analysis, while Espinoza and Pelletier took turns pushing the Italian's wheelchair since Morini wasn't in the best of health this time, but rather in paltry health, so that his two friends and colleagues considered that a little bit of fresh air would do him no harm, and in fact might do him good.

Only Pelletier and Espinoza attended the next German literature conference, held in Paris in January 1992. Morini, who had been invited too, was in worse health than usual just then, causing his doctor to advise him, among other things, to avoid even short trips. It wasn't a bad conference, and despite their full schedules, Pelletier and Espinoza found time to eat together at a little restaurant on the Rue Galande, near Saint-Julien-le-Pauvre, where, besides talking about their respective projects and interests, during dessert they speculated about the health (the ill health, the delicate health, the miserable health) of the melancholy Italian, ill health that nevertheless hadn't prevented him from beginning a book on Archimboldi, a book that might be the grand Archimboldian opus, the pilot fish that would swim for a long time beside the great black shark of the German's oeuvre, or so Pelletier explained that Morini had told him on the phone, whether seriously or in jest he wasn't sure. Both Pelletier and Espinoza respected Morini's work, but Pelletier's words (spoken as if from inside an old castle or a dungeon dug under the moat of an old castle) sounded like a threat in the peaceful little restaurant on the Rue Galande and hastened the end of an evening that had begun in an atmosphere of cordiality and contentment.

•

None of this soured Pelletier's and Espinoza's relations with Morini.

The three met again at a German-language literature colloquium held in Bologna in 1993. And all three contributed to Number 46 of the Berlin journal *Literary Studies*, a monograph devoted to the work of Archimboldi. It wasn't the first time they'd contributed to the journal. In Number 44, there'd been a piece by Espinoza on the idea of God in the work of Archimboldi and Unamuno. In Number 38, Morini had published an article on the state of German literature instruction in Italy. And in Number 37, Pelletier had presented an overview of the most important German writers of the twentieth century in France and Europe, a text that incidentally sparked more than one protest and even a couple of scoldings.

But it's Number 46 that matters to us, since not only did it mark the formation of two opposing groups of Archimboldians—Pelletier, Morini, and Espinoza versus Schwarz, Borchmeyer, and Pohl—it also contained a piece by Liz Norton, incredibly brilliant, according to Pelletier, well argued, acording to Espinoza, interesting, according to Morini, a piece that aligned itself (and not at anyone's bidding) with the theses of the three friends, whom it cited on various occasions, demonstrating a thorough knowledge of their studies and monographs published in specialized journals or issued by small presses.

Pelletier thought about writing her a letter, but in the end he didn't. Espinoza called Pelletier and asked whether it wouldn't be a good idea to get in touch with her. Unsure, they decided to ask Morini. Morini abstained from comment. All they knew about Liz Norton was that she taught German literature at a university in London. And that, unlike them, she wasn't a full professor.

•

The Bremen German literature conference was highly eventful. Pelletier, backed by Morini and Espinoza, went on the attack like Napoleon at Jena, assaulting the unsuspecting German Archimboldi scholars, and the downed flags of Pohl, Schwarz, and Borchmeyer were soon routed to the cafés and taverns of Bremen. The young German professors participating in the event were bewildered at first and then took the side of Pelletier and his friends, albeit cautiously. The audience, consisting mostly of university students who had traveled from Göttingen by train or in vans, was also won over by Pelletier's fiery and uncompromising interpretations, throwing caution to the winds and enthusiastically yielding to the festive, Dionysian vision of ultimate carnival (or penultimate carnival) exegesis upheld by Pelletier and Espinoza. Two days later, Schwarz and his minions counterattacked. They compared Archimboldi to Heinrich Böll. They spoke of suffering. They compared Archimboldi to Günter Grass. They spoke of civic duty. Borchmeyer even compared Archimboldi to Friedrich Dürrenmatt and spoke of humor, which seemed to Morini the height of gall. Then Liz Norton appeared, heavensent, and demolished the counterattack like a Desaix, like a Lannes, a blond Amazon who spoke excellent German, if anything too rapidly, and who expounded on Grimmelshausen and Gryphius and many others, including Theophrastus Bombastus von Hohenheim, better known as Paracelsus.

•

That same night they ate together in a long, narrow tavern near the river, on a dark street flanked by old Hanseatic buildings, some of which looked like abandoned Nazi offices, a tavern they reached by going down stairs wet from the drizzle.

The place couldn't have been more awful, thought Liz Norton, but the evening was long and agreeable, and the friendliness of Pelletier, Morini, and Espinoza, who weren't standoffish at all, made her feel at ease. Naturally, she was familiar with most of their work, but what surprised her (pleasantly, of course) was that they were familiar with some of hers, too. The conversation proceeded in four stages: first they laughed about the flaying Norton had given Borchmeyer and about Borchmeyer's growing dismay at Norton's increasingly ruthless attacks, then they talked about future conferences, especially a strange one at the University of Minnesota, supposedly to be attended by five hundred professors, translators, and German literature specialists, though Morini had reason to believe the whole thing was a hoax, then they discussed Benno von Archimboldi and his life, about which so little was known. All of them, from Pelletier to Morini (who was talkative that night, though he was usually the quietest), reviewed anecdotes and gossip, compared old, vague information for the umpteenth time, and speculated about the secret of the great writer's whereabouts and life like people endlessly analyzing a favorite movie, and finally, as they walked the wet, bright streets (bright only intermittently, as if Bremen were a machine jolted every so often by brief, powerful electric charges), they talked about themselves.

All four were single and that struck them as an encouraging sign. All four lived alone, although Liz Norton sometimes shared her London flat with a globe-trotting brother who worked for an NGO and who came back to England only a few times a year. All four were devoted to their careers, although Pelletier, Espinoza, and Morini had doctorates and Pelletier and Espinoza also chaired their respective departments, whereas Norton was just preparing her dissertation and had no expectation of becoming the head of her university's German department.

That night, before he fell asleep, Pelletier didn't think back on the squabbles at the conference. Instead he thought about walking along the streets near the river and about Liz Norton walking beside him as Espinoza pushed Morini's wheelchair and the four of them laughed at the little animals of Bremen, which watched them or watched their shadows on the pavement while mounted harmoniously, innocently, on each other's backs.

•

From that day on or that night on, not a week went by without the four of them calling back and forth regularly, sometimes at the oddest hours, without a thought for the phone bill.

Sometimes it was Liz Norton who would call Espinoza and ask about Morini, whom she'd talked to the day before and whom she'd thought seemed a little depressed. That same day Espinoza would call Pelletier and inform him that according to Norton, Morini's health had taken a turn for the worse, to which Pelletier would respond by immediately calling Morini, asking him bluntly how he was, laughing with him (because Morini did his best never to talk seriously about his condition), exchanging a few unimportant remarks about work, and later telephoning Norton, maybe at midnight, after putting off the pleasure of the call with a frugal and exquisite dinner, and assuring her that as far as could be hoped, Morini was fine, normal, stable, and what Norton had taken for depression was just the Italian's natural state, sensitive as he was to changes in the weather (maybe the weather had been bad in Turin, maybe Morini had dreamed who knows what kind of horrible dream the night before), thus ending a cycle that would begin again a day later, or two days later, with Morini calling Espinoza for no reason, just to say hello, that was all, to talk for a while, the call invariably taken up with unimportant things, remarks about the weather (as if Morini and even Espinoza were adopting British conversational habits), film recommendations, dispassionate commentary on recent books, in short, a generally soporific or at best listless phone conversation, but one that Espinoza followed with odd enthusiasm, or feigned enthusiasm, or fondness, or at least civilized interest, and that Morini attended to as if his life depended on it, and which was succeeded two days or a few hours later by Espinoza calling Norton and having a conversation along essentially the same lines, and Norton calling Pelletier, and Pelletier calling Morini, with the whole process starting over again days later, the call transmuted into hyperspecialized code, signifier and signified in Archimboldi, text, subtext, and paratext, reconquest of the verbal and physical territoriality in the final pages of *Bitzius*, which under the circumstances was the same as talking about film or problems in the German department or the clouds that passed incessantly over their respective cities, morning to night.

●

They met again at the postwar European literature colloquium held in Avignon at the end of 1994. Norton and Morini went as spectators, although their trips were funded by their universities, and Pelletier and Espinoza presented papers on the import of Archimboldi's work. Pelletier's paper focused on insularity, on the rupture that seemed to separate the whole of Archimboldi's oeuvre from the German tradition, though not from a larger European tradition. Espinoza's paper, one of the most engaging he ever wrote, revolved around the mystery veiling the figure of Archimboldi, about whom virtually no one, not even his publisher, knew anything: his books appeared with no author photograph on the flaps or back cover; his biographical data was minimal (German writer born in Prussia in 1920); his place of residence was a mystery, although at some point his publisher let slip in front of a *Spiegel* reporter that one of his manuscripts had arrived from Sicily; none of his surviving fellow writers had ever seen him; no biography of him existed in German even though sales of his books were rising in Germany as well as in the rest of Europe and even in the United States, which likes vanished writers (vanished writers or millionaire writers) or the legend of vanished writers, and where his work was beginning to circulate widely, no longer just in German departments but on campus and off campus, in the vast cities with a love for the oral and the visual arts.

●

At night Pelletier, Morini, Espinoza, and Norton would have dinner together, sometimes accompanied by one or two German professors whom they'd known for a long time, and who would usually retire early to their hotels or stay until the end of the evening but remain discreetly in the background, as if they understood that the four-cornered figure formed by the Archimboldians was inviolable and also liable to react violently to any outside interference at that hour of the night. By the end it was always just the four of them walking the streets of Avignon, as blithely and happily as they'd walked the grimy, bureaucratic streets of Bremen and as they would walk the many streets awaiting them in the future, Norton pushing Morini with Pelletier to her left and Espinoza to her right, or

Pelletier pushing Morini with Espinoza to his left and Norton walking backward ahead of them and laughing with all the might of her twenty-six years, a magnificent laugh that they were quick to imitate although they would surely have preferred not to laugh but just to look at her, or the four of them abreast and halted beside the low wall of a storied river, in other words a river tamed, talking about their German obsession without interrupting one another, testing and savoring one another's intelligence, with long intervals of silence that not even the rain could disturb.

•

When Pelletier returned from Avignon at the end of 1994, when he opened the door to his apartment in Paris and set his bag on the floor and closed the door, when he poured himself a glass of whiskey and opened the drapes and saw the usual view, a slice of the Place de Breteuil with the UNESCO building in the background, when he took off his jacket and left the whiskey in the kitchen and listened to the messages on the answering machine, when he felt drowsiness, heaviness in his eyelids, but instead of getting into bed and going to sleep he undressed and took a shower, when wrapped in a white bathrobe that reached almost to his ankles he turned on the computer, only then did he realize that he missed Liz Norton and that he would have given anything to be with her at that moment, not just talking to her but in bed with her, telling her that he loved her and hearing from her lips that she loved him too.

Espinoza experienced something similar, though slightly different in two respects. First, the need to be near Liz Norton struck some time before he got back to his apartment in Madrid. By the time he was on the plane he'd realized that she was the perfect woman, the one he'd always hoped to find, and he began to suffer. Second, among the ideal images of Norton that passed at supersonic speed through his head as the plane flew toward Spain at four hundred miles an hour, there were more sex scenes than Pelletier had imagined. Not many more, but more.

Meanwhile, Morini, who traveled by train from Avignon to Turin, spent the trip reading the cultural supplement of *Il Manifesto*, and then he slept until a couple of ticket collectors (who would help him onto the platform in his wheelchair) let him know that they'd arrived.

As for what passed through Liz Norton's head, it's better not to say.

Still, the friendship of the four Archimboldians continued in the same fashion as ever, unshakable, shaped by a greater force that the four didn't resist, even though it meant relegating their personal desires to the background.

In 1995 they met at a panel discussion on contemporary German literature held in Amsterdam, a discussion within the framework of a larger discussion that was taking place in the same building (although in separate lecture halls), encompassing French, English, and Italian literature.

It goes without saying that most of the attendees of these curious discussions gravitated toward the hall where contemporary English literature was being discussed, next door to the German literature hall and separated from it by a wall that was clearly not made of stone, as walls used to be, but of fragile bricks covered with a thin layer of plaster, so that the shouts, howls, and especially the applause sparked by English literature could be heard in the German literature room as if the two talks or dialogues were one, or as if the Germans were being mocked, when not drowned out, by the English, not to mention by the massive audience attending the English (or Anglo-Indian) discussion, notably larger than the sparse and earnest audience attending the German discussion. Which in the final analysis was a good thing, because it's common knowledge that a conversation involving only a few people, with everyone listening to everyone else and taking time to think and not shouting, tends to be more productive or at least more relaxed than a mass conversation, which runs the permanent risk of becoming a rally, or, because of the necessary brevity of the speeches, a series of slogans that fade as soon as they're put into words.

But before coming to the crux of the matter, or of the discussion, a rather petty detail that nonetheless affected the course of events must be noted. On a last-minute whim, the organizers—the same people who'd left out contemporary Spanish and Polish and Swedish literature for lack of time or money—earmarked most of the funds to provide luxurious accommodations for the stars of English literature, and with the money left over they brought in three French novelists, an Italian poet, an Italian short story writer, and three German writers, the first two of them novelists from West and East Berlin, now reunified, both vaguely renowned (and both of whom arrived in Amsterdam by train and made no complaint when they were put up at a three-star hotel), and the third a rather shadowy figure about whom no one knew anything, not even Morini, who, presenter or not, knew quite a bit about contemporary German literature.

And when the shadowy writer, who was Swabian, began to reminisce during his talk (or discussion) about his stint as a journalist, as an editor of arts pages, as an interviewer of all kinds of writers and artists wary of interviews, and then began to recall the era in which he had served as cultural promoter in towns that were far-flung or simply forgotten but interested in culture, suddenly, out of the blue, Archimboldi's name cropped up (maybe prompted by the previous talk led by Espinoza and Pelletier), since the Swabian, as it happened, had met Archimboldi while he was cultural promoter for a Frisian town, north of Wilhelmshaven, facing the North Sea coast and the East Frisian islands, a place where it was cold, very cold, and even wetter than it was cold, with a salty wetness that got into the bones, and there were only two ways of making it through the winter, one, drinking until you got cirrhosis, and two, listening to music (usually amateur string quartets) in the town hall auditorium or talking to writers who came from elsewhere and who were given very little, a room at the only boardinghouse in town and a few marks to cover the return trip by train, those trains so unlike German trains today, but on which the people were perhaps more talkative, more polite, more interested in their neighbors, but anyway, writers who, after being paid and subtracting transportation costs, left these places and went home (which was sometimes just a room in Frankfurt or Cologne) with a little money and possibly a few books sold, in the case of those writers or poets (especially poets) who, after reading a few pages and answering the townspeople's questions, would set up a table and make a few extra marks, a fairly profitable activity back then, because if the audience liked what the writer had read, or if the reading moved them or entertained them or made them think, then they would buy one of his books, sometimes to keep as a souvenir of a pleasant evening, as the wind whistled along the narrow streets of the Frisian town, cutting into the flesh it was so cold, sometimes to read or reread a poem or story, back at home now, weeks after the event, maybe by the light of an oil lamp because there wasn't always electricity, of course, since the war had just ended and there were still gaping wounds, social and economic, anyway, more or less the same as a literary reading today, with the exception that the books displayed on the table were self-published and now it's the publishing houses that set up the table, and one of these writers who came to the town where the Swabian was cultural promoter was Benno von Archimboldi, a writer of the stature of Gustav Heller or Rainer Kuhl or Wilhelm Frayn (writers whom Morini would later look up in his encyclopedia of German authors, without success), and he didn't bring books, and he read two chapters from a novel in progress, his second novel, the first, remembered the Swabian, had been published in Hamburg that year, although he didn't read anything from it, but that first novel did exist, said the Swabian, and Archimboldi, as if anticipating doubts, had brought a copy with him, a little novel about one hundred pages long, maybe longer, one hundred and twenty, one hundred and twenty-five pages, and he carried the novel in his jacket pocket, and, strangely, the Swabian remembered Archimboldi's jacket more clearly than the novel crammed into its pocket, a little novel with a dirty, creased cover that had once been deep ivory or a pale wheat color or gold shading into invisibility, but now was colorless and dull, just the title of the novel and the author's name and the colophon of the publishing house, whereas the jacket was unforgettable, a black leather jacket with a high collar, providing excellent protection against the snow and rain and cold, loose fitting, so it could be worn over heavy sweaters or two sweaters without anyone noticing, with horizontal pockets on each side, and a row of four buttons, neither very large nor very small, sewn on with something like fishing line, a jacket that brought to mind, why I don't know, the jackets worn by some Gestapo officers, although back then black leather jackets were in fashion and anyone who had the money to buy one or had inherited one wore it without stopping to think about what it suggested, and the writer who had come to that Frisian town was Benno von Archimboldi, the young Benno von Archimboldi, twenty-nine or thirty years old, and it had been he, the Swabian, who had gone to wait for him at the train station and who had accompanied him to the boardinghouse, talking about the weather, which was bad, and then had brought him to city hall, where Archimboldi hadn't set up any table and had read two chapters from a novel that wasn't finished yet, and then the Swabian had gone to dinner with him at the local tavern, along with the teacher and a widow who preferred music or painting to literature, but who, once resigned to not having music or painting, was in no way averse to a literary evening, and it was she who somehow or other kept up the conversation during dinner (sausages and potatoes and beer: neither the times, recalled the Swabian, nor the town's budget allowed for anything more extravagant), although it might be truer to say that she steered it with a firm hand on the rudder, and the men who were around the table, the mayor's secretary, a man in the salted fish business, an old schoolteacher who kept falling asleep even with his fork in his hand, and a town employee, a very nice boy named Fritz who was a good friend of the Swabian's, nodded or were careful not to contradict the redoubtable widow whose knowledge of the arts was much greater than anyone else's, even the Swabian's, and who had traveled in Italy and France and had even, on one of her voyages, an unforgettable ocean crossing, gone as far as Buenos Aires, in 1927 or 1928, when the city was a meat emporium and the refrigerator ships left port laden with meat, a sight to see, hundreds of ships arriving empty and leaving laden with tons of meat headed all over the world, and when she, the lady, went out on deck, say at night, half asleep or seasick or ailing, all she had to do was lean on the rail and let her eyes grow accustomed to the dark and then the view of the port was startling and it instantly cleared away any vestiges of sleep or seasickness or other ailments, the nervous system having no choice but to surrender unconditionally to such a picture, the parade of immigrants like ants loading the flesh of thousands of dead cattle into the ships' holds, the movements of pallets piled with the meat of thousands of sacrificed calves, and the gauzy tint that shaded every corner of the port from dawn until dusk and even during the night shifts, the red of barely cooked steak, of T-bones, of filet, of ribs grilled rare, terrible, thank goodness the lady, who wasn't a widow at the time, had to see it only the first night, then they disembarked and took rooms at one of the most expensive hotels in Buenos Aires, and they went to the opera and then to a ranch where her husband, an expert horseman, agreed to race with the rancher's son, who lost, and then with a ranch hand, the son's right-hand man, a gaucho, who also lost, and then with the gaucho's son, a little sixteen-year-old gaucho, thin as a reed and with bright eyes, so bright that when the lady looked at him he lowered his head and then lifted it a little and gave her such a wicked look that she was offended, what an insolent urchin, while her husband laughed and said in German: you've made quite an impression on the boy, a joke the lady didn't find the least bit funny, and then the little gaucho mounted his horse and they set off, the boy could really gallop, he clung to the horse so tightly it was as if he were glued to its neck, and he sweated and thrashed it with his whip, but in the end her husband won the race, he hadn't been captain of a cavalry regiment for nothing, and the rancher and the rancher's son got up from their seats and clapped, good losers, and the rest of the guests clapped too, excellent rider, this German, extraordinary rider, although when the little gaucho reached the finish line, or in other words the porch, he didn't look like a good loser, a dark, angry expression on his face, his head down, and while the men, speaking French, scattered along the porch in search of glasses of ice-cold champagne, the lady went up to the little gaucho, who was left standing alone, holding his horse's reins in his left hand (at the other end of the long yard the little gaucho's father headed off toward the stables with the horse the German had ridden), and told him, in an incomprehensible language, not to be sad, that he had ridden an excellent race but her husband was good too and more experienced, words that to the little gaucho sounded like the moon, like the passage of clouds across the moon, like a slow storm, and then the little gaucho looked up at the lady with the eyes of a bird of prey, ready to plunge a knife into her at the navel and slice up to the breasts, cutting her wide open, his eyes shining with a strange intensity, like the eyes of a clumsy young butcher, as the lady recalled, which didn't stop her from following him without protest when he took her by the hand and led her to the other side of the house, to a place where a wrought-iron pergola stood, bordered by flowers and trees that the lady had never seen in her life or which at that moment she thought she had never seen in her life, and she even saw a fountain in the park, a stone fountain, in the center of which, balanced on one little foot, a creole cherub with smiling features danced, part European and part cannibal, perpetually bathed by three jets of water that spouted at its feet, a fountain sculpted from a single piece of black marble, a fountain that the lady and the little gaucho admired at length, until a distant cousin of the rancher appeared (or a mistress whom the rancher had lost in the deep folds of memory), telling her in brusque and serviceable English that her husband had been looking for her for some time, and then the lady walked out of the enchanted park on the distant cousin's arm, and the little gaucho called to her, or so she thought, and when she turned he spoke a few hissing words, and the lady stroked his head and asked the cousin what the little gaucho had said, her fingers lost in the thick curls of his hair, and the cousin seemed to hesitate for a moment, but the lady, who wouldn't tolerate lies or half-truths, demanded an immediate, direct translation, and the cousin said: he says . . . he says the boss . . . arranged it so your husband would win the last two races, and then the cousin was quiet and the little gaucho went off toward the other end of the park, dragging on his horse's reins, and the lady rejoined the party but she couldn't stop thinking about what the little gaucho had confessed at the last moment, the sainted lamb, and no matter how much she thought, his words were still a riddle, a riddle that lasted the rest of the party, and tormented her as she tossed and turned in bed, unable to sleep, and made her listless the next day during a long horseback ride and barbecue, and followed her back to Buenos Aires and all through the days she was at the hotel or went out to receptions at the German embassy or the English embassy or the Ecuadorean embassy, and was solved only days after her ship set sail for Europe, one night, at four in the morning, when the lady went out to stroll the deck, not knowing or caring what parallel or longitude they were at, surrounded or partially surrounded by forty-one million square miles of salt water, just then, as the lady lit a cigarette on the first-class passengers' first deck, with her eyes fixed on the expanse of ocean that she couldn't see but could hear, the riddle was miraculously solved, and it was then, at that point in the story, said the Swabian, that the lady, the once rich and powerful and intelligent (in her fashion, at least) Frisian lady, fell silent, and a religious, or worse, superstitious hush fell over that sad postwar German tavern, where everyone began to feel more and more uncomfortable and hurried to mop up what was left of their sausage and potatoes and swallow the last drops of beer from their mugs, as if they were afraid that at any moment the lady would begin to howl like a Fury and they judged it wise to prepare themselves to face the cold journey home with full stomachs.

And then the lady spoke. She said:

"Can anyone solve the riddle?"

That's what she said, but she didn't look at any of the townspeople or address them directly.

"Does anyone know the answer to the riddle? Does anyone understand it? Is there by chance a man in this town who can tell me the solution, even if he has to whisper it in my ear?"

She said all of this with her eyes on her plate, where her sausage and her serving of potatoes remained almost untouched.

And then Archimboldi, who had kept his head down, eating, as the lady talked, said, without raising his voice, that it had been an act of hospitality, that the rancher and his son were sure the lady's husband would lose the first race, and they had rigged the second and third races so the former cavalry captain would win. Then the lady looked him in the eye and laughed and asked why her husband had won the first race.

"Why? why?" asked the lady.

"Because the rancher's son," said Archimboldi, "who surely rode better and had a better mount than your husband, was overcome at the last minute by selflessness. In other words, he chose extravagance, carried away by the impromptu festivities that he and his father had arranged. Everything had to be squandered, including his victory, and somehow everyone understood it had to be that way, including the woman who came looking for you in the park. Everyone except the little gaucho."

"Was that all?" asked the lady.

"Not for the little gaucho. If you'd spent any longer with him, I think he would have killed you, which would have been an extravagant gesture in its own right, though certainly not the kind the rancher and his son had in mind."

Then the lady got up, thanked everyone for a pleasant evening, and left.

"A few minutes later," said the Swabian, "I walked Archimboldi back to the boardinghouse. The next morning, when I went to get him to take him to the station, he was gone."

•

Astounding Swabian, said Espinoza. I want him all to myself, said Pelletier. Try not to overwhelm him, try not to seem too interested, said Morini. We have to treat the man with kid gloves, said Norton. Which means we have to be very nice to him.

•

But the Swabian had already said everything he had to say, and even though they coddled him and took him out to the best restaurant in Amsterdam and complimented him and talked to him about hospitality and extravagance and the fate of cultural promoters trapped in small provincial towns, it was impossible to get anything interesting out of him, although the four were careful to record every word he spoke, as if they'd met their Moses, a detail that didn't go unnoticed by the Swabian and in fact heightened his shyness (which, according to Espinoza and Pelletier, was such an unusual trait in a former cultural promoter that they thought the Swabian must be some kind of impostor), his reserve, his discretion, which verged on the improbable *omertà* of an old Nazi who smells danger.

•

Fifteen days later, Espinoza and Pelletier took a few days' leave and went to Hamburg to visit Archimboldi's publisher. They were received by the editor in chief, a thin, upright man in his sixties by the name of Schnell, which means quick, although Schnell was on the slow side. He had sleek dark brown hair, sprinkled with gray at the temples, which only accentuated his youthful appearance. When he got up to shake hands, it occurred to both Espinoza and Pelletier that he must be gay.

"That faggot is the closest thing to an eel I've ever seen," Espinoza said afterward, as they strolled through Hamburg.

Pelletier chided him for his comment, with its markedly homophobic overtones, although deep down he agreed, there was something eellike about Schnell, something of the fish that swims in dark, muddy waters.

Of course, there was little Schnell could tell them that they didn't already know. He had never seen Archimboldi, and the money, of which there was more and more, was deposited in a Swiss bank account. Once every two years, instructions were received from the writer, the letters usually postmarked Italy, although there were also letters in the publisher's files with Greek and Spanish and Moroccan stamps, letters, incidentally, that were addressed to Mrs. Bubis, the owner of the publishing house, and that he, naturally, hadn't read.

"There are only two people left here, besides Mrs. Bubis, of course, who've met Benno von Archimboldi in person," Schnell told them. "The publicity director and the copy chief. By the time I came to work here, Archimboldi had long since vanished."

Pelletier and Espinoza asked to speak to both women. The publicity director's office was full of plants and photographs, not necessarily of the house authors, and the only thing she could tell them about the vanished writer was that he was a good person.

"A tall man, very tall," she said. "When he walked beside the late Mr. Bubis they looked like a *ti*. Or a *li*."

Espinoza and Pelletier didn't understand what she meant and the publicity director wrote the letter *l* and then the letter *i* on a scrap of paper. Or maybe more like a *le*. Like this.

And again she wrote something on the scrap of paper.

Le

"The *l* is Archimboldi, the *e* is the late Mr. Bubis."

Then the publicity director laughed and watched them for a while, reclining in her swivel chair in silence. Later they talked to the copy chief. She was about the same age as the publicity director but not as cheery.

She said yes, she had met Archimboldi many years ago, but she didn't remember his face anymore, or what he was like, or any story about him that would be worth telling. She couldn't remember the last time he was at the publishing house. She advised them to speak to Mrs. Bubis, and then, without a word, she busied herself editing a galley, answering the other copy editors' questions, talking on the phone to people who might—Espinoza and Pelletier thought with pity—be translators. Before they left, refusing to be discouraged, they returned to Schnell's office and talked to him about Archimboldian conferences and colloquiums planned for the future. Schnell, attentive and cordial, told them they could count on him for whatever they might need.

•

Since they didn't have anything to do except wait for their flights back to Paris and Madrid, Pelletier and Espinoza went walking around Hamburg. The walk inevitably took them to the district of streetwalkers and peep shows, and then they both lapsed into gloom and began telling each other stories of love and disillusionment. Of course, they didn't give names or dates, they spoke in what might be called abstract terms, but despite the seemingly detached presentation of their misfortunes, the conversation and the walk only sank them deeper into a state of melancholy, to such a degree that after two hours they both felt as if they were suffocating.

They took a taxi back to the hotel in silence.

A surprise awaited them there. At the desk there was a note from Schnell addressed to both of them, in which he explained that after their conversation that morning, he'd decided to talk to Mrs. Bubis and she had agreed to see them. The next morning, Espinoza and Pelletier called at the publisher's apartment, on the third floor of an old building in Hamburg's upper town. As they waited they looked at the framed photographs on one wall. On the other two walls there were canvases by Soutine and Kandinsky, and several drawings by Grosz, Kokoschka, and Ensor. But Espinoza and Pelletier were much more interested in the photographs, which were almost all of writers they disdained or admired, and in any case had read: Thomas Mann with Bubis, Heinrich Mann with Bubis, Klaus Mann with Bubis, Alfred Döblin with Bubis, Hermann Hesse with Bubis, Walter Benjamin with Bubis, Anna Seghers with Bubis, Stefan Zweig with Bubis, Bertolt Brecht with Bubis, Feuchtwanger with Bubis, Johannes Becher with Bubis, Oskar Maria Graf with Bubis, bodies and faces and vague scenery, beautifully framed. With the innocence of the dead, who no longer mind being observed, the people in the photographs gazed out on the professors' barely contained enthusiasm. When Mrs. Bubis appeared, the two of them had their heads together trying to decide whether a man next to Bubis was Fallada or not.

Indeed, it is Fallada, said Mrs. Bubis. When they turned, Pelletier and Espinoza saw an older woman in a white blouse and black skirt, a woman with a figure like Marlene Dietrich, as Pelletier would say much later, a woman who despite her years was still as strong willed as ever, a woman who didn't cling to the edge of the abyss but plunged into it with curiosity and elegance. A woman who plunged into the abyss *sitting down*.

"My husband knew all the German writers and the German writers loved and respected my husband, even if a few of them said horrible things about him later that weren't always even accurate," said Mrs. Bubis, with a smile.

They talked about Archimboldi and Mrs. Bubis had tea and cakes brought in, although she drank vodka, which surprised Espinoza and Pelletier, not that she would start to drink so early, but that she wouldn't offer them a drink too, a drink they would in any case have refused.

"The only person at the press who knew Archimboldi's work to perfection," said Mrs. Bubis, "was Mr. Bubis, who published all his books."

But she asked herself (and by extension, the two of them) how well anyone could really know another person's work.

"For example, I love Grosz's work," she said, gesturing toward the Grosz drawings on the wall, "but do I really know it? His stories make me laugh, often I think Grosz drew what he did to make me laugh, sometimes I laugh to the point of hilarity, and hilarity becomes helpless mirth, but once I met an art critic who of course liked Grosz, and who nevertheless got very depressed when he attended a retrospective of his work or had to study some canvas or drawing in a professional capacity. And these bouts of depression or sadness would last for weeks. This art critic was a friend, but we'd never discussed Grosz. Once, however, I mentioned the effect Grosz had on me. At first he refused to believe me. Then he started to shake his head. Then he looked me up and down as if he'd never laid eyes on me before. I thought he'd gone mad. That was the end of our friendship. A while ago I was told that he still says I know nothing about Grosz and I have the aesthetic sense of a cow. Well, as far as I'm concerned he can say whatever he likes. Grosz makes me laugh, Grosz depresses him, but who can say they really know Grosz?

"Let's suppose," said Mrs. Bubis, "that at this very moment there's a knock on the door and my old friend the art critic comes in. He sits here on the sofa beside me, and one of you brings out an unsigned drawing and tells us it's by Grosz and you want to sell it. I look at the drawing and smile and I take out my checkbook and buy it. The art critic looks at the drawing and *isn't* depressed and tries to make me reconsider. He thinks it isn't a Grosz. I think it is. Which of us is right?

"Or let's tell the story a different way. You," said Mrs. Bubis, pointing to Espinoza, "present an unsigned drawing and say it's by Grosz and try to sell it. I don't laugh, I look at it coldly, I appreciate the line, the control, the satire, but nothing about it tickles me. The art critic examines it carefully and gets depressed, in his normal way, and then and there he makes an offer, an offer that exceeds his savings, and that if accepted will condemn him to endless afternoons of melancholy. I try to change his mind. I tell him the drawing strikes me as suspicious because it doesn't make me laugh. The critic says finally I'm looking at Grosz like an adult and gives me his congratulations. Which of the two of us is right?"

•

Then they went back to talking about Archimboldi and Mrs. Bubis showed them a very odd review that had appeared in a Berlin newspaper after the publication of *Lüdicke*, Archimboldi's first novel. The review, by someone named Schleiermacher, tried to sum up the novelist's personality in a few words.

Intelligence: average.

Character: epileptic.

Scholarship: sloppy.

Storytelling ability: chaotic.

Prosody: chaotic.

German usage: chaotic.

Average intelligence and sloppy scholarship are easy to understand. What did he mean by epileptic character, though? that Archimboldi had epilepsy? that he wasn't right in the head? that he suffered attacks of a mysterious nature? that he was a compulsive reader of Dostoevsky? There was no physical description of the writer in the piece.

"We never knew who this man Schleiermacher was," said Mrs. Bubis, "and sometimes my late husband would joke that Archimboldi himself had written the review. But he knew as well as I did that it wasn't true."

Near midday, when it was time to leave, Pelletier and Espinoza dared to ask the only question they thought really mattered: could she help them get in touch with Archimboldi? Mrs. Bubis's eyes lit up. As if she were at the scene of a fire, Pelletier told Liz Norton later. Not a raging blaze, but a fire that was about to go out, after burning for months. Her no came as a slight shake of the head that made Pelletier and Espinoza abruptly aware of the futility of their plea.

Still, they stayed a while longer. From somewhere in the house came the muted strains of an Italian popular song. Espinoza asked whether she knew Archimboldi, whether she had ever seen him in person while her husband was alive. Mrs. Bubis said she had and then, under her breath, she sang the song's final chorus. Her Italian, according to the two friends, was very good.

"What is Archimboldi like?" asked Espinoza.

"Very tall," said Mrs. Bubis, "very tall, a man of truly great height. If he'd been born in this day and age he likely would have played basketball."

Although by the way she said it, Archimboldi might as well have been a dwarf. In the taxi back to the hotel the two friends thought about Grosz and about Mrs. Bubis's cruel, crystalline laugh and about the impression left by that house full of photographs, where nevertheless the photograph of the only writer they cared about was missing. And although neither wanted to admit it, both believed (or sensed) that the flash of insight granted to them in the red-light district was more important than any revelation they might have scented as the guests of Mrs. Bubis.

•

In a word, and bluntly: as they walked around Sankt Pauli, it came to Pelletier and Espinoza that the search for Archimboldi could never fill their lives. They could read him, they could study him, they could pick him apart, but they couldn't laugh or be sad with him, partly because Archimboldi was always far away, partly because the deeper they went into his work, the more it devoured its explorers. In a word: in Sankt Pauli and later at Mrs. Bubis's house, hung with photographs of the late Mr. Bubis and his writers, Pelletier and Espinoza understood that what they wanted to make was love, not war.

•

That afternoon, and without indulging in any confidences beyond the strictly necessary—confidences in general, or maybe abstract, terms— they shared another taxi to the airport, and as they waited for their planes they talked about love, about the need for love. Pelletier was the first to go. When Espinoza was left alone (his flight was an hour later), his thoughts turned to Liz Norton and his real chances of wooing her. He imagined her and then he imagined himself, side by side, sharing an apartment in Madrid, going to the supermarket, both of them working in the German department. He imagined his office and her office, separated by a wall, and nights in Madrid next to her, eating with friends at good restaurants, and, back at home, an enormous bathtub, an enormous bed.

•

But Pelletier got there first. Three days after the meeting with Archimboldi's publisher, he showed up in London unannounced, and after telling Liz Norton the latest news, he invited her to dinner at a restaurant in Hammersmith that a colleague in the Russian department had recommended, where they ate goulash and chickpea puree with beets and fish macerated in lemon with yogurt, a dinner with candles and violins and real Russian waiters and Irish waiters disguised as Russians, all of it excessive from any point of view, and somewhat rustic and dubious from a gastronomic point of view, and they had vodka with their dinner and a bottle of Bordeaux, and the whole meal cost Pelletier an arm and a leg, but it was worth it because then Norton invited him home, officially to discuss Archimboldi and the few things that Mrs. Bubis had revealed, including, of course, the critic Schleiermacher's contemptuous appraisal of Archimboldi's first book, and then both of them started to laugh and Pelletier kissed Norton on the lips, with great tact, and she kissed him back much more ardently, thanks possibly to the dinner and the vodka and the Bordeaux, but Pelletier thought it showed promise, and then they went to bed and screwed for an hour until Norton fell asleep.

•

That night, while Liz Norton was sleeping, Pelletier remembered a long-ago afternoon when he and Espinoza had watched a horror film in a room at a German hotel.

The film was Japanese, and in one of the early scenes there were two teenage girls. One was telling a story. The story was about a boy spending his holidays in Kobe who wanted to go out to play with friends at the same time that his favorite TV show was on. So the boy found a video-cassette and set the machine to record the show and went outside. The problem was that the boy was from Tokyo and in Tokyo his show was on Channel 34, whereas in Kobe, Channel 34 is blank, a channel on which all you see is snow.

And after he came back in, when he sat down in front of the TV and started the player, instead of his favorite show he saw a white-faced woman telling him he was going to die.

And that was all.

And then the phone rang and the boy answered and he heard the same woman's voice asking him did he think it was a joke. A day later they found him in the yard, dead.

And the first girl told the second girl this story, and the whole time she was talking it looked like she was about to crack up. The second girl was obviously scared. But the first girl, the one who was telling the story, looked like she was about to roll on the floor laughing.

And then, remembered Pelletier, Espinoza said the first girl was a two-bit psychopath and the second girl was a silly bitch, and the film could have been good if the second girl, instead of staring openmouthed and looking horrified, had told the first one to shut up. And not gently, not politely, instead she should have told the girl: "Shut up, you cunt, what's so funny? does it turn you on telling the story of a dead boy? does it make you come telling the story of a dead boy, you imaginary-dick-sucking bitch?"

And so on, in the same vein. And Pelletier remembered that Espinoza spoke so vehemently, he even did the voice the second girl should have used and the way she should have stood, that he thought it best to turn off the TV and take him to the bar for a drink before they went back to their rooms. And he also remembered that he felt tenderness toward Espinoza at that moment, a tenderness that brought back adolescence, adventures fiercely shared, and small-town afternoons.

•

That week, Liz Norton's home phone rang three or four times every afternoon and her cell phone rang two or three times every morning. The calls were from Pelletier and Espinoza, and although both produced elaborate Archimboldian pretexts, the pretexts were exhausted in a minute and the two professors proceeded to say what was really on their minds.

Pelletier talked about his colleagues in the German department, about a young Swiss poet and professor who was badgering him for a scholarship, about the sky in Paris (shades of Baudelaire, Verlaine, Banville), about the cars at dusk, their lights already on, heading home. Espinoza talked about his library, where he arranged his books in the strictest solitude, about the distant drums that he sometimes heard coming from a neighboring apartment that seemed to be home to a group of African musicians, about the neighborhoods of Madrid, Lavapiés, Malasaña, and about the area around the Gran Vía, where you could go for a walk at any time of night.

•

During this period, both Espinoza and Pelletier completely forgot about Morini. Only Norton called him now and then, carrying on the same conversations as ever.

In his way, Morini had vanished from sight.

•

Soon Pelletier got used to traveling to London whenever he wanted, though it must be emphasized that in terms of proximity and ready modes of transportation, he had it easiest.

These visits lasted only a single night. Pelletier would arrive just after nine, meeting Norton at ten at a restaurant where he had made reservations from Paris, and by one they were in bed.

Liz Norton was a passionate lover, although her passion was of limited duration. Not having much imagination of her own, she abandoned herself to any game her lover suggested, without ever taking the initiative, or thinking she ought to. These sessions rarely lasted more than three hours, a fact that occasionally saddened Pelletier, who would gladly have screwed till daybreak.

After the sexual act, and this was what frustrated Pelletier most, Norton preferred to talk about academic matters rather than to look frankly at what was developing between them. To Pelletier, Norton's coldness seemed a particularly feminine mode of self-protection. Hoping to get through to her, one night he decided to tell her the story of his own sentimental adventures. He drew up a long list of women he had known and exposed them to her frosty or indifferent gaze. She seemed unimpressed and showed no desire to repay his confession with one of her own.

In the mornings, after he called a cab, Pelletier slipped soundlessly into his clothes so as not to wake her and headed for the airport. Before he left he would spend a few seconds watching her, sprawled on the sheets, and sometimes he felt so full of love he could have burst into tears.

•

An hour later Liz Norton's alarm would sound and she'd jump out of bed. She'd take a shower, put water on to boil, drink tea with milk, dry her hair, and launch a thorough inspection of her apartment as if she were afraid that her nocturnal visitor had purloined some object of value. The living room and bedroom were almost always a wreck, and that bothered her. Impatiently, she would gather up the dirty glasses, empty the ashtrays, change the sheets, put back the books that Pelletier had taken down from the shelves and left on the floor, return the bottles to the rack in the kitchen, and then get dressed and go to the university. If she had a meeting with her department colleagues, she would go to the meeting, and if she didn't have a meeting she would shut herself up in the library to work or read until it was time for class.

•

One Saturday Espinoza told her that she must come to Madrid, she would be his guest, Madrid at this time of year was the most beautiful city in the world, and there was a Bacon retrospective on, too, which wasn't to be missed.

"I'll be there tomorrow," said Norton, which caught Espinoza off guard, since what his invitation had expressed was more a wish than any real hope that she might accept.

The certain knowledge that she would appear at his apartment the next day naturally sent Espinoza into a state of growing excitement and rampant insecurity. And yet they had a wonderful Sunday (Espinoza did everything in his power to assure they would), and that night they went to bed together, listening for the sound of the drums next door but hearing nothing, as if that day the African band had packed up for a tour of other Spanish cities. Espinoza had so many questions to ask that when the time came he didn't ask a single one. He didn't need to. Norton told him that she and Pelletier were lovers, although she put it another way, using some more ambiguous word, friends maybe, or maybe she said they'd been seeing each other, or words to that effect.

Espinoza would have liked to ask how long they'd been lovers, but all that came out was a sigh. Norton said she had many friends, without specifying whether she meant friend-friends or lover-friends, and always had ever since she was sixteen, when she made love for the first time with a thirty-four-year-old, a failed Pottery Lane musician, and this was how she saw things. Espinoza, who had never talked to a woman about love (or sex) in German, the two of them naked in bed, wanted to know how exactly she *did* see things, because he wasn't quite clear on that, but all he did was nod.

Then came the great surprise. Norton looked him in the eye and asked whether he thought he knew her. Espinoza said he wasn't sure, maybe in some ways he thought he did and in other ways he didn't, but he felt great respect for her and admired her work as a scholar and critic of the Archimboldian oeuvre. That was when Norton told him she'd been married and was now divorced.

"I had no idea," said Espinoza.

"Well, it's true," said Norton. "I'm a divorcée."

When Liz Norton flew back to London, Espinoza was left even more nervous than he'd been during her two days in Madrid. On the one hand, the encounter had been as successful as he could have hoped, of that there was no doubt. In bed, especially, the two of them seemed to understand each other, to be in sync, well matched, as if they'd known each other for a long time, but when the sex was over and Norton was in the mood to talk, everything changed. She entered a hypnotic state, as if she didn't have any woman friend to turn to, thought Espinoza, who in his heart believed that such confessions weren't intended for men's ears but should be heard by other women: Norton talked about menstrual cycles, for example, and the moon and black-and-white movies that turned without warning into horror films, which thoroughly depressed Espinoza, to the extent that when she stopped talking it took a superhuman effort for him to dress and go out for dinner or meet friends, arm in arm with Norton, not to mention the business with Pelletier, which when you really thought about it was chilling, and now who'll tell Pelletier that I'm sleeping with Liz?, all of which unsettled Espinoza and, when he was alone, gave him knots in his stomach and made him want to run to the bathroom, just as Norton had explained happened to her (how could I have let her tell me these things!) when she saw her ex-husband, six foot three and not very stable, a danger to himself and others, somebody who might have been a small-time thug or hooligan, the extent of his cultural education the old songs he sang in the pub with his mates from childhood, a bastard who believed in television and had the shrunken and shriveled soul of a religious fundamentalist. To put it plainly, the worst husband a woman could inflict on herself, no matter how you looked at it.

•

And even though Espinoza calmed himself with the promise that he wouldn't take things any further, four days later, once he was recovered, he called Norton and said he wanted to see her. Norton asked whether he'd rather meet in London or Madrid. Espinoza said it was up to her. Norton chose Madrid. Espinoza felt like the happiest man in the world.

Norton arrived Saturday evening and left Sunday night. Espinoza drove her to El Escorial and then they went to a flamenco show. He thought she seemed happy, and he was glad. Saturday night they made love for three hours, after which Norton, instead of starting to talk as she had before, said that she was exhausted and went to sleep. The next day, after they showered, they made love again and left for El Escorial. On the way back Espinoza asked her whether she'd seen Pelletier. Norton said she had, that Jean-Claude had been in London.

"How is he?" asked Espinoza.

"Fine," said Norton. "I told him about us."

Espinoza got nervous and concentrated on the road.

"So what did he think?" he asked.

"That it's my business," said Norton, "but sooner or later I'll have to choose."

Though he made no comment, Espinoza admired Pelletier's attitude. There's a man who knows how to play fair, he thought. Then Norton asked him how he felt about it.

"More or less the same," lied Espinoza, without taking his eyes off the road.

For a while they were silent and then Norton started to talk about her husband. This time the horror stories she told didn't affect Espinoza in the slightest.

•

Pelletier called Espinoza that Sunday night, just after Espinoza had dropped Norton off at the airport. He got straight to the point. He said he knew Espinoza knew what was going on. Espinoza said he appreciated the call, and whether Pelletier believed it or not, he'd been planning to call him that very night and the only reason he hadn't was because Pelletier had beaten him to it. Pelletier said he believed him.

"So what do we do now?" asked Espinoza.

"Leave it all in the hands of fate," answered Pelletier.

Then they started to talk—and laughed quite a bit—about a strange conference that had just been held in Salonika, to which only Morini had been invited.

•

In Salonika, Morini had a mild attack. One morning he woke up in his hotel room and couldn't see anything. He had gone blind. He panicked at first, but after a while he managed to regain control. He lay in bed without moving, trying to go back to sleep. He thought of pleasant things, trying out childhood scenes, a few films, still shots of faces, but nothing worked. He sat up in bed and felt around for his wheelchair. He unfolded it and swung into it with less effort than he had expected. Then, very slowly, he tried to turn himself toward the room's only window, a French door that opened onto a balcony with a view of bare, yellowish-brown hills and an office building topped with a neon sign for a real estate company advertising chalets in an area presumably near Salonika.

The development (which had yet to be built) boasted the name Apollo Residences, and the night before, Morini had been watching the sign from his balcony, a glass of whiskey in his hand, as it blinked on and off. When he reached the window at last and managed to open it, he felt dizzy, as if he were about to faint. First he thought about trying to find the door to the hallway and maybe calling for help or letting himself fall in the middle of the corridor. Then he decided that it would be best to go back to bed. An hour later he was woken by the light coming in the open window and by his own perspiration. He called the reception desk and asked whether there were any messages for him. He was told there were none. He undressed in bed and got back in the wheelchair sitting ready beside him. It took him half an hour to shower and dress himself in clean clothes. Then he closed the window, without looking out, and left the room for the conference.

•

The four of them met again at the contemporary German literature symposium held in Salzburg in 1996. Espinoza and Pelletier seemed very happy. Norton, on the other hand, was like an ice queen, indifferent to the city's cultural offerings and beauty. Morini showed up loaded with books and papers to grade, as if the Salzburg meeting had caught him at one of his busiest moments.

All four were put up at the same hotel. Morini and Norton were on the third floor, in rooms 305 and 311, respectively. Espinoza was on the fifth floor, in room 509. And Pelletier was on the sixth floor, in room 602. The hotel was literally overrun by a German orchestra and a Russian choir, and there was a constant musical hubbub in the hallways and on the stairs, sometimes louder and sometimes softer, as if the musicians never stopped humming overtures or as if a mental (and musical) static had settled over the hotel. Espinoza and Pelletier weren't bothered in the least by it, and Morini seemed not to notice, but this was just the sort of thing, Norton exclaimed, one of many others she wouldn't mention, that made Salzburg such a shithole.

Naturally, neither Pelletier nor Espinoza visited Norton in her room a single time. Instead, the room that Espinoza visited (once) was Pelletier's, and the room that Pelletier visited (twice) was Espinoza's, the two of them as excited as children at the news spreading like wildfire, like a nuclear conflagration, along the hallways and through the symposium gatherings in *petit comité*, to wit, that Archimboldi was a candidate for the Nobel that year, not only cause for great joy among Archimboldians everywhere but also a triumph and a vindication, so much so that in Salzburg, at the Red Bull beer hall, on a night of many toasts, peace was declared between the two main factions of Archimboldi scholars, that is, between Pelletier and Espinoza and Borchmeyer, Pohl, and Schwarz, who from then on decided, with respect for each other's differences and methods of interpretation, to pool their efforts and forswear sabotage, which in practical terms meant that Pelletier would no longer veto the publication of Schwarz's essays in the journals where he held sway, and Schwarz would no longer veto the publication of Pelletier's studies in the journals where he, Schwarz, was held in godlike esteem.

•

Morini, less excited than Pelletier and Espinoza, was the first to point out that until now, at least as far as he knew, Archimboldi had never received an important prize in Germany, no booksellers' award, or critics' award, or readers' award, or publishers' award, assuming there was such a thing, which meant that one might reasonably expect that, knowing Archimboldi was up for the biggest prize in world literature, his fellow Germans, even if only to play it safe, would offer him a national award or a symbolic award or an honorary award or at least an hour-long television interview, none of which happened, incensing the Archimboldians (united this time), who, rather than being disheartened by the poor treatment that Archimboldi continued to receive, redoubled their efforts, galvanized in their frustration and spurred on by the injustice with which a civilized state was treating not only—in their opinion—the best living writer in Germany, but the best living writer in Europe, and this triggered an avalanche of literary and even biographical studies of Archimboldi (about whom so little was known that it might as well be nothing at all), which in turn drew more readers, most captivated not by the German's work but by the life or nonlife of such a singular figure, which in turn translated into a word-of-mouth movement that increased sales considerably in Germany (a phenomenon not unrelated to the presence of Dieter Hellfeld, the latest acquisition of the Schwarz, Borchmeyer, and Pohl group), which in turn gave new impetus to the translations and the reissues of the old translations, none of which made Archimboldi a bestseller but did boost him, for two weeks, to ninth place on the bestseller list in Italy, and to twelfth place in France, also for two weeks, and although it never made the lists in Spain, a publishing house there bought the rights to the few novels that still belonged to other Spanish publishers and the rights to all of the writer's books that had yet to be translated into Spanish, and in this way a kind of Archimboldi Library was begun, which wasn't a bad business.

•

In the British Isles, it must be said, Archimboldi remained a decidedly marginal writer.

•

In these heady days, Pelletier happened on a piece written by the Swabian whom they'd had the pleasure of meeting in Amsterdam. In the piece the Swabian basically repeated what he'd already told them about Archimboldi's visit to the Frisian town and the dinner afterward with the lady who had traveled to Buenos Aires. The piece was published in the *Reutlingen Morning News* and differed from the Swabian's original account in that it reproduced an exchange between the lady and Archimboldi, pitched in a key of sardonic humor. The conversation began with her asking him where he was from. Archimboldi replied that he was Prussian. The lady asked whether his was a noble name, of the Prussian landed gentry. Archimboldi replied that it probably was. Then the lady murmured the name Benno von Archimboldi, as if biting a gold coin to test it. Immediately she said it didn't sound familiar and she mentioned a few other names, to see whether Archimboldi recognized them. He said he didn't, all he'd known of Prussia were its forests.

"And yet your name is of Italian origin," said the lady.

"French," replied Archimboldi. "It's Huguenot."

At this, the lady laughed. She had once been very beautiful, said the Swabian. Even then, in the dim light of the tavern, she looked beautiful, although when she laughed her false teeth slipped and she had to adjust them with her hand. Still, the operation was not ungraceful, as performed by her. The lady was so easy and natural with the fishermen and peasants that she inspired only respect and affection. She had been a widow for a long time. Sometimes she would go out riding on the dunes.

Other times she would wander down side roads buffeted by the wind off the North Sea.

•

When Pelletier discussed the Swabian's article with his three friends one morning as they were having breakfast at the hotel before going out into Salzburg, opinions and interpretations varied considerably.

According to Espinoza and Pelletier, the Swabian had probably been the lady's lover at the time when Archimboldi came to give his reading. According to Norton, the Swabian had a different version of events depending on his mood and his audience, and it was possible that he himself didn't even remember anymore what was really said and what had really happened on that momentous occasion. According to Morini, the Swabian was a grotesque double of Archimboldi, his twin, the negative image of a developed photograph that keeps looming larger, becoming more powerful, more oppressive, without ever losing its link to the negative (which undergoes the reverse process, gradually altered by time and fate), the two images somehow still the same: both young men in the years of terror and barbarism under Hitler, both World War II veterans, both writers, both citizens of a bankrupt nation, both poor bastards adrift at the moment when they meet and (in their grotesque fashion) recognize each other, Archimboldi as a struggling writer, the Swabian as "cultural promoter" in a town where culture was hardly a serious concern.

Was it even conceivable that the miserable and (why not?) contemptible Swabian was really Archimboldi? It wasn't Morini who asked this question, but Norton. And the answer was no, since the Swabian, to begin with, was short and of delicate constitution, which didn't match Archimboldi's physical description at all. Pelletier's and Espinoza's explanation was much more plausible: the Swabian as the noble lady's lover, even though she could have been his grandmother. The Swabian trudging each afternoon to the house of the lady who had traveled to Buenos Aires, to fill his belly with charcuterie and biscuits and cups of tea. The Swabian massaging the back of the former cavalry captain's widow, as the rain lashed the windows, a sad Frisian rain that made one want to weep, and although it didn't make the Swabian weep, it made him pale, and he approached the nearest window, where he stood looking out at what was beyond the curtains of frenzied rain, until the lady called him, peremptorily, and the Swabian turned his back on the window, not knowing why he had gone to it, not knowing what he hoped to see, and just at that moment, when there was no one at the window anymore and only a little lamp of colored glass at the back of the room flickering, it appeared.

•

So the days in Salzburg were generally pleasant, and although Archimboldi didn't receive the Nobel Prize that year, life for our four friends proceeded smoothly, flowing along on the placid river of European university German departments, not without racking up one upset or another that in the end simply added a dash of pepper, a dash of mustard, a drizzle of vinegar to orderly lives, or lives that looked orderly from without, although each of the four had his or her own cross to bear, like anyone, a strange cross in Norton's case, ghostly and phosphorescent, for Norton made frequent and rather tasteless references to her ex-husband as a lurking threat, ascribed to him the vices and defects of a monster, a horribly violent monster but one who never materialized, a monster all evocation and no action, although with her words Norton managed to give substance to a being whom neither Espinoza nor Pelletier had ever seen, as if her ex existed only in their dreams, until Pelletier, sharper than Espinoza, understood that Norton's unthinking diatribe, that endless list of grievances, was more than anything a punishment inflicted on herself, perhaps for the shame of having fallen in love with such a cretin and married him. Pelletier, of course, was wrong.

•

Around this time, Pelletier and Espinoza, worried about the current state of their mutual lover, had two long conversations on the phone.

Pelletier made the first call, which lasted an hour and fifteen minutes. The second was made three days later by Espinoza and lasted two hours and fifteen minutes. After they'd been talking for an hour and a half, Pelletier told Espinoza to hang up, the call would be expensive and he'd call right back, but Espinoza firmly refused.

The first conversation began awkwardly, although Espinoza had been expecting Pelletier's call, as if both men found it difficult to say what sooner or later they would have to say. The first twenty minutes were tragic in tone, with the word *fate* used ten times and the word *friendship* twenty-four times. Liz Norton's name was spoken fifty times, nine of them in vain. The word *Paris* was said seven times, *Madrid*, eight. The word *love* was spoken twice, once by each man. The word *horror* was spoken six times and the word *happiness* once (by Espinoza). The word *solution* was said twelve times. The word *solipsism* seven times. The word *euphemism* ten times. The word *category*, in the singular and the plural, nine times. The word *structuralism* once (Pelletier). The term *American literature* three times. The words *dinner* or *eating* or *breakfast* or *sandwich* nineteen times. The words *eyes* or *hands* or *hair* fourteen times. Then the conversation proceeded more smoothly. Pelletier told Espinoza a joke in German and Espinoza laughed. In fact, they both laughed, wrapped up in the waves or whatever it was that linked their voices and ears across the dark fields and the wind and the snow of the Pyrenees and the rivers and the lonely roads and the separate and interminable suburbs surrounding Paris and Madrid.

•

The second conversation, radically longer than the first, was a conversation between friends doing their best to clear up any murky points they might have overlooked, a conversation that refused to become technical or logistical and instead touched on subjects connected only tenuously to Norton, subjects that had nothing to do with surges of emotion, subjects easy to broach and then drop when they wished to return to the main subject, Liz Norton, whom, by the time the second call was nearing its close, both had recognized not as the Fury who destroyed their friendship, black clad with bloodstained wings, nor as Hecate, who began as an au pair, caring for children, and ended up learning witchcraft and turning herself into an animal, but as the angel who had fortified their friendship, forcibly shown them what they'd known all along, what they'd assumed all along, which was that they were civilized beings, beings capable of noble sentiments, not two dumb beasts debased by routine and regular sedentary work, no, that night Pelletier and Espinoza discovered that they were generous, so generous that if they'd been together they'd have felt the need to go out and celebrate, dazzled by the shine of their own virtue, a shine that might not last (since virtue, once recognized in a flash, has no shine and makes its home in a dark cave amid cave dwellers, some dangerous indeed), and for lack of celebration or revelry they hailed this virtue with an unspoken promise of eternal friendship, and sealed the vow, after they hung up their respective phones in their respective apartments crammed with books, by sipping whiskey with supreme slowness and watching the night outside their windows, maybe seeking unconsciously what the Swabian had sought outside the widow's window in vain.

•

Morini was the last to know, as one would expect, although in Morini's case the sentimental mathematics didn't always work out.

Even before Norton first went to bed with Pelletier, Morini had felt it coming. Not because of the way Pelletier behaved around Norton but because of her own detachment, a generalized detachment, Baudelaire would have called it spleen, Nerval melancholy, which left Norton liable to embark on an intimate relationship with anyone who came along.

Espinoza, of course, he hadn't predicted. When Norton called and told him she was involved with the two of them, Morini was surprised (although he wouldn't have been surprised if Norton had said she was involved with Pelletier and a colleague at the University of London or even a student), but he hid it well. Then he tried to think of other things, but he couldn't.

He asked Norton whether she was happy. Norton said she was. He told her he had received an e-mail from Borchmeyer with fresh news. Norton didn't seem very interested. He asked her whether she'd heard from her husband.

"Ex-husband," said Norton.

No, she hadn't heard from him, although an old friend had called to tell her that her ex was living with another old friend. Morini asked whether the woman had been a very close friend. Norton didn't understand the question.

"What close friend?"

"The one who's living with your ex now," said Morini.

"She doesn't live with him, she's supporting him, it's completely different."

"Ah," said Morini, and he tried to change the subject, but he drew a blank.

Maybe I should talk to her about my illness, he thought bitterly. But that he would never do.

•

Around this time, Morini was the first of the four to read an article about the killings in Sonora, which appeared in *Il Manifesto* and was written by an Italian reporter who had gone to Mexico to cover the Zapatista guerrillas. The news was horrible, he thought. In Italy there were serial killers, too, but they hardly ever killed more than ten people, whereas in Sonora the dead numbered well over one hundred.

Then he thought about the reporter from *Il Manifesto* and it struck him as odd that she had gone to Chiapas, which is at the southern tip of the country, and that she had ended up writing about events in Sonora, which, if he wasn't mistaken, was in the north, the northwest, on the border with the United States. He imagined her traveling by bus, a long way from Mexico City to the desert lands of the north. He imagined her talking to Subcomandante Marcos. He imagined her in the Mexican capital. Someone there must have told her what was happening in Sonora. And instead of getting on the next plane to Italy, she had decided to buy a bus ticket and set off on a long trip to Sonora. For an instant, Morini felt a wild desire to travel with the reporter.

I'd love her until the end of time, he thought. An hour later he'd already forgotten the matter completely.

•

A little later he got an e-mail from Norton. He thought it was strange that Norton would write and not call. Once he had read the letter, though, he understood that she needed to express her thoughts as precisely as possible and that was why she'd decided to write. In the letter she asked his forgiveness for what she called her egotism, an egotism that expressed itself in the contemplation of her own misfortunes, real or imaginary. She went on to say that she'd finally resolved her lingering quarrel with her ex-husband. The dark clouds had vanished from her life. Now she wanted to be happy and sing [*sic*]. Until probably the week before, she added, she'd loved him still, and now she could attest that the part of her past that included him was behind her for good. I'm suddenly keen on my work, she said, and on all those little everyday things that make human beings happy. And she also said: I wanted you, my patient Piero, to be the first to know.

Morini read the letter three times. With a heavy heart, he thought how wrong Norton was when she said her love and her ex-husband and everything they'd been through were behind her. Nothing is ever behind us.

Pelletier and Espinoza, meanwhile, received no such confidences. But Pelletier noticed something that Espinoza didn't. The London–Paris trips had become more frequent than the Paris–London trips. And as often as not, Norton would show up with a gift—a collection of essays, an art book, catalogs of exhibitions that Pelletier would never see, even a shirt or a handkerchief—which had never happened before.

Otherwise, everything was the same. They screwed, went out to dinner, discussed the latest news about Archimboldi. They never talked about their future as a couple. Each time Espinoza came up in conversation (which was rare), both adopted a strictly impartial, cautious, and above all friendly tone. Some nights they even fell asleep in each other's arms without making love, something Pelletier was sure didn't happen with Espinoza. But he was wrong, because relations between Norton and Espinoza were often a faithful simulacrum of Norton's relations with Pelletier.

The meals were different, better in Paris; the setting and the scenery were different, more modern in Paris; and the language was different, because with Espinoza Norton spoke mostly German and with Pelletier mostly English, but overall the similarities outweighed the differences. Naturally, with Espinoza there had also been nights without sex.

•

If Norton's closest friend (she had none) had asked which of the two friends she had a better time with in bed, Norton wouldn't have known what to say.

Sometimes she thought Pelletier was the more skillful lover. Other times, Espinoza. Viewed from outside, say from a rigorously academic standpoint, one could maintain that Pelletier had a longer bibliography than Espinoza, who relied more on instinct than intellect in such matters, and who had the disadvantage of being Spanish, that is, of belonging to a culture that tended to confuse eroticism with scatology and pornography with coprophagy, a confusion evident (because unaddressed) in Espinoza's mental library, for he had only just read the Marquis de Sade in order to check (and refute) an article by Pohl in which the latter drew connections from *Justine* and *Philosophy in the Boudoir* to one of Archimboldi's novels of the 1950s.

Pelletier, on the other hand, had read the divine Marquis when he was sixteen and at eighteen had participated in a ménage à trois with two female fellow students, and his adolescent predilection for erotic comics had flowered into a reasonable, restrained adult collection of licentious literature of the seventeenth and eighteenth centuries. In figurative terms: Pelletier was more intimately acquainted than Espinoza with Mnemosyne, mountain goddess and mother of the nine muses. In plain speech: Pelletier could screw for six hours (without coming) thanks to his bibliography, whereas Espinoza could go for the same amount of time (coming twice, sometimes three times, and finishing half dead) sheerly on the basis of strength and force of will.

•

And speaking of the Greeks, it would be fair to say that Espinoza and Pelletier believed themselves to be (and in their perverse way, were) incarnations of Ulysses, and that both thought of Morini as Eurylochus, the loyal friend about whom two very different stories are told in the *Odyssey*. The first, in which he escapes being turned into a pig, suggests shrewdness or a solitary and individualistic nature, careful skepticism, the craftiness of an old seaman. The second, however, involves an impious and sacrilegous adventure: the cattle of Zeus or another powerful god are grazing peacefully on the island of the Sun when they wake the powerful appetite of Eurylochus, so that with clever words he cajoles his friends to kill the cattle and prepare a feast, which angers Zeus or whichever god it is no end, who curses Eurylochus for putting on airs and presuming to be enlightened or atheistic or Promethean, since the god in question is more incensed by Eurylochus's attitude, by the dialectic of his hunger, than by the act itself of eating the cattle, and because of this act, or because of the feast, the ship that bears Eurylochus capsizes and all the sailors die, which was what Pelletier and Espinoza believed would happen to Morini, not in a conscious way, of course, but in a kind of disjointed or instinctual way, a dark thought in the form of a microscopic sign throbbing in a dark and microscopic part of the two friends' souls.

•

Near the end of 1996, Morini had a nightmare. He dreamed that Norton was diving into a pool as he, Pelletier, and Espinoza played cards around a stone table. Espinoza and Pelletier had their backs to the pool, which seemed at first glance to be an ordinary hotel pool. As they played, Morini watched the other tables, the parasols, the deck chairs lined up along both sides of the pool. In the distance there was a park with deep green hedges, shining as if with fresh rain. Little by little people began to leave, vanishing through the different doors connecting the outdoor space, the bar, and the building's rooms or little suites, suites that Morini imagined consisted of a double room with kitchenette and bathroom. Soon there was no one left outside, not even the bored waiters he'd seen earlier bustling around. Pelletier and Espinoza were still absorbed in the game. Next to Pelletier he saw a pile of poker chips, as well as coins from various countries, so he guessed Pelletier was winning. And yet Espinoza didn't look ready to give up. Just then, Morini glanced at his cards and saw he had nothing to play. He discarded and asked for four cards, which he left facedown on the stone table, without looking at them, and with some difficulty he set his wheelchair in motion. Pelletier and Espinoza didn't even ask where he was going. He rolled the wheelchair to the edge of the pool. Only then did he realize how enormous it was. It must have been at least a thousand feet wide and more than two miles long, calculated Morini. The water was dark and in some places there were oily patches, the kind you see in harbors. There was no trace of Norton. Morini shouted.

"Liz."

He thought he saw a shadow at the other end of the pool, and he moved his wheelchair in that direction. It was a long way. The one time he looked back, Pelletier and Espinoza had vanished from sight. A fog had settled over that part of the terrace. He went on. The water in the pool seemed to scale the edges, as if somewhere a squall were brewing or worse, although where Morini was heading everything was calm and silent, and there was no sign of a storm. Soon the fog settled over Morini. At first he tried to keep going, but then he realized that he was in danger of tipping his wheelchair into the pool, and he decided not to risk it. When his eyes had adjusted, he saw a rock jutting from the pool, like a dark and iridescent reef. This didn't seem strange to him. He went over to the edge and shouted Liz's name once more, afraid now that he would never see her again. A half turn of the wheels was all it would take to topple him in. Then he saw that the pool had emptied and was enormously deep, as if a gulf of moldy black tiles were opening at his feet. At the bottom he seemed to make out the figure of a woman (though it was impossible to be sure) heading toward the slope of rock. Morini was about to shout again and wave when he sensed someone at his back. Two things were instantly certain: the thing was evil and it wanted Morini to turn around and see its face. Carefully, he backed away and continued around the pool, trying not to look at whoever was following him, searching for the ladder that might take him down to the bottom. But of course the ladder, which should logically be in a corner, never appeared, and after he had rolled a few feet Morini stopped and turned and looked into the stranger's face, controlling his fear, a fear all the worse for his dawning certainty that he knew the person following him, who gave off a stench of evil that Morini could hardly bear. In the fog, Liz Norton's face appeared. A younger Norton—twenty, if that—staring so seriously and intently that Morini had to look away. Who was the person at the bottom of the pool? Morini could still see him or her, a tiny speck trying to climb the rock that had now become a mountain, and the sight of this person, so far away, filled his eyes with tears and made him deeply and inconsolably sad, as if he were seeing his first love wandering in a labyrinth. Or himself, with legs that still worked, lost on a hopeless climb. Also, and he couldn't help it, and it was good that he didn't, he thought it looked like a painting by Gustave Moreau or Odilon Redon. Then he swung around to face Norton and she said:

"There's no turning back."

He heard the sentence not with his ears but in his head. Norton has acquired telepathic powers, Morini thought. She isn't bad, she's good. It isn't evil that I sensed, it's telepathy, he told himself to alter the course of a dream that in his heart of hearts he knew was fixed and inevitable. Then Norton repeated, in German, there's no turning back. And, paradoxically, she turned and walked off away from the pool and was lost in a forest that could barely be seen through the fog, a forest that gave off a red glow, and it was into this red glow that Norton disappeared.

•

A week later, having interpreted the dream in at least four different ways, Morini traveled to London. The decision to make the trip was a complete break from his usual routine, since normally he traveled only to conferences and meetings, his plane ticket and hotel room paid for by the organization in question. This time there was no professional excuse and he paid the hotel and transportation costs out of his own pocket. Nor can it be said that he was answering a call of help from Liz Norton. He had talked to her just four days before and told her he was planning to come to London, a city he hadn't visited in a long time.

Norton was delighted and invited him to stay with her, but Morini lied, saying he'd already made a reservation at a hotel. When he landed at Gatwick, Norton was waiting for him. That day they had breakfast together, in a restaurant near Morini's hotel, and that night they had dinner in Norton's apartment. During dinner, bland but praised politely by Morini, they talked about Archimboldi, about his growing renown and the innumerable gaps in his story that remained to be filled, but later, over dessert, the conversation took a more personal turn, tending more toward reminiscence, and until three in the morning, when they called a cab and Norton helped Morini into her building's old elevator, then down a flight of six steps, everything was, as the Italian reviewed it in his mind, much more pleasant than he'd expected.

Between breakfast and dinner, Morini was alone, hardly daring at first to leave his room, although later, driven by boredom, he decided to go out and went as far as Hyde Park, where he wandered aimlessly, lost in thought, without noticing or seeing anyone. Some people gazed after him in curiosity, because they had never seen a man in a wheelchair moving with such determination and at such a steady pace. When he finally came to a stop he found himself outside the Italian Gardens, or so they were called, although nothing about them struck him as Italian, but who knows, he mused, sometimes people are staggeringly ignorant of what's under their very noses.

He pulled a book out of his jacket pocket and began to read as he regained his strength. Soon he heard a voice saying hello, then the noise a heavy body makes when it drops to a wooden bench. He returned the greeting. The stranger had straw-colored hair, graying and dirty, and must have weighed at least two hundred and fifty pounds. They sat a moment looking at each other and the stranger asked whether he was a foreigner. Morini said he was Italian. The stranger wanted to know whether he lived in London, and then what the book he was reading was called. Morini answered that he didn't live in London and that the book he was reading was called *Il libro di cucina di Juana Inés de la Cruz*, by Angelo Morino, and that it was written in Italian, of course, although it was about a Mexican nun. About the nun's life and some of her recipes.

"So this Mexican nun liked to cook?" asked the stranger.

"In a way she did, although she also wrote poems," Morini replied.

"I don't trust nuns," said the stranger.

"Well, this nun was a great poet," said Morini.

"I don't trust people who cook from recipes," said the stranger, as if he hadn't heard him.

"So whom do you trust?" asked Morini.

"People who eat when they're hungry, I guess," said the stranger.

Then he went on to explain that a long time ago he had worked for a company that made mugs, just mugs, the plain kind and the kind decorated with phrases or mottoes or jokes: *Sorry, I'm On My Coffee Break!* or *Daddy Loves Mummy* or *Last Round Today, Last Round Forever*, that sort of thing, mugs with anodyne captions, and one day, surely due to demand, the inscriptions on the mugs changed drastically and they started using pictures, black-and-white at first, but then the venture did so well they switched to pictures in color, some humorous but some dirty, too.

"They even gave me a raise," the stranger said. "Do mugs like that exist in Italy?" he asked then.

"Yes," said Morini, "some with phrases in English and others with phrases in Italian."

"Well, it was everything we could have asked for," said the stranger. "We all worked more happily. The managers worked more happily, too, and the boss looked happy. But after a few months of making those mugs I realized that my happiness was artificial. I felt happy because I saw the others were happy and because I knew I should feel happy, but I wasn't really happy. In fact, I felt worse than before they'd given me a raise. I thought I was going through a bad patch and I tried not to think about it, but after three months I couldn't keep pretending nothing was wrong. I was in a terrible mood, I was much more violent than I'd been before, any little thing would make me angry, I started to drink. So I faced up to the problem, and finally I realized that I didn't like to make that particular kind of mug. At night, I swear, I suffered like a dog. I thought I was going crazy, that I didn't know what I was doing or thinking. Some of the thoughts I had back then still scare me. One day I confronted one of the managers. I told him I was sick of making those idiotic mugs. This manager was a good man, his name was Andy, and he always tried to make conversation with the workers. He asked me whether I'd preferred making the mugs we'd made before. That's right, I said. Are you serious, Dick? he asked me. Completely serious, I answered. Are the new mugs more work? Not at all, I said, the work is the same, but the fucking mugs didn't do damage to me this way before. What do you mean? said Andy. That the bloody mugs didn't bother me before and now they're destroying me inside. So what the hell makes them different, aside from being more modern? asked Andy. That's it exactly, I answered, the mugs weren't so modern before, and even if they tried to hurt me, they couldn't, I didn't feel their sting, but now the fucking mugs are like samurais armed with those fucking samurai swords and they're driving me insane. Anyway, it was a long conversation," said the stranger. "The manager listened to me, but he didn't understand a single word I was saying. The next day I asked for the pay I was due and I left the company. I haven't worked since. What do you think of that?"

Morini hesitated before answering.

"I don't know," he said finally.

"That's what everyone says: they don't know," said the stranger.

"What do you do now?" asked Morini.

"Nothing, I don't work anymore, I'm a London bum," the stranger said.

It's as if he's pointing out a tourist attraction, thought Morini, but he was careful not to say this out loud.

"So what do you think of that book?" asked the stranger.

"What book?" asked Morini.

The stranger pointed one of his thick fingers at the book, published by Sellerio, in Palermo, that Morini was holding delicately in one hand.

"Oh, I think it's very good," he said.

"Read me some recipes," said the stranger, in a tone of voice that struck Morini as threatening.

"I don't know whether I have time," he said, "I have to meet a friend."

"What's your friend's name?" asked the stranger in the same tone of voice.

"Liz Norton," said Morini.

"Liz, pretty name," said the stranger. "And what's your name, if you don't mind me asking?"

"Piero Morini," said Morini.

"Odd," said the stranger, "your name is almost the same as the name of the author of the book."

"No," said Morini, "my name is Piero Morini, and his name is Angelo Morino."

"If you wouldn't mind," said the stranger, "at least read me the names of some recipes. I'll close my eyes and imagine them."

"All right," said Morini.

The stranger closed his eyes and Morini began to read some of the names of the recipes attributed to Sor Juana Inés de la Cruz, slowly and with an actor's intonation.

Sgonfiotti al formaggio
Sgonfiotti alla ricotta
Sgonfiotti di vento
Crespelle
Dolce di tuorli di uovo
Uova regali
Dolce alla panna
Dolce alle noci
Dolce di testoline di moro
Dolce alle barbabietole
Dolce di burro e zucchero
Dolce alla crema
Dolce di mamey

By the time he got to *dolce di mamey*, the stranger seemed to have fallen asleep and Morini left the Italian Gardens.

•

The next day was much like the first. This time Norton came to meet him at the hotel, and as Morini was paying the bill she put his only suitcase in the boot of her car. When they left, she drove the same way he'd taken to Hyde Park the day before.

Morini realized it and watched the streets in silence, and then the appearance of the park, which looked to him like a film of the jungle, the colors wrong, terribly sad, exalted, until the car turned and disappeared down other streets.

They ate together in a neighborhood that Norton had discovered, a neighborhood near the river, where there had once been a few factories and dry docks and where boutiques and food shops and fashionable restaurants had now opened in the renovated buildings. A small boutique occupied the same number of square feet as four workers' houses, calculated Morini. The restaurant, twelve or sixteen. Liz Norton's voice praised the neighborhood and the efforts of the people who were setting it back afloat.

Morini thought that *afloat* was wrong, despite its maritime ring. In fact, as they ate dessert he felt like weeping, or better yet, fainting, sliding gently out of his chair with his eyes fixed on Norton's face, and never waking up. But now Norton was telling a story about a painter, the first to settle in the neighborhood.

He was a young man, thirty-three or so, known on the scene but not what you'd call famous. The real reason he came was because it was cheaper to rent a studio here than anywhere else. The neighborhood was less lively in those days. There were still old workmen living here on their pensions, but no young people or children. Women were notably absent: they had either died or spent all day inside, never going out. There was just one pub, as tumbledown as the rest of the neighborhood. In short, a lonely, decrepit place. But it seemed this sparked the painter's imagination and inspired him to work. He was a solitary kind of person, too. Or else just comfortable being alone.

So the neighborhood didn't frighten him. He fell in love with it, actually. He liked to come home at night and walk for blocks and blocks without seeing anyone. He liked the color of the streetlamps and the light that spilled over the fronts of the houses. The shadows that moved as he moved. The ashen, sooty dawns. The men of few words who gathered in the pub, where he became a regular. The pain, or the memory of pain, that here was literally sucked away by something nameless until only a void was left. The knowledge that this question was possible: pain that turns finally into emptiness. The knowledge that the same equation applied to everything, more or less.

The point is, he set to work more eagerly than ever. A year later he had a show at the Emma Waterson gallery, an alternative space in Wapping, and it was an enormous success. He ushered in something that would later be known as the *new decadence* or *English animalism*. The paintings in the inaugural show of this school were big, ten feet by seven, and they portrayed the remains of the shipwreck of his neighborhood, awash in a mingling of grays. It was as if painter and neighborhood had achieved total symbiosis. As if, in other words, the painter were painting the neighborhood or the neighborhood were painting the painter, in savage, gloomy strokes. The paintings weren't bad. Still, the show wouldn't have been so successful or had such an impact if not for the central painting, much smaller than the rest, the masterpiece that years later led so many British artists down the path of new decadence. This painting, viewed properly (although one could never be sure of viewing it properly), was an ellipsis of self-portraits, sometimes a spiral of self-portraits (depending on the angle from which it was seen), seven feet by three and a half feet, in the center of which hung the painter's mummified right hand.

It happened like this. One morning, after two days of feverish work on the self-portraits, the painter cut off his painting hand. He immediately applied a tourniquet to his arm and took the hand to a taxidermist he knew, who'd already been informed of the nature of the assignment. Then he went to the hospital, where they stanched the bleeding and proceeded to suture his arm. At some point someone asked how the accident had happened. He answered that he had cut off his hand with a machete blow while he was working, by mistake. The doctors asked where the amputated hand was, because there was always the possibility that it might be reattached. He said he'd thrown it in the river on his way to the hospital, out of sheer rage and pain.

Although the prices were astronomical, the show sold out. The masterpiece, it was said, went to an Arab who worked in the City, as did four of the big paintings. Shortly thereafter, the painter went mad and his wife (he was married by then) had no choice but to send him to a convalescent home on the outskirts of Lausanne or Montreux.

He lives there to this day.

Other painters, meanwhile, began to move into the neighborhood. Mostly because it was cheap, but also because they were attracted by the legend of the man who had painted the most radical self-portrait of our time. Then came the architects, then some families who bought houses that had been renovated and remodeled. Then came the boutiques, the black-box theaters, the cutting-edge restaurants, until it was one of the trendiest neighborhoods in London, nowhere near as cheap as it was reputed to be.

"What do you think of that story?"

"I don't know what to think," said Morini.

The urge to weep—or else, faint—persisted, but he restrained it.

•

They had tea at Norton's apartment. Only then did she begin to talk about Espinoza and Pelletier, but casually, as if the matter was too familiar to be worthy of interest or discussion with Morini (whom she had noticed was upset, although she was careful not to pry, knowing there was rarely anything soothing about being pestered with questions), and not even something she cared to discuss herself.

It was a very pleasant afternoon. From his armchair, Morini admired Norton's sitting room—her books and her framed prints hanging on white walls, her mysterious photographs and souvenirs, her preferences expressed in things as simple as the choice of furniture, which was tasteful, comfortable, and modest, and even in the sliver of tree-lined street that she surely saw each morning before she left the apartment—and he began to feel good, as if he were swaddled in these various manifestations of his friend, as if they were also an expression of affirmation, the words of which he might not understand but that brought him comfort nevertheless.

Shortly before he left, he asked the name of the painter whose story he'd just heard and whether there'd been a catalog for that terrible show. His name is Edwin Johns, said Norton. Then she got up and searched one of the bookcases. She found a large catalog and handed it to Morini. Before he opened it he asked himself whether it was a good idea to insist on this, precisely now that he was so relaxed. But if I don't do it I'll die, he told himself, and he opened the catalog, which more than a catalog was an art book that covered or tried to cover the trajectory of Johns's career. There was a photograph of Johns on the first page, from before his self-mutilation, which showed a young man of about twenty-five looking straight at the camera and smiling a half smile that might be shy or mocking. His hair was dark and straight.

"It's a gift," he heard Norton say.

"Thank you," he heard himself answer.

An hour later they left together for the airport, and an hour after that Morini was on his way back to Italy.

•

Around this time, a previously insignificant Serbian critic, a German professor at the University of Belgrade, published a strange article in the journal overseen by Pelletier, an article reminiscent in a certain sense of the minuscule findings on the Marquis de Sade published many years ago by a French critic, which comprised the facsimile reproduction of loose papers testifying vaguely to the Marquis's visit to a laundry, an aide-mémoire of his relations with a certain theater impresario, a doctor's bill complete with medicines prescribed, an order for a doublet specifying buttonwork and color, etc., all of it accompanied by lengthy notes from which only a single conclusion could be drawn: Sade had existed, Sade had washed his clothes and bought new clothes and maintained a correspondence with beings now definitively wiped from the slate of time.

The Serb's text was very similar. In this case, the person traced was Archimboldi, not Sade, and the article consisted of a painstaking and often frustrating investigation that began in Germany, continued through France, Switzerland, Italy, Greece, returned to Italy, and ended at a travel agency in Palermo, where it seemed Archimboldi had bought a plane ticket to Morocco. An old man, a German, said the Serbian. The words *old man* and *German* he waved like magic wands to uncover a secret, and at the same time they supplied the stamp of ultraconcrete critical literature, a nonspeculative literature free of ideas, assertions, denials, doubts, free of any intent to serve as guide, neither pro nor con, just an eye seeking out the tangible elements, not judging them but simply displaying them coldly, archaeology of the facsimile, and, by the same token, of the photocopier.

•

To Pelletier it seemed an odd text. Before he published it, he sent copies to Espinoza, Morini, and Norton. Espinoza said it could lead somewhere, and even though researching and writing that way might seem like drudge work, like the lowest of menial tasks, he thought, and said, that it was good to have a place in the Archimboldian project for these single-minded fanatics. Norton said she'd always had the feeling (feminine intuition) that sooner or later Archimboldi would show up somewhere in the Maghreb, and that the only part of the Serb's paper that was worth anything was the ticket in the name of Benno von Archimboldi, bought a week before the Italian plane was scheduled to depart for Rabat. From now on we can imagine him lost in a cave in the Atlas Mountains, she said. Morini held his tongue.

•

Here we should clarify in the interest of properly (or improperly) understanding the Serb's text. A reservation was indeed made in the name of Benno von Archimboldi. And yet, that reservation was never confirmed and at the departure time no Benno von Archimboldi appeared at the airport. By the Serb's lights, the matter couldn't be clearer. Archimboldi had doubtless made the reservation himself. We can imagine him at his hotel, likely upset about something or other, maybe drunk, perhaps even half asleep, at that abysslike hour (with its ineffably nauseating scent) when momentous decisions are made, speaking to the girl at Alitalia and mistakenly giving her his pen name instead of booking the seat under the name on his passport, an error that later, the next day, he would rectify by going in person to the airline office and buying a ticket in his own name. This explained the absence of an Archimboldi on the flight to Morocco. Of course, there were other possibilities: at the last minute, after having second (or fourth) thoughts, Archimboldi may have decided not to take the trip, or to travel somewhere else instead, say the United States, or maybe it was all simply a joke or misunderstanding.

The Serb's text contained a physical description of Archimboldi. This description was plainly based on the Swabian's account. Of course, in the Swabian's account Archimboldi was a young postwar writer. All the Serbian had done was age him, turning that same young man, who had traveled with his single published book to Friesland in 1949, into an old man, seventy-five or eighty, who now had a substantial oeuvre behind him but the same attributes more or less, as if Archimboldi, unlike most people, hadn't changed and were still the same person. To judge by his work, our writer is unquestionably a stubborn man, said the Serb, he's stubborn as a mule, as a pachyderm, and if during the saddest stretch of a Sicilian afternoon he hatched a plan to travel to Morocco, no matter that he made the reservation under the name Archimboldi by mistake, instead of his legal name, there's no reason to think he might not have changed his mind the very next day and gone personally to the travel agency to buy the ticket, this time under his legal name and with his legal passport, and that he didn't set off, like any of the thousands of old men, German bachelors, who each day cross the skies alone heading for any of the countries of North Africa.

•

Old and alone, thought Pelletier. Just one of thousands of old men on their own. Like the *machine célibataire*. Like the bachelor who suddenly grows old, or like the bachelor who, when he returns from a trip at light speed, finds the other bachelors grown old or turned into pillars of salt.

Thousands, hundreds of thousands of *machines célibataires* crossing an amniotic sea each day, on Alitalia, eating *spaghetti al pomodoro* and drinking Chianti or grappa, their eyes half closed, positive that the paradise of retirees isn't in Italy (or, therefore, anywhere in Europe), bachelors flying to the hectic airports of Africa or America, burial ground of elephants. The great cemeteries at light speed. I don't know why I'm thinking this, thought Pelletier. Spots on the wall and spots on the skin, thought Pelletier, looking at his hands. Fuck the Serb.

•

In the end, after the article came out, Espinoza and Pelletier were forced to recognize flaws in the Serb's approach. There had to be research, literary criticism, interpretive essays, even informational pamphlets if required, but not this hybrid between science fiction and half-finished *roman noir*, said Espinoza, and Pelletier was in complete agreement.

•

Around this time, at the beginning of 1997, Norton felt a desire for change. To get away. To visit Ireland or New York. To distance herself abruptly from Espinoza and Pelletier. She summoned them both to London. Pelletier had a feeling that nothing serious would happen, nothing irrevocable at least, and he arrived calm, ready to listen and say little. By contrast, Espinoza feared the worst (that Norton had summoned them to tell them she preferred Pelletier, but also to assure him that they'd still be friends, maybe even to ask if he'd give her away at her approaching wedding).

Pelletier was the first to show up at Norton's apartment. He asked whether anything serious was wrong. Norton said she'd rather discuss it when Espinoza got there, to keep from making the same speech twice. As they had nothing else important to say, they began to talk about the weather. Pelletier soon rebelled and changed the subject. Then Norton started to talk about Archimboldi. This new subject of conversation almost did Pelletier in. He thought again about the Serb, he thought again about that poor writer, old and alone and possibly misanthropic (Archimboldi), he thought again about the lost years of his own life before Norton had appeared.

Espinoza was late. Life is shit, thought Pelletier in astonishment, all of it. And then: if we hadn't teamed up, she would be mine now. And then: if there hadn't been mutual understanding and friendship and affinity and alliance, she would be mine now. And a little later: if there hadn't been anything, I wouldn't even have met her. And: I might have met her, since each of us has an independent interest in Archimboldi that doesn't spring from our mutual friendship. And: it's possible, too, that she might have hated me, found me pedantic, cold, arrogant, narcissistic, an intellectual elitist. The term *intellectual elitist* amused him. Espinoza was late. Norton seemed very calm. Actually, Pelletier seemed very calm too, but that was far from how he felt.

Norton said there was nothing strange about Espinoza's lateness. Planes get delayed, she said. Pelletier imagined Espinoza's plane engulfed in flames, crashing onto a runway at the Madrid airport in a screech of twisted steel.

"Maybe we should turn on the television," he said.

Norton looked at him and smiled. I never turn on the television, she said, smiling, surprised that Pelletier didn't already know that. Of course, Pelletier did know it. But he hadn't had the spirit to say: let's watch the news, let's see whether some plane wreck appears on the screen.

"Can I turn it on?" he asked.

"Of course," said Norton, and as Pelletier bent over the knobs of the set, he saw her out of the corner of his eye, luminous, so natural, making a cup of tea or moving from one room to another, putting away a book that she had just shown him, answering the phone and talking to someone who wasn't Espinoza.

He turned on the television. He clicked through different channels. He saw a man with a beard dressed in cheap clothes. He saw a group of blacks walking along a dirt track. He saw two men in suits and ties talking slowly and deliberately, both with their legs crossed, both glancing every so often at a map that appeared and disappeared behind their backs. He saw a chubby woman saying: daughter . . . factory . . . meeting . . . doctors . . . inevitable, and then smiling a little and lowering her gaze. He saw the face of a Belgian minister. He saw the smoldering remains of a plane next to a runway, surrounded by ambulances and fire trucks. He shouted for Norton. She was still talking on the phone.

•

Espinoza's plane has crashed, said Pelletier, this time not raising his voice, and Norton, instead of looking at the television screen, looked at

58

him. It took her only a few seconds to realize that the plane in flames wasn't a Spanish plane. In addition to the firemen and rescue teams, passengers could be seen walking away, some limping, others wrapped in blankets, their faces contorted in fear or shock, but apparently unharmed.

•

Twenty minutes later, Espinoza arrived, and during lunch Norton told him that Pelletier had thought he was in the plane that went down. Espinoza laughed but gave Pelletier a strange look, which Norton didn't notice, but Pelletier caught immediately. It was a sad meal, all things considered, although Norton's behavior was perfectly normal, as if she had run into the two of them by chance and hadn't expressly asked them to come to London. They guessed what she had to tell them before she said anything: Norton wanted to end her romantic involvement with both of them, at least for the time being. The reason she gave was that she needed to think and get her bearings. Then she said she didn't want to stop being friends with either of them. She needed to think, that was all.

Espinoza accepted Norton's explanation without asking a single question. Pelletier would have liked to ask whether her ex-husband had anything to do with her decision, but following Espinoza's example, he kept quiet. After they ate they went out for a drive around London in Norton's car. Pelletier insisted on sitting in back, until he saw a sarcastic flash in Norton's eyes, and then he said he would sit anywhere, which happened to be the backseat.

As she drove along Cromwell Road, Norton said that maybe that night it would make most sense for her to sleep with both of them. Espinoza laughed and said something meant to be funny, a continuation of the joke, but Pelletier wasn't sure Norton was joking and he was even less sure he was ready to participate in a ménage à trois. Then they went to watch the sun set near the Peter Pan statue in Kensington Gardens. They sat on a bench by a giant oak tree, Norton's favorite spot, a place she'd been drawn to ever since she was a child. At first there were people lying on the grass, but little by little the area began to empty. Couples or elegantly dressed single women passed briskly, toward the Serpentine Gallery or the Albert Memorial, and in the opposite direction men with crumpled newspapers or mothers pushing baby carriages headed toward Bayswater Road.

As dusk fell, they watched a young Spanish-speaking couple approach the Peter Pan statue. The woman had black hair and was very pretty, and she reached out as if to touch Peter Pan's leg. The man beside her was tall and had a beard and mustache and pulled a notepad out of his pocket and jotted something down. Then he said out loud:

"Kensington Gardens."

The woman wasn't looking at the statue anymore but at the lake, or rather at something moving in the grass and weeds that separated the little path from the lake.

"What's she looking at?" asked Norton in German.

"It seems to be a snake," said Espinoza.

"There aren't any snakes here!" said Norton.

Then the woman called to the man: Rodrigo, come see this, she said. The man seemed not to hear. He had put the little notepad away in a pocket of his leather jacket and he was gazing silently at the statue of Peter Pan. The woman bent down and something beneath the leaves slithered toward the lake.

"It does actually seem to be a snake," said Pelletier.

"That's what I thought," said Espinoza.

Norton didn't answer but she stood to get a better look.

•

That night Pelletier and Espinoza slept for a few hours in Norton's sitting room. Although they had the sofa bed and the rug at their disposal, they had difficulty dozing off. Pelletier tried to talk, explain the plane wreck thing to Espinoza, but Espinoza said there was no need for explanations, he understood everything.

At four in the morning, by common accord, they turned on the light and started to read. Pelletier opened a book on the work of Berthe Morisot, the first woman impressionist, but soon he felt like hurling it against the wall. Espinoza, meanwhile, pulled Archimboldi's latest novel, *The Head*, out of his bag and started to go over the notes he had written in the margins, notes that were the nucleus of an essay he planned to publish in the journal edited by Borchmeyer.

Espinoza's thesis, also espoused by Pelletier, was that with this novel Archimboldi was drawing his literary adventures to a close. After *The Head*, said Espinoza, there'll be no new books on the market, an opinion that another illustrious Archimboldian, Dieter Hellfeld, considered too risky, based as it was on no more than the writer's age, and the same thing had been said when Archimboldi came out with *Railroad Perfection*; a few Berlin professors had even said it when *Bitzius* was published. At five in the morning Pelletier took a shower, then made coffee. At six Espinoza was asleep again but at six-thirty he woke in a foul mood. At a quarter to seven they called a cab and straightened up the sitting room.

Espinoza wrote a goodbye note. Pelletier glanced at it and after thinking for a few seconds, decided to leave another note himself. Before they left he asked Espinoza whether he didn't want to shower. I'll shower in Madrid, Espinoza answered. The water is better there. True, said Pelletier, although his reply struck him as stupid and appeasing. Then the two of them left without making a sound and had breakfast at the airport, as they'd done so many times before.

•

On the plane back to Paris, Pelletier began to think, inexplicably, about the Berthe Morisot book he'd wanted to slam against the wall the night before. Why? Pelletier asked himself. Was it that he didn't like Berthe Morisot or something she stood for in some momentary way? Actually, he liked Berthe Morisot. All at once it struck him that Norton hadn't bought the book, that he'd been the one who traveled from Paris to London with the gift-wrapped volume, that the first Berthe Morisot reproductions Norton had ever seen were the ones in that book, with Pelletier next to her, massaging the back of her neck and walking her through each painting. Did he regret having given her the book now? No, of course not. Did the painter have anything to do with their separation? The idea was ridiculous. Then why had he wanted to slam the book against the wall? And more to the point: why was he thinking about Berthe Morisot and the book and Norton's neck and not about the real possibility of a ménage à trois that had hovered in Norton's apartment that night like a howling Indian witch doctor without ever materializing?

•

On the plane back to Madrid, Espinoza, unlike Pelletier, thought about the book he believed to be Archimboldi's last novel, and how—if he was right, which he thought he was—there would be no more novels by Archimboldi, and he thought about all that entailed, and about a plane in flames and Pelletier's hidden desires (the son of a bitch could be oh so modern, but only when it was to his advantage), and every once in a while he looked out the window and glanced at the engines and dearly wished he was back in Madrid.

•

For a while Pelletier and Espinoza didn't call each other. Pelletier called Norton occasionally, although their conversations were increasingly, how to put it, stilted, as if good manners were the only thing sustaining their relationship, and he called Morini just as frequently as ever, for with him nothing had changed.

It was the same for Espinoza, although it took him a little longer to realize that Norton meant what she said. Naturally, Morini noticed something wrong, but out of discretion or laziness, the awkward and sometimes painful laziness that gripped him now and then, he preferred to behave as if he hadn't noticed, for which Pelletier and Espinoza were grateful.

Even Borchmeyer, who in some ways feared the tandem of Espinoza and Pelletier, noticed something new in the correspondence he maintained with each, veiled insinuations, tiny retractions, the faintest of doubts (all extremely eloquent, naturally, coming from them) about the methodology they had previously shared.

•

Then came an assembly of Germanists in Berlin, a twentieth-century German literature congress in Stuttgart, a symposium on German literature in Hamburg, and a conference on the future of German literature in Mainz. Norton, Morini, Pelletier, and Espinoza attended the Berlin assembly, but for one reason or another all four of them were able to meet only once, at breakfast, where they were surrounded by other Germanists fighting doggedly over the butter and jam. Pelletier, Espinoza, and Norton attended the congress, and just as Pelletier managed to speak to Norton alone (while Espinoza was exchanging views with Schwarz), when it was Espinoza's turn to talk to Norton, Pelletier went off discreetly with Dieter Hellfeld.

This time Norton noticed that her friends were doing their best not to speak to each other, sometimes even avoiding each other's company, which couldn't help affecting her since she felt in some way responsible for the rift between them.

Only Espinoza and Morini attended the symposium, and since they were in Hamburg anyway and killing time they went to visit the Bubis publishing house and paid their compliments to Schnell, but they couldn't see Mrs. Bubis, for whom they'd brought a bouquet of roses, since she was on a trip to Moscow. That woman, Schnell said to them, I don't know where she gets her energy, and then he gave a pleased laugh that Espinoza and Morini thought was a bit much. Before they left the publishing house they gave the roses to Schnell.

Only Pelletier and Espinoza attended the conference, and this time they had no choice but to meet and lay their cards on the table. At first, as was natural, they tried to avoid each other, politely most of the time or brusquely on a few occasions, but in the end there was nothing to do but talk. This event took place at the hotel bar, late at night, when only one waiter was left, the youngest one, a tall, blond, sleepy boy.

Pelletier was sitting at one end of the bar and Espinoza at the other. Then the bar began gradually to empty, and when only the two of them were left Pelletier got up and sat down next to Espinoza. They tried to discuss the conference, but after a few minutes it came to seem ridiculous going on, or pretending to go on, in that vein. Once again it was Pelletier, better versed in the art of conciliation and confidences, who took the first step. He asked how Norton was. Espinoza confessed he didn't know. Then he said that he called her sometimes and it was like talking to a stranger. This last part Pelletier inferred, because Espinoza, who at times expressed himself in unintelligible ellipses, didn't call Norton a stranger but used the word *busy*, then the word *distracted*. For a while, the phone in Norton's apartment floated in their conversation. A white telephone in the grasp of a white hand, the white forearm of a stranger. But she wasn't a stranger. Not insofar as both had slept with her. Oh white hind, little hind, white hind, murmured Espinoza. Pelletier assumed he was quoting a classic, but without comment asked him whether they were really going to become enemies. The question seemed to surprise Espinoza, as if the possibility had never occurred to him.

"That's absurd, Jean-Claude," he said, although Pelletier noticed he thought for a long time before he answered.

By the end of the night, they were drunk and the young waiter had to help them both out of the bar. What Pelletier remembered best was the strength of the waiter who hauled them, one on each side, to the elevators in the lobby, as if he and Espinoza were adolescents, no older than

63

fifteen, two weedy adolescents clamped in the powerful arms of this young German who had stayed until closing time, when all the veteran waiters had already gone home, a country boy, to judge by his face and build, or a laborer, and he also remembered something like a whisper that he later understood was a kind of laugh, Espinoza's laugh as he was lugged by the peasant waiter, a soft chuckle, a discreet laugh, as if the situation weren't merely ridiculous but also an escape valve for his unspoken sorrows.

•

One day, when more than three months had gone by since their visit to Norton, one of them called the other and suggested a weekend in London. It's unclear whether Pelletier or Espinoza made the call. In theory, it must have been the one with the strongest sense of loyalty, or of friendship, which amounts to the same thing, but in truth neither Pelletier nor Espinoza had a strong sense of any such virtue. Both of them paid it lip service, of course. But in practice, neither believed in friendship or loyalty. They believed in passion, they believed in a hybrid form of social or public happiness (both voted Socialist, albeit with the occasional abstention), they believed in the possibility of self-realization.

The salient point is that one called and the other said yes, and one Friday afternoon they met at the London airport and got a cab to a hotel, then another cab, now very close to dinnertime (they had made a reservation for three at Jane & Chloe), to Norton's apartment.

From the sidewalk, after they paid the driver, they looked up at the lighted windows. Then, as the cab drove off, they saw Liz's silhouette, the beloved silhouette, and then, as if a breath of foul air had wafted into a commercial for sanitary pads, the silhouette of a man that made them freeze, Espinoza with a bouquet of flowers in his hand, Pelletier with a Jacob Epstein book wrapped in the finest paper. But the pantomime above didn't end there. In one window, Norton's silhouette gestured, as if trying to explain something that her interlocutor refused to understand. In the other window, the man's silhouette, to the horror of its two gaping spectators, made a kind of hula-hooping motion, or what looked to Pelletier and Espinoza like a hula-hooping motion, first the hips, then the legs, the torso, even the neck! a motion that contained a hint of sarcasm and mockery, unless behind the curtains the man was undressing or melting, which seemed very unlikely; the motion, or the series of motions, expressed not only sarcasm but cruelty and assurance too, the assurance plain, since he was the strongest one in the apartment, the tallest, the most muscular, the hula-hooper.

And yet there was something strange about Liz's silhouette. To the extent that they knew her, and they thought they knew her well, Norton wasn't the sort to stand for slights, especially in her own apartment. So it was possible, they decided, that the man's silhouette wasn't actually hula-hooping or insulting Liz but laughing, and laughing with her, not at her. But Liz's silhouette didn't seem to be laughing. Then the man's silhouette disappeared: maybe he had gone to look at books, maybe to the bathroom or the kitchen. Maybe he had dropped onto the sofa, still laughing. And just then Norton's silhouette drew near the window, seeming to shrink, and then pushed back the curtains and opened the window. Norton's eyes were closed, as if she needed to breathe the night air of London, and then she opened her eyes and looked down, into the abyss, and saw them.

•

They called hello as if the taxi had just left them there. Espinoza waved his bouquet of flowers in the air and Pelletier his book, and then, without waiting to see Norton's confused face, they headed to the door of the building and waited for Liz to buzz them in.

They were sure all was lost. As they climbed the stairs, without talking, they heard a door being opened, and although they didn't see her, both sensed Norton's luminous presence on the landing. The apartment smelled of Dutch tobacco. Leaning in the doorway, Norton looked at them as if they were two friends who had died long ago, ghosts returning from the sea. The man waiting for them in the sitting room was younger, probably born in the seventies, not the sixties—even the midseventies. He was wearing a turtleneck sweater, although the neck seemed to sag, and faded jeans and sneakers. He looked like a student of Norton's or a substitute teacher.

Norton said his name was Alex Pritchard. A friend. Pelletier and Espinoza shook his hand and smiled, knowing their smiles would be pathetic. Pritchard didn't smile. Two minutes later they were all sitting drinking whiskey in silence. Pritchard, who was drinking orange juice, sat next to Norton and slung an arm over her shoulders, a gesture she didn't seem to mind at first (in fact, Pritchard's long arm was resting on the back of the sofa and only his fingers, long as a spider's or a pianist's, occasionally brushed Norton's blouse), but as the minutes went by Norton became more and more nervous and her trips to the kitchen or bedroom became more frequent.

Pelletier attempted a few subjects of conversation. He tried to talk about film, music, recent theater productions, without getting any help even from Espinoza, who seemed to vie with Pritchard in his muteness, although Pritchard's muteness was at least that of the observer, equal parts distracted and engaged, and Espinoza's muteness was that of the observed, sunk in misery and shame. Suddenly, without anyone being able to say for sure who had started it, they began to talk about Archimboldian studies. It was probably Norton, from the kitchen, who mentioned the work they all did. Pritchard waited for her to come back and then, his arm stretched once again along the back of the sofa and his spider fingers on Norton's shoulder, said he thought German literature was a scam.

Norton laughed, as if someone had told a joke. Pelletier asked him what he, Pritchard, knew about German literature.

"Not much, really," he said.

"Then you're a cretin," said Espinoza.

"Or an ignoramus, at least," said Pelletier.

"In any case, a *badulaque*," said Espinoza.

Espinoza had said *badulaque* in Spanish, and Pritchard didn't know what it meant. Norton didn't understand it either and wanted to know what it was.

"A *badulaque*," said Espinoza, "is someone of no consequence. It's a word that can also be applied to fools, but there are fools of consequence, and *badulaque* applies only to fools of no consequence."

"Are you insulting me?" Pritchard wanted to know.

"Do you feel insulted?" asked Espinoza, who had begun to sweat profusely.

Pritchard took a swallow of his orange juice and said that he did, he really did feel insulted.

"Then you have a problem, sir," said Espinoza.

"Typical reaction of a *badulaque*," added Pelletier.

Pritchard got up from the sofa. Espinoza got up from his armchair. Norton said that's enough, you're behaving like stupid children. Pelletier started to laugh. Pritchard went over to Espinoza and tapped him on the chest with his index finger, which was almost as long as his middle finger. He tapped his chest, one, two, three, four times, as he said:

"First: I don't like to be insulted. Second: I don't like to be taken for a fool. Third: I don't like it when some Spanish fucker takes the piss. Fourth: if you have anything else to say to me, let's go outside."

Espinoza looked at Pelletier and asked him, in German, of course, what he should do.

"Don't go outside," said Pelletier.

"Alex, leave now," said Norton.

And since Pritchard didn't really intend to hit anyone, he kissed Norton on the cheek and left without saying goodbye.

•

That night the three of them ate at Jane & Chloe. At first they were a little subdued, but the dinner and wine cheered them up and in the end they went home laughing. Still, they were reluctant to ask Norton who Pritchard was and she didn't say anything that might cast light on the lanky figure of that disagreeable youth. Instead, toward the end of dinner, they talked about themselves, about how close they'd come to destroying, possibly forever, the friendship they felt for one another.

Sex, they agreed, was too wonderful (although almost immediately they regretted the adjective) to get in the way of a friendship based as much on emotional as intellectual affinities. Pelletier and Espinoza took pains, however, to make it clear there in front of each other that the ideal thing for them, and they imagined for Norton too, was that she ultimately and in a nontraumatic way (try to make it a soft landing, said Pelletier) choose one of them, or neither of them, said Espinoza, either way the decision was in her hands, Norton's hands, and it was a decision she could make whenever she wanted, whenever was most convenient for her, or never make, put off, defer, postpone, draw out, delay, adjourn until her deathbed, they didn't care, because they were as in love with her now, while Liz was keeping them in limbo, as they had been before, when they were her active lovers or colovers, as in love with her as they would be when she chose one of them or the other, or when she (in a possible future that was only slightly more bitter, a future of shared bitterness, of somehow mitigated bitterness), if such was her wish, chose neither of them. To which Norton replied with a question, no doubt partly rhetorical, but a plausible question all the same: what would happen if, while she took her time considering the options, one of them, Pelletier for example, suddenly fell in love with a student who was younger and prettier than she, and richer, too, and more charming? Should she consider the pact broken and automatically give up on Espinoza? Or should she take the Spaniard, since he was the only one left? To which Pelletier and Espinoza responded that the real possibility of such a thing happening was extremely remote, and anyway she could do as she liked, even become a nun if she so desired.

"The only thing either of us wants is to marry you, live with you, have children with you, grow old with you, but at this point in our lives, what matters to us is preserving your friendship."

•

After that night, the plane trips to London began again. Sometimes it would be Espinoza who came to visit, other times Pelletier, and once in a while both. When this happened they would always stay at the same place, a small, uncomfortable hotel on Foley Street, near the Middlesex Hospital. When they left Norton's apartment, they would often take a walk near the hotel, usually in silence, frustrated, somehow exhausted by the goodwill and cheer they felt required to display during these joint visits. Many times they would just stand there under the streetlight on the corner, watching the ambulances going in and out. The English nurses spoke at the top of their lungs, although from where they stood the sound of the braying voices was muted.

One night, as they were watching the unusually quiet entrance to the hospital, they asked themselves why, when they came to London together, neither of them stayed at Liz's apartment. Out of politeness, probably, they said. But neither one of them believed in that kind of politeness anymore. And they also asked themselves, at first hesitantly and then vehemently, why the three of them didn't sleep together. That night a green, sickly light seeped from under the hospital doors, a transparent green swimming pool light, and an orderly smoked a cigarette, standing on the curb, and among the parked cars there was one with its light on, a yellow light as in a nest, though not just any nest but a post-nuclear nest, a nest with no room for any certainties but cold, despair, and apathy.

One night, while talking to Norton on the phone from Paris or Madrid, one of them brought the subject up. Surprisingly, Norton said she'd been asking herself the same question for a while.

"I don't think we'll ever suggest it," said the person on the phone.

"I know," said Norton. "You're afraid to. You're waiting for me to make the first move."

"I don't know," said the person on the phone, "maybe it isn't as simple as that."

They saw Pritchard again a few times. The lanky youth didn't seem as ill-humored as before, although in truth their encounters were fleeting, too brief for rudeness or violence. Espinoza was on his way into Norton's apartment as Pritchard was leaving; Pelletier crossed paths with him once on the stairs. Brief though it was, however, this latter encounter was significant. Pelletier said hello to Pritchard. Pritchard said hello to Pelletier, and after they had passed each other Pritchard turned around and called after Pelletier.

"Do you want some advice?" he asked. Pelletier gazed at him in alarm. "I know you don't, old man, but here it is. Be careful," said Pritchard.

"Careful of what?" Pelletier managed to ask.

"Of the Medusa," said Pritchard. "Beware of the Medusa."

And then, before he continued down the stairs, he added: "When you've got her in your hands she'll blow you to pieces."

For a while Pelletier stood there motionless, listening to Pritchard's footsteps on the stairs, then the noise of the street door opening and closing. Only when the silence became unbearable did he continue upstairs, thoughtful and in the dark.

•

He said nothing to Norton about the incident with Pritchard, but on his return to Paris he wasted no time calling Espinoza and telling him the story of the enigmatic encounter.

"Odd," said the Spaniard. "It sounds like a warning but also a threat."

"There's this, too," said Pelletier. "Medusa is one of the three daughters of Phorcys and Ceto, the so-called Gorgons, three sea monsters. According to Hesiod, the other two sisters, Stheno and Euryale, were immortal. But not Medusa."

"Have you been reading the Greek myths?" asked Espinoza.

"It's the first thing I did when I got home," said Pelletier. "Listen to this: when Perseus cut Medusa's head off, Chrysaor, father of the monster Geryon, emerged, and so did the horse Pegasus."

"Pegasus came out of Medusa's body? Fuck," said Espinoza.

"That's right. The winged horse Pegasus, which to me stands for love."

"You think Pegasus stands for love?"

"That's right."

"Strange," said Espinoza.

"It's a lycée thing," said Pelletier.

"And you think Pritchard knows this stuff?"

"Impossible," said Pelletier. "Although who's to say, but no, I doubt it."

"Then what do you think it all means?"

"I'd say Pritchard is alerting me, alerting us, to a danger we can't see. Or rather, he was trying to tell me that only after Norton's death would I, or we, find true love."

"After Norton's death?" said Espinoza.

"Of course, don't you understand? Pritchard sees himself as Perseus, Medusa's assassin."

•

For a while, Espinoza and Pelletier wandered around as if possessed. Archimboldi, who was again rumored to stand a clear chance for the Nobel, left them cold. They resented their work at the university, their periodic contributions to the journals of German departments around the world, their classes, and even the conferences they attended like sleepwalkers or drugged detectives. They were there but they weren't there. They talked, but their minds were on something else. Only Pritchard held their interest, the ominous presence of Pritchard, Norton's constant companion. A Pritchard who saw Norton as the Medusa, as a Gorgon, a Pritchard about whom, as reticent spectators, they knew almost nothing at all.

To fill in the gaps, they began to question the one person who could give them answers. At first Norton was reluctant to talk. He was a teacher, as they had suspected, though not at the university but at a secondary school. He wasn't from London but a town near Bournemouth. He had studied at Oxford for a year, and then, incomprehensibly to Espinoza and Pelletier, had moved to London and finished his studies there. He was on the Left, the *pragmatic* Left, and, according to Norton, on occasion he had mentioned plans (which never hardened into action) to become active in the Labour Party. The school where he taught was a council school with a good number of students from immigrant families.

He was headstrong and generous and lacked imagination, something Pelletier and Espinoza had already gathered. But that didn't make them feel any better.

"A bastard may have no imagination and then do one imaginative thing when you least expect it," said Espinoza.

"England is full of swine like him," was Pelletier's opinion.

Talking on the phone one night, they discovered without surprise (without even a shadow of surprise) that both of them hated Pritchard, and that they hated him more each day.

•

During the next conference they attended ("Reflecting the Twentieth Century: The Work of Benno von Archimboldi," a two-day event in Bologna packed with young Italian Archimboldians and a crop of Archimboldian neostructuralists from all over Europe), they decided to tell Morini everything that had happened to them in the last few months and all the fears they harbored concerning Norton and Pritchard.

Morini, whose health had deteriorated slightly since the last time (although neither Espinoza nor Pelletier knew), listened patiently at the hotel bar and at a trattoria near the conference headquarters and at an extremely expensive restaurant in the old part of the city and also as they strolled aimlessly along the streets of Bologna, Espinoza and Pelletier pushing Morini's wheelchair and talking nonstop. In the end, when they requested his opinion on the romantic imbroglio, real or imaginary, in which they found themselves, Morini only asked if either of them, or both, had asked Norton whether she loved Pritchard or was attracted to him. They had to confess that out of delicacy, tact, and good taste—out of consideration for Norton, essentially—they hadn't asked.

"Well, that's where you should have begun," said Morini, who, although he felt ill, and dizzy, too, after taking so many turns, breathed not a sigh of complaint.

•

(And at this point it must be said that there's truth to the saying *make your name, then sleep and reap fame*, because Espinoza's and Pelletier's participation in the conference "Reflecting the Twentieth Century: The Work of Benno von Archimboldi," not to mention their contribution to it, was at best null, at worst catatonic, as if they were suddenly spent or ab-

sent, prematurely aged or in a state of shock, a fact that didn't pass unnoticed by the attendees used to Espinoza's and Pelletier's displays of
energy [sometimes brazen] at this sort of event, nor did it go unnoticed
by the latest litter of Archimboldians, recent graduates, boys and girls,
their doctorates tucked still warm under their arms, who planned, by any
means necessary, to impose their particular readings of Archimboldi, like
missionaries ready to instill faith in God, even if to do so meant signing
a pact with the devil, for most were what you might call rationalists, not
in the philosophical sense but in the pejorative literal sense, denoting
people less interested in literature than in literary criticism, the one
field, according to them—some of them, anyway—where revolution was
still possible, and in some way they behaved not like youths but like *nouveaux* youths, in the sense that there are the rich and the *nouveaux
riches*, all of them generally rational thinkers, let us repeat, although often incapable of telling their asses from their elbows, and although they
noticed a there and a not-there, an absence-presence in the fleeting passage of Pelletier and Espinoza through Bologna, they were incapable of
seeing what was really important: Pelletier's and Espinoza's absolute
boredom regarding everything said there about Archimboldi or their neg-
ligent disregard for the gaze of others, as if the two were so much cannibal fodder, a disregard lost on the young conferencegoers, those eager
and insatiable cannibals, their thirtysomething faces bloated with success, their expressions shifting from boredom to madness, their coded
stutterings speaking only two words: *love me*, or maybe two words and a
phrase: *love me, let me love you*, though obviously no one understood.)

•

So Pelletier and Espinoza, who drifted through Bologna like two ghosts,
asked Norton on their next visit to London, almost panting, as if they'd
been running or jogging (without pause, in dreams or in reality), whether
she, their beloved Liz who hadn't been able to go to Bologna, loved or
lusted after Pritchard.

And Norton told them no. And then she said maybe she did, it was
hard to give a conclusive answer in that regard. And Pelletier and Espinoza said they needed to know, that is, they needed definitive confirmation. And Norton asked them why now, precisely, they were so
interested in Pritchard.

And Pelletier and Espinoza said, almost on the verge of tears, if not
now, when?

And Norton asked whether they were jealous. And they said that was simply too much, jealousy had nothing to do with it, it was almost an insult to accuse them of being jealous considering the nature of their friendship.

And Norton said it was only a question. And Pelletier and Espinoza said they weren't prepared to answer such a hurtful or captious or ill-intentioned question. And then they went out to dinner and the three of them drank too much, happy as children, talking about jealousy and its disastrous consequences. And they also talked about the inevitability of jealousy. And about the need for jealousy, as if jealousy were a middle-of-the-night urge. Not to mention the sweetness and the open, in some cases, to some people, delectable wounds. And on the way out they got in a cab and the discourse went on.

And for the first few minutes, the driver, a Pakistani, watched them in his rearview mirror, in silence, as if he couldn't believe what his ears were hearing, and then he said something in his language and the cab passed Harmsworth Park and the Imperial War Musuem, heading along Brook Drive and then Austral Street and then Geraldine Street, driving around the park, an unnecessary maneuver no matter how you looked at it. And when Norton told him he was lost and said which streets he should take to find his way, the driver fell silent again, with no more murmurings in his incomprehensible tongue, until he confessed that London was such a labyrinth, he really had lost his bearings.

Which led Espinoza to remark that he'd be damned if the cabbie hadn't just quoted Borges, who once said London was like a labyrinth—unintentionally, of course. To which Norton replied that Dickens and Stevenson had used the same trope long before Borges in their descriptions of London. This seemed to set the driver off, for he burst out that as a Pakistani he might not know this Borges, and he might not have read the famous Dickens and Stevenson either, and he might not even know London and its streets as well as he should, that's why he'd said they were like a labyrinth, but he knew very well what decency and dignity were, and by what he had heard, the woman here present, in other words Norton, was lacking in decency and dignity, and in his country there was a word for what she was, the same word they had for it in London as it happened, and the word was *bitch* or *slut* or *pig*, and the gentlemen here present, gentlemen who, to judge by their accents, weren't English, also had a name in his country and that name was *pimp* or *hustler* or *whoremonger*.

This speech, it may be said without exaggeration, took the Archimboldians by surprise, and they were slow to respond. If they were on Geraldine Street when the driver let them have it, they didn't manage to speak till they came to Saint George's Road. And then all they managed to say was: stop the cab right here, we're getting out. Or rather: stop this filthy car, we're not going any farther. Which the Pakistani promptly did, punching the meter as he pulled up to the curb and announcing to his passengers what they owed him, a fait accompli or final scene or parting token that seemed more or less normal to Norton and Pelletier, no doubt still reeling from the ugly surprise, but which was absolutely the last straw for Espinoza, who stepped down and opened the driver's door and jerked the driver out, the latter not expecting anything of the sort from such a well-dressed gentleman. Much less did he expect the hail of Iberian kicks that proceeded to rain down on him, kicks delivered at first by Espinoza alone, but then by Pelletier, too, when Espinoza flagged, despite Norton's shouts at them to stop, despite Norton's objecting that violence didn't solve anything, that in fact after this beating the Pakistani would hate the English even more, something that apparently mattered little to Pelletier, who wasn't English, and even less to Espinoza, both of whom nevertheless insulted the Pakistani in English as they kicked him, without caring in the least that he was down, curled into a ball on the ground, as they delivered kick after kick, shove Islam up your ass, which is where it belongs, this one is for Salman Rushdie (an author neither of them happened to think was much good but whose mention seemed pertinent), this one is for the feminists of Paris (will you fucking stop, Norton was shouting), this one is for the feminists of New York (you're going to kill him, shouted Norton), this one is for the ghost of Valerie Solanas, you son of a bitch, and on and on, until he was unconscious and bleeding from every orifice in the head, except the eyes.

•

When they stopped kicking him they were sunk for a few seconds in the strangest calm of their lives. It was as if they'd finally had the ménage à trois they'd so often dreamed of.

Pelletier felt as if he had come. Espinoza felt the same, to a slightly different degree. Norton, who was staring at them without seeing them in the dark, seemed to have experienced multiple orgasms. A few cars were passing by on St. George's Road, but the three of them were invisible to anyone traveling in a vehicle at that hour. There wasn't a single star in the sky. And yet the night was clear: they could see everything in great detail, even the outlines of the smallest things, as if an angel had suddenly clapped night-vision goggles on their eyes. Their skin felt smooth, extremely soft to the touch, although in fact the three of them were sweating. For a moment Espinoza and Pelletier thought they'd killed the Pakistani. A similar idea seemed to be passing through Norton's mind, because she bent over the cabbie and felt for his pulse. To move, to kneel down, hurt her as if the bones of her legs were dislocated.

A group of people came from Garden Row singing a song. They were laughing. Three men and two women. Without moving, Norton, Pelletier, and Espinoza turned their heads toward them and waited. The group began to walk in their direction.

"The cab," said Pelletier, "they want the cab."

Only at that moment did they realize the interior light of the cab was still on.

"Let's go," said Espinoza.

Pelletier took Norton by the shoulders and helped her up. Espinoza had gotten behind the wheel and was urging them to hurry. Pelletier pushed Norton into the backseat and then got in himself. The group from Garden Row headed straight toward the spot where the driver lay.

"He's alive, he's breathing," said Norton.

Espinoza started the car and they drove away. On the other side of the Thames, on a little street near Old Marylebone, they left the cab and walked for a while. They wanted to talk to Norton, explain what had happened, but she wouldn't even let them take her home.

•

The next day, as they ate a big breakfast at the hotel, they searched the papers for news about the Pakistani cabbie, but he wasn't mentioned anywhere. After breakfast they went out to get the tabloids. They didn't find anything there either.

They called Norton, who didn't seem as angry as she had the night before. They said they had to see her that afternoon. There was something important they needed to tell her. Norton said she had something important to tell them, too. To kill time they went out for a walk around the neighborhood. For a few minutes they entertained themselves by watching the ambulances coming in and out of Middlesex Hospital, imagining that each sick or hurt person who went in looked like the Pakistani they'd beaten so badly, until they got bored and went for a walk, their minds calmer, along Charing Cross toward the Strand. They confided in each other, as is natural. They shared their innermost feelings. What worried them most was that the police would come after them and catch them in the end.

"Before I got out of the cab," confessed Espinoza, "I wiped my fingerprints away with a handkerchief."

"I know," said Pelletier, "I saw you do it and I did the same. I wiped my fingerprints away, and Liz's, too."

More calmly each time, they went over and over the concatenation of events that had driven them, finally, to give the cabbie a beating. Pritchard, no question about it. And the Gorgon, that innocent and mortal Medusa, set apart from her immortal sisters. And the veiled or not so veiled threat. And nerves. And the rudeness of that ignorant wretch. They wished they had a radio so they could hear the latest news. They talked about what they'd felt as they rained blows on the fallen body. A combination of sleepiness and sexual desire. Desire to fuck the poor bastard? Not at all! More as if they were fucking themselves. As if they were digging into themselves. With long nails and empty hands. Though if your fingernails are long enough your hands are never really empty. But in this dreamlike state, they dug and dug, rending fabric and ripping veins and puncturing vital organs. What were they looking for? They didn't know. Nor, at that stage, did they care.

●

In the afternoon they saw Norton and they told her everything they knew or feared about Pritchard. The Gorgon, the death of the Gorgon. The exploding woman. She let them talk until they ran out of words. Then she soothed them. Pritchard couldn't hurt a fly, she said. They thought of Anthony Perkins, who claimed he wouldn't hurt a fly and look what happened, but they were content not to argue and they accepted her arguments, unconvinced. Then Norton sat down and said that the thing that couldn't be explained was what had happened the night before.

As if to divert blame, they asked her whether she'd heard anything about the Pakistani. Norton said she had. There'd been something on a local television station. A group of friends, probably the people they saw coming from Garden Row, had found the driver's body and called the police. He had four broken ribs, a concussion, a broken nose, and he'd lost all his top teeth. Now he was in the hospital.

"It was my fault," said Espinoza. "When he said what I did, I lost control."

"It would be best if we didn't see each other for a while," said Norton, "I have to think this over."

Pelletier agreed, but Espinoza kept blaming himself: it seemed fair that Norton should stop seeing him but not that she should stop seeing Pelletier.

"Stop talking nonsense," Pelletier said to him in a low voice, and only then did Espinoza realize that what he was saying was, in fact, stupid.

That night they both flew home.

•

When he got back to Madrid, Espinoza had a minor breakdown. In the cab home he started to cry, discreetly, covering his eyes with his hand, but the driver saw him crying and asked him if anything was wrong, whether he felt ill.

"I feel all right," said Espinoza, "I'm just a little on edge."

"Are you from here?" asked the driver.

"Yes," said Espinoza, "I was born in Madrid."

For a while neither of them said anything. Then the driver renewed his attack and asked whether he was interested in soccer. Espinoza said no, he'd never been interested in soccer or any other sport. And he added, as if not to put an abrupt end to the conversation, that the night before he had almost killed a man.

"Really," said the driver.

"That's right," said Espinoza, "I almost killed him."

"How's that?" asked the driver.

"It was in a rage," said Espinoza.

"Abroad?" asked the driver.

"Yes," said Espinoza, laughing for the first time, "far from here, and the man had a strange job, too."

Pelletier, meanwhile, neither had a breakdown nor talked to the driver who brought him back to his apartment. When he got home he took a shower and made himself some pasta with olive oil and cheese.

Then he checked his e-mail, answered a few messages, and went to bed with a novel by a young French author, nothing of great significance but amusing, and a journal of literary studies. A little while later he was asleep and he had the following extremely strange dream: he was married to Norton and they lived in a big house, near a cliff from which one could see a beach full of people in bathing suits lying in the sun or swimming, though never getting too far from shore.

The days were short. From his window he watched an almost unending succession of sunrises and sunsets. From time to time Norton would approach the room he was in and say something to him, but she never crossed the threshold. The people on the beach were always there. Sometimes he had the impression that at night they didn't go home, or that they all left together when it was dark, returning in a long procession before the sun came up. Other times, if he closed his eyes, he could soar over the beach like a seagull and see the bathers from up close. They came in every shape and size, although most were adults, in their thirties, forties, fifties, and all gave the impression of being focused on foolish activities, like rubbing oil on themselves, eating sandwiches, listening with more politeness than interest to the conversation of friends, relatives, or towel mates. Sometimes, however, the bathers would get up circumspectly and gaze at the horizon, even if for only a second or two. It was a calm horizon, cloudless, of a transparent blue.

When Pelletier opened his eyes he thought about the bathers' behavior. It was clear they were waiting for something, but you couldn't say there was anything desperate in their waiting. Every once in a while they'd simply look more alert, their eyes scanning the horizon for a second or two, and then they would once again become part of the flow of time on the beach, fluidly, without a moment of hesitation. Absorbed in watching the bathers, Pelletier forgot about Norton, trusting, perhaps, in her presence in the house, a presence evidenced by the noises that occasionally drifted from within, from the rooms that had no windows or windows that overlooked the fields or the mountains, not the sea or the crowded beach. He slept, or so he discovered deep into the dream, sitting in a chair, near his desk and the window. And he didn't seem to do much sleeping. Even when the sun set he tried to stay awake as long as possible, with his eyes fixed on the beach, now a black canvas or the bottom of a well, watching for any light, the trace of a flashlight, the flickering flame of a bonfire. He lost all notion of time. He vaguely remembered a confusing scene, at once embarrassing and exciting. The papers he had on the table were manuscripts by Archimboldi, or at least that was what he'd been told when he bought them, although when he looked through them he realized that they were written in French, not German. Next to him was a phone that never rang. The days grew hotter and hotter.

One morning, near midday, he saw the bathers halt their activities and turn to watch the horizon, all at once, in the usual way. Nothing happened. But then, for the first time, the bathers turned around and began to leave the beach. Some headed along a dirt road between two hills. Others struck off cross-country, clinging to bushes and stones. A few moved toward the cliff and Pelletier couldn't see them but he knew they were beginning a slow climb. All that was left on the beach was a mass, a dark form projecting from a yellow pit. For an instant Pelletier wondered whether he should go down to the beach and bury the mass at the bottom of the hole, taking all necessary precautions. But just imagining how far he would have to walk to get to the beach made him sweat, and he kept sweating more and more, as if once you turned the spigot you couldn't turn it off.

And then he spied a tremor in the sea, as if the water were sweating too, or as if it were about to boil. A barely perceptible simmer that spilled into ripples, building into waves that came to die on the beach. And then Pelletier felt dizzy and a hum of bees came from outside. And when the hum faded, a silence that was even worse fell over the house and everywhere around. And Pelletier shouted Norton's name and called to her, but no one answered his calls, as if the silence had swallowed up his cries for help. And then Pelletier began to weep and he watched as what was left of a statue emerged from the bottom of the metallic sea. A formless chunk of stone, gigantic, eroded by time and water, though a hand, a wrist, part of a forearm could still be made out with total clarity. And this statue came out of the sea and rose above the beach and it was horrific and at the same time very beautiful.

•

For a few days, Pelletier and Espinoza were, quite independently, filled with remorse by the business with the Pakistani driver, which circled in their guilty consciences like a ghost or an electric charge.

Espinoza wondered whether his behavior didn't reveal what he truly was, in other words a violent, xenophobic reactionary. Pelletier's guilt, on the other hand, was driven by having kicked the Pakistani when he was already on the ground, which was frankly unsportsmanlike. What need was there for that? he asked himself. The cabbie had already got what he deserved and there was no need to heap violence on violence.

One night the two of them talked on the phone for a long time. They expressed their respective fears. They comforted each other. But after a few minutes they were again lamenting what had happened, even though deep inside they were convinced that it was the Pakistani who was the real reactionary and misogynist, the violent one, the intolerant and offensive one, that the Pakistani had asked for it a thousand times over. The truth is that at moments like these, if the Pakistani had materialized before them, they probably would have killed him.

•

For a long time they forgot their weekly trips to London. They forgot Pritchard and the Gorgon. They forgot Archimboldi, whose renown continued to grow while their backs were turned. They forgot their papers, which they wrote in a perfunctory and uninspired way and which were really the work of their acolytes or of assistant professors from their respective departments recruited for the Archimboldian cause on the basis of vague promises of tenure-track positions or higher pay.

During a conference, as Pohl was giving a brilliant lecture on Archimboldi and shame in postwar German literature, the two visited a brothel in Berlin, where they slept with two tall and long-legged blondes. Upon leaving, near midnight, they were so happy they began to sing like children in the pouring rain. The experience, something new in their lives, was repeated several times in different European cities and finally ended up becoming part of their daily routine in Paris and Madrid. Others might have slept with students. They, afraid of falling in love, or of falling out of love with Norton, turned to whores.

In Paris, Pelletier went looking for them on the Internet, with excellent results. In Madrid, Espinoza found them by reading the sex ads in *El País*, which provided a much more reliable and practical service than the newspaper's arts pages, where Archimboldi was hardly ever mentioned and Portuguese heroes abounded, just as in the arts pages of *ABC*.

"You know," complained Espinoza in his conversations with Pelletier, perhaps seeking some consolation, "we Spaniards have always been provincials."

"True," replied Pelletier, after considering his answer for exactly two seconds.

Nor did they emerge unscathed from their adventures in prostitution.

•

Pelletier met a girl called Vanessa. She was married and had a son. Sometimes she would go weeks without seeing her husband and son. According to her, her husband was a saint. He had some flaws—for example he was an Arab, Moroccan to be precise, plus he was lazy—but overall, according to Vanessa, he was a good person, who almost never got angry about anything, and when he did, he wasn't violent or cruel like other men but instead melancholy, sad, filled with sorrow in the face of a world that suddenly struck him as overwhelming and incomprehensible. When Pelletier asked whether the Arab knew she worked as a prostitute, Vanessa said he did, that he knew but didn't care, because he believed in the freedom of individuals.

"Then he's your pimp," said Pelletier.

To this Vanessa replied that he might be, that if you thought about it he probably was, but he wasn't like other pimps, who were always demanding too much of their women. The Moroccan made no demands. There were periods, said Vanessa, when she, too, lapsed into a kind of habitual laziness, a persistent languor, and then money was tight. At times like these, the Moroccan contented himself with what there was and tried, without much luck, to find odd jobs so the three of them could scrape by. He was a Muslim, and sometimes he prayed toward Mecca, but clearly he was his own kind of Muslim. According to him, Allah permitted everything, or almost everything. To consciously hurt a child was not allowed. To abuse a child, kill a child, abandon a child to certain death, was forbidden. Everything else was relative and, in the end, permitted.

At some point, Vanessa told Pelletier, they had traveled to Spain. She, her son, and the Moroccan. In Barcelona they met up with the Moroccan's younger brother, who lived with another Frenchwoman, a tall, fat girl. They were musicians, the Moroccan told Vanessa, but really they were beggars. She had never seen the Moroccan so happy. He was constantly laughing and telling stories and he never got tired of walking around Barcelona, all the way to the suburbs or the mountains with views of the whole city and the gleam of the Mediterranean. Never, according to Vanessa, had she seen a man with such energy. Children, yes. A few, not many. But no adults.

When Pelletier asked Vanessa whether her son was the Moroccan's son too, she answered that he wasn't, and something about the way she said it made it plain that the question struck her as offensive or hurtful, an insult to her son. He was light-skinned, almost blond, she said, and he had turned six by the time she met the Moroccan, if she remembered correctly. A terrible time in my life, she said without going into details. The Moroccan's appearance could hardly be called providential. When she met him, it was a bad time for her, but he was literally starving.

Pelletier liked Vanessa and they saw each other several times. She was a tall girl, with a straight Greek nose and a steely, arrogant gaze. Her disdain for culture, especially book culture, was schoolgirlish somehow, a combination of innocence and elegance so thoroughly immaculate, or so Pelletier believed, that Vanessa could make the most idiotic remarks without provoking the slightest annoyance. One night, after they had made love, Pelletier got up naked and went looking among his books for a novel by Archimboldi. After hesitating for a moment he decided on *The Leather Mask*, thinking that with some luck Vanessa might read it as a horror novel, might be attracted by the sinister side of the book. She was surprised at first by the gift, then touched, since she was used to her clients giving her clothes or shoes or lingerie. Really, she was very happy with it, especially when Pelletier explained who Archimboldi was and the role the German writer played in his life.

"It's as if you were giving me a part of you," said Vanessa.

This remark left Pelletier a bit confused, since in a way it was perfectly true, Archimboldi was by now a part of him, the author belonged to him insofar as Pelletier had, along with a few others, instituted a new reading of the German, a reading that would endure, a reading as ambitious as Archimboldi's writing, and this reading would keep pace with Archimboldi's writing for a long time, until the reading was exhausted or until Archimboldi's writing—the capacity of the Archimboldian oeuvre to spark emotion and revelations—was exhausted (but he didn't believe that would happen), though in another way it wasn't true, because sometimes, especially since he and Espinoza had given up their trips to London and stopped seeing Norton, Archimboldi's work, his novels and stories, that is, seemed completely foreign, a shapeless and mysterious verbal mass, something that appeared and disappeared capriciously, literally a pretext, a false door, a murderer's alias, a hotel bathtub full of amniotic liquid in which he, Jean-Claude Pelletier, would end up committing suicide for no reason, gratuitously, in bewilderment, just because.

As he expected, Vanessa never told him what she thought of the book. One morning he went home with her. She lived in a working-class neighborhood full of immigrants. When they got there, her son was watching TV and Vanessa scolded him because he hadn't gone to school. The boy said he had a stomachache and Vanessa immediately made him some herbal tea. Pelletier watched her move around the kitchen. The energy Vanessa expended was boundless and ninety percent of it was lost in wasted movement. The house was a complete mess, which he attributed in part to the boy and the Moroccan, though it was essentially her fault.

Soon, drawn by the noise from the kitchen (spoons dropping on the floor, a broken glass, shouts demanding to know of no one in particular where the hell the tea was), the Moroccan appeared. Without anyone introducing them, they shook hands. The Moroccan was small and thin. Soon the boy would be taller and stronger than he was. He had a heavy mustache and he was balding. After greeting Pelletier he sat on the sofa, still half asleep, and began to watch cartoons with the boy. When Vanessa came out of the kitchen, Pelletier told her he had to leave.

"That's fine with me," she said.

He thought there was something belligerent about her reply, but then he remembered Vanessa was like that. The boy took a sip of the tea and said it needed sugar, then he left the steaming glass untouched. A few leaves floated in the liquid, leaves that struck Pelletier as strange and suspicious.

That morning, while he was at the university, he spent his idle moments thinking about Vanessa. When he saw her again they didn't make love, though he paid her as if they had, and they talked for hours. Before he fell asleep, Pelletier had come to some conclusions. Vanessa was perfectly suited to live in the Middle Ages, emotionally as well as physically. For her, the concept of "modern life" was meaningless. She had much more faith in what she could see than in the media. She was mistrustful and brave, although paradoxically her bravery made her trust people—

waiters, train conductors, friends in trouble, for example—who almost always let her down or betrayed her trust. These betrayals drove her wild and could lead her into unthinkably violent situations. She held grudges, too, and she boasted of saying things to people's faces without beating around the bush. She considered herself a free woman and had an answer for everything. Whatever she didn't understand didn't interest her. She never thought about the future, even her son's future, but only the present, a perpetual present. She was pretty but didn't consider herself pretty. More than half her friends were Moroccan immigrants, but she, who never got around to voting for Le Pen, saw immigration as a danger to France.

"Whores are there to be fucked," Espinoza said the night Pelletier talked to him about Vanessa, "not psychoanalyzed."

•

Espinoza, unlike his friend, didn't remember any of their names. On one side were the bodies and faces, and on the other side, flowing in a kind of ventilation tube, the Lorenas, the Lolas, the Martas, the Paulas, the Susanas, names without bodies, faces without names.

He never saw the same girl twice. He was with a Dominican, a Brazilian, three Andalusians, a Catalan woman. He learned from the start to be the silent type, the well-dressed man who pays and makes it known what he wants, sometimes with a gesture, and then gets dressed and leaves as if he'd never been there. He met a Chilean who advertised herself as a Chilean and a Colombian who advertised herself as a Colombian, as if the two nationalities held a special fascination. He did it with a Frenchwoman, two Poles, a Russian, a Ukrainian, a German. One night he slept with a Mexican and that was the best.

As always, they went to a hotel, and when he woke up in the morning the Mexican was gone. That day was strange. As if something inside of him had burst. He spent a long time sitting in bed, naked, with his feet resting on the floor, trying to remember something vague. When he got in the shower he realized that he had a mark on his inner thigh. It was as if someone had sucked there or set a leech on his left leg. The bruise was as big as a child's fist. The first thing he thought was that the whore had given him a love bite, and he tried to remember it, but he couldn't, the only images that came were of him on top of her, her legs around his shoulders, and some vague, indecipherable words, whether spoken by him or the Mexican he wasn't sure, probably obscene.

For a few days he thought he'd forgotten her, until one night he found himself searching for her along the streets of Madrid where the whores went or in the Casa de Campo. One night he thought he saw her and he followed her and touched her shoulder. The woman who turned around was Spanish and didn't look like the Mexican whore at all. Another night, in a dream, he thought he remembered what she'd said. He realized that he was dreaming, realized the dream was going to end badly, realized there was a good chance he would forget her words and maybe that was for the best, but he resolved to do everything he could to remember them before he woke up. In the middle of the dream, with the sky spinning in slow motion, he even tried to force himself awake, to turn on the light, to shout so that the sound of his own voice would return him to wakefulness, but the bulbs in the house seemed to have burned out and instead of a shout all he heard was a distant moan, as if of a boy or a girl or maybe an animal sheltering in a faraway room.

When he woke up, of course, he couldn't remember a thing, except that he had dreamed about the Mexican, that she was standing in the middle of a long, dimly lit hallway and he was watching her, unseen. The Mexican seemed to read something written in felt-tip pen on the wall, graffiti or obscene messages that she was spelling out slowly, as if she didn't know how to read. He kept looking for her for a few more days, but then he got tired of it and slept with a Hungarian, two Spanish women, a Gambian, a Senegalese, and an Argentinian. He never dreamed of her again, and finally he managed to forget her.

•

Time, which heals all wounds, finally erased the sense of guilt that had been instilled in them by the violent episode in London. One day they returned to their respective labors as fresh as daisies. They began writing and attending conferences again with uncommon energy, as if the time of the whores had been a Mediterranean rest cruise. They got back in touch with Morini, whom they'd somehow sidelined at first during their adventures and then forgotten altogether. They found the Italian in slightly worse health than usual, but just as warm, intelligent, and discreet, which meant that he didn't ask a single question, didn't demand a single confidence. One night, to their mutual surprise, Pelletier said to Espinoza that Morini was like a gift. A gift from the gods to the two of them. It was a silly thing to say and to argue it would have been to wade directly into a swamp of sentimentalism, but Espinoza, who felt the same way, even if he'd have put it differently, instantly agreed. Life smiled on them once again. They traveled to conferences here and there. They partook of the pleasures of gastronomy. They read and were lighthearted. Everything around them that had stopped and grown creaky and rusted sprang into motion again. The lives of other people grew visible, to a point. Their remorse vanished like laughter on a spring night. Once more they began to call Norton.

•

Deeply affected by their reunion, Pelletier, Espinoza, and Norton met at a bar, or rather at the tiny cafeteria (truly Lilliputian: two tables and a counter at which no more than four people fit shoulder to shoulder) of an unorthodox gallery only a little bigger than the bar, which exhibited paintings but also sold used books and clothes and shoes, located on Hyde Park Gate, very near the Dutch embassy. The three expressed their admiration for the Netherlands, a thoroughly democratic country.

At this bar, according to Norton, they made the best margaritas in London, a distinction of little interest to Pelletier and Espinoza, although they feigned enthusiasm. They were the only ones there, of course, and despite the time of day, the single employee or owner looked as if he were asleep or had just woken up, in contrast to Pelletier and Espinoza, who, though each had woken at seven and taken a plane, then separately endured the delays of their respective flights, were fresh and full of energy, ready to make the most of their London weekend.

Conversation, it's true, was difficult at first. In the silence, Pelletier and Espinoza watched Norton: she was as pretty and seductive as ever. Sometimes they were distracted by the little ant steps of the gallery owner, who was taking dresses off a rack and carrying them into a back room, returning with identical or very similar dresses, which he left where the others had been hanging.

Though the silence didn't bother Pelletier or Espinoza, Norton found it stifling and felt obliged to tell them, quickly and rather ferociously, about her teaching activities during the time they hadn't seen each other. It was a boring subject, and soon exhausted, so Norton went on to describe everything she had done the day before and the day before that, but once again she was left with nothing to say. For a while, smiling like squirrels, the three of them turned to their margaritas, but the quiet became more and more unbearable, as if within it, in the interregnum of silence, cutting words and cutting ideas were slowly being formed, never a performance or dance to be observed with indifference. So Espinoza decided it would be a good idea to describe a trip to Switzerland, a trip that hadn't involved Norton and that might amuse her.

•

In his telling, Espinoza didn't leave out the tidy cities or the rivers that invited contemplation or the springtime mountainsides clothed in green. And then he spoke of a trip by train, once the work that had brought the three friends together was finished, into the countryside, toward one of the towns halfway between Montreux and the foothills of the Bernese Alps, where they hired a car that took them along a winding but scrupulously paved road toward a rest clinic that bore the name of a late nineteenth-century Swiss politician or financier, the Auguste Demarre Clinic, an unobjectionable name behind which lay concealed a civilized and discreet lunatic asylum.

It hadn't been Pelletier's or Espinoza's idea to visit such a place. It was Morini's idea, because Morini had somehow learned that a man he considered to be one of the most disturbing painters of the twentieth century was living there. Or not. Maybe Morini hadn't said that. Either way, the name of this painter was Edwin Johns and he had cut off his right hand, the hand he painted with, then had it embalmed, and attached it to a kind of multiple self-portrait.

"How is it you never told me this story?" interrupted Norton.

Espinoza shrugged his shoulders.

"I thought you'd heard it from me," said Pelletier.

Although after a few seconds he realized that in fact she hadn't.

Norton, to everyone's surprise, burst into inappropriate laughter and ordered another margarita. For a while, as they were waiting for their drinks to be brought by the owner, who was still taking down and hanging up dresses, the three of them sat in silence. Then, at Norton's pleading, Espinoza had to resume his tale. But he didn't want to.

"You tell it," he said to Pelletier, "you were there, too."

Pelletier's story then began with the three Archimboldians contemplating the iron gate that rose in welcome to the Auguste Demarre lunatic asylum, while also blocking the way out (and preventing the entrance of any importunate guests). Or rather, the story begins seconds before, with Espinoza and Morini in his wheelchair surveying the iron gate and the iron railings that vanished to right and left, shaded by a venerable and well-tended grove of trees, as Pelletier, half in and half out of the car, paid the driver and arranged a reasonable time for him to drive up from the town to retrieve them. Then the three turned to face the bulk of the asylum, which could just be seen at the end of the road, like a fifteenth-century fortress, not in its architecture but in the effect of its inertness.

And what was this effect? An odd conviction. The certainty that the American continent, for example, had never been discovered, or in other words had never *existed*, and that this had in no way impeded the sustained economic growth or normal demographic growth or democratic advancement of the Helvetian republic. Just one of those strange and pointless ideas, said Pelletier, that people exchange on trips, especially if the trip is manifestly pointless, as this one was shaping up to be.

Next they made their way through all the formalities and red tape of a Swiss lunatic asylum. At last, without having seen a single one of the mental patients taking the cure, they were led by a middle-aged nurse with an inscrutable face to a small cottage in the rear grounds of the clinic, huge grounds that enjoyed a splendid view but sloped downward, which Pelletier, who was pushing Morini's wheelchair, thought must not be very calming for the disturbed or the severely disturbed.

To their surprise, the cottage turned out to be a cozy place, surrounded by pine trees, with rosebushes along a low wall, and armchairs within that mimicked the comfort of the English countryside, a fireplace, an oak table, a half-empty bookcase (the titles were almost all in German and French, besides a few in English), a special table with a computer and modem, a Turkish divan that clashed with the rest of the furnishings, a bathroom containing a toilet, a sink, and even a shower with a sliding plastic door.

"They don't have it too bad," said Espinoza.

Pelletier went over to a window and looked out at the view. At the foot of the mountains, he thought he saw a city. Maybe it's Montreux, he said to himself. Or maybe it was the town where they'd hired the car. After all, you couldn't see the lake. When Espinoza came over to the window he thought the houses were the town, certainly not Montreux. Morini sat still in his wheelchair, his gaze fixed on the door.

•

When the door opened, Morini was the first to see him. Edwin Johns had straight hair, starting to thin on top, and pale skin. He wasn't especially tall, but he was still thin. He wore a gray turtleneck sweater and a leather blazer. The first thing he noticed was Morini's wheelchair, which evinced pleasant surprise, as if clearly he hadn't been expecting anything quite so concrete. Morini, meanwhile, couldn't help glancing at Johns's right arm, where the hand was missing, and to his own great surprise, not at all pleasant, he discovered that where there should only have been emptiness, a hand emerged from Johns's jacket cuff, plastic of course, but so well made that only a careful and informed observer could tell it was artificial.

Behind Johns a nurse came in, not the one who had attended them but another one, a little younger and much blonder, who sat in a chair by one of the windows and took out a fat paperback, which she began to read, oblivious to Johns and the visitors. Morini introduced himself as a professor of literature from the University of Turin and an admirer of Johns's work, and then proceeded to introduce his friends. Johns, who had remained standing all this time, offered his hand to Espinoza and Pelletier, who shook it carefully, then sat in a chair at the table and watched Morini, as if they were the only two people in the cottage.

At first Johns made a slight, almost imperceptible effort to start a conversation. He asked whether Morini had bought any of his art. Morini replied in the negative. He said no, then he added that he couldn't afford Johns's work. Espinoza noticed then that the book the nurse was reading so intently was an anthology of twentieth-century German literature. He elbowed Pelletier, and the latter asked the nurse, more to break the ice than because he was curious, whether Benno von Archimboldi was included in the anthology. At that moment they all heard the caw or squawk of a crow. The nurse said yes. Johns began to blink and then he closed his eyes and ran his prosthetic hand over his face.

"It's my book," he said, "I loaned it to her."

"Unbelievable," said Morini, "what a coincidence."

"But of course I haven't read it, I don't speak German."

Espinoza asked why he'd bought it, then.

"For the cover," said Johns. "The drawing is by Hans Wette, a fine painter. And as far as coincidence is concerned, it's never a question of believing in it or not. The whole world is a coincidence. I had a friend who told me I was wrong to think that way. My friend said the world isn't a coincidence for someone traveling by rail, even if the train should cross foreign lands, places the traveler will never see again in his life. And it isn't a coincidence for the person who gets up at six in the morning, exhausted, to go to work; for the person who has no choice but to get up and pile more suffering on the suffering he's already accumulated. Suffering is accumulated, said my friend, that's a fact, and the greater the suffering, the smaller the coincidence."

"As if coincidence were a luxury?" asked Morini.

At that moment, Espinoza, who had been following Johns's monologue, noticed Pelletier next to the nurse, one elbow propped on the window ledge as with the other hand, in a polite gesture, he helped her find the page where the story by Archimboldi began. The blond nurse, sitting in the chair with the book on her lap, and Pelletier, standing by her side, in a pose not lacking in gallantry. And the window ledge and the roses outside and beyond them the grass and the trees and the evening advancing across ridges and ravines and lonely crags. The shadows that crept imperceptibly across the inside of the cottage, creating angles where none had existed before, vague sketches that suddenly appeared on the walls, circles that faded like mute explosions.

"Coincidence isn't a luxury, it's the flip side of fate, and something else besides," said Johns.

"What else?" asked Morini.

"Something my friend couldn't grasp, for a reason that's simple and easy to understand. My friend (if I may still call him that) believed in humanity, and so he also believed in order, in the order of painting and the order of words, since words are what we paint with. He believed in redemption. Deep down he may even have believed in progress. Coincidence, on the other hand, is total freedom, our natural destiny. Coincidence obeys no laws and if it does we don't know what they are. Coincidence, if you'll permit me the simile, is like the manifestation of God at every moment on our planet. A senseless God making senseless gestures at his senseless creatures. In that hurricane, in that osseous implosion, we find communion. The communion of coincidence and effect and the communion of effect with us."

Then, just then, Espinoza—and Pelletier, too—heard or sensed that Morini was formulating the question he had come to ask, his voice low, his torso so far inclined they feared he would tumble out of his wheelchair.

"Why did you mutilate yourself?"

Morini's face seemed to be pierced by the last lights rolling across the grounds of the asylum. Johns listened impassively. His attitude suggested a presentiment that the man in the wheelchair had come on this visit in search of an answer, like so many others before him. Then Johns smiled and posed a question of his own.

"Are you going to publish this conversation?"

"Certainly not," said Morini.

"Then why ask me a question like that?"

"I want to hear you say it yourself," whispered Morini.

In a movement that to Pelletier seemed slow and rehearsed, Johns lifted his right hand and held it an inch or so from Morini's expectant face.

"Do you think you're like me?" asked Johns.

"No, I'm not an artist," answered Morini.

"I'm not an artist either," said Johns. "Do you think you're like me?"

Morini shook his head back and forth, and his wheelchair moved too. For a few seconds Johns looked at him with a faint smile on his thin, bloodless lips.

"Why do you think I did it?" he asked.

"Honestly, I don't know," said Morini, looking him in the eye.

Dusk had settled around Morini and Johns now. The nurse made a move as if to get up and turn on the light, but Pelletier lifted a finger to his lips and stopped her. The nurse sat down again. The nurse's shoes were white. Pelletier's and Espinoza's shoes were black. Morini's shoes were brown. Johns's shoes were white and made for running long distance, on the paved streets of a city or cross-country. That was the last thing Pelletier saw, the color of the shoes and their shape and stillness, before night plunged them into the cold nothingness of the Alps.

"I'll tell you why I did it," said Johns, and for the first time his body relaxed, abandoning its stiff, martial stance, and he bent toward Morini, saying something into his ear.

Then he straightened up and went over to Espinoza and shook his hand very politely and then he shook Pelletier's hand too, and then he left the cottage and the nurse went out after him.

As he turned on the light, Espinoza pointed out, in case they hadn't noticed, that Johns hadn't shaken Morini's hand at the beginning or end of the interview. Pelletier answered that he had noticed. Morini said nothing. After a time the first nurse came and led them to the exit. As they crossed the grounds she told them a car was waiting for them at the gate.

The car took them back to Montreux, where they spent the night at the Hotel Helvetia. All three were tired and they decided not to go out to dinner. A few hours later, however, Espinoza called Pelletier's room and said he was hungry and was going to see whether he could find anything open. Pelletier told him to wait, he'd come too. When they met in the lobby, Pelletier asked whether he'd called Morini.

"I did," said Espinoza, "but no one answered."

They decided the Italian must already be asleep. That night they got back to the hotel late and slightly tipsy. The next morning they went to Morini's room to get him and he wasn't there. The clerk told them that according to the computer Mr. Piero Morini had settled his bill and left the hotel at midnight (as Pelletier and Espinoza were having dinner at an Italian restaurant). Around that time he had come down to the reception desk and asked for a car.

"He left at midnight? Where was he going?"

The clerk, of course, didn't know.

That morning, after they made sure Morini wasn't at any of the hospitals in or around Montreux, Pelletier and Espinoza took the train to Geneva. From the Geneva airport they called Morini's apartment in Turin. All they got was the answering machine, which they lavished with abuse. Then each caught a flight back to his city.

As soon as he got to Madrid Espinoza called Pelletier. The latter, who had been home for an hour, said he had nothing new to report. All day long, both Espinoza and Pelletier left short and increasingly hopeless messages on Morini's answering machine. By the second day they were in a state of anguish and even considered catching the next flights to Turin and notifying the authorities if they couldn't find Morini. But they didn't want to be rash or look foolish, and they didn't do anything.

The third day was the same as the second: they called Morini, they called each other, they weighed several courses of action, they considered Morini's mental health, his undeniable maturity and common sense, and did nothing. On the fourth day, Pelletier called the University of Turin directly. He spoke to a young Austrian who was working temporarily in the German department. The Austrian had no idea where Morini might be. Pelletier asked him to put the department secretary on the phone. The Austrian informed him that the secretary had gone out for breakfast and wasn't back yet. Pelletier immediately called Espinoza and gave him a detailed account of the phone call. Espinoza said he would try his luck.

This time it wasn't the Austrian who answered the phone but a German literature student. The student's German wasn't the best, so Espinoza switched to Italian. He asked whether the department secretary had come back yet. The student replied that he was alone, that everyone had gone out, presumably for breakfast, and there was no one in the department. Espinoza wanted to know what time people had breakfast at the University of Turin and how long breakfast usually lasted. The student didn't understand Espinoza's poor Italian and Espinoza had to repeat the question twice, the second time in slightly offensive terms.

The student said that he, for example, almost never had breakfast, but that didn't mean anything, everyone did things their own way. Did he understand or not?

"I understand," said Espinoza, gritting his teeth, "but I need to talk to someone in a position of authority."

"Talk to me," said the student.

Espinoza asked whether Dr. Morini had missed any of his classes.

"Let's see, let me think," said the student.

And then Espinoza heard someone, the student himself, whispering Morini . . . Morini . . . Morini, in a voice that didn't sound like his but rather like the voice of a sorcerer, or more specifically, a sorceress, a soothsayer from the times of the Roman Empire, a voice that reached Espinoza like the dripping of a basalt fountain but that soon swelled and overflowed with a deafening roar, with the sound of thousands of voices, the thunder of a great river in flood comprising the shared fate of every voice.

"Yesterday he had a class and he wasn't here," said the student after some thought.

Espinoza thanked him and hung up. That afternoon he tried Morini again at home and then he called Pelletier. There was no one at either place and he had to content himself with leaving messages. Then he began to reflect. But his thoughts only returned to what had just happened, the strict past, the past that seems deceptively like the present. He remembered the voice on Morini's answering machine, which is to say Morini's own recorded voice, saying briefly but politely that this was

Piero Morini's number and to please leave a message, and Pelletier's voice, which, instead of saying this is Pelletier, repeated the number to eliminate any uncertainty, then urged whoever was calling to leave his name and phone number, promising vaguely to call back.

That night Pelletier called Espinoza and they agreed, after each had dispelled the other's forebodings, to let a few days go by, not to fall into vulgar hysteria, and to bear in mind that whatever Morini might do, he was free to do it and there was nothing they could (or should) do to prevent it. That night, for the first time since they'd returned from Switzerland, they had a good night's sleep.

The next morning both men left for work rested in body and easy in mind, although by eleven, a little before he went out for lunch with colleagues, Espinoza broke down and called the German department at the University of Turin, with the same futile results as before. Later Pelletier called from Paris and they discussed the advisability of letting Norton know what was going on.

They weighed the pros and cons and decided to shield Morini's privacy behind a veil of silence, at least until they had more concrete information. Two days later, almost reflexively, Pelletier called Morini's apartment and this time someone picked up the phone. Pelletier's first words expressed the astonishment he felt upon hearing his friend's voice at the other end of the line.

"It can't be," shouted Pelletier, "how can it be, it's impossible."

Morini's voice sounded the same as always. Then came the delight, the relief, the waking from a bad dream, a baffling dream. In the middle of the conversation, Pelletier said he had to let Espinoza know right away.

"You won't go anywhere, will you?" he asked before he hung up.

"Where would I go?" asked Morini.

But Pelletier didn't call Espinoza. Instead he poured himself some whiskey and went into the kitchen and then the bathroom and then his office, turning on all the lights in the apartment. Only then did he call Espinoza and tell him he'd found Morini safe and sound and that he'd just talked to him on the phone, but he couldn't talk any longer. After he hung up he drank more whiskey. Half an hour later Espinoza called from Madrid. It was true, Morini was fine. He wouldn't say where he'd been over the last few days. He said he'd needed to rest. To collect his thoughts. According to Espinoza, who'd been reluctant to bombard him with questions, Morini seemed to be trying to hide something. Why? Espinoza hadn't the remotest idea.

"We really know very little about him," said Pelletier, who was beginning to tire of Morini, Espinoza, the phone.

"Did you ask him how he felt?" Pelletier asked.

Espinoza said yes and that Morini had assured him he was fine.

"There's nothing we can do now," concluded Pelletier in a tone of sadness that wasn't lost on Espinoza.

A little later they hung up and Espinoza picked up a book and tried to read, but he couldn't.

•

Then, as the gallery employee or owner kept taking down dresses and hanging them up, Norton told them that during the time he disappeared, Morini had been in London.

"He spent the first two days alone, without calling me once."

When she saw him he said he'd spent his time going to museums and wandering through unfamiliar neighborhoods, neighborhoods that were vaguely reminiscent of Chesterton stories but no longer had anything to do with Chesterton, although the spirit of Father Brown still hovered over them, not in a religious way, said Morini, as if he were trying not to overdramatize his solitary ramblings, but really Norton imagined him shut in his hotel room, with the drapes open, staring at the drab backs of buildings and reading for hour after hour. Then he called her and invited her out to lunch.

Naturally, Norton was happy to hear from him and to learn he was in the city and at the agreed-upon time she appeared in the hotel lobby, where Morini, sitting in his wheelchair with a package on his lap, was patiently and impassively deflecting the flow of guests and visitors that convulsed the lobby in an ever-changing display of luggage, tired faces, perfumes trailing after meteoridian bodies, bellhops with their stern jitters, the philosophical circles under the eyes of the manager or associate manager, each with his brace of assistants radiating freshness, the same freshness of eager sacrifice emitted by young women (in the form of ghostly laughter), which Morini tactfully chose to ignore. When Norton got there they left for a restaurant in Notting Hill, a Brazilian vegetarian restaurant she had recently discovered.

When Norton learned that Morini had spent two days in London already, she demanded to know what on earth he'd been doing and why he hadn't called. That was when Morini brought up Chesterton, said he'd spent the time wandering, praised the way the city accommodated the handicapped, unlike Turin, which was full of obstacles for wheelchairs, said he'd been to some secondhand bookshops where he'd bought a few books he didn't name, mentioned two visits to Sherlock Holmes's house, Baker Street being one of his favorite streets, a street that for him, a middle-aged Italian, cultured and crippled and a reader of detective novels, was timeless or outside time, lovingly (although the word wasn't lovingly but immaculately) preserved in Dr. Watson's tales. Then they went to Norton's house and there Morini gave her the gift he'd bought her, a book on Brunelleschi, with excellent photographs by photographers from four different countries of the same buildings by the great Renaissance architect.

"They're interpretations," said Morini. "The French photographer is the best," he said. "The one I like least is the American. Too showy. He's too eager to discover Brunelleschi. To *be* Brunelleschi. The German isn't bad, but the French one is best, I'd say. You'll have to tell me what you think."

Although she'd never seen the book, exquisite in paper and binding alone, something about it struck Norton as familiar. The next day they met in front of a theater. Morini had two tickets that he'd bought at the hotel, and they saw a bad, vulgar comedy that made them laugh, Norton more than Morini, who couldn't follow some of the cockney slang. That night they went to dinner and when Norton asked how Morini had spent his day he said he'd visited Kensington Gardens and the Italian Gardens in Hyde Park and roamed around, although Norton, for some reason, imagined him sitting still in the park, sometimes craning to see something he couldn't quite make out, most of the time with his eyes closed, pretending to sleep. Over dinner, Norton explained the parts of the play he hadn't understood. Only then did Morini realize it had been worse than he'd thought. The acting, however, rose greatly in his esteem, and back at the hotel, as he partially undressed without getting out of the wheelchair, in front of the silent television where he and the room were mirrored like ghostly figures in a performance that prudence and fear would keep anyone from staging, he concluded that the play hadn't been so bad after all, it had been good, he had laughed, the actors were good, the seats comfortable, the price of the tickets not too high.

The next day he told Norton he had to leave. Norton drove him to the airport. As they were waiting, Morini, adopting a casual tone of voice, said he thought he knew why Johns had cut off his right hand.

"Johns who?" asked Norton.

"Edwin Johns, the painter you told me about," said Morini.

"Oh, Edwin Johns," said Norton. "Why?"

"For money," said Morini.

"Money?"

"Because he believed in investments, the flow of capital, one has to play the game to win, that kind of thing."

Norton looked doubtful and then said: maybe.

"He did it for money," said Morini.

Then Norton asked him (for the first time) how Pelletier and Espinoza were.

"I'd prefer it if they didn't know I was here," said Morini.

Norton looked at him quizzically and told him not to worry, his secret was safe. Then she asked him to call when he got to Turin.

"Of course," said Morini.

A flight hostess asked to speak with them and a few minutes later she went away smiling. The line of passengers began to move. Norton gave Morini a kiss on the cheek and departed.

•

Before they left the gallery, thoughtful but hardly downcast, the owner and only attendant told them that the establishment would soon be closing its doors. With a lamé dress over one arm, he said that the house, of which the gallery was part, had belonged to his grandmother, a very respectable lady, ahead of her times. When she died the house was passed down to her three grandchildren, in theory equally. But back then, he, who was one of the grandchildren, lived in the Caribbean, where in addition to learning to make margaritas he did intel and spy work. A hippie spy with some rather bad habits, was how he described himself. When he got back to England he discovered that his cousins had taken over the entire house. That's when the quarreling began. Lawyers cost money, though, and in the end he had to settle for three rooms, where he set up his gallery. But the business was a flop: he didn't sell paintings or used clothes and hardly anyone came to try his cocktails. This neighborhood is too chic for my customers, he said, now the galleries are in the old working-class neighborhoods, the bars are on the traditional bar circuit, and people in this part of town don't buy used clothes. When Norton, Pelletier, and Espinoza had gotten up and were heading down the little metal staircase that led to the street, the gallery owner told them that, on top of it all, he'd recently begun to see his grandmother's ghost. This confession piqued the interest of Norton and her companions.

Have you seen her? they asked. I have, said the gallery owner, though at first I just heard strange noises, like water and bubbles. Noises he'd never heard in this house, although since it had been divided up to be sold as flats and new bathrooms had been installed, there might be some logical explanation for the sounds. But next came the moans, expressions not exactly of pain but more of puzzlement and frustration, as if the ghost of his grandmother were moving around her old house and not recognizing it, converted as it was into several smaller homes, with walls she didn't remember and modern furniture that must have struck her as common and mirrors where there never used to be mirrors.

Sometimes the owner got so depressed he slept in the store. What depressed him wasn't the sounds the ghost made, of course, but his business on the brink of ruin. On those nights he could clearly hear his grandmother's steps and her moans as she moved about upstairs as if she understood nothing about the world of the dead or the world of the living. One night, before he closed the gallery, he saw her reflected in the only mirror, an old full-length Victorian looking glass that stood in a corner for the use of customers trying on dresses. His grandmother peered at one of the paintings on the wall, then shifted her gaze to the clothing on hangers, then she looked at the gallery's two lone tables, as if they were the ultimate indignity.

She shuddered in horror, said the owner. That was the first and last time he'd seen her, though every now and then he heard her wandering on the upper floors, where surely she was moving through walls that hadn't used to exist. When Espinoza asked what his old job in the Caribbean had been like, the owner smiled sadly and promised them he wasn't mad, as anyone might think. He'd been a spy, he told them, in the same way that others work for the census bureau or in some statistics department. His words saddened them greatly, though they couldn't say why.

•

During a seminar in Toulouse they met Rodolfo Alatorre, a young Mexican whose scattershot reading included the work of Archimboldi. The Mexican, who was living on a creative writing scholarship and spent his days striving, apparently in vain, to write a modern novel, attended a few lectures then introduced himself to Norton and Espinoza, who lost no time giving him the brush-off, and then to Pelletier, who supremely ignored him, since nothing distinguished Alatorre from the hordes of generally irritating young European university students who swarmed around the Archimboldian apostles. To his greater discredit, Alatorre didn't speak German, which disqualified him from the outset. Meanwhile, the Toulouse seminar was a great success, and amid the fauna of critics and specialists who knew each other from previous conferences and who, at least on the surface, seemed happy to see each other again and eager to resume old discussions, the Mexican could either go home, which was something he was loath to do because home was a dreary scholarship student's room where only his books and papers awaited him, or stand in a corner and smile right and left pretending to be deep in thought, which is what in the end he did. As it happened, it was thanks to this position or pose that he noticed Morini, who, confined to his wheelchair and responding distractedly to everyone's greetings, displayed—or so it seemed to Alatorre—a forlornness resembling his own. A little while later, after Alatorre had introduced himself, the Mexican and the Italian went out for a walk along the streets of Toulouse.

First they discussed Alfonso Reyes, with whom Morini was reasonably well acquainted, then Sor Juana, Morini unable to forget the book by Morino—that Morino who might almost have been Morini himself—on the Mexican nun's recipes. Then they talked about Alatorre's novel, the novel he planned to write and the one novel he'd written so far, and they talked about the life of a young Mexican in Toulouse, about the winter days that dragged on, short but endless, Alatorre's few French friends (the librarian, another scholarship student from Ecuador he saw only every so often, the barman whose image of Mexico struck Alatorre as half bizarre, half offensive), about the friends he'd left behind in Mexico City and to whom he daily wrote long monothematic e-mails about his novel in progress, and about melancholy.

One of these Mexico City friends, said Alatorre, and he said it innocently, with that slight hint of clumsy boasting typical of minor writers, had met Archimboldi *just the other day.*

At first Morini, who wasn't paying close attention and was letting himself be dragged to all the places Alatorre considered worthy of interest, places that in fact, while not being obligatory tourist stops, were in some way interesting, as if Alatorre's secret calling was to be a tour guide, not a novelist, decided that the Mexican, who had in any case read only two novels by Archimboldi, was bragging or mistaken or else didn't know that Archimboldi had vanished long ago.

The story Alatorre told was in short as follows: his friend, an essayist and novelist and poet by the name of Almendro, a man in his forties better known to his friends as El Cerdo, or the Pig, had received a phone call at midnight. El Cerdo, after a brief conversation in German, got dressed and set off in his car to a hotel near the Mexico City airport. Even though there wasn't much traffic at that time of night, it was past one when he reached the hotel. A clerk and a policeman were in the lobby. El Cerdo showed his credentials, identifying him as a top government official, and then he accompanied the policeman to a room on the third floor. There were two other policemen there and an old German who was sitting on the bed, his hair uncombed, dressed in a gray T-shirt and jeans, barefoot, as if the arrival of the police had caught him sleeping. Evidently the German, thought El Cerdo, slept in his clothes. One of the two policemen was watching TV. The other was smoking, leaning against the wall. The policeman who had arrived with El Cerdo turned off the TV and told them to follow him. The policeman leaning against the wall demanded an explanation, but the policeman who had come up with El Cerdo told him to keep his mouth shut. Before the policemen left the room, El Cerdo asked, in German, whether they had stolen anything from him. The old man said no. They wanted money, but they hadn't stolen anything.

"That's good," said El Cerdo in German. "That's progress."

Then he asked the policemen which station they were from and let them go. When the policemen had gone, El Cerdo sat down next to the TV and said he was sorry. The old German got up from the bed without saying anything and went into the bathroom. He was huge, El Cerdo wrote to Alatorre. Nearly seven feet tall. Six foot six at least. In any case: enormous and imposing. When the old man came out of the bathroom, El Cerdo realized that now he had his shoes on and he asked him whether he felt like taking a drive around Mexico City or going out for a drink.

"If you're tired," he added, "just tell me and I'll leave this instant."

"My flight is at seven in the morning," the old man said.

El Cerdo looked at his watch. It was after two. He didn't know what to say. He, like Alatorre, hardly knew the old man's work. Any of his books that were translated into Spanish were published in Spain and were late coming to Mexico. Three years ago, when he was the head of a publishing house, before he became one of the top cultural officials in the new government, he had tried to publish *The Berlin Underworld*, but the rights already belonged to a house in Barcelona. He wondered how the old man had gotten his phone number, who had given it to him. Simply posing the question, a question to which he didn't expect an answer, made him happy, filled him with a happiness that somehow vindicated him as a person and a writer.

"We can go out," he said. "I'm game."

The old man put on a leather jacket over his gray T-shirt and followed him. El Cerdo took him to Plaza Garibaldi. There weren't many people there when they arrived, most of the tourists had gone back to their hotels, leaving only drunks and night owls, people on their way to supper, and mariachi bands rehashing the latest soccer match. Shadowy figures slunk around the streets leading into the plaza, occasionally halting to scrutinize them. El Cerdo fingered the pistol he had begun to carry since he began to work for the government. They went into a bar and El Cerdo ordered pork tacos. The old man was drinking tequila and he had a beer. As the old man ate, El Cerdo thought about the changes life brings. Not even ten years ago, if he'd walked into this same bar and started speaking in German to a gangling old man, someone would inevitably have insulted him or taken offense on the slenderest of pretexts. Then the looming fight would have been staved off by El Cerdo begging someone's pardon or making explanations or buying a round of tequila. Now no one bothered him, as if the act of wearing a gun under his shirt or working high up in the government gave him an aura of sainthood that even the killers and drunks could sense from a distance. Pussies, thought El Cerdo. They smell me, they smell me and they're shitting in their pants. Then he started to think about Voltaire (why Voltaire, for fuck's sake?) and then he started to think about an old idea he'd been mulling over for a while, requesting an ambassadorship in Europe, or at least a post as cultural attaché, although with his connections the least they could make him was ambassador. The problem was that at an embassy he would make only a salary, an ambassador's salary. As the German ate, El Cerdo weighed the pros and cons of leaving Mexico. One of the pros, absolutely, would be the chance to write again. He was attracted by the idea of living in Italy or near Italy and spending long periods in Tuscany and Rome writing an essay on Piranesi and his imaginary prisons, which he saw extrapolated not exactly in Mexican prisons but in the imaginary and iconographic versions of some Mexican prisons. One of the cons, no question about it, was the physical separation from power. Distancing oneself from power is never good, he'd discovered that early on, before he'd been granted real power, when he was head of the house that tried to publish Archimboldi.

"Listen," he said suddenly, "weren't you supposed to have disappeared?"

The old man looked at him and smiled politely.

•

That same night, after Alatorre had repeated his story for Pelletier, Espinoza, and Norton, they called Almendro, alias El Cerdo, who had no trouble relating to Espinoza what, along general lines, Alatorre had already told him. In a certain sense, the relationship between Alatorre and El Cerdo was teacher-student or big brother–little brother. In fact, it had been El Cerdo who had gotten Alatorre the scholarship in Toulouse, which in a sense testified to the degree of El Cerdo's regard for his little brother, since it was in his power to grant flashier scholarships in more prestigious locales, to say nothing of appointing a cultural attaché in Athens or Caracas, which might not have been much but would've been something, and Alatorre would have thanked him for the appointment with all his heart, although God knows he didn't turn up his nose at the little scholarship in Toulouse. The next time around, he was sure, El Cerdo would be more munificent. Almendro, meanwhile, wasn't yet fifty, and outside the limits of Mexico City his work was widely unknown. But in Mexico City, and, to be fair, at some American universities, his name was familiar, even overfamiliar. How, then, did Archimboldi, supposing that the old German really was Archimboldi and not a prankster, get his number? El Cerdo believed it had come from Archimboldi's German editor, Mrs. Bubis. Espinoza asked, not without some perplexity, whether he knew the great lady.

"Of course," said El Cerdo. "I was at a party in Berlin, a cultural *charreada* with some German editors, and we were introduced there."

What the hell is a cultural *charreada*? wrote Espinoza on a piece of paper, the question seen by all but deciphered by Alatorre alone, for whom it was intended.

"I must have given her my card," said El Cerdo from Mexico City.

"And your home phone number was on your card."

"That's right," said El Cerdo. "I must have given her my A card. The B card only has my office number. And it's just my secretary's number on the C card."

"I understand," said Espinoza, mustering patience.

"There's nothing on the D card, it's blank, just my name, that's all," said El Cerdo, laughing.

"I see, I see," said Espinoza, "just your name."

"Exactly," said El Cerdo. "My name, period. No phone number or title or street where I live or anything, you know what I'm saying?"

"I do," said Espinoza.

"So obviously I gave the A card to Mrs. Bubis."

"And she must have given it to Archimboldi," said Espinoza.

"Correct," said El Cerdo.

•

El Cerdo was with the German until five in the morning. After they ate (the old man was hungry and ordered more tacos and more tequila, while El Cerdo buried his head like an ostrich in reflections on melancholy and power), they went for a walk around the Zócalo, visiting the plaza and the Aztec ruins springing like lilacs from wasteland, as El Cerdo put it, stone flowers among other stone flowers, a chaos that would surely lead nowhere, only to further chaos, said El Cerdo, as he and the German walked the streets around the Zócalo, toward the Plaza Santo Domingo, where, during the day, under the arches, scribes with their typewriters set up shop to type letters or legal claims. Then they went to see the Angel on Reforma, but that night the Angel was dark and as they drove around the traffic circle, El Cerdo could only describe it to the German, who looked up from his open window.

At five in the morning they returned to the hotel. El Cerdo waited in the lobby, smoking a cigarette. When the old man emerged from the elevator he was carrying a single suitcase and was dressed in the same gray T-shirt and jeans. The streets leading to the airport were empty and El Cerdo ran several red lights. He hunted around for a topic of conversation, but couldn't come up with one. He had already asked the old man, as they were eating, whether he had been to Mexico before, and the old man had answered no, which was odd, because almost every European writer had been there at some time or other. But the old man said this was his first time. Near the airport there were more cars and the traffic no longer moved smoothly. When they drove into the parking lot, the old man tried to say goodbye, but El Cerdo insisted on accompanying him.

"Give me your suitcase," he said.

The suitcase had wheels and hardly weighed a thing. The old man was flying from Mexico City to Hermosillo.

"Hermosillo?" said Espinoza. "Where's that?"

"The state of Sonora," said El Cerdo. "It's the capital of Sonora, in northwestern Mexico, on the border with the United States."

"What are you going to do in Sonora?" asked El Cerdo.

The old man hesitated a moment before answering, as if he'd forgotten how to talk.

"I'm going to see what it's like," he said.

Although El Cerdo wasn't sure. Maybe what he actually said was that he was going to learn something.

"Hermosillo?" said El Cerdo.

"No, Santa Teresa," said the old man. "Do you know it?"

"No," said El Cerdo. "I've been to Hermosillo a few times, giving talks on literature, a while ago, but never to Santa Teresa."

"I think it's a big city," said the old man.

"It's big, yes," said El Cerdo. "There are factories there, and problems too. I don't think it's a nice place."

El Cerdo pulled out his ID and was able to accompany the old man to the departure gate. Before they parted he gave him a card. An A card.

"In case you run into any trouble," he said.

"Many thanks," said the old man.

Then they shook hands and El Cerdo never saw him again.

•

They decided not to tell anyone else what they knew. By keeping quiet, they reasoned, they weren't betraying anyone, merely behaving with prudence and discretion, as the case merited. They soon convinced themselves that it was best not to raise false hopes. According to Borchmeyer, Archimboldi had come up again as a possible Nobel candidate this year. His name had been in the prize pool the year before, too. False hopes.

According to Dieter Hellfeld, a member of the Swedish Academy or the secretary of a member of the academy had been in touch with Archimboldi's publisher to get an idea how the writer would respond if he were awarded the prize. What could a man past eighty have to say? What could the Nobel mean to such a man, with no family, no heirs, no public face? Mrs. Bubis said he would be delighted. Probably on her own recognizance, thinking of sales. But did the baroness concern herself with sales, with the books piling up in the warehouses of the Bubis publishing house in Hamburg? No, surely not, said Dieter Hellfeld. The baroness was nearing ninety, and warehouses were of no interest to her. She traveled a lot, Milan, Paris, Frankfurt. Sometimes she could be seen talking to Signora Sellerio at the Bubis stand in Frankfurt. Or at the German embassy in Moscow, in a Chanel suit, with two Russian poets in her retinue, declaiming on Bulgakov and the (incomparable) beauty of Russian rivers in the fall, before the winter frosts. Sometimes, said Pelletier, it's as if Mrs. Bubis has forgotten that Archimboldi even exists. That's the way it always is in Mexico, said young Alatorre. In any case, according to Schwarz, Archimboldi was on the short list, so the Nobel was within the realm of possibility. And maybe the Swedish academicians wanted a change. A veteran, a World War II deserter still on the run, a reminder of the past for Europe in troubled times. A writer on the Left whom even the situationists respected. A person who didn't pretend to reconcile the irreconcilable, as was the fashion these days. Imagine, said Pelletier, Archimboldi wins the Nobel and at that very moment we appear, leading him by the hand.

●

They couldn't explain to themselves what Archimboldi was doing in Mexico. Why would someone in his eighties travel to a country he had never visited before? Sudden interest? Research for the setting of a novel in progress? It was improbable, they thought, not least because the four believed there would be no more books by Archimboldi.

Tacitly, they inclined toward the simplest but also the most outlandish answer: Archimboldi had gone to Mexico as a tourist, like so many retired Germans and other Europeans. The explanation didn't hold water. They imagined a misanthropic old Prussian waking up one morning, out of his head. They weighed the possibilities of senile dementia. They discarded their hypotheses and cleaved strictly to what El Cerdo had said. What if Archimboldi were fleeing? What if Archimboldi had suddenly found a new reason to flee?

At first Norton was least eager to go tracking him down. The image of them returning to Europe with Archimboldi by the hand seemed to her the image of a gang of kidnappers. Of course, no one planned to kidnap Archimboldi. Or even barrage him with questions. Espinoza would be satisfied just to see him. Pelletier would be satisfied if he could ask him whose skin the leather mask was made of in his homonymous novel. Morini would be satisfied if he could see the pictures they took of him in Sonora.

Alatorre, whose opinion no one had requested, would be satisfied to strike up an epistolary friendship with Pelletier, Espinoza, Morini, and Norton, and maybe, if it wasn't too much bother, visit them every so often in their respective cities. Only Norton had reservations. But in the end she decided to make the trip. I think Archimboldi lives in Greece, said Dieter Hellfeld, and the author we know by the name of Archimboldi is really Mrs. Bubis.

"Yes, of course," said our four friends, "Mrs. Bubis."

•

At the last minute, Morini decided not to travel. His ill health, he said, made it impossible. Marcel Schwob, whose health was equally fragile, had set off in 1901 on a more difficult trip to visit Stevenson's grave on an island in the Pacific. Schwob's trip lasted many days, first on the *Ville de la Ciotat*, then on the *Polynésienne*, and then on the *Manapouri*. In January 1902 he fell ill with pneumonia and nearly died. Schwob was traveling with his Chinese manservant, Ting, who got seasick at the drop of a hat. Or maybe he got seasick only if the sea was rough. In any case the trip was plagued by rough seas and seasickness. At one point, Schwob, in bed in his stateroom and convinced he was on the verge of death, felt someone lie down beside him. When he turned to see who the intruder was he discovered his Oriental servant, his skin as green as grass. Only then did he realize what kind of venture he had embarked on. When he got to Samoa, after many hardships, he didn't visit Stevenson's grave. Partly because he was too sick, and partly because what's the point of visiting the grave of someone who hasn't died? Stevenson—and Schwob owed this simple revelation to his trip—lived inside him.

Morini, who admired Schwob (or, more precisely, felt a great fondness for him), thought at first that his trip to Sonora could be a kind of lesser homage to the French writer and also to the English writer whose grave the French writer had gone to visit, but when he got back to Turin he saw that travel was beyond him. So he called his friends and lied, saying the doctor had strictly forbidden anything of the kind. Pelletier and Espinoza accepted his explanation and promised they would call regularly to keep him posted on the search they were undertaking, the definitive search this time.

With Norton it was different. Morini repeated that he wasn't going. That the doctor had forbidden it. That he planned to write them every day. He even laughed and indulged in a silly joke that Norton didn't understand. A joke on Italians. An Italian, a Frenchman, and an Englishman are in a plane with only two parachutes. Norton thought it was a political joke. Actually, it was a children's joke, although because of the way Morini told it, the Italian in the plane (which first lost one engine then the other and then went into a tailspin) resembled Berlusconi. Norton hardly opened her mouth. She said mm-hmm, mm-hmm, mm-hmm. And then she said good night, Piero, in English and very sweetly, or at least in a way that seemed to Morini unbearably sweet, and then she hung up.

Norton felt somehow insulted by Morini's decision not to go with them. They didn't call each other again. Morini might have called Norton, but before his friends set off on their search for Archimboldi, he, in his own way, like Schwob in Samoa, had already begun a voyage, a voyage that would end not at the grave of a brave man but in a kind of resignation, what might be called a new experience, since this wasn't resignation in any ordinary sense of the word, or even patience or conformity, but rather a state of meekness, a refined and incomprehensible humility that made him cry for no reason and in which his own image, what Morini saw as Morini, gradually and helplessly dissolved, like a river that stops being a river or a tree that burns on the horizon, not knowing that it's burning.

•

Pelletier, Espinoza, and Norton traveled from Paris to Mexico City, where El Cerdo was waiting. They spent the night in a hotel, and the next morning they flew to Hermosillo. El Cerdo, who didn't understand much of what was going on, was thrilled to play host to such distinguished European academics even though, to his disappointment, they refused to give a lecture at Bellas Artes or UNAM or the Colegio de México.

The night they spent in Mexico City, Espinoza and Pelletier went with El Cerdo to the hotel where Archimboldi had stayed. The clerk had no problem letting them see the computer. With the mouse, El Cerdo scrolled over the names that appeared on the glowing screen under the date he'd met Archimboldi. Pelletier noticed that his fingernails were dirty and understood why he'd been given his nickname.

"Here he is," said El Cerdo, "this is it."

Pelletier and Espinoza searched for the name the Mexican was pointing to. Hans Reiter. One night. Paid in cash. He hadn't used a credit card or taken anything from the minibar. Then they went back to their own hotel, although El Cerdo asked them whether they'd like to see any tourist sites. No, said Espinoza and Pelletier, we're not interested.

Norton, meanwhile, was at the hotel, and although she wasn't tired she had turned off the lights and left just the television on with the volume turned down low. Through the open windows of her room came a distant buzzing, as if many miles away, in a neighborhood on the outskirts of the city, people were being evacuated. She thought it was the television and turned it off, but the noise persisted. She sat on the windowsill and looked out at the city. A sea of flickering lights stretched toward the south. If she leaned half her body out the window, the humming stopped. The air was cold and felt good.

At the entrance to the hotel a couple of doormen were arguing with a guest and a taxi driver. The guest was drunk. One of the doormen was propping him up with one arm and the other doorman was listening to the taxi driver, who, to judge by his gestures, was getting more and more upset. Soon afterward a car stopped in front of the hotel and Norton watched as Espinoza and Pelletier climbed out, followed by the Mexican. From up above she wasn't entirely sure they were her friends. In any case, if they were, they seemed different, they were walking differently, in a more virile way, if such a thing were possible, although the word *virile*, especially applied to a form of walking, sounded grotesque to Norton, completely absurd. The Mexican handed the car keys to one of the doormen and then the three men went into the hotel. The doorman who had El Cerdo's keys got in the car, then the taxi driver directed his arm waving at the doorman propping up the drunk. Norton had the impression that the taxi driver was demanding more money and the drunk hotel guest didn't want to pay. From where she was, Norton thought the drunk might be American. He was wearing an untucked white shirt over his khaki trousers, the color of cappuccino or milky iced coffee. She couldn't tell his age. When the other doorman came back, the taxi driver retreated two steps and said something.

His attitude, thought Norton, was menacing. Then one of the doormen, the one who was supporting the drunk guest, leaped forward and grabbed him by the neck. The taxi driver wasn't expecting this reaction and barely managed to step back, but he couldn't shake off the doorman. In the sky, presumably full of black clouds heavy with pollution, the lights of a plane appeared. Norton lifted her gaze, surprised, because then all the air began to buzz, as if millions of bees were surrounding the hotel. For an instant the idea of a suicide bomber or a plane accident passed through her mind. At the entrance to the hotel, the two doormen were beating the taxi driver, who was on the ground. It wasn't a sustained attack. They might kick him four or six times, then stop and give him the chance to talk or go, but the taxi driver, doubled over, would open his mouth and swear at them, then another round of blows would follow.

The plane descended a little farther in the dark and Norton thought she could see the expectant faces of the passengers through the windows. Then it turned and climbed again, and a few seconds later it disappeared into the belly of the clouds. The taillights, red and blue sparks, were the last thing she saw before it disappeared. When she looked down, one of the hotel clerks had come out and was helping the drunk guest, who could hardly walk, as if he were wounded, while the two doormen dragged the taxi driver not toward the taxi but toward the underground parking garage.

•

Her first impulse was to go down to the bar, where she would find Pelletier and Espinoza talking to the Mexican, but in the end she decided to close the window and go to bed. The hum continued and Norton thought it must be the air-conditioning.

•

"There's a kind of war between taxi drivers and doormen," said El Cerdo. "An undeclared war, with its ups and downs, moments of tension and moments of truce."

"So what will happen now?" asked Espinoza.

They were sitting at the hotel bar, next to one of the big windows that overlooked the street. Outside the air had a liquid texture. Black water, jet-black, that made one want to reach out and stroke its back.

"The doormen will teach the taxi driver a lesson and it'll be a long time before he comes back to the hotel," said El Cerdo. "It's about tips."

Then El Cerdo pulled out his electronic organizer and they copied the phone number of the rector at the University of Santa Teresa into their address books.

"I talked to him today," said El Cerdo, "and I asked him to give you all the help he could."

"Who'll get the taxi driver out of here?" asked Pelletier.

"He'll walk out on his own two feet," said El Cerdo. "They'll beat the shit out of him in the garage and then they'll wake him up with buckets of cold water so that he gets in his car and hightails it out of here."

"But if the doormen and the taxi drivers are at war, what do the guests do when they need a taxi?" asked Espinoza.

"Oh, then the hotel calls a radio taxi. The radio taxis are at peace with everyone," said El Cerdo.

When they went out to say goodbye to him at the entrance to the hotel they saw the taxi driver emerge limping from the garage. His face was unmarked and his clothes didn't seem to be wet.

"He probably cut a deal," said El Cerdo.

"A deal?"

"A deal with the doormen. Money," said El Cerdo, "he must have given them money."

For a second, Pelletier and Espinoza imagined that El Cerdo would leave in the taxi, which was parked a few feet away, across the street, with an abandoned look about it, but El Cerdo nodded to one of the doormen, who went to get his car.

•

The next morning they flew to Hermosillo and from the airport they called the rector of the University of Santa Teresa, then they rented a car and set off toward the border. As they left the airport, the three of them noticed how bright it was in Sonora. It was as if the light were buried in the Pacific Ocean, producing an enormous curvature of space. It made a person hungry to travel in that light, although also, and maybe more insistently, thought Norton, it made you want to bear your hunger until the end.

•

They drove into Santa Teresa from the south and the city looked to them like an enormous camp of gypsies or refugees ready to pick up and move at the slightest prompting. They took three rooms on the fourth floor of the Hotel México. The three rooms were the same, but they were full of small distinguishing characteristics. In Espinoza's room there was a giant painting of the desert, with a group of men on horseback to the left, dressed in beige shirts, as if they were in the army or a riding club. In Norton's room there were two mirrors instead of one. The first mirror was by the door, as it was in the other rooms. The second was on the opposite wall, next to the window overlooking the street, hung in such a way that if one stood in a certain spot, the two mirrors reflected each other. In Pelletier's bathroom the toilet bowl was missing a chunk. It wasn't visible at first glance, but when the toilet seat was lifted, the missing piece suddenly leaped into sight, almost like a bark. How the hell did no one notice this? wondered Pelletier. Norton had never seen a toilet in such bad shape. Some eight inches were missing. Under the white porcelain was a red substance, like brick wafers spread with plaster. The missing piece was in the shape of a half-moon. It looked as if someone had ripped it off with a hammer. Or as if someone had picked up another person who was already on the floor and smashed that person's head against the toilet, thought Norton.

•

The rector of the University of Santa Teresa had a pleasant, timid appearance. He was very tall, with lightly tanned skin, as if every day he took long meditative walks in the country. He offered them coffee and listened to their story with patience and feigned interest. Then he gave them a tour of the university, pointing out the buildings and telling them which departments were housed in each. When Pelletier, to change the subject, talked about the light in Sonora, the rector waxed poetic about sunsets in the desert and mentioned a few painters, with names they didn't recognize, who had come to live in Sonora or nearby Arizona.

When they got back to his office he offered them more coffee and asked where they were staying. When they told him he wrote down the name of the hotel on a slip of paper that he tucked into the breast pocket of his jacket, then he invited them to dinner at his house. They left soon afterward. As they made their way from the rector's office to the parking lot they saw a group of students of both sexes walking across a lawn just as the sprinklers came on. The students screamed and scattered.

•

Before they went back to the hotel they took a drive around the city. It made them laugh it seemed so chaotic. Until then they hadn't been in good spirits. They had looked at things and listened to the people who could help them, but only as part of a grander scheme. On the ride back to the hotel, they lost the sense of being in a hostile environment, although *hostile* wasn't the word, an environment whose language they refused to recognize, an environment that existed on some parallel plane where they couldn't make their presence felt, imprint themselves, unless they raised their voices, unless they argued, something they had no intention of doing.

At the hotel they found a note from Augusto Guerra, the dean of the Faculty of Arts and Letters. The note was addressed to his "colleagues" Espinoza, Pelletier, and Norton. Dear Colleagues, he had written without a hint of irony. This made them laugh even more, although then they were immediately sad, since the ridiculousness of "colleague" somehow erected bridges of reinforced concrete between Europe and this drifters' retreat. It's like hearing a child cry, said Norton. In his note, after wishing them a pleasant and enjoyable stay in his city, Augusto Guerra talked about a certain Professor Amalfitano, "an expert on Benno von Archimboldi," who would diligently present himself at the hotel that very afternoon to help them as best he could. In a poetic turn of phrase, the flowery closing compared the desert to a petrified garden.

They decided not to leave the hotel as they waited for the Archimboldi expert. According to what they could see out the windows of the bar, this was a decision shared by a group of American tourists who were getting deliberately drunk on the terrace, which was decorated with some surprising varieties of cactus, some almost ten feet tall. Every once in a while one of the tourists would get up from the table and go over to the railing draped in half-dead plants and glance out into the street.

Then, stumbling, he would return to his friends and after a while they would all laugh, as if the one who had gotten up was telling them a dirty and very funny joke. None of them was young, though none was old either. They were a group of tourists in their forties and fifties who would probably return to the United States that same day. Little by little the hotel terrace filled up, until there wasn't a single empty table. As night began to creep in from the east, the first notes of a Willie Nelson song sounded on the terrace speakers.

When one of the drunks recognized the song, he gave a shout and rose to his feet. Espinoza, Pelletier, and Norton thought he was about to start dancing, but instead he went over to the terrace railing and looked up and down the street, craning his neck, then went calmly back to sit with his wife and friends. These people are crazy, said Espinoza and Pelletier. But Norton thought something strange was going on, on the street, on the terrace, in the hotel rooms, even in Mexico City with those unreal taxi drivers and doormen, unreal or at least logically ungraspable, and even in Europe something strange had been happening, something she didn't understand, at the Paris airport where the three of them had met, and maybe before, with Morini and his refusal to accompany them, with that slightly repulsive young man they had met in Toulouse, with Dieter Hellfeld and his sudden news about Archimboldi. And something strange was going on even with Archimboldi and everything Archimboldi had written about, and with Norton, unrecognizable to herself, if only intermittently, who read and made notes on and interpreted Archimboldi's books.

•

"Have you said the toilet in your room needs to be fixed?" asked Espinoza.

"I did tell them to do something about it," said Pelletier. "But at the desk they suggested I change rooms. They wanted to put me on the third floor. So I told them I was fine, I planned to stay in *my* room and they could fix the toilet when I left. I'd rather we stick together," said Pelletier with a smile.

"You did the right thing," said Espinoza.

"The clerk told me they were planning to replace the toilet but they couldn't find the right model. He didn't want me to leave with a negative impression of the hotel. A nice person, after all," said Pelletier.

•

The first impression the critics had of Amalfitano was mostly negative, perfectly in keeping with the mediocrity of the place, except that the place, the sprawling city in the desert, could be seen as something authentic, something full of local color, more evidence of the often terrible richness of the human landscape, whereas Amalfitano could only be considered a castaway, a carelessly dressed man, a nonexistent professor at a nonexistent university, the unknown soldier in a doomed battle against barbarism, or, less melodramatically, as what he ultimately was, a melancholy literature professor put out to pasture in his own field, on the back of a capricious and childish beast that would have swallowed Heidegger in a single gulp if Heidegger had had the bad luck to be born on the Mexican-U.S. border. Espinoza and Pelletier saw him as a failed man, failed above all because he had lived and taught in Europe, who tried to protect himself with a veneer of toughness but whose innate gentleness gave him away in the act. But Norton's impression was of a sad man whose life was ebbing swiftly away and who would rather do anything than serve them as guide to Santa Teresa.

•

That night the three critics went to bed on the early side. Pelletier dreamed of his toilet. A muffled noise woke him and he got up naked and saw from under the door that someone had turned on the bathroom light. At first he thought it was Norton, even Espinoza, but as he came closer he knew it couldn't be either of them. When he opened the door the bathroom was empty. On the floor he saw big smears of blood. The bathtub and the shower curtain were crusted with a substance that wasn't entirely dry yet and that Pelletier at first thought was mud or vomit, but which he soon discovered was shit. He was much more revolted by the shit than frightened by the blood. As he began to retch he woke up.

Espinoza dreamed about the painting of the desert. In the dream Espinoza sat up in bed, and from there, as if watching TV on a screen more than five feet square, he could see the still, bright desert, such a solar yellow it hurt his eyes, and the figures on horseback, whose movements—the movements of horses and riders—were barely perceptible, as if they were living in a world different from ours, where speed was different, a kind of speed that looked to Espinoza like slowness, although he knew it was only the slowness that kept whoever watched the painting from losing his mind. And then there were the voices. Espinoza listened to them. Barely audible voices, at first only syllables, brief moans shooting like meteorites over the desert and the framed space of the hotel room and the dream. He recognized a few stray words. *Quickness, urgency, speed, agility.* The words tunneled through the rarefied air of the room like virulent roots through dead flesh. Our culture, said a voice. Our freedom. The word *freedom* sounded to Espinoza like the crack of a whip in an empty classroom. He woke up in a sweat.

In Norton's dream she saw herself reflected in both mirrors. From the front in one and from the back in the other. Her body was slightly aslant. It was impossible to say for sure whether she was about to move forward or backward. The light in the room was dim and uncertain, like the light of an English dusk. No lamp was lit. Her image in the mirrors was dressed to go out, in a tailored gray suit and, oddly, since Norton hardly ever wore such things, a little gray hat that brought to mind the fashion pages of the fifties. She was probably wearing black pumps, although they weren't visible. The stillness of her body, something reminiscent of inertia and also of defenselessness, made her wonder, nevertheless, what she was waiting for to leave, what signal she was waiting for before she stepped out of the field between the watching mirrors and opened the door and disappeared. Had she heard a noise in the hall? Had someone passing by tried to open her door? A confused hotel guest? A worker, someone sent up by reception, a chambermaid? And yet the silence was total, and there was a certain calm about it, the calm of long early-evening silences. All at once Norton realized that the woman reflected in the mirror wasn't her. She felt afraid and curious, and she didn't move, watching the figure in the mirror even more carefully, if possible. Objectively, she said to herself, she looks just like me and there's no reason why I should think otherwise. She's me. But then she looked at the woman's neck: a vein, swollen as if to bursting, ran down from her ear and vanished at the shoulder blade. A vein that didn't seem real, that seemed drawn on. Then Norton thought: I have to get out of here. And she scanned the room, trying to pinpoint the exact spot where the woman was, but it was impossible to see her. In order for her to be reflected in both mirrors, she said to herself, she must be just between the little entryway and the room. But she couldn't see her. When she watched her in the mirrors she noticed a change. The woman's head was turning almost imperceptibly. I'm being reflected in the mirrors too, Norton said to herself. And if she keeps moving, in the end we'll see each other. Each of us will see the other's face. Norton clenched her fists and waited. The woman in the mirror clenched her fists too, as if she were making a superhuman effort. The light coming into the room was ashen. Norton had the impression that outside, in the streets, a fire was raging. She began to sweat. She lowered her head and closed her eyes. When she looked in the mirrors again, the woman's swollen vein had grown and her profile was beginning to appear. I have to escape, she thought. She also thought: where are Jean-Claude and Manuel? She thought about Morini. All she saw was an empty wheelchair and behind it an enormous, impenetrable forest, so dark green it was almost black, which it took her a while to recognize as Hyde Park. When she opened her eyes, the gaze of the woman in the mirror and her own gaze intersected at some indeterminate point in the room. The woman's eyes were just like her eyes. The cheekbones, the lips, the forehead, the nose. Norton started to cry in sorrow or fear, or thought she was crying. She's just like me, she said to herself, but she's dead. The woman smiled tentatively and then, almost without transition, a grimace of fear twisted her face. Startled, Norton looked behind her, but there was no one there, just the wall. The woman smiled at her again. This time the smile grew not out of a grimace but out of a look of despair. And then the woman smiled at her again and her face became anxious, then blank, then nervous, then resigned, and then all the expressions of madness passed over it and after each she always smiled. Meanwhile, Norton, regaining her composure, had taken out a small notebook and was rapidly taking notes about everything as it happened, as if her fate or her share of happiness on earth depended on it, and this went on until she woke up.

•

When Amalfitano told them he had translated *The Endless Rose* for an Argentinian publishing house in 1974, the critics' opinion of him changed. They wanted to know where he had learned German, how he had discovered Archimboldi, which books of his he had read, what he thought of him. Amalfitano said he had learned German in Chile, at the German School, which he had attended from the time he was small, although when he turned fifteen he had moved, for reasons that were neither here nor there, to a public high school. He had come into contact with Archimboldi's work, as far as he could recall, at the age of twenty, when he read *The Endless Rose, The Leather Mask*, and *Rivers of Europe* in German, books he borrowed from a library in Santiago. The library had only those three and *Bifurcaria Bifurcata*, but this last he had begun and couldn't finish. It was a public library, augmented by the collection of a German man who had accumulated many books in German and who had donated them before he died to the municipality of Ñuñoa, in Santiago.

Of course, Amalfitano admired Archimboldi, although he felt nothing like the adoration the critics felt for him. Amalfitano, for example, thought that Günter Grass or Arno Schmidt was just as good. When the critics wanted to know whether the translation of *The Endless Rose* had been his idea or an assignment, Amalfitano said that as far as he remembered, it had been the Argentinian publisher's idea. In those days, he said, I translated everything I could and I worked as a proofreader, too. As far as he knew, it had been a pirate edition, although the possibility didn't occur to him till much later and he couldn't say for sure.

When the critics, much more kindly disposed toward him now, asked what he was doing in Argentina in 1974, Amalfitano looked at them and then at his margarita and said, as if he had repeated it many times, that in 1974 he was in Argentina because of the coup in Chile, which had obliged him to choose the path of exile. And then he apologized for expressing himself so grandiloquently. Everything becomes a habit, he said, but none of the critics paid much attention to this last remark.

"Exile must be a terrible thing," said Norton sympathetically.

"Actually," said Amalfitano, "now I see it as a natural movement, something that, in its way, helps to abolish fate, or what is generally thought of as fate."

"But exile," said Pelletier, "is full of inconveniences, of skips and breaks that essentially keep recurring and interfere with anything you try to do that's important."

"That's just what I mean by abolishing fate," said Amalfitano. "But again, I beg your pardon."

•

The next morning Amalfitano was waiting for them in the hotel lobby. If the Chilean professor hadn't been there they would surely have told one another the nightmares they'd had the night before and who knows what might have come to light. But there was Amalfitano, and the four set off together to have breakfast and plan the day's activities. They went over the possibilities. In the first place, it was clear that Archimboldi hadn't stopped by the university. At least not the Faculty of Arts and Letters. There was no German consulate in Santa Teresa, so any steps in that direction could be ruled out from the start. They asked Amalfitano how many hotels there were in town. He said he didn't know, but he could find out right away, as soon as they were done with breakfast.

"How?" Espinoza wanted to know.

"By asking at the reception desk," said Amalfitano. "They must have a list of all the hotels and motels in the area."

"Of course," said Pelletier and Norton.

As they finished breakfast they speculated again about the motives that might have compelled Archimboldi to travel to Santa Teresa. That was when Amalfitano learned that no one had ever seen Archimboldi in person. The story struck him as amusing, though he couldn't say exactly why, and he asked why they wanted to find him when it was clear Archimboldi didn't want to be seen. Because we're studying his work, said the critics. Because he's dying and it isn't right that the greatest German writer of the twentieth century should die without being offered the chance to speak to the readers who know his novels best. Because, they said, we want to convince him to come back to Europe.

"I thought," said Amalfitano, "that Kafka was the greatest German writer of the twentieth century."

Well, then the greatest postwar German writer or the greatest German writer of the second half of the twentieth century, said the critics.

"Have you read Peter Handke?" Amalfitano asked them. "And what about Thomas Bernhard?"

Ugh, said the critics, and until breakfast was over Amalfitano was attacked until he resembled the bird in Azuela's *Mangy Parrot*, gutted and plucked to the last feather.

•

At the reception desk they were given the list of every hotel in the city. Amalfitano suggested that they call from the university, since it appeared that Guerra and the critics were on such excellent terms, or that Guerra felt a respect for them bordering on reverence and even fear, a fear, in turn, not without its element of vanity or coquetry, although cunning, to be fair, crouched behind the coquetry and fear, since even if Guerra's co-operation came down to the wishes of Rector Negrete, it was no secret to Amalfitano that Guerra planned to get something out of the visit of the distinguished European professors, for as we all know the future is a mystery and we never know when we may come to a bend in the road or what unexpected places our steps may lead us. But the critics didn't want to use the university phone and they made calls on their room accounts. To save time, Espinoza and Norton called from Espinoza's room, and Amalfitano and Pelletier called from Pelletier's room. After an hour the results couldn't have been more disheartening. No Hans Reiter was registered at any hotel. After two hours they decided to give up calling and go down to the bar for a drink. All they had left were a few hotels and some motels on the outskirts of the city. Looking over the list more carefully, Amalfitano said most of the motels on the list rented rooms by the hour or were really brothels, places where it was hard to imagine a German tourist.

"We aren't looking for a German tourist, we're looking for Archimboldi," Espinoza replied.

"True," said Amalfitano, and the truth was he could imagine Archimboldi at one of the motels.

•

The question is, what did Archimboldi come to this city to do, said Norton. After some argument, the three critics concluded, and Amalfitano agreed, that he could have come to Santa Teresa only to see a friend or to collect information for a novel in progress or for both reasons at once. Pelletier inclined toward the possibility of the friend.

"An old friend," he conjectured. "In other words, a German like himself."

"A German he hasn't seen for years, maybe since the end of the war," said Espinoza.

"An army friend, someone who meant a lot to Archimboldi and disappeared as soon as the war ended, maybe even before it ended," said Norton.

"But it must be someone who knows Archimboldi is Hans Reiter," said Espinoza.

"Not necessarily. Maybe Archimboldi's friend has no idea that Hans

Reiter and Archimboldi are the same person. He only knows Reiter and how to get in touch with Reiter and that's it," said Norton.

"Which isn't likely," said Pelletier.

"No, it isn't, since it assumes that Reiter has been at the same address since the last time he saw his friend, say in 1945," said Amalfitano.

"Statistically speaking, there isn't a single German born in 1920 who hasn't changed addresses at least once in his life," said Pelletier.

"So maybe it isn't this friend who got in touch with Archimboldi but Archimboldi himself who got in touch with him," said Espinoza.

"Him or her," said Norton.

"I'm more inclined to think it's a man than a woman," said Pelletier.

"Unless it's neither a man nor a woman and we're all groping in the dark," said Espinoza.

"But then why would Archimboldi come here?" asked Norton.

"It must be a friend, a dear friend, dear enough that Archimboldi felt he had to make the trip," said Pelletier.

"What if we're wrong? What if Almendro lied to us or was confused or someone lied to him?" said Norton.

"Almendro who? Héctor Enrique Almendro?" said Amalfitano.

"That's the one. You know him?" asked Espinoza.

"Not personally, but I wouldn't bet much on a tip from Almendro," said Amalfitano.

"Why?" asked Norton.

"Well, because he's a typical Mexican intellectual, his main concern is getting by," said Amalfitano.

"Isn't that the main concern of all Latin American intellectuals?" asked Pelletier.

"I wouldn't say that. Some of them are more interested in writing, for example," said Amalfitano.

"Tell us what you mean," said Espinoza.

"I don't really know how to explain it," said Amalfitano. "It's an old story, the relationship of Mexican intellectuals with power. I'm not saying they're all the same. There are some notable exceptions. Nor am I saying that those who surrender do so in bad faith. Or even that they surrender completely. You could say it's just a job. But they're working for the state. In Europe, intellectuals work for publishing houses or for the papers or their wives support them or their parents are well-off and give them a monthly allowance or they're laborers or criminals and they make an honest living from their jobs. In Mexico, and this might be true across Latin America, except in Argentina, intellectuals work for the state. It was like that under the PRI and it'll be the same under the PAN. The intellectual himself may be a passionate defender of the state or a critic of the state. The state doesn't care. The state feeds him and watches over him in silence. And it puts this giant cohort of essentially useless writers to use. How? It exorcises demons, it alters the national climate or at least tries to sway it. It adds layers of lime to a pit that may or may not exist, no one knows for sure. Not that it's always this way, of course. An intellectual can work at the university, or, better, go to work for an American university, where the literature departments are just as bad as in Mexico, but that doesn't mean they won't get a late-night call from someone speaking in the name of the state, someone who offers them a better job, better pay, something the intellectual thinks he deserves, and intellectuals *always* think they deserve better. This mechanism somehow crops the ears off Mexican writers. It drives them insane. Some, for example, will set out to translate Japanese poetry without knowing Japanese and others just spend their time drinking. Take Almendro—as far as I know he does both. Literature in Mexico is like a nursery school, a kindergarten, a playground, a kiddie club, if you follow me. The weather is good, it's sunny, you can go out and sit in the park and open a book by Valéry, possibly the writer most read by Mexican writers, and then you go over to a friend's house and talk. And yet your shadow isn't following you anymore. At some point your shadow has quietly slipped away. You pretend you don't notice, but you have, you're missing your fucking shadow, though there are plenty of ways to explain it, the angle of the sun, the degree of oblivion induced by the sun beating down on hatless heads, the quantity of alcohol ingested, the movement of something like subterranean tanks of pain, the fear of more contingent things, a disease that begins to become apparent, wounded vanity, the desire just for once in your life to be on time. But the point is, your shadow is lost and you, momentarily, forget it. And so you arrive on a kind of stage, without your shadow, and you start to translate reality or reinterpret it or sing it. The stage is really a proscenium and upstage there's an enormous tube, something like a mine shaft or the gigantic opening of a mine. Let's call it a cave. But a mine works, too. From the opening of the mine come unintelligible noises. Onomatopoeic noises, syllables of rage or of seduction or of seductive rage or maybe just murmurs and whispers and moans. The point is, no one sees, really sees, the mouth of the mine. Stage machinery, the play of light and shadows, a trick of time, hides the real shape of the opening from the gaze of the audience. In fact, only the spectators who are closest to the stage, right up against the orchestra pit, can see the shape of something behind the dense veil of camouflage, not the real shape, but at any rate it's the shape of something. The other spectators can't see anything beyond the proscenium, and it's fair to say they'd rather not. Meanwhile, the shadowless intellectuals are always facing the audience, so unless they have eyes in the backs of their heads, they can't see anything. They only hear the sounds that come from deep in the mine. And they translate or reinterpret or re-create them. Their work, it goes without saying, is of a very low standard. They employ rhetoric where they sense a hurricane, they try to be eloquent where they sense fury unleashed, they strive to maintain the discipline of meter where there's only a deafening and hopeless silence. They say cheep cheep, bowwow, meow meow, because they're incapable of imagining an animal of colossal proportions, or the absence of such an animal. Meanwhile, the stage on which they work is very pretty, very well designed, very charming, but it grows smaller and smaller with the passage of time. This shrinking of the stage doesn't spoil it in any way. It simply gets smaller and smaller and the hall gets smaller too, and naturally there are fewer and fewer people watching. Next to this stage there are others, of course. New stages that have sprung up over time. There's the painting stage, which is enormous, and the audience is tiny, though all elegant, for lack of a better word. There's the film stage and the television stage. Here the capacity is huge, the hall is always full, and year after year the proscenium grows by leaps and bounds. Sometimes the performers from the stage where the intellectuals give their talks are invited to perform on the television stage. On this stage the opening of the mine is the same, the perspective slightly altered, although maybe the camouflage is denser and, paradoxically, bespeaks a mysterious sense of humor, but it still stinks. This humorous camouflage, naturally, lends itself to many interpretations, which are finally reduced to two for the public's convenience or for the convenience of the public's collective eye. Sometimes intellectuals take up permanent residence on the television proscenium. The roars keep coming from the opening of the mine and the intellectuals keep misinterpreting them. In fact, they, in theory the masters of language, can't even enrich it themselves. Their best words are borrowings

that they hear spoken by the spectators in the front row. These spectators are called *flagellants*. They're sick, and from time to time they invent
hideous words and there's a spike in their mortality rate. When the workday ends the theaters are closed and they cover the openings of the
mines with big sheets of steel. The intellectuals retire for the night. The
moon is fat and the night air is so pure it seems edible. Songs can be
heard in some bars, the notes reaching the street. Sometimes an intellectual wanders off course and goes into one of these places and drinks
mezcal. Then he thinks what would happen if one day he. But no. He
doesn't think anything. He just drinks and sings. Sometimes he thinks
he sees a legendary German writer. But all he's really seen is a shadow,
sometimes all he's seen is his *own* shadow, which comes home every
night so that the intellectual won't burst or hang himself from the lintel.
But he swears he's seen a German writer and his own happiness, his
sense of order, his bustle, his spirit of revelry rest on that conviction. The
next morning it's nice out. The sun shoots sparks but doesn't burn. A
person can go out reasonably relaxed, with his shadow on his heels, and
stop in a park and read a few pages of Valéry. And so on until the end."

"I don't understand a word you've said," said Norton.

"Really I've just been talking nonsense," said Amalfitano.

•

Later they called the remaining hotels and motels and Archimboldi
wasn't at any of them. For a few hours they thought Amalfitano was
right, that Almendro's tip was probably the product of an overheated
imagination, that Archimboldi's trip to Mexico existed only in the recesses of El Cerdo's brain. The rest of the day they spent reading and
drinking, and none of the three could muster the energy to leave the
hotel.

•

That night, while Norton was checking her e-mail on the hotel computer, she found a message from Morini. In his message Morini talked
about the weather, as if he had nothing better to say, about the slanting
rain that had begun to fall on Turin at eight and hadn't stopped until one
in the morning, and he sincerely wished Norton better weather in the
north of Mexico, where he believed it never rained and it was cold only
at night, and then only in the desert. That night, too, after replying to

some messages (not Morini's), Norton went up to her room, combed her hair, brushed her teeth, put moisturizing cream on her face, sat on the edge of the bed for a while, thinking, and then went out into the hallway and knocked at Pelletier's door and next at Espinoza's door and without a word she led them to her room, where she made love to both of them until five in the morning, at which time the critics, at Norton's request, returned to their rooms, where they soon fell into a deep sleep, a sleep that eluded Norton, who straightened the sheets of her bed a little and turned out the lights but remained wide awake.

●

She thought about Morini, or rather she saw Morini sitting in his wheelchair at a window in his apartment in Turin, an apartment she had never been to, looking out at the street and the façades of the surrounding buildings and watching the rain falling incessantly. The buildings across the street were gray. The street was dark and wide, a boulevard, although not a single car went by, with a spindly tree planted every sixty feet, like a bad joke on the part of the mayor or city planner. The sky was a blanket on top of a blanket, with another blanket on top of that, even thicker and wetter. The window Morini looked out was big, almost like a French door, narrower than it was wide but very tall, and so clean that the glass, with the raindrops sliding over it, was like pure crystal. The window frame was wooden, painted white. The lights were on in the room. The parquet shone, the bookshelves looked meticulously organized, and just a few paintings, in impeccable taste, hung on the walls. There were no rugs, and the furniture—a black leather sofa and two white leather armchairs—in no way impeded the passage of the wheelchair. Through double doors, half open, stretched a dark hallway.

And what to say about Morini? His position in the wheelchair expressed a certain degree of surrender, as if watching the night rain and the sleeping neighborhood fulfilled all his expectations. Sometimes he would rest his two arms on the chair, other times he would rest his head in one hand and prop his elbow on the chair's armrest. His useless legs, like the legs of an adolescent near death, were clothed in jeans possibly too big for him. He was wearing a white shirt with the top buttons undone, and on his left wrist his watch strap was too loose, though not so loose that the watch would fall off. He wasn't wearing shoes but rather very old slippers, of a cloth as black and shiny as the night. Everything he had on was comfortable, intended for wearing around the house, and by Morini's attitude it seemed clear that he had no intention of going in to work the next day, or that he planned to go in late.

The rain out the window, as he'd said in his e-mail, was falling obliquely, and there was something of the peasant fatalist in Morini's lassitude, his stillness and surrender, his uncomplaining and total abandonment to insomnia.

●

The next day they went to see the crafts market, which had been meant as a trading post for everyone living near Santa Teresa, where craftspeople and peasants from all over the region would bring their goods by cart or burro, even cattlemen came from Nogales and Vicente Guerrero and horse dealers from Agua Prieta and Cananea, but now the market was kept up solely for American tourists from Phoenix, who arrived by bus or in caravans of three or four cars and left the city before nightfall. Still, the critics liked the market, and even though they weren't planning to buy anything, in the end Pelletier picked up a clay figurine of a man sitting on a stone reading the newspaper, for next to nothing. The man was blond and two little devil horns sprouted from his forehead. Espinoza bought an Indian rug from a girl who had a rug and serape stall. He didn't actually like the rug very much, but the girl was nice and he spent a long time talking to her. He asked her where she was from, because he had the sense that she'd traveled from somewhere far away with her rugs, but the girl said she was from right here, Santa Teresa, from a neighborhood west of the market. She also said she was in high school and that if things went well, she planned to study to become a nurse. She wasn't just pretty but intelligent, too, thought Espinoza, though possibly too thin and delicate for his taste.

Amalfitano was waiting for them at the hotel. They took him out to lunch and then the four of them went to visit the offices of all the newspapers in Santa Teresa. At each place they looked through the papers dating from a month before Almendro saw Archimboldi in Mexico City to the previous day. They couldn't find a single sign to indicate that Archimboldi had passed through the city. First they looked in the death notices. Then they plowed through Society and Politics and they even read the items in Agriculture and Livestock. One of the papers didn't have an arts section. Another devoted one page a week to book reviews and listings of arts events in Santa Teresa, although it would have been better off allotting the page to sports. At six that evening they left the Chilean professor outside one of the newspaper offices and went back to the hotel. They showered and then each checked his or her e-mail. Pelletier and Espinoza wrote to Morini informing him of their meager findings. In both messages they announced that if nothing changed soon, they would return to Europe within the next few days. Norton didn't write to him. She hadn't answered his previous message and she didn't feel like facing up to that motionless Morini watching the rain, as if he had something to tell her and at the last moment had decided not to. Instead, and without saying anything to her two friends, she called Almendro's number in Mexico City and, after some fruitless efforts (El Cerdo's secretary and then his maid couldn't speak English, although both tried) she managed to reach him.

With enviable patience, and in English polished at Stanford, El Cerdo once again told her everything that had happened, beginning with the call from the hotel where Archimboldi was being interrogated by three policemen. Without contradicting himself, he again described his first meeting with Archimboldi, the time they spent in Plaza Garibaldi, the return to the hotel where Archimboldi collected his suitcase, the mostly silent trip to the airport, and then Archimboldi's departure for Hermosillo, after which he never saw him again. Following this, Norton's questions were all about Archimboldi's physical appearance. Nearly six and a half feet tall; his hair gray and thick, though he had a bald spot in back; thin; obviously strong.

"An old, old man," said Norton.

"No, I wouldn't say that," said El Cerdo. "When he opened his suitcase I saw lots of medicine. His skin was covered in age spots. Sometimes he seemed to get very tired but then he would recover easily or pretend to."

"What were his eyes like?" asked Norton.

"Blue," said El Cerdo.

"No, I already know they're blue, I've read all his books many times and they couldn't not be blue, I mean what were they like, what was your impression of them."

At the other end of the line there was a long silence, as if the question were completely unexpected or as if it were something El Cerdo had asked himself many times, and still couldn't answer.

"That's a hard question," said El Cerdo.

"You're the only person who can answer it. No one has seen him in a long time, and your situation is privileged, if I may say so," said Norton.

"Christ," said El Cerdo.

"What?" said Norton.

"Nothing, nothing, I'm thinking," said El Cerdo.

And after a while he said:

"He had the eyes of a blind man, I don't mean he couldn't see, but his eyes were just like the eyes of the blind, though I could be wrong about that."

•

That night they went to the party that Rector Negrete had planned in their honor, although it was only later that they discovered it was in their honor. Norton strolled through the gardens and admired the plants as the rector's wife named them one by one, although afterward she forgot all the names. Pelletier chatted for a long time with Guerra, the dean, and with another professor from the university who had written his thesis in Paris about a Mexican who wrote in French (a Mexican who wrote in French?), yes indeed, a most extraordinary, peculiar, excellent writer whose name the university professor mentioned several times (Fernández? García?), a man who came to a rather bad end because he had been a collaborator, yes indeed, a close friend of Céline and Drieu La Rochelle and a disciple of Maurras, shot by the Resistance, the Mexican writer, that is, not Maurras, a man who stood firm until the end, yes indeed, a real man, not like so many of his French counterparts who fled to Germany with their tails between their legs, this Fernández or García (or López or Pérez?) didn't leave home, he waited like a Mexican for them to come after him and his knees didn't buckle when they brought him (dragged him?) down the stairs and flung him against a wall, where they shot him.

Espinoza, meanwhile, was sitting the whole time next to Rector Negrete and various distinguished gentlemen of the same age as the host, men who spoke only Spanish and a very little bit of English, and he had to endure a conversation in praise of the latest signs of Santa Teresa's unstoppable progress.

None of the three critics failed to notice Amalfitano's constant companion that night. He was a handsome and athletic young man with very fair skin, who clung to the Chilean professor like a limpet and every so often gestured theatrically and grimaced like a madman, and other times just listened to what Amalfitano was saying, constantly shaking his head, small movements of almost spasmodic denial, as if he were abiding only grudgingly by the universal rules of conversation or as if Amalfitano's words (reprimands, to judge by his face) never hit their mark.

•

They left dinner having received a number of proposals, and with a suspicion. The proposals were: to give a class at the university on contemporary Spanish literature (Espinoza), to give a class on contemporary French literature (Pelletier), to give a class on contemporary English literature (Norton), to give a master class on Benno von Archimboldi and postwar German literature (Espinoza, Pelletier, and Norton), to take part in a panel discussion on economic and cultural relations between Europe and Mexico (Espinoza, Pelletier, and Norton, plus Dean Guerra and two economics professors from the university), to visit the foothills of the Sierra Madre, and, finally, to attend a lamb barbecue at a ranch near Santa Teresa, a barbecue that was predicted to be massive, with many professors in attendance, in a landscape, according to Guerra, of extraordinary beauty, although Rector Negrete declared that it was really quite severe and that some found it unsettling.

The suspicion was: that Amalfitano might be gay, and the vehement young man his lover, a dreadful suspicion since by the end of the night they had learned that the young man in question was the only son of Dean Guerra, Amalfitano's direct boss and the rector's right-hand man, and unless they were greatly mistaken, Guerra had no idea what kind of business his son was mixed up in.

"This could end in a hail of bullets," said Espinoza.

Then they talked about other things and afterward they went to sleep, exhausted.

•

The next day they went for a drive around the city, letting themselves be carried by chance, in no hurry, as if they were really hoping to find a tall old German man walking the streets. The western part of the city was very poor, with most streets unpaved and a sea of houses assembled out of scrap. The city center was old, with three- or four-story buildings and arcaded plazas in a state of neglect and young office workers in shirt-sleeves and Indian women with bundles on their backs hurrying down cobblestoned streets, and they saw streetwalkers and young thugs loitering on the corners, Mexican types straight out of a black-and-white movie. Toward the east were the middle- and upper-class neighborhoods. There they saw streets with carefully pruned trees and public playgrounds and shopping centers. The university was there, too. To the north were abandoned factories and sheds, and a street of bars and souvenir shops and small hotels, where it was said no one ever slept, and farther out there were more poor neighborhoods, though they were less crowded, and vacant lots out of which every so often there rose a school. To the south they discovered rail lines and slum soccer fields surrounded by shacks, and they even watched a match, without getting out of the car, between a team of the terminally ill and a team of the starving to death, and there were two highways that led out of the city, and a gully that had become a garbage dump, and neighborhoods that had grown up lame or mutilated or blind, and, sometimes, in the distance, the silhouettes of industrial warehouses, the horizon of the maquiladoras.

The city, like all cities, was endless. If you continued east, say, there came a moment when the middle-class neighborhoods ended and the slums began, like a reflection of what happened in the west but jumbled up, with a rougher orography: hills, valleys, the remains of old ranches, dry riverbeds, all of which went some way toward preventing overcrowding. To the north they saw a fence that separated the United States from Mexico and they gazed past it at the Arizona desert, this time getting out of the car. In the west they circled a couple of industrial parks that were in their turn being surrounded by slums.

They were convinced the city was growing by the second. On the far edge of Santa Teresa, they saw flocks of black vultures, watchful, walking through barren fields, birds that here were called turkey vultures, and also turkey buzzards. Where there were vultures, they noted, there were no other birds. They drank tequila and beer and ate tacos at a motel on the Santa Teresa–Caborca highway, at outdoor tables with a view. The sky, at sunset, looked like a carnivorous flower.

•

They returned to find Amalfitano waiting for them with Guerra's son, who invited them to dinner at a restaurant specializing in the food of northern Mexico. The place had a certain ambience, but the food didn't agree with them at all. They discovered, or believed they discovered, that the bond between the Chilean professor and the dean's son was more socratic than homosexual, and this in some way put their minds at ease, since the three of them had grown inexplicably fond of Amalfitano.

•

For three days they lived as if submerged in an undersea world. They watched television, seeking out the strangest and most random news, they reread novels by Archimboldi that suddenly they didn't understand, they took long naps, they were the last to leave the terrace at night, they talked about their childhoods as they had never done before. For the first time, the three of them felt like siblings or like the veterans of some shock troop who've lost their interest in most things of this world. They got drunk and they got up late and only every so often did they deign to go out with Amalfitano on walks around the city, to visit any attractions that might possibly be of interest to a hypothetical German tourist getting on in years.

•

And yes, in fact, they went to the lamb barbecue, and their movements were measured and cautious, as if they were three astronauts recently arrived on a planet about which nothing was known for sure. On the patio where the barbecue was being held they gazed at several smoke pits. The professors of the University of Santa Teresa displayed a rare talent for feats of country living. Two of them raced on horseback. Another sang a *corrido* from 1915. In a practice ring for bullfights some of them tried their luck with the lasso, with mixed results. Upon the appearance of Rector Negrete, who had been shut up in the main house with a man who seemed to be the ranch foreman, they dug up the barbecue, and a smell of meat and hot earth spread over the patio in a thin curtain of smoke that enveloped them all like the fog that drifts before a murder, and vanished mysteriously as the women carried the plates to the table, leaving clothing and skin impregnated with its aroma.

•

That night, maybe because of the barbecue and all they'd had to drink, the three had nightmares, which they couldn't remember when they woke, no matter how hard they tried. Pelletier dreamed of a page, a page that he tried to read forward and backward, every which way, turning it and sometimes turning his head, faster and faster, unable to decipher it at all. Norton dreamed of a tree, an English oak that she picked up and moved from place to place in the countryside, no spot entirely satisfying her. Sometimes the oak had no roots, other times it trailed long roots like snakes or the locks of a Gorgon. Espinoza dreamed about a girl who sold rugs. He wanted to buy a rug, any rug, and the girl showed him lots of rugs, one after the other, without stopping. Her thin, dark arms were never still and that prevented him from speaking, prevented him from telling her something important, from seizing her by the arm and getting her out of there.

•

The next morning Norton didn't come down for breakfast. They called her, thinking she was sick, but Norton assured them she just felt like sleeping in, and they should do without her. Gloomily, they waited for Amalfitano and then drove out to the northeast of the city, where a circus was setting up. According to Amalfitano, there was a German magician with the circus who went by the name of Doktor Koenig. He'd heard about the circus the night before, on his way back from the barbecue, when he saw leaflets that someone had gone to the trouble of leaving in all the yards in the neighborhood. The next day, on the corner where he waited for the bus to the university, he saw a color poster pasted on a sky-blue wall that announced the stars of the circus. Among them was the German magician, and Amalfitano thought this Doktor Koenig might be Archimboldi in disguise. Examined coolly, it was a stupid idea, he realized, but the critics were in such low spirits that he thought it wouldn't hurt to suggest a visit to the circus. When he told them, they looked at him the way students look at the class idiot.

"What would Archimboldi be doing in a circus?" said Pelletier when they were in the car.

"I don't know," said Amalfitano, "you're the experts, all I know is this is the first German who's come our way."

•

The circus was called Circo Internacional and some men who were raising the big top with a complicated system of cords and pulleys (or so it

131

seemed to the critics) directed them to the trailer where the owner lived. The owner was a Chicano in his fifties who had worked a long time in European circuses that crossed the continent from Copenhagen to Málaga, performing in small towns and with middling success, until he decided to go back to Earlimart, California, where he was from, and start a circus of his own. He called it Circo Internacional because one of his original ideas was to have performers from all over the world, although in the end they were mostly Mexican and American, except that every so often some Central American came looking for work and once he had a Canadian lion tamer in his seventies whom no other circus in the United States would employ. His circus wasn't fancy, he said, but it was the first circus owned by a Chicano.

When they weren't traveling they could be found in Bakersfield, not far from Earlimart, where he had his winter quarters, although sometimes he set up camp in Sinaloa, Mexico, not for long, just so he could travel to Mexico City and sign deals for sites in the south, all the way to the Guatemalan border, and from there they'd head back up to Bakersfield. When the foreigners asked him about Doktor Koenig, the impresario wanted to know whether they had some dispute or money problem with his magician, to which Amalfitano was quick to reply that they didn't, certainly not, these gentlemen were highly respected university professors from Spain and France respectively, and he himself, not to put too fine a point on it and with all due respect, was a professor at the University of Santa Teresa.

"Oh, well then," said the Chicano, "if that's the way it is I'll take you to see Doktor Koenig. I think he used to be a professor too."

The critics' hearts leaped at his words. Then they followed the impresario past the circus trailers and cages on wheels until they came to what was, for all intents and purposes, the edge of the camp. Farther out there was only yellow earth and a black hut or two and the fence along the Mexican-American border.

"He likes the quiet," said the impresario, though they hadn't asked.

He rapped with his knuckles on the door of the magician's little trailer. Someone opened the door and a voice from the darkness asked what he wanted. The impresario said it was him and he had some European friends with him who wanted to say hello. Come in, then, said the voice, and they went up the single step and into the trailer, where the curtains were drawn over the only two windows, which were just a little bigger than portholes.

"I don't know how we're all going to fit in here," said the impresario, and immediately he pulled back the curtains.

Lying on the only bed they saw an olive-skinned bald man wearing only a pair of enormous black shorts, who looked at them, blinking with difficulty. He couldn't have been more than sixty, if that, which ruled him out immediately, but they decided to stay for a while and at least thank him for seeing them. Amalfitano, who was in a better mood than the other two, explained that they were looking for a German friend, a writer, and they couldn't find him.

"So you thought you'd find him in my circus?" said the impresario.

"Not him, but someone who might know him," said Amalfitano.

"I've never hired a writer," said the impresario.

"I'm not German," said Doktor Koenig. "I'm American. My name is Andy López."

With these words he pulled his wallet out of a bag hanging on a hook and held out his driver's license.

"What's your magic act?" Pelletier asked him in English.

"I start by making fleas disappear," said Doktor Koenig, and the five of them laughed.

"It's the truth," said the impresario.

"Then I make pigeons disappear, then I make a cat disappear, then a dog, and I end the act by disappearing a kid."

•

After they left the Circo Internacional, Amalfitano invited them to his house for lunch.

Espinoza went out into the backyard and saw a book hanging from a clothesline. He didn't want to go over and see what book it was, but when he went back into the house he asked Amalfitano about it.

"It's Rafael Dieste's *Testamento geométrico*," said Amalfitano.

"Rafael Dieste, the Galician poet," said Espinoza.

"That's right," said Amalfitano, "but this is a book of geometry, not poetry, ideas that came to Dieste while he was a high school teacher."

Espinoza translated what Amalfitano had said for Pelletier.

"And it's hanging outside?" said Pelletier with a smile.

"Yes," said Espinoza as Amalfitano looked in the refrigerator for something to eat, "like a shirt left out to dry."

"Do you like beans?" asked Amalfitano.

"Anything is fine. We're used to everything now," said Espinoza.

Pelletier went over to the window and looked at the book, its pages stirring almost imperceptibly in the slight afternoon breeze. Then he went outside and spent a while examining it.

"Don't take it down," he heard Espinoza say behind him.

"This book wasn't left out to dry, it's been here a long time," said Pelletier.

"That's what I thought," said Espinoza, "but we'd better leave it alone and go home."

Amalfitano watched them from the window, biting his lip, although the look on his face (just then at least) wasn't of desperation or impotence but of deep, boundless sadness.

When the critics showed the first sign of turning around, Amalfitano retreated, returning rapidly to the kitchen, where he pretended to be intent on making lunch.

·

When they got back to the hotel, Norton told them she was leaving the next day and they received the news without surprise, as if they'd been expecting it for a while. The flight Norton had found was out of Tucson, and despite her protests—she'd been planning to take a taxi—they decided to drive her to the airport. That night they talked until late. They told Norton about their visit to the circus and promised that if nothing changed, they would spend three more days there at most. Then Norton got up to go to bed and Espinoza suggested they spend their last night in Santa Teresa together. Norton misunderstood and said that she was the only one who was leaving, they still had more nights in the city.

"I mean the three of us together," said Espinoza.

"In bed?" asked Norton.

"Yes, in bed," said Espinoza.

"I don't think that's a good idea," said Norton, "I'd rather sleep alone."

So they walked her to the elevator and then they went to the bar and ordered two Bloody Marys and sat waiting for them in silence.

"I really put my foot in it this time," said Espinoza when the bartender brought them their drinks.

"It seems that way," said Pelletier.

"Have you realized," said Espinoza, after another silence, "that during this whole trip we've only been to bed with her once?"

"Of course I've realized," said Pelletier.

"And whose fault is that," asked Espinoza, "hers or ours?"

"I don't know," said Pelletier, "the truth is I haven't been much in the mood for making love these days. What about you?"

"I haven't either," said Espinoza.

They were quiet again for a while.

"She probably feels more or less the same," said Pelletier.

•

They left Santa Teresa very early. First they called Amalfitano and told him they were going to the United States and probably wouldn't be back all day. At the border the American customs officer wanted to see the car's papers and then he let them pass. Following the instructions of the hotel clerk, they took a dirt road and for a while they drove through a patch of woods and streams, as if they'd stumbled into a dome with its own ecosystem. For a while they thought they'd never get to the airport, or anywhere else. But the dirt road ended in Sonoita and from there they took Route 83 to Interstate 10, which brought them straight to Tucson. At the airport there was still time for them to have coffee and talk about what they'd do when they saw each other again in Europe. Then Norton had to go to the boarding gate and half an hour later her plane took off for New York, where she would catch a connecting flight to London.

To get back they took Interstate 19 to Nogales, although they turned off a little after Rio Rico and followed the border on the Arizona side, to Lochiel, where they entered Mexico again. They were hungry and thirsty but they didn't stop in any town. At five in the afternoon they got back to the hotel and after they showered they went down to have a sandwich and call Amalfitano. He told them not to leave the hotel, he'd take a taxi and be there in ten minutes. We're in no hurry, they said.

•

After that moment, reality for Pelletier and Espinoza seemed to tear like paper scenery, and when it was stripped away it revealed what was behind it: a smoking landscape, as if someone, an angel, maybe, was tending hundreds of barbecue pits for a crowd of invisible beings. They stopped getting up early, they stopped eating at the hotel, among the American tourists, and they moved to the center of the city, choosing dark bars for breakfast (beer and fiery *chilaquiles*) and bars with big windows for lunch, where the waiters wrote the specials in white ink on the glass. Dinner they had wherever they happened to be.

They accepted the rector's offer and gave lectures on contemporary French and Spanish literature, lectures that were more like massacres and that at least had the virtue of striking fear into their listeners, mostly young men, readers of Michon and Rolin or Marías and Vila-Matas. Then, and this time together, they gave a master class on Benno von Archimboldi, feeling less like butchers than like gutters or disembowelers, but something in them urged restraint, something undetectable at first, though silently they sensed a fated encounter: in the audience, not counting Amalfitano, there were three young readers of Archimboldi who almost brought them to tears. One of them, who could speak French, even had one of the books translated by Pelletier. So miracles were possible, after all. The Internet bookstores worked. Culture, despite the disappearances and guilt, was still alive, in a permanent state of transformation, as they soon discovered when, after the lecture and at the express request of Pelletier and Espinoza, the young readers of Archimboldi accompanied them to the university's reception hall, where there was a love fest, or rather a cocktail hour, or maybe a cocktail half hour, or possibly just a polite nod to the distinguished lecturers, and where, for lack of a better subject, people talked about what good writers the Germans were, all of them, and about the historic significance of universities like the Sorbonne or the University of Salamanca, where, to the astonishment of the critics, two of the professors (one who taught Roman law and another who taught twentieth-century penal law) had studied. Later, Dean Guerra and one of the administration secretaries took them aside and gave them their checks and a little later, under cover of a fainting fit suffered by one of the professors' wives, they slipped out.

•

They were accompanied by Amalfitano, who hated these parties though he had no choice but to endure them from time to time, and the three readers of Archimboldi. First they had dinner in the center and then they drove up and down the street that never slept. The rental car was big, but they still had to sit almost on top of each other and the people on the sidewalks gave them curious looks, the kind of looks they gave everyone on the street, until they saw Amalfitano and the three students crammed in the backseat and then they quickly averted their eyes.

They went into a bar that one of the boys knew. The bar was big and in the back was a yard with trees and a little fenced-in space for cock-fights. The boy said his father had brought him there once. They talked politics, and Espinoza translated what the boys said for Pelletier. None of them was older than twenty and they had a fresh, healthy look. They seemed eager to learn. Amalfitano, in contrast, seemed more tired and defeated than ever that night. In a low voice, Pelletier asked him whether something was the matter. Amalfitano shook his head and said no, although back at the hotel, the critics remarked that the way their friend had chain-smoked and hardly spoken a word all night, he was either extremely depressed or a nervous wreck.

The next day, when he got up, Espinoza found Pelletier sitting on the hotel terrace, dressed in Bermuda shorts and leather sandals, reading that day's Santa Teresa papers, armed with a Spanish-French dictionary he'd probably bought that very morning.

"Are we going to the center for breakfast?" asked Espinoza.

"No," said Pelletier, "enough alcohol and rotgut meals. I want to find out what's going on in this city."

Then Espinoza remembered that the night before, one of the boys had told them the story of the women who were being killed. All he remembered was that the boy had said there were more than two hundred of them and he'd had to repeat it two or three times because neither Espinoza nor Pelletier could believe his ears. Not believing your ears, though, thought Espinoza, is a form of exaggeration. You see something beautiful and you can't believe your eyes. Someone tells you something about . . . the natural beauty of Iceland . . . people bathing in thermal springs, among geysers . . . in fact you've seen it in pictures, but still you say you can't believe it . . . Although obviously you believe it . . . Exaggeration is a form of polite admiration . . . You set it up so the person you're talking to can say: it's true . . . And then you say: incredible. First you can't believe it and then you think it's incredible.

That was probably what he and Pelletier had said the night before when the boy, healthy and strong and pure, told them that more than two hundred women had died. But not over a short period of time, thought Espinoza. From 1993 or 1994 to the present day . . . And many more women might have been killed. Maybe two hundred and fifty or three hundred. No one will ever know, the boy had said in French. The boy had read a book by Archimboldi translated by Pelletier and obtained thanks to the good offices of an Internet bookstore. He didn't speak much French, thought Espinoza. But a person can speak a language badly or not at all and still be able to read it. In any case, there were lots of dead women.

"So who's guilty?" asked Pelletier.

"There are people who've been in prison a long time, but women keep dying," said one of the boys.

Amalfitano, Espinoza remembered, was quiet, with an absent look on his face, probably plastered. At a nearby table there were three men who kept looking at them as if they were very interested in what they were talking about. What else do I remember? Espinoza thought. Someone, one of the boys, talked about a murder epidemic. Someone said something about the copycat effect. Someone spoke the name Albert Kessler. At a certain moment Espinoza got up and went to the bathroom to vomit. As he was doing it he heard someone outside, someone who was probably washing his hands or his face or primping in front of the mirror, say to him:

"That's all right, buddy, go ahead and puke."

The voice soothed me, thought Espinoza, but that implies I was upset, and why should I have been upset? When he left the stall there was no one there, just the music from the bar drifting in faintly and the sound of the plumbing, deeper and spasmodic. Who brought us back to the hotel? he wondered.

"Who drove us back?" he asked Pelletier.

"You did," said Pelletier.

•

That day Espinoza left Pelletier reading newspapers at the hotel and went out on his own. Although it was late for breakfast he went into a bar on Calle Arizpe that was always empty and asked for something restorative.

"This is the best thing for a hangover, sir," said the bartender, and he put a glass of cold beer in front of him.

From inside came the sound of frying. He asked for something to eat.

"Quesadillas, sir?"

"Just one," said Espinoza.

The bartender shrugged his shoulders. The bar was empty and it wasn't quite as dark as the bars where he usually went in the morning. The door to the bathroom opened and a very tall man came out. Espinoza's eyes hurt and he was starting to feel sick again, but the appearance of the tall man startled him. In the darkness he couldn't see his face or tell how old he was. But the tall man sat down next to the window, and yellow and green light illuminated his features.

Espinoza realized it couldn't be Archimboldi. He looked like a farmer or a rancher on a visit to the city. The bartender put a quesadilla in front of him. When he picked it up in his hands he burned himself and he asked for a napkin. Then he asked the bartender to bring him three more quesadillas. When he left the bar he headed for the crafts market. Some of the vendors were gathering up their wares and stowing their folding tables. It was lunchtime and there weren't many people. At first he had a hard time finding the stall of the girl who sold rugs. The streets of the market were dirty, as if food or fruit and vegetables were sold there instead of crafts. When he saw the girl she was busy rolling up rugs and tying the ends. The smallest ones, the handwoven ones, she put in a long cardboard box. She had a vacant expression, as if she was far away. Espinoza approached and stroked one of the rugs. He asked whether she remembered him. The girl showed no sign of surprise. She raised her eyes, looked at him, and said yes with a naturalness that made him smile.

"Who am I?" asked Espinoza.

"The Spanish man who bought a rug from me," said the girl, "we talked for a while."

•

After deciphering the newspapers, Pelletier felt like showering and washing off all the filth that clung to his skin. He saw Amalfitano approaching from a long way off. He watched him come into the hotel and speak to the desk clerk. Before he came out onto the terrace, Amalfitano raised one hand weakly in a sign of recognition. Pelletier got up and told him to order whatever he liked, he was going to take a shower. As he left he noticed that Amalfitano's eyes were red and there were circles under them, as if he hadn't slept. Crossing the lobby he changed his mind and turned on one of the two computers that the hotel provided for its guests in a little room next to the bar. When he checked his e-mail he found a long message from Norton in which she gave him what she believed to be her real reasons for leaving so abruptly. He read it as if he were still drunk. He thought about the young Archimboldi readers from the night before, and he wanted, vaguely, to be like them, to exchange his life for one of theirs. This wish was, he told himself, a form of lassitude. Then he pressed the button for the elevator and rode up with an American woman in her seventies who was reading a Mexican paper, one of the same ones he'd read that morning. As he was undressing he thought about how he would tell Espinoza. There was probably a message waiting for him from Norton. What can I do? he wondered.

The bite out of the toilet bowl was still there and for a few seconds he stared at it and let the warm water run over his body. What's the reasonable thing to do? he thought. The most reasonable thing would be to go back and postpone any conclusion as long as possible. Only when soap got in his eyes was he able to look away from the toilet. He turned his face into the stream of water and closed his eyes. I'm not as sad as I'd have thought, he told himself. This is all unreal, he said to himself. Then he turned off the shower, dressed, and went down to join Amalfitano.

•

He went with Espinoza to check his e-mail. He stood behind him until he'd made sure there was a message from Norton, and when he saw that there was, certain it would say the same thing his had, he sat in an armchair a few feet away from the computers and leafed through a tourist magazine. Every so often he would lift his eyes and look at Espinoza, who didn't seem about to get up. He would've liked to pat him on the back, but he chose not to move. When Espinoza turned around to look at him, he said he'd gotten one just like it.

"I can't believe it," said Espinoza in a thread of a voice.

Pelletier left the magazine on the glass table and went over to the computer, where he glanced through Norton's letter. Then, without sitting down, and typing with one finger, he found his own e-mail and showed Espinoza the message he'd gotten. He asked him, very gently, to read it. Espinoza turned toward the screen again and read Pelletier's letter several times.

"It's almost exactly the same," he said.

"What does it matter?" said the Frenchman.

"She could have shown a bit more decency in that regard, at least," said Espinoza.

"In these cases, decency is informing the person at all," said Pelletier.

When they went out onto the terrace there was almost no one there.

A waiter, dressed in a white jacket and black pants, was gathering up glasses and bottles from the empty tables. At one end, near the railing, a couple in their twenties looked out at the silent, deep green street, holding hands. Espinoza asked Pelletier what he was thinking about.

"About her," said Pelletier, "of course."

He also said it was strange, or at least curious, that they were here, in this hotel, in this city, when Norton finally came to a decision. Espinoza gave him a long look and then said in disgust that he felt like throwing up.

●

The next day Espinoza went back to the crafts market and asked the girl what her name was. She said it was Rebeca, and Espinoza smiled, because the name, he thought, suited her perfectly. He stood there for three hours, talking to Rebeca, as tourists and browsers wandered around looking halfheartedly at the merchandise, as if under duress. Only twice did customers come up to Rebeca's stall, but both times they left without buying anything, which made Espinoza feel guilty because in some sense he blamed the girl's bad luck on himself, on his stubborn presence at the stall. He decided to make up for it by buying what he imagined the others would have bought. He chose a big rug, two small rugs, a serape that was mostly green, another that was mostly red, and a kind of knapsack made of the same cloth and with the same pattern as the serapes. Rebeca asked whether he was going back to his country soon and Espinoza smiled and said he didn't know. Then the girl called a boy, who loaded all of Espinoza's purchases onto his back and went with him to where he had parked the car.

Rebeca's voice when she called the boy (who had appeared out of nowhere or out of the crowd, which was essentially the same thing), her tone, the calm authority she projected, made Espinoza shudder. As he was walking behind the boy he noticed that most of the vendors were beginning to pack up. When he got to the car they put the rugs in the trunk and Espinoza asked the boy how long he'd been working with Rebeca. She's my sister, he said. They don't look alike at all, thought Espinoza. Then he glanced at the boy, who was short but also seemed strong, and gave him a ten-dollar bill.

●

When he got to the hotel, Pelletier was on the terrace reading Archimboldi. Espinoza asked him what book it was and Pelletier smiled and answered that it was *Saint Thomas*.

"How many times have you read it?" asked Espinoza.

"I've lost count, although this is one of the ones I've read least."

Just like me, thought Espinoza, just like me.

•

Rather than two letters, it was really a single one albeit with variations, brusque personalized twists that opened onto the same abyss. Santa Teresa, that horrible city, said Norton, had made her think. Think in the strict sense, for the first time in years. In other words: she had begun to think about practical, real, tangible things, and she had also begun to remember. She had thought about her family, her friends, and her job, and nearly simultaneously she had remembered family scenes or work scenes, scenes in which her friends raised their glasses and made toasts, maybe to her, maybe to someone she'd forgotten. Mexico is unbelievable (here she digressed, but only in Espinoza's letter, as if Pelletier wouldn't understand or as if she knew beforehand that they would compare letters), a place where one of the big fish in the cultural establishment, someone presumably refined, a writer who has reached the highest levels of government, is called El Cerdo, and no one even questions it, she said, and she saw a connection between this, the nickname or the cruelty of the nickname or the resignation to the nickname, and the criminal acts that had been occurring for some time in Santa Teresa.

When I was little there was a boy I liked. I don't know why I liked him, but I did. I was eight and so was he. He was called James Crawford. I think he was a very shy boy. He would speak only to other boys and kept his distance from the girls. He had dark hair and brown eyes. He always wore short pants, even when the other boys began to wear trousers. The first time I talked to him—this I remembered just a little while ago—I called him Jimmy instead of James. No one called him that. Only me. The two of us were eight years old. His face was very serious. What was my excuse for talking to him? I think he left something on the desk, maybe an eraser or a pencil, I can't remember now, and I said: Jimmy, you forgot your eraser. I do remember smiling. I do remember why I called him Jimmy and not James or Jim. Out of fondness. Because it made me happy. Because I liked Jimmy and I thought he was very handsome.

•

The next day Espinoza went to the crafts market first thing in the morning. The vendors and craftspeople were just beginning to set up their stalls and the cobblestoned street was still clean. His heart was beating faster than normal. Rebeca was arranging her rugs on a folding table and she smiled when she saw him. Some vendors were standing around drinking coffee or soda and chatting from stall to stall. Behind the stalls, on the sidewalk, under the old arches and the awnings of some of the more traditional stores, men were milling around arguing over wholesale batches of pottery that were guaranteed to sell in Tucson or Phoenix. Espinoza said hello to Rebeca and helped her set out the last rugs. Then he asked whether she'd like to have breakfast with him and the girl said she couldn't and anyway she'd already had breakfast at home. Refusing to give up, Espinoza asked where her brother was.

"At school," said Rebeca.

"So who helps you bring everything here?"

"My mother," said Rebeca.

For a while, Espinoza was silent, his eyes on the ground, not knowing whether to buy another rug from her or leave without a word.

"Have lunch with me," he said finally.

"All right," said the girl.

•

When Espinoza got back to the hotel he found Pelletier reading Archimboldi. Seen from the distance, Pelletier's face, and in fact not just his face but his whole body, radiated an enviable calm. When he got a little closer he saw that the book wasn't *Saint Thomas* but rather *The Blind Woman*, and he asked Pelletier whether he'd had the patience to reread the other book from start to finish. Pelletier looked up at him and didn't answer. He said instead that it was surprising, or that it would never cease to surprise him, the way Archimboldi depicted pain and shame.

"Delicately," said Espinoza.

"That's right," said Pelletier. "Delicately."

•

In Santa Teresa, in that horrible city, said Norton's letter, I thought about Jimmy, but mostly I thought about me, about what I was like at eight, and at first the ideas leaped, the images leaped, it was as if there were an earthquake in my head, I couldn't focus clearly or precisely on any single memory, but when I finally could it was worse, I saw myself saying Jimmy, I saw my smile, Jimmy Crawford's serious face, the flock of children, their backs, the sudden swell of them in the calm waters of the schoolyard, I saw my lips announcing to the boy that he'd forgotten something, I saw the eraser, or maybe it was a pencil, I saw the way my eyes looked then, saw them with the eyes I have now, and I heard my cry once more, the timbre of my voice, the extreme politeness of a girl of eight who shouts after a boy of eight to remind him not to forget his eraser and yet can't call him by his name, James, or Crawford, the way we do in school, and opts, consciously or unconsciously, for the diminutive Jimmy, which indicates fondness, a verbal fondness, a personal fondness, since only she, in that world-encompassing instant, calls him that, a name that somehow casts in a new light the fondness or solicitude implicit in the gesture of warning him he's forgotten something, don't forget your eraser, or your pencil, though in the end it's simply an expression, verbally poor or verbally rich, of happiness.

●

They ate at a cheap restaurant near the market, while Rebeca's little brother watched the cart that was used each morning to transport the rugs and folding table. Espinoza asked Rebeca whether it wasn't possible to leave the cart unguarded so the boy could eat with them, but Rebeca told him not to worry. If the cart was left unguarded then someone would probably take it. From the window of the restaurant Espinoza could see the boy on top of the heap of rugs like a bird, scanning the horizon.

"I'll take him something," he said, "what does your brother like?"

"Ice cream," said Rebeca, "but they don't have ice cream here."

For a few seconds Espinoza considered going out to find ice cream somewhere else, but he gave up the idea for fear the girl would be gone by the time he got back. She asked him what Spain was like.

"Different," said Espinoza, thinking about the ice cream.

"Different from Mexico?" she asked.

"No," said Espinoza, "different in different places, diverse."

Suddenly it occurred to Espinoza to take the boy a sandwich.

"They're called *tortas* in Mexico," said Rebeca, "and my brother likes ham."

She was like a princess or an ambassadress, thought Espinoza. He asked the waitress to bring him a ham sandwich and a soda. The waitress asked him how he wanted the sandwich.

"Tell her you want it with everything," said Rebeca.

"With everything," said Espinoza.

Later he went outside with the sandwich and the soda and handed them to the boy, who was still perched atop the cart. At first the boy shook his head and said he wasn't hungry. Espinoza saw that there were three slightly bigger boys on the corner watching them, holding back laughter.

"If you're not hungry, just drink the soda and keep the sandwich," he said, "or give it to the dogs."

When he sat back down with Rebeca he felt good. In fact, he felt replete.

"This won't work," he said, "it isn't right. Next time, the three of us will eat together."

Rebeca looked him in the eye, her fork halted in the air, and then a half smile appeared on her face and she conveyed the food to her mouth.

•

At the hotel, stretched out on a deck chair beside the empty pool, Pelletier was reading, and Espinoza knew, even before he saw the title, that it wasn't *Saint Thomas* or *The Blind Woman*, but another book by Archimboldi. When he sat down next to Pelletier he could see it was *Lethaea*, not one of his favorites, although to judge by Pelletier's face, the rereading was fruitful and thoroughly enjoyable. When he sat down in the next deck chair he asked Pelletier what he'd done all day.

"I read," answered Pelletier, who in turn asked him the same question.

"Not much," said Espinoza.

That night, as they ate together at the hotel restaurant, Espinoza told him he'd bought some souvenirs, including something for Pelletier. Pelletier was happy to hear it and asked what kind of souvenir Espinoza had bought for him.

"An Indian rug," said Espinoza.

•

When I reached London after an exhausting trip, said Norton in her letter, I started to think about Jimmy Crawford, or maybe I started to think about him as I was waiting for the New York–London flight, but either way Jimmy Crawford and my eight-year-old voice calling after him were already with me at the moment when I found the keys to my flat and turned on the light and left my bags on the floor in the hall. I went into the kitchen and made tea. Then I showered and went to bed. I had a feeling that I wouldn't be able to sleep, so I took a sleeping pill. I remember I started to leaf through a magazine, I remember I thought about the two of you, wandering that horrible city, I remember I thought about the hotel. In my room at the hotel there were two very odd mirrors that frightened me the last few days. When I felt myself dropping off, I barely had the strength to reach out and turn off the light.

I had no dreams at all. When I woke up I didn't know where I was, but the feeling lasted just a second or two, because straightaway I recognized the usual street noises. Everything's over, I thought. I feel rested, I'm home, I have lots to do. When I sat up in bed, though, all I did was start to cry like a fool, for no apparent reason. All day I was like that. At moments I wished I hadn't left Santa Teresa, that I'd stayed there with you until the end. More than once I felt the urge to rush to the airport and catch the first plane to Mexico. These urges were followed by other, more destructive ones: to set fire to my apartment, slit my wrists, never return to the university, and live on the streets forever after.

But in England at least, women who live on the streets are often subjected to terrible humiliations, I just read an article about it in some magazine or other. In England these street women are gang-raped, beaten, and it isn't unusual for them to be found dead outside hospitals. The people who do these things to them aren't, as I might have thought at eighteen, the police or gangs of neo-Nazi thugs, but other street people, which makes it seem somehow even worse. Feeling confused, I went out, hoping to cheer up and thinking I might call some friend to meet for dinner. How I don't know, but suddenly I found myself in front of a gallery hosting a retrospective of the work of Edwin Johns, the artist who cut off his right hand to display it in a self-portrait.

•

On his next visit, Espinoza managed to persuade the girl to let him take her home. They left the cart safe in the back room of the restaurant where they'd eaten before, among empty bottles and stacks of canned chiles and meat, after Espinoza paid a meager rent to a fat woman in an old factory worker's apron. Then they put the rugs and serapes in the backseat of the car and the three of them squeezed up in front. The boy was happy and Espinoza told him he could decide where they went to eat that day. They ended up at a McDonald's in the city center.

The girl's house was in one of the neighborhoods to the west, the area where most crimes were committed, according to what he'd read in the papers, but the neighborhood and the street where Rebeca lived just seemed like a poor neighborhood and a poor street, there was nothing ominous about them. He left the car parked in front of the house. There was a tiny garden in front, with three planter boxes made of cane and wire, full of pots of flowers and plants. Rebeca told her brother to stay outside and watch the car. The house was built of wood and when anyone walked on the floorboards they made a hollow sound, as if a drain ran underneath, or as if there was a secret room below.

Contrary to Espinoza's expectations, Rebeca's mother greeted him in a friendly way and offered him a soda. Then she herself introduced the rest of her children. Rebeca had two brothers and three sisters, although the oldest didn't live at home anymore because she'd gotten married. One of the sisters was just like Rebeca but younger. Her name was Cristina and everyone said she was the smartest in the family. Once a reasonable amount of time had passed, Espinoza asked Rebeca to go for a walk with him around the neighborhood. As they left they saw the boy up on the roof of the car. He was reading a comic book and had something in his mouth, probably candy. When they got back from the walk the boy was still there, although he wasn't reading anymore and his candy was gone.

•

When he returned to the hotel Pelletier was reading *Saint Thomas* again. When he sat down beside him Pelletier looked up from the book and said there were still things he didn't understand and probably never would. Espinoza laughed and said nothing.

"Amalfitano was here today," said Pelletier.

In his opinion, the Chilean professor's nerves were shot. Pelletier had invited him to take a dip in the pool. Since he didn't have bathing trunks Pelletier had picked up a pair for him at the reception desk. Everything seemed to be going fine. But when Amalfitano got in the pool, he froze, as if he'd suddenly seen the devil. Then he sank. Before he went under, Pelletier remembered, he covered his mouth with both hands. In any case, he made no attempt to swim. Fortunately, Pelletier was there and it was easy to dive down and bring him back up to the surface. Then they each had a whiskey, and Amalfitano explained that it had been a long time since he swam.

"We talked about Archimboldi," said Pelletier.

Then Amalfitano got dressed, returned the swimming trunks, and left.

"And what did you do?" asked Espinoza.

"I showered, got dressed, came down to eat, and kept reading."

•

For an instant, said Norton in her letter, I felt like a derelict dazzled by the sudden lights of a theater. I wasn't in the best state of mind to go into a gallery, but the name Edwin Johns drew me like a magnet. I went up to the gallery door, which was glass, and inside I saw many people and I saw waiters dressed in white who could scarcely move, balancing trays laden with glasses of champagne or red wine. I decided to wait and went back across the street. Little by little the gallery emptied and the moment came when I thought I could go in and at least see part of the retrospective.

When I opened the glass door I felt something strange, as if everything I saw or felt from that moment on would determine the course of my life to come. I stopped in front of a kind of landscape, a Surrey landscape from Johns's early period, that looked to me at once sad and sweet, profound and not at all grandiloquent, an English landscape as only the English can paint them. All at once I decided that seeing this one painting was enough and I was about to leave when a waiter, maybe the last of the waiters from the catering company, came over to me with a single glass of wine on his tray, a glass especially for me. He didn't say anything. He just offered it to me and I smiled at him and took the glass. Then I saw the poster for the show, across the room from where I was standing, a poster that showed the painting with the severed hand, Johns's masterpiece, and in white numerals gave his dates of birth and death.

I hadn't known he was dead, said Norton in her letter, I thought he was still living in Switzerland, in a comfortable asylum, laughing at himself and most of all at us. I remember the glass of wine fell from my hands. I remember that a couple, both tall and thin, turned away from a painting and peered over as if I might be an ex-lover or a living (and unfinished) painting that had just got news of the painter's death. I know I walked out without looking back and that I walked for a long time until I realized I wasn't crying, but that it was raining and I was soaked. That night I didn't sleep at all.

•

In the mornings Espinoza would pick Rebeca up at her house. He'd park the car out front, have a coffee, and then, without saying anything, he'd put the rugs in the backseat and occupy himself polishing the trim. If he'd been at all mechanically inclined he would have lifted the hood and looked at the engine, but he wasn't, and in any case the car ran perfectly. Then the girl and her brother would come out of the house and Espinoza would open the passenger door for them, without a word, as if they'd had the same routine for years, and then he would get in the driver's side, put the dust rag away in the glove compartment, and head to the crafts market. Once they were there he helped set up the stall and once they finished he'd go to a nearby restaurant and buy two coffees and one Coca-Cola to go, which they drank standing up, looking at the other booths or the squat but proud horizon of colonial buildings surrounding them. Sometimes Espinoza scolded the girl's brother, telling him that drinking Coca-Cola in the morning was a bad habit, but the boy, whose name was Eulogio, laughed and ignored him because he knew Espinoza's anger was ninety percent put-on. The rest of the morning Espinoza would spend at an outdoor café in the neighborhood, the only neighborhood in Santa Teresa he liked, besides Rebeca's, reading the local papers and drinking coffee and smoking. When he went into the bathroom and looked at himself in the mirror, he thought his features were changing. I look like a gentleman, he said to himself sometimes. I look younger. I look like someone else.

•

At the hotel, when he got back, Pelletier was always on the terrace or at the pool or sprawled in an armchair in one of the lounges, rereading *Saint Thomas* or *The Blind Woman* or *Lethaea*, which were, it seemed,

the only books by Archimboldi he'd brought with him to Mexico. Espinoza asked whether he was preparing some article or essay on those
three books in particular and Pelletier's answer was vague. At first he had
been. Not anymore. He was reading them just because they were the
ones he had. Espinoza considered lending him one of his, and all at once
he realized with alarm that he'd forgotten all about the books by Archimboldi hidden away in his suitcase.

•

That night I didn't sleep a wink, said Norton in her letter, and it occurred to me to call Morini. It was very late, it was rude to bother him at
that hour, it was rash of me, it was a terrible imposition, but I called
him. I remember I dialed his number and immediately I turned out the
light in the room, as if so long as I was in the dark Morini couldn't see
my face. To my surprise, he picked up the phone instantly.

"Piero, it's me, Liz," I said. "Did you know Edwin Johns is dead?"

"Yes," said Morini's voice from Turin. "He died a few months ago."

"But I only found out just now, tonight," I said.

"I thought you already knew," said Morini.

"How did he die?" I asked.

"It was an accident," said Morini, "he went out for a walk, he wanted
to sketch a little waterfall near the sanatorium, he climbed up on a rock
and slipped. They found his body at the bottom of a ravine, one hundred
and fifty feet down."

"It can't be," I said.

"It can," said Morini.

"He went for a walk alone? With no one watching him?"

"He wasn't alone," said Morini, "a nurse was with him, and one of
those strong young men from the sanatorium, the kind who can pin a
raving lunatic in no time."

I laughed—for the first time—at the expression *raving lunatic*, and
Morini, at the other end of the line, laughed with me, although only for
an instant.

"The word for those men is orderlies," I said.

"Well, he had a nurse and an orderly with him," he said. "Johns
climbed up on a rock and the man climbed up too. The nurse sat on a
stump, as Johns asked her to do, and pretended to read a book. Then
Johns started to draw with his left hand, with which he had become

quite proficient. He drew the waterfall, the mountains, the outcroppings of rock, the forest, and the nurse reading her book, far away from it all. Then the accident happened. Johns stood up on the rock and slipped, and although the man tried to catch him, he fell into the abyss."

That was all.

We were quiet for a time, said Norton in her letter, until Morini broke the silence and asked how things had gone in Mexico.

"Badly," I said.

He didn't ask any more questions. I listened to his steady breathing, and he listened to my breathing, which was growing steadily calmer.

"I'll call you tomorrow," I said to him.

"All right," he said, but for a few seconds neither of us was able to hang up the phone.

That night I thought about Edwin Johns, I thought about his hand, now doubtless on display in his retrospective, the hand that the sanatorium orderly couldn't grasp to prevent his fall, although this was too obvious, a false representation, having nothing to do with what Johns had actually been. Much more real was the Swiss landscape, the landscape that you two saw and I've never seen, with its mountains and forests, its iridescent stones and waterfalls, its deadly ravines and reading nurses.

•

One night Espinoza took Rebeca dancing. They went to a club in the center of Santa Teresa where the girl had never been but that her friends highly recommended. As they drank Cuba libres, Rebeca told him that two of the girls who later showed up dead had been kidnapped on their way out of the club. Their bodies were dumped in the desert.

Espinoza thought it was a bad omen that she'd told him the killer made a habit of frequenting the club. When he'd brought her home he kissed her. Rebeca smelled like alcohol and her skin was very cold. He asked if she wanted to make love and she nodded, several times, without saying anything. Then they moved from the front seat into the back and did it. It was a quick fuck. But then she rested her head on his chest, without saying a word, and for a long time he stroked her hair. The smell of chemicals came in waves on the night air. Espinoza wondered whether there was a paper factory nearby. He asked Rebeca and she said there were only houses built by the people who lived in them and empty fields.

•

No matter what time he got back to the hotel, Pelletier was always awake, reading a book and waiting for him. This was his way of reaffirming their friendship, Espinoza thought. It was also possible that Pelletier couldn't sleep and his insomnia drove him to read in the empty hotel lounges until dawn.

Sometimes Pelletier was by the pool, in a sweater or wrapped in a towel, sipping whiskey. Other times Espinoza found him in a room presided over by an enormous border landscape, painted, one could see instantly, by someone who had never been to the border: there was more wishfulness than realism in the industriousness and harmony of the landscape. The waiters, even those on the night shift, made sure Pelletier lacked for nothing, because he was a decent tipper. When Espinoza got in, the two men spent a few minutes exchanging brief, pleasant remarks.

Sometimes, before he went to look for Pelletier in the hotel's empty lounges, he would go check his e-mail, in the hope of finding letters from Europe, from Hellfeld or Borchmeyer, that might shed some light on Archimboldi's whereabouts. Then he would go in search of Pelletier and later both of them would head silently up to their rooms.

•

The next day, said Norton in her letter, I tidied my apartment and put my papers in order. This was done much sooner than I expected. In the afternoon I went to see a film, and on the way out, though I felt calm, I couldn't reconstruct the plot or think who the actors had been. That night I had dinner with a friend and went to bed early, though it was midnight before I fell asleep. As soon as I got up, early in the morning and with no ticket, I went to the airport and booked a seat on the next flight to Italy. I flew from London to Milan, then I took the train to Turin. When Morini opened the door I told him I'd come to stay, that it was up to him to decide whether I should go to a hotel or stay with him. He didn't answer my question. He just moved aside in the wheelchair and asked me in. I went to the bathroom to wash my face. When I returned Morini had made tea and put three little biscuits on a plate, which he urged me to try. I tasted one and it was delicious. It was like a Greek pastry, filled with pistachio and fig paste. I made short work of all three and had two cups of tea. Morini, meanwhile, made a phone call, and then he sat listening to me, stopping me every now and then to ask a question, which I was happy to answer.

We talked for hours. We talked about the Italian Right, about the resurgence of fascism in Europe, about immigrants, about Islamic terrorists, about British and American politics, and as we talked I felt better and better, which is odd because the subjects we were discussing were depressing, until I couldn't go on any longer and I asked him for another magic biscuit, just one, and then Morini looked at the clock and said it was only natural I should be hungry, and he'd do better than give me a pistachio biscuit, he'd made us a reservation at a restaurant in Turin and he was going to take me there for dinner.

The restaurant was in the middle of a garden where there were benches and stone statues. I remember that I pushed Morini's chair and he showed me the statues. Some were of mythological figures, but others were of simple peasants lost in the night. In the park there were other couples strolling and sometimes we crossed paths with them and other times we only glimpsed their shadows. As we ate Morini asked about the two of you. I told him the tip we'd gotten about Archimboldi being in the north of Mexico was false, and that he'd probably never set foot in the country. I told him about your Mexican friend, the great intellectual El Cerdo, and we laughed for a long time. I really was feeling better and better.

•

One night, after making love with Rebeca for the second time in the backseat of the car, Espinoza asked what her family thought of him. The girl said her sisters thought he was handsome and her mother had said he had a responsible look. The smell of chemicals seemed to lift the car from the ground. The next day Espinoza bought five rugs. She asked him why he wanted so many rugs and Espinoza answered that he planned to give them as gifts. When he got back to the hotel he left the rugs on the bed he didn't sleep in, then he sat on his bed and for a fraction of a second the shadows retreated and he had a fleeting glimpse of reality. He felt dizzy and he closed his eyes. Without knowing it he fell asleep.

When he woke up his stomach hurt and he wanted to die. In the afternoon he went shopping. He went into a lingerie shop and a women's clothing shop and a shoe shop. That night he brought Rebeca to the ho-

tel and after they had showered together he dressed her in a thong and
garters and black tights and a black teddy and black spike-heeled shoes
and fucked her until she was no more than a tremor in his arms. Then
he ordered dinner for two from room service and after they ate he gave
her the other gifts he'd bought her and then they fucked again until the
sun began to come up. Then they both got dressed, she packed her gifts
in the bags, and he took her home first and then to the crafts market, where he helped her set up. Before he said goodbye she asked
him whether she would see him again. Espinoza, without knowing why,
maybe just because he was tired, shrugged his shoulders and said you
never know.

"You do know," said Rebeca, in a sad voice he didn't recognize. "Are
you leaving Mexico?" she asked him.

"Someday I have to go," he answered.

•

When he got back to the hotel, Pelletier wasn't on the terrace or at the
pool or in any of the lounges where he usually hid away to read. He
asked at the desk whether it had been long since his friend went out and
they told him that Pelletier hadn't left the hotel at all. He went up to
Pelletier's room and knocked on the door, but no one answered. He
knocked again, banging several times, to no avail. He told the clerk he
was afraid something had happened to his friend, that he might have
had a heart attack, and the clerk, who knew them both, went up with
Espinoza.

"I doubt anything bad has happened," he said to Espinoza in the
elevator.

After opening the door with the passkey, the clerk didn't cross the
threshold. The room was dark and Espinoza turned on the light. On one
of the beds he saw Pelletier with the bedspread pulled up to his chin.
He was on his back, his face turned slightly to one side, and he had his
hands folded on his chest. There was a peaceful expression on his face
that Espinoza had never seen before. Espinoza called out to him:

"Pelletier, Pelletier."

The clerk, his curiosity getting the better of him, advanced a few
steps and advised him not to touch Pelletier.

"Pelletier," shouted Espinoza, and he sat down beside him and shook
him by the shoulders.

Then Pelletier opened his eyes and asked what was going on.

"We thought you were dead," said Espinoza.

"No," said Pelletier, "I was dreaming I was on vacation in the Greek islands and I rented a boat and I met a boy who spent the whole day diving.

"It was a beautiful dream," he said.

"It sure does sound relaxing," said the clerk.

"The strangest part of the dream," said Pelletier, "was that the water was alive."

●

The first few hours of my first night in Turin, said Norton in her letter, I spent in Morini's guest room. I had no trouble falling asleep, but all of a sudden a thunderclap, real or in my dream, woke me, and I thought I saw Morini and his wheelchair silhouetted at the end of the hallway. At first I ignored him and tried to go back to sleep, until suddenly it struck me what I'd seen: to one side the outline of the wheelchair in the hallway and to the other side the figure of Morini, not in the hallway but in the sitting room, with his back to me. I started awake, grabbed an ashtray, and turned on the light. The hallway was deserted. I went to the sitting room and no one was there. Months before, I would've just drunk a glass of water and gone back to bed, but nothing would ever be the same again. So I went to Morini's room. When I opened the door the first thing I saw was the wheelchair to one side of the bed, and then the bulk of Morini, who was breathing steadily. I whispered his name. He didn't move. I raised my voice and Morini's voice asked me what was wrong.

"I saw you in the hallway," I said.

"When?" asked Morini.

"A minute ago, when I heard the thunder."

"Is it raining?" asked Morini.

"It must be," I said.

"I wasn't in the hallway, Liz," said Morini.

"I saw you there. You had gotten up. The wheelchair was in the hallway, facing me, but you were at the end of the hallway, in the sitting room, with your back to me," I said.

"It must have been a dream," said Morini.

"The wheelchair was facing me and you had your back to me," I said.

"Calm down, Liz," said Morini.

"Don't tell me to calm down, don't treat me like a fool. The wheel-chair was looking at me, and you were standing there cool as can be, not looking at me. Do you understand?"

Morini allowed himself a few minutes to think, propped on his elbows.

"I think so," he said. "My chair was watching you while I was ignoring you, yes? As if the chair and I were a single person or a single being. And the chair was bad precisely because it was watching you, and I was bad too, because I had lied to you and I wasn't looking at you."

Then I started to laugh and I said that really, as far as I was concerned, he could never be bad, and neither could the wheelchair, since it was of such great use to him.

The rest of the night we spent together. I told him to move over and make room for me and Morini obeyed without a word.

"How could it have taken me so long to realize you loved me?" I asked him afterward. "How could it have taken me so long to realize I loved you?"

"It's my fault," said Morini in the dark, "I'm hopeless at these things."

•

In the morning Espinoza gave the clerks and the guards and the waiters at the hotel some of the rugs and serapes he'd been accumulating. He also gave rugs to the two women who cleaned his room. The last serape—a very pretty one, with a red, green, and lavender geometric motif—he put in a bag and told the clerk to have it sent up to Pelletier.

"An anonymous gift," he said.

The clerk winked at him and said he would take care of it.

When Espinoza got to the crafts market she was sitting on a wooden bench reading a pop magazine full of color photos, with articles on Mexican singers, their weddings, divorces, tours, their gold and platinum albums, their stints in prison, their deaths in poverty. He sat down next to her, on the curb, and wondered whether to greet her with a kiss or not. Across the way was a new stall that sold little clay figurines. From where he was Espinoza could make out some tiny gallows and he smiled sadly. He asked the girl where her brother was, and she said he'd gone to school, like every morning.

A woman with very wrinkled skin, dressed in white as if she were about to get married, stopped to talk to Rebeca, so he picked up the magazine, which the girl had left under the table on a lunch box, and leafed through it until Rebeca's friend was gone. A few times he tried to say something, but he couldn't. Her silence wasn't unpleasant, nor did it imply resentment or sadness. It was transparent, not dense. It took up almost no space. A person could even get used to silence like this, thought Espinoza, and be happy. But he would never get used to it, he knew that too.

When he got tired of sitting he went to a bar and asked for a beer at the counter. Around him there were only men and no one was alone. Espinoza swept the bar with a terrible gaze and immediately he saw that the men were drinking but eating too. He muttered the word *fuck* and spat on the floor, less than an inch from his own shoes. Then he had another beer and went back to the stall with the half-empty bottle. Rebeca looked at him and smiled. Espinoza sat on the sidewalk next to her and told her he was going home. The girl didn't say anything.

"I'll be coming back to Santa Teresa," he said, "in less than a year, I swear."

"Don't swear," said the girl, smiling in a pleased way.

"I'll come back to you," said Espinoza, swallowing the last of his beer. "And maybe we'll get married and you'll come to Madrid with me."

It sounded as if the girl said: that would be nice, but Espinoza couldn't hear her.

"What? What?" he asked.

Rebeca was silent.

•

When he got back that night, Pelletier was reading and drinking whiskey by the pool. Espinoza sat in the deck chair next to him and asked what their plans were. Pelletier smiled and set his book on the table.

"I found your gift in my room," he said, "and it's perfect. Even charming."

"Ah, the serape," said Espinoza, and he let himself fall back on the deck chair.

There were many stars in the sky. The green-blue water of the pool danced on the tables and on the pots of flowers and cacti, in a chain of reflections stretching off to a cream-colored brick wall, behind which lay a tennis court and a sauna that Espinoza had successfully avoided. Every so often the *pock* of a racquet could be heard, and muted voices commenting on the game.

Pelletier stood up and said let's walk. He headed toward the tennis

court, followed by Espinoza. The court lights were on and two men with
big bellies were struggling through an inept game, making the two
women watching them laugh. The women were sitting on a wooden
bench, under an umbrella like those around the pool. Beyond them, behind a wire fence, was the sauna, a cement box with two tiny windows
like the portholes of a sunken ship. Sitting on the brick wall, Pelletier
said:

"We aren't going to find Archimboldi."

"I've known that for days," said Espinoza.

Then he leaped and leaped again until he was sitting on the wall, his
legs dangling down toward the tennis court.

"And yet," said Pelletier, "I'm sure Archimboldi is here, in Santa
Teresa."

Espinoza looked at his hands, as if he feared he had hurt himself.
One of the women got up from her seat and ran onto the court. When
she reached one of the men, she said something in his ear and then she
ran back off the court. The man she'd spoken to lifted his arms, opened
his mouth, and threw back his head, all without making the slightest
sound. The other man, dressed just like the first in spotless white,
waited until his opponent had finished his silent rejoicing and was calm,
and then he tossed the ball. The match started up again and the women
laughed some more.

"Believe me," said Pelletier in a very soft voice, like the breeze that
was blowing just then, suffusing everything with the scent of flowers, "I
know Archimboldi is here."

"Where?" asked Espinoza.

"Somewhere, either in Santa Teresa or else nearby."

"So why haven't we found him?" asked Espinoza.

One of the tennis players fell and Pelletier smiled.

"That doesn't matter. Because we've been clumsy or because Archimboldi is extraordinarily good at self-concealment. It means nothing. The
important thing is something else entirely."

"What?" asked Espinoza.

"That he's here," said Pelletier, and he motioned toward the sauna,
the hotel, the court, the fence, the dry brush that could be glimpsed in
the distance, on the unlit hotel grounds. The hair rose on the back of
Espinoza's neck. The cement box where the sauna was looked like a
bunker holding a corpse.

"I believe you," he said, and he really did believe what his friend was saying.

"Archimboldi is here," said Pelletier, "and we're here, and this is the closest we'll ever be to him."

•

I don't know how long we'll last together, said Norton in her letter. It doesn't matter to me or to Morini either (I think). We love each other and we're happy. I know the two of you will understand.

2
THE PART ABOUT AMALFITANO

I don't know what I'm doing in Santa Teresa, Amalfitano said to himself after he'd been living in the city for a week. Don't you? Don't you really? he asked himself. Really I don't, he said to himself, and that was as eloquent as he could be.

•

He had a little single-story house, three bedrooms, a full bathroom and a half bathroom, a combined kitchen–living room–dining room with windows that faced west, a small brick porch where there was a wooden bench worn by the wind that came down from the mountains and the sea, the wind from the north, the wind through the gaps, the wind that smelled like smoke and came from the south. He had books he'd kept for more than twenty-five years. Not many. All of them old. He had books he'd bought in the last ten years, books he didn't mind lending, books that could've been lost or stolen for all he cared. He had books that he sometimes received neatly packaged and with unfamiliar return addresses, books he didn't even open anymore. He had a yard perfect for growing grass and planting flowers, but he didn't know what flowers would do best there—flowers, as opposed to cacti or succulents. There would be time (so he thought) for gardening. He had a wooden gate that needed a coat of paint. He had a monthly salary.

•

He had a daughter named Rosa who had always lived with him. Hard to believe, but true.

•

Sometimes, at night, he remembered Rosa's mother and sometimes he laughed and other times he felt like crying. He thought of her while he was shut in his office with Rosa asleep in her room. The living room was empty and quiet, and the lights were off. Anyone listening carefully on the porch would have heard the whine of a few mosquitoes. But no one was listening. The houses next door were silent and dark.

•

Rosa was seventeen and she was Spanish. Amalfitano was fifty and Chilean. Rosa had had a passport since she was ten. On some of their trips, remembered Amalfitano, they had found themselves in strange situations, because Rosa went through customs by the gate for EU citizens and Amalfitano went by the gate for non-EU citizens. The first time, Rosa threw a tantrum and started to cry and refused to be separated from her father. Another time, since the lines were moving at different speeds, the EU citizens' line quickly and the noncitizens' line more slowly and laboriously, Rosa got lost and it took Amalfitano half an hour to find her. Sometimes the customs officers would see Rosa, so little, and ask whether she was traveling alone or whether someone was waiting for her outside. Rosa would answer that she was traveling with her father, who was South American, and she was supposed to wait for him right there. Once Rosa's suitcase was searched because they suspected her father of smuggling drugs or arms under cover of his daughter's innocence and nationality. But Amalfitano had never trafficked in drugs, or for that matter arms.

•

It was Lola, Rosa's mother, who always traveled with a weapon, never going anywhere without her stainless-steel spring-loaded switchblade, Amalfitano remembered as he smoked a Mexican cigarette, sitting in his office or standing on the dark porch. Once they were stopped in an airport, before Rosa was born, and Lola was asked what she was doing with the knife. It's for peeling fruit, she said. Oranges, apples, pears, kiwis, all kinds of fruit. The officer gave her a long look and let her go. A year and a few months after that, Rosa was born. Two years later, Lola left, still carrying the knife.

•

Lola's pretext was a plan to visit her favorite poet, who lived in the insane asylum in Mondragón, near San Sebastián. Amalfitano listened to her explanations for a whole night as she packed her bag and promised she'd come home soon to him and Rosa. Lola, especially toward the end, used to claim that she knew the poet, that she'd met him at a party in Barcelona before Amalfitano became a part of her life. At this party, which Lola described as a wild party, a long overdue party that suddenly sprang to life in the middle of the summer heat and a traffic jam of cars with red lights on, she had slept with him and they'd made love all night, although Amalfitano knew it wasn't true, not just because the poet was gay, but because Lola had first heard of the poet's existence from him, when he'd given her one of his books. Then Lola took it upon herself to buy everything else the poet had written and to choose friends who thought the poet was a genius, an alien, God's messenger, friends who had themselves just been released from the Sant Boi asylum or had flipped out after repeated stints in rehab. The truth was, Amalfitano knew that sooner or later she would make her way to San Sebastián, so he chose not to argue but offered her part of his savings, begged her to come back in a few months, and promised to take good care of Rosa. Lola seemed not to hear a thing. When she had finished, she went into the kitchen, made coffee, and sat in silence, waiting for dawn, although Amalfitano tried to come up with subjects of conversation that might interest her or at least help pass the time. At six-thirty the doorbell rang and Lola jumped. They've come for me, she said, and since she didn't move, Amalfitano had to get up and ask over the intercom who it was. He heard a weak voice saying it's me. Who is it? asked Amalfitano. Let me in, it's me, said the voice. Who? asked Amalfitano. The voice, while still barely audible, seemed indignant at the interrogation. Me me me me, it said. Amalfitano closed his eyes and buzzed the door open. He heard the sound of the elevator cables and he went back to the kitchen. Lola was still sitting there, sipping the last of her coffee. I think it's for you, said Amalfitano. Lola gave no sign of having heard him. Are you going to say goodbye to Rosa? asked Amalfitano. Lola looked up and said it was better not to wake her. There were dark circles under her blue eyes. Then the doorbell rang twice and Amalfitano went to open the door. A small woman, no more than five feet tall, gave him a brief glance and murmured an unintelligible greeting, then brushed past him and went straight to the kitchen, as if she knew Lola's habits better than Amalfitano did. When he returned to the kitchen he noticed the woman's knapsack, which she had left on the floor by the refrigerator, smaller than Lola's, almost a miniature. The woman's name was Inmaculada, but Lola called her Imma. Amalfitano had encountered her a few times in the apartment when he came home from work, and then the woman had told him her name and what she liked to be called. Imma was short for Immaculada, in Catalan, but Lola's friend wasn't Catalan and her name wasn't Immaculada with a double *m*, either, it was Inmaculada, and Amalfitano, for phonetic reasons, preferred to call her Inma, although each time he did his wife scolded him, until he decided not to call her anything. He watched them from the kitchen door. He felt much calmer than he had expected. Lola and her friend had their eyes fixed on the Formica table, although Amalfitano couldn't help noticing that both looked up now and then and stared at each other with an intensity unfamiliar to him. Lola asked whether anyone wanted more coffee. She means me, thought Amalfitano. Inmaculada shook her head and said there was no time, they should get moving, since before long there would be no way out of Barcelona. She talks as if Barcelona were a medieval city, thought Amalfitano. Lola and her friend stood up. Amalfitano stepped forward and opened the refrigerator door to get a beer, driven by a sudden thirst. To do so, he had to move Imma's backpack. It was so light it might've held just two shirts and another pair of black pants. It's like a fetus, was what Amalfitano thought, and he dropped it to one side. Then Lola kissed him on both cheeks and she and her friend were gone.

•

A week later Amalfitano got a letter from Lola, postmarked Pamplona. In the letter she told him that their trip so far had been full of pleasant and unpleasant experiences. Mostly pleasant. And although the unpleasant experiences could certainly be called unpleasant, *experiences* might not be the right word. Nothing unpleasant that happens to us can take us by surprise, said Lola, because Imma has lived through all of this already. For two days, said Lola, we were working at a roadside restaurant in Lérida, for a man who also owned an apple orchard. It was a big orchard and there were already green apples on the trees. In a little while the apple harvest would begin, and the owner had asked them to stay till then. Imma had gone to talk to him while Lola read a book by the Mondragón poet (she had all the books he'd published so far in her backpack), sitting by the Canadian tent where the two of them slept. The tent was pitched in the shade of a poplar, the only poplar she'd seen in the orchard, next to a garage that no one used anymore. A little while later, Imma came back, and she didn't want to explain the deal the restaurant owner had offered her. The next day they headed back out to the highway to hitchhike, without telling anyone goodbye. In Zaragoza they stayed with an old friend of Imma's from university. Lola was very tired and she went to bed early and in her dreams she heard laughter and loud voices and scolding, almost all Imma's but some her friend's, too. They talked about the old days, about the struggle against Franco, about the women's prison in Zaragoza. They talked about a pit, a very deep hole from which oil or coal could be extracted, about an underground jungle, about a commando team of female suicide bombers. Then Lola's letter took an abrupt turn. I'm not a lesbian, she said, I don't know why I'm telling you this, I don't know why I'm treating you like a child by saying it. Homosexuality is a lie, it's an act of violence committed against us in our adolescence, she said. Imma knows this. She knows it, she knows it, she's too clearsighted not to, but all she can do is help. Imma is a lesbian, every day hundreds of thousands of cows are sacrificed, every day a herd of herbivores or several herds cross the valley, from north to south, so slowly but so fast it makes me sick, right now, now, now, do you understand, Óscar? No, thought Amalfitano, I don't, as he held the letter in his two hands like a life raft of reeds and grasses, and with his foot he steadily rocked his daughter in her seat.

•

Then Lola described again the night when she'd made love with the poet, who lay in majestic and semisecret repose in the Mondragón asylum. He was still free back then, he hadn't yet been committed to any institution. He lived in Barcelona, with a gay philosopher, and they threw parties together once a week or once every two weeks. This was before I knew you. I don't know whether you'd come to Spain yet or whether you were in Italy or France or some filthy Latin American hole. The gay philosopher's parties were famous in Barcelona. People said the poet and the philosopher were lovers, but it never looked that way. One had an apartment and ideas and money, and the other had his legend and his poetry and the fervor of the true believer, a doglike fervor, the fervor of the whipped dog that's spent the night or all its youth in the rain, Spain's endless storm of dandruff, and has finally found a place to lay its head, no matter if it's a bucket of putrid water, a vaguely familiar bucket of water. One day fortune smiled on me and I attended one of these parties. To say I met the philosopher would be an exaggeration. I saw him. In a corner of the room, talking to another poet and another philosopher. He appeared to be giving a lecture. Then everything seemed slightly off. The guests were waiting for the poet to make his entrance. They were waiting for him to pick a fight. Or to defecate in the middle of the living room, on a Turkish carpet like the threadbare carpet from the *Thousand and One Nights*, a battered carpet that sometimes functioned as a mirror, reflecting all of us from below. I mean: it turned into a mirror at the command of our spasms. Neurochemical spasms. When the poet showed up, though, nothing happened. At first all eyes turned to him, to see what could be had. Then everybody went back to what they'd been doing and the poet said hello to certain writer friends and joined the group around the gay philosopher. I had been dancing with myself and I kept dancing with myself. At five in the morning I went into one of the bedrooms. The poet was leading me by the hand. Without getting undressed, I began to make love with him. I came three times, feeling the poet's breath on my neck. It took him quite a while longer. In the semidarkness I made out three shadowy figures in a corner of the room. One of them was smoking. Another one never stopped whispering. The third was the philosopher and I realized that the bed was his and the room was the room where, the gossip was, he and the poet made love. But now I was the one making love and the poet was gentle with me and the only thing I didn't understand was why the other three were watching, although I didn't much care, in those days, if you remember, nothing really mattered. When the poet finally came, crying out and turning his head to look at his three friends, I was sorry it wasn't the right time of month, because I would've loved to have his baby. Then he got up and went over to the shadowy figures. One of them put a hand on his shoulder. Another one gave him something. I got up and went to the bathroom without even looking at them. The last party guests were in the living room. In the bathroom, a girl was asleep in the tub. I washed my face and hands. I combed my hair. When I came out the philosopher was kicking everyone out who could still walk. He didn't look the least bit drunk or high. He looked fresh, as if he'd just got up and drunk a big glass of orange juice. I left with a couple of people I'd met at the party. At that hour only the Drugstore on Las Ramblas was open and we headed there without a word. At the Drugstore I ran into a girl I'd known a few years before who was a reporter for *Ajoblanco*, although it disgusted her to work there. She started to talk to me about moving to Madrid. She asked if I felt like I needed a change. I shrugged my shoulders. All cities are more or less the same, I said. What I was really thinking about was the poet and what he and I had just done. A gay man doesn't do that. Everyone said he was gay, but I knew it wasn't true. Then I thought about the confusion of the senses and I understood everything. I knew the poet had lost his way, he was a lost child and I could save him, give him back a small part of all he'd given me. For almost a month I kept watch outside the philosopher's building hoping one day I'd see the poet and he'd ask me to make love with him again. I didn't see him, but one night I saw the philosopher. I noticed that something was wrong with his face. When he got closer (he didn't recognize me) I could see he had a black eye and was covered in bruises. No sign of the poet. Sometimes I tried to guess, by the lights, what floor the apartment was on. Sometimes I saw shadows behind the curtains. Sometimes someone, an older woman, a man in a tie, a long-faced adolescent, would open a window and look out at the grid of Barcelona at dusk. One night I discovered I wasn't the only one there, spying on the poet or waiting for him to appear. A kid, maybe eighteen, maybe younger, was quietly keeping watch from the opposite sidewalk. He hadn't noticed me because clearly he was the heedless type, a dreamer. He would sit at a bar, at an outside table, and he always ordered a can of Coca-Cola, sipping it slowly as he wrote in a school notebook or read books that I recognized at a glance. One night, before he could get up from the table and dash away, I went over and sat down next to him. I told him I knew what he was doing. Who are you? he asked me, terrified. I smiled and said I was someone like him. He looked at me the way you look at a crazy person. Don't get the wrong idea, I said, I'm not crazy, I'm in full possession of my faculties. He laughed. You look crazy, he said, even if you aren't. Then he motioned for the check and he was about to get up when I confessed that I was looking for the poet, too. He sat down again abruptly, as if I'd clapped a gun to his head. I ordered a chamomile tea and told him my story. He told me that he wrote poetry, too, and he wanted the poet to read his poems. There was no need to ask to know that he was gay and very lonely. Let me see them, I said, and I pulled the notebook out of his hands. His poems weren't bad. His only problem was that he wrote just like the poet. These things can't have happened to you, I said, you're too young to have suffered this much. He made a gesture as if to say that he didn't care whether I believed him or not. What matters is that it's well written, he said. No, I told him, you know that isn't what matters. Wrong, wrong, wrong, I said, and finally he had to cede the point. His name was Jordi and today he may be teaching at the university or writing reviews for *La Vanguardia* or *El Periódico*.

•

Amalfitano received the next letter from San Sebastián. In it, Lola told him that she'd gone with Imma to the asylum at Mondragón to visit the poet, who lived there, raving and demented, and that the guards, priests disguised as security guards, wouldn't let them in. In San Sebastián they had plans to stay with a friend of Imma's, a Basque girl named Edurne, who had been an ETA commando and had given up the armed struggle when democracy came, and who didn't want them in her house for more than one night, saying she had lots to do and her husband didn't like unexpected guests. Her husband's name was Jon, and guests really did make him nervous, as Lola had opportunity to observe. He shook, he flushed as red as a glowing clay pot, he always seemed about to burst out shouting although he never spoke a word, he was sweaty and his hands shook, he was constantly moving, as if he couldn't sit still for two minutes at a time. Edurne herself was very relaxed. She had a little boy (though Lola and Imma never saw him, because Jon always found a reason to keep them out of his room) and she worked almost full-time as a street educator, with junkie families and the street people who huddled on the steps of the cathedral of San Sebastián and only wanted to be left alone, as Edurne explained, laughing, as if she'd just told a joke that only Imma understood, because neither Lola nor Jon laughed. That night they had dinner together and the next day they left. They found a cheap boardinghouse that Edurne had told them about and they hitchhiked back to Mondragón. They weren't allowed into the asylum this time either, but they settled for studying it from the outside, noting and committing to memory all the dirt and gravel roads they could see, the gray walls, the rises and curves of the land, the walks taken by the inmates and their caretakers, whom they watched from a distance, the curtains of trees following one after the other at unpredictable intervals or in a pattern they didn't understand, and the brush where they thought they saw flies, by which they deduced that some of the inmates and maybe even a worker or two urinated there in the dark or as night fell. Then they sat together by the side of the road and ate the cheese sandwiches they'd brought from San Sebastián, without talking, or musing as if to themselves on the fractured shadows that the asylum of Mondragón cast over its surroundings.

•

For their third try, they called to make an appointment. Imma passed herself off as a reporter from a Barcelona newspaper and Lola claimed to be a poet. This time they got to see him. Lola thought he looked older, his eyes sunken, his hair thinner than before. At first they were accompanied by a doctor or priest, who led them down the endless corridors, painted blue and white, until they came to a nondescript room where the poet was waiting. It was Lola's impression that the asylum people were proud to have him as a patient. All of them knew him, all of them greeted him as he headed to the garden or went to receive his daily dose of tranquilizers. When they were alone she told him that she'd missed him, that for a while she'd kept watch over the philosopher's apartment in the Ensanche, and that despite her perseverance she'd never seen him again. It's not my fault, she said, I did everything I could. The poet looked her in the eyes and asked for a cigarette. Imma was standing next to the bench where they were sitting and wordlessly she handed him a cigarette. The poet said thank you and then he said perseverance. I was, I was, I was, said Lola, who was turned toward him, her gaze fixed on him, although out of the corner of her eye she saw that Imma, after flicking her lighter, had taken a book out of her bag and begun to read, standing there like a tiny and infinitely patient Amazon, the lighter still visible in one of her hands as she held the book. Then Lola started to talk about the trip they had made together. She spoke of highways and back roads, problems with chauvinist truck drivers, cities and towns, nameless forests where they had pitched camp, rivers and gas station bathrooms where they had washed. The poet, meanwhile, blew smoke out of his mouth and nose, making perfect rings, bluish nimbuses, gray cumulonimbuses that dissolved in the park breeze or were carried off toward the edge of the grounds where a dark forest rose, the branches of the trees silver in the light falling from the hills. As if to gain time, Lola described the two previous visits, fruitless but eventful. And then she told him what she had really come to say: that she knew he wasn't gay, she knew he was a prisoner and wanted to escape, she knew that love, no matter how mistreated or mutilated, always left room for hope, and that hope was her plan (or the other way around), and that its materialization, its objectification, consisted of his fleeing the asylum with her and heading for France. What about her? asked the poet, who was taking sixteen pills a day and recording his visions, and he pointed at Imma, who read on undaunted, still standing, as if her skirts and underskirts were made of concrete and she couldn't sit down. She'll help us, said Lola. In fact, the plan was hers in the first place. We'll cross into France over the mountains, like pilgrims. We'll make our way to Saint-Jean-de-Luz and take the train to Paris, traveling through the countryside, which is the prettiest in the world at this time of year. We'll live in hostels. That's Imma's plan. She and I will work cleaning or taking care of children in the wealthy neighborhoods of Paris while you write poetry. At night you'll read us your poems and make love to me. That's Imma's plan, worked out to the last detail. After three or four months I'll be pregnant, and that will prove for once and for all that you aren't a nonbreeder, the last of your line. What more can our enemy families want! I'll keep working a few more months, but when the time comes, Imma will have to work twice as hard. We'll live like mendicants or child prophets while Paris trains a distant eye on fashion, movies, games of chance, French and American literature, gastronomy, the gross domestic product, arms exports, the manufacture of massive batches of anesthesia, all mere backdrop for our fetus's first few months. Then, when I'm six months pregnant, we'll go back to Spain, though this time we won't cross over at Irún but at La Jonquera or Port Bou, into Catalan country. The poet looked at her with interest (and also at Imma, who never took her eyes off his poems, poems he'd written perhaps five years ago, he thought), and he began to blow smoke rings again, in the most unlikely shapes, as if he'd spent his long stay in Mondragón perfecting that peculiar art. How do you do it? asked Lola. With the tongue, and by pursing the lips a certain way, he said. Sometimes by making a kind of fluted shape. Sometimes like someone who's burned himself. Sometimes like sucking a small to medium dick. Sometimes like shooting a Zen arrow with a Zen bow into a Zen pavilion. Ah, I understand, said Lola. You, read a poem, said the poet. Imma looked at him and raised the book a little higher, as if she was trying to hide behind it. Which poem? Whichever one you like best, said the poet. I like them all, said Imma. So read one, said the poet. When Imma had finished reading a poem about a labyrinth and Ariadne lost in the labyrinth and a young Spaniard who lived in a Paris garret, the poet asked if they had any chocolate. No, said Lola. We don't smoke these days, said Imma, we're focusing all our efforts on getting you out of here. The poet smiled. I didn't mean that kind of chocolate, he said, I meant the other kind, the kind made with cocoa and milk and sugar. Oh, I see, said Lola, and they both were forced to admit they hadn't brought anything like that either. They remembered that they had cheese sandwiches in their bags, wrapped in napkins and aluminum foil, and they offered them to him, but the poet seemed not to hear. Before it began to get dark, a flock of big blackbirds flew over the park, vanishing northward. A doctor approached along the gravel path, his white robe flapping in the evening breeze. When he reached them he asked the poet how he felt, calling him by his first name as if they'd been friends since adolescence. The poet gave him a blank look, and, calling him by his first name too, said he was a little tired. The doctor, whose name was Gorka and who couldn't have been more than thirty, sat down beside him and put a hand on his forehead, then took his pulse. You're doing fucking great, man, he said. And how are the ladies? he asked, with a smile full of health and cheer. Imma didn't answer. Lola had the sense that Imma was dying behind her book. Just fine, she said, it's been a while since we saw each other and we're having a wonderful time. So you knew each other already? asked the doctor. Not me, said Imma, and she turned the page. I knew him, said Lola, we were friends a few years ago, in Barcelona, when he lived in Barcelona. In fact, she said, looking up at the last blackbirds, the stragglers, taking flight just as someone turned on the park lights from a hidden switch in the asylum, we were more than friends. How interesting, said Gorka, his eyes on the birds, which at that time of day and in the artificial light had a burnished glow. What year was that? asked the doctor. It was 1979 or 1978, I can't remember now, said Lola in a faint voice. I hope you won't think I'm indiscreet, said the doctor, but I'm writing a biography of our friend and the more information I can gather on his life, the better, wouldn't you say? Someday he'll leave here, said Gorka, smoothing his eyebrows, someday the Spanish public will have to recognize him as one of the greats, I don't mean they'll give him a prize, hardly, no Príncipe de Asturias or Cervantes for him, let alone a seat in the Academy, literary careers in Spain are for social climbers, operators, and ass kissers, if you'll pardon the expression. But someday he'll leave here. There's no question about that. Someday I'll leave, too. And so will my patients and my colleagues' patients. Someday all of us will finally leave Mondragón, and this noble institution, ecclesiastical in origin, charitable in aim, will stand abandoned. Then my biography will be of interest and I'll be able to publish it, but in the meantime, as you can imagine, it's my duty to collect information, dates, names, confirm stories, some in questionable taste, even damaging, others more picturesque, stories that revolve around a chaotic center of gravity, which is our friend here, or what he's willing to reveal, the ordered self he presents, ordered verbally, I mean, according to a strategy I think I understand, although its purpose is a mystery to me, an order concealing a verbal disorder that would shake us to the core if ever we were to experience it, even as spectators of a staged performance. Doctor, you're a sweetheart, said Lola. Imma ground her teeth. Then Lola began to tell Gorka about her heterosexual experience with the poet, but her friend sidled over and kicked her in the ankle with the pointed toe of her shoe. Just then, the poet, who had begun to blow smoke rings again, remembered the apartment in Barcelona's Ensanche and remembered the philosopher, and although his eyes didn't light up, part of his bone structure did: the jaws, the chin, the hollow cheeks, as if he'd been lost in the Amazon and three Sevillian friars had rescued him, or a monstrous three-headed friar, which held no terror for him either. So, turning to Lola, he asked her about the philosopher, said the philosopher's name, talked about his stay in the philosopher's apartment, the months he'd spent in Barcelona with no job, playing stupid jokes, throwing books that he hadn't bought out the window (as the philosopher ran down the stairs to retrieve them, which wasn't always possible), playing loud music, practically never sleeping and laughing all the time, taking the occasional assignment as a translator or lead reviewer, a liquid star of boiling water. And then Lola was afraid and she covered her face with her hands. And Imma, who had at last put the book of poems away in her pocket, did the same, covering her face with her small, knotty hands. And Gorka looked from the two women to the poet and laughter bubbled up inside him. But before the laughter could fade in his placid heart, Lola said the philosopher had recently died of AIDS. Well, well,

well, said the poet. He who laughs last, laughs best, said the poet. The early bird doesn't always catch the worm, the poet said. I love you, said Lola. The poet got up and asked Imma for another cigarette. For tomorrow, he said. The doctor and the poet made their way down one path toward the asylum. Lola and Imma took a different path toward the gate, where they ran into the sister of another lunatic and the son of a laborer, also mad, and a woman with a sorrowful look whose cousin was interned in the asylum.

•

They returned the next day but were told that the patient was on bedrest. The same thing happened the following days. One day their money ran out, and Imma decided to take to the road again, this time heading south, to Madrid, where she had a brother who had done well for himself under the democracy and whom she planned to ask for a loan. Lola didn't have the strength to travel and the two women agreed that she should wait at the boardinghouse, as if nothing had happened, and Imma would be back in a week. Alone, Lola killed time writing long letters to Amalfitano in which she described her daily life in San Sebastián and the area around the asylum, which she visited every day. Clinging to the fence, she imagined that she was establishing telepathic contact with the poet. Most of the time she would find a clearing in the nearby woods and read or pick little flowers and bunches of grasses with which she made bouquets that she dropped through the railings or took back to the boardinghouse. Once one of the drivers who picked her up on the highway asked if she wanted to see the Mondragón cemetery and she said she did. He parked the car outside, under an acacia tree, and for a while they walked among the graves, most of them with Basque names, until they came to the niche where the driver's mother was buried. Then he told Lola that he'd like to fuck her right there. Lola laughed and warned him that they would be in plain view of any visitor coming along the cemetery's main path. The driver thought for a few seconds, then he said: Christ, you're right. They went looking for a more private spot and it was all over in less than fifteen minutes. The driver's last name was Larrazábal, and although he had a first name, he didn't want to tell her what it was. Just Larrazábal, like my friends call me, he said. Then he told Lola that this wasn't the first time he'd made love in the cemetery. He'd been there with a sort-of girlfriend before, with a girl he'd met at a club, and with two prostitutes from San Sebastián. As they were leaving, he tried to give her money, but she wouldn't take it. They talked for a long time in the car. Larrazábal asked her whether she had a relative at the asylum, and Lola told him her story. Larrazábal said he'd never read a poem. He added that he didn't understand Lola's obsession with the poet. I don't understand your fascination with fucking in the cemetery either, said Lola, but I don't judge you for it. True, Larrazábal admitted, everyone's got obsessions. Before Lola got out of the car, at the entrance to the asylum, Larrazábal snuck a five-thousand-peseta note into her pocket. Lola noticed but didn't say anything and then she was left alone under the trees, in front of the iron gate to the madhouse, home to the poet who was supremely ignoring her.

•

After a week Imma still wasn't back. Lola imagined her tiny, impassively staring, with her face like an educated peasant's or a high school teacher's looking out over a vast prehistoric field, a woman near fifty, dressed in black, walking without looking to either side, without looking back, through a valley where it was still possible to distinguish the tracks of the great predators from the tracks of the scurrying herbivores. She imagined her stopped at a crossroads as the trucks with their many tons of cargo passed at full speed, raising dust clouds that didn't touch her, as if her hesitance and vulnerability constituted a state of grace, a dome that protected her from the inclemencies of fate, nature, and her fellow beings. On the ninth day the owner of the boardinghouse kicked her out. After that she slept at the railroad station, or in an abandoned warehouse where some tramps slept, each keeping to himself, or in the open country, near the border between the asylum and the outside world. One night she hitchhiked to the cemetery and slept in an empty niche. The next morning she felt happy and lucky and she decided to wait there for Imma to come back. She had water to drink and wash her face and brush her teeth, she was near the asylum, it was a peaceful spot. One afternoon, as she was laying a shirt that she had just washed out to dry on a white slab propped against the cemetery wall, she heard voices coming from a mausoleum, and she went to see what was happening. The mausoleum belonged to the Lagasca family, and judging by the state it was in, the last of the Lagascas had long since died or moved far away. Inside the crypt she saw the beam of a flashlight and she asked who was there.

Christ, it's you, she heard a voice say inside. She thought it might be thieves or workers restoring the mausoleum or grave robbers, then she heard a kind of meow and when she was about to turn away she saw Larrazábal's sallow face at the barred door of the crypt. Then a woman came out. Larrazábal ordered her to wait for him by his car, and for a while he and Lola talked and strolled arm in arm along the cemetery paths until the sun began to drop behind the worn edges of the niches.

•

Madness is contagious, thought Amalfitano, sitting on the floor of his front porch as the sky grew suddenly overcast and the moon and the stars disappeared, along with the ghostly lights that are famously visible without binoculars or telescope in northern Sonora and southern Arizona.

•

Madness really is contagious, and friends are a blessing, especially when you're on your own. It was in these words, years before, in a letter with no postmark, that Lola had told Amalfitano about her chance encounter with Larrazábal, which ended with him forcing her to accept a loan of ten thousand pesetas and promising to come back the next day, before he got in his car, motioning to the prostitute who was waiting impatiently for him to do the same. That night Lola slept in her niche, although she was tempted to try the open crypt, happy because things were looking up. The next morning, she scrubbed herself all over with a wet rag, brushed her teeth, combed her hair, put on clean clothes, then went out to the highway to hitchhike to Mondragón. In town she bought some goat cheese and bread and had breakfast in the square, hungrily, since she honestly couldn't remember the last time she'd eaten. Then she went into a bar full of construction workers and had coffee. She'd forgotten when Larrazábal had said he'd come to the cemetery, but that didn't matter, and in the same distant way, Larrazábal and the cemetery and the town and the tremulous early morning landscape didn't matter to her either. Before she left the bar she went into the bathroom and looked at herself in the mirror. She walked back to the highway and stood there waiting until a woman stopped and asked where she was going. To the asylum, said Lola. Her reply clearly took the woman aback, but she told her to get in nevertheless. That's where she was going. Are you visiting someone or are you an inmate? she asked Lola. I'm visiting, answered Lola. The woman's face was thin and long, her almost nonexistent lips giving her a cold, calculating look, although she had nice cheekbones and she dressed like a professional woman who is no longer single, who has a house, a husband, maybe even a child to care for. My father is there, she confessed. Lola didn't say anything. When they reached the entrance, Lola got out of the car and the woman went on alone. For a while Lola wandered along the edge of the asylum grounds. She heard the sound of horses and she guessed that somewhere, on the other side of the woods, there must be a riding club or school. At a certain point she spotted the red-tiled roof of a house that wasn't part of the asylum. She retraced her steps. She returned to the section of fence that gave the best view of the grounds. As the sun rose higher in the sky she saw a tight knot of patients emerge from a slate outbuilding, then they scattered to the benches in the park and lit cigarettes. She thought she saw the poet. He was with two inmates and he was wearing jeans and a very tight white T-shirt. She waved to him, shyly at first, as if her arms were stiff from the cold, then openly, tracing strange patterns in the still-cold air, trying to give her signals a laserlike urgency, trying to transmit telepathic messages in his direction. Five minutes later, she watched as the poet got up from his bench and one of the lunatics kicked him in the legs. With an effort she resisted the urge to scream. The poet turned around and kicked back. The lunatic, who was sitting down again, took it in the chest and dropped like a little bird. The inmate smoking next to him got up and chased the poet for thirty feet, aiming kicks at his ass and throwing punches at his back. Then he returned calmly to his seat, where the other inmate had revived and was rubbing his chest, neck, and head, which anyone would call excessive, since he had been kicked only in the chest. At that moment Lola stopped signaling. One of the lunatics on the bench began to masturbate. The other one, the one in exaggerated pain, felt in one of his pockets and pulled out a cigarette. The poet approached them. Lola thought she heard his laugh. An ironic laugh, as if he were saying: boys, you can't take a joke. But maybe the poet wasn't laughing. Maybe, Lola said in her letter to Amalfitano, it was my madness that was laughing. In any case, whether it was her madness or not, the poet went over to the other two and said something to them. Neither of the lunatics answered. Lola saw them: they were looking down, at the life throbbing at ground level, between the blades of grass and under the loose clumps of dirt. A blind life in which everything had the transparency of water. The poet, however, must have scanned the faces of his companions in misfortune, first one and then the other, looking for a sign that would tell him whether it was safe for him to sit down on the bench again. Which he finally did. He raised his hand in a gesture of truce or surrender and he sat between the other two. He raised his hand the way someone might raise a tattered flag. He moved his fingers, each finger, as if his fingers were a flag in flames, the flag of the unvanquished. And he sat between them and then he looked at the one who was masturbating and said something into his ear. This time Lola couldn't hear him but she saw clearly how the poet's left hand groped its way into the other inmate's robe. And then she watched the three of them smoke. And she watched the artful spirals issuing from the poet's mouth and nose.

●

The next and final letter Amalfitano received from his wife wasn't postmarked but the stamps were French. In it Lola recounted a conversation with Larrazábal. Christ, you're lucky, said Larrazábal, my whole life I've wanted to live in a cemetery, and look at you, the minute you get here, you move right in. A good person, Larrazábal. He invited her to stay at his apartment. He offered to drive her each morning to the Mondragón asylum, where Spain's greatest and most self-deluding poet was studying osteology. He offered her money without asking for anything in return. One night he took her to the movies. Another night he went with her to the boardinghouse to ask whether there was any word from Imma. Once, late one Saturday night, after they'd made love for hours, he proposed to her and he didn't feel offended or stupid when Lola reminded him that she was already married. A good person, Larrazábal. He bought her a skirt at a little street fair and he bought her some brand-name jeans at a store in downtown San Sebastián. He talked to her about his mother, whom he'd loved dearly, and about his siblings, to whom he wasn't close. None of this had much of an effect on Lola, or rather it did, but not in the way he had hoped. For her, those days were like a prolonged parachute landing after a long space flight. She went to Mondragón once every three days now, instead of once a day, and she looked through the fence with no hope at all of seeing the poet, seeking at most some sign, a sign that she knew beforehand she would never understand or that she would understand only many years later, when none of it mattered anymore. Sometimes, without calling first or leaving a note, she wouldn't sleep at Larrazábal's apartment and he would go looking for her at the cemetery, the asylum, the old boardinghouse where she'd stayed, the places where the tramps and transients of San Sebastián gathered. Once he found her in the waiting room of the train station. Another time he found her sitting on a seafront bench at La Concha, at an hour when the only people out walking were two opposite types: those running out of time and those with time to burn. In the morning it was Larrazábal who made breakfast. At night, when he came home from work, he was the one who made dinner. During the day Lola drank only water, lots of it, and ate a little piece of bread or a roll small enough to fit in her pocket, which she would buy at the corner bakery before she went roaming. One night, as they were showering, she told Larrazábal that she was planning to leave and asked him for money for the train. I'll give you everything I've got, he answered, but I can't give you money to go away so I never see you again. Lola didn't insist. Somehow, though she didn't tell Amalfitano how she did it, she scraped together just enough money for a ticket, and one day at noon she took the train to France. She was in Bayonne for a while. She left for Landes. She returned to Bayonne. She was in Pau and in Lourdes. One morning she saw a train full of sick people, paralyzed people, adolescents with cerebral palsy, farmers with skin cancer, terminally ill Castilian bureaucrats, polite old ladies dressed like Carmelite nuns, people with rashes, blind children, and without knowing how she began to help them, as if she were a nun in jeans stationed there by the church to aid and direct the desperate, who one by one got on buses parked outside the train station or waited in long lines as if each person were a scale on a giant and old and cruel but vigorous snake. Then trains came from Italy and from the north of France, and Lola went back and forth like a sleepwalker, her big blue eyes unblinking, moving slowly, since the weariness of her days was beginning to weigh on her, and she was permitted entry to every part of the station, some rooms converted into first aid posts, others into resuscitation posts, and just one, discreetly located, converted into an improvised morgue for the bodies of those whose strength hadn't been equal to the accelerated wear and tear of the train trip. At night she slept in the most modern building in Lourdes, a functionalist monster of steel and glass that buried its head, bristling with antennas, in the white clouds that floated down from the north, big and sorrowful, or marched from the west like a ragtag army whose only strength was its numbers, or dropped down from the Pyrenees like the ghosts of dead beasts. There she would sleep in the trash compartments, which she entered through a tiny door. Other times she would stay at the station, at the station bar, when the chaos of the trains subsided, and let the old men buy her coffee and talk to her about movies and crops. One afternoon she thought she saw Imma get off the train from Madrid escorted by a troop of cripples. She was the same height as Imma, she was wearing long black skirts like Imma, her doleful Castilian nun's face was just like Imma's face. Lola sat still until she had gone by and didn't call out to her, and five minutes later she elbowed her way out of the Lourdes station and the town of Lourdes and walked to the highway and only then did she try to thumb a ride.

•

For five years, Amalfitano had no news of Lola. One afternoon, when he was at the playground with his daughter, he saw a woman leaning against the wooden fence that separated the playground from the rest of the park. He thought she looked like Imma and he followed her gaze and was relieved to discover that it was another child who had attracted her madwoman's attention. The boy was wearing shorts and was a little older than Amalfitano's daughter, and he had dark, very silky hair that kept falling in his face. Between the fence and the benches that the city had put there so parents could sit and watch their children, a hedge struggled to grow, reaching all the way to an old oak tree outside the playground. Imma's hand, her hard, gnarled hand, roughened by the sun and icy rivers, stroked the freshly clipped top of the hedge as one might stroke a dog's back. Next to her was a big plastic bag. Amalfitano walked toward her, willing himself futilely to be calm. His daughter was in line for the slide. Suddenly, before he could speak to Imma, Amalfitano saw that the boy had at last noticed her watchful presence, and once he had brushed a lock of hair out of his eyes he raised his right arm and waved to her several times. Then Imma, as if this were the sign she'd been waiting for, silently raised her left arm, waved, and went walking out of the park through the north gate, which led onto a busy street.

•

Five years after she left, Amalfitano heard from Lola again. The letter was short and came from Paris. In it Lola told him that she had a job cleaning big office buildings. It was a night job that started at ten and ended at four or five or six in the morning. Paris was pretty then, like all big cities when everyone is asleep. She would take the metro home. The metro at that hour was the saddest thing in the world. She'd had another child, a son, named Benoît, with whom she lived. She'd also been in the hospital. She didn't say why, or whether she was still sick. She didn't mention any man. She didn't ask about Rosa. For her it's as if Rosa doesn't exist, thought Amalfitano, but then it struck him that this might not be the case at all. He cried for a while with the letter in his hands. It was only as he was drying his eyes that he noticed the letter was typed. He knew, without a doubt, that Lola had written it from one of the offices she said she cleaned. For a second he thought it was all a lie, that Lola was working as an administrative assistant or secretary in some big company. Then he saw it clearly. He saw the vacuum cleaner parked between two rows of desks, saw the floor waxer like a cross between a mastiff and a pig sitting next to a plant, he saw an enormous window through which the lights of Paris blinked, he saw Lola in the cleaning company's smock, a worn blue smock, sitting writing the letter and maybe taking slow drags on a cigarette, he saw Lola's fingers, Lola's wrists, Lola's blank eyes, he saw another Lola reflected in the quicksilver of the window, floating weightless in the skies of Paris, like a trick photograph that isn't a trick, floating, floating pensively in the skies of Paris, weary, sending messages from the coldest, iciest realm of passion.

•

Two years after she sent this last letter, seven years after she'd abandoned Amalfitano and her daughter, Lola came home and found them gone. She spent three weeks asking around at old addresses for her husband's whereabouts. Some people didn't let her in, because they couldn't figure out who she was or they had forgotten her long ago. Others kept her standing in the doorway, because they didn't trust her or because Lola had simply got the address wrong. A few asked her in and offered her a cup of coffee or tea that Lola never accepted, since she was apparently in a hurry to see her daughter and Amalfitano. At first the search was discouraging and unreal. She talked to people even she had forgotten. At night she slept in a boardinghouse near Las Ramblas, where foreign workers crammed into tiny rooms. She found the city changed but she couldn't say what exactly was different. In the afternoons, after walking all day, she would sit on the steps of a church to rest and listen to the conversations of the people going in and out, mostly tourists. She read books in French about Greece or witchcraft or healthy living. Sometimes she felt like Electra, daughter of Agamemnon and Clytemnestra, wandering in disguise through Mycenae, the killer mingling with the plebes, the masses, the killer whose mind no one understands, not even the FBI special agents or the charitable people who dropped coins in her hands. Other times she saw herself as the mother of Medon and Strophius, a happy mother who watches her children play from the window while behind them the blue sky struggles in the white arms of the Mediterranean. She whispered: Pylades, Orestes, and those two names stood in her mind for the faces of many men, except Amalfitano's, the face of the man she was looking for now. One night she met an ex-student of her husband's, who recognized her at once, as if in his university days he had been in love with her. The ex-student took her home, told her she could stay as long as she wanted, fixed up the guest room for her exclusive use. The second night, as they were having dinner together, the ex-student embraced her and she let him embrace her for a few seconds, as if she needed him too, and then she said something into his ear and the ex-student moved away and went to sit on the floor in a corner of the living room. They were like that for hours, she sitting in her chair and he sitting on the floor, which was a very odd parquet, dark yellow, so that it looked more like a tightly woven straw rug. The candles on the table went out and only then did she go and sit in the living room, in the opposite corner. In the dark she thought she heard faint sobs. She supposed the young man was crying and she fell asleep, lulled by his weeping. For the next few days she and the ex-student redoubled their efforts. When she saw Amalfitano at last she didn't recognize him. He was fatter than before and he'd lost some of his hair. She spotted him from a distance and didn't hesitate for a second as she approached him. Amalfitano was sitting under a larch and smoking with an absent look on his face. You've changed a lot, she said. Amalfitano recognized her instantly. You haven't, he said. Thank you, she said. Then Amalfitano stood up and they left.

•

In those days, Amalfitano was living in Sant Cugat and teaching philosophy classes at Barcelona's Universidad Autónoma, not far away. Rosa went to a public elementary school in town and left at eight-thirty in the morning and didn't come home until five. Lola saw Rosa and told her she was her mother. Rosa screamed and hugged her and then almost immediately ran away to hide in her bedroom. That night, after showering and making up her bed on the sofa, Lola told Amalfitano that she was very sick, she would probably die, and she had wanted to see Rosa one last time. Amalfitano offered to take her to the hospital the next day, but Lola refused, saying French doctors had always been better than Spanish doctors, and she took some papers out of her bag that stated in no uncertain terms and in French that she had AIDS. The next day, when he got back from the university, Amalfitano spotted Lola and Rosa walking near the station holding hands. He didn't want to disturb them and he followed them from a distance. When he got home they were sitting together watching TV. Later, when Rosa was asleep, he asked Lola about her son Benoît. For a while she was silent, recalling with near photographic memory each part of her son's body, each gesture, each expression of astonishment or surprise, then she said that Benoît was an intelligent and sensitive boy, and that he had been the first to know she was going to die. Amalfitano asked her who had told him, although he thought, with resignation, that he knew the answer. He realized it without anyone telling him, said Lola, just by looking. It's terrible for a child to know his mother is going to die, said Amalfitano. It's worse to lie to them, children should never be lied to, said Lola. On her fifth morning with them, when the medicine she had brought with her from France was about to run out, Lola told them she had to leave. Benoît is little and he needs me, she said. Actually, he doesn't need me, but that doesn't mean he isn't little, she said. I don't know who needs who, she said at last, but the fact is I have to go see how he is. Amalfitano left a note on the table and an envelope containing a good part of his savings. When he got back from work he thought Lola would be gone. He picked Rosa up at school and they walked home. When they got there Lola was sitting in front of the TV, which was on but with the sound off, reading her book on Greece. They had dinner together. Rosa went to bed near midnight. Amalfitano took her to her bedroom, undressed her, and tucked her in. Lola was waiting for him in the living room, with her suitcase packed. You should stay the night, said Amalfitano. It's too late to go. There aren't any more trains to Barcelona, he lied. I'm not taking the train, said Lola. I'm going to hitchhike. Amalfitano bowed his head and said she could go whenever she wanted. Lola gave him a kiss on the cheek and left. The next day Amalfitano got up at six and turned on the radio, to make sure no hitchhiker on any highway nearby had been murdered or raped. Nothing.

•

And yet this vision of Lola lingered in his mind for many years, like a memory rising up from glacial seas, although in fact he hadn't seen anything, which meant there was nothing to remember, only the shadow of his ex-wife projected on the neighboring buildings in the beam of the streetlights, and then the dream: Lola walking off down one of the highways out of Sant Cugat, walking along the side of the road, an almost deserted road since most cars took the new toll highway to save time, a woman bowed by the weight of her suitcase, fearless, walking fearlessly along the side of the road.

•

The University of Santa Teresa was like a cemetery that suddenly begins to think, in vain. It also was like an empty dance club.

•

One afternoon Amalfitano went into the yard in his shirtsleeves, like a feudal lord riding out on horseback to survey his lands. The moment before, he'd been sitting on the floor of his study opening boxes of books with a kitchen knife, and in one of the boxes he'd found a strange book, a book he didn't remember ever buying or receiving as a gift. The book was Rafael Dieste's *Testamento geométrico*, published by Ediciones del Castro in La Coruña, in 1975, a book evidently about geometry, a subject that meant next to nothing to Amalfitano, divided into three parts, the first an "Introduction to Euclid, Lobachevsky and Riemann," the second concerning "The Geometry of Motion," and the third titled "Three Proofs of the V Postulate." This last was the most enigmatic by far since Amalfitano had no idea what the V Postulate was or what it consisted of, nor did he mean to find out, although this was probably owing not to a lack of curiosity, of which he possessed an ample supply, but to the heat that swept Santa Teresa in the afternoons, the dry, dusty heat of a bitter sun, inescapable unless you lived in a new apartment with air-conditioning, which Amalfitano didn't. The publication of the book had been made possible thanks to the support of some friends of the author, friends who'd been immortalized, in a photograph that looked as if it was taken at the end of a party, on page 4, where the publisher's information usually appears. What it said there was: *The present edition is offered as a tribute to Rafael Dieste by: Ramón BALTAR DOMÍNGUEZ, Isaac DÍAZ PARDO, Felipe FERNÁNDEZ ARMESTO, Francisco FERNÁNDEZ DEL RIEGO, Álvaro GIL VARELA, Domingo GARCÍA-SABELL, Valentín PAZ-ANDRADE and Luis SEOANE LÓPEZ.* It struck Amalfitano as odd, to say the least, that the friends' last names had been printed in capitals while the name of the man being honored was in small letters. On the front flap, the reader was informed that the *Testamento geométrico* was really three books, "each independent, but functionally correlated by the sweep of the whole," and then it said "this work representing the final distillation of Dieste's reflections and research on Space, the notion of which is involved in any methodical discussion of the fundamentals of Geometry." At that moment, Amalfitano thought he remembered that Rafael Dieste was a poet. A Galician poet, of course, or long settled in Galicia. And his friends and patrons were also Galician, naturally, or long settled in Galicia, where Dieste probably gave classes at the University of La Coruña or Santiago de Compostela, or maybe he was a high school teacher, teaching geometry to kids of fifteen or sixteen and looking out the window at the permanently overcast winter sky of Galicia and the pouring rain. And on the back flap there was more about Dieste. It said: "Of the books that make up Dieste's varied but in no way uneven body of work, which always cleaves to the demands of a personal process in which poetic creation and speculative creation are focused on a single object, the closest forerunners of the present book are *Nuevo tratado del paralelismo* (Buenos Aires, 1958) and more recent works: *Variaciones sobre Zenón de Elea* and *¿Qué es un axioma?* this followed by *Movilidad y Semejanza* together in one volume." So, thought Amalfitano, his face running with sweat to which microscopic particles of dust adhered, Dieste's passion for geometry wasn't something new. And his patrons, in this new light, were no longer friends who got together every night at the club to drink and talk politics or football or mistresses. Instead, in a flash, they became distinguished university colleagues, some doubtless retired but others fully active, and all well-to-do or relatively well-to-do, which of course didn't mean that they didn't meet up every so often like provincial intellectuals, or in other words like deeply self-sufficient men, at the La Coruña club to drink good cognac or whiskey and talk about intrigues and mistresses while their wives, or in the case of the widowers, their housekeepers, were sitting in front of the TV or preparing supper. But the question for Amalfitano was how this book had ended up in one of his boxes. For half an hour he searched his memory, leafing distractedly through Dieste's book. Finally he concluded that for the moment it was a mystery beyond his powers to solve, but he didn't give up. He asked Rosa, who was in the bathroom putting on makeup, if the book was hers. Rosa looked at it and said no. Amalfitano begged her to look again and tell him for sure whether it was hers or not. Rosa asked him if he was feeling all right. I feel fine, said Amalfitano, but this book isn't mine and it showed up in one of the boxes of books I sent from Barcelona. Rosa told him, in Catalan, not to worry, and kept putting on her makeup. How can I not worry, said Amalfitano, also in Catalan, when it feels like I'm losing my memory. Rosa looked at the book again and said: it might be mine. Are you sure? asked Amalfitano. No, it isn't mine, said Rosa, I'm sure it isn't, in fact, I've never seen it before. Amalfitano left his daughter in front of the bathroom mirror and went back out into the desolate yard, where everything was a dusty brown, as if the desert had settled around his new house, with the book dangling from his hand. He thought back on the bookstores where he might have bought it. He looked at the first page and the last page and the back cover for some sign, and on the first page he found a stamp reading Librería Follas Novas, S.L., Montero Ríos 37, phone 981-59-44-06 and 981-59-44-18, Santiago. Clearly it wasn't Santiago de Chile, the only place in the world where Amalfitano could see himself in a state of total catatonia, walking into a bookstore, choosing some book without even looking at the cover, paying for it, and leaving. Obviously, it was Santiago de Compostela, in Galicia. For an instant Amalfitano envisioned a pilgrimage along the Camino de Santiago. He walked to the back of the yard, where his wooden fence met the cement wall surrounding the house behind his. He had never really looked at it. Glass shards, he thought, the owners' fear of unwanted guests. The edges of the shards were reflecting the afternoon sun when Amalfitano resumed his walk around the desolate yard. The wall of the house next door was also bristling with glass, here mostly green and brown glass from beer and liquor bottles. Never, even in dreams, had he been in Santiago de Compostela, Amalfitano had to acknowledge, halting in the shadow of the left-hand wall. But that hardly mattered. Some of the bookstores he frequented in Barcelona carried stock bought directly from other bookstores in Spain, from bookstores that were selling off their inventories or closing, or, in a few cases, that functioned as both bookstore and distributor. I probably picked it up at Laie, he thought, or maybe at La Central, the time I stopped in to buy some philosophy book and the clerk was excited because Pere Gimferrer, Rodrigo Rey Rosa, and Juan Villoro were all there, arguing about whether it was a good idea to fly, and plane accidents, and which was more dangerous, taking off or landing, and she mistakenly put this book in my bag. La Central, that makes sense. But if that was the way it happened I'd have discovered the book when I got home and opened the bag or the package or whatever it was, unless, of course, something terrible or upsetting happened to me on the walk home that eliminated any desire or curiosity I had to examine my new book or books. It's even possible that I might have opened the package like a zombie and left the new book on the night table and Dieste's book on the bookshelf, shaken by something I'd just seen on the street, maybe a car accident, maybe a mugging, maybe a suicide in the subway, although if I had seen something like that, thought Amalfitano, I would surely remember it now or at least retain a vague memory of it. I wouldn't remember the *Testamento geométrico*, but I would remember whatever had made me forget the *Testamento geométrico*. And as if this wasn't enough, the biggest problem wasn't really where the book had come from but how it had ended up in Santa Teresa in one of Amalfitano's boxes of books, books he had chosen in Barcelona before he left. At what point of utter obliviousness had he put it there? How could he have packed a book without noticing what he was doing? Had he planned to read it when he got to the north of Mexico? Had he planned to use it as the starting point for a desultory study of geometry? And if that was his plan, why had he forgotten the moment he arrived in this city rising up in the middle of nowhere? Had the book disappeared from his memory while he and his daughter were flying east to west? Or had it disappeared from his memory as he was waiting for his boxes of books to arrive, once he was in Santa Teresa? Had Dieste's book vanished as a side effect of jet lag?

•

Amalfitano had some rather idiosyncratic ideas about jet lag. They weren't consistent, so it might be an exaggeration to call them ideas. They were feelings. Make-believe ideas. As if he were looking out the window and forcing himself to see an extraterrestrial landscape. He believed (or liked to think he believed) that when a person was in Barcelona, the people living and present in Buenos Aires and Mexico City didn't exist. The time difference only masked their nonexistence. And so if you suddenly traveled to cities that, according to this theory, didn't exist or hadn't yet had time to put themselves together, the result was the phenomenon known as jet lag, which arose not from your exhaustion but from the exhaustion of the people who would still have been asleep if you hadn't traveled. This was something he'd probably read in some science fiction novel or story and that he'd forgotten having read.

•

Anyway, these ideas or feelings or ramblings had their satisfactions. They turned the pain of others into memories of one's own. They turned pain, which is natural, enduring, and eternally triumphant, into personal memory, which is human, brief, and eternally elusive. They turned a brutal story of injustice and abuse, an incoherent howl with no beginning or end, into a neatly structured story in which suicide was always held out as a possibility. They turned flight into freedom, even if freedom meant no more than the perpetuation of flight. They turned chaos into order, even if it was at the cost of what is commonly known as sanity.

•

And although Amalfitano later found more information on the life and works of Rafael Dieste at the University of Santa Teresa library—information that confirmed what he had already guessed or what Don Domingo García-Sabell had insinuated in his prologue, titled "Enlightened Intuition," which went so far as to quote Heidegger (*Es gibt Zeit: there is time*)—on the afternoon when he'd ranged over his humble and barren lands like a medieval squire, as his daughter, like a medieval princess, finished applying her makeup in front of the bathroom mirror, he could in no way remember why or where he'd bought the book or how it had ended up packed and sent with other more familiar and cherished volumes to this populous city that stood in defiance of the desert on the border of Sonora and Arizona. And it was then, just then, as if it were the pistol shot inaugurating a series of events that would build upon each other with sometimes happy and sometimes disastrous consequences, Rosa left the house and said she was going to the movies with a friend and asked if he had his keys and Amalfitano said yes and he heard the door bang shut and then he heard his daughter's footsteps along the path of uneven paving stones to the tiny wooden gate that didn't even come up to her waist and then he heard his daughter's footsteps on the sidewalk, heading off toward the bus stop, and then he heard the engine of a car starting. And then Amalfitano walked into his devastated front yard and looked up and down the street, craning his neck, and didn't see any car or Rosa and he gripped Dieste's book tightly, which he was still holding in his left hand. And then he looked up at the sky and saw the moon, too big and too wrinkled, although it wasn't night yet. And then he returned to his ravaged backyard and for a few seconds he stopped, looking left and right, ahead and behind, trying to see his shadow, but although it was still daytime and the sun was still shining in the west, toward Tijuana, he couldn't see it. And then his eyes fell on the four rows of cord, each tied at one end to a kind of miniature soccer goal, two posts perhaps six feet tall planted in the ground, and a third post bolted horizontally across the top, making them sturdier, the cords strung from this top bar to hooks fixed in the side of the house. It was the clothesline, although the only things he saw hanging on it were a shirt of Rosa's, white with ocher embroidery around the neck, and a pair of underpants and two towels, still dripping. In the corner, in a brick hut, was the washing machine. For a while he didn't move, breathing with his mouth open, leaning on the horizontal bar of the clothesline. Then he went into the hut as if he were short of oxygen, and from a plastic bag with the logo of the supermarket where he went with his daughter to do the weekly shopping, he took out three clothespins, which he persisted in calling *perritos*, as they were called in Chile, and with them he clamped the book and hung it from one of the cords and then he went back into the house, feeling much calmer.

•

The idea, of course, was Duchamp's.

•

All that exists, or remains, of Duchamp's stay in Buenos Aires is a readymade. Though of course his whole life was a readymade, which was his way of appeasing fate and at the same time sending out signals of distress. As Calvin Tomkins writes: *As a wedding present for his sister Suzanne and his close friend Jean Crotti, who were married in Paris on April 14, 1919, Duchamp instructed the couple by letter to hang a geometry book by strings on the balcony of their apartment so that the wind could "go through the book, choose its own problems, turn and tear out the pages."* Clearly, then, Duchamp wasn't just playing chess in Buenos Aires. Tompkins continues: *This* Unhappy Readymade, *as he called it, might strike some newlyweds as an oddly cheerless wedding gift, but Suzanne and Jean carried out Duchamp's instructions in good spirit; they took a photograph of the open book dangling in midair (the only existing record of the work, which did not survive its exposure to the elements), and Suzanne later painted a picture of it called* Le Readymade malheureux de Marcel. *As Duchamp later told Cabanne, "It amused me to bring the idea of happy and unhappy into readymades, and then the rain, the wind, the pages flying, it was an amusing idea."* I take it back: all Duchamp did while he was in Buenos Aires was play chess. Yvonne, who was with him, got sick of all his play-science and left for France. According to Tompkins: *Duchamp told one interviewer in later years that he had liked disparaging "the seriousness of a book full of principles," and suggested to another that, in its exposure to the weather, "the treatise seriously got the facts of life."*

•

That night, when Rosa got back from the movies, Amalfitano was watching television in the living room and he told her he'd hung Dieste's book on the clothesline. Rosa looked at him as if she had no idea what he was talking about. I mean, said Amalfitano, I didn't hang it out because it got sprayed with the hose or dropped in the water, I hung it there just because, to see how it survives the assault of nature, to see how it survives this desert climate. I hope you aren't going crazy, said Rosa. No, don't worry, said Amalfitano, in fact looking quite cheerful. I'm telling you so you don't take it down. Just pretend the book doesn't exist. Fine, Rosa said, and she shut herself in her room.

•

The next day, as his students wrote, or as he himself was talking, Amalfitano began to draw very simple geometric figures, a triangle, a rectangle, and at each vertex he wrote whatever name came to him, dictated by fate or lethargy or the immense boredom he felt thanks to his students and the classes and the oppressive heat that had settled over the city. Like this:

Drawing 1

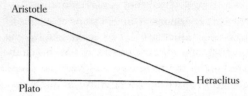

Or like this:

Drawing 2

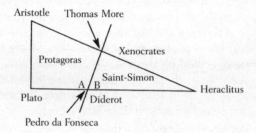

Or like this:

Drawing 3

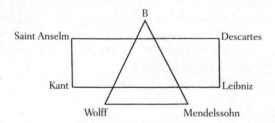

When he returned to his cubicle he discovered the paper and before he threw it in the trash he examined it for a few minutes. The only possible explanation for Drawing 1 was boredom. Drawing 2 seemed an extension of Drawing 1, but the names he had added struck him as insane. Xenocrates made sense, there was a fleeting logic there, and Protagoras, too, but why Thomas More and Saint-Simon? Why Diderot, what was he doing there, and God in heaven, why the Portuguese Jesuit Pedro da Fonseca, one of the thousands of commentators on Aristotle, who by no amount of forceps wiggling could be taken for anything but a very minor thinker? In contrast, there was a certain logic to Drawing 3, the logic of a teenage moron, or a teen bum in the desert, his clothes in tatters, but clothes even so. All the names, it could be said, were of philosophers who concerned themselves with ontological questions. The B that appeared at the apex of the triangle superimposed on the rectangle could be God or the existence of God as derived from his essence. Only then did Amalfitano notice that an A and a B also appeared in Drawing 2, and he no longer had any doubt that the heat, to which he was unaccustomed, was affecting his mind as he taught his classes.

•

That night, however, after he had finished his dinner and watched the TV news and talked on the phone to Professor Silvia Pérez, who was outraged at the way the Sonora police and the local Santa Teresa police were carrying out the investigation of the crimes, Amalfitano found three more diagrams on his desk. It was clear he had drawn them himself. In fact, he remembered doodling absentmindedly on a blank sheet of paper as he thought other things. Drawing 1 (or Drawing 4) was like this:

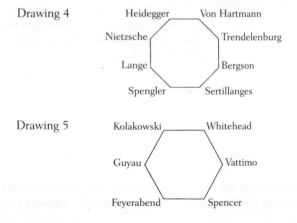

193

And Drawing 6

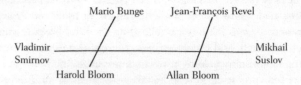

Drawing 4 was odd. Trendelenburg—it had been years since he thought about Trendelenburg. Adolf Trendelenburg. Why now, precisely, and why in the company of Bergson and Heidegger and Nietzsche and Spengler? Drawing 5 was even odder. The appearance of Kolakowski and Vattimo. The presence of Whitehead, forgotten until now. But especially the unexpected materialization of poor Guyau, Jean-Marie Guyau, dead at thirty-four in 1888, called the French Nietzsche by some jokers, with no more than ten disciples in the whole world, although really there were only six, and Amalfitano knew this because in Barcelona he had met the only Spanish Guyautist, a professor from Gerona, shy and a zealot in his own way, whose great quest was to find a text (it might have been a poem or a philosophical piece or an article, he wasn't sure) that Guyau had written in English and published in a San Francisco newspaper sometime around 1886–1887. Finally, Drawing 6 was the oddest of all (and the least "philosophical"). What said it all was the appearance at opposite ends of the horizontal axis of Vladimir Smirnov, who disappeared in Stalin's concentration camps in 1938 (not to be confused with Ivan Nikitich Smirnov, executed by the Stalinists in 1936 after the first Moscow show trial), and Suslov, party ideologue, prepared to countenance any atrocity or crime. But the intersection of the horizontal by two slanted lines, reading Bunge and Revel above and Harold Bloom and Allan Bloom below, was something like a joke. And yet it was a joke Amalfitano didn't understand, especially the appearance of the two Blooms. There had to be something funny about it, but whatever it might be, he couldn't put his finger on it, no matter how he tried.

•

That night, as his daughter slept, and after he listened to the last news broadcast on Santa Teresa's most popular radio station, Voice of the Border, Amalfitano went out into the yard. He smoked a cigarette, staring into the deserted street, then he headed for the back, moving hesitantly, as if he feared stepping in a hole or was afraid of the reigning darkness. Dieste's book was still hanging with the clothes Rosa had washed that day, clothes that seemed to be made of cement or some very heavy material, because they didn't move at all, while the fitful breeze swung the book back and forth, as if it were grudgingly rocking it or trying to detach it from the clothespins holding it to the line. Amalfitano felt the breeze on his face. He was sweating and the irregular gusts of air dried the little drops of perspiration and occluded his soul. As if I were in Trendelenburg's study, he thought, as if I were following in Whitehead's footsteps along the edge of a canal, as if I were approaching Guyau's sickbed and asking him for advice. What would his response have been? Be happy. Live in the moment. Be good. Or rather: Who are you? What are you doing here? Go away.

•

Help.

•

The next day, searching in the university library, he found more information on Dieste. Born in Rianxo, La Coruña, in 1899. Begins writing in Galician, although later he switches to Castilian or writes in both. Man of the theater. Anti-Fascist during the Civil War. After his side's defeat he goes into exile, ending up in Buenos Aires, where he publishes *Viaje, duelo y perdición: tragedia, humorada y comedia*, in 1945, a book made up of three previously published works. Poet. Essayist. In 1958 (Amalfitano is seven), he publishes the aforementioned *Nuevo tratado del paralelismo*. As a short story writer, his most important work is *Historia e invenciones de Félix Muriel* (1943). Returns to Spain, returns to Galicia. Dies in Santiago de Compostela in 1981.

•

What's the experiment? asked Rosa. What experiment? asked Amalfitano. With the hanging book, said Rosa. It isn't an experiment in the literal sense of the word, said Amalfitano. Why is it there? asked Rosa. It occurred to me all of a sudden, said Amalfitano, it's a Duchamp idea, leaving a geometry book hanging exposed to the elements to see if it learns something about real life. You're going to destroy it, said Rosa. Not me, said Amalfitano, nature. You're getting crazier every day, you know, said Rosa. Amalfitano smiled. I've never seen you do a thing like that to a book, said Rosa. It isn't mine, said Amalfitano. It doesn't matter, Rosa said, it's yours now. It's funny, said Amalfitano, that's how I should feel, but I really don't have the sense it belongs to me, and anyway I'm almost sure I'm not doing it any harm. Well, pretend it's mine and take it down, said Rosa, the neighbors are going to think you're crazy. The neighbors who top their walls with broken glass? They don't even know we exist, said Amalfitano, and they're a thousand times crazier than me. No, not them, said Rosa, the other ones, the ones who can see exactly what's going on in our yard. Have any of them bothered you? asked Amalfitano. No, said Rosa. Then it's not a problem, said Amalfitano, it's silly to worry about it when much worse things are happening in this city than a book being hung from a cord. Two wrongs don't make a right, said Rosa, we're not animals. Leave the book alone, pretend it doesn't exist, forget about it, said Amalfitano, you've never been interested in geometry.

•

In the mornings, before he left for the university, Amalfitano would go out the back door to watch the book while he finished his coffee. No doubt about it: it had been printed on good paper and the binding was stoically withstanding nature's onslaught. Rafael Dieste's old friends had chosen good materials for their tribute, a tribute that amounted to an early farewell from a circle of learned old men (or old men with a patina of learning) to another learned old man. In any case, nature in northwestern Mexico, and particularly in his desolate yard, thought Amalfitano, was in short supply. One morning, as he was waiting for the bus to the university, he made firm plans to plant grass or a lawn, and also to buy a little tree in some store that sold that kind of thing, and plant flowers along the fence. Another morning he thought that any work he did to make the yard nicer would ultimately be pointless, since he didn't plan to stay long in Santa Teresa. I have to go back now, he said to himself, but where? And then he asked himself: what made me come here? Why did I bring my daughter to this cursed city? Because it was one of the few hellholes in the world I hadn't seen yet? Because I really just want to die? And then he looked at Dieste's book, the *Testamento geométrico*, hanging impassively from the line, held there by two clothespins, and he felt the urge to take it down and wipe off the ocher dust that had begun to cling to it here and there, but he didn't dare.

•

Sometimes, after he came home from the University of Santa Teresa or while he sat on the porch and read his students' essays, Amalfitano remembered his father, who followed boxing. Amalfitano's father used to say that all Chileans were faggots. Amalfitano, who was ten, said: but Dad, it's really the Italians who are faggots, just look at World War II. Amalfitano's father gave his son a very serious look when he heard him say that. His own father, Amalfitano's grandfather, was born in Naples. And he himself always felt more Italian than Chilean. But anyway, he liked to talk about boxing, or rather he liked to talk about fights that he'd only read about in the usual articles in boxing magazines or the sports page. So he would talk about the Loayza brothers, Mario and Rubén, nephews of El Tani, and about Godfrey Stevens, a stately faggot with no punch, and about Humberto Loayza, also a nephew of El Tani, who had a good punch but no stamina, about Arturo Godoy, a wily fighter and martyr, about Luis Vicentini, a powerfully built Italian from Chillán who was defeated by the sad fate of being born in Chile, and about Estanislao Loayza, El Tani, who was robbed of the world title in the United States in the most ridiculous way, when the referee stepped on his foot in the first round and El Tani fractured his ankle. Can you imagine? Amalfitano's father asked. I can't imagine, Amalfitano said. Let's give it a try, said Amalfitano's father, shadowbox around me and I'll step on your foot. I'd rather not, said Amalfitano. You can trust me, you'll be fine, said Amalfitano's father. Some other time, said Amalfitano. It has to be now, said his father. Then Amalfitano put up his fists and moved around his father with surprising agility, throwing a few jabs with his left and hooks with his right, and suddenly his father moved in and stepped on his foot and that was the end of it, Amalfitano stood still or tried to go in for a clinch or pulled away, but in no way fractured his ankle. I think the referee did it on purpose, said Amalfitano's father. You can't fuck up somebody's ankle by stomping on his foot. Then came the rant: Chilean boxers are all faggots, all the people in this shitty country are faggots, every one of them, happy to be cheated, happy to be bought, happy to pull down their pants the minute someone asks them to take off their watches. It was at this point that Amalfitano, who at ten read history magazines, especially military history magazines, not sports magazines, answered that the Italians had already claimed that role, all the way back to World War II. His father was silent then, looking at his son with frank admiration and pride, as if asking himself where the hell the kid had come from, and then he was silent for a while longer and afterward he said in a low voice, as if telling a secret, that Italians were brave individually. In large numbers, he admitted, they were hopeless. And this, he explained, was precisely what gave a person hope.

•

By which you might guess, thought Amalfitano, as he went out the front door and paused on the porch with his whiskey and then looked out into the street where a few cars were parked, cars that had been left there for hours and smelled, or so it seemed to him, of scrap metal and blood, before he turned and headed around the side of the house to the backyard where the *Testamento geométrico* was waiting for him in the stillness and the dark, by which you might guess that he himself, deep down, very deep down, was still a hopeful person, since he was Italian by blood, as well as an individualist and a civilized person. And it was even possible that he wasn't a coward. Although he didn't like boxing. But then Dieste's book fluttered and the black handkerchief of the breeze dried the sweat beading on his forehead and Amalfitano closed his eyes and tried to conjure up any image of his father, in vain. When he went back inside, not through the back door but through the front door, he peered over the gate and looked both ways down the street. Some nights he had the feeling he was being spied on.

•

In the mornings, when Amalfitano came into the kitchen and left his coffee cup in the sink after his obligatory visit to Dieste's book, Rosa was the first to leave. They didn't usually speak, although sometimes, if Amalfitano came in sooner than usual or put off going into the backyard, he would say goodbye, remind her to take care of herself, or give her a kiss. One morning he managed only to say goodbye, then he sat at the table looking out the window at the clothesline. The *Testamento geométrico* was moving imperceptibly. Suddenly, it stopped. The birds that had been singing in the neighboring yards were quiet. Everything was plunged into complete silence for an instant. Amalfitano thought he heard the sound of the gate and his daughter's footsteps receding. Then he heard a car start. That night, as Rosa watched a movie she'd rented, Amalfitano called Professor Pérez and confessed that he was turning into a nervous wreck. Professor Pérez soothed him, told him not to worry so much, all you had to do was be careful, there was no point giving in to paranoia. She reminded him that the victims were usually kidnapped in other parts of the city. Amalfitano listened to her talk and all of a sudden he laughed. He told her his nerves were in tatters. Professor Pérez didn't get the joke. Nobody gets anything here, thought Amalfitano angrily. Then Professor Pérez tried to convince him to come out that weekend, with Rosa and Professor Pérez's son. Where to, asked Amalfitano, almost inaudibly. We could go eat at a *merendero* ten miles out of the city, she said, a very nice place, with a pool for the kids and lots of outdoor tables in the shade with a view of the slopes of a quartz mountain, a silver mountain with black streaks. At the top of the mountain there was a chapel built of black adobe. The inside was dark, except for the light that came in through a kind of skylight, and the walls were covered in ex-votos written by travelers and Indians in the nineteenth century who had risked the pass between Chihuahua and Sonora.

·

Amalfitano's first few days in Santa Teresa and at the University of Santa Teresa were miserable, although Amalfitano was only half aware of the fact. He felt ill, but he thought it was jet lag and ignored it. A faculty colleague, a young professor from Hermosillo who had only recently finished his degree, asked what had made him choose the University of Santa Teresa over the University of Barcelona. I hope it wasn't the climate, he said. The climate here seems wonderful, answered Amalfitano. Oh, I agree, said the young professor, I just meant that the people who come here for the climate are usually ill and I sincerely hope that's not the case with you. No, said Amalfitano, it wasn't the climate, my contract had run out in Barcelona and Professor Pérez convinced me to take a job here. He had met Professor Silvia Pérez in Buenos Aires and then they had seen each other twice in Barcelona. It was she who had rented the house and bought some furniture for him. Amalfitano paid her back even before he collected his first paycheck to prevent any misunderstandings. The house was in Colonia Lindavista, an upper-middle-class neighborhood of one- and two-story houses with yards. The sidewalk, cracked by the roots of two enormous trees, was shady and pleasant, although behind the gates some of the houses were in advanced states of disrepair, as if the neighbors had left in a hurry, with no time even to sell, which would suggest that it hadn't been so hard to rent in the neighborhood, no matter what Professor Pérez claimed. He took a dislike to the dean of the Faculty of Literature, to whom Professor Pérez introduced him on his second day in Santa Teresa. The dean's name was Augusto Guerra and he had the pale, shiny skin of a fat man, but he was actually thin and wiry. He didn't seem very sure of himself, although he tried to disguise it with a combination of folk wisdom and a military air. He didn't really believe in philosophy either, or, by extension, in the teaching of philosophy, a discipline frankly on the decline in the face of the current and future marvels that science has to offer, he said. Amalfitano asked politely whether he felt the same way about literature. No, literature does have a future, believe it or not, and so does history, Augusto Guerra had said, take biographies, there used to be almost no supply or demand and today all anybody does is read them. Of course, I'm talking about biographies, not memoirs. People have a thirst to learn about other people's lives, the lives of their famous contemporaries, the ones who made it big or came close, and they also have a thirst to know what the old *chincuales* did, maybe even learn something, although they aren't prepared to jump through the same hoops themselves. Amalfitano asked politely what *chincuales* meant, since he had never heard the word. Really? asked Augusto Guerra. I swear, said Amalfitano. Then the dean asked Professor Pérez: Silvita, do you know what *chincuales* means? Professor Pérez took Amalfitano's arm, as if they were lovers, and confessed that really she didn't have the slightest idea, although the word rang a bell. What a pack of imbeciles, thought Amalfitano. The word *chincuales*, said Augusto Guerra, like all the words in the Mexican tongue, has a number of senses. First, it means flea or bedbug bites, those little red welts, you know? The bites itch, and the poor victims can't stop scratching, as you can readily imagine. Hence the second meaning, which is restless people who squirm and scratch and can't sit still, to the discomfort of anyone who's forced to watch them. Like European scabies, say, like all those people with scabies in Europe, who pick it up in public restrooms or in those horrendous French, Italian, and Spanish latrines. Related to this is the final sense, call it the Guerrist sense, which applies to a certain class of traveler, to adventurers of the mind, those who can't keep still *mentally*. Ah, said Amalfitano. Magnificent, said Professor Pérez. Also present at this impromptu gathering in the dean's office, which Amalfitano thought of as a welcome meeting, were three other professors from the literature department, and Guerra's secretary, who uncorked a bottle of Californian champagne and passed out paper cups and crackers. Then Guerra's son came in. He was maybe twenty-five years old, in sunglasses and a track suit, his skin very tanned. He spent all his time in a corner talking to his father's secretary and glancing every so often at Amalfitano with an amused look on his face.

•

The night before the excursion, Amalfitano heard the voice for the first time. Maybe he'd heard it before, in the street or while he was asleep, and thought it was part of someone else's conversation or that he was having a nightmare. But that night he heard it and he had no doubt whatsoever that it was addressing him. At first he thought he'd gone crazy. The voice said: hello, Óscar Amalfitano, please don't be afraid, there's nothing wrong. Amalfitano was afraid. He got up and rushed to his daughter's room. Rosa was sleeping peacefully. Amalfitano turned on the light and checked the window latch. Rosa woke up and asked what was wrong with him. Not what was wrong, what was wrong with him. I must look terrible, thought Amalfitano. He sat in a chair and told her he was ridiculously nervous, he'd thought he heard a noise, he was sorry he'd brought her to this disgusting city. Don't worry, it's no big deal, said Rosa. Amalfitano gave her a kiss on the cheek, stroked her hair, and went out but didn't turn off the light. After a while, as he was looking out the living room window at the yard and the street and the still branches of the trees, he heard Rosa turn off the light. He went out the back door, without making a sound. He wished he had a flashlight, but he went out anyway. No one was there. Hanging on the clothesline were the *Testamento geométrico* and some of his socks and a pair of his daughter's pants. He circled the yard. There was no one on the porch. He went over to the gate and inspected the street, without going out, and all he saw was a dog heading calmly toward Avenida Madero, to the bus stop. A dog on its way to the bus stop, Amalfitano said to himself. From where he was he thought he could tell that it was a mutt, not a purebreed. A *quiltro*, thought Amalfitano. He laughed to himself. Those Chilean words. Those cracks in the psyche. That hockey rink the size of Atacama where the players never saw a member of the opposing team and only every so often saw a member of their own. He went back into the house. He locked the door and windows, took a short, sturdy knife out of a drawer in the kitchen and set it down next to a history of German and French philosophy from 1900 to 1930, then sat back down at the table.

The voice said: don't think this is easy for me. If you think it's easy for me, you're one hundred percent wrong. In fact, it's hard. Ninety percent hard. Amalfitano closed his eyes and thought he was going crazy. He didn't have any tranquilizers in the house. He got up. He went into the kitchen and splashed water on his face with both hands. He dried himself with the kitchen towel and his sleeves. He tried to remember the psychiatric name for the auditory phenomenon he was experiencing. He went back into his office and after closing the door he sat down again, with his head bowed and his hands on the table. The voice said: I beg you to forgive me. I beg you to relax. I beg you not to consider this a violation of your freedom. Of my freedom? thought Amalfitano, surprised, as he sprang to the window and opened it and looked out at the side yard and the wall of the house next door, spiky with glass, and the reflection of the streetlights in the shards of broken bottles, very faint green and brown and orange gleams, as if at this time of night the wall stopped being a barricade and became or played at becoming ornamental, a tiny element in a choreography the basic features of which even the ostensible choreographer, the feudal lord next door, couldn't have identified, features that affected the stability, color, and offensive or defensive nature of his fortification. Or as if there was a vine growing on the wall, Amalfitano thought before he closed the window.

•

That night there were no further manifestations of the voice and Amalfitano slept very badly, his sleep plagued by jerks and starts, as if someone was scratching his arms and legs, his body drenched in sweat, although at five in the morning the torment ceased and Lola appeared in his sleep, waving to him from a park behind a tall fence (he was on the other side), along with the faces of two friends he hadn't seen for years (and would probably never see again), and a room full of philosophy books covered in dust but still magnificent. At that same moment the Santa Teresa police found the body of another teenage girl, half buried in a vacant lot in one of the neighborhoods on the edge of the city, and a strong wind from the west hurled itself against the slope of the mountains to the east, raising dust and a litter of newspaper and cardboard on its way through Santa Teresa, moving the clothes that Rosa had hung in the backyard, as if the wind, young and energetic in its brief life, were trying on Amalfitano's shirts and pants and slipping into his daughter's underpants and reading a few pages of the *Testamento geométrico* to see whether there was anything in it that might be of use, anything that might explain the strange landscape of streets and houses through which it was galloping, or that would explain it to itself as wind.

•

At eight o'clock Amalfitano dragged himself into the kitchen. His daughter asked how he'd slept. A rhetorical question that Amalfitano answered with a shrug. When Rosa went out to buy provisions for their day in the country, he made himself a cup of tea with milk and went into the living room to drink it. Then he opened the curtains and asked himself whether he was up to the trip planned by Professor Pérez. He decided that he was, that what had happened to him the night before might have been his body's response to the attack of a local virus or the onset of the flu. Before he got in the shower he took his temperature. He didn't have a fever. For ten minutes he stood under the spray, thinking about his behavior the night before, which embarrassed him and even made him blush. Every so often he lifted his head so that the water streamed directly onto his face. The water tasted different from the water in Barcelona. The water in Santa Teresa seemed much denser, as if it weren't filtered at all but came loaded with minerals, tasting of earth. In the first few days he had acquired the habit, which he shared with Rosa, of brushing his teeth twice as often as he had in Barcelona, because it seemed to him that his teeth were turning brown, as if they were being covered in a thin film of some substance from the underground rivers of Sonora. As time passed, though, he went back to brushing them three or four times a day. Rosa, more concerned about her appearance, kept brushing six or seven times. In his class he noticed some students with ocher-colored teeth. Professor Pérez had white teeth. Once he asked her: was it true that the water in that part of Sonora stained the teeth? Professor Pérez didn't know. It's the first I've heard of it, she said, and she promised to find out. It's not important, said Amalfitano, alarmed, it's not important, forget I asked. In the expression on Professor Pérez's face he had detected a hint of unease, as if the question concealed some other question, this one highly offensive and wounding. You have to watch what you say, sang Amalfitano in the shower, feeling completely recovered, sure proof of his frequent irresponsibility.

•

Rosa came back with two newspapers that she left on the table, then she started to make ham or tuna sandwiches with lettuce and slices of tomato and mayonnaise or *salsa rosa*. She wrapped the sandwiches in paper towels and aluminum foil and put them all in a plastic bag that she stowed in a small brown knapsack with the words *University of Phoenix* printed on it in an arc, and she also put in two bottles of water and a dozen paper cups. At nine-thirty they heard Professor Pérez's horn. Professor Pérez's son was sixteen and short, with a square face and broad shoulders, as if he played some sport. His face and part of his neck were covered in pimples. Professor Pérez was wearing jeans and a white shirt and a white bandanna. Sunglasses, possibly too big, hid her eyes. From a distance, thought Amalfitano, she looked like a Mexican actress from the seventies. When he got in the car the illusion vanished. Professor Pérez drove and he sat next to her. They headed east. For the first few miles the highway ran through a little valley dotted with rocks that seemed to have fallen from the sky. Chunks of granite with no origin or context. There were some fields, plots where invisible peasants grew crops that neither Professor Pérez nor Amalfitano could make out. Then they were in the desert and the mountains. There were the parents of the orphan rocks they'd just passed. Granitic formations, volcanic formations, peaks silhouetted against the sky in the shape and fashion of birds, but birds of sorrow, thought Amalfitano, as Professor Pérez talked to her son and Rosa about the place where they were going, painting it in colors that shaded from fun (a pool carved out of living rock) to mystery, exemplified for her by the voices to be heard from the lookout point, sounds clearly made by the wind. When Amalfitano turned his head to see the expression on Rosa's face and on the face of Professor Pérez's son, he saw four cars trailing them, waiting to pass. Inside each car he imagined a happy family, a mother, a picnic basket full of food, two children, and a father driving with the window rolled down. He smiled at his daughter and turned back to watch the road. Half an hour later they went up a hill, from the top of which he could see a wide expanse of desert behind them. They saw more cars. He supposed that the roadside bar or café or restaurant or by-the-hour motel was a fashionable destination for the inhabitants of Santa Teresa. He regretted having accepted the invitation. At some point he fell asleep. By the time he woke up, they were there. Professor Pérez's hand was on his face, a gesture that might have been a caress or not. Her hand was like a blind woman's hand. Rosa and Rafael were no longer in the car. He saw a parking lot, almost full, the sun glittering on the chrome-plated surfaces, an open terrace on a slightly higher level, a couple with their arms around each other's shoulders looking at something he couldn't see, the blinding sky full of small, low, white clouds, distant music and a voice that sang or muttered at great speed, so that it was impossible to understand the words. An inch away he saw Professor Pérez's face. He took her hand and kissed it. His shirt was damp with sweat, but what surprised him most was that the professor was sweating too.

•

Despite everything, they had a pleasant day. Rosa and Rafael swam in the pool and then joined Amalfitano and Professor Pérez, who were watching them from one of the tables. After that they all bought sodas and went out to walk around. In some places the mountain dropped straight down, and in the depths or on the cliff sides there were big gashes with different-colored rock showing through, or rock that looked different colors in the sun as it fled westward, lutites and andesites sandwiched between sandstone formations, vertical outcrops of tuff and great trays of basaltic rock. Here and there, a Sonora cactus dangled from the mountainside. And farther away there were more mountains and then tiny valleys and more mountains, finally giving way to an expanse veiled in haze, in mist, like a cloud cemetery, behind which were Chihuahua and New Mexico and Texas. Sitting on rocks and surveying this view, they ate in silence. Rosa and Rafael spoke only to exchange sandwiches. Professor Pérez seemed lost in her own thoughts. And Amalfitano felt tired and overwhelmed by the landscape, a landscape that seemed best suited to the young or the old, imbecilic or insensitive or evil and old who meant to impose impossible tasks on themselves and others until they breathed their last.

•

That night Amalfitano was up until very late. The first thing he did when he got home was go out into the backyard to see whether Dieste's book was still there. On the ride home Professor Pérez had tried to be nice and start a conversation in which all four of them could participate, but her son fell asleep as soon as they began the descent and soon afterward Rosa did, too, with her head against the window. It wasn't long before

Amalfitano followed his daughter's example. He dreamed of a woman's voice, not Professor Pérez's but a Frenchwoman's, talking to him about signs and numbers and something Amalfitano didn't understand, something the voice in the dream called "history broken down" or "history taken apart and put back together," although clearly the reassembled history became something else, a scribble in the margin, a clever footnote, a laugh slow to fade that leaped from an andesite rock to a rhyolite and then a tufa, and from that collection of prehistoric rocks there arose a kind of quicksilver, the American mirror, said the voice, the sad American mirror of wealth and poverty and constant useless metamorphosis, the mirror that sails and whose sails are pain. And then Amalfitano switched dreams and stopped hearing voices, which must have meant he was sleeping deeply, and he dreamed he was moving toward a woman, a woman who was only a pair of legs at the end of a dark hallway and then he heard someone laugh at his snoring, Professor Pérez's son, and he thought: good. As they were driving into Santa Teresa on the westbound highway, crowded at that time of day with dilapidated trucks and small pickups on their way back from the city market or from cities in Arizona, he woke up. Not only had he slept with his mouth open, but he had drooled on the collar of his shirt. Good, he thought, excellent. When he looked in satisfaction at Professor Pérez, he detected an air of sadness about her. Out of sight of their respective children, she lightly stroked Amalfitano's leg as he turned his head and looked at a taco stand where a couple of policemen with guns on their hips were drinking beer and talking and watching the red and black dusk, like a thick chili whose last simmer was fading in the west. When they got home it was dark but the shadow of Dieste's book hanging from the clothesline was clearer, steadier, more reasonable, thought Amalfitano, than anything they'd seen on the outskirts of Santa Teresa or in the city itself, images with no handhold, images freighted with all the orphanhood in the world, fragments, fragments.

•

That night he waited, dreading the voice. He tried to prepare for a class, but he soon realized it was a pointless task to prepare for something he knew backward and forward. He thought that if he drew on the blank piece of paper in front of him, the basic geometric figures would appear again. So he drew a face and erased it and then immersed himself in the memory of the obliterated face. He remembered (but fleetingly, as one remembers a lightning bolt) Ramon Llull and his fantastic machine. Fantastic in its uselessness. When he looked at the blank sheet again he had written the following names in three columns:

Pico della Mirandola	Hobbes	Boecio
Husserl	Locke	Alexander of Hales
Eugen Fink	Erich Becher	Marx
Merleau-Ponty	Wittgenstein	Lichtenberg
Bede	Llull	Sade
St. Bonaventure	Hegel	Condorcet
John Philoponus	Pascal	Fourier
Saint Augustine	Canetti	Lacan
Schopenhauer	Freud	Lessing

For a while, Amalfitano read and reread the names, horizontally and vertically, from the center outward, from bottom to top, skipping and at random, and then he laughed and thought that the whole thing was a truism, in other words a proposition too obvious to formulate. Then he drank a glass of tap water, water from the mountains of Sonora, and as he waited for the water to make its way down his throat he stopped shaking, an imperceptible shaking that only he could feel, and he began to think about the Sierra Madre aquifers running toward the city in the middle of the endless night, and he also thought about the aquifers rising from their hiding places closer to Santa Teresa, and about the water that coated teeth with a smooth ocher film. And when he'd drunk the whole glass of water he looked out the window and saw the long shadow, the coffinlike shadow, cast by Dieste's book hanging in the yard.

•

But the voice returned, and this time it asked him, begged him, to be a man, not a queer. Queer? asked Amalfitano. Yes, queer, faggot, cocksucker, said the voice. Ho-mo-sex-u-al, said the voice. In the next breath it asked him whether he happened to be one of those. One of what? asked Amalfitano, terrified. A ho-mo-sex-u-al, said the voice. And before Amalfitano could answer, it hastened to make clear that it was speaking figuratively, that it had nothing against faggots or queers, in fact it felt boundless admiration for certain poets who had professed such sexual leanings, not to mention certain painters and government clerks. Government clerks? asked Amalfitano. Yes, yes, yes, said the voice, young government clerks with short life spans. Clerks who stained official documents with senseless tears. Dead by their own hand. Then the voice was silent and Amalfitano remained sitting in his office. Much later, maybe a quarter of an hour later, maybe the next night, the voice said: let's say I'm your grandfather, your father's father, and let's say that as your grandfather I can ask you a personal question. You're free to answer or not, but I can ask the question. My grandfather? said Amalfitano. Yes, your grandfather, said the voice, you can call me *nono*. And my question for you is: are you a queer, are you going to go running out of this room, are you a ho-mo-sex-u-al, are you going to go wake up your daughter? No, said Amalfitano. I'm listening. Tell me what you have to say.

•

And the voice said: are you a queer? are you? and Amalfitano said no and shook his head, too. I'm not going to run away. You won't be seeing my back or the soles of my shoes. Assuming you see at all. And the voice said: see? as in *see*? to tell the truth, I can't. Not much, anyway. It's enough work just keeping one foot in. Where? asked Amalfitano. At your house, I suppose, said the voice. This is my house, said Amalfitano. Yes, I realize, said the voice, now why don't we relax. I'm relaxed, said Amalfitano, I'm here in my house. And he wondered: why is it telling me to relax? And the voice said: I think this is the first day of what I hope will be a long and mutually beneficial relationship. But if it's going to work out, it's absolutely crucial that we stay calm. Calm is the one thing that will never let us down. And Amalfitano said: everything else lets us down? And the voice: yes, that's right, it's hard to admit, I mean it's hard to have to admit it to you, but that's the honest-to-God truth. Ethics lets us down? The sense of duty lets us down? Honesty lets us down? Curiosity lets us down? Love lets us down? Bravery lets us down? Art lets us down? That's right, said the voice, everything lets us down, everything. Or lets you down, which isn't the same thing but for our purposes it might as well be, except calm, calm is the one thing that never lets us down, though that's no guarantee of anything, I have to tell you. You're wrong, said Amalfitano, bravery never lets us down. And neither does our love for our children. Oh no? said the voice. No, said Amalfitano, suddenly feeling calm.

·

And then, in a whisper, like everything he had said so far, he asked whether calm was therefore the opposite of madness. And the voice said: no, absolutely not, if you're worried that you've lost your mind, don't worry, you haven't, all you're doing is having a casual conversation. So I haven't lost my mind, said Amalfitano. No, absolutely not, said the voice. So you're my grandfather, said Amalfitano. Call me pops, said the voice. So everything lets us down, including curiosity and honesty and what we love best. Yes, said the voice, but cheer up, it's fun in the end.

·

There is no friendship, said the voice, there is no love, there is no epic, there is no lyric poetry that isn't the gurgle or chuckle of egoists, the murmur of cheats, the babble of traitors, the burble of social climbers, the warble of faggots. What is it you have against homosexuals? whispered Amalfitano. Nothing, said the voice. I'm speaking figuratively, said the voice. Are we in Santa Teresa? asked the voice. Is this city part of the state of Sonora? A pretty significant part of it, in fact? Yes, said Amalfitano. Well, there you go, said the voice. It's one thing to be a social climber, say, for example, said Amalfitano, tugging at his hair as if in slow motion, and something very different to be a faggot. I'm speaking figuratively, said the voice. I'm talking so you understand me. I'm talking like I'm in the studio of a ho-mo-sex-u-al painter, with you there behind me. I'm talking from a studio where the chaos is just a mask or the faint stink of anesthesia. I'm talking from a studio with the lights out, where the sinew of the will detaches itself from the rest of the body the way the snake tongue detaches itself from the body and slithers away, self-mutilated, amid the rubbish. I'm talking from the perspective of the simple things in life. You teach philosophy? said the voice. You teach Wittgenstein? said the voice. And have you asked yourself whether your hand is a hand? said the voice. I've asked myself, said Amalfitano. But now you have more important things to ask yourself, am I right? said the voice. No, said Amalfitano. For example, why not go to a nursery and buy seeds and plants and maybe even a little tree to plant in the middle of your backyard? said the voice. Yes, said Amalfitano. I've thought about my possible and conceivable yard and the plants and tools I need to buy. And you've also thought about your daughter, said the voice, and about the murders committed daily in this city, and about Baudelaire's faggoty

(I'm sorry) clouds, but you haven't thought seriously about whether your hand is really a hand. That isn't true, said Amalfitano, I have thought about it, I have. If you had thought about it, said the voice, you'd be dancing to the tune of a different piper. And Amalfitano was silent and he felt that the silence was a kind of eugenics. He looked at his watch. It was four in the morning. He heard someone starting a car. The engine took a while to turn over. He got up and went over to the window. The cars parked in front of the house were empty. He looked behind him and then put his hand on the doorknob. The voice said: be careful, but it said it as if it were very far away, at the bottom of a ravine revealing glimpses of volcanic rock, rhyolites, andesites, streaks of silver and gold, petrified puddles covered with tiny little eggs, while red-tailed hawks soared above in the sky, which was purple like the skin of an Indian woman beaten to death. Amalfitano went out onto the porch. To the left, some thirty feet from his house, the lights of a black car came on and its engine started. When it passed the yard the driver leaned out and looked at Amalfitano without stopping. He was a fat man with very black hair, dressed in a cheap suit with no tie. When he was gone, Amalfitano came back into the house. I didn't like the looks of him, said the voice the minute Amalfitano was through the door. And then: you'll have to be careful, my friend, things here seem to be coming to a head.

•

So who are you and how did you get here? asked Amalfitano. There's no point going into it, said the voice. No point? asked Amalfitano, laughing in a whisper, like a fly. There's no point, said the voice. Can I ask you a question? said Amalfitano. Go ahead, said the voice. Are you really the ghost of my grandfather? The things you come up with, said the voice. Of course not, I'm the spirit of your father. Your grandfather's spirit doesn't remember you anymore. But I'm your father and I'll never forget you. Do you understand? Yes, said Amalfitano. Do you understand that you have nothing to fear from me? Yes, said Amalfitano. Do something useful, then check that all the doors and windows are shut tight and go to sleep. Something useful like what? asked Amalfitano. For example, wash the dishes, said the voice. And Amalfitano lit a cigarette and began to do what the voice had suggested. You wash and I'll talk, said the voice. All is calm, said the voice. There's no bad blood between us. The headache, if you have a headache, will go away soon, and so will the buzzing in your ears, the racing pulse, the rapid heartbeat. You'll relax, you'll think some and relax, said the voice, while you do something use-ful for your daughter and yourself. Understood, whispered Amalfitano. Good, said the voice, this is like an endoscopy, but painless. Got it, whis-pered Amalfitano. And he scrubbed the plates and the pot with the re-mains of pasta and tomato sauce and the forks and the glasses and the stove and the table where they'd eaten, smoking one cigarette after an-other and also taking occasional gulps of water straight from the faucet. And at five in the morning he took the dirty clothes out of the bathroom hamper and went out into the backyard and put the clothes in the wash-ing machine and pushed the button for a normal wash and looked at Dieste's book hanging motionless and then he went back into the living room and his eyes, like the eyes of an addict, sought out something else to clean or tidy or wash, but he couldn't find anything and he sat down, whispering yes or no or I don't remember or maybe. Everything is fine, said the voice. It's all a question of getting used to it. Without making a fuss. Without sweating and flailing around.

•

It was past six when Amalfitano fell into bed without undressing and slept like a baby. Rosa woke him at nine. It had been a long time since Amalfitano felt so good, although his classes that morning were entirely incomprehensible. At one o'clock he ate at the cafeteria and sat at one of the farthest, most out-of-the-way tables. He didn't want to see Professor Pérez, and he didn't want to run into any other colleagues either, least of all the dean, who made a habit of eating there every day, surrounded by professors and a few students who ceaselessly fawned over him. He or-dered at the counter, almost stealthily, boiled chicken and salad, and he hurried to his table, dodging the students who crowded the cafeteria at that time of day. Then he sat down to eat and think some more about what had happened the previous night. He realized with astonishment that he was excited by what he had experienced. I feel like a nightingale, he thought happily. It was a simple and antiquated and ridiculous senti-ment, but it was the only thing that fully expressed his current state of mind. He tried to relax. The students' laughter, their shouts to each other, the clatter of plates, made it a less than ideal spot for reflection. And yet after a few seconds he realized there could be no better place. Equally good, yes, but not better. So he took a long drink of bottled wa-ter (it didn't taste the same as the tap water, but it didn't taste very dif-ferent either) and he began to think. First he thought about madness.

About the possibility—great—that he was losing his mind. It came as a surprise to him to realize that the thought (and the possibility) in no way diminished his excitement. Or his happiness. My excitement and my happiness are growing under the wing of a storm, he said to himself. I may be going crazy, but I feel good, he said to himself. He contemplated the possibility—great—that if he really was going crazy it would get worse, and then his excitement would turn into pain and helplessness and, especially, a source of pain and helplessness for his daughter. As if he had X-ray eyes he reviewed his savings and calculated that with what he had saved, Rosa could go back to Barcelona and still have money to start with. To start what? That was a question he preferred not to answer. He imagined himself locked up in an asylum in Santa Teresa or Hermosillo with Professor Pérez as his only occasional visitor, and every so often receiving letters from Rosa in Barcelona, where she would be working or finishing her studies, and where she would meet a Catalan boy, responsible and affectionate, who would fall in love with her and respect her and take care of her and be nice to her and with whom Rosa would end up living and going to the movies at night and traveling to Italy or Greece in July or August, and the scenario didn't seem so bad. Then he considered other possibilities. Of course, he said to himself, he didn't believe in ghosts or spirits, although during his childhood in the south of Chile people talked about the *mechona* who waited for riders on a tree branch, dropping onto horses' haunches, clinging to the back of the cowboy or smuggler without letting go, like a lover whose embrace maddened the horse as well as the rider, both of them dying of fright or ending up at the bottom of a ravine, or the *colocolo*, or the *chonchones*, or the *candelillas*, or so many other little creatures, lost souls, incubi and succubi, lesser demons that roamed between the Cordillera de la Costa and the Andes, but in which he didn't believe, not exactly because of his training in philosophy (Schopenhauer, after all, believed in ghosts, and it was surely a ghost that appeared to Nietzsche and drove him mad) but because of his materialist leanings. So he rejected the possibility of ghosts, at least until he had exhausted other lines of inquiry. The voice could be a ghost, he wouldn't rule it out, but he tried to come up with a different explanation. After much reflection, though, the only thing that made sense was the theory of the lost soul. He thought about the seer of Hermosillo, Madame Cristina, La Santa. He thought about his father. He decided that his father would never use the Mexican words the voice had used, no matter what kind of roving spirit he had become, whereas the slight tinge of homophobia suited him perfectly. With a happiness hard to disguise, he asked himself what kind of mess he had gotten himself into. That afternoon he taught another few classes and then he went walking home. As he passed the central plaza of Santa Teresa he saw a group of women protesting in front of the town hall. On one of the posters he read: No to impunity. On another: End the corruption. A group of policemen were watching the women from under the adobe arches of the colonial building. They weren't riot police but plain Santa Teresa uniformed policemen. As he walked past he heard someone call his name. When he turned he saw Professor Pérez and his daughter on the sidewalk across the street. He offered to buy them a soda. At the coffee shop they explained that the protest was to demand transparency in the investigation of the disappearances and killings of women. Professor Pérez said she had three feminists from Mexico City staying at her house, and that night she planned to have a dinner for them. I'd like you to come, she said. Rosa said yes. Amalfitano expressed no objection. Then his daughter and Professor Pérez returned to the protest and Amalfitano continued on his way.

•

But before he got home someone called his name again. Professor Amalfitano, he heard someone saying. He turned around and didn't see anyone. He wasn't in the center of the city anymore. He was walking along Avenida Madero, and the four-story buildings had given way to ranch houses, imitations of a kind of California house from the fifties, houses that had begun to suffer the ravages of time long ago, when their occupants moved to the neighborhood where Amalfitano now lived. Some houses had been converted into garages that also sold ice cream and others had become businesses dealing in bread or clothes, without any modifications whatsoever. Many of them displayed signs advertising doctors, lawyers specializing in divorce or criminal law. Others offered rooms by the day. Some had been divided without much skill into two or three separate shops, where newspapers and magazines or fruit and vegetables were sold, or passersby were promised a good deal on dentures. As Amalfitano was about to keep walking, someone called his name again. Then he saw who it was. The voice was coming from a car parked at the curb. At first he didn't recognize the young man who was calling him. He thought it was a student. Whoever it was had on sunglasses and a black shirt unbuttoned over his chest. He was very tan, like a singer or a Puerto Rican playboy. Get in, Professor, I'll give you a ride home. Amalfitano was about to tell him he'd rather walk when the young man identified himself. I'm Dean Guerra's son, he said as he got out of the car on the side of the street where the traffic thundered by, not looking either way, ignoring the danger in a way that struck Amalfitano as extremely bold. Walking around the car, he came up to Amalfitano and offered his hand. I'm Marco Antonio Guerra, he said, and he reminded him of their champagne toast at his father's office, Amalfitano's welcome to the department. You have nothing to fear from me, Professor, he said, and Amalfitano couldn't help but be surprised by the remark. The young Guerra stopped in front of him. He was smiling just as he had been the first time they met. A confident, mocking smile, like the smile of a cocksure sniper. He wore jeans and cowboy boots. Inside the car, on the backseat, lay a pearl-gray designer jacket and a folder full of papers. I was just driving by, said Marco Antonio Guerra. They headed toward Colonia Lindavista, but before they got there the dean's son suggested they get a drink. Amalfitano politely declined the invitation. Then let's go to your place and have a drink, said Marco Antonio Guerra. I don't have anything to offer, apologized Amalfitano. Then that's settled, said Marco Antonio Guerra, and he took the first turn. Soon there was a change in the urban scenery. West of Colonia Lindavista the houses were new, surrounded in some places by wide-open fields, and some streets weren't even paved. People say these neighborhoods are the city's future, said Marco Antonio Guerra, but in my opinion this shithole has no future. He drove straight onto a soccer field, across which were a pair of enormous sheds or warehouses surrounded by barbed wire. Beyond them ran a canal or creek carrying the neighborhood trash away to the north. Near another open field they saw the old railroad line that had once connected Santa Teresa to Ures and Hermosillo. A few dogs approached timidly. Marco Antonio rolled down the window and let them sniff his hand and lick it. To the left was the highway to Ures. They began to head out of Santa Teresa. Amalfitano asked where they were going. Guerra's son answered that they were on their way to one of the few places around where you could still drink real Mexican mezcal.

•

The place was called Los Zancudos and it was a rectangle three hundred feet long by one hundred feet wide, with a small stage at the end where *corrido* or *ranchera* groups performed on Fridays and Saturdays. The bar was at least one hundred and fifty feet long. The toilets were outside, and they could be entered directly from the outdoor patio or by way of a narrow passageway of galvanized tin connecting them to the restaurant. There weren't many people there. They were greeted by the waiters, whom Marco Antonio Guerra called by name, but no one came to wait on them. Only a few lights were on. I recommend the Los Suicidas, said Marco Antonio. Amalfitano smiled pleasantly and said yes, but just a small one. Marco Antonio raised his arm and snapped his fingers. The bastards must be deaf, he said. He got up and went to the bar. Some time passed before he came back with two glasses and a half-filled bottle of mezcal. Try it, he said. Amalfitano took a sip and thought it tasted good. There should be a worm at the bottom of the bottle, said Marco Antonio, but those scum probably ate it. It sounded like a joke and Amalfitano laughed. But I guarantee it's genuine Los Suicidas, drink up and enjoy, said Marco Antonio. At the second sip Amalfitano thought it really was an extraordinary drink. They don't make it anymore, said Marco Antonio, like so much in this fucking country. And after a while, fixing his gaze on Amalfitano, he said: we're going to hell, I suppose you've realized, Professor? Amalfitano answered that the situation certainly wasn't anything to applaud, without specifying what he meant or going into detail. It's all falling apart in our hands, said Marco Antonio Guerra. The politicians don't know how to govern. All the middle class wants is to move to the United States. And more and more people keep coming to work in the maquiladoras. You know what I would do? No, said Amalfitano. Burn a few of them down, you know? A few what? asked Amalfitano. A few maquiladoras. Interesting, said Amalfitano. I'd also send the army out into the streets, well, not the streets, the highways, to keep more scum from coming here. Highway checkpoints? asked Amalfitano. That's right. I can't see any other solution. There must be other solutions, said Amalfitano. People have lost all respect, said Marco Antonio Guerra. Respect for others and self-respect. Amalfitano glanced toward the bar. Three waiters were whispering, casting sidelong glances at their table. I think we should leave, said Amalfitano. Marco Antonio Guerra noticed the waiters and made an obscene gesture, then he laughed. Amalfitano took him by the arm and dragged him out into the parking lot. By now it was night and a huge glowing sign featuring a long-legged mosquito shone brightly on a metal scaffolding. I think these people have some problem with you, said Amalfitano. Don't worry, Professor, said Marco Antonio Guerra, I'm armed.

·

When he got home, Amalfitano immediately forgot about Marco Antonio Guerra and decided that maybe he wasn't as crazy as he'd thought he was, and that the voice he'd been hearing wasn't a bereaved soul. He thought about telepathy. He thought about the telepathic Mapuches or Araucanians. He remembered a very short book, scarcely one hundred pages long, by a certain Lonko Kilapán, published in Santiago de Chile in 1978, that an old friend, a wiseass of long standing, had sent him while he was living in Europe. This Kilapán presented himself with the following credentials: Historian of the Race, President of the Indigenous Confederation of Chile, and Secretary of the Academy of the Araucanian Language. The book was called *O'Higgins Is Araucanian*, and it was subtitled *17 Proofs, Taken from the Secret History of Araucanía*. Between the title and the subtitle was the following phrase: Text approved by the Araucanian History Council. Then came the prologue, which read like this: "*Prologue*. If proof were desired that any of the heroes of Chile's Independence shared kinship with the Araucanians, it would be difficult to find and harder to verify. Only Iberian blood flowed in the veins of the Carrera brothers, Mackenna, Freire, Manuel Rodríguez. But the dazzling light of Araucanian parentage shines bright in Bernardo O'Higgins, and to prove it we present these 17 proofs. Bernardo is not the illegitimate son described by historians, some with pity, others unable to hide their satisfaction. He is the dashing legitimate son of Irishman Ambrosio O'Higgins, Governor of Chile and Viceroy of Peru, and of an Araucanian woman who belonged to one of the principal tribes of Araucanía. The marriage was celebrated according to Admapu law, with the traditional Gapitun (abduction ceremony). The biography of the Liberator exposes the millenarian Araucanian secret on the very bicentenary of his birth; it springs from the Litrang* to paper, as faithfully as only an Epeutufe can render it." And that was the end of the prologue, by José R. Pichiñual, Cacique of Puerto Saavedra.

·

Odd, thought Amalfitano, with the book in his hands. Odd, extremely odd. For example, the single asterisk. *Litrang*: stone tablets on which the Araucanians engraved their writings. But why footnote *litrang* and not *admapu* or *epeutufe*? Did the Cacique of Puerto Saavedra assume that everyone would know what they meant? And then the sentence about whether or not O'Higgins was a bastard: *Bernardo is not the illegitimate son described by historians, some with* pity, *others unable to hide their* satisfaction. There you had the day-to-day history of Chile, the private history, the history behind closed doors. Pitying the father of the country because he was a bastard. Or being unable to conceal a certain satisfaction when discussing the subject. So telling, thought Amalfitano, and he thought about the first time he'd read Kilapán's book, laughing out loud, and the way he was reading it now, with something like laughter but also something like sorrow. Ambrosio O'Higgins as an Irishman was definitely a good joke. Ambrosio O'Higgins marrying an Araucanian woman, but under the aegis of *admapu* and even going so far as to cap it off with the traditional *gapitun* or abduction ceremony, struck him as a macabre joke that could point only to abuse, rape, a further mockery staged by fat Ambrosio to fuck the Indian woman in peace. I can't think of anything without the word *rape* popping up to stare with its helpless little mammal eyes, thought Amalfitano. Then he fell asleep in his chair, with the book in his hands. Maybe he dreamed something. Something short. Maybe he dreamed about his childhood. Maybe not.

•

Then he woke up and made himself and his daughter something to eat. Back in his office he felt extremely tired, unable to prepare a class or read anything serious, so he returned resignedly to Kilapán's book. Seventeen proofs. Proof number 1 was titled *He was born in the Araucanian state*. It went like this: "The Yekmonchi,[1] called Chile,[2] was geographically and politically identical to the Greek state, and, like it, forming a delta, between the respective latitudes of the 35th and 42nd parallels." Ignoring the construction of the sentence (where it read *forming* it should have read *formed*, and there were at least two commas too many), the most interesting thing about the first paragraph was what might be called its military slant. It began with a straight jab to the chin or a full artillery assault on the center of the enemy line. Note 1 clarified that *Yekmonchi* meant State. Note 2 stated that *Chile* was a Greek word whose translation was "distant tribe." Then came the geographic description of the Yekmonchi of Chile: "It stretched from the Maullis to the Chiligüe rivers, including the west of Argentina. The reigning Mother City, or that is Chile, properly speaking, was located between the Butaleufu and Toltén rivers; like the Greek state, it was surrounded by allied and interrelated peoples, those who were subject to the Küga Chiliches (that is to say the Chilean (or Chiliches: people of Chile) tribe (Küga). Che: people, as Kilapán meticulously took care to recall), who taught them the sciences, the arts, sports, and especially the science of war." Farther along Kilapán confessed: "In 1947," although Amalfitano suspected that this was an erratum and that the year was actually 1974, "I opened the tomb of Kurillanka, which was under the main Kuralwe, covered by a flat stone. All that remained was a katankura, a metawe, duck, an obsidian ornament, like an arrowhead to pay the 'toll' that the soul of Kurillanka had to pay to Zenpilkawe, the Greek Charon, to take him across the sea to his place of origin: a remote island in the sea. These pieces were distributed among the Araucanian museums of Temuco, the future Museo Abate Molina of Villa Alegre, and the Museo Araucano of Santiago, which will soon be open to the public." The mention of Villa Alegre prompted Kilapán to add the oddest note. It read: "In Villa Alegre, formerly Warakulen, lie the remains of Abate Juan Ignacio Molina, brought from Italy to his native city. He was a professor at the University of Bologna, where his statue presides over the entrance to the Pantheon of the Distinguished Sons of Italy, between the statues of Copernicus and Galileo. According to Molina, there is an unquestionable kinship between Greeks and Araucanians." This Molina was a Jesuit and a naturalist, and he lived from 1740 to 1829.

•

Shortly after the episode at Los Zancudos, Amalfitano saw Dean Guerra's son again. This time he was dressed like a cowboy, although he had shaved and he smelled of Calvin Klein cologne. Even so, all he lacked to look like a real cowboy was the hat. There was something mysterious about the way he accosted Amalfitano. It was late in the day, and as Amalfitano walked along a ridiculously long corridor at the university, deserted and dark at that hour, Marco Antonio Guerra burst out from a corner like someone playing a bad joke or about to attack him. Amalfitano jumped, then struck out automatically with his fist. It's me, Marco

Antonio, said the dean's son, after he was hit again. Then they recognized each other and relaxed and set off together toward the rectangle of light at the end of the hallway, which reminded Marco Antonio of the stories of people who'd been in comas or declared clinically dead and who claimed to have seen a dark tunnel with a white or dazzling brightness at the end, and sometimes these people even testified to the presence of loved ones who had passed away, who took their hands or soothed them or urged them to turn back because the hour or microfraction of a second in which the change took effect hadn't yet arrived. What do you think, Professor? Do people on the verge of death make this shit up, or is it real? Is it all just a dream, or is it within the realm of possibility? I don't know, said Amalfitano curtly, since he still hadn't gotten over his fright, and he wasn't in the mood for a repeat of their last meeting. Well, said Marco Antonio Guerra, if you want to know what I think, I don't believe it. People see what they want to see and what people want to see never has anything to do with the truth. People are cowards to the last breath. I'm telling you between you and me: the human being, broadly speaking, is the closest thing there is to a rat.

•

Despite what he had hoped (to get rid of Marco Antonio Guerra as soon as they emerged from the hallway with its aura of life after death), Amalfitano had to follow him without complaint because the dean's son was the bearer of an invitation to dinner that very evening at the house of the rector of the University of Santa Teresa, the august Dr. Pablo Negrete. So he climbed in Marco Antonio's car, and Marco Antonio drove him home, then chose, in an unwonted display of shyness, to wait for him outside, watching the car, as if there were thieves in Colonia Lindavista, while Amalfitano cleaned up and changed clothes, and his daughter, who of course was invited too, did the same, or not, since his daughter could go dressed as she liked, but he, Amalfitano, had better show up at Dr. Negrete's house in a jacket and tie at the very least. The dinner, as it happened, was nothing to worry about. Dr. Negrete simply wanted to meet him and had assumed, or been advised, that a first meeting in his office at the administration building would be much chillier than a first meeting in the comfort of his own home, a grand old two-story house surrounded by a lush garden with plants from all over Mexico and plenty of shady nooks where guests could gather in *petit comité*. Dr. Negrete was a man of silence and reserve who was happier listening to others than leading the conversation himself. He asked about Barcelona, recollected that in his youth he had attended a conference in Prague, mentioned a former professor at the University of Santa Teresa, an Argentinian who now taught at one of the branches of the University of California, and the rest of the time he was quiet. His wife, who carried herself with a distinction that the rector lacked, though to judge by her features she had never been a beauty, was much nicer to Amalfitano and especially to Rosa, who reminded her of her youngest daughter, whose name was Clara, like her mother's, and who had been living in Phoenix for years. At some point during the dinner Amalfitano thought he noticed a rather murky exchange of glances between the rector and his wife. In her eyes he glimpsed something that might have been hatred. At the same time, a sudden fear flitted as swiftly as a butterfly across the rector's face. But Amalfitano noticed it and for a moment (the second flutter of wings) the rector's fear nearly brushed his own skin. When he recovered and looked at the other dinner guests he realized that no one had noticed the slight shadow, like a hastily dug pit that gives off an alarming stench.

•

But he was wrong. Young Marco Antonio Guerra had noticed. And he had also noticed that Amalfitano had noticed. Life is worthless, he said into Amalfitano's ear when they went out into the garden. Rosa sat with the rector's wife and Professor Pérez. The rector sat in the gazebo's only rocking chair. Dean Guerra and two philosophy professors took seats near the rector's wife. A third professor, a bachelor, remained standing, next to Amalfitano and Marco Antonio Guerra. A servant, an almost elderly woman, came in after a while carrying an enormous tray of glasses that she set on a marble table. Amalfitano considered helping her, but then he thought it might be seen as disrespectful if he did. When the old woman reappeared, carrying more than seven bottles in precarious equilibrium, Amalfitano couldn't stop himself and went to help her. When she saw him, the old woman's eyes widened and the tray began to slip from her hands. Amalfitano heard a shriek, the ridiculous little shriek of one of the professors' wives, and at that same moment, as the tray was falling, he glimpsed the shadow of young Guerra setting everything right again. Don't worry, Chachita, he heard the rector's wife say.

Then he heard young Guerra, after he had set the bottles on the table, ask Doña Clara whether she kept any Los Suicidas mezcal in her liquor cabinet. And he heard Dean Guerra saying: pay no attention to my son and his foolish notions. And he heard Rosa say: Los Suicidas mezcal, what a pretty name. And he heard a professor's wife say: it certainly is unusual. And he heard Professor Pérez: what a fright, I thought she was going to drop them. And he heard a philosophy professor talking about *norteño* music, to change the subject. And he heard Dean Guerra say that the difference between *norteño* groups and groups from anywhere else in the country was that *norteño* groups were always made up of an accordion and a guitar, with the accompaniment of a *bajo sexto*, the twelve-string guitar, and some kind of *brinco*. And he heard the same philosophy professor asking what a *brinco* was. And he heard the dean answer that a *brinco* could be drums, for example, like a rock group's drum kit, or kettledrums, and in *norteño* music a proper *brinco* might be the *redova*, a hollow wooden block, or more commonly a pair of sticks. And he heard Rector Negrete saying: that's right. And then he accepted a glass of whiskey and sought the face of the person who had put it in his hand and found the face of young Guerra, pale in the moonlight.

•

Proof number 2, by far the most interesting to Amalfitano, was called *He was born to an Araucanian woman* and it began like this: "Upon the arrival of the Spaniards, the Araucanians established two channels for communication from Santiago: telepathy and Adkintuwe.[55] Lautaro,[56] because of his notable telepathic skills, was taken north with his mother when he was still a child to enter the service of the Spaniards. It was in this way that Lautaro contributed to the defeat of the Spaniards. Since telepaths could be eliminated and communications cut, Adkintuwe was created. Only after 1700 did the Spaniards become aware of this method of sending messages by the movement of branches. They were puzzled by the fact that the Araucanians knew everything that happened in the city of Concepción. Although they managed to discover Adkintuwe, they were never able to decipher it. They never suspected that the Araucanians were telepathic, believing instead that they had 'traffic with the devil,' who informed them of events in Santiago. There were three lines of Adkintuwe from the capital: one along the buttresses of the Andes, another along the coast, and a third along the central valley. Primitive man was ignorant of language; he communicated by brainwaves, as animals and plants do. When he resorted to sounds and gestures and hand signals to communicate, he began to lose the gift of telepathy, and this loss was accelerated when he went to live in cities, distancing himself from nature. Although the Araucanians had two kinds of writing— the rope knotting known as Prom,[57] and the triangle writing known as Adentunemul[58]—they never gave up telecommunication; on the contrary, some Kügas whose families were scattered all over America, the Pacific Islands, and the deepest south specialized in it so that no enemy would ever take them by surprise. By means of telepathy they kept in permanent contact with the Chilean migrants who first settled in the north of India, where they were called Aryans, then headed to the fields of ancient Germania and later descended to the Peloponnese, traveling from there to Chile along the traditional route to India and across the Pacific Ocean." Immediately following this and apropos of nothing, Kilapán wrote: "Killenkusi was a Machi[59] priestess. Her daughter Kinturay had to choose between succeeding her or becoming a spy; she chose the latter and her love for the Irishman; this opportunity afforded her the hope of having a child who, like Lautaro and mixed-race Alejo, would be raised among the Spaniards, and like them might one day lead the hosts of those who wished to push the conquistadors back beyond the Maule River, because Admapu law prohibited the Araucanians from fighting outside of Yekmonchi. Her hope was realized and in the spring[60] of the year 1777, in the place called Palpal, an Araucanian woman endured the pain of childbirth in a standing position because tradition decreed that a strong child could not be born of a weak mother. The son arrived and became the Liberator of Chile."

•

The footnotes made it very clear in what kind of drunken ship Kilapán had set sail, if it wasn't clear already. Note 55, *Adkintuwe*, read: "After many years the Spaniards became aware of its existence, but they were never able to decipher it." Note 56: "*Lautaro*, swift noise (*taros* in Greek means swift)." Note 57: "*Prom*, word handed down from the Greek by way of Prometheus, the Titan who stole writing from the gods to give to man." Note 58: "*Adentunemul*, secret writing consisting of triangles." Note 59: "*Machi*, seer. From the Greek verb *mantis*, which means to divine." Note 60: "*Spring*, Admapu law ordered that children should be conceived in summer, when all fruits were ripe; thus they would be born in spring when the land awakens in the fullness of its strength; when all the animals and birds are born."

•

From this one could conclude that: (1) all Araucanians or most of them were telepathic, (2) the Araucanian language was closely linked to the language of Homer, (3) Araucanians had traveled all over the globe, especially to India, ancient Germania, and the Peloponnese, (4) Araucanians were amazing sailors, (5) Araucanians had two kinds of writing, one based on knots and the other on triangles, the latter secret, (6) the exact nature of the mode of communication that Kilapán called Adkintuwe (and that had been discovered by the Spaniards, although they were unable to decipher it) wasn't very clear. Maybe it was the sending of messages by the movement of tree branches located in strategic places, like at the tops of hills? Something like the smoke signals of the Plains Indians of America? (7) in contrast, telepathic communication was never discovered and if at some point it stopped working this was because the Spaniards killed the telepaths, (8) telepathy also permitted the Araucanians of Chile to remain in permanent contact with Chilean migrants scattered in places as far-flung as populous India or green Germany, (9) should one deduce from this that Bernardo O'Higgins was also a telepath? Should one deduce that the author himself, Lonko Kilapán, was a telepath? Yes, in fact, one should.

•

One could also deduce (and, with a little effort, see) other things, thought Amalfitano as he diligently gauged his mood, watching Dieste's book hanging in the dark in the backyard. One could see, for example, the date that Kilapán's book was published, 1978, in other words during the military dictatorship, and deduce the atmosphere of triumph, loneliness, and fear in which it was published. One could see, for example, a gentleman of Indian appearance, half out of his head but hiding it well, dealing with the printers of the prestigious Editorial Universitaria, located on Calle San Francisco, number 454, in Santiago. One could see the sum that the publication of the little book would cost the Historian of the Race, the President of the Indigenous Confederation of Chile, and the Secretary of the Academy of the Araucanian Language, a sum that Mr. Kilapán tries to bargain down more wishfully than effectively, although the manager of the print shop knows that they aren't exactly overrun with work and that he could very well give this Mr. Kilapán a little discount, especially since the man swears he has two more books already finished and edited (*Araucanian Legends and Greek Legends* and *Origins of the American Man and Kinship Between Araucanians, Aryans, Early Germans, and Greeks*) and he swears up and down that he'll bring them here, because, gentlemen, a book published by the Editorial Universitaria is a book distinguished at first glance, a book of distinction, and it's this final argument that convinces the printer, the manager, the office drudge who handles these matters, to let him have his little discount. The word *distinguished*. The word *distinction*. Ah, ah, ah, ah, pants Amalfitano, struggling for breath as if he's having a sudden asthma attack. Ah, Chile.

•

Although it was possible to imagine other scenarios, of course, or it was possible to see the same sad picture from different angles. And just as the book began with a jab to the jaw ("the Yekmonchi, called Chile, was geographically and politically identical to the Greek state"), the active reader—the reader as envisioned by Cortázar—could begin his reading with a kick to the author's testicles, viewing him from the start as a straw man, a factotum in the service of some colonel in the intelligence services, or maybe of some general who fancied himself an intellectual, which wouldn't be so strange either, this being Chile, in fact the reverse would be stranger, in Chile military men behaved like writers, and writers, so as not to be outdone, behaved like military men, and politicians (of every stripe) behaved like writers and like military men, and diplomats behaved like cretinous cherubim, and doctors and lawyers behaved like thieves, and so on ad nauseam, impervious to discouragement. But picking up the thread where he had left off, it seemed possible that Kilapán hadn't been the one who wrote the book. And if Kilapán hadn't written the book, it might be that Kilapán didn't exist, in other words that there was no President of the Indigenous Confederation of Chile, among other reasons because perhaps the Indigenous Confederation didn't exist, nor was there any Secretary of the Academy of the Araucanian Language, among other reasons because perhaps said Academy of the Araucanian Language never existed. All fake. All nonexistent. Kilapán, from that perspective, thought Amalfitano, moving his head in time to the (very slight) swaying of Dieste's book outside the window, might easily be a nom de plume for Pinochet, representing Pinochet's long sleepless nights or his productive mornings, when he got up at six or five-thirty and after he showered and performed a few calisthenics he shut himself in his library to review international slights, to meditate on Chile's negative reputation abroad. But there was no reason to get too excited. Kilapán's prose could be Pinochet's, certainly. But it could also be Aylwin's or Lagos's. Kilapán's prose could be Frei's (which was saying something) or the prose of any right-wing neo-Fascist. Not only did Lonko Kilapán's prose encapsulate all of Chile's styles, it also represented all of its political factions, from the conservatives to the Communists, from the new liberals to the old survivors of the MIR. Kilapán was the high-grade Spanish spoken and written in Chile, its cadences revealing not only the leathery nose of Abate Molina, but also the butchery of Patricio Lynch, the endless shipwrecks of the *Esmeralda*, the Atacama desert and cattle grazing, the Guggenheim Fellowships, the Socialist politicians praising the economic policy of the junta, the corners where pumpkin fritters were sold, the *mote con huesillos*, the ghost of the Berlin Wall rippling on motionless red flags, the domestic abuse, the good-hearted whores, the cheap housing, what in Chile they called grudge holding and Amalfitano called madness.

•

But what he was really looking for was a name. The name of O'Higgins's telepathic mother. According to Kilapán: Kinturay Treulen, daughter of Killenkusi and Waramanke Treulen. According to the official story: Doña Isabel Riquelme. Having reached this point, Amalfitano decided to stop watching Dieste's book swaying (ever so slightly) in the darkness and sit down and think about his own mother's name: Doña Eugenia Riquelme (actually Doña Filia Maria Eugenia Riquelme Graña). He was briefly startled. For five seconds, his hair stood on end. He tried to laugh but he couldn't.

•

I understand you, Marco Antonio Guerra said to him. I mean, if I'm right, I think I understand you. You're like me and I'm like you. We aren't happy. The atmosphere around us is stifling. We pretend there's nothing wrong, but there is. What's wrong? We're being fucking stifled. You let off steam your own way. I beat the shit out of people or let them beat the shit out of me. But the fights I get into aren't just any fights, they're fucking apocalyptic mayhem. I'm going to tell you a secret. Sometimes I go out at night, to bars you can't even imagine. And I pretend to be a faggot. But not just any kind of faggot: smooth, stuck-up, sarcastic, a daisy in the filthiest pigsty in Sonora. Of course, I don't have a gay bone in me, I can swear that on the grave of my dead mother. But I pretend that's what I am. An arrogant little faggot with money who looks down on everyone. And then the inevitable happens. Two or three vultures ask me to step outside. And then the shit kicking begins. I know it and I don't care. Sometimes they're the ones who get the worst of it, especially when I have my gun. Other times it's me. I don't give a fuck. I need the fucking release. Sometimes my friends, the few friends I have, guys my age who are lawyers now, tell me I should be careful, I'm a time bomb, I'm a masochist. One of them, someone I was really close to, told me that only somebody like me could get away with what I did because I had my father to bail me out. Pure coincidence, that's all. I've never asked my father for a thing. The truth is, I don't have friends. I don't want any. At least, I'd rather not have friends who're Mexicans. Mexicans are rotten inside, did you know? Every last one of them. No one escapes. From the president of the republic to that clown Subcomandante Marcos. If I were Subcomandante Marcos, you know what I'd do? I'd launch an attack with my whole army on any city in Chiapas, so long as it had a strong military garrison. And there I'd sacrifice my poor Indians. And then I'd probably go live in Miami. What kind of music do you like? asked Amalfitano. Classical music, Professor, Vivaldi, Cimarosa, Bach. And what books do you read? I used to read everything, Professor, I read all the time. Now all I read is poetry. Poetry is the one thing that isn't contaminated, the one thing that isn't part of the game. I don't know if you follow me, Professor. Only poetry—and let me be clear, only some of it—is good for you, only poetry isn't shit.

●

Young Guerra's voice, breaking into flat, harmless shards, issued from a climbing vine, and he said: Georg Trakl is one of my favorites.

●

The mention of Trakl made Amalfitano think, as he went through the motions of teaching a class, about a drugstore near where he lived in Barcelona, a place he used to go when he needed medicine for Rosa. One of the employees was a young pharmacist, barely out of his teens, extremely thin and with big glasses, who would sit up at night reading a book when the pharmacy was open twenty-four hours. One night, while the kid was scanning the shelves, Amalfitano asked him what books he liked and what book he was reading, just to make conversation. Without turning, the pharmacist answered that he liked books like *The Metamorphosis*, *Bartleby*, *A Simple Heart*, *A Christmas Carol*. And then he said that he was reading Capote's *Breakfast at Tiffany's*. Leaving aside the fact that *A Simple Heart* and *A Christmas Carol* were stories, not books, there was something revelatory about the taste of this bookish young pharmacist, who in another life might have been Trakl or who in this life might still be writing poems as desperate as those of his distant Austrian counterpart, and who clearly and inarguably preferred minor works to major ones. He chose *The Metamorphosis* over *The Trial*, he chose *Bartleby* over *Moby-Dick*, he chose *A Simple Heart* over *Bouvard and Pécuchet*, and *A Christmas Carol* over *A Tale of Two Cities* or *The Pickwick Papers*. What a sad paradox, thought Amalfitano. Now even bookish pharmacists are afraid to take on the great, imperfect, torrential works, books that blaze paths into the unknown. They choose the perfect exercises of the great masters. Or what amounts to the same thing: they want to watch the great masters spar, but they have no interest in real combat, when the great masters struggle against that something, that something that terrifies us all, that something that cows us and spurs us on, amid blood and mortal wounds and stench.

•

That night, as young Guerra's grandiloquent words were still echoing in the depths of his brain, Amalfitano dreamed that he saw the last Communist philosopher of the twentieth century appear in a pink marble courtyard. He was speaking Russian. Or rather: he was singing a song in Russian as his big body went weaving toward a patch of red-streaked majolica that stood out on the flat plane of the courtyard like a kind of crater or latrine. The last Communist philosopher was dressed in a dark suit and sky-blue tie and had gray hair. Although he seemed about to collapse at any moment, he remained miraculously upright. The song wasn't always the same, since sometimes he mixed in words in English or French, words to other songs, pop ballads or tangos, tunes that celebrated drunkenness or love. And yet these interruptions were brief and sporadic and he soon returned to the original song, in Russian, the words of which Amalfitano didn't understand (although in dreams, as in the Gospels, one usually possesses the gift of tongues). Still, he sensed that the words were sad, the story or lament of a Volga boatman who sails all night and commiserates with the moon about the sad fate of men condemned to be born and to die. When the last Communist philosopher finally reached the crater or latrine, Amalfitano discovered in astonishment that it was none other than Boris Yeltsin. This is the last Communist philosopher? What kind of lunatic am I if this is the kind of nonsense I dream? And yet the dream was at peace with Amalfitano's soul. It wasn't a nightmare. And it also granted him a kind of featherlight sense of well-being. Then Boris Yeltsin looked at Amalfitano with curiosity, as if it were Amalfitano who had invaded his dream, not the other way around. And he said: listen carefully to what I have to say, comrade. I'm going to explain what the third leg of the human table is. I'm going to tell you. And then leave me alone. Life is demand and supply, or supply and demand, that's what it all boils down to, but that's no way to live. A third leg is needed to keep the table from collapsing into the garbage pit of history, which in turn is permanently collapsing into the garbage pit of the void. So take note. This is the equation: supply + demand + magic. And what is magic? Magic is epic and it's also sex and Dionysian mists and play. And then Yeltsin sat on the crater or the latrine and showed Amalfitano the fingers he was missing and talked about his childhood and about the Urals and Siberia and about a white tiger that roamed the infinite snowy spaces. And then he took a flask of vodka out of his suit pocket and said:

"I think it's time for a little drink."

And after he had drunk and given the poor Chilean professor the sly squint of a hunter, he began to sing again, if possible with even more brio. And then he disappeared, swallowed up by the crater streaked with red or by the latrine streaked with red, and Amalfitano was left alone and he didn't dare look down the hole, which meant he had no choice but to wake.

3
THE PART ABOUT FATE

hen did it all begin? he thought. When did I go under? A dark, vaguely familiar Aztec lake. The nightmare. How do I get away? How do I take control? And the questions kept coming: Was getting away what he really wanted? Did he really want to leave it all behind? And he also thought: the pain doesn't matter anymore. And also: maybe it all began with my mother's death. And also: the pain doesn't matter, as long as it doesn't get any worse, as long as it isn't unbearable. And also: fuck, it hurts, fuck, it hurts. Pay it no mind, pay it no mind. And all around him, ghosts.

•

Quincy Williams was thirty when his mother died. A neighbor called him at work.

"Honey," she said, "Edna's dead."

He asked when she'd died. He heard the woman sobbing at the other end of the line, and other voices, probably other women. He asked how. No one said anything and he hung up. He dialed his mother's number.

"Who is this?" he heard a woman say angrily.

He thought: my mother is in hell. He hung up again. He called again. It was a young woman.

"This is Quincy, Edna Miller's son," he said.

There was an exclamation he couldn't make out, and a moment later another woman came to the phone. He asked to speak to the neighbor. She's in bed, the woman said, she just had a heart attack, Quincy, we're waiting for an ambulance to come and take her to the hospital. He didn't dare ask about his mother. He heard a man's voice cursing. The man must be in the hallway and his mother's door must be open. He put his hand to his forehead and waited, without hanging up, for someone to explain what was going on. Two women's voices scolded the man who had sworn. They spoke a man's name, but he couldn't hear it clearly.

The woman who was typing at the next desk asked whether something was wrong. He raised his hand as if he was listening to something important and shook his head. The woman went back to typing. Quincy waited awhile and hung up, put on the jacket that was hanging on the back of his chair, and said he had to leave.

•

When he got to his mother's apartment, the only person there was a fifteen-year-old girl who was sitting on the couch watching TV. She got up when she saw him come in. She must have been six feet tall and she was very thin. She was wearing jeans and over them a black dress with yellow flowers, very loose, like a robe.

"Where is she?" he asked.

"In the bedroom," said the girl.

His mother was on the bed with her eyes closed, dressed as if to go out. They'd even put lipstick on her. All she was missing was her shoes. Quincy stood for a time in the doorway, looking at her feet: there were corns on her two big toes and calluses on the soles of her feet, big calluses that must have hurt her. But he remembered that his mother went to a podiatrist on Lewis Street, a Dr. Johnson, always the same person, so they must not have bothered her too much after all. Then he looked at her face: it seemed to have been carved out of wax.

"I'm leaving," said the girl from the living room.

Quincy came out of the bedroom and tried to give her a twenty, but the girl said she didn't want money. He insisted. Finally the girl took the bill and put it in the pocket of her jeans. To do that she had to hitch her dress up to her hip. She looks like a nun, thought Quincy, or like she belongs to a dangerous cult. The girl gave him a piece of paper where someone had written the phone number of a neighborhood funeral home.

"They'll take care of everything," she said gravely.

"All right," he said.

He asked about the neighbor woman.

"She's in the hospital," said the girl. "I think they're putting in a pacemaker."

"A pacemaker?"

"Yes," said the girl, "in her heart."

When the girl left, Quincy thought that the people in the building and the neighborhood had loved his mother, but they had loved his mother's neighbor, whose face he couldn't remember clearly, even more.

•

He called the funeral home and talked to someone by the name of Tremayne. He said he was Edna Miller's son. Tremayne consulted his notes and expressed his condolences several times, until he found the paper he was looking for. Then he put him on hold and transferred him to someone called Lawrence. Lawrence asked him what kind of ceremony he wanted.

"Something simple and intimate," said Quincy. "Very simple, very intimate."

In the end they agreed that his mother would be cremated, and the ceremony, barring unforeseen circumstances, would take place the next evening, at the funeral home, at seven. By seven forty-five it would all be over. He asked whether it was possible to do it sooner. It wasn't. Then Mr. Lawrence delicately approached the matter of payment. There was no problem. Quincy wanted to know whether he should call the police or the hospital. No, said Mr. Lawrence, Miss Holly already took care of that. Quincy asked himself who Miss Holly was and drew a blank.

"Miss Holly is your late mother's neighbor," said Mr. Lawrence.

"That's right," said Quincy.

For a moment they were both silent, as if they were trying to remember or piece together the faces of Edna Miller and her neighbor. Mr. Lawrence cleared his throat. He asked whether Quincy knew what church his mother belonged to. He asked whether he himself had any religious preferences. Quincy said his mother belonged to the Christian Church of Fallen Angels. Or no, maybe it had another name. He couldn't remember. You're right, said Mr. Lawrence, it does have a different name, it's the Christian Church of Angels Redeemed. That's the one, said Quincy. And he also said he had no religious leanings. So long as it was a Christian ceremony, that would be enough.

That night he slept on the couch in his mother's house. He went into her room just once and had a glance at the body. The next day, first thing in the morning, the people from the funeral home came and took her away. He got up to let them in, gave them a check, and watched how they carried the pine coffin down the stairs. Then he went back to sleep on the couch.

When he woke up he thought he'd dreamed about a movie he'd seen the other day. But everything was different. The characters were black, so the movie in the dream was like a negative of the real movie. And different things happened, too. The plot was the same, what happened was the same, but the ending was different or at some moment things took an unexpected turn and became something completely different. Most terrible of all, though, was that as he was dreaming he knew it didn't necessarily have to be that way, he noticed the resemblance to the movie, he thought he understood that both were based on the same premise, and that if the movie he'd seen was the real movie, then the other one, the one he had dreamed, might be a reasoned response, a reasoned critique, and not necessarily a nightmare. All criticism is ultimately a nightmare, he thought as he washed his face in the apartment where his mother's body no longer was.

He also thought about what she would have said to him. Be a man and bear your cross.

•

At work everybody called him Oscar Fate. When he came back no one said anything to him. There was no reason for anyone to say anything. He spent some time looking over his notes on Barry Seaman. The girl at the next desk wasn't there. Then he locked his notes in a drawer and went out to eat. In the elevator he ran into the editor of the magazine, who was with a fat young woman who wrote about teen killers. They nodded to each other and went their separate ways.

He had French onion soup and an omelet at a good, cheap restaurant two blocks away. He hadn't eaten anything since the day before and the food made him feel better. When he'd paid and was about to leave, a man who worked for the sports section called him over and offered to buy him a beer. As they were sitting waiting at the bar, the man told him that the chief boxing correspondent had died that morning outside Chicago. *Chief* was really an honorary term, since the dead man was the only boxing correspondent they had.

"How did he die?" asked Fate.

"Some black guys from Chicago stabbed him to death," said the other man.

The waiter set a hamburger on the bar. Fate finished his beer, clapped the man on the shoulder, and said he had to go. When he got to the glass door he turned around and contemplated the crowded restaurant and the back of the man from the sports section and the people in pairs, gazing into each other's eyes as they ate or talked, and the three waiters who were never still. Then he opened the door and went out. He looked back into the restaurant, but with the glass in between everything was different. He walked away.

•

"When are you heading out, Oscar?" asked his editor.

"Tomorrow."

"You got everything you need, are you set?"

"All set," said Fate. "Everything's ready to go."

"That's what I like to hear, son," said the boss. "Did you hear that Jimmy Lowell got whacked?"

"I heard something."

"It was in Paradise City, near Chicago," said the boss. "They say Jimmy had a girl there. Some bitch twenty years younger and married."

"How old was Jimmy?" asked Fate without the least interest.

"He must've been fifty-five or sixty," said the boss. "The police arrested the girl's husband, but our man in Chicago says she was probably mixed up in it too."

"Was Jimmy a big guy? Weighed about two hundred and fifty pounds?" asked Fate.

"No, Jimmy wasn't big, and he didn't weigh two hundred and fifty neither. He was five ten, maybe, maybe one seventy-five," said the boss.

"I must be mixing him up with someone else," said Fate, "a big guy who had lunch with Remy Burton sometimes. I used to see him in the elevator."

"No," said the boss, "Jimmy almost never came into the office. He stayed on the road. He showed up here once a year tops. I think he lived in Tampa, he may not even have had a place, spent his life in hotels and airports."

•

He showered and didn't shave. He listened to the messages on the answering machine. He left the Barry Seaman file that he'd brought from the office on the table. He put on clean clothes and went out. Since he still had time, he went to his mother's apartment first. He noticed that something there smelled bad. He went into the kitchen and when he didn't find anything rotten he tied up the garbage bag and opened the window. Then he sat on the couch and turned on the TV. On a shelf near the TV there were some videotapes. For a few seconds he thought about checking them out, but he gave up the idea almost as soon as it came to him. They had probably just been used to record shows that his mother watched later, at night. He tried to think about something pleasant. He tried to mentally run through all the things he had to do. He couldn't. After sitting absolutely still for a while, he turned off the TV, picked up the keys and the garbage bag, and left the apartment. Before he went down the stairs he knocked at the neighbor's door. No one answered. Outside he tossed the garbage bag into an overflowing Dumpster.

The ceremony was simple and businesslike. He signed a few papers. He wrote another check. He accepted the condolences first of Mr. Tremayne, then of Mr. Lawrence, who appeared at the end as Quincy was leaving with the urn that held his mother's ashes. Was the service satisfactory? asked Mr. Lawrence. During the ceremony, sitting at one end of the room, he saw the tall girl again. She was dressed just as she had been before, in jeans and the black dress with yellow flowers. He looked at her and tried to give her a friendly wave, but she wasn't looking his way. The rest of the people there were strangers, although they were mostly women, so he supposed they must be friends of his mother's. At the end, two of them came up to him and spoke words he didn't understand, words of consolation or rebuke. He went walking back to his mother's apartment. He set the urn next to the videotapes and turned the TV back on. The apartment had stopped smelling bad. The whole building was silent, as if no one was there, as if everyone had gone out on urgent business. From the window he saw teenagers playing and talking (or plotting) but doing the one thing on its own. In other words, they would play for a minute, stop, gather, talk for a minute, and go back to playing, and after that they'd stop and do the same thing over and over again.

He asked himself what kind of game it was and whether the pauses to talk were part of the game or a clear sign that they didn't know the rules. He made up his mind to take a walk. After a while he felt hungry and went into a little Middle Eastern restaurant (Egyptian or Jordanian, he didn't know which), where they served him a sandwich of ground lamb. When he came out he felt sick. In a dark alley he threw up the lamb and was left with a taste of bile and spices in his mouth. He saw a man pushing a hot dog cart. He caught up to him and asked for a beer. The man looked at him as if Fate was high and told him he wasn't allowed to sell alcoholic beverages.

"Give me whatever you have," Fate said.

The man handed him a Coke. He paid and drank the whole thing as the man with the cart went off down the dimly lit street. After a while he saw a movie theater marquee. He remembered that as a teenager he used to spend many evenings there. He decided to go in, even though the movie had already started some time ago, as the ticket seller informed him.

•

He sat through only one scene. A white man is arrested by three black cops. Instead of taking him to the police station, the cops take him to an airfield. There, the man who's been arrested sees the chief of police, who's also black. The man is no fool and he figures out they're working for the DEA. Through unspoken assurances and eloquent silences, they reach a kind of deal. As they talk, the man looks out a window. He sees the landing strip and a Cessna taxiing toward one end of it. They unload a shipment of cocaine. The cop opening the crates and unpacking the bricks is black. Next to him, another black cop is tossing the bricks into a fire barrel, like the kind the homeless use to keep warm on winter nights. But these cops aren't bums. They're DEA agents, neatly dressed, government employees. The man turns away from the window and points out to the chief that all his men are black. They're more motivated, says the chief. And then he says: you can go now. When the man leaves, the chief smiles, but his smile quickly turns into a scowl. At that moment Fate rose and went to the men's room, where he vomited up the rest of the lamb in his stomach. Then he left and went back to his mother's.

Before he went in, he knocked at the neighbor's door. A woman more or less his own age opened the door. She was wearing glasses and her hair was up in a green African turban. He explained who he was and inquired after the neighbor. The woman looked him in the eye and asked him in. The living room looked like his mother's. Even the furniture was similar. In the room he saw six women and three men. Some were standing or leaning in the kitchen doorway, but most were sitting down.

"I'm Rosalind," said the woman in the turban. "Your mother and mine were very close friends."

Fate nodded. Sobs came from the back of the apartment. One of the women got up and went into the bedroom. When she opened the door the sobs got louder, but when the door closed the sound vanished.

"It's my sister," Rosalind said wearily. "Would you like some coffee?"

Fate said yes. When the woman went into the kitchen, one of the men who was standing came over and asked whether he wanted to see Miss Holly. He nodded. The man led him to the bedroom but remained outside, on the other side of the door. The neighbor lady's body was laid out on the bed, and beside it he saw a woman on her knees, praying. Sitting in a rocking chair next to the window was the girl in jeans and the black dress with yellow flowers. Her eyes were red and she looked at him as if she'd never seen him before.

When he came out he sat on the edge of a couch occupied by women speaking in monosyllables. When Rosalind put a cup of coffee in his hands he asked when her mother had died. This afternoon, said Rosalind in a calm voice. What did she die of? She was old, said Rosalind with a smile. When he got home, Fate realized he was still holding the coffee cup. For an instant he thought about going back to the neighbor's apartment and returning it, but then he thought it would be better to leave it for the next day. He couldn't drink the coffee. He set it next to the videotapes and the urn containing his mother's ashes, then he turned on the TV and turned off the lights and stretched out on the couch. He muted the sound.

•

The next morning, when he opened his eyes, the first thing he saw was a cartoon. Rats were streaming through a city, silently squealing.

He grabbed the remote control and changed channels. When he found the news, he turned on the sound, though not very loud, and got up. He washed his face and neck and when he dried himself he realized that the towel, hanging on the towel rack, was almost certainly the last towel his mother had used. He smelled it but didn't detect any familiar scent. In the bathroom cabinet there were various bottles of pills and some jars of moisturizing or anti-inflammatory cream. He called in to work and asked to speak to his editor. The only person there was the girl at the next desk and he talked to her. He told her he wasn't coming into the magazine because he planned to leave in a few hours for Detroit. She said she already knew and she wished him good luck.

"I'll be back in three days, maybe four," he said.

Then he hung up, smoothed his shirt, put on his jacket, looked at himself in the mirror by the door, and tried and failed to pull himself together. It was time to get back to work. He stood with his hand on the doorknob, wondering whether he should take the urn with the ashes home with him. I'll do it when I get back, he thought, and he opened the door.

•

He was home just long enough to put the Barry Seaman file, a few shirts, a few pairs of socks, and some underwear in a bag. He sat in a chair and realized he was a nervous wreck. He tried to relax. When he went outside, it was raining. When had it started to rain? All the taxis that went by had fares. He slung the bag over his shoulder and began to walk along the curb. At last a taxi stopped. When he was about to close the door he heard something like a shot. He asked the taxi driver whether he'd heard it. The taxi driver was Hispanic and spoke very bad English.

"Every day you hear more fantastic things in New York," the driver said.

"What do you mean, fantastic?" he asked.

"Exactly what I say, fantastic," said the taxi driver.

After a while Fate fell asleep. Every now and then he opened his eyes and watched buildings go by where no one seemed to live, or gray streets slicked with rain. Then he closed his eyes and went back to sleep. He woke up when the taxi driver asked him what terminal he wanted.

"I'm going to Detroit," he said, and he went back to sleep.

•

The two people sitting in front of him were discussing ghosts. Fate couldn't see their faces, but he imagined them as older, maybe sixty or seventy. He asked for an orange juice. The stewardess was blond, about forty, and she had a mark on her neck covered with a white scarf that had slipped as she bustled up and down assisting passengers. The man in the seat next to him was black and was drinking from a bottle of water. Fate opened his bag and took out the Seaman file. Instead of ghosts, now the passengers in front of him were talking about a person they called Bobby. This Bobby lived in Jackson Tree, Michigan, and had a cabin on Lake Huron. One time this Bobby had gone out in a boat and capsized. He managed to cling to a log that was floating nearby and waited for morning. But as night went on, the water kept getting colder and Bobby was freezing and started to lose his strength. He felt weaker and weaker, and even though he did his best to tie himself to the log with his belt, he couldn't no matter how hard he tried. It may sound easy, but in real life it's hard to tie your own body to a floating log. So he gave up hope, turned his thoughts to his loved ones (here they mentioned someone called Jig, which might have been the name of a friend or a dog or a pet frog he had), and clung to the branch as tightly as he could. Then he saw a light in the sky. He thought it was a helicopter coming to find him, which was foolish, and he started to shout. But then it occurred to him that helicopters clatter and the light he saw wasn't clattering. A few seconds later he realized it was an airplane. A great big plane about to crash right where he was floating, clinging to that log. Suddenly all his tiredness vanished. He saw the plane pass just overhead. It was in flames. Maybe a thousand feet from where he was, the plane plunged into the lake. He heard two explosions, possibly more. He felt the urge to get closer to the site of the disaster and that's what he did, very slowly, because it was hard to steer the log. The plane had split in half and only one part was still floating. Before Bobby got there he watched it sinking slowly down into the waters of the lake, which had gone dark again. A little while later the rescue helicopters arrived. The only person they found was Bobby and they felt cheated when he told them he hadn't been on the plane, that he'd capsized his boat when he was fishing. Still, he was famous for a while, said the person telling the story.

"And does he still live in Jackson Tree?" asked the other man.

"No, I think he lives in Colorado now," was the response.

Then they started to talk about sports. The man next to Fate finished his water and belched discreetly, covering his mouth with his hand.

"Lies," he said softly.

"What?" asked Fate.

"Lies, lies," said the man.

Right, said Fate, and he turned away and stared out the window at the clouds that looked like cathedrals or maybe just little toy churches abandoned in a labyrinthine marble quarry one hundred times bigger than the Grand Canyon.

•

In Detroit, Fate rented a car, and after he checked a map from the car rental agency, he headed to the neighborhood where Barry Seaman lived.

Seaman wasn't home, but a boy told him he was almost always at Pete's Bar, not far from there. The neighborhood looked like a neighborhood of Ford and General Motors retirees. As he walked he looked at the buildings, five and six stories high, and all he saw were old people sitting on the stoops or leaning out the windows smoking. Every so often he passed a group of boys hanging out on the corner or girls jumping rope. The parked cars weren't nice cars or new cars, but they looked cared for.

The bar was next to a vacant lot full of weeds and wildflowers growing over the ruins of the building that had once stood there. On the side of a neighboring building he saw a mural that struck him as odd. It was circular, like a clock, and where the numbers should have been there were scenes of people working in the factories of Detroit. Twelve scenes representing twelve stages in the production chain. In each scene, there was one recurring character: a black teenager, or a long-limbed, scrawny black man-child, or a man clinging to childhood, dressed in clothes that changed from scene to scene but that were invariably too small for him. He had apparently been assigned the role of clown, intended to make people laugh, although a closer look made it clear that he wasn't there only to make people laugh. The mural looked like the work of a lunatic. The last painting of a lunatic. In the middle of the clock, where all the scenes converged, there was a word painted in letters that looked like they were made of gelatin: *fear*.

Fate went into the bar. He took a stool and asked the man behind the bar who had painted the mural outside. The bartender, a heavy black man in his sixties with a scar, said he didn't know.

"Probably some kid from the neighborhood," he muttered.

Fate ordered a beer and cast a glance around the bar. He didn't see anyone who might have been Seaman. Beer in hand, he asked loudly whether anyone knew Barry Seaman.

"Who wants to know?" asked a short guy in a Pistons T-shirt and a sky-blue tweed jacket.

"Oscar Fate," said Fate, "of the magazine *Black Dawn*, from New York."

The bartender came over and asked whether he was really a reporter. I'm a reporter. For *Black Dawn*.

"Man," said the short guy without getting up from his table, "that's a fucked-up name for a magazine." His two fellow cardplayers laughed. "Personally I'm sick of all these dawns," said the short guy. "Why don't the brothers in New York do something with the sunset for once, that's the best time of day, at least in this goddamn neighborhood."

"When I get back I'll tell them. I just write stories," he said.

"Barry Seaman didn't come in today," said an old man who was sitting at the bar, like Fate.

"I think he's sick," said another.

"That's right, I did hear something like that," said the old man at the bar.

"I'll wait for him awhile," said Fate, and he finished his beer.

The bartender settled across from him and told him that in his day he'd been a fighter.

"My last fight was in Athens, in South Carolina. I fought a white boy. Who do you think won?" he asked.

Fate looked him in the eye, frowned noncommittally, and ordered another beer.

"It was four months since I saw my manager. I just went around with my trainer, this old man called Johnny Bird, we went from one town to another in South Carolina, North Carolina, sleeping in these shitty-ass motels. He was wobbly and so was I, you know what I'm saying, me because I'd got hit so much and old Bird because by then he was eighty at least. That's right, eighty, maybe he was eighty-three. We used to argue about that before we went to sleep, with the lights out. Bird said he'd just hit eighty. I said he was eighty-three. They fixed the fight. The promoter told me to go down in the fifth. And to let myself get knocked around some in the fourth. For that, they'd give me double what they'd promised, which wasn't much. I told Bird about it that night, eating supper. It don't matter none to me, he said. I don't give a damn. The problem is, most times these people don't pay their bills. So it's up to you. That's what he said."

•

On the way back to Seaman's house Fate felt a little dizzy. An enormous moon was rising over the roofs. Near the entrance to a building a man came up to him and said something that either he didn't understand or that struck him as unacceptable. I'm Barry Seaman's friend, motherfucker, said Fate as he tried to grab the man by the lapels of his leather jacket.

"Relax," said the man. "Easy, brother."

Inside the doorway he saw four pairs of yellow eyes shining in the dark, and in the dangling hand of the man he was gripping he saw the fleeting reflection of the moon.

"Get out of here or I'll kill you," he said.

"Relax, brother, let me go first," said the man.

Fate let go of him and looked for the moon over the roofs ahead. He followed it. As he walked he heard noises on the side streets, steps, running, as if part of the neighborhood had just woken up. Next to Seaman's building he made out his rental car. He examined it. Nothing had happened to it. Then he rang the buzzer and an irritated voice asked what he wanted. Fate identified himself and said he'd been sent from *Black Dawn*. Over the intercom he heard a little laugh of satisfaction. Come in, said the voice. Fate crawled up the stairs. At some point he understood he wasn't well. Seaman was waiting for him on the landing.

"I need to use the bathroom," said Fate.

"Jesus," said Seaman.

The living room was small and modest and he saw books strewn everywhere and also posters taped to the walls and little photographs scattered along the shelves and the table and on top of the TV.

"The second door," said Seaman.

Fate went in and began to vomit.

•

When he woke up he saw Seaman writing with a pen. Next to him were four thick books and several folders full of papers. Seaman wore glasses when he wrote. Fate noticed that three of the four books were dictionaries and the fourth was a huge tome called *The Abridged French Encyclopedia*, which he'd never heard of, in college or ever. The sun was coming in the window. He threw off the blanket and sat up on the couch. He asked Seaman what had happened. The old man looked at him over his glasses and offered him a cup of coffee. Seaman was six feet tall, at least, but he stood slightly stooped, which made him seem smaller. He made a living giving lectures, which tended to be badly paid, since he was hired most often by educational organizations operating in the ghetto and sometimes by small progressive colleges with tiny budgets. Years ago he had published a book called *Eating Ribs with Barry Seaman*, in which he collected all the recipes he knew for ribs, mostly grilled or barbecued, adding strange or notable facts about the places where he'd learned each recipe, who had taught it to him, and under what circumstances. The best part of the book had to do with the ribs and mashed potatoes or applesauce he'd made in prison: how he'd got hold of the ingredients and how he'd cooked them in a place where cooking, like so many other things, was forbidden. The book wasn't a bestseller, but it put Seaman back in circulation and he appeared on a few morning shows, cooking some of his famous recipes live. Now he had fallen into obscurity again, but he kept giving lectures and traveling the country, sometimes in exchange for a return ticket and three hundred dollars.

Next to the table where he wrote and where the two of them sat to have coffee, there was a black-and-white poster of two young men in black jackets and black berets and dark glasses. Fate shivered, not because of the poster but because he felt so sick, and after the first swallow of coffee he asked whether one of the boys was Seaman. That's right, said Seaman. Fate asked which one. Seaman smiled. He didn't have a single tooth.

"Hard to tell, isn't it?"

"I don't know, I don't feel very well, if I felt better I'm sure I could figure it out," said Fate.

"The one on the right, the shorter one," said Seaman.

"Who's the other one?" asked Fate.

"Are you sure you don't know?"

Fate looked at the poster again for a while.

"It's Marius Newell," he said.

"That's right," said Seaman.

•

Seaman put on a jacket. Then he went into the bedroom and when he came out he was wearing a narrow-brimmed dark green hat. He picked his dentures out of a glass in the dark bathroom and fit them in carefully. Fate watched him from the living room. He rinsed his mouth with a red liquid, spat in the sink, rinsed again, and said he was ready.

They left in the rental car for Rebecca Holmes Park, some twenty blocks away. Since they had time to kill, they stopped the car on the edge of the park and spent a while talking as they stretched their legs. Rebecca Holmes Park was big and in the middle, surrounded by a half-collapsed fence, was a playground called Temple A. Hoffman Memorial Playground, where they didn't see any children playing. In fact, the playground was completely empty, except for a couple of rats that took off when they saw Seaman and Fate. Next to a cluster of oaks stood a vaguely Oriental-looking gazebo, like a miniature Russian Orthodox church. Hip-hop sounded from the other side of the gazebo.

"I hate this shit," said Seaman, "make sure you get that in your article."

"Why?" asked Fate.

They headed toward the gazebo and next to it they saw the dried-up bed of a pond. A pair of Nike sneakers had left frozen tracks in the dry mud. Fate thought about dinosaurs and felt sick again. They walked around the gazebo. On the other side, on the ground next to some shrubs, they saw a boom box, the source of the music. There was no one nearby. Seaman said he didn't like rap because the only out it offered was suicide. But not even meaningful suicide. I know, I know, he said. It's hard to imagine meaningful suicide. It isn't a common thing. Although I've seen or been near two meaningful suicides. At least I think I have. I could be wrong, he said.

"How does rap lead to suicide?" asked Fate.

Seaman didn't answer and led him on a shortcut through the trees, which brought them out into an open space. On the pavement three girls were jumping rope. The song they were singing seemed highly unusual. There was something about a woman whose legs and arms and tongue had been amputated. There was something about the Chicago sewers and the sanitation boss or a city worker called Sebastian D'Onofrio, and then came a refrain, repeating Chi-Chi-Chi-Chicago. There was something about the pull of the moon. Then the woman grew wooden legs and wire arms and a tongue made of braided grasses and plants. Completely disoriented, Fate asked where his car was, and the old man said it was on the other side of the park. They crossed the street, talking about sports. They walked one hundred yards and went into a church.

·

There, from the pulpit, Seaman spoke about his life. The Reverend Ronald K. Foster introduced him, in a way that made it clear Seaman had been there before. I'm going to address five subjects, said Seaman, no more and no less. The first subject is DANGER. The second, MONEY. The third, FOOD. The fourth, STARS. The fifth and last, USEFULNESS. People smiled and some nodded their heads in approval, as if to say all right, as if to inform the speaker they had nothing better to do than listen to him. In a corner Fate saw five boys in black jackets and black berets and dark glasses, none of them older than twenty. They were watching Seaman with impassive faces, ready to applaud him or jeer. On the stage the old man paced back and forth, his back hunched, as if he had suddenly forgotten his speech. Unexpectedly, at a sign from the preacher, the choir sang a gospel hymn. The hymn was about Moses and the captivity of the people of Israel in Egypt. The preacher himself accompanied them on the piano. Then Seaman returned to center stage and raised a hand (he had his eyes closed), and in a few seconds the choir's singing ceased and the church was silent.

·

DANGER. Despite what the congregation (or most of it) expected, Seaman began by talking about his childhood in California. He said that for those who hadn't been to California, what it was most like was an enchanted island. The spitting image. Just like in the movies, but better. People live in houses, not apartment buildings, he said, and then he embarked on a comparison of houses (one-story, at most two-story), and four- or five-story buildings where the elevator is broken one day and out of order the next. The only way buildings compared favorably to houses was in terms of proximity. A neighborhood of buildings makes distances shorter, he said. Everything is closer. You can go walking to buy groceries or you can walk to your local tavern (here he winked at Reverend Foster), or the local church you belong to, or a museum. In other words, you don't need to drive. You don't even need a car. And here he recited a list of statistics on fatal car accidents in a county of Detroit and a county of Los Angeles. And that's even considering that cars are made in Detroit, he said, not Los Angeles. He raised a finger, felt for something in the pocket of his jacket, and brought out an inhaler. Everyone waited in silence. The two spurts of the inhaler could be heard all the way to the farthest corner of the church. Pardon me, he said. Then he said he had learned to drive at thirteen. I don't drive anymore, he said, but I learned at thirteen and it's not something I am proud of. At that point he stared out into the room, at a vague spot in the middle of the sanctuary, and said he had been one of the founders of the Black Panthers. Marius Newell and I, he said, to be precise. After that, the speech subtly drifted from its course. It was as if the doors of the church had opened, wrote Fate in his notebook, and the ghost of Newell had come in. But just then, as if to avoid a certain awkwardness, Seaman began to talk not about Newell but about Newell's mother, Anne Jordan Newell. He described her appearance (pleasing), her work (she had a job at a factory that made irrigation systems), her faith (she went to church every Sunday), her industriousness (she kept the house as neat as a pin), her kindness (she always had a smile for everyone), her common sense (she gave good advice, wise advice, without forcing it on anyone). A mother is a precious thing, concluded Seaman. Marius and I founded the Panthers. We worked whatever jobs we could get and we bought shotguns and handguns for the people's self-defense. But a mother is worth more than the Black Revolution. That I can promise you. In my long and eventful life, I've seen many things. I was in Algeria and I was in China and in several prisons in the United States. A mother is a precious thing. This I say here and I'll say anywhere, anytime, he said in a hoarse voice. He excused himself again and turned toward the altar, then he turned back to face the audience. As you all know, he said, Marius Newell was killed. A black man like you and like me killed him one night in Santa Cruz, California. I told him, Marius, don't go back to California, there are too many cops there, cops out to get us. But he didn't listen. He liked California. He liked to go to the rocky beaches on a Sunday and breathe the smell of the Pacific. When we were both in prison, I got postcards from him in which he told me he'd dreamed he was breathing that air. Which is strange, because I haven't met many black folks who took to the sea the way he did. Maybe none, definitely none in California. But I know what he was talking about, I know what he meant. As it happens, I have a theory about this, about why we don't like the sea. We do like it. Just not as much as other folks. But that's for another occasion. Marius told me things had changed in California. There were many more black police now, for example. It was true. It had changed in that way. But in other ways it was still the same. And yet there was no denying that some things had changed. And Marius recognized that and he knew we deserved part of the credit. The Panthers had helped bring the change. With our grain of sand or our dump truck. We had contributed. So had his mother and all the other black mothers who wept at night and saw visions of the gates of hell when they should have been asleep. So he decided he'd go back to California and live the rest of his life there, in peace, out of harm's way, and maybe he'd start a family. He always said he would call his first son Frank, after a friend who lost his life in Soledad Prison. Truth is, he would've had to have at least thirty children to pay tribute to all the friends who'd been taken from him. Or ten, and give each of them three names. Or five, and give them each six. But as it happened he didn't have any children because one night, as he was walking down the street in Santa Cruz, a black man killed him. They say it was for money. They say Marius owed him money and that was why he was killed, but I find that hard to believe. I think someone hired that man to kill him. At the time, Marius was fighting the drug trade in town and someone didn't like that. Maybe. I was still in prison so I don't really know. I have my theories, too many of them. All I know is that Marius died in Santa Cruz, where he had gone to spend a few days. He didn't live there and it's hard to imagine the killer lived there. The killer followed Marius, is what I'm saying. And the only reason I can think of why Marius was in Santa Cruz is the ocean. Marius went to see the Pacific Ocean, went to smell it. And the killer tracked him down to Santa Cruz. And you all know what happened next. Oftentimes I think about Marius. More than I want to, to tell you the truth. I see him on the beach in California. A beach in Big Sur, maybe, or in Monterey north of Fisherman's Wharf, up Highway 1. He's standing at a lookout point, looking away. It's winter, off-season. The Panthers are young, none of us even twenty-five. We're all armed, but we've left our weapons in the car, and you can see the deep dissatisfaction on our faces. The sea roars. Then I go up to Marius and I say let's get out of here now. And at that moment Marius turns and he looks at me. He's smiling. He's beyond it all. And he waves his hand toward the sea, because he's incapable of expressing what he feels in words. And then I'm afraid, even though it's my brother there beside me, and I think: the danger is the sea.

•

MONEY. In a word, Seaman believed that money was necessary, but not as necessary as some people claimed. He talked about what he called "economic relativism." At Folsom Prison, he said, a cigarette was worth one-twentieth of a little jar of strawberry jam. Meanwhile, at Soledad, a cigarette was worth one-thirtieth of a jar. And at Walla-Walla, a cigarette was worth the same as a jar of jam, for one thing because the prisoners at Walla-Walla—who knows why, maybe because of some brainwashing against food, maybe because they were hooked on that nicotine—would have nothing to do with anything that was sweet, and all they wanted was to breathe that smoke into their lungs. Money, said Seaman, was ultimately a mystery, and as an uneducated man, he was hardly the right person to try to explain it. Still, he had two things to say. The first was that he didn't approve of the way poor people spent their money, especially poor African Americans. It makes my blood boil, he said, when I see a pimp cruising around the neighborhood in a limousine or a Lincoln Continental. I can't stand it. When poor people make money, they should behave with greater dignity, he said. When poor people make money, they should help their neighbors. When poor people make money, they should send their children to college and adopt an orphan, or more than one. When poor people make money, they should admit publicly to having made only half as much. They shouldn't even tell their children how much they really have, because then their children will want the whole inheritance and won't be willing to share it with their adopted siblings. When poor people make money, they should establish secret funds, not just to help the black people rotting in this country's prisons, but to start small businesses like laundries, bars, video stores, the profits to be fully reinvested in the community. Scholarships. Never mind if the scholarship students come to a bad end. Never mind if the scholarship students end up killing themselves because they listened to too much rap, or killing their white teacher and five classmates in a rage. The road to wealth is sown with false starts and failures that should in no way discourage the poor who make good or our neighbors with new-found riches. We have to give it our all. We have to squeeze water from the rocks, and from the desert too. But we can never forget that money remains a problem to be solved, Seaman said.

•

FOOD. As you all know, said Seaman, pork chops saved my life. First I was a Panther and I faced down the police in California and then I traveled all over the world and then I lived for years on the tab of the U.S. government. When they let me out I was nobody. The Panthers no longer existed. In the minds of some, we were old terrorists. In the minds of others, we were a vague memory of sixties blackness, we were picturesque. Marius Newell had died in Santa Cruz. Some comrades had died in prison and others had made public apologies and started new lives. Now there weren't just black cops. There were black people in public office, black mayors, black businessmen, famous black lawyers, black TV and movie stars, and the Panthers were a hindrance. So when they let me out there was nothing left, or next to nothing, the smoldering remains of a nightmare we had plunged into as youths and that as grown men we were leaving behind now, practically old men, you could say, with no future ahead of us, because during the long years in prison we'd forgotten what we knew and we'd learned nothing, nothing but cruelty from the guards and sadism from our fellow inmates. That was my situation. So those first months out on parole were sad and gray. Sometimes I would sit at the window for hours watching the lights blink on a nameless street, just smoking. I won't lie to you, terrible thoughts crossed my mind more than once. Only one person helped me selflessly: my older sister, God rest her soul. She invited me to stay at her house in Detroit, which was small, but for me it was as if a princess in Europe had offered me her castle for a resting place. My days were all alike, but they had something that today, in hindsight, I don't hesitate to call happiness. Back then I saw only two people regularly: my sister, who was the world's most good-hearted human being, and my parole officer, a fat man who used to pour me a shot of whiskey in his office and he'd say: tell me, Barry, how could you be so bad? Sometimes I thought he said it to get me going. Sometimes I thought: this man is on the payroll of the California police and he wants to get me going and then he'll shoot me in the gut. Tell me about your b——, Barry, he would say, referring to my manly attributes, or: tell me about the guys you killed. Talk, Barry. Talk. And he would open his desk drawer, where I knew he kept his gun, and wait. And what could I do? Well, I would say, I didn't meet Chairman Mao, but I did meet Lin Piao, and later on he wanted to kill Chairman Mao and he was killed in a plane crash when he was trying to get away to Russia. A little man, wise as a serpent. Do you remember Lin Piao? And Lou would say he had never heard of Lin Piao in his life. Well, Lou, I would say, he was something like a Chinese cabinet member or like the Chinese secretary of state. And in those days we didn't have a whole lot of Americans in China, I can tell you. You could say we paved the way for Kissinger and Nixon. And Lou and I could go on like that for three hours, him asking me to tell him about the guys I'd shot in the back, and me talking about the politicians I'd met and the countries I'd seen. Until I was finally able to get rid of him, with a little Christian patience, and I've never seen him since. Lou probably died of cirrhosis. And my life went on, with the same uncertainties and the same feeling of impermanence. Then, one day I realized there was one thing I hadn't forgotten. I hadn't forgotten how to cook. I hadn't forgotten my pork chops. With the help of my sister, who was one of God's angels and who loved to talk about food, I started writing down all the recipes I remembered, my mother's recipes, the ones I'd made in prison, the ones I'd made on Saturdays at home on the roof for my sister, though she didn't care for meat. And when I'd finished the book I went to New York and took it to some publishers and one of them was interested and you all know the rest. The book put me back in the public eye. I learned to combine cooking with history. I learned to combine cooking with the thankfulness and confusion I felt at the kindness of so many people, from my late sister to countless others. And let me explain something. When I say confusion, I also mean awe. In other words, the sense of wonderment at a marvelous thing, like the lilies that bloom and die in a single day, or azaleas, or forget-me-nots. But I also realized this wasn't enough. I couldn't live forever on my recipes for ribs, my famous recipes. Ribs were not the answer. You have to change. You have to turn yourself around and change. You have to know how to look even if you don't know what you're looking for. So those of you who are interested can take out pencil and paper now, because I'm going to read you a new recipe. It's for *duck à l'orange*. This is not something you want to eat every day, because it isn't cheap and it will take you an hour and a half, maybe more, to make, but every two months or when a birthday comes around, it isn't bad. These are the ingredients, for four: a four-pound duck, two tablespoons of butter, four cloves of garlic, two cups of broth, a few sprigs of herbs, a tablespoon of tomato paste, four oranges, four tablespoons of sugar, three tablespoons of brandy, black pepper, oil, and salt. Then Seaman explained the preparation, step by step, and when he had finished explaining he said that duck made a fine meal, and that was all.

·

STARS. He said that people knew many different kinds of stars or thought they knew many different kinds of stars. He talked about the stars you see at night, say when you're driving from Des Moines to Lincoln on Route 80 and the car breaks down, the way they do, maybe it's the oil or the radiator, maybe it's a flat tire, and you get out and get the jack and the spare tire out of the trunk and change the tire, maybe half an hour, at most, and when you're done you look up and see the sky full of stars. The Milky Way. He talked about star athletes. That's a different kind of star, he said, and he compared them to movie stars, though as he said, the life of an athlete is generally much shorter. A star athlete might last fifteen years at best, whereas a movie star could go on for forty or fifty years if he or she started young. Meanwhile, any star you could see from the side of Route 80, on the way from Des Moines to Lincoln, would live for probably millions of years. Either that or it might have been dead for millions of years, and the traveler who gazed up at it would never know. It might be a live star or it might be a dead star. Sometimes, depending on your point of view, he said, it doesn't matter, since the stars you see at night exist in the realm of semblance. They are semblances, the same way dreams are semblances. So the traveler on Route 80 with a flat tire doesn't know whether what he's staring up at in the vast night are stars or whether they're dreams. In a way, he said, the traveler is also part of a dream, a dream that breaks away from another dream like one drop of water breaking away from a bigger drop of water that we call a wave. Having reached this point, Seaman warned that stars were one thing, meteors another. Meteors have nothing to do with stars, he said. Meteors, especially if they're on a direct collision course with the earth, have nothing to do with stars or dreams, though they might have something to do with the notion of breaking away, a kind of breaking away in reverse. Then he talked about starfish, he said he didn't know how, but each time Marius Newell walked along a beach in California he came upon a starfish. But he also said that the starfish you find on the beach are usually dead, corpses tossed up by the waves, with exceptions, of course. Newell, he said, could always tell the dead starfish from the ones that were still alive. I don't know how he did it, but he told them apart. And he left the dead on the beach and returned the living to the sea, tossing them near the rocks to give them a chance. Except once, when he brought a starfish home and put it in a tank, with some of that Pacific brine. This was in the early days of the Panthers, when we spent our time directing traffic in the community so cars wouldn't speed through and kill the children. A couple of stoplights would have come in handy, but the city wouldn't help us. So that was one of the first of the Panthers' roles, as traffic cops. And meanwhile Marius Newell saw to his starfish. Naturally, before too long he realized that he needed a pump for his tank. One night he went out with Seaman and little Nelson Sánchez to steal one. None of them was armed. They went to a store that specialized in the sale of rare fish in Colchester Sun, a white neighborhood, and they went in through the back door. When Marius had the pump in his hands, there came a man with a shotgun. I thought that was the end of us, said Seaman, but then Marius said: don't shoot, don't shoot, it's for my starfish. The man with the gun didn't move. We stepped back. He stepped forward. We stopped. He stopped. We took another step back. He came after us. At last we got to the car that little Nelson was driving and the man stopped less than ten feet away. When Nelson started the car the man lifted the shotgun to his shoulder and he took aim. Step on it, I said. No, said Marius. Go slow. The car rolled out toward the main street and the man came walking after us, his gun raised. Now you can hit it, said Marius, and when little Nelson stepped on the gas the man stood still, shrinking until I saw him disappear in the rearview mirror. Of course, the pump didn't do Marius any good, and a week or two later, for all the care he'd lavished on that starfish, it died and ended up in the trash. Really, when you talk about stars you're speaking figuratively. That's metaphor. Call someone a movie star. You've used a metaphor. Say: the sky is full of stars. More metaphors. If somebody takes a hard right to the chin and goes down, you say he's seeing stars. Another metaphor. Metaphors are our way of losing ourselves in semblances or treading water in a sea of seeming. In that sense a metaphor is like a life jacket. And remember, there are life jackets that float and others that sink to the bottom like lead. Best not to forget it. But really, there's just one star and that star isn't semblance, it isn't metaphor, it doesn't come from any dream or any nightmare. We have it right outside. It's the sun. The sun, I am sorry to say, is our only star. When I was young I saw a science fiction movie. A rocket ship drifts off course and heads toward the sun. First, the astronauts start to get headaches. Then they're all dripping sweat and they take off their spacesuits and even so they can't stop sweating and before long they're dehydrated. The sun's gravity keeps pulling them ceaselessly in. The sun begins to melt the hull of the ship. Sitting in his seat, the viewer can't help feeling hot, too hot to bear. Now I've forgotten how it ends. At the last minute they get saved, I seem to recall, and they correct the course of that rocket ship and turn it around toward the earth, and the huge sun is left behind, a frenzied star in the reaches of space.

•

USEFULNESS. But the sun has its uses, as any fool knows, said Seaman. From up close it's hell, but from far away you'd have to be a vampire not to see how useful it is, how beautiful. Then he began to talk about things that were useful back in the day, things once generally appreciated but now distrusted instead, like smiles. In the fifties, for example, he said, a smile opened doors for you. I don't know if it could get you places, but it could definitely open doors. Now nobody trusts a smile. Before, if you were a salesman and you went in somewhere, you'd better have a big smile on your face. It was the same thing no matter whether you were a waiter or a businessman, a secretary, a doctor, a scriptwriter, a gardener. The only folks who never smiled were cops and prison guards. That hasn't changed. But everybody else, they all did their best to smile. It was a golden age for dentists in America. Black folks, of course, were always smiling. White folks smiled. Asian folks. Hispanic folks. Now, as we know, our worst enemy might be hiding behind a smile. Or to put it another way, we don't trust anybody, least of all people who smile, since we know they want something from us. Still, American television is full of smiles and more and more perfect-looking teeth. Do these people want us to trust them? No. Do they want us to think they're good people, that they'd never hurt a fly? No again. The truth is they don't want anything from us. They just want to show us their teeth, their smiles, and admiration is all they ask for in return. Admiration. They want us to look at them, that's all. Their perfect teeth, their perfect bodies, their perfect manners, as if they were constantly breaking away from the sun and they were little pieces of fire, little pieces of blazing hell, here on this planet simply to be worshipped. When I was little, said Seaman, I don't remember children wearing braces. Today I've hardly met a child who doesn't wear them. Useless things are forced upon us, and it isn't because they improve our quality of life but because they're the fashion or markers of class, and fashionable people and high-class people require admiration and worship. Naturally, fashions don't last, one year, four at most, and then they pass through every stage of decay. But markers of class rot only when the corpse that was tagged with them rots. Then he began to talk about useful things the body needs. First, a balanced diet. I see lots of fat people in this church, he said. I suspect few of you eat green vegetables. Maybe now is the time for a recipe. The name of the recipe is: Brussels Sprouts with Lemon. Take note, please. Four servings calls for: two pounds of brussels sprouts, juice and zest of one lemon, one onion, one sprig of parsley, three tablespoons of butter, black pepper, and salt. You make it like so. One: Clean sprouts well and remove outer leaves. Finely chop onion and parsley. Two: In a pot of salted boiling water, cook sprouts for twenty minutes, or until tender. Then drain well and set aside. Three: Melt butter in frying pan and lightly sauté onion, add zest and juice of lemon and salt and pepper to taste. Four: Add brussels sprouts, toss with sauce, reheat for a few minutes, sprinkle with parsley, and serve with lemon wedges on the side. So good you'll be licking your fingers, said Seaman. No cholesterol, good for the liver, good for the blood pressure, very healthy. Then he dictated recipes for Endive and Shrimp Salad and Broccoli Salad and then he said that man couldn't live on healthy food alone. You have to read books, he said. Not watch so much TV. The experts say TV doesn't hurt the eyes. I'm not so sure. It won't do your eyes any good, and cell phones are still a mystery. Maybe they cause cancer, as some scientists say. I'm not saying they do or they don't, but there you have it. What I'm saying is, you have to read books. The preacher knows I'm telling you the truth. Read books by black writers. But don't stop there. This is my real contribution tonight. Reading is never a waste of time. I read in jail. That's where I started to read. I read a lot. I went through books like they were barbecue. In prison they turn the lights out early. You get in bed and hear sounds. Footsteps. People yelling. As if instead of being in California, the prison was inside the planet Mercury, the planet closest to the sun. You feel cold and hot at the same time and that's a clear sign you're lonely or sick. You try to think about other things, sure, nice things, but sometimes you just can't do it. Sometimes a guard at the nearest desk turns on a lamp and light from that lamp shines through the bars of your cell. This happened to me any number of times. The light from a lamp set in the wrong place, or from the fluorescent bulbs in the corridor above or the next corridor over. Then I would pick up my book and hold it in the light and get to reading. It wasn't easy, because the letters and the paragraphs seemed frenzied or spooked in that unpredictable, under-ground world. But I read and read anyway, sometimes so fast that even I was surprised, and sometimes very slowly, as if each sentence or word were something good for my whole body, not just my brain. And I could read like that for hours, not caring whether I was tired and not dwelling on the inarguable fact that I was in prison because I had stood up for my brothers, most of whom couldn't care less whether I rotted or not. I knew I was doing something useful. That was all that counted. I was do-ing something useful as the guards marched back and forth or greeted each other at the change of shift with friendly words that sounded like obscenities to my ear and that, thinking about it now, might actually have been obscene. I was doing something useful. Something useful no matter how you look at it. Reading is like thinking, like praying, like talk-ing to a friend, like expressing your ideas, like listening to other people's ideas, like listening to music (oh yes), like looking at the view, like taking a walk on the beach. And you, who are so kind, now you must be asking: what did you read, Barry? I read everything. But I especially remember a certain book I read at one of the most desperate moments of my life and it brought me peace again. What book do I mean? What book do I mean? Well, it was a book called *An Abridged Digest of the Complete Works of Voltaire*, and I promise you that is one useful book, or at least it was of great use to me.

•

That night, after he dropped Seaman off at home, Fate slept at the hotel where the magazine had booked him a room from New York. The receptionist told him that he'd been expected the day before and handed him a message from his editor asking how everything had gone. He called the magazine from his room, knowing no one would be there, and left a message vaguely explaining his meeting with the old man.

He showered and got in bed. He turned on the TV, looking for porn. He found a movie in which a German woman was making love with two black men. The German woman was speaking German and so were the black men. Were there black people in Germany, too? he wondered. Then he got bored and switched to a free channel. He saw part of a trashy show on which a hugely fat woman in her early forties had to sit and listen to her husband, a hugely fat man in his midthirties, and her husband's new girlfriend, a slightly less fat woman in her early thirties, insult her. The man, he thought, was clearly a faggot. The show was shot in Florida. Everyone was in short sleeves, except for the host, who was wearing a white blazer, khaki pants, a gray-green shirt, and an ivory tie. At moments, the host looked uncomfortable. The fat man gestured and bobbed like a rapper, egged on by his slightly less fat girlfriend. The fat man's wife, meanwhile, was quiet, gazing at the audience until, without a word, she started to cry.

This must be the end, thought Fate. But the show or this segment of the show didn't end there. At the sight of his wife in tears, the fat man stepped up his verbal attack. Among the things he called her Fate thought he heard the word *fat*. He also told her that he wasn't going to let her keep ruining his life. I don't belong to you, he said. His slightly less fat girlfriend said: he doesn't belong to you, why don't you get that through your head? After a while, the seated woman reacted. She got up and said she'd heard enough. She didn't say it to her husband or to her husband's girlfriend but directly to the host. He told her to pull herself together and take her turn saying what she needed to say. I was tricked into coming on this show, said the woman, still in tears. No one's tricked into coming here, said the host. Don't be a coward, listen to what he has to say to you, said the fat man's girlfriend. Listen to what I have to say to you, said the fat man, circling her. The woman raised her hand to fend him off and left the set. The girlfriend took a seat. After a while, the fat man sat down, too. The host, who was sitting in the audience, asked the fat man what he did for a living. I'm unemployed now, but I used to be a security guard, he said. Fate changed the channel. He took a little bottle of Tennessee Bull bourbon from the minibar. After the first swallow he

257

felt like throwing up. He put the cap back on the bottle and returned it to the minibar. After a while he fell asleep with the TV on.

•

While Fate was sleeping, there was a report on an American who had disappeared in Santa Teresa, in the state of Sonora in the north of Mexico. The reporter, Dick Medina, was a Chicano, and he talked about the long list of women killed in Santa Teresa, many of whom ended up in the common grave at the cemetery because no one claimed their bodies. Medina was talking in the desert. Behind him was a highway and off in the distance was a rise that Medina gestured toward at some point in the broadcast, saying it was Arizona. The wind ruffled the reporter's smooth black hair. He was wearing a short-sleeved shirt. Then came a shot of some assembly plants and Medina's voice-over saying that unemployment was almost nonexistent along that stretch of the border. People standing in line on a narrow sidewalk. Pickup trucks covered in a fine dust the brown color of baby shit. Hollows in the ground, like World War I bomb craters, that gradually gave way to dumping sites. The smiling face of some kid who couldn't have been more than twenty, thin and dark-skinned, with prominent cheekbones, whom Medina identified in a voice-over as a *pollero* or *coyote* or person who leads illegal immigrants over the border. Medina said a name. The name of a girl. Then there was a shot of the streets of an Arizona town where the girl was from. Houses with scorched yards and dirty silver-colored chicken-wire fences. The sad face of the mother. Exhausted with crying. The face of the father, a tall man with broad shoulders who stared into the camera saying nothing. Behind the two of them were the shadowy figures of three teenage girls. Our other three daughters, said the mother in accented English. The three girls, the oldest no more than fifteen, went running into the dark of the house.

•

As this report was showing on TV, Fate dreamed of a man he'd written a story about, the first story he'd had published in *Black Dawn*, after three other pieces were rejected. He was an old black man, much older than Seaman, who lived in Brooklyn and was a member of the Communist Party. When Fate met him there wasn't a single Communist left in Brooklyn, but the man was keeping his cell operative. What was his name? Antonio Ulises Jones, although the kids in the neighborhood called him Scottsboro Boy. They also called him Old Freak or Bones or Skin, but they usually called him Scottsboro Boy, among other reasons because Antonio Jones often talked about what had happened in Scottsboro, about the Scottsboro trials, about the blacks who were almost lynched in Scottsboro, people no one in his Brooklyn neighborhood remembered.

When Fate met him, purely by chance, Antonio Jones must have been eighty years old and he lived in a two-room apartment in one of the poorest parts of Brooklyn. In the living room there were a table and more than fifteen chairs, those old folding wooden bar stools with long legs and low backs. On the wall there was a photograph of a huge man, well over six feet tall, dressed like a worker of the period, receiving a diploma from a boy who looked straight into the camera and smiled, showing perfect, gleaming white teeth. The face of the giant worker, in its way, also resembled a child's face.

"That's me," Antonio Jones told Fate the first time Fate visited him, "and the big man is Robert Martillo Smith, a Brooklyn city maintenance worker, a specialist at going down into the sewers and wrestling with thirty-foot alligators."

In the three conversations they had, Fate asked Jones many questions, some intended to prick the old man's conscience. He asked about Stalin, and Antonio Jones answered that Stalin was a son of a bitch. He asked about Lenin, and Antonio Jones answered that Lenin was a son of a bitch. He asked about Marx, and Antonio Jones said now he was talking, that was where he should have started: Marx was a wonderful man. After that, Antonio Jones began to speak of Marx in glowing terms. There was only one thing he didn't like about Marx: his temper. This he blamed on poverty, because according to Jones, poverty didn't cause only illness and resentment, it caused bad temper. Fate's next question was what he thought about the fall of the Berlin Wall and the resulting collapse of the real-world Socialist regimes. It was foreseeable, I predicted it ten years before it happened, was Antonio Jones's response. Then, out of the blue, he began to sing the "Internationale." He opened the window and in a deep voice that took Fate by surprise, he intoned the first few lines: Arise, you prisoners of starvation! Arise, you wretched of the earth! When he had finished singing he asked Fate whether it didn't strike him as an anthem made especially for black people. I don't know, said Fate, I never thought of it that way. Later, Jones gave him an off-the-cuff accounting of the Communists of Brooklyn. During World War II, there were more than a thousand. After the war, the number rose to thirteen hundred. At the start of McCarthyism, there were only about seven hundred, and when it ended there were scarcely two hundred Communists in Brooklyn. In the sixties there were just half as many and by the seventies there were no more than thirty Communists scattered in five hardy cells. At the end of the seventies, there were ten left. By the beginning of the eighties, there were only four. During the eighties, two of the four who were left died of cancer and one vanished without saying anything to anyone. Maybe he just went on a trip and died on the way there or the way back, mused Antonio Jones. Whatever it was, he never showed up again, not at headquarters or at his apartment or at the bars where he was a regular. Maybe he went to live with his daughter in Florida. He was Jewish and he had a daughter there. The fact of the matter is that by 1987 there was only one left. And here I still am, he said. Why? asked Fate. Antonio Jones hesitated for a few seconds, considering his answer. Then he looked Fate in the eye and said:

"Because someone has to keep the cell operative."

Jones's eyes were small and black as coal, and his eyelids were heavy with folds. He had hardly any eyelashes. His eyebrows were sparse, and sometimes, when he and Fate went out to take walks around the neighborhood, he put on big sunglasses and picked up a cane, which he left by the door when they got back. He could go whole days without eating. Once you get to be a certain age, he said, food is no good. He wasn't in contact with any other Communists in the United States or abroad, except for a retired UCLA professor, Dr. Minski, with whom he corresponded occasionally. Until fifteen years ago I belonged to the Third International, and Minski convinced me to join the Fourth, he said. Then he said:

"Son, I'm going to give you a book that will be of great use to you."

Fate thought it would be *The Communist Manifesto*, maybe because in the living room, piled in corners and under chairs, he had seen several copies published by Antonio Jones himself—who knew where he'd gotten the money or how he'd fast-talked the printers—but when the old man put the book in his hands he saw with surprise that it wasn't the *Manifesto* but a fat volume titled *The Slave Trade* by someone called Hugh Thomas, whose name he had never heard before. At first he refused to take it.

"It's an expensive book and this must be your only copy," he said.

Jones's answer was that he shouldn't worry, that it had cost him only cunning, not money, by which Fate deduced that Jones had stolen the book, though this also struck him as unlikely, since the old man wasn't in any shape for such things, though he might conceivably have an accomplice at the bookstore where he pocketed his finds, a young black man who turned a blind eye when Jones slipped a book under his jacket.

Flipping through the book in his apartment hours later, he realized that the author was white. A white Englishman who had also been a professor at Sandhurst, the Royal Military Academy, which for Fate made him more or less the equivalent of a drill sergeant, an English motherfucking sergeant in short pants, so he put the book aside and didn't read it. People responded to the interview with Antonio Ulises Jones. To most of his colleagues, Fate noted, the story was little more than a venture into the African-American picturesque. A loony preacher, a loony ex–jazz musician, the loony last member of the Brooklyn Communist Party (Fourth International). Sociological curiosities. But they liked it and soon afterward he became a staff writer. He never saw Antonio Jones again, just as in all likelihood he would never see Barry Seaman again.

When he woke up it was still dark.

•

Before he left Detroit he went to the only decent bookstore in the city and bought *The Slave Trade* by Hugh Thomas, the former professor at Sandhurst. Then he headed down Woodward Avenue and checked out the downtown. He had a cup of coffee and toast for breakfast at a Greektown diner. When he said he didn't want anything else, the waitress, a blond woman in her forties, asked him if he was sick. He said he had an upset stomach. Then the waitress took away the cup of coffee she'd poured him and told him she had something better for him. A little while later she came back with a tea brewed from anise and an herb called boldo that Fate had never tasted and at first he was reluctant to try it.

"This is what you need, not coffee," said the waitress.

She was a tall, thin woman, with very large breasts and nice hips. She was wearing a black skirt and a white blouse and flat-heeled shoes. For a while neither of them said anything, both waiting expectantly, until Fate shrugged and took a sip of the tea. Then the waitress smiled and went to wait on other customers.

•

At the hotel, as he was about to pay his bill, he discovered he had a phone message from New York. A voice he didn't recognize asked him to get in touch with his editor or the editor of the sports section as soon as possible. He made the call from the lobby. He talked to the girl at the next desk and she told him to hold on while she tried to find the editor. After a while an unfamiliar voice came on. The speaker introduced himself as Jeff Roberts, editor of the sports section, and he began to talk to Fate about a boxing match. Count Pickett is fighting, he said, and we don't have anybody to cover the event. The editor called him Oscar as if they had known each other for years, and he talked on and on about Count Pickett, a promising Harlem light heavyweight.

"So what does this have to do with me?" asked Fate.

"Well, Oscar," said the sports editor, "you know Jimmy Lowell died and we still haven't found anyone to replace him."

Fate thought the fight must be in Detroit or Chicago and it didn't strike him as a bad idea to spend a few days away from New York.

"You want me to write up the fight?"

"That's right, kid," said Roberts, "say five pages, a short profile of Pickett, the match, and some local color."

"Where is the fight?"

"In Mexico," said the sports editor, "and keep in mind that we give a bigger travel allowance than they do in your section."

•

With his suitcase packed, Fate headed to Seaman's apartment for the last time. He found the old man reading and taking notes. From the kitchen came the smell of spices and frying onion and garlic.

"I'm leaving," he said. "I just stopped to say goodbye."

Seaman asked if he could give him something to eat first.

"No, I don't have time," said Fate.

They embraced and Fate headed down the stairs, taking them in threes as if he were dashing for the street, like a boy heading out for a free afternoon with his friends. As he drove toward the Detroit–Wayne County airport, he thought about Seaman's strange books, *The Abridged French Encyclopedia* and the one he hadn't seen but that Seaman had claimed to have read in prison, *The Abridged Digest of the Complete Works of Voltaire*, which made him laugh out loud.

•

At the airport he bought a ticket to Tucson. While he was waiting, leaning on the counter at a coffee place, he remembered the dream he'd had
the night before about Antonio Jones, who had been dead for several
years now. As before, he asked himself what Jones could have died of,
and the one answer that occurred to him was old age. One day, walking
down some street in Brooklyn, Antonio Jones had felt tired, sat down on
the sidewalk, and a second later stopped existing. Maybe it happened
that way for my mother, thought Fate, but deep down he knew otherwise. When the airplane took off from Detroit a storm had begun to
break over the city.

Fate opened the book by the white man who had been a professor at
Sandhurst and started to read it on page 361. It said: *Beyond the delta of
the Niger, the coast of Africa at last begins to turn south again and there, in
the Cameroons, in the late eighteenth century, Liverpool merchants from
England pioneered a new branch of the slave trade. Further on, and well to
the south, the River Gabon, just north of Cape Lopez, was also coming into
full activity as a slave region in the 1780s. This area seemed to the Reverend John Newton to possess "the most humane and moral people I ever
met with in Africa," perhaps "because they were the people who had least
intercourse with Europe at that time." But off the coast the Dutch had for
a long time used the island of Corisco (the word in Portuguese means "flash
of lightning") as a trading center, though not specifically for slaves.* Then he
saw an illustration—there were quite a few in the book—showing a Portuguese fort on the Gold Coast, called Elmina, captured by the Danes in
1637. For three hundred and fifty years Elmina was a center of the slave
trade. Over the fort, and over a small nearby fort built at the top of a hill,
flew a flag that Fate couldn't identify. What kingdom did it belong to?
he wondered before his eyes closed and he fell asleep with the book on
his lap.

•

At the Tucson airport he rented a car, bought a road map, and drove
south out of the city. He planned to stop at the first roadside diner he
came to, because his appetite seemed to have sharpened in the dry
desert air. Two Camaros of the same model and the same color passed
him, honking. He thought they must be in a race. The cars probably had
souped-up engines, and their bodies shone in the Arizona sun. He

passed a little ranch that sold oranges, but he didn't stop. The ranch was about three hundred feet from the highway, and the orange stand, an old cart with an awning and big wooden wheels, stood by the side of the road, tended by two Mexican kids. A few miles down the road he saw a place called Cochise's Corner and he parked in a big lot, next to a gas station. The two Camaros were parked next to a flag with a red stripe on top and a black stripe on the bottom. In the middle was a white circle emblazoned with the words Chiricahua Auto Club. For an instant he thought the Camaro drivers must be two Indians, but then the idea struck him as absurd. He sat in a corner of the restaurant next to a window, where he could keep an eye on his car. There were two men at the next table. One was tall and young and looked like a teacher of computer science. He had an easy smile and sometimes he clapped his hands to his face in what might have been astonishment or horror, or anything at all. Fate couldn't see the other man's face, but he was clearly quite a bit older than his companion. His neck was thick, his hair was white, and he wore glasses. Whether he was talking or listening he remained impassive, without gesturing or moving.

·

The girl who came to wait on him was Mexican. He ordered coffee and scanned the menu for a few minutes. He asked whether they had club sandwiches. The waitress shook her head. A steak, said Fate. With salsa? asked the waitress. What's in the salsa? asked Fate. Chile, tomato, onion, and cilantro. And we put some spices in, too. All right, he said, I'll try it. When the waitress left he looked around the restaurant. At one table he saw two Indians, one an adult and the other a teenager, maybe father and son. At another he saw two white men with a Mexican woman. The men were exactly alike, identical twins of about fifty. The Mexican woman must have been forty-five or so, and it was clear the twins were crazy about her. They're the Camaro owners, thought Fate. He also realized that no one in the whole restaurant was black except for him.

·

The young man at the next table said something about inspiration. All Fate heard was: you've been an inspiration to us. The white-haired man said it was really nothing. The young man raised his hands to his face and said something about willpower, about the power to hold a gaze. Then he removed his hands from his face and with shining eyes he said: I don't mean a natural gaze, a gaze from the natural realm, I mean a gaze in the abstract. The white-haired man said: of course. When you caught Jurevich, said the young man, and then his voice was drowned out by the deafening roar of a diesel engine. A semi was parking in the lot. The waitress brought Fate's coffee and the steak with salsa. The young man was still talking about the person called Jurevich who'd been caught by the white-haired man.

"It wasn't hard," said the white-haired man.

"A killer who's sloppy," said the young man, and he raised his hand to his mouth as if he were about to sneeze.

"No," said the white-haired man, "a careful killer."

"Oh, I thought he was sloppy," said the young man.

"No, no, he was careful," said the white-haired man.

"Which is worse?" asked the young man.

Fate cut a piece of meat. It was thick and tender and it tasted good. The salsa was tasty, especially once you got used to the heat.

"The sloppy ones are worse," said the white-haired man. "It's harder to establish a pattern of behavior."

"But can it it be established?" asked the young man.

"Given the means and the time, you can do anything," said the white-haired man.

Fate beckoned for the waitress. The Mexican woman rested her head on the shoulder of one of the twins and the other twin smiled as if this were a common occurrence. Fate imagined that she was married to the twin who had his arm around her, but that their marriage hadn't extinguished the other brother's love or dashed his hopes. The Indian father asked for the check. Meanwhile, the young Indian had pulled out a comic book from somewhere and was reading it. Out in the lot Fate saw the truck driver who had just parked his truck. He was on his way back from the gas station bathroom and he was combing his blond hair with a tiny comb. The waitress asked him what he wanted. Another coffee and a big glass of water.

"We've gotten used to death," he heard the young man say.

"It's always been that way," said the white-haired man, "always."

•

In the nineteenth century, toward the middle or the end of the nineteenth century, said the white-haired man, society tended to filter death through the fabric of words. Reading news stories from back then you might get the idea that there was hardly any crime, or that a single murder could throw a whole country into tumult. We didn't want death in the home, or in our dreams and fantasies, and yet it was a fact that terrible crimes were committed, mutilations, all kinds of rape, even serial killings. Of course, most of the serial killers were never caught. Take the most famous case of the day. No one knew who Jack the Ripper was. Everything was passed through the filter of words, everything trimmed to fit our fear. What does a child do when he's afraid? He closes his eyes. What does a child do when he's about to be raped and murdered? He closes his eyes. And he screams, too, but first he closes his eyes. Words served that purpose. And the funny thing is, the archetypes of human madness and cruelty weren't invented by the men of our day but by our forebears. The Greeks, you might say, invented evil, the Greeks saw the evil inside us all, but testimonies or proofs of this evil no longer move us. They strike us as futile, senseless. You could say the same about madness. It was the Greeks who showed us the range of possibilities and yet now they mean nothing to us. Everything changes, you say. Of course everything changes, but not the archetypes of crime, not any more than human nature changes. Maybe it's because polite society was so small back then. I'm talking about the nineteenth century, eighteenth century, seventeenth century. No doubt about it, society was small. Most human beings existed on the outer fringes of society. In the seventeenth century, for example, at least twenty percent of the merchandise on every slave ship died. By that I mean the dark-skinned people who were being transported for sale, to Virginia, say. And that didn't get anyone upset or make headlines in the Virginia papers or make anyone go out and call for the ship captain to be hanged. But if a plantation owner went crazy and killed his neighbor and then went galloping back home, dismounted, and promptly killed his wife, two deaths in total, Virginia society spent the next six months in fear, and the legend of the murderer on horseback might linger for generations. Or look at the French. During the Paris Commune of 1871, thousands of people were killed and no one batted an eye. Around the same time a knife sharpener killed his wife and his elderly mother and then he was shot and killed by the police. The story didn't just make all the French newspapers, it was written up in papers across Europe, and even got a mention in the New York *Examiner*. How come? The ones killed in the Commune weren't part of society, the dark-skinned people who died on the ship weren't part of society, whereas the woman killed in a French provincial capital and the murderer on horseback in Virginia were. What happened to them could be written, you might say, it was legible. That said, words back then were mostly used in the art of avoidance, not of revelation. Maybe they revealed something all the same. I couldn't tell you.

•

The young man covered his face with his hands.

"This isn't your first trip to Mexico," he said, uncovering his face and smiling a catlike smile.

"No," said the white-haired man. "I was there for a while a few years ago and I tried to help, but the situation was impossible."

"And why did you come back this time?"

"To have a look, I guess," said the white-haired man. "I was staying at a friend's house, a friend I made last time. The Mexicans are a hospitable people."

"It wasn't an official trip?"

"Oh, no," said the white-haired man.

"And what's your unofficial opinion about what's going on there?"

"I have several opinions, Edward, and I'd prefer that none of them be published without my consent."

The young man covered his face with his hands and said:

"Professor Kessler, my lips are sealed."

"All right, then," said the white-haired man. "I'll tell you three things I'm sure of: (a) everyone living in that city is outside of society, and everyone, I mean everyone, is like the ancient Christians in the Roman circus; (b) the crimes have different signatures; (c) the city seems to be booming, it seems to be moving ahead in some ineffable way, but the best thing would be for every last one of the people there to head out into the desert some night and cross the border."

When the sun began to set in a blaze of red, and the twins, the Indians, and the men at the next table had been gone for a long time, Fate decided to ask for the check. A chubby, dark-skinned girl who wasn't the waitress he'd had before brought it and asked whether everything had been to his liking.

"Everything," said Fate, as he felt in his pocket for money.

Then he went back to watching the sunset. He thought about his mother, about his mother's neighbor, about the magazine, about the streets of New York, all with an unspeakable sadness and weariness. He opened the book by the former Sandhurst professor and read a paragraph at random. *Many captains of slave ships looked on their task as, as a rule, complete, when they had delivered their slaves to the West Indies. But it was often impossible to realize the proceeds of the sale of slaves fast enough to provide the ship concerned with a return cargo of sugar. Merchants and captains could not be certain of the prices which they would receive at home for goods taken on their own account. Planters might take several years to pay for the slaves. Sometimes the European merchant preferred to have remittances from the West Indies in bills of exchange than to have sugar, indigo, cotton, or ginger in exchange for the slaves, because the prices of these goods in London were unpredictable or low.* What pretty names, he thought. Indigo, sugar, ginger, cotton. The reddish flowers of the indigo bush. The dark blue paste, with copper glints. A woman painted indigo, washing herself in the shower.

When he got up, the chubby waitress came over and asked him where he was headed. To Mexico, said Fate.

"I guessed that," said the waitress, "but where in Mexico?"

Leaning on the counter, a cook smoked a cigarette and watched them, waiting for his answer.

"To Santa Teresa," said Fate.

"It isn't a very nice place," said the waitress, "but it's big and there are lots of clubs and places to have fun."

Fate looked at the ground, smiling, and realized that the desert sunset had tinted the tiles a soft red.

"I'm a reporter," he said.

"You're going to write about the crimes," said the cook.

"I don't know what you're talking about. I'm going to cover the boxing match this Saturday," said Fate.

"Who's fighting?" asked the cook.

"Count Pickett, the New York light heavyweight."

"I used to follow the fights," said the cook. "I'd bet and check out the boxing digests, but one day I made up my mind to give it up. Now I don't know the names. Do you want a drink? It's on the house."

Fate sat at the counter and asked for a glass of water. The cook smiled and said he knew for a fact all reporters drank.

"I do, too," said Fate, "but I think there's something wrong with my stomach."

After bringing him a glass of water the cook wanted to know who was up against Count Pickett.

"I don't remember the name," said Fate. "I have it written down somewhere, a Mexican, I think."

"Strange," said the cook. "There're never any good Mexican light heavyweights. Once every twenty years you get a heavyweight, who usually winds up crazy or shot dead, but never a light heavyweight."

"I could be wrong, maybe it's not a Mexican," admitted Fate.

"Maybe he's Cuban or Colombian," said the cook, "although the Colombians don't have a tradition of light heavyweights either."

Fate drank the water and got up and stretched. It's time for me to go, he said, though in fact he was happy at the restaurant.

"How far is it to Santa Teresa?" he asked.

"That depends," said the cook. "Sometimes there are lots of trucks at the border and you can spend half an hour waiting. Say three hours from here to Santa Teresa and then half an hour or forty-five minutes at the border, four hours all together."

"From here to Santa Teresa it's only an hour and a half," said the waitress.

The cook looked at her and said that depended on the car and how well the driver knew the terrain.

"Have you ever driven in the desert?"

"No," said Fate.

"Well, it isn't easy. It looks easy. It looks like the simplest thing in the world, but there's nothing simple about it," said the cook.

"You're right about that," said the waitress, "especially at night, driving at night in the desert scares me."

"Make a mistake, take a wrong turn, and you're liable to go thirty miles in the wrong direction," said the cook.

"Maybe I should go now while it's still light out," said Fate.

"It won't do you much good," said the cook, "it'll be dark in five minutes. Sunsets in the desert seem like they'll never end, until suddenly, before you know it, they're done. It's like someone just turned out the lights," said the cook.

Fate asked for another glass of water and went to drink it by the window. Don't you want something else to eat before you go? he heard the cook say. He didn't answer. The desert began to disappear.

•

He drove for two hours along dark roads, with the radio on, listening to a Phoenix jazz station. He passed places where there were houses and restaurants and yards with white flowers and crookedly parked cars, but there were no lights on in the houses, as if the inhabitants had died that very night and a breath of blood still lingered in the air. He made out the shapes of hills silhouetted against the moon and the shapes of low clouds sitting motionless or speeding west at a given moment as if driven by a sudden, fitful wind that lifted dust clouds, clouds adorned in fabulous human garb by the car's headlights or the shadows created by the headlights, as if the dust clouds were tramps or ghosts looming up alongside the road.

He got lost twice. Once he was tempted to turn back, toward the restaurant or Tucson. The other time he came to a town called Patagonia where a boy at the gas station told him the easiest way to get to Santa Teresa. On his way out of Patagonia he saw a horse. When the headlights swept over it the horse lifted its head and looked at him. Fate stopped the car and waited. The horse was black and after a moment it moved and vanished into the dark. He passed a mesa, or what he took to be a mesa. It was huge, completely flat on top, and from one end of the base to the other it must have been at least three miles long. There was a gully next to the road. He got out of the car, leaving the lights on, and urinated at length, breathing the cool night air. Then the road sloped down into a kind of valley that at first glimpse struck him as gigantic. In the farthest corner of the valley he thought he saw a glow. But it could have been anything. A convoy of trucks moving very slowly, the first lights of a town. Or maybe just his desire to escape the darkness, which in some way reminded him of his childhood and adolescence. At some point in between childhood and adolescence, he thought, he had dreamed of this landscape or one like it, less dark, less desertlike. He was in a bus with his mother and one of his mother's sisters and they were taking a short trip, from New York to a town near New York. He was next to the window and the view never changed, just buildings and highways, until suddenly they were in the country. At that exact moment, or maybe earlier, the sun had begun to set and he watched the trees, a small wood, though in his eyes it looked bigger. And then he thought he saw a man walking along the edge of the little wood. In great strides, as if he didn't want night to overtake him. He wondered who the man was. The only way he could tell it was a man and not a shadow was because he wore a shirt and swung his arms as he walked. The man's loneliness was so great, Fate remembered, that he wanted to look away and cling to his mother, but instead he kept his eyes open until the bus was out of the woods, and buildings, factories, and warehouses once again lined the sides of the road.

The valley he was crossing was lonelier now, and darker. He saw himself striding along the roadside. He shivered. Then he remembered the urn holding his mother's ashes and the neighbor's cup that he hadn't returned, the coffee infinitely cold now, and his mother's videotapes that no one would ever watch again. He thought about stopping the car and waiting until the sun came up. He knew without being told that for a black man to sleep in a rental car parked on the shoulder wasn't the best idea in Arizona. He changed stations. A voice in Spanish began to tell the story of a singer from Gómez Palacio who had returned to his city in the state of Durango just to commit suicide. Then he heard a woman's voice singing *rancheras*. For a while, as he drove through the valley, he listened. Then he tried to go back to the jazz station in Phoenix and couldn't find it.

•

On the American side of the border stood a town called Adobe. It had once been an adobe factory, but now it was a collection of houses and appliance stores, almost all strung along a long main street. At the end of the street you came out into a brightly lit empty lot and immediately after that was the American border post.

The customs officer asked for his passport and Fate handed it to him. With the passport was his press ID. The customs officer asked if he was coming to write about the killings.

"No," said Fate, "I'm going to cover the fight on Saturday."

"What fight?" asked the customs officer.

"Count Pickett, the light heavyweight from New York."

"Never heard of him," said the officer.

"He's going to be world champ," said Fate.

"I hope you're right," said the officer.

Then Fate advanced three hundred feet to the Mexican border and he had to get out of the car and open his suitcase, then show his car papers, his passport, and his press ID. He was asked to fill out some forms. The faces of the Mexican policemen were numb with exhaustion. From the window of the customshouse he saw the long, high fence that divided the two countries. Four birds were perched on the farthest stretch of the fence, their heads buried in their feathers. It's cold, said Fate. Very cold, said the Mexican official, who was studying the form Fate had just filled out.

"The birds. They're cold."

The official looked in the direction Fate was pointing.

"They're turkey buzzards, they're always cold at this time of night," he said.

•

Fate got a room at a motel called Las Brisas, in the northern part of Santa Teresa. Every so often, trucks passed along the highway, headed to Arizona. Sometimes they stopped on the other side of the highway, next to the gas pumps, and then they set off again or their drivers got out and had something to eat at the service station, which was painted sky blue. In the morning there were hardly any big trucks, just cars and pickups. Fate was so tired that he didn't even notice what time it was when he fell asleep.

When he woke up he went out to talk to the motel clerk and asked him for a map of the city. The clerk was a guy in his midtwenties and he told Fate that they'd never had maps at Las Brisas, at least not since he'd been working there. He asked where Fate wanted to go. Fate said he was a reporter and he was there to cover the Count Pickett fight. Count Pickett versus El Merolino Fernández, said the clerk.

"Lino Fernández," said Fate.

"Here we call him El Merolino," said the clerk with a smile. "So who do you think will win?"

"Pickett," said Fate.

"We'll see, but I bet you're wrong."

Then the clerk ripped out a piece of paper and drew him a map with precise directions to the Arena del Norte boxing stadium, where the fight would be held. The map was much better than Fate expected. The Arena del Norte looked like an old theater from 1900, with a boxing ring set in the middle of it. At one of the offices there, Fate picked up his credentials and asked where Pickett was staying. They told him the American fighter hadn't come to town yet. Among the reporters he met were a couple of men who spoke English and who planned to interview Fernández. Fate asked whether he could go along with them and the reporters shrugged their shoulders and said it was fine with them.

When they got to the hotel where Fernández was giving the press conference, the fighter was talking to a group of Mexican reporters. The Americans asked him in English whether he thought he could beat Pickett. Fernández understood the question and said yes. The Americans asked him whether he had ever seen Pickett fight. Fernández didn't understand the question and one of the Mexican reporters translated.

"The important thing is to trust your own strength," said Fernández, and the American reporters wrote his answer in their notebooks.

"Do you know Pickett's record?" they asked him.

Fernández waited for the question to be translated, then he said that kind of thing didn't interest him. The American reporters snickered, then asked him for his own record. Thirty fights, said Fernández. Twenty-five wins. Eighteen of them knockouts. Three losses. Two draws. Not bad, said one of the reporters, and he went on asking questions.

•

Most of the reporters were staying at the Hotel Sonora Resort, in the center of Santa Teresa. When Fate told them he was staying at a motel on the edge of town, they said he should check out and try to get a room at the Sonora Resort. Fate stopped by the hotel, where he got the sense that he'd stepped into a convention of Mexican sportswriters. Most of the Mexican reporters spoke English and they were much friendlier than the American reporters he'd met, or so it seemed at first. At the bar, some were placing bets on the fight and as a group they seemed generally cheerful and laid-back, but in the end Fate decided to stay at his motel.

From a phone at the Sonora Resort, he made a collect call to the magazine and asked to speak to the sports editor. The woman he talked to said no one was there.

"The offices are empty," she said.

She had a hoarse, nasal voice and she didn't talk like a New York secretary but like a country person who has just come from the cemetery. This woman has firsthand knowledge of the planet of the dead, thought Fate, and she doesn't know what she's saying anymore.

"I'll call back later," he said before he hung up.

•

Fate's car was following the car of the Mexican reporters who wanted to interview Merolino Fernández. The Mexican fighter had set up camp at a ranch on the edge of Santa Teresa, and without the help of the reporters Fate could never have found it. They drove through a neighborhood on the edge of town along a web of unpaved, unlit streets. At moments, after passing fields and vacant lots where the garbage of the poor piled up, it seemed as if they were about to come out into the open countryside, but then another neighborhood would appear, this time older, with adobe houses surrounded by shacks built of cardboard, of corrugated tin, of old packing crates, shacks that provided shelter from the sun and the occasional showers, that seemed petrified by the passage of time. Here not only the weeds were different but even the flies seemed to belong to a different species. Then a dirt track came into sight, camouflaged by the darkening horizon. It ran parallel to a ditch and was bordered by dusty trees. The first fences appeared. The road grew narrower. This used to be a cart track, thought Fate. In fact, he could see the wheel ruts, but maybe they were just the tracks of old cattle trucks.

The ranch where Merolino Fernández was staying was a cluster of three low, long buildings around a courtyard of earth as dry and hard as cement, where someone had set up a flimsy-looking ring. When they got to the ring it was empty and the only person in the courtyard was a man sleeping on a wicker chaise who woke at the sound of the engines. The man was big and heavy and his face was covered in scars. The Mexican reporters knew him and they began to talk to him. His name was Víctor García and he had a tattoo on his right shoulder that Fate thought was interesting. A naked man, seen from behind, was kneeling in the vestibule of a church. Around him at least ten angels in female form came flying out of the darkness, like butterflies summoned by his prayers. Everything else was darkness and vague shapes. The tattoo, although it was technically accomplished, looked as if it had been done in prison by a tattoo artist who for all his skill lacked tools and inks, but the scene it depicted was unsettling. When Fate asked the reporters who the man was, they answered that he was one of Merolino's sparring partners. Then, as if someone had been observing them from the window, a woman came out into the courtyard with a tray of soft drinks and cold beers.

After a while, the trainer of the Mexican fighter showed up in a white shirt and white sweater and asked whether they'd rather interview Merolino before or after the training session. Whatever you want, López, said one of the reporters. Have they brought you anything to eat? asked the trainer as he sat down within reach of the soft drinks and beer. The reporters shook their heads, and the trainer, without getting up from his seat, sent García to the kitchen to bring some snacks. Before García returned they saw Merolino appear along one of the paths that vanished into the desert, followed by a black guy dressed in sweatpants who tried to speak Spanish but could only curse. They didn't greet anyone as they walked into the courtyard, and they headed to a cement watering trough where they used a bucket to wash their faces and torsos. Only then did they come to say hello, not bothering to dry themselves or put on the tops of their sweat suits.

The black guy was from Oceanside, California, or at least he had been born there and had later grown up in Los Angeles, and his name was Omar Abdul. He worked as Merolino's sparring partner and he told Fate he was thinking of staying in Mexico to live for a while.

"What'll you do after the fight?" asked Fate.

"Get along as best I can," said Omar, "like we do, right?"

"Where will you get the money?"

"Anywhere," said Omar, "this country is cheap."

Every few minutes, for no reason, Omar would smile. He had a nice smile, set off with a goatee and a fancy little mustache. But every few minutes he would scowl, too, and then the goatee and the little mustache took on a menacing look, a look of supreme and ominous indifference. When Fate asked whether he was a professional or had been in any matches, he answered that he'd "fought," without deigning to explain further. When Fate asked him about Merolino Fernández's chances of winning, he said you never knew until the bell.

As the fighters dressed, Fate took a stroll around the courtyard and surveyed his surroundings.

"What you looking at?" Omar Abdul said to him.

"The landscape," he said, "it's one sad landscape."

Next to him, the fighter scanned the horizon and then he said:

"That's just how it is here. It's always sad at this time of day. It's a goddamn landscape for women."

"It's getting dark," said Fate.

"There's still light enough to spar," said Omar Abdul.

"What do you do at night, when you're done training?"

"All of us?" asked Omar Abdul.

"Yeah, the whole team or whatever you call it."

"We eat, we watch TV, then Mr. López goes to bed and Merolino goes to bed and the rest of us can go to bed too or watch more TV or head over into town, if you know what I'm saying," he said with a smile that might have meant anything.

"How old are you?" Fate asked suddenly.

"Twenty-two," said Omar Abdul.

•

When Merolino climbed into the ring the sun was sinking in the west and the trainer turned on the lights, which were fed by an independent generator that supplied the house with electricity. In a corner, García stood motionless with his head bowed. He had changed and put on knee-length black boxing shorts. He seemed to be asleep. Only when the lights came on did he raise his head and look at López for a few seconds, as if waiting for a signal. One of the reporters, who never stopped smiling, rang a bell, and García assumed a defensive stance and moved into the center of the ring. Merolino was wearing a safety helmet and he circled García, who threw a couple of left jabs, no more, trying to land a hit or two. Fate asked one of the reporters whether sparring partners usually wore safety helmets.

"Usually," said the reporter.

"So why isn't he wearing one?" asked Fate.

"Because no matter how much anybody hits him they won't do any damage," said the reporter. "Do you see what I mean? He doesn't feel anything, he's out of it."

In the third round García left the ring and Omar Abdul stepped up. The kid was bare chested but he hadn't taken off his warm-up pants. His movements were much quicker than those of the Mexican fighter, and he dodged away easily when Merolino tried to corner him, although it was clear that the fighter and his sparring partner had no intention of hurting each other. Every so often they would talk, while still moving, and laugh.

"You off in Costa Rica?" Omar Abdul asked him. "Come on, baby, open your eyes."

Fate asked the reporter what the fighter was saying.

"Nothing," said the reporter, "all the son of a bitch knows are curse words."

After three rounds the trainer stopped the fight and disappeared into the house, followed by Merolino.

"The masseur is waiting for them," said the reporter.

"Who is the masseur?" asked Fate.

"We haven't seen him, I think he never comes out into the yard, he's a blind guy, you know, he was born blind, and he spends all day in the kitchen eating, or in the bathroom shitting, or lying on the floor in his room reading books for blind people, in that blind people's language, what's it called?"

"Braille," said the other reporter.

Fate imagined the masseur reading in a dark room and a shudder passed through him. It must be something like happiness, he thought. At the watering trough, García dumped a bucket of cold water on Omar Abdul's back. The fighter from California winked at Fate.

"What did you think?" he asked.

"Not bad," said Fate, to be nice, "but I get the feeling Pickett's in better condition."

"Pickett's a punk," said Omar Abdul.

"Do you know him?"

"I've seen him fight on TV a couple times. Motherfucker doesn't know how to move."

"Well, I guess I've never actually seen him," said Fate.

Omar Abdul stared at him in astonishment.

"You've never seen Pickett fight?" he asked.

"No, the truth is the boxing guy at my magazine died last week and since we didn't have anyone else, they sent me."

"Put your money on Merolino," said Omar Abdul after a moment of silence.

"Good luck," said Fate before he left.

The ride back seemed shorter. For a while he followed the rear lights of the reporters' car, until he saw them park outside a bar when they were back on the paved streets of Santa Teresa. He pulled up next to them and asked what the plan was. We're getting something to eat, said one of the reporters. Although he wasn't hungry, Fate agreed to come for a beer. One of the reporters, Chucho Flores, worked for a local paper and radio station. The other one, Ángel Martínez Mesa, who had rung the bell when they were at the ranch, worked for a Mexico City sports paper. Martínez Mesa was short and must have been around fifty. Chucho Flores was only a little shorter than Fate. He was thirty-five and he was always smiling. The relationship between Flores and Martínez Mesa, Fate sensed, was that of grateful disciple and largely indifferent master. And yet Martínez Mesa's indifference seemed less a matter of arrogance or any sense of superiority than of exhaustion, an exhaustion that showed even in his disheveled clothing, a stained suit and scuffed shoes, while his disciple wore a designer suit and designer tie and gold cuff links and possibly saw himself as a man of style. As the Mexicans ate grilled meat with fried potatoes, Fate thought about García's tattoo. Then he compared the loneliness of the ranch to the loneliness of his mother's apartment. He thought about her ashes, which were still there. He thought about the dead neighbor. He thought about Barry Seaman's neighborhood. And everywhere his memory alighted as the Mexicans ate seemed bleak.

•

After they dropped Martínez Mesa off at the Sonora Resort, Chucho Flores insisted on going out for a last drink. There were several reporters at the bar, among them a few Americans Fate would've liked to talk to, but Chucho Flores had other plans. They went to a bar on a narrow street in the center of Santa Teresa, a bar with walls painted fluorescent colors and a zigzagging bar. They ordered whiskey and orange juice. The bartender knew Chucho Flores. The man looked more like the owner than a bartender, thought Fate. His movements were brusque and commanding, even when he began to dry glasses with the apron tied around his waist. And yet he wasn't very old, twenty-five at most, and Chucho Flores, who was busy talking to Fate about New York and reporting in New York, didn't pay him much attention.

"I'd like to go live there," confessed Chucho Flores, "and work for some Hispanic radio station."

"There are lots of them," said Fate.

"I know, I know," said Chucho Flores, as if he'd already done plenty of research, and then he mentioned names of two stations that broadcast in Spanish, stations Fate had never heard of before.

"So what's the name of your magazine?" asked Chucho Flores.

Fate told him, and after thinking awhile, Chucho Flores shook his head.

"I don't know it," he said, "is it big?"

"No, it isn't big," said Fate, "it's a Harlem magazine, if that means anything to you."

"No," said Chucho Flores, "it doesn't."

"It's a magazine where the owners are African American and the editor is African American and almost all the reporters are African American," said Fate.

"Really?" asked Chucho Flores. "Can you do objective reporting that way?"

It was then that Fate realized Chucho Flores was a little drunk. He thought about what he'd just said. In fact, he didn't really have any basis to claim that *almost* all the reporters were black. He had seen only African Americans at the office, although of course he didn't know the correspondents. Maybe there was some Chicano in California, he thought. Or maybe in Texas. But it also seemed likely that there was *no one* in Texas, because otherwise why send him from Detroit and not give the job to the person in Texas or California?

Some girls came up to say hello to Chucho Flores. They were dressed for a night out, in high heels and club clothes. One of them had bleached blond hair and the other one was very dark, quieter and shy. The blonde said hello to the bartender and he nodded back, as if he knew her well and didn't trust her. Chucho Flores introduced Fate as a famous sportswriter from New York. Fate chose that moment to tell the Mexican that he wasn't really a sports reporter, he covered political and social issues, which Chucho Flores found very interesting. After a while another man showed up and was introduced by Chucho Flores as the biggest film buff south of the Arizona border. His name was Charly Cruz, and with a big smile he told Fate not to believe a word Chucho Flores had said. He owned a video store and in his line of work he had to watch lots of movies, but that was all, I'm no expert, he said.

"How many stores do you have?" Chucho Flores asked him. "Go on, tell my friend Fate."

"Three," said Charly Cruz.

"The dude is loaded," said Chucho Flores.

The girl with bleached blond hair was Rosa Méndez, and according to Chucho Flores, she had been his girlfriend. She had also been Charly Cruz's girlfriend and now she was dating the owner of a dance hall.

"That's Rosita," said Charly Cruz, "that's just the way she is."

"What way is that?" Fate asked.

In not very good English the girl answered that she liked to have fun. Life is short, she said, and then she was quiet, looking back and forth between Fate and Chucho Flores, as if reflecting on what she'd just said.

"Rosita is a little bit of a philosopher, too," said Charly Cruz.

Fate nodded his head. Two other girls came up to them. They were even younger and they knew only Chucho Flores and the bartender. Fate calculated that neither of them could be over eighteen. Charly Cruz asked him if he liked Spike Lee. Yes, said Fate, although he didn't really.

"He seems Mexican," said Charly Cruz.

"Maybe," said Fate. "That's an interesting way to look at it."

"And what about Woody Allen?"

"I like him," said Fate.

"He seems Mexican too, but Mexican from Mexico City or Cuernavaca," said Charly Cruz.

"Mexican from Cancún," said Chucho Flores.

Fate laughed, although he had no idea what they were talking about. He guessed they were making fun of him.

"What about Robert Rodriguez?"

"I like him," said Fate.

"That shithead is one of ours," said Chucho Flores.

"I have a movie on video by Robert Rodriguez," said Charly Cruz, "a movie hardly anyone has ever seen."

"*El Mariachi*?" asked Fate.

"No, everybody's seen that one. An earlier one, from when Robert Rodriguez was a nobody. When he was just a piss-poor Chicano motherfucker. A fuckup who took any gig he could get," said Charly Cruz.

"Let's sit down and you can tell us the story," said Chucho Flores.

"Good idea," said Charly Cruz. "I was getting tired of standing."

The story was simple and implausible. Two years before he shot *El Mariachi*, Robert Rodriguez took a trip to Mexico. He spent a few days wandering along the Texas-Chihuahua border and then he went south, to Mexico City, where he spent his time drinking and getting high. He sank so low, said Charly Cruz, that he would go into a *pulquería* before noon and leave only when it was closing and they kicked him out. In the end, he was living in a bordello or a brothel or a whorehouse, where he got to be friends with a whore and her pimp, a guy who went by the name El Perno, which for a pimp was like being called the Penis or the Cock. This Perno guy hit it off with Robert Rodriguez and was a good friend to him. Sometimes he had to drag him up to the room where he slept. Other times he and the whore had to undress him and put him in the shower, because Robert Rodriguez was always passing out. One morning, one of those rare mornings when the future movie director was half sober, the pimp told him he had some friends who wanted to make a movie and asked whether he could shoot it. Robert Rodriguez, as you might imagine, said sure thing, and El Perno took care of the practical details.

The shooting lasted three days, it seems, and Robert Rodriguez was always drunk and high when he got behind the camera. Naturally, his name doesn't appear in the credits. The director is listed as Johnny Swiggerson, which is obviously a joke, but if you know Robert Rodriguez's movies, the way he frames a scene, his takes and overhead shots, his sense of speed, there's no doubt it's his work. The only thing missing is his personal editing style, which makes it clear the film was edited by someone else. But he's the director, that much I'm sure of.

•

Fate wasn't interested in Robert Rodriguez or the story of his first film, first or last, he couldn't care less, and also he was starting to feel like eating some dinner or having a sandwich and then going to bed at the motel and getting some sleep, but still he had to hear scraps of the plot, a story of whores who gave wise advice or maybe they were just whores with hearts of gold, especially a whore called Justina, who, for reasons that escaped him but weren't too hard to figure out, was acquainted with some vampires in Mexico City who roamed at night disguised as policemen. He ignored the rest of the story. As he and the dark-haired girl who had come with Rosita Méndez were kissing, he heard something about pyramids, Aztec vampires, a book written in blood, the inspiration for *From Dusk Till Dawn*, the recurring nightmare of Robert Rodriguez. The girl with dark hair didn't know how to kiss. Before he left he gave Chucho Flores the phone number of the motel where he was staying and then he stumbled out to where he had parked the car.

As he was opening the car door he heard someone ask if he felt all right. He took a deep breath and turned around. Chucho Flores was ten feet away with the knot of his tie loosened and his arm around Rosa Méndez. Rosa was looking at Fate as if he were some kind of exotic specimen, what kind? he didn't know, but he didn't like the look in her eye.

"I'm fine," he said, "there's no problem."

"Do you want me to drive you to your motel?" asked Chucho Flores.

Rosa Méndez smiled more broadly. It occurred to him that Chucho Flores might be gay.

"No need," he said, "I can handle it."

Chucho Flores let go of Rosa Méndez and took a step in his direction. Fate got into the car and started the engine, looking away from them. Goodbye, amigo, he heard the Mexican say, his voice somehow muted. Rosa Méndez had her hands on her hips in what struck him as a completely artificial pose, and she wasn't looking at him or his car as he drove away but at her companion, who stood motionless, as if the night air had frozen him.

•

There was a new kid at the front desk of the motel, and Fate asked him whether he could get something to eat. The boy said they didn't have a kitchen but he could buy cookies or a candy bar from the machine out front. Outside, trucks passed by now and then heading north and south, and across the road were the lights of the service station. Fate headed that way. When he was crossing the road, a car almost hit him. For a moment he thought it was because he was drunk, but then he told himself that before he crossed, drunk or not, he had looked both ways and he hadn't seen any lights on the road. So where had the car come from? The service station was brightly lit and almost empty. Behind the counter, a fifteen-year-old girl was reading a magazine. It looked to Fate as if she had a very small head. Next to the register was a woman, maybe twenty years old, who watched him as he went over to a machine that sold hot dogs.

"You have to pay first," said the woman in Spanish.

"I don't understand," said Fate, "I'm American."

The woman repeated what she had said in English.

"Two hot dogs and a beer," said Fate.

The woman took a pen out of the pocket of her uniform and wrote down the amount of money Fate had to give her.

"Dollars or pesos?" asked Fate.

"Pesos," said the woman.

Fate left some money next to the cash register and went to get a beer out of the refrigerator case and then he held up two fingers to show the small-headed teenager how many hot dogs he wanted. The girl brought him the hot dogs and Fate asked her how the condiments machine worked.

"Push the button for the one you want," said the teenager in English.

Fate put ketchup, mustard, and something that looked like guacamole on one of the hot dogs and ate it right there.

"Nice," he said.

"Good," said the girl.

Then he repeated the operation with the other hot dog and went to the register to get his change. He took some coins and went back over to where the teenager was and tipped her.

"Gracias, señorita," he said in Spanish.

Then he went out with his beer and hot dog. As he waited by the highway for three trucks to go by on their way from Santa Teresa to Arizona, he remembered what he'd said to the cashier. I'm American. Why didn't I say I was African American? Because I'm in a foreign country? But can I really consider myself to be in a foreign country when I could go walking back to my own country right now if I wanted, and it wouldn't even take very long? Does this mean that in some places I'm American and in some places I'm African American and in other places, by logical extension, I'm nobody?

•

When he got up he called the editor of the sports section at the magazine and told him Pickett wasn't in Santa Teresa.

"That's no surprise," said the editor of the sports section, "he's probably at some ranch outside Vegas."

"So how the hell am I supposed to interview him?" asked Fate. "You want me to go to Vegas?"

"Interview? You don't need any fucking interview, all we need is somebody to cover the fight, you know, the atmosphere, the mood in the ring, the shape Pickett's in, the impression he makes on the Mexicans."

"The mise-en-scène," said Fate.

"Mise-what?" asked the editor of the sports section.

"Shit, man, the atmosphere," said Fate.

"In plain English," said the editor of the sports section, "like you're telling a story at a bar and all your friends are there and people are gathered around to listen to what you have to say."

"I hear you," said Fate, "I'll get it to you the day after tomorrow."

"If there's anything you don't understand, don't worry about it, we'll edit it here so it sounds like you spent your whole life ringside."

"All right, I hear you," said Fate.

•

When he stepped onto the landing outside his room he saw three blond kids, almost albinos, playing with a white ball, a red bucket, and some red plastic shovels. The oldest must have been five and the youngest three. It wasn't a safe place for children to play. If they weren't careful they might try to cross the road and be run over by a truck. He looked around: sitting on a wooden bench in the shade, a very blond woman in sunglasses was watching them. He waved to her. She glanced at him for a second and jerked her chin as if she couldn't take her eyes off the kids.

Fate went down the stairs and got in his car. The heat inside was unbearable and he opened both windows. Without knowing why, he thought about his mother again, the way she had watched him when he was a boy. When he started the car one of the albino children got up and stared at him. Fate smiled at him and waved. The boy dropped his ball and stood to attention like a soldier. As the car turned out of the motel parking lot, the boy lifted his right hand to his visor and stood that way until Fate's car disappeared to the south.

As he was driving he thought about his mother again. He saw her walking, saw her from behind, saw the back of her head as she watched a TV show, heard her laugh, saw her washing dishes in the sink. Her face, however, was always in shadows, as if in some way she were already dead or as if she were telling him, in actions instead of words, that faces weren't important in this life or the next. There weren't any reporters at the Sonora Resort, and he had to ask the clerk how to get to the Arena del Norte. When he got to the stadium he noticed some kind of commotion. He asked a shoeshine man who had set up shop in one of the corridors what was going on and the shoeshine man said that the American fighter had arrived.

He found Count Pickett in the ring, dressed in a suit and tie and flashing a broad, confident smile. The photographers were shooting pictures and the reporters around the ring called to him by his first name and barked questions. When'll you be up for the championship? Is it true Jesse Brentwood is scared of you? What did you get to come to Santa Teresa? Is it true you eloped in Las Vegas? Pickett's manager was standing next to him. He was a short, fat little man and he was the one who answered most of the questions. The Mexican reporters addressed him in Spanish and called him by name, Sol, Mr. Sol, and Mr. Sol answered them in Spanish and sometimes he called the Mexican reporters by name too. An American reporter, a big guy with a square face, asked whether bringing Pickett to fight in Santa Teresa was politically correct.

"What do you mean politically correct?" asked the manager.

The reporter was about to answer, but the manager cut him off.

"Boxing," he said, "is a sport, and sports, like art, are beyond politics. Let's not mix sports and politics, Ralph."

"So what you're saying is," said the reporter called Ralph, "you aren't worried about bringing Count Pickett to Santa Teresa."

"Count Pickett isn't afraid of anybody," said the manager.

"There's no man alive who can beat me," said Count Pickett.

"Well, Count's a man, that's for sure. So I guess the question ought to be: has he brought any women with him?" asked Ralph.

A Mexican reporter at the other end of the ring got up and told him to go fuck himself. Somebody not far from Fate shouted that he'd better not talk shit about Mexicans if he didn't want to get his ass kicked.

"Shut your mouth, man, or I'll shut it for you."

Ralph seemed not to hear what they were saying and he stood there calmly, waiting for the manager's answer. Some American reporters who were in a corner of the ring, near the photographers, gave the manager a questioning look. The manager cleared his throat and then he said:

"We don't have any women with us, Ralph, you know we never travel with women."

"Not even Mrs. Alversohn?"

The manager laughed and so did some of the reporters.

"You know very well my wife doesn't like boxing, Ralph," said the manager.

•

"What the hell were they talking about?" Fate asked Chucho Flores as they were eating breakfast at a bar near the Arena del Norte.

"About the women who've been killed," said Chucho Flores glumly. "The numbers are up," he said. "Every so often the numbers go up and it's news again and the reporters talk about it. People talk about it too, and the story grows like a snowball until the sun comes out and the whole damn ball melts and everybody forgets about it and goes back to work."

"They go back to work?" asked Fate.

"The fucking killings are like a strike, amigo, a brutal fucking strike."

The comparison of the killings to a strike was odd. But Fate nodded his head and didn't say anything.

"This is a big city, a real city," said Chucho Flores. "We have everything. Factories, maquiladoras, one of the lowest unemployment rates in Mexico, a cocaine cartel, a constant flow of workers from other cities, Central American immigrants, an urban infrastructure that can't support the level of demographic growth. We have plenty of money and poverty, we have imagination and bureaucracy, we have violence and the desire to work in peace. There's just one thing we haven't got," said Chucho Flores.

Oil, thought Fate, but he didn't say it.

"What don't you have?" he asked.

"Time," said Chucho Flores. "We haven't got any fucking time."

Time for what? thought Fate. Time for this shithole, equal parts lost cemetery and garbage dump, to turn into a kind of Detroit? For a while they didn't talk. Chucho Flores took out a pencil and notebook and started to draw women's faces. He did it very quickly, completely absorbed in the effort, and also, it seemed to Fate, with some talent, as if before he'd become a sportswriter Chucho Flores had studied drawing and spent many hours sketching from life. None of his women were smiling. Some had their eyes closed. Others were old and had their heads turned as if they were waiting for something or someone to call their names. None of them was pretty.

"You're good," said Fate as Chucho Flores started on his seventh portrait.

"It's nothing," said Chucho Flores.

Then, more than anything because it embarrassed him to keep talking about how well the Mexican could draw, Fate asked about the dead women.

"Most of them are workers at the maquiladoras. Young girls with long hair. But that isn't necessarily the mark of the killer. In Santa Teresa almost all the girls have long hair," said Chucho Flores.

"Is there a single killer?" asked Fate.

"That's what they say," said Chucho Flores, still drawing. "A few people have been arrested. Some cases have been solved. But according to the legend, there's just one killer and he'll never be caught."

"How many women have been killed?"

"I don't know," said Chucho Flores, "lots, more than two hundred."

Fate watched as the Mexican began to sketch his ninth portrait.

"That's a lot for one person," he said.

"That's right, amigo. Too many. Even for a Mexican killer."

"And how are they killed?" asked Fate.

"Nobody's sure. They disappear. They vanish into thin air, here one minute, gone the next. And after a while their bodies turn up in the desert."

•

As they were driving to the Sonora Resort, where he planned to check his e-mail, it occurred to Fate that it would be much more interesting to write a story about the women who were being killed than about the Pickett-Fernández fight. That was what he wrote to his editor. He asked if he could stay in the city for another week and asked them to send a photographer. Then he went out to have a drink at the bar, joining some American reporters. They were talking about the fight and all of them agreed that Fernández wouldn't last more than four rounds. One of them told the story of the Mexican fighter Hércules Carreño. Carreño was almost six and a half feet tall, unusually tall for Mexico, where people tend to be short. And he was strong, too. He worked unloading sacks at a market or butcher's, and someone convinced him to try boxing. He got a late start. He might have been twenty-five. But in Mexico heavyweights are few and far between, and he won all his fights. This is a country with good bantamweights, good flyweights, good featherweights, even the occasional welterweight, but no heavyweights or light heavyweights. It has to do with tradition and nutrition. Morphology. Now Mexico has a president who's taller than the president of the United States. This is the first time it's ever happened. Gradually, the presidents here are getting taller. It used to be unthinkable. A Mexican president would come up to the American president's shoulder, at most. Sometimes the Mexican president's head would be barely an inch or two above our president's belly button. That's just how it was. But now the Mexican upper class is changing. They're getting richer and they go looking for wives north of the border. That's what you call *improving the race*. A short Mexican sends his short son to college in California. The kid has money and does whatever he wants and that impresses some girls. There's no place on earth with more dumb girls per square foot than a college in California. Bottom line: the kid gets himself a degree and a wife, who moves to Mexico with him. So then the short Mexican grandkids aren't so short anymore, they're medium, and meanwhile their skin's getting lighter too. These grandkids, when the time comes, set off on the same journey of initiation as their father. American college, American wife, taller and taller kids. What this means is that the Mexican upper class, of its own accord, is doing what the Spaniards did, but backward. The Spaniards, who were hot-blooded and didn't think too far ahead, mixed with the Indian women, raped them, forced them to practice their religion, and thought that meant they were turning the country white. Those Spaniards believed in a mongrel whiteness. But they overestimated their semen and that was their mistake. You just can't rape that many people. It's mathematically impossible. It's too hard on the body. You get tired. Plus, they were raping from the bottom up, when what would've made more sense would be raping from the top down. They might have gotten some results if they'd been capable of raping their own mongrel children and then their mongrel grandchildren and even their bastard great-grandchildren. But who's going to go out raping people when you're seventy and you can hardly stand on your own two feet? You can see the results all around you. The semen of those Spaniards, who thought they were titans, just got lost in the amorphous mass of thousands of Indians. The first mongrels, the ones with fifty-fifty blood, took charge of the country, those were your ministers, your soldiers, your shopkeepers, your founders of new cities. And they kept on raping, but it didn't yield the same fruits, since the Indian women they were raping gave birth to mestizos with a smaller percentage of white blood. And so on. Until we come to this fighter, Hércules Carreño, who started out winning, either because his rivals were even worse than he was or because the matches were fixed, which got some Mexicans to boast about having a real heavyweight champion, and one fine day Hércules Carreño was taken to the United States, and they matched him with a drunken Irishman and then a black guy who'd been smoking pot and then a fat Russian, and he beat them all, and it filled the Mexicans with happiness and pride: now their champion had hit the big time. And then they set up a fight against Arthur Ashley, in Los Angeles. Any of you guys see that fight? I did. They called Arthur Ashley the Sadist. That's the fight where he got the name. Poor Hércules Carreño was wiped right off the map. From round one you could tell it was going to be a massacre. The Sadist took his time, he was in no hurry, picking the perfect spots to land his hooks, turning each round into a monograph, round three on the subject of the face, round four on the liver. In the end, it was all Hércules Carreño could do to hang in till round eight. After that you could still see him fighting in third-rate rings. He almost always went down in round two. Then he tried to get work as a bouncer, but he was in such a fog he couldn't hold down a job for more than a week. He never went back to Mexico. Maybe he'd forgotten he was Mexican. The Mexicans, of course, forgot him. They say he started to beg on the streets and that one day he died under a bridge. The pride of the Mexican heavyweights, said the reporter.

The others laughed and then they all assumed expressions of penitence. Twenty seconds of silence to remember the unfortunate Carreño. The faces, suddenly solemn, made Fate think of a masked ball. For a brief instant he couldn't breathe, he saw his mother's empty apartment, he had a premonition of two people making love in a miserable room, all at the same time, a moment defined by the word *climacteric*. What are you, flacking for the Klan? Fate asked the reporter who had told the story. Watch out, looks like we got ourselves another touchy jig, said the reporter. Fate tried to lunge at him and get a punch in (though a slap in the face would've been better), but he was blocked by the reporters surrounding the man. He's just fucking around, he heard someone say. We're all American here. There's nobody here from the Klan. At least I don't think so. Then he heard more laughter. When he calmed down and went to sit by himself in a corner of the bar, one of the reporters who'd been listening to the story of Hércules Carreño came up to him and held out his hand.

"Chuck Campbell, *Sport Magazine*, Chicago."

Fate shook the reporter's hand and told him his name and the name of the magazine he worked for.

"I heard your sports guy was killed," said Campbell.

"That's right," said Fate.

"Woman trouble, I bet," said Campbell.

"I don't know," said Fate.

"I knew Jimmy Lowell," said Campbell, "at least we saw each other forty times or so, which is more than some men see a mistress, or even a wife. He was a good person. He liked his beer and he liked his dinner. A hardworking man, he used to say, has to eat, and the food has to be good. Sometimes we flew together. I can't sleep on planes. Jimmy Lowell would sleep through the whole flight, only time he'd wake up was to eat or tell some story. The truth is, he didn't really give a shit about boxing, his sport was baseball, but for you guys he covered everything, even tennis. He never had a bad word for anybody. He respected people and people respected him. Wouldn't you say?"

"I never met Lowell in my life," said Fate.

"Don't let yourself get upset by what you just heard," said Campbell. "Sports is a boring beat and guys shoot off their mouths without thinking about it, they make up stories just to have something different to talk about. Sometimes we say stupid things without meaning to. The guy who told the story about that Mexican fighter, he isn't a bad guy. Compared to the others, he's pretty decent, has an open mind. It's just that every so often, to pass the time, we act like assholes. But we don't mean anything by it," said Campbell.

"It's not a problem," said Fate.

"How many rounds you think it'll take Count Pickett to win?"

"I don't know," said Fate, "I saw Merolino Fernández training at his place yesterday and he didn't look like a loser to me."

"He'll go down before the third," said Campbell.

Another reporter asked where Fernández was staying.

"Not far from the city," said Fate, "although I don't actually know, I didn't go alone, some Mexicans took me."

•

When Fate checked his e-mail again, he found a reply from his editor. There was no interest in the story he'd pitched, or no budget. His editor suggested that Fate limit himself to completing the assignment from the sports editor and then return immediately. Fate spoke to a clerk at the Sonora Resort and asked to place a call to New York.

While he waited he thought about other pitches the magazine had turned down. The most recent had been about a political group in Harlem, the Mohammedan Brotherhood. He'd met them during a pro-Palestine demonstration. The turnout was mixed, groups of Arabs, New York lefties, new antiglobalization activists. But the Mohammedan

Brotherhood caught his attention because they were marching under a big poster of Osama bin Laden. They were all black and they were all wearing black leather jackets and black berets and sunglasses, which gave them a vague resemblance to the Panthers, except that the Panthers had been teenagers and the ones who weren't teenagers had a youthful look, an aura of youthfulness and tragedy, whereas the members of the Mohammedan Brotherhood were grown men, broad shouldered with huge biceps, people who spent hours and hours at the gym, lifting weights, people born to be bodyguards, but whose bodyguards? true human tanks whose very presence was intimidating, although there were no more than twenty at the demonstration, possibly fewer, but somehow the poster of bin Laden had a magnifying effect, first and foremost because it was less than six months since the attack on the World Trade Center and walking around with bin Laden, even just in effigy, was an extreme provocation. Of course, Fate wasn't the only one who took notice of the small, defiant presence of the Brotherhood: the television cameras followed them, their spokesman was interviewed, and the photographers from several papers documented the attendance of the group, which looked as if it was asking to be crushed.

Fate observed them from a distance. He watched them talk to the television crews and some local radio reporters, he watched them yell slogans, he watched them march through the crowd, and he followed them. Before the demonstration began to break up, the members of the Mohammedan Brotherhood exited in a planned maneuver. A couple of vans were waiting for them on a corner. Only then did Fate realize that there were no more than fifteen of them. They ran. He ran after them. He explained that he wanted to interview them for his magazine. They talked next to the vans, on a side street. The one who seemed to be the leader, a tall, fat guy with a shaved head, asked him what magazine he worked for. Fate told him and the man smirked.

"No one reads that shit today," he said.

"It's a magazine for brothers," said Fate.

"It's a motherfucking sellout," said the man, still smiling. "It's played."

"I don't think so," said Fate.

A Chinese kitchen worker came out to leave some garbage bags. An Arab watched them from the corner. Strange, remote faces, thought Fate, as the man who seemed to be the leader gave him a time, a date, a place in the Bronx where they would see each other in a few days.

Fate kept the appointment. Three members of the Brotherhood and a black van were waiting for him. They drove to a basement near Baychester. The fat guy with the shaved head was waiting for them there. He said to call him Khalil. The others didn't give their names. Khalil talked about the Holy War. Explain what the hell you mean by Holy War, said Fate. The Holy War speaks for us when our mouths are parched, said Khalil. The Holy War is the language of the mute, of those who've lost the power of speech, of those who never knew how to speak. Why do you march against Israel? asked Fate. The Jew is keeping us down, said Khalil. You won't see a Jew in the Klan, said Fate. That's what the Jews want us to think. In fact, the Klan is everywhere. In Tel Aviv, in London, in Washington. Many leaders of the Klan are Jews, said Khalil. It's always been that way. Hollywood is full of Klan leaders. Who? asked Fate. Khalil warned him that what he was about to say was off the record.

"The Jew tycoons have good Jew lawyers," he said.

Who? asked Fate. Khalil named three movie directors and two actors. Then Fate had an inspiration. He asked: is Woody Allen a member of the Klan? He is, said Khalil, look at his movies, have you ever seen a black man in them? Not many, said Fate. Not one, said Khalil. Why were you carrying a poster of bin Laden? asked Fate. Because Osama bin Laden was the first to understand the nature of the fight we face today. Then they talked about bin Laden's innocence and Pearl Harbor and about how convenient the attack on the Twin Towers had been for some people. Stockbrokers, said Khalil, people with incriminating papers hidden in their offices, people who sell arms and needed something like that to happen. According to you, said Fate, Mohamed Atta was an undercover agent for the CIA or the FBI. What happened to Mohamed Atta's body? Khalil asked. Who can be sure Mohamed Atta was on one of those planes? I'll tell you what I think. I think Atta is dead. He died under torture, or he was shot in the back of the head. Then I think they chopped him into little pieces and ground his bones down until they looked like chicken bones. After that they put the little bones and cutlets in a box, filled it with cement, and dropped it in some Florida swamp. And they did the same thing to the men he was with.

So who flew the planes? asked Fate. Klan lunatics, nameless inmates from mental hospitals in the Midwest, volunteers brainwashed to face suicide. Thousands of people disappear in this country every year and nobody tries to find them. Then they talked about the Romans and the Roman circus and the first Christians who were eaten by lions. But the lions will choke on our black flesh, he said.

·

The next day Fate met them at a Harlem club and there he was introduced to Ibrahim, a man of average height with a scarred face, who set about describing to him in great detail all the charitable work the Brotherhood did in the neighborhood. They ate together at a diner next door to the club. The diner was run by a woman. A boy helped her, and in the kitchen there was an old man who never stopped singing. In the afternoon Khalil joined them and Fate asked the two men where they'd met. In prison, they said. Prison is where black brothers meet. They talked about the other Muslim groups in Harlem. Ibrahim and Khalil didn't think very highly of them, but they tried to be fair and maintain a dialogue with them. Sooner or later the good Muslims would end up finding their way to the Mohammedan Brotherhood.

Before he left, Fate told them that they would probably never be forgiven for having marched under the effigy of Osama bin Laden. Ibrahim and Khalil laughed. He thought they looked like two black stones quaking with laughter.

"They'll probably never *forget* it," said Ibrahim.

"Now they know who they're dealing with," said Khalil.

·

His editor told him to forget writing a story about the Brotherhood.

"Those guys, how many of them are there?" he asked.

"Twenty, more or less," said Fate.

"Twenty niggers," said his editor. "At least five of them must be FBI."

"Maybe more," said Fate.

"What makes them interesting to us?" asked his editor.

"Stupidity," said Fate. "The endless variety of ways we destroy ourselves."

"Have you become a masochist, Oscar?" asked his editor.

"Could be," said Fate.

"You need to get more pussy," said the editor. "Get out more, listen to music, make friends, talk to them."

"I've thought about it," said Fate.

"Thought about what?"

"About getting more pussy," said Fate.

"That isn't the kind of thing you think about, it's the kind of thing you do," said the editor.

"First you have to think about it," said Fate. Then he added: "Can I do the story?"

The editor shook his head.

"Forget about it," he said. "Sell it to a philosophy quarterly or an urban anthropology journal, or write a fucking script if you want and let Spike Lee shoot the motherfucker, but it's not going to run in any magazine of mine."

"All right," said Fate.

"Motherfuckers marched with a poster of bin Laden," said his editor.

"It takes balls," said Fate.

"Balls of steel, plus you have to be a complete goddamn moron."

"You know some undercover cop came up with it," said Fate.

"Makes no difference," said the editor, "whoever came up with it, it's a sign."

"A sign of what?" asked Fate.

"That we're living on a planet of lunatics," said the editor.

•

When his editor came to the phone, Fate explained what was going on in Santa Teresa. He gave a synopsis of the story he wanted to write. He talked about the women being killed, about the possibility that all the crimes had been committed by one or two people, which made them the biggest serial killings in history, he talked about drug trafficking and the border, about police corruption and the city's boundless growth, he promised that all he wanted was another week to get all the material needed and then he'd come back to New York and in five days he'd file the story.

"Oscar," said his editor, "you're there to cover a goddamn boxing match."

"This is more important," said Fate, "the fight is just a little story. What I'm proposing is so much more."

"What are you proposing?"

"A sketch of the industrial landscape in the third world," said Fate, "a piece of *reportage* about the current situation in Mexico, a panorama of the border, a serious crime story, for fuck's sake."

"*Reportage?*" asked his editor. "Is that French, nigger? Since when do you speak French?"

"I don't speak French," said Fate, "but I know what fucking *reportage* is."

"I know what fucking *reportage* is, too," said the editor, "and I also know *merci* and *au revoir* and *faire l'amour*, which is the same as *coucher avec moi*. And I think that you, nigger, want to *coucher avec moi,* but you've forgot the *voulez-vous*, which in this case ought to have been your first move. You hear me? You say *voulez-vous* or you can get the fuck out."

"It's a great story," said Fate.

"How many black men are involved in this shit?" asked the editor.

"Black men? Say what?" asked Fate.

"How many niggers have ropes around their neck?" asked the editor.

"How should I know? I'm talking about a great story," said Fate, "not some riot in the ghetto."

"So in other words, there are no black men," said the editor.

"No black men, but more than two hundred Mexican women killed," said Fate.

"How're Pickett's odds?" asked the editor.

"Take Count Pickett and stick him up your black ass," said Fate.

"You seen the other guy?" asked the editor.

"You can stick Count Pickett up your black faggot ass," said Fate, "and ask him to watch it for you because when I get back to New York I'm going to kick the shit out of you."

"You do your job and hold on to your receipts, nigger," said the editor. Fate hung up.

Next to him, smiling at him, was a woman in jeans and a leather jacket. She was wearing sunglasses and she had a nice bag and a camera slung over her shoulder. She looked like a tourist.

"Are you interested in the Santa Teresa killings?" she asked.

Fate looked at her and it took him a moment to realize that she had listened to his phone conversation.

"My name's Guadalupe Roncal," said the woman, holding out her hand.

He shook it. It was a delicate hand.

"I'm a reporter," said Guadalupe Roncal when Fate let go of her hand.

"But I'm not here to cover the fight. Boxing doesn't interest me, though I know some women find it sexy. To be honest, it's always struck me as vulgar and pointless. How about you? Do you like to watch two grown men hit each other?"

Fate shrugged his shoulders.

"You won't tell? Fine, I'm not one to judge what you like to watch. Actually, I don't like any sports. Not boxing, for the reasons I mentioned, or soccer, or basketball, not even track and field. So you may wonder what I'm doing in a hotel full of sports reporters instead of someplace quieter, somewhere I wouldn't have to hear all these pathetic stories of great forgotten fights every time I come down to the bar. I'll tell you if you come sit at my table and let me buy you a drink."

As he followed her it occurred to him that he might be in the company of a crazy person or maybe a hooker, but Guadalupe Roncal didn't look like a crazy person or a hooker, although Fate didn't really know what Mexican crazy people or hookers looked like. For that matter, she didn't look like a reporter. They sat at an outside table, with a view of a building under construction, a building more than ten stories high. Another hotel, the woman informed him with indifference. Some workmen leaning on beams or sitting on piles of bricks were looking at them, or so Fate thought, although it was impossible to say for sure because the figures moving around the unfinished building were so small.

"As I said already, I'm a reporter," said Guadalupe Roncal. "I work for one of the big Mexico City newspapers. And I'm staying at this hotel out of fear."

"Fear of what?" asked Fate.

"Fear of everything. When you work on something that involves the killings of women in Santa Teresa, you end up scared of everything. Scared you'll be beaten up. Scared of being kidnapped. Scared of torture. Of course, the fear lessens with experience. But I don't have experience. No experience whatsoever. I'm cursed by a lack of experience. You might even say I'm here undercover, as an undercover reporter, if there is such a thing. I know everything about the killings. But I'm not really an expert on the subject. What I mean is, until a week ago this wasn't my subject. I wasn't up on it, I hadn't written anything about it, and suddenly, out of the blue, the file landed on my desk and I was in charge of the investigation. Do you want to know why?"

Fate nodded.

"Because I'm a woman and women can't turn down assignments. Of course, I already knew what had happened to my predecessor. Everybody at the paper knew it. The case got a lot of attention. You might even have heard about it." Fate shook his head. "He was killed, of course. He got in too deep and they killed him. Not here, in Santa Teresa, but in Mexico City. The police said it was a robbery that went wrong. You want to know how it happened? He got in a taxi. The taxi drove off. Then it stopped at a corner and two strangers got in. For a while they drove around to different cash machines, maxing out my predecessor's credit card, then they headed somewhere on the edge of the city and stabbed him. He wasn't the first reporter to be killed for what he wrote. Going through his papers I found information on two others. A woman, a radio correspondent, who was kidnapped in Mexico City, and a Chicano who worked for an Arizona paper called *La Raza*, who disappeared. The two of them were investigating the killings of women in Santa Teresa. I'd met the radio correspondent at journalism school. We were never friends. We might've exchanged a few words at most. But I think I'd met her. Before they killed her they raped her and tortured her."

"Here, in Santa Teresa?" asked Fate.

"No, man, in Mexico City. The arm of the killers is long, very long," said Guadalupe Roncal in a dreamy voice. "I used to work for the city section. I almost never got a byline. I was a complete unknown. When my predecessor was killed, two of the big bosses at the paper came to see me. They invited me out to lunch. Of course, I thought I'd done something wrong. Or that one of them wanted to sleep with me. I knew who they were, but I had never talked to either of them. It was a nice lunch. They were proper and polite, I was quick and careful. It would've been better if I hadn't made such a good impression. Then we went back to the paper and they told me to follow them, they had something important to discuss with me. We went into one of their offices. The first thing they did was ask me if I'd like a raise. By that point I had figured out that something strange was going on and I was tempted to say no, but I said yes, and then they pulled out a piece of paper and named a figure, which was exactly what I was making as a city reporter, and then they looked straight at me and named another figure, which was like offering me a forty percent raise. I almost jumped for joy. Then they handed me the file my predecessor had put together and told me that from then on I would work solely and exclusively on the story of the women who'd been killed in Santa Teresa. I realized that if I said no I'd lose everything. It came out almost as a whisper when I asked why me. Because you're smart, Lupita, said one of them. Because no one knows you, said the other."

The woman gave a long sigh. Fate smiled in understanding. They ordered another whiskey and another beer. The workmen on the building under construction had disappeared. I'm drinking too much, said the woman.

"Since I read my predecessor's file, I've been drinking lots of whiskey, much more than I used to, and I drink vodka and tequila, too, and now I've discovered this Sonoran drink called *bacanora*, and I drink that, too," said Guadalupe Roncal. "And every day I'm more afraid and sometimes I can't help being a nervous wreck. You've probably heard that Mexicans never get scared." She laughed. "It's a lie. We get scared all right, we just know how to hide it. When I got to Santa Teresa, for example, I was so scared I thought I was going to die. On the flight here from Hermosillo I wouldn't have minded if the plane crashed. At least it's a quick death, or so they say. Luckily someone I work with in Mexico City had given me the address of this hotel. He told me he was going to be at the Sonora Resort to cover the fight and that no one could hurt me here around all these sportswriters. So here I am. The problem is that when the fight is over I can't leave with the reporters and I'll have to stay a few more days in Santa Teresa."

"Why?" asked Fate.

"I have to interview the chief suspect in the killings. He's from the United States, too."

"I had no idea," said Fate.

"How were you going to write about the crimes if you didn't know that?" asked Guadalupe Roncal.

"I thought I'd do some research. On the phone just now I was asking for more time."

"My predecessor was the one who knew most about all of this. It took him seven years to get a general sense of what was going on. Life is unbearably sad, don't you think?"

Guadalupe Roncal massaged both temples, as if suddenly she felt a migraine coming on. She whispered something Fate couldn't hear, and then she tried to flag the waiter but they were the only two at the outside tables. When she realized, she shivered.

"I have to go visit him in prison," she said. "The chief suspect—your countryman—has been in prison for years."

"So how can he be the chief suspect?" asked Fate. "I thought the crimes were still being committed."

"Mysteries of Mexico," said Guadalupe Roncal. "Do you want to come along? Would you like to come with me and interview him? The truth is I'd feel better if a man came with me, which goes against my beliefs as a feminist. Do you have anything against feminists? It's hard to be a feminist in Mexico. Not if you have money, maybe, but if you're middle class, it's hard. At first it isn't, of course, at first it's easy, in college it's easy, for example, but as the years go by it gets harder and harder. Mexican men, I can tell you, find feminism charming only in young women. But we age quickly here. We're built to age quickly. Thank goodness I'm still young."

"You're pretty young," said Fate.

"But I'm scared. And I need company. This morning I drove past the Santa Teresa prison and I almost had a panic attack."

"Is it that bad?"

"It's like a dream," said Guadalupe Roncal. "It looks like something alive."

"Alive?"

"I don't know how to explain it. More alive than an apartment building, for example. Much more alive. Don't be shocked by what I'm about to say, but it looks like a woman who's been hacked to pieces. Who's been hacked to pieces but is still alive. And the prisoners are living *inside* this woman."

"I understand," said Fate.

"No, I don't think you do, but it doesn't matter. You're interested, so I'm offering you the chance to meet the chief suspect in the killings in exchange for your company and protection. I think that seems fair and equitable. Do we have a deal?"

"It is fair," said Fate. "And very kind of you. What I don't understand is what you're afraid of. No one can hurt you in prison. In theory, anyhow, prisoners can't hurt anyone. They only hurt each other."

"You've never seen a picture of the chief suspect."

"No," said Fate.

Guadalupe Roncal looked up at the sky and smiled.

"I must seem crazy," she said, "or like a hooker. But I'm neither. I'm just nervous and lately I've been drinking too much. Do you think I want to get you in bed?"

"No. I believe what you've told me."

"Among my poor predecessor's papers there were several photographs. A few of the suspect. Three, to be precise. All three taken in prison. In two of them, the gringo—sorry, I didn't mean that to be offensive—is sitting and looking at the camera, probably in a visitor's room. He has very blond hair and very blue eyes. Eyes so blue he looks blind. In the third picture he's standing up, looking to the side. He's hugely tall and thin, very thin, but not feeble looking at all. He has the face of a dreamer. I don't know if that makes sense. He doesn't look uncomfortable. He's in prison, but I don't get the sense he's uncomfortable. He doesn't seem calm or relaxed, either. And he doesn't seem angry. He has the face of a dreamer, but of a dreamer who's dreaming at great speed. A dreamer whose dreams are far out ahead of our dreams. And that scares me. Do you understand?"

"I can't say I do," said Fate. "But you can count on me to go with you to interview him."

"All right, then," said Guadalupe Roncal. "I'll be waiting for you the day after tomorrow, at the entrance to the hotel, at ten. Does that sound good?"

"Ten in the morning. I'll be there," said Fate.

"Ten a.m. Okay," said Guadalupe Roncal. Then she shook his hand and walked off. Her gait was unsteady, Fate noticed.

●

He spent the rest of the day drinking with Campbell in the bar at the Sonora Resort. They complained about sportswriting, a dead-end profession that never got anyone a Pulitzer and that most people thought involved little more than showing up at games. Then they began to reminisce about their college years, Fate's at New York University, Campbell's at a college in Sioux City.

"In those days all I cared about was baseball and ethics," said Campbell.

For a second Fate imagined Campbell on his knees in the corner of a dark room, clutching a Bible and weeping. But then Campbell started to talk about women, about a bar in a place called Smithland, a kind of country inn near the Little Sioux River. First you got to Smithland and then you went a few miles east and there, under some trees, was the bar and the bar girls, whose clients were mostly farmers and a few students who came by car from Sioux City.

"We always did the same thing," said Campbell, "first we fucked the girls, then we went outside and played baseball until we were exhausted, and then, when it started to get dark, we would get drunk and sing cowboy songs on the porch."

When Fate was a student at NYU, he never got drunk or slept with prostitutes (in fact, he had never in his life been with a woman he had to pay). His free time was spent working and reading. Once a week, on Saturdays, he went to a creative writing workshop and for a while, not long, just a few months, he imagined that maybe he could make a living writing fiction, until the writer who led the workshop told him he'd do better to focus on journalism.

But that wasn't what he told Campbell.

When it began to get dark, Chucho Flores came in to find him. Fate noticed that Chucho Flores didn't invite Campbell along. He didn't know why, but this made him happy, though it made him unhappy too. For a while they drove aimlessly around Santa Teresa, at least that was how it seemed to Fate, as if Chucho Flores had something to tell him and couldn't find the right moment. The city lights at night changed the Mexican's face. The muscles under his skin grew tense. An ugly profile, thought Fate. Only then did he realize that at some point he would have to go back to the Sonora Resort, because that was where he'd parked his car.

"Let's not go too far," he said.

"Are you hungry?" the Mexican asked him. Fate said he was. The Mexican laughed and put on music. Fate heard an accordion and some far-off shouts, not of sorrow or joy, but of pure energy, self-sufficient and self-consuming. Chucho Flores smiled and his smile remained stamped on his face as he kept driving, not looking at Fate, facing forward, as if he'd been fitted with a steel neck brace, as the wails came closer and closer to the microphones and the voices of people who Fate imagined as savage beasts began to sing or kept howling, less than at first, and shouting *viva* for no clear reason.

"What is this?" asked Fate.

"Sonoran jazz," said Chucho Flores.

•

When he got back to the motel it was four in the morning. Over the course of the night he had gotten drunk and then sobered up and then gotten drunk again, and now, outside his room, he was sober again, as if instead of drinking real alcohol Mexicans drank water with short-term hypnotic effects. For a while, sitting on the trunk of his car, he watched the trucks going by on the highway. The night was cool and full of stars. He thought about his mother and what she must have thought about at night in Harlem, not looking out the window to see the few stars shining in the sky, sitting in front of the TV or washing dishes in the kitchen with laughter coming from the TV, black people and white people laughing, telling jokes that she might have thought were funny, although probably she didn't even pay much attention to what was being said, busy washing the dishes she had just used and the pot she had just used and the fork and spoon she had just used, peaceful in a way that seemed to go beyond simple peacefulness, thought Fate, or maybe not, maybe her peacefulness was just peacefulness and a hint of weariness, peacefulness and banked embers, peacefulness and tranquillity and sleepiness, which is ultimately (sleepiness, that is) the wellspring and also the last refuge of peacefulness. But then peacefulness isn't just peacefulness, thought Fate. Or what we think of as peacefulness is wrong and peacefulness or the realms of peacefulness are really no more than a gauge of movement, an accelerator or a brake, depending.

•

The next day he got up at two in the afternoon. The first thing he remembered was that before he went to bed he'd felt sick and thrown up. He checked on both sides of the bed and then he went into the bathroom but he couldn't find a single trace of vomit. Still, while he was sleeping he had woken up twice and both times he had smelled vomit: a foul odor that emanated from every corner of the room. He had been too tired to get up and had opened the windows and gone back to sleep.

Now the smell was gone and there was no sign that he had vomited the night before. He showered and then he got dressed, thinking that after the fight that night he would head straight back to Tucson, where he would try to catch a red-eye to New York. He wouldn't keep his appointment with Guadalupe Roncal. Why interview a suspected serial killer if he couldn't write about it? He thought about calling and making a reservation from the motel, but at the last minute he decided to do it later, from one of the phones at the Arena del Norte or the Sonora Resort. Then he packed his suitcase and went to the desk to check out. You don't have to leave now, the clerk told him, I'll charge you the same price to keep the room until midnight. Fate thanked him and put the key back in his pocket, but he didn't take his suitcase out of the car.

"Who do you think will win?" the clerk asked him.

"I don't know. Anything could happen in a fight like this," said Fate, as if he'd been a sportswriter all his life.

The sky was a deep blue, broken only by a few cylindrical clouds floating in the east and moving toward the city.

"They look like tubes," said Fate from the open door of the lobby.

"They're cirrus clouds," said the clerk. "By the time they reach the heights of Santa Teresa they'll have disappeared."

"It's funny," said Fate, still standing in the doorway, "*cirrus* means hard, it comes from the Greek *skirrhós*, which means hard, and it refers to tumors, hard tumors, but those clouds don't look hard at all."

"No," said the clerk, "they're clouds in the top layer of the atmosphere, and if they drop or rise a little, just a tiny bit, they disappear."

•

There was no one at the Arena del Norte. The main door was closed. On the walls were some posters, already faded, advertising the Fernández-Pickett fight. Some had been torn down and others had been covered by new posters pasted up by unknown hands, posters advertising concerts, folk dances, and even a circus calling itself Circo Internacional.

Fate walked around the building. He ran into a woman who was pushing a juice cart. The woman had long black hair and was wearing an ankle-length skirt. Among the jugs of water and buckets of ice the heads of two children bobbed. When she got to the corner the woman stopped and began to set up a kind of parasol with metal tubes. The children got off the cart and sat on the pavement, against the wall. For a while Fate stood watching them and the utterly deserted street. When he walked on, another cart appeared from around the opposite corner and Fate stopped again. The man who was pushing the new cart waved to the woman. She barely nodded in recognition and began to take huge glass jars out of the side of her cart, setting them on a makeshift counter. The man who had just arrived was selling corn, and steam rose from his cart. Fate discovered a back door and looked for a bell, but there was no bell of any kind so he had to knock. The children had gone up to the corn vendor, who got two cobs, spread them with thick cream, sprinkled them with cheese and then chile powder, and handed them to the children. As he waited, Fate imagined that the man with the corn was the children's father and that he was on bad terms with the mother, the juice woman, in fact maybe they were divorced and they saw each other only when they ran into each other on the job. But that couldn't possibly be the case, he thought. Then he knocked again and no one came to let him in.

•

At the bar at the Sonora Resort he found almost all of the reporters who were covering the fight. He saw Campbell talking to a man who looked Mexican and walked toward them, but before he reached them he realized that Campbell was working and decided not to interrupt. He saw Chucho Flores by the bar and waved from across the room. Chucho Flores was with three men who looked like ex-fighters and his wave back seemed halfhearted. Fate found an empty table outside and sat down. For a while he watched people get up from their tables and greet each other with long hugs or shout back and forth, and he watched the bustle of photographers shooting pictures, arranging and rearranging groups to their liking, and the procession of Santa Teresa notables, faces that weren't familiar to him at all, well-dressed young women, tall men in cowboy boots and Armani suits, young men with bright eyes and stiff jaws who didn't talk and just shook their heads yes or no, until he got tired of waiting for the waiter to bring him a drink and he elbowed his way out without looking back, not caring that two or three rude remarks were dropped behind him, remarks in Spanish that he didn't understand and that wouldn't have given him reason to stay even if he had understood them.

•

He ate at a restaurant in the eastern part of the city, on a cool patio under a vine-covered arbor. At the back of the patio, on the dirt floor next to a chain-link fence, there were three foosball tables. For a few minutes he looked at the menu, not understanding anything. Then he tried to explain what he wanted with gestures, but the woman who was waiting on him just smiled and shrugged her shoulders. After a while a man came over, but the English he spoke was even more unintelligible. The only word Fate understood was bread. And beer.

Then the man vanished and he was left alone. He got up and went over to the edge of the arbor, next to the foosball tables. One team was dressed in white T-shirts and green shorts and had black hair and very light-colored skin. The other team was in red, with black shorts, and all the players had full beards. The strangest thing, though, was that the players on the red team had tiny horns on their foreheads. The other two tables were exactly the same.

He could see hills on the horizon. The hills were dark yellow and black. Past the hills, he guessed, was the dessert. He felt the urge to leave and drive into the hills, but when he got back to his table the woman had brought him a beer and a very thick kind of sandwich. He took a bite and it was good. The taste was strange, spicy. Out of curiosity, he lifted the piece of bread on top: the sandwich was full of all kinds of things. He took a long drink of beer and stretched in his chair. Through the vine leaves he saw a bee, perched motionless. Two slender rays of sun fell vertically on the dirt floor. When the man came back he asked how to get to the hills. The man laughed. He spoke a few words Fate didn't understand and then he said not pretty, several times.

"Not pretty?"

"Not pretty," said the man, and he laughed again.

Then he took Fate by the arm and dragged him into a room that served as kitchen and that looked very tidy to Fate, each thing in its place, not a spot of grease on the white-tiled wall, and he pointed to the garbage can.

"Hills not pretty?" asked Fate.

The man laughed again.

"Hills are garbage?"

The man couldn't stop laughing. He had a bird tattoed on his left forearm. Not a bird in flight, like most tattoos of birds, but a bird perched on a branch, a little bird, possibly a swallow.

"Hills a garbage dump?"

The man laughed even more and nodded his head.

•

At seven that night Fate showed his press pass and went into the Arena del Norte. There were crowds outside and vendors selling food, soft drinks, and boxing souvenirs. Inside, the second-tier fights had already started. A bantamweight Mexican was fighting another bantamweight Mexican with only a few people watching. Others were buying sodas, talking, greeting each other. Ringside, he saw two television cameras. One of them seemed to be recording what was happening in the main aisle. The other cameraman was sitting on a bench, trying to get a snack cake out of its plastic wrapping. He headed down one of the covered side passageways. He saw people placing bets, two short men each with an arm around a tall woman in a tight dress, men smoking or drinking beer, men with loosened ties making signs with their fingers, as if they were playing a children's game. Above the awning that covered the passageway were the cheap seats and there the noise was even louder. He decided to go check out the dressing rooms and the pressroom. The only people in the pressroom were two Mexican reporters who stared at him like dying men. Both were seated and their shirts were damp with sweat. At the entrance to Merolino Fernández's dressing room he saw Omar Abdul. He said hello but the fighter pretended not to recognize him and kept talking to some Mexicans. The people outside the door were talking about blood, or so Fate thought he understood.

"What are you talking about?" he asked them.

"Bullfighting," one of the Mexicans said in English.

As he was leaving he heard someone call his name. Mr. Fate. He turned around and was met with Omar Abdul's broad smile.

"Don't you say hello to your friends, man?"

From up close he could see that both of the fighter's cheekbones were bruised.

"I guess Merolino's been working out," he said.

"Hazards of the trade," said Omar Abdul.

"Can I see the boss?"

Omar Abdul looked over his shoulder, through the door to the dressing room, and then he shook his head.

"If I let you in, brother, I'd have to let in all these other punks."

"Are they reporters?"

"Some of them are reporters, but most of them just want their picture taken with Merolino, want to kiss his hand, kiss his ass."

"How you doing?"

"Can't complain, can't really complain," said Omar Abdul.

"What do you plan to do after the fight?"

"Celebrate, I guess," said Omar Abdul.

"No, I don't mean tonight, but after it's all over," said Fate.

Omar Abdul smiled. A cocky, teasing smile. A Cheshire cat smile, as if instead of being perched on a tree branch, the Cheshire cat were out in an open field in a storm. The smile of a young black man, thought Fate, but also a very American smile.

"I don't know," he said, "look for work, hang out in Sinaloa on the beach, we'll see."

"Good luck," said Fate.

As he was walking away he heard Omar say: Count Pickett is the one who's going to need luck tonight. When he got back to the hall two different fighters were in the ring and there were hardly any empty seats left. He headed down the main aisle to the press pit. There was a fat man in his seat who looked at him, not understanding what he was saying. Fate showed him his ticket and the man got up and searched his pockets until he found his own ticket. The two of them had the same seat number. Fate smiled and the fat man smiled. Just then one of the fighters landed a hook that knocked his opponent down and most of the audience stood up and roared.

"What should we do?" Fate asked the fat man. The fat man shrugged and kept his eyes on the referee as the countdown proceeded. The fallen fighter got up and the audience roared again.

Fate raised a hand, with his palm toward the fat man, and retreated. When he was back in the main aisle, he heard someone calling him. He looked all around but he couldn't see anyone. Fate, Oscar Fate, the voice shouted. The fighter who had just gotten up threw his arms around his opponent. His opponent tried to get out of the clinch by aiming a flurry of blows at the first fighter's stomach and backing away. Here, Fate, here, the voice shouted. The referee broke up the clinch. The fighter who had just gotten up made a move as if to attack but danced slowly backward waiting for the bell. His opponent backed away, too. The first fighter was wearing white shorts and his face was covered in blood. The second fighter was wearing black, purple, and red striped shorts and looked surprised that the other fighter wasn't still on the ground. Oscar, Oscar, we're over here, shouted the voice. When the bell rang, the referee headed for the corner of the fighter in white shorts and motioned for a doctor to come up. The doctor, or whatever he was, examined the boxer's eyebrow and said the fight could go on.

Fate turned around and tried to find the people who were calling him. Most of the fans had gotten up from their seats and he couldn't see anybody. When the next round began, the fighter in striped shorts went on the offensive, looking for a knockout. For the first few seconds the other fighter stood his ground, but then he threw his arms around the fighter in striped shorts. The referee separated them several times. The shoulder of the fighter with striped shorts was stained with the other fighter's blood. Fate walked slowly toward the ringside seats. He saw Campbell reading a basketball magazine, he saw another American reporter coolly taking notes. One of the cameramen had set his camera up on a tripod, and the lighting boy next to him chewed gum and every so often checked out the legs of a girl in the first row.

He heard his name again and turned around. He thought he saw a blond woman motioning to him. The fighter in the white shorts fell again. His mouth guard popped out and flew across the ring, falling right next to Fate. For a moment Fate thought about bending down and picking it up, but then he was disgusted by the idea and didn't move, watching the sprawled body of the fighter and listening to the referee's count. Then, before the referee got to nine, the fighter stood again. He's going to fight without a mouth guard, thought Fate, and then he bent down and felt for the mouth guard but he couldn't find it. Who took it? he thought. I haven't moved and I haven't seen anybody else move, so who the fuck took the mouth guard?

•

When the fight was over, a song played over the loudspeakers that Fate recognized as one Chucho Flores had called Sonoran jazz. The fans in the cheap seats howled in delight and then they started to sing along. Three thousand Mexicans up in the gallery of the arena singing the same song in unison. Fate tried to get a look at them, but the lights, focused on the ring, left the upper part of the hall in darkness. The tone, he thought, was solemn and defiant, the battle hymn of a lost war sung in the dark. In the solemnity there was only desperation and death, but in the defiance there was a hint of corrosive humor, a humor that existed only in relation to itself and in dreams, no matter whether the dreams were long or short. Sonoran jazz. In the seats below, some people were singing along, but not many. Most were talking or drinking beer. He saw a boy in a white shirt and black pants run down the aisle. He saw the man who sold beer walk up the aisle singing to himself. A woman with her hands on her hips laughed at what a short man with a little mustache was saying. The short man was shouting but his voice was barely audible. A group of men seemed to converse just by clenching their jaws (and their jaws expressed only scorn or indifference). A man stared at the floor and talked to himself and smiled. Everyone seemed happy. Just then, as if he'd had a revelation, Fate understood that almost everybody at the arena thought Merolino Fernández would win the fight. What made them so sure? For a moment he thought he knew, but the knowledge slipped like water through his fingers. All for the best, he thought, because the fleeting shadow of the idea (another stupid idea) might destroy him on the spot.

•

Then, at last, he saw them. Chucho Flores was motioning him to come sit with them. He recognized the blond girl next to him. He'd seen her before, but now she was much more nicely dressed. He bought a beer and made his way through the crowd. The blond girl gave him a kiss on the cheek. She told him her name, which he'd already forgotten: Rosa Méndez. Chucho Flores introduced him to the other two: a man he'd never seen before, Juan Corona, who was probably another reporter, and an extremely beautiful girl, Rosa Amalfitano. This is Charly Cruz, the video king, you know him, said Chucho Flores. Charly Cruz shook Fate's hand. He was the only one still sitting, oblivious to what was going on around him. They were all very well dressed, as if after the fight they planned to attend a gala. One of the seats was empty and Fate sat down once they had moved their coats and jackets. He asked whether they were waiting for someone.

"We were expecting a friend," Chucho Flores said into his ear, "but she seems to have stood us up at the last minute."

"If she comes, it's no problem," said Fate, "I'll get up and go."

"No, man, you're with us now," said Chucho Flores.

Corona asked him what part of the United States he was from. New York, said Fate. And what do you do? I'm a reporter. After that, Corona's English was exhausted, and he didn't ask anything else.

"You're the first black man I've ever met," said Rosa Méndez.

Charly Cruz translated. Fate smiled. Rosa Méndez smiled too.

"I like Denzel Washington," she said.

Charly Cruz translated and Fate smiled again.

"I've never been friends with a black man," said Rosa Méndez, "I've seen them on TV and walking around sometimes, but there aren't many black people in the city."

That's Rosita for you, said Charly Cruz, a good person, a little bit naïve. Fate didn't understand what he meant by a little bit naïve.

"The truth is, there aren't many black people in Mexico," said Rosa Méndez. "Just a few in Veracruz. Have you ever been to Veracruz?"

Charly Cruz translated. He said that Rosita wanted to know whether he'd ever been to Veracruz. No, I've never been there, said Fate.

"Me neither. I was there on the way somewhere else, when I was fifteen," said Rosa Méndez, "but I've forgotten everything about it. It's like something bad happened to me in Veracruz and my brain erased it. Do you know what I mean?"

This time it was Rosa Amalfitano who translated. She didn't smile like Charly Cruz but just translated what the other woman said in complete seriousness.

"Sure," said Fate, though he didn't understand at all.

Rosa Méndez looked him in the eye and he couldn't have said whether she was making small talk or sharing an intimate secret with him.

"Something must have happened to me there," said Rosa Méndez, "because I really don't remember a thing. I know I was there—not for long, maybe three days or only two—but I don't have a single memory of the city. Has anything like that ever happened to you?"

It probably has, Fate thought, but instead of admitting it he asked whether she liked boxing. Rosa Amalfitano translated the question and Rosa Méndez said that sometimes it was exciting, but only sometimes, especially when the fighter was handsome.

"And what about you?" he asked the girl who spoke English.

"I don't care either way," said Rosa Amalfitano, "this is the first time I've come to something like this."

"The first time?" asked Fate, forgetting that he wasn't a boxing expert either.

Rosa Amalfitano smiled and nodded. Then she lit a cigarette and Fate chose that moment to look in the other direction, and his eyes met the eyes of Chucho Flores. Chucho Flores was looking at him as if he'd never seen him before. Pretty girl, said Charly Cruz next to him. Fate remarked that it was hot. A drop of perspiration was rolling down Rosa Méndez's right temple. She was wearing a low-cut dress revealing large breasts and a cream-colored bra. Let's drink to Merolino, said Rosa Méndez. Charly Cruz, Fate, and Rosa Méndez clinked bottles. Rosa Amalfitano lifted a paper cup, probably full of water or vodka or tequila. Fate thought about asking her which it was, but right away he realized it was a bad idea. You didn't ask women like Rosa Amalfitano that kind of question. Chucho Flores and Corona were the only two members of the group still standing, as if they hadn't yet lost hope of seeing the missing girl appear. Rosa Méndez asked him whether he liked Santa Teresa a lot or too much. Rosa Amalfitano translated. Fate didn't understand the question. Rosa Amalfitano smiled. Fate thought she smiled like a goddess. The beer tasted worse than before, bitter and warm. He was tempted to ask to take a sip from her cup, but that, he knew, was something he'd never do.

"A lot or too much? Which is the right answer?"

"Too much, I think," said Rosa Amalfitano.

"Too much, then," said Fate.

"Have you been to see a bullfight?" asked Rosa Méndez.

"No," said Fate.

"What about a soccer game? A baseball game? Have you been to see our basketball team play?"

"Your friend is very interested in sports," said Fate.

"Not really," said Rosa Amalfitano, "she's just trying to make conversation."

So she's just making conversation? thought Fate. All right, then she's trying to play dumb or act natural. No, she's just trying to be nice, he thought, but he could feel there was more to it.

"I haven't gone to see any of those things," said Fate.

"Aren't you a sportswriter?" asked Rosa Méndez.

Oh, thought Fate, she isn't trying to play dumb or act natural, she's not even trying to be nice, she thinks I'm a sportswriter and so these things must interest me.

"I'm an accidental sportswriter," said Fate, and then he told the two Rosas and Charly Cruz the story of the real sportswriter and his death, and how he'd been sent to cover the Pickett-Fernández fight.

"So what do you write about, then?" asked Charly Cruz.

"Politics," said Fate. "Political things that affect the African-American community. Social things."

"That must be very interesting," said Rosa Méndez.

Fate watched Rosa Amalfitano's lips as she translated. He felt happy to be there.

•

The fight was short. First Count Pickett came out. Polite applause, some boos. Then Merolino Fernández came out. Thundering applause. In the first round, they sized each other up. In the second, Pickett went on the offensive and knocked his opponent out in less than a minute. Merolino Fernández's body didn't even move where it lay on the canvas. His seconds hauled him into his corner and when he didn't recover the medics came in and took him off to the hospital. Count Pickett raised an arm, without much enthusiasm, and left surrounded by his people. The fans began to empty out of the arena.

•

They ate at a place called El Rey del Taco. At the entrance there was a neon sign: a kid wearing a big crown mounted on a burro that regularly kicked up its hind legs and tried to throw him. The boy never fell, although in one hand he was holding a taco and in the other a kind of scepter that could also serve as a riding crop. The inside was decorated like a McDonald's, but in an unsettling way. The chairs were straw, not plastic. The tables were wooden. The floor was covered in big green tiles, some of them printed with desert landscapes and episodes from the life of El Rey del Taco. From the ceiling hung piñatas featuring more adventures of the boy king, always accompanied by the burro. Some of the scenes depicted were charmingly ordinary: the boy, the burro, and a one-eyed old woman, or the boy, the burro, and a well, or the boy, the burro, and a pot of beans. Other scenes were set firmly in the realm of the fantastic: in some the boy and the burro fell down a ravine, in others, the boy and the burro were tied to a funeral pyre, and there was even one in which the boy threatened to shoot his burro, holding a gun to its head. It was as if El Rey del Taco weren't the name of a restaurant but a character in a comic book Fate happened never to have heard of. Still, the feeling of being in a McDonald's persisted. Maybe the waitresses and waiters, very young and dressed in military uniforms (Chucho Flores told him they were dressed up as *federales*), helped create the impression. This was certainly no victorious army. The young waiters radiated exhaustion, although they smiled at the customers. Some of them seemed lost in the desert that was El Rey del Taco. Others, fifteen-year-olds or fourteen-year-olds, tried in vain to joke with some of the diners, men on their own or in pairs who looked like government workers or cops, men who eyed them grimly, in no mood for jokes. Some of the girls had tears in their eyes, and they seemed unreal, faces glimpsed in a dream.

"This place is like hell," he said to Rosa Amalfitano.

"You're right," she said, looking at him sympathetically, "but the food isn't bad."

"I've lost my appetite," said Fate.

"As soon as they put a plate of tacos in front of you it'll come back," said Rosa Amalfitano.

"I hope you're right," said Fate.

•

They had come to the restaurant in three separate cars. Rosa Amalfitano was riding with Chucho Flores. Charly Cruz and Rosa Méndez were riding with silent Corona. Fate drove alone, following the other two cars closely, and more than once, when they seemed to be driving in endless circles around the city, he thought about honking his horn and abandoning the convoy—there was something absurd and childish about it, though he couldn't say exactly what—and heading for the Sonora Resort to write his story about the brief fight he'd just witnessed. Maybe Campbell would still be there and could explain whatever it was he'd missed. Although it's not as if there was anything to understand, if you thought about it. Pickett knew how to fight and Fernández didn't, it was that simple. Or maybe it would be better to skip the Sonora Resort and just drive straight to the border, to Tucson, where he was sure to find a cybercafé at the airport, and write his story, exhausted and without thinking about what he was writing, and then fly to New York, where everything would take on the consistency of reality again.

But instead Fate followed the convoy of cars driving around and around an alien city, with the faint suspicion that the only object of all that driving was to wear him down and get rid of him, although they'd been the ones to ask him along, they'd been the ones who'd said come eat with us and then you can leave for the United States, a last supper in Mexico, speaking without conviction or sincerity, trapped by the formulas of hospitality, a Mexican rite, to which he should have responded by thanking them (effusively!) and then driving away down a nearly empty street with his dignity intact.

But he accepted the invitation. Good idea, he said, I'm hungry. Let's all go get some dinner. As if it was the most natural thing in the world. And although he saw the expression in Chucho Flores's eyes change, and the way Corona was looking at him, even more coldly than Chucho, as if trying to scare him off with his stare or blaming him for the defeat of the Mexican fighter, he insisted on going to eat something typical, my last night in Mexico, what do you say we get some *Mexican* food? Only Charly Cruz seemed amused by the idea that he would stick around with them for dinner, Charly Cruz and the two girls, although in different ways, in keeping with their different personalities, although it was also possible, thought Fate, that the girls were just plain happy, whereas Charly Cruz found himself presented with unexpected possibilities in a landscape that up until then had seemed fixed and devoid of surprise.

•

Why am I here, eating tacos and drinking beer with some Mexicans I hardly know? thought Fate. The answer, he knew, was simple. I'm here for her. They were all speaking Spanish. Only Charly Cruz addressed him in English. Charly Cruz liked to talk about film and he liked to talk in English. His English was fast, as if he were trying to imitate a college student, and full of mistakes. He mentioned the name of a Los Angeles director, Barry Guardini, whom he'd met personally, but Fate had never seen any of Guardini's movies. Then he started to talk about DVDs. He said that in the future everything would be on DVD, or something like DVDs but better, and there'd be no such thing as movie theaters.

The only movie theaters that were worth anything, said Charly Cruz, were the old ones, remember them? those huge theaters where your heart leaped when they turned out the lights. Those places were great, they were real movie theaters, more like churches than anything else, high ceilings, red curtains, pillars, aisles with worn carpeting, box seats, orchestra seats, balcony seats, theaters built at a time when going to the movies was still a religious experience, routine but religious, theaters that were gradually demolished to build banks or supermarkets or multiplexes. Today, said Charly Cruz, there are only a few left, today all movie theaters are multiplexes, with small screens, less space, comfortable seats. Seven of these smaller multiplex theaters would fit into one of the old theaters, the real ones. Or ten. Or even fifteen. And there's no sense of the *abyss* anymore, there's no *vertigo* before the movie begins, no one feels *alone* inside a multiplex. Then, Fate remembered, he began to talk about the end of the *sacred*.

The end had begun somewhere, Charly Cruz didn't care where, maybe in the churches, when the priests stopped celebrating the Mass in Latin, or in families, when the fathers (terrified, believe me, brother) left the mothers. Soon the end of the sacred came to the movies. The big theaters were torn down and up went the hideous boxes called multiplexes, practical, functional. The cathedrals were felled by the wrecking balls of demolition teams. Then the VCR came along. A TV set isn't the same as a movie screen. Your living room isn't the same as the old endless rows of seats. But look carefully and you'll see it's the closest thing to it. In the first place, because with videos you can watch a movie *all by yourself.* You close the windows and you turn on the TV. You pop in the video and you sit in a chair. First off: do it alone. No matter how big or small your house is, it feels bigger with no one else there. Second: be prepared. In other words, rent the movie, buy the drinks you want, the snacks you want, decide what time you're going to sit down in front of the TV. Third: don't answer the phone, ignore the doorbell, be ready to spend an hour and a half or two hours or an hour and forty-five minutes in complete and utter solitude. Fourth: have the remote control within reach in case you want to see a scene more than once. And that's it. After that it all depends on the movie and on you. If things work out, and sometimes they don't, you're back in the presence of the *sacred*. You burrow your head into your own chest and open your eyes and watch, pronounced Charly Cruz.

•

What's sacred to me? thought Fate. The vague pain I feel at the passing of my mother? An understanding of what can't be fixed? Or the kind of pang in the stomach I feel when I look at this woman? And why do I feel a pang, if that's what it is, when she looks at me and not when her friend looks at me? Because her friend is nowhere near as beautiful, thought Fate. Which seems to suggest that what's sacred to me is beauty, a pretty girl with perfect features. And what if all of a sudden the most beautiful actress in Hollywood appeared in the middle of this big, repulsive restaurant, would I still feel a pang each time my eyes surreptitiously met this girl's or would the sudden appearance of a superior beauty, a beauty enhanced by recognition, relieve the pang, diminish her beauty to ordinary levels, the beauty of a slightly odd girl out to have a good time on a weekend night with three slightly peculiar men and a woman who basically seems like a hooker? And who am I to think that Rosita Méndez seems like a hooker? thought Fate. Do I really know enough about Mexican hookers to be able to recognize them at a glance? Do I know anything about innocence or pain? Do I know anything about women? I like to watch videos, thought Fate. I also like to go to the movies. I like to sleep with women. Right now I don't have a steady girl-friend, but I know what it's like to have one. Do I see the *sacred* any-where? All I register is practical experiences, thought Fate. An emptiness to be filled, a hunger to be satisfied, people to talk to so I can finish my article and get paid. And why do I think the men Rosa Amalfitano is out with are *peculiar*? What's peculiar about them? And why am I so sure that if a Hollywood actress appeared all of a sudden Rosa Amalfitano's beauty would fade? What if it didn't? What if it sped up? And what if everything began to accelerate from the instant a Hollywood actress crossed the threshold of El Rey del Taco?

●

Later, he remembered vaguely, they were at a few clubs, maybe three. Actually, it might have been four. No: three. But they were also at a fourth place, which wasn't exactly a club or a private house either. The music was loud. One of the clubs, not the first one, had a patio. From the patio, where they stacked boxes of soft drinks and beer, you could see the sky. A black sky like the bottom of the sea. At some point Fate threw up. Then he laughed because something on the patio struck him as funny. What? He didn't know. Something that was moving or crawling along the chain-link fence. Maybe a sheet of newspaper. When he went back inside he saw Corona kissing Rosa Méndez. Corona's right hand was squeezing one of her breasts. When he passed them, Rosa Méndez opened her eyes and looked at him as if she didn't recognize him. Charly Cruz was leaning on the bar talking to the bartender. Fate asked him where Rosa Amalfitano was. Charly Cruz shrugged. He repeated the question. Charly Cruz looked him in the eyes and said she might be in the ladies' room.

"Where is the ladies' room?" asked Fate.

"Upstairs," said Charly Cruz.

Fate went up the only stairs he could find: a metal staircase that wobbled a little, as if the base were loose. It seemed to him like the staircase on an old-time boat. The staircase ended in a green-carpeted hallway. At the end of the hallway there was an open door. Music was playing. The light that came from the room was green, too. Standing in the middle of the hallway was a skinny kid, who looked at him and then moved toward him. Fate thought he was going to be attacked and he prepared himself mentally to take the first punch. But the kid let him pass and then went down the stairs. His face was very serious, Fate remembered. Then he kept walking until he came to a room where he saw Chucho Flores talking on a cell phone. Next to him, sitting at a desk, was a man in his forties, dressed in a checkered shirt and a bolo tie, who stared at Fate and gestured inquiringly. Chucho Flores caught the gesture and glanced toward the door.

"Come on in, Fate," he said.

The lamp hanging from the ceiling was green. Next to a window, sitting in an armchair, was Rosa Amalfitano. She had her legs crossed and she was smoking. When Fate came through the door she lifted her eyes and looked at him.

"We're doing some business here," said Chucho Flores.

Fate leaned against the wall, feeling short of breath. It's the green color, he thought.

"I see," he said.

Rosa Amalfitano seemed to be high.

•

Fate thought he remembered that someone, at some point, announced it was someone's birthday that night, the birthday of a person who wasn't with them but whom Chucho Flores and Charly Cruz apparently knew. As he drank tequila a woman started to sing "Happy Birthday" in English. Then three men (was Chucho Flores one of them?) started to sing the Mexican birthday song "Las Mañanitas." Many voices joined in. Next to him, standing at the bar, was Rosa Amalfitano. She wasn't singing, but she translated the words of the song. Fate asked her what the connection was between King David and birthdays.

"I don't know," said Rosa. "I'm not Mexican, I'm Spanish."

Fate thought about Spain. He was going to ask her what part of Spain she was from when he saw a man hit a woman in a corner of the room. The first blow made the woman's head snap violently and the second blow knocked her down. Without thinking, Fate tried to move toward them, but someone grabbed his arm. When he turned to see who it was, no one was there. In the opposite corner of the club the man who had hit the woman stepped next to where she was huddled on the ground and kicked her in the stomach. A few feet away from him he saw Rosa Méndez smiling happily. Next to her was Corona, who was looking in a different direction with the usual serious expression on his face. Corona's arm was around Rosa Méndez's shoulders. Every so often she would lift Corona's hand to her mouth and bite his finger. Sometimes Rosa Méndez's teeth bit too hard and then Corona's brow furrowed slightly.

•

At the last place they went Fate saw Omar Abdul and Merolino's other sparring partner. They were drinking alone in a corner of the bar and he went over to say hello. The fighter named García barely nodded in recognition. Omar Abdul, however, gave him a broad smile. Fate asked them how Merolino Fernández was doing.

"Fine, just fine," said Oscar Abdul. "He's at the ranch."

Before Fate said goodbye, Omar Abdul asked him why he hadn't left yet.

"I like this city," said Fate, to say something.

"Brother, this city is a shithole," said Omar Abdul.

"Well, there are some beautiful women here," said Fate.

"The women here aren't worth shit," said Omar Abdul.

"Then you should go back to California," said Fate.

Omar Abdul looked him in the eye and nodded several times.

"I wish I was a goddamn reporter," he said, "you people don't miss a thing."

Fate pulled out some money and beckoned to the bartender. Whatever my friends are having, it's on me, he said. The bartender took the money and looked at the fighters.

"Two more mezcals," said Omar Abdul.

When Fate went back to his table, Chucho Flores asked him whether the fighters were his friends.

"They aren't fighters," said Fate, "they're Merolino's sparring partners."

"García was a fairly well-known fighter in Sonora," said Chucho Flores. "He wasn't very good, but he could stand there and take it better than anybody else."

Fate looked toward the end of the bar. Omar Abdul and García were still there, silent, staring at the rows of bottles.

"One night he went crazy and killed his sister," said Chucho Flores. "His lawyer argued temporary insanity and all he did was eight years in the prison at Hermosillo. When he got out he didn't want to box anymore. For a while he was with the Arizona Pentecostalists. But God never gave him the gift of speech and one day he stopped preaching the Word and started working the door at some clubs. Until López, Merolino's trainer, showed up, and hired him as a sparring partner."

"A couple of fuckups," said Corona.

"Yes," said Fate, "judging by the fight, a couple of fuckups."

•

Then, and this he did remember clearly, they ended up at Charly Cruz's house. He remembered because of the videos. Specifically, the video that was supposed to be by Robert Rodriguez. Charly Cruz's house was big, as solid as a two-story bunker—that he also remembered clearly— and it cast its shadow over a vacant lot. There was no yard, but there was a garage for four or maybe five cars. At some point during the night, although this was much less clear, a fourth man had joined the convoy. The fourth man didn't talk much but he kept smiling for no reason and he seemed nice. He was dark-skinned and he had a mustache. And he rode with Fate, in his car, sitting next to him, smiling at every word Fate said. Every so often he looked behind them and every so often he checked his watch. But he didn't say a single word.

"Can't you talk?" Fate asked him in English after several attempts to start a conversation. "Cat got your tongue? Motherfucker, why do you keep looking at your watch?" And the man invariably smiled and nodded.

Charly Cruz's car led the way, followed by Chucho Flores's car. Sometimes Fate could see the shapes of Chucho and Rosa Amalfitano. Usually when they stopped at a stoplight. Sometimes the two shapes were very close together, as if they were kissing. Other times all he saw was the shape of the driver. At one point he tried to pull up alongside Chucho Flores's car, but he couldn't.

"What time is it?" he asked the man with the mustache, and the man shrugged his shoulders.

In Charly Cruz's garage there was a mural painted on one of the cement walls. The mural was six feet tall and maybe ten feet long and showed the Virgin of Guadalupe in the middle of a lush landscape of rivers and forests and gold mines and silver mines and oil rigs and giant cornfields and wheat fields and vast meadows where cattle grazed. The Virgin had her arms spread wide, as if offering all of these riches in exchange for nothing. But despite being drunk, Fate noticed right away there was something wrong about her face. One of the Virgin's eyes was open and the other eye was closed.

●

The house had many rooms. Some were used just for storage and were stacked full of videos and DVDs from Charly Cruz's video stores or his private collection. The living room was on the first floor. Two armchairs and two leather sofas and a wooden table and a TV. The armchairs were good but old. The floor was yellow tile edged with black and it was dirty. Not even a couple of multicolored Indian rugs could hide it. A full-length mirror hung on one wall. On the other wall there was a poster for a Mexican movie from the 1950s, framed and protected behind glass. Charly Cruz said it was the original poster for a very rare film, of which almost all the copies had been lost. Bottles of liquor were kept in a glass cabinet. Next to the living room was an apparently unused room where there was a latest-generation music system and a cardboard box full of CDs. Rosa Méndez knelt next to the box and began to dig through it.

"Women go crazy for music," Charly Cruz said into Fate's ear, "I go crazy for movies."

The nearness of Charly Cruz startled Fate. Only then did he realize that the room had no windows and it struck him as odd that anyone would choose it for the living room, especially since the house was so big and there had to be lots of rooms with more light. When the music started, Corona and Chucho Flores each took a girl by the arm and left the living room. The man with the mustache sat in an armchair and looked at his watch. Charly Cruz asked Fate whether he was interested in seeing the Robert Rodriguez movie. Fate nodded. The man with the mustache, because of the angle of his chair, couldn't see the movie without craning his neck exaggeratedly, but he showed no curiosity at all. He just sat there looking at them and every so often looking at the ceiling.

The movie, according to Charlie Cruz, was half an hour long at most.

An old woman with a heavily made-up face looked into the camera. After a while she began to whisper incomprehensible words and weep. She looked like a whore who'd retired and, Fate thought at times, was facing death. Then a thin, dark-skinned young woman with big breasts took off her clothes while seated on a bed. Out of the darkness came three men who first whispered in her ear and then fucked her. At first the woman resisted. She looked straight at the camera and said something in Spanish that Fate didn't understand. Then she faked an orgasm and started to scream. After that, the men, who until that moment had been taking turns, joined in all together, the first penetrating her vagina, the second her anus, and the third sticking his cock in her mouth. The effect was of a perpetual-motion machine. The spectator could see that the machine was going to explode at some point, but it was impossible to say what the explosion would be like and when it would happen. And then the woman came for real. An unforeseen orgasm that she was the last to expect. The woman's movements, constrained by the weight of the three men, accelerated. Her eyes were fixed on the camera, which in turn zoomed in on her face. Her eyes said something, although they spoke in an unidentifiable language. For an instant, everything about her seemed to shine, her breasts gleamed, her chin glistened, half hidden by the shoulder of one of the men, her teeth took on a supernatural whiteness. Then the flesh seemed to melt from her bones and drop to the floor of the anonymous brothel or vanish into thin air, leaving just a skeleton, no eyes, no lips, a death's-head laughing suddenly at everything. Then there was a street in a big Mexican city at dusk, probably Mexico City, a street swept by rain, cars parked along the curb, stores with their metal gates lowered, people walking fast so as not to be soaked. A puddle of rainwater. Water washing clean a car coated in a thick layer of dust. The lighted-up windows of government buildings. A bus stop next to a small park. The branches of a sick tree stretching vainly toward nothing. The face of the old whore, who smiles at the camera now as if to say: did I do it right? did I look good? is everybody happy? A redbrick staircase comes into view. A linoleum floor. The same rain, but filmed from inside a room. A plastic table with nicked edges. Glasses and a jar of Nescafé. A frying pan with the remains of scrambled eggs. A hallway. The body of a half-dressed woman sprawled on the floor. A door. A room in complete disarray. Two men sleeping in the same bed. A mirror. The camera zooms in on the mirror. The tape ends.

"Where's Rosa?" asked Fate when the movie ended.

"There's a second tape," said Charly Cruz.

"Where's Rosa?"

"In some room," said Charly Cruz, "sucking Chucho's dick."

Then he got up and went out of the room, and when he came back he had the remaining tape in his hand. As he rewound the video, Fate said he had to use the bathroom.

"End of the hall, fourth door," said Charly Cruz. "But you don't want to use the bathroom, you want to look for Rosa, you lying gringo."

Fate laughed.

"Well, maybe Chucho needs some help," he said as if he were asleep and drunk at the same time.

When he got up, the man with the mustache started. Charly Cruz said something to him in Spanish and he settled comfortably back in the armchair. Fate walked along the hallway, counting doors. When he got to the third door he heard a noise from the floor above. He paused. The noise stopped. The bathroom was big and looked like something straight out of a design magazine. The walls and floor were white marble. At least four people could fit into the bathtub, which was circular. Next to the bathtub was a big oak box in the shape of a coffin. A coffin from which the head would protrude, and that Fate would have said was a sauna, if the box weren't so narrow. The toilet was black marble. Next to it was a bidet and next to the bidet was a marble protuberance a foot and a half high whose purpose Fate was unable to discern. By a stretch of the imagination, you might say it looked like a chair or a saddle. But he couldn't imagine anyone sitting there, not in a normal position. Maybe it was used to hold towels for the bidet. As he urinated, he gazed at the wooden box and the marble sculpture. For an instant he thought both things were alive. Behind him was a mirror that covered the whole wall and made the bathroom seem bigger than it was. Looking to the left, Fate saw the wooden coffin, and turning his head to the right, he saw the protuberant marble fixture. At one point he looked behind him and saw his own back, standing in front of the toilet, flanked by the coffin and the useless-seeming saddle. The sense of unreality that dogged him that night was heightened.

He climbed the stairs trying not to make a sound. In the living room Charly Cruz and the man with the mustache were talking in Spanish. Charly Cruz's voice was soothing. The voice of the man with the mustache was squeaky, as if his vocal cords were atrophied. The noise he'd heard in the hallway repeated itself. The stairs ended in a room with a big window behind the dark brown plastic slats of a venetian blind. Fate went down another hallway. He opened a door. Rosa Méndez was lying facedown on a military-looking bed. She was dressed and had high heels on, but she seemed to be asleep or to have passed out. The room was furnished with only a bed and chair. The floor, unlike the floor downstairs, was carpeted, so his steps made almost no sound. He went over to the girl and turned her head. Rosa Méndez smiled without opening her eyes. This hallway led to another. Fate could see light coming from under one of the doors. He heard Chucho Flores and Corona arguing, but he didn't know what they were arguing about. He thought they both wanted to fuck Rosa Amalfitano. Then he thought maybe they were arguing about him. Corona sounded truly angry. He opened the door without knocking and the two men turned around at once, their faces stamped with a mixture of surprise and sleepiness. Now I have to try to be what I am, thought Fate, a black guy from Harlem, a terrifying Harlem motherfucker. Almost immediately he realized that neither of the Mexicans was impressed.

"Where's Rosa?" he asked.

Chucho Flores managed to point to a corner of the room that Fate hadn't seen. I've lived this scene before, thought Fate. Rosa was sitting in an armchair, with her legs crossed, snorting cocaine.

"Let's go," he said.

He didn't order her or plead with her. He just asked her to come with him, but he put all his soul into the words. Rosa smiled at him sympathetically, but she didn't seem to understand. He heard Chucho Flores say in English: get out of here, amigo, wait for us downstairs. Fate held out his hand to the girl. Rosa got up and took it. Her hand felt warm, its temperature evoking other scenarios but also evoking or encompassing their current sordid circumstances. When he took it he became conscious of the coldness of his own hand. I've been dying all this time, he thought. I'm as cold as ice. If she hadn't taken my hand I would've died right here and they would've had to send my body back to New York.

•

As they left the room he felt Corona grab his arm and saw him lift his free hand, which seemed to be holding a blunt instrument. He turned around and dealt Corona an uppercut to the chin, in the style of Count Pickett. Like Merolino Fernández earlier, Corona dropped to the floor without a sound. Only then did Fate realize Corona was holding a gun. He took it away from him and asked Chucho Flores what he planned to do.

"I'm not jealous, amigo," said Chucho Flores with his hands raised at chest height so that Fate could see he wasn't carrying a weapon.

Rosa Amalfitano looked at Corona's gun as if it were a sex-shop contraption.

"Let's go," he heard her say.

"Who's the guy downstairs?" asked Fate.

"Charly, your friend Charly Cruz," said Chucho Flores, smiling.

"No, you son of a bitch, the other one, the one with the mustache."

"A friend of Charly's," said Chucho Flores.

"Is there another way out of this goddamn house?"

Chucho Flores shrugged.

"Listen, man, aren't you taking this too far?" he asked.

"Yes, there's a back door," said Rosa Amalfitano.

Fate looked at Corona's fallen body and seemed to reflect for a few seconds.

"The car is in the garage," he said, "we can't leave without it."

"Then you'll have to go out the front door," said Chucho Flores.

"What about him?" asked Rosa Amalfitano, pointing to Corona, "is he dead?"

Fate looked again at the limp body on the floor. He could have stared for hours.

"Let's go," he said in a decisive voice.

They went down the stairs, passed through an enormous kitchen that smelled of neglect, as if it had been a long time since anyone cooked there, crossed a hallway with a view of a courtyard where there was a pickup truck covered by a black tarp, and then walked entirely in the dark until they reached the door that led down to the garage. When Fate turned on the lights, two big fluorescent tubes hanging from the ceiling, he took another look at the mural of the Virgin of Guadalupe. When he moved to open the garage door he realized that the Virgin's single open eye seemed to follow him wherever he went. He put Chucho Flores in the front passenger seat and Rosa got in the back. As they drove out of the garage he caught a glimpse of the man with the mustache. He had appeared at the top of the stairs and was looking around for them with the expression of a startled adolescent.

They left Charly Cruz's house behind and turned down unpaved streets. Without realizing it, they crossed an empty stretch that gave off a strong smell of weeds and rotting food. Fate stopped the car, cleaned the gun with a handkerchief, and threw it into the lot.

"What a pretty night," murmured Chucho Flores.

Neither Rosa nor Fate said anything.

•

They left Chucho Flores at a bus stop on a deserted and brightly lit street. Rosa got in the front seat, giving Chucho Flores a parting slap in the face. Then they headed down a labyrinth of streets that neither Rosa nor Fate recognized, until they came out onto another street that led straight to the center of the city.

"I think I've been an idiot," said Fate.

"I was the idiot," said Rosa.

"No, I was," said Fate.

They started to laugh, and after circling the city center a few times, they let themselves be caught up in the stream of cars with Mexican and American license plates heading out of the city.

"Where are we going?" asked Fate. "Where do you live?"

She said she didn't want to go home yet. They passed Fate's motel, and for a few seconds he didn't know whether to keep going to the border or stay there. Half a mile farther down the road he turned around and headed south again, toward the motel. The clerk recognized him. He asked how the fight had gone.

"Merolino lost," said Fate.

"Of course," said the clerk.

Fate asked whether his room was still vacant. The clerk said it was. Fate stuck his hand in his pocket and pulled out the key to the room, which he had kept.

"That's right," he said.

He paid for another night and then he went out. Rosa was waiting for him in the car.

"You can stay here for a while," said Fate, "and whenever you say I'll take you home."

Rosa nodded and they went in. The bed was made and the sheets were clean. The two windows were open a crack. Maybe the cleaning person had noticed a trace of vomit smell, thought Fate. But the room smelled fine. Rosa turned on the TV and sat in a chair.

"I've been watching you," she said.

"I'm flattered," said Fate.

"Why did you clean the gun before you got rid of it?" asked Rosa.

"You never know," said Fate, "but I'd rather not go around leaving fingerprints on firearms."

Then Rosa focused her attention on the TV show, a Mexican talk show that was essentially just an old woman talking. She had long white hair. Sometimes she smiled and you could tell she was a nice, harmless little old lady, but most of the time she had a grave expression on her face, as if she were addressing matters of great importance. Of course, he didn't understand a thing she said. Then Rosa got up from the chair, turned off the TV, and asked whether she could take a shower. Fate nodded. When Rosa went into the bathroom and closed the door he began to think about everything that had happened that night and his stomach hurt. He felt a wave of heat rise to his face. He sat on the bed, covered his face with his hands, and thought of what an idiot he'd been.

•

When she came out of the bathroom, Rosa told him that she had been Chucho Flores's girlfriend, or something like that. She was lonely in Santa Teresa and one day she met Rosa Méndez at Charly Cruz's video store, where she went to rent movies. She couldn't say why, but she liked Rosa Méndez from the moment she met her. During the day, according to Rosa Méndez, she worked at a supermarket and at night she worked as a waitress at a restaurant. She liked movies and she loved thrillers. Maybe what Rosa Amalfitano liked about Rosa Méndez was her perpetual cheerfulness and also her bleached-blond hair, which contrasted strongly with her dark skin.

One day Rosa Méndez introduced her to Charly Cruz, the owner of the video store, whom she'd seen only a few times, and Charly Cruz struck her as a relaxed person, someone who took things easy, and sometimes he loaned her movies or didn't charge her for the movies she rented. Often she would spend whole afternoons at the video store, talking to them or helping Charly Cruz unpack new shipments of movies.

One night, when the store was about to close, she met Chucho Flores. That same night Chucho Flores took them all out to dinner and later he gave her a ride home, although when she invited him in he said he'd rather pass, because he didn't want to bother her father. But she gave him her phone number and Chucho Flores called the next day and asked her out to the movies. When Rosa got to the theater, Chucho Flores was there with Rosa Méndez and her date, an older man around fifty who said he was in the real estate business and who treated Chucho like a nephew. After the movie they had dinner at a fancy restaurant and later Chucho Flores dropped her off at home, claiming that the next day he had to get up early because he was going to Hermosillo to interview someone for the radio.

Around that time, Rosa Amalfitano saw Rosa Méndez not just at Charly Cruz's video store but also at her place in Colonia Madero, in an apartment on the fourth floor of an old five-story building with no elevator, for which Rosa Méndez paid lots of money. At first, Rosa Méndez had shared the apartment with two friends, so the rent wasn't too bad. But one friend left to try her luck in Mexico City and she had a fight with the other friend, and after that she lived alone. Rosa Méndez liked to live alone, even though she had to work a second job to afford it. Sometimes Rosa Amalfitano would spend hours at Rosa Méndez's apartment, not talking, lying on the couch drinking *agua fresca* and listening to her friend's stories. Sometimes they talked about men. Here, as elsewhere, Rosa Méndez's experience was richer and more varied than Rosa Amalfitano's. She was twenty-four and she'd had, in her own words, four lovers who'd changed her in some way. The first was when she was fifteen, a guy who worked at a maquiladora and left her to go to the United States. She remembered him fondly, but of all her lovers he was the one who'd left the least mark on her. When she said this Rosa Amalfitano laughed and Rosa Méndez laughed too without knowing exactly why.

"You sound like a *bolero*," Rosa Amalfitano told her.

"Oh, so that's it," answered Rosa Méndez, "well, *boleros* are true, *mana*, the words of the songs come from deep inside all of us and they're always right."

"No," said Rosa Amalfitano, "they *seem* right, they *seem* authentic, but they're actually full of shit."

At this point, Rosa Méndez would give up arguing. Tacitly she acknowledged that her friend, who was in college, after all, knew more about these things than she did. The boyfriend who'd left for the United States, she explained again, was the one who'd left the least mark on her but also the one she missed the most. How was that possible? She didn't know. The other ones, the ones who came later, were different. And that was all. One day Rosa Méndez told Rosa Amalfitano what it felt like to make love with a policeman.

"It's the best," she said.

"Why, what difference does it make?" her friend wanted to know.

"It's hard to explain, *mana*," said Rosa Méndez, "but it's like fucking a man who isn't exactly a man. It's like becoming a little girl again, if that makes sense. It's like being fucked by a rock. A mountain. You know you'll be there, on your knees, until the mountain says it's over. And that in the end you'll be full."

"Full of what?" asked Rosa Amalfitano, "full of semen?"

"No, *mana*, don't be disgusting, full of something else, it's like you're fucking a mountain but you're fucking *inside* a cave, know what I mean?"

"In a cave?" asked Rosa Amalfitano.

"That's right," said Rosa Méndez.

"In other words it's like being fucked by a mountain in a cave inside the mountain itself," said Rosa Amalfitano.

"Exactly," said Rosa Méndez.

And then she said:

"I love how you say *follar* for fuck; people from Spain talk so pretty."

"You're weird, you know," said Rosa Amalfitano.

"I always have been, ever since I was little," said Rosa Méndez.

And she added:

"Want me to tell you something else?"

"What?" asked Rosa Amalfitano.

"I've fucked *narcos*. I swear. Do you want to know what it feels like? Well, it feels like being fucked by the air. That's exactly how it feels."

"So fucking a policeman is like being fucked by a mountain and fucking a *narco* is like being fucked by the air."

"Yes," said Rosa Méndez, "but not the air we breathe or the air we feel when we go outside, but the desert air, a blast of air, air that doesn't taste the same as the air here and doesn't smell like nature or the country, air that smells the way it smells, that has its own smell, a smell you can't explain, it's just air, pure air, so much air that sometimes it's hard to breathe and you feel like you're going to suffocate."

"So," concluded Rosa Amalfitano, "if a policeman fucks you it's like being fucked by a mountain inside the mountain itself, and if a *narco* fucks you it's like being fucked by the desert air."

"That's right, *mana*, if a *narco* fucks you it's always out in the open."

Around that time, Rosa Amalfitano started to officially date Chucho Flores. He was the first Mexican she slept with. At the university there had been two or three boys who tried to flirt with her, but nothing happened. She did go to bed with Chucho Flores, though. The courtship period wasn't long, but it lasted longer than Rosa expected. When he came back from Hermosillo, Chucho Flores brought her a pearl necklace. Alone, in front of the mirror, Rosa tried it on, and although the necklace had a certain appeal (and had probably cost a lot), she couldn't imagine ever wearing it. Rosa had a long, beautiful neck, but that necklace required a different kind of wardrobe. Other gifts followed: sometimes, as they walked along the streets where the fashionable stores were, Chucho Flores would stop in front of a window and point out something she should try on, telling her that if she liked it he'd buy it for her. Usually Rosa would try on the thing he'd suggested and then she'd try on other things and in the end she'd end up with something to her taste. Chucho Flores also gave her art books, since he'd once heard her talk about painting, and about painters whose works she'd seen in famous European museums. Other times he gave her CDs, mostly of classical music, although sometimes, like a tour guide with an eye for local color, he mixed in music from the north of Mexico or Mexican folk music, which later, alone at home, Rosa listened to distractedly as she washed the dishes or loaded the dirty clothes in the washing machine.

At night they would go out to eat at nice restaurants, where they invariably ran into men and, less often, women, who knew Chucho Flores, and to whom Chucho Flores introduced her as his friend, Miss Rosa Amalfitano, daughter of the philosophy professor Óscar Amalfitano, my friend Rosa, Miss Amalfitano, immediately prompting a paean to her beauty and elegance, and then commentary on Spain and Barcelona, a city they had all visited as tourists, every one of them, the distinguished citizens of Santa Teresa, and for which they had nothing but words of praise and admiration. One night, instead of driving her home, Chucho Flores asked her if she wanted to go for a ride with him. Rosa expected he would take her to his apartment, but they headed west out of Santa

Teresa, and after driving for half an hour along a lonely highway they came to a motel where Chucho Flores got a room. The motel was in the middle of the desert, just before a slight rise, and alongside the highway there was only gray brush, sometimes with its wind-scoured roots exposed. The room was big and in the bathroom there was a Jacuzzi like a small pool. The bed was round and the mirrors on the walls and part of the ceiling made it seem bigger. The carpet on the floor was thick, almost like a cushion. Instead of a minibar there was a small real bar stocked with all kinds of liquor and soft drinks. When Rosa asked him why he'd brought her to a place like this, the kind of place rich men brought their whores, Chucho Flores thought for a while and then he said it was for the mirrors. He sounded apologetic. Then he undressed her and they fucked on the bed and on the carpet.

At first, Chucho Flores was more gentle than anything else, more concerned about his partner's satisfaction than his own. Finally Rosa came and then Chucho Flores stopped fucking and took a little metal box out of his jacket. Rosa thought it would be cocaine, but instead of white powder the box held tiny yellow pills. Chucho Flores took out two pills and swallowed them with a little bit of whiskey. For a while they talked, lying in bed, until he got on top of her again. This time he wasn't gentle at all. Surprised, Rosa didn't protest or say anything. It seemed as if Chucho Flores would put her in every possible position, and some of them—this Rosa realized later—she liked. When the sun came up they stopped fucking and left the motel.

There were other cars in the courtyard parking lot, shielded from the highway by a redbrick wall. The air was cool and dry and had a faintly musky smell. The motel and everything around it seemed sealed in a pocket of silence. As they walked through the parking lot to the car they heard a rooster crow. The noise of the car doors opening, the engine starting, and the tires crunching the gravel seemed to Rosa like the sound of a drum. No trucks went by on the highway.

•

After that, things with Chucho Flores got stranger and stranger. There were days when it seemed he couldn't live without her, and other days when he treated her like his slave. Some nights they slept at his apartment and when she woke up in the morning he'd be gone, because there were times he got up very early to do a live radio show called *Good Morning, Sonora*, or *Good Morning, Friends*, she wasn't sure because she never heard it from the beginning, a show for truck drivers crossing the border in either direction and bus drivers carrying workers to the factories and anyone who had to get up early in Santa Teresa. When Rosa got up she made herself breakfast, usually a glass of orange juice and a piece of toast or a cookie, and then she washed the plate, the glass, the juicer, and left. Other times she stayed for a while, looking out the windows at the sprawl of the city under the cobalt-blue sky, and then she made the bed and wandered around the apartment, with nothing to do except think about her life and the strange Mexican she was involved with. She wondered whether he loved her, whether what he felt for her was love, whether she loved him herself, or whether she was just attracted to him, whether she felt anything for him at all, and whether this was all she could expect from being with another person.

Some afternoons they got in his car and sped east to a mountain overlook from which Santa Teresa was visible in the distance, the first lights of the city, the enormous black parachute that dropped gradually over the desert. Each time they went, after silently watching day change to night, Chucho Flores would unzip his pants and push her head down to his crotch. Then Rosa would take his penis in her mouth, barely sucking it until it got hard, and then she would begin to run her tongue over it. When Chucho Flores was about to come, she could tell by the pressure of his hand on her head, forcing her down. Rosa would stop moving her tongue and be still, as if having his whole penis in her mouth had choked her, until she felt the spurt of semen in her throat, and even then she didn't move, although she could hear her lover's moans and his exclamations, often bizarre, because he liked to say crude things and swear as he came, not at her but at unspecified people, ghosts who appeared for just a moment and were as quickly lost in the night. Then, with a salty, bitter taste still in her mouth, she would light a cigarette as Chucho Flores took a folded cigarette paper out of his silver cigarette case, tipping the cocaine it held onto the inner lid of the case, the outside of which was engraved with bucolic ranching motifs, and then, in no hurry, he would cut three lines with one of his credit cards and snort them with a business card, one that read Chucho Flores, reporter and radio correspondent, and then the address of the radio station.

One of those evenings, without having been asked (since Chucho had never once offered to share his coke with her), Rosa told him to leave her the last line as she wiped a few drops of semen from her lips with the palm of her hand. Chucho Flores asked whether she was sure, and then, with a gesture of indifference but also of deference, he handed her the cigarette case and a fresh business card. Rosa snorted all the cocaine that was left and then lay back in her seat and looked up at the black clouds, indistinguishable from the black sky.

That night, when she got home, she went out into the yard and saw her father talking to the book that for some time had been hanging from the clothesline in the backyard. Then, before her father noticed she was there, she shut herself in her room to read a novel and think about her relationship with the Mexican.

●

Of course, the Mexican and her father had met. Chucho Flores came away from this meeting with a positive feeling, although Rosa thought he was lying, since it didn't make sense for a person to like anyone who looked at him the way her father had looked at Chucho Flores. That night Amalfitano asked the Mexican three questions. The first was what he thought of hexagons. The second was whether he knew how to construct a hexagon. The third was what he thought about the killings of women in Santa Teresa. Chucho Flores's reply to the first question was that he didn't think anything. The second question he answered with an honest no. In response to the third question, he said that it was regrettable, but the police were catching the killers one by one. Rosa's father didn't ask any more questions and sat motionless in his chair as his daughter walked Chucho Flores to the door. When Rosa came back in, and before the sound of her boyfriend's car engine had faded in the distance, Óscar Amalfitano told his daughter to be careful, he had a bad feeling about that man, offering no further explanation.

"So what you mean is," said Rosa from the kitchen, laughing, "I should dump him."

"Dump him," said Óscar Amalfitano.

"Oh, Dad, you just keep getting crazier," said Rosa.

"It's true," said Óscar Amalfitano.

"So what are we going to do? What can we do?"

"You: leave that ignorant, lying piece of shit. Me: I don't know, maybe when we get back to Europe I'll check into the Clínico for an electroshock treatment."

●

The second time Chucho Flores and Óscar Amalfitano met face-to-face, Chucho Flores had come to drop Rosa off at home, along with Charly Cruz and Rosa Méndez. Actually, Óscar Amalfitano should have been at the university teaching classes, but that afternoon he had pleaded illness and come home much earlier than usual. It was a brief encounter, since Rosa made sure her friends left as soon as possible, but her father happened to be unusually sociable, and a conversation was struck up between him and Charly Cruz, which if not pleasant at least wasn't boring, and in fact, as the days went by, in Rosa's memory the conversation between her father and Charly began to take on sharper outlines, as if time, in the classic embodiment of an old man, were blowing incessantly on a flat gray stone covered in dust, until the black grooves of the letters carved into the stone were perfectly legible.

Everything began, Rosa guessed—since at the time she was in the kitchen, not the living room, pouring four glasses of mango juice—with one of the mischievous questions her father often sprang on guests, her guests, of course, not his own guests, or maybe it all began with some declaration of principles by innocent Rosa Méndez, since her voice seemed to dominate the conversation in the living room in the first few moments. Maybe Rosa Méndez was talking about how much she loved movies and then Óscar Amalfitano asked her if she knew what apparent movement was. But inevitably it was Charly Cruz, not Rosa Méndez, who answered, saying that apparent movement was the illusion of movement caused by the persistence of images on the retina.

"Exactly," said Óscar Amalfitano, "images linger on the retina for a fraction of a second."

And then, brushing aside Rosa Méndez, who might have said wow, because her ignorance was great but so was her capacity for astonishment and her desire to learn, her father asked Charly Cruz directly if he knew who had discovered this thing, this persistence of the image, and Charly Cruz said he didn't remember the name, but he was sure it had been a Frenchman. To which her father replied:

"That's right, a Frenchman by the name of Professor Plateau."

Who, once the principle had been discovered, launched himself ferociously into experiments with different devices he built himself, with the object of creating the effect of movement from the rapid succession of fixed images. Then the zoetrope was born.

"Do you know what that is?" asked Óscar Amalfitano.

"I had one when I was a boy," said Charly Cruz. "And I had a magic disk, too."

"A magic disk," said Óscar Amalfitano. "Interesting. Do you remember it? Could you describe it to me?"

"I could make one for you right now," said Charly Cruz, "all I need is a piece of cardboard, two colored pencils, and a piece of string, if I'm not mistaken."

"Oh no, oh no, oh no, no need for that," said Óscar Amalfitano. "A good description is enough for me. In a way, we all have millions of magic disks floating or spinning in our brains."

"Oh, really?" said Charly Cruz.

"Wow," said Rosa Méndez.

"Well, there was a little old drunk, laughing. That was the picture on one side of the disk. And on the other side was a picture of a prison cell, or the bars of a cell. When you spun the disk the laughing drunk looked like he was behind bars."

"Which isn't really a laughing matter, is it?" said Óscar Amalfitano.

"No, it isn't," said Charly Cruz with a sigh.

"Still, the drunk (by the way, why do you call him a little old drunk and not just a drunk?) was laughing, maybe because *he* knew he wasn't in jail."

For a few seconds, remembered Rosa, Charly Cruz's gaze altered, as if he were trying to see where her father was going with all this. Charly Cruz, as we've already said, was a relaxed man, and for those few seconds, although his poise and natural calm were unshaken, something did happen behind his face, as if the lens through which he was observing her father, Rosa remembered, had stopped working and he was proceeding, *calmly*, to change it, an operation that took less than a fraction of a second, but during which his gaze was necessarily left naked or empty, *vacant*, in any case, since one lens was being removed and another inserted, and both operations couldn't be carried out simultaneously, and for that fraction of a second, which Rosa remembered as if she had invented it herself, Charly Cruz's face was empty or it emptied, and the speed at which this happened was startling, say the speed of light, to put it in exaggerated but nevertheless roughly accurate terms, and the emptying of the face was complete, hair and teeth included, although to say hair and teeth in the presence of that blankness was like saying nothing, all of Charly Cruz's features emptied, his wrinkles, his veins, his pores, everything left defenseless, everything acquiring a dimension to which the only response, remembered Rosa, could be vertigo and nausea, although it wasn't.

"The *little old drunk* is laughing because he thinks he's free, but he's really in prison," said Óscar Amalfitano, "that's what makes it funny, but in fact the prison is drawn on the other side of the disk, which means one could also say that the *little old drunk* is laughing because we think he's in prison, not realizing that the prison is on one side and the *little old drunk* is on the other, and that's reality, no matter how much we spin the disk and it looks to us as if the *little old drunk* is behind bars. In fact, we could even guess what the *little old drunk* is laughing about: he's laughing at our credulity, you might even say at our eyes."

•

A little later something happened that upset Rosa quite a bit. She was on her way back from the university, walking along, and suddenly she heard someone calling her name. A boy her age, a classmate, pulled up at the curb and offered her a ride home. Instead of getting in the car, she said she'd rather go have a soda at a nearby coffee shop that had air-conditioning. The boy offered to take her and Rosa accepted. She got in the car and gave him directions. The coffee shop was new and spacious, in the shape of an L, American-style with rows of tables and big windows that let in the sun. For a while they talked about random things. Then the boy said he had to go and he got up. They kissed each other goodbye on the cheek and Rosa asked the waitress to bring her a cup of coffee. Then she opened a book on Mexican painting in the twentieth century and began to read a chapter on Paalen. At that time of day, the coffee shop was half empty. Voices could be heard coming from the kitchen, a woman giving another woman advice, the steps of the waitress who came by every so often to offer more coffee to the few customers scattered around the big space. Suddenly someone she hadn't heard approach her said: you whore. The voice startled her and she looked up, thinking it was a bad joke or that she'd been mistaken for someone else. Standing there was Chucho Flores. Flustered, all she could do was tell him to sit down, but Chucho Flores, his lips barely moving, told her to get up and follow him. She asked him where he planned to go. Home, said Chucho Flores. He was sweating and his face was flushed. Rosa told him she wasn't going anywhere. Then Chucho Flores asked her who the boy was who had kissed her.

"A classmate," said Rosa, and she noticed that Chucho Flores's hands were shaking.

"You whore," he said again.

And then he began to mutter something that Rosa couldn't understand at first, but after a moment she realized he was repeating the same words over and over again: you whore, uttered with teeth clenched, as if saying it cost him a huge effort.

"Let's go," shouted Chucho Flores.

"I'm not going anywhere with you," said Rosa, and she looked around to see whether anyone had noticed the scene they were making. But no one was looking at them and she felt better.

"Have you slept with him?" asked Chucho Flores.

For a few seconds Rosa didn't know what he was talking about. The air-conditioning seemed too cold. She wanted to go outside and stand in the sun. If she'd brought a sweater or a vest she would've put it on.

"You're the only person I sleep with," she said, trying to soothe him.

"Lies," shouted Chucho Flores.

The waitress appeared at the other end of the room and came toward them, but she changed her mind halfway and went to stand at the counter.

"Don't be ridiculous, please," Rosa said, and she fixed her gaze on the Paalen article but all she saw were black ants and then black spiders on a bed of salt. The ants were battling the spiders.

"Let's go home," she heard Chucho Flores say. She felt cold.

When she looked up she saw he was about to cry.

"You're my only love," said Chucho Flores. "I'd give everything for you. I'd die for you."

For a few seconds she didn't know what to say. Maybe the time has come to end things, she thought.

"I'm nothing without you," said Chucho Flores. "You're all I have. All I need. You're all I've ever dreamed of. If I lost you I would die."

The waitress watched them from behind the counter. Some twenty tables away, a man was drinking coffee and reading the paper. He was wearing a short-sleeved shirt and a tie. The sun seemed to vibrate against the windows.

"Sit down, please," said Rosa.

Chucho Flores pulled out the chair he was leaning on and sat down. Immediately he covered his face with his hands and Rosa thought he was going to shout again or cry. What a spectacle, she thought.

"Do you want something to drink?"

Chucho Flores nodded.

"Coffee," he whispered without moving his hands from his face.

Rosa turned to the waitress and beckoned to her.

"Two coffees," she said.

"Yes, miss," said the waitress.

"The guy you saw me with is just a friend. Not even a friend: a class-mate. The kiss he gave me was on the cheek. It's normal," said Rosa. "It's something people do."

Chucho Flores laughed and shook his head from side to side without moving his hands from his face.

"Of course, of course," he said. "It's normal, I know. I'm sorry."

The waitress came back with the coffeepot and a cup for Chucho Flores. First she filled Rosa's cup and then the other cup. As she moved away, her eyes met Rosa's and she made a sign, or that was what Rosa thought later. A sign with her eyebrows. She arched them. Or maybe she moved her lips. A word articulated in silence. She couldn't remember. But the waitress was trying to tell her something.

"Drink your coffee," said Rosa.

"I will," said Chucho Flores, but he didn't move, his hands still over his face.

Another man had come in and sat next to the door. The waitress was standing at his table and they were talking. The man was wearing a baggy denim jacket and a black sweatshirt. He was thin and probably no older than twenty-five. Rosa looked at him and the man noticed that she was looking at him, but he ignored her and drank his soda, not returning her gaze.

•

"Three days later I met you," said Rosa.

"Why did you come to the fight?" asked Fate. "Do you like boxing?"

"No, I already told you it was the first time I'd been, but it was Rosa who convinced me to come."

"The other Rosa," said Fate.

"Yes, Rosita Méndez," said Rosa.

"But after the fight you were going to make love with Chucho Flores," said Fate.

"No," said Rosa. "I took his cocaine, but I had no intention of going to bed with him. I can't stand jealous men, but I was willing to be his friend. We had talked about it on the phone and he seemed to understand. But I did think he was acting strange. In the car, looking for a restaurant, he wanted me to give him a blow job. He said: blow me one last time. Or maybe he didn't say it like that, in those words, but that was more or less what he meant. I asked him if he'd gone crazy and he laughed. I laughed, too. It all seemed like a joke. For two days he'd been calling me and when it wasn't him it was Rosita Méndez calling and giving me messages from him. She said I shouldn't break up with him. She said he was a good catch. But I told her I considered our relationship or whatever it was over."

"He understood things were over between you," said Fate.

"We had talked on the phone, I'd explained that I don't like jealous men, I'm not a jealous person," said Rosa, "I can't stand jealousy."

"He thought he'd lost you," said Fate.

"Probably," said Rosa, "or he wouldn't have asked me to give him a blow job. I never would've done it, especially not in the middle of town, even if it was dark out."

"But he didn't seem sad," said Fate, "or at least I didn't get that impression."

"No, he seemed happy," said Rosa. "He was always a happy man."

"Yes, that's what I thought," said Fate, "a happy man looking to have a good time with his girlfriend and his friends."

"He was high," said Rosa, "he kept taking pills."

"He didn't seem high to me," said Fate, "he seemed a little strange, as if he had something too big in his head. And as if he didn't know what to do with it, even though it would blow up on him in the end."

"So is that why you stayed?" asked Rosa.

"Maybe," said Fate, "I don't really know, I should be in the United States right now or writing my article, but here I am, in a motel, talking to you. I don't understand it."

"Did you want to go to bed with my friend Rosita?" asked Rosa.

"No," said Fate. "Not at all."

"Did you stay for me?" asked Rosa.

"I don't know," said Fate.

They both yawned.

"Have you fallen in love with me?" asked Rosa with disarming naturalness.

"Maybe," said Fate.

•

When Rosa fell asleep he took off her high-heeled shoes and covered her with a blanket. He turned off the lights and for a while he stood looking out through the blinds at the parking lot and the highway lights. Then he put on his jacket and quietly left the room. At the desk, the clerk was watching TV and he smiled at Fate when he saw him come in. They talked for a while about Mexican and American TV shows. The clerk said that American shows were better made but Mexican shows were funnier. Fate asked if he had cable. The clerk said cable was only for rich people or faggots. Real life was on the free channels, and that was where you had to look for it. Fate asked if he thought anything was really free in the end, and the clerk started to laugh and said he knew where Fate was heading but he wasn't about to be convinced. Fate said he wasn't trying to convince him of anything, and then he asked whether he had a computer he could use to send an e-mail. The clerk shook his head and looked through a pile of papers on the desk until he found the card of a Santa Teresa cybercafé.

"It's open all night," he said, which surprised Fate, because even in New York he'd never heard of cybercafés that stayed open twenty-four hours.

The card for the Santa Teresa cybercafé was a deep red, so red that it was hard to read what was printed on it. On the back, in a lighter red, was a map that showed exactly where the café was located. He asked the receptionist to translate the name of the place. The clerk laughed and said it was called Fire, Walk With Me.

"It sounds like the title of a David Lynch film," said Fate.

The clerk shrugged and said that all of Mexico was a collage of diverse and wide-ranging homages.

"Every single thing in this country is an homage to everything in the world, even the things that haven't happened yet," he said.

After he told Fate how to get to the cybercafé, they talked for a while about Lynch's films. The clerk had seen all of them. Fate had seen only three or four. According to the clerk, Lynch's greatest achievement was the TV series *Twin Peaks*. Fate liked *The Elephant Man* best, maybe because he'd often felt like the elephant man himself, wanting to be like other people but at the same time knowing he was different. When the clerk asked him whether he'd heard that Michael Jackson had bought or tried to buy the skeleton of the elephant man, Fate shrugged and said that Michael Jackson was sick. I don't think so, said the clerk, watching something presumably important that was happening on TV just then.

"In my opinion," he said with his eyes fixed on the TV Fate couldn't see, "Michael knows things the rest of us don't."

"We all know things we think nobody else knows," said Fate.

Then he said good night, put the cybercafé card in his pocket, and went back to his room.

•

For a long time Fate stood with the lights out, looking through the blinds at the gravel lot and the incessant lights of the trucks going by on the highway. He thought about Chucho Flores and Charly Cruz. Once again he saw the shadow that Charly Cruz's house cast over the vacant lot next door. He heard Chucho Flores's laugh and he saw Rosa Méndez stretched out on the bed in a bare, narrow room like a monk's cell. He thought about Corona, Corona's gaze, the way Corona had looked at him. He thought about the man with the mustache who had joined them at the last minute and who didn't speak, and then he remembered the man's voice when they were fleeing, as shrill as a bird's. When he was tired of standing he pulled a chair over to the window and kept watching. Sometimes he thought about his mother's apartment and he remembered concrete courtyards where children shouted and played. If he closed his eyes he could see a white dress lifted by the wind on the streets of Harlem as invincible laughter spilled down the walls, running along the sidewalks, cool and warm as the white dress. He felt sleep trickling in his ears or rising from his chest. But he didn't want to close his eyes and instead he kept scanning the lot, the two streetlights in front of the motel, the shadows dispersed by the flashes of car lights like comet tails in the dark.

Sometimes he turned his head and glanced at Rosa sleeping. But the third or fourth time he realized he didn't need to turn and look. It simply wasn't necessary. For a second he thought he would never be sleepy again. Suddenly, as he was following the wake of the taillights of two

trucks that seemed to be in a race, the telephone rang. When he answered he heard the clerk's voice and he knew immediately that this was
what he'd been waiting for.

"Mr. Fate," said the clerk, "someone just called to ask if you were
staying here."

He asked who had called.

"A policeman, Mr. Fate," said the clerk.

"A policeman? A Mexican policeman?"

"I just talked to him. He wanted to know if you were a guest here."

"And what did you tell him?" asked Fate.

"The truth, that you were here, but that you'd left," said the clerk.

"Thanks," said Fate, and he hung up.

He woke up Rosa and told her to put on her shoes. He packed the
few things he had unpacked and put the suitcase in the trunk of his car.
Outside it was cold. When he went back into the room Rosa was combing her hair in the bathroom, and Fate told her they didn't have time for
that. They got in the car and drove to the motel reception. The clerk was
standing there polishing his Coke-bottle glasses with the tail of his shirt.
Fate took out a fifty-dollar bill and slid it across the counter.

"If they come, tell them I went home," he said.

"They'll come," said the clerk.

As they turned onto the highway, he asked Rosa whether she was carrying her passport.

"Of course not," said Rosa.

"The police are looking for me," said Fate, and he told her what the
clerk had said.

"Why are you so sure it's the police?" asked Rosa. "It could be
Corona, or Chucho."

"You're right," said Fate, "maybe it's Charly Cruz or maybe it's Rosita
Méndez putting on a man's voice, but I'd rather not wait to find out."

•

They drove around the block to see whether anyone was lying in wait for
them, but everything was calm (the calm of quicksilver or the calm that
heralds border dawns), and the second time around they parked the car
under a tree in front of a neighbor's house. For a while they sat there,
alert to any sign, any movement. When they crossed the street they were
careful to stay away from the streetlights. Then they hopped over the

fence and headed straight for the backyard. As Rosa searched for her keys, Fate saw the geometry book hanging from the clothesline. Without thinking, he went over and touched it with the tip of his fingers. Then, not because he cared but to defuse the tension, he asked Rosa what *Testamento geométrico* meant and Rosa translated it for him without comment.

"It's odd that someone would hang a book out like a shirt," he whispered.

"It was my father's idea."

The house, although shared by father and daughter, had a clearly feminine air. It smelled of incense and blond tobacco. Rosa turned on a lamp and for a time they sat back in armchairs draped in multicolored Mexican blankets, neither one speaking a word. Then Rosa made coffee, and while she was in the kitchen, Fate saw Óscar Amalfitano appear in the doorway, barefoot, his hair uncombed, dressed in a very wrinkled white shirt and jeans, as if he'd slept in his clothes. For a moment the two of them looked at each other, wordless, as if they were asleep and their dreams had converged on common ground, a place where sound was alien. Fate got up and introduced himself. Amalfitano asked whether he spoke Spanish. Fate apologized and smiled and Amalfitano repeated the question in English.

"I'm a friend of your daughter's," said Fate, "she asked me in."

From the kitchen came Rosa's voice, telling her father in Spanish not to worry, that he was a reporter from New York. Then she asked him if he wanted coffee too and Amalfitano said yes without taking his eyes off the stranger. When Rosa appeared with a tray, three cups of coffee, a little pitcher of milk, and the sugar bowl, her father asked her what was going on. Nothing right now, I think, said Rosa, but some strange things happened earlier. Amalfitano looked down then and studied his bare feet. He added milk and sugar to his coffee and asked his daughter to explain everything. Rosa looked at Fate and translated what her father had just said. Fate smiled and sat down again in his chair. He took a cup of coffee and began to sip it as Rosa proceeded to tell her father, in Spanish, what had happened that night, from the boxing match to the moment when she had to leave the American's motel. When Rosa finished her story the sun was beginning to come up, and Amalfitano, who had interrupted his daughter only a very few times asking questions and pressing for explanations, suggested that they call the motel and ask the

clerk whether the police had shown up or not. Rosa translated her father's suggestion, and more out of politeness than because he thought it
would do any good, Fate called the number of the motel. No one answered. Óscar Amalfitano got up from his chair and went over to the
window. The street was silent. You'd both better go, he said. Rosa looked
at him without saying a word.

"Can you get her to the United States and then take her to an airport
and put her on a plane to Barcelona?"

Fate said he could. Óscar Amalfitano left the window and disappeared into his room. When he came back he handed Rosa a roll of bills.
It isn't much but it'll be enough for your ticket and the first few days in
Barcelona. I don't want to go, Papa, said Rosa. Yes, yes, I know that, said
Amalfitano, and he made her take the money. Where's your passport? Go
get it. Pack a suitcase. But hurry, he said, and then he went back to his
post at the window. Behind the Spirit that belonged to the neighbors
across the street, he saw the black Peregrino he was looking for. He
sighed. Fate set his coffee on a table and went over to the window.

"I'd like to know what's going on," said Fate. His voice was hoarse.

"Get my daughter out of this city and then forget everything. Or no,
don't forget anything, just take her away."

At that moment Fate remembered his appointment with Guadalupe
Roncal.

"Does it have to do with the killings?" he asked. "Do you think this
Chucho Flores is mixed up in that?"

"They're all mixed up in it," said Amalfitano.

A tall young man in jeans and a denim jacket got out of the Peregrino
and lit a cigarette. Rosa looked over her father's shoulder.

"Who is it?" she asked.

"Haven't you ever seen him before?"

"No, I don't think so."

"He's a cop," said Amalfitano.

Then he took his daughter by the hand and pulled her into her room.
They closed the door. Fate guessed they were saying their goodbyes and
he looked out the window again. The man in the Peregrino was smoking,
leaning on the hood of his car. Every so often he looked up at the sky,
which was gradually growing brighter. He seemed relaxed, in no hurry, at
ease, happy to be watching another sunrise in Santa Teresa. A man came
out of one of the neighboring houses and started his car. The man in the

Peregrino tossed the end of his cigarette on the sidewalk and got in his car. He never once looked toward the house. When Rosa came out of her room she was carrying a small suitcase.

"How will we leave?" Fate wanted to know.

"By the door," said Amalfitano.

Then Fate saw, as if it were a movie he didn't entirely understand but that in a strange way took him back to his mother's death, how Amalfitano kissed and hugged his daughter and then strode purposefully outside. First Fate watched him walk through the front yard, then he watched him open the peeling wooden gate, then he watched him cross the street, barefoot, his hair uncombed, to the black Peregrino. When he got there the man rolled down the window and they talked for a while, Amalfitano in the street and the man in his car. They know each other, thought Fate, this isn't the first time they've talked.

"It's time, let's go," said Rosa.

Fate followed her. They crossed the yard and the street and their bodies cast extremely fine shadows that every five seconds were shaken by a tremor, as if the sun were spinning backward. When he got in the car Fate thought he heard a laugh behind him and he turned around, but all he saw was Amalfitano and the young man still talking in the same position as before.

•

It didn't take Guadalupe Roncal and Rosa Amalfitano more than a minute to share their respective woes. The reporter offered to drive with them to Tucson. Rosa said there was no need to go overboard. They deliberated for a while. As they spoke in Spanish, Fate looked out the window, but everything was normal around the Sonora Resort. All the reporters were gone, no one was talking about boxing matches, the waiters seemed to have stirred from a long lethargy and were less friendly, as if waking put them out of sorts. Rosa called her father from the hotel. Fate watched her head toward the reception desk with Guadalupe Roncal, and while he was waiting for them to come back he smoked a cigarette and took some notes for the story he still hadn't filed. In the light of day the previous night's events seemed unreal, invested with childish gravity. As his thoughts drifted, Fate saw Merolino's two sparring partners, Omar Abdul and García. He imagined them taking a bus to the coast. He saw them get off the bus, he saw them take a few steps through the scrub. The oneiric wind whipped grains of sand that stuck to their faces. A golden bath. So peaceful, thought Fate. How simple it all is. Then he saw the bus and he imagined it black, like a huge hearse. He saw Abdul's arrogant smile, Garcia's impassive face, his strange tattoos, and he heard the sudden sound of dishes breaking, not many of them, or a crash of boxes falling, and only then did Fate realize that he was asleep and looked around for the waiter, to ask for another coffee, but he didn't see anyone. Guadalupe Roncal and Rosa Amalfitano were still on the phone.

•

"They're good people, friendly, hospitable. Mexicans are hardworking, they're hugely curious about everything, they care about people, they're brave and generous, their sadness isn't destructive, it's life giving," said Rosa Amalfitano as they crossed the border into the United States.

"Will you miss them?" asked Fate.

"I'll miss my father and I'll miss the people," said Rosa.

•

When they were in the car on the way to the Santa Teresa prison, Rosa said no one had answered the phone at her father's. After she called Amalfitano several times, Rosa had called Rosa Méndez's house, and there was no one there either. I think Rosa's dead, she said. Fate shook his head as if he couldn't believe it.

"We're still alive," he said.

"We're alive because we haven't seen anything and we don't know anything," said Rosa.

The reporter's car was ahead of them. It was a yellow Little Nemo. Guadalupe Roncal drove carefully, although every once in a while she stopped, as if she didn't quite remember the way. Fate thought it might be better to stop following her and head straight for the border. When he suggested it, Rosa was strongly opposed. He asked her whether she had friends in the city. Rosa said no, she didn't really have any friends. Chucho Flores and Rosa Méndez and Charly Cruz, but he wouldn't call them friends, would he?

"No, those aren't friends," said Fate.

•

They saw a Mexican flag flying in the desert, on the other side of the fence. One of the border police on the American side scrutinized Fate and Rosa. He wondered what a white girl, and a pretty white girl at that, was doing with a black man. Fate held his gaze. Reporter? asked the officer. Fate nodded. A big fish, thought the officer. Every night he must knock her around. Spanish? Rosa smiled at the officer. A shadow of frustration crossed the officer's face. When they pulled away the flag disappeared and all they could see was the fence and warehouses surrounded by walls.

"The problem is bad luck," said Rosa.

Fate didn't hear her.

•

As they were waiting in a windowless room, Fate felt his penis getting harder and harder. For a moment he thought he hadn't had an erection since his mother's death, but then he rejected the idea, it couldn't have been that long, he thought, but it could have, the irremediable was possible, the unsalvageable was possible, so why couldn't the blood flow to his cock have stopped for what really was a fairly short period of time? Rosa Amalfitano looked at him. Guadalupe Roncal was busy with her notes and her tape recorder, sitting in a chair bolted to the floor. Every once in a while the everyday sounds of the prison reached them. Shouted names, muted music, footsteps receding in the distance. Fate sat on a wooden bench and yawned. He thought he would fall asleep. He imagined Rosa's legs on his shoulders. He saw his room at the motel again and wondered whether or not they'd made love. Of course not, he said to himself. Then he heard shouts, as if a bachelor party were being held in one of the prison chambers. He thought about the killings. He heard distant laughter. Roars. He heard Guadalupe Roncal say something to Rosa and he heard Rosa answer. Sleep overtook him and he saw himself peacefully sleeping on the sofa in his mother's apartment in Harlem, with the TV on. I'll sleep for half an hour, he said to himself, and then I'll get back to work. I have to write the fight story. I have to drive all night. When the sun comes up everything will be over.

•

After they crossed the border, the few tourists they saw on the streets of El Adobe seemed to be sleepwalking. A woman in her seventies, in a flowered dress and Nike sneakers, was kneeling down to examine some Indian rugs. She looked like an athlete from the 1940s. Three children holding hands watched some objects displayed in a shop window. The objects were moving almost imperceptibly, and Fate couldn't tell whether they were animals or machines. Outside a bar some men in cowboy hats who looked like Chicanos were gesticulating and pointing in opposite directions. At the end of the street there were some wooden sheds and metal containers on the pavement and beyond them was the desert. All of this is like somebody else's dream, thought Fate. Next to him, Rosa's head rested delicately on the seat and her big eyes were fixed on some point on the horizon. Fate looked at her knees, which struck him as perfect, and then her hips and then her shoulders and her collarbones, which seemed to have a life of their own, a dark, suspended life that gave signs of itself only now and then. Then he concentrated on driving. The highway out of El Adobe headed into a kind of swirl of shades of ocher.

"I wonder how Guadalupe Roncal is doing," said Rosa in a dreamy voice.

"By now she must be flying home," said Fate.

"Strange," said Rosa.

•

Rosa's voice woke him.

"Listen," she said.

Fate opened his eyes but he didn't hear anything. Guadalupe Roncal had gotten up and she was standing next to them now, her eyes very wide, as if her worst nightmares had come true. Fate went over to the door and opened it. One of his legs had fallen asleep and he couldn't quite manage to wake up yet. He saw a hallway and at the end of the hallway he saw a rough cement staircase, as if the builders had left it half finished. The hallway was dimly lit.

"Don't leave," Rosa said to him.

"Let's get out of this trap," said Guadalupe Roncal.

A prison official appeared at the end of the hallway and headed toward them. Fate showed his press ID. The official nodded without looking at the ID and he smiled at Guadalupe Roncal, who remained standing in the doorway. Then the official closed the door and said something about a storm. Rosa translated into Fate's ear. A sandstorm or a rainstorm or an electric storm. High clouds dropping down from the mountains, clouds that wouldn't burst over Santa Teresa but that cast a pall on the landscape. A miserable morning. The inmates always get nervous, said the official. He was a young man, with a skimpy mustache, maybe a little bit soft around the middle for his age, and you could tell he didn't like his job. They're bringing the killer now.

●

You have to listen to women. You should never ignore a woman's fears. It was something like that, remembered Fate, that his mother or her neighbor, the deceased Miss Holly, used to say when both of them were young and he was a boy. For an instant he imagined a set of scales, like the scales of Blind Justice, except that instead of two platters, there were two bottles, or something like two bottles. The bottle on the left was clear and full of desert sand. There were several holes in it through which the sand escaped. The bottle on the right was full of acid. There were no holes in it, but the acid was eating away at the bottle from the inside. On the way to Tucson, Fate didn't recognize any of the things he'd seen a few days before, when he'd traveled the same road in the opposite direction. What used to be my right is my left, and there are no points of reference. Everything is erased. Toward noon they stopped at a diner on the highway. A group of Mexicans who looked like jobless migrant workers watched them from the counter. They were drinking bottled water and local sodas, the names and logos odd to Fate. New businesses that would soon fail. The food was bad. Rosa was sleepy and when they got back to the car she fell asleep. Fate remembered the words of Guadalupe Roncal. No one pays attention to these killings, but the secret of the world is hidden in them. Did Guadalupe Roncal say that, or was it Rosa? At moments, the highway was like a river. The suspected killer said it, thought Fate. The giant fucking albino who appeared along with the black cloud.

●

When Fate heard footsteps approaching he thought they were the footsteps of a giant. Guadalupe Roncal must have thought something similar, because she seemed about to faint, but instead of fainting, she clung to the prison official's hand and then his lapel. Rather than pull away, he put his arm around her shoulders. Fate felt Rosa's body next to him. He heard voices. As if the inmates were egging someone on. He heard laughter and calls to order, and then the black clouds from the east passed over the prison and the air seemed to darken. The footsteps came closer. He heard laughter and pleas. Suddenly a voice began to sing a song. It sounded like a woodcutter chopping down trees. The voice wasn't singing in English. At first Fate couldn't figure out what the language was, until Rosa, beside him, said it was German. The voice grew louder. It occurred to Fate that he might still be dreaming. The trees fell one by one. I'm a giant lost in the middle of a burned forest. But someone will come to rescue me. Rosa translated the suspect's string of curses for him. A polyglot woodcutter, thought Fate, who speaks English as well as he speaks Spanish and who sings in German. I'm a giant lost in the middle of a charred forest. And yet only I know where I'm going, only I know my destiny. And then the footsteps and the laughter could be heard once more, and the goading and words of encouragement of the inmates and the guards escorting the giant. And then an enormous and very blond man came into the visitors' room, ducked his head, as if he were afraid of knocking it on the ceiling, and smiled as if he had just done something naughty, singing the German song about the lost woodcutter and fixing them all with an intelligent and mocking gaze. Then the guard accompanying him asked Guadalupe Roncal if she would prefer that he be handcuffed to the chair and Guadalupe Roncal shook her head and the guard gave the tall man a little pat on the shoulder and left and the official who was standing with Fate and the women went out too, though not before saying something into Guadalupe Roncal's ear, and they were left alone.

"Good morning," said the giant in Spanish. He sat down and stretched his legs under the table so that his feet stuck out the other side.

He was wearing black tennis shoes and white socks. Guadalupe Roncal took a step back.

"Ask whatever you want," said the giant.

Guadalupe Roncal raised her hand to her mouth, as if she were inhaling a toxic gas, and she couldn't think what to ask.

THE PART ABOUT THE CRIMES

The girl's body turned up in a vacant lot in Colonia Las Flores. She was dressed in a white long-sleeved T-shirt and a yellow knee-length skirt, a size too big. Some children playing in the lot found her and told their parents. One of the mothers called the police, who showed up half an hour later. The lot was bordered by Calle Peláez and Calle Hermanos Chacón and it ended in a ditch behind which rose the walls of an abandoned dairy in ruins. There was no one around, which at first made the policemen think it was a joke. Nevertheless, they pulled up on Calle Peláez and one of them made his way into the lot. Soon he came across two women with their heads covered, kneeling in the weeds, praying. Seen from a distance, the women looked old, but they weren't. Before them lay the body. Without interrupting, the policeman went back the way he'd come and motioned to his partner, who was waiting for him in the car, smoking. Then the two of them returned (the one who'd waited in the car had his gun in his hand) to the place where the women were kneeling and they stood there beside them staring at the body. The policeman with the gun asked whether they knew her. No, sir, said one of the women. We've never seen her before. She isn't from around here, poor thing.

This happened in 1993. January 1993. From then on, the killings of women began to be counted. But it's likely there had been other deaths before. The name of the first victim was Esperanza Gómez Saldaña and she was thirteen. Maybe for the sake of convenience, maybe because she was the first to be killed in 1993, she heads the list. Although surely there were other girls and women who died in 1992. Other girls and women who didn't make it onto the list or were never found, who were buried in unmarked graves in the desert or whose ashes were scattered in the middle of the night, when not even the person scattering them knew where he was, what place he had come to.

•

The identification of Esperanza Gómez Saldaña was relatively easy. First the body was brought to one of the three Santa Teresa police stations, where it was seen by a judge and examined by more policemen and photographed. After a while, as an ambulance waited outside the station, Pedro Negrete, the police chief, arrived, followed by a pair of deputies, and he proceeded to examine her again. When he had finished he met with the judge and three policemen who were waiting for him in an office and asked what conclusion they had reached. She was strangled, said the judge, it's clear as day. The policemen just nodded. Do we know who she is? asked the chief. They all said no. All right, we'll find out, said Pedro Negrete, and he left with the judge. One of his deputies stayed behind at the station and asked to see the officers who had found the dead girl. They've gone back out on patrol, he was told. Well, get them back here, shitheads, he said. Then the body was taken to the morgue at the city hospital, where the medical examiner conducted an autopsy. According to the autopsy, Esperanza Gómez Saldaña had been strangled to death. There was bruising on her chin and around her left eye. Severe bruising on her legs and rib cage. She had been vaginally and anally raped, probably more than once, since both orifices exhibited tears and abrasions, from which she had bled profusely. At two in the morning the examiner concluded the autopsy and left. A black orderly, who had moved north from Veracruz years ago, put the body away in a freezer.

•

Five days later, before the end of January, Luisa Celina Vázquez was strangled. She was sixteen years old, sturdily built, fair-skinned, and five months pregnant. The man she lived with and a friend of his were small-time thieves who stole from stores and appliance warehouses. The police were alerted by a call from neighbors in the couple's building, located on Avenida Rubén Darío, in Colonia Mancera. After breaking down the door, they found Luisa Celina strangled with a television cord. That night, her lover, Marcos Sepúlveda, and his partner, Ezequiel

Romero, were arrested. Both were locked up at Precinct #2 and subjected to an interrogation that lasted all night, conducted by the police chief's right-hand man, Officer Epifanio Galindo, with optimal results, since before the sun came up Romero confessed to having maintained intimate relations with the deceased behind the back of his friend and partner. Upon learning that she was pregnant, Luisa Celina had decided to put an end to these relations, which Romero refused to accept, because he thought that he, not Marcos Sepúlveda, was the father of the unborn child. After a few months, when Luisa Celina wouldn't change her mind, he decided in a fit of insanity to kill her, which he finally did one night when Sepúlveda was away. Two days later, Sepúlveda was released, and Romero, rather than being sent to prison, remained locked up at Precinct #2, where the interrogations continued, their object this time not to clear up any lingering questions regarding the murder of Luisa Celina but to incriminate Romero in the murder of Esperanza Gómez Saldaña, whose body had by now been identified. Despite what the police expected, deceived as they were by the speed with which they had obtained the first confession, Romero stood firm and refused to implicate himself in the earlier crime.

•

Midway through February, in an alley in the center of the city, some garbagemen found another dead woman. She was about thirty and dressed in a black skirt and low-cut white blouse. She had been stabbed to death, although contusions from multiple blows were visible about her face and abdomen. In her purse was a ticket for the nine a.m. bus to Tucson, a bus she would never catch. Also found were a lipstick, powder, eyeliner, Kleenex, a half-empty pack of cigarettes, and a package of condoms. There was no passport or appointment book or anything that might identify her. Nor was she carrying a lighter or matches.

•

In March, the female reporter for the radio station El Heraldo del Norte, sister company of the newspaper *El Heraldo del Norte*, left the broadcast studio at ten with a male reporter and the sound engineer. They headed to the Italian restaurant Piazza Navona, where they ordered three slices of pizza and three small bottles of California wine. The male reporter was the first to leave. The female reporter, Isabel Urrea, and the sound engineer, Francisco Santamaría, decided to stay and talk a little longer. They discussed work matters, scheduling, and programs, and then they began to talk about a friend who had left the station, gotten married, and gone to live with her husband in a town near Hermosillo, the name of which they couldn't recall but which they were sure was near the ocean and which for six months out of the year, according to this friend, was the closest thing to paradise. They both left the restaurant. The sound engineer didn't have a car, so Isabel Urrea offered to give him a ride home. No need, said the engineer, his house was nearby and anyway he would rather walk. As the engineer set off down the street, Isabel walked toward the place where she had left her car. As she got out her keys to unlock it, a shadowy figure appeared on the sidewalk and fired at her three times. The keys fell. A passerby some twenty feet away dropped to the ground. Isabel tried to get up but she could only lean her head against the front tire. She felt no pain. The shadowy figure approached and shot her in the forehead.

•

The murder of Isabel Urrea, covered the first three days by her radio station and paper, was explained as a frustrated robbery, the work of a lunatic or drug addict who probably meant to steal her car. The theory also circulated that the perpetrator might be a Guatemalan or Salvadorean veteran of the wars in Central America, someone desperate to get the money to move on to the United States. There was no autopsy, in deference to the family, and the ballistic analysis, which was never made public, was later lost for good somewhere in transit between the courts of Santa Teresa and Hermosillo.

•

A month later, a knife sharpener making his way along Calle El Arroyo between Colonia Ciudad Nueva and Colonia Morelos saw a woman clinging drunkenly to a wooden post. A black Peregrino with tinted windows passed by. At the other end of the street, the knife sharpener spotted an ice cream vendor approaching, covered in flies. The two men converged on the wooden post, but the woman had slipped or lost the strength to hold on. Her face, half hidden by her forearm, was a pulpy mass of red and purple flesh. The knife sharpener said they had to call an ambulance. The ice cream vendor stared at the woman and said she looked as if she'd gone fifteen rounds with El Torito Ramírez. The knife sharpener realized the ice cream vendor wasn't going to budge and he said to watch his cart, he would be right back. After he crossed the dirt road he turned around to check that the ice cream vendor was obeying, and he saw all the flies that had been circling the vendor settle around the woman's battered head. A few women were watching from the windows across the street. Somebody needs to call an ambulance, said the knife sharpener. That woman is dying. After a while an ambulance came from the hospital and the medics wanted to know who would pay for the ride. The knife sharpener explained that he and the ice cream vendor had found the woman lying on the ground. I know, said the medic, but what I care about now is finding out who will take responsibility for her. How can I take responsibility for a person when I don't even know her name? asked the knife sharpener. Well, somebody has to, said the medic. Is there something wrong with your ears, dumbfuck? asked the knife sharpener, pulling a giant carving knife out of a drawer in his cart. Hey now, hey now, hey now, said the medic. Go on, get her in the ambulance, said the knife sharpener. The other medic, who had knelt to examine the fallen woman, swatting away the flies, said there was no point in anyone losing his shit, the woman was already dead. The knife sharpener's eyes narrowed until they looked like two lines drawn with charcoal. Goddamn motherfucking asshole, it's your fault, he said, and he started after the medic. The other medic tried to intervene, but when he saw the knife in the knife sharpener's hand, he decided to lock himself in the ambulance and call the police. For a while the knife sharpener chased the medic until his fury, exasperation, and bloodlust abated, or until he got tired. And then he stopped, took his cart, and headed off down Calle El Arroyo until the onlookers who had gathered around the ambulance lost sight of him.

•

The woman's name was Isabel Cansino, though she went by Elizabeth, and she was a prostitute. The blows she'd received had destroyed her spleen. The police blamed the crime on one or several dissatisfied customers. She lived in Colonia San Damián, quite a bit farther south than she'd been found, and she wasn't known to have a steady boyfriend, although a neighbor woman talked about someone called Iván who came by often, and who couldn't be located on subsequent visits. An attempt was also made to discover the whereabouts of the knife sharpener, whose name was Nicanor, according to the statements of residents of Colonia Ciudad Nueva and Colonia Morelos, where he came around approximately once a week or once every two weeks, but all efforts to find him were in vain. Either he had changed jobs or he'd moved from the west of Santa Teresa to the south or east or he'd left the city altogether. In any case, he was never seen again.

•

The next month, in May, a dead woman was found in a dump between Colonia Las Flores and the General Sepúlveda industrial park. In the complex stood the buildings of four maquiladoras where household appliances were assembled. The electric towers that supplied power to the maquiladoras were new and painted silver. Next to them, amid some low hills, were the roofs of shacks that had been built a little before the arrival of the maquiladoras, stretching all the way to the train tracks and across, along the edge of Colonia La Preciada. In the plaza there were six trees, one at each corner and two in the middle, so dusty they looked yellow. At one end of the plaza was the stop for the buses that brought workers from different neighborhoods of Santa Teresa. Then it was a long walk along dirt roads to the gates where the guards checked the workers' passes, after which they were allowed into their various workplaces. Only one of the maquiladoras had a cafeteria. At the others the workers ate next to their machines or in small groups in a corner, talking and laughing until the siren sounded that signaled the end of lunch. Most were women. In the dump where the dead woman was found, the trash of the slum dwellers piled up along with the waste of the maquiladoras. The call informing the authorities of the discovery of the dead woman came from the manager of one of the plants, Multizone-West, a subsidiary of a multinational that manufactured TVs. The policemen who came to get her found three executives from the maquiladora waiting for them by the dump. Two were Mexican and the other was American. One of the Mexicans said they hoped the body would be removed as soon as possible. One of the policemen asked where the body was, while his partner called an ambulance. The three executives accompanied the policeman into the dump. The four of them held their noses, but when the American stopped holding his nose the Mexicans followed his example. The dead woman had dark skin and straight black hair past her shoulders. She was wearing a black sweat-shirt and shorts. The four men stood looking at her. The American crouched down and moved the hair from her neck with a pen. It would be better if the gringo didn't touch her, said the policeman. I'm not touching her, said the American in Spanish, I just want to see her neck. The two Mexican executives crouched down and peered at the marks on the dead woman's neck. Then they got up and looked at their watches. The ambulance is taking a long time, said one of them. It'll be here in a second, said the policeman. Well, said one of the executives, you'll take care of everything, won't you? The policeman said yes, of course, and tucked the money the other man handed him into the pocket of his regulation pants. The dead woman spent that night in a refrigerated compartment in the Santa Teresa hospital and the next day one of the medical examiner's assistants performed the autopsy. She had been strangled. She had been raped. Vaginally and anally, noted the medical examiner's assistant. And she was five months pregnant.

•

The first dead woman of May was never identified, so it was assumed she was a migrant from some central or southern state who had stopped in Santa Teresa on her way to the United States. No one was traveling with her, no one had reported her missing. She was approximately thirty-five years old and she was pregnant. Maybe she was going to the United States to join her husband or her lover, the father of the child she was expecting, some poor fuck who lived there illegally and maybe never knew he had gotten this woman pregnant or that she, when she found out, would come looking for him. But this first death wasn't the only one. Three days later, Guadalupe Rojas (her identity clear from the start) was killed. She was twenty-six, a resident of Calle Jazmín, one of the streets parallel to Avenida Carranza, in Colonia Carranza, and employed at the File-Sis maquiladora, recently built on the road to Nogales, some five miles from Santa Teresa. As it happened, Guadalupe Rojas didn't die on her way to work, which might have made sense, since the area around the maquiladora was deserted and dangerous, best crossed in a car and not by bus and then on foot since the factory was at least a mile from the nearest bus stop, but at the door to her building on Calle Jazmín. The cause of death was three gunshot wounds, two of them pronounced fatal. The killer turned out to be her boyfriend, who tried to flee that very night and was caught by the train tracks, not far from a nightspot called Los Zancudos where he had gotten drunk earlier. It was the owner of the bar, a former city police officer, who called the police. Once the suspect had been questioned, it was revealed that the motive of the crime was jealousy, warranted or not, and after an appearance before the judge and upon the agreement of all present, he was sent without further delay to the Santa Teresa jail to await transfer or trial. The last dead woman of May was found on the slopes of Cerro Estrella, the hills that lend their name to the Colonia that surrounds them unevenly, as if nothing could easily grow or expand there. Only the eastern side of the hills faced mostly open country. That was where they found her. According to the medical examiner, she had been stabbed to death. There was unmistakable evidence of rape. She must have been twenty-five or twenty-six. Her skin was fair and her hair light colored. She was wearing jeans, a blue shirt, and Nike sneakers. She wasn't carrying any identifying documents. Whoever killed her had taken the trouble to dress her, because neither her jeans nor her shirt were torn. There were no indications of anal rape. The only mark on her face was a faint bruise on her upper jaw, near her right ear. In the days after the discovery, *El Heraldo del Norte* as well as *La Tribuna de Santa Teresa* and *La Voz de Sonora*, the three city papers, published pictures of the unknown victim of Cerro Estrella, but no one came forward to identify her. On the fourth day after her death, the Santa Teresa police chief, Pedro Negrete, went in person to Cerro Estrella, not accompanied by anyone, even Epifanio Galindo, and examined the place where the dead woman had been found. Then he left the low slopes and began to climb to the top of the Cerro. Among the volcanic rocks were supermarket bags full of trash. He remembered that his son, who was studying in Phoenix, had once told him that plastic bags took hundreds, maybe thousands of years to disintegrate. Not these, he thought, noting the rapid pace of decomposition here. At the top some children went running and vanished down the hill, toward Colonia Estrella. It began to get dark. To the west he saw houses with zinc and cardboard roofs, the streets winding through an anarchic sprawl. To the east he saw the highway that led to the mountains and the desert, the lights of the trucks, the first stars, real stars, stars that crept in with the night from the far side of the mountains. To the north he didn't see anything, just a vast monotonous plain, as if life ended beyond Santa Teresa, despite what he hoped and believed. Then he heard dogs, the sounds coming closer and closer until he saw them. They were probably starving and wild, like the children he'd caught a glimpse of when he arrived. He pulled his gun out of his shoulder holster. He counted five dogs. He took off the safety and shot. Instead of leaping in the air, the dog collapsed, and the force of the shot sent it skidding through the dust, curled in a ball. The other four dogs ran off. Pedro Negrete watched them go. Two had their tails between their legs and ran in a crouch. Of the other two, one ran stiff tailed, and the fourth, for some unknown reason, wagged its tail, as if it had been given a treat. He went over to the dead dog and touched it with his foot. The bullet had gone into its head. Without glancing behind him he walked on down the hill, to the place where the body of the victim had been found. There he stopped and lit a cigarette. A Ducados, unfiltered. Then he continued on to his car. From here, he thought, everything looked different.

•

There were no other deaths of women in May, with the exception of those who died of natural causes, that is, of illness or old age, or in childbirth. But the end of the month marked the appearance of the church desecrator. One day a stranger came into the church of San Rafael, on Calle Patriotas Mexicanos, in the center of Santa Teresa, during the early service. The church was almost empty. There were just a few of the faithful clustered together in the front pews, and the priest was in the confessional. The church smelled of incense and cheap cleaning products. The stranger sat in one of the last pews and got right down on his knees, his head buried in his hands as if it ached or he felt ill. Some of the elderly parishioners turned to look at him and whispered among themselves. One little old lady came out of the confessional and stood motionless staring at the stranger, as a young woman with Indian features went in to confess. When the priest had absolved the Indian woman of her sins, the service would start. But the little old lady who had come out of the confessional just stood there staring at the stranger, although sometimes she shifted her weight from one foot to the other, doing a kind of dance step. She knew immediately that something was wrong with the man and she intended to go and warn the other old ladies. As she walked up the main aisle, she saw a pool of liquid spread across the floor from the pew where the stranger was sitting and she smelled urine. Then, instead of moving on toward where the old ladies were clustered, she turned around and returned to the confessional. She knocked several times on the priest's little window. I'm busy, my child, he said. Father, said the little old lady, there's a man here who's polluting the house of the Lord. Yes, child, I'll be with you in a moment, said the priest. Father, I don't like this one bit, do something, for the love of God. As she talked, the little old lady seemed to dance. I'm coming, my child, be patient, I'm busy, said the priest. Father, there's a man doing his business in the church, said the little old lady. The priest poked his head out between the threadbare curtains and peered through the sepia dusk at the stranger, and then he stepped out of the confessional and the woman with Indian features also stepped out of the confessional and the three of them stood frozen watching the stranger who was moaning faintly and kept urinating, wetting his pants and loosing a river of urine that ran toward the vestibule, confirming that the aisle, as the priest had feared, was worryingly uneven. Then the priest went to call the sexton, who was having his coffee at the sacristy table and looked tired, and the two of them went up to the stranger to scold him and throw him out of the church. The stranger saw them coming and gazed at them with his eyes full of tears and asked them to leave him alone. Almost at the same moment, a blade appeared in his hand, and as the old ladies in the front pews screamed, he stabbed the sexton.

•

The case was entrusted to Inspector Juan de Dios Martínez, who was reputed to be capable and discreet, a quality some policemen associated with religious faith. Juan de Dios Martínez talked to the priest, who described the stranger as a man of about thirty, average height, dark-skinned, sturdy, your average Mexican. Then he talked to the old ladies. To them, the stranger was no average Mexican, he was the devil incarnate. So what was the devil doing at the early service? asked the inspector. He was there to kill us all, said the old ladies. At two in the afternoon, accompanied by a sketch artist, Juan de Dios Martínez went to the hospital to take the sexton's statement. The sexton's description matched the priest's. The stranger smelled of liquor. The smell was strong, as if he had washed his shirt the night before in a basin of ninety-proof alcohol. He hadn't shaved for days, although you couldn't really tell because he didn't have much of a beard. How did the sexton know he didn't have much of a beard? Juan de Dios Martínez wanted to know. By the way the hairs grew on his face, skimpy and every which way, like they were stuck there in the dark by his bitch of a mother and his cocksucking faggot of a father, said the sexton. Also: he had big, strong hands. Hands maybe too big for his body. And he was crying, no question about that, but he also seemed to be laughing, crying and laughing at the same time. Do you know what I mean? asked the sexton. Like he was high? asked the inspector. Exactly. That's it. Later Juan de Dios Martínez called the Santa Teresa asylum and asked whether they had an inmate who matched the description he had compiled. They said they had two, but neither was violent. He asked if they were allowed out. One is and the other isn't, he was told. I'm coming to see them, said the inspector. At five, after eating lunch at a coffee shop where cops never went, Juan de Dios Martínez parked his metallic gray Cougar in the asylum parking lot. He was received by the director, a woman of about fifty, with her hair dyed blond, who had coffee brought in for him. The director's office was pretty and struck him as tastefully decorated. On the walls there were two prints, a Picasso and a Diego Rivera. Juan de Dios Martínez spent a long time gazing at the Rivera print as he waited for the director. On the desk were two photographs: one was of the director, when she was younger, with her arms around a girl looking straight into the camera. The girl had a sweet, blank expression on her face. In the other photograph the director was even younger. She was sitting next to an older woman, regarding her with an amused expression. The older woman had a serious air about her and stared at the camera as if she thought it was frivolous to have her picture taken. When the director came in at last, the inspector could see immediately that many years had gone by since the pictures were taken. He observed further that the director was still very attractive. For a while they talked about the mental patients. The dangerous ones weren't allowed out, the director informed him. And there weren't many dangerous ones, anyway. The inspector showed her the sketch the artist had made and the director examined it carefully for a few seconds. Juan de Dios Martínez stared at her hands. Her nails were painted and her fingers were long and looked soft to the touch. On the back of her hands he counted a few freckles. The director said the sketch wasn't good and it might be anyone. Then they went to see the two patients. They were in the yard, an enormous yard with no trees, a dirt yard like a soccer field in a slum. A guard dressed in white T-shirt and trousers brought out the first inmate. Juan de Dios Martínez heard the director ask how he felt. Then they talked about food. The patient said he could hardly eat meat anymore, but he said it in such a scattered way that the inspector couldn't tell whether he was complaining about the menu or informing the director of a recently acquired aversion. She talked about protein. The breeze in the yard ruffled the patients' hair. We need to build a wall, he heard the doctor say. When the wind blows it makes them nervous, said the guard dressed in white. Then they brought out the other inmate. Juan de Dios Martínez thought at first that they were brothers, although when the two were side by side he realized the resemblance was deceptive. From a distance, he thought, maybe all madmen look alike. Back in the director's office, he asked how long she'd been the head of the asylum. For ages, she said, laughing. I can't even remember how long. As they drank more coffee, of which the director was clearly very fond, he asked if she was from Santa Teresa. No, said the director. I was born in Guadalajara and I studied in Mexico City and then in San Francisco, at Berkeley. Juan de Dios Martínez would have liked to keep talking and drinking coffee, and maybe ask whether she was married or divorced, but he didn't have time. Can I take them with me? he asked. The director looked at him uncomprehendingly. Can I take the patients with me? he asked. The director laughed in his face and asked if he was right in the head. Where do you want to take them? To be part of a kind of lineup, said the inspector. The victim is in the hospital and can't go anywhere. You lend me your patients for a few hours, I'll take them on a ride to the hospital, and you'll have them back before dark. You're asking me? said the director. You're the boss, said the inspector. Bring me a court order from the judge, said the director. I can get one, but it's just red tape. Also, if I come with a court order, your patients will be brought in to the station, they might be kept a night or two, it won't be any fun for them. But if I take them with me now, it'll be easy. They ride in the car with me, I'm the only cop, and if the victim makes a positive identification, you still get your boys back, both of them. Doesn't that seem easier? No, not to me it doesn't, said the director, bring me a court order from the judge and then we'll see. I didn't mean to offend you, said the inspector. I'm shocked, said the director. Juan de Dios Martínez laughed. Well, I won't take them, then, and that's the end of it, he said. But will you promise to do your best to make sure neither of them leaves the asylum? The director got up and for a moment he thought she was going to kick him out. Then she called her secretary and asked for another cup of coffee. Would you like one? Juan de Dios Martínez nodded. Tonight I won't be able to sleep, he thought.

•

That night the stranger from San Rafael found his way to the church of San Tadeo, in Colonia Kino, a neighborhood springing up amid the scrub and rolling hills of southeastern Santa Teresa. Inspector Juan de Dios Martínez got a call at midnight. He was watching TV and after he hung up he collected the dirty plates on the table and put them in the sink. From the drawer of the night table he took his gun and the sketch, which he had folded in four, and went down the steps to the garage where his red Chevy Astra was parked. When he got to San Tadeo some women were sitting on the adobe steps. There weren't many of them. Inside the church he caught a glimpse of Inspector José Márquez questioning the priest. He asked a policeman whether the ambulance had come yet. The policeman looked at him with a smile and said there were no casualties. What the fuck was all this? Two crime scene technicians were trying to find prints on a statue of Christ next to the altar, on the floor. This time the freak didn't hurt anyone, José Márquez told him when he was done with the priest. Juan de Dios Martínez wanted to know what had happened. Some tripped-out asshole showed up here around ten, said Márquez. He was carrying a switchblade or a knife. He sat in the last row. There. Where it's darkest. An old woman heard him crying. Because he was sad or happy, I don't know. He was pissing. Then the old woman went to call the priest and he jumped up and started to smash statues. Christ, the Virgin of Guadalupe, and a couple of other saints. Then he left. And that's all? asked Inspector Juan de Dios Martínez. End of story, said Márquez. For a while the two of them talked to the witnesses. The description of the perpetrator matched the description of the perpetrator at San Rafael. Juan de Dios Martínez showed the priest the sketch. The priest was young and seemed tired, not because of what had happened that night but because of something that had been wearing him down for years. Looks like him, the priest said indifferently. The church smelled of incense and urine. The chunks of plaster scattered across the floor reminded him of a movie, but he couldn't remember which one. With the tip of his foot he nudged one of the fragments. It looked like a piece of a hand and it was soaked. Have you noticed? asked Márquez. What? asked Juan de Dios Martínez. The bastard must have a huge bladder. Or else he holds it as long as he can and waits until he's inside a church to let go. When Juan de Dios Martínez came out, he saw some reporters from *El Heraldo del Norte* and *La Tribuna de Santa Teresa* talking to bystanders. He went for a walk through the nearby streets. It didn't smell of incense there, although at times the air seemed to waft directly from a septic tank. The streets were barely lit. I've never been here before, Juan de Dios Martínez said to himself. At the end of the street he spotted the shadow of a big tree. It stood in a poor imitation of a plaza, the tree the only thing that gave the barren semicircle any resemblance to a public space. Around the tree were some clumsily built benches where the neighborhood residents could sit and get a breath of fresh air. There used to be an Indian settlement here, remembered the inspector. A policeman who'd lived in the colonia had told him so. He dropped onto a bench and gazed up at the imposing shadow of the tree silhouetted menacingly against the starry sky. Where are the Indians now? He thought about the director of the asylum. He would've liked to talk to her just then, but he knew he wouldn't dare call her.

•

The attacks on San Rafael and San Tadeo got more attention in the local press than the women killed in the preceding months. The next day, Juan de Dios Martínez and two policemen went back to Colonia Kino and Colonia La Preciada and showed people the sketch of the attacker. No one recognized him. At lunchtime the policemen went downtown and Juan de Dios Martínez called the director of the asylum. The director hadn't read the papers and didn't know anything about what had happened the night before. Juan de Dios asked her out to lunch. Unexpectedly, the director accepted the invitation and they agreed to meet at a vegetarian restaurant on Calle Río Usumacinta, in Colonia Podestá. He'd never been to the restaurant, and when he got there he asked for a table for two and a whiskey while he waited, but they didn't serve alcohol. The waiter was wearing a checkered shirt and sandals and looked at him as if something was wrong with him or he'd come to the wrong restaurant. It was a nice place, he thought. The people at the other tables talked in low voices and there was the sound of music like water tumbling over smooth stones. The director saw him as soon as she came in, but she didn't say hello. She went to talk to the waiter, who was preparing fresh-squeezed juice behind the bar. After exchanging a few words with him, she came over to the table. She was wearing gray pants and a low-cut pearl-colored sweater. Juan de Dios Martínez got up when she reached him and thanked her for agreeing to have lunch with him. The director smiled: she had small, even teeth, very white and sharp, which made her smile look carnivorous in a way that was out of keeping with the restaurant. The waiter asked what they wanted to eat. Juan de Dios Martínez looked at the menu and then said she should choose for him. As they were waiting for their food he told her about San Tadeo. The director listened carefully and at the end she asked if there was anything else. That's the whole story, said the inspector. My two patients spent the night at the center, she said. I know, he said. How? After I left the church I went to the asylum. I asked the guard and the nurse on duty to take me to their rooms. Both were asleep. There were no urine-stained clothes. No one let them out. What you're describing is illegal, said the director. But now they aren't suspects anymore, said the inspector. And I didn't even wake them up. They didn't realize a thing. For a while the director ate in silence. Juan de Dios Martínez was beginning to like the water-sounds music more and more. He told her so. I'd like to buy the album, he said. He meant it sincerely. The director seemed not to hear him. For dessert they were served figs. Juan de Dios Martínez said it had been years since he ate figs. The director ordered a coffee and wanted to pay for the meal herself, but he wouldn't let her. It wasn't easy. He had to insist more than once, and the director seemed to turn to stone. When they left the restaurant they shook hands as if they would never see each other again.

•

Two days later, the stranger got into the church of Santa Catalina, in Colonia Lomas del Toro, late at night when the building was closed, and he urinated and defecated on the altar, as well as decapitating almost all the statues in his path. This time, the story made the national news and a reporter from *La Voz de Sonora* dubbed the attacker the Demon Penitent. As far as Juan de Dios Martínez knew, the culprit might be anyone, but the police decided it had been the Penitent and he thought it best to go along with the official story. It didn't strike him as odd that nobody living near the church had heard anything, even though it would have taken time to break all those sacred objects and would've made lots of noise. No one lived at the church. The officiating priest was there from nine in the morning till one in the afternoon, and then he went to work at a parochial school in Colonia Ciudad Nueva. There was no sexton and the altar boys who helped at Mass sometimes came and sometimes didn't. In fact, Santa Catalina was a church with almost no parishioners, and the things inside were cheap, bought by the diocese at a store downtown that sold cassocks and saints, wholesale and retail. The priest was an open-minded man, a freethinker, or so it seemed to Juan de Dios Martínez. They talked for a while. There was nothing missing from the church. The priest didn't seem scandalized or upset by the outrage. He made a rapid calculation of the damages and said that for the diocese it was a drop in the bucket. He wasn't startled by the shit on the altar. After you leave this will all be cleaned up in a few hours, he said. But the quantity of urine alarmed him. Shoulder to shoulder, like Siamese twins, the inspector and the priest examined every corner where the Penitent had urinated, and the priest said at last that the man must have a bladder the size of a watermelon. That night, Juan de Dios Martínez thought to himself that he was beginning to like the Penitent. The first attack was violent and the sexton was almost killed, but as the days went by he was perfecting his technique. With the second attack he had only frightened some churchgoers, and with the third no one saw him and he was able to work in peace.

•

Three days after the desecration of the church of Santa Catalina, in the early morning hours, the Penitent slipped into the church of Nuestro Señor Jesucristo, in Colonia Reforma, the oldest church in the city, built in the mideighteenth century and once the seat of the diocese of Santa Teresa. Three priests and two young Pápago Indian seminarians who were studying anthropology and history at the University of Santa Teresa slept in an adjacent building, located at the corner of Calle Soler and Calle Ortiz Rubio. In addition to pursuing their studies, the seminarians performed some minor cleaning tasks, like washing the dishes each night or gathering up the priests' dirty laundry and delivering the load to the woman who did the washing. That night, one of the seminarians wasn't asleep. He had tried to study in his room and then he got up to get a book from the library, where, for no reason, he sat reading in an armchair until he fell asleep. The building was connected to the church by a passageway that led straight to the rectory office. It was said that there was another underground passageway that the priests had used during the Revolution and the Cristero War, but the Pápago student had never heard of it. Suddenly he was woken by the sound of breaking glass. First, oddly enough, he thought it was raining, but then he realized the noise was coming from inside the church, not outside, and he went to investigate. When he got to the rectory office he heard moans and he thought someone had gotten locked inside one of the confessionals, which was entirely unlikely, since the doors didn't lock. The Pápago student, despite what was commonly believed about people of his ancestry, wasn't brave at all and was afraid to go into the church alone. First he went to wake up the other seminarian and then the two of them knocked very discreetly at the door of Father Juan Carrasco, who at that hour was asleep, like everybody else in the building. Father Juan Carrasco listened to the Pápago's story in the hallway and since he read the news he said: it must be the Penitent. Immediately he went back into his room, put on pants and sneakers that he wore to go jogging or to play *frontón*, and got an old baseball bat out of a cupboard. Then he sent one of the Pápagos to wake up the caretaker, who slept in a little room on the first floor, next to the stairs, and, followed by the Pápago who had raised the alert, he headed for the church. At first glance both had the impression that no one was there. The opalescent smoke of the candles rose slowly toward the vaulted ceiling and a dense, tawny cloud hovered motionless inside the sanctuary. A moment later they heard the moan, like a child trying not to vomit, then another and another, and then the familiar sound of the first retch. It's the Penitent, whispered the seminarian. Father Carrasco furrowed his brow and headed resolutely toward the place the noise was coming from, gripping the baseball bat in two hands, as if he were about to step up to the plate. The Pápago didn't follow him. Maybe he took a small step or two in the direction the priest had gone, but then he stood still, prey to a divine terror. Even his teeth were chattering. He could neither advance nor retreat. So, as he later explained to the police, he began to pray. What did you pray? asked Inspector Juan de Dios Martínez. The Pápago didn't understand the question. The Lord's Prayer? asked the inspector. No, oh no, my mind went blank, said the Pápago, I prayed for my soul, I prayed to the Holy Mother, I begged the Holy Mother not to abandon me. From where he was he heard the sound of the baseball bat slamming against a column. It might have been (he thought or he remembered having thought) the Penitent's spinal column or the six-foot column on which stood the wooden carving of the Archangel Gabriel. Then he heard someone panting. He heard the Penitent moan. He heard Father Carrasco swear at someone, but the words were strange, and he couldn't tell whether it was the Penitent who was being sworn at, or he himself for not following, or an unknown person from Father Carrasco's past, someone the Pápago would never know and the priest would never see again. Then came the sound of a baseball bat dropping on stones cut with skill and precision. The wood, the bat, bounced several times until at last the noise ceased. Almost at the same instant he heard the scream, which brought back the sense of divine terror. Unthinking terror. Or a terror expressed in shaky images. Then he thought he saw, as if by candlelight, though it might just as easily have been a ray of lightning, the figure of the Penitent shattering the shinbones of the archangel in a single blow and knocking it off its pedestal with the baseball bat. Again the sound of wood, this time very old wood, hitting stone, as if in that place wood and stone were strictly antagonistic terms. And more blows. And then the footsteps of the caretaker, who came running and plunged into the darkness too, and the voice of his Pápago brother asking him, in Pápago, what was wrong, what hurt. And then more shouting and more priests and voices calling for the police and a flurry of white shirts and an acid smell, as if someone had mopped the stones of the old church with a gallon of ammonia, the smell of piss, as he was informed by Inspector Juan de Dios Martínez, too much urine for one man, for a man with a normal bladder.

•

This time the Penitent went berserk, said Inspector José Márquez as he knelt to look at the bodies of Father Carrasco and the caretaker. Juan de Dios Martínez examined the window the Penitent had come in through and then he went outside and spent a while walking along Calle Soler and then Calle Ortiz Rubio and through a plaza the residents used as free parking at night. When he got back to the church, Pedro Negrete and Epifanio were there, and as soon as he came in the police chief motioned for him to join them. For a while they talked and smoked sitting in the last row of pews. Under his leather jacket Negrete was wearing a pajama shirt. He smelled of expensive cologne and he didn't seem tired. Epifanio was wearing a light blue suit that looked good in the dim light of the church. Juan de Dios Martínez told the police chief the Penitent must have a car. What makes you say that? He can't get around on foot without attracting attention, said the inspector. His piss stinks. It's a long way from Kino to Reforma. It's a long way from Reforma to Lomas del Toro, too. Let's say the Penitent lives downtown. You could walk downtown from Reforma, and if it was nighttime, no one would notice you smelled like piss. But to walk downtown from Lomas del Toro, that would take, I don't know, at least an hour. Or more, said Epifanio. And how far is it from Lomas del Toro to Kino? At least forty-five minutes, assuming you don't get lost, said Epifanio. And that's not to mention Reforma to Kino, said Juan de Dios Martínez. So the bastard gets around by car, said the police chief. It's the only thing we can be sure of, said Juan de Dios Martínez. And he probably carries a change of clothes in the car. What for? asked the police chief. As a safety precaution. So in other words you think the Penitent is nobody's fool, said Negrete. He only goes crazy when he's in a church, when he comes out he's just like anybody else, whispered Juan de Dios Martínez. Goddamn, said the police chief. What do you think, Epifanio? Could be, said Epifanio. If he lives alone, he can come back smelling like shit, since it doesn't take him more than a minute to get from his car to his base of operations. If he's got some woman at home or his folks, he must change his clothes before he goes in. Makes sense, said the police chief. But the question is how we stop all this. Any ideas? For now, station an officer in each church and wait for the Penitent to make his next move, said Juan de Dios Martínez. My brother's a churchgoer, said the police chief, as if thinking out loud. I have to ask him a few things. What about you, Juan de Dios, where do you think the Penitent lives? I don't know, Chief, said the inspector, anywhere, although if he has a car I doubt he lives in Kino.

At five in the morning, when Inspector Juan de Dios Martínez got home, there was a message from the asylum director on his answering machine. The person you're looking for, said the director's voice, is sacraphobic. Call me and I'll explain. Late as it was, he called her right away. The director's recorded voice answered. Martínez here, from the Policía Judicial, said Juan de Dios Martínez, sorry to call so early . . . I got your message . . . I just got in . . . Tonight the Penitent . . . Anyway, I'll call you tomorrow . . . Or today, I guess . . . Good night and thanks for the message. Then he took off his shoes and pants and fell into bed, but he couldn't sleep. By six he was at the station. A group of patrolmen were celebrating the birthday of a colleague and they offered him a drink, but he said no. From the offices of the judicial police inspectors, which were empty, he heard them singing "Happy Birthday" over and over again on the floor above. He made a list of the officers he wanted to work with him. He wrote a report for the Hermosillo office and then he stood out by the vending machine and drank a cup of coffee. He watched two patrolmen come down the stairs with their arms around each other and he followed them. In the hallway he saw several cops talking, in groups of two, three, four. Every so often one group laughed loudly. A man dressed in white, but wearing jeans, pushed a stretcher. On the stretcher, covered in a gray plastic sheet, lay the body of Emilia Mena Mena. Nobody noticed.

•

Emilia Mena Mena died in June. Her body was found in the illegal dump near Calle Yucatecos, on the way to the Hermanos Corinto brick factory. The medical examiner's report stated that she had been raped, stabbed, and burned, without specifying whether the stab wounds or the burns had been the cause of death, and without specifying whether Emilia Mena Mena was already dead when the burns were inflicted. Fires were constantly being reported in the dump where she was found, most of them set on purpose, others flaring up by chance, so there was some possibility the body had been charred by a random blaze, not set alight by the murderer. The dump didn't have a formal name, because it wasn't supposed to be there, but it had an informal name: it was called El Chile. During the day there wasn't a soul to be seen in El Chile or the surrounding fields soon to be swallowed up by the dump. At night those who had nothing or less than nothing ventured out. In Mexico City they call them *teporochos*, but a *teporocho* is a survivor, a cynic and a humorist, compared to the human beings who swarmed alone or in pairs around El Chile. There weren't many of them. They spoke a slang that was hard to understand. The police conducted a roundup the night after the body of Emilia Mena Mena was found and all they brought in was three children hunting for cardboard in the trash. The night residents of El Chile were few. Their life expectancy was short. They died after seven months, at most, of picking their way through the dump. Their feeding habits and their sex lives were a mystery. It was likely they had forgotten how to eat or fuck. Or that food and sex were beyond their reach by then, unattainable, indescribable, beyond action and expression. All, without exception, were sick. To strip the clothes from a body in El Chile was to skin it. The population was stable: never fewer than three, never more than twenty.

•

The main suspect in the killing of Emilia Mena Mena was her boyfriend. When the police came looking for him at the house where he lived with his parents and three brothers, he was already gone. According to the family he had gotten on a bus a day or two before the body was found. The father and two brothers spent a few days in a cell, but the only coherent information that could be extracted from them was the address of the father's brother, in Ciudad Guzmán, the suspect's ostensible destination. When the police in Ciudad Guzmán were alerted, some officers made a visit to the residence in question, equipped with the necessary warrants, but they found no trace of the alleged boyfriend and killer. The case remained open and was soon forgotten. Five days later, while the investigation was still unconcluded, the janitor at Morelos Preparatory School found the body of another dead woman. It was on a piece of ground where the students sometimes played soccer and baseball, a field with a view of Arizona and the shells of the maquiladoras on the Mexican side of the border and the dirt roads leading from the factories to the network of paved roads. Along one side, separated from the field by a barbed-wire fence, were the school yards, and farther off were the two three-story school buildings, where classes were taught in big, sunny rooms. The school had opened in 1990 and the janitor had been there since the beginning. He was the first to arrive each morning and one of the last to leave. The morning he found the dead woman, something caught his attention while he was picking up the master keys from the principal's office. At first he wasn't sure what it was. By the time he came into the supply room he realized. Buzzards. Buzzards were flying over the field next to the yard. But he still had plenty to do, and he decided to investigate later. Shortly afterward, the cook and the kitchen boy arrived, and he went to have coffee with them in the kitchen. They talked for ten minutes about the usual things, until the janitor asked if they had seen buzzards over the school when they came in. Both of them answered that they hadn't. Then the janitor finished his coffee and said he was going to take a walk out to the field. He was afraid he would find a dead dog. If he did, he would have to come back to the school, to the room where the tools were kept, and get a shovel and go back to the field and bury the dog deep enough so the students wouldn't dig it up. But what he found was a woman. She was dressed in a black shirt and black shoes and her skirt was rolled up around her waist. She didn't have anything on underneath. That was the first thing he saw. Then he got a look at her face and saw she hadn't died that night. One of the buzzards landed on the fence but he shooed it off. The woman had long black hair at least halfway down her back. Some strands were stuck together with coagulated blood. On her stomach and between her legs there was dried blood. He crossed himself twice and stood up slowly. When he got back to the school he told the cook what had happened. The kitchen boy was scrubbing a pot and the janitor spoke in a low voice, so he wouldn't hear. He called the principal from the office, but the principal had already left home. He found a blanket and went to cover up the dead woman. Only then did he realize a stake had been driven straight through her. His eyes filled with tears as he returned to the school. The cook was there, sitting in the yard, smoking a cigarette. She made a gesture as if to ask how it had gone. The janitor responded with another gesture, impossible to decipher, and went out to wait for the principal by the main door. When he arrived they both went out to the field. From the yard the cook watched as the principal lifted one side of the blanket and stared from different angles at the scarcely visible shape on the ground. A little later they were joined by two teachers, and, about thirty feet away, by a group of students. At noon, two police cars, a third, unmarked car, and an ambulance arrived, and the dead woman was taken away. Her name was never learned. The medical examiner stated that she had been dead for several days, without specifying how many. The stab wounds to the chest were the probable cause of death, but the examiner couldn't rule out a fractured skull as the principal cause. The dead woman was probably somewhere between twenty-three and twenty-five. She was five feet seven inches tall.

•

The last dead woman to be discovered in June 1993 was Margarita López Santos. She had disappeared more than forty days before. The second day she was gone, her mother filed a report at Precinct #2. Margarita López worked at K&T, a maquiladora in the El Progreso industrial park near the Nogales highway and the last houses of Colonia Guadalupe Victoria. The day of her disappearance she was working the third shift at the maquiladora, from nine at night to five in the morning. According to her fellow workers, she had come in on time, as always, because Margarita was more dependable and responsible than most, which meant that her disappearance could be fixed around the time of the shift change and her walk home. But no one saw anything then, in part because it was dark at five or five-thirty in the morning, and there wasn't enough public lighting. Most of the houses in the northern part of Colonia Guadalupe Victoria had no electricity. The roads out of the industrial park, except the one leading to the Nogales highway, also lacked adequate lighting, paving, and drainage systems: almost all the waste from the park ended up in Colonia Las Rositas, where it formed a lake of mud that bleached white in the sun. So Margarita López left work at five-thirty. That much was established. And then she set out along the dark streets of the industrial park. Maybe she saw the pickup that parked each night in an empty plaza next to the parking lot of the WS-Inc. maquiladora, a truck that sold coffee and soft drinks and different kinds of sandwiches to the workers on their way into or out of work. Most of them women. But she wasn't hungry or she knew there was a meal waiting for her at home and she didn't stop. She left the park and the ever more distant glow of the lights of the maquiladoras. She crossed the Nogales highway and turned down the first streets of Colonia Guadalupe Victoria. Crossing Guadalupe Victoria would take her no more than half an hour. Then she would be in Colonia San Bartolomé, where she lived. All in all, a fifty-minute walk, more or less. But somewhere along the way something happened or something went permanently wrong and afterward her mother was told there was a chance she had run off with a man. She's only sixteen, said her mother, and she's a good girl. Forty days later some children found her body near a shack in Colonia Maytorena. Her left hand rested on some guaco leaves. Due to the state of the body, the medical examiner was unable to determine the cause of death. One of the policemen present at the removal of the body, however, was able to identify the guaco plant. It's good for mosquito bites, he said, crouching down and plucking some little green leaves, pointed and tough.

•

There were no deaths in July. None in August either.

•

Around this time the Mexico City newspaper *La Razón* sent Sergio González to write a story on the Penitent. Sergio González was thirty-five and recently divorced, and he was looking to make money any way he could. Normally he wouldn't have accepted the assignment, because he was an arts writer, not a crime reporter. He wrote reviews of philosophy books that no one read, not the books or his reviews, and sometimes he wrote about art shows or music. He had been on staff at *La Razón* for four years and his financial situation was acceptable, if not comfortable, until the divorce, when suddenly he was in constant need of money. Since there was nothing else he could write for his own section (where he sometimes used a pseudonym so readers wouldn't be able to tell that all the articles were his), he badgered the editors of the other sections to give him extra assignments to help boost his income. Hence the proposal to travel to Santa Teresa and write the story of the Penitent. The person who offered him the story was the editor of the paper's Sunday magazine, who held González in high regard and thought that with his offer he would kill two birds with one stone: on the one hand, González would make some money, and on the other hand, he could take three or four days of vacation up north, somewhere with good food and clean air, and forget about his wife. So in July 1993, Sergio González flew to Hermosillo and took the bus to Santa Teresa. And in fact, the change of scene suited him perfectly. Hermosillo's bright blue skies, almost a metallic blue, lit from beneath, cheered him up instantly. The people in the airport and later on the city streets struck him as friendly, relaxed, as if he were in a foreign country and seeing only the good side of its inhabitants. In Santa Teresa, which he thought of as a hardworking city with very little unemployment, he got a room at a cheap hotel called El Oasis in the center of town, on a street where the paving stones dated back to the time of the Reform, and a little later he visited the offices of *El Heraldo del Norte* and *La Voz de Sonora* and spoke at length with the reporters who were covering the story of the Penitent. They told him how to get to the desecrated churches, which he visited in a single day, in the company of a taxi driver who waited for him out front. He managed to talk to two priests, at San Tadeo and Santa Catalina, who had little new to add, although the priest at Santa Catalina suggested he take a good look around, because in his opinion the church-desecrator-turned-killer wasn't the worst scourge of Santa Teresa. The police let him have a copy of the sketch of the perpetrator and he made an appointment to talk to

Juan de Dios Martínez, the inspector in charge of the case. In the afternoon he talked to the mayor, who invited him to lunch at the restaurant next door to the city council building, a restaurant with stone walls that strove and failed to look colonial. But the food was very good, and the mayor and two other lower-ranking members of the city administration made it their business to keep things lively with gossip and dirty jokes. The next day he tried to interview the chief of police, but it was a staff member who met with him, probably the police department's press officer, a kid straight out of law school who handed him a folder with all the information a reporter might need to write a story about the Penitent. The kid's last name was Zamudio and he had nothing better to do that night than keep Sergio González company. They had dinner together. Then they went to a club. Sergio González couldn't remember having been in a club since he was seventeen years old. He told Zamudio, who laughed. They bought drinks for lots of girls. The girls were from Sinaloa and it was immediately clear by their clothes that they were factory workers. Sergio González asked one girl he ended up with whether she liked to dance, and she said she liked it more than anything in the world. The answer struck him as illuminating, though he couldn't say why, and also devastatingly sad. In turn, the girl asked him what a *chilango* from Mexico City was doing in Santa Teresa, and he said he was a reporter and he was writing a story on the Penitent. She didn't seem impressed by the revelation. She had never read *La Razón* either, which González found hard to believe. At some point, Zamudio took him aside and said they could sleep with the girls. Zamudio's face was distorted by the strobe lights and he looked like a madman. González shrugged.

•

The next day he woke up alone in his hotel room with the sensation of having seen or heard something forbidden. Or at least inappropriate, awkward. He tried to interview Juan de Dios Martínez. The only people in the office were two men playing dice, while a third watched. All three were judicial police inspectors. Sergio González introduced himself and then sat down in a chair to wait, since they'd told him that Juan de Dios Martínez would be in soon. The inspectors were dressed in warm-up jackets and sweats. Each of the players had a cup of beans and at each toss of the dice they took a few beans out of their respective cups and placed them in the middle of the table. It seemed strange to González that grown men would bet with beans, but even stranger when he saw that some of the beans in the middle of the table were jumping. He looked carefully, and it was true, every so often one or sometimes two of the beans jumped, not very high, maybe half an inch or a quarter of an inch, but they really were jumping. The players paid no attention to the beans. They dropped the dice, of which there were five, into the barrel, shook it, and, with a sharp knock, spilled them onto the table. At each throw, they spoke words González didn't understand. They said: *engarróteseme ahí*, or *metateado*, or *peladeaje*, or *combiliado*, or *biscornieto*, or *bola de pinole*, or *despatolado*, or *sin desperdicio*, as if they were uttering the names of gods or steps in a ceremony that even they didn't understand but everyone had to obey. The inspector who wasn't playing wagged his head in unison. Sergio González asked if the beans were jumping beans. The inspector looked at him and nodded. I've never seen so many, he said. In fact, he had never even seen one. When Juan de Dios Martínez came in, the inspectors kept playing. Juan de Dios Martínez was wearing a gray suit, slightly wrinkled, and a dark green tie. They sat down at a desk, which from what González could see was the neatest in the office, and talked about the Penitent. According to the inspector, although he asked that this be off the record, the Penitent was sick. What kind of sickness does he have? whispered González, realizing as they spoke that Juan de Dios Martínez didn't want his colleagues to hear. Sacraphobia, said the inspector. And what's that? asked González. Fear and hatred of sacred objects, said the inspector. According to him, the Penitent didn't desecrate churches with the premeditated intent to kill. The deaths were accidental. The Penitent just wanted to vent his rage on the images of the saints.

·

It wasn't long before the churches desecrated by the Penitent were tidied up and the damages fully repaired, except at Santa Catalina, which for a while remained just as the Penitent had left it. We need money for many things, Sergio González was told by the Ciudad Nueva priest who came once a day to Colonia Lomas del Toro to say Mass and clean, his words implying that there were higher or more urgent priorities than the replacement of the sacred objects that had been destroyed. It was thanks to this priest, the second and last time they met at the church, that Sergio González learned that crimes other than the Penitent's were being committed in Santa Teresa, crimes against women, still mostly unsolved. For a while, as he swept, the priest talked and talked: about the city, about the trickle of Central American immigrants, about the hundreds of Mexicans who arrived each day in search of work at the maquiladoras or hoping to cross the border, about the human trafficking by *polleros* and *coyotes*, about the starvation wages paid at the factories, about how those wages were still coveted by the desperate who arrived from Querétaro or Zacatecas or Oaxaca, desperate Christians, said the priest (which was an odd way to describe them, especially for a priest), who embarked on the most incredible journeys, sometimes alone and sometimes with their families in tow, until they reached the border and only then did they rest or cry or pray or get drunk or get high or dance until they fell down exhausted. The priest sounded like he was chanting a litany, and for a moment, as he listened, Sergio González closed his eyes and nearly fell asleep. Later they went outside and sat on the brick steps of the church. The priest offered him a Camel and they smoked, gazing at the horizon. So besides being a reporter, what other things do you do in Mexico City? the priest asked. For a few seconds, as he breathed in the smoke of his cigarette, Sergio González thought about what to answer and couldn't come up with anything. I just got divorced, he said, and I read a lot. What kind of books? the priest wanted to know. Philosophy, more than anything, said González. Do you like to read, too? A couple of girls came running by and greeted the priest by name, without stopping. González watched them cut through a lot where big red flowers were blooming and then cross a street. Of course, said the priest. What kind of books? asked González. Liberation theology, especially, said the priest. I like Boff and the Brazilians. But I read detective novels, too. González got up and stubbed out his cigarette on the sole of his shoe. It's been a pleasure, he said. The priest shook his hand and nodded.

•

The next morning, Sergio González took the bus to Hermosillo and then, after a four-hour wait, flew back to Mexico City. Two days later he filed his story on the Penitent with the Sunday magazine editor and promptly forgot the whole business.

•

What is sacraphobia exactly? Juan de Dios Martínez asked the director. Teach me a little about it. The director said her name was Elvira Campos and she ordered a whiskey. Juan de Dios Martínez ordered a beer and glanced around the bar. On the terrace an accordion player, followed by a violinist, was trying in vain to attract the attention of a man dressed like a rancher. A *narco*, thought Juan de Dios Martínez, although since the man had his back to him, he couldn't say who it was. Sacraphobia is fear or hatred of the sacred, of sacred objects, especially from your own religion, said Elvira Campos. He thought about making a reference to Dracula, who fled crucifixes, but he was afraid the director would laugh at him. And you believe the Penitent suffers from sacraphobia? I've given it some thought, and I do. A few days ago he disemboweled a priest and another person, said Juan de Dios Martínez. The accordion player was very young, twenty at most, and round as an apple. The way he held himself, however, made him look at least twenty-five, except when he smiled, which was often, and then all of a sudden it was clear how young and inexperienced he was. He doesn't carry the knife to hurt anyone, any living thing, I mean, but to destroy the sacred images he finds in churches, said the director. Shall we call each other by our first names? Juan de Dios Martínez asked her. Elvira Campos smiled and nodded. You're a very attractive woman, said Juan de Dios Martínez. Thin and attractive. You don't like thin women, Inspector? asked the director. The violinist was taller than the accordionist and she was wearing a black blouse and black leggings. She had long straight hair down to her waist and sometimes she closed her eyes, especially when the accordionist sang and played. The saddest thing, thought Juan de Dios Martínez, was that the *narco*, or the suited back of the man he thought was a *narco*, was hardly paying any attention to them, busy as he was talking to a man with the face of a mongoose and a hooker with the face of a cat. Weren't we going to call each other by our first names? asked Juan de Dios Martínez. You're right, said the director. So are you sure the Penitent suffers from sacraphobia? The director said she'd been looking through the archives at the asylum to see whether she could find some former patient with a case history like the Penitent's. She hadn't come up with anything. If he's as old as you say he is, I'd guess he's been institutionalized at some point. The accordion player suddenly started to stamp in time to the music. From where they were sitting they couldn't hear him, but he was making faces, working his mouth and eyebrows, and then he ruffled his hair with one hand and seemed to howl with laughter. The violinist had her eyes closed. The *narco*'s head swiveled. Juan de Dios Martínez thought to himself that the boy had finally gotten what he wanted. There's probably a file on him in some psychiatric center in Hermosillo or Tijuana. It can't be such a rare case. Maybe he was on medication until recently. Maybe he stopped taking it, said the director. Are you married, do you live with anyone? asked Juan de Dios Martínez in an almost inaudible voice. I live alone, said the director. But you have children, I saw the pictures in your office. I have a daughter, she's married. Juan de Dios Martínez felt something release inside of him and he laughed. Don't tell me you're already a grandmother. That's not the kind of thing you say to a woman, Inspector. How old are you? asked the director. Thirty-four, said Juan de Dios Martínez. Seventeen years younger than me. You don't look more than forty, said the inspector. The director laughed: I exercise every day, I don't smoke, I drink very little, I eat right, I used to go running every morning. Not anymore? No, now I've bought myself a treadmill. The two of them laughed. I listen to Bach on my headphones and I almost always run three or four miles a day. Sacraphobia. If I tell my colleagues the Penitent is suffering from sacraphobia, they'll laugh at me. The man with the mongoose face rose from his chair and said something into the accordionist's ear. Then he sat down again and the accordionist's mouth screwed up into a pout. Like a child on the verge of tears. The violinist had her eyes open and she was smiling. The *narco* and the woman with the cat face bent their heads together. The *narco*'s nose was big and bony and aristocratic looking. But aristocratic looking how? There was a wild expression on the accordionist's face, except for his lips. Unfamiliar currents surged through the inspector's chest. The world is a strange and fascinating place, he thought.

·

There are odder things than sacraphobia, said Elvira Campos, especially if you consider that we're in Mexico and religion has always been a problem here. In fact, I'd say all Mexicans are essentially sacraphobes. Or take gephyrophobia, a classic fear. Lots of people suffer from it. What's gephyrophobia? asked Juan de Dios Martínez. The fear of crossing bridges. That's right, I knew someone once, well, it was a boy, really, who was afraid that when he crossed a bridge it would collapse, so he'd run across it, which was much more dangerous. A classic, said Elvira Campos. Another classic: claustrophobia. Fear of confined spaces. And another: agoraphobia. Fear of open spaces. I've heard of those, said Juan de Dios Martínez. And one more: necrophobia. Fear of the dead, said Juan de Dios Martínez, I've known people like that. It's a handicap for a policeman. Then there's hemophobia, fear of blood. That's right, said Juan de Dios Martínez. And peccatophobia, fear of comitting sins. But there are other, rarer, fears. For instance, clinophobia. Do you know what that is? No idea, said Juan de Dios Martínez. Fear of beds. Can anyone really fear beds, or hate them? Actually, yes, there are people who do. But they can deal with the problem by sleeping on the floor and never going into a bedroom. And then there's tricophobia, or fear of hair. That's a little more complicated, isn't it? Yes, very much so. There are cases of tricophobia that end in suicide. And there's verbophobia, fear of words. Which must mean it's best not to speak, said Juan de Dios Martínez. There's more to it than that, because words are everywhere, even in silence, which is never complete silence, is it? And then we have vestiphobia, which is fear of clothes. It sounds strange but it's much more widespread than you'd expect. And this one is relatively common: iatrophobia, or fear of doctors. Or gynophobia, which is fear of women, and naturally afflicts only men. Very widespread in Mexico, although it manifests itself in different ways. Isn't that a slight exaggeration? Not a bit: almost all Mexican men are afraid of women. I don't know what to say to that, said Juan de Dios Martínez. Then there are two fears that are really very romantic: ombrophobia and thalassophobia, or fear of rain and fear of the sea. And two others with a touch of the romantic: anthophobia, or fear of flowers, and dendrophobia, fear of trees. Some Mexican men may be gynophobes, said Juan de Dios Martínez, but not all of them, it can't be that bad. What do you think optophobia is? asked the director. Opto, opto, something to do with the eyes, my God, fear of the eyes? Even worse: fear of opening the eyes. In a figurative sense, that's an answer to what you just said about gynophobia. In a literal sense, it leads to violent attacks, loss of consciousness, visual and auditory hallucinations, and generally aggressive behavior. I know, though not personally, of course, of two cases in which the patient went so far as to mutilate himself. He put his eyes out? With his fingers, the nails, said the director. Good God, said Juan de Dios Martínez. Then we have pedophobia, of course, which is fear of children, and ballistophobia, fear of bullets. That's my phobia, said Juan de Dios Martínez. Yes, I suppose it's only common sense, said the director. And another phobia, this one on the rise: tropophobia, or the fear of making changes or moving. Which can be aggravated if it becomes agyrophobia, fear of streets or crossing the street. Not to forget chromophobia, which is fear of certain colors, or nyctophobia, fear of night, or ergophobia, fear of work. A common complaint is decidophobia, the fear of making decisions. And there's a fear that's just beginning to spread, which is anthrophobia, or fear of people. Some Indians suffer from a heightened form of astrophobia, which is fear of meteorological phenomena like thunder and lightning. But the worst phobias, in my opinion, are pantophobia, which is fear of everything, and phobophobia, fear of fear itself. If you had to suffer from one of the two, which would you choose? Phobophobia, said Juan de Dios Martínez. Think carefully, it has its drawbacks, said the director. Between being afraid of everything and being afraid of my own fear, I'd take the latter. Don't forget I'm a policeman and if I was scared of everything I couldn't work. But if you're afraid of your own fears, you're forced to live in constant contemplation of them, and if they materialize, what you have is a system that feeds on itself, a vicious cycle, said the director.

•

A few days before Sergio González came to Santa Teresa, Juan de Dios Martínez and Elvira Campos went to bed together. This isn't anything serious, the director warned him, I don't want you to get the wrong idea about where things are going. Juan de Dios Martínez promised that she would set the limits and he would simply abide by her decisions. The director found the first sexual encounter satisfactory. The next time they saw each other, fifteen days later, the results were even better. Sometimes he was the one who called, usually in the afternoon, while she was still at work, and they would talk for five minutes, sometimes ten, about the events of the day. It was when she called him that they made plans to see each other, always at Elvira's apartment in a new building in Colonia Michoacán, on a street of upper-middle-class houses where doctors and lawyers, a few dentists, and one or two college professors lived. Their meetings always followed the same pattern. The inspector left his car parked on the street and took the elevator up, checking in the mirror to make sure his appearance was impeccable, at least to the extent possible, considering his limitations, which he would be the first to enumerate, and then he would ring the director's doorbell. She would open the door, they would greet each other with a handshake or without touching, and immediately they would have a drink sitting in the living room, watching the dark move over the mountains to the east through the glass doors that led onto the big terrace where, in addition to a couple of wooden and canvas chairs and a sun umbrella furled for the night, there was only a steel-gray exercise bicycle. Then, with no preliminaries, they would go into the bedroom and make love for three hours. When they were done, the director would put on a black silk bathrobe and go shower. When she came out, Juan de Dios Martínez would already be dressed, sitting in the living room, gazing not at the mountains but at the stars visible from the terrace. The silence was absolute. Sometimes there would be a party going on in the yard of one of the nearby houses and they would watch the lights and the people walking or embracing next to the pool or coming in and out, as if at random, of the tents erected for the occasion or the gazebos of wood and wrought iron. The director wouldn't talk and Juan de Dios Martínez would contain the urge he sometimes felt to rattle off questions or tell her things about his life that he'd never told anyone. Then she would remind him, as if he'd asked her to, that he had to go and the inspector would say you're right or glance pointlessly at his watch and leave at once. Fifteen days later they would see each other again and everything would be just as it had been the time before. Of course, there wasn't always a party at a house nearby and sometimes the director couldn't or didn't want to drink, but the dim light was always the same, the shower was always repeated, the sunsets and the mountains never changed, the stars were the same stars.

•

Around this time, Pedro Negrete traveled to Villaviciosa to hire someone trustworthy for his old friend Pedro Rengifo. He saw several young men. He scrutinized them, asked some questions. He asked if they knew how to shoot. He asked if he could rely on them. He asked if they wanted to make money. It had been a while since he'd been back to Villaviciosa and the town looked the same as it had the last time he was there. Low adobe houses with small front yards. Two bars and a grocery store. To the east, the foothills of mountains that seemed to shrink or grow depending on the progression of the sun and shadows. When he'd made his choice, he called Epifanio over and asked privately what he thought. Which one is it, boss? The youngest one, said Negrete. Epifanio let his gaze drift over the boy and then he glanced at the others and before he went back to the car he said the kid wasn't bad, but you never knew. Then Negrete let a couple of old men from Villaviciosa buy him a drink. One was very thin, dressed in white, and wearing a gold-plated watch. Judging by the wrinkles on his face, he was over seventy. The other man was even older and thinner and wasn't wearing a shirt. He was short and his torso was covered in scars partly hidden by the folds of his skin. They drank pulque and every so often huge glasses of water because the pulque was salty and made them thirsty. They talked about goats lost in the Blue Hills and about holes in the mountains. During a pause, without fanfare, Negrete called the boy over and told him he'd been chosen. Go on, say goodbye to your mother, said the shirtless old man. The boy looked at Negrete and then looked at the floor, as if thinking what to say, but suddenly he changed his mind, said nothing, and went out. When Negrete left the bar, the boy and Epifanio were leaning on the fender of the car, talking.

•

The boy sat beside him, in the back. Epifanio was at the wheel. When they had left the dirt streets of Villaviciosa behind and were driving through the desert, the police chief asked what his name was. Olegario Cura Expósito, said the boy. Olegario Cura Expósito, said Negrete, staring up at the stars, strange name. For a while they were silent. Epifanio tried to tune in a Santa Teresa radio station but he couldn't get it and turned off the radio. From his window the police chief glimpsed a flash of lightning many miles away. Just then the car shuddered and Epifanio braked and got out to see what he had hit. The police chief watched him head down the highway and then he saw the beam of Epifanio's flashlight. He rolled down the window and asked what it was. They heard a gunshot. The chief opened the door and got out. He took a few steps to stretch his stiff legs, and Epifanio came ambling back. I killed a wolf, he said. Let's see, said the police chief, and the two of them set out into the darkness again. There were no headlights visible on the highway. The air was dry but sometimes there were gusts of salty wind, as if before it made its way into the desert the air had brushed across a salt marsh. The boy looked at the lighted dashboard of the car and then he covered his face with his hands. A few yards away the police chief ordered Epifanio

to pass him the flashlight and he shone it on the body of the animal lying in the road. It isn't a wolf, said the police chief. Oh, no? Look at its
coat, wolves' coats are shinier, sleeker, not to mention they aren't dumb
enough to get themselves run over by a car in the middle of a deserted
highway. Let's see, let's measure it, you hold the flashlight. Epifanio
trained the beam on the animal as the chief laid it straight and eyeballed
it. Coyotes, he said, are twenty-eight to thirty-six inches long, counting
the head. What would you say this one measures? About thirty-two?
asked Epifanio. Correct, said the police chief. And he went on: coyotes
weigh between twenty-two and thirty-five pounds. Pass me the flashlight
and pick it up, it won't bite you. Epifanio picked up the dead animal,
cradling it in his arms. How much would you say it weighs? Somewhere
between twenty-six and thirty-three, maybe, said Epifanio. Like a coyote. Because it is a coyote, jackass, said the police chief. They shone the
flashlight in its eyes. Maybe it was blind and that's why it didn't see me,
said Epifanio. No, it wasn't blind, said the police chief, looking at the
coyote's big dead eyes. Then they left the animal by the side of the road
and went back to the car. Epifanio tried to get a Santa Teresa station
again. All he heard was static and he turned the radio off. He imagined
that the coyote he'd hit was a female coyote and it was looking for a safe
place to give birth. That's why it didn't see me, he thought, but he
wasn't satisfied by the explanation. At El Altillo, when the first lights of
Santa Teresa appeared, the police chief broke the silence into which the
three of them had fallen. Olegario Cura Expósito, he said. Yes, sir, said
the boy. So what do your friends call you? Lalo, said the boy. Lalo? Yes,
sir. Did you hear that, Epifanio? I heard, said Epifanio, still thinking
about the coyote. Lalo Cura? asked the police chief. Yes, sir, said the
boy. You're kidding, right? No sir, that's what my friends call me, said the
boy. Did you hear that, Epifanio? asked the police chief. Sure, I heard,
said Epifanio. His name is Lalo Cura, said the police chief, and he
started to laugh. La locura, lunacy, get it? Of course I get it, said Epifanio, and he started to laugh too. Soon the three of them were laughing.

•

That night the Santa Teresa police chief slept soundly. He dreamed
about his twin brother. They were fifteen and they were poor and they
had gone out to roam the scrub hills where many years later Colonia
Lindavista would rise. They crossed a gully where boys sometimes went

in the rainy season to hunt toads, which were poisonous and had to be killed with stones, although he and his brother were interested in lizards, not toads. At dusk they returned to Santa Teresa, children scattering through the countryside like defeated soldiers. On the edge of the city there was always traffic, trucks going to Hermosillo or heading north or on their way to Nogales. Some were inscribed with odd phrases. One said: *In a hurry? Go right on under me.* Another one said: *Passing on the left? Just pump my horn.* And another one: *Like the ride?* In the dream neither he nor his brother talked, but all of their movements were identical, the same stride, the same pace, the arm swinging. His brother was already quite a bit taller, but they still looked alike. Then they were back on the streets of Santa Teresa and they strolled along the sidewalk and the dream vanished little by little in a comfortable yellow haze.

•

That night Epifanio dreamed about the female coyote left by the side of the road. In the dream he was sitting a few yards away, on a chunk of basalt, staring alertly into the dark and listening to the whimpering of the coyote, whose insides were torn up. She probably already knows she lost her pup, thought Epifanio, but instead of getting up and putting a bullet in her brain he sat there and did nothing. Then he saw himself driving Pedro Negrete's car along a long track that came to an end on the slopes of a mountain bristling with sharp rocks. There were no passengers in the car. He couldn't tell whether he had stolen the car or the chief had loaned it to him. The track was straight and he could easily get up to ninety miles an hour, although whenever he hit the accelerator he heard a strange noise from under the chassis, like something jumping. Behind him rose a giant plume of dust, like the tail of a hallucinogenic coyote. But the mountains still looked just as far away, so Epifanio braked and got out to inspect the car. At first glance everything looked all right. The suspension, the engine, the battery, the axles. Suddenly, with the car stopped, he heard the knocks again and turned around. He opened the trunk. There was a body inside. Its hands and feet were tied. A black cloth was wrapped around its head. What the fuck is this? shouted Epifanio in the dream. When he had checked that the body was still alive (its chest was rising and falling, though perhaps too violently), he closed the trunk without daring to remove the black cloth and see who it was. He got back in the car, which leaped forward at the first thrust. On the horizon the mountains seemed to be burning or crumbling, but he kept driving toward them.

•

That night Lalo Cura slept well. The cot was too soft, but he closed his eyes and started to think about his new job, and soon he was asleep. He'd been to Santa Teresa only once before, with some old women who had come to the market to sell herbs. He could hardly remember the trip now, because he'd been very small. This time he hadn't seen much either. The lights of the highway ramps and then a neighborhood of dark streets and then a neighborhood of big houses behind high walls bristling with glass. And later another road, heading east, and the sounds of the country. He slept in a bungalow next to the gardener's house, on a cot in a corner that no one used. The blanket smelled of rancid sweat. There was no pillow. On the cot there had been a stack of old newspapers and magazines with pictures of naked women, which he put under the bed. At one in the morning the two men who slept on the cots next to his came in. They were both wearing suits and wide ties and fancy cowboy boots. They turned on the light and looked at him. One of them said: he's a little guy. Lalo smelled them without opening his eyes. They smelled of tequila and *chilaquiles* and rice pudding and fear. Then he fell asleep and didn't dream about anything. The next morning the two men were sitting at the table in the kitchen of the gardener's house. They were eating eggs and smoking. He sat down next to them and drank a glass of orange juice and a cup of black coffee. He didn't want anything to eat. Pedro Rengifo's security chief was an Irishman named Pat and he was the one who made the formal introductions. The two men weren't from Santa Teresa or anywhere nearby. The bigger one was from the state of Jalisco. The other was from Ciudad Juárez, in Chihuahua. Lalo met their eyes and thought they didn't seem like gunmen, they seemed like cowards. When he was done with breakfast the security chief took him to the farthest corner of the yard and gave him a Desert Eagle .50 Magnum pistol. He asked Lalo if he knew how to use it. Lalo said he didn't. The chief put a seven-round magazine on the gun and then found some cans in the weeds that he set on the roof of a car up on blocks. For a while the two of them shot. Then the chief explained how to load a gun, how to use the safety, how to carry it. He said his job would be to watch out for Mrs. Rengifo, the boss's wife, and he would be working with the two men he'd just met. He asked if he knew how much he would be paid. He told him that payday was every fifteen days, that he personally paid everyone, and no one ever had any complaints in that regard. He asked him his name. Lalo Cura, said Lalo. The Irishman didn't laugh or give him a strange look or think it was a joke. He wrote down the name in a little black book that he kept in the back pocket of his jeans, and then their meeting was over. Before he left he told Lalo his name was Pat O'Bannion.

•

In September another dead woman was found, this time in a car in the Buenavista subdivision, past Colonia Lindavista. It was a lonely place. The only building there was a prefab house used as an office by the salesmen who showed the plots. The rest of the subdivision was bare, with a few sickly trees, their trunks painted white, the last survivors of an old meadow and woods that drew water from an aquifer. Sunday was the day when the most people bustled around the subdivision. Whole families or developers came to see the plots, although without much enthusiasm, because the most promising spaces were already sold, although no one had started to build yet. The rest of the week, visits were by appointment, and by eight there was no one left except the occasional pack of kids or dogs who had come down from Colonia Maytorena and couldn't find their way back up. The discovery was made by one of the salesmen. He got to the subdivision at nine in the morning and parked in his usual spot, next to the prefab house. As he was about to go in he noticed another car parked in a lot that hadn't been sold yet, just behind a rise in the ground, which had hidden it until then. He thought it might be another salesman's car but dismissed the idea as absurd, because who would leave his car so far away when he could park right next to the office? So instead of going inside, he headed toward the strange car. He thought maybe the driver was a drunk who had parked there to sleep, or someone lost, because the exit for the southbound highway wasn't far away. He even thought it might be an overeager buyer. The car, when he came around the rise (excellent plot, with nice views and enough land to build a pool on later), struck him as too old to belong to a buyer. He was leaning again toward the idea that it was a drunk and was tempted to turn back, but then he saw a woman's head resting against one of the rear windows and decided to keep going. The woman was wearing a white dress and she was barefoot. She was about five foot seven. There were three cheap rings on her left hand, on the index finger, middle finger, and ring finger. On her right hand she was wearing a couple of bracelets and two big rings with fake stones. According to the medical examiner's report, she had been vaginally and anally raped and then strangled. She wasn't carrying any identification. The case was assigned to Inspector Ernesto Ortiz Rebolledo, who first made inquiries among Santa Teresa's high-class hookers to see whether anyone knew the dead woman, and then, when his questioning yielded scant results, among the cheap hookers, but no one from either group had seen her before. Ortiz Rebolledo visited hotels and boardinghouses, checked out some motels on the edge of town, mobilized his informers. His efforts were unsuccessful, and the case was soon closed.

•

In the same month, two weeks after the discovery of the dead woman in the Buenavista subdivision, another body turned up. The victim was Gabriela Morón, eighteen, shot by her boyfriend, Feliciano José Sandoval, twenty-seven, both of them workers at the maquiladora Nip-Mex. The events, according to the police investigation, revolved around a fight caused by Gabriela Morón's refusal to immigrate to the United States. The suspect, Feliciano José Sandoval, had already made two attempts and had been sent back each time by the American border police, which hadn't diminished his desire to try his luck for a third time. According to some friends, Sandoval had relatives in Chicago. Gabriela Morón, on the other hand, had never crossed the border, and after finding work at Nip-Mex, where she was well liked by her bosses, which meant she had hopes of a quick promotion and a raise, her interest in seeking her fortune across the border dropped to practically zero. For a few days the police looked for Feliciano José Sandoval in Santa Teresa and Lomas de Poniente, the Tamaulipas town he was from, and an arrest order was also issued by the proper American authorities, in case the suspect, his dream come true, had made it to the United States, although oddly enough no *coyote* or *pollero* who might have helped him cross over was questioned. To all intents and purposes, the case was closed.

•

The next dead woman appeared in October, at the dump in the Arsenio Farrell industrial park. Her name was Marta Navales Gómez. She was twenty years old, five foot seven, and she had long brown hair. She had been missing from home for two days. She was dressed in a bathrobe and stockings that her parents didn't recognize as hers. She had been anally and vaginally raped several times. The cause of death was strangulation. The odd thing about the case was that Marta Navales Gómez worked at Aiwo, a Japanese maquiladora located in the El Progreso industrial park, but her body was found in the Arsenio Farrell industrial park, in the dump, a difficult place to reach unless you were driving a garbage truck. The body was found by some children in the morning, and by noon, when it was taken away, a considerable number of workers had gathered around the ambulance to see whether the victim was a friend, coworker, or acquaintance.

•

In October, too, the body of another woman was found in the desert, a few yards from the highway between Santa Teresa and Villaviciosa. The body, which was in an advanced state of decomposition, was facedown, and the victim was dressed in a sweatshirt and synthetic-fabric pants, in the pocket of which was found an ID card in the name of Elsa Luz Pintado, an employee at Hipermercado Del Norte. The killer or killers didn't bother to dig a grave. Nor did they bother to venture too far into the desert. They just dragged the body a few yards and left it there. Subsequent questioning at Hipermercado Del Norte yielded the following results: none of the cashiers or saleswomen had gone missing recently; Elsa Luz Pintado had been on the payroll, yes, but it had been a year and a half since she lent her services to that branch or any other branch of the superstore chain that stretched across the north of Sonora; those who had known Elsa Luz Pintado described her as a tall woman, five foot seven and a half, and the body found in the desert probably measured five foot three at most. An unsuccessful attempt was made to discover the whereabouts of Elsa Luz Pintado in Santa Teresa. The officer in charge of the case was Inspector Ángel Fernández. The forensic report failed to establish the cause of death, alluding vaguely to the possibility of strangulation, but it did confirm that the body had been in the desert for at least seven days and no more than one month. Sometime later Inspector Juan de Dios Martínez joined the investigation and issued a request for a search for Elsa Luz Pintado, who had presumably also disappeared. He wanted an official letter to be sent to police stations all over the state, but his request was returned with the recommendation that he focus on the specific case under investigation.

•

In the middle of November, Andrea Pacheco Martínez, thirteen, was kidnapped on her way out of Vocational School 16. Although the street was far from deserted, there were no witnesses, except for two of Andrea's classmates who saw her head toward a black car, probably a Peregrino or a Spirit, where a person in sunglasses was waiting for her. There may have been other people in the car, but Andrea's classmates didn't get a look at them, partly because the car windows were tinted. That afternoon Andrea didn't come home and her parents filed a police report a few hours later, after they had called some of her friends. The city police and the judicial police took charge of the case. When she was found, two days later, her body showed unmistakable signs of strangulation, with a fracture of the hyoid bone. She had been anally and vaginally raped. There was tumefaction of the wrists, as if they had been bound. Both ankles presented lacerations, by which it was deduced that her feet had also been tied. A Salvadorean immigrant found the body behind the Francisco I School, on Madero, near Colonia Álamos. It was fully dressed, and the clothes, except for the shirt, which was missing several buttons, were intact. The Salvadorean was accused of the homicide and spent two weeks in the cells of Police Precinct #3, at the end of which he was released. When he got out he was a broken man. A little later he crossed the border with a *pollero*. In Arizona he got lost in the desert and after walking for three days, he made it to Patagonia, badly dehydrated, where a rancher beat him up for vomiting on his land. He was picked up by the sheriff and spent a day in jail and then he was sent to a hospital, where the only thing left for him to do was die in peace, which he did.

•

On December 20, the last violent death of a woman was recorded for the year 1993. The victim was fifty years old and, as if to contradict some voices that were timidly beginning to be raised, she died at home and her body was found at home, not in a vacant lot, or a dump, or the yellow scrub of the desert. Her name was Felicidad Jiménez Jiménez and she worked at the Multizone-West maquiladora. The neighbors found her on the bedroom floor, naked from the waist down, with a piece of wood jammed in her vagina. The cause of death was multiple stab wounds, more than sixty as counted by the medical examiner, delivered by her son, Ernesto Luis Castillo Jiménez, with whom she lived. The boy, according to the testimony of some of the neighbors, suffered from attacks of madness, which sometimes, depending on the state of the family finances, were treated with antianxiety medication or stronger drugs. The police found him that very night, hours after the macabre deed, wandering the dark streets of Colonia Morelos. In his statement he admitted without any coercion whatsoever that he had killed his mother. He also admitted to being the Penitent, the desecrator of churches. When he was asked what made him jam the piece of wood in his mother's vagina, first he answered that he didn't know, and then, after thinking about it more carefully, that he had done it to teach her. Teach her what? asked the policemen, among whom were Pedro Negrete, Epifanio Galindo, Ángel Fernández, Juan de Dios Martínez, and José Márquez. To take him seriously. Then he lapsed into incoherence and was transferred to the city hospital. Felicidad Jiménez Jiménez had another son, an older son, who had immigrated to the United States. The police tried to contact him, but no one could provide a reliable address. In the subsequent search of the house they found no letters from this son, or any personal objects left behind after his departure, or anything that testified to his existence. Just two photographs: in one, Felicidad appears with two boys between the ages of ten and thirteen, both of them staring seriously into the camera. In the other picture, dating farther back, Felicidad appears again with two children, one just a few months old, gazing up at her (her killer, years later), and the other, about three, who would immigrate to the United States and never come back to Santa Teresa. When he was released from the psychiatric hospital, Ernesto Luis Castillo Jiménez was taken to the Santa Teresa prison, where he proved to be unusually talkative. He didn't like to be alone and he was always requesting the presence of policemen or reporters. The police tried to pin other unsolved murders on him. The prisoner's willing nature invited it. Juan de Dios Martínez was sure Castillo Jiménez wasn't the Penitent. Probably the only person he had killed was his mother, and he couldn't even be held responsible for that, because it was clear he was mentally unstable. And this was the last death of 1993, which was the year the killings of women began in the Mexican state of Sonora, under Governor José Andrés Briceño of the Partido de Acción Nacional (PAN), and Santa Teresa Mayor José Refugio de las Heras of the Partido Revolucionario Institucional (PRI), decent and upright men who did the right thing, without fear of reprisals, prepared for any unpleasantness.

•

Before the end of the year, however, another lamentable event occurred that had nothing to do with the killings of women, assuming the killings were related to one another, which had yet to be proved. Around this time, Lalo Cura and his two sorry partners worked every day protecting Pedro Rengifo's wife. Lalo had seen Pedro Rengifo only once, from far away. And yet by now he knew several of the bodyguards who worked for him. There were some who seemed interesting. Pat O'Bannion, for example. Or a Yaqui Indian who almost never talked. But all he felt for the two men he worked with was distrust. There was nothing to be learned from them. The tall one from Tijuana liked to talk about California and the women he had met there. He mixed Spanish and English. He told lies, stories appreciated only by his partner, the man from Juárez, who was quieter but struck Lalo as the less trustworthy of the two. One morning, like so many others, Pedro Rengifo's wife took the children to school. They left in two cars, the wife's light green Mercedes, and a brown Jeep Grand Cherokee that stood parked at the corner outside the school all morning with two other bodyguards inside. These two were called the *kids' bodyguards,* in the same way that Lalo and his two partners were called the *wife's bodyguards,* all of them inferior to the three on Pedro Rengifo's team, who were called the *boss's bodyguards* or the *boss's men,* thus indicating a hierarchy not only of pay and duties but also of bravery, daring, and disregard for personal safety. After she dropped the children off at school, Pedro Rengifo's wife went shopping. First she stopped at a boutique and then she went into a drugstore and later she decided to visit a friend on Calle Astrónomos, in Colonia Madero. For almost an hour Lalo Cura and the two bodyguards waited for her, the man from Tijuana in the car and Lalo and the man from Juárez leaning on the fender, in silence. When Pedro Rengifo's wife came out (her friend accompanied her to the door), the man from Tijuana got out of the car and Lalo and the other bodyguard straightened. There were a few people on the street. Not many, but a few. People walking into town to run some errand or another, people getting ready for the Christmas holidays, people going out to buy tortillas for lunch. The sidewalk was gray but the sun coming through the branches of the trees made it look bluish, like a river. Pedro Rengifo's wife gave her friend a kiss and stepped out onto the sidewalk. The man from Juárez hurried to open the gate for her. On one side of the street, the sidewalk was empty. On the other side, two maids were walking toward them. As Pedro Rengifo's wife came through the gate, she turned and said something to her friend, who was still in the doorway. Then the bodyguard from Tijuana spotted two men walking behind the two maids and he stiffened. Lalo Cura saw his face and he saw the men and he knew instantly that they were gunmen and they were there to kill Pedro Rengifo's wife. The man from Tijuana sidled up to the man from Juárez, who was still holding open the gate, and said something, though it wasn't clear whether it was in words or gestures. Pedro Rengifo's wife smiled. Her friend gave a laugh that Lalo heard like something coming from very far away, from the top of a hill. Then he saw the way the man from Juárez was looking at the man from Tijuana: up and down, like a pig staring into the sun. With his left hand he released the safety of his Desert Eagle and then he heard the clack of heels, Pedro Rengifo's wife heading to the car, and the voices of the two maids, full of question marks, as if instead of chatting they were constantly interrogating each other and lapsing into astonishment, as if not even they could believe what they were saying. Neither of them was over twenty. They were wearing ocher skirts and yellow blouses. The friend, who was waving goodbye from the doorway, was wearing tight pants and a green sweater. Pedro Rengifo's wife was wearing a white suit and her high-heeled shoes were white too. Lalo thought about his boss's wife's outfit just as the other two bodyguards took off down the street. He wanted to shout: don't run, you fucking pussies, but he could only murmur pussies. Pedro Rengifo's wife didn't notice anything. The gunmen shoved the maids aside. One was carrying an Uzi submachine gun. He was thin and his skin was very dark. The other was carrying a pistol and wearing a dark suit and a white shirt, without a tie, and he looked like a professional. Just as the maids were pushed aside to clear the line of fire, Pedro Rengifo's wife felt someone tugging on her suit and pulling her to the ground. As she went down she saw the maids fall in front of her and she thought there had been an earthquake. Out of the corner of her eye, she also saw Lalo, kneeling with his gun in his hand, and she heard a noise and saw a shell leap from the gun in Lalo's grasp and then she didn't see anything because her forehead hit the cement of the sidewalk. Her friend, who was still standing in the doorway and therefore had a broader view of the scene, started to scream, frozen in place, although in the back of her mind a little voice was saying that instead of screaming she should go inside and lock the door, or if she couldn't do that, at least get down and hide behind the geraniums. By now, the man from Tijuana and the man from Juárez had covered quite a distance and although they were sweating and panting since they weren't used to physical exercise, they didn't stop running. As for the maids, from the moment they hit the ground, they both curled up and began to pray or scan the faces of their loved ones and both closed their eyes and didn't open them until everything was over. Meanwhile, for Lalo Cura the problem was deciding which of the two gunmen would shoot him first, the one with the Uzi or the one who looked more like a professional. He should have fired at the latter, but he fired at the former. The bullet struck the thin, dark-skinned man in the chest and felled him instantly. The other gunman shifted imperceptibly to the right and experienced his own moment of uncertainty. How was it that the boy was armed? Why hadn't he gone running off with the other two bodyguards? The professional's bullet lodged in Lalo Cura's left shoulder, severing blood vessels and fracturing the bone. A shudder ran through Lalo Cura, and without changing position he fired again. The professional fell flat on his face on the ground and his second shot went wide. He was still alive. He could see the cement sidewalk, the blades of grass growing through the cracks, the white suit of Pedro Rengifo's wife, the sneakers of the boy coming toward him to shoot him dead. Fucking kid, he whispered. Then Lalo Cura turned and saw the figures of his two ex-partners in the distance. He aimed carefully and fired. The man from Juárez realized they were being shot at and ran faster. At the first corner they disappeared.

•

Twenty minutes later a patrol car showed up. Pedro Rengifo's wife had a cut on her forehead but she wasn't bleeding anymore and it was she who directed the policemen's first steps. Her initial concern was for her friend, who was in a state of shock. Then she realized that Lalo Cura was wounded and she demanded they call another ambulance for him and that both Lalo and her friend be taken to the Pérez Guterson clinic. Before the ambulances came, more policemen arrived and several recognized the professional, who was lying dead on the sidewalk, as a state judicial police inspector. Just as Lalo Cura was about to be put in an ambulance, a couple of officers grabbed him by the arms, shoved him in a car, and drove him to Precinct #1. When Pedro Rengifo's wife got to the clinic, after leaving her friend settled in one of the best rooms, she went to check on the state of her bodyguard and was told he had never arrived. She demanded that the medics from the other ambulance be fetched immediately, and they confirmed that Lalo Cura had been arrested. Pedro Rengifo's wife picked up the phone and called her husband. An hour later the Santa Teresa police chief appeared at Precinct #1. With him was Epifanio, looking as if he hadn't slept for three days. Neither of the two seemed pleased. They found Lalo in one of the basement cells. There was blood on the boy's face. The policemen who were questioning him wanted to know why he had finished off the two gunmen, and when they saw Pedro Negrete come in they stood up. The chief sat in one of the vacated chairs and made a sign to Epifanio. Epifanio grabbed one of the policemen by the neck, pulled a switchblade from his jacket, and slashed the man's face from mouth to ear. He did it in such a way that not a single drop of blood landed on him. Is this the one who fucked you up? asked Epifanio. The boy shrugged. Take off his handcuffs, said Pedro Negrete. The other policeman took off the handcuffs, all the while muttering *ay, ay, ay*. What's wrong, man? asked Pedro Negrete. We made a mistake, boss, said the policeman. Get Pepe into a chair, it looks like he's about to pass out, said Pedro Negrete. Between Epifanio and the other policeman they sat the wounded officer down. How are you? Fine, boss, it's nothing, I'm just dizzy, that's all, said the officer as he felt in his pockets for something to press against the wound. Pedro Negrete handed him a tissue. Why did you arrest him? he asked. One of the guys he shot was Patricio López, from the state judicial police, said the other policeman. Well, what do you know, so it was Patricio López, but why did you think it was the kid who did it and not one of his partners? asked Pedro Negrete. His partners ran off, said the other policeman. Goddamn, that's what I call partners, said Pedro Negrete. So what did my boy do then? The policemen said that as far as they could establish, it seemed Lalo Cura had proceeded to shoot at them. At his own partners? That's right, his own partners, but before that, wounded in the shoulder and seemingly for no good reason, he had finished off Patricio López and a shithead with an Uzi. It must have been the shock, said Pedro Negrete. I'm sure you're right, said the officer with the cut face. Anyway, what else could he do? asked Pedro Negrete. If Patricio López had gotten the chance, he would have finished the kid off too. That's true, said the other policeman. Then they talked and smoked for a while longer, with a few brief interruptions for the officer with the cut face to change tissues, and then Epifanio escorted Lalo Cura out of the cell and helped him to the door of the police station where Pedro Negrete's car was waiting for him, the same car that had driven him away from Villaviciosa a few months before.

●

A month later, Pedro Negrete visited Pedro Rengifo's ranch, southeast of Santa Teresa, and demanded the return of Lalo Cura. I gave him to you, Pedro, and now I'm taking him back, he said. And why is that, Pedro? asked Pedro Rengifo. Because of the way you've treated him, Pedro, said Pedro Negrete. Instead of putting him with someone experienced, like your Irishman, so my boy could learn, you put him with a couple of faggots. You're right about that, Pedro, said Pedro Rengifo, but I'd like to remind you that one of those faggots came to me on your recommendation. True, I admit it, and as soon as I get my hands on him I'll right the wrong, Pedro, said Pedro Negrete, but now we're here to right your wrong. Well, as far as I'm concerned there's no problem, Pedro, if you want the boy back, he's yours, and Pedro Rengifo gave orders to one of his men to bring Lalo Cura from the gardener's house. While they were waiting, Pedro Negrete asked about Pedro Rengifo's wife and children. About the livestock. About Pedro Rengifo's grocery businesses in Santa Teresa and other northern cities. The wife spends all her time in Cuernavaca, said Pedro Rengifo, and we sent the children away to the United States for school (he was careful not to say where), the livestock is more a worry than a business, and the superstores have their ups and downs. Then Pedro Negrete wanted to know how Lalo Cura's shoulder was. It's just like new, Pedro, said Pedro Rengifo. The work is easy. The kid spends all day sleeping and reading magazines. He's happy here. I know he is, Pedro, said Pedro Negrete, but the way things are, one of these days he might get killed. Don't make it sound worse than it is, Pedro, said Pedro Rengifo with a laugh, but then he turned pale. On their way back to Santa Teresa, Pedro Negrete asked the boy if he'd like to be on the police force. Lalo Cura nodded. Shortly after they left the ranch they passed an enormous black stone. On the stone Lalo thought he saw a Gila monster, motionless, staring into the endless west. They say that stone is really a meteorite, said Pedro Negrete. In a gully, farther to the north, the Río Paredes curved, and from the road the tops of trees were visible like a green-black carpet with a cloud of dust hanging over them where Pedro Rengifo's cattle came to drink each afternoon. But if it was a meteorite, said Pedro Negrete, it would've left a crater, and where's the crater? When Lalo Cura looked at the black stone again in the rearview mirror, the Gila monster was gone.

·

The first dead woman of 1994 was found by some truck drivers on a road off the Nogales highway, in the middle of the desert. The truckers, both Mexican, worked for the maquiladora Key Corp., and that afternoon, despite having full loads, they decided to stop for food and drinks at a bar called El Ajo, where one of the truck drivers, Antonio Villas Martínez, was a regular. On their way to the bar in question, the other truck driver, Rigoberto Reséndiz, was dazzled for a few seconds by a flash in the desert. Thinking it was a joke, he radioed his friend Villas Martínez and the trucks pulled over. The road was deserted. Villas Martínez tried to convince Reséndiz that it had probably been the reflection of the sun off a bottle or some broken glass, but then Reséndiz saw a shape about three hundred yards from the highway and strode toward it. After a while, Villas Martínez heard Reséndiz whistle and he set off after him, not without first checking that both trucks were locked. When he got to where his friend was waiting he saw the body, which was clearly a woman's, though her face was a bloody mess. Oddly, the first thing he noticed were the woman's shoes. She was wearing nice tooled-leather sandals. Villas Martínez crossed himself. What do we do, *compadre*? he heard Reséndiz ask. By the tone of his friend's voice he understood that the question was rhetorical. Call the police, he said. Good idea, said Reséndiz. Villas Martínez spotted a belt with a big metal buckle around the dead woman's waist. That's what was flashing, *compadre*, he said. Yes, I saw, said Reséndiz. The dead woman was wearing hot pants and a silky yellow shirt with a big black flower stamped on the chest and a red flower on the back. When the body reached the medical examiner, he discovered, in astonishment, that under the hot pants the woman still had on white underpants with little bows on the sides. He also noted that she had been anally and vaginally raped, and that the cause of death was massive craniocerebral trauma, although she had been stabbed twice too, once in the chest and once in the back, wounds that had caused her to lose blood but weren't necessarily fatal. Her face, as the truck drivers had observed, was unrecognizable. The date of death was fixed, in a general way, between January 1 and January 6, 1994, although there was some possibility that the body had been dumped in the desert on December 25 or 26 of the previous year, now fortunately past.

•

The next dead woman was Leticia Contreras Zamudio. The police reported to La Riviera, a nightclub between Calle Lorenzo Sepúlveda and Calle Álvaro Obregón, in the center of Santa Teresa, after receiving an anonymous call. In one of the private rooms at La Riviera, they found the body, which exhibited multiple wounds to the abdomen and chest, as well as to the forearms, which led to the conclusion that Leticia Contreras had fought for her life to the last. The dead woman was twenty-three and had been working as a prostitute for more than four years, without a single brush with the police. After being questioned, none of the other girls could say who was with Leticia Contreras in the private room. At the time she was killed, some thought she had been in the bathroom. Others said she was in the basement, where there were four pool tables, because Leticia couldn't resist a game of pool and she wasn't a bad player. One girl even went so far as to suggest she had been alone, but what would a whore be doing alone in a private room? At four in the morning the whole staff of La Riviera was brought in to Precinct #1. Around this time, Lalo Cura was learning the traffic cop beat. He worked at night, on foot, and he drifted like a ghost through Colonia Álamos and Colonia Rubén Darío, from south to north, in no hurry, until he reached the center of the city, and then he could go back to Precinct #1 or do whatever he liked. He heard the screams as he was taking off his uniform. He got in the shower without paying much attention, but when he turned off the water he heard them again. They were coming from the cells. He tucked his gun in his belt and went out into the corridor. At that time of night, Precinct #1 was almost empty, except for the waiting room. In the antitheft task force office he found another policeman, asleep. He woke him and asked if he knew what was going on. The policeman said there was a party in the cells, and he could go down if he wanted. When Lalo Cura left, the policeman went back to sleep. From the stairs Lalo Cura smelled alcohol. There were twenty people jammed into one of the cells. He stared at them without blinking. Some were asleep on their feet. One who was up against the bars had his pants undone. The ones in the back were a shapeless mass of darkness and hair. It smelled of vomit. The cell must not have been more than ten feet square. In the corridor he saw Epifanio, who was watching what was happening in the other cells with a cigarette between his lips. He moved toward him to tell him the men were going to suffocate or be crushed to death, but with his first step he was silenced. In the other cells policemen were raping the whores from La Riviera. How's it rolling, Lalito? said Epifanio, going to get in on the action? No, said Lalo Cura, you? Me neither, said Epifanio. When they'd seen enough they went out for some fresh air. What did those whores do? asked Lalo. It looks like they bumped off another girl, said Epifanio. Lalo Cura was quiet. The early morning breeze along the streets of Santa Teresa really was fresh and cool. The scarred moon still shone in the sky.

•

Two of the girls who worked with Leticia Contreras Zamudio were formally accused of her murder, although there was no proof they were guilty, except for their presence at La Riviera at the time of events. Nati Gordillo was thirty years old and had known the dead woman since the latter came to work at the nightclub. At the moment in question she was in the bathroom. Rubí Campos was twenty-one and she hadn't been at La Riviera for more than five months. At the moment in question she was waiting for Nati in the bathroom, with only the door of the stall between them. The two of them, it was established, had a very close relationship. And it was proved that Rubí had been verbally attacked by Leticia two days before Leticia was killed. Another girl had heard Rubí say that Leticia would pay. The suspect didn't deny this, although she made it clear that she had planned to beat her up, not murder her. The two whores were transferred to Hermosillo and locked up at Paquita Avendaño, the women's prison, where they remained until their case was handed over to another judge, who was quick to declare them innocent.

In all, they spent two years in prison. When they got out they said they were going to try their luck in Mexico City, or maybe they went to the United States. The one thing certain is that they were never seen in the state of Sonora again.

•

The next victim was Penélope Méndez Becerra. She was eleven years old. Her mother worked at the maquiladora Interzone-Berny. Her older sister, sixteen, was also an Interzone-Berny employee. Her older brother, fifteen, worked as a delivery boy and messenger for a bakery not far from Calle Industrial, where they lived, in Colonia Veracruz. Penélope was the youngest and the only one in school. Seven years before, the children's father had left home. At the time, they all lived in Colonia More-los, near the Arsenio Farrell industrial park, in a house Penélope's father had built himself from cardboard and stray bricks and sheets of zinc, next to a trench that two of the maquiladora companies had dug to build a drainage system that in the end was never completed. Both parents were from the state of Hidalgo, in the middle of the country, and both had migrated north in 1985, in search of work. But one day Penélope's father decided that the family's living conditions weren't going to improve with what he earned at the maquiladoras and he decided to cross the border. He left with nine others, all from Oaxaca. One had made the trip three times already and said he knew how to dodge the *migra*. For the others it was the first attempt. The *pollero* who led them across told them not to worry. If they were unlucky enough to be arrested, he said, they should give themselves up without a struggle. Penélope Méndez's father spent all his savings on that trip. He promised he would write as soon as he got to California. He planned to bring his family to join him in less than a year. They never heard from him again. Penélope's mother imagined that maybe he had found another woman, American or Mexican, and they were doing well for themselves. She also wondered, especially in the first few months, whether he had died in the desert, at night, alone, listening to the coyotes howl or thinking of his children, or on an American street, killed by a driver who left him to die, but these thoughts paralyzed her (in them everyone, including her husband, spoke a different, incomprehensible, language), and she decided not to think them. Also, if he had died, she reasoned, someone would have let her know, wouldn't they? In any case she had enough problems at home without speculating about her husband's fate. It was hard to keep her family afloat. But since she was a neighborly and circumspect woman, optimistic by nature, and since she knew how to listen, she had plenty of friends. Especially women, who found her story familiar, nothing strange or out of the ordinary. One of these friends got her the job at Interzone-Berny. At first she walked a long way to work. Her older daughter took care of the other children. Her name was Livia, and one afternoon a drunken neighbor tried to rape her. When her mother got home from work, Livia told her what had happened and her mother went to call on the neighbor with a knife in her apron pocket. She talked to him and she talked to his wife and then she talked to him again: pray to the Virgencita that nothing happens to my daughter, she said, because if it does I'll blame you and I'll kill you with this knife. The neighbor said that from then on everything would change. But by this point she didn't trust the word of men and she worked hard and put in overtime and even sold sandwiches to her own coworkers at lunch until she had enough money to rent a little house in Colonia Veracruz, which was farther from Interzone than the shack by the trench, but it was a real little house, with two rooms, sturdy walls, a door that could be locked. She didn't mind having to walk twenty minutes longer each morning. In fact, she almost sang as she walked. She didn't mind spending nights without sleeping, working two shifts back to back, or staying up until two in the morning in the kitchen when she had to leave for the factory at six, making the chile-spiked sandwiches her fellow workers would eat the next day. In fact, the physical effort filled her with energy, her exhaustion was transformed into vivacity and grace, the days were long, slow, and the world (perceived as an endless shipwreck) showed her its brightest face and made her aware, as a matter of course, of the brightness of her own. At fifteen, her older daughter started work. They still walked to the factory, but the trip seemed shorter with all their talking and laughing. Her son left school at fourteen. He worked at Interzone-Berny for a few months, but after several warnings he was fired for not being quick enough. The boy's hands were too big and clumsy. Then his mother got him a job at a neighborhood bakery. The only child still in school was Penélope. Her school was called Aquiles Serdán Primary School and it was on Calle Aquiles Serdán. There were children there from Colonia Carranza and Colonia Veracruz and Colonia Morelos and even a few children from the center of the city. Penélope Méndez Becerra was in the fifth grade. She was a quiet girl, and she always got good grades. She had long straight black hair. One day she left school and was never seen again. That very evening her mother requested permission from Interzone to go to Precinct #2 to file a missing person report. Her son went with her. At the precinct a policeman wrote down her name and told her she would have to wait a few days. Her older daughter, Livia, wasn't able to come with her because Interzone was of the opinion that it was sufficient to have given her mother leave. The next day Penélope Méndez Becerra was still missing. Her mother and brother and sister showed up at the police station again and wanted to know what progress had been made. The policeman behind the desk told them not to be insolent. The Aquiles Serdán principal and three teachers were at the station, inquiring about Penélope, and it was they who led the family away before they could be fined for disorderly conduct. The next day Penélope's brother talked to some of her classmates. One said she thought Penélope had gotten into a car with tinted windows and hadn't gotten out again. By the description it sounded like a Peregrino or a MasterRoad. Penélope's brother and her teacher talked to the girl for a long time, but the only thing they could get clear was that it was an expensive black car. For three days her brother crisscrossed Santa Teresa on exhausting walks looking for a black car. He found many, even some with tinted windows, gleaming as if they had just come from the factory, but the people in them didn't look like kidnappers, or were young couples (their happiness made Penélope's brother cry) or women. Still, he noted down all the license plate numbers. At night the family would gather at home and talk about Penélope in words that meant nothing or whose ultimate meaning only they could understand. A week later her body turned up. It was found by some city maintenance workers in a drainage pipe that ran beneath the city from Colonia San Damián to the El Ojito ravine, near the Casas Negras highway, past the clandestine dump El Chile. The body was immediately removed to the medical examiner's office, where it was established that the girl had been anally and vaginally raped, with considerable tearing of both orifices, and then strangled. After a second autopsy, however, it was declared that Penélope Méndez Becerra had died of a heart attack while being subjected to the abuses described above.

•

Around this time, Lalo Cura turned seventeen, six years older than Penélope Méndez when she was killed, and Epifanio found him a place to live. It was in one of the tenement buildings that still stood in the center of the city. The tenement was on Calle Obispo, and after crossing a hall where the stairs began, the visitor came out into a huge courtyard, with a big fountain in the middle, around which rose three floors of flaking arcades where children played or neighbor women talked, arcades half covered by wooden roofs supported by very narrow iron columns, rusted with the passage of time. Lalo Cura's room was big, with enough space for a bed, a table and three chairs, a refrigerator (next to the table), and a wardrobe too large for the few items of clothing he possessed. There was also a little stove and a new cement sink where he could wash dirty pots and dishes or splash his face. The toilet, like the shower, was communal, and there were two latrines on each floor and three more on the roof. Epifanio showed him his own room first, which was on the first floor. His clothes hung from a cord strung from one wall to the other and next to the unmade bed Lalo Cura spotted a stack of old newspapers, almost all Santa Teresa papers. The bottom ones were yellowing. The stove didn't seem to have been used in a long time. Epifanio said it was best for a policeman to live alone, but that he should do as he liked. Then he took Lalo Cura up to his room, which was on the third floor, and gave him the keys. Now you have a home, Lalito, he said. If you want to sweep, borrow a broom from your neighbor. Someone had written a name on the wall: Ernesto Arancibia. Arancibia was spelled with a *v* instead of a *b*. Lalo pointed to the name and Epifanio shrugged his shoulders. Rent is due at the end of the month, he said, and he left without further explanations.

•

Around this time, too, Juan de Dios Martínez was ordered to stop working on the Penitent case and look into a series of armed robberies that had taken place in Colonia Centeno and Colonia Podestá. When he asked whether this meant the Penitent case was closed, he was told it didn't, but since the Penitent seemed to have vanished and the investigation was stalled, and given that a limited number of investigators were assigned to Santa Teresa, they would have to prioritize more urgent cases. Of course, this didn't mean they had forgotten about the Penitent or that Juan de Dios Martínez was no longer in charge of the investigation, but the officers under his command, who were wasting their time watching the city's churches twenty-four hours a day, would have to devote themselves to matters of greater benefit to public security. Juan de Dios Martínez accepted the assignment without protest.

•

The next dead woman was Lucy Anne Sander. She lived in Huntsville, about thirty miles from Santa Teresa, in Arizona, and she had been to El Adobe first, with a friend, and then they had driven across the border, ready for a sampling, at least, of Santa Teresa's nonstop nightlife. Her friend, Erica Delmore, was the owner and driver of the car. They both worked at a crafts factory in Huntsville that made Indian beads sold wholesale to tourist gift shops in Tombstone, Tucson, Phoenix, and Apache Junction. They were the only two white women at the factory, because all the other workers were Mexican or Indian. Lucy Anne had been born in a little town in Mississippi. She was twenty-six and her dream was to live near the ocean. Sometimes she talked about going back home, but usually only when she was tired or upset, which wasn't often. Erica Delmore was forty and she had been married twice. She was from California, but she was happy in Arizona, where there weren't many people and life was more relaxed. When they got to Santa Teresa they headed straight to the downtown clubs, first El Pelícano and then Domino's. Along the way they were joined by a twenty-two-year-old Mexican who said his name was Manuel or Miguel. He was a nice guy, according to Erica, who tried to hook up with Lucy Anne, and then, when Lucy Anne turned him down, with Erica, and in no way could be called a stalker or a bully. At some point, while they were at Domino's, Manuel or Miguel (Erica couldn't remember his name exactly) went off and they were left alone at the bar. Then they drove randomly around the center, visiting the city's historic landmarks: the cathedral, the town hall, some old colonial buildings, the colonnaded Plaza de Armas. According to Erica, no one bothered them, nor were they followed. As they circled the plaza, an American tourist called out: girls, you have to see the bandstand, it's amazing. Then he vanished into the bushes and they decided it might not be a bad idea to walk for a while. The night was bright, cool, full of stars. As Erica was looking for a place to park, Lucy Anne got out, took off her shoes, and went running through the grass, which had just been watered. After she parked, Erica went to look for Lucy Anne but couldn't find her. She decided to head into the plaza, toward the famous bandstand. Some of the paths were dirt, but the main ones were still paved with old stone. On the benches she saw couples talking or kissing. The bandstand was wrought iron, and in it, though it was late at night, insomniac children played. The lights, Erica noted, were dim, just bright enough to let you see where you were going, but with so many people around, there was no sense of threat. She couldn't find Lucy Anne, but she did think she recognized the American tourist who had shouted to them from the plaza. He was with three others and they were drinking tequila, passing the bottle around. She went up to them and asked whether they had seen her friend. The American tourist looked at her as if she had escaped from a mental institution. They were all drunk and very young, but Erica knew how to handle drunks and she explained the situation. Since they had nothing better to do, they decided to help her. After a while the plaza echoed with shouts for Lucy Anne. Erica went back to where she had parked the car. No one was there. She got in, locked the doors, and honked the horn several times. Then she started to smoke until the air inside became unbreathable and she had to roll down a window. At dawn, she went to the police station and asked if there was an American consulate in the city. The policeman attending her didn't know and had to ask some other policemen. One of them said there was. Erica filed a missing person report and then she headed to the consulate with a copy of it. The consulate was on Calle Verdejo, in Colonia Centro-Norte, not far from where she'd been the night before, and it was still closed. A few steps away was a coffee shop, and Erica went in to have breakfast. She ordered a vegetable sandwich and pineapple juice and then she used the phone to call Huntsville, Lucy Anne's house, but no one answered. From her table she watched the slow stirrings of the street as it came to life. When she had finished her juice she called Huntsville again, but this time she dialed the sheriff's number. A kid called Rory Campuzano, someone she knew well, picked up the phone. He said the sheriff wasn't in yet. Erica told him that Lucy Anne Sander had disappeared in Santa Teresa, and the way things looked, she was going to spend all morning at the consulate or making the rounds of hospitals. Tell him to call me at the consulate, she said. Will do, Erica, sit tight, said Rory, and then he hung up. She sat there for an hour, picking at her vegetable sandwich, until she saw activity around the door of the consulate. She was helped by a man who said his name was Kurt A. Banks and who asked her all kinds of questions about her friend and herself, as if he didn't believe Erica's story. Only after she left did Erica realize he suspected the two of them of being whores. Then she went back to the police station, where she had to tell the same story twice more to policemen who knew nothing about the report she had filed and was finally informed that there was no news of her missing friend, who might very well have crossed back over the border. One of the policemen recommended that she do likewise, best to leave the matter in the hands of the consulate and go home. Erica stared at him. He looked like a good person and his advice seemed well-intentioned. The rest of the morning and much of the afternoon she spent visiting hospitals. Until that moment she hadn't stopped to think how Lucy Anne might have ended up at a hospital. She ruled out the possibility of an accident, because Lucy Anne had disappeared in the plaza or somewhere nearby and she hadn't heard any noise at all, no shout, no squealing of brakes, no skid. After trying to come up with other reasons that might explain why Lucy Anne would be in a hospital, all she could think of was an amnesia attack. The likelihood was so remote that her eyes filled with tears. Anyway, none of the hospitals she visited had any record of having admitted an American woman. At the last one, a nurse suggested she try the Clínica América, a private hospital, but she answered with a burst of sarcasm. We're blue-collar workers, honey, she said in English. Like me, said the nurse, also in English. The two of them talked for a while and then the nurse invited Erica to have coffee at the hospital cafeteria, where she informed her that many women disappeared in Santa Teresa. It's the same in the United States, said Erica. The nurse met her eyes and shook her head. It's worse here, she said. When they parted they exchanged phone numbers and Erica promised to keep the nurse posted on any developments. She ate outside at a restaurant in the center of the city and twice she thought she saw Lucy Anne walking along the sidewalk, once coming toward her and once heading away, but it wasn't really Lucy Anne either time. Almost without knowing what she was ordering, she pointed at random to a couple of dishes that weren't too expensive. Both were seasoned with lots of hot pepper and after a while tears came to her eyes, but she kept eating anyway. Then she drove her car to the plaza where Lucy Anne had disappeared, parked in the shade of a big oak, and went to sleep with both hands clutching the steering wheel. When she woke she headed to the consulate, and the man named Kurt A. Banks introduced her to another man who said his name was Henderson. He told her it was still too

soon for there to be any progress in the matter of her friend's disappearance. She asked when it wouldn't be too soon. Henderson gazed at her
impassively and said: three more days. And he added: at least. As she
was leaving, Kurt A. Banks said the Huntsville sheriff had called asking
for her and inquiring about Lucy Anne Sander's disappearance. She
thanked him and left. When she got outside she found a public phone
and called Huntsville. Rory Campuzano answered and told her the sheriff had tried to get in touch with her three times. He's out now, said
Rory, but when he comes back I'll tell him to call you. No, said Erica, I
still don't have a place to stay, I'll call back in a little while. Before it got
dark she checked out several hotels. The ones that seemed good were
too expensive and finally she got a room at a boardinghouse in Colonia
Rubén Darío, without private bath or television. The shower was down
the hall and there was a little bolt to lock the door from inside. She took
her clothes off, but not her shoes, afraid of catching a fungus, and stood
under the water for a long time. Half an hour later, still wrapped in the
towel with which she'd dried herself, she fell into bed and forgot about
calling the Huntsville sheriff and the consulate and slept deeply until
the next day.

•

That day they found Lucy Anne Sander not far from the border fence, a
few yards past some gas tanks in a ditch running alongside the Nogales
highway. The body exhibited stab wounds, most them very deep, to the
neck, chest, and abdomen. It was discovered by some workers who immediately alerted the police. In the forensic examination a significant
sampling of semen was found in the vagina, and it was established that
Lucy Anne Sander had been raped several times. Death was caused by
one of five stab wounds, any of which might have been fatal. Erica Delmore was given the news when she called the American consulate.
Kurt A. Banks asked her to come in immediately, saying he had some
sad news for her, but so insistent was she and so loud did her voice grow
that he had no choice but to tell her the whole truth without further pre-
amble. Before she went to the consulate, Erica called the Huntsville
sheriff and this time she was able to reach him. She told him Lucy Anne
had been murdered in Santa Teresa. Do you want me to come get you?
asked the sheriff. I'd like that, but it's all right if you can't, I have my car,
said Erica. I'll come get you, said the sheriff. Then she called the nurse

who had befriended her and gave her the latest and presumably final up-
date. They'll probably want you to identify the body, said the nurse. The
morgue was in one of the hospitals she'd visited the day before. She
went with Henderson, who was nicer than Kurt A. Banks, but she would
really have preferred to go alone. As they were waiting in a corridor in
the basement, the nurse appeared. They hugged and kissed each other
on the cheek. Then she introduced the nurse to Henderson, who
greeted her distractedly but wanted to know how long they'd known
each other. Twenty-four hours, said the nurse. Or less. It's true, thought
Erica, just a day, but I already feel as if I've known her for a long time.
When the medical examiner turned up, he said Henderson couldn't
come in with her. Believe me, I'd rather not, said Henderson, with a half
smile, but it's my duty. The nurse gave her a hug and the two women
went in together, followed by the American official. Two Mexican policemen were in the room examining the dead woman. Erica went to look
and said it was her friend. The policemen asked her to sign some papers.
Erica tried to read them but they were in Spanish. It's nothing, said
Henderson, sign them. The nurse read the papers and told her she could
sign. Is that all? asked Henderson. That's all, said one of the Mexican
policemen. Who did this to Lucy Anne? she asked. The policemen
looked at her uncomprehendingly. The nurse translated and the police
said they didn't know yet. Past noon, the Huntsville sheriff drove up to
the American consulate. Erica was smoking in her car with the doors
locked when he arrived. The sheriff spotted her from the distance and
they talked, she still sitting in the car and he bent toward her, one hand
resting on the open door and the other on his belt. Then he went to request more information from the consulate and Erica stayed in the car
with the doors locked again, chain-smoking. When the sheriff came out
he said they should go home. Erica waited for the sheriff to start his car
and then, as if in a dream, she followed him along the Mexican streets
and across the border and through the desert, in Arizona now, until the
sheriff honked his horn and waved and both cars stopped at an old gas
station that also served food. But Erica wasn't hungry and she just listened to what the sheriff had to tell her: that Lucy Anne's body would be
sent to Huntsville in three days, that the Mexican police had promised
to catch the killer, that the whole thing stank like shit. Then the sheriff
ordered scrambled eggs with refried beans and a beer and she got up
from the table and went to buy more cigarettes. When she got back the

sheriff was cleaning his plate with a piece of sandwich bread. His hair was thick and black and made him look younger than he was. Do you think they told you the truth, Harry? she asked. No, I don't, said the sheriff, but I plan to make it my business to find it out. I believe you, Harry, she said, and started to cry.

●

The next dead woman was found near the Hermosillo highway, five miles from Santa Teresa, two days after Lucy Anne Sander's body turned up. The discovery fell to four ranch hands and the ranch owner's nephew. They had been searching for runaway cattle for more than twenty hours. The five trackers were on horseback, and when they could see that it was a dead woman, the nephew sent one of the hands back to the ranch with orders to tell the boss, while the rest of them stayed behind, perplexed by the bizarre position of the body. Its head was buried in a hole. As if the killer, clearly a lunatic, had thought it was enough to bury the head. Or as if he'd thought that by covering the head with earth the rest of the body would be invisible. The body was facedown with its hands pressed to its body. Both hands were missing the index and little finger. There were stains of coagulated blood in the chest region. The woman wore a light dress, purple, the kind that fastens in front. She wasn't wearing stockings or shoes. In the subsequent forensic examination it was determined that despite multiple cuts to the chest and arms, the cause of death was strangulation, with a fracture of the hyoid bone. There were no signs of rape. The case was assigned to Inspector José Márquez, who soon identified the dead woman as América García Cifuentes, twenty-three, a waitress at Serafino's, a bar belonging to Luis Chantre, a pimp with a long police record who was said to be a police informer. América García Cifuentes shared a house with two friends, both waitresses, who had nothing of substance to contribute to the investigation. The only thing established beyond a doubt was that América García Cifuentes had left home at five for Serafino's, where she worked until four in the morning, when the bar closed. She never came home, said her friends. Inspector José Márquez held Luis Chantre for a few days, but his alibi was impeccable. América García Cifuentes was from the state of Guerrero and had been living in Santa Teresa for five years, where she had come with a brother, who was in the United States now, according to the testimony of friends, and with whom she never corre-

sponded. For a few days, Inspector José Márquez investigated some Serafino's patrons but didn't come up with anything.

•

Two weeks later, in May 1994, Mónica Durán Reyes was kidnapped on
her way out of the Diego Rivera School in Colonia Lomas del Toro. She
was twelve years old and she was a little scatterbrained but a good student. It was her first year of secondary school. Both her mother and
father worked at Maderas de México, a maquiladora that built colonial-
and rustic-style furniture that was exported to the United States and
Canada. She had a younger sister who was in school, and two older siblings, a sixteen-year-old sister who worked at a maquiladora that made
wiring, and a fifteen-year-old brother who worked with his parents at
Maderas de México. Her body appeared two days after the kidnapping,
alongside the Santa Teresa–Pueblo Azul highway. She was dressed and
next to her was her schoolbag full of books and notebooks. According to
the forensic examination, she had been raped and strangled. In the subsequent investigation, some friends said they had seen Mónica get into a
black car with tinted windows, maybe a Peregrino or a MasterRoad or
a Silencioso. It didn't look as if she was taken by force. She had time to
scream, but she didn't scream. When she saw one of her friends, she
even waved goodbye. She didn't seem to be afraid.

•

In Colonia Lomas del Toro once again, a month later, the body of Rebeca Fernández de Hoyos, thirty-three, was found. She had long dark
hair down to her waist, and she had been a waitress at El Catrín, a bar
on Calle Xalapa, in nearby Colonia Rubén Darío. Previously she had
worked at the Holmes & West and Aiwo maquiladoras, where she was
fired for trying to organize a union. Rebeca Fernández de Hoyos was
from Oaxaca, although she had been living in the north of Sonora for
more than ten years now. When she was eighteen, she had lived in Tijuana, where she appeared on a register of prostitutes, and she had made
several unsuccessful attempts to settle in the United States, brought
back to Mexico four times by the *migra*. Her body was discovered by a
friend who had a key to her house and was surprised Rebeca hadn't
come in to work at El Catrín, because, as she stated later, the deceased
was a responsible woman and missed work only when she was sick. The
house, according to her friend, was the same as always, or in other words

at first glance she didn't see anything to suggest what she was about to find. It was a small house, with a living room, bedroom, kitchen, and bathroom. When she went into the bathroom, she discovered her friend's body, which was sprawled on the floor as if Rebeca had fallen and knocked herself on the head, though there was no blood. Only when she tried to revive her, patting water on her face, did she realize that Rebeca was dead. She called the police and the Red Cross from a public phone and then she went back to the house, moved her friend's body to the bed, sat in one of the two armchairs in the living room, and watched a TV show while she waited. The Red Cross came much more quickly than the police. There were two medics, one of them very young, twenty at most, and the other about forty-five, who might have been his father. It was the older man who told her there was nothing they could do. Rebeca was dead. Then he asked her where she'd found the body and she said in the bathroom. Well, let's put her back in the bathroom, you don't want trouble with the cops, said the man, motioning to the boy to take the dead woman by the feet as he lifted her by the shoulders, returning her to the original scene of death. Then the medic asked her what position she had found her friend in: sitting on the toilet, propped against it, on the floor, huddled in a corner? She turned off the TV and came to the door of the bathroom and gave instructions until the two men had left Rebeca just as she'd found her. The three of them stared from the doorway. Rebeca seemed to be drowning in a sea of white tiles. When they were tired of the sight or felt queasy, they sat down, she in the armchair and the medics at the table, and lit some cigarettes that the medic took out of the back pocket of his pants. You must be used to this, she said, somewhat incoherently. That depends, said the medic, who didn't know whether she was talking about the cigarettes or about hauling dead and injured people every day. The next morning the medical examiner wrote in his report that the cause of death had been strangulation. The dead woman had had sexual relations in the hours before her murder, although the examiner couldn't certify whether she'd been raped or not. Probably not, he said when a final opinion was demanded. The police tried to arrest her lover, a man by the name of Pedro Pérez Ochoa, but when they at last found where he lived, a week later, the person in question had been gone for days. Pedro Pérez Ochoa lived at the end of Calle Sayuca, in Colonia Las Flores, in a shack built, rather skillfully, of adobe and bits of trash, with room for a mattress and a table, a few yards from the waste pipe of the EastWest maquiladora, where he had worked. The neighbors described him as a polite and generally clean-looking man, from which it was deduced that he had showered at Rebeca's house, at least in recent months. No one knew where he was, so no arrest warrant was sent anywhere. At EastWest his file had been lost, which wasn't unusual at the maquiladoras, since workers were constantly coming and going. Inside the shack, several sports magazines were found, as well as a biography of Flores Magón, some sweatshirts, a pair of sandals, two pairs of shorts, and three photographs of Mexican boxers cut out of a magazine and stuck to the wall next to the mattress, as if Pérez Ochoa had wanted to burn the faces and fighting stances of those champions onto his retina before he went to sleep.

•

In July 1994 no woman died, but a man showed up asking questions. He came on Saturdays around noon and left late Sunday night or early Monday morning. The man was of average height and had black hair and brown eyes and dressed like a cowboy. He began by pacing the central plaza, as if he were taking measurements, but then he became a regular at some clubs, especially El Pelícano and Domino's. He never asked any direct questions. He looked Mexican, but he spoke Spanish with a gringo accent and his vocabulary was limited. He didn't understand puns, although when people saw his eyes they were careful not to kid him. He said his name was Harry Magaña, or at least that's how he wrote it, but he pronounced it Magana, so that when he said it you heard Macgana, as if the self-sucking faggot was of Scottish descent. The second time he came by Domino's he asked for somebody called Miguel or Manuel, a young guy, in his early twenties, about so tall, built like so, a nice kid with an honest face, but no one could or would tell him anything. Another night he made friends with one of the bartenders, and when the bartender left work Harry Magaña was waiting for him outside, sitting in his car. The next day the bartender couldn't come in to work, supposedly because he'd been in an accident. When he came back to Domino's four days later with his face covered in bruises and scabs, everyone was shocked. He was missing three teeth, and if he lifted his shirt he revealed countless bruises in the most outrageous colors on his back and chest. He didn't show his testicles, but there was still a cigarette burn on the left one. Of course, he was asked what kind of accident he'd gotten into and his answer was that on the night in question he had been out drinking until late, with Harry Magaña, as it happened, and that after he left the gringo and was on his way home to Calle Tres Vírgenes, a group of maybe five bastards had attacked him and beaten the shit out of him. The next weekend Harry Magaña wasn't seen at Domino's or El Pelícano. Instead, he visited a whorehouse called Internal Affairs, on Avenida Madero-Norte, where he spent a while drinking highballs and then settled in at a pool table and played Demetrio Águila, a big man, six foot three and over two hundred and fifty pounds, with whom he got to be friendly, because the big man had lived in Arizona and New Mexico, working as a fieldhand, by which he meant tending livestock, and then he had come back to Mexico because he didn't want to die far from home, he said, although later he admitted he didn't really have much family in the usual sense, a sister who must be around sixty by now and a niece who had never married and lived in Cananea, where he was from too, but Cananea could start to feel small, stifling, tiny, and sometimes he needed a trip to the big city that never sleeps, so then he hopped in his pickup without a word to anyone, or maybe with a see-you-later to his sister, and no matter what time it was he turned onto the Cananea–Santa Teresa highway, which was one of the prettiest highways he had ever seen in his life, especially at night, and drove nonstop to Santa Teresa, where he had a cozy little house on Calle Luciérnaga, in Colonia Rubén Darío, you're welcome to stay any-time, Harry, my friend, one of the few old houses still standing after all the change and the mostly shoddy redevelopment projects that had been carried out. Demetrio Águila must have been about sixty-five and he struck Harry Magaña as a good person. Sometimes he went to a room with a whore, but most of the time he preferred to drink and watch the crowd. Harry asked if he knew a girl called Elsa Fuentes. Demetrio Águila wanted to know what she looked like. About so tall, said Harry Magaña, raising his hand to just over five feet. Blond dye job. Pretty. Nice tits. I know her, said Demetrio Águila, Elsita, that's right, nice kid. Is she here? Harry Magaña wanted to know. Demetrio Águila said he'd seen her on the dance floor a while ago. I want you to point her out to me, Señor Demetrio, said Harry, can you do that? Certainly, my friend. As they went up the stairs to the dance club, Demetrio Águila inquired whether he had some score to settle with her. Harry Magaña shook his head. Elsa Fuentes was sitting at a table with two other whores and three clients, laughing at something one of the girls said in her ear. Harry Magaña leaned on the table with one hand, his other hand resting on his belt, behind his back. He told her to get up. The whore stopped laughing and raised her head to get a good look at him. The clients were about to say something, but when they saw Demetrio Águila behind Harry they shrugged it off. Where can we talk? Let's go to a room, he said into Elsa's ear. As they were on their way up the stairs Harry Magaña paused and told Demetrio Águila it wasn't necessary for him to come along. Of course not, said Demetrio Águila, and he started back down. In Elsa Fuentes's room everything was red: the walls, the bedspread, the sheets, the pillow, the lamp, the lightbulbs, even half the tiles. Through the window you could see the bustle of Madero-Norte late at night, cars crawling by and people overflowing the sidewalks between the food carts and juice carts and the cheap restaurants jostling for business, the prices of their daily specials scrawled on big blackboards that were constantly revised. When Harry Magaña turned to look at Elsa, she had taken off her blouse and bra. She does have big tits, he thought, but he didn't plan to make love to her that night. Don't get undressed, he said. The girl sat on the bed and crossed her legs. Do you have cigarettes? she asked. He pulled out a pack of Marlboros and offered her one. Give me a light, said the girl in English. He lit a match and held it out to her. Elsa Fuentes's eyes were a brown so light they looked yellow like the desert. Stupid kid, he thought. Then he asked her about Miguel Montes, where he was, what he was doing, the last time she'd seen him. So you're looking for Miguel? asked the whore. Do you mind telling me why? Harry Magaña didn't answer: he undid his belt and then rolled it up in his right hand, letting the buckle dangle like a bell. I don't have time, he said. The last time I saw him was about a month ago, maybe two, she said. Where was he working? Nowhere and everywhere. He wanted to get a degree, I think he was going to night school. Where did he make the money? Odd jobs here and there, said the girl. Don't lie to me, said Harry Magaña. The girl shook her head and blew a stream of smoke up to the ceiling. Where does he live? I don't know, he's always moving. The belt whistled through the air and left a red mark on the whore's arm. Before she could scream, Harry Magaña covered her mouth with one hand and pushed her down on the bed. If you scream, I'll kill you, he said. When the whore sat up again the mark on her arm was bleeding. It'll be your face next time, said Harry Magaña. Where does he live?

•

The next dead woman turned up in August 1994, on Callejón Las Ánimas, almost at the end of the alley, where there were four abandoned
houses, five counting the victim's house. She wasn't a stranger, but,
oddly, no one could say what her name was. No personal papers or anything that might lead to a rapid identification were found in the house,
where she had lived alone for three years. A few people, not many, knew
her first name was Isabel, but almost everyone called her La Vaca. She
was a solidly built woman, five foot five, dark-skinned, with short curly
hair. She must have been about thirty. According to some of her neighbors, she worked as a hooker at a club downtown or in Madero-Norte.
According to others, La Vaca had never worked. And yet it couldn't be
said she was short of money. When her house was searched, the kitchen
shelves were found to be full of canned food. She also had a refrigerator
(she stole electricity from the city lines, like most of her neighbors on
the alley), well stocked with meat, milk, eggs, and vegetables. She
dressed carelessly, and no one could say she put on airs. She had a new
TV and a video player, and the police counted more than sixty tapes,
most of them romances or melodramas, that she'd bought over the last
few years. Behind the house was a little yard full of plants, and, in a corner, a wire chicken coop with a rooster and ten hens. The case was handled jointly by Epifanio Galindo and Inspector Ernesto Ortiz Rebolledo,
with Juan de Dios Martínez joining them as backup, neither side particularly happy about the arrangement. It didn't take much digging to discover that La Vaca's life was unpredictable and full of contradictions.
According to an old lady who lived at the head of the alley, women like
Isabel were few and far between. She was the real thing. One night a
drunken neighbor was hitting his wife. Everyone who lived on the alley
heard her screams, which rose or fell in intensity as time passed, as if
the battered woman was in the throes of a difficult childbirth, the kind
that often ends in the death of the mother and the little angel. But the
woman wasn't giving birth, she was just being beaten. Then the old
woman heard footsteps and went to the window. In the gloom of the alley she glimpsed the unmistakable silhouette of Isabelita. Anyone else
would have walked on home, but the old woman saw how La Vaca
stopped and stood there. Listening. Just then the screams weren't very
loud, but after a few minutes the volume rose again and during all that
time, the old woman said to the police with a smile, La Vaca stood motionless, waiting, like someone who walks down a random street and

suddenly hears her favorite song, the saddest song in the world, coming from a window. And it's clear which window it is. What happened next is hard to believe. La Vaca went into the house and when she came back out she was dragging the man by the hair. I saw it myself, said the old woman, and maybe everyone saw it, but they were too embarrassed to say so. She hit like a man, and if the drunk's wife hadn't come out of the house and asked her for the love of God to stop hitting him, La Vaca would've killed him for sure. Another neighbor testified that she was a violent woman, that she came home late, usually drunk, and then no one would see hide nor hair of her until after five in the afternoon. It didn't take Epifanio long to establish a connection between La Vaca and two men who had recently been visiting her, one of them called El Mariachi and the other El Cuervo, who often stayed to sleep or stopped by every day, and other times vanished as if they had never existed. La Vaca's friends were probably musicians, not just because of the first one's nickname, but because they were occasionally seen walking down the alley with their guitars. While Epifanio visited clubs with live music in the center of Santa Teresa and around Madero-Norte, Inspector Juan de Dios Martínez kept investigating in the alley. The conclusions he drew were the following: (1) La Vaca was a good person, according to the majority opinion of the women; (2) La Vaca didn't work, but she always had plenty of money; (3) La Vaca could be extremely violent and she had strong ideas about right and wrong, rudimentary ideas, but ideas nonetheless; (4) someone was giving La Vaca money in exchange for something. Four days later El Mariachi and El Cuervo were arrested. They turned out to be the musicians Gustavo Domínguez and Renato Hernández Saldaña, respectively, and after being questioned at Precinct #3 they declared that they had committed the murder on Callejón Las Ánimas. As it happened, it was a movie that triggered the crime, a movie La Vaca wanted to watch and couldn't because her friends kept bursting out laughing. All three of them were pretty drunk. La Vaca started it, punching El Mariachi. At first El Cuervo didn't want to get involved, but when La Vaca started swinging at him he had to defend himself. The fight was long and fair, said El Mariachi. La Vaca had asked them to step out into the street so they wouldn't damage the furniture, and they obeyed. Once they were outside, La Vaca informed them that it would be a clean fight, fists only, and they agreed, although they knew how strong their friend was. After all, she weighed almost one hundred and eighty pounds. And it wasn't fat, it was muscle, said El Cuervo. Outside, in the dark, they really started to give each other hell. They kept it up for almost half an hour, back and forth, without a pause. When the fight was over, El Mariachi's nose was broken and he was bleeding from both eyebrows, and El Cuervo was complaining of a rib he said was broken. La Vaca was on the ground. Only when they tried to hoist her up did they realize she was dead. The case was closed.

•

Shortly afterward, Inspector Juan de Dios Martínez went to visit the musicians at the Santa Teresa penitentiary. He brought them cigarettes and a few magazines and asked how things were going. We can't complain, boss, said El Mariachi. The inspector said he had some friends inside and he could help them if they wanted. What do you want from us in return? asked El Mariachi. Just some information, said the inspector. What kind of information? Very simple. You and La Vaca were friends, close friends. I'll ask you some questions, you answer them, that's all. Let's hear the questions, said El Mariachi. Did you sleep with La Vaca? No, said El Mariachi. And what about you? Never, said El Cuervo. Well, now, said the inspector. And why is that? La Vaca didn't like men, she was already macho enough herself, said El Mariachi. Do you know her full name? asked the inspector. No idea, said El Mariachi, we just called her Vaca. Real close friends, weren't you? said the inspector. It's the honest truth, boss, said El Mariachi. So do you know where she got her money from? asked the inspector. We wondered that ourselves, boss, said El Cuervo, because we would've liked to make a few extra pesos, but La Vaca never talked about it. And didn't she have any friends, I mean besides you and the old women in the alley? asked the inspector. Sure, once when we were in my car she pointed out a friend of hers, said El Mariachi, some girl who worked in a coffee shop downtown, nothing special, on the skinny side, but La Vaca pointed and asked if I had ever seen such a pretty woman. I said no, so she wouldn't get mad, but really the girl wasn't anything special. What was her name? asked the inspector. She didn't tell me her name, said El Mariachi, and she didn't introduce me to her either.

•

While the police were working to solve the murder of La Vaca, Harry Magaña found the house where Miguel Montes lived. One Saturday afternoon he kept watch, and after two hours, tired of waiting, he forced the lock and went in. The house had only one room and a kitchen and a bathroom. On the walls were pictures of Hollywood actors and actresses. On a shelf were two framed photographs of Miguel himself, and he really was a kid with an honest face, good-looking, the kind of man women like. He went through all the drawers. In one he found a checkbook and a knife. When he lifted the mattress on the bed he found some magazines and letters. He flipped through the magazines. In the kitchen, under a cupboard, he came upon an envelope containing four Polaroids. One was of a house in the middle of the desert, a modest-looking adobe house, with a little porch and two tiny windows. A four-wheel-drive pickup was parked next to the house. Another picture was of two girls with their arms around each other's shoulders, their heads tilted to the left, gazing at the camera with similar expressions of incredible assurance, as if they had just set foot on this planet or their suitcases were already packed to leave. This picture was taken on a crowded street, which might have been in downtown Santa Teresa. The third picture was of a little plane on a dirt landing strip, in the desert. Behind the little plane was a hill. Everything else was flat, nothing but sand and scrub. The last picture was of two men who weren't looking at the camera and were probably drunk or high, dressed in white shirts, one of them in a hat, shaking hands as if they were great friends. He looked everywhere for the Polaroid camera but couldn't find it. He put the pictures, the letters, and the knife in his pocket, and after searching the house once more he sat down in a chair to wait. Miguel Montes didn't come back that night or the next. He thought maybe he'd had to leave town in a hurry or maybe he was dead. He felt depressed. Luckily for him, ever since he'd met Demetrio Águila he no longer stayed at a boardinghouse or hotel or spent sleepless nights wandering from dive bar to dive bar and drinking. Instead, he slept at the house on Calle Luciérnaga, in Colonia Rubén Darío, owned by his friend, who had given him a key. The little house, despite what a person might expect, was always clean, but its cleanliness, its neatness, lacked any feminine touch: it was a stoic cleanliness, utterly graceless, like the cleanliness of a prison or monastery cell, a cleanliness that tended toward sparseness, not abundance. Sometimes when he came in he found Demetrio Águila making *café de olla* in the kitchen and the two of them would sit in the living room and talk. Talking to the Mexican relaxed him. The Mexican talked about the days when he'd been a cowboy at the Triple T ranch and about the ten ways to tame a wild colt. Sometimes Harry told him he should come to Arizona to visit and the Mexican answered that it was all the same, Arizona, Sonora, New Mexico, Chihuahua, it's all the same, and Harry thought about it and in the end he couldn't accept that it was all the same, but it made him sad to contradict Demetrio Águila and so he didn't. Other times they would go out together and the Mexican was able to observe the gringo's methods from close up. He didn't like their harshness in principle, but he believed they were justified. That night, when Harry got back to the house on Calle Luciérnaga, he found Demetrio Águila up, and as he made coffee he told him he thought his last lead had disappeared. Demetrio Águila didn't say anything. He poured the coffee and made scrambled eggs with bacon. The two of them began to eat in silence. I think nothing ever disappears, said the Mexican. There are people, and animals, too, and even objects, that for one reason or another sometimes seem to want to disappear, to vanish. Whether you believe it or not, Harry, sometimes a stone wants to vanish, I've seen it. But God won't let it happen. He won't let it happen because He can't. Do you believe in God, Harry? Yes, Señor Demetrio, said Harry Magaña. Well, then, trust in God, He won't let anything disappear.

•

Around this time, Juan de Dios Martínez was still sleeping with Dr. Elvira Campos every two weeks. Sometimes the inspector thought it was a miracle the relationship had survived. There were difficulties, there were misunderstandings, but they were still together. In bed, or so he believed, the attraction was mutual. He had never wanted a woman the way he wanted her. If it had been up to him he would have married the director without a second thought. Sometimes, when it had been a long time since he saw her, he began to mull over their cultural differences, which he saw as the main hurdle. The director liked art and could look at a painting and say who the painter was, for example. The books she read he had never heard of. The music she listened to just made him pleasantly drowsy, and after a while all he wanted was to lie down and sleep which, of course, he was careful not to do at her apartment. Even the food the director liked was different from the food he liked. He tried to adapt to these new circumstances and sometimes he would go to a record store and buy some Beethoven or Mozart, which he would then listen to alone at home. Usually he fell asleep. But his dreams were peaceful and happy. He dreamed that he and Elvira Campos lived together in a cabin in the mountains. The cabin didn't have electricity or running water or anything to remind them of civilization. They slept on a bearskin, with a wolf skin over them. And sometimes Elvira Campos laughed, a ringing laugh, as she went running into the woods and he lost sight of her.

•

Let's read the letters, Harry, said Demetrio Águila. I'll read them to you as many times as you need me to. The first letter was from an old friend of Miguel's who lived in Tijuana, although the envelope wasn't postmarked, and it was a catalog of memories of the happy times they'd had together. It made reference to baseball, hookers, stolen cars, fights, alcohol, and it mentioned in passing at least five crimes for which Miguel Montes and his friend could have gotten jail time. The second letter was from a woman. It had been postmarked in Santa Teresa itself. The woman demanded money and insisted on swift payment. Otherwise beware the consequences, it said. The third letter, to judge by the handwriting, since it wasn't signed either, was from the same woman, with whom Miguel still hadn't settled his debt, and it said he had three days to show up with the money, you know where, and if not—and here, according to Demetrio Águila and also Harry Magaña, it was possible to discern a hint of sympathy, the hint of feminine sympathy Miguel could always count on, even at the worst of moments—the woman recommended that he leave town as soon as possible and without a word to anybody. The fourth letter was from another friend, and it might have come from Mexico City, although the postmark was illegible. The friend, a northerner who had recently arrived in the capital, described his impressions of the big city: he talked about the metro, which he compared to a mass grave, about the coldness of the residents of Mexico City, who never lifted a finger to help anyone, about how hard it was to get around, since in Mexico City there was no point having a badass car because the traffic jams were endless, about the pollution and how ugly the women were. Regarding this he made some tasteless jokes. The last letter was from a girl from Chucarit, near Navojoa, in the south of Sonora, and, predictably, it was a love letter. It said of course she would wait, she would be patient, that even though she was dying to see him it was up to him to take the first step, and she was in no hurry. It sounds like a letter from a hometown girlfriend, said Demetrio Águila. Chucarit, said Harry

Magaña. I have a hunch our man was born there, Señor Demetrio. Will you believe that's just what I was thinking? said Demetrio Águila.

•

Sometimes Juan de Dios Martínez would sit and think how he wished he knew more about the director's life. For example, her friendships. Who were her friends? He didn't know any of them, except for a few employees at the psychiatric center, people the director treated warmly but also kept at arm's length. Did she have friends? He suspected she did, although she never talked about it. One night, after they had made love, he told her he wanted to know more about her life. The director said he already knew more than enough. Juan de Dios Martínez didn't insist.

•

La Vaca was killed in August 1994. In October the next victim was found at the new city dump, a festering heap a mile and a half long and half a mile wide in a gully south of the El Ojito ravine, off the Casas Negras highway, where a fleet of more than one hundred trucks came each day to drop their loads. Despite its size, the dump would soon be too small and there was already talk, given the proliferation of illegal sites, about creating a new dump on the edge or to the west of Casas Negras. The dead girl was between fifteen and seventeen years old, according to the medical examiner, although the final word was left to the pathologist, who examined her three days later and concurred with his colleague. She had been anally and vaginally raped and then strangled. She was four foot seven. The scavengers who found her said she was dressed in a bra, denim skirt, and Reebok sneakers. By the time the police got there the bra and denim skirt were gone. On the ring finger of her right hand she was wearing a gold ring with a black stone, inscribed with the name of an English academy in the center of the city. She was photographed and later the police visited the language academy, but no one recognized the dead girl. The photograph was published in *El Heraldo del Norte* and *La Voz de Sonora*, with the same lack of results. Inspector José Márquez and Inspector Juan de Dios Martínez questioned the head of the school for three hours and apparently they went too far, because his lawyer sued them for harassment. The suit didn't go anywhere but it got them each a reprimand from the state representative and the chief of police. A report was also issued on the conduct of the head of the judicial police in Hermosillo. Two weeks later the body of the unidentified girl was sent to swell the supply of corpses for medical school students at the University of Santa Teresa.

•

Sometimes Inspector Juan de Dios Martínez was surprised how well Elvira Campos could fuck and how inexhaustible she was in bed. She fucks like someone on the brink of death, he thought. More than once he would have liked to tell her it wasn't necessary, she didn't need to work so hard, that just feeling her nearby, brushing against him, was enough, but when it came to sex the director was practical and businesslike. Darling, Juan de Dios Martínez would say to her sometimes, sweetheart, love, and in the darkness she would tell him to be quiet and then suck every last drop from him—of semen? of his soul? of the little life he felt, at the time, remained to him? They made love, at her express request, in semidarkness. A few times he was tempted to turn on the light and look at her, but he didn't, not wanting to upset her. Don't turn on the light, she said to him once, and it seemed to him Elvira Campos could read his mind.

•

In November, on the second floor of a building under construction, some workers found the body of a woman of about thirty, five feet tall, dark-skinned, bleached blond, two gold crowns on her teeth, dressed in only a sweater and hot pants or shorts. She had been raped and strangled. No identification was found on the body. The building was on Calle Alondra, in Colonia Podestá, in the upper part of Santa Teresa. Because of where it was, the workers didn't stay to sleep, as they would at other construction sites. At night a private security guard kept watch over the building. When he was questioned, he confessed that despite the terms of his contract, he usually slept at night, since during the day he worked at a maquiladora, and some nights he would be at the site until two in the morning and then go home, to Avenida Cuauhtémoc, in Colonia San Damián. The interrogation, conducted by the chief's right-hand man, Epifanio Galindo, was tough, but from the beginning it was clear the watchman was telling the truth. It was assumed, not without reason, that the victim was a recent arrival and there must be a suitcase somewhere with her clothes in it. With this in mind, inquiries were made at boardinghouses and hotels in the center, but none was missing a guest. Her picture was published in the city papers, to no avail: either no one knew her or the picture wasn't good or no one wanted trouble with the police. Missing person reports from other states were checked for matches, but no description fit the dead woman who had turned up in the building on Calle Alondra. Only one thing was clear, or at least clear to Epifanio: the woman wasn't from the neighborhood, she hadn't been strangled and raped in the neighborhood, so why dump the body in the upper part of the city, on streets assiduously patrolled at night by the police or private security guards? why go to the effort to leave the body on the second floor of a building under construction, with all the risks that entailed, including a fall down stairs still missing a railing, when the logical thing would be to dispose of it in the desert or at the edge of a dump? For two days he thought about it. As he ate, as he listened to his companions talk about sports or women, as he drove Pedro Negrete's car, as he slept. Until he decided that no matter how much he thought about it he wasn't going to come up with a good answer, and then he didn't think about it anymore.

•

Sometimes, especially on his days off, Inspector Juan de Dios Martínez would have liked to go out with the director. That is, he wanted to be seen in public with her, eat at a downtown restaurant with her, neither a cheap nor a very expensive restaurant but a normal restaurant where normal couples went and where he would almost certainly run into someone he knew, to whom he would introduce the director naturally, casually, coolly, this is my girlfriend, Elvira Campos, she's a psychiatrist. After they ate they'd probably go back to her apartment to make love and then nap. And at night they'd go out again, in her BMW or his Cougar, to the movies or some outdoor café for a soda or to dance at one of Santa Teresa's many clubs. The perfect happiness, goddamn it, thought Juan de Dios Martínez. But Elvira Campos wouldn't even hear of a public relationship. Phone calls to the psychiatric center, yes, so long as they were short. Meetings in person every two weeks. A glass of whiskey or Absolut vodka and nocturnal landscapes. Sterile goodbyes.

•

That same month of November 1994, the partially charred body of Silvana Pérez Arjona was found in a vacant lot. She was fifteen and thin, dark-skinned, five foot three. Her black hair fell below her shoulders, although when she was found half her hair was scorched off. The body was discovered by some women from Colonia Las Flores who had hung their washing on the edge of the lot, and it was they who called the Red Cross. When the ambulance arrived the older man, the ambulance driver, asked the women and the onlookers milling around the body if anyone knew the dead woman. Some filed by, gazed at her face, and shook their heads. No one knew her. Then my friends if I were you I'd move along, said the older medic, because the cops will want to question you all. He didn't say it loudly, but his voice carried and everyone backed away. Now it looked as if there was no one in the lot, but the two medics smiled because they knew people were watching from their hiding places. While one of them, the younger one, radioed the police from the ambulance, the older one went off on foot down the dirt roads of Colonia Las Flores to a taco stand where the owner knew him. He ordered six pork tacos, three with sour cream and three without, all six of them extra hot, and two cans of Coca-Cola. Then he paid and strolled back to the ambulance, where the kid who looked like his son was reading a comic book, leaning on the fender. By the time the police showed up, both of them had finished eating and they were having a smoke. For three hours the body lay in the vacant lot. According to the medical examiner, the girl had been raped. Two direct stabs to the heart were the cause of death. Then the killer had tried to burn the body to erase his tracks, but apparently he was a fuckup or else someone had sold him water for gasoline or else he'd lost his nerve. The next day it was learned that the dead girl was Silvana Pérez Arjona, a machine operator at a maquiladora in the General Sepúlveda industrial park, not far from where the body had been found. Until a year ago Silvana had been living with her mother and four siblings, all workers at different maquiladoras around the city. She had been the only one in school, at Profesor Emilio Cervantes, a high school in Colonia Lomas del Toro. For financial reasons, however, she'd had to drop out and one of her sisters found her a job at Horizon W&E, where she met Carlos Llanos, thirty-five, started to date him, and finally moved into his house on Calle Prometeo. According to his friends, Llanos was a good-natured man, a drinker but not a drunk, and a person who read books in his spare time, which was unusual and gave him the aura of someone exceptional. According to Silvana's mother, it was this that seduced her daughter, who had never even had a boyfriend, not counting some innocent romances at school. They were together for seven months. Llanos read, yes, and sometimes the two of them would sit in his little living room and talk about what they were reading, but he drank more than he read and he was an extremely jealous and insecure man. When Silvana visited her mother, sometimes she would confess that Llanos hit her. Mother and daughter often spent hours in each other's arms, crying in the dark. Llano's arrest, which presented no difficulties, was the first in which Lalo Cura took part. Two Santa Teresa patrol cars drove up, the police knocked, Llanos came to the door, the police beat him to the ground without a word, handcuffed him, and took him in to the station, where they tried to stick him with the murder of the woman on Calle Alondra, or at least of the girl they'd found at the new city dump, but it wouldn't work, Silvana Pérez herself was his alibi, since he'd been seen with her on the dates in question, strutting around Colonia Carranza's ramshackle park, where there'd been a carnival, and even Silvana's relatives had seen the two of them together. As far as nights were concerned, until barely a week ago he'd spent them on the night shift at the maquiladora and his fellow workers could vouch for him. Of Silvana's murder he declared himself guilty and was only sorry he had tried to burn her. Silvana was a good kid, he said, and she didn't deserve to be treated like that.

•

Around this time, too, a seer appeared on Sonora TV. Her name was Florita Almada, but her followers, whose numbers were small, called her La Santa. Florita Almada was seventy and it was only recently, ten years before, that she had been granted the gift of sight. She saw things no one else saw. She heard things no one else heard. And she knew how to find a meaningful explanation for everything that happened to her. Before she became a seer she had been an herbalist, which was her true calling, or so she said, because seer meant someone who sees, and sometimes she didn't see anything, the picture was fuzzy, the sound faulty, as if the antenna that had sprung up in her brain wasn't installed right or had been shot full of holes or was made of aluminum foil and blew every which way in the wind. So even though she called herself a seer or let her followers call her one, she put more faith in herbs and flowers, in healthy eating and prayer. She recommended that people with high blood pressure give up eggs and cheese and white bread, for example, because those were foods high in sodium, and sodium attracts

427

water and causes extra fluid to build up in the body, which raises blood pressure. Plain as day, said Florita Almada. No matter how much you like to eat huevos rancheros or huevos a la mexicana for breakfast, if you have high blood pressure you'd better give up eggs. And if you've given up eggs, you might as well give up meat and fish, too, and eat nothing but rice and fruit. Rice and fruit are very good for you, especially when you're over forty. She also denounced the excessive consumption of fat. Your total intake of fat, she said, should never be more than twenty-five percent of the total energy quotient of the food you eat. Ideally, the consumption of fat should settle at between fifteen and twenty percent. But the employed sometimes consume up to eighty or ninety percent of fat, and if their employment is stable, consumption rises to one hundred percent, which is disgraceful, she said. In contrast, consumption of fat by the unemployed is between thirty and fifty percent, which is an affliction, too, because those poor people aren't just undernourished, they're also malnourished, if you follow me, said Florita Almada, and really, being undernourished is an affliction in itself, and being malnourished doesn't help, maybe I haven't made myself clear, what I'm trying to say is that a tortilla with chile is better for you than pork rinds that are actually dog or cat or rat, she said, sounding apologetic. Then, too, she was against cults and healers and all those despicable people who tried to swindle the poor. She thought botanomancy, or the art of predicting the future through plants, was trickery. Still, she knew how it worked, and once she explained to a third-rate healer the different branches of the divinatory art of botanomancy, namely: floromancy, or the study of the shapes, movements, and reactions of plants, subdivided in turn into cromniomancy and fructomancy, the reading of sprouting onions or fruits, and also dendromancy, the interpretation of trees, and phyllomancy, the study of leaves, and xylomancy, or divination using wood and tree branches, which, she said, is lovely, poetic, but has more to do with laying the past to rest and nurturing and pacifying the present than with predicting the future. Then came cleromantic botanomancy, subdivided into favomancy, practiced with several white beans and a black bean, as well as the disciplines of rhabdomancy and belomancy, in which wooden rods were used. She had nothing against any of these arts and hence nothing to say about them. Then came plant pharmacology, or the use of hallucinogenic and alkaloid plants, which she had nothing against either. Everyone was free to mess with their own heads. It worked well for some people and not for others, especially lazy youths with regrettable habits. She'd rather not rule in favor or against. Then came meteorological botanomancy, which really was interesting but which very few people had mastered, no more than could be counted on the fingers of one hand, and which was based on observation of the reactions of plants. For example: if the poppy lifts its petals, the weather will be fine. For example: if a poplar begins to quiver, something unexpected will happen. For example: if the little flower with white petals and a tiny yellow corolla, called the *pijulí*, bows its head, it will be hot. For example: if another flower, the kind with yellowish and sometimes pink petals, called camphor in Sonora—why I don't know—and crow's beak in Sinaloa because from a distance it looks like a hummingbird, well, if the little rascal shuts, then rain is coming. And finally we have radiesthesia, a practice that originally required a hazel rod, now replaced by a pendulum, and about which Florita Almada had nothing to say. When you know something, you know it, and when you don't, you'd better learn. And in the meantime, you should keep quiet, or at least speak only when what you say will advance the learning process. Her own life, as she explained, had been a constant apprenticeship. She didn't learn to read or write until she was twenty, more or less. She was born in Nácori Grande and she couldn't go to school like a normal child because her mother was blind and the task of caring for her fell to Florita. About her brothers and sisters, of whom she preserved fond, vague recollections, she knew nothing. The gale forces of life had scattered them to the four corners of Mexico and they might be in their graves by now. Her childhood, despite the hardships and misfortunes typical of a peasant family, was happy. I loved the country, she said, although now it bothers me a little because I've stopped being used to the bugs. Life in Nácori Grande, believe it or not, could sometimes be very involving. Taking care of her blind mother could be fun. Tending the chickens could be fun. Washing the clothes could be fun. Cooking could be fun. The only thing she regretted was not having gone to school. Then they moved, for reasons not worth discussing, to Villa Pesqueira, where her mother died and where she, eight months later, married a man she barely knew, a hardworking and honorable man, who treated everyone with respect, someone quite a bit older than she was, incidentally, thirty-eight to her seventeen the day they stood before the altar, in other words twenty-one years her senior, a livestock dealer who mostly bought and sold goats and sheep, although every once in a while he also dealt in cattle or even pigs, and who was obliged by the circumstances of his work to travel constantly in the area, to towns like San José de Batuc, San Pedro de la Cueva, Huépari, Tepache, Lampazos, Divisaderos, Nácori Chico, El Chorro, and Napopa, along dirt roads or animal tracks and on shortcuts that skirted the mazelike mountains. Business wasn't bad. Sometimes she went with him on his trips, not often, because it was considered unseemly for a dealer to travel with a woman, especially his own wife, but she did go occasionally. It was a unique opportunity to see the world. To get a glimpse of other landscapes, which, though they might seem familiar, when you looked carefully were very different from the landscapes of Villa Pesqueira. Every hundred feet the world changes, said Florita Almada. The idea that some places are the same as others is a lie. The world is a kind of tremor. Of course, she would have liked to have children, but nature (nature in general or her husband's nature, she said, laughing) denied her that responsibility. The time she would have devoted to a baby she used to study. Who taught her to read? Children taught me, said Florita Almada, there are no better teachers. Children with their alphabet books, who came to her house for toasted cornmeal. Such is life that just when she thought her chances of taking classes or going back to school (unlikely, since in Villa Pesqueira they thought Night School was the name of a brothel outside San José de Pimas) had vanished forever, she learned almost effortlessly to read and write. From that moment on she read everything that fell into her hands. In a notebook, she jotted down thoughts and impressions inspired by her reading. She read old magazines and newspapers, she read political flyers distributed every so often from pickups by young men with mustaches, she read the daily papers, she read the few books she could find and the books her husband got into the habit of bringing back each time he returned from his buying and selling trips to neighboring towns, books he purchased sometimes by the pound. Ten pounds of books. Fifteen pounds of books. Once he came back with twenty-five pounds. And she read every single one, and from each, without exception, she drew some lesson. Sometimes she read magazines from Mexico City, sometimes she read history books, sometimes she read religious books, sometimes she read dirty books that made her blush, sitting alone at the table, the pages lit by an oil lamp's light that seemed to dance and assume demonic shapes, sometimes she read technical books about the cultivation of vineyards or the construction of prefabricated houses, sometimes she read horror stories or ghost stories, any kind of reading that providence placed within her reach, and she learned something each time, sometimes very little, but something was left behind, like a gold nugget in a trash heap, or, to refine the metaphor, said Florita, like a doll lost and found in a heap of somebody else's trash. Anyway, she wasn't an educated person, at least she didn't have what you might call a classical education, for which she apologized, but she wasn't ashamed of being what she was, because what God takes away the Virgin restores, and when that's the way it is, it's impossible not to be at peace with the world. And so the years went by. One day, by the miraculous laws of symmetry, her husband went blind. Luckily she was already experienced in the care of the sightless and the livestock dealer's last years were peaceful, because his wife looked after him with skill and tenderness. Then she was alone and by that time she had turned forty-four. She didn't marry again, not for lack of suitors but because she found she liked being alone. What she did was buy herself a .38 revolver, because the shotgun her husband had left her seemed unwieldy, and, for the moment, she took over the business of buying and selling livestock. But the problem, she explained, was that to buy and especially to sell livestock a certain sensibility was required, a certain training, a certain propensity to blindness that she in no way possessed. Traveling with the animals along the mountain trails was lovely; auctioning them at the market or the slaughterhouse was a nightmare. So she soon abandoned the business and kept traveling, with her late husband's dog and her revolver and sometimes her animals, which began to age with her, but this time she went as a healer, one of the many in the blessed state of Sonora, and on her travels she foraged for herbs or recorded her thoughts while the animals grazed, as Benito Juárez had done when he was a shepherd boy, oh, Benito Juárez, what a great man, so honorable, so wise, and what a charming boy, too, little was said about that period of his life, in part because little was known, in part because Mexicans were aware that when they talked about children they tended to speak nonsense. Mind you, she had something to say on the subject. Of the thousands of books she had read, among them books on the history of Mexico, the history of Spain, the history of Colombia, the history of religion, the history of the popes of Rome, the advances of NASA, she had come across only a few pages that depicted with complete faithfulness, utter faithfulness, what the boy Benito Juárez must have felt, more

than thought, when he went out to pasture with his flock and was sometimes gone for several days and nights, as is the way of these things. Inside that book with a yellow cover everything was expressed so clearly
that sometimes Florita Almada thought the author must have been a
friend of Benito Juárez and that Benito Juárez had confided all his childhood experiences in the man's ear. If such a thing were possible. If it
were possible to convey what one feels when night falls and the stars
come out and one is alone in the vastness, and life's truths (night truths)
begin to march past one by one, somehow swooning or as if the person
out in the open were swooning or as if a strange sickness were circulat-
ing in the blood unnoticed. What are you doing, moon, up in the sky?
asks the little shepherd in the poem. What are you doing, tell me, silent
moon? Aren't you tired of plying the eternal byways? The shepherd's life
is like your life. He rises at first light and moves his flock across the field.
Then, weary, he rests at evening and hopes for nothing more. What good
is the shepherd's life to him or yours to you? Tell me, the shepherd
muses, said Florita Almada in a transported voice, where is it heading,
my brief wandering, your immortal journey? Man is born into pain, and
being born itself means risking death, said the poem. And also: But why
bring to light, why educate someone we'll console for living later? And
also: If life is misery, why do we endure it? And also: This, unblemished
moon, is the mortal condition. But you're not mortal, and what I say may
matter little to you. And also, and on the contrary: You, eternal solitary
wanderer, you who are so pensive, it may be you understand this life on
earth, what our suffering and sighing is, what this death is, this last pal-
ing of the face, and leaving Earth behind, abandoning all familiar, loving
company. And also: What does the endless air do, and that deep eternal
blue? What does this enormous solitude portend? And what am I? And
also: This is what I know and feel: that from the eternal motions, from
my fragile being, others may derive some good or happiness. And also:
But life for me is wrong. And also: Old, white haired, weak, barefoot,
bearing an enormous burden, up mountain and down valley, over sharp
rocks, across deep sands and bracken, through wind and storm, when it's
hot and later when it freezes, running on, running faster, crossing rivers,
swamps, falling and rising and hurrying faster, no rest or relief, battered
and bloody, at last coming to where the way and all effort has led: terrible, immense abyss into which, upon falling, all is forgotten. And also:
This, O virgin moon, is human life. And also: O resting flock, who don't,

I think, know your own misery! How I envy you! Not just because you travel as if trouble free and soon forget each need, each hurt, each deathly fear, but more because you're never bored. And also: When you lie in the shade, on the grass, you're calm and happy, and you spend the great part of the year this way and feel no boredom. And also: I sit on the grass, too, in the shade, but an anxiousness invades my mind as if a thorn is pricking me. And also: Yet I desire nothing, and till now I have no reason for complaint. And at this point, after sighing deeply, Florita Almada would say that several conclusions could be drawn: (1) that the thoughts that seize a shepherd can easily gallop away with him because it's human nature; (2) that facing boredom head-on was an act of bravery and Benito Juárez had done it and she had done it too and both had seen terrible things in the face of boredom, things she would rather not recall; (3) that the poem, now she remembered, was about an Asian shepherd, not a Mexican shepherd, but it made no difference, since shepherds are the same everywhere; (4) that if it was true that all effort led to a vast abyss, she had two recommendations to begin with, first, not to cheat people, and, second, to treat them properly. Beyond that, there was room for discussion. And that was what she did, listen and talk, until the day Reinaldo stopped by to consult her about a lost love and left with a diet plan and some calming herbal infusions and other aromatic herbs that he tucked in the corners of his apartment, herbs that made it smell like a church and a spaceship at the same time, as Reinaldo told his friends when they came to visit, a glorious smell, a smell that soothes and gladdens the spirit, it even makes you want to listen to classical music, don't you think? And Reinaldo's friends began to insist that he introduce them to Florita, *ay*, Reinaldo, I need Florita Almada, one after the other, like a procession of penitents with their purple or fabulous vermillion or checkered hoods, and Reinaldo weighed the pros and cons, all right, boys, you win, I'm going to introduce you to Florita, and when Florita met them, one Saturday night, at Reinaldo's apartment, so thoroughly decked out for the occasion that there was even a lonely piñata on the terrace, she didn't turn up her nose or look displeased but instead said why, you've gone to so much trouble for me, these amazing treats, who made them, I want to compliment the cook, this delicious cake, I never had anything like it in my life, it's pineapple, no? the fresh-squeezed juices, the perfectly laid table, what charming young men, so thoughtful, look, you brought me presents, and it's not even my birthday, and then she went into Reinaldo's bedroom and the boys trooped in one by one to tell her their woes, and those who went in bowed with care came out full of hope, that woman, Reinaldo, where did you find her? she's a saint, she's a miracle worker, I wept and she wept with me, I couldn't find the words and she guessed what was wrong, she told me to try sulphured glycosides, because they're supposed to stimulate the renal epithelium and they're a diuretic, I was told to try a course of colon hydrotherapy, I saw her sweat blood, I saw her forehead studded with rubies, she rocked me on her breast and sang me a lullaby and when I woke up it was like I'd just gotten out of the sauna, La Santa understands Hermosillo's unfortunates better than anyone, La Santa has a feeling for those who've been hurt, for sensitive and abused children, for those who've been raped and humiliated, for those who are the butt of jokes and laughter, everyone gets a kind word, a bit of practical advice, the freaks feel like divas when she speaks to them, the scatterbrained feel sensible, the fat lose weight, the AIDS patients smile. So it wasn't many years before Florita Almada, beloved of all, made her TV debut. But the first time Reinaldo asked her, she said no, she wasn't interested, she didn't have time, if worse came to worst someone might think to ask her how she made her money, and she wasn't about to pay taxes, absolutely not! better to leave it for another day, she was no one. But months later, when Reinaldo had stopped insisting, it was she who called and told him she wanted to come on the show because she had a message she'd like to make public. Reinaldo wanted to know what kind of message and she said something about visions, the moon, pictures in the sand, the reading she did at home, in the kitchen, sitting at the kitchen table when her visitors had gone, the newspaper, the newspapers, the things she read, the shadows that watched her through the window, though they weren't shadows, which meant they weren't watching, it was the night, the night that sometimes seemed pixilated. She was going on in such a way that Reinaldo had no idea what she meant, but since he really did love her, he found a spot for her on his next show. The television studios were in Hermosillo and sometimes the signal was strong in Santa Teresa, but other times the broadcast was interrupted by ghostly images and fog and background noise. The first time Florita Almada was on, the reception in Santa Teresa was terrible, and almost no one in the city saw her, although *An Hour with Reinaldo* was one of Sonora's most popular shows. She was scheduled to speak after a ventriloquist from Guaymas, an autodidact who had made a name for himself in Mexico City, Acapulco, Tijuana, and San Diego, and who thought his dummy was a living creature. He came right out and said so. He's alive, the little bastard. There've been times he tried to escape, times he tried to kill me. But his little hands aren't strong enough to hold a gun or a knife, let alone strangle me. When Reinaldo, looking straight into the camera and smiling his trademark wicked smile, said that in films about ventriloquists the same thing always happened, in other words, the dummy rebelled against its master, the ventriloquist from Guaymas, in the broken voice of the infinitely misunderstood, answered that he was well aware of it, he had seen those films, and probably many more of them than Reinaldo or anyone in the live audience had seen, and all he could think was that the reason there were so many films was that the rebellion was much more widespread than he had first believed, so that by now it extended all over the world. Deep inside, all of us ventriloquists, one way or another, know that once the bastards reach a certain level of animation, they come to life. They suck life from the performances. They suck it from the ventriloquist's capillaries. They suck it from the applause. And especially from the gullibility of the audience! Isn't that right, Andresito? Yes, sir. And are you good or are you sometimes an evil little bastard, Andresito? Good, very good, very very good. And you've never tried to kill me, Andresito? Never, never, never! It so happened that Florita Almada was impressed by the wooden dummy's profession of innocence and the story of the ventriloquist, to whom she took an immediate liking, and when it was her turn the first thing she did was offer the man a few words of encouragement, despite surreptitious hints from Reinaldo, who smiled and winked at her as if to say the ventriloquist wasn't quite right in the head and she should ignore him. But Florita didn't ignore him, she asked about his health, asked how many hours a night he slept, how many meals a day he ate and where, and although the ventriloquist's replies were mostly ironic, addressed to the audience in a bid for applause or fleeting sympathy, La Santa got more than enough information to recommend (quite vehemently, too) that he visit an acupuncturist with some knowledge of craniopuncture, an excellent technique for treating neuropathies originating in the central nervous system. Then she glanced at Reinaldo, who was fidgeting in his chair, and began to talk about her latest vision. She said she had seen dead women and dead girls. A desert. An oasis. Like in films about the French Foreign Legion and the Arabs.

A city. She said that in this city they killed little girls. As she talked, trying to recall her vision as exactly as possible, she realized she was about to go into a trance and she was mortified, since sometimes, not often, her trances could be violent and end with the medium crawling on the ground, which she didn't want to happen since it was her first time on television. But the trance, the possession, was progressing, she felt it in her chest and in the blood coursing through her, and there was no way to stop it no matter how much she fought and sweated and smiled at Reinaldo, who asked her if she felt all right, Florita, if she wanted the assistants to bring her a glass of water, if the glare and the spotlights and the heat were bothering her. She was afraid to speak, because sometimes the first thing to be seized was her tongue. And even though she wanted to, because it would have been a great relief, she was afraid to close her eyes, since it was precisely when they were closed that she saw what the spirit possessing her saw, so Florita kept her eyes open and her mouth shut (though curved in a pleasant and enigmatic smile), watching the ventriloquist, who looked back and forth between her and his dummy, as if he had no idea what was going on but he could smell danger, the moment of revelation, unsolicited and afterward uncomprehended, the kind of revelation that flashes past and leaves us with only the certainty of a void, a void that very quickly escapes even the word that contains it. And the ventriloquist knew this was dangerous. Dangerous especially for people like him, hypersensitive, of artistic temperament, their wounds still open. And Florita glanced at Reinaldo too when she got tired of looking at the ventriloquist, and he said to her: don't be afraid, Florita, don't be shy, think of this show as your home away from home. And she also glanced, though less often, at the audience, where several friends of hers were seated, waiting to hear what she had to say. Poor things, she thought, they must be feeling so sorry for me. And then she couldn't help it and she went into a trance. She closed her eyes. She opened her mouth. Her tongue began to work. She repeated what she had already said: a big desert, a big city, in the north of the state, girls killed, women killed. What city is it? she asked herself. Come now, what city is it? I must know the name of this infernal city. She concentrated for a few seconds. It's on the tip of my tongue. I don't censor myself, ladies, especially not at times like this. It's Santa Teresa! It's Santa Teresa! I see it clearly now. Women are being killed there. They're killing my daughters! My daughters! My daughters! she screamed as she threw an imaginary shawl over her head and Reinaldo felt a shiver descend his spine like an elevator, or maybe rise, or both at once. The police do nothing, she said after a few seconds, in a different voice, deeper and more masculine, the fucking police do nothing, they just watch, but what are they watching? what are they watching? At this point Reinaldo tried to call her to order and get her to stop talking, but he couldn't. Away from me, you bootlicker, said Florita. The state governor must be informed, she said in a hoarse voice. This is no joke. José Andrés Briceño must hear about this, he must know what's being done to the women and girls of beautiful Santa Teresa. Beautiful and hardworking too. The silence must be broken, friends. José Andrés Briceño is a good man and a wise man and he won't let so many killers go unpunished. Such terrible apathy and such terrible darkness. Then, in a little girl's voice, she said: some are driven away in black cars, but they kill them anywhere. Then she said, in a normal voice: can't they at least leave the virgins in peace? A moment later, she leaped from her chair, perfectly captured by the cameras of Sonora TV's Studio 1, and dropped to the floor as if felled by a bullet. Reinaldo and the ventriloquist hurried to her aid, but when they tried to help her up, each taking an arm, Florita roared (never in his life had Reinaldo seen her like this, a real fury): don't touch me, you coldhearted wretches! Don't worry about me! Haven't you understood what I've said? Then she got up, turned toward the audience, went to Reinaldo and asked him what had happened, and a moment later she apologized, gazing straight into the camera.

•

Around this time, Lalo Cura found some books at the precinct, books no one read that seemed destined to be rat food, on top of shelves of forgotten reports and files. He took them home. There were eight books, and at first, so as not to make trouble, he took three: *Techniques for Police Instructors* by John C. Klotter, *The Informer in Law Enforcement* by Malachi L. Harney and John C. Cross, and *Modern Criminal Investigation* by Harry Söderman and John J. O'Connell. One afternoon he told Epifanio what he'd done and Epifanio said they were books sent from Mexico City or Hermosillo, books no one read. So he ended up bringing home the five he'd left behind. The one he liked best (and the first one he read) was *Modern Criminal Investigation*. Despite its title, the book had been written long ago. The first Mexican edition was dated 1965.

The copy he had was the tenth edition, published in 1992. In fact, in the reprinted preface to the fourth edition, Harry Söderman complained that the death of his dear friend, the late Inspector General John O'Connell, had placed the burden of revision on his own shoulders. And later he said: in the process of reworking [this book] I've sorely missed the inspiration, the rich experience, and the valued collaboration of the late Inspector O'Connell. Probably, thought Lalo Cura as he read the book in the dim light of a single bulb at night in the tenement or by the first rays of sunlight that filtered in the open window, Söderman himself had been dead for some time and he would never know it. But it didn't matter. In fact, the lack of certainty was just one more thing spurring him on to read. And he read and sometimes he laughed at what the Swede and the gringo had to say and other times he was dumbstruck, as if he'd been shot in the head. Around this time, too, the speed with which the murder of Silvana Pérez was solved obscured the previous police failures and the news was on Santa Teresa TV and in the two city papers. Some officers seemed happier than usual. In a coffee shop Lalo Cura ran into a few young cops, nineteen or twenty years old, who were discussing the case. How could Llanos rape her, one of them asked, if he was her husband? The others laughed, but Lalo Cura took the question seriously. He raped her because he forced her, because he made her do something she didn't want to do, he said. Otherwise, it wouldn't be rape. One of the young cops asked if he planned to go to law school. Do you want to be a lawyer, man? No, said Lalo Cura. The others looked at him like he was some kind of idiot. Meanwhile, in December 1994 there were no more killings of women, at least that anyone knew of, and the year ended peacefully.

•

Before the year was over, Harry Magaña traveled to Chucarit and found the girl who had been writing love letters to Miguel Montes. Her name was María del Mar Enciso Montes and she was Miguel's cousin. She was sixteen and she had been in love with him since she was twelve. She was very thin and she had chestnut hair, bleached by the sun. She asked Harry Magaña why he wanted to see her cousin, and Harry said he was a friend and talked about some money Miguel had lent him one night. Then the girl introduced him to her parents, who had a little grocery store where they also sold salted fish that they went to buy themselves from the fishermen, driving along the coast from Huatabampo to Los Médanos and sometimes farther north, to Isla Lobos, where almost all the fishermen were Indians and had skin cancer, which didn't seem to bother them, and when they'd filled their pickup with fish they came back to Chucarit and then they did the salting themselves. Harry Magaña liked María del Mar's parents. That night he stayed for dinner. But first he went out and drove around Chucarit with the girl, looking for a place to buy something, a small gift for her parents, who had shown him such hospitality. The only place he could find anything was a bar, where he tried to buy a bottle of wine. The girl waited for him outside. When he came out she asked if he wanted to see Miguel's house. Harry said yes. They drove to the edge of Chucarit. In the shade of some trees stood an old adobe house. No one lives here anymore, said María del Mar. Harry Magaña got out of the car and saw a pigsty, a corral with a rotting, broken wooden fence, a henhouse where something moved, maybe a rat or a snake. Then he pushed open the door of the house and the smell of dead animal hit him in the face. He had a presentiment. He went back to the car, got his flashlight, and returned to the house. This time María del Mar followed. In the room were many dead birds. He shone the flashlight upward. Through beams made of branches you could see part of the attic, where there were piles of unidentifiable objects or natural excrescences. The first to leave was Miguel, said María del Mar in the darkness. Then his mother died and his father held on for a year here alone. One day he was gone. My mother says he killed himself. My father says he went north to look for Miguel. Didn't they have any other children? They did, said María del Mar, but they died when they were babies. Are you an only child too? asked Harry Magaña. No, it was the same in my family. All of my older brothers and sisters got sick and died before any of them were six. I'm sorry, said Harry Magaña. The other room was even darker. But it didn't smell of death. Strange, thought Harry. It smelled of life. Maybe life suspended, fleeting visits, cruel laughter, but life. When they came out the girl pointed up at the Chucarit sky full of stars. Do you hope Miguel will come back someday? Harry Magaña asked her. I hope he comes back, but I don't know if he will. Where do you think he is now? I don't know, said María del Mar. In Santa Teresa? No, she said, if he was there you wouldn't have come to Chucarit, would you? True, said Harry Magaña. Before they left, he took her hand and told her Miguel Montes didn't deserve her. The girl

smiled. She had small teeth. But I deserve him, she said. No, said Harry
Magaña, you deserve much better. That night, after dinner at the girl's
house, he headed north again. Early in the morning he got to Tijuana. All
he knew was that Miguel Montes's friend in Tijuana was called Chucho.
He thought about searching the bars and clubs for a waiter or bartender
by that name, but he didn't have time. Nor did he know anyone in the
city who could help him. At noon he called an old acquaintance from
California. It's me, Harry Magaña, he said. The man said he didn't know
any Harry Magaña. Five years ago we took a course together in Santa
Barbara, said Harry Magaña, do you remember? Fuck, of course, it's the
sheriff from Huntsville, Arizona. Are you still sheriff? Yes, said Harry
Magaña. Then they asked about each other's wives. The cop from East
L.A. said his was fine, getting fatter every day. Harry said his had died
four years ago, a few months after he'd finished the course in Santa Barbara. I'm sorry, said the other man. It's all right, said Harry Magaña, and
there was an uncomfortable silence until the cop asked how she had
died. Cancer, said Harry, it was quick. Are you in Los Angeles, Harry?
the other man wanted to know. No, no, I'm nearby, in Tijuana. So what
are you doing in Tijuana? Are you on vacation? No, no, said Harry Magaña. I'm looking for somebody. I'm looking in an unofficial capacity, if
you know what I mean. But I only have a name. Do you need help?
asked the cop. It wouldn't hurt, said Harry. Where are you calling from?
I'm at a phone booth. Put in more coins and wait a couple of minutes,
said the policeman. As he waited, Harry didn't think about his wife. Instead, he thought about Lucy Anne Sander and then he stopped thinking about Lucy Anne and he watched the people on the street, some in
cardboard sombreros painted black or purple or orange, all with big bags
and smiles, and the idea passed through his head (but so fleetingly it
didn't even register) of going back to Huntsville and forgetting the whole
thing. Then he heard the voice of the cop from East L.A. giving him a
name: Raúl Ramírez Cerezo, and an address: 401 Calle Oro. Do you
speak Spanish, Harry? asked the voice from California. Less and less,
answered Harry Magaña. At three in the afternoon, under a blazing sun,
he rang the bell at 401 Calle Oro. A ten-year-old girl in a school uniform
opened the door. I'm looking for Mr. Raúl Ramírez Cerezo, said Harry.
The girl smiled, left the door open, and disappeared into the darkness.
At first Harry wasn't sure whether to go in or wait outside. Maybe it was
the sun that propelled him inside. It smelled of water and plants that

had just been watered and hot, wet clay pots. Two hallways led from the room. At the end of one of them was a gray-tiled patio and a vine-covered wall. The other hallway was even darker than the entranceway or whatever this room was called. What do you want? asked a man's voice. I'm looking for Mr. Ramírez, said Harry Magaña. And who are you? asked the voice. A friend of Don Richardson, of the LAPD. Well, now, said the voice, isn't that interesting. And how can Mr. Ramírez help you? I'm looking for a man, said Harry. You and everybody else, said the voice, sounding equal parts melancholy and tired. That afternoon Harry Magaña went with Raúl Ramírez Cerezo to a police station in downtown Tijuana, where the Mexican left him alone with more than one thousand files. Check these out, he said. After two hours Harry Magaña found one that seemed a perfect match. This guy's a small-time crook, Ramírez said when he came back and took a look at the file. Occasionally works as a pimp. We can find him tonight at Wow, a club where he hangs out, but first let's get some dinner, said Ramírez. As they ate at an outdoor restaurant, the Mexican cop told his life story. I don't come from money, he said, and for the first twenty-five years of my life it was one obstacle af-ter another. Harry Magaña didn't feel much like listening. He would rather have been talking to Chucho, but he pretended to pay attention. Spanish could slide off his skin when he wanted it to and not leave a trace. It wasn't the same with English, although he'd tried that too. He gathered vaguely that Ramírez's life had not, in fact, been easy. Opera-tions, surgeons, an unhappy mother accustomed to misfortune. The bad rap policemen got, sometimes deserved, sometimes not, the cross we all have to bear. A cross, thought Harry Magaña. Then Ramírez talked about women. Women with their legs spread. Spread wide. What do you see when a woman spreads her legs? What do you see? For Christ's sake, this wasn't dinner conversation. A goddamn hole. A goddamn hole. A goddamn gash, like the crack in the earth's crust they've got in Califor-nia, the San Bernardino fault, I think it's called. Is there something like that in California? First I've heard, but I live in Arizona, said Harry. Far from here, yes, sir, said Ramírez. No, right around the corner, tomorrow I'm going home, said Harry. Then came a long story about children. Have you ever listened carefully to a child cry, Harry? No, he said, I don't have children. True, said Ramírez, forgive me, I'm sorry. Why is he apologizing? wondered Harry. A decent woman, a good woman. A woman you treat badly, without meaning to. Out of habit. We become blind (or at least partly blind) out of habit, Harry, until suddenly, when there's no turning back, this woman falls ill in our arms. A woman who took care of everyone, except herself, and she begins to fade away in our arms. And even then we don't realize, said Ramírez. Did I tell him my story? wondered Harry Magaña. Have I sunk that low? Things aren't the way they seem, whispered Ramírez. Do you think things are the way they seem, as simple as that, no complicating factors, no questions asked? No, said Harry Magaña, it's always important to ask questions. Correct, said the Tijuana cop. It's always important to ask questions, and it's important to ask yourself why you ask the questions you ask. And do you know why? Because just one slip and our questions take us places we don't want to go. Do you see what I'm getting at, Harry? Our questions are, by definition, suspect. But we have to ask them. And that's the most fucked-up thing of all. That's life, said Harry Magaña. Then the Mexican cop was silent and both of them watched the people walking by, feeling the breeze on their hot cheeks. A breeze that smelled of motor oil, withered plants, oranges, a cemetery of cyclopean proportions. Should we have another couple of beers or should we go find our man Chucho right now? Let's have another beer, said Harry Magaña. When they got to the club he let Ramírez take the lead. Ramírez called over one of the bouncers, a man with the build of a weight lifter and a sweatshirt that clung to his torso like a leotard, and said something into his ear. The bouncer listened with his eyes on the ground, then he looked up and seemed about to say something, but Ramírez said come and he disappeared into the lights of the club. Harry Magaña followed Ramírez to the back corridor. They went into the men's room. There were two men there, but when they saw the cop they left in a hurry. For a while Ramírez gazed at himself in the mirror. He washed his hands and face and then he took out a comb and proceeded to carefully comb his hair. Harry Magaña didn't do anything. He stood leaning against the bare cement wall, until Chucho appeared in the doorway and asked what they wanted. Come here, Chucho, said Ramírez. Harry Magaña closed the door. Ramírez asked the questions and Chucho answered all of them. He knew Miguel Montes. He was a friend of Miguel Montes. As far as he knew, Miguel Montes was still in Santa Teresa, where he lived with some whore. He didn't know the whore's name, but he did know she was young and she'd worked for a while at a club called Internal Affairs. Elsa Fuentes? asked Harry Magaña, and Chucho turned around, looked at him, and nodded. He had the resentful gaze of the poor bastard who never gets a break. I think that's her name, he said. So how do I know you're not lying to me, Chuchito? asked Ramírez. Because I never lie to you, boss, said the pimp. But I have to know for sure, Chuchito, said the Mexican cop, taking a knife out of his pocket. It was a switchblade, with a mother-of-pearl handle and a slender six-inch blade. I never lie to you, boss, whined Chucho. This is important to my friend, Chuchito, how do I know you aren't going to call Miguel Montes as soon as we're gone? I would never do that, never, never, not if it was you asking me not to, boss, the thought would never even cross my mind. What should we do, Harry? asked the Mexican cop. I don't think the bastard's lying, said Harry Magaña. When he opened the door, two whores and the bouncer were just outside. The whores were short and fleshy and they must have been the sentimental type because when they saw Chucho safe and sound they ran to hug him, laughing and crying. Ramírez was the last to leave the washroom. Anything wrong? he asked the bouncer. No, said the bouncer in a thin voice. Everything okay, then? We're cool, said the bouncer. Outside was a line of kids waiting to get into the club. At the end of the sidewalk, Harry Magaña spotted Chucho walking with his arms around his two whores. Above him hung a full moon that reminded Harry of the ocean, an ocean he had seen only three times. He's off to bed, said Ramírez when he came up next to Harry Magaña. When you've been that scared and on a roller coaster of emotions all you want is a nice comfortable chair, a nice cocktail, a nice TV show, and a nice meal cooked by your two old ladies. Really, cooking is all they're good for, said the Mexican cop as if he'd known the whores since school. There were some American tourists in the line, too, talking in shouts. What do you plan to do now, Harry? asked Ramírez. I'm going to Santa Teresa, said Harry Magaña, looking at the ground. That night he followed the path of the stars. As he crossed the Río Colorado he saw a meteor in the sky, or a shooting star, and he made a silent wish as his mother had taught him. He drove the lonely road from San Luis to Los Vidrios, where he stopped and had two cups of coffee, his mind blank, feeling the hot liquid burning his esophagus as it went down. Then he turned onto the Los Vidrios–Sonoyta road and after that he headed south, toward Caborca. Trying to find the exit, he drove through the center of town and everything looked closed, except the gas station. He turned east and passed through Altar, Pueblo Nuevo, and Santa Ana, finally ending up on the four-lane highway to Nogales and Santa Teresa. It was four in the morning when he got to the city. There was no one home at Demetrio Águila's, so he didn't even lie down for a moment. He washed his face and arms, scrubbed his chest and armpits with cold water, and took a clean shirt out of his suitcase. Internal Affairs hadn't closed yet when he arrived, and he asked to talk to the madam. The man he spoke to gave him a mocking look. He was in a carved wooden booth, a stage designed for a single person, a master of ceremonies or a barker, and he looked taller than he was. There's no madam here, sir, he said. Then I'd like to talk to the manager, said Harry Magaña. There's no manager, sir. Who's in charge? asked Harry Magaña. There's a *manageress*, sir. Our manageress of public relations, sir. Miss Isela. Harry Magaña tried to smile and said he wanted to speak to Miss Isela for a moment. Go up to the club and ask for her, the master of ceremonies said. Harry Magaña went into a lounge and saw a man with a white mustache asleep in an armchair. The walls were covered with a red quilted fabric as if the lounge were a padded cell in a madhouse for whores. On the stairs, the banister covered in the same red fabric, he passed a whore with a client and grabbed her by the arm. He asked if Elsa Fuentes still worked there. Let me go, said the whore, and she went on down the stairs. There were quite a few people on the dance floor, although the music playing was *boleros* or sad *danzones* from the south. The couples scarcely moved in the darkness. With difficulty he located a waiter and asked where he could find Miss Isela. The waiter pointed to a door at the other end of the club. Miss Isela was with a man of about fifty, dressed in a black suit and yellow tie. When she asked Harry Magaña to sit down, the man went to lean on the windowsill. Harry Magaña said he was looking for Elsa Fuentes. And why is that? Miss Isela wanted to know. For no good reason, said Harry Magaña with a smile. Miss Isela laughed. She was thin and had a nice body, a tattoo of a blue butterfly on her left shoulder, and she couldn't have been more than twenty-two. The man by the window tried to laugh too but all he could manage was a smirk that barely made his upper lip quiver. She doesn't work here anymore, said Miss Isela. How long has it been since she left? asked Harry Magaña. About a month, said Miss Isela. And do you know where I might find her? Miss Isela looked over at the man by the window and asked whether they could tell him. Why not? said the man. If we don't spill the beans our-selves, he'll find out some other way. This gringo looks stubborn. It's true, said Harry Magaña, I'm stubborn. So fuck the suspense, Iselita, tell him where Elsa Fuentes lives, said the man. Miss Isela took a narrow, hardcover ledger out of a drawer and flipped through it. Elsa Fuentes, as far as we know, lives at 23 Calle Santa Catarina. And where is that? asked Harry Magaña. In Colonia Carranza, said Miss Isela. If you ask around you'll find it, said the man. Harry Magaña got up and thanked them. Before he left he turned and was about to ask them if they knew Miguel Montes or had heard the name, but he changed his mind in time and said nothing.

·

He had a hard time finding Calle Santa Catarina, but he got there at last. Elsa Fuentes's house had whitewashed walls and a steel door. He knocked twice. The nearby houses were completely silent, although he had passed three women on the street on their way to work. The three of them flocked together as soon as they left their houses and vanished rapidly after glancing at his car. He pulled out his knife, crouched down, and got the door open with no trouble. On the inside of the door was an iron bar that served as a bolt and wasn't in place, by which he guessed no one was home. He closed the door, ran the bolt, and began to search. The rooms gave no sense of having been abandoned; instead they had an air of decorum, with a hint of coquettishness. The walls were hung with jugs, a guitar, bundles of medicinal herbs that gave off a pleasant scent. The bed in Elsa Fuentes's room was unmade, but otherwise the room was impeccable. The clothes in the closet were neatly put away, there were several photographs on a night table (two of Elsa with Miguel Montes), the dust hadn't had time to build up on the floor. There was plenty of food in the refrigerator. Nothing was turned on, not even the electric candle next to the picture of a saint. Everything seemed set to wait for Elsa Fuentes to return. He looked for signs that Miguel Montes had been staying there but found nothing. He sat in a chair in the living room and prepared to wait. He couldn't say exactly when he fell asleep. By the time he woke up, it was noon and no one had tried to get in. He went into the kitchen and looked for something to eat for breakfast. He drank a big glass of milk after checking the expiration date on the carton. Then he took an apple from a plastic basket near the window and ate it as he searched every corner of the house again. He didn't want to light the stove, so he didn't make coffee. The only thing in the kitchen that

445

had spoiled was the bread, which was stale. He looked for an address book, a bus ticket, the least sign of a struggle that he might have missed. He checked the bathroom, he looked under Elsa Fuentes's bed, he rummaged in the trash. He opened three boxes of shoes and found only shoes. He looked under the mattress. He lifted the three small rugs, all Oriental, coquettish in Elsa Fuentes's particular way, and didn't find anything. Then it occurred to him to look up at the ceiling. In the bathroom and the living room there was nothing. In the kitchen, however, he spotted a crack. He got on a chair and dug with the knife until plaster fell to the floor. He made the hole bigger and stuck in his hand. He found a plastic bag with ten thousand dollars and a notebook inside. He put the money in his pocket and began to leaf through the notebook. There were phone numbers without name or label, seemingly set down at random. He guessed they were clients. A few numbers were attached to names, Mamá, Miguel, Lupe, Juana, and some nicknames, possibly friends from work. Among the Mexican telephone numbers he recognized a few Arizona numbers. He put the notebook in his pocket with the money and decided it was time to go. He was nervous and his body was crying out for coffee. When he started the car he had the feeling that he was being spied on. And yet everything was quiet, except for some boys playing soccer in the middle of the street. He honked the horn and the boys took a long time to get out of the way. In the rearview mirror he saw a Rand Charger appear at the other end of the street. He coasted along and let the Rand Charger catch up. The driver and his companion showed not the least interest in him and at the corner the Rand Charger passed his car and left him behind. He drove downtown and stopped in front of a fairly crowded restaurant. He ordered a plate of scrambled eggs with ham and a cup of coffee. As he was waiting for his food he went up to the counter and asked a boy if he could make a call. The boy, who was wearing a white shirt and black bow tie, asked if he planned to call the United States or Mexico. Here, in Sonora, said Harry Magaña, and he brought out the notebook and showed him the numbers. Okay, said the boy, you call where you want and then I'll charge you, all right? Sure, said Harry Magaña. The boy brought over the telephone and then went to wait on other customers. First Harry Magaña called Elsa Fuentes's mother. A woman answered. He asked for Elsa. Elsita isn't here, said the woman. But isn't this her mother? he asked. I'm her mother, yes, but Elsita lives in Santa Teresa, said the woman. So where am I calling then? asked Harry Magaña. Excuse me? said the woman. Where do you live, señora? In Toconilco, said the woman. And where is that, señora? asked Harry Magaña. In Mexico, señor, said the woman. But where in Mexico? Near Tepehuanes, said the woman. And where is Tepehuanes? yelled Harry Magaña. Why, in Durango, señor. The state of Durango? asked Harry Magaña as he wrote the words Toconilco and Tepehuanes and finally Durango on a sheet of paper. Before he hung up, he asked for her address. The woman gave it to him, all garbled, but without any hesitation. I'll send you some money on your daughter's behalf, said Harry Magaña. God bless you, said the woman. No, señora, bless your daughter, said Harry Magaña. So be it, then, said the woman, God bless my daughter, and you too. Then he motioned to the boy in the bow tie, indicating that he hadn't finished yet, and returned to the table, where his scrambled eggs and coffee were waiting for him. Before he made another call he asked for a refill of coffee and with the cup in his hand he went back up to the counter. He called Miguel Montes's number (although it might be a different Miguel, he thought), and just as he'd feared, no one answered. Then he called the number of the woman named Lupe and the conversation was even more chaotic than the one he'd just had with Elsa Fuentes's mother. What he managed to get straight was that Lupe lived in Hermosillo, she didn't want to have anything to do with Elsa Fuentes or Santa Teresa, she had indeed known Miguel Montes but she didn't want to have anything to do with him either (if he was still alive), her life in Santa Teresa had been a mistake from start to finish and she didn't plan to make the same mistake twice. Next he called two other women, the one listed as Juana and the woman (though it might have been a man, it wasn't clear) tagged Vaca. Both numbers, a prerecorded voice informed him, had been disconnected. The last attempt he made almost at random. He called one of the numbers in Arizona. A man's voice, distorted by the answering machine, asked him to leave a message and promised to return the call. He asked for the bill. The boy with the bow tie did some math on a paper he took out of his pocket and asked whether he had enjoyed his meal. Very much, said Harry Magaña. He took a nap at Demetrio Águila's, on Calle Luciérnaga, and dreamed of a street in Huntsville, the main street, pounded by a sandstorm. We have to get the girls at the bead factory! shouted someone behind him, but he paid no attention and remained immersed in a file, photocopied documents that seemed to be written in a language not of this world. When he woke he took a cold shower and dried himself with a big white towel, pleasing to the touch. Then he called information and gave them Miguel Montes's number. He asked what address the number belonged to. The woman made him wait a moment and then read the name of a street and a number. Before he hung up he asked whose name the number was registered in. Francisco Díaz, sir, said the operator. Night was falling fast in Santa Teresa when Harry Magaña got to Calle Portal de San Pablo, parallel to Avenida Madero-Centro, in a neighborhood that still retained traces of what it had once been: one- and two-story cement and brick houses, middle-class, formerly inhabited by government employees or young professionals. The only people to be seen on the street now were old men and women and gangs of adolescents who went by at a run or on bikes or in beat-up cars, always in a hurry, as if they had something very urgent to do that night. In fact, the only one with anything urgent to do is me, thought Harry Magaña, and he sat in his car, motionless, until everything was dark. He crossed the street without being seen. The door was wooden and didn't seem hard to crack. He went to work with the knife and the lock soon gave way. From the living room a long hallway led to a small yard lit by the lights of a neighboring yard. Everything was a complete wreck. He heard the muted sounds of a TV in another house and a grunt. He knew immediately that he wasn't alone. It was then that Harry Magaña regretted not having his gun with him. He peered into the first bedroom. A man, short and broad backed, was pulling a bundle out from under a bed. The bed was low and it was hard to get the bundle out. When the man managed it at last and began to drag it into the hallway, he turned and looked at Harry Magaña without surprise. The bundle was wrapped in plastic and Harry Magaña felt choked by nausea and rage. For an instant the two of them stood frozen. The short man was wearing a black zip-up overall, probably the official overall of a maquiladora, and his expression was angry and even embarassed. I always get stuck with the dirty work, it seemed to say. With a sense of fatalism, Harry Magaña imagined that he was somewhere else, not a few minutes from downtown, at Francisco Díaz's house, which was like being at no one's house, but in the country, in the dust and brush, at a shack with a corral and a henhouse and a woodstove, in the Santa Teresa desert or any other desert. He heard someone closing the front door and then steps in the living room. A voice calling the short man. And he heard the latter reply: I'm over here, with our friend. His rage grew. He wanted to bury his knife in the man's heart. He lunged at him, glancing desperately out of the corner of his eye at the two shadowy figures he had seen in the Rand Charger, coming down the hallway.

●

The year 1995 began with the discovery, on January 5, of another dead woman. This time it was a skeleton shallowly buried in a field belonging to the Hijos de Morelos farming cooperative. The farmworkers who dug it up didn't know it was a woman. They assumed it was a small man. There were no clothes or anything buried with the skeleton that might have helped to identify the remains. The cooperative alerted the police, who showed up six hours later. In addition to taking statements from everyone who had been present when the skeleton was found, they asked whether any worker was missing, whether there had been fights lately, whether there had been a change in anyone's behavior in recent days. As might be expected, two young men had left the cooperative, like every year, for Santa Teresa or Nogales or the United States. Fights happened all the time, but they were never serious. The workers' behavior varied depending on the season, the harvest, the little livestock they had left, in sum, on the economy, like everyone else's. The Santa Teresa medical examiner soon established that the skeleton was a woman's. If to this one added the fact that there were no clothes or scraps of cloth in the hole where she was buried, the verdict was plain: it was murder. How had she been killed? It was impossible to say now. And when? Probably about three months before, although on this last point the medical examiner preferred not to venture any definitive conclusion, since corpses decompose at different rates. If anyone required an exact date, they would have to send the bones to the Institute of Forensic Anatomy in Hermosillo, or better yet, to Mexico City. The Santa Teresa police issued a public statement in which it ultimately and vaguely evaded any responsibility. The killer might easily have been a driver headed to Chihuahua from Baja California, and the dead woman might have been a hitchhiker picked up in Tijuana, killed in Saric, and randomly buried here.

●

On January 15 the next dead woman turned up. Her name was Claudia Pérez Millán. The body was found on Calle Sahuaritos. The deceased was dressed in a black sweater and had two cheap rings on each hand, plus an engagement ring. She wasn't wearing a skirt or panties, although she did have on red imitation-leather flats. She had been raped and strangled and wrapped in a white blanket, as if the killer had planned to move the body elsewhere and had suddenly decided, or been obliged by circumstance, to leave it behind a dumpster on Calle Sahuaritos. Claudia Pérez Millán was thirty-one and lived with her husband and two children on Calle Marquesas, not far from where the body was found. When the police paid a visit to her place of residence, no one came to the door, although crying and shouts could be heard from inside. Equipped with the proper warrant, the police broke down the door of the dead woman's residence, and, locked in one of the bedrooms, they found the minors Juan Aparicio Pérez and his brother Frank Aparicio Pérez. In the room were two loaves of sandwich bread and a bucket of drinking water. Questioned in the presence of a child psychologist, the minors both admitted that it had been their father, Juan Aparicio Regla, who had locked them in the night before. Then they had heard noises and shouting until they fell asleep, though they hadn't been able to tell who was shouting or where the noises came from. The next morning the house was empty and when they heard the police they began to scream. The suspect owned a car, which wasn't found either, leading to the conclusion that he had fled after killing his wife. Claudia Pérez Millán worked as a waitress in a coffee shop in the center of the city. Juan Aparicio Regla had no known occupation. Some thought he worked at a maquiladora, others that he was a *pollero*, leading migrants across the border into the United States. An urgent arrest warrant was issued, but those in the know were sure he would never set foot in the city again.

•

In February María de la Luz Romero died. She was fourteen, and five foot three, with long hair down to her waist, although she planned to cut it someday soon, as she had revealed to one of her sisters. She had just started working at EMSA, one of the oldest maquiladoras in Santa Teresa, which wasn't in any industrial park but in the middle of Colonia La Preciada, like a melon-colored pyramid, its sacrificial altar hidden behind smokestacks and two enormous hangar doors though which workers and trucks entered. María de la Luz Romero left home at seven in the evening, accompanied by some friends who had stopped by for her. She told her siblings she was going out dancing at La Sonorita, a cheap club on the border of Colonia San Damián and Colonia Plata, and she would get something to eat near the club. Her parents were working the night shift and weren't home. María de la Luz did, in fact, eat with her girlfriends, on foot next to a van that sold tacos and quesadillas, parked across the street from the club. It was eight when they went in, and the club was full of kids they knew, either because they worked at EMSA too or because they lived in the neighborhood. According to one of her friends, María de la Luz danced alone, unlike the other girls, who had boyfriends or acquaintances there. Twice, however, she was approached by different boys who wanted to buy her a drink or a soda, which María de la Luz refused, the first time because she didn't like the boy and the second time out of shyness. At eleven-thirty, she left with a friend. Both of them lived more or less nearby and walking home together was much nicer than making the trip alone. They parted about five blocks from María de la Luz's house. There her trail vanished. When some of the neighbors who lived along the final stretch of her walk were questioned, all declared they hadn't heard any cries, much less a call for help. Her body appeared two days later, by the Casas Negras highway. She had been raped and hit multiple times in the face. A few of the blows were particularly violent, and she also exhibited a fracture of the palatine bone, which was highly unusual for a beating and led the medical examiner to conjecture (although of course he just as quickly abandoned the idea) that the car in which María de la Luz was picked up had been in an accident. The cause of death was stab wounds to the torso and neck, which had pierced both lungs and multiple arteries. The case was handled by Inspector Juan de Dios Martínez, who once again questioned the friends with her at the club, the owner of the club and some of the bartenders, and the people who lived along the five blocks María de la Luz had walked or tried to walk alone before she was snatched. The results were disappointing.

•

In March no dead woman turned up in the city, but in April two appeared just a few days apart, as did the first complaints about the police, who were incapable not only of stopping the wave (or incessant drip) of sex crimes but also of apprehending the killers and restoring peace and quiet to a hardworking city. The first dead woman was found in a room at Mi Reposo, a hotel in the center of Santa Teresa. She was under the bed, wrapped in a sheet, wearing only a white bra. According to the manager of Mi Reposo, the dead woman's room was registered to a guest by the name of Alejandro Peñalva Brown, who had taken it three days before and hadn't been seen since. When the cleaning women and the two clerks were questioned, all were in agreement that the only glimpse they'd had of the aforementioned Peñalva Brown was on the first day of his stay at the hotel. The cleaning women, meanwhile, swore that on the second and third day they hadn't found anything under the bed, although this, according to the police, could easily be a fib to cover up the sloppy job they did on the rooms. In the hotel registry, Peñalva Brown had left an Hermosillo address. When the Hermosillo police were alerted, it was discovered that no Peñalva Brown had ever lived at that address. The arms of the dead woman, who was about thirty-five, dark and solidly built, were covered in needle tracks, so the police delved into the city's drug scene, without turning up any clues that might lead to the identification of the body. According to the medical examiner, the cause of death was an overdose of bad cocaine. The possibility wasn't ruled out that the cocaine had been supplied by the suspected killer, and that Peñalva Brown knew he was giving her poison. Two weeks later, when all efforts were focused on solving the second murder, two women appeared at the precinct station, where they stated that they had known the dead woman. Her name was Sofía Serrano and she had worked at three maquiladoras and as a waitress, and most recently as a whore in the vacant lots of Colonia Ciudad Nueva, behind the cemetery. She had no family in Santa Teresa, just some friends, all of them poor, so her body was handed over to the University of Santa Teresa medical school.

•

The second dead woman turned up next to a trash can in Colonia Estrella. She had been raped and strangled. Shortly afterward she was identified as Olga Paredes Pacheco, twenty-five, salesgirl at a clothing store on Avenida Real, near the center of the city, single, five foot three, resident of Calle Hermanos Redondo, in Colonia Rubén Darío, where she lived with her younger sister, Elisa Paredes Pacheco, both of them well-known in the neighborhood for their warmth, friendliness, and trustworthiness. Their parents had died five years before, scarcely two months apart, first their father, of cancer, and then their mother, of a heart attack, and Olga had taken charge of the household smoothly and easily. She wasn't known to be dating anyone. Her sister, twenty, was engaged to be married. Elisa's fiancé, a young lawyer recently graduated from the University of Santa Teresa, worked in the offices of a well-known corporate lawyer, and also possessed an alibi for the night when it was believed Olga had been kidnapped. Shaken by the death of his future sister-in-law, he confessed during the (informal) questioning to which he was subjected to not having the least idea who could wish Olga ill, let alone want to kill her, and he appeared to be obsessed by the bad luck, the tragic fate, that, according to him, had beset his fiancée's family, first with the death of her parents and then the death of her sister. Olga's few friends confirmed what her sister and the young lawyer had said. Everybody loved her, she was the kind of woman you didn't often come across in Santa Teresa anymore, that is, virtuous, true to her word, honest, and responsible. And she knew how to dress, too, with elegance and good taste. Concerning her taste in clothing the medical examiner was in agreement. He also discovered something odd about the body: the skirt she was wearing the night of her death—the skirt in which she was found—was on backward.

•

In May the American consul visited the mayor of Santa Teresa and then, along with the latter, paid an informal visit to the police chief. The consul's name was Abraham Mitchell, but his wife and friends called him Conan. He was a tall man, six foot three, two hundred and thirty pounds, his face lined and his ears perhaps too big, who loved living in Mexico and camping in the desert and who intervened personally only in serious matters. In other words, he almost never had anything to do, except attend parties as his country's representative and make occasional surreptitious visits, once every two months, along with a few fellow countrymen of great drinking prowess, to the two most famous *pulquerías* in Santa Teresa. The Huntsville sheriff had disappeared and all available reports indicated that he had last been seen in Santa Teresa. The police chief wanted to know whether he had been in Santa Teresa on official business or as a tourist. As a tourist, of course, said the consul. Well, then, what do you expect me to know? asked Pedro Negrete, hundreds of tourists come through here every day. The consul reflected for an instant and ultimately agreed that the police chief was right. Better not to stir things up, he thought. Still, as a courtesy to the mayor, who was Pedro Negrete's friend, permission was granted for the consul or whomever he deemed appropriate to go through the photographs of unidentified dead bodies found in the city from November 1994 to the present, and none of the bodies were identified by Rory Campuzano, assistant to the sheriff, who came from Huntsville for that express purpose. Probably the sheriff flipped out, said Kurt A. Banks, and killed himself in the desert. Or now he's living with a transvestite in Florida, said Henderson, the other consular officer. Conan Mitchell frowned and said it wasn't respectful to talk that way about a United States sheriff. In May, meanwhile, no woman was killed in Santa Teresa and the same was true of June. But in July two dead women turned up, and the first protests were staged by a feminist organization, Women of Sonora for Democracy and Peace (WSDP), a group whose headquarters were in Hermosillo and that had only three members in Santa Teresa. The first dead woman appeared in the yard of an auto repair shop, at the end of Calle Refugio, near the Nogales highway. The woman was nineteen and had been raped and strangled. Her body was found in a car about to be scrapped. She was dressed in jeans, a low-cut white blouse, and cowboy boots. Three days later it was learned that she was Paula García Zapatero, resident of Colonia Lomas del Toro, machine operator at the maquiladora TECNOSA, born in the state of Querétaro. She lived with three other women from Querétaro, and she wasn't known to have a boyfriend, although she'd been involved with two fellow workers from the same maquiladora. The men were found and questioned for several days and both could substantiate their alibis, although one of them ended up in the hospital with nervous shock and three broken ribs. While the case of Paula García Zapatero was still under investigation, the second dead woman of July turned up. Her body was found behind some Pemex tanks along the Casas Negras highway. She was nineteen, thin and dark-skinned, with long black hair. She had been raped repeatedly, anally and vaginally, according to the medical examiner, and the presence of multiple hematomas testified to the excessive violence employed against her. Her body, however, was found fully clothed, jeans, black panties, panty hose, white bra, white blouse, garments without a single rip or tear, from which it was deduced that the killer or killers, after stripping and molesting and killing her, had proceeded to dress her before dumping her body behind the Pémex tanks. The Paula García Zapatero case was handled by Inspector Efraín Bustelo of the state judicial

police, and the Rosaura López Santana case was assigned to Inspector
Ernesto Ortiz Rebolledo, and both cases soon hit a wall, since there
were no witnesses or leads.

•

In August 1995, the bodies of seven women were found, Florita Almada
made her second appearance on Sonora television, and two Tucson cops
came to Santa Teresa asking questions. The Tucson cops spoke with the
consular officers Kurt A. Banks and Dick Henderson, since the consul
was spending some time at his ranch in Sage, California, actually a rotting wooden cabin, on the far side of the Ramona Indian Reservation,
while his wife took a few months' break with her sister in Escondido,
near San Diego. There had once been land with the cabin, but the land
was sold by Conan Mitchell's father and all that was left now was a
quarter acre of overgrown yard where Conan Mitchell spent his time
shooting field mice with a Remington 870 Wingmaster and reading cowboy novels and watching porn videos. When he was bored he would get
in his car and go down to Sage, to the bar, where some of the old men
had known him since he was a boy. At times Conan Mitchell would stare
at the old men and think it was impossible they could remember his
childhood so well, since some of them didn't seem much older than he
was. But the old men clattered their false teeth and recalled the young
Abe Mitchell's pranks as if they were occurring before their eyes and
Conan had no choice but to pretend he was laughing too. The truth is,
he didn't have clear memories of his childhood. He remembered his father and his older brother and sometimes he remembered thunder-
storms, but the rain had been somewhere else he'd lived, not Sage. He'd
had the superstition since childhood that he would die struck by lightning, and he did remember that, although he hadn't told many people
about it, except his wife. The truth is, Conan Mitchell wasn't much of a
talker. That was one of the reasons he liked to live in Mexico, where he
had two small transport companies. Mexicans like to talk, but they'd
rather not talk to higher-ups, especially if they're American. This idea,
which he'd come up with himself, though God knows how it had taken
shape in his head, soothed him when he was south of the border. Sometimes, though, and always at his wife's insistence, he had to spend periods in California or Arizona, which he accepted with resignation. The
first few days the change didn't seem to affect him. Two weeks later, un-

able to bear the noise (noise directed at him and requiring answers), he left for Sage, to hole up in his old cabin. When the Tucson police came to Santa Teresa, Conan had been gone for twenty days, which the policemen were secretly glad of, because they'd heard talk of his incompetence. Henderson and Banks acted as guides. The policemen traveled all over the city, visited bars and clubs, were introduced to Pedro Negrete, with whom they had a long conversation about drug trafficking, held a meeting with Inspector Ortiz Rebolledo and Inspector Juan de Dios Martínez, spoke to two medical examiners from the city morgue, examined some files of nameless bodies found in the desert, and visited the brothel Internal Affairs, where they each slept with a whore. Then, as suddenly as they had come, they went away.

•

As for Florita Almada, her second television appearance was less spectacular than the first. She spoke, at Reinaldo's particular request, about the three books she'd written and published. They might not be good books, she said, but for a woman who'd been illiterate until she was past twenty, they weren't entirely lacking in merit. Everything in this world, she said, no matter how big, was the tiniest speck compared to the universe. What did she mean by that? Why, that human beings, if they put their minds to it, could better themselves. She didn't mean that a peasant, to give an example, would be capable from one day to the next of running NASA, or even of working for NASA, but who could say that the peasant's son, guided by his father's love and example, might not end up working there one day? She, to give another example, would have liked to go to school and become a teacher, because in her modest understanding, teaching children might be the best job in the world, gently opening children's eyes, even the tiniest bit, to the treasures of life and culture, which were ultimately one and the same. But it wasn't to be and she was at peace with the world. Sometimes she dreamed she was a schoolteacher and she lived in the country. Her school was at the top of a hill with a view of the town, the brown and white houses, the dusky yellow roofs where the old folks sometimes settled to gaze down on the dirt streets. From the schoolyard she could see the girls on their way to class. Black hair gathered in ponytails or braids or held back with bands. Dark-skinned faces and white smiles. In the distance, the peasants worked the land, reaped fruit from the desert, tended flocks of goats.

She could hear them, the way they said good morning or good night, how clearly, effortlessly, she could hear them, every word they spoke, the words that never changed and the words that changed each day, each hour, each minute. Well, that was the way it was in dreams. There were dreams in which everything fit together and other dreams in which nothing fit and the world was like a creaky coffin. For all that, she was at peace with the world, since even though she hadn't studied to become a schoolteacher, which was her dream, now she was an herbalist and, in the view of some, a seer, and many people were grateful to her for a few little things she had done for them, nothing important, bits of advice, small suggestions, like for example recommending that they incorporate vegetable fiber into their diets, vegetable fiber isn't food for human beings, in other words our digestive system can't break it down and absorb it, but it helps us go to the toilet, or make number two or, begging the pardon of Reinaldo and this distinguished audience, defecate. Only the digestive system of herbivorous animals, said Florita, is equipped with substances capable of digesting cellulose and therefore of absorbing the glucose molecules that make up cellulose. Vegetable fiber is the name we give to cellulose and other similar substances. The consumption of vegetable fiber, even though it doesn't provide us with usable energy-producing elements, is beneficial. When it isn't absorbed, the fiber causes the bolus, in its passage through the digestive tract, to retain its volume. And that causes pressure to be generated inside the intestine, which stimulates intestinal activity, assuring the easy passage of waste through the whole digestive tract. Diarrhea is hardly ever a good thing, but going to the bathroom once or twice a day brings serenity and balance, a kind of inner peace. Not great inner peace, why exaggerate, but a small and shining inner peace. What a difference between vegetable fiber and iron and what they represent! Vegetable fiber is the food of herbivores and it's small and provides us not with nourishment but with peace the size of a jumping bean. Iron, in contrast, represents harshness in our treatment of others and ourselves, harshness in its most extreme form. What iron am I talking about? Why, the iron that swords are made from. Or that swords used to be made from and that stands for inflexibility. Either way, iron was the dealer of death. King Solomon was a wise king, probably the wisest in history, son himself of the king from Las Mañanitas, our birthday song, and protector of childhood, although it's said he once wanted to slice a child in two. When King Solomon ordered the Temple of Jerusalem to be built, he strictly forbade the use of iron as a support in the construction, even in the smallest details, and he also forbade the use of iron in circumcision, a practice, let it be said in passing and with no intention to offend, that might've had its purposes in those days and those deserts, but now, with modern hygiene, strikes me as unnecessary. I think men should circumcise themselves at twenty-one if they want, and if they don't want to, fine. Getting back to iron, said Florita, let it also be said that neither the Greeks nor the Celts used it in the collection of medicinal or magical herbs. Because iron signified death, inflexibility, power. And this was at odds with healing practices. Though later the Romans attributed a long series of therapeutic virtues to iron, believing it relieved or cured various afflictions, like the bites of rabid dogs, hemorrhage, dysentery, hemorrhoids. This notion carried over into the Middle Ages, in which it was also believed that demons, witches, and wizards fled from iron. And why shouldn't they when iron was the instrument of their deaths! They would have been complete idiots if they hadn't run away! In those dark years iron was used in the practice of the divinatory art called sideromancy. This consisted of heating a piece of iron in the forge until it was red-hot and then tossing bits of straw on it, which burned with a blinding brightness, like the stars. The metal, well polished, served to protect the eyes from the venomous glare of witches. That makes me think, if you'll pardon the digression, said Florita Almada, about the dark glasses worn by some of our political leaders or labor bosses or policemen. Why do they cover their eyes, I ask? Have they been up all night studying how to help the country advance, how to promise workers greater job security or pay raises, how to fight crime? Maybe so. It's not for me to say otherwise. Maybe that's why they have circles under their eyes. But what would happen if I went up to one of them and took off his glasses and saw that he *didn't have* circles under his eyes? It frightens me to imagine it. It makes me angry. Very angry, dear friends. But it made her even more frightened and angry, and this she had to say here, in front of the cameras, on Reinaldo's lovely show, so fittingly called *An Hour with Reinaldo*, a nice, wholesome program that gave everyone a chance to laugh and enjoy themselves and learn something new in the process, because Reinaldo was a cultured young man and he always took the trouble to find interesting guests, a singer, a painter, a retired fire-eater from Mexico City, an interior designer, a ventriloquist and his dummy, a mother of fifteen children, a composer of romantic ballads, and now that she was here, she said, it was her duty to take this opportunity to speak of other things, by which she meant that she couldn't talk about herself, she couldn't let herself succumb to that temptation of the ego, that frivolity, which might not be frivolity or sin or anything of the sort if she were a girl of seventeen or eighteen, but would be unforgivable in a woman of seventy, although my life, she said, could furnish material for several novels or at least a soap opera, but God and especially the blessed Virgin would deliver her from talking about herself, Reinaldo will have to forgive me, he wants me to talk about myself, but there's something more important than me and my so-called miracles, which aren't miracles, as I never get tired of saying, but the fruit of many years of reading and handling plants, in other words my miracles are the product of work and observation, and, possibly, I say *possibly*, also of a natural talent, said Florita. And then she said: it makes me very angry, it makes me frightened and angry what's happening in the lovely state of Sonora, which is my homeland, the place I was born and will probably die. And then she said: I'm talking about visions that would take away the breath of the bravest of brave men. In dreams I see the crimes and it's as if a television set had exploded and I keep seeing, in the little shards of screen scattered around my bedroom, horrible scenes, endless tears. And she said: after these visions I can't sleep. No matter what I take for my nerves, nothing helps. The shoemaker's son always goes barefoot. So I stay up until dawn and I try to read and do something useful and practical, but in the end I sit down at the kitchen table and start to mull over the problem. And finally she said: I'm talking about the women brutally murdered in Santa Teresa, I'm talking about the girls and the mothers of families and the workers from all walks of life who turn up dead each day in the neighborhoods and on the edges of that industrious city in the northern part of our state. I'm talking about Santa Teresa. I'm talking about Santa Teresa.

•

As for the dead women of August 1995, the first was Aurora Muñoz Álvarez and her body was found on the pavement of the Santa Teresa–Cananea highway. She had been strangled. She was twenty-eight and she was dressed in green leggings, a white T-shirt, and pink tennis shoes. According to the medical examiner, she had been beaten and whipped: the marks of a wide belt were still visible on her back. She had worked as a waitress at a café in the center of the city. The first to take the rap was her boyfriend, with whom she often fought, according to some witnesses. The man's name was Rogelio Reinosa and he worked at the maquiladora Rem&Co. and didn't have an alibi for the evening Aurora Muñoz was kidnapped. He spent a week in one interrogation session after another. A month later, after he had already been moved to the Santa Teresa jail, he was released for lack of evidence. There were no other arrests. According to the eyewitnesses, who had no idea it was a kidnapping, Aurora Muñoz had gotten into a black Peregrino with two men she seemed to know. Two days after the appearance of the first August victim, the body of Emilia Escalante Sanjuán, thirty-three, was found, presenting multiple hematomas over the chest and neck. The body was discovered at the intersection of Michoacán and General Saavedra, in Colonia Trabajadores. The medical examiner's report stated that the cause of death was strangulation, after the victim had been raped countless times. The report of Inspector Ángel Fernández, who took charge of the case, indicated, on the contrary, that the cause of death was alcohol poisoning. Emilia Escalante Sanjuán lived in Colonia Morelos, in the west of the city, and worked at the maquiladora New-Markets. She had two young children and lived with her mother, whom she had sent for from Oaxaca, where she was from. She didn't have a husband, although once every two months she went out to clubs downtown, with friends from work, where she usually drank and went off with some man. Practically a whore, said the police. A week later the body of Estrella Ruiz Sandoval, seventeen, turned up next to the Casas Negras highway. She had been raped and strangled. She was dressed in jeans and a dark blue blouse. Her arms were tied behind her back. Her body showed no signs of torture or beating. She had disappeared from home, where she lived with her parents and siblings, three days before. The case was handled by Epifanio Galindo and Noé Velasco, of the Santa Teresa police department, to ease the burden on the judicial police inspectors, who were complaining about having too much work. One day after Estrella Ruiz Sandoval's body was found, the body of Mónica Posadas, twenty, was discovered in a vacant lot near Calle Amistad, in Colonia La Preciada. According to the medical examiner, Mónica had been anally and vaginally raped, although traces of semen were also found in her throat, which led to talk in police circles of a "three-way" rape. There was one cop, however, who said a full rape meant a rape of all five orifices. Asked what the other two were, he said the ears. Another cop said he'd heard of a man from Sinaloa who raped seven ways. That is, the five known orifices, plus the eyes. And another cop said he'd heard of a man from Mexico City who did it eight ways, which meant the seven orifices previously mentioned, call it the seven classics, plus the navel, where the man from Mexico City would make a small incision with his knife, then stick in his dick, although to do that, of course, you had to be out of your tree. Anyway, the story of the "three-way" rape spread and became a favorite among the Santa Teresa police, acquiring semiofficial status and occasionally cropping up in reports, interrogations, and off-the-record conversations with the press. In the case of Mónica Posadas, the victim hadn't only been raped "three ways," but also strangled. The body, which was found half hidden behind some cardboard boxes, was naked from the waist down. The legs were stained with blood. So much blood that if seen from a distance, or from a certain height, a stranger (or an angel, since there was no nearby building from which to look down) might have said the girl was wearing red tights. Her vagina was torn. Her vulva and thighs showed clear signs of bites and tears, as if a street dog had gnawed at her. The inspectors centered their investigation on the family circle and among the acquaintances of Mónica Posadas, who lived with her family on Calle San Hipólito, about six blocks from the vacant lot where the body was found. Her mother and stepfather, as well as her older brother, worked at Overworld, a maquiladora where Mónica had worked for three years, after which she'd left to try her luck at Country&SeaTech. Mónica's family came from a little town in Michoacán and had moved to Santa Teresa ten years ago. At first, life seemed to get worse instead of better, and Mónica's father decided to cross the border. He was never heard from again and after a while his family gave him up for dead. Then Mónica's mother met a hardworking, responsible man whom she ended up marrying. Three children were born of this marriage. One worked at a small boot factory and the other two went to school. Upon being questioned, it wasn't long before Mónica's stepfather began to flagrantly contradict himself, and in the end, he admitted he was guilty of the murder. According to his confession, he had loved Mónica in secret from the time she was fifteen. His life since then had been a living hell, he told Inspector Juan de Dios Martínez, Inspector Ernesto Ortiz Rebolledo, and Inspector Efraín Rebolledo, but he had controlled himself and stayed away from her, partly because she was his stepdaughter and partly because her mother was also the mother of his own children. His account of the day of the crime was vague, full of holes and forgotten details. In his first statement he said it was late at night. In the second he said it was early morning, and only he and Mónica were in the house because they were both working the afternoon shift that week. He hid the body in a wardrobe. In my wardrobe, he told the inspectors, a wardrobe no one touched because it was my wardrobe and I demanded respect for my things. At night, while the family was asleep, he wrapped the body in a blanket and left it in the nearest vacant lot. Asked about the bites and the blood covering Mónica's legs, he didn't know what to answer. He said he had strangled her and that was all he remembered. The rest had been erased from his memory. Two days after Mónica's body was discovered in the vacant lot on Calle Amistad, the body of another dead woman appeared on the Santa Teresa–Caborca highway. According to the medical examiner, the woman was probably between eighteen and twenty-two, although she might well have been between sixteen and twenty-three. The cause of death, at least, was clear. She had been shot. One hundred feet from where she was found, the skeleton of another woman was discovered, half buried in a decumbent position, still wearing a blue jacket and good-quality leather shoes with a small heel. The state of the body made it impossible to determine the cause of death. A week later, when August was nearing an end, the body of Jacqueline Ríos, twenty-five, salesgirl at a drugstore in Colonia Madero, was found next to the Santa Teresa–Cananea highway. She was dressed in jeans and a light gray blouse, white tennis shoes, and black underwear. She had been shot in the chest and the abdomen. She had an apartment with a friend on Calle Bulgaria, in Colonia Madero, and both dreamed of going to live in California someday. Found in her bedroom, which she shared with her friend, were clippings of Hollywood actresses and actors and pictures of places around the world. First we wanted to move to California, find decent, well-paying jobs, and then, once we were settled, see the world on our vacations, said her friend. Both of them studied English at a private academy in Colonia Madero. The case remained unsolved.

•

Those fucking *judiciales* never solve a case, Epifanio said to Lalo Cura. Then he began to rummage through his papers until he found a little notebook. What do you think this is? he asked. An address book, said Lalo Cura. No, said Epifanio, it's an unsolved case. This happened before you came to Santa Teresa. I don't remember the year. A little before Don Pedro brought you, that I do remember, but I'm not sure about the exact year. Maybe 1993. What year did you come? In '93, said Lalo Cura. Is that so? Yes, said Lalo Cura. Well, then this was months before you got here, said Epifanio. A radio reporter was killed. Her name was Isabel Urrea. She was shot to death. No one ever figured out who the killer was. They tried to find him, but they couldn't. Of course, it didn't occur to anyone to look at Isabel Urrea's appointment book. The assholes thought it was a mugging gone wrong. There was talk about a Central American. Some desperate fuck who needed money to cross the border, an illegal, see? An illegal even in Mexico, which is saying a lot, because we're all potential illegals here and one more or one less hardly makes a difference. I was there when they searched her house to see if they could find some clue. Of course, they found nothing. I remember I sat in an armchair, with a glass of tequila next to me, Isabel Urrea's tequila, and I glanced through the appointment book. An inspector asked me where I had gotten the tequila. But no one asked me where I had gotten the appointment book or whether there was anything important in it. I glanced through it, some of the names sounded familiar, and then I left it with the rest of the evidence. A month later I went into the archives at the precinct, and there was the appointment book, along with a few other things belonging to the reporter. I slipped it into my pocket and took it. That way I could study it in my own time. I found the phone numbers of three *narcos*. One of them was Pedro Rengifo. I also found the numbers of several *judiciales*, including a big boss in Hermosillo. What were those phone numbers doing in an ordinary reporter's appointment book? Had she interviewed them, put them on the air? Was she friends with them? And if she wasn't, who had given her the numbers? A mystery. I could have done something. I could've called some of the names I'd found and asked for money. But money doesn't do it for me. So I kept the notebook, fuck it, and didn't do anything.

•

Early in September, the body of a girl later identified as Marisa Hernández Silva appeared. She was seventeen and had vanished at the beginning of July on her way to the Vasconcelos Preparatory School, in Colonia Reforma. According to the forensic report, she had been raped and strangled. One of her breasts was almost completely severed and the other was missing the nipple, which had been bitten off. The body was found at the entrance to the illegal dump El Chile. The call that alerted the police was made by a woman who had come to the dump to dispose of a refrigerator, at noon, a time of day when there were no tramps, just the occasional pack of children or dogs. Marisa Hernández Silva was sprawled between two big gray plastic bags full of scraps of synthetic fiber. She was wearing the same clothes she'd had on when she disappeared: denim pants, yellow blouse, and sneakers. The mayor of Santa Teresa ordered that the dump be closed, although he later changed the order (informed by his secretary of the legal impossibility of closing something that, for all intents and purposes, had never been open) to decree the dismantling, removal, and destruction of that pestilential no-man's-land. For a week a police guard was posted on the edge of El Chile and for three days a few garbage trucks, aided by the two city dump trucks, ferried trash to the dump in Colonia Kino, but faced with the magnitude of the job and their own lack of manpower, they soon gave up.

•

Around this time, Sergio González, the reporter from Mexico City, had moved up the ranks of his paper's arts page and his salary was higher, which meant he could send monthly support payments to his ex-wife and still live comfortably, and he even had a lover, a reporter from the international news section, with whom he slept occasionally, but to whom he couldn't talk, because they were so different. He hadn't forgotten—although he wondered himself why the memory persisted—the days he'd spent in Santa Teresa or the killings of women, or the priest-killer called the Penitent, who had vanished as mysteriously as he'd appeared. Sometimes, he thought, being an arts reporter in Mexico was the same as reporting on crime. And being on the police beat was the same as working for the arts page, although in the minds of the crime reporters, all the arts reporters were faggots (*assthetes*, they called them), and in the minds of the arts reporters, all the crime reporters were scum. Some nights after work he went for drinks with a few older reporters from the crime page, which, as it happened, had the highest percentage of the oldest reporters at the newspaper, trailed distantly by national news and sports. Usually they ended up at a bar frequented by whores in Colonia

Guerrero, a huge lounge presided over by a seven-foot-tall plaster statue of Aphrodite, probably, he thought, a place that had enjoyed a certain louche glory back in Tin-Tan's day, and since then had been in perpetual decline, one of those interminable Mexican declines, meaning a decline stitched together here and there with a muted laugh, a muted shot, a muted whimper. A Mexican decline? More like a Latin American decline. The crime reporters liked to drink there, but they hardly ever slept with the whores. They talked about old cases, recalled tales of corruption, extortion, and bloodshed, greeted the cops who dropped by too, or took them aside to talk, as they put it, on background, but they hardly ever went with a whore. At first, Sergio González followed their example, until he figured out that the reason the older reporters didn't sleep with the whores was essentially because they had already been with all of them, years ago, and because they weren't of an age to throw their money around. So he stopped following their example, found a pretty young whore, and took her to a nearby hotel. Once, he asked one of the oldest reporters what he thought about the killings of women up north. The reporter answered that Santa Teresa was a center of the drug trade and most likely nothing happened there that wasn't related to the phenomenon one way or another. This struck him as an obvious answer, an answer anyone might have given him, but every so often he pondered it, as if despite the obviousness or simplicity of what the reporter had said, the answer was orbiting his brain and emitting signals. His few writer friends, those who came to visit him at the arts department, had no idea what was happening in Santa Teresa, although news of the dead women reached Mexico City at a steady rate, and Sergio imagined they probably didn't care much what was happening in some distant corner of the country. His fellow reporters, even those on the police beat, were indifferent too. One night, after making love with the whore, as they lay smoking in bed, he asked her what she thought about all the kidnappings and all the bodies of women found in the desert, and she said she had only a vague idea what he was talking about. Then Sergio told her everything he knew about the dead women and described the trip he'd taken to Santa Teresa, and why he took it, because he needed the money, because he'd just gotten divorced, and then he talked about the killings, which he, as a newspaper reader, had followed, and about the press releases from a women's organization whose initials, WSDP, he remembered, although he'd forgotten what they stood for, Women of

Sonora for Democracy and the People?, and as he was talking the whore yawned, not because she wasn't interested in what he was saying but because she was tired, which irritated Sergio and made him say, in exasperation, that in Santa Teresa they were killing whores, so why not show a little professional solidarity, to which the whore replied that he was wrong, in the story as he had told it the women dying were factory workers, not whores. Workers, workers, she said. And then Sergio apologized, and, as if a lightbulb had gone on over his head, he glimpsed an aspect of the situation that until now he'd overlooked.

•

The month of September still held surprises for the citizens of Santa Teresa. Three days after the discovery of Marisa Hernández Silva's mutilated body, the body of an unidentified woman turned up next to the Santa Teresa–Cananea highway. The dead woman must have been about twenty-five and she had a congenital dislocation of the right hip. And yet, no one missed her, and even after the details of her deformity were published in the press, no one came to the police with new information that might lead to an identification. She was found with her hands bound, the strap of a woman's purse used for the purpose. Her neck was broken and both arms displayed knife wounds. But most significant of all was that, just like young Marisa Hernández Silva, one of her breasts had been severed and the nipple of the other breast had been bitten off.

•

The same day that the victim with the hip dislocation was found next to the Santa Teresa–Cananea highway, city workers who were trying to move the El Chile dump discovered the rotting body of a woman. It was impossible to determine the cause of death. She had long black hair. She was dressed in a light-colored blouse with dark patterns that couldn't be made out because of the body's state of decay. She was wearing Jokko brand jeans. No one came to the police with information that might lead to an identification.

•

At the end of September, the body of a thirteen-year-old girl was found on the east side of Cerro Estrella. Like Marisa Hernández Silva and the woman by the Santa Teresa–Cananea highway, her right breast had been severed and the nipple of her left breast had been bitten off. She was dressed in Lee jeans, a sweatshirt, and a red vest. She was very thin. She had been raped numerous times and stabbed, and the cause of death was a fracture of the hyoid bone. But what surprised the reporters most was that no one claimed or acknowledged the body. As if the girl had come to Santa Teresa alone and lived there invisibly until the murderer or murderers took notice of her and killed her.

•

As the crimes followed one after the other, Epifanio carried on alone with his investigation of the death of Estrella Ruiz Sandoval. He talked to her parents and the siblings still living at home. They didn't know anything. He talked to an older sister, who was married and lived on Calle Esperanza now, in Colonia Lomas del Toro. He looked at pictures of Estrella. She was a pretty girl, tall, with beautiful hair and nice features. Her sister told him who her friends were at the maquiladora where she'd worked. He waited for them outside. He noticed that he was the only older person waiting; the others were children, some even carrying schoolbooks. Near the children was a man with a green ice cream cart. The cart had a white umbrella. As if Epifanio wanted to make them disappear, he whistled to the children and bought all of them ice cream bars, except one who wasn't even three months old yet, a baby in the arms of her sister, who might have been six. The names of Estrella's friends were Rosa Márquez and Rosa María Medina. He asked how to find them, and one of the women leaving work pointed out Rosa Márquez. He told her he was a cop and asked her to find her friend. Then they went walking out of the industrial park. As they talked about Estrella, the one called Rosa María Medina started to cry. The three liked the movies and on Sundays, though not every Sunday, they would go downtown, where they usually saw the double feature at the Rex. Other times they just window-shopped, looking at women's clothes especially, or they went to a mall in Colonia Centeno. There was live music there on Sundays and it was free. He asked if Estrella had plans for the future. Of course she had plans, she wanted to study, not spend her whole life working at the maquiladora. What did she want to study? She wanted to learn how to use a computer, said Rosa María Medina. Then Epifanio asked if they wanted to learn a trade too and they said they did, but it wasn't easy. Did she only go out with you or did she have any other friends? he wanted to know. We were her best friends, they answered. She didn't have a boyfriend. Once she did. But that was a long time ago. They didn't know him. When Epifanio asked how old Estrella was then, the two girls thought a little and said she was at least twelve. How can it be that such a pretty girl didn't have any boys chasing her? he wanted to know. The friends laughed and said there had been lots of men who would've liked to date Estrella, but she didn't want to waste her time. What do we need men for when we have our own jobs and make money and can do what we want? Rosa Márquez asked him. True, said Epifanio, you're right, although sometimes, especially when you're young, there's nothing wrong with going out and having fun, sometimes you need to. We have fun by ourselves, the girls told him, and we never feel the need. When they had almost reached the house of one of the girls, he asked them, even though it might not do any good, to describe the men who had wanted to date Estrella or be her friend. They stopped on the street and Epifanio wrote down five names, no last names, all of them workers at the same maquiladora. Then he walked a few more blocks with Rosa María Medina. I don't think it was any of them, said the girl. Why do you say that? Because they seem like nice people, said the girl. I'll talk to them, said Epifanio, and after I've talked to them I'll let you know. In three days he had tracked down the five men on the list. None of them looked like a bad person. One of them was married, but the night Estrella disappeared he had been at home with his wife and three children. The other four had more or less solid alibis, and, most important, none had a car. He talked to Rosa María Medina again. This time he sat outside her house waiting for her. When the girl got home she asked, scandalized, why he hadn't knocked. I knocked, said Epifanio, and your mother came to the door and asked me in for a cup of coffee, but then she had to go to work and I came out here to wait for you. The girl invited him in but Epifanio said he would rather sit outside, claiming it was too hot indoors. He asked her whether she smoked. At first the girl remained standing to one side, and then she sat on a flat stone and said she didn't smoke. Epifanio gazed at the stone: it was very odd, shaped like a chair, but with no back, and the fact that Rosa María Medina's mother or someone in the family had set it there, in that little yard, showed good taste and even sensitivity. He asked the girl where the stone had come from. My father found it, said Rosa María Medina, in Casas Negras, and he carried it back all by himself. That's where Estrella's body was found, said Epifanio. On the highway, said the girl, closing her eyes. My father found this stone right in Casas Negras, at a party, and he fell in love with it. That's how he was. Then she said her father had died. Epifanio wanted to know when. Years and years ago, said the girl, with a shrug. He lit a cigarette and asked her to tell him again, any way she wanted, about her outings with Estrella and the other girl, what was her name? Rosa Márquez, on Sundays. The girl started to talk, with her gaze fixed on the few potted plants her mother kept in the tiny front yard, although from time to time she lifted her eyes and glanced at him as if to gauge whether what she was telling him was useful or a waste of time. When she was finished Epifanio had gotten one thing clear: they didn't go out only on Sundays, sometimes they went to the movies on Mondays or Thursdays, or out dancing, it all depended on the shifts at the maquiladora, which followed no set pattern and obeyed production schedules beyond the workers' comprehension. Then he changed the line of questioning and wanted to know what they did for fun on Tuesdays, say, if that was the day of the week they had off. The routine, according to the girl, was similar, although in some ways it was a little better, because the stores downtown were all open, which wasn't the case on Sundays. Epifanio pushed a little. He wanted to know what their favorite movie theater was, besides the Rex, what other theaters they had gone to, whether anyone had approached Estrella anywhere, what businesses they had visited even if they hadn't gone in and just stood looking in the windows, what coffee shops they had been to, the names of the coffee shops, whether they had ever been to any club. The girl said they had never been to a club, Estrella didn't like that kind of place. But you do, said Epifanio. You and your friend Rosa Márquez. The girl wouldn't look him in the face and she said that sometimes, when they went out without Estrella, they went to the clubs downtown. And not Estrella? Estrella never went with you? Never, said the girl. Estrella wanted to know things about computers, she wanted to learn, she wanted to get ahead, said the girl. Computers, computers, I don't believe a word you're saying, cupcake, said Epifanio. I'm not your fucking cupcake, said the girl. For a while they sat there without speaking. Epifanio laughed a little and then lit another cigarette, sitting there at the door to the house, watching people come and go. There's a place, said the girl, but now I don't remember where it is, it's downtown, a computer store. We went there a few times. Rosa and I waited for her outside and she went in by herself and talked to a tall man, really tall, much taller than you, said the girl. Tall, and what else? asked Epifanio. Tall and blond, a *güero*, said the girl. And what else? Well, at first Estrella seemed excited, I mean, the first time she went in and talked to that man. She said he was the owner of the store and he knew a lot about computers and also you could tell he had money. The second time we went to see him Estrella was mad when she came out. I asked her what had happened and she didn't want to say. It was just the two of us and then we went to the carnival in Colonia Veracruz and we forgot all about it. And when was that, cupcake? asked Epifanio. I already told you I'm not your fucking cupcake, you pig, said the girl. When was that? asked Epifanio, who could already see a very tall, very blond man walking in the dark, along a long, dark passageway, back and forth, as if waiting for him. A week before she was killed, said the girl.

•

Life is hard, said the mayor of Santa Teresa. We have three clear-cut cases, said Inspector Ángel Fernández. Everything has to be examined with a magnifying glass, said the man from the chamber of commerce. I do examine everything with a magnifying glass, over and over, until I can't see straight, said Pedro Negrete. The important thing is not to stir up any shit, said the mayor. We have to do what it takes, said Pedro Negrete. We have a serial killer, like in the gringo movies, said Inspector Ernesto Ortiz Rebolledo. We have to watch our step, said the man from the chamber of commerce. What's the difference between a serial killer and an ordinary killer? asked Inspector Ángel Fernández. Very simple: the serial killer has a signature, you see? he doesn't have a motive but he does have a signature, said Inspector Ernesto Ortiz Rebolledo. What do you mean he doesn't have a motive? Is he moved by electrical charges? asked the mayor. In this kind of business you have to be careful what you say, or else you end up somewhere you don't want to be, said the man from the chamber of commerce. There are three dead women, said Inspector Ángel Fernández, holding up his thumb, index finger, and middle finger. If only it were just three, said Pedro Negrete. Three dead women whose right breasts were cut off and whose left nipples were bitten off, said Inspector Ernesto Ortiz Rebolledo. What does that sound like to all of you? asked Inspector Ángel Fernández. A serial killer? asked the mayor. Well, of course, said Inspector Ángel Fernández. It would be too much of a coincidence if three bastards chose the same way to carve up their victims, said Inspector Ernesto Ortiz Rebolledo. Sounds logical, said the mayor. But that might not be the whole story, said Inspector Ángel Fernández. If we let our imaginations run wild there's no knowing where it'll lead us, said the man from the chamber of commerce. I know what you're trying to get at, said Pedro Negrete. And do you think we're right? asked the mayor. If the three women with their right breasts sliced off were killed by the same person, wouldn't that person have killed other women too? asked Inspector Ángel Fernández. It's only scientific, said Inspector Ernesto Ortiz Rebolledo. The killer is a scientist? asked the man from the chamber of commerce. No, I'm talking about the modus operandi, the way this son of a bitch is warming up to his work, said Inspector Ernesto Ortiz Rebolledo. Let me explain: he began by raping and strangling, which is what you might call a normal way to kill. When he wasn't caught, his murders became more personalized. The monster was unleashed. Now each crime bears his personal signature, said Inspector Ángel Fernández. What do you think, Judge? asked the mayor. Anything is possible, said the judge. Anything is possible, but there's no need to descend into chaos, no need to lose our bearings, said the man from the chamber of commerce. What does seem clear is that the person who killed and mutilated those three poor women is the same person, said Pedro Negrete. Well, find him and put an end to this goddamn business, said the mayor. But discreetly, if I may make one request, without sending anyone into a panic, said the man from the chamber of commerce.

•

Juan de Dios Martínez wasn't invited to the meeting. He knew it was being held, he knew Ortiz Rebolledo and Ángel Fernández would be there, and he knew he was being left out. But when Juan de Dios Martínez closed his eyes, all he saw was Elvira Campos's body in the half-light of her apartment in Colonia Michoacán. Sometimes he saw her in bed, naked, leaning toward him. Other times he saw her on the terrace, surrounded by metallic objects, phallic objects, that turned out to be all kinds of telescopes (there were really only three), through which she scanned the starry sky of Santa Teresa and then took notes in pencil. When he came up behind her and looked at the notebook, all he saw were telephone numbers, most of them Santa Teresa numbers. The pencil was an ordinary pencil. The notebook was a school notebook. Both objects struck him as nothing like the kind of thing the director would own. That night, after he heard about the meeting from which he'd been excluded, he called her and said he needed to see her. A moment of weakness. She replied that she couldn't and hung up. Sometimes the doctor treated him like a patient, he thought. He remembered that once she had talked to him about age, her age and his. I'm fifty-one, she'd told him, and you're thirty-four. Before long, no matter how well I take care of myself, I'll be a lonely old hag and you'll still be young. Do you really want to sleep with someone like your mother? It was the first time Juan de Dios had heard her talk like that. An old hag? Honestly it had never crossed his mind to think of her as old. Because I kill myself exercising, she said. Because I take care of myself. Because I keep thin and I buy the most expensive antiwrinkle products on the market. Antiwrinkle products? Lotions, moisturizing creams, woman things, she said in a neutral voice that frightened him. I like you the way you are, he said. His voice didn't sound convincing to him. If he opened his eyes, though, and gazed at the real world and tried to control his own jitters, everything stayed more or less in place.

·

So Pedro Rengifo is a *narco*? asked Lalo Cura. That's right, said Epifanio. I can hardly believe it, said Lalo Cura. Because you're still a fledgling, said Epifanio. A fat old Indian woman brought them each a dish of posole. It was five in the morning. Lalo Cura had worked all night on traffic duty. While he and his partner were stopped at a corner, someone knocked on the window. Neither Lalo Cura nor the other cop had seen anyone coming. It was Epifanio, up late and looking drunk, although he wasn't. I'm taking the kid, he told the other patrolman. The patrolman shrugged and was left alone on the corner, under some oaks with white-painted trunks. Epifanio was on foot. The night was cool and all the stars were out in the desert breeze. They walked downtown, without talking, until Epifanio asked if he was hungry. Lalo Cura said he was. Then let's get something to eat, said Epifanio. When the fat old Indian woman served them the posole, Epifanio sat looking at the earthenware dish as if he'd seen someone else's face reflected in its surface. Do you know where posole comes from, Lalito? he asked. No idea, said Lalo Cura. It's from the middle of the country, not the north. It's a Mexico

City specialty. The Aztecs invented it, he said. The Aztecs? well, it's good, said Lalo Cura. Did you eat posole in Villaviciosa? asked Epifanio. Lalo Cura thought about it, as if Villaviciosa were very far away, and then he said no, in fact he hadn't, although now it seemed strange to him that he hadn't tried it before he came to live in Santa Teresa. Maybe I did try it and now I don't remember, he said. Well, this posole isn't quite the same as the original posole, said Epifanio. It's missing an ingredient. What ingredient is that? asked Lalo Cura. Human flesh, said Epifanio. Don't fuck with me, said Lalo Cura. It's true, the Aztecs cooked posole with pieces of human flesh, said Epifanio. I don't believe it, said Lalo Cura. Well, it doesn't matter, maybe I'm wrong or the guy who told me was wrong, although he knew all kinds of shit, said Epifanio. Then they talked about Pedro Rengifo, and Lalo Cura asked how it was possible he hadn't realized Don Pedro was a *narco*. Because you're still an infant, said Epifanio. And then he said: why did you think he had so many bodyguards? Because he's rich, said Lalo Cura. Epifanio laughed. Come on, he said, let's get to bed, you're half asleep already.

·

In October no dead women turned up in Santa Teresa, in the city or the desert, and work to get rid of the illegal dump El Chile was permanently halted. A reporter for *La Tribuna de Santa Teresa* who was covering the relocation or demolition of the dump said he'd never seen so much chaos in his life. Asked whether the chaos was caused by the city workers involved in the futile effort, he answered that it wasn't, it came from the inertia of the festering place itself. In October five judicial police inspectors were sent from Hermosillo to supplement the team of inspectors already in the city. One of them came from Caborca, another from Ciudad Obregón, and the remaining three from Hermosillo. They seemed to be up to the task. In October, Florita Almada made another appearance on *An Hour with Reinaldo* and said she had consulted with her friends (sometimes she called them friends and other times protectors) and they had told her the crimes would continue. They had also told her to be careful, there were people who wished her ill. But I'm not worried, she said, why should I be, when I'm already an old woman. Then, in front of the cameras, she tried to talk to the spirit of one of the victims, but she couldn't and she fainted. Reinaldo thought the faint was faked and tried to rouse her himself, patting her cheeks and giving her sips of water to drink, but it wasn't faked at all (it was a real blackout) and Florita ended up in the hospital.

•

Blond and very tall. Owner or possibly trusted employee at a computer store. Downtown. It didn't take Epifanio long to find the place. The man's name was Klaus Haas. He was six foot three and he had canary-yellow hair, as if he dyed it once a week. The first time Epifanio visited the store, Klaus Haas was sitting at his desk talking to a customer. A short, very dark boy came up to him and asked if he needed help. Epifanio pointed to Haas and asked who he was. The boss, said the boy. I want to talk to him, he said. He's busy now, said the boy, if you tell me what you want maybe I can find it for you. No, said Epifanio. He sat down, lit a cigarette, and prepared to wait. Two other customers came in. Then a man in blue overalls came in and left some cardboard boxes in a corner. Haas waved to him from his desk. His arms are long and strong, thought Epifanio. The boy went over and left him an ashtray. At the back of the store there was a girl typing. When the customers left, a woman who looked like a secretary came in and began to look at the laptops. As she looked she noted down prices and features. She was wearing a skirt and high heels, and Epifanio thought she must definitely be fucking her boss. Then two other customers came in and the boy left the woman and went to wait on them. Haas, removed from it all, kept talking to the man Epifanio could see only from behind. Haas's eyebrows were almost white and sometimes he laughed or smiled at something the other man said and his teeth gleamed like a movie actor's. Epifanio put out his cigarette and lit another. The woman turned and glanced at the street, as if someone was waiting for her outside. Her face seemed familiar, as if a long time ago he had arrested her. How long ago? he wondered. Years and years. But the woman didn't look older than twenty-five, so she couldn't have been more than seventeen at the time. Might be, thought Epifanio. And then he thought that business wasn't bad for the *güero*. He had steady customers and he could permit himself the luxury of sitting behind his desk, carrying on a leisurely conversation. Then Epifanio thought about Rosa María Medina and her credibility. It isn't worth shit, he said to himself. Half an hour later there was no one in the store. When the woman left she glanced at him as if she recognized him too. Haas and his friend weren't laughing anymore. Behind the counter, which was horseshoe shaped, the *güero* was waiting for him with a smile. Epifanio took the picture of Estrella Ruiz Sandoval out of his pocket and showed it to him. The *güero* looked at it without touching it and then made a strange face, jutting his lower lip over his upper lip, and glanced at him as if to ask what this was all about. Do you know her? I don't think so, said Haas, but lots of people come through the store. Then Epifanio introduced himself: Epifanio Galindo, of the Santa Teresa police. Haas held out his hand and when Epifanio shook it he got the feeling the blond man's bones were made of steel. He would have liked to tell him not to lie, that he had witnesses, but instead he smiled. Behind Haas, sitting at the other desk, the boy pretended to go through some papers, but he hadn't missed a word.

●

After he locked up the store, the boy got on a Japanese motorcycle and took a slow spin around the city center, as if he expected to see someone. When he came to Calle Universidad he accelerated and headed off in the direction of Colonia Veracruz. He stopped in front of a two-story house and locked the motorcycle again. His mother had been waiting for him for ten minutes with dinner ready. The boy gave her a kiss and turned on the television. His mother went into the kitchen. She took off her apron and picked up an imitation-leather purse. She gave the boy a kiss and left. I'll be right back, she said. The boy thought about asking where she was going but he didn't say anything. From one of the bedrooms came the wail of a child. At first the boy ignored it and kept watching television, but when the wailing got louder he got up, went into the bedroom, and came out with a little baby in his arms. The baby was white and pudgy, the complete opposite of his brother. The boy sat him on his knee and kept eating. There was a news program on TV. He saw a group of blacks running along the streets of an American city, a man talking about Mars, a group of women who strode out of the ocean and burst into laughter in front of the cameras. He changed the channel with the remote. A couple of kids boxing. He changed the channel again, because he didn't like boxing. His mother seemed to have vanished, but the baby had stopped crying and the boy didn't mind holding him. The doorbell rang. The boy had time to change the channel—a soap opera—and then he got up with the baby in his arms and opened the door. So this is where you live, said Epifanio. Yes, said the boy. Behind Epifanio was a cop, a short cop, though he was taller than the boy, and he sat in the armchair without asking permission. Were you having dinner? asked Epifanio. Yes, said the boy. Keep eating, keep eating, said Epifanio as he popped in and out of the other rooms, as if with a single glance he could search every corner of the house. What's your name? asked Epifanio. Juan Pablo Castañón, said the boy. Well, Juan Pablo, first sit down and keep eating, said Epifanio. Yes, sir, said the boy. And don't be nervous or you'll drop the baby, said Epifanio. The other policeman smiled.

●

An hour later they left and everything was much clearer to Epifanio. Klaus Haas was German but he had acquired American citizenship. He owned two stores in Santa Teresa where he sold everything from Walkmans to computers, and he had another similar store in Tijuana, which meant he had to travel once a month to check the books, pay the employees, and replenish stock. He also traveled to the United States every two months, although not on a fixed date or in a regular way, except that none of his trips ever lasted more than three days. He had lived for a while in Denver and left because of woman trouble. He liked women, but as far as anyone knew he wasn't married and he didn't have a girlfriend. He frequented clubs and brothels downtown, and he was friendly with a few of the owners, for whom he had at some point installed security cameras or computer accounting programs. In one case, at least, the boy knew this for a fact, because he had been the programmer. As a boss Haas was fair and reasonable and he didn't pay badly, although sometimes he got angry for no good reason and might hit anyone, no matter who it was. The boy had never been hit, but he had been scolded for coming in late to work a few times. Who had Haas hit, then? A secretary, the boy said. Asked if the secretary he'd hit was the current secretary, the boy said no, it was the previous one, a woman he hadn't met. Then how did he know she'd been hit? Because that was what the oldest employees said, the ones at the warehouse, where the *güero* stored part of his stock. The names of the employees were all neatly recorded. Finally, Epifanio showed the boy the picture of Estrella Ruiz Sandoval. Have you seen her around the store? The boy looked at the picture and said yes, her face was somehow familiar.

●

The next time Epifanio visited Klaus Haas it was close to midnight. He rang the bell and had to wait a long time before anyone came to the door, although there were lights on in the house. The place was in Colonia El Cerezal, a middle-class neighborhood of one- and two-story houses, not all of them new, where you could walk to buy bread or milk along quiet, tree-lined sidewalks, far from the noise of Colonia Madero, which was a little farther out, and away from the din of the center. It was Haas himself who opened the door. He was wearing a white shirt, untucked, and at first he didn't recognize Epifanio or pretended not to recognize him. Epifanio showed his credentials, as if it were a joke, and asked Haas whether he remembered him. Haas asked what he wanted. Can I come in? asked Epifanio. The living room was nicely furnished, with armchairs and a big white sofa. Haas took a bottle of whiskey from a liquor cabinet and poured himself a glass. He asked Epifanio if he wanted some. Epifanio shook his head. I'm on duty, he said. Haas shook with a strange laugh. It was as if he'd said ahhh, or haaah, or sneezed, but only once. Epifanio sat in one of the armchairs and asked if he had a good alibi for the day Estrella Ruiz Sandoval was killed. Haas looked him up and down and after a few seconds he said sometimes he didn't even remember what he'd done the night before. His face turned red and his eyebrows seemed whiter than they really were, as if he was making an effort to control himself. I have two witnesses who say they saw you with the victim, said Epifanio. Who? asked Haas. Epifanio didn't answer. He looked around the living room and nodded. This must have cost you a fortune, he said. I work hard and I don't do badly for myself, said Haas. Will you show me around? asked Epifanio. What? asked Haas. The house, said Epifanio. Don't fuck with me, man, said Haas, if you want to search my house, come with a warrant. Before he left, Epifanio said: I think you killed that girl. Her and who knows how many others. Don't fuck with me, said Haas. See you later, said Epifanio, and he held out his hand. Don't fuck with me, said Haas. You've got balls, said Epifanio from the door. For God's sake, man, for God's sake, quit fucking with me and leave me alone, said Haas.

●

From a friend on the El Adobe police force, Epifanio got Klaus Haas's police record. That's how he found out that Haas had never lived in Denver, but in Tampa, where he had been accused of attempted rape by a woman named Laurie Enciso. He was locked up for a month and then

Laurie Enciso dropped the charges and they let him go. He had also been charged with exhibitionism and indecency. When Epifanio asked what the hell the gringos meant by indecency he was told that it basically referred to groping, off-color verbal insinuations, and a third offense that was a combination of the first two. In Tampa, too, Haas had been fined several times for soliciting sex with prostitutes, nothing very serious. He was born in Bielefeld, in the former West Germany, in 1955, and he immigrated to the United States in 1980. In 1990 he decided to switch countries again, this time as an American citizen. Coming to live in Mexico, in northern Sonora, was evidently a fortunate choice, because he soon opened a second store in Santa Teresa, where his client portfolio continued to grow, and another in Tijuana, which seemed to be doing well. One night, accompanied by two Santa Teresa policemen and an inspector, Epifanio paid a visit to Haas's downtown store (the other store was in Colonia Centeno). The place was much bigger than he'd thought. Several rooms in the back were full of boxes of computer parts that Haas himself would later assemble. In one of the rooms there was a bed, a candlestick with a candle, and a big mirror next to the bed. The light didn't work, but the inspector who had come with Epifanio realized right away that the only reason it didn't work was because someone had unscrewed the bulb. There were two bathrooms. One was very neat, with soap, toilet paper, and a clean floor. Next to the toilet was a toilet brush that Haas required his employees—accustomed to just pulling the chain—to use. The other bathroom was so dirty that it might have been abandoned, even though the water was running and the toilet worked, but instead it seemed set there on purpose to illustrate an asymmetrical and incomprehensible phenomenon. Then came a long hallway that led to a door onto an alley. The alley was full of trash and cardboard boxes, but from the door you could see one of the busiest corners in the city, the center of Santa Teresa's nightlife. Then they went down to the basement.

•

Two days later, Epifanio, two inspectors, and three Santa Teresa policemen showed up at the store bearing warrants authorizing the arrest of Klaus Haas, forty-year-old American citizen, as a suspect in the rape, torture, and murder of Estrella Ruiz Sandoval, seventeen-year-old Mexican citizen, but when they got to the store, they were told by the employees that the boss hadn't come in that day, so the party split up, and while one inspector and two Santa Teresa cops drove to the other store, located in Colonia Centeno, Epifanio, one inspector, and the remaining cop left for the German-American's house in Colonia El Cerezal, where they scattered strategically, the Santa Teresa officer covering the back of the house while Epifanio and the inspector rang the doorbell. To their surprise, Haas himself came to the door, looking as if he was in the throes of a cold or the flu, or at least showing clear signs of having spent a bad night. The policemen declined his invitation to come in, and Haas was immediately informed that he was under arrest, then shown the arrest warrant and given a brief glance at the search warrants for his house and two stores. The cuffs went straight on after that, because the suspect was a big man and no one knew how he might react once he had gathered what was happening. Then they put him in the back of the patrol car and drove immediately to Precinct #1, leaving the Santa Teresa cop guarding the suspect's residence.

•

The interrogation of Klaus Haas lasted four days and was performed by Epifanio Galindo and Tony Pintado of the Santa Teresa police and Ernesto Ortiz Rebolledo, Ángel Fernández, and Carlos Marín of the judicial police. Present at the interrogation was Santa Teresa police chief Pedro Negrete, who brought as special guests two city judges and César Huerta Cerna, head of the Deputy Attorney General's Office of Sonora's Northern Zone. The suspect was seized by two attacks of uncontrollable rage, during which he had to be subdued by the officers interrogating him. After this, Haas acknowledged having had dealings with Estrella Ruiz Sandoval, who had visited him at his store on three occasions. Five Hermosillo officers from the Special Anti-Kidnapping Group of Sonora's Policía Judicial searched for incriminating evidence at Haas's house as well as at his two Santa Teresa stores, paying special attention to the basement of the downtown store, and found traces of blood on one of the blankets in the basement room and on the floor. Estrella Ruiz Sandoval's family members came in for DNA testing, but the blood samples were lost before they got to Hermosillo, from where they were supposed to be sent to a lab in San Diego. Asked about the blood, Haas said it was probably from one of the women with whom he'd had relations during her menstrual period. When Haas relayed this information, Inspector

Ortiz Rebolledo asked what kind of man he thought he was. An ordinary man, said Haas. An ordinary man doesn't fuck a woman when she's bleeding, said Ortiz Rebolledo. I do, was Haas's answer. Only swine behave like that, said the inspector. In Europe we're all swine, answered Haas. Then Inspector Ortiz Rebolledo got too agitated and was replaced in the interrogation room by Ángel Fernández and Santa Teresa police officer Epifanio Galindo. The crime scene technicians from the Anti-Kidnapping Group didn't find fingerprints in the basement room, but they did find several sharp instruments in Haas's garage, including a machete with a thirty-inch blade, old but in a perfect state of preservation, and two big hunting knives. These weapons were clean and not a single trace of blood or fabric could be found on them. During his interrogation, Klaus Haas had to be taken to the General Sepúlveda Hospital twice, first when his flu took a turn for the worse and he developed a high fever, and the second time so he could be treated for cuts and bruises to his eye and right eyebrow, incurred on the way from the interrogation room to his cell. On the third day of his stay, at the suggestion of the Santa Teresa police themselves, Haas agreed to call his consul in the city, Abraham Mitchell, whose whereabouts were revealed to be unknown. Another official, Kurt A. Banks, took the call, and the next day he came by the precinct, where he spoke for ten minutes to his fellow countryman, after which he left without filing a single complaint. Shortly afterward, Klaus Haas was put in a van and driven to the city jail.

•

While Haas was at the precinct, some cops came to look at him. Most stopped by the cells, but all Haas did there was sleep or pretend to sleep, his face covered with a blanket, and the only thing they could do was ogle his huge bony feet. Sometimes he deigned to talk to the officer who brought him his meals. They talked about food. The cop asked if he liked Mexican food and Haas said it wasn't bad and then he was silent. Epifanio Galindo brought Lalo Cura to see Haas during one of the interrogations. Lalo thought Haas seemed sharp. He didn't look sharp, but Lalo guessed he was by the way he answered the questions the inspectors asked him. And he seemed to have endless stores of energy, too, making the men who were shut in the soundproof room with him sweat and lose their patience as they swore friendship or understanding and told him to talk, unburden yourself, in Mexico there's no death penalty, get it off your chest, and then hit him and insulted him. But Haas was unwearying and he appeared to escape reality (or try to make the inspectors lose their grip on it) with unexpected remarks and incoherent questions. For half an hour Lalo Cura watched the interrogation, and he could have stayed two or three hours longer, but Epifanio told him to leave because the boss and some other important people were coming soon and they didn't want the questioning to turn into a spectacle.

•

At the Santa Teresa jail Haas was placed in a private cell until his fever went down. There were only four private cells. One of them was occupied by a *narco* accused of killing two American policemen, another by a mercantile lawyer accused of fraud, the third by the *narco's* two bodyguards, and the fourth by a rancher from El Alamillo who had strangled his wife and shot and killed his two children. To make room for Haas, they moved the *narco's* bodyguards to Cell Block Three, into a five-inmate cell. The private cells were furnished with only a bed, bolted to the floor, and when Haas was left in his new home he could tell by the smell that two people had been there, one who slept on the bed and another who slept on a pallet on the floor. The first night he spent in prison he had a hard time sleeping. He paced the cell and every once in a while he slapped himself on the arms. The rancher, who was a light sleeper, called out to him to stop making noise and go to sleep. Haas asked, in the darkness, who had spoken. The rancher didn't answer and for a minute Haas stood motionless, silent, waiting for someone to say something. When he realized no one was going to answer he kept circling the cell and slapping his arms, as if he were killing mosquitoes, until the rancher demanded again that he stop making noise. This time Haas didn't pause or ask who had spoken. Nights are made for sleeping, you gringo son of a bitch, he heard the rancher say. Then he heard him tossing and turning and he imagined the man covering his head with his pillow, which triggered an attack of hilarity. Don't cover your head, he said aloud and in a booming voice, you're still going to die. And who's going to kill me, you gringo son of a bitch? You? Not me, motherfucker, said Haas, a giant is coming and the giant is going to kill you. A giant? asked the rancher. You heard me right, motherfucker, said Haas. A giant. A big man, very big, and he's going to kill you and everybody else. You crazy-ass gringo son of a bitch, said the rancher. For a moment no one said anything and the rancher seemed to fall asleep again. A little while later, however, Haas called out to say he heard footsteps. The giant was coming. He was covered in blood from head to toe and he was coming now. The mercantile lawyer woke up and asked what they were talking about. His voice was soft, sharp, and frightened. Our friend here has lost his mind, said the rancher's voice.

•

When Epifanio came to visit Haas, one of the guards told him the gringo wouldn't let the other prisoners sleep in peace. He talked about a monster and was up all night. Epifanio wanted to know what kind of monster and the guard said a giant, a friend of Haas's, probably, who would come to rescue him and kill everyone who had done him wrong. Since he can't sleep he won't let anybody else sleep, the guard said, and he showed no respect for Mexicans either, he called them Indians or greasers. Epifanio wanted to know why greasers, and the guard, very serious, answered that, according to Haas, Mexicans didn't wash, didn't bathe. He added that, according to Haas, Mexicans had a gland that made them secrete a kind of oily sweat, more or less like blacks, who, according to Haas, exuded a particular and unmistakable smell. In fact, the only one who didn't bathe was Haas, since the prison officials preferred not to make him visit the showers until they received orders from the judge or the warden in person, who, it seemed, was handling the business with kid gloves. When Epifanio came face-to-face with Haas, Haas didn't recognize him. He had big circles under his eyes and he seemed much thinner than the first time Epifanio had seen him, but none of the injuries he'd suffered during the interrogation were visible. Epifanio offered him a cigarette, but Haas said he didn't smoke. Then Epifanio talked about the Hermosillo prison, which was new, with spacious cell blocks and huge yards with exercise equipment. If Haas pleaded guilty, he said, he would see to it that he be transferred to Hermosillo, where he would have a cell to himself, a much better one than this. Only then did Haas look him in the eye and say don't fuck with me. Epifanio realized that Haas had recognized him and he smiled. Haas didn't return the smile. The expression on his face, Epifanio thought, was strange, I don't know, scandalized somehow. Morally scandalized. He asked him about the monster, the giant, he asked whether the giant was Haas himself, and then Haas did laugh. Me? You have no clue, he spat. Go fuck your goddamn mother.

The inmates in the private cells could go out into the cell block yard or spend their days inside, venturing out only very early, from six-thirty to seven-thirty in the morning, when the yard was off-limits to the rest of the inmates, or then after nine at night, when in theory the night count had been taken and the prisoners had returned to their cells. The rancher who had killed his wife and children and the mercantile lawyer would go out alone at night, after dinner. They would stroll around the yard, talk business and politics, and then go back to their cells. The *narco* kept to the same schedule as the rest of the inmates and could spend hours leaning against a wall, smoking and gazing at the sky, as his bodyguards, never far away, traced an invisible boundary around their boss with their presence. Klaus Haas, when his fever subsided, decided to go out during "regular hours," as they were described to him by the guard. When the guard asked whether he wasn't afraid he would be killed in the yard, Haas made a scornful gesture and said something about the corpselike pallor of the rancher and lawyer, whose faces were never touched by the sunlight. The first time he went out into the yard, the *narco*, who until then had shown no interest in him, asked who he was. Haas gave his name and introduced himself as a computer expert. The *narco* looked him up and down and kept walking as if his curiosity had been instantly exhausted. Some prisoners, just a few, wore mended remnants of what had been the prison uniform, but most wore whatever they wanted. Some sold sodas that they kept in coolers, the box carried under one arm and later set on the ground next to the four-on-four soccer matches or basketball games. Others sold cigarettes and porn shots. The most discreet dealt drugs. The yard was V-shaped. Half was cement and the other half was dirt and it was flanked by two walls topped by watchtowers, with bored guards staring out smoking marijuana. At the narrow end of the V were the windows of some cells, with clothes strung on lines between the bars. Across the open end, there was a chain-link fence some thirty feet high, behind which ran a paved road leading to other prison buildings, and beyond that there was another fence, not as high but topped with a coil of razor wire, a fence that seemed to rise straight out of the desert. The first time he went out into the yard, Haas had the momentary sense that he was walking through a park in a foreign city where no one knew him. For an instant he felt free. But everybody knows everything here, he said to himself, and he waited patiently for the first inmate to approach him. Within an hour he was offered drugs and cigarettes, but all he bought was a soda. As he was drinking it, watching the basketball game, a few inmates came up to him and asked whether it was true he had killed all those women. Haas said no. Then the inmates asked about his job and whether selling computers was good money. Haas said it had its ups and downs. And that businessmen were always taking a gamble. So you're a businessman, said the prisoners. No, said Haas, I'm a computer expert who started his own business. He said it so seriously and with such conviction that some of the prisoners nodded. Then Haas wanted to know what they did outside, and most of them started to laugh. Hang out, was the only answer he understood. He laughed too and bought sodas for the five or six of them who were gathered around him.

·

The first time he went to the showers, an inmate they called El Anillo tried to rape him. He was a big man, but compared to Haas he was small, and by his expression it was clear he was doing this only because circumstances required him to play the role. If it had been up to him, his expression said, he would have jerked off peacefully in his cell. Haas stared him in the face and asked what kind of an adult would do such a thing. El Anillo didn't understand a word he said and laughed. He had a wide face and smooth skin and his laugh wasn't unpleasant. The prisoners around him laughed too. El Anillo's friend, a younger prisoner called El Guajolote, pulled a shiv out from under a towel and told Haas to shut his mouth and come with them to a corner. A corner? asked Haas. A motherfucking corner? Two of the friends Haas had made in the yard got behind El Guajolote and grabbed his arms. Haas's face was scandalized. El Anillo laughed again and said it was no big deal. In a corner is no big deal? shouted Haas. In a corner like dogs is no big deal? Another of Haas's friends stood in the doorway so no one could come in or out of the showers. Make him suck your dick, gringo, shouted one of the prisoners. Make the fucker give you a blow job, gringo. Now. Destroy him. The voices of the prisoners rose. Haas took the shiv away from El Guajolote and told El Anillo to get down on all fours. If you don't move, cocksucker, nothing will happen. If you move or you're scared, you'll end up with two holes to shit from. El Anillo took off his towel and got down on the floor on all fours. No, not there, said Haas, under the shower. El Anillo got up impassively and moved under the water. His hair, wavy and

484

combed backward, fell over his eyes. Discipline, motherfucker, all I ask for is a little discipline and respect, said Haas as he stepped into the line of stalls. Then he kneeled behind El Anillo, whispered to him to spread his legs, and pushed in the shiv slowly all the way to the handle. Some could see that every so often El Anillo choked back a little cry. Others could see the very dark drops of blood fall, drops that dissolved in the water in seconds.

•

Haas's friends were called El Tormenta, El Tequila, and El Tutanramón. El Tormenta was twenty-two and was serving time for having killed the bodyguard of a *narco* who wanted to take advantage of his sister. Twice in prison someone had tried to kill him. El Tequila was thirty and was infected with HIV, although not many knew it because he hadn't yet developed the disease. El Tutanramón was eighteen and his nickname came from a film. His real name was Ramón, but he had gone three times to see *The Revenge of the Mummy*, which was his favorite movie, and his friends had christened him Tutanramón, or maybe he'd given himself the name, as Haas believed. Haas kept them happy by buying them canned food and drugs. They ran errands for him or served as bodyguards. Sometimes Haas listened to them talk about the things that mattered to them, their business, their family life, what they most desired and feared, and he didn't understand a thing. They seemed like extraterrestrials. Other times it was Haas who talked and his three friends listened in affecting silence. Haas talked about self-control, hard work, self-help, every individual controls his own fate, a man could become Lee Iacocca if he put his mind to it. They had no idea who Lee Iacocca was. They imagined he was a Mafia boss. But they didn't ask any questions for fear Haas would lose his train of thought.

•

When Haas was moved to the cell block with the rest of the prisoners, the *narco* came over to say goodbye, a courtesy for which Haas thanked him, touched. If you have any problem, let me know, the *narco* said, but only if it's serious, don't bother me with little shit. I do my best not to get in the way, said Haas. I've noticed, said the *narco*. On her visit the next day, Haas's lawyer asked if he wanted to initiate proceedings to be returned to a private cell. Haas told her he was fine as he was, that before long he was going to have to leave the cell and the sooner he accepted the reality the better. What can I do for you? asked his lawyer. Bring me a cell phone, said Haas. It won't be easy to get them to let you keep a phone in prison, his lawyer said. Oh yes it will, said Haas. Bring me one.

•

A week later he asked his lawyer for another cell phone, and, shortly afterward, another. The first he sold to a man who was serving time for killing three people. He was an ordinary-looking guy, on the short side, who was regularly sent money from the outside, probably so he would keep his mouth shut. Haas told him that the best way to handle business was with a cell phone and the man paid three times what the phone had cost. The other he sold to a butcher who had killed one of his employees, a fifteen-year-old boy, with a cleaver. When the butcher was asked, half in jest, why he had killed the boy, he answered that the boy was a thief and had taken advantage of him. Then the inmates laughed and asked if it hadn't really been because the boy wouldn't let himself be fucked. Then the butcher hung his head and shook it several times, stubbornly, but not a word issued from his lips to deny the calumny. He wanted to keep running his two butcher shops from prison, because he thought his sister, who was in charge now, was stealing from him. Haas sold him the phone and showed him how to use the address book and send messages. He charged him five times the original price.

•

Haas shared his cell with five other inmates. Farfán was the boss. He was about forty and Haas had never seen an uglier man. His hair grew down to the middle of his forehead and he had the eyes of a bird of prey, set as if at random in the middle of a porcine face. He was potbellied and he smelled bad. He had a straggly mustache to which tiny bits of food often clung. On the rare occasions when he laughed he sounded like a donkey and only then did his face seem bearable. When Haas moved into the cell he thought it wouldn't be long before Farfán picked a fight with him, but not only did Farfán not pick a fight, he seemed lost in a kind of labyrinth where all the prisoners were insubstantial figures. He had friends on the cell block, other tough guys who liked to have him around to watch their backs, but the only company he sought was that of a prisoner as ugly as himself, a man named Gómez, skinny and clam-faced, with a birthmark the size of a fist on his left cheek and the glassy stare of someone permanently high. They would see each other in the yard and the cafeteria. In the yard they nodded to each other, and even if they joined larger groups, in the end they would split off and end up leaning against the wall in the sun or walking pensively from the basketball court to the fence. They didn't talk much, maybe because they had little to say to each other. Farfán was so poor when he got to prison that not even the public defender came to see him. Gómez, who was there for robbing trucks, did have a lawyer, and after he and Farfán met he got his lawyer to handle Farfán's paperwork. The first time they fucked was in one of the kitchen buildings. Actually, Farfán raped Gómez. He hit him, pushed him down on some sacks, and raped him twice. Gómez's rage was so great that he tried to kill Farfán. One afternoon he waited for him in the kitchen, where Farfán worked washing dishes and hauling sacks of beans, and tried to stab him with a shiv, but it wasn't hard for Farfán to wrestle him down. Farfán raped him again, and then, while he was still on top of Gómez, he said a situation like this had to be resolved somehow. To make amends, he let Gómez fuck him. What's more, he gave him back the shiv in token of his trust, and then he pulled down his pants and dropped onto the pallet. Lying there with his ass in the air, Farfán looked like a sow, but Gómez fucked him regardless and they resumed their friendship.

•

Since Farfán was the strongest, sometimes he forced the others to leave the cell. Soon afterward, Gómez would come by and the two of them would fuck and then, when they had finished, they would smoke and talk or lie in silence, Farfán on his cot and Gómez on another inmate's cot, staring at the ceiling or at the plumes of smoke that drifted out the open window. Sometimes it seemed to Farfán that the smoke assumed strange forms: snakes, arms, bent legs, belts cracking in the air, submarines from another dimension. He narrowed his eyes and said: that's cool shit, that's a fucking trip. Gómez, who was more pragmatic, asked what was a trip, what was he talking about, and Farfán couldn't explain. Then Gómez would get up and look all around, as if searching for his friend's ghosts, and finally he would say: you're seeing things.

•

Haas didn't understand how a cock could get hard when faced with an asshole like Farfán's or Gómez's. He could understand that a man might be turned on by an adolescent, a youth, he thought, but not that a man or a man's brain could signal for blood to fill the spongy tissue of the penis, difficult as that was, with the sole enticement of an asshole like Farfán's or Gómez's. Animals, he thought. Filthy beasts attracted by filth. In his dreams he saw himself walking the corridors of the prison, the different cell blocks, and he could see his eyes like a hawk's as he strode that labyrinth of snores and nightmares, aware of what was going on in each cell, until suddenly he could go no farther and he came to a stop at the edge of an abyss (since the prison of his dreams was like a castle built on the edge of a bottomless abyss). There, unable to retreat, he lifted his arms, as if beseeching the heavens (which were as dark as the abyss), and tried to say something to a legion of miniature Klaus Haases, speak to them, warn them, impart advice, but he realized, or for an instant he had the impression, that someone had sewn his lips shut. And yet he could feel something inside his mouth. Not his tongue, not his teeth. A piece of flesh that he tried not to swallow as with one hand he ripped out the threads. Blood ran down his chin. His gums were numb. When at last he could open his mouth he spat out the piece of flesh and then he got on his knees in the dark and searched for it. When he found it, after feeling it carefully, he realized it was a penis. Alarmed, he put his hand to his crotch, afraid his own penis would be gone, but it was there, so the penis in his hands was someone else's. Whose? he wondered as blood kept dripping from his lips. Then he felt very tired and curled up on the edge of the abyss and fell asleep. More dreams usually followed.

•

Raping women and then killing them seemed more *attractive* to him, more *sexy*, than plunging a cock into Farfán's oozing hole or Gómez's hole full of shit. If they keep fucking each other, I'm going to kill them, he thought sometimes. First I'll kill Farfán, then I'll kill Gómez, the three Ts will help me, they'll provide the weapon and the alibi, the logistics, then I'll throw the bodies into the abyss and that will be the last of them.

•

Fifteen days after his arrival at the Santa Teresa prison, Haas held what could be called his first press conference, attended by four reporters from Mexico City and almost all the print media of the state of Sonora. During the question-and-answer period Haas reaffirmed his innocence. He said that when he was interrogated he had been given "strange substances" to break his will. He didn't remember having signed anything, any self-incriminating statement, but he indicated that if he had it had been achieved after four days of physical, psychological, and "medical" torture. He warned the reporters that "things" were happening in Santa Teresa that would prove he wasn't the killer. Among the reporters who had come from Mexico City was Sergio González. His presence this time wasn't due, as it had been the first time, to a need for money and his eagerness to take on extra work. When he found out that Haas had been arrested, he talked to the editor of the crime page and asked him, as a special favor, to let him follow the case. The editor raised no objection and when he found out that Haas planned to speak to the press, he called Sergio at the arts page and told him he should go if he wanted. It's finished business, he said, I'm not sure I understand why you're interested. Sergio González didn't really understand either. Was it simply morbid fascination, or was it perhaps the certainty that in Mexico nothing was ever finished business? When the improvised press conference was over, Haas's lawyer shook each reporter's hand. When it was Sergio's turn he felt the lawyer slip him a piece of paper. He put his hand holding the paper in his pocket. Outside the prison, while he was waiting for a taxi, he examined it. The only thing on the paper was a phone number.

•

Haas's press conference was a minor scandal. Since when, it was asked in some circles, could an inmate call a meeting with the press and talk to reporters as if he were in the comfort of his own home and not the place the state and justice system had sent him to pay for a crime, or, as the legal documents reminded, to *serve a sentence*. It was said Haas had paid off the warden. It was said Haas was the heir, the sole heir, of a very wealthy European family. According to this dispatch, Haas was swimming in cash and had the whole Santa Teresa prison at his beck and call.

•

That night, after the press conference, Sergio González called the number the lawyer had given him. Haas answered. Sergio didn't know what to say. Hello? said Haas. You have a phone, said Sergio. Who is this? asked Haas. I'm one of the reporters you saw today. The one from Mexico City, said Haas. Yes, said Sergio. Who did you think would pick up? asked Haas. Your lawyer, admitted Sergio. Well, well, well, said Haas. For a moment both were silent. Do you want me to tell you something? said Haas. Here in prison, the first few days, I was afraid. I thought the other inmates, when they saw me, would come after me to avenge the death of all those girls. For me, being in prison was exactly like being dumped on a Saturday at noon in a neighborhood like Colonia Kino, San Damián, Colonia Las Flores. A lynching. Being torn to pieces. Do you understand? The mob spitting on me and kicking me and tearing me to pieces. With no time for explanations. But I soon realized that in prison no one would tear me to pieces. At least not for what I was accused of. What does this mean? I asked myself. That these shitheads are impervious to murder? No. Here, to a greater or lesser degree, everyone is sensitive to what happens outside, to the heartbeat of the city, you might say. What was it, then? I asked an inmate. I asked him what he thought about the dead women, the dead girls. He looked at me and said they were whores. So in other words, they deserved to die? I asked. No, said the inmate. They deserved to be fucked as many times as anyone wanted to fuck them, but they didn't deserve to die. Then I asked him if he thought I had killed them and the bastard said no, not you, gringo, as if I was a fucking gringo, which inside maybe I am, although I'm becoming less and less of one. What are you trying to say to me? asked Sergio González. That here in prison they know I'm innocent, said Haas. And how do they know it? asked Haas. That was a little harder for me to figure out. It's like a noise you hear in a dream. The dream, like everything dreamed in enclosed spaces, is contagious. Suddenly someone dreams it and after a while half the prisoners dream it. But the *noise* you hear isn't part of the dream, it's real. The noise belongs to a separate order of things. Do you understand? First someone and then everyone hears a noise in a dream, but the noise is from real life, not the dream. The noise is real. Do you understand? Is that clear to you, Señor Reporter? I think so, said Sergio González. I think I follow you. Do you, are you sure? asked Haas. You mean there's someone in the prison who knows for a fact that you couldn't have done the murders, said Sergio. That's it, said Haas. And do you know who the person is? I have some ideas, said Haas, but I need time, which in my case is paradoxical, don't you think? Why? asked Sergio. Because all I have here is plenty of time. But I need even more time, much more, said Haas. Then Sergio wanted to ask Haas about his confession, the trial date, his treatment by the police, but Haas said they would talk about that on another occasion.

•

That same night, Inspector José Márquez told Inspector Juan de Dios Martínez about a conversation he'd overheard without meaning to at one of the Santa Teresa police stations. Those present were Pedro Negrete, Inspector Ortiz Rebolledo, Inspector Ángel Fernández, and Negrete's watchdog, Epifanio Galindo, although as it happened Epifanio Galindo was the only one who never opened his mouth. The subject of the conversation was Klaus Haas's press conference. Ortiz Rebolledo believed it was the warden's fault. Haas must have given him money. Ángel Fernández agreed. Pedro Negrete said there was probably something more to it. An extra peso or two to tip the warden in the right direction. Then the name of Enrique Hernández came up. I think Enriquito Hernández twisted the warden's arm, said Negrete. Could be, said Ortiz Rebolledo. Son of a fucking bitch, said Ángel Fernández. And that was all. Then José Márquez came into the office, said hello, and was about to sit down, but Ortiz Rebolledo waved him away, making it clear he should leave, and when he went out Ortiz Rebolledo himself closed and locked the door so no one else would bother them.

•

Enrique Hernández was thirty-six. For a while he had worked for Pedro Rengifo and then for Estanislao Campuzano. He was born in Cananea, and when he had enough money he bought a ranch nearby, where he raised cattle, and a house, the best he could get, in the center of town, steps from the market square. All his right-hand men were from Cananea, too. He had a fleet of five trucks and three Suburbans, and it was believed he was in charge of transporting the drugs that came by sea to Sonora and were dropped at some point between Guaymas and Cabo Tepoca. His mission was to deliver the shipments safely to Santa Teresa, then another person took charge of transporting them to the United States. But one day Enriquito Hernández met up with a Salvadorean who was in the business and who, like him, wanted to go independent, and the Salvadorean put him in touch with a Colombian, and all of a sudden Estanislao Campuzano found he no longer had a transport manager in Mexico and Enriquito had become a competitor. Not that the volume of sales bore any comparison. For each kilo Enriquito moved, Campuzano moved twenty, but wrath doesn't recognize differences of magnitude, so Campuzano, patiently and without haste, waited for his time to come. Of course, it wasn't to his advantage to turn Enriquito in, for reasons to do with the trade. Instead, he wanted to put him out of circulation by legal means, then quietly take back the route himself. When the right moment came (a wrangle over a woman in which Enriquito went too far and ended up killing four people from the same family), Campuzano notified the Sonora attorney general's office and doled out money and clues, and Enriquito wound up in prison. For the first two weeks nothing happened, but during the third week four gunmen showed up at a warehouse outside of San Blas, in northern Sinaloa, and after killing the two watchmen they carted off a shipment of one hundred kilos of coke. The warehouse belonged to a peasant from Guaymas, in the south of Sonora, who had been dead for more than five years. Campuzano sent one of his trusted deputies to investigate the matter, a man by the name of Sergio Cansino (alias Sergio Carlos, alias Sergio Camargo, alias Sergio Carrizo), who, after asking at the gas station and around the warehouse, was able to learn only that during the robbery more than one person had seen a black Suburban in the area, like the ones Enriquito Hernández's men used. Then Sergio went around to the ranches in the area, on the off chance he might find the Suburban's owner. He got as far as El Fuerte, but no one there and none of the few ranchers he came across had the money to buy a Suburban. The fact wasn't reassuring, but that was all it was, thought Estanislao Campuzano, a fact to be considered in context. The Suburban might easily have belonged to an American tourist lost in the billowing dust or a *judicial* passing through, or a high official on vacation with his family. Soon afterward, as one of Estanislao Campuzano's trucks, loaded with twenty kilos of coke, was driving along the dirt road from La Discordia to the border town of El Sasabe, it was attacked and the driver and his companion were killed. They were unarmed, because they had planned to cross over into Arizona that evening and no one crosses the border armed when he's transporting drugs. You carry either arms or drugs, but not both at the same time. That was the last anyone heard of the men in the truck. Or the drugs. The truck turned up two months later in a scrapyard in Hermosillo. According to Sergio Cansino, the owner of the scrapyard had bought the truck, which was a wreck, from three junkies, petty criminals and police informers. He talked to one of them, called El Elvis. El Elvis told him that a player from Sinaloa had let him have the truck for four pesos. When Sergio asked how he knew the man was from Sinaloa, El Elvis said he could tell by the way he talked. When Sergio asked how he knew he was a player, El Elvis said it was his eyes, the way he looked at you, like a player, openhanded, not afraid of anybody. He was no weekend cowboy, he was the real thing, somebody who would just as soon shoot you in the guts as trade you his truck for a Marlboro or a toke of weed. He gave you the truck in exchange for a joint? Sergio asked, laughing. Half a stick, said El Elvis. This time Campuzano really was angry.

•

Why is Enriquito Hernández, in his own way, of course, protecting Haas? Inspector Juan de Dios Martínez asked himself. What does he get out of it? Who does he hurt by protecting Haas? And he asked himself, too: how long does he plan to protect him? A month, two months, as long as he thinks he needs to? And why rule out affection, friendship? Wasn't it possible that Enriquito had befriended Haas? Couldn't it be a decision based solely on friendship? But no, said Juan de Dios Martínez to himself, Enriquito Hernández didn't have friends.

•

In October 1995, no dead woman turned up in Santa Teresa or the surrounding area. Since the middle of September, the city had been able to breathe easy, as they say. In November, however, a girl subsequently identified as Adela García Estrada, fifteen, a worker at the EastWest maquiladora, was found in the El Ojito ravine. She had disappeared a week before. According to the medical examiner, the cause of death was a fracture of the hyoid bone. She was dressed in a gray rock band sweatshirt with a white bra underneath. And yet, her right breast had been severed and the nipple of her left breast bitten off. The case was handled by Inspector Lino Rivera and later by Inspector Ortiz Rebolledo and Inspector Carlos Marín.

•

On November 20, a week after the discovery of the body of Adela García Estrada, the body of an unidentified woman was found in a vacant lot in Colonia La Vistosa. The woman seemed to be about nineteen and the cause of death was various stab wounds to the chest, all or almost all potentially fatal, produced by a double-edged blade. The woman was wearing a pearl-gray vest and black pants. When her pants were removed in the forensic lab, it was discovered that underneath she had on another pair of pants, gray. Human behavior is a mystery, declared the medical examiner. The case was assigned to Inspector Juan de Dios Martínez. No one claimed the body.

•

Four days later, the mutilated corpse of Beatriz Concepción Roldán appeared by the side of the Santa Teresa–Cananea highway. The cause of death was a gash that sliced her open from navel to chest, presumably inflicted with a machete or big knife. Beatriz Concepción Roldán was twenty-two, five foot five, thin, and dark-skinned. She had long hair halfway down her back. She worked as a waitress in Madero-Norte and she lived with Evodio Cifuentes and his sister, Eliana Cifuentes, although no one had reported her disappearance. Various parts of the body showed evidence of bruising, but a single knife wound was the cause of death, by which the medical examiner concluded that the victim hadn't defended herself or was unconscious at the moment of the fatal attack. After her picture appeared in *La Voz de Sonora*, an anonymous call identified her as Beatriz Concepción Roldán, resident of Colonia Sur. Four days later, when the police paid a visit to the victim's residence, the property—four hundred square feet, two small bedrooms, a living room outfitted with vinyl-covered furniture—was completely abandoned. According to the neighbors, the man who called himself Evodio Cifuentes and his sister Eliana had been gone for six days. One of the neighbor women saw them leave, each dragging two suitcases. When the house was searched, few personal effects of the Cifuentes siblings were found. From the beginning the case was handled by Inspector Efraín Bustelo, who soon discovered that the Cifuentes siblings were hardly any more substantial than a pair of ghosts. There were no photographs of them. The descriptions he could come up with were vague, when not contradictory: Cifuentes was short and thin and his sister was nondescript looking. One neighbor thought he remembered that Evodio Cifuentes worked at the maquiladora File-Sis, but the plant had no payroll record of anyone by that name, now or in the last three months. When Efraín

Bustelo asked for the lists of workers going back six months, he was told that a filing error had regrettably caused them to be lost or mislaid. Before Efraín Bustelo could ask when they might locate the lists so he could take a look at them, a File-Sis executive handed him an envelope full of cash and Bustelo forgot the whole business. Even if the lists did exist, even if no one had burned them, he thought, he probably wouldn't find any trace of Evodio Cifuentes. An arrest warrant was issued for the two siblings that circled various police stations around the country like a mosquito around a campfire. The case remained unsolved.

•

In December, in a vacant lot in Colonia Morelos, up by Calle Colima and Calle Fuensanta, not far from the Morelos Preparatory School, the body of Michelle Requejo was found. The victim had disappeared a week before. The discovery was made by some children who often played baseball in the lot. Michelle Requejo lived in Colonia San Damián, in the south of the city, and worked for the maquiladora HorizonW&E. She was fourteen, a thin, friendly girl. She wasn't known to have a boyfriend. Her mother worked for the same company and in her free time she earned a few extra pesos as a fortune-teller and healer. Her clients were mostly the neighborhood women or a few of her coworkers with romantic troubles. Her father worked at the maquiladora Aguilar&Lennox. He put in double shifts most weeks. She had two sisters under ten who were in school and a sixteen-year-old brother who worked with her father at Aguilar&Lennox. Michelle Requejo had been stabbed several times in the arms and the chest. She was wearing a black blouse torn in a number of places, presumably by the same knife. Her pants were tight, of synthetic fabric, and were pulled down to her knees. She was wearing black Reebok tennis shoes. Her hands were tied behind her back and a little later someone noticed that the rope was knotted the same way as the rope that had bound Estrella Ruiz Sandoval, which made some policemen smile. The case was handled by José Márquez, who discussed some of its peculiarities with Juan de Dios Martínez. The latter pointed out that the knots weren't the only strange coincidence, and that in fact another crime had been committed in a field next to the Morelos Preparatory School. José Márquez didn't remember the case. The victim, said Juan de Dios Martínez, was a woman who was never identified. That night the two inspectors stopped by the vacant lot where Michelle Requejo's body had been found. For a while they watched the play of shadows in the lot. Then they got out of the car and walked through the brush, treading on plastic bags with soft things inside. They lit cigarettes. There was a smell of dead flesh. José Márquez said he was getting sick of this work, he talked about a job as a security chief in Monterrey, and he asked where the school was. Juan de Dios Martínez pointed to a spot in the dark. There, he said. They walked in that direction. They crossed several dirt roads and felt as if they were being watched. José Márquez put his hand on the holster of his gun and although he didn't draw it this calmed him. They got to the school fence, lit by a single lamp. That's where the dead woman was, said Juan de Dios Martínez, indicating a vague spot near the Nogales highway. The school janitor found the body. The killer or the killers must have come by car. They hauled the dead woman out of the trunk and left her in the vacant lot. It must have taken them at least five minutes. I calculate about ten, because the spot isn't near the highway. They were either on their way to Cananea or coming from Cananea. Based on where they left the body, I would say they were heading to Cananea. Why, *mano?* asked José Márquez. Because if you're coming from Cananea, there are lots of better places to dispose of a body before you get to Santa Teresa. Also, I think they took their time. According to what I was told, a stake had been driven partway through the body. Shit, said José Márquez. That's right, Pepito, and it isn't easy to stow a body like that, looking like that, all set to go, you might say, in the trunk of a car. Chances are they drove the stake into her by the school. Those people were animals, *mano*, said José Márquez. They dumped her on the ground and then they shoved a stake up her ass, what do you think of that? Brutal, *mano*, said José Márquez. But she was dead by then, wasn't she? That's right, she was already dead, said Juan de Dios Martínez.

•

The next two dead women were also found in December 1995. The first was Rosa López Larios, nineteen. Her body was discovered behind a Pemex tower where couples met at night to make love. At first they came in cars or vans, but then it became fashionable to arrive by motorcycle or bicycle, and it wasn't even unusual to spot young working couples on foot, since there was a bus stop nearby. There had been plans to put up another building behind the Pemex tower, but in the end the plans were scrapped, and now there was just an esplanade and beyond it some pre-fab barracks, now empty, which had housed company workers for a while. Each night, sometimes brazenly, with radios blasting, but most of the time quietly, cars lined up along the esplanade and the kids who had come by motorcycle or bike pushed open the falling-down doors of the barracks, where they turned on flashlights and lit candles and put on music and sometimes even made dinner. Behind the barracks, on a gentle slope, stood a grove of stunted pines that Pemex had planted when it built the tower. Some kids, seeking greater privacy, made their way into the grove, equipped with blankets. That was where Rosa López Larios's body was discovered. It was a seventeen-year-old couple who found it. The girl thought it was someone sleeping, but when they shone the flashlight on the body they realized she was dead. The girl screamed and went running, terrified. The boy had the fortitude, or was curious enough, to turn the body over and look at the dead woman's face. The girl's screams alerted the people on the esplanade. Some cars drove off immediately. In one of the cars was a city cop, and it was he who reported the discovery and tried, unsuccessfully, to prevent the general flight. When the police showed up, only a few frightened teenagers were still there and the city cop had them all at gunpoint. At three in the morning Inspector Ortiz Rebolledo and Officer Epifanio Galindo arrived on the scene. By then the other policemen had managed to get the city cop to put away his nonregulation Taurus Magnum and calm down. On the esplanade, leaning against a patrol car, Epifanio questioned the girl, while Ortiz Rebolledo went up to the grove to take a look at the body. Rosa López had died of multiple wounds inflicted with a sharp instrument that also ripped up her blouse and sweater. She had no identification on her, so at first she was classified as an anonymous victim. Two days later, however, after her picture was published in the three Santa Teresa newspapers, a woman who claimed to be her cousin identified her as Rosa López Larios and gave the police all the information she could, including the address of the deceased, on Calle San Mateo, in Colonia Las Flores. The Pemex tower was near the Cananea highway, which, while not close to Colonia Las Flores, wasn't terribly far either, which meant the victim might have made her way to the tower on foot or by bus, maybe to meet someone. Rosa López Larios lived with two friends, veterans like herself of several maquiladoras located in the General Sepúlveda industrial park. Her friends said Rosa had a boyfriend,

Ernesto Astudillo, from Oaxaca, who worked delivering soft drinks for Pepsi. At the Pepsi warehouse the police were told that, in fact, Astudillo had worked as a loader on a truck on the Colonia Las Flores–Colonia Kino route, but he hadn't shown up for work for four days, which meant, as far as the company was concerned, that he could consider himself fired. Once his place of residence was located, a raid was conducted, but the only person present was a friend of Astudillo's who shared the house, a shack barely two hundred feet square. The friend was questioned, and it turned out that Astudillo had a cousin or a friend, someone he loved like a brother, who worked as a *pollero*. This case is shot to hell, said Epifanio Galindo. Still, there was a search among the *polleros* for Astudillo's friend, but no one would talk and nothing was discovered. Ortiz Rebolledo dropped the case. Epifanio pursued other lines of investigation. He asked himself what it would mean if Astudillo were dead. If he had died, say, three days before his girlfriend's body was found. He asked himself what she had gone to look for, whom Rosa López Larios had gone to meet at the Pemex tower, the day or night she was killed. Sure enough, the case was shot to hell.

•

The second dead woman of December was Ema Contreras, and this time the killer was easy to find. Ema Contreras lived on Calle Pablo Cifuentes, in Colonia Álamos. One night the neighbors heard a man shouting. As they described it later, it was as if he was alone and had lost his mind. Around two in the morning the man stopped his ranting and was quiet. The house was plunged into silence. Around three in the morning two shots woke the neighbors. The lights were off in the house, but no one had the slightest doubt where the noise had come from. Then two more shots were fired and they heard someone shout. A few minutes later they saw a man come out, get in a car parked in front of the house, and disappear. One of the neighbors called the police. A patrol car showed up at about three-thirty in the morning. The door to the house was ajar and the police walked right in. In the biggest bedroom they found the body of Ema Contreras, her hands and feet bound. She had been shot four times, and two of the shots had destroyed her face. The case was handled by Inspector Juan de Dios Martínez, who, after reaching the scene of the crime at four in the morning and searching the house, quickly came to the conclusion that the killer was the victim's housemate (or paramour), Officer Jaime Sánchez, who, days before and equipped with a Brazilian Magnum Taurus, had tried to prevent the flight of couples from the Pemex tower. Juan de Dios Martínez radioed a search order. At six in the morning Jaime Sánchez was found at Serafino's. It was late enough that the place was closed, but a poker game was in progress inside. Near the table of players and spectators, a group of late-night drinkers, more than one policeman among them, were talking at the bar. Jaime Sánchez was in this group. When he got the tip, Juan de Dios Martínez gave orders that the bar be surrounded and Jaime Sánchez not be allowed to leave under any pretext, but also that no one should go in until he got there. Jaime Sánchez was talking about women when he saw the inspector come into the bar with two other officers. He kept talking. At the poker table, among the spectators, was Inspector Ortiz Rebolledo, who got up when he saw Juan de Dios and asked what brought him to Serafino's so early in the day. I've come to make an arrest, said Juan de Dios, and Ortiz Rebolledo stared at him, smiling broadly. You and these two? he asked. And then: don't be a dick, why don't you go suck cock somewhere else? Juan de Dios Martínez looked at him as if he didn't know him, shook him off, and went over to Jaime Sánchez. From there he could see that Ortiz Rebolledo had hold of the arm of one of the two policemen, who was talking his ear off. He must be telling him who I'm here to arrest, thought Juan de Dios. Jaime Sánchez gave himself up without a struggle. Juan de Dios felt under his jacket until he found the holster and the Magnum Taurus. Is this what you killed her with? he asked. I flipped out and lost control, said Sánchez. Don't make me look bad in front of my friends, he added. I don't give a flying fuck about your friends, said Juan de Dios as he handcuffed him. When they left the bar the poker match resumed as if nothing had happened.

•

In January 1996, Klaus Haas convened the press again. Not as many reporters came this time, but those who showed up at the prison were able to go about their business in the normal way, undisturbed. Haas asked the reporters how it could be that with the killer (him, in other words) behind bars, murders were still being committed. In particular, he talked about the identical knots in the ropes binding Michelle Requejo and Estrella Ruiz Sandoval, and pointed out that Estrella Ruiz Sandoval was the only one of the dead women who'd had direct contact with him, due, he specified, to her interest in computer science and computers. The newspaper *La Razón*, where Sergio González worked, sent a novice crime reporter, who read the case file on the plane to Hermosillo. In the file were Sergio González's stories. Sergio stayed behind in Mexico City writing a long article on new Mexican and Latin American fiction. Before the novice was assigned the story, the crime editor went up the five floors to the arts section, despite the fact that he almost never took the elevator, and asked Sergio if he wanted to go. Sergio looked at him without answering and finally shook his head. In January, too, the Santa Teresa branch of Women of Sonora for Democracy and Peace held a press conference, which was attended by just two reporters from Santa Teresa, at which they talked about the degrading and inconsiderate treatment suffered by the family members of the dead women and showed the letters they planned to send to the state governor, José Andrés Briceño, of the PAN, and to the attorney general of the republic. The letters were never answered. The Santa Teresa branch of the WSDP grew from three to twenty activists and supporters. And yet, January 1996 wasn't a bad month for the city police. Three men were shot to death in a bar near the old rail line, apparently in a settling of scores between *narcos*. The body of a Central American with his throat cut appeared on a route used by *polleros*. A fat, short little man wearing a strange tie printed with rainbows and naked women with the heads of animals shot himself in the roof of the mouth while playing Russian roulette in a night club in Madero-Norte. But no bodies of women were found in the city's vacant lots, or on its outskirts, or in the desert.

•

At the beginning of February, however, an anonymous call notified the police of a body abandoned inside an old railroad shed. The body, as the medical examiner established, was a woman of about thirty, although to look at her anyone might have said she was forty. She had been stabbed twice fatally, and her forearms were marked with deep cuts. According to the medical examiner, the weapon was probably a bowie knife like those seen in American films. Asked about this, the medical examiner explained that he meant Westerns, and the kind of knife used for bear hunting. In other words, a *very* big knife. On the third day of the investigation, the medical examiner supplied another important clue. The dead woman was an Indian. She might be a Yaqui, but he didn't think so, and she might be a Pima, but he didn't think that was it either. It was possible she was a Mayo, from the south of the state, but frankly he didn't think so. What kind of Indian was she, then? Well, she might be a Seri, but based on certain physical characteristics it was unlikely. She might also be a Pápago, which would be only natural, since the Pápagos were the Indians geographically closest to Santa Teresa, but he didn't think she was a Pápago either. On the fourth day, after much deliberation and measuring, the medical examiner, whose students had begun to call him the Dr. Mengele of Sonora, said the dead woman was definitely a Tarahumara. What was a Tarahumara doing in Santa Teresa? Probably working as a maid for some upper- or middle-class family. Or waiting her turn to cross over to the United States. The investigation centered on *pollero* informers and households whose maids had left their jobs unexpectedly. It was soon neglected and forgotten.

•

The next dead girl was found between the Casas Negras highway and the bottom of a valley without a name, full of brush and wildflowers. She was the first dead girl or woman found in March 1996, a terrible month in which five more bodies would be discovered. Among the six policemen who reported to the scene was Lalo Cura. The dead girl was ten years old, more or less. She was four foot three. She was wearing clear plastic sandals fastened with a metal buckle. She had brown hair, lighter where it fell over her forehead, as if it had been dyed. She'd been stabbed eight times, three times in the chest. One of the policemen started to cry when he saw her. The ambulance men climbed down into the valley and proceeded to tie her to the stretcher, because the climb up could be rough and if they tripped, her little body might tumble to the ground. No one came to claim the body. According to the official police statement, she hadn't lived in Santa Teresa. What was she doing there? How had she come there? That they didn't say. Her physical description was sent by fax to police stations around the country. The investigation was handled by Inspector Ángel Fernández and the case was soon closed.

•

A few days later, also down in the valley but on the other side of the Casas Negras highway, the body of another girl was found, this one approximately thirteen years old, strangled to death. Like the previous victim, she wasn't carrying anything that might have helped to identify her. She was dressed in white shorts and a gray sweatshirt with the logo of an American football team. According to the medical examiner, she had been dead for at least four days, which meant it was possible that both bodies had been dumped the same day. According to Juan de Dios Martínez, this was a rather odd idea, to put it mildly, because in order to leave the first body in the valley the killer would've had to park his vehicle not far from the Casas Negras highway, with the second body inside, running the risk not only that a patrol car would stop, but even that some unsuspecting persons might come by and steal it, and the same would be true if he had dumped the first body on the opposite side of the highway, in other words near the settlement of El Obelisco, which was neither a village nor exactly a suburb of Santa Teresa, but a way station for the poorest of the poor who came each day from the south, people who slept there at night and even died in hovels that they didn't think of as homes but as one more stop along the road to something different or at least a place where they would be fed. Instead of El Obelisco, some called it El Moridero. And in a way they were right, because there was no obelisk and people did die much faster there than in other places. But there had once been an obelisk, when the city limits were different, farther off, and Casas Negras was what might be called an independent town. A stone obelisk, or rather three stones, one set on top of the other, stones stacked in a haphazard column, though with imagination or a sense of humor the stack could be seen as a primitive obelisk or an obelisk drawn by a child learning to draw, a monstrous baby who lived outside of Santa Teresa and crawled through the desert eating scorpions and lizards and never sleeping. The most practical thing, thought Juan de Dios Martínez, would have been to dispose of the two bodies in the same place, first one and then the other. And not drag the first body down into the valley, which was too far from the highway, but dump it right by the road, a few yards from the pavement. And the same with the second body. Why walk to the edge of El Obelisco, with all the risks that entailed, when you could leave it anywhere else? Unless, he said to himself, there were three killers in the car, one to drive and the other two to dispose quickly of the dead girls, who hardly weighed anything, and who, if carried between two men, surely were each no heavier than a small suitcase. The choice of El Obelisco, then, appeared in a new light, acquired new dimensions. Did the killers want the police to turn their suspicions on the inhabitants of that sea of paper houses? But then why not dump both bodies in the same place? In the interests of *verisimilitude*? And why not suppose that both girls had lived in El Obelisco? Where else in Santa Teresa could there be ten-year-old girls no one claimed? So then the killers didn't have a car? They crossed the highway with the first girl to the valley near Casas Negras and left her there? And why, if they went to so much trouble, didn't they bury the body? Because the ground was hard in the valley and they didn't have tools? The case was handled by Inspector Ángel Fernández, who conducted a raid in El Obelisco and arrested twenty people. Four were convicted of theft and sent to prison. Another died in the cells of Precinct #2, of tuberculosis, according to the medical examiner. No one admitted to the murder of either of the two girls.

•

A week after the discovery of the corpse of the thirteen-year-old girl on the outskirts of El Obelisco, the body of a girl of about sixteen was found by the Cananea highway. The dead girl was a little under five foot four and slightly built, and she had long black hair. She had been stabbed only once, in the abdomen, a stab so deep that the blade had literally pierced her through. But her death, according to the medical examiner, was caused by strangulation and a fracture of the hyoid bone. From the place where the body was found there was a view of a succession of low hills and scattered white and yellow houses with low roofs, and a few industrial sheds where the maquiladoras stored their reserve parts, and paths off the highway that melted away like dreams, without rhyme or reason. The victim, according to the police, was probably a hitchhiker who had been raped on her way to Santa Teresa. All attempts to identify her were in vain and the case was closed.

•

Almost at the same time, the body of another girl, approximately sixteen years old, was found, stabbed and mauled (although the mauling might have been the work of the dogs in the area), on the slopes of Cerro Estrella, to the northeast of the city, many miles from where the first three victims of March had appeared. Slightly built and with long black hair, the dead girl, said some policemen, looked like the twin sister of the presumed hitchhiker found by the Cananea highway. Like the other girl, she wasn't carrying anything that might have helped to identify her. In the Santa Teresa press there was talk about the *cursed sisters*, and then, picking up on the police version, the *ill-fated twins*. The case was handled by Inspector Carlos Marín and was soon filed as unsolved.

•

As March came to an end, the last two victims were found on the same day. The first was Beverly Beltrán Hoyos. She was sixteen and she worked at a maquiladora in General Sepúlveda industrial park. She had disappeared three days before the discovery of the body. Her mother, Isabel Hoyos, had gone to a police station downtown and after she waited for five hours she was attended and her report was processed, signed, and passed on to the next stage, albeit grudgingly. Beverly, unlike the previous March victims, had brown hair. Otherwise, there were some similarities: slight build, five foot four, long hair. She was found by some children on a stretch of open ground to the west of General Sepúlveda industrial park, in a place that was hard to reach by car. The body exhibited multiple stab wounds to the chest and abdominal area. Beverly had been vaginally and anally raped and then dressed by her killers, since her clothes, the same ones she'd been wearing when she disappeared, were entirely free of rips or holes or bullet scorch marks. The case was handled by Inspector Lino Rivera, who initiated and exhausted his inquiries by questioning her coworkers and trying to find a nonexistent boyfriend. No one combed the crime scene, nor did anyone make casts of the numerous tracks around the site.

•

The second victim of the day, and the last of March, was found in a vacant lot west of Colonia Remedios Mayor and the illegal dump El Chile, and south of General Sepúlveda industrial park. According to Inspector José Márquez, who was assigned the case, she was very attractive. She was thin but not skinny, and she had long legs, full breasts, and hair past her shoulders. There was both vaginal and anal abrasion. After she was raped she had been stabbed to death. According to the medical examiner, she must have been between eighteen and twenty. She wasn't carrying identification and no one came forward to claim the body, so she was buried, after a reasonable waiting period, in the public grave.

On April 2, Florita Almada made an appearance on Reinaldo's show along with some activists from the WSDP. Florita said she was there only to introduce the other women, who had something important to say. Then the WSDP activists stepped up to talk about the climate of impunity in Santa Teresa, the laxity of the police, the corruption, and the number of dead women, which had been constantly on the rise since 1993. After that they gave their thanks to the kind audience and their friend Florita Almada and said their goodbyes, not without first calling upon the state governor, José Andrés Briceño, to find a solution to this unsustainable situation in a country that claimed to respect human rights and the law. The station head called Reinaldo and came close to suspending him. Reinaldo had a nervous fit and told him to go ahead and fire him if that was what he'd been ordered to do. The station head called him a faggot and an agitator. Reinaldo shut himself in his dressing room and spent a while on the phone with some people in L.A. who owned a radio station and wanted to hire him. The show's producer told the station head he'd better go easy on Reinaldo. The station head sent his secretary for Reinaldo. Reinaldo refused to go and stayed on the phone. The Chicano he was talking to told him the story of an L.A. serial killer, a man who killed only homosexuals. My God, said Reinaldo, we've got somebody here who only kills women. The L.A. killer liked to prowl gay bars. There are people like that everywhere, said Reinaldo, wolves who prey on the flock. The L.A. guy seduced homosexuals in gay bars or on the street where male prostitutes hung out and then took them somewhere and killed them. He was as bloodthirsty as Jack the Ripper. He literally chopped up his victims. Are they going to make a movie about him? asked Reinaldo. They already have, said the Chicano at the other end of the line. So in other words the police caught him? Of course, said the Chicano. What a relief! said Reinaldo. And who was in the movie? Keanu Reeves, said the Chicano. Keanu as the killer? No, as the policeman who catches him. So who played the killer? That blond guy, what's his name? said the Chicano, he has the same name as a character from a Salinger novel. *Ay*, there's an author I haven't read, said Reinaldo. You haven't read Salinger? asked the Chicano. That, my friend, is a giant gap in your education, said the Chicano. The thing is, lately I read only gay writers, said Reinaldo. And, if possible, gay writers with a literary background like mine. You'll have to explain that to me when you get to L.A., said the Chicano. When they hung up Reinaldo closed his eyes and imagined himself living in a neighborhood of big palm trees, with pretty little bungalows, and aspiring actors for neighbors, whom he would interview long before they became famous. Then he talked to the show's producer and the station head and both of them, standing in the doorway of his dressing room, asked him to forget what had happened and stay. Reinaldo said he would think about it, he had other offers. That night he threw a party at his apartment and near dawn some friends suggested they go to the beach to watch the sunrise. Reinaldo shut himself in his bedroom and called Florita Almada. On the third ring, the seer answered. Reinaldo asked if he'd woken her. Florita Almada said yes, but it didn't matter because she'd been dreaming about him. Reinaldo asked her to tell him the dream. Florita Almada talked about a meteor shower on a beach in Sonora and described a boy who looked like him. And that boy was watching the falling stars? asked Reinaldo. That's right, said Florita Almada, he was watching them fall as the waves lapped his shins. What a nice dream, said Reinaldo. I thought so too, said Florita Almada. Such a very nice dream, Florita, said Reinaldo. Yes, she said.

•

The show with Florita Almada and the women from the WSDP was seen by many people. Elvira Campos, the director of the Santa Teresa psychiatric hospital, saw it and mentioned it to Juan de Dios Martínez, who hadn't seen it. Don Pedro Rengifo, Lalo Cura's old boss, who almost never left his ranch outside of Santa Teresa, saw it too, but he didn't discuss it with anyone, even though his right-hand man, Pat O'Bannion, was sitting next to him. El Tequila, one of Klaus Haas's friends, saw it in the Santa Teresa penitentiary and mentioned it to Haas, but Haas shrugged it off. It doesn't matter what those old bitches say or think, he said. The killer keeps killing and I'm locked up. *That's* an incontrovertible fact. Someone should consider *that* and draw *conclusions*. That same night, in bed in his cell, Haas said: the killer is on the outside and I'm on the inside. But someone worse than me and worse than the killer is coming to this motherfucking city. Do you hear his footsteps getting closer? Do you hear them? Shut the fuck up, *güero*, said Farfán from his cot. Haas was quiet.

The first week of April the body of another dead woman was found on the open ground east of the old rail sheds. The dead woman had no identification on her except for a card without a photograph certifying her as a worker at the maquiladora Dutch&Rhodes, in the name of Sagrario Baeza López. She had been stabbed several times, and evidence of rape was present. She was approximately twenty years old. When the police visited the offices of Dutch&Rhodes, it turned out that Sagrario Baeza López was alive. Upon being questioned, she stated that she didn't know the dead woman, had never even seen her before. She'd lost her card at least six months ago. And, finally, she led an orderly life, devoted to her job and her family, with whom she lived in Colonia Carranza, and she'd never had trouble with the law, which was confirmed by some of her coworkers. And in fact, a record was found in the Dutch&Rhodes files of the exact date when Sagrario Baeza had been issued a new card, with the warning to be more careful and not lose it again. What was the dead woman doing with someone else's work ID? wondered Inspector Efraín Bustelo. For a few days the Dutch&Rhodes employees were questioned, in case the dead woman was another worker at the company, but the women who'd left didn't match the dead woman's physical description. Three workers, ranging in age from twenty-five to thirty, had chosen to cross over into the United States. Another one, a short, fat woman, had been fired for trying to start a union. The case was quietly closed.

•

The last week in April another dead woman was found. According to the medical examiner, before she died she had been beaten all over. The cause of death, however, was strangulation and a fracture of the hyoid bone. The body was found in the desert, some fifty yards from a secondary road that headed east, toward the mountains, in a place where it wasn't unusual to see small drug planes land. The case was handled by Ángel Fernández. The dead woman wasn't carrying identification and her disappearance hadn't been reported at any Santa Teresa police station. Her picture wasn't published in the papers, even though the police supplied photographs of her mutilated face to *El Heraldo del Norte*, *La Voz de Sonora*, and *La Tribuna de Santa Teresa*.

•

In May 1996, no more bodies of women were found. Lalo Cura took part in an auto theft investigation, which ended in five arrests. Epifanio Galindo went to visit Haas in prison. Their conversation was brief. The mayor of Santa Teresa announced to the press that the city could relax, the killer was behind bars and the subsequent killings of women were the work of common criminals. Juan de Dios Martínez took charge of a case of aggravated robbery. In two days he apprehended the guilty parties. In the Santa Teresa penitentiary a twenty-one-year-old prisoner held in preventive custody committed suicide. The American consul Conan Mitchell went hunting at a ranch owned by businessman Conrado Padilla in the foothills of the Sierra. Also present were his friends, university rector Pablo Negrete and banker Juan Salazar Crespo, and a third individual no one knew, a fat, short man with red hair, named René Alvarado, who didn't spend a single day hunting with them because he said guns made him nervous and what's more he had a heart condition. This René Alvarado was from Guadalajara and according to what he said he had interests in the stock market. In the morning, when they went out to hunt, Alvarado wrapped himself up in a blanket and sat on the terrace, facing the mountains, always with a book.

•

In June a dancer at the bar El Pelícano was killed. According to eyewitnesses, she was in the lounge, dancing half clothed, when her husband, Julián Centeno, came in, and without exchanging a word with the victim, fired four bullets into her. The dancer, known as Paula or Paulina, although at other bars in Santa Teresa she went by the name Norma, collapsed and never recovered consciousness, although two of the other dancers tried to revive her. By the time the ambulance appeared she was dead. The case was handled by Inspector Ortiz Rebolledo. Before dawn he was at Julián Centeno's residence, which was deserted and exhibited clear signs of a hasty flight. Julián Centeno was forty-eight, and the dancer, according to the girls she worked with, was no more than twenty-three. He was from Veracruz and she was from Mexico City and they had come to Sonora a few years ago. According to the dancer herself, they were legally married. At first, no one could say what Paula or Paulina's last name was. At her small, sparsely furnished apartment at

79 Calle Lorenzo Covarrubias in Colonia Madero-Norte, no documents were found that might clear up the identity of the victim. There was a chance Centeno had burned them, but Ortiz Rebolledo inclined toward the possibility that the woman called Paulina had lived the last few years without a single document testifying to her existence, which wasn't uncommon among showgirls and whores with no fixed address. But a fax from the Mexico City Police Identification Bureau informed them that Paulina's real name was Paula Sánchez Garcés. Her record showed that she had been arrested several times for prostitution, a line of work she seemed to have pursued from the age of fifteen. According to her friends at El Pelícano, the victim had recently fallen in love with a client, a man they knew only by his first name, and she was planning to leave Centeno to live with him. The search for Centeno was fruitless.

·

A few days after the murder of Paula Sánchez Garcés, the body of a girl of about seventeen, five foot seven, long hair, and slight build, appeared by the Casas Negras highway. She had been stabbed three times, and there were abrasions on her wrists and ankles and marks on her neck. The cause of death, according to the medical examiner, was one of the stab wounds. She was dressed in a red T-shirt, white bra, black panties, and red high heels. She wasn't wearing pants or a skirt. After vaginal and anal swabs were taken, it was concluded that the victim had been raped. Later, one of the medical examiner's assistants discovered that the shoes the victim was wearing were at least two sizes too big for her. No identification of any kind was found, and the case was closed.

·

At the end of June, the body of another woman, approximately twenty-one, was found on the way out of Colonia El Cerezal, near the Pueblo Azul highway. The body was literally riddled with knife wounds. Later the medical examiner would count twenty-seven, superficial and severe. The day after the discovery of the body, the parents of Ana Hernández Cecilio, seventeen, visited the police station and identified the dead woman as their daughter, who had disappeared a week before. Three days later, however, when the presumed Ana Hernández Cecilio had already been buried in the Santa Teresa cemetery, the real Ana Hernández Cecilio showed up at the police station, saying she had run away with her boyfriend. The two of them still lived in Santa Teresa, in Colonia San Bartolomé, and both worked at a maquiladora in Arsenio Farrell industrial park. Ana Hernández's parents corroborated their daughter's statement. Then an exhumation order was issued for the body found on the Pueblo Azul highway and the investigation continued, under the direction of Inspector Juan de Dios Martínez and Inspector Ángel Fernández and Epifanio Galindo of the Santa Teresa police. The latter occupied himself walking around Colonia Maytorena and Colonia Cerezal, accompanied by an old shopkeeper who had been a policeman. That was how he learned that a man named Arturo Olivárez had been abandoned by his wife. The strange thing was that the woman hadn't taken her children, a two-year-old boy and a girl just a few months old. While they were following other leads, Epifanio asked the ex-cop shopkeeper to keep him informed of Olivárez's movements. This led to the discovery that the suspect was occasionally visited by a man by the name of Segovia, who turned out to be a first cousin of Olivárez. Segovia lived in a neighborhood on the west side of Santa Teresa and had no known occupation. Until a month ago, he had hardly ever been seen in Colonia Maytorena. Segovia was put under surveillance and witnesses were found who said they had seen him come home with bloodstains on his shirt. The witnesses were Segovia's neighbors, and they weren't on the best of terms with him. Segovia made a living acting as a middleman for the dogfights held in a few yards in Colonia Aurora. Juan de Dios Martínez and Ángel Fernández stopped by Segovia's house when he wasn't there. They didn't find anything to implicate him directly in the killing of the woman discovered by the Pueblo Azul highway. They asked a cop who kept fighting dogs whether he knew Segovia. The cop said he did. They assigned him to watch Segovia. Two days later the cop told them that lately Segovia wasn't just organizing fights, he was betting, too. He's getting money from someone, said Ángel Fernández. They shadowed Segovia. At least once a week he went to see his cousin. Epifanio Galindo shadowed Olivárez. He discovered that he was selling off the house's furnishings. Olivárez plans to skip town, said Epifanio. On Sundays Olivárez played soccer with a neighborhood team. The soccer field was on a lot near the Pueblo Azul highway. When Olivárez saw the policemen approaching, two in plain clothes and three in uniform, he stopped playing and waited for them on the field, as if it were a mental space that would protect him from harm. Epifanio asked him his name and handcuffed him. Olivárez didn't put up a fight. The other players and some thirty spectators watching the match were paralyzed. The silence, Epifanio would tell Lalo Cura that night, was total. The policeman pointed to the desert that stretched off on the other side of the road and asked if he had killed her there or at home. It was there, said Olivárez. The children were with the wife of a friend of Olivárez's, who watched them on Sundays when he played soccer. Did you do it alone or did your cousin help? He helped, said Olivárez, but not much.

•

Every life, Epifanio said that night to Lalo Cura, no matter how happy it is, ends in pain and suffering. That depends, said Lalo Cura. Depends on what, champ? On lots of things, said Lalo Cura. Say you're shot in the back of the head, for example, and you don't hear the motherfucker come up behind you, then you're off to the next world, no pain, no suffering. Goddamn kid, said Epifanio. Have you ever been shot in the back of the head?

•

The dead woman's name was Erica Mendoza. She was the mother of two young children. She was twenty-one. Her husband, Arturo Olivárez, was a jealous man and often hit her. The night Olivárez decided to kill her he was drunk and his cousin was with him. They were watching a soccer game on TV and talking about sports and women. Erica Mendoza wasn't watching TV because she was cooking. The children were asleep. Suddenly Olivárez stood up, got a knife, and asked his cousin to come with him. The two of them led Erica to the other side of the Pueblo Azul highway. According to Olivárez, she didn't protest at first. Then they made their way into the desert and proceeded to rape her. First Olivárez raped her. Then he ordered his cousin to rape her too, which his cousin refused to do at first. Olivárez's manner, however, convinced him that opposition could be fatal. After the two of them had raped her, Olivárez attacked his wife with the knife, stabbing her over and over. Then, with their hands, they dug a hole, inadequate by any measure, and that was where they left the body. On the way back to the house, Segovia was afraid Olivárez would come after him or the children, but it was as if Olivárez had been freed of a weight and he seemed relaxed, or at least as relaxed as the circumstances permitted. They went back to watching TV and then they had dinner and three hours later Segovia left for home. Because it was so late, it was a long, slow trip. He walked for forty-five minutes to Colonia Madero, where he waited half an hour for the Avenida Madero–Avenida Carranza bus. He got off in Colonia Carranza and walked north, crossing Colonia Veracruz and Colonia Ciudad Nueva, until he came to Avenida Cementerio. From there it was a straight shot to where he lived in Colonia San Bartolomé. All in all, more than four hours. By the time he got home the sun had come up, although since it was Sunday there weren't many people on the streets. The happy ending of the Erica Mendoza case earned the Santa Teresa police a modicum of trust in the media.

·

In the Sonora media, that is, because in Mexico City a feminist group called Women in Action (WA) made a TV appearance denouncing the endless trickle of deaths in Santa Teresa and asking the government to send Mexico City investigators to Santa Teresa to resolve the situation, since by all accounts the problem was too much for the Sonora police, who were incapable of handling it, if not complicit. On the same show the question of the serial killer was addressed. Was there a serial killer behind the murders? Two serial killers? Three? The show's host mentioned Haas, who was in prison and whose trial date still hadn't been set. The Women in Action said Haas was probably a scapegoat and they challenged the show's host to come up with a single piece of evidence incriminating him. They also talked about the WSDP, the Sonora feminists, comrades whose fight for justice was being waged in the most adverse circumstances, and they cast aspersions on the seer who had appeared with the WSDP on a regional TV show, just some old woman who apparently wanted to exploit the crimes for her own benefit.

·

Sometimes Elvira Campos suspected that the whole of Mexico had gone crazy. When she saw the WA women, she recognized one of them as an old friend from college. She looked different, *much older*, she thought in astonishment, *more wrinkled, sunken cheeks*, but she was the same person. Dr. González León. Was she still practicing medicine? And why this scorn for the seer from Hermosillo? The director of the Santa Teresa psychiatric center would have liked to ask Juan de Dios Martínez more about the crimes, but she knew that doing so would only deepen the relationship, lead them, *together*, into a locked room to which she alone held the key. Sometimes Elvira Campos thought it would be best to leave Mexico. Or kill herself before she turned fifty-five. Maybe fifty-six?

•

In July, the body of a girl was found some five hundred yards from the pavement of the Cananea highway. The victim was naked, and, according to Juan de Dios Martínez, who oversaw the case until he was replaced by Inspector Lino Rivera, the murder took place right there, because clenched in the victim's hand was a kind of grass called *zacate*, the only thing that grew in the area. According to the medical examiner, the cause of death was craniocerebral trauma or one of three stab wounds to the chest, but he was unable to give a conclusive answer because the body's state of putrefaction made it impossible to say without conducting further pathological studies. Those studies were carried out by three students of forensic medicine at the University of Santa Teresa, and their conclusions were filed and then lost. The victim was between fifteen and sixteen years old. She was never identified.

•

Shortly afterward, near the border, in a spot similar to where Lucy Anne Sander was found, Inspector Francisco Álvarez and Inspector Juan Carlos Reyes, of the narcotics squad, came upon the body of a girl of approximately seventeen. Questioned by Inspector Ortiz Rebolledo, the agents claimed to have received a phone call from the American side, from some border patrol buddies who let them know there was something strange near the border. Álvarez and Reyes thought it might be a bag of cocaine, presumably lost by a group of illegals, and they headed for the spot indicated by the Americans. According to the forensic scientist, the victim's hyoid bone was fractured, which meant she had been strangled to death. Before that she had been subjected to sexual abuses that included anal and vaginal rape. The missing person reports were checked and the dead woman turned out to be Guadalupe Elena Blanco. She had arrived in Santa Teresa from Pachuca less than a week before, with her father, mother, and three younger siblings. The day of her disappearance she had a job interview at a maquiladora in the El Progreso industrial park and that was the last anyone saw of her. According to the maquiladora employees, she didn't show up for the interview. That same day her parents filed a missing person report. Guadalupe was thin, five foot four, with long black hair. The day of her interview at the maquiladora she was wearing jeans and a newly purchased dark green blouse.

•

A little later, in an alley behind a movie theater, the knifed body of Linda Vázquez, sixteen, was found. According to her parents, Linda had gone to the movies with a friend, María Clara Soto Wolf, seventeen, a classmate of the victim. Questioned at home by Inspector Juan de Dios Martínez and Inspector Efraín Bustelo, María Clara stated that she had gone to the theater with her friend to see a Tom Cruise movie. When the show was over, María Clara offered to drive Linda home, but Linda said she was meeting her boyfriend, so María Clara left and Linda stood waiting at the entrance to the theater, looking at the posters for coming attractions. When María Clara passed the theater again, now in her car, Linda was still there. It wasn't quite dark yet. There was no difficulty locating the boyfriend, sixteen-year-old Enrique Sarabia, who denied he had planned to meet Linda. Not only his parents, but also the maid and two of his friends, were able to testify that Enrique hadn't left the house, where he'd spent the day playing on the computer and then swimming in the pool. That night, two couples, friends of his father, had stopped by, and they could also confirm his alibi. Around the theater no one had seen or heard anything, although by Linda's wounds it was easy to deduce that she had put up a fight. Juan de Dios Martínez and Efraín Bustelo decided to give the ticket taker at the theater the third degree. She said she had seen a girl waiting at the entrance and a little while later the girl had been approached by a boy who didn't seem to be of the same social class. The ticket taker got the impression they were more than friends. That was all she could say, because when she wasn't selling tickets she sat reading in the booth. They had more luck at a photo shop. The owner was pulling down the shutters when he saw Linda and the boy. For some reason he thought they were planning to attack him and he hurried to lock up and leave. The description he provided of the boy was fairly complete: five foot eight, denim jacket with an insignia on the back, black jeans, and cowboy boots. The inspectors asked him about the insignia. The owner of the photo shop said he didn't remember it very well, but it looked to him like a skull. Juan de Dios Martínez brought him a book assembled by the youth gang task force (two policemen who for the moment had been transferred to the narcotics squad) and showed him more than twenty insignias. The man recognized the one on the boy's jacket with no hesitation. That same night the police staged an operation that rounded up two dozen members of the Los Caciques gang. Both the ticket taker and the shop owner were able to pick Jesús Chimal out of a lineup. Chimal was eighteen, worked off and on at a motorcycle repair shop in Colonia Rubén Darío, had a record of minor offenses. Chimal's interrogation was conducted by the police chief in person, along with Epifanio Galindo and Inspector Ortiz Rebolledo. Within an hour, Chimal confessed to having killed Linda Vázquez. As he told it, he had been dating the victim for three weeks, since they'd met at a rock concert outside of El Adobe. Chimal fell in love with her as he'd never fallen in love with anyone else before. They saw each other behind Linda's parents' backs. Twice Chimal had visited her house while her parents were away in California. According to Chimal, Linda's parents traveled to Disneyland at least once a year. There, in the empty house, they made love for the first time. The evening of the crime Chimal invited Linda to another concert, this one at El Arenas, a club where boxing matches were also held. Linda said she couldn't go. They walked for a while: they went around the block and then turned into the alley. Waiting there were Chimal's friends, four men and a woman, in a black Peregrino they had just stolen. Linda knew the woman and two of the men. They talked about the concert. They smoked pot. Linda smoked too. They talked about an abandoned house near a farming cooperative where no farmworkers lived anymore. One of the boys suggested they go there. Linda refused. Someone complained about something Linda had done. Someone accused her of something. Linda wanted to leave but Chimal wouldn't let her. He asked her to get in the car and make love. Linda didn't want to. Then Chimal and the others started to hit her. After that, so she wouldn't say anything to her parents, they knifed her. That same night, thanks to the information supplied by Chimal, the others were arrested, except for one who, according to his parents, had fled Santa Teresa a few hours after the crime. All of those arrested pleaded guilty.

•

At the end of July some children found the remains of Marisol Camarena, twenty-eight, owner of the nightclub Los Héroes del Norte. Her
body had been dropped into a fifty-gallon drum of corrosive acid. Only
her hands and feet were still whole. Identification was possible thanks to
her silicone implants. Two days before, she had been kidnapped by seventeen men from her apartment above the nightclub. Her maid, Carolina Arancibia, eighteen, managed to escape a presumably similar fate
by hiding in the attic with the daughter of the deceased, a tiny two-
month-old baby. From up above she heard the men talk, heard laughter,
shouts, curses, the sound of several cars starting. The case was handled
by Inspector Lino Rivera, who questioned a few regulars at the nightclub, but the seventeen kidnappers and killers were never found.

•

From the first to the fifteenth of August there was a heat wave, and two
more victims were found. The first was thirteen-year-old Marina Rebolledo. Her body was discovered behind Secondary School 30, in Colonia Félix Gómez, a few yards from the state judicial police building. She
was dark, long haired, slightly built, five foot two. She was wearing the
same clothes she'd had on at the moment of her disappearance: yellow
shorts, white blouse, white socks, and black shoes. The girl had left her
house, at 38 Calle Mistula, in Colonia Veracruz, at six in the morning to
walk her sister to work at a maquiladora in Arsenio Farrell industrial
park, and she never came back. That same day her family filed a missing
person report. Two of the girl's male friends, fifteen and sixteen years
old, were arrested, but after a week in jail they were both released. On
August 15, the body of Angélica Nevares, twenty-three, was found near
a sewage ditch west of General Sepúlveda industrial park. Angélica
Nevares, better known as Jessica, lived in Colonia Plata and was a
dancer at the nightclub Mi Casita. She had also worked as a dancer at
the nightclub Los Héroes del Norte, whose owner, Marisol Camarena,
had been found not long ago in a drum of acid. Angélica Nevares was
from Culiacán, in the state of Sinaloa, and she had been living in Santa
Teresa for five years. On August 16, the heat broke, and a slightly cooler
wind began to blow from the mountains.

•

On August 17, Perla Beatriz Ochoterena, a twenty-eight-year-old
teacher, was found hanged in her room. She was from the town of More-

los, near the Sonora-Chihuahua border. She taught classes at Secondary School 20 and was, according to her friends and acquaintances, a pleasant, easygoing person. She lived in an apartment on Calle Jaguar, two blocks from Avenida Carranza, shared with two other teachers. In her room were many books, especially poetry collections and essays, which she ordered COD from bookstores in Mexico City or Hermosillo. According to her roommates, she was a sensitive and intelligent woman, who had started from almost nothing (the town of Morelos, in Sonora, is pretty but tiny, with virtually nothing but scenic views) and who had gotten where she was by dint of hard work and stubbornness. They also said she liked to write and that an Hermosillo literary magazine had published some of her poems under a pseudonym. The case was handled by Juan de Dios Martínez, and from the beginning he had no doubt it was suicide. An unaddressed letter was found in her desk, in which she tried to explain that she couldn't stand what was happening in Santa Teresa anymore. In the letter it said: all those dead girls. It was a heartfelt letter, thought Juan de Dios, and also slightly sappy. In the letter it said: I can't take it anymore. It also said: I try to make a life for myself, like everyone, but how? The inspector searched through the teacher's papers for some of her poems but couldn't find any. He noted down several titles of books from her collection. He asked her roommates whether the teacher had a boyfriend. Her roommates said they had never seen her with a man. She led such a quiet life, it got on her friends' nerves. All she seemed to care about were her classes, her students, her books. She didn't have many clothes. She was neat and hardworking and she never complained about anything. Juan de Dios asked what they meant by that. Her roommates gave him an example: sometimes they would forget to do their share of the housework, like washing the dishes or sweeping, that kind of thing, and she would do it and not give them a hard time about it. In fact she never gave anyone a hard time about anything. Her life seemed devoid of scolding and blame.

·

On August 20 the body of a new victim was found in a field near the western cemetery. She was between sixteen and eighteen years old and wasn't carrying any kind of identification. Except for a white blouse, she was naked, wrapped in an old yellow blanket printed with black and red elephants. After the forensic examination, it was established that death had been caused by two stab wounds to the neck and another very

517

near the right auricle. In their first statement, the police said she hadn't been raped. Four days later, they issued a correction and said she had been raped. The medical examiner in charge of conducting the autopsy declared to the press that they, the team of police and university pathologists, had never had the slightest doubt she'd been raped, and they had made this clear in the first (and only) official report. The police spokesperson reported that the misunderstanding was due to a problem in the interpretation of said report. The case was handled by Inspector José Márquez and soon shelved. The victim was buried in the public grave in the second week of September.

·

Why did Perla Beatriz Ochoterena kill herself? According to Elvira Campos, she was probably depressed. Maybe she was heading toward a breakdown. She was clearly a lonely and hypersensitive woman. Juan de Dios Martínez read her some of the titles of the teacher's books that he'd jotted down at random. Have you read any of those? the director asked him. Juan de Dios admitted he hadn't. They're good books, said the director, and some of them are hard to find, at least here in Santa Teresa. She had them sent from the D.F., said Juan de Dios.

·

The next dead woman was Adela García Ceballos, twenty, a worker at the maquiladora Dun-Corp., stabbed to death in her parents' house. The killer was Rubén Bustos, twenty-five, with whom Adela had been living at 56 Calle Taxqueña in Colonia Mancera, and with whom she had a one-year-old son. For a week the couple had been fighting, and Adela had moved in with her parents. According to Bustos, she planned to leave him for another man. The capture of Bustos was relatively easy. He holed up in his house in Colonia Mancera, but he had only a knife to defend himself. Inspector Ortiz Rebolledo came in shooting and Bustos hid under his bed. The police surrounded the bed, with Bustos refusing to come out, and threatened to pump him full of lead. Lalo Cura was part of the group. Every so often Bustos's arm swept out from under the bed, the same knife in his hand with which he'd killed Adela, and tried to slash them in the ankles. The policemen laughed and jumped back. One of them stepped up on the bed and Bustos tried to stab the soles of his feet through the mattress. Another cop, a man by the name of

Cordero, famous at Precinct #3 for the size of his dick, began to urinate, aiming straight under the bed. Seeing the urine running along the floor toward him, Bustos started to sob. Finally Ortiz Rebolledo got tired of laughing and told him that if he didn't come out they would kill him right there. The policemen watched as he crawled out, a wreck, and they dragged him into the kitchen. There one of them filled a pot with water and dumped it over him. Ortiz Rebolledo grabbed Cordero by the neck and warned him that if the slightest trace of piss smell lingered in his car he would be sorry. Cordero, though he was near choking, laughed and promised it wouldn't happen. But what if he pisses, boss? he said. I can tell different kinds of piss, said Ortiz Rebolledo. This faggot's piss would smell like fear and yours stinks of tequila. When Cordero came into the kitchen, Bustos was crying. Between sobs he said something about his son. He talked about his parents, although it wasn't clear whether he meant his own parents or Adela's, who had witnessed the murder. Cordero filled the pot of water and slopped it over him, hard. Then he filled it again and doused him again. The pant legs of the two cops guarding Bustos were wet, and so were their black shoes.

●

What was it the teacher couldn't stand anymore? asked Elvira Campos. Life in Santa Teresa? The deaths in Santa Teresa? The underage girls who died without anyone doing anything to stop it? Would that be enough to drive a young woman to suicide? Would a college student have killed herself for that? Would a peasant girl who'd had to work hard to become a teacher have killed herself for that? One in a thousand? One in one hundred thousand? One in a million? One in one hundred million Mexicans?

●

In September there were almost no killings of women. There were fights. There were drug deals and arrests. There were parties and long hot nights. There were trucks loaded with cocaine crossing the desert. There were Cessna planes flying low over the desert like the spirits of Catholic Indians ready to slit everyone's throats. There were whispered conversations and laughter and *narcocorridos* as background music. On the last day of September, however, the bodies of two women were found near Pueblo Azul. The place they were discovered was a spot the motorcyclists of Santa Teresa used for races. The two women were dressed in house clothes, one even wearing slippers and a bathrobe. No identification was found on the bodies. The case was handled by Inspector José Márquez and Inspector Carlos Marín, who, based on the brands of the women's clothing, suspected they might be American. After the American police were informed, the dead women were revealed to be the Reynolds sisters, from Rillito, outside of Tucson, Lola and Janet Reynolds, thirty and forty-four respectively, both with drug-trafficking records. Márquez and Marín guessed the rest: the sisters owed money for some purchase, not a big one, because they never moved large quantities, and then they never paid up. Maybe they had liquidity problems, maybe they got cocky (according to the Tucson police, Lola was a woman to be reckoned with), maybe their suppliers came looking for them, showed up at night and found them on their way to bed, maybe they crossed the border with their victims and killed them when they got to Sonora, or maybe they killed them in Arizona, two shots each to the head, the women still half asleep, and then crossed the border and left them near Pueblo Azul.

•

In October the body of another woman was found in the desert, south of Santa Teresa, between two country roads. The body was in a state of decomposition and the forensic scientists said it would take days to determine the cause of death. The victim had red-painted nails, which led the first officers on the scene to think she was a whore. By the clothes— jeans and a low-cut blouse—they deduced she was young. Although plenty of sixty-year-olds dressed that way too. When the forensic report finally arrived (the cause of death probably some kind of stab wound), everyone had forgotten the case, even the media, and the body was tossed without further ado into the public grave.

•

In October, too, Jesús Chimal of Los Caciques, responsible for the death of Linda Vázquez, was admitted to the Santa Teresa prison. Although new people were brought in every day, the arrival of the young killer roused unusual interest among the inmate population, as if they were being visited by a famous singer or a banker's son, someone who would provide at least a weekend's worth of entertainment. Klaus Haas could feel the excitement in the cell blocks and he asked himself if it had been the same when he arrived. No, this time the expectation was different. There was something terrifying about it, and also stirring. The prisoners didn't discuss it directly, but somehow they alluded to it when they talked about soccer or baseball. About their families. About bars and whores who existed only in their imagination. Even the behavior of some of the most disruptive inmates improved. As if they wanted to be worthy. But worthy in whose eyes? Haas asked himself. They were *waiting* for Chimal. They knew he was on his way. They knew which cell he would be in and they knew he had killed the daughter of a man with money. According to El Tequila, the prisoners who were former Caciques were the only ones steering clear of all this drama. The day Chimal arrived they were also the only ones who came out to greet him. Chimal, for his part, didn't come alone. The other three who'd been arrested for the killing of Linda Vázquez were with him and they never left each other's side, even to go to the can. One of the Caciques who'd been inside for a year slipped Chimal a steel shiv. Another slipped him three amphetamine capsules under the table. The first two days Chimal acted like a madman. He kept turning around to see what was going on behind his back. He slept with the shiv in his hand. He carried the amphetamines everywhere, like a tiny talisman that would protect him from evil. His three companions were never far behind. When they walked in the yard, it was two by two. They moved like commandos lost on a toxic island on another planet. Sometimes Haas watched them from a distance and thought: poor boys, poor kids lost in a dream. On their eighth day in prison, the four were forced into the laundry room. Suddenly, the guards disappeared. Four inmates kept watch over the door. When Haas arrived they let him in as if he was one of them, one of the family, something for which Haas thanked them tacitly, although he never stopped despising them. Chimal and his three partners were pinned in the middle of the laundry room. Their mouths had been taped shut. Two of the Caciques were already naked. One of them was shaking. From the fifth row, leaning on a pillar, Haas watched Chimal's eyes. It seemed clear he wanted to say something. If they had taken off the tape, he thought, he might've harangued his very captors. From a window some guards were looking down on the events under way in the laundry room. The light coming from the window was yellow and dim compared to the light radiated by the laundry room's fluorescent tubes. The guards, noted Haas, had taken off their caps. One had a camera. An inmate by the name of Ayala went up to the naked Caciques and slit their scrotums. The prisoners who were holding the Caciques immobile grew tense. Electricity, thought Haas, pure life force. Ayala seemed to milk the two Caciques until their balls dropped, encased in fat, blood, and something crystalline he couldn't identify (and didn't want to identify). Who is that guy? asked Haas. It's Ayala, whispered El Tequila, the steel gut of the border. Steel gut? wondered Haas. Later El Tequila explained that among the many deaths Ayala could claim were those of eight immigrants he had ferried to Arizona in a pickup. After three days away, Ayala returned to Santa Teresa, but nothing was heard of the pickup and the immigrants until the gringos found the wreckage of the truck, with blood everywhere, as if Ayala, before he turned back, had sliced the bodies into bits. Something ugly happened here, said the border patrol, but since there were no bodies, the whole thing was easy to write off. What did Ayala do with the bodies? According to El Tequila, he ate them, that's how crazy and evil he was, although Haas doubted there was anyone capable of wolfing down eight illegal immigrants, no matter how demented or ravenous he might be. One of the castrated Caciques fainted. The other one had his eyes closed and the veins in his neck looked as if they were about to burst. Next to Ayala now was Farfán, and the two of them shared the role of master of ceremonies. Get rid of those, said Farfán. Gómez scooped the balls off the floor and remarked that they looked like turtle eggs. Nice and tender, he said. Some of the spectators murmured in agreement and no one laughed. Then Ayala and Farfán, each with a two-foot length of broomstick, headed for Chimal and the other Cacique.

•

At the beginning of November, María Sandra Rosales Zepeda, thirty-one, a prostitute who worked the sidewalk outside the Pancho Villa bar, was killed. María Sandra had been born in a town in the state of Nayarit and at eighteen she had come to Santa Teresa, where she worked at the HorizonW&E maquiladora and El Mueble Mexicano. At twenty-two she became a streetwalker. The night she was killed there were at least five other girls outside. According to the eyewitnesses, a black Suburban pulled up near the women. Inside there were at least three men. Music was blasting from the Suburban's speakers. The men called to one of the women and talked to her for a while. Then the woman moved away from the Suburban and the men called María Sandra. She leaned on the open window of the Suburban, as if ready to get into a long discussion about her rates. But the conversation lasted barely a minute. One of the men pulled out a gun and shot her from close range. María Sandra toppled backward, and for the first few seconds the whores waiting on the sidewalk didn't know what had happened. Then they saw an arm come out the window and fire again at María Sandra, who was sprawled on the ground. After that the Suburban started and disappeared in the direction of downtown. The case was handled by Inspector Ángel Fernández, later joined by Epifanio Galindo, who signed up on his own initiative. No one remembered the Suburban's license plate number. The whore who had talked to the strangers said they asked about María Sandra. They talked about her as if they knew her by reputation, as if someone had spoken highly of her. There were three of them and the three wanted to do some business with her. She didn't remember their faces well. They were Mexicans, they sounded like they were from Sonora, and they seemed loose, ready to party all night. According to one of Epifanio Galindo's informers, three men showed up at the bar Los Zancudos an hour after María Sandra's murder. They were in high spirits and they drank shots of mezcal the way other people eat peanuts. At a certain point one of them pulled a gun from his belt and aimed at the ceiling, as if to blow away a spider. No one said a thing and he put the gun away. According to the informer, it was an Austrian Glock with a fifteen-shot clip. Later they were joined by a fourth person, a tall, thin man in a white shirt, with whom they drank for a while, and then they left in a bright red Dodge. Epifanio asked his source whether they had come in a Suburban. The source said he didn't know, all he knew was that they had left in a bright red Dodge. The bullets that ended María Sandra's life were from a 7.65mm Browning. The Glock was a 9mm Parabellum. They probably killed the poor thing with a Skorpion submachine gun, Czech made, thought Epifanio, a weapon he didn't like, though some models had begun to be seen regularly in Santa Teresa, especially among the small groups involved in drug trafficking or among kidnappers out of Sinaloa.

•

The news barely filled an inside column in the Santa Teresa newspapers and few media outlets in the rest of the country picked it up. Prison scores settled, read the headline. Four members of the gang Los

Caciques, in custody while awaiting trial, were massacred by inmates at the Santa Teresa penitentiary. Their bodies were found piled in the laundry supply room. Later the bodies of two other former members of Los Caciques were found in the sanitary facilities. The police and members of the penal institution itself launched an investigation but were unable to uncover the motives or identity of those responsible.

·

When his lawyer came to see him at noon, Haas told her he had witnessed the killing of the Caciques. The whole cell block was there, said Haas. The guards watched from a kind of skylight on the floor above. They took pictures. No one did anything. The Caciques got reamed. Their assholes were shredded. Are those bad words? asked Haas. Chimal, the leader, was screaming for them to kill him. They splashed him with water five times to wake him up. The executioners stood aside so the guards could take good pictures. They stood aside and moved the spectators aside. I wasn't in the first row. I could see it all because I'm tall. Strange: it didn't turn my stomach. Strange, very strange: I watched all the way to the end. The executioner seemed happy. His name is Ayala. He was helped by another man, an ugly guy who's in my cell, named Farfán. Farfán's lover, Gómez, also took part. I don't know who killed the Caciques they found later in the bathroom, but the first four were killed by Ayala, Farfán, and Gómez, with the help of another six men who held them down. Maybe there were more. Scratch six, make it twelve. And all of us from the cell block who watched the action and didn't do anything. And you think, asked the lawyer, that they don't know all this on the outside? Oh, Klaus, you're so naïve. No, just stupid, said Haas. But if they know, why don't they say anything? Because people are discreet, Klaus, said the lawyer. The reporters too? asked Haas. They're the most discreet of all, said the lawyer. For them, discretion equals money. Discretion is money? asked Haas. Now you're getting it, said the lawyer. Do you know why they killed the Caciques? I don't know, said Haas, all I know is it wasn't a walk in the park. The lawyer laughed. For money, she said. Those animals killed the daughter of a man with money. Everything else is beside the point. Just babble, said the lawyer.

·

In the middle of November the body of another dead woman was discovered in the Podestá ravine. She had multiple fractures of the skull, with loss of brain matter. Some marks on the body indicated that she had put up a struggle. She was found with her pants down around her knees, by which it was assumed that she'd been raped, although after a vaginal swab was taken this hypothesis was discarded. Five days later the dead woman was identified. She was Luisa Cardona Pardo, thirty-four, from the state of Sinaloa, where she had worked as a prostitute from the age of seventeen. She had been living in Santa Teresa for four years and she was employed at the EMSA maquiladora. Previously she had worked as a waitress and kept a little flower stall in the center of the city. She lived with a friend in a modest house, though it had electricity and running water, in Colonia La Preciada. Her friend, who also worked at EMSA, told the police that at first Luisa had talked about immigrating to the United States and had even had dealings with a *pollero*, but in the end she decided to stay in the city. The police questioned some of the other workers at the maquiladora and then closed the case.

·

Three days after the discovery of Luisa Cardona's body, the body of another woman was found in the same Podestá ravine. The patrolmen Santiago Ordóñez and Olegario Cura found the body. What were Ordóñez and Cura doing there? Taking a look around, as Ordóñez admitted. Later he said they were there because Cura had insisted on going. The area they were assigned to that day stretched from Colonia El Cerezal to Colonia Las Cumbres, but Lalo Cura said he wanted to see the place where they'd found Luisa Cardona's body, and Ordóñez, who was driving, didn't object. They parked the patrol car at the top of the ravine and headed down a steep path. The Podestá ravine wasn't very big. The tape that had cordoned off the area for the crime scene investigators was still there, tangled in the brush and the yellow and gray stones. For a while, according to Ordóñez, Lalo Cura did strange things, like measuring the ground and the height of the walls, looking up toward the top of the ravine and calculating the arc that Laura Cardona's body must have traced as it fell. After a while, when Ordóñez was getting bored, Lalo Cura told him that the killer or killers had disposed of the body in that particular spot so it would be found as soon as possible. When Ordóñez objected that there weren't exactly many people around, Lalo Cura pointed to the edge of the ravine. Ordóñez looked up and saw three children, or maybe an adolescent and two children, all wearing shorts, who were watching them closely. Then Lalo Cura began to walk toward the south end of the ravine and Ordóñez sat on a rock, smoking and thinking that maybe he should have gone to work for the fire department instead. A little while later, with Lalo out of sight, he heard a whistle and headed after his partner. When he reached him he saw the woman's body lying at his feet. She was dressed in something that looked like a blouse, torn on one side, and she was naked from the waist down. According to Ordóñez, the expression on Lalo Cura's face was very odd, not a look of surprise but of happiness. What did he mean by happiness? Was he laughing? Smiling? they asked. He wasn't smiling, said Ordóñez, he looked serious, like he was concentrating, like he wasn't there, not right then, like he was in the Podestá ravine, but at a different time, when the bitch got it. When Ordóñez came up to him Lalo Cura told him not to move. He was holding a little notebook and he had taken out a pencil and was writing down everything he could see. She has a tattoo, he heard Lalo Cura say. A good tattoo. By her position I'd say her neck was broken. But first she was probably raped. Where is the tattoo? asked Ordóñez. On her left thigh, he heard his companion say. Then Lalo Cura got up and searched for the missing clothes. All he found were old newspapers, rusted cans, burst plastic bags. Her pants aren't here, he said. Then he told Ordóñez to go up to the car and call the police. The dead woman was five foot seven and she had long black hair. She didn't have any kind of identification on her. No one claimed the body. The case was soon shelved.

•

When Epifanio asked why he'd gone to the Podestá ravine, Lalo Cura answered that it was because he was a cop. You little shit, Epifanio said, don't go where you're not called, do you hear me? Then Epifanio took him by the arm and looked him in the face and said he wanted to know the truth. I thought it was strange, said Lalo Cura, that in all this time a dead woman had never turned up in the Podestá ravine. And how did you know that, ass wipe? asked Epifanio. Because I read the papers, said Lalo Cura. Do you really, you little cocksucking son of a bitch? Yes, said Lalo Cura. And you read books, too, I suppose. That's right, said Lalo Cura. The faggot books for faggots that I gave you? *Modern Criminal Investigation* by the late chief director of Sweden's National Institute of Technical Police, Mr. Harry Söderman, and the former president of the International Association of Chiefs of Police, ex-Inspector John J.

O'Connell, said Lalo Cura. And if those supercops were so fucking great how come they're ex-fuckers now? asked Epifanio. Answer me that, you little punk. Don't you know, you snot-nose bastard, that there is no such thing as modern criminal investigation? You're not even twenty years old yet, are you? Or am I wrong? You aren't wrong, Epifanio, said Lalo Cura. Well, be careful, champ, that's the first and only rule, said Epifanio, letting go of his arm and smiling and giving him a hug and taking him out to eat at the only place that served posole in the center of Santa Teresa at that murky time of night.

•

In December—and these were the last victims of 1996—the bodies of Estefanía Rivas, fifteen, and Herminia Noriega, thirteen, were found in an empty house on Calle García Herrero, in Colonia El Cerezal. They were half sisters. Estefanía's father had disappeared soon after she was born. Herminia's father lived with his wife and daughters and worked as a night watchman at the MachenCorp. maquiladora, where the girls' mother was also on the payroll, as a machine operator. The girls themselves were still in school and helped with the housework, although Estefanía planned to quit the following year and go to work. The morning they were kidnapped they were both on their way to school, along with two younger sisters, one eleven and the other eight. The two little girls and Herminia went to José Vasconcelos Primary School. Every day, after Estefania left them, she walked the same fifteen blocks to her own school. The day of the kidnapping, however, a car stopped next to the four sisters, and a man got out and pushed Estefanía into the car and then got out again and thrust Herminia in and then the car disappeared. The two little girls stood frozen on the sidewalk and then they walked home, but no one was there, so they knocked at the house next door, where they told their story and finally burst into tears. The woman who took them in, a worker at the HorizonW&E maquiladora, went to get another neighbor and then she called the MachenCorp. maquiladora trying to find the girls' parents. At MachenCorp. she was told that personal calls were forbidden and the operator hung up on her. The woman called again and gave the name and job title of the girls' father, since it occurred to her that their mother, being an ordinary worker like herself, must be considered of lower rank, meaning disposable at any moment or for any reason or hint of a reason, and this time the operator kept her waiting for so long that she ran out of coins and the call was cut off. That was all the money she had. Despondent, she went back to her house, to the other neighbor woman and the girls, and for a while the four of them experienced what it was like to be in purgatory, a long, helpless wait, a wait that begins and ends in neglect, a very Latin American experience, as it happened, and all too familiar, something that once you thought about it you realized you experienced daily, minus the despair, minus the shadow of death sweeping over the neighborhood like a flock of vultures and casting its pall, upsetting all routines, leaving everything overturned. So, as they waited for the girls' father to get home, the neighbor woman (to kill time and master her fear) thought how she would like to have a gun and go out in the street. And then what? Well, then she would fire a few shots in the air to express her anger and shout *viva Mexico* to pluck up her courage or feel a last surge of warmth and then dig a hole with her hands, with mindless speed, a hole in the packed-dirt street, and bury herself in it, soaked to the bone, for ever and ever. When the girls' father finally arrived they all went together to the nearest police station. There, after giving a brief (or scattered) explanation of the problem, they were made to wait for more than an hour until two inspectors arrived. The inspectors asked them the same questions all over again and some new ones, all about the car that picked up Estefanía and Herminia. After a while, there were four inspectors in the office where the girls were being questioned. One of them, who seemed nice, asked the neighbor woman to come along and took the girls to the police station garage, where they were asked which car, of the ones parked there, looked most like the car that had taken away their sisters. With the information they got from the girls, the inspector said the car to look for was a black Peregrino or Arquero. At five the girls' mother arrived at the station. One of the neighbors had left by then and the other couldn't stop crying and hugging the littlest girl. At eight that night Ortiz Rebolledo arrived and organized two search teams, one to question the friends and family of the girls, headed by Inspector Juan de Dios Martínez and Lino Rivera, and the other to locate, with the assistance of the city police, the Peregrino or Arquero or Lincoln in which it seemed the girls had been kidnapped, this team coordinated by Inspector Ángel Fernández and Inspector Efraín Bustelo. Juan de Dios Martínez took a public stand against this approach, since in his opinion the two teams should unite their efforts to find the car. His chief argument was that few if any of the circle of friends, acquaintances, and coworkers of the Noriega family owned a car at all, let alone a black Peregrino or a black Chevy Astra, since virtually all of them could be classed as pedestrians, some so poor they didn't even take the bus to work, preferring to walk and save a few pennies. Ortiz Rebolledo's answer was unequivocal: anyone could steal a Peregrino, anyone could steal an Arquero or a Bocho or a Jetta, you didn't need money or a driver's license, all you needed to know was how to break into a car and start it. So the teams remained divided as Ortiz Rebolledo had ordered, and the policemen, moving wearily, like soldiers trapped in a time warp who march over and over again to the same defeat, got to work. That same night, after making some inquiries, Juan de Dios Martínez learned that Estefanía had a boyfriend or a suitor, a kid with a wild streak, nineteen years old, called Ronald Luis Luque, aka Lucky Strike, aka Ronnie, aka Ronnie el Mágico, who had been arrested twice for car theft. When he got out of prison, Ronald Luis had shared a house with a man by the name of Felipe Escalante, someone he'd met in prison. Escalante was a professional car thief and he had also been under investigation, though never charged, for rape of a minor. For five months Ronald Luis lived with Escalante and then he moved out. Juan de Dios Martínez went to see Escalante that same night. According to Escalante, his former cell mate hadn't left of his own accord but had been kicked out because he didn't pay his share of anything. Escalante was currently stocking shelves at a supermarket and no longer led a life of crime. It's been years since I stole a car, boss, I swear, he said, kissing his fingers held up in the sign of the cross. In fact, he didn't even have wheels, anyplace he went he took the bus, what choice did he have, or hoofed it, which was cheaper and anyway made him feel like a free man. Asked whether Lucky Strike, as he was called, ever stole even the occasional car, Escalante said he didn't think so, although honest to God he couldn't say for sure, because the fucker wasn't exactly predictable in these matters. Others who were questioned seemed to confirm what Escalante had said: El Mágico was a freeloader and a lazy bastard, but not a thief or a thug, or at least not into violence for the sake of violence, and most of them thought he would piss himself if he went so far as to kidnap his girlfriend and his girlfriend's sister. Now Ronald Luis lived with his parents and still couldn't find a job. It was to his parents' house that Juan de Dios Martínez headed, where he talked to Ronnie's father, who resignedly let him in and said that his son had left shortly after the kidnapping of Estefanía and Herminia. The inspector asked if he could take a look around the place. Make yourself at home, said Ronnie's father. For a while Juan de Dios Martínez poked around the room that Ronnie shared with three younger siblings, although from the start he could see he wouldn't find anything there. Then he went out into the yard and lit a cigarette as he watched the orange and violet sunset over the ghost city. Did he say where he was going? he asked. Yuma, answered his father. And have you ever been to Yuma? Many times, as a young man: I crossed over, found work, got caught by the border cops, was sent back to Mexico, and then I crossed over again, many times, said Ronnie's father. Until I got tired of it and settled down to work here and take care of my old lady and the kids. And do you think the same thing will happen to Ronald Luis? I pray to God it won't, said Ronnie's father. Three days had gone by when Juan de Dios Martínez learned that the team assigned to find the black car used in the kidnapping had been disbanded. When he went to demand an explanation from Ortiz Rebolledo he was told that the order came from above. It seemed the police had fallen afoul of some big fish whose sons, the Jrs. of Santa Teresa, owned almost the entire fleet of the city's Peregrinos (it was a car of choice for rich kids, like the Arcángel or Desertwind convertible), and they pulled strings to get the cops to stop fucking with them. Four days later an anonymous call alerted the police to some shots fired inside a house on Calle García Herrero. A patrol car showed up half an hour later. The officers rang the bell several times and no one answered. When the neighbors were questioned, they said they hadn't heard anything, although their sudden deafness might have had something to do with the volume of their TV sets, turned up so loud they could be heard from the street. But a boy said that while he was riding by on his bicycle he had heard shots. When the neighbors were asked who lived in the house, their answers were contradictory, which made the patrolmen think it could be *narcos* and they'd better leave and not make trouble. One of the neighbors, however, said he'd seen a black Peregrino parked outside the house. Then the police drew their guns and knocked again at 677 Calle García Herrero, with the same results. Next they radioed the station and waited. Half an hour later another pair of cops appeared, to act as backup, they said, and shortly afterward Juan de Dios Martínez and Lino Rivera arrived. According to the latter, orders were to wait for the rest of the inspectors. But Juan de Dios Martínez said there wasn't time and the patrolmen, on his express instructions, broke down the door. Juan de Dios Martínez was the first to go in. The house smelled of semen and alcohol, he said. What do semen and alcohol smell like? Bad, said Juan de Dios Martínez, just plain bad. But then you get used to it. It isn't like the smell of decomposing flesh, which you never get used to and which worms its way into your head, even into your thoughts, and no matter whether you shower and change your clothes three times a day you keep smelling it for days, sometimes weeks, sometimes whole months. Behind him came Lino Rivera and nobody else. Don't touch anything, Lino remembers Juan de Dios said. First they scanned the living room. Normal. Cheap but decent furniture, a table with newspapers on it, don't touch them, said Juan de Dios, two empty bottles of Sauza tequila and an empty bottle of Absolut vodka in the dining room. Clean kitchen. Normal. Food wrappers from McDonald's in the garbage can. Clean floor. Through the kitchen window a small yard, half paved, the other half dried up, with a few shrubs clinging to the wall that separated the yard from another yard. Normal. Then they went back the other way. First Juan de Dios and behind him Lino Rivera. The hallway. The bedrooms. Two bedrooms. In one of them, lying facedown on the bed, Herminia's naked body. Oh, shit, Juan de Dios heard Lino Rivera murmur. In the bathroom, curled up in the shower, her hands tied behind her back, Estefanía's body. Stay in the hallway, don't come in, said Juan de Dios. He himself did go into the bathroom. He went in and kneeled down next to Estefanía's body and examined it carefully, until he lost all sense of time. Behind his back he heard Lino talking on the radio. Get the medical examiner here, said Juan de Dios. According to the medical examiner, Estefanía had been shot twice in the back of the head. Before that she had been beaten and it looked as if she'd been strangled. But she wasn't strangled to death, said the medical examiner. They played at strangling her. Abrasion marks were visible on her ankles. I'd say she was hung by her feet, said the medical examiner. Juan de Dios looked for a beam or a hook in the ceiling. The house was full of cops. Someone had covered Herminia with a sheet. In the other bedroom he found an iron hook bolted to the ceiling between the two beds. He closed his eyes and imagined Estefanía hanging upside down. He called two cops and ordered them to find the rope. The medical examiner was in Herminia's room. She was shot in the back of the head, too, he said when Juan de

Dios came up next to him, but I don't think that was the cause of death. So why did they shoot her then? asked Juan de Dios. To make sure she was dead. I want everybody out of the house who isn't a tech, shouted Juan de Dios. The cops filed out slowly. In the living room two hunched men, looking exhausted, searched for fingerprints. Everybody out! shouted Juan de Dios. Lino Rivera was sitting on the sofa reading a boxing magazine. Here are the ropes, boss, said one of the cops. Thanks, said Juan de Dios, and now get out, man, I only want the techs here. The photographer lowered his camera and winked at him. There's no end to it, is there, Juan de Dios? No end, no end, answered Juan de Dios as he dropped onto the sofa where Lino Rivera was sitting and lit a cigarette. Take it easy, the inspector said. Before he was done smoking his cigarette, the medical examiner called him into the bedroom. Each girl was raped several times, I'd say, with penetration of both orifices, although there might have been penetration of three orifices in the case of the girl in the bathroom. Both of them were tortured. In one instance, the cause of death is clear. Less so in the other. Tomorrow I'll give you an official report. Now clear the street for me because I'm taking them to the morgue, said the medical examiner. Juan de Dios went out into the yard and told a policeman that the bodies were going to be moved. The sidewalk was full of gawkers. It's strange, thought Juan de Dios as the ambulance disappeared in the direction of the Institute of Forensic Anatomy, suddenly, in a few seconds, everything has changed. An hour later, when Ortiz Rebolledo and Ángel Fernández showed up, Juan de Dios was questioning the neighbors. Some said it was a couple who lived at 677, others said it was three boys, or rather a man and two boys, who came there only to sleep, and others said it was a strange man who didn't speak to anyone in the neighborhood and sometimes didn't appear for days, as if he worked outside of Santa Teresa, and other times spent days without leaving the house, watching TV until very late or listening to *corridos* and *danzones* and then sleeping past noon. Those who claimed it was a couple living at 677 said they owned a Combi or some other kind of van and they drove back and forth together from work. What kind of work? They didn't know, although one of them said they were probably waiters. Those who believed it was a man with two boys living in the house thought that the man drove a van, which might, in fact, be a Combi. Those who said it was a single man living there were unable to remember whether he had a car or not, although they said he was often visited by friends who did. So in the end, who the fuck lives here? asked Ortiz Rebolledo. We'll have to investigate, answered Juan de Dios before he left the house. The next day, once the autopsies were completed, the medical examiner confirmed his initial assessments and added that what had killed Herminia wasn't the bullet lodged in the back of her head but a heart attack. The poor little thing, the medical examiner said to a group of inspectors, the torture and abuse were more than she could stand. She didn't have a chance. The gun used was probably a Smith & Wesson 9mm pistol. The house where the bodies were found belonged to an old woman who had no clue about anything, a Santa Teresa society lady who lived off the rents of her properties, including most of the neighboring houses. The properties were managed by a real estate company that belonged to one of the old lady's grandsons. According to papers held by the agent, all of them in order, incidentally, the tenant at 677 was a man named Javier Ramos and he paid his monthly bills through the bank. Inquiries at the bank revealed that Javier Ramos had made a couple of big deposits, enough to cover six months of rent as well as the electricity and hot water bills, and no one had seen him since. A curious bit of information, worth filing away for future reference, was turned up at the Property Registration Office by Juan de Dios Martínez, namely that the houses on the next block of Calle García Herrero belonged, in their entirety, to Pedro Rengifo, and the houses on Calle Tablada, which ran parallel to García Herrero, were the property of someone called Lorenzo Juan Hinojosa, who was a straw man for the *narco* Estanislao Campuzano. In addition, all the buildings on Calle Hortensia and Calle Licenciado Cabezas, parallel to Tablada, were registered in the name of the mayor of Santa Teresa or one or another of his children. Also: two blocks to the north, the houses and buildings on Calle Ingeniero Guillermo Ortiz were the property of Pablo Negrete, brother of Pedro Negrete and distinguished rector of the University of Santa Teresa. It's an odd thing, Juan de Dios said to himself. The bodies are there and you shake. Then they take the bodies away and you stop shaking. Is Rengifo mixed up in this business with the girls? Is Campuzano up to his eyebrows in it? Rengifo was the good drug lord. Campuzano was the bad drug lord. Odd, genuinely odd, Juan de Dios said to himself. No one rapes and kills on his own property. No one rapes and kills *near* his own property. Unless he's crazy and wants to be caught. Two nights after the discovery of the bodies there was a meeting at the country club, attended by the mayor of Santa Teresa, José Refugio de las Heras, the police chief Pedro Negrete, and Mr. Pedro Rengifo and Mr. Estanislao Campuzano. The meeting lasted until four in the morning and a few things were cleared up. The next day it seemed as if all the police in the city were on the hunt for Javier Ramos. No stone in the desert was left unturned. But in the end they couldn't come up with so much as a convincing sketch of him.

•

For many days Juan de Dios Martínez thought about the four heart attacks Herminia Noriega had suffered before she died. Sometimes he thought about it while he was eating or while he was urinating in the men's room at a coffee shop or one of the inspector's regular lunch spots, or before he went to sleep, just at the moment he turned off the light, or maybe seconds before he turned off the light, and when that happened he simply *couldn't* turn off the light and then he got out of bed and went over to the window and looked out at the street, an ordinary, ugly, silent, dimly lit street, and then he went into the kitchen and put water on to boil and made himself coffee, and sometimes, as he drank the hot coffee with no sugar, shitty coffee, he turned on the TV and watched late-night shows broadcast across the desert from the four cardinal points, at that late hour he could get Mexican channels and American channels, channels with crippled madmen who galloped under the stars and uttered unintelligible greetings, in Spanish or English or Spanglish, every last fucking word unintelligible, and then Juan de Dios Martínez set his coffee cup on the table and covered his face with his hands and a faint and precise sob escaped his lips, as if he were weeping or trying to weep, but when finally he removed his hands, all that appeared, lit by the TV screen, was his old face, his old skin, stripped and dry, and not the slightest trace of a tear.

•

When he told Elvira Campos what was happening to him, the asylum director listened in silence and then, for a long time afterward, as they lay naked in the dusk of the bedroom, she confessed that she sometimes dreamed of giving up everything. In other words, making a drastic break, no holds barred. She dreamed, for example, of selling her apartment and two other properties she owned in Santa Teresa, and her car and her jewelry, selling everything until she had collected a decent sum of money, and then she dreamed about flying to Paris, where she would rent a tiny apartment, a studio, say between Villiers and Porte de Clichy, and then she would go to see a famous doctor, a wonder-working plastic surgeon, get a face-lift, get her nose and cheekbones fixed, have her breasts enlarged, in short, when she got off the operating table she would look like someone else, a different woman, not fiftysomething anymore but fortysomething, or better yet, just over forty, unrecognizable, new, changed, rejuvenated, although of course for a while she would go everywhere wrapped in bandages, like a mummy, not an Egyptian mummy but a Mexican mummy, which would be something she enjoyed, walking to the metro, for example, knowing that all the Parisians were watching her surreptitiously, some of them even giving up their seats for her, imagining the horrible suffering, burns, traffic accident, that this silent and stoic stranger had undergone, and then getting off the metro and going into a museum or an art gallery or a Montparnasse bookstore, and studying French for two hours a day, with joy, with excitement, French is so pretty, such a musical language, it has a certain je ne sais quoi, and then, one rainy morning, taking off her bandages, slowly, like an archaeologist who has just discovered an incredible bone, like a girl who carefully unwraps, bit by bit, a present that she wants to make last, forever? nearly forever, until finally the last bandage falls, where does it fall? to the floor, to the rug or the wooden floor, in any case a top-quality floor, and on the floor all the bandages slither like snakes, or all the bandages open their sleepy eyes like snakes, although she knows they aren't snakes but rather the guardian angels of snakes, and then someone brings her a mirror and she stares at herself, she nods at herself, she approves of herself, with a gesture in which she rediscovers the sovereignty of childhood, the love of her father and mother, and then she signs something, a paper, a document, a check, and she steps out into the streets of Paris. Into a new life? asked Juan de Dios Martínez. I suppose so, said the director. I like you the way you are, said Juan de Dios Martínez. A new life without Mexicans or Mexico or Mexican patients, said the director. I'm crazy about you the way you are, said Juan de Dios Martínez.

·

At the end of 1996, it was reported or hinted at in some Mexican media that films of real murders, snuff films, were being shot in the north, and that the capital of snuff was Santa Teresa. One night two reporters talked to General Humberto Paredes, the former police chief of Mexico City, in his walled castle in Colonia del Valle. The reporters were old Macario López Santos, who had been on the crime beat for more than forty years, and Sergio González. The dinner with which the general regaled them consisted of pork tacos with extra chile sauce and La Invisible tequila. Anything else the general tried to eat at night only gave him heartburn. When inroads had been made on the food, Macario López asked the general what he thought about the snuff industry in Santa Teresa, and the general told them that over the course of his long career he had seen many terrible things, but he'd never seen films like that and he wasn't sure they existed. But they do exist, said the old reporter. Maybe they do, maybe they don't, answered the general, but what's strange is that I never saw one, when I saw and was informed of everything. The two reporters agreed that it was strange, although they hinted that maybe, back when the general was on the job, this particular brand of horror hadn't yet emerged. The general begged to differ: according to him, pornography had reached its fullest flowering slightly before the French Revolution. Everything you might see today in a film from the Netherlands or a collection of photographs or a dirty book had already been *set* before the year 1789, and for the most part was a repetition, a filip on an already-gazing gaze. General, said Macario López Santos, sometimes you talk just like Octavio Paz, you wouldn't happen to be reading him, would you? The general burst out laughing and said the only thing he'd read by Paz, and this was many years ago, was *The Labyrinth of Solitude*, and he hadn't understood a single word. I was very young back then, said the general, eyeing the reporters, I must have been forty. Oh, *mi general*, said Macario López. Then they talked about freedom and evil, about the highways of freedom where evil is like a Ferrari, and after a while, when an elderly maid cleared the table and asked whether the gentlemen would be having coffee, they returned to the subject of snuff films. According to Macario López, the situation in Mexico had changed. On the one hand there had never been so much corruption. To this you had to add the problem of the drug trade and the heaps of money revolving around it. The snuff industry, in this context, was just a symptom. A virulent symptom in the case of Santa Teresa, but ultimately just a symptom. The general's reply was dismissive. He said he didn't think corruption today was any worse than under past governments. It wasn't as bad as it was during Miguel Alemán's administration, for example, or López Mateos's presidency. The desperation might be worse now, but not the corruption. The drug trade, he conceded, was something new, but the real burden of the drug trade on Mexican society (and on American society) was overstated. All you needed to make a snuff film, he said, was money, nothing but money, and there was money before the drug lords made their fortunes, and also a pornography industry, and still, the films, the famous films, weren't made. You may not have seen them, General, said Macario López. The general laughed and his laughter was lost among the flower beds in the dark yard. I saw everything, Macario my friend, he answered. Before they left, the old crime reporter remarked that he hadn't had the pleasure of saluting any bodyguard when they got to the walled house in Colonia del Valle. The general answered that this was because he didn't have bodyguards anymore. And why is that, *mi general*? asked the reporter. Have your enemies given up? Security is getting more and more expensive, Macario, said the general as he walked them to the gate along a path lined with bougainvilleas, and I would rather spend my few pesos on pleasanter indulgences. And if you're attacked? The general reached behind him and showed the two reporters an Israeli Desert Eagle .50 Magnum with a seven-shot clip. In his pocket, he told them, he always carried two replacement clips. But I don't think I'll have to use the gun, he said, I'm so old my enemies must think I'm already pushing up daisies. Some people hold grudges for a long time, observed Macario López Santos. True, Macario, said the general, in Mexico we don't know how to be good sports. Of course, if you lose you die and if you win sometimes you die too, which makes it hard to keep up a sporting attitude, but still, the general reflected, some of us try to fight the good fight. Oh, *mi general,* said Macario López Santos, laughing.

•

In January 1997, five members of the Los Bisontes gang were arrested. They were accused of several murders committed after Haas was caught. Those arrested were Sebastián Rosales, nineteen, Carlos Camilo Alonso, twenty, René Gardea, seventeen, Julio Bustamante, nineteen, and Roberto Aguilera, twenty. All five had previous convictions for sexual abuse and two of them, Sebastián Rosales and Carlos Camilo Alonso, had been held in custody for the rape of a minor, María Inés Rosales, a first cousin of Sebastián, who withdrew the charges a few months after

Sebastián was sent to the Santa Teresa penitentiary. It was said that Carlos Camilo Alonso had been renting the house on Calle García Herrero where the bodies of Estefanía and Herminia were found. All five were accused of having kidnapped, raped, tortured, and killed the two women found dead in the Podestá ravine, in addition to being charged with the murder of Marisol Camarena, whose body was found in a drum of acid, and the murder of Guadalupe Elena Blanco, plus the killings of Estefanía and Herminia. During the interrogation to which they were subjected, Carlos Camilo Alonso lost all his teeth and suffered a fracture of the nasal septum, supposedly in a suicide attempt. Roberto Aguilera ended up with four broken ribs. Julio Bustamante was locked in a cell with two butch queers, who sodomized him until they were tired, as well as beating the shit out of him every three hours and breaking the fingers of his left hand. A lineup was assembled, and out of ten residents of Calle García Herrero only two recognized Carlos Camilo Alonso as the tenant at 677. Two witnesses, one of whom was a known police informer, stated that they had seen Sebastián Rosales in a black Peregrino during the week when Estefanía and Herminia were kidnapped. According to Rosales's own testimony, it was a car he had just stolen. Three firearms were found in the possession of the Bisontes: two CZ model 85 9mm pistols and a German Heckler & Koch. Another witness, however, said that Carlos Camilo Alonso had bragged about owning a Smith & Wesson like the one that had been used to kill the two sisters. Where was the gun? According to the same witness, Carlos Camilo had told him he'd sold it to some gringo drug traffickers he knew. Meanwhile, after the Bisontes were arrested, it was discovered by chance that one of them, Roberto Aguilera, was the younger brother of a certain Jesús Aguilera, an inmate at the Santa Teresa penitentiary who went by the nickname El Tequila and was a good friend and protégé of Klaus Haas. It wasn't long before conclusions were drawn. Very likely, said the police, the series of killings carried out by the Bisontes were murders for hire. According to this version, Haas paid three thousand dollars for each dead woman who resembled his own victims. The news was soon leaked to the press. Voices were raised demanding the resignation of the warden. It was said that the prison was under the control of organized crime gangs, in turn reigned over by Enriquito Hernández, the Cananea drug lord and true boss of the prison, from which he continued to manage his affairs with impunity. An article appeared in *La Tribuna de Santa Teresa* that linked Enriquito Hernández to Haas in the trafficking of drugs disguised as a legal cross-border import/export business in computer parts. The article wasn't attributed and the reporter who wrote it had seen Haas only once in his life, which didn't stop him from putting statements in Haas's mouth that Haas had never made. The serial killings of women have been successfully resolved, said José Refugio de las Heras, mayor of Santa Teresa, on Hermosillo television (and his declaration was rebroadcast on the news programs of the big Mexico City stations). Everything that happens from now on falls under the category of ordinary crimes, what you'd naturally find in a city in a constant state of growth and development. This is the end of the psychopaths.

●

One night, as he was reading George Steiner, he got a call from someone he at first couldn't identify. A very agitated voice with a foreign accent said it's all a lie, it's all a con, not as if this were the start of a conversation but as if they'd been talking for half an hour. What do you want? he asked, who is this? Is that Sergio González? asked the voice. Speaking. Well, then, you son of a bitch, how are you? said the voice. It sounded as if it came from very far away, thought Sergio. Who is this? he asked. What the fuck, you don't recognize me? asked the voice with a hint of astonishment. Klaus Haas? asked Sergio. At the other end of the line he heard a laugh and then a kind of metallic wind, the sound of the desert and of prisons at night. That's right, I see you haven't forgotten me. No, said Sergio. How could I forget you? I don't have much time, said Haas. I just wanted to tell you that the bullshit about how I paid off the Bisontes isn't true. I'd need serious cake to cover all those deaths. Cake? asked Sergio. Money, said Haas. I'm friends with a crazy bastard everybody calls El Tequila, and one of the Bisontes is El Tequila's brother. But that's all. There's nothing else, I swear, said the voice with the foreign accent. Tell it to your lawyer, said Sergio, I don't write about the killings in Santa Teresa anymore. At the other end of the line Haas laughed. That's what everybody says. Tell this person, tell that person. My lawyer already knows, he said. I can't do anything for you, said Sergio. Well, I'm telling you, I think you can, said Haas. Again Sergio heard the sound of pipes, scratches, a hurricane wind that came in gusts. What would I do if I were locked up? Sergio wondered. Would I hide in a corner, wrapped in my blanket, like a child? Would I shake? Would I beg for help, cry, try to kill myself? They want to destroy me, said Haas. They're postponing the trial. They're afraid of me. They want to destroy me. Then Sergio heard the sound of the desert and something like the tread of an animal. We're all losing our minds, he thought. Haas? Are you still there? No one answered.

•

After the arrest of the Bisontes gang in January, the city got a break. The best Christmas present, read the headline of the story in *La Voz de Sonora* describing the capture of the five pachucos. True, there were deaths. A longtime thief whose stage of operations was the city center was stabbed to death, two men with ties to the drug trade died, a dog breeder died, but no one found any women who had been raped and tortured and then killed. This was in January. And it was the same in February. There were the usual deaths, yes, those to be expected, people who started off celebrating and ended up killing each other, uncinematic deaths, deaths from the realm of folklore, not modernity: deaths that didn't scare anybody. The serial killer was officially behind bars. His imitators or followers or hirelings were, too. The city could breathe easy.

•

In January, the correspondent for a Buenos Aires newspaper spent three days in Santa Teresa on his way to Los Angeles and wrote a story about the city and the killings of women. He tried to visit Haas in prison but was refused permission. He went to a bullfight. He was at a brothel, Internal Affairs, and he slept with a whore called Rosana. He visited Domino's, the club, and Serafino's, the bar. He met a fellow reporter from *El Heraldo del Norte* and consulted the paper's file on disappeared, kidnapped, and murdered women. The reporter at *El Heraldo* introduced him to a friend who introduced him to another friend who claimed to have seen a snuff film. The Argentinean told him he wanted to see it. The friend of the friend of the reporter asked how much he was willing to pay in dollars. The Argentinean said he wouldn't give half a mango for filth like that, he wanted to see it only as a matter of professional interest, and also, he had to admit, out of curiosity. The Mexican made an appointment with him at a house in the northern part of the city. The Argentinean had green eyes and was six foot three and weighed almost two hundred and twenty pounds. He came at the appointed time and saw the movie. The Mexican was short and on the heavy side, and as they watched the movie he was very still, sitting on the sofa next to the Argentinean, like a young lady. Through the whole movie the Argentinean was waiting for the moment when the Mexican would touch his cock. But the Mexican didn't do anything except breathe heavily, as if he didn't want to miss a cubic inch of the oxygen previously breathed by the Argentinean. When the movie was over the Argentinean asked politely for a copy, but the Mexican refused even to consider it. That night they went to a place called El Rey del Taco for beers. As they were drinking, the Argentinean thought for a moment that all the waiters were zombies. It didn't surprise him. The place was huge, full of murals and paintings depicting the childhood of El Rey del Taco, and the heaviness of a petrified nightmare hung over the tables. At one point the Argentinean thought someone had put something in his beer. He left abruptly and went back to his hotel by taxi. The next day he took a bus to Phoenix and caught a plane from there to Los Angeles, where he spent his days interviewing any actors who would agree to be interviewed, which wasn't many, and his nights writing a long article about the killings of women in Santa Teresa. The article centered on the porn film industry and the underground subindustry of snuff films. The term *snuff film*, according to the Argentinean, had been invented in Argentina, although not by an Argentinean but by an American couple who had come there to make a movie. The Americans were called Mike and Clarissa Epstein and they hired two relatively famous Buenos Aires actors who had fallen on hard times, and several young people, some of whom were later very well-known. The crew was also Argentinean, except for the cameraman, a buddy of Epstein's called JT Hardy, who got to Buenos Aires a day before the filming began. This was in 1972, when there was still talk in Argentina about revolution, about Peronist revolution, about Socialist revolution and even mystical revolution. Psychoanalysts and poets roamed the streets and were watched from the windows by psychics and practitioners of the dark arts. When JT arrived in Buenos Aires he was met at the airport by Mike and Clarissa Epstein, who were more excited about Argentina with each passing day. As they rode in a taxi to the house they had rented on the edge of the city, Mike confessed that all of this, and in explanation he spread his arms wide, was like the West, the American West, but better than the American West, because in the West, when you thought about it, all the cowboys did was herd cattle, and here, on the pampa, as he had come to see more and more clearly, the cowboys were zombie hunters. Is the movie about zombies? JT wanted to know. There are one or two, said Clarissa. That night, in honor of the cameraman, a traditional Argentinean barbecue was held in the Epsteins' yard, next to the pool, with the actors and crew in attendance. Two days later they left for Tigre. After a week of filming the whole team returned to Buenos Aires. They took a break for a few days. The actors, who were mostly younger, went to visit their parents and friends, and JT, sitting next to the Epsteins' pool, read the script. He didn't understand much of it, and what was worse, he didn't recognize any of the scenes he'd shot in Tigre. A little later, in a fleet of two trucks and a pickup, they left for the pampa. They looked, said one of the Argentinean actors, like a troupe of gypsies heading into the unknown. The trip was endless. The first night they slept at a kind of truck stop and Mike and Clarissa had their first fight. An eighteen-year-old Argentinean actress started to cry and said she wanted to go home, back to her mother and little brothers and sisters. An Argentinean actor who looked like a leading man got drunk and fell asleep in the bathroom and the other actors had to drag him to his room. The next day Mike woke them up very early and they got back on the road, looking sheepish. To save money, they ate on riverbanks, as if they were picnicking. The girls were good cooks and even the boys seemed skilled at grilling. Their diet was based on meat and wine. Almost everyone had a camera and during the meal breaks they took pictures of one another. Some spoke in English with Clarissa and JT, to practice, they said. Mike, meanwhile, talked to everybody in Spanish, a Spanish riddled with the Argentinean slang *lunfardo* that made the kids smile. On the fourth day of the trip, when JT thought he was lost in a nightmare, they arrived at a ranch, where they were received by the only two employees, a couple in their fifties who looked after the house and stables. Mike talked to them for a while, explaining that he was a friend of the boss, and then everyone got out of the trucks and took possession of the house. That same afternoon work started up again. They filmed an outdoors scene, a man making a fire, a woman tied to a barbed-wire fence, two men talking business while they sat on the ground eating big pieces of meat. The meat was hot, and the men tossed it from hand to hand so as not to burn themselves. That night they had a party. There was talk about politics, the need for agricultural reform, landowners, the future of Latin America, and the Epsteins and JT were quiet, partly because they weren't interested and partly because they had more important things to think about. That night JT had discovered that Clarissa was cheating on Mike with one of the actors, although Mike didn't seem to care. The next day they filmed inside the ranch. Sex scenes, which was what JT was best at, since he was an expert in indirect lighting, in the art of hints and suggestion. The ranch caretaker slaughtered a calf, which they ate at noon, and Mike went along, equipped with several plastic bags. When he came back the bags were full of blood. The filming that morning resembled nothing so much as a massacre. It was supposed to look as if two of the actors had killed one of the actresses and then chopped her to pieces, wrapped the remains in sacking, and gone out onto the pampa to bury them. Pieces of the calf slaughtered that morning were used, and almost all of its innards. One of the Argentinean girls cried and said the movie they were making was disgusting trash. The housekeeper, however, seemed highly amused. On Sunday, the third day of filming, the woman who owned the ranch drove up in a Bentley. The only Bentley JT remembered having seen was one that belonged to a Hollywood producer, in a far-off time when he still thought he could make a life for himself in Hollywood. The owner might have been forty-five and she was an attractive, elegant blonde who spoke much more proper English than the three Americans. The Argentinean kids were cautious around her at first. As if they didn't trust her and as if she, necessarily, would distrust them, which wasn't the case. Also, she turned out to be a very practical kind of person: she reorganized the pantry in such a way that there was always enough food, sent for another woman to help the housekeeper with the cleaning, set a schedule for meals, put her Bentley at the director's disposal. Suddenly the ranch was no longer an Indian camp. Or to put it another way: the ranch lost on the pampa stopped being Sparta and became Athens, as one of the young actors resoundingly declared during one of the evening gatherings that since the owner's arrival were held daily on the large, comfortable veranda. Of these gatherings, which sometimes lasted until three or four in the morning, JT would remember the hostess's readiness to listen, her bright eyes, the way her skin glowed in the moonlight, the stories she told about her childhood in the country and her adolescence at a Swiss boarding school. Sometimes, especially when he was alone, in his room, in bed and with a blanket pulled up to his chin, JT thought that she might be the woman he'd been looking for all his life. What am

I here for, he asked himself, if not to meet her? What's the point of Mike's disgusting and incomprehensible film if not to give me the chance to come to this godforsaken country and meet her? Does it mean anything that I was out of work when Mike called me? Of course it does! It means I had no choice but to accept his offer and meet her. The ranch owner's name was Estela and JT could repeat it until his mouth was parched. Estela, Estela, he said over and over again, under the blankets, like a worm or an insomniac mole. During the day, however, when they met or talked, the cameraman was all circumspection and prudence. He didn't allow himself yearning looks, he didn't allow himself suggestive hints or romantic swoons. His relationship with their hostess never once departed from the strict pathways of courtesy and respect. When the filming was over, the ranch owner offered to drive the Epsteins and JT back to Buenos Aires in her Bentley, but JT said he would rather make the return trip with the team. Three days later the Epsteins dropped him off at the airport and JT didn't dare ask them directly about Estela. Nor did he ask anything about the film. In New York he tried in vain to forget her. The first few days were tinged with melancholy and regret and JT thought he would never recover. Anyway: recover *why*? And yet, with the passage of time, in his heart he understood that he'd gained much more than he'd lost. At least, he said to himself, I've *met* the woman of my dreams. Other people, most people, glimpse something in films, the shadow of great actresses, the gaze of true love. But I saw her in the flesh, heard her voice, saw her silhouetted against the endless pampa. I talked to her and she talked *back*. What do I have to complain about? In Buenos Aires, meanwhile, Mike edited the film in a cheap studio that he rented by the hour, on Calle Corrientes. A month after the filming had ended, one of the young actresses fell in love with an Italian revolution-ary on his way through Buenos Aires and left with him for Europe. No one could say why, but word spread that the actress had died while Ep-stein's film was being shot, and a little later it was rumored, although it must be emphasized that no one took this seriously, that Epstein and his troupe had killed her. According to this last version Epstein wanted to film a real murder and to that end he had selected, with the acquies-cence of the other actors and the crew—everyone, at the peak of the madness, immersed in satanic rituals—the least well-known and most defenseless actress in the cast. Hearing these rumors, Epstein took it upon himself to spread them, and the story, with slight variations, reached some cinephile circles in the United States. The following year the film opened in Los Angeles and New York. It was a total flop, dubbed as it was into English, chaotic, with a weak script and pitiful performances. Epstein, who returned to the United States, tried to exploit the gruesome element, but a TV commentator demonstrated, frame by frame, that the purportedly real crime had been faked. The actress, concluded the critic, deserved to die for her poor acting, but the truth is, in this film at least, no one had the good sense to do away with her. After *Snuff*, Epstein shot two more films, both low budget. Clarissa, his wife, stayed in Buenos Aires, where she moved in with an Argentinean movie producer. Her new companion, a Peronist, later became an active member of a death squad that began by killing Trotskyites and guerrillas and ended up orchestrating the disappearance of children and housewives. During the military dictatorship Clarissa returned to the United States. A year later, while he was shooting what would be his last film (his name doesn't appear in the credits), Epstein was killed when he fell down an elevator shaft. After a fall of fourteen flights, the state of the body, according to witnesses, was indescribable.

•

The second week of March 1997, the macabre round began again with the discovery of a body on some desert land in the southern part of the city, designated El Rosario on city blueprints, where there was a plan to build a neighborhood of Phoenix-style houses. The body was found half buried some fifty yards from the road that crossed El Rosario and intersected a dirt track that ran from the eastern end of the Podestá ravine. It was discovered by a local ranch hand who was passing by on horseback. According to the medical examiners, the cause of death was strangulation, with a fracture of the hyoid bone. Despite the body's state of decomposition, signs of battery with a blunt object were still evident about the head, hands, and legs. The victim had probably also been raped. As indicated by the fauna found on the body, the date of death was approximately the first or second week of February. There was nothing to identify the victim, although her particulars matched those of Guadalupe Guzmán Prieto, eleven years old, disappeared the evening of February 8, in Colonia San Bartolomé. Anthropometric and odontologic tests were carried out to establish her identity, with positive results. Later a new autopsy was performed and there was confirmation of the cranial trauma and hematomas, as well as of the ecchymosis of the neck and the fracture of the hyoid. According to one of the inspectors in charge of the case, it was possible that the killer had hanged the girl with his hands. Trauma to the right thigh and gluteal muscles was also detected. The parents recognized the body as that of their daughter Guadalupe. According to *La Voz de Sonora*, the corpse was well preserved, which helped with the identification, its skin cured as if the arid yellow earth of El Rosario were a kind of medium for mummification.

•

Four days after the discovery of the body of Guadalupe Guzmán Prieto, the body of Jazmín Torres Dorantes, also eleven years old, was found on the eastern slopes of Cerro Estrella. The cause of death was determined to be hypovolemic shock, occasioned by the more than fifteen stabs she had been dealt by her attacker or attackers. The vaginal and anal swabs established that she had been raped several times. The body was fully dressed: khaki sweatshirt, jeans, and cheap sneakers. The girl lived in the western part of the city, in Colonia Morelos, and she had been kidnapped twenty days before, although the case hadn't been publicized. The police arrested eight young men from Colonia Estrella, members of a gang involved in car theft and small-time drug dealing, as the perpetrators of the crime. Three were transferred to juvenile court and the other five ended up being held in the Santa Teresa penitentiary, although there was no conclusive evidence against them.

•

Two days after Jazmín was discovered, a group of children found the lifeless body of Carolina Fernández Fuentes, nineteen, worker at the WS-Inc. maquiladora, on a stretch of wasteland to the west of General Sepúlveda industrial park. According to the medical examiner, it had been two weeks since she was killed. The body was completely naked, although a bloodstained blue bra was found fifteen yards away, and a pair of black nylon stockings some fifty yards away. When Carolina's roommate, also a worker at WS-Inc., was interviewed, she declared that the bra belonged to the deceased but the stockings certainly did not, because her friend and beloved roommate wore only panties and had never used stockings, an item of clothing she considered more suitable for a whore than a factory worker. When the requisite tests were completed, however, it turned out that there were traces of Carolina Fernández Fuentes's blood on both the stockings and the bra, which started a rumor that Carolina had led a double life, or that the night when she was killed she had participated voluntarily in an orgy, since traces of semen were also found in her vagina and rectum. For two days some men at WS-Inc. were questioned about their possible connection to the dead woman, to no avail. Carolina's parents, who were from the town of San Miguel de Horcasitas, made the trip to Santa Teresa. They didn't issue any statements. They claimed their daughter's body, signed the papers that were put in front of them, and returned by bus to Horcasitas with what was left of Carolina. The cause of death was five stab wounds to the neck. According to the experts, she wasn't killed in the place she was found.

•

Three days after the discovery of Carolina's body, in the calamitous month of March 1997, a girl of between sixteen and twenty was found on some stony ground near the Pueblo Azul highway. The body was in an advanced state of decomposition, by which it was assumed that she had been dead for at least fifteen days. She was completely naked, wearing only brass earrings in the shape of little elephants. Several families of girls and women who had disappeared were brought in to view the body, but no one recognized her as a daughter, sister, cousin, or wife. According to the medical examiner, the right breast had been mutilated and the nipple of the left breast had been torn off, probably bitten or cut with a knife, though the putrefaction of the body made it impossible to say for sure. The official cause of death: fracture of the hyoid.

•

In the last week of March the skeleton of another woman was discovered some four hundred yards from the Cananea highway, essentially in the middle of the desert. It was three students and an American history professor from the University of Los Angeles who found it. They were on a motorcycle trip in the north of Mexico, and according to them, they had turned down a back road looking for a Yaqui village and gotten lost. According to the Santa Teresa police, the gringos had left the road to commit indecent acts, in other words to fuck each other, and they put the four in a cell to await developments. Late that night, when the students and their professor had been locked up for more than eight hours, Epifanio Galindo arrived at the police station and asked to hear their story. The Americans repeated it and even drew a map that showed the exact spot where they'd found the half-buried body. When asked whether they might not have mistaken the bones of a cow or a coyote for those of a human being, the professor responded that there was no animal, except possibly a primate, with a human skull. The tone in which he said this irritated Epifanio, who decided to make a trip to the scene the next day, at dawn, along with the gringos, which meant that in order to facilitate the process they would have to remain on hand, in other words as guests of the Santa Teresa police, though of course in their very own cell, not to mention that they would be fed on the public dime, and not jailhouse slop but decent food that a policeman went to fetch for them at the nearest coffee shop. And despite the foreigners' protests, that was that. The next day, Epifanio Galindo, several policemen, and two inspectors, with the Americans in tow, made their way to the spot, a place called El Pajonal, a name that was clearly more the expression of a wish than a reality, since there were no grasslands nearby or anything of the kind, only desert and stones and, here and there, gray-green shrubs, the mere sight of which made the heart sink. There, poorly buried, in the exact spot marked by the gringos, they found the bones. According to the medical examiner, the victim was a young woman with a fractured hyoid. She wasn't wearing clothes or shoes or anything that might have helped to identify her. Either they carried the naked body here or they stripped her before they buried her, said Epifanio. Do you call this burying? asked the medical examiner. Why, no, sir, they didn't try very hard, said Epifanio, they didn't try very hard.

•

The next day the body of Elena Montoya, twenty, was found by the side of a local road from the cemetery to the La Cruz ranch. She had been missing from home for three days and a report had been filed. The body exhibited multiple stab wounds to the abdomen, abrasions to the wrists and ankles, and marks around the neck, as well as trauma to the head produced by a blunt object, possibly a hammer or a stone. The case was handled by Inspector Lino Rivera and his first step was to question the husband of the deceased, Samuel Blanco Blanco, who remained under interrogation for four days, at the end of which he was released for lack of evidence. Elena Montoya worked at the Cal&Son maquiladora and had a three-month-old son.

•

The last day of March some scavenger children discovered a body in the El Chile dump, in a complete state of decomposition. What was left of it was removed to the city's Institute of Forensic Anatomy, where all the usual procedures were performed. It appeared that the victim was somewhere between fifteen and twenty years old. According to the medical examiners, she had died more than twelve months ago, and the cause of death was unable to be determined. This information nevertheless caught the attention of the González Reséndiz family, of Guanajuato, whose daughter had disappeared around that time, and the Guanajuato police requested the forensic report for the El Chile victim from the Santa Teresa police, putting special emphasis on the dental evidence. Once the evidence was received, it was confirmed that the victim was Irene González Reséndiz, sixteen, who had run away from home in January 1996 after a quarrel with her family. Her father was a well-known local PRI politician and her mother had appeared on a popular TV show, live before the cameras, asking her daughter to come home. Even a passport-style picture of Irene was printed on the labels of milk bottles, with her physical description and a telephone number. No Santa Teresa policeman ever saw the picture. No Santa Teresa policeman drank milk. None but Lalo Cura.

•

The three medical examiners of Santa Teresa bore no resemblance to one another. The oldest of them, Emilio Garibay, was big and fat and suffered from asthma. Sometimes he had an asthma attack at the morgue, while he was performing an autopsy, and he ignored it. If Doña Isabel, his assistant, was nearby, she would get his inhaler out of his jacket, hanging on the coatrack, and Garibay would open his mouth, like a baby bird, and let himself be given a spurt. But when he was alone he ignored it and kept working. He had been born in Santa Teresa, and everything seemed to indicate he would die there. His family were upper-middle-class landowners, and many had gotten rich selling desert plots to the maquiladoras that set up shop this side of the border in the eighties. Emilio Garibay, however, hadn't sold anything. Or not much. He was a professor at the medical school, and as a medical examiner he unfortunately never lacked for work, so he simply didn't have time for other things, like business, for example. He was an atheist and it had been years since he'd read a book, despite the fact that he had amassed a more than decent library of works in his specialty, as well as volumes of philosophy and Mexican history and a novel or two. Sometimes he thought it was precisely because he was an atheist that he didn't read anymore. Not reading, it might be said, was the highest expression of atheism or at least of atheism as he conceived of it. If you don't believe in God, how do you believe in a fucking book? he asked himself.

The name of the second medical examiner was Juan Arredondo and he was from Hermosillo, the capital of Sonora. Unlike Garibay, who had studied in Mexico City, he got his degree at the medical school of the University of Hermosillo. He was forty-five, married to a native of Santa Teresa with whom he had three children, and his political sympathies lay on the left, with the PRD, although he was never active in the party. Like Garibay, he alternated his work as a medical examiner with teaching duties at the University of Santa Teresa, where he was well liked by the students, who saw him as a friend, not just a professor. What he liked best was watching TV and eating at home with his family, although when invitations came to conferences abroad he went wild and did everything he could to get his hands on them. The dean, who was a friend of Garibay's, despised Arredondo, and sometimes, out of pure contempt, tossed him a bone. As a result, Arredondo had traveled three times to the United States, once to Spain, and once to Costa Rica. On one occasion he represented the Institute of Forensic Anatomy and the University of Santa Teresa at a symposium held in Medellín, Colombia, and when he got back, he was a changed man. We have no idea what's going on there, he told his wife, and that was all he would say.

The third medical examiner was Rigoberto Frías and he was thirty-two. He was from Irapuato, Irapuato, and for a while he had worked in Mexico City, then left his job abruptly and without explanation. He had been in Santa Teresa for two years, hired on the recommendation of a former classmate of Garibay, and he was, in the opinion of his colleagues, meticulous and skillful. He worked as a teaching assistant at the medical school and lived alone on a quiet street in Colonia Serafín Garabito. His apartment was small but tastefully furnished. He had many books and almost no friends. Outside of class he hardly ever talked to his students, and he had no social life, at least not in university circles. Sometimes, at an order from Garibay, the three medical examiners would meet for breakfast in the early morning hours. At that time of day, the only place open was a twenty-four-hour American-style coffee shop, which drew people from the area who had been up all night: orderlies and nurses at the General Sepúlveda Hospital, ambulance drivers, relatives and friends of patients, whores, students. The coffee shop was called Runaway, and on the sidewalk next to one of the windows there was a vent from which big gusts of steam billowed. The Runaway sign was green and sometimes the steam was tinted green, an intense green, like a tropical forest, and when Garibay saw it he invariably said: fuck, that's pretty. Then he would fall silent and the three medical examiners would wait for the waitress, a chubby, dark-skinned teenager from Aguascalientes, or at least that's where they thought she was from, to bring them coffee and ask what they wanted for breakfast. Young Frías hardly ever ordered anything, at most a doughnut. Arredondo usually asked for a piece of cake with ice cream. And Garibay had a steak, rare. A while back, Arredondo had told him it was terrible for his joints. At your age, you shouldn't, he'd said. He no longer remembered Garibay's answer, but it was sharp and succinct. While they were waiting for their breakfast to come, the medical examiners sat in silence, Arredondo staring at the back of his hands, as if searching for some tiny drop of blood, Frías staring at the table or with his eyes fixed on Runaway's ocher ceiling, and Garibay watching the street and the few cars that went by. Sometimes, very rarely, two students who made extra money as lab or office assistants came along, and then they usually talked a little more, but as a general rule they were silent, sunk deep in what Garibay called the knowledge of a job well done. Then each paid his bill and they slunk out like vultures, and one of them, whoever's turn it was, walked back to the institute, and the other two went down to the underground parking garage and parted without saying goodbye, and shortly afterward a Renault drove out, Arredondo gripping the wheel with both hands, and vanished into the city, and shortly after that another car drove out, Garibay's Grand Marquis, and the streets swallowed it up like a commonplace lament.

•

At the same time of day, cops at the end of their shifts met for breakfast at Trejo's, a long coffee shop like a coffin, with few windows. There they drank coffee and ate huevos rancheros or eggs and bacon or scrambled eggs. And they told jokes. Sometimes they were monographic, the jokes. And many of them were about women. For example, one cop would say: what's the perfect woman? *Pues* she's two feet tall, big ears, flat head, no teeth, and hideously ugly. Why? *Pues* two feet tall so she comes right up to your waist, big ears so you can steer her, a flat head so you have a place to set your beer, no teeth so she can't bite your dick, and hideously ugly so no bastard steals her away. Some laughed. Others kept eating their eggs and drinking their coffee. And the teller of the first joke continued. He asked: why don't women know how to ski? Silence. *Pues* because it never snows in the kitchen. Some didn't get it. Most of the cops had never skied in their lives. Where do you ski in the middle of the desert? But some laughed. And the joke teller said: all right, friends, what's the definition of a woman? Silence. And the answer: *pues* a vagina surrounded by a more or less organized bunch of cells. And then someone laughed, an inspector, good one, González, a bunch of cells, yes, sir. And another joke, international this time: why is the Statue of Liberty a woman? Because they needed an empty head for the observation deck. And another: how many parts is a woman's brain divided into? *Pues* that depends, *valedores*! Depends on what, González? Depends how hard you hit her. And on a roll now: why can't women count to seventy? Because by the time they get to sixty-nine their mouths are full. And still going strong: what's dumber than a dumb man? (An easy one.) *Pues* a smart woman. And full throttle: why don't men lend their cars to women? *Pues* because there's no road from the bedroom to the kitchen. And in the same vein: what does a woman do outside the kitchen? *Pues* wait for the floor to dry. And a variation: what do you call a neuron in a woman's brain? *Pues* a tourist. And then the same inspector laughed again and said excellent, González, brilliant, neuron, yes, sir, tourist, brilliant. And González, tireless, went on: how do you pick the three dumbest women in the world? *Pues* at random. Get it? At random! It makes no difference! And: how do you give a woman more freedom? *Pues* get her a bigger kitchen. And: how do you give a woman even more freedom? *Pues* plug the iron into an extension cord. And: how long does it take a woman to die who's been shot in the head? *Pues* seven or eight hours, depending on how long it takes the bullet to find the brain. Brain, yes, sir, mused the inspector. And if someone complained to González about all the chauvinist jokes, González responded that God was the chauvinist, because he made men superior. And he went on: what do you call a woman who's lost ninety-nine percent of her IQ? *Pues* speechless. And: what happens to a woman's brain in a spoon of coffee? *Pues* it floats. And: why do women have one more brain cell than dogs? *Pues* so that when they're cleaning the bathroom they don't drink the water out of the toilet. And: what's a man doing when he throws a woman out of the window? *Pues* polluting the environment. And: how is a woman like a squash ball? *Pues* the harder you hit her, the faster she comes back. And: why do kitchens have windows? *Pues* so that women can see the world. Until at last González wore himself out and got a beer and dropped into a chair and the rest of the policemen went back to their eggs. Then the inspector, exhausted after a night's work, wondered to himself how much of God's truth lay hidden in ordinary jokes. And he scratched his crotch and dropped his Smith & Wesson Model 686, which weighed almost two and a half pounds, on the plastic table, and it made a muffled sound like thunder in the distance when it hit the tabletop, attracting the attention of the five or six nearest cops, who were listening, no, who *glimpsed* his words, the words the inspector meant to utter, as if they were wetbacks lost in the desert and they had *glimpsed* an oasis or a town or a pack of wild horses. God's truth, said the inspector. Who the fuck comes up with jokes? asked the inspector. And sayings? Where the fuck do they come from? Who's the first to *think them up*? Who's the first to *tell them*? And after a few seconds of silence, with his eyes closed, as if he'd fallen asleep, the inspector half opened his left eye and said: listen to the one-eyed man, you bastards. A woman's path lies from the kitchen to the bedroom, with a beating along the way. Or he said: women are like laws, they were made to be broken. And the laughter was general. A great blanket of laughter rose over the long room, as if death were being tossed in it. Not all of the cops laughed, of course. Some, at the farthest tables, polished off their eggs with chile or their eggs with meat or their eggs with beans in silence or talked among themselves, about their own business, separate from the others. They ate, it might be said, hunched over in anguish and doubt. Hunched over in contemplation of essential questions, which doesn't get you anywhere. Numb with sleep: in other words with their backs turned to the laughter that invited a different kind of sleep. Meanwhile, leaning at the ends of the bar, others drank without a word, just watching the commotion, or murmuring what a load of shit, or not murmuring a thing, simply taking a mental snapshot of the crooked cops and inspectors.

•

The morning of the jokes about women, for example, when González and his partner, patrolman Juan Rubio, left Trejo's, Lalo Cura was waiting for them. And when González and his partner tried to shake him off, Epifanio emerged from a corner and said they'd better listen to the kid. According to Juan Rubio they'd been working the night shift and they were tired and who was Epifanio to tell them what to do. This kind of event was as popular among Santa Teresa cops as jokes about women. Even more so, in fact. The two cars drove off to a secluded spot. Slowly. After all, why hurry to a shit kicking. First González's car, followed a few yards back by Epifanio's. They left behind the paved streets and any buildings over three stories high. They watched the sun rise through the windows. They put on sunglasses. News of the event was radioed from one of the cars, and soon after they got to the field some ten police cars showed up. The men got out of their cars and offered each other cigarettes or laughed or kicked at stones. Those who had flasks took swallows and made innocent remarks about the weather or their private affairs. After half an hour all the cars drove off, leaving a cloud of yellow dust hanging in the air behind them.

•

Talk to me about your family history, said the bastards. Explain your family tree, the assholes said. Self-sucking pieces of shit. Lalo Cura didn't get angry. Faggot sons of bitches. Tell me about your coat of arms. That's enough now. The kid's going to blow. Stay calm. Respect the uniform. Don't show you're scared or back down, don't let them think they're getting to you. Some nights, in the dim light of the tenement, when he was done with the books on criminology (don't lose it now, man), dizzy from all the fingerprints, blood and semen stains, principles of toxicology, investigations of thefts, breaking and entering, footprints, how to make sketches and take photographs of the crime scene, half asleep, drifting between sleep and wakefulness, he heard or remembered voices talking to him about the first Expósito, the family tree dating back to 1865, the nameless orphan, fifteen years old, raped by a Belgian soldier in a one-room adobe house outside Villaviciosa. The next day the soldier got his throat cut and nine months later a girl was born, called María Expósito. The orphan, the first one, said the voice, or several voices taking turns, died in childbirth and the girl grew up in the same house where she was conceived, which became the property of some peasants who took her in and treated her like another member of the family. In 1881, when María Expósito was fifteen, on the feast day of San Dimas, a drunk from another town carried her off on his horse, singing at the top of his lungs: *Qué chingaderas son estas / Dimas le dijo a Gestas*. On the slope of a hill that looked like a dinosaur or a Gila monster he raped her several times and disappeared. In 1882, María Expósito gave birth to a child who was baptized María Expósito Expósito, said the voice, and the girl was the wonder of the peasants of Villaviciosa. From early on she showed herself to be clever and spirited, and although she never learned to read or write she was known as a wise woman, learned in the ways of herbs and medicinal salves. In 1898, after she had been away for seven days, María Expósito appeared one morning in the Villaviciosa plaza, a bare space in the center of town, with a broken arm and bruises all over her body. She would never explain what had happened to her, nor did the old women who tended to her insist that she tell. Nine months later a girl was born and given the name María Expósito, and her mother, who never married or had more children or lived with any man, initiated her into the secret art of healing. But the young María Expósito resembled her mother only in her good nature, a quality shared by all the María Expósitos of Villaviciosa. Some were quiet and others liked to talk, but common to them all was their good nature and the fortitude to endure periods of violence or extreme poverty. But young María Expósito's childhood and adolescence were more carefree than her mother's and grandmother's had been. In 1914, at sixteen, her thoughts and actions were still those of a girl whose only tasks were to accompany her mother once a month in search of rare herbs and to wash the clothes, not at the public washhouse, which was too far away, but behind the house, in an old wooden trough. That was the year Colonel Sabino Duque (who in 1915 would be shot to death for cowardice) came to town looking for brave men—and the men of Villaviciosa were famous for being braver than anyone—to fight for the Revolution. Several boys from the town joined up. One of them, whom until then María Expósito had thought of only as an occasional playmate, the same age as she and seemingly as naïve, decided to declare his love the night before he marched to war. For the purpose, he chose a grain shed that no one used anymore (the people of Villaviciosa had grown poorer and poorer), and when his declaration only made the girl laugh he proceeded to rape her on the spot, desperately and clumsily. In the morning, before he left, he promised he would come back and marry her, but seven months later he died in a skirmish with the federal troops and he and his horse were swept away by the Río Sangre de Cristo. So he never returned to Villaviciosa, like so many other boys who had gone away to war or found work as guns for hire, boys who were never heard of again or who cropped up here and there in stories that might or might not have been true. In any case, nine months later María Expósito Expósito was born, and young María Expósito, now a mother herself, set to work selling potions and the eggs from her own henhouse in the neighboring towns and she didn't do badly. In 1917, there was an unusual development in the Expósito family: María, after one of her trips, got pregnant again and this time she had a boy. He was named Rafael. His eyes were green like those of his distant Belgian great-grandfather and there was something strange about his gaze, the same strangeness that outsiders noted in the townspeople of Villaviciosa: they had the opaque, intense stare of killers. The few times she was asked who the father was, María Expósito, who had gradually adopted her mother's witchlike language and manner, although all she did was sell the potions, fumbling among the little rheumatism bottles and the varicose vein flasks, answered that his father was the devil and Rafael his spitting image. In 1934, after a Homeric bender, the bullfighter Celestino Arraya and his comrades from the club Los Charros de la Muerte came to Villaviciosa in the early morning hours and took rooms at a tavern that no longer exists and that in those days offered beds for travelers. They shouted for roast goat, which they were served by three village girls. One of those girls was María Expósito. By twelve the next day they were gone, and three months later María Expósito confessed to her mother that she was going to have a baby. Who's the father? asked her brother. The women were silent and the boy set out to retrace his sister's steps on his own. A week later Rafael Expósito borrowed a rifle and went walking to Santa Teresa. He had never been in such a big place, and the paved streets, the Teatro Carlota, the movie theaters, the city hall, and the whores who back then walked the streets of Colonia México, near the border and the American town of El Adobe, surprised him greatly. He decided to stay in the city for three days and learn his way around before he did what he had come to do. The first day he spent searching for Celestino Arraya's haunts and a place to sleep for free. He discovered that in certain neighborhoods night was the same as day and he told himself he simply wouldn't sleep. On the second day, as he was walking up and down the street in Colonia México, a short, shapely Yucatecan girl, with jet-black hair down to her waist, took pity on him and brought him home with her. In a room in a boardinghouse she made him rice soup and then they made love until night. For Rafael Expósito it was the first time. When they parted the whore ordered him to wait for her in the room, or, if he went out, in the café on the corner or on the stairs. The boy said he was in love with her and the whore went off happily. On the third day they went to Teatro Carlota to hear the ballads of Pajarito de la Cruz, the Dominican *trovador* who was touring Mexico, and José Ramírez's *rancheras*, but what the boy liked best were the chorus girls and the magic numbers by a Chinese conjurer from Michoacán. At sunset on the fourth day, well fed and calm in mind and heart, Rafael Expósito said goodbye to the whore, retrieved the rifle from where he had hidden it, and headed resolutely for the bar Los Primos Hermanos, where he found Celestino Arraya. Seconds after he shot him he knew without a shadow of a doubt that he had killed him and he felt avenged and happy. He didn't shut his eyes when the bullfighter's friends emptied their revolvers into him. He was buried in the public grave in Santa Teresa. In 1935 another María Expósito was born. She was shy and sweet, and so tall that even the tallest men in town looked short next to her. From the time she was ten she spent her days helping her mother and grandmother to sell her great-grandmother's remedies, and going along with her great-grandmother at dawn to gather herbs. Sometimes the peasants of Villaviciosa saw her silhouette against the horizon, climbing up and down hills, and it struck them as extraordinary that such a tall, long-legged girl could exist. She was the first of her lineage, said the voice, or the voices, who learned to read and write. At eighteen she was raped by a peddler, and in 1953 a girl was born who was called María Expósito. By then there were five generations of María Expósitos living outside Villaviciosa, and the little house had grown, with rooms added on and a big kitchen with a gas stove and a wood fire where the eldest prepared her brews and medicaments. At night, when it was time for dinner, the five always sat down together, the girl, her lanky mother, Rafael's melancholy sister, the childlike one, and the witch, and often they talked about saints and illnesses that they never caught, about the weather and men, which they considered equally troublesome, and they thanked heaven, though not too enthusiastically, said the voice, that they were only women. In 1976, the young María Expósito met two students from Mexico City in the desert who said they were lost but appeared to be fleeing something and who, after a dizzying week, she never saw again. The students lived in their car and one of them seemed to be sick. They looked as if they were high on something and they talked a lot and didn't eat anything, although she brought them tortillas and beans that she snuck from home. They talked, for example, about a new revolution, an invisible revolution that was already brewing but wouldn't hit the streets for at least fifty years. Or five hundred. Or five thousand. The students had been to Villaviciosa but what they wanted was to find the highway to Ures or Hermosillo. Each night they made love to her, in the car or on the warm desert sand, until one morning she came to meet them and they were gone. Three months later, when her great-grandmother asked her about the father of the child she was expecting, the young María Expósito had a strange vision: she saw herself small and strong, she saw herself fucking two men in the middle of a salt lake, she saw a tunnel full of potted plants and flowers. Against the wishes of the family, who wanted to baptize the boy Rafael, María Expósito called him Olegario, the patron saint of hunters and a Catalan monk in the twelfth century, bishop of Barcelona and archbishop of Tarragona, and she also decided that the first half of her son's last name wouldn't be Expósito, which was a name for orphans, as the students from Mexico City had explained to her one of the nights she spent with them, said the voice, but Cura, and that was how she entered it in the register at the parish of San Cipriano, twenty miles from Villaviciosa, Olegario Cura Expósito, despite the questioning to which she was subjected by the priest and his incredulity about the identity of the alleged father. Her great-grandmother said it was pure arrogance to put the name Cura before Expósito, which was the name she'd always had, and a little while later she died, when Lalo was two and walking naked in the yard, contemplating the yellow or white houses of Villaviciosa, always shut tight. And when Lalo was four, the other old woman, the childish one, died, and when he turned fifteen, Rafael Expósito's sister died, said the voice or the voices. And when Pedro Negrete came to get him to put him to work for Don Pedro Rengifo, only the lanky Expósito and Lalo Cura's mother were still alive.

Living in this desert, thought Lalo Cura as the car, with Epifanio at the wheel, left the field behind, is like living at sea. The border between Sonora and Arizona is a chain of haunted or enchanted islands. The cities and towns are boats. The desert is an endless sea. This is a good place for fish, especially deep-sea fish, not men.

•

The dead women of March prompted the Mexico City papers to ask some questions out loud. If the murderer was behind bars, who had killed all these other women? If the killer's lackeys or accomplices were behind bars, too, who was responsible for all the deaths? To what extent were Los Bisontes, that terrible and improbable youth gang, a real phenomenon and to what extent were they a police creation? Why had Haas's trial been postponed over and over again? Why didn't the federal authorities send a special prosecutor to lead the investigations? On April 4, Sergio González got his paper to send him to write a new story about the killings in Santa Teresa.

•

On April 6 the body of Michele Sánchez Castillo was found, next to the storage sheds of a soft drink bottling plant. The discovery was made by two company employees assigned to clean the area. Some fifty yards from the body an iron bar was recovered, bloodstained and with bits of scalp adhering to it, which led to the conclusion that it was the murder weapon. Michele Sánchez was wrapped in old quilts, next to a stack of tires, a place where it wasn't unusual to find people on their way through town or neighborhood drunks asleep, more or less tolerated by the bottling plant. Peaceable people, according to the night watchmen, but if they got angry they might set fire to the tires, which could make the situation even more difficult. The victim exhibited facial trauma and minor lacerations to the chest, as well as a fatal fracture of the skull just behind the right ear. She was wearing white-beaded black pants, which the police found pulled down to her knees, and a pink blouse with big black buttons, pulled up over her breasts. Her shoes were heavy, with tractor-tire soles. She had on a bra and panties. By ten in the morning the place was full of onlookers. According to Inspector José Márquez, who was in charge of the investigation, the woman had been attacked and killed where she was found. The reporters who knew him asked to be allowed to come closer and take pictures and the inspector didn't object. It wasn't known who she was because she wasn't carrying any kind of identification. But she seemed to be under twenty, said José Márquez. Among the reporters who approached the body was Sergio González. He had never seen a corpse. At intervals, the stacks of tires formed something like caves. On a cold night, it wouldn't be a bad place to sleep. You'd have to crawl in. And it was probably even harder to get out. He saw two legs and a blanket. He heard the Santa Teresa reporters asking José Márquez to uncover the body and he heard José Márquez laugh. Sergio González had seen enough. He walked back to the highway where the Beetle he had rented was parked. The next day the victim was identified as Michele Sánchez Castillo, sixteen. According to the forensic report, the autopsy had determined that death was due to severe head trauma and that she hadn't been sexually assaulted. Bits of skin were found under her fingernails, so it could be argued that she had fought her attacker to the end. The trauma to her face and ribs was more evidence of the fight she had put up. And the vaginal swab proved conclusively that she hadn't been raped. Her family said Michele had visited a friend on April 5 and gone from there to look for work at a maquiladora. According to the police press release, she was probably attacked and killed sometime between the night of the fifth and the early morning of the sixth. No fingerprints were found on the iron bar.

•

Sergio González interviewed Inspector José Márquez. He arrived just as night was falling over the city and the judicial police offices were almost empty. A man who acted as custodian showed him the way to José Márquez's desk. He didn't pass anyone in the hall. The doors to most of the offices were open and the sound of a photocopier could be heard coming from somewhere. José Márquez talked to him with one eye on the clock and after a while he asked Sergio to come with him to the locker room, to save time. As the inspector undressed, Sergio asked how it was that Michele Sánchez could have reached the rear grounds of the bottling plant alive. Why not? answered Márquez. As I understand it, said Sergio, the women are kidnapped in one place, raped and killed somewhere else, and finally dumped in a third place, in this case behind the storage sheds. Sometimes it's like that, Márquez said, but the killings don't all follow the same pattern. Márquez put his suit in a bag and changed into sweatpants and a warm-up jacket. You must be wondering, he said as he adjusted his Desert Eagle .357 Magnum in its holster under his jacket, why the building is so empty. Sergio said the logical answer was that the inspectors were all out working. Not at this time of day, said Márquez. Why, then? asked Sergio. Because today is the indoor soccer match between the Santa Teresa police and our boys. Are you going to play? asked Sergio. Maybe, maybe not, I'm a substitute, said Márquez. As they were leaving the locker room, the inspector told him he shouldn't try to find a logical explanation for the crimes. It's fucked up, that's the only explanation, said Márquez.

•

The next day he visited Haas and Michele Sánchez's parents. Haas struck him as even colder than before, if possible. And taller, too, as if in prison his hormones had gone haywire and he had finally attained his true height. He asked about Michele Sánchez, whether Haas had any opinion on the subject, and he asked about the Bisontes and all the dead women who had been springing up in the Santa Teresa desert since his arrest. Haas replied listlessly, with a smile, and Sergio thought that even if he hadn't been guilty of the most recent killings, he was guilty of *something*. Then, when he left, he asked himself how he could size someone up by his smile or his eyes. Who was he to judge?

•

Michele Sánchez's mother told him that for a year she had been having terrible dreams. She would wake up in the middle of the night or the day (when she worked the night shift) with the certainty that she had lost her little girl forever. Sergio asked if Michele was her youngest. No, I have two younger children, said the woman. But in my dreams the one I lost was Michele. And why is that? I guess I don't know, said the woman, in my dreams Michele was a baby, not the age she is now, she was two or three at most, and suddenly she would disappear. I never saw the person who took her from me. All I saw was an empty street or yard or room. One moment my little girl was there. And when I looked again she was gone. Sergio asked her if people were afraid. The mothers are, said the woman. Some fathers, too. But not people in general, I don't think. Before he said goodbye, at the approach to the Arsenio Farrell industrial park, the woman said her dreams had begun around the time she first saw Florita Almada on TV, Florita Almada, La Santa, as she was called. A crowd of women arrived on foot or got off the buses run by the park's different maquiladoras. Are the buses free? asked Sergio, distracted. Nothing here is free, said the woman. Then he asked her who Florita Almada was. She's an old woman who's on Hermosillo TV every so often, on Reinaldo's show. She knows what's hidden behind the crimes and she tried to tell us, but we didn't listen, no one listens to her. She's seen the faces of the killers. If you want to know more, go and see her, and when you've seen her call me or write me. I'll do that, said Sergio.

•

Haas liked to sit on the ground, against the wall, in the shady part of the yard. And he liked to think. He liked to imagine that God didn't exist. For three minutes, at least. He also liked to think about the insignificance of human beings. Five minutes. If pain didn't exist, he thought, we would be perfect. Insignificant and ignorant of pain. Fucking perfect. But there was pain to fuck everything up. Finally he would think about luxury. The luxury of memory, the luxury of knowing a language or several languages, the luxury of thinking and not running away. Then he opened his eyes and contemplated, as if in a dream, some of the Bisontes, who were moving around the sunny part of the yard, the other side, as if they were grazing. The Bisontes graze in the prison yard, he thought, and that calmed him like a fast-acting tranquilizer, because sometimes, though not often, Haas started the day as if his head had been pierced with the point of a knife. El Tequila and El Tormenta were next to him. Sometimes he felt like a shepherd misunderstood by the very stones. Some inmates seemed to move in slow motion. The one with the sodas, for example, who came over with three cold Coca-Colas. Or the ones playing basketball. The previous night, before he went to bed, a guard had come to get him and told him that Don Enrique Hernández wanted to see him. The drug lord wasn't alone. With him were the warden and a man who turned out to be his lawyer. They had just eaten and Enriquito Hernández offered him a cup of coffee that Haas turned down, saying it kept him awake. Everyone laughed except the lawyer, who gave no indication of having heard. I like you, gringo, said the drug lord, and I just want you to know that someone's looking into this business with the Bisontes. Is that clear? Totally clear, Don Enrique. After that they invited him to sit down and asked him how life was for the prisoners. The next day he told El Tequila that the whole affair was in Enriquito Hernández's hands. Tell your brother. El Tequila nodded and said: that's good. Isn't it nice to sit here in the shade, said Haas.

•

According to Santa Teresa's Department of Sex Crimes, a government agency barely a year old, the male-female ratio of killings in Mexico was ten to one, whereas in Santa Teresa it was ten to four. The head of the department, Yolanda Palacio, was a woman of about thirty, fair-skinned and brown haired, formal in manner, although her formality betrayed glimpses of a yearning for happiness, a yearning for good times. But what are *good times*? Sergio González asked himself. Maybe they're what separate certain people from the rest of us, who live in a state of perpetual sadness. The will to live, the will to fight, as his father used to say, but fight what? The inevitable? Fight *who*? And what for? More time, certain knowledge, the glimpse of something essential? As if there were anything essential in this shitty country, he thought, anything essential on this whole self-sucking motherfucker of a planet. Yolanda Palacio had studied law at the University of Santa Teresa, and then she had specialized in penal law at the University of Hermosillo, but she didn't like trials, as she had discovered a little too late, and didn't want to become a litigator, so she had gone into research. Do you know how many women are the victims of sex crimes in this city? More than two thousand a year. And almost half of them are underage. And probably at least that many don't report being attacked, which means we're talking about four thousand rapes a year. In other words, every day more than ten women are raped here, she said, gesturing as if the women were being assaulted in the corridor. A corridor dimly lit by a yellow fluorescent tube, exactly like the fluorescent tube that was turned off in Yolanda Palacio's office. Some of the rapes end in murder, of course. But I don't mean to exaggerate, most rapists just do their thing and move on, that's all folks, next customer. Sergio didn't know what to say. Do you know how many people work here in the Department of Sex Crimes? Just me. There used to be a secretary. But she got fed up and moved to Ensenada, where she has family. Shit, said Sergio. That's right, shit, it's always shit, it's always Jesus, fuck, you're shitting me, but when it comes down to it no one remembers, not a word, and no one has the balls to do anything about it.

Sergio looked at the floor and then he looked at Yolanda Palacio's tired face. And speaking of shit, she said, want to get something to eat? I'm starving, there's a restaurant near here called El Rey del Taco, you should try it if you like Tex-Mex. Sergio got up. My treat, he said. I assumed that, said Yolanda Palacio.

•

On April 12 the remains of a woman were found in a field near Casas Negras. The people who came upon the corpse realized it was a woman by the hair, black and waist length. The body was discovered in an advanced state of decomposition. After the forensic examination, it was determined that the victim was between twenty-eight and thirty-three, five foot six, and that the cause of death was massive cerebral contusion. She wasn't carrying identification. She was dressed in black pants, a green blouse, and tennis shoes. Car keys were found in one of her pockets. Her description didn't match that of any women missing from Santa Teresa. She had probably been dead for a few months. The case was shelved.

•

Without knowing very well why, since he didn't believe in seers, Sergio González went looking for Florita Almada at Hermosillo's Channel 7 studios. He talked to one secretary, then another, then to Reinaldo, who told him it wasn't easy to get to see Florita. Her friends, said Reinaldo, protect her. We protect her privacy. We're a human shield around La Santa. Sergio explained that he was a reporter and said Florita's privacy was guaranteed. Reinaldo set a time to meet with him that same night. Sergio went back to his hotel and tried to write a draft of his article about the killings, but after a while he realized he couldn't write anything. He went down to the hotel bar and spent a while drinking and reading the local papers. Then he went up to his room, took a shower, and came back down again. Half an hour before the time Reinaldo had indicated, he hailed a taxi and asked the driver to circle around the center of town a few times before taking him to his appointment. The driver asked where he was from. Mexico City, said Sergio. Crazy city, said the driver. Once I was attacked seven times in the same day. The only thing they didn't do was rape me, said the driver, laughing in the rearview mirror. Things have changed, said Sergio, now it's the taxi drivers who attack people. So I hear, said the driver, and about time, too. Depends how you look at it, said Sergio. The meeting was at a bar with a male clientele. The place was called Popeye and the bouncer outside was well over six feet tall and weighed more than two hundred pounds. Inside there was a zigzagging bar and tiny tables lit by little lamps and chairs upholstered in purple velvet. New Age music was playing over the speakers and the waiters were dressed as sailors. Reinaldo and a stranger were waiting for him on overly tall stools at the bar. The stranger had a fashionable haircut and was well dressed. His name was José Patricio and he was Reinaldo's and Florita's lawyer. So Florita Almada needs a lawyer? Everybody needs one, said José Patricio very seriously. Sergio didn't want a drink and soon afterward the three of them got in José Patricio's BMW and drove down darker and darker streets to Florita's house. Along the way José Patricio wanted to know what it was like to be a crime reporter in Mexico City and Sergio had to confess that he actually worked for the arts page. He gave a very general explanation of how he had come to write about the killings in Santa Teresa and José Patricio and Reinaldo listened with rapt attention, like children hearing the same story for the thousandth time, a story that terrifies and paralyzes them, nodding seriously, in on the secret. Later, however, when it wasn't much farther to Florita's house, Reinaldo asked whether Sergio knew a certain famous Televisa talk show host. Sergio said he knew him by name but had never run into him at a party. Then Reinaldo said that this host had been in love with José Patricio. For a while he came to Hermosillo every weekend and took José Patricio and his friends to the beach, spending money right and left. At the time, José Patricio was in love with a gringo, a law professor at Berkeley, and completely ignored him. One night, said Reinaldo, the famous host asked me up to his hotel room and told me he had a proposal to make. He'd just been rejected, and I thought he wanted to sleep with me or take me under his wing and launch me on a new TV career in Mexico City, but he only wanted to talk, with me as audience. At first, said Reinaldo, all I felt was disgust. He isn't an attractive man and he looks even worse in person than he does on TV. At the time I hadn't met Florita Almada yet and I was living the life of a sinner. (Laughter.) The point is: I despised him and I was probably also a little envious, since I thought he'd gotten luckier than he deserved. Anyway, I went with him to his room, said Reinaldo, the best suite at the best hotel in Bahía Kino, our base for sailing trips to Tiburón or Turner Island, every possible luxury, as you can imagine, said Reinaldo, as he stared out the window of José Patricio's BMW at the modest houses they were passing, and there was the famous host, Televisa's star of the moment, sitting at the foot of the bed, with a drink in his hand, his hair a mess, and his eyes so squinty they almost vanished, and when his gaze fell on me, when he realized I was in the room, standing there, waiting, he blurted out that this would probably be his last night on earth. As you can imagine, I was petrified, because immediately I thought: this fucker is going to kill me first and then kill himself, all to teach José Patricio a posthumous lesson. (Laughter.) That's the word, isn't it, posthumous? More or less, said José Patricio. So I said to him, said Reinaldo, listen, don't be ridiculous. Listen, maybe we should go for a walk. And as I was talking, my eyes were searching for the gun. But I didn't see a gun anywhere, although he could easily have had it under his shirt, like a hit man, although he didn't look like a hit man just then, he looked desperate and alone. I remember I turned on the TV and found a late-night show out of Tijuana, a talk show, and I said to him: I'm sure you could've done a better job, given the same resources, but he wouldn't so much as glance at the TV. All he did was stare at the floor and whisper that life was meaningless and he might as well be dead. Blah blah blah. Anything I might say, I realized then, would be useless. He wasn't even listening to me, he just wanted me nearby, in case, but in case of what? I don't know, but definitely in case of something. I remember I went out onto the balcony and gazed at the bay. There was a full moon. It's so pretty, the coast, I reflected, but the sad thing is we notice it only at the worst of times, when we can scarcely enjoy it. The coast and the beach and the sky full of stars, all so pretty. But then I got bored and came back in and sat in the chair in the bedroom, and so I wouldn't have to look at the host's face I started watching TV again, where some guy was saying that he stood in possession, those were his words, *stood in possession*, like somebody talking about medieval history or politics, or the record for most expulsions from the United States. Do you know how many times he had entered the United States illegally? Three hundred and forty-five! And three hundred and forty-five times he had been arrested and deported to Mexico. All within a span of four years. I admit that suddenly my interest was piqued. I imagined him on my show. I imagined the questions I would ask. I began to think about how to get in touch with him, because there's no denying it was a very interesting story. The guy from Tijuana TV asked a key question: where did he get the money to pay the *coyotes* to take him to the other side? Because considering the frantic rate at which he was expelled it was clear there was no way he had time to work and save up money in the United States. His answer was breathtaking. He said at first he paid what they asked, but later, maybe after the tenth deportation, he bargained and asked for discounts, and after the fiftieth deportation the *polleros* and *coyotes* brought him along out of friendship, and after the hundredth they probably felt sorry for him, he thought. Now, he said to the Tijuana talk show host, they brought him as a good-luck charm, because his presence in some way relieved the stress for everyone else: if anyone was caught that someone would be him, not the others, at least if they knew to steer clear of him once they had crossed the border. Put it this way: he had become the marked card, the marked bill, as he said himself. Then the host, who was bad, asked him one stupid question and one good question. The stupid question was whether he planned to get into the *Guinness Book of World Records*. The man didn't even know what the fuck he was talking about, he'd never heard of the *Guinness Book of World Records*. The good question was whether he was going to keep trying. Trying what? asked the man. Trying to get across, said the host. God willing, the man said, so long as he was in good health he would never give up on the idea of living in the United States. Aren't you tired? asked the host. Don't you want to go back to your village or look for a job here in Tijuana? The guy smiled like he was embarrassed and said that once he had an idea in his head he couldn't get rid of it. He was a crazy guy, crazy, crazy, really crazy, said Reinaldo, but I was in the craziest hotel in Bahía Kino and next to me, sitting at the foot of the bed, was the craziest talk show host in Mexico City, so what was I supposed to think, really? Of course, the host had given up the idea of killing himself. He was still sitting at the foot of the bed, but his eyes, the eyes of a tired dog, were fixed on the TV. What do you think? I asked him. Can a person like that really exist? Isn't he the most charming thing? Isn't he innocence personified? Then the host got up holding the gun that all this time he'd had hidden under his leg or a buttock, and the color drained from my face again and he made a gesture, a barely perceptible gesture, as if to say I had nothing to worry about anymore and he went into the bathroom without shutting the door and I thought oh, fuck, now he's going to kill himself, but all he did was take a long piss, everything was so cozy, everything made sense, the TV on, the open door, the night like a glove over the hotel, the perfect wetback, the wetback I wanted to have on my show and who maybe the host in love with José Patricio wanted to have on his show, the appalling wetback, the king of bad luck, the man carrying the fate of Mexico on his shoulders, the smiling wetback, that toadlike creature, that dumb, helpless greasy illegal, that lump of coal who in some other reincarnation could have been a diamond, that untouchable born in Mexico instead of India, everything made sense, suddenly everything made sense, so why commit suicide now? From where I was I saw the Televisa host put the gun away in his toilet kit and then he closed the kit and put it in a bathroom drawer. I asked him if he wanted to get a drink at the hotel bar. All right, he said, but first he wanted to see the end of the show. On TV they were already talking to someone else, a cat trainer, I think. What channel is this? asked the host. Tijuana 35, I answered. Tijuana 35, like someone talking in his sleep. Then we left the room. In the hallway the host stopped and took a comb out of his back pocket and combed his hair. How do I look? he asked. Divine, I said. Then we pressed the button for the elevator and waited. What a day, said the host. I nodded. When the elevator came we got in and went down to the bar without saying a word. Shortly afterward we parted and each of us went to bed.

•

After they had eaten, as both of them stared out at the night through the windows of El Rey del Taco, Yolanda Palacio said it wasn't all bad in Santa Teresa. It wasn't all bad, where women were concerned. As if, with their stomachs full, tired and ready for bed, both of them could appreciate the good, the fabricated hopeful details. They smoked. Do you know which Mexican city has the lowest female unemployment rate? Sergio González glimpsed the desert moon, a fragment, a helicoidal slice, rising above the roofs. Santa Teresa? he asked. That's right, Santa Teresa, said the head of the Department of Sex Crimes. Here almost all the women have work. Badly paid and exploitative work, with ridiculous hours and no union protections, but work, after all, which is a blessing for so many women from Oaxaca or Zacatecas. A helicoidal slice? It can't be, thought Sergio. It must be an optical illusion, strange clouds in the shape of little cigars, clothes fluttering in the night breeze, Poe's fly or mosquito. So there's no female unemployment? he asked. Don't be an asshole, said Yolanda Palacio, of course there's unemployment, female and male; it's just that the rate of female unemployment is much lower than in the rest of the country. So in fact you might say, speaking broadly, that all the women here have work. Ask for the figures and see for yourself.

•

In May, Aurora Cruz Barrientos, eighteen, was killed in her own home. She was found in the conjugal bed, with multiple stab wounds, mainly to the chest, in the middle of a big slick of coagulated blood, her arms flung wide as if she was beseeching the heavens. The discovery was made by a neighbor and friend, who thought it was strange that the curtains were still drawn. The door was open and the neighbor walked into the house, where immediately she sensed that something was wrong, though she couldn't say what. When she got to the bedroom and saw what had been done to Aurora Cruz she fainted. The house was located at 870 Calle Estepa, in Colonia Félix Gómez, a lower-middle-class neighborhood. The case was assigned to Inspector Juan de Dios Martínez, who showed up at the scene an hour after the house had been occupied by the police. Aurora Cruz's husband, Rolando Pérez Mejía, was at work at the City Keys maquiladora and hadn't yet been notified of his wife's death. The police who searched the house found some blood-stained undershorts, presumably belonging to Pérez Mejía, discarded in the bathroom. Early that afternoon a couple of officers stopped by City Keys and brought Pérez Mejía in to Precinct #2. In his statement he maintained that before he left for work he'd had breakfast with his wife, like every morning, and that they got along well together because they didn't let their problems (which were mostly financial) interfere with their lives. They had been married, according to Pérez Mejía, for a year and a few months and they never fought. When he was shown the bloodstained undershorts, Pérez Mejía recognized them as his own, or similar to a pair that belonged to him, and Juan de Dios Martínez thought he would collapse. But although he wept bitterly when he saw them, which struck Juan de Dios Martínez as odd, since a pair of shorts isn't a picture or a letter, just a pair of shorts, he didn't collapse. In any case, he remained under arrest in anticipation of new developments, which weren't long in coming. First a witness appeared who said he had seen a man prowling around Aurora Cruz's house. The prowler, according to this witness, was an athletic-looking young man who rang door-bells and peered in windows as if he wanted to check which houses were empty. At least that was what he did at three houses, one of them Aurora Cruz's, and then he disappeared. What happened after that, the witness didn't know, because he had left for work, not without first warning his wife and his wife's mother, who lived with them, of the intruder's presence. According to the witness's wife, shortly after her husband left, she spent a while looking out the window but didn't see anything. Then she went to work too, and the only person left at home was her mother, who, like her daughter and son-in-law before her, scanned the street from the window, without noticing anything suspicious, until her grandchildren got up and she had to fix them breakfast before she sent them to school. No one else in the neighborhood, for that matter, saw the athletic-looking prowler. At the maquiladora where the victim's husband worked, several workers testified that Rolando Pérez Mejía had arrived at the same time as he did every morning, a little before his shift began. According to the forensic report, Aurora Cruz had been anally and vaginally raped. The rapist and killer, said the medical examiner, was a person of great vitality, undoubtedly a young man, someone completely unrestrained. Asked by Juan de Dios Martínez what he meant by unrestrained, the medical examiner replied that the quantity of semen found in the victim's body and on the sheets was abnormal. It might have been two people, said Juan de Dios Martínez. Possibly, said the medical examiner, and to find out he had already sent samples to the crime lab analysts in Hermosillo for confirmation if not of the attacker's DNA then at least of his blood type. Based on the anal tearing, the medical examiner was inclined to believe that the anal rape took place after the victim was dead. For a few days, feeling sicker and sicker, Juan de Dios investigated some neighborhood kids with gang ties. One night he had to go to the doctor, who confirmed that he had the flu and prescribed decongestants and patience. The flu took a more serious turn a few days later when he came down with strep throat and was put on antibiotics. The victim's husband spent a week in the cells of Precinct #2 and then was released. The semen samples sent to Hermosillo were lost, whether on the way there or the way back it wasn't clear.

•

Florita herself came to the door. Sergio hadn't expected her to be so old. Florita gave Reinaldo and José Patricio each a kiss on the cheek and shook Sergio's hand. We've been dying of boredom, he heard Reinaldo say. Florita's hand was creased, like the hand of someone who had spent a lot of time working with chemicals. The living room was small, with two armchairs and a TV set. Black-and-white photographs hung on the walls. In one of the photographs he saw Reinaldo and some other men, all smiling, dressed as if for a picnic, gathered around Florita: the members of a sect gathered around their priestess. He was offered tea or beer. Sergio requested a beer and asked Florita whether it was true that she could *see* the deaths that had taken place in Santa Teresa. La Santa seemed uncomfortable and took a while to answer. She tugged at the neck of her blouse and her little wool jacket, possibly too tight. Her answer was vague. She said that sometimes, like anybody, she saw things, and the things she saw weren't necessarily visions but things she imagined, like anybody, things that sprang into her head, which was supposedly the price you paid to live in modern society, although she believed that anybody, no matter where they lived, at certain moments *saw* or *pictured* things, and all she could picture recently, as it happened, were the killings of women. A charlatan with a heart of gold, thought Sergio. Why a heart of gold? Because all little old Mexican ladies had hearts of gold? More like a heart of flint, thought Sergio, to endure so much. Florita, as if she'd read his mind, nodded several times. So how do you know these killings are the Santa Teresa killings? asked Sergio. Because they're such a burden, said Florita. And because they come one after the other. Urged to explain herself better, she said that an ordinary murder (although there was no such thing as an ordinary murder) almost always ended with a liquid image, a lake or a well that after being disturbed grew calm again, whereas serial killings, like the killings in the border city, projected a *heavy* image, metallic or mineral, a smoldering image, say, that burned curtains, dancing, but the more curtains it burned the darker it grew in the bedroom or the living room or the shed or the barn where the killings took place. And can you see the killers' faces? asked Sergio, feeling suddenly weary. Sometimes, said Florita, sometimes I see their faces, but when I wake up I forget them. What would you say their faces are like, Florita? They're ordinary faces (although there's no such thing as an ordinary face, at least not in Mexico). So you wouldn't say these people look like killers? No, I'd just say they have big faces. Big? Yes, big, somehow swollen, or inflated. Like masks? I wouldn't say that, said Florita; they're faces, not masks or disguises, they're just swollen, as if the killers were taking too much cortisone. Cortisone? Or any other kind of corticosteroid that makes you swell up, said Florita. So they're sick? I don't know, it depends. Depends on what? On the way you see them. Do they consider themselves sick people? No, not at all. They know they're healthy, then? If by knowing you mean they really *know*, no one in this world knows anything for sure, child. But they think they're healthy? Let's say they do, said Florita. And their voices, have you ever heard them? asked Sergio (she called me *child*, it's the oddest thing, she called me *child*). Not often, but I have heard them talk once or twice. And what do they say, Florita? I don't know, they speak Spanish, a mixed-up Spanish that doesn't sound like Spanish, it isn't English either, sometimes I think they speak a made-up language, but it can't be made up because I understand some words, so I'd say it's Spanish and they're Mexican, except that most of their words are incomprehensible to me. She called me *child*, thought Sergio. Just once, which means it's fair to think it isn't only rhetoric. A charlatan with a heart of gold. He was offered another beer, which he refused. He said he was tired. He said he had to get back to his hotel. Reinaldo looked at him with poorly disguised resentment. What have I done? wondered Sergio. He went to the bathroom: it smelled like old lady, but on the floor there were two potted plants, so dark green they were almost black. Not a bad idea, plants in the bathroom, thought Sergio as he listened to the voices of Reinaldo and José Patricio and Florita, who seemed to be arguing in the living room. From the tiny bathroom window he could see a small cement yard, wet as if it had just rained, where, among the potted plants, he spied red and blue flowers, of an unknown variety. When he got back to the living room he didn't sit down again. He shook Florita's hand and promised her he would send her the article he planned to publish, although he knew very well he wouldn't send her anything. One thing I do understand, said La Santa as she walked them to the door. As she spoke, she looked Sergio in the eye and then Reinaldo. What is it you understand, Florita? asked Sergio. Don't tell, Florita, said Reinaldo. When a person speaks, his joys and sorrows shine through, even if only in part, wouldn't you say? That's God's truth, said José Patricio. Well, when these figments of mine speak among themselves, even though I don't understand their words, I can tell for a fact that their joys and sorrows are *big*, said Florita. How big? asked Sergio. Florita fixed him with her gaze. She opened the door. He could feel the Sonora night brushing his back like a ghost. *Huge*, said Florita. As if they know they're beyond the law? No, no, no, said Florita, it has nothing to do with the law.

On June 1, Sabrina Gómez Demetrio, fifteen, arrived on foot at IMSS Gerardo Regueira Hospital. She'd been stabbed multiple times and shot twice in the back. She was admitted immediately to the emergency ward, where she expired a few minutes later. She didn't say much before she died. She gave her name and the street where she lived with her sisters and brothers. She said she had been locked in a Suburban. She said something about a man with the face of a pig. One of the nurses who was trying to stop her from hemorrhaging asked if he was the man who had kidnapped her. Sabrina Gómez said she was sorry she would never see her brothers and sisters again.

In June, Klaus Haas made some phone calls and convened a press conference at the Santa Teresa penitentiary, attended by six reporters. His lawyer had advised against the conference, but by now Haas seemed to have lost his previous composure and he refused to listen to a single argument against his plan. Nor did he, according to his lawyer, advise her of the subject of the conference. All he said was that he was now in possession of a piece of information that he'd been lacking before, something he wanted to make public. The reporters who came weren't expecting anything new, let alone something that would illuminate the dark chasm that the regular appearance of dead women—in the city or just outside the city or in the desert that closed around Santa Teresa like an iron fist—had become, but they came because ultimately Haas and the dead women were their news. The big Mexico City papers didn't send any representatives.

In June, a few days after Haas, by phone, had promised the reporters a statement, a stunning revelation, as he put it, Aurora Ibáñez Medel, whose disappearance had been reported a few weeks ago by her husband, appeared dead by the side of the Casas Negras highway. Aurora Ibáñez was thirty-four and worked at the Interzone-Berny maquiladora. She had four children between the ages of fourteen and three and she had been married since she was seventeen to Jaime Pacheco Pacheco, a mechanic, who at the moment of his wife's disappearance was unemployed, a victim of factory-floor layoffs at Interzone-Berny. According to the forensic report, the cause of death was asphyxiation, and despite the passage of time, lesions were still visible around the victim's neck. The hyoid wasn't fractured. It was likely that Aurora had been raped. The case was handled by Inspector Efraín Bustelo, in consultation with Inspector Ortiz Rebolledo. Following inquiries among the victim's acquaintances, they proceeded to arrest Jaime Pacheco, who, after being subjected to an interrogation, confessed to the crime. The motive, Ortiz Rebolledo told the press, was jealousy. Not of any man in particular, but of all the men she might have encountered or because of his new situation, which was intolerable. Poor Pacheco thought his wife was going to leave him. Asked about the means of transportation he had used to get his unwitting wife out past the fifteen-mile marker on the Casas Negras highway or to dispose of the body there, supposing he had killed her elsewhere, which was a matter Pacheco refused to discuss despite the harshness of the interrogation, he stated that a friend had loaned him his car, an '87 Coyote, yellow with red flames on the sides, but the police were unable to find this friend or failed to search for him as diligently as the case warranted.

●

Sitting stiffly next to Haas and looking straight ahead, as if images of a rape were passing through her head, was his lawyer, and gathered around them were reporters from the three local papers, *El Heraldo del Norte*, *La Voz de Sonora*, and *La Tribuna de Santa Teresa*, as well as reporters from *El Independiente de Phoenix*, *El Sonorense de Hermosillo*, and *La Raza de Green Valley*, a small weekly (sometimes biweekly or monthly) paper that got by with almost no advertising on the subscriptions of some lower-middle-class Chicanos from the area between Green Valley and Sierra Vista, old farmworkers settled in Río Rico, Carmen, Tubac, Sonoita, Amado, Sahuarita, Patagonia, San Xavier, a paper that published nothing but crime stories, the more gruesome the better. *La Voz de Sonora* had only sent a photographer, Chuy Pimentel, who stood just behind the circle of reporters. Every so often the door would open and a guard would come in and glance at Haas or his lawyer, as if to inquire whether they needed anything. At one point the lawyer asked the guard to bring water. The guard nodded and said right away and disappeared. After a while he showed up with two bottles of water and several cans of cold soda. The reporters thanked him and almost all of them took sodas, except for Haas and his lawyer, who preferred to drink water. For a few minutes no one said anything, not a word, and everyone drank.

•

In July, the body of a woman was found in a sewage ditch to the east of Colonia Maytorena, not far from a dirt track and some high-voltage electrical towers. The woman was somewhere between twenty and twenty-five, and according to the forensic team she had been dead for at least three months. Her hands were tied behind her back with plastic cord, the kind used to tie up big packages. On her left hand she was wearing a long black glove that reached halfway up her arm. It wasn't a cheap glove either, but a velvet one, like the kind used by the highest-class exotic dancers. When the glove was removed they found two rings, one on the middle finger, of real silver, and the other on the ring finger, worked in the shape of a snake. On her right foot she was wearing a man's sock, brand name Tracy. And most surprising of all: tied around her head, like a strange but not entirely implausible hat, was an expensive black bra. Otherwise the woman was naked and had no identification on her. After the necessary procedures, the case was shelved and her body was tossed into the public grave in the Santa Teresa cemetery.

•

At the end of July, the Santa Teresa authorities, in collaboration with Sonora state officials, invited the investigator Albert Kessler to the city. When the news was made public some reporters, especially from Mexico City, asked the mayor, José Refugio de las Heras, if the hiring of the former FBI agent was a tacit acknowledgment that the Mexican police had failed. De las Heras replied that it wasn't, not at all, that Mr. Kessler was coming to Santa Teresa to give a fifteen-hour professional training course to a select group of students chosen from among Sonora's best officers and that Santa Teresa had been picked as the site for this course— over Hermosillo, for example—for its status as an industrial powerhouse as well as its sad record of serial killings, a blight previously unheard-of or almost unheard-of in Mexico, that they, the country's top officials, wanted to halt in time, and what better way to eliminate a blight than by forming a police corps with expertise in the matter?

•

I'm going to tell you who killed Estrella Ruiz Sandoval, of whose death I've been unjustly accused, said Haas. It's the same people who've killed at least thirty of this city's young women. Haas's lawyer bowed her head. Chuy Pimentel took his first picture. It shows the faces of the reporters, who look at Haas or consult their notebooks with no excitement, no enthusiasm.

•

In September, the body of Ana Muñoz Sanjuán was found behind some trash cans on Calle Javier Paredes, between Colonia Félix Gómez and Colonia Centro. The body was completely naked and showed evidence of strangulation and rape, which would later be confirmed by the medical examiner. After an initial investigation her identity was determined. The victim's name was Ana Muñoz Sanjuán and she was eighteen. She lived on Calle Maestro Caicedo in Colonia Rubén Darío, where she shared a house with three other women, and she worked as a waitress at El Gran Chaparral, a coffee shop in the historic district of Santa Teresa. Her disappearance hadn't been reported to the police. The last people she was seen with were three men known as El Mono, El Tamaulipas, and La Vieja. The police tried to find them, but it was as if the earth had swallowed them up. The case was shelved.

•

Who's bringing in Albert Kessler? asked the reporters. Who's going to pay for Mr. Kessler's services? And how much? The city of Santa Teresa, the state of Sonora? Where will the money come from for Mr. Kessler's fees? From the University of Santa Teresa, from the illicit funds of the state police? Will private sources be part of it? Is there some benefactor behind the visit of the eminent American investigator? And why now, why bring in a serial killer expert precisely now and not sooner? And also, aren't there any Mexican criminologists capable of collaborating with the police? Professor Silverio García Correa, for example, isn't he good enough? Wasn't he the best psychologist of his year at UNAM? Didn't he get a master's in criminology from NYU and another master's from Stanford? Wouldn't it have been cheaper to hire Professor García Correa? Wouldn't it have been more patriotic to entrust a Mexican affair to a Mexican, rather than an American? And, incidentally, does Albert Kessler speak Spanish? And if he doesn't, who'll interpret for him? Is he bringing his own interpreter, or will he be supplied one from here?

·

Haas said: I've been investigating. He said: I've gotten tips. He said: nothing's secret in prison. He said: friends of friends are your friends and they tell you things. He said: friends of friends of friends get around and do you favors. No one laughed. Chuy Pimentel kept taking pictures. They show the lawyer, who seems about to shed a few tears. Of rage. The reporters have the gaze of reptiles: they watch Haas, who stares at the gray walls as if his lines are written on the crumbling cement. The name, said one of the reporters, whispering, but loudly enough for everyone to hear. Haas stopped staring at the wall and contemplated the person who had spoken. Instead of answering directly, he explained once more that he was innocent of the murder of Estrella Ruiz Sandoval. I didn't know her, he said. Then he covered his face with his hands. A lovely girl, he said. I wish I had known her. He feels sick. He imagines a street full of people, at sunset, a street that slowly empties until there's no one to be seen, just a car parked on a corner. Then night falls and Haas feels the lawyer's fingers on his hand. Fingers that are too thick, too short. The name, says another reporter, we won't get anywhere without the name.

·

In September, on an empty lot in Colonia Sur, wrapped in a quilt and black plastic bags, the naked body of María Estela Ramos was found. Her feet were bound with a cord and she showed signs of having been tortured. Inspector Juan de Dios Martínez handled the case, and he determined that the body had been dumped between midnight and one-thirty on Saturday, since the rest of the time the field had been used as a meeting point for drug dealers and their clients and packs of teenagers who came there to listen to music. After comparing various statements, it was established that, for one reason or another, no one had been there between twelve and one-thirty. María Estela Ramos lived in Colonia Veracruz, and these weren't her usual haunts. She was twenty-three and she had a four-year-old son and she shared a house with two fellow workers at the maquiladora, one of them unemployed at the time, since, as the woman told Juan de Dios, she had tried to organize a union. What do you think of that? she asked. They kicked me out for demanding my rights. The inspector shrugged his shoulders. He asked her who would take charge of María Estela's son. Me, said the thwarted union organizer. Isn't there any family, doesn't the boy have grandparents? I don't think so, said the woman, but we'll try to find out. According to the medical examiner, the cause of death had been blunt trauma to the head, although the victim also had five broken ribs and superficial cuts on her arms. She had been raped. And the killing had taken place at least four days before the drug addicts found her among the trash and weeds of the vacant lot in Colonia Sur. According to her friends, María Estela had or had had a boyfriend, called El Chino. No one knew his real name, but they did know where he worked. Juan de Dios went to look for him at a hardware store in Colonia Serafin Garabito. He asked for El Chino and they told him they didn't know anyone by that name. He described El Chino as he had been described by María Estela's friends, but the response was the same: no one who answered to that name or fit that description had ever worked there, at the counter or in the back. He sent out his informants and for a few days he did nothing but search. But it was like looking for a phantom.

•

Mr. Albert Kessler is a highly qualified professional, said Professor García Correa. Mr. Kessler, according to what I'm told, was one of the first to draw up psychological profiles of serial killers. I understand that he's worked for the FBI and before that he worked for the United States military police or army intelligence, which is almost an oxymoron, since the word *intelligence* rarely sits comfortably with the word *army*, said Professor García Correa. No, I don't feel offended or supplanted because I wasn't given the job. The Sonora authorities know me very well and they know I'm a man whose only god is Truth, said Professor García Correa. In Mexico it takes frighteningly little to dazzle us. It makes me cringe when I see or hear or read certain adjectives in the press, certain praise that seems to have been spouted by a tribe of deranged monkeys, but there's nothing to be done, that's Mexico for you, and in time a person gets used to it, said Professor García Correa. Being a criminologist in this country is like being a cryptographer at the North Pole. It's like being a child in a cell block of pedophiles. It's like being a beggar in the country of the deaf. It's like being a condom in the realm of the Amazons, said Professor García Correa. If you're mistreated, you get used to it. If you're snubbed, you get used to it. If your life savings vanish, the money you were putting aside for retirement, you get used to it. If your son swindles you, you get used to it. If you have to keep working when by law you should be doing whatever you please, you get used to it. If on top of that your salary is cut, you get used to it. If you have to work for crooked lawyers and corrupt detectives to supplement your pay, you get used to it. But you'd better not put any of this in your articles, boys, because if you do, my job will be on the line, said Professor García Correa. Mr. Albert Kessler, as I was saying, is a highly qualified investigator. As I understand it, he works with computers. Interesting work. He's also a consultant or adviser on some action movies. I haven't seen any of them, because it's been a long time since I went to the movies and Hollywood trash just puts me to sleep. But according to my grandson, they're plenty of fun and the good guys always win, said Professor García Correa.

•

The name, said the reporter. Antonio Uribe, said Haas. The reporters exchanged glances, to see whether any of them recognized it, but they all shrugged their shoulders. Antonio Uribe, said Haas, that's the name of the killer of women in Santa Teresa. After a silence, he added: and the surrounding area. And the surrounding area? asked one of the reporters. The killer of women in Santa Teresa, said Haas, and also of the dead women who've turned up just outside the city. And do you know this Uribe? asked one of the reporters. I met him once, just once, said Haas. Then he took a breath, as if he were about to tell a long story, and Chuy Pimentel chose that moment to take a picture of him. In it, because of the light and the angle, Haas looks much thinner, his neck long like a turkey's, though not just any turkey but a singing turkey or a turkey about to *break into song*, not just sing, but *break into song*, a piercing song, a grating song, a song of shattered glass, but of glass bearing a strong resemblance to crystal, that is, to purity, to self-abnegation, to a total lack of deceitfulness.

•

On October 7, the body of a girl somewhere between the ages of fourteen and sixteen was discovered thirty yards from the railroad tracks, in the bushes bordering some baseball fields. She showed clear signs of torture. Her arms, chest, and legs were covered with bruises and stab wounds (a policeman set out to count them and got bored when he reached thirty-five), none of which, however, had injured or pierced any vital organ. The victim wasn't carrying identification. According to the medical examiner, the cause of death was strangulation. There were bite marks on the left nipple and it was half torn off, attached by just a few strands of tissue. Another piece of information supplied by the medical examiner: one of the victim's legs was shorter than the other, which at first seemed likely to speed the identification process, though this turned out not to be the case, since none of the women reported missing in Santa Teresa fit the description. The day the body was discovered (by a group of teenage baseball players), Epifanio and Lalo Cura paid a visit to the scene. The place was crawling with cops. There were inspectors, city policemen, crime scene technicians, the Red Cross, reporters. Epifanio and Lalo Cura took a stroll around until they came to the exact spot where the body still lay. The girl wasn't short. She was at least five foot six. She was naked except for a white bra and a white blouse covered with smudges of dirt and bloodstains. As they walked away, Epifanio asked Lalo Cura what he thought. About the dead woman? asked Lalo. No, the crime scene, said Epifanio, lighting a cigarette. There is no crime scene, said Lalo. It's been deliberately wiped clean. Epifanio started the car. Not deliberately, he said, stupidly, but it doesn't matter. It's been wiped clean.

•

Nineteen ninety-seven was a good year for Albert Kessler. He had given lectures in Virginia, Alabama, Kentucky, Montana, California, Oregon, Indiana, Maine, Florida. He had been to different universities and talked to former students who were professors now and had grown children, some of them even married, which never failed to surprise him. He had traveled to Paris (France), London (England), Rome (Italy), where his name was known and those who attended his lectures brought along his book, translated into French, Italian, German, Spanish, so he could scrawl some warm or clever remark, which he was happy to do. He had traveled to Moscow (Russia) and St. Petersburg (Russia) and Warsaw (Poland), and he had been invited to many other places, which suggested that 1998 would be another busy year. The world really is small, thought Albert Kessler sometimes, especially when he was flying, in first or business class, and for a few seconds he forgot the lecture he was going to give in Tallahassee or Amarillo or New Bedford and looked out at the fanciful shapes of the clouds. He almost never dreamed about killers. He had known many of them and tracked down many others, but he hardly ever dreamed about any of them. The truth was, he didn't dream much or he was lucky enough to forget his dreams as soon as he woke up. His wife, with whom he'd lived for more than thirty years, often remembered her dreams, and sometimes, when Albert Kessler was home, she would tell them to him as they had breakfast together. They would put on the radio, a classical station, and have coffee, orange juice, frozen bread that his wife put in the microwave and that came out delicious, better than any other bread he'd ever had anywhere. As he spread butter on his bread his wife would tell him what she'd dreamed the night before, almost always about relatives of hers, most of them dead, or about mutual friends they hadn't seen for a long time. Then his wife would shut herself in the bathroom and Albert Kessler would go out into the front yard and scan the horizon of red, gray, and yellow roofs, the tidy sidewalks, the late-model cars that his neighbors' younger children left parked in the gravel driveways. In the neighborhood people knew who he was and they respected him. If a neighbor came by while Albert Kessler was in the yard, he would wave and say good morning, Mr. Kessler, before he got in his car and drove off. They were all younger than he was. Not too young, doctors or midlevel executives, professionals who worked hard for a living and tried to do no harm, although on this last point one never did know for sure. Almost all of them were married and had one or two children. Sometimes they had poolside barbecues in their backyards, and once, because his wife begged him to, he came along to one and drank half a Bud and a whiskey. No policemen lived in the neighborhood and the only person who seemed to have his wits about him was a college professor, a bald, lanky man who ultimately turned out to be an idiot, someone who could only talk sports. A cop or an ex-cop, he thought sometimes, is most at home with a woman or another cop, a cop of his same rank. In his case, only the second part of that statement was true. It had been a long time since women interested him, unless they were cops and they worked on murder cases. At some point, a Japanese colleague suggested he spend his free time gardening. The man was a retired policeman like him and for a while, or so it was said, he had been the ace of Osaka's crime squad. Kessler followed his advice and when he got home he told his wife to let the gardener go, because from then on he would personally take charge of the gardening. Of course, it wasn't long before he made a mess of everything and the gardener came back. Why did I try to cure myself of stress I didn't feel, through gardening, no less? he asked himself. Sometimes, when he got home after twenty or thirty days on tour, promoting his book or advising crime writers and thriller directors or hosted by universities or police departments mired in insoluble murder cases, he gazed at his wife and had the vague impression he didn't know her. But he knew her, there could be no doubt about that. Maybe it was the way she walked, the way she moved around the house, the way she invited him to come with her, in the evenings, when it was beginning to get dark, to the supermarket where she always went and where she bought the frozen bread they ate in the mornings, bread that seemed to have come straight from a European oven, not an American microwave. Sometimes, after they'd done the shopping, they would stop, each with his or her cart, in front of a bookstore that carried the paperback edition of his book. His wife would point to it and say: you're still there. Invariably, he would nod and then they would continue browsing the mall stores. Did he know her or didn't he? He knew her, of course he did, it was just that sometimes reality, the same little reality that served to anchor reality, seemed to fade around the edges, as if the passage of time had a porous effect on things, and blurred and made more insubstantial what was itself already, by its very nature, insubstantial and satisfactory and real.

•

I saw him only once, said Haas. It was at a club or a place like a club that might just have been a bar with the music turned up too loud. I was with some friends. Friends and clients. And there was this kid, sitting at a table, with people who knew some of the people with me. Next to him was his cousin, Daniel Uribe. I was introduced to both of them. They seemed like two polite kids, they both spoke English and they dressed like ranchers, but it was clear they weren't ranchers. They were strong and tall, Antonio Uribe taller than his cousin, you could tell they went to the gym and lifted weights and took care of themselves. You could tell they cared about their appearance. They had three-day-old beards, but they smelled good, they had the right haircuts, clean shirts, clean pants, everything brand-name, their cowboy boots shiny, their underwear probably clean and brand-name too, two modern kids, all in all. I talked to them for a while (about boring things, the kind of things you talk about in a place like that, men's things, as they say, new cars, DVDs, CDs of *rancheras*, Paulina Rubio, *narcocorridos*, that black woman, what's her name, Whitney Houston? no, not her, Lana Jones? not her either, a black woman, now I can't remember who), and I had a drink with them and the others and then we all left the club, I can't remember why, everybody was outside all of a sudden, and there in the dark I lost sight of the Uribes, it was the last time I saw them, but it was them, and then one of my friends hustled me into his car and we got out of there like a bomb was about to go off.

•

On October 10, near the Pemex soccer fields, between the Cananea highway and the railroad, the body of Leticia Borrego García, eighteen, was found, half buried and in an advanced state of decomposition. The body was wrapped in an industrial plastic bag, and, according to the forensic report, the cause of death was strangulation with a fracture of the hyoid bone. The body was identified by the girl's mother, who had reported her disappearance a month before. Why did the killer bother to dig a little hole and try to bury her? Lalo Cura asked himself as he poked around the site. Why not just dump her by the side of the Cananea highway or in the rubble of the old railroad warehouses? Didn't the killer notice he was leaving his victim's body next to the soccer fields? For a while, until he was asked to leave, Lalo Cura stood there staring at the spot where the body had been found. A child's or a dog's body might have just fit in the hole, but never a woman's. Was the killer in a hurry to get rid of his victim? Was it nighttime, and was he in an unfamiliar place?

•

The night before Albert Kessler arrived in Santa Teresa, at four in the morning, Sergio González Rodríguez got a call from Azucena Esquivel Plata, reporter and PRI congresswoman. When he answered the phone, afraid it would be some family member calling to tell him there had been an accident, he heard a woman's voice, firm, imperious, commanding, a voice that wasn't used to apologizing or accepting excuses. The voice asked whether he was alone. Sergio said he'd been asleep. But are you alone, man, or not? asked the voice. Then he recognized it, or his auditory memory was triggered. It could only be Azucena Esquivel Plata, the María Félix of Mexican politics, the grande dame, the Dolores del Rio of the PRI, the Tongolele of the lustful fantasies of some congressmen and nearly every political reporter over fifty, or actually closer to sixty, all of them sinking like crocodiles in the swamp, more mental than real, presided over—some might say invented—by Azucena Esquivel Plata. I'm alone, he said. And in your pajamas, yes? That's right. Well, get dressed and come downstairs, I'm picking you up in ten minutes. Actually, Sergio wasn't in his pajamas, but it seemed hardly tactful to contradict her from the start, so he put on jeans, socks, and a sweater and went down to the building entrance. At the door was a Mercedes with its lights off. Someone in the Mercedes had seen him too, because one of the back doors opened and a hand with bejeweled fingers beckoned for him to get in. In a corner of the backseat, bundled in a plaid blanket, was Congresswoman Azucena Esquivel Plata, the grande dame, who despite the darkness, and as if she were the bastard daughter of Fidel Velázquez, hid her eyes behind black-framed sunglasses with wide black bows, like the kind Stevie Wonder wore occasionally and that some blind people used so the inquisitive couldn't see their vacant eyeballs.

•

First he flew to Tucson and in Tucson he boarded a small plane that landed at the Santa Teresa airport. The Sonora state attorney general remarked that soon, in a year or maybe a year and a half, construction work would begin on the new Santa Teresa airport, which would be big enough for Boeings. The mayor welcomed him and as they were clearing customs a mariachi began to play in his honor, singing a song in which his name was mentioned, or so he thought. He decided it was best not to ask and smiled. The mayor pushed aside the customs officer who was stamping passports and it was he himself who stamped in the illustrious guest. As he did, he froze in place, stamp raised and smile stretched from ear to ear, so the photographers gathered could take their pictures at leisure. The state attorney general made a joke and everyone laughed, except for the customs officer, who didn't look happy. Then they all climbed into a convoy of cars and headed for city hall, where, in the main assembly room, the former FBI agent proceeded to give his first press conference. He was asked whether the case file for the killings of women in Santa Teresa, or something like it, was already in his hands. He was asked whether it was true that Terry Fox, the star of the movie *Stained*, was really a psychopath—in real life, that is—as his third wife had announced before she divorced him. He was asked whether he had been to Mexico before, and, if so, whether he liked it. He was asked whether it was true that R. H. Davis, the author of *Stained* and *Killer Among the Children* and *Code Name*, couldn't sleep without the lights on. He was asked whether it was true that Ray Samuelson, the director of *Stained*, had barred Davis from the film set. He was asked whether anything like the Santa Teresa serial killings would be possible in the United States. No comment, said Kessler, and then, in very deliberate fashion, he paid his respects to the reporters, thanked them, and left for his hotel, where he had reserved the best suite, which wasn't called the presidential suite or the honeymoon suite, as it would be in most hotels, but the desert suite, since from the terrace, which faced south and west, there was a sweeping view of the Sonora desert in all its grandeur and solitude.

•

They're from Sonora, said Haas, and also from Arizona. How does that work? asked one of the reporters. They're Mexican but also American. They have joint citizenship. Is there such a thing as Mexican-U.S. joint citizenship? The lawyer nodded without lifting her head. So where do they live? asked one of the reporters. In Santa Teresa, but they have another house in Phoenix. Uribe, said one of the reporters, the name sounds familiar. It sounds familiar to me, too, said another reporter. They wouldn't be related to that Uribe from Hermosillo, would they? Which Uribe? The dude from Hermosillo, said the reporter from *El Sonorense*, the shipping guy. The one with the fleet of trucks. At this point Chuy Pimentel got a picture of the reporters. Young, poorly dressed, some looking ready to sell themselves to the highest bidder, hardworking kids with tired faces who exchanged glances and set in motion a kind of shared memory. Even the envoy from *La Raza de Green Valley*, who looked more like a ranch hand than a reporter, understood and applied himself readily to the task of remembering, of tightening the focus a few degrees. Uribe from Hermosillo. The Uribe with the trucks. What's his name? Pedro Uribe? Rafael Uribe? Pedro Uribe, said Haas. Does he have anything to do with the Uribes you're talking about? He's

Antonio Uribe's father, said Haas. And then he said: Pedro Uribe has more than one hundred cargo trucks. He transports merchandise from various maquiladoras in Hermosillo, and Santa Teresa too. His trucks cross the border every hour or half hour. He also owns property in Phoenix and Tucson. His brother, Joaquín Uribe, has several hotels in Sonora and Sinaloa and a chain of coffee shops in Santa Teresa. He's Daniel's father. The two Uribes are married to Americans. Antonio and Daniel are the oldest children. Antonio has two sisters and a brother. Daniel is an only child. Antonio used to work at his father's offices in Hermosillo, but he hasn't worked anywhere for a while. Daniel was always a fuckup. Both are protégés of Fabio Izquierdo, a *narco* who himself works for Estanislao Campuzano. It's said that Estanislao Campuzano was Antonio's godfather. Their friends are other children of millionaires, but also Santa Teresa cops and *narcos*. Wherever they go they spend money like water. They are the Santa Teresa serial killers.

•

On October 10, the same day Leticia Borrego García's body was found near the Pemex soccer fields, the body of Lucía Domínguez Roa was found in Colonia Hidalgo, on the sidewalk along Calle Perséfone. The first police report stated that Lucía worked as a prostitute and was a drug addict and that the cause of death had probably been an overdose. The next morning, however, a distinctly different statement was issued. It said that Lucía Domínguez Roa had worked as a waitress at a bar in Colonia México and that the cause of death was a gunshot wound to the abdomen. The bullet was a .44, probably from a revolver. There were no witnesses to the killing and the possibility that the killer might have shot from inside a moving vehicle hadn't been ruled out. Nor had the possibility that the bullet was intended for someone else. Lucía Domínguez Roa was thirty-three and separated, and she lived alone in a room in Colonia México. No one knew what she was doing in Colonia Hidalgo, although it was most likely, according to the police, that she'd been taking a walk and had come upon death purely by chance.

•

The Mercedes entered Colonia Tlalpan, circled around several times, and finally turned down a cobblestone street of moonlit houses behind high walls, houses that appeared to be uninhabited or in ruins. During the ride, Azucena Esquivel Plata sat in silence, smoking swathed in her plaid blanket, and Sergio stared out the window. The congresswoman's house was big and low, with courtyards where in the old days there had been carriages and stables and watering troughs carved directly into the stone. He followed her to a big room where a Tamayo and an Orozco hung. The Tamayo was red and green, the Orozco black and gray. The stark white walls of the room somehow called up visions of a private clinic or death. The congresswoman asked him what he would like to drink. Sergio said coffee. Coffee and a tequila, said the congresswoman without raising her voice, as if she were simply commenting on what each would like at that early hour. Sergio looked behind him, in case there was a maid, but he didn't see anyone. After a few minutes, however, a middle-aged woman of more or less the same generation as the congresswoman but much more worn by work and the years, appeared with tequila and a steaming cup of coffee. The coffee was wonderful and Sergio told his hostess so. Azucena Esquivel Plata laughed (actually, she just bared her teeth and let out a sound bearing some resemblance to laughter, a sound like the croak of a night bird) and said he wouldn't know what good was until he tried her tequila. But let's get down to business, she said without taking off her enormous dark glasses. Have you heard of Kelly Rivera Parker? No, said Sergio. I was afraid of that, said the congresswoman. Have you heard of me? Of course, said Sergio. But not of Kelly? No, said Sergio. That's this fucking country for you, said Azucena, and for a few minutes she was silent, gazing at her glass of tequila, shot through by the light of a table lamp, or staring at the floor or with her eyes closed, because she could do all of that, and more, under cover of her glasses. I met Kelly when we were girls, the congresswoman said, as if in a dream. At first I didn't like her, she was too prissy, or so I thought at the time. Her father was an architect and he worked for the city's nouveaux riches. Her mother was a gringa and her father had met her when he was at Harvard or Yale, one of the two. Of course, it wasn't his own parents, Kelly's grandparents, who paid his way. He went on a government scholarship. I suppose he must have been a good student, mustn't he? No doubt, said Sergio, seeing that silence seemed about to descend once again on the congresswoman. He was a fine student of architecture, yes, but a miserable architect. Do you know La Casa Elizondo? No, said Sergio. It's in Coyoacán, said the congresswoman. It's a hideous house. Kelly's father built it. I've never heard of it, said Sergio. A film producer lives there now, a hopeless drunk, a has-been who doesn't make movies anymore. Sergio shrugged his shoulders. One of these days he'll turn up dead and his nephews will sell La Casa Elizondo to a developer and they'll put up an apartment block. In fact, fewer and fewer traces are left of Rivera's passage through this world. Isn't reality an insatiable AIDS-riddled whore? Sergio nodded and said of course, she was right. Rivera, Rivera, said the congresswoman. After a moment of silence, she said: her mother was a lovely woman, beautiful is the word, very beautiful. Mrs. Parker. A beautiful and modern woman who, incidentally, her husband treated like a queen. As well he should have, because when men saw her they lost their heads and if she had wanted to leave the architect, she wouldn't have lacked for willing part-ners. But the truth is she never left him, although when I was little it was said that a general and a politician were wooing her and she wasn't averse to their attentions. But she must have loved Rivera because she never left him. They had only the one child, Kelly, whose real name was Luz María, like her grandmother. Mrs. Parker got pregnant many times, but she had trouble with her pregnancies. I suppose there was some-thing wrong with her womb. Maybe it couldn't stand any more Mexican children and the babies were aborted naturally. It could be. Stranger things have happened. Anyway, Kelly was an only child, and that misfor-tune or stroke of luck left its stamp on her. On the one hand, she was or seemed to be a prissy girl, the typical pampered daughter of an arriviste, and on the other hand, from the time she was little she was strong-willed, determined, I would even say an original. Anyway, I didn't get along with her at first, but later, as I got to know her, when she invited me to her house and I invited her to mine, I grew to like her more and more, until we became inseparable. These things tend to leave a lasting imprint, said the congresswoman, as if she were spitting in the face of a man or a ghost. I can imagine, said Sergio. Won't you have more coffee?

•

On the very day he arrived in Santa Teresa, Kessler left the hotel on his own. First he went down to the lobby. He talked for a while to the recep-tionist, asked her about the hotel computer and Internet connection, then he went to the bar, where he ordered a whiskey, which he left half finished to get up and go to the bathroom. When he came out he seemed to have washed his face, and he headed to the restaurant, not

glancing at anyone at the bar tables or in the lounge. He ordered a Cae-
sar salad and whole wheat bread and butter and a beer. As he was waiting for his food he got up and made a phone call from the phone at the
entrance to the restaurant. Then he sat down again and took an English-
Spanish dictionary out of his jacket pocket and looked up some words.
Then a waiter set his salad on the table and Kessler drank a few swallows of Mexican beer and spread butter on a piece of bread. He got up
again and headed to the bathroom. But he didn't actually go in. Instead
he gave a dollar to the attendant and exchanged a few words in English
with him, then he turned down a side corridor and opened a door and
crossed another corridor. At last he came to the hotel kitchens, above
which floated a cloud that smelled like hot salsa and *carne en adobo*, and
Kessler asked one of the kitchen boys for the exit. The boy showed him
to a door. Kessler gave him a dollar and left by the back way. On the corner a taxi was waiting for him and he got in. Let's take a ride around the
slums, he told the driver in English. The driver said okay and they set
off. The tour lasted approximately two hours. They circled the center of
the city, driving through Colonia Madero-Norte and Colonia México and
almost to the border, where you could make out El Adobe, which was on
American soil. Then they went back to Madero-Norte and cruised the
streets of Colonia Madero and Colonia Reforma. This isn't what I want,
said Kessler. What do you want, boss? asked the driver. Shantytowns,
the area around the maquiladoras, the illegal dumps. The driver headed
back across Colonia Centro and set off in the direction of Colonia Félix
Gómez, where he turned onto Avenida Carranza and drove through
Colonia Veracruz, Colonia Carranza, and Colonia Morelos. At the end of
the street there was a kind of plaza or big open space, of an intense yellow, with an accumulation of trucks and buses and stalls at which people sold and bought everything from vegetables and chickens to cheap
jewelry. Kessler told the driver to stop, he wanted to look around. The
driver said better not, boss, a gringo's life isn't worth much here. Do you
think I was born yesterday? asked Kessler. The driver didn't understand
the expression and insisted he stay in the car. Stop here, damn it, said
Kessler. The driver braked and asked him to pay up. Are you planning to
leave? asked Kessler. No, said the driver, I'll wait for you, but there's no
guarantee you'll come back with money in your pocket. Kessler laughed.
How much do you want? Twenty dollars will do, said the driver. Kessler
gave him a twenty-dollar bill and got out of the taxi. For a while, with his

hands in his pockets and his tie undone, he wandered around the makeshift market. He asked a little old woman who was selling pineapple with chile powder which way the buses went, since they all headed in the same direction. They end up in Santa Teresa, said the old woman. And what's over there? he asked in Spanish, pointing in the opposite direction. That would be the park, said the old woman. Out of politeness, he bought a piece of pineapple with chile, which he dropped on the ground as soon as he was out of sight. You see, nothing happened to me, he told the driver when he got back to the car. By some miracle, said the driver, smiling in the rearview mirror. Let's go to the park, said Kessler. At the edge of the dirt plaza, the road split, each branch in turn splitting in two. The six roads were paved and met at Arsenio Farrell industrial park. The factory buildings were tall and each plant was surrounded by a wire fence and the light of the big streetlights bathed everything in a vague aura of haste, of momentousness, which was false, since it was just another workday. Kessler got out of the taxi again and breathed the air of the maquila, the industrial air of northern Mexico. Buses arrived with workers and other buses left. Damp, fetid air, smelling of scorched oil, struck him in the face. He thought he heard laughter and accordion music on the wind. North of the industrial park stretched a sea of scrap roofs. South, past the distant shacks, he spotted an island of light and knew right away that it was another industrial park. He asked the driver what it was called. The driver got out and looked for a while in the direction Kessler had pointed. That must be General Sepúlveda industrial park, he said. Dusk began to fall. It had been a while since Kessler saw such a beautiful sunset. The colors swirled in the evening sky and he was reminded of a sunset he had seen many years ago in Kansas. It wasn't exactly the same, but the colors were identical. He was there, he remembered, on the highway, with the sheriff and another FBI man, and the car stopped for a moment, maybe because one of the three had to get out to pee, and then he saw it. Bright colors in the west, giant butterflies dancing as night crept like a cripple toward the east. Let's go, boss, said the driver, let's not push our luck.

●

So what proof do you have, Klaus, that the Uribes are the serial killers? asked the reporter from *El Independiente de Phoenix*. You hear everything in prison, said Haas. Some reporters nodded in agreement. The reporter from Phoenix said that was impossible. It's just a legend, Klaus. A legend invented by inmates. A false substitute for freedom. In prison you hear the little that gets past the prison walls and that's it. Haas gave her an angry look. I meant, he said, that in prison you know everything that happens outside the law. Not true, Klaus, said the reporter. It is true, said Haas. No, it isn't, said the reporter. It's an urban legend, a movie invention. The lawyer ground her teeth. Chuy Pimentel took her picture: black hair, dyed, covering her face, her nose slightly aquiline in profile, her eyes lined with pencil. If it had been up to her, everyone around her, the shadowy figures on the edges of the photograph, would have disappeared instantly, and so would the room, the prison, jailers and jailed, the hundred-year-old walls of the Santa Teresa penitentiary, and all that was left would be a crater, and in the crater there would be only silence and the vague presence of the lawyer and Haas, chained in the depths.

●

On October 14, by the side of a dirt road leading from Colonia Estrella to the ranches on the outskirts of Santa Teresa, the body of another dead woman was found. She was dressed in a long-sleeved dark blue T-shirt, a pink jacket with black and white vertical stripes, Levi's, a wide belt with a velvet-covered buckle, calf-length spike-heeled boots, white socks, black panties, and a white bra. Death, according to the forensic report, was due to asphyxiation caused by strangulation. There was still a three-foot-long electrical cord around her neck, doubled and knotted in the middle, that had likely been used to strangle her. External signs of violence were also visible around her neck, as if before using the cable someone had tried to strangle her with his hands, and there was excoriation of the left arm and right leg, and bruises to the gluteal region, as if she had been kicked. According to the forensic report, she had been dead for three or four days. Her age was calculated to be between twenty-five and thirty. Later she was identified as Rosa Gutiérrez Centeno, thirty-eight, a former maquila worker, and, at the time of her death, a waitress at a coffee shop in the center of Santa Teresa. She had disappeared four days previously. She was identified by her daughter, seventeen, same name, with whom she had lived in Colonia Álamos. The young Rosa Gutiérrez Centeno viewed her mother's corpse in one of the rooms at the morgue and said it was her. Lest any doubt remain, she also stated that the pink jacket with black and white vertical stripes was hers, it belonged to her, and she and her mother had shared it, as they shared so many things.

•

There were times, said the congresswoman, when we saw each other every day. Of course, as girls, in school, we didn't have any choice. We spent our recesses together and played and talked about our lives. Sometimes she invited me to visit and I loved to go, although my parents and grandparents weren't eager for me to spend time with girls like Kelly, not because of her, of course, but because of her parents, for fear her architect father would in some way take advantage of his daughter's friendship to gain access to what my family considered sacrosanct, the iron circle of our private life, which had resisted the onslaughts of revolution and repression that came after the Cristero uprising and the marginalization when the remnants of Porfirism—in fact, the remnants of Mexican Iturbidism—were roasted over a slow fire. To give you an idea: things weren't bad for my family under Porfirio Díaz, but they were better under Emperor Maximilian, and they would have been at their best under Iturbide, under an Iturbidist monarchy without upheavals or interruptions. In my family's view, I can tell you, real Mexicans were few and far between. Three hundred families in the whole country. Fifteen hundred or two thousand people. The rest were embittered Indians or resentful whites or violent people come from who knows where to destroy Mexico. Thieves, most of them. Upstarts. Fortune hunters. People without scruples. In their minds, as you can imagine, Kelly's father was the prototype of the social climber. They took it for granted that his wife wasn't Catholic. Probably, judging by what I heard later, they considered her a whore. Anyway, that was the charming attitude they took. But they never forbade me to visit her (although, as I say, it wasn't to their liking) or to have her over to my house, more and more often. The truth is, Kelly liked my house, I'd say she liked it better than her own, and ultimately it makes sense that she should have, and it says a great deal about the clarity of her taste, even as a girl. Or stubbornness, which might be the more fitting word. In this country we've always confused clarity with stubbornness, don't you think? We think we're clear-sighted when in fact we're stubborn. In that sense, Kelly was very Mexican. She was stubborn, obstinate. More stubborn than me, which is saying a lot. Why did she like my house better than hers? Well, because mine had class and hers only had style, do you see the difference? Kelly's house was pretty, much more comfortable than mine, with more amenities, I mean, a light-filled house, with a big, pleasant main room, perfect for receiving guests or throwing parties, and a modern yard, with a lawn and lawn mower, a rational house, as they were called back then. Mine, you can see for yourself, was this very house, although of course not as well kept as it is now, a big, rambling house that smelled of mummies and candles, more like a giant chapel than a house, but with all the attributes of Mexican wealth and permanence. It was a house with no style, sometimes as ugly as a sunken ship, but it had class. And do you know what it means to have class? To be, in the final instance, a sovereign entity. Not to owe anything to anyone. Not to have to make explanations to anyone. And that was Kelly. I don't mean she was conscious of that. Nor was I. The two of us were children and as children we were simple and complicated and we didn't get tangled up in words. But that was how she was. Pure will, pure explosive force, pure thirst for pleasure. Do you have daughters? No, said Sergio. No sons and no daughters. Well, if you ever have daughters you'll know what I mean. The congresswoman was silent for a while. I have just one child, a son, she said. He's in school in the United States. Sometimes I hope he never comes back to Mexico. I think that would be best for him.

•

That night Kessler was escorted from the hotel to a gala dinner at the mayor's house. At the table were the Sonora attorney general, the assistant attorney general, two inspectors, Dr. Emilio Garibay, head of the forensics department and professor of pathology and forensic medicine at the University of Santa Teresa, the U.S. consul Mr. Abraham Mitchell, whom everyone called Conan, the businessmen Conrado Padilla and René Alvarado, and the university rector, Don Pablo Negrete, all either with their wives, if they were married, or alone, though one or two who were married had been invited without their wives. The bachelors were far gloomier and quieter than the married men, although a few seemed content with their status and laughed and told stories. During the meal the talk was of business, not crime (the economic situation along their strip of border was good and still improving), and of movies, especially those on which Kessler had served as adviser. After coffee and the near-instantaneous disappearance of the women, following prior instruction by their spouses, the men gathered in the library, which looked more like a trophy room or the gun room of a fancy ranch, where they touched on the main subject, at first with excessive delicacy. To the surprise of some, Kessler answered the initial questions with other questions. Questions, in addition, that were addressed to the wrong people. For example, he asked Conan Mitchell what he, as an American citizen, thought was going on in Santa Teresa. Those who spoke English translated. Some felt it was in bad taste to begin with the American. Not to mention addressing him specifically in his capacity as an American citizen. Conan Mitchell said he had formed no opinion on the matter. Immediately afterward Kessler asked Rector Pablo Negrete the same question. The rector shrugged his shoulders, smiled faintly, said his business was the world of culture, and then coughed and was silent. Finally Kessler wanted to know what Dr. Garibay thought. Do you want me to answer as a resident of Santa Teresa or as a forensic scientist? asked Garibay in return. As an ordinary citizen, said Kessler. Not much chance a forensic scientist can ever be an ordinary citizen, said Garibay, too many bodies. The mention of bodies dimmed the enthusiasm of those present. The Sonora attorney general presented Kessler with a file. One of the inspectors said he believed there was, in fact, a serial killer, but he was already in prison. The assistant attorney general told Kessler the story of Haas and the Bisontes gang. The other inspector wanted to know what Kessler thought about killers who imitated other killers. Kessler had a hard time understanding the question until Conan Mitchell whispered *copycats*. The university rector invited him to teach a couple of master classes. The mayor said once again how happy they were to have him there, in the city. On his way back to the hotel, in one of the city council's official cars, Kessler thought how nice and hospitable these people really were, just as he had believed Mexicans to be. That night, tired, he dreamed of a crater and a man pacing around it. That man is probably me, he said to himself in the dream, but it didn't strike him as important and the image was lost.

•

It was Antonio Uribe who started the killing, said Haas. Daniel went along with him and helped to dispose of the bodies afterward. But little by little Daniel got interested, though *interested* isn't the right word, said Haas. What is the right word? asked the reporters. I'd say it if there were no women in the room, said Haas. The reporters laughed. The woman reporter from *El Independiente de Phoenix* said he shouldn't hold back for her sake. Chuy Pimentel got a shot of the lawyer. A good-looking woman, in her own way, thought the photographer: nice posture, tall, proud looking, what is it that drives a woman like that to spend her life at trials and visiting clients in prison? Say it, Klaus, said the lawyer. Haas looked at the ceiling. The right word, he said, is *aroused*. Aroused? asked the reporters. Watching what his cousin did, Daniel Uribe got *aroused*, said Haas, and it wasn't long before he started to rape and kill, too. Damn, exclaimed the reporter from *El Independiente de Phoenix*.

•

At the beginning of November, a group of hikers from a Santa Teresa private school found the remains of a woman on the steepest side of Cerro La Asunción, also known as Cerro Dávila. The teacher in charge used his cell phone to call the police, who showed up five hours later, just as it was getting dark. As they climbed the hill, one of the policemen, Inspector Élmer Donoso, slipped and broke both legs. With the help of the hikers, who were still there, the inspector was taken to a Santa Teresa hospital. Before dawn the next morning, Inspector Juan de Dios Martínez, assisted by several policemen, returned to Cerro La Asunción along with the teacher who had reported the discovery of the bones, which were located this time with no problem, and proceeded to collect them and remove them to the city's forensic facilities, where it was determined that the remains were those of a woman, though the cause of death couldn't be established. There was no soft tissue left, and not even any microorganisms. Near where the remains were discovered, Inspector Juan de Dios Martínez found a pair of pants, threadbare from exposure. As if the killers had removed the victim's pants before tossing her in the bushes. Or as if they had brought her up there naked, with her pants in a bag, and later discarded the pants a few yards from the body. The truth is, none of it made any sense.

•

When we were twelve we stopped seeing each other. The architect had the nerve to die unexpectedly, and all of a sudden Kelly's mother found herself not only husbandless but deep in debt. The first measure she took was to find Kelly a new school and then she sold their house in

Coyoacán and they went to live in an apartment in Colonia Roma. But Kelly and I still talked on the phone and we saw each other two or three times. Then they left the Roma apartment and moved to New York. I remember when she left I spent two whole days crying. I thought I would never see her again. At eighteen I went to college. I think I was the first woman in my family to go. Probably they let me stay in school because I threatened to kill myself if they didn't. First I studied law, then journalism. That was when I realized that if I wanted to keep living, that is to keep living as who I was, as Azucena Esquivel Plata, I had to shift my priorities one hundred and eighty degrees, priorities that up until then hadn't differed substantially from my family's. I, like Kelly, was an only child, and my family members were languishing and expiring one after the other. It wasn't in my nature, as you might suppose, to languish or expire. I liked life too much. I liked what life had to offer me, and me alone, and I was convinced I deserved every bit of it. At college I started to change. I met different kinds of people. The young sharks of the PRI in the law department, the bird dogs of Mexican politics in the journalism department. Everybody taught me something. My professors loved me. At first that disconcerted me. Why me, someone who seemed to have stepped off a country estate anchored in the early nineteenth century? Was there something special about me? Was I particularly attractive or intelligent? I wasn't stupid, true, but I wasn't a genius either. Why, then, did I inspire this fondness in my professors? Because I was the last of the Esquivel Platas with blood in my veins? And if that was the case, who cared, why did that make me different? I could write a treatise on the secret sources of Mexican sentimentalism. What twisted people we are. How simple we seem, or pretend to be in front of others, and how twisted we are deep down. How paltry we are and how spectacularly we contort ourselves before our own eyes and the eyes of others, we Mexicans. And all for what? To hide what? To make people believe what?

•

At seven in the morning he got up. At seven-thirty, showered and dressed in a dove-gray suit, white shirt, and green tie, he went down to breakfast. He ordered orange juice, coffee, and two pieces of toast with butter and strawberry jam. The jam was good, the butter wasn't. At eight-thirty, as he was glancing over the crime reports, two policemen came to get him. The policemen were utterly submissive in manner. They were like two whores allowed for the first time to dress their pimp, but Kessler didn't notice. At nine he gave a closed-door lecture to an exclusive audience of twenty-four handpicked officers, most in plain clothes, although a few were in uniform. At ten-thirty he visited the judicial police offices and spent a while examining the computers, playing with them and the programs for identifying suspects, under the satisfied gaze of the retinue of policemen accompanying him. At eleven-thirty they all went to eat at a restaurant specializing in Mexican and *norteña* food that wasn't far from the judicial building. Kessler ordered coffee and a cheese sandwich, but the inspectors insisted that he try some Mexican *antojitos*, or snacks, which the owner of the restaurant brought out in person on two big trays. Seeing the *antojitos*, Kessler was reminded of Chinese food. After his coffee, though he hadn't ordered it, a little glass of pineapple juice was set in front of him. He tried it and immediately tasted alcohol. Very little, just enough to heighten or serve as counterpoint to the scent of pineapple. The glass was full of finely crushed ice. Some of the *antojitos* were crunchy, with unidentifiable fillings, others were smooth on the outside, like boiled fruit, but full of meat. On one tray were the hot things and on the other tray the milder things. Kessler tried a few from the second tray. Nice, he said, very nice. Then he tried the hot things and drank the rest of his pineapple juice. These sons of bitches eat well, he thought. At one o'clock he left with two English-speaking inspectors to visit ten places Kessler had chosen beforehand from the files he'd been given. Another car carrying more inspectors followed. First they stopped at the Podestá ravine. Kessler got out, went over to the ravine, took out a map of the city, and made some notes. Then he asked the inspectors to take him to the Buenavista subdivision. When they arrived he didn't even get out of the car. He spread the map in front of him, scrawled four notes that the inspectors couldn't make out, and then asked to be taken to Cerro Estrella. They drove up from the south, through Colonia Maytorena, and when Kessler asked what this neighborhood was called and the inspectors told him, he insisted that they stop and walk for a while. The car following them pulled up beside them and the driver looked inquiringly at the officers in the main car. The inspector who was standing in the street with Kessler shrugged his shoulders. In the end they all got out and set off walking behind the American, with people stealing glances at them, some of them fearing the worst, others thinking it was a party of *narcos*, although some of them recognized the old man who was walking ahead of the group as the great FBI detective. After two blocks Kessler discovered a little place with tables outside, under a creeping vine and some blue-and-white-striped pieces of canvas tied to sticks. The floor was scuffed wood and the place was empty. Let's sit for a while, he said to one of the inspectors. From the patio you could see Cerro Estrella. The inspectors pushed two tables together and sat down and lit cigarettes, and they couldn't help smiling among themselves, as if to say here we are, sir, at your orders. Young, energetic faces, thought Kessler, the faces of healthy youths, some would die before they reached old age, before they grew wrinkled with age or fear or useless fretting. A middle-aged woman in a white apron appeared at the back of the patio. Kessler said he wanted pineapple juice with ice, like the kind he'd had that morning, but the policemen advised him to order something different, you couldn't trust the water in this neighborhood. It took them a while to come up with the English word *drinkable*. What are you having, friends? asked Kessler. *Bacanora*, said the policemen, and they explained that it was a drink distilled only in Sonora, from a kind of agave that grew here and nowhere else in Mexico. Let's try the *bacanora*, then, said Kessler, as some children peeked in and stared at the group of policemen and then went running off. When the woman came back she was carrying a tray with five glasses and a bottle of *bacanora*. She herself poured and stood waiting for Kessler's approval. Very nice, said the American detective as the blood rushed to his head. Are you here because of the dead women, Mr. Kessler? asked the woman. How do you know my name? asked Kessler. I saw it yesterday on TV. I've seen your movies too. Ah, my movies, said Kessler. Are you going to stop the killings? asked the woman. That's a hard question, I'll try, that's all I can promise you, said Kessler, and the inspector translated for the woman. From where they were, under the blue-and-white-striped canvas, Cerro Estrella looked like a plaster cast. The black veins must be garbage. The brown veins were houses or shacks perched in precarious and bizarre equilibrium. The red veins might have been scraps of metal rusted from contact with the elements. Good *bacanora*, said Kessler as he got up from the table and left a ten-dollar bill that the inspectors handed right back to him. You're our guest here, Mr. Kessler. We want you to feel at home, Mr. Kessler. It's an honor to have you here. To patrol with you. Are we on patrol? asked

Kessler with a smile. From the far end of the patio the woman watched them go, half veiled, like a statue, by a blue curtain that separated the kitchen or whatever it was from the tables. Who got that metal up the hill? wondered Kessler.

•

And you, Klaus, how long have you known all this? For a long time, said Haas. So why didn't you say anything earlier? Because I had to verify the information, said Haas. How can you verify anything in prison? asked the reporter from *El Independiente*. Let's not start that again, said Haas. I have my sources, I have friends, I have people who hear things. And according to your sources, where are the Uribes now? They disappeared six months ago, said Haas. Disappeared from Santa Teresa? That's right, from Santa Teresa, although there are people who claim to have seen them in Tucson, Phoenix, even Los Angeles, said Haas. How can *we* verify this? Very simple: get their parents' phone numbers and ask where they are, said Haas with a smile of triumph.

•

On November 12, Inspector Juan de Dios Martínez heard over the police scanner that the body of another woman had been found in Santa Teresa. Though he hadn't been assigned to the case, he headed to the scene, between Calle Caribe and Calle Bermudas, in Colonia Félix Gómez. The dead woman's name was Angélica Ochoa and, as he was told by the policemen who were cordoning off the street, it looked more like a settling of scores than a sex crime. Shortly before the crime was committed, two cops saw a couple arguing heatedly on the sidewalk, next to the club El Vaquero, but they didn't want to intervene, thinking it was a normal lovers' spat. Angélica Ochoa had been shot through the left temple, the bullet exiting her right ear. A second bullet had pierced her cheek and exited the right side of her neck. There was a third bullet in her right knee. A fourth in her left thigh. And a fifth and last bullet in her right thigh. The sequence of shots, thought Juan de Dios Martínez, was probably fifth to first, the coup de grâce delivered to the left temple. At the moment the shots were fired, where were the policemen who had seen the couple fighting? When they were questioned, they couldn't give a coherent explanation. They said they'd heard the shots, turned around, returned to Calle Caribe, and by that time the only people there were

Angélica, on the ground, and a few onlookers who were beginning to come to the doors of nearby businesses. The day after the occurrence the police declared that it was a crime of passion and that the likely murderer was Rubén Gómez Arancibia, a local pimp also known as La Venada, not because he looked like a deer but because he claimed to have *venadeado* many men, which was like saying he had hunted them down, treacherously and at an advantage, as befitted a second- or third-rate pimp. Angélica Ochoa was his wife, and it seems La Venada had heard she was planning to leave him. Most likely, thought Juan de Dios sitting behind the wheel of his car, parked on a dark corner, the murder hadn't been premeditated. At first La Venada probably just wanted to hurt or scare or warn her, thus the bullet in the right thigh, then, upon seeing Angélica's expression of pain or surprise, he felt not only rage but amusement, the darkest expression of humor, which manifested itself in a desire for symmetry, and then he shot her in the left thigh. After that he lost control. The floodgates were open. Juan de Dios rested his head on the steering wheel and tried to cry but couldn't. The attempts of the police to find La Venada were in vain. He had disappeared.

•

At nineteen I began to take lovers. My sex life is legendary all over Mexico, but legends are always false, especially in this country. The first time I slept with a man it was out of curiosity. That's right. Not love or admiration or fear, the way it is for most women. I could have slept with him out of pity, because ultimately I pitied the kid I fucked that first time, but the honest truth is it was curiosity. After two months I left him and went off with someone else, an asshole who thought he was a revolutionary. Mexico has an abundance of these assholes. Hopelessly stupid, arrogant men, who lose their wits when they come across an Esquivel Plata, want to fuck her right away, as if the act of possessing a woman like me were the equivalent of storming the Winter Palace. The Winter Palace! They, who couldn't even cut the grass of the Summer Dacha! Well, I got rid of that one soon enough, too, and now he's a fairly well-known reporter who, every time he gets drunk, likes to talk about how he was my first love. My next lovers were chosen because they were good in bed or because I was bored and they were witty or entertaining or strange, so extravagantly strange that only I found them amusing. For a while, as I'm sure you know, I was someone with a certain stake in the university Leftist movement. I even visited Cuba. Then I got married, had my son. My husband, who was also on the Left, joined the PRI. I began to work in journalism. On Sundays I would go home, I mean to my old house, where my family was slowly rotting away, and I would wander the hallways, the garden, look at photo albums, read the diaries of unknown forebears, which were more like missals than diaries, sit quietly for hours next to the stone well in the courtyard, deep in an expectant silence, smoking one cigarette after another, not reading, not thinking, sometimes even unable to remember anything. The truth is I was bored. I wanted to do things, but I didn't know exactly what. Months later I got divorced. My marriage didn't last two years. Of course, my family tried to dissuade me, they threatened to leave me in the street, saying, and it was completely true, incidentally, that I was the first Esquivel to profane the holy sacrament of marriage, one of my uncles, a ninety-year-old priest, Don Ezequiel Plata, wanted to have a talk with me, an informational chat or two, but then, when they least expected it, I was overtaken by the demon of command or leadership, as it's called now, and I put them in their place, each and every one of them and all together. In short: beneath these walls I became what I am and what I'll be until I die. I told them that the time for pieties and mealymouthed platitudes was over. I told them I wasn't going to stand for any more limp wrists in the family. I told them that the fortune and properties of the Esquivels had only dwindled with the years and that at this pace my son, say, or my grandchildren, if my son turned out like me and not like them, would be left without a penny. I told them I didn't want to hear any muttering while I was talking. I told them that if they didn't agree with what I had to say, they should leave, the door was wide open and Mexico itself was open even wider. Beginning this stormy night, I said (because lightning really was flashing all over the city, and we could see it from the windows), there would be no more alms for the church, which promised us heaven but for more than one hundred years had been bleeding us here on earth. I told them I wouldn't marry again, and I warned them to expect even worse gossip about me. I told them they were dying and I didn't want them to die. They all turned pale and gaped, but no one had a heart attack. When it comes down to it, we Esquivels are tough. A few days later, I remember it as if it were yesterday, I saw Kelly again.

•

That same day Kessler was at Cerro Estrella and he walked around Colonia Estrella and Colonia Hidalgo and explored the area along the Pueblo Azul highway and saw the ranches empty like shoe boxes, solid structures, graceless, functionless, that stood at the bends of the roads that ran into the Pueblo Azul highway, and then he wanted to see the neighborhoods along the border, Colonia México, next to El Adobe, at which point you were back in the United States, the bars and restaurants and hotels of Colonia México and its main street, where there was a permanent thunder of trucks and cars on their way to the border crossing, and then he made his entourage turn south along Avenida General Sepúlveda and the Cananea highway, where they took a detour into Colonia La Vistosa, a place the police almost never ventured, one of the inspectors told him, the one who was driving, and the other one nodded sorrowfully, as if the absence of police in Colonia La Vistosa and Colonia Kino and Colonia Remedios Mayor was a shameful stain that they, zealous young men, bore with sorrow, and why sorrow? well, because impunity pained them, they said, whose impunity? the impunity of the gangs that controlled the drug trade in these godforsaken neighborhoods, something that made Kessler think, since in principle, looking out the car window at the fragmented landscape, it was hard to imagine any of the residents buying drugs, easy to imagine them using, but hard, very hard, to imagine them buying, digging in their pockets to come up with enough change to make a purchase, something easy enough to imagine in the black and Hispanic ghettos up north, neighborhoods that looked placid in comparison to this dismal chaos, but the two inspectors nodded, their strong, young jaws, that's right, there's lots of coke around here and all the filth that comes with it, and then Kessler looked out again at the landscape, fragmented or in the constant process of fragmentation, like a puzzle repeatedly assembled and disassembled, and told the driver to take him to the illegal dump El Chile, the biggest illegal dump in Santa Teresa, bigger than the city dump, where waste was disposed of not only by the maquiladora trucks but also by garbage trucks contracted by the city and some private garbage trucks and pickups, subcontracted or working in areas that public services didn't cover, and then the car was back on paved streets and they seemed to head the way they'd come, returning to Colonia La Vistosa and the highway, but then they turned down a wider street, just as desolate, where even the brush was covered with a thick layer of dust, as if an atomic bomb had dropped nearby and no one had noticed, except the victims, thought Kessler, but they didn't count because they'd lost their minds or were dead, even though they still walked and stared, their eyes and stares straight out of a Western, the stares of Indians or bad guys, of course, in other words lunatics, people living in another dimension, their gazes no longer able to touch us, we're aware of them but they don't touch us, they don't adhere to our skin, they shoot straight through us, thought Kessler as he moved to roll down the window. No, don't open it, said one of the inspectors. Why not? The smell, it smells like death. It stinks. Ten minutes later they reached the dump.

•

So what do you think of all this? one of the reporters asked the lawyer. The lawyer bent her head and then looked at the reporter and at Haas. Chuy Pimentel took her picture: she seemed short of breath, as if her lungs were about to burst, although she wasn't red in the face but deeply pale. This was Mr. Haas's idea, she said, and I don't pretend to have anything to do with it. Then she talked about Mr. Haas's vulnerable position, about the trials that kept being postponed, about the evidence lost, the witnesses coerced, the limbo in which her defendant was living. Anyone in his place would lose his head, she murmured. The reporter from El Independiente looked at her mockingly and with interest. You're romantically involved with Klaus, aren't you? she asked. The reporter was young, still in her twenties, and she was used to dealing with people who spoke bluntly and sometimes harshly. The lawyer was past forty and she seemed tired, as if she had gone several days without sleeping. I'm not going to answer that question, she said. It has no bearing.

•

On November 16, the body of another woman was found on the back lot of the Kusai maquiladora, in Colonia San Bartolomé. According to the initial examination, the victim was between eighteen and twenty-two and the cause of death, according to the forensic report, was asphyxiation due to strangulation. She was completely naked and her clothes were found five yards away, hidden in the bushes. Actually, not all of her clothes were found, just a pair of black leggings and red panties. Two days later, she was identified by her parents as Rosario Marquina, nineteen, who disappeared on November 12 while she was out dancing at

Salón Montana, on Avenida Carranza, not far from Colonia Veracruz, where they lived. It just so happened that both the victim and her parents worked at the Kusai maquiladora. According to the medical examiners, the victim was raped several times before she died.

•

Kelly's reappearance was like a gift. The first night we saw each other we were up till dawn telling each other our life stories. Hers had been mostly a disaster. She tried to be a theater actress in New York, a movie actress in Los Angeles, tried to be a model in Paris, a photographer in London, a translator in Spain. She set out to study modern dance but gave it up the first year. She set out to be a painter and at her first show she realized she had made the worst mistake of her life. She wasn't married, she had no children, no family (her mother had just died after a long illness), no projects. It was the perfect moment to return to Mexico. In Mexico City it would be easy for her to find work. She had friends and she had me, her best friend, don't you doubt that for a second. But she wasn't obliged to turn to anyone (at least anyone I knew) because she soon found work on what you might call the gallery circuit. In other words, she planned openings, designed and printed catalogs, slept with artists, talked to buyers, all of this for four art dealers who in those days were *the* dealers in Mexico City, the phantom figures behind the galleries and the painters, pulling all the strings. By that time I had given up my activities in support of the ineffectual Left, no offense intended, and was nudging closer and closer to certain sectors of the PRI. Once my ex-husband said to me: if you keep writing what you're writing you're going to be ostracized or worse. And I didn't stop to think what he meant by *worse* but kept writing and turning out articles. As it happened, not only was I not ostracized, I received signals that the people on top were increasingly interested in me. It was an incredible time. We were young, we didn't have many responsibilities, we were independent, and we had plenty of money. It was in those days that Kelly decided that the name that suited her best was Kelly. I still called her Luz María, though everybody else called her Kelly, until one day she brought it up. She said: Azucena, I don't like Luz María Rivera, I don't like how it sounds, I prefer Kelly, that's what everybody calls me, will you too? And I said: fine. If you want me to call you Kelly, I will. And from then on I started to call her Kelly. At first I thought it was funny. A typically American affectation. But then I realized that the name suited her. Maybe because Kelly had a hint of Grace Kelly about her. Or because Kelly is a short name, two syllables, whereas Luz María was longer. Or because Luz María had religious associations and Kelly had no associations, or its association was a photograph. Somewhere I must have letters from her signed Kelly R. Parker. I think that was even how she signed her checks. Kelly Rivera Parker. There are people who think our names are our destiny. I don't believe that. But if they are, when Kelly chose that name she somehow took the first step into invisibility, into a nightmare. Do you think our names are our destiny? No, said Sergio, but then I wouldn't. Why not? asked the congresswoman with a sigh, without curiosity. I have an ordinary name, said Sergio, fixing his gaze on his hostess's dark glasses. For a moment, the congresswoman put her hands to her head, as if she had a migraine. Do you want me to tell you something? All names are ordinary, they're all vulgar. Whether your name is Kelly or Luz María, it makes no difference in the end. All names disappear. Children should be taught that in elementary school. But we're afraid to teach them.

●

The El Chile dump made less of an impression on Kessler than the neighborhoods he drove through—always in a police car escorted by another police car—where the snatchings most often took place. Colonia Kino, La Vistosa, Remedios Mayor, and La Preciada to the southeast, Colonia Las Flores, Colonia Plata, Álamos, Lomas del Toro to the west, the neighborhoods near the industrial parks and along both sides of Avenida Rubén Darío and Avenida Carranza like a double spinal cord, and Colonia San Bartolomé, Guadalupe Victoria, Ciudad Nueva, Colonia Las Rositas to the northeast. Walking the streets in broad daylight, he told the press, is frightening. I mean: frightening for a man like me. The reporters, none of whom lived in those neighborhoods, nodded. The officers, however, hid smiles. They thought Kessler sounded naïve. He sounded like a gringo. A good gringo, of course, because bad gringos sounded different, spoke differently. For a woman, said Kessler, it's dangerous to be out at night. Reckless. Most of the streets, except for the main thoroughfares with bus routes, are poorly lit or not lit at all. The police keep out of some neighborhoods, he told the mayor, who squirmed in his seat as if he'd been bitten by a snake and assumed an expression of infinite regret and infinite comprehension. The Sonora state attorney general, the assistant attorney general, the inspectors, said that the problem might be, perhaps was, could conceivably be, you might say, a problem of the city police, headed by Don Pedro Negrete, twin brother of the university rector. And Kessler asked who Pedro Negrete was, whether he had been introduced to him, and the two energetic young officers who had escorted him everywhere and whose English wasn't bad, said no, in fact Mr. Kessler and Don Pedro hadn't crossed paths, and Kessler asked them to describe him, since maybe he'd seen him the first day, at the airport, and the inspectors gave a brief description of the police chief, not very enthusiastically, a poor sketch, as if after having mentioned Pedro Negrete they regretted having done so. And the sketch didn't suggest anything to Kessler. It remained mute. Crafted of hollow words. A tough guy, the real thing, said the energetic young inspectors. A former member of the judicial police. He must look like his brother, the rector, mused Kessler. But the inspectors laughed and offered him a last shot of *bacanora* and said no, he shouldn't get that idea, Don Pedro didn't look anything like Don Pablo, nothing at all like him, the rector was a tall, thin man, practically skin and bones, whereas Don Pedro was on the short side, broad shouldered but short, and carrying a few extra pounds because he liked to eat well and didn't turn up his nose at either *norteña* food or American hamburgers. And then Kessler wondered whether he should talk to the man. Whether he should visit him. And he also wondered why the police chief hadn't come to visit him, when after all he was the guest. So he wrote down the name in his notebook. Pedro Negrete, former *judicial*, municipal police chief, highly regarded, didn't come to welcome me. And then he turned to other matters. He busied himself studying the killings one by one. He busied himself drinking shots of *bacanora*, Christ it was good. He busied himself preparing his two lectures to be given at the university. And one afternoon he went out the back way, as he'd done the day he arrived, and took a taxi to the crafts market, which some called the Indian market and others the *norteño* market, to buy a souvenir for his wife. And just like the first time, unknown to him, an unmarked police car followed the whole way.

•

When the reporters left the Santa Teresa penitentiary, the lawyer laid her head on the table and began to sob very softly, so unobtrusively that she didn't seem like a white woman. Indian women cried like that. Some mestizas. But not white women and certainly not college-educated white women. When she felt Haas's hand on her shoulder, his touch not a caress or even friendly, maybe just a token gesture, the few tears she'd let fall on the tabletop (a table that smelled of disinfectant and, strangely, of cordite) dried and she lifted her head and gazed at the pale face of her defendant, her beloved, her friend, a haughty and at the same time relaxed face (how could anyone be haughty and relaxed at the same time?), observing her with scientific rigor, not from that prison room but from the sulphurous vapors of another planet.

•

On November 25, the body of María Elena Torres, thirty-two, was found in her house on Calle Sucre in Colonia Rubén Darío. Two days earlier, on November 23, there had been a march of women across Santa Teresa, from the university to city hall, protesting the killings of women and the climate of impunity. The march was organized by the WSDP, along with several NGOs, plus the PRD and some student groups. According to the authorities, no more than five thousand people took part. According to the organizers, there had been more than sixty thousand people marching the streets of Santa Teresa. María Elena Torres was among them. Two days later she was knifed in her own home, stabbed through the neck so that she bled to death. María Elena Torres lived alone, since she and her husband had separated not long before. She had no children. According to the neighbors she had fought with her husband that week. When the police showed up at the boardinghouse where her husband lived, he had already fled. The case was assigned to Inspector Luis Villaseñor, recently arrived from Hermosillo, who after a week of interrogations came to the conclusion that the killer wasn't the fugitive husband but María Elena's boyfriend, Augusto or Tito Escobar, whom the victim had been seeing for a month. This Escobar lived in Colonia La Vistosa and had no known occupation. When they went to look for him, he was gone. Three men were found in the house. Upon interrogation, they declared that they had seen Escobar come home one night with bloodstains on his shirt. Inspector Villaseñor had to say that he'd never interrogated three worse-smelling individuals. Shit, he said, was like their second skin. The three men worked picking through the trash at El Chile, the illegal dump. Not only was there no shower where they lived, but no running water either. How the fuck, Inspector Villaseñor asked himself, had Escobar managed to become María Elena's lover? At the end of the interrogation, Villaseñor took the three men out to the courtyard and gave them a beating with a length of hose. Then he made them undress, threw them some soap, and sprayed them down for fifteen minutes. Later, as he was throwing up, it occurred to him that there was a logical connection between the two acts. As if one led to the other. The beating with the piece of green hose. The water gushing from the black hose. Thinking this made him feel better. From the scavengers' combined descriptions a police sketch was made of the suspected killer and police stations around the country were alerted. But the case went nowhere. María Elena's ex-husband and boyfriend simply disappeared and were never heard of again.

•

Of course, one day the work dried up. Dealers and galleries come and go. Mexican painters don't. Mexican painters are always what they are, like mariachis, say, but dealers fly off one day to the Cayman Islands, and galleries close or cut their employees' salaries. Something like that had to happen to Kelly. Afterward she turned to managing fashion shows. The first few months she did well. Fashion is like art but easier. Clothes are cheaper, no one has any illusions when she buys a dress, and at first she did well, she had experience and friends, people trusted her taste even if they didn't trust her, her shows were a success. But she was bad at managing herself and her money, and always, for as long as I can remember, she was strapped for cash. Sometimes the way she lived drove me crazy and we had huge fights. Several times I introduced her to men, single or more often divorced, who would have married her and financed her lifestyle, but in that regard Kelly was irreproachably independent. By this I don't mean she was a saint. There was nothing saintly about her. I know of men (because those same men told me so with tears in their eyes) she took for everything she could get. But never under legal cover. If they gave her what she asked for it was because she, Kelly Rivera Parker, had asked for it, not because they felt an obligation to their wife or the mother of their children (by this point in her life Kelly had decided she would never have children) or their official lover. There was something in her nature that rejected any notion of romantic commitment, even if her perpetual lack of commitment left her in a precarious position, a position that Kelly, meanwhile, never attributed to her own actions but to unforeseen twists of fate. She lived, like Oscar Wilde, above her means. The most incredible thing of all was that this never made her bitter. Well, once or twice it did, once or twice I saw her furious, raging, but these attacks would be over in minutes. Another of her good points, one of mine, too, was loyalty to her friends. Well, this might not be exactly a good point. But Kelly was like that, friends were sacred and she would always stand up for a friend. For example, when I joined the PRI there was a slight domestic upheaval, to call it something. Some reporters who had known me for years stopped talking to me. Others, the worst, still talked, but mostly behind my back. As you're well aware, this is a macho country full of faggots. The history of Mexico wouldn't make sense otherwise. But Kelly was always on my side, never asked me to explain, never reproached me for a thing. The others, as you know, said I had joined the party out of self-interest. Of course I joined out of self-interest. But there are all kinds of self-interest and I was tired of preaching in a vacuum. I wanted power, that I won't deny. I wanted free rein to change some things in this country. I won't deny that either. I wanted to improve public health and the public schools and do my bit to prepare Mexico to enter the twenty-first century. If that's self-interest, so be it. Of course, I didn't achieve much. I brought more hopes than hardheadedness to it, I'm sure, and it wasn't long before I realized my mistake. You think that from the inside you might change some things for the better. First you work from the outside, then you think that if you were inside the real possibilities for change would be greater. You think that inside, at least, you'll have more freedom to act. Not true. There are things that can't be changed from outside or inside. But here comes the funniest part. The really unbelievable part of the story (the sad story of Mexico or Latin America, it makes no difference). The part you can't *believe*. When you make mistakes from inside, the mistakes stop mattering. Mistakes stop being mistakes. Making a mistake, butting your head against the wall, becomes a political virtue, a political tactic, gives you political *presence*, gets you media attention. At the moment of truth— which is every moment, or at least every moment from eight a.m. to five p.m.—it makes just as much sense to be present and to err as to hunker down and wait. You can do nothing, you can fuck things up—it doesn't matter, so long as you're there. Where? Why, there, the place to be. And that was how I went from being well-known to being famous. I was an attractive woman, I didn't mince words, the dinosaurs of the PRI laughed at my jabs, the sharks of the PRI considered me one of their own, the Left wing of the party unanimously cheered my brazenness. I wasn't aware of the half of it. The truth is like a strung-out pimp. Wouldn't you agree?

•

Albert Kessler's first lecture at the University of Santa Teresa was a popular success like few in memory. If you didn't count the two talks given in the same place years ago, by a PRI candidate for president, or another by a president-elect, never before had the fifteen-hundred-seat university hall been completely filled. According to the most conservative estimates, the number of people who came to listen to Kessler far exceeded three thousand. It was a social occasion, because everybody who was anybody in Santa Teresa wanted to meet Kessler, shake the distinguished visitor's hand, or at least see him from up close, and it was also a political occasion, because even the most stubborn opposition groups seemed to relax or assume a more diplomatic and less antagonistic stance than they had adopted thus far, and even the feminists and the groups of relatives of disappeared women and girls settled down to wait for the scientific miracle, the miracle of the human mind set in motion by that modern-day Sherlock Holmes.

•

The story of Haas's denunciation of the Uribes came out in the six papers that had sent their correspondents to the Santa Teresa penitentiary. Before publication, five of the reporters called the police for comment, and the police, like the big national papers, expressly denied there was any credibility to the account. The reporters also called the Uribe residence and talked to family members who said that Antonio and Daniel were traveling or didn't live in Mexico anymore or had moved to Mexico City, where they were studying at one of the universities there. The reporter from *El Independiente de Phoenix*, Mary-Sue Bravo, even managed to get the address of Daniel Uribe's father and tried to interview him, but all her attempts were in vain. Joaquín Uribe always had something to do or wasn't in Santa Teresa or had just stepped out. While Mary-Sue Bravo was in Santa Teresa, she happened to run into the reporter from *La Raza de Green Valley*, who was the only reporter to cover

Haas's press conference who hadn't called the police for their official response, thus risking a lawsuit from the Uribe family and the Sonora state agencies handling the case. Mary-Sue Bravo spotted him through the window of a cheap restaurant in Colonia Madero where the reporter from *La Raza* was eating. He wasn't alone. Sitting with him was a brawny man who Mary-Sue thought looked like a policeman. At first she shrugged it off and kept walking, but a few yards farther on she had a presentiment and turned back. She found the reporter from *La Raza* alone, polishing off some *chilaquiles*. They said hello and she asked if she could sit down. The reporter from *La Raza* said of course. Mary-Sue ordered a Diet Coke and for a while they talked about Haas and the slippery Uribe family. Then the reporter from *La Raza* paid the bill and left, leaving Mary-Sue alone in a restaurant full of men who, like the reporter, looked like farmworkers and wetbacks.

•

On December 1, the body of a young woman between eighteen and twenty-two was found in a dry streambed near Casas Negras. The discovery was made by Santiago Catalán, who was out hunting and noticed that his dogs were behaving strangely as they approached the stream. Suddenly, in the words of the witness, the dogs began to quiver as if they'd scented a tiger or a bear. But since there are no tigers or bears around here I got it in my head that they'd scented the *ghost* of a tiger or a bear. I know my dogs and I know when they start to quiver and whine it's for a reason. Then I got curious, so after I had kicked the dogs to get them to stop acting like a bunch of pussies, I strode toward the stream. When he stepped down into the dry streambed, which was no more than a foot and a half deep, Santiago Catalán didn't see or smell anything and even the dogs seemed to relax. But when he got to the first bend he heard a noise and the dogs started to bark again and quiver. The body was enveloped in a cloud of flies. Santiago Catalán was so startled that he let the dogs go and fired a burst of birdshot in the air. The flies rose for a moment and he could see it was the body of a woman. At the same time, he remembered that the bodies of other young women had been found in the area. For a few seconds he was afraid the killers might still be there and he regretted having fired his gun. Then he stepped very carefully out of the streambed and scanned the scene. Just cholla and biznaga cactuses and in the distance a saguaro or two, and a whole spectrum of yellows, one shading into another. When he got back to his ranch, El Jugador, outside of Casas Negras, he called the police and described the exact place he'd made the discovery. Then he washed his face and changed his shirt, thinking about the dead woman, and before he went out again he ordered one of his employees to accompany him. When the police got to the streambed, Catalán was still carrying his rifle and ammunition belt. The body was faceup, with pants on just one leg, caught around the ankle. There were four stab wounds to the abdomen and three to the chest, as well as marks around the neck. The victim was dark-skinned with shoulder-length hair dyed black. A few yards away they found her shoes: black Converse sneakers with white laces. The rest of her clothes had disappeared. The police combed the streambed for clues but they failed to find anything or didn't know how to go about it. Four months later, purely by chance, an identification was made. She was Úrsula González Rojo, twenty or twenty-one, no family, resident for the last three years of the city of Zacatecas. She had been in Santa Teresa for three days when she was kidnapped and then killed. This last bit of information came from a friend in Zacatecas, whom Ursula had called. She sounded happy, said the friend, because she was about to get work at a maquiladora. Identification was possible thanks to the Converse and a small scar on the victim's back in the shape of a lightning bolt.

•

The truth is like a strung-out pimp in the middle of a storm, said the congresswoman. Then she was quiet for a while, as if listening for thunder in the distance. And then she picked up her glass of tequila, which was full again, and said: every day I had more work, that's the honest truth. Every day I was busy with dinners, trips, meetings, planning sessions that achieved nothing except my utter exhaustion, busy with interviews, busy with denials, television appearances, lovers, men I fucked, why? to keep the legend alive, maybe, or because I liked them, or because it was to my advantage to fuck them, but just once, so they got a taste and nothing else, or maybe simply because I like to fuck when and where I please, and I had no time for anything, my affairs in the hands of my lawyers, the Esquivel Plata fortune—no longer dwindling, I won't lie, but growing—in the hands of my lawyers, my son in the hands of his teachers, and me with more and more work: water problems in the state of Michoacán, highways in Querétaro, interviews, equestrian statues, public sewage systems, all the local shit passing through my hands. Around this time, I suppose I neglected my friends a little. Kelly was the only one I saw. Whenever I had time I visited her at her apartment in Colonia Condesa and we tried to talk. But really, I was so tired when I got there that communication was a problem. She told me things, I remember that clearly, she told me things about her life, more than once she would explain something and then ask me for money and what I did was take out my checkbook and write a check for the amount she needed. Sometimes I would fall asleep while we were talking. Other times we would go out for dinner and have a good time, but my head was almost always elsewhere, mulling over a problem yet to be solved, it was hard for me to follow the thread of the conversation. Kelly never blamed me for it. Each time I was on television, for example, the next day she would send me a bouquet of roses and a note telling me how well I'd done and how proud of me she was. She never stopped sending me a present for my birthday. Thoughtful gestures like that. Of course, as time went by I noticed a few things. The fashion shows Kelly organized were fewer and farther between. The modeling agency she ran was no longer the elegant, bustling place it had once been, but a dark office, almost always closed. Once I stopped by the agency with Kelly and was struck by its state of abandonment. I asked her what was wrong. She looked at me with a smile, one of her carefree smiles, and said that the best Mexican models would rather sign up with American or European agencies. That's where the money was. I wanted to know what had happened to her business. Then Kelly spread her arms and said this is it, encompassing the darkness, the dust, the lowered shades. I had a shiver of foreboding. It had to be foreboding. I'm not the kind of woman who shivers at just anything. I sat down in a chair and tried to reason. The rent for those offices was expensive and it seemed to me it wasn't worth paying all that for a business that was going under. Kelly told me she still put together some shows, and she named places that struck me as picturesque, unlikely or unthinkable spots for high fashion, although I suppose high fashion didn't enter into it, and then she said she was making enough to keep the office open. She also explained that now she organized parties, not in Mexico City but in provincial capitals. What does that mean? I asked. It's very simple, said Kelly, suppose for a moment that you're a rich lady from Aguascalientes. You're going to throw a party.

Suppose you want this party to be a great party. In other words, a party that will impress your friends. What makes a party memorable? There's the buffet, of course, and the waiters, the band, lots of things, but there's one thing in particular that makes all the difference. What is it, do you know? The guests, I said. Exactly, the guests. If you're a lady from Aguascalientes and you've got lots of money and you want a party to remember, then you get in touch with me. I oversee everything. As if it were a fashion show. I take care of the food, the staff, the decorating, the music, but especially, and depending on how much money I have to work with, the guests. If you want the star from your favorite soap opera, you have to talk to me. If you want a talk show host, you have to talk to me. Put it this way: I handle the famous guests. It's all about the money. Bringing a famous talk show host to Aguascalientes maybe isn't possible. But if the party is in Cuernavaca, I might be able to get him to show up. I'm not saying it's easy or cheap, but I can try. Getting a soap star to Aguascalientes *is* possible, though that won't come cheap either. But if the star is in a slump, say, if he hasn't worked in the last year and a half, there's more of a chance he'll make an appearance. And it won't cost too much. What's my job? Well, to convince them to come. First I call them, I take them out for coffee, I sound them out. Then I talk to them about the party. I tell them there's money in it for them if they make a cameo. At this point, there's usually some bargaining. I offer a small sum. They ask for more. We approach an agreement. I reveal the names of the hosts. I say these are important people, provincials, but important. I make them repeat the husband's and wife's names several times. They ask me whether I'll be there. Of course I'll be there. Supervising everything. They ask me about the hotels in Aguascalientes, Tampico, Irapuato. Nice hotels. And anyway, all the houses we're at have lots of guest rooms. Finally we make a deal. The day of the party I show up with two or three or four famous guests and the party is a success. And you make enough doing that? More than enough, said Kelly, the only problem is that there are dry spells, when no one has any interest in fancy parties, and since I don't know how to save, then things are tight. After that we went out, I don't know where, to a party, maybe, or the movies, or dinner with some friends, and that was the last we spoke of the matter. Anyway, I never heard her complain. I imagine sometimes things were all right and other times they weren't. But one night she called and said she had a problem. I thought it had to do with money and I told her she could count on me. But it wasn't money. I've gotten myself into a mess, she said. Are you in debt? I asked her. No, it isn't that, she said. I was in bed, half asleep, and her voice sounded different, it was Kelly's voice, of course, but it sounded strange, as if she were alone, I thought, in her offices, with the lights out, sitting in a chair not knowing what to say or how to begin. I think I've gotten myself into trouble, she said. If it's trouble with the police, I said, tell me where you are and I'll come get you right away. She told me it wasn't that kind of trouble. For God's sake, Kelly, speak plainly or let me sleep, I said. For a few seconds I thought she'd hung up or that she'd left the phone on the chair and walked away. Then I heard her voice, like the voice of a child, saying I don't know, I don't know, I don't know, several times, and I was sure, too, that her *I don't know* was addressed not to me but to herself. I asked then if she was drunk or high. At first she didn't answer, as if she hadn't heard me, then she laughed, she wasn't drunk or high, she promised, maybe she'd had a couple of whiskey sodas, but that was all. Then she apologized for calling so late. She was about to hang up. Wait, I said, there's something wrong, you can't kid me. She laughed again. There's nothing wrong, she said. I'm sorry, we get emotional as we get older, she said, good night. Wait, don't hang up, don't hang up, I said. Something's wrong, don't lie to me. I've never lied to you, she said. There was a silence. Except when we were girls, said Kelly. Oh, really? When I was a girl I lied to everyone, not all the time, of course, but I lied. Not anymore.

•

A week later, as she was leafing idly through *La Raza de Green Valley*, Mary-Sue Bravo learned that the reporter who had covered Haas's vaunted and ultimately disappointing declaration had disappeared. So it said in her own paper, too, which was the only outside source to pick up the news, a vague, local piece of news, so local that the only people who seemed interested were the publishers of *La Raza*. According to the article, Josué Hernández Mercado—that was his name—had disappeared five days before. He had covered the killings of women in Santa Teresa. He was thirty-two. He lived alone, in a small house in Sonoita. He was born in Mexico City, but he had lived in the United States since the age of fifteen, and he was an American citizen. He was the author of two books of poetry, both in Spanish, published by a small company in Hermosillo, probably at his own expense, and two plays, written in Chicano or Spanglish and printed in a Texas magazine, *La Windowa*, which sheltered in its tumultuous breast an unpredictable group of writers in this neolanguage. As a reporter for *La Raza* he had published a long series of pieces on farmworkers in the area, a job he knew from watching his parents and working at it himself. He had pulled himself up by his bootstraps, the profile ended by saying, though it seemed less like a profile, thought Mary-Sue, than an obituary.

•

On December 3, the body of another woman was found dumped in an open field in Colonia Maytorena, near the Pueblo Azul highway. The body was clothed and no external signs of violence were visible. Later the victim was identified as Juana Marín Lozada. According to the medical examiner, the cause of death was a fracture of the cervical vertebrae. Or what amounted to the same thing: her neck had been snapped. The case was handled by Inspector Luis Villaseñor, who, as a first step, interrogated the victim's husband and then arrested him as the prime suspect. Juana Marín lived in Colonia Centeno, in a middle-class neighborhood, and worked at a computer store. According to Villaseñor's report, she was probably killed somewhere indoors, possibly in her own home, and then her body was tossed in the field in Colonia Maytorena. It wasn't clear whether she'd been raped or not, although the vaginal swab revealed that she'd had sexual relations in the previous twenty-four hours. According to Villaseñor's report, Juana Marín was reportedly involved with a computer teacher from an academy near the store where she worked. Another version had it that her lover worked for the University of Santa Teresa television station. Her husband remained in custody for two weeks and then was released for lack of evidence. The case remained unsolved.

•

Three months later, Kelly disappeared in Santa Teresa, Sonora. I hadn't seen her since the phone call. Her partner, an ugly young woman who adored her, called me. After many tries she had managed to reach me. She told me that Kelly should have been back from Santa Teresa two weeks ago and had never shown up. I asked if she'd tried to call her. She said Kelly's cell phone was dead. It rings and rings and rings and no one answers, she said. I could see Kelly having a fling and disappearing for a few days, in fact she'd done it more than once, but I couldn't see her not calling her partner, if only to advise her how to handle business during the time she planned to be away. I asked her if she had gotten in touch with the people Kelly was working for in Santa Teresa. She said yes. According to the man who'd hired her, Kelly had left for the airport the day after the party, to catch the Santa Teresa–Hermosillo flight, and then she had planned to fly from Hermosillo to Mexico City. When did this happen? I asked. Two weeks ago, she said. I imagined her sniffling, clinging to the phone, nicely but plainly dressed, her makeup smudged, and then it occurred to me that this was the first time she had called me, the first time we had talked this way, and I got worried. Have you called the Santa Teresa hospitals or the police? I asked. She said she had and no one knew anything. Kelly left the ranch for the airport and disappeared, simply vanished into thin air, she said in a shrill voice. The ranch? The party was at a ranch, she said. So in other words she had to be driven, someone dropped her off at the airport. No, she said. Kelly had rented a car. And where's the car? They found it in the airport parking lot, she said. So she made it to the airport, I said. But she didn't get on the plane, she said. I asked her for the name of the people who had hired Kelly. She said it was the Salazar Crespo family and she gave me a phone number. I'll see what I can find out, I said. Actually, I figured Kelly would turn up before long. Probably she was off with some man, and the way things were unfolding, almost definitely a married man. I imagined her in Los Angeles or San Francisco, two perfect cities for lovers looking to have a good time and not attract attention. So I tried to be calm and wait. A week later, however, her partner called me again and told me she still had no news of my friend. She talked to me about one or two lost contracts, said she didn't know what to do. In short, what she was trying to say was that she felt alone. I imagined her more disheveled than ever, pacing that dark office, and it made me shudder. I asked her what news she had from Santa Teresa. She had talked to the police, but the police didn't know or wouldn't tell her anything. She's just vanished, she said. That afternoon, from my office, I called a trusted friend who had worked for me for a while, and explained the problem. He said it would be best if we spoke in person and we agreed to meet at El Rostro Pálido, a fashionable coffee shop, I don't know whether it still exists or whether it's closed now, fads in Mexico, as you know, disappear or go underground like people and no one misses them. I explained Kelly's story to my friend. He asked some questions. He wrote down the name Salazar Crespo in a notebook and told me he'd give me a call later that night. When we said goodbye and I got in my car I thought that anybody else would be afraid by now or beginning to be afraid, but all I felt, increasingly, was anger, an immense rage, all the rage the Esquivel Platas had stored up for decades or centuries, now suddenly lodged in my nervous system, and I also thought, with bitterness and remorse, that this anger or rage should have set in sooner, that it shouldn't have been driven, if that's the word, propelled by personal friendship, even though that personal friendship undoubtedly exceeded the very definition of personal friendship, that it should have been triggered by so many other things I'd seen since I was old enough to take notice, but no, no, no, that's fucking life, I said to myself, weeping and gnashing my teeth. That night, around eleven, my friend called and the first thing he asked was whether it was a secure line. Bad sign, bad news, I thought instantly. In any case, I turned ice-cold again. I said the line was utterly secure. Then my friend told me that the name I'd given him (he was careful not to speak it) belonged to a banker who, according to his sources, laundered money for the Santa Teresa cartel, which was like saying the Sonora cartel. All right, I said. Then he said that this banker, in fact, owned not one ranch outside the city but several, although according to his sources there hadn't been a party at any of them on the days my friend was in the area. In other words, there was no public party, he said, with society photos and that kind of thing. Do you understand what I mean? Yes, I said. Then he said that to his knowledge, and this had been confirmed by his sources, the banker in question had good relations with the party. How good? I asked. Exemplary, he whispered. To what degree? I pressed. They go deep, very deep, said my friend. Then we said good night and I sat there thinking. Deep meant reaching far back in time, very far back, in other words millions of years back, in other words to the dinosaurs. Who were the dinosaurs of the PRI? I mused. Several names came to my head. Two of them, I remembered, were from the north or had interests there. I didn't know either one personally. For a while I thought about the friends we might have in common. But I didn't want to get any friend in trouble. The night, I remember as if it were yesterday and not years ago, was pitch-dark, with no stars, no moon, and the house, this house, was silent, no sound even from the night birds in the garden, although I knew my bodyguard was nearby, awake, maybe playing dominoes with the chauffeur, and if I rang a bell one of my maids wouldn't be long in coming. The next day, first thing, after spending a sleepless night, I got on a plane to Hermosillo and then another to Santa Teresa. When the mayor, José Refugio de las Heras, was informed that Congresswoman Esquivel Plata was waiting for him, he dropped everything and was with me in a flash. Probably we had met at some point. In any case, I didn't remember him. When I saw him, smiling and sniveling like a lap dog, I felt like smacking him, but I controlled myself. One of those dogs that stand up on their hind legs, if you know what I mean. I do, said Sergio. Then he asked me if I'd had breakfast. I said no. He had a Sonora breakfast brought in, a typical border breakfast, and as we were waiting, two city workers dressed as waiters busied themselves preparing a table next to the window of his office. From the window you could see the old plaza of Santa Teresa and people going back and forth, on their way to work or idling along. It struck me as a terrible place, despite the light, which glowed golden, very faint in the morning and strong and dense in the afternoon, as if the air, at sunset, was laden with desert dust. Before we ate I told him I was there about Kelly Rivera. I told him she had disappeared and I wanted her to be found. The mayor called his secretary, who began to take notes. What is your friend's name, Congresswoman? Kelly Rivera Parker. And more questions: the day she disappeared, the reason for her stay in Santa Teresa, age, profession, and the secretary took down everything I said, and when I had finished answering the questions, the mayor ordered the secretary to run and get the top boss of the state judicial police, a man by the name of Ortiz Rebolledo, and bring him straight back to city hall. I didn't mention Salazar Crespo. I wanted to see what would happen. The mayor and I had huevos a la ranchera.

•

Mary-Sue Bravo asked her editor to let her investigate the disappearance of the reporter from *La Raza*. Her editor said that Hernández Mercado had probably gone completely out of his head and now he might be wandering one of the state parks, Tubac or Patagonia Lake, eating berries and talking to himself. There aren't any berries in those parks, said Mary-Sue. Well, then, drooling and talking to himself, said her editor, but in the end he let her cover the story. First she was in Green Valley, at the offices of *La Raza*, and she talked to the editor, another man who looked like a farmworker, and to the reporter who had written up Hernández Mercado's disappearance, a boy of eighteen, maybe seventeen, who took his job very seriously. Then she went to Sonoita with the boy. Before they visited the sheriff's office they stopped at Hernández Mercado's house and the boy let her in with a key he said was kept at the offices of *La Raza*, although to Mary-Sue it looked like a picklock. The sheriff told her that Hernández Mercado was probably in California by now. Mary-Sue wanted to know why he thought that. The sheriff said the reporter had lots of debts (for example, he owed six months' rent and the landlord planned to evict him) and with what he made working on the paper he could barely feed himself. The boy, to his chagrin, confirmed what the sheriff had said: *La Raza* didn't pay much because it was a paper for the people, he said. The sheriff laughed. Mary-Sue wanted to know whether Hernández had a car. The sheriff said no, that when Hernández had to leave Sonoita, he took the bus. The sheriff was a friendly man and he went with her to the bus stop and they asked whether anyone had seen Hernández, but the information they got was confused and useless. The day of his disappearance, according to the old man who sold tickets and the few people who rode the bus daily, Hernández might have gotten on the bus and then again he might not have. Before she left Sonoita, Mary-Sue wanted to see the reporter's house once more. Everything was orderly, there were no traces of violence, dust was gathering on the few pieces of furniture. Mary-Sue asked the sheriff whether he had checked Hernández's computer. The sheriff said he hadn't. Mary-Sue turned it on and began to go through the files of the reporter and poet of *La Raza de Green Valley*, more or less at random. She didn't find anything interesting. The beginning of a novel, a mystery by the look of it, written in Spanglish. Published articles. Sketches of the daily life of seasonal laborers and farmworkers on the ranches in southern Arizona. The articles about Haas, almost all sensationalistic. And little else.

•

On December 10, some workers at the ranch La Perdición informed the police of the discovery of some bones at the edge of the ranch, around mile fifteen of the Casas Negras highway. At first they thought it was an animal, but when they found the skull they realized their mistake. According to the forensic report, it was a woman, and the cause of death, due to the time elapsed, remained undetermined. Some three yards from the body a pair of leggings and a pair of tennis shoes were found.

•

In total, I spent two nights in Santa Teresa, staying at the Hotel México, and although everybody claimed to be eager to indulge my slightest whim, we didn't actually get anywhere. Ortiz Rebolledo struck me as a fudge packer. The mayor seemed to play for the other team. The assistant attorney general looked limp in the wrist. They all lied to me or said things that didn't add up. To start with, they assured me that no one had reported Kelly missing, when I knew for a fact her partner had. The name Salazar Crespo never came up. No one talked to me about the killings of women, which were public knowledge by then, let alone connected Kelly's disappearance to those shameful cases. The night before I left I called three local reporters and announced that I was going to hold a press conference at my hotel. There I told Kelly's story, which was later picked up by the national press, and I said that as a politician and feminist, as well as a friend, I would be unflagging in my determination to uncover the truth. Inside I thought: you don't know whom you've crossed, you pack of cowards, you're going to piss your pants. That night, after I had given the press conference, I went up to my room and made phone calls. I talked to two PRI deputies, good friends, who told me I could count on their support. Of course I expected no less. Then I called Kelly's partner and told her I was in Santa Teresa. The poor girl, so ugly, so hopelessly ugly, burst into tears and thanked me, I have no idea what for. Then I called home and asked if anyone had tried to reach me in the last few days. Rosita read me the list of calls. Nothing out of the ordinary. Everything was the same as always. I tried to sleep but couldn't. I spent a while looking out the window at the city's dark buildings, the yards, and the streets, empty except for the occasional new-looking car. I paced the room. I noticed there were two mirrors. One at one end and the other by the door, and they didn't reflect each other. But if you stood in a certain place, you could see one mirror in the other. What you couldn't see was me. Strange, I said to myself, and for a while, as sleep began to overtake me, I made calculations and experimented with positions. That was where I was when five o'clock struck. The more I studied the mirrors, the more uneasy I felt. I realized it was ridiculous to go to bed at that hour. I showered, changed clothes, packed my suit-case. At six I went down to the restaurant for breakfast, but it wasn't open yet. One of the hotel employees went into the kitchen and made me orangeade and a cup of strong coffee. I tried to eat but couldn't. At seven a taxi took me to the airport. As I passed through different parts of the city, I thought about Kelly, about what Kelly had thought as she gazed at the same things I was gazing at now, and then I knew I'd be back. The first thing I did when I got to Mexico City was go to see a friend who had worked for the Mexico City attorney general's office and ask him to recommend a good detective, a man above suspicion, some-one who had what it takes. My friend asked me what the problem was. I told him. He recommended Luis Miguel Loya, who had worked for the federal attorney general. Why did he leave? I asked. Because he could make more in the private sector, said my friend. I couldn't help thinking my friend hadn't told me the whole story, because since when is private business incompatible with public employment in Mexico? But I just thanked him and went to visit Loya. He, of course, had been alerted by my friend and was expecting me. Loya was an odd character. On the short side, but with a boxer's build, not an ounce of fat, although when I met him he must have been fifty. Good manners, well dressed, big of-fice, and he had at least ten people working for him, between the secre-taries and the men with the look of hired thugs. Once again I told Kelly's story, I talked about the banker Salazar Crespo, his dealings with drug traffickers, the attitude of the authorities in Santa Teresa. He didn't ask stupid questions. He didn't take notes. Not even when he asked me for a phone number where he could reach me. I suppose he was recording it all. When I left, when we shook hands, he told me he'd have news of Kelly in three days. He smelled of aftershave and a cologne I didn't rec-ognize. Lavender, with a faint underlying scent of imported coffee, barely noticeable. He walked me to the door. Three days. When he told me that, it didn't seem very long. Making it through those days, waiting for them to go by, was like an eternity. I went halfheartedly back to work. The second day of the wait I was visited by a group of feminists who be-lieved that the stance I'd taken after Kelly's disappearance was admirable and most fitting for a woman. There were three of them, and by what I understood, the group's membership wasn't large. Ordinarily I would have gotten rid of them, but I must have been depressed, not sure ex-actly what to do, and I invited them to sit down and stay for a while. So long as we didn't talk politics, they were even pleasant. And one of them had gone to the same convent school Kelly and I had, although this woman had been two years behind us, and we shared many memories. We drank tea, talked about men, our jobs, the three of them were college professors, two of them divorced. They asked why I had never married again, and I laughed. Because deep inside, I confessed, I'm the biggest feminist of all. On the third day Loya called me at ten at night. He told me he had prepared an initial report and if I wanted he could show it to me right away. I can't wait much longer, I said. Where are you? In my car, said Loya, no need for you to come anywhere, I'm on my way to your house. Loya's report was ten pages long. His work had consisted of compiling a detailed account of Kelly's professional activities. There were names, people from Mexico City, parties in Acapulco, Mazatlán, Oaxaca. According to Loya, most of Kelly's jobs could simply be considered veiled prostitution. High-level prostitution. Her models were whores, the parties she organized were for men only, even her percentage of the take was that of a high-class madam. I told him I couldn't believe it. I flung the papers in his face. Loya bent down and picked them up and handed them back to me. Read it all, he said. I kept reading. Garbage, complete garbage. Until the name Salazar Crespo appeared. According to Loya, Kelly had worked for Salazar Crespo before, four times in all. I also read that between 1990 and 1994 Kelly had flown at least ten times to Hermosillo, and of those ten times, on seven occasions she had traveled on to Santa Teresa. The meetings with Salazar Crespo were classified under the heading "party planning." To judge by the flights from Hermosillo to Mexico City, she never spent more than two nights in Santa Teresa. The number of models she took with her to the city varied. At first, in '90 and '91, she might travel with four or five. Then there would be only two, and she made the final trips alone. Maybe those times she really was planning parties. Another name appeared alongside that of Salazar Crespo. Conrado Padilla, a Sonora businessman with interests in a few maquiladoras, a few transport companies, and the Santa Teresa slaughterhouse. Kelly had worked for this Conrado Padilla on three occasions, according to Loya. I asked who Conrado Padilla was. Loya shrugged his shoulders and said he was a man with lots of money, in other words somebody exposed to every kind of threat, every kind of unpleasantness. I asked Loya if he'd gone to Santa Teresa. No, he said. I asked if he'd sent someone there. No, he said. I told him to go to Santa Teresa, I wanted to see him there, at the heart of things, and he should keep investigating. For a while he seemed to consider my proposal, or rather search for the right words for what he had to say. Then he said he didn't want to see me waste my money or my time. Do you mean you think Kelly is dead? I shouted. More or less, he said without losing his composure in the slightest. What do you mean, more or less? I shouted. For fuck's sake, you're either dead or you're not! In Mexico a person can be more or less dead, he answered very seriously. I stared at him, wanting to hit him. What a cold, detached man he was. No, I said, almost hissing, no one can be more or less dead, in Mexico or anywhere else in the world. Stop talking like a tour guide. Either my friend is alive, which means I want you to find her, or my friend is dead, which means I want the people who killed her. Loya smiled. What are you laughing at? I asked him. The tour guide part was funny, he said. I'm sick of Mexicans who talk and act as if this is all *Pedro Páramo*, I said. Maybe it is, said Loya. No, it isn't, I can assure you, I said. For a while Loya was silent, sitting with his legs crossed, very dignified, thinking about what I'd just said. It might take me months, even years, he said at last. And also, he added, I don't think they'll let me do my job. Who? Your own people, Congresswoman, your own party colleagues. I'll be behind you every step of the way and I'll back you up, I said to him. I think you overestimate yourself, said Loya. Fuck it all, of course I overestimate myself, if I didn't I wouldn't be where I am, I said. Loya was silent again. For a moment I thought he'd fallen asleep, but his eyes were wide open. If you won't do it, I'll find someone else, I said, not looking at him. After a while he got up. I went with him to the door. Are you going to take the job? I'll see what I can do, but I'm not promising anything, he said, and he disappeared down the path to the street, where my bodyguard and my chauffeur were trading puns like a couple of zombies.

●

One night Mary-Sue Bravo dreamed that a woman was sitting at the foot of her bed. She felt the weight of a body on the mattress, but when she stretched her legs she didn't touch anything. That night, before she went to bed, she had read a few online news stories about the Uribes. In one of them, by a reporter from a well-known Mexico City daily, it said that Antonio Uribe really had disappeared. His cousin Daniel Uribe was in Tucson, it seemed. The reporter had talked to him on the phone. According to Daniel Uribe, all the information provided by Haas was a pack of lies, easily disproved. Regarding the whereabouts of Antonio, however, he gave no hint or the hints the reporter got out of him were ambiguous, imprecise, evasive. When Mary-Sue woke up she didn't entirely lose the feeling that there was another woman in the room until she got out of bed and went to the kitchen to drink a glass of water. The next day she called Haas's lawyer. She didn't know exactly what she wanted to ask her, what she wanted to be told, but the need to hear her voice overrode any logical imperative. After identifying herself, she asked the lawyer how her client was. Isabel Santolaya said he was the same as he'd been the last few months. Mary-Sue asked if she'd read Daniel Uribe's statements. The lawyer said she had. I'm going to try to interview him, said Mary-Sue. Can you think of anything I should ask? No, I can't, said the lawyer. To Mary-Sue it seemed as if the lawyer were talking like someone in a trance. Then, for no reason, she asked the lawyer about herself. My life isn't important, said the lawyer. She said it haughtily, as if addressing an impertinent teenager.

·

On December 15, Esther Perea Peña, twenty-four, was shot to death at the dance hall Los Lobos. The victim was sitting at a table with three friends. At one of the next tables, a good-looking man in a black suit and white shirt pulled out a gun and started to fool around with it. It was a Smith & Wesson Model 5906 with a fifteen-round clip. According to some witnesses the same man had danced with Esther and one of her friends, and everything had been relaxed and friendly. The man's two friends, according to the version of one of the witnesses, warned him to put away the gun. The man ignored them. Apparently he wanted to impress someone, presumably the victim herself or the victim's friend, the one he'd danced with before. According to other witnesses, the man claimed to be a *judicial* assigned to the narcotics squad. He looked like a *judicial*. He was tall and strong, and he had a good haircut. At a certain moment, as he was handling the gun, it went off and Esther was fatally wounded. By the time the ambulance arrived, the girl was dead and the shooter had disappeared. Inspector Ortiz Rebolledo took personal charge of the case and the next morning he was able to inform the press that the police had found the body of a man (whose clothing and physical description matched those of Esther's killer) on the old Pemex sports fields, with a Smith & Wesson just like the one Esther's killer had been carrying and a bullet in his right temple. His name was Francisco López Ríos and he had a long record of auto theft. But he wasn't a natural killer and shooting someone, even if it was accidental, must have upset him considerably. The man committed suicide, said Ortiz Rebolledo. Case closed. Later Lalo Cura would comment to Epifanio that it was strange there hadn't been a lineup to identify the body. And it was strange, too, that the killer's companions hadn't come forward. And that the Smith & Wesson, once it was locked away in the police archives, had disappeared. And strangest of all was that a car thief should commit suicide. Did you know this Francisco López Ríos? Epifanio asked him. I saw him once and I wouldn't say he was handsome, said Lalo Cura. No, he looked more like a rat. All very strange, said Epifanio.

•

For two years I had Loya on the case. Over those two years I had time to craft an image that little by little began filtering into the media: of a woman sensitive to violence, a woman who represented change in the heart of the party, not just generational change but a change in attitude, with a view of Mexican reality that was open-minded, not dogmatic. Really, I was just burning with rage at Kelly's disappearance, at the macabre joke made at her expense. I cared less and less about the opinion of what we call the public, my constituents, whom I didn't truly see or if I did see, accidentally or sporadically, I despised. As I learned about other cases, however, as I heard other voices, my rage began to assume what you might call mass stature, my rage became collective or the expression of something collective, my rage, when it allowed itself to show, saw itself as the instrument of vengeance of thousands of victims. Honestly, I think I was losing my mind. Those voices I heard (voices, never faces or shapes) came from the desert. In the desert, I roamed with a knife in my hand. My face was reflected in the blade. I had white hair and sunken cheeks covered with tiny scars. Each scar was a little story that I tried and failed to recall. I ended up taking pills for my nerves. Every three months I saw Loya. At his express wish I never visited him at his office. Sometimes he would call me or I would call him, on a secure line, but we never said much when we talked on the phone, because nothing, Loya would say, is one hundred percent secure. Thanks to Loya's reports I began to create a map or piece together the puzzle of the place where Kelly had disappeared. From his reports I learned that the parties thrown by the banker Salazar Crespo were in fact orgies and that Kelly's job had presumably been to put these orgies together. Loya had talked to a model who worked for Kelly for a few months and now lived in San Diego. The model told him that Salazar Crespo's parties would be held at either of the two ranches he owned, showplace properties, pieces of land that the rich bought and neither cultivated nor used to keep livestock. Just expanses of land, a sprawling house in the middle, a big living room and lots of bedrooms, sometimes but not always a pool, they aren't comfortable places, really, there's no feminine touch. In the north they call them *narcorranchos*, because lots of drug traffickers own similar estates, less like ranches than garrisons in the middle of the desert, some even with watchtowers where they post their best marksmen. Sometimes these *narcorranchos* sit empty for long stretches of time. One employee might be left there, without keys to the main house, with orders to do little, to wander the barren, stony grounds, to watch so that packs of wild dogs don't take up residence. All these poor men are given is a cell phone and some vague instructions that they gradually forget. According to Loya, it isn't unusual for one of them to die with no one the wiser, or simply to disappear, drawn by the simurgh, the mythical giant flying creature of the desert. Then, all at once, the *narcorrancho* stirs to life. First to arrive are some of the peons, say three or four, in a Combi, and they spend a day getting the big house ready. Then come the bodyguards, the muscle, in their black Suburbans or Spirits or Peregrinos, and the first thing they do when they show up, besides strut around, is set a security perimeter. Finally the boss and his right-hand men make their appearance. Armored Mercedes-Benzes or Porsches snaking through the desert. At night the lights never go out. You see all kinds of cars, even Lincoln Continentals and vintage Cadillacs, ferrying people to and from the ranch. Trackers loaded with meat, baked goods in Chevy Astras. And music and shouting all night long. These were the parties, as Loya told me, that Kelly would help to plan on her trips north. According to Loya, at first Kelly took along models who wanted to make good money fast. The girl who lived in San Diego had told him there were never more than three. At the parties there were other women, women Kelly in theory didn't know, young girls, younger than the models, girls Kelly dressed appropriately for the parties. Little whores from Santa Teresa, I guess. What happened at night? The usual. The men would get drunk or high, watch videotaped soccer or baseball games, play cards, go out to the courtyard for target shooting, talk business. No one ever shot a porn film, or at least that's what the girl from San Diego told Loya. Sometimes, in a bedroom, the guests would watch porn, the model had walked in once by mistake and she saw the familiar sight, stony-faced men, their profiles lit by the glow of the screen. It's always that way. I mean: stony-faced, as if watching a film where people fuck turns the viewers into statues. But no one, according to the model, ever shot a film like that at the *narcorranchos*. Sometimes, a few guests would sing *rancheras* and *corridos*. Sometimes, those same guests would go out into the courtyard and parade around the ranch, singing at the top of their lungs. And once they went out naked, maybe one or two covered their private parts, wore a thong or leopard- or tiger-print briefs, braving the cold, which was intense at four in the morning, singing and laughing, from one caper to the next, like Satan's helpers. Those aren't my words. They're the words of the model who lived in San Diego, spoken to Loya. But no porn films, nothing like that. Then Kelly stopped relying on the models and didn't call them anymore. According to Loya, the decision was probably Kelly's, because the models' rates were high and the little whores of Santa Teresa didn't charge much and Kelly's finances weren't in very good shape. She made her first trips for Salazar Crespo, but through him she met important people in the area and it was possible that she had also organized parties for Sigfrido Catalán, who owned a fleet of garbage trucks and was said to have an exclusive contract with most of the maquiladoras in Santa Teresa, and for Conrado Padilla, a businessman with interests in Sonora, Sinaloa, and Jalisco. Salazar Crespo, Sigfrido Catalán, and Padilla, according to Loya, all had connections to the Santa Teresa cartel, which meant Estanislao Campuzano, who occasionally, though not often, in truth, had attended these parties. Evidence, or what a civilized jury would consider evidence, was lacking, but during the time Loya worked for me he collected a vast number of testimonies, drunken conversations or talk in brothels, with people saying Campuzano didn't come, or that sometimes he did. Whatever the case, there were plenty of *narcos* at Kelly's orgies, especially two of them, considered Campuzano's lieutenants, one by the name of Muñoz Otero, Sergio Muñoz Otero, the boss of the Nogales *narcos*, and Fabio Izquierdo, who for a while was the boss of the Hermosillo *narcos* and later worked creating routes for the transport of drugs from Sinaloa to

Santa Teresa or from Oaxaca or Michoacán or even Tamaulipas, which was the territory of the Ciudad Juárez cartel. There was no question, Loya believed, that Muñoz Otero and Fabio Izquierdo were present at some of Kelly's parties. So there was Kelly, without models, working with girls of humble origin or simply with whores, at *narcorranchos* in the middle of nowhere, and at her parties we have a banker, Salazar Crespo, a businessman, Catalán, a millionaire, Padilla, and, if not Campuzano, at least two of his most notorious men, Fabio Izquierdo and Muñoz Otero, as well as other personages from the worlds of society, crime, and politics. A collection of worthies. And one morning or night my friend vanishes into thin air.

•

For a few days, from the offices of *El Independiente de Phoenix*, Mary-Sue tried to get in touch with the reporter from Mexico City who had interviewed Daniel Uribe. He was almost never at the paper and the people she talked to refused to give her his cell phone number. When she was finally able to speak to him, the reporter, who sounded like a drunk and an asshole, thought Mary-Sue, or at least arrogant, wouldn't give her Daniel Uribe's phone number, claiming he had to protect the privacy of his sources. Mary-Sue unwisely reminded him that they were colleagues, they both worked for the press, and the reporter from Mexico City told her they could have been lovers for all he cared. There was no news about Josué Hernández Mercado, the vanished reporter from *La Raza*. One night Mary-Sue searched through her file on the Haas case until she came up with the story Hernández Mercado had written after the poorly attended press conference at the Santa Teresa penitentiary. Hernández Mercado's style wavered between sensationalism and flatness. The story was riddled with clichés, inaccuracies, sweeping statements, exaggerations, and flagrant lies. Sometimes Hernández Mercado painted Haas as the scapegoat of a conspiracy of rich Sonorans and sometimes Haas appeared as an avenging angel or a detective locked in a cell but by no means defeated, gradually cornering his tormentors solely by dint of intelligence. At two in the morning, as she drank her last cup of coffee before she left the paper, Mary-Sue thought that no one with half a brain would have bothered to kill a person and hide the body over trash like that. But then what had happened to Hernández Mercado? Her editor, who was also working late, supplied various possi-

629

ble answers. He got fed up and ran off. He flipped out and ran off. He ran off, period. A week later the boy reporter who had traveled with her to Sonoita called. He wanted to know what kind of progress Mary-Sue had made on the story she planned to write about Hernández Mercado. I'm not going to write anything, she told him. The boy reporter wanted to know why. Because there's nothing to write about, said Mary-Sue. Hernández is probably living and working in California. I don't think so, said the boy reporter. It sounded to Mary-Sue as if he'd shouted. In the background she heard the noise of a truck or several trucks, as if he were making the call from the yard of a trucking company. Why won't you believe it? she asked. Because I've been to his house, said the boy. So have I, and I didn't see anything to make me think he'd been taken by force. He left because he wanted to. No, she heard the boy say. If he'd left of his own accord, he would have brought his books. Books are heavy, said Mary-Sue, and anyway you can always buy new ones. There are more bookstores in California than in Sonoita, she said; intending it as a joke, but almost as she spoke she realized it wasn't funny. No, I'm not talking about those books, I'm talking about *his* books, said the boy. What do you mean *his books*? asked Mary-Sue. The ones he wrote and published. He wouldn't have left those behind even if the world was coming to an end. For a while Mary-Sue tried to remember Hernández Mercado's house. There were books in the living room, and some in the bedroom too. All together there couldn't have been more than one hundred volumes. It wasn't a big collection, but for someone like the farmworker-reporter, maybe it was more than enough. It hadn't occurred to her to think that among them might be the books Hernández Mercado had written. And you think he wouldn't have left without them? No chance, said the boy, they were like his children. Mary-Sue thought that the books Hernández Mercado had written must not have weighed much and there was no way he could have bought new copies in California.

•

On December 19, on some land near Colonia Kino, a few miles from the Gavilanes del Norte farming cooperative, the remains of a woman were found in a plastic bag. According to the police statement, she was another victim of the Bisontes gang. According to the medical examiners, the victim was between fifteen and sixteen years old, five foot two or five foot three, and it had been approximately a year since she'd been killed.

In the bag were a pair of cheap navy blue pants, like the kind women wore to work at the maquiladoras, a shirt, and a black plastic belt with a big plastic buckle, of the decorative variety. The case was handled by Inspector Marcos Arana, recently transferred from Hermosillo, where he was attached to the narcotics squad, but on the first day Inspector Ángel Fernández and Inspector Juan de Dios Martínez showed up at the scene. The latter, when told to leave the case to Arana because they wanted to break him in, took a stroll around the area until he came to the gates of the Gavilanes del Norte farming cooperative. The main house still had its roof and windows, but the other buildings looked as if they'd been flattened by a hurricane. For a while, Juan de Dios wandered around the ghost farm, to see if he could at least find a farmworker or a child or a dog, if nothing else, but even the dogs were gone.

•

What is it I want you to do? asked the congresswoman. I want you to write about this, keep writing about this. I've read your articles. They're good, but too often you pull your punches. I want you to strike hard, strike human flesh, unassailable flesh, not shadows. I want you to go to Santa Teresa and sniff around. I want you to sink in your teeth. At first I didn't know much about Santa Teresa. I had some general ideas, like anybody, but I think it was after my fourth visit that I began to understand the city and the desert. Now I can't get them out of my head. I know everybody's names, or almost everybody's. I know of some illicit activities. But I can't go to the Mexican police. At the attorney general's office they would think I was crazy. And I can't hand over my information to the gringo police. Out of patriotism, ultimately, because no matter whom it disturbs (myself first of all), I'm a Mexican. And also a Mexican congresswoman. We'll fight it out among ourselves, as always, or we'll go down together. There are people I don't want to hurt, but I know I'll hurt them. I accept it, because times are changing and the PRI has to change too. So all I have left is the press. Maybe because of my years as a reporter, I've kept my faith in some of you. Also, the system may be full of flaws, but at least we have freedom of expression, which is something the PRI has almost always respected. I said *almost* always, don't look so incredulous, said the congresswoman. Here people publish what they want with no trouble. Anyway, we aren't going to argue about this, are we? You published a so-called political novel in which all you do is toss around unfounded accusations, and nothing happened to you, did it? You weren't censored or taken to court. It was my first novel, said Sergio, and it's very bad. Did you read it? I read it, said the congresswoman, I've read everything you've written. It's very bad, said Sergio, and then he said: books aren't censored or read here, but the press is another story. Newspapers are read. At least the headlines. And after a silence: what happened to Loya? Loya died, said the congresswoman. No, he wasn't killed and he didn't disappear. He just died. He had cancer and no one knew it. He was a private man. Now someone else runs his agency, maybe it doesn't even exist anymore, maybe it's a corporate consulting firm now. I have no idea. Before he died, Loya gave me all his files on Kelly. What he couldn't turn over he destroyed. I sensed something was wrong, but he wouldn't tell me anything. He went off to the United States, to a clinic in Seattle, where he held out for three months and then he died. He was a strange man. I visited him only once, he lived alone in an apartment in Colonia Nápoles. From the outside it was an ordinary middle-class place, but inside it was something else, I don't know how to describe it, like a mirror image of Loya or a self-portrait, but an unfinished self-portrait. He had lots of records and art books. The doors were armored. He had a photograph of an older woman in a gold frame, a melodramatic touch. The kitchen was completely redone and it was big and full of professional kitchen gadgets. When he found out he didn't have long to live he called me from Seattle and in his own way he said goodbye. I remember I asked whether he was afraid. I don't know why I asked him that. He answered with another question. He asked whether I was afraid. No, I'm not afraid, I said. Then neither am I, he said. Now I want you to use everything that Loya and I gathered between us and stir up the hive. Naturally, you won't be alone. I'll be with you always, though you can't see me, helping you every step of the way.

•

The last case of 1997 was fairly similar to the second to last, except that the bag containing the body wasn't found on the western edge of the city but on the eastern edge, by the dirt road that runs along the border and then forks and vanishes when it reaches the first mountains and steep passes. The victim, according to the medical examiners, had been dead for a long time. She was about eighteen, five foot two and a half or three. She was naked, but a pair of good-quality leather high heels were found in the bag, which led the police to think she might be a whore. Some white thong panties were also found. Both this case and the previous case were closed after three days of generally halfhearted investigations. The Christmas holidays in Santa Teresa were celebrated in the usual fashion. There were *posadas*, piñatas were smashed, tequila and beer were drunk. Even on the poorest streets people could be heard laughing. Some of these streets were completely dark, like black holes, and the laughter that came from who knows where was the only sign, the only beacon that kept residents and strangers from getting lost.

THE PART ABOUT ARCHIMBOLDI

His mother was blind in one eye. She had blond hair and was blind in one eye. Her good eye was sky blue and placid, which made her seem slow but sweet natured, truly good. His father was lame. He had lost his leg in the war and spent a month in a military hospital near Düren, thinking he was done for and watching as the patients who could move (he couldn't!) stole cigarettes from the others. When they tried to steal his cigarettes, though, he grabbed the thief by the neck, a freckled boy with broad cheekbones and broad hips, and said: halt! a soldier's tobacco is sacred! Then the freckled boy went away and night fell and he had the sense that someone was watching him.

In the next bed there was a mummy. He had black eyes like two deep wells.

"Do you want a smoke?" the man with one leg asked.

The mummy didn't answer.

"It's good to have a smoke," said the man with one leg, and he lit a cigarette and tried to find the mummy's mouth among the bandages.

The mummy shuddered. Maybe he doesn't smoke, thought the man, and he took the cigarette away. The moon illuminated the end of the cigarette, which was stained with a kind of white mold. Then he put it back between the mummy's lips, saying: smoke, smoke, forget all about it. The mummy's eyes remained fixed on him, maybe, he thought, it's a comrade from the battalion and he's recognized me. But why doesn't he say anything? Maybe he can't talk, he thought. Suddenly, smoke began to filter out between the bandages. He's boiling, he thought, boiling, boiling.

Smoke came out of the mummy's ears, his throat, his forehead, his eyes, which remained fixed on the man with one leg, until the man plucked the cigarette from the mummy's lips and blew, and kept blowing for a while on the mummy's bandaged head until the smoke had disappeared. Then he stubbed the cigarette out on the floor and fell asleep.

When he woke, the mummy was no longer there. Where's the mummy? he asked. He died this morning, said someone from a different bed. Then he lit a cigarette and settled down to wait for breakfast. When he was released he went stumping toward the city of Düren. There he boarded a train that brought him to another city.

In this city he waited twenty-four hours in the station, eating army soup. The man distributing the soup was a one-legged sergeant like himself. They talked for a while, as the sergeant ladled soup into the soldiers' tin plates and he ate, sitting on a nearby wooden bench like a carpenter's. According to the sergeant, everything was about to change. The war was coming to an end and a new era was about to begin. He answered, as he ate, that nothing would ever change. Not even the two of them had changed, and each had lost a leg.

Whenever he spoke, the sergeant laughed. If the sergeant said white, he said black. If the sergeant said day, he said night. And the sergeant laughed at his answers and asked whether the soup needed salt, whether it was very bland. Then the man got tired of waiting for a train that seemed as if it would never come, and he set off again on foot.

He roamed the countryside for three weeks, eating stale bread and stealing fruit and chickens from farmyards. During his wanderings, Germany surrendered. When he was told, he said: good. One afternoon he came to his town and knocked at the door of his house. His mother came to the door and upon seeing him in such a state she didn't recognize him. Then everyone hugged him and fed him. He asked if the girl who was blind in one eye had married. They said no. That night he went to see her, without changing clothes or washing, despite his mother's pleas that he at least shave. When the girl saw him standing at the door to her house, she recognized him instantly. The one-legged man saw her too, looking out the window, and he raised a hand in a formal salute, even a stiff salute, though it could also have been interpreted as a way of saying such is life. From that moment on he told whoever would listen that in his town everyone was blind and the one-eyed girl was a queen.

•

In 1920 Hans Reiter was born. He seemed less like a child than like a strand of seaweed. Canetti, and Borges, too, I think—two very different men—said that just as the sea was the symbol or mirror of the English, the forest was the metaphor the Germans inhabited. Hans Reiter defied this rule from the moment he was born. He didn't like the earth, much less forests. He didn't like the sea either, or what ordinary mortals call the sea, which is really only the surface of the sea, waves kicked up by the wind that have gradually become the metaphor for defeat and madness. What he liked was the seabed, that other earth, with its plains that weren't plains and valleys that weren't valleys and cliffs that weren't cliffs.

•

When his one-eyed mother bathed him in a washtub, the child Hans Reiter always slipped from her soapy hands and sank to the bottom, with his eyes open, and if her hands hadn't lifted him back up to the surface he would have stayed there, contemplating the black wood and the black water where little particles of his own filth floated, tiny bits of skin that traveled like submarines toward an inlet the size of an eye, a calm, dark cove, although there was no calm, and all that existed was movement, which is the mask of many things, calm among them.

•

Once, his one-legged father, who sometimes watched as his one-eyed mother bathed him, told her not to lift him out, to see what he would do. From the bottom of the washtub Hans Reiter's blue eyes gazed up at his mother's blue eye, and then he turned on his side and remained very still, watching the fragments of his body drift away in all directions, like space probes launched at random across the universe. When he ran out of breath he stopped watching the tiny particles as they were lost in the distance and set out after them. He turned red and understood that he was passing through a region very like hell. But he didn't open his mouth or make the slightest attempt to come up, although his head was only four inches below the surface and the seas of oxygen. Finally his mother's arms lifted him out and he began to cry. His father, wrapped in an old military cloak, looked down at the floor and spat into the center of the hearth.

•

At three Hans Reiter was taller than all the other three-year-olds in his town. He was also taller than any four-year-old, and not all the five-year-olds were taller than he was. At first he was unsteady on his feet and the town doctor said it was because of his height and advised that he be given more milk to strengthen his bones. But the doctor was wrong. Hans Reiter was unsteady on his feet because he moved across the surface of the earth like a novice diver along the seafloor. He actually lived and ate and slept and played at the bottom of the sea. Milk wasn't a problem. His mother kept three cows and hens and the boy was given plenty to eat.

His one-legged father sometimes watched him walking in the fields and wondered whether anyone in his family had ever been so tall. The brother of a great-great-grandfather or great-grandfather, it was said, had served under Frederick the Great in a regiment composed only of men over five foot ten or six feet. This select regiment or battalion had suffered many losses, because the soldiers were such easy targets.

At some point, thought the one-legged man as he watched his son move clumsily along the edges of the neighboring gardens, the Prussian regiment found itself face-to-face with a similar Russian regiment, peasants five foot ten or six feet tall, clad in the green jackets of the Russian Imperial Guard, and they clashed and the carnage was terrible. Even when both armies had retreated, the two regiments of giants remained locked in hand-to-hand combat that ceased only when the top generals sent unconditional orders to retreat to new positions.

Before Hans Reiter's father went off to war, he was five foot five. When he came back, perhaps because he was missing a leg, he was only five foot four. A regiment of giants is madness, he thought. Hans's one-eyed mother was five foot two and she believed that men could never be too tall.

•

At six Hans Reiter was taller than all the other six-year-olds, taller than all the seven-year-olds, taller than all the eight-year-olds, taller than all the nine-year-olds, and taller than half the ten-year-olds. At age six, too, he stole his first book. The book was called *Animals and Plants of the European Coastal Region*. He hid it under his bed although no one at school ever noticed it was missing. Around the same time he began to dive. This was in 1926. He had been swimming since he was four and he would put his head underwater and open his eyes and then his mother scolded him because his eyes were red all day and she was afraid that when people saw him they would think he was always crying. But until he was six, he didn't learn to dive. He would duck underwater, swim down a few feet, and open his eyes and look around. That much he did. But he didn't dive. At six he decided that a few feet wasn't enough and he plunged toward the bottom of the sea.

The book *Animals and Plants of the European Coastal Region* was stamped on his brain, and while he dove he would slowly page through it. This was how he discovered *Laminaria digitata*, a giant seaweed with a sturdy stem and broad leaves, as the book said, shaped like a fan with numerous sections of strands that really did look like fingers. *Laminaria digitata* is native to cold waters like the Baltic, the North Sea, and the Atlantic. It's found in large masses, at low tide, and off rocky shores. The tide often uncovers forests of this seaweed. When Hans Reiter saw a seaweed forest for the first time he was so moved that he began to cry underwater. It may be hard to believe that a human being could cry while diving with his eyes open, but let us not forget that Hans was only six at the time and in a sense he was a singular child.

Laminaria digitata is light brown and resembles *Laminaria hyperborea*, which has a rougher stalk, and *Saccorhiza polyschides*, which has a stem with bulbous protuberances. The latter two, however, live in deep waters, and although sometimes, on summer afternoons, Hans Reiter would swim far from the beach or the rocks where he had left his clothes and then dive down, he could never spot them, only fantasize that he'd seen them there in the depths, a still and silent forest.

•

Around this time he began to draw all kinds of seaweed in a notebook. He drew *Chorda filum*, made up of thin strands that could nevertheless grow to be twenty-five feet long. It had no branches and looked delicate but was really very strong. It grew below the low-tide mark. He also drew *Leathesia difformis*, rounded bulbs of olive brown that grew on rocks and other seaweed. A strange-looking plant. He never saw it, but he often dreamed about it. He drew *Ascophyllum nodosum*, a dun-colored, irregularly patterned seaweed with oval blisters along its branches. There were male and female varieties of *Ascophyllum nodosum*, which produced fruitlike growths akin to raisins. In the male, they were yellow. In the female, they were a greenish color. He drew *Laminaria saccharina*, a single long frond in the shape of a belt. When it was dry, crystals of a sweet substance called mannitol were visible on its surface. It grew on rocky coasts, clinging to various solid objects, though it was often washed out to sea. He drew *Padina pavonia*, an uncommon seaweed, small and fan shaped. It was a warm-water species found from the southern coasts of Great Britain to the Mediterranean. There were no related species. He drew *Sargassum vulgare*, a seaweed that lived on the stony beaches of the Mediterranean and possessed small pedunculated reproductive organs among its fronds. It was found in shallow water as well as in the deepest seas. He drew *Porphyra umbilicalis,* a particularly lovely seaweed, nearly eight inches long and reddish purple in color. It grew in the Mediterranean, the Atlantic, the English Channel, and the North Sea. There were various species of *Porphyra* and all of them were edible. The Welsh, in particular, were fond of them.

•

"The Welsh are swine," said the one-legged man in reply to a question from his son. "Absolute swine. The English are swine, too, but not as bad as the Welsh. Though really they're the same, but they make an effort not to seem it, and since they know how to pretend, they succeed. The Scots are bigger swine than the English and only a little better than the Welsh. The French are as bad as the Scots. The Italians are little swine. Little swine ready and willing to gobble up their own swine mother. The same can be said of the Austrians: swine, swine, swine. Never trust a Hungarian. Never trust a Bohemian. They'll lick your hand while they devour your little finger. Never trust a Jew: he'll eat your thumb and leave your hand covered in slobber. The Bavarians are also swine. When you talk to a Bavarian, son, make sure you keep your belt fastened tight. Better not to talk to Rhinelanders at all: before the cock crows they'll try to saw off your leg. The Poles look like chickens, but pluck four feathers and you'll see they've got the skin of swine. Same with the Russians. They look like starving dogs but they're really starving swine, swine that'll eat anyone, without a second thought, without the slightest remorse. The Serbs are the same as the Russians, but miniature. They're like swine disguised as Chihuahuas. Chihuahuas are tiny dogs, the size of a sparrow, that live in the north of Mexico and are seen in some American movies. Americans are swine, of course. And Canadians are big ruthless swine, although the worst swine from Canada are the French-Canadians, just as the worst swine from America are the Irish-American swine. The Turks are no better. They're sodomite swine, like the Saxons and the Westphalians. All I can say about the Greeks is that they're the same as the Turks: bald, sodomitic swine. The only people who aren't swine are the Prussians. But Prussia no longer exists. Where is Prussia? Do you see it? I don't. Sometimes I imagine that while I was in the hospital, that filthy swine hospital, there was a mass migration of Prussians to some faraway place. Sometimes I go out to the rocks and gaze at the Baltic and try to guess where the Prussian ships sailed. Sweden? Norway? Finland? Not on your life: those are swine lands. Where, then? Iceland, Greenland? I try but I can't make it out. Where are the Prussians, then? I climb up on the rocks and search for them on the gray horizon. A churning gray like pus. And I don't mean once a year. Once a month! Every two weeks! But I never see them, I can never guess what point on the horizon they set sail to. All I see is you, your head in the waves as they wash back and forth, and then I have a seat on a rock and for a long time I don't move, watching you, as if I've become another rock, and even though sometimes I lose sight of you, or your head comes up far away from where you went under, I'm never afraid, because I know you'll come up again, there's no danger in the water for you. Sometimes I actually fall asleep, sitting on a rock, and when I wake up I'm so cold I don't so much as look up to make sure you're still there. What do I do then? Why, I get up and come back to town, teeth chattering. And as I turn down the first streets I start to sing so that the neighbors tell themselves I've been out drinking down at Krebs's."

•

Young Hans Reiter also liked to walk, like a diver, but he didn't like to sing, for divers never sing. Sometimes he would walk east out of town, along a dirt road through the forest, and he would come to the Village of Red Men, where all they did was sell peat. If he walked farther east, there was the Village of Blue Women, in the middle of a lake that dried up in the summer. Both places looked like ghost towns, inhabited by the dead. Beyond the Village of Blue Women was the Town of the Fat. It smelled bad there, like blood and rotting meat, a dense, heavy smell very different from the smell of his own town, which smelled of dirty clothes, sweat clinging to the skin, pissed-upon earth, which is a thin smell, a smell like *Chorda filum*.

In the Town of the Fat, as was to be expected, there were many animals and several butcher shops. Sometimes, on his way home, moving like a diver, he watched the Town of the Fat citizens wander the streets of the Village of Blue Women or the Village of Red Men and he thought that maybe the villagers, those who were ghosts now, had died at the hands of the inhabitants of the Town of the Fat, who were surely fearsome and relentless practitioners of the art of killing, no matter that they never bothered him, among other reasons because he was a diver, which is to say he didn't belong to their world, where he came only as an explorer or a visitor.

On other occasions his steps took him west, and he walked down the main street of Egg Village, which each year was farther and farther from the rocks, as if the houses could move on their own and chose to seek a safer place near the dells and forests. It wasn't far from Egg Village to Pig Village, a village he imagined his father never visited, where there were many pigstys and the happiest herds of pigs for miles around, pigs that seemed to greet the passerby regardless of his social standing or age or marital status, with friendly grunts, almost musical, or in fact entirely musical, while the villagers stood frozen with their hats in their hands or covering their faces, whether out of modesty or shame it wasn't clear.

And farther on was the Town of Chattering Girls, girls who went to parties and dances in even bigger towns whose names the young Hans Reiter heard and immediately forgot, girls who smoked in the streets and talked about sailors at a big port who served on this or that ship, the names of which the young Hans Reiter immediately forgot, girls who went to the movies and saw the most thrilling films, with actors who were the handsomest men on the planet and actresses who, if one wanted to be fashionable, one had to imitate, and whose names the young Hans Reiter immediately forgot. When he got home, like a night diver, his mother asked him where he'd spent the day and the young Hans Reiter told her the first thing that came to mind, anything but the truth.

Then his mother stared at him with her blue eye and the boy held her gaze with his two blue eyes, and from the corner near the hearth, the one-legged man watched them both with his two blue eyes and for three or four seconds the island of Prussia seemed to rise from the depths.

•

At eight Hans Reiter lost interest in school. By then he had twice come close to drowning. The first time was during the summer and he was saved by a young tourist from Berlin who was spending his holidays in the Town of Chattering Girls. The young tourist saw a boy near some rocks, his head bobbing up and down, and after confirming that it was in fact a boy, since the tourist was shortsighted and at first glance thought it was a clump of seaweed, he removed his jacket, in which he was carrying some important papers, climbed down the rocks as far as he could go, and plunged into the water. In four strokes he was beside the boy, and once he'd scanned the shore for the best place to make for land, he began to swim toward a spot some thirty yards from where he'd gone in.

The tourist's name was Vogel and he was a man of incredible optimism. Though perhaps he wasn't optimistic so much as mad, and he was on holiday in the Town of Chattering Girls on the orders of his doctor, who, concerned about his health, endeavored to get him out of Berlin on the slightest pretext. If one was on anything like intimate terms with Vogel, his presence soon became unbearable. He believed in the intrinsic goodness of humankind, he claimed that a person who was pure of heart could walk from Moscow to Madrid without being accosted by anyone, whether beast or police officer, to say nothing of a customs official, because the traveler would take the necessary precautions, among them leaving the road from time to time and striking off across country. He was easily smitten and awkward, with the result that he didn't have a girl. Sometimes he talked, not caring who might be listening, about the healing properties of masturbation (he cited Kant as an example), to be practiced from the earliest years to the most advanced age, which mostly tended to provoke laughter in the girls from the Town of Chattering Girls who happened to hear him, and which exceedingly bored and disgusted his acquaintances in Berlin, who were already overfamiliar with this theory and who thought that Vogel, in explaining it with such stubborn zeal, was really masturbating in front of them or using them as masturbation aids.

But bravery was another thing he held in high esteem, and when he saw that a boy, though at first he mistook him for seaweed, was drowning, he didn't hesitate a second before throwing himself into the sea, which wasn't exactly calm near the rocks just there, to rescue him. One further thing must be noted, which is that Vogel's blunder (mistaking a boy with brown skin and blond hair for a tangle of seaweed) tormented him that night, after it was all over. In bed, in the dark, Vogel relived the day's occurrences just as he always did, that is, with great satisfaction, until suddenly he saw the drowning boy again and himself watching, not sure whether it was a human being or seaweed. Sleep deserted him. How could he have mistaken a boy for seaweed? he asked himself. And then: in what sense can a boy resemble seaweed? And then: can a boy and seaweed have anything in common?

Before he formulated a fourth question, Vogel thought that possibly his doctor in Berlin was right and he was going mad, or perhaps not mad in the usual sense, but he was approaching the path of madness, so to speak, because a boy, he thought, has nothing in common with seaweed, and an observer from the rocks who mistakes a boy for seaweed is a person with a half-loosened screw, not a madman, exactly, with a screw altogether loose, but a man whose screw is loosening, and who, as a result, must tread more carefully in all matters regarding his mental health.

Then, since he knew he wouldn't be able to sleep all night, he began to think about the boy he had saved. He was very thin, he remembered, very tall for his age, and his speech was confoundedly garbled. When Vogel asked what had happened, the boy answered:

"Nut."

"What?" asked Vogel. "What did you say?"

"Nut," repeated the boy. And Vogel understood that nut meant: nothing, nothing happened.

And so it was with the rest of his vocabulary, which struck Vogel as highly picturesque and amusing, so he began to ask all kinds of pointless questions, just for the pleasure of listening to the boy, who answered everything in the most natural manner, for example, what do you call this wood, Vogel asked, and the boy answered Stavs, which meant Gustav's wood, and: what's the name of that wood over there, and the boy answered Retas, which meant Greta's wood, and: what's the name of that dark wood, to the right of Greta's wood, and the boy answered annaname, which meant the wood that has no name, until they got to the top of the rocks where Vogel had left his jacket with the important papers in the pocket, and at the urging of Vogel, who wouldn't let him get back in the water, the boy retrieved his clothes from a cave a little farther down the shore, a kind of resting place for gulls, and then they said goodbye, not without first introducing themselves:

"My name is Heinz Vogel," Vogel said as if he were addressing an idiot, "what is your name?"

The boy told him it was Hans Reiter, pronouncing the name clearly, and then they shook hands and each went his separate way. All of this Vogel recalled as he tossed and turned in bed, reluctant to turn on the light and unable to sleep. What was it about the boy that made him look like seaweed? he asked himself. Was it his thinness, his sun-bleached hair, his long, placid face? And he wondered: should I return to Berlin, should I take my doctor more seriously, should I embark on a course of self-examination? Finally he grew tired of all the questions and jerked off, and fell asleep.

•

The second time young Hans Reiter almost drowned was in winter, when he went with some fishermen to cast nets across from the Village of Blue Women. It was getting dark and the fishermen began to talk about the lights that moved at the bottom of the sea. One said it was dead fishermen searching for the way to their villages, their cemeteries on dry land. Another said it was shining lichens, lichens that shone only once a month, as if in a single night they gave off all the light it had taken them thirty days to build up. Another said it was a kind of anemone particular to that coast, and the female anemones lit up to attract the male anemones, although everywhere else in the world anemones were hermaphrodites, neither male nor female, but male and female in a single body, as if the mind lapsed into sleep and when it woke, a part of the anemone had fucked the other part, as if inside each of us there were a woman and a man, or a faggot and a man in the cases where the anemone was sterile. Another said it was electric fish, a very strange kind of fish that required great vigilance, because if they landed in your nets they looked no different from any other kind of fish, but when people ate them they fell ill, with terrible electric shocks in the stomach, which at times could even be deadly.

And as the fishermen talked, young Hans Reiter's irrepressible curiosity, or madness, which at times made him do things he shouldn't, led him to drop off the boat with no warning, and he dove down after the lights or light of those singular fish or that singular fish, and at first the fishermen weren't alarmed, nor did they shout or cry out, because they were all aware of young Reiter's peculiarities, and yet, after a few seconds without a sighting of his head, they grew worried, because even though they were uneducated Prussians they were also men of the sea and they knew that no one can hold his breath for more than two minutes (or thereabouts), certainly not a boy, whose lungs—no matter how tall he is—aren't strong enough to survive the strain.

And finally two of them plunged into that dark sea, a sea like a pack of wolves, and they dove around the boat trying to find young Reiter's body, with no success, until they had to come up for air, and before they dove again, they asked the men on the boat whether the brat had surfaced. And then, under the weight of the negative response, they disappeared once more among the dark waves like forest beasts and one of the men who hadn't been in before joined them, and it was he who some fifteen feet down spotted the body of young Reiter floating like uprooted seaweed, upward, a brilliant white in the underwater space, and it was he who grabbed the boy under the arms and brought him up, and also he who made the young Reiter vomit all the water he had swallowed.

●

When Hans Reiter was ten, his one-eyed mother and one-legged father had their second child. It was a girl and they called her Lotte. She was a beautiful child and she might have been the first person on the surface of the earth who interested (or moved) Hans Reiter. Often his parents left her in his care. In no time at all he learned to change diapers, fix bottles, walk with the baby in his arms until she fell asleep. As far as Hans was concerned, his sister was the best thing that had ever happened to him, and many times he tried to draw her in the same notebook where he'd drawn different kinds of seaweed, but the results were always unsatisfactory: sometimes the baby looked like a bag of rubbish left on a pebbly beach, other times like *Petrobius maritimus*, a marine insect that lives in crevices and rocks and feeds on scraps, or *Lipura maritima*, another insect, very small and dark slate or gray, its habitat the puddles among rocks.

In time, by stretching his imagination or his tastes or his own artistic nature, he managed to draw her as a little mermaid, more fish than girl, closer to fat than thin, but always smiling, always with an enviable tendency to smile and see the positive side of things, which was a faithful reflection of his sister's character.

●

At thirteen Hans Reiter left school. This was 1933, the year Hitler came to power. At twelve Hans had begun to attend a school in the Town of

Chattering Girls. But for various reasons, all of them perfectly sensible, he didn't like it there, and he dawdled on his way, finding the path neither flat nor flat with hills nor flat with switchbacks, but vertical, a prolonged fall toward the bottom of the sea where everything, trees, grass, swamps, animals, fences, was transformed into marine insects or crustaceans, into suspended and *remote* forms of life, into starfish and sea spiders, whose bodies, the young Reiter knew, were so tiny that the animal's stomach didn't fit inside and extended into its legs, which were themselves enormous and mysterious, or in other words contained an enigma (or at least for him they did), because the sea spider has eight legs, four on each side, plus another pair, much smaller, in fact infinitely smaller *and useless*, at the end nearest its head, and those legs or tiny appendages struck Reiter not as legs but as hands, as if the sea spider, over a long process of evolution, had finally developed two arms and therefore two hands but didn't know yet that it had them. How long would the sea spider be unaware that it had hands?

"Probly," the young Reiter said to himself out loud, "nuffer a thousings, nuffer two thousings, nuffer ten thousings year. Nuffer long, long time."

And that was how he walked to school in the Town of Chattering Girls, and of course he was always late, his mind elsewhere, too.

•

In 1933, the headmaster of the school summoned Hans Reiter's parents. Only Hans's mother came. The headmaster ushered her into his office and explained briefly that the boy wasn't fit for school. Then he spread his arms, as if to take the sting out of what he'd said, and suggested that she apprentice him in a trade.

This was the year Hitler seized power. The same year, before Hitler seized power, a propaganda committee passed through Hans Reiter's town. The committee stopped first in the Town of Chattering Girls, where it held a rally at the movie theater, a success, and the next day it moved on to Pig Village and Egg Village and in the afternoon it reached Hans Reiter's town, where the members of the committee drank beer at the tavern with the local farmers and fishermen, bringing glad tidings and explanations of National Socialism, a movement that would raise Germany up from its ashes and Prussia from its ashes, too, the talk open and friendly, until someone who couldn't keep his mouth shut men-

tioned Hans Reiter's one-legged father, the only townsman who had returned alive from the front, a hero, a seasoned veteran, every inch a
Prussian, although perhaps a bit lazy, a countryman who told war stories
that gave you goose bumps, stories he had lived himself, the townspeople put special emphasis on this, he had lived them, they were true, and
not only were they true but the storyteller had lived them, and then one
member of the committee, a man who put on lordly airs (this must be
stressed, because his companions certainly didn't put on lordly airs, they
were ordinary men, happy to drink beer and eat fish and sausages and
fart and laugh and sing, and they didn't put on airs, which is only fair to
say and bears repeating because in fact they were like villagers, salesmen
who traveled from village to village and sprang from the common herd
and lived as part of the common herd, and who, when they died, would
fade from common memory), said that perhaps, just perhaps, it would
be interesting to meet this soldier, and then he asked why Reiter wasn't
there, at the tavern, conversing with his National Socialist comrades
who had only Germany at heart, and one of the townspeople, a man who
had a one-eyed horse that he looked after more carefully than Reiter
looked after his one-eyed wife, said that the aforementioned wasn't at
the tavern because he didn't have the money to buy even a mug of beer,
which led the members of the committee to protest that they would buy
the soldier a beer, and then the man who put on lordly airs singled out
one of the townsmen and ordered him to go to Reiter's house and bring
the old soldier to the tavern, and the townsman hurried off, but when he
returned, fifteen minutes later, he informed those present that Reiter
had refused to come, with the excuse that he wasn't dressed properly to
be introduced to the distinguished members of the committee, and also
that he was alone with his daughter, because his one-eyed wife was still
at work, and naturally his daughter couldn't be left alone, an argument
that nearly moved the members of the committee (who were swine) to
tears, because in addition to being swine they were sentimentalists, and
the fate of this veteran and war cripple touched their hearts, but not so
the lordly man, who got up and, after saying, as evidence of his great
learning, that if Mohammed couldn't come to the mountain, the mountain would come to Mohammed, motioned for the townsman to lead
him to the soldier's house and forbade any of the other members of the
committee to accompany them, and so this National Socialist Party
member dirtied his boots in the mud of the town streets and followed

the townsman nearly to the edge of the forest, where the Reiter family house stood, which the lordly man scanned with a knowing eye for an instant before he went in, as if to weigh the character of the paterfamilias by the harmony or strength of the house's lines, or as if he were tremendously interested in rustic architecture in that part of Prussia, and then they went into the house and there really was a girl of three asleep in a wooden cot and her one-legged father really was dressed in rags, because his military cloak and only pair of decent trousers were in the washtub that day or hanging wet in the yard, which didn't prevent the old soldier from offering his visitor a warm welcome, and surely at first he felt proud, privileged, that a member of the committee had come all the way to his house expressly to meet him, but then things took a wrong turn or seemed to take a wrong turn, because the questions asked by the lordly man began gradually to displease the one-legged man, and the lordly man's remarks, which were more like prophecies, also began to displease him, and then the one-legged man answered each question with a statement, generally outlandish or outrageous, and countered each of the other man's remarks with a question that somehow discredited the remark itself or cast it in doubt or made it seem puerile, completely lacking in common sense, which in turn began to exasperate the lordly man, and in a vain effort to find common ground he told the one-legged man that he had been a pilot during the war and shot down twelve French planes and eight English planes and he knew very well the suffering one experienced at the front, to which the one-legged man replied that his worst suffering hadn't come at the front but at the cursed military hospital near Düren, where his comrades stole not only cigarettes but whatever they could lay their hands on, they even stole men's souls to sell, since there were a disproportionate number of satanists in German military hospitals, which, after all, said the one-legged man, was understandable, because a long stay in a military hospital drove people to become satanists, a claim that exasperated the self-avowed aviator, who had also spent three weeks in a military hospital, in Düren? asked the one-legged man, no, in Belgium, said the lordly man, and the treatment he had received not only met but very often exceeded every expectation of sacrifice but also of kindness and understanding, marvelous and manly doctors, skilled and pretty nurses, an atmosphere of solidarity and endurance and courage, even a group of Belgian nuns had shown the highest sense of duty, in short, everyone had done his or her part to make the patient's stay as pleasant as possible, taking into account the circumstances, of course, because naturally a hospital isn't a cabaret or a brothel, and then they moved on to other topics, like the creation of Greater Germany, the construction of a Hinterland, the cleansing of the state institutions, to be followed by the cleansing of the nation, the creation of new jobs, the struggle for modernization, and as the ex-pilot talked Hans Reiter's father grew more and more nervous, as if he were afraid little Lotte would start to cry at any moment, or as if all at once he had realized that he wasn't a worthy interlocutor for this lordly man, and that perhaps it would be best to throw himself at the feet of this dreamer, this centurion of the skies, and plead what was already obvious, his ignorance and poverty and the courage he had lost, but he did nothing of the sort, instead he shook his head at each word the other uttered, as if he wasn't convinced (in fact he was terrified), as if it were difficult for him to understand the full scope of the other man's dreams (in fact he didn't understand them at all), until suddenly both of them, the former pilot who put on lordly airs and the old soldier, witnessed the arrival of young Hans Reiter, who, without a word, lifted his sister from her cot and carried her into the yard.

"And who is that?" asked the former pilot.

"My son," said the one-legged man.

"He looks like a giraffe fish," said the former pilot, and he laughed.

•

So in 1933 Hans Reiter left school, charged with apathy and poor attendance, which was strictly true, and his parents and relatives found him a job on a fishing boat, which lasted three months, until the skipper let him go, because young Reiter was more interested in gazing at the bottom of the sea than helping to cast the nets, and then he worked for a little while as a farm laborer, until he was let go for idling, and as a gatherer of peat and an apprentice at a tool shop in the Town of the Fat and as a helper to a farmer who traveled to Stettin to sell his vegetables, until he was once again let go because he was more of a burden than a help, and finally he was put to work at the country house of a Prussian baron, a house in the middle of a forest, near a lake of black waters, where his one-eyed mother also worked, dusting the furniture and paintings and enormous curtains and Gobelins and the different rooms, each with a mysterious name of its own that evoked the rites of a secret sect, where the dust inevitably built up, rooms that had to be aired to be rid of the smell of damp and neglect that crept in every so often, and there was also dusting to be done of the books in the huge library, books the baron hardly ever read, old tomes his father had tended and that had been handed down by the baron's grandfather, seemingly the only member of that vast family who read books and who had inculcated the love of books in his descendants, a love that translated not into reading but into the preservation of the library, which was exactly as the baron's grandfather had left it, no bigger and no smaller.

And Hans Reiter, who had never in his life seen so many books all together, dusted them one by one and handled them with care, but didn't read them either, partly because he was satisfied with his book of marine life and partly because he feared the sudden appearance of the baron, who rarely visited the country house, busy as he was with his affairs in Berlin and Paris, although every so often his nephew came to stay, the son of the baron's younger sister, prematurely deceased, and a painter who had settled in the south of France, despised by the baron. This nephew was a boy of twenty who often spent a week at the country house, entirely alone, never getting in anyone's way, retreating to the library for hours on end to read and drink cognac until he fell asleep in his chair.

Other times the baron's daughter came, but her visits were shorter, no longer than a weekend, although for the servants that weekend was like a month because the baron's daughter never came alone but with a retinue of friends, sometimes more than ten, all gay, all voracious, all untidy, who turned the house into a chaotic and noisy place, with parties every night that lasted until dawn.

Sometimes the daughter's arrival coincided with one of the visits from the baron's nephew, and then the baron's nephew almost always left immediately, despite his cousin's urging, sometimes even without waiting for the cart drawn by a draft horse that in such cases usually conveyed him to the train station in the Town of Chattering Girls.

With the arrival of his cousin, the baron's nephew, already timid, was thrown into a state of such stiffness and awkwardness that the servants, when they discussed the day's events, were unanimous in their verdict: he loved her or desired her or yearned for her or was pining away for her, opinions that the young Hans Reiter listened to, sitting cross-legged and eating bread and butter, without saying a word or adding any commentary of his own, although the truth is he knew the baron's nephew, whose name was Hugo Halder, much better than the other servants, who seemed blind to reality and saw only what they wanted to see, which was a young orphan in love and distress and a young orphan girl (although the baron's daughter had a father and mother, as everyone well knew), headstrong and awaiting a vague, dense redemption.

A redemption that smelled of peat smoke, of cabbage soup, of the wind tangled in the forest undergrowth. A redemption that smelled of mirror, thought young Reiter, nearly choking on his bread.

•

And why did the boy Reiter know Hugo Halder, a youth of some twenty years, better than the rest of the servants? Well, for one very simple reason. Or two very simple reasons, which, intertwined or combined, supply a fuller and also more complicated portrait of the baron's nephew.

First: he had watched him in the library as he ran his feather duster over the books, he had watched, from the top of the rolling ladder, as the baron's nephew slept, breathing deeply or snoring, talking to himself, though not in whole sentences, like sweet Lotte, but in monosyllables, scraps of words, particles of insults, defensive, as if in his sleep he were about to be killed. He had also seen the titles of the books the baron's nephew read. Most were history books, which meant the baron's nephew loved history or found it interesting, which at first struck the young Reiter as repulsive. Nights spent drinking cognac and smoking and reading history books. Repulsive. Which led him to wonder: all that silence for this? And he'd heard the words uttered by the baron's nephew when he was woken by the least sound, the rustle of a mouse or the soft scrape of a leather-bound book as it was returned to its place between two other books, words of total confusion, as if the world had shifted on its axis, not the words of a man in love but words of total confusion, the words of a sufferer, words issuing from a trap.

The second reason was even more solid. On one of the several occasions when Hugo Halder had decided to make a quick exit from the country house upon the sudden appearance of his cousin, young Hans Reiter had accompanied him, carrying his valise. There were two paths from the country house to the train station in the Town of Chattering Girls. One, the longest, passed Pig Village and Egg Village and occasionally ran along the rocks and the sea. The other, much shorter, cut through a huge forest of oaks and beeches and poplars and emerged on the edge of the Town of Chattering Girls, near an abandoned pickle factory, very near the station.

The scene is the following: Hugo Halder walks ahead of Hans Reiter with his hat in his hand and carefully scans the forest canopy, a dark underbelly alive with the stealthy movement of animals and birds he doesn't recognize. Thirty feet behind walks Hans Reiter with the nephew's valise, which is too heavy and which every so often he shifts from hand to hand. Suddenly both hear the grunt of a wild boar or what they believe is a wild boar. Maybe it's just a dog. Maybe what they've heard is the distant engine of a car about to crash. These two last scenarios are highly improbable but not impossible. In any case, both quicken their step, without a word, and suddenly Hans Reiter trips and falls and the valise falls too and it opens and its contents are scattered over the dark path through the dark forest. And in the tangle of Hugo Halder's clothes, as Hugo Halder keeps walking, not noticing the boy has fallen, the exhausted young Hans Reiter sees silver cutlery, candelabras, little lacquered wooden boxes, medallions forgotten in the many chambers of the country house, which the baron's nephew will surely pawn or sell for a pittance in Berlin.

•

Of course, Hugo Halder knew Hans Reiter had found him out and the result of this was to bring him closer to the young servant. The first sign came the same afternoon Hans Reiter carried his valise to the train station. When Halder took his leave, he dropped a few coins into Hans's hand (it was the first time he'd given him money and also the first time Hans Reiter had received money over and above his meager wage). On Halder's next visit to the country house he gave Hans a sweater. He said it was his and it didn't fit him anymore because he'd gained a little weight, though it was plain at a glance that this was untrue. In a word, Hans Reiter was no longer invisible and his presence merited some sort of notice.

Sometimes, when Halder was in the library reading or pretending to read his history books, he sent for Reiter, with whom he held longer and longer conversations. At first he asked about the other servants. He wanted to know what they thought of him, whether they were inconvenienced by his presence, whether they minded having him, whether anyone bore him a grudge. Next came the monologues. Halder talked about his life, his dead mother, his uncle the baron, his only cousin (that unattainable and headstrong girl), about the temptations of Berlin, a city he loved but that also caused him untold suffering, at times unbearably fierce, about the state of his nerves, always near the breaking point.

Then, in turn, he wanted the young Hans Reiter to talk about his own life, what did he do? what did he want to do? what were his dreams? what did he think the future held for him?

Regarding the future, naturally, Halder had ideas of his own. He believed that someone would soon invent and sell a kind of artificial stomach. The idea was so outrageous that he was the first to laugh at it (it was the first time Hans Reiter had heard him laugh and he found Halder's laugh deeply disagreeable). About his father, the painter who lived in France, Halder never spoke, but at the same time he liked to hear about other people's parents. He was amused by young Reiter's response to his questions on the subject. Hans said he didn't know anything about his father.

"True," said Halder, "one never knows anything about one's father."

A father, he said, is a passageway immersed in the deepest darkness, where we stumble blindly seeking a way out. Still, he insisted that the boy at least tell him what his father looked like, but the young Hans Reiter replied that he sincerely didn't know. At this point Halder wanted to know whether he lived with his father or not. I've always lived with him, answered Hans Reiter.

"So what does he look like? Can't you describe him?"

"I can't because I don't know," answered Hans Reiter.

For a few seconds both were silent, one examining his nails and the other gazing up at the library's high ceiling. It may have been hard to believe this reply, but Halder did.

•

Speaking very loosely, one might call Halder Hans Reiter's first friend. Each time Halder came to the country house he spent more time with Hans, whether shut in the library or walking and talking in the parkland that surrounded the estate.

Halder, too, was the first to get Hans to read something other than *Animals and Plants of the European Coastal Region*. It wasn't easy. First he asked whether he knew how to read. Hans Reiter said yes. Then he asked whether he'd ever read a good book. He stressed the word *good*. Hans Reiter said yes. He had a good book, he said. Halder asked what the book was. Hans Reiter told him it was *Animals and Plants of the European Coastal Region*. Halder said that must be a reference book and he meant a good literary book. Hans Reiter said he didn't know the difference between a good refnts (reference) book and a good litchy (literary) book. Halder said the difference lay in beauty, in the beauty of the story and the beauty of the language in which the story was told. Immediately he began to cite examples. He talked about Goethe and Schiller, he talked about Hölderlin and Kleist, he raved about Novalis. He said he had read all these authors and each time he reread them he wept.

"Wept," he said, "wept, do you understand, Hans?"

To which Hans Reiter replied that the only books he had seen Halder with were history books. Halder's answer took him by surprise. Halder said:

"It's because I don't have a proper grasp of history and I need to brush up."

"What for?" asked Hans Reiter.

"To fill a void."

"Voids can't be filled," said Hans Reiter.

"Yes, they can," said Halder, "with a little effort everything in this world can be filled. When I was your age," said Halder, clearly exaggerating, "I read Goethe until I couldn't read anymore (although Goethe, of course, is infinite), but anyway, I read Goethe, Eichendorff, Hoffman, and I neglected my studies of history, which are also needed in order to hone both edges of the blade, so to speak."

Then, as dusk fell and they listened to the crackling of the fire, they tried to decide which book Hans Reiter should read first and were unable to agree. When night had come, Halder finally told him to take any book he wanted and return it in a week. The young servant agreed that this was the best solution.

•

Soon afterward there was an increase in small thefts by the baron's nephew at the country estate, due, in his words, to gambling debts and inescapable obligations to certain ladies he was duty-bound to assist. Halder's clumsiness in disguising his purloinings was great and the young Hans Reiter decided to help. To keep the pilfered objects from being missed he suggested that Halder order the other servants to shift things around arbitrarily, to empty rooms under the pretext of airing them, to bring up old trunks from the cellars and carry them back down. In a word: to make rearrangements.

He also suggested, and in this he actively participated, that Halder devote his attention to the rare objects, taking only the really old and therefore forgotten antiques, diadems of no apparent value that had belonged to his great-grandmother or great-great-grandmother, silver-handled walking sticks of precious wood, swords that his forebears had used in the Napoleonic wars or against the Danes or the Austrians.

Meanwhile, Halder was always generous. Upon each new visit he gave Hans what he called his share of the booty, which was really no more than a rather large tip, but which for Hans Reiter constituted a fortune. He didn't show his parents this fortune, of course, because they would have been quick to accuse him of stealing. Nor did he buy anything for himself. He found a biscuit tin, into which he put the few bills and many coins, wrote on a paper "this money belongs to Lotte Reiter," and buried it in the forest.

•

Chance or the devil had it that the book Hans Reiter chose to read was Wolfram von Eschenbach's *Parzival*. When Halder saw him with it he smiled and told him he wouldn't understand it, but he also said he wasn't surprised he had chosen that book and none other, because in fact, he said, though he might never understand it, it was the perfect book for him, just as Wolfram von Eschenbach was the author in whom he would find the clearest resemblance to himself or his inner being or what he aspired to be, and, regrettably, never would become, though he might come this close, said Halder, holding his thumb and index finger a fraction of an inch apart.

Wolfram, Hans discovered, said of himself: I fled the pursuit of letters. Wolfram, Hans discovered, broke with the archetype of the courtly knight and was denied (or denied himself) all training, all clerical schooling. Wolfram, Hans discovered, unlike the troubadours and the minnesingers, declined to serve a lady. Wolfram, Hans discovered, declared that he was untutored in the arts, not to boast of a lack of education, but as a way of saying he was free from the burden of Latin learning and that he was a lay and independent knight. Lay and independent.

Of course, there were German medieval poets more important than Wolfram von Eschenbach. Like Friedrich von Hausen or Walther von der Vogelweide. But Wolfram's pride (*I fled the pursuit of letters, I was untutored in the arts*), a pride that stands aloof, a pride that says *die, all of you, but I'll live*, confers on him a halo of dizzying mystery, of terrible indifference, which attracted the young Hans the way a giant magnet attracts a slender nail.

Wolfram had no lands. Wolfram therefore lived in a state of vassalage. Wolfram had some protectors, counts who allowed their vassals—or at least some of them—to be visible. Wolfram said: *my hereditary office is the shield*. And as Halder told Hans all these things about Wolfram, as if to place him at the scene of the crime, Hans read *Parzival* from beginning to end, sometimes aloud, out in the fields or on his way along the path home from work, and not only did he understand it, he liked it. And what he liked most, what made him cry and roll laughing in the grass, was that Parzival sometimes rode (*my hereditary office is the shield*) wearing his madman's garb under his suit of armor.

•

The years he spent in Hugo Halder's company were profitable for him. The thefts continued, now at a furious pace, now slowing, in part because there was little left to rob anymore that wouldn't be noticed by Hugo's cousin or the other servants. Only once did the baron make an appearance. He drove up in a black sedan, with the curtains drawn, and stayed one night.

Hans thought he would see him, thought perhaps the baron would speak to him, but nothing happened like that. The baron spent only a single night at the estate, roaming the most neglected wings of the house, in constant motion (and constant silence), making no demands on the servants, as if he were lost in a dream and couldn't communicate verbally with anyone. At night he dined on black bread and cheese and went down to the cellars himself to choose the bottle of wine he opened to accompany his frugal meal. The next morning he was gone by the first light of day.

The baron's daughter, however, he saw many times. Always in the company of her friends. On three occasions during the time Hans worked at the house she came to stay while Halder was visiting, and each time Halder, profoundly ill at ease in his cousin's presence, was quick to pack his bags and leave. The last time, as they were crossing the forest that had in some sense sealed their complicity, Hans asked what made him so nervous. Halder's response was curt and ill-tempered. He said Hans wouldn't understand and strode along under the leafy forest roof.

In 1936 the baron closed the country house and let the servants go, retaining only the groundskeeper. For a while Hans had nothing to do and then he moved on to swell the ranks of the laborers who built the Reich's highways. Each month he sent his family almost his entire salary, because his needs were few, although on his free days he went down with his fellow workers to the taverns in the nearest towns, where they drank themselves insensible with beer. Among the young workers he undoubtedly held his liquor best, and a few times he took part in impromptu contests to see who could drink the most in the shortest time. But he didn't like alcohol, or he didn't like it any more than food, and when his team was stationed near Berlin he gave his notice and headed off.

It didn't take him long to find Halder in the big city, and he turned up at his door in search of assistance. Halder got him a job as a clerk in a stationery shop. Hans lived in a room in a house of workmen, where he was let a bed. He shared the room with a man of about forty who worked as a night watchman at a factory. The man's name was Füchler and he suffered from an affliction, possibly of nervous origin, as he admitted, that some nights manifested itself in the form of rheumatism and other nights as heart trouble or sudden attacks of asthma.

He and Füchler didn't see each other often, because Füchler worked at night and Hans worked during the day, but when they did meet they got along marvelously. As Füchler confessed, long ago he had been married and had a child. When his son was five the boy fell ill, and soon afterward he died. The child's death was more than Füchler could bear, and after three months of mourning in the cellar, he filled a pack and left without a word to anyone. For a time he wandered the roads of Germany, living on charity or whatever chance saw fit to offer him. A number of years later he came to Berlin, where a friend recognized him on the street and offered him a job. This friend, who was dead now, worked as a supervisor at the factory where Füchler was still employed as a watchman. The factory wasn't very big and it used to make shotguns, but lately it had been converted to the production of rifles.

One night, when he got back from work, Hans Reiter found the watchman in bed. The landlady had brought up a plate of soup. The stationer's apprentice knew at once that his roommate was going to die.

•

Healthy people flee contact with the diseased. This rule applies to almost everyone. Hans Reiter was an exception. He feared neither the healthy nor the diseased. He never got bored. He was always eager to help and he greatly valued the notion—so vague, so malleable, so warped—of friendship. The diseased, anyway, are more interesting than the healthy. The words of the diseased, even those who can manage only a murmur, carry more weight than those of the healthy. Then, too, all healthy people will in the future know disease. That sense of time, ah, the diseased man's sense of time, what treasure hidden in a desert cave. Then, too, the diseased truly bite, whereas the healthy pretend to bite but really only snap at the air. Then, too, then, too, then, too.

•

Before he died, Füchler told Hans he could have his job if he wanted it. He asked how much he earned at the stationer's. Hans told him. A pittance. Füchler wrote Hans a letter of introduction to the new supervisor, in which he vouched for the young man's conduct, saying he had known Hans since he was born. Hans thought about it all day, as he unloaded boxes of pencils and erasers and notebooks and swept the sidewalk in front of the shop. When he got home he told Füchler he liked the idea, he would change jobs. That same night he showed up at the rifle factory, which was on the edge of the city, and after a brief conversation with the supervisor they agreed on a two-week trial period. Shortly afterward, Füchler died. Since there was no one to give his belongings to, Hans kept them. A coat, two pairs of shoes, a wool scarf, four shirts, various undershirts, seven pairs of socks. Füchler's razor he presented to the landlord. Under the bed, in a cardboard box, he found several cowboy novels. He kept those for himself.

•

From then on Hans Reiter had much more free time. At night he paced the flagstone factory yard and the cold corridors of long rooms with big glass windows designed to let in as much sunlight as possible, and in the mornings, after breakfasting at some cart in the working-class neighborhood where he lived, he slept between four and six hours and then he had his afternoons free to ride the tram to the center of Berlin, where he would drop in on Hugo Halder, with whom he would go for a walk or to cafés and restaurants where the baron's nephew invariably came upon acquaintances and proposed deals that were never made.

In those days Hugo Halder was living on a backstreet near the Himmelstrasse, in a small flat crammed with old furniture and dusty paintings, and his best friend, besides Hans, was a Japanese who worked as assistant to the chargé of agricultural affairs at the Japanese legation. The Japanese man's name was Noburo Nisamata, but Halder, and Hans, too, called him Nisa. He was twenty-eight and good-natured, ready to laugh at the most innocent jokes and willing to listen to the most outrageous ideas. Generally they met at the Stone Virgin Café, a few steps from Alexanderplatz, where Halder and Hans usually arrived first and had something to eat, perhaps sausage with a bit of sauerkraut. An hour or two later, the Japanese man would meet them, impeccably dressed, and they would scarcely drink a glass of whiskey neat before leaving in a hurry and losing themselves in the Berlin night.

Then Halder would take charge. They went by taxi to the Eclipse, a cabaret with the worst performers in Berlin, a group of talentless old women who had found success in the unadorned exhibition of failure, and where, despite the laughter and whistles, if one knew a waiter well enough to be given an out-of-the-way table, one could converse without too much difficulty. The Eclipse was cheap, too, although Halder didn't concern himself with money during these nights of Berlin revelry, among other reasons because his Japanese friend always paid. Then, well lubricated, they would go to the Café des Artistes, where there were no variety acts but one could catch a glimpse of some of the Reich's painters, and—this was something Nisa greatly enjoyed—share a table with an art world celebrity or two, many of whom Halder had long known and some of whom he even called by their first names.

It was generally three in the morning when they left the Café des Artistes for the Danube, a fancy cabaret, where the dancers were very tall and beautiful and where they more than once had trouble convincing the doorman or maître d' to let Hans in, since he was as poor as a church mouse and his attire didn't conform to the dress code. On weekdays, anyway, Hans left his friends at ten to run to the tram stop and make it just on time to the factory where he worked as night watchman. On these days, if the weather was good, they spent hours sitting on the terrace of some fashionable restaurant, talking about the inventions Halder came up with. Halder swore that someday, when he had time, he would patent them and make his fortune, which provoked strange attacks of hilarity in his Japanese friend. There was something hysterical about Nisa's laughter: he laughed not only with his lips and eyes and throat but also with his hands and neck and feet, stamping delicately on the floor.

Once, after explaining the usefulness of a machine that would make artificial clouds, Halder asked Nisa abruptly whether his mission in Germany was what he claimed it to be or whether he was really a secret agent. The question, so unexpected, took Nisa by surprise, and at first he didn't fully understand it. Then, when Halder seriously explained the mission of a secret agent, Nisa exploded in an attack of laughter like nothing Hans had witnessed in his life, going so far as to fall in a faint onto the table, and Hans and Halder had to carry him off to the washroom, where they splashed water on his face and managed to revive him.

Nisa didn't talk much himself, whether out of discretion or because he didn't want to offend with his heavily accented German. And yet sometimes he said interesting things. He said, for example, that Zen was a mountain that bites its own tail. He said the language he had studied was English and it was just another of the ministry's many mistakes that he was stationed in Berlin. He said that samurais were like fish in a waterfall but the best samurai in history was a woman. He said his father had known a Christian monk who lived for fifteen years without ever leaving the island of Endo, a few miles from Okinawa, an island of volcanic rock with no water.

When he said these things it was often with a smile. Halder, in turn, baited him by announcing that Nisa was a Shintoist, that he liked only German whores, that in addition to German and English he could speak and write Finnish, Swedish, Norwegian, Danish, Dutch, and Russian. When Halder said these things, Nisa laughed slowly, hee hee hee, and showed Hans his teeth, his eyes shining.

•

Sometimes, however, as they sat on a café terrace or around a dark cabaret table, an obstinate silence descended inexplicably over the trio. They seemed suddenly to freeze, lose all sense of time, and turn completely inward, as if they were bypassing the abyss of daily life, the abyss of people, the abyss of conversation, and had decided to approach a kind of lakeside region, a late-romantic region, where the borders were clocked from dusk to dusk, ten, fifteen, twenty minutes, an eternity, like the minutes of those condemned to die, like the minutes of women who've just given birth and are condemned to die, who understand that more time isn't more eternity and nevertheless wish with all their souls for more time, and their wails are birds that come flying every so often across the double lakeside landscape, so calmly, like luxurious excrescences or heartbeats. Then, naturally, the three men would emerge stiff from the silence and go back to talking about inventions, women, Finnish philology, the building of highways across the Reich.

·

On no few occasions they ended their nights at the flat of Grete von Joachimsthaler, an old friend with whom Halder maintained relations full of subterfuge and misunderstandings.

Musicians often visited Grete, including an orchestra conductor who claimed that music was the fourth dimension and whom Halder respected greatly. The orchestra conductor was thirty-five and was admired (women swooned over him) as if he were twenty-five and venerated as if he were eighty. As a general rule, when he came to conclude an evening at Grete's flat he sat at the piano, though he didn't touch it with even the tip of his little finger, and immediately he was surrounded by a court of spellbound friends and followers, until he decided to get up and go forth like the keeper of a swarm of bees, except that this beekeeper wasn't protected by a mesh suit or a helmet and woe betide the bee that tried to sting him, even if only in thought.

The fourth dimension, he liked to say, encompasses the three dimensions and consequently puts them in their place, that is, it obliterates the dictatorship of the three dimensions and thereby obliterates the three-dimensional world we know and live in. The fourth dimension, he said, is the full richness of the senses and the (capital S) Spirit, it's the (capital E) Eye, in other words the open Eye that obliterates the eyes, which compared to the Eye are just poor orifices of mud, absorbed in contemplation or the equation birth-training-work-death, whereas the Eye sails up the river of philosophy, the river of existence, the (fast-flowing) river of fate.

The fourth dimension, he said, was expressible only through music. Bach, Mozart, Beethoven.

It was hard to get near the conductor. That is, it wasn't hard to get near him physically, but it was hard to get him to see one, blinded as he was by the footlights, separated from others by the pit. One night, however, the picturesque trio composed of Halder, Nisa, and Hans caught his attention and he asked the hostess who they were. She told him that Halder was a friend, the son of a once-promising painter, nephew of Baron Von Zumpe, and that the Japanese gentleman worked at the Japanese embassy and the tall, shabby, poorly dressed young man was doubtless an artist, perhaps a painter, Halder's protégé.

The conductor then wanted to meet them, and the hostess, with great delicacy, beckoned to the surprised trio and led them to a quiet corner of the flat. For a while, as might be expected, they didn't know what to say. Again, because it was his favorite subject at the time, the conductor talked about music or the fourth dimension, it wasn't exactly clear where one ended and the other began, though perhaps, to judge by certain mysterious words of the conductor, the point of union was the conductor himself, in whom mysteries and answers spontaneously coincided. Halder and Nisa nodded agreement at everything. Not so Hans. According to the director, life qua life in the fourth dimension was of an unimaginable richness, etc., etc., but the truly important thing was the distance from which one, immersed in this harmony, could contemplate human affairs, with equanimity, in a word, and free of the artificial travails that oppress the spirit devoted to work and creation, to life's only transcendent truth, the truth that creates more and more life, an inexhaustible torrent of life and happiness and brightness.

The conductor talked and talked, about the fourth dimension and some symphonies he had conducted or planned soon to conduct, never once taking his eyes off his listeners. His eyes were like the eyes of a hawk that flies and delights in its flight, but that also maintains a watchful gaze, capable of discerning even the slightest movement down below, on the scrambled pattern of earth.

Perhaps the conductor was slightly drunk. Perhaps the conductor was tired and his thoughts were elsewhere. Perhaps the conductor's words didn't at all express his state of mind, his manner of being, his worshipful regard for the artistic phenomenon.

•

That night, however, Hans asked or wondered aloud (it was the first time he had spoken) what those who inhabited or visited the fifth dimension must think. At first the conductor didn't quite understand him, although

665

Hans's German had improved considerably since he left home to join the road crews and even more since he came to live in Berlin. Then he got the idea and turned from Halder and Nisa to focus his hawk's or eagle's or carrion bird's gaze on the calm blue eyes of the young Prussian, who was already formulating another question: what would those who had ready access to the sixth dimension think of those who were settled in the fifth or fourth dimension? What would those who lived in the tenth dimension, that is, those who perceived ten dimensions, think of music, for example? What would Beethoven mean to them? What would Mozart mean to them? What would Bach mean to them? Probably, the young Reiter answered himself, music would just be noise, noise like crumpled pages, noise like burned books.

At this point the conductor raised a hand and said or rather whispered confidentially:

"Don't speak of burned books, my dear young man."

To which Hans responded:

"Everything is a burned book, my dear maestro. Music, the tenth dimension, the fourth dimension, cradles, the production of bullets and rifles, Westerns: all burned books."

"What are you talking about?" asked the director.

"I was just stating my opinion," said Hans.

"An opinion like any other," said Halder, doing his best to end the conversation on a humorous note, one that would leave them all on good terms, he and the conductor and Hans and the conductor, "a typically adolescent pronouncement."

"No, no, no," said the conductor, "what do you mean by Westerns?"

"Cowboy novels," said Hans.

This declaration seemed to relieve the director, who, after exchanging a few friendly words with them, soon took his leave. Later, he would tell their hostess that Halder and the Japanese man seemed like decent people, but Halder's young friend was a time bomb, no question about it: an untrained, powerful mind, irrational, illogical, capable of exploding at the moment least expected. Which was untrue.

•

After the musicians had gone home, nights at Grete von Joachimsthaler's flat usually ended in bed or the bathtub, a bathtub like few in Berlin, eight feet long and five feet wide, black enamel with claw feet, where Halder and then Nisa endlessly massaged Grete, from temples to toes, the two of them fully dressed, even sometimes with their coats on (at Grete's express request), while Grete cavorted like a mermaid, sometimes on her back, sometimes on her belly, other times underwater! her nakedness covered only by foam.

During these amorous interludes Hans waited in the kitchen, where he made a snack and poured a beer, and then walked, glass of beer in one hand and snack in the other, along the flat's wide hallways or went to stand by the big windows in the salon from which he watched the sunrise as it washed like a wave over the city, drowning them all.

Sometimes Hans felt feverish and he thought it was desire that made his face burn, but he was wrong. Sometimes Hans left the windows open to clear the smell of smoke from the salon and turned out the lights and sat in an armchair, bundled in his coat. Then he felt the cold and he was tired and closed his eyes. An hour later, when the sun was fully up, he felt Halder and Nisa shaking him, telling him they had to go.

Grete von Joachimsthaler never appeared at that hour. Only Halder and Nisa. And Halder always had a bundle that he tried to hide under his coat. Once out in the street, still half asleep, he saw that his friends' trouser legs were wet and the sleeves of their suits, too, and that the legs and sleeves steamed in the cold, the vapor only a little less dense than the clouds breathed out by Nisa and Halder and Hans himself, and in the early morning his friends spurned taxis to walk to the nearest café and eat a big breakfast.

•

In 1939 Hans Reiter was drafted. After a few months of training he was assigned to the 310th, a light infantry regiment whose base was twenty miles from the Polish border. The 310th, as well as the 311th and 312th, was part of the 79th Light Infantry Division, commanded at the time by General Kruger, which in turn was part of the 10th Infantry Corps, commanded by General Von Bohle, one of the Reich's leading philatelists. The 310th was commanded by Colonel Von Berenberg, and it consisted of three battalions. Hans Reiter belonged to the 3rd Battalion, assigned first to serve as an assistant machine gun operator and then to an assault company.

The captain responsible for this second assignment was Paul Gercke, an aesthete who believed that Reiter's height would do very well to instill respect and even fear during, say, a practice charge or military parade, but who knew that in the case of real as opposed to simulated combat the same height that had got him the post would, in the long run, be his undoing, because in practice the best assault soldier is short and thin as a sprig and darts along like a squirrel. Of course, before becoming an infantryman with the 310th Regiment, 79th Division, Hans Reiter, presented with the dilemma of choosing, tried to get himself selected for service on a submarine. This ambition, encouraged by Halder, who called on or claimed to have called on all of his friends in the military and government, most of whom, Hans suspected, were more imaginary than real, only provoked fits of laughter in the officers in charge of the German navy's priority lists, especially among those familiar with the real dimensions of submarines and the living conditions aboard, where a man who was six foot five would surely become the bane of his comrades.

Whatever the case, despite Halder's connections, real or not, Hans was rejected by the German navy in the most ignominious fashion (it was even recommended to him, in jest, that he join a tank company), and he had to content himself with his original assignment, the light infantry.

A week before he left for basic training, Halder and Nisa took him out for a farewell dinner that ended at a brothel, where they begged him to lose his virginity once and for all, in honor of their friendship. The whore he was assigned (chosen by Halder and probably a friend of Halder's and also probably a disappointed partner in one of Halder's multiple business schemes) was a peasant from Bavaria, very sweet and quiet, although when she talked, which she did infrequently as if to conserve words, she seemed to be a practical woman in every sense, including the sexual, even showing signs of avarice that thoroughly repelled Hans. Of course, he didn't make love that night, although he told his friends he had, but the next day he went back to see the whore, whose name was Anita. On this second visit Hans lost his virginity, and there were two more visits, enough to inspire Anita to expound on her life and her philosophy of life.

When the time came for him to go, he left alone. He noted that it was odd no one saw him off at the train station. He'd said his goodbyes to Anita the night before. Of Halder and Nisa he'd heard nothing since the first visit to the brothel, as if both friends had taken it for granted that he was leaving the next morning, which wasn't the case. For a week now, he thought, Halder has been living in Berlin as if I were already gone. The only person he bade farewell the day he left was his landlady, who told him it was an honor to serve his country. All he carried in his new kit bag were a few items of clothing and the book *Animals and Plants of the European Coastal Region*.

•

In September the war began. Reiter's division advanced to the border and crossed behind the Panzer divisions and the motorized infantry divisions that cleared the way. By forced marches they made their way into Polish territory, seeing no combat and taking few precautions: the three regiments moved almost as one in a general atmosphere of festivity, as if the men were on a journey of pilgrimage and not a march toward a war in which some would inevitably be killed.

They passed through several towns, without plundering them, in orderly fashion, but not arrogantly at all, smiling at the children and young women, and every so often they crossed paths with soldiers on motorcycles flying along the road, sometimes heading east and sometimes west, carrying orders for the division or the corps general staff. They forged ahead of the artillery. Sometimes, when they reached the top of a hill, they gazed east, toward where they imagined the front to be, and they didn't see anything, just a landscape slumbering in summer's last splendor. Toward the west, however, they could make out the dust cloud of the regimental and divisional artillery as it strove to catch up with them.

On the third day of traveling, Hans's regiment turned onto another dirt road. Just before nightfall they reached a river. Past the river rose a forest of pines and poplars, and past the forest, they were told, was a village where a group of Poles had taken a stand. They assembled the machine guns and mortars and shot up flares, but there was no response. Two assault companies crossed the river after midnight. In the forest Hans and his comrades heard the hoot of an owl. When they came out on the far side, they spied the village, like a black lump set or encrusted in the darkness. The two companies divided into several groups and continued their advance. At fifty yards from the first house the captain gave the order and they all went running toward the village and one or two even seemed surprised when they found it was deserted. The next day the regiment continued eastward, along three different roads, parallel to the main route taken by the larger part of the division.

Reiter's battalion came upon a detachment of Poles occupying a bridge. The Germans demanded the surrender of the Poles. The Poles refused and opened fire. After the battle, which lasted scarcely ten minutes, one of Reiter's comrades returned with a broken nose, which bled copiously. As he told it, after he had crossed the bridge he had walked on with ten soldiers to the edge of the forest. Just at that moment, a Pole dropped from a tree branch and began to beat him with his fists. Naturally, Reiter's comrade didn't know what to do, because in the worst or best of cases, call it the most extreme of cases, he had imagined being attacked with a knife or a bayonet, if not shot, but he had never imagined being punched. When the Pole hit him in the face, he felt anger, of course, but stronger than anger was the surprise, the shock of it, which left him powerless to respond, whether with his fists, like his attacker, or with his gun. He just stood there and took a blow to the stomach, which didn't hurt, and then to the nose, which half stunned him, and then, as he fell, he saw the Pole, the hazy silhouette of the Pole, who instead of taking his gun, as someone more intelligent might have, tried to run back into the forest, and the silhouette of one of his companions shooting at the Pole, and then more shots and the silhouette of the Pole falling riddled with bullets. When Hans and the rest of the battalion crossed the bridge there were no enemy bodies lying by the side of the road and the battalion's only casualties were two lightly wounded soldiers.

•

It was around this time, as they walked under the sun or the gray clouds, enormous, endless gray clouds that brought tidings of a fall to remember, and his battalion left behind village after village, that Hans imagined that under his Wehrmacht uniform he was wearing the suit or garb of a madman.

•

One afternoon his battalion encountered a group of general staff officers. Which general staff? He didn't know, but they were general staff officers. As his battalion marched along the road, the officers had gathered on a hill very near the road and were gazing at the sky, across which at that moment a squadron of planes was flying east, maybe Stukas, maybe fighter planes; some of the officers pointed with their index finger or with their whole hand, as if they were giving the planes the Heil Hitler salute, while a few steps away, another officer, seemingly lost in thought, watched as an orderly carefully laid out refreshments on a folding table, refreshments that he unpacked from a large black box, like a special box from some pharmaceutical company, the kind of box that holds dangerous medicines or medicines that haven't been thoroughly tested, or even worse, like a box from some scientific research center where glove-wearing German scientists pack away something with the power to destroy the world and Germany too.

Near the orderly and the officer who watched as the orderly arranged the refreshments on the table was another officer, this one in a Luftwaffe uniform, his back to everyone, bored with watching the planes fly overhead, who held a long cigarette in one hand and a book in the other, a simple operation but one that seemed to demand untold efforts, because the breeze on the hill where everyone stood was constantly fluttering the pages of the book so that the officer was unable to read and had to use the hand that held the long cigarette to keep the pages from fluttering (or ruffling or flipping), which only managed to make the situation worse, because the cigarette or the cigarette's ash unfailingly scorched the pages or the breeze scattered ash across them, which bothered the officer no end, causing him to bend his head and blow, very carefully, because he was facing into the wind and when he blew there was a risk the ashes would fly into his eyes.

Near this Luftwaffe officer, but sitting in two folding chairs, were a couple of old soldiers. One of them looked like a general of the land forces. The other seemed to be dressed as a lancer or hussar. They looked at each other and laughed, first the general and then the lancer, and so on, back and forth, as if they had no idea what was happening or as if they understood something that none of the general staff officers stationed on the hill knew. Three cars were parked at the bottom of the hill. Next to the cars, the drivers stood and smoked, and in one of the cars was a woman, lovely and elegantly dressed, who bore a strong resemblance, or so Reiter thought, to the daughter of the Baron Von Zumpe, Hugo Halder's uncle.

•

The first real battle in which Reiter took part was on the outskirts of Kutno, where the Poles were few and poorly armed but showed no inclination to surrender. The clash didn't last long, because in the end it turned out that the Poles did want to surrender and the problem was they didn't know how. Reiter's assault group attacked a farm and a forest where the enemy had concentrated the remains of its artillery. As he watched the group leave, Captain Gercke thought that Reiter would probably be killed. For the captain it was like seeing a giraffe go off in a pack of wolves, coyotes, and hyenas. Reiter was so tall that any Polish conscript, even the clumsiest, would surely target him.

Two German soldiers were killed in the attack on the farm and five others were wounded. In the attack on the forest, another German soldier was killed and three more were wounded. Nothing happened to Reiter. That night, the sergeant who commanded the group told the captain that far from serving as an easy target, Reiter had somehow frightened the other side. How? asked the captain, by shouting? by cursing? by his ruthlessness? maybe he had frightened them because in combat he was transformed? transformed into a Teutonic warrior without fear or mercy? or maybe a hunter, the primal hunter inside all of us, wily, fast, always a step ahead of his prey?

To which the sergeant, after thinking a moment, replied no, it wasn't exactly that, Reiter, he said, was different, but actually he was the same person as always, the person everyone knew, what happened was that he had gone into combat as if he wasn't going into combat, as if he wasn't there or the quarrel wasn't with him, which didn't mean he failed to follow orders or disobeyed orders, it wasn't that at all, nor was he in a trance, some soldiers, paralyzed by fear, go into a trance, but it isn't a trance, it's just fear, anyway, he, the sergeant, wasn't sure what it was, but Reiter had something evident even to the enemy, who shot at him several times and never hit him, to their increasing dismay.

•

The 79th Division kept fighting on the outskirts of Kutno, but Reiter didn't take part in another skirmish. Before the end of September the whole division was transferred, this time by train, to the western border, to join the rest of the 10th Infantry Corps.

•

From October 1939 to June 1940 they didn't budge. Ahead was the Maginot Line, though they couldn't see it from where they lay hidden in forests and orchards. Life grew calm: the soldiers listened to the radio, ate, drank beer, wrote letters, slept. Some talked about the day they would have to march straight for the concrete fortifications of the French. Those who listened laughed nervously, told jokes, swapped stories about their families.

One night someone told them that Denmark and Norway had surrendered. That night Hans dreamed of his father. He saw the one-legged man, wrapped in his old military cloak, staring out at the Baltic and wondering where the island of Prussia had hidden itself.

Sometimes Captain Gercke came to talk to Hans for a while. The captain asked whether he was afraid of dying. What kind of question is that, Captain? said Reiter, of course I'm afraid. When the captain heard this, he gave him a long stare and then said in a low voice, as if talking to himself:

"You goddamn liar, I don't believe you, you can't fool me. You're not afraid of anything!"

Then the captain would go talk to other soldiers and his mood changed depending on the soldier he was talking to. Around this time his sergeant was awarded the Iron Cross Second Class, for valor in combat in Poland. They celebrated by drinking beer. At night Hans left the makeshift barracks and lay on his back on the cold grass outside to watch the stars. The chill didn't seem to bother him much. He often thought about his family, about little Lotte, who by then would be ten, in school. Sometimes, without bitterness, he regretted having abandoned his studies so early, because he sensed vaguely that he might have had a better life if he had kept at them.

At the same time, he wasn't unhappy as a soldier and he felt no need or perhaps wasn't able to think seriously about the future. Sometimes, alone or with his companions, he pretended he was a diver, strolling along the bottom of the sea again. No one noticed, of course, although if they had watched Reiter's movements more carefully, something might have given him away: a slight difference in the way he walked, the way he breathed, the way he gazed around him. A certain prudence, each step premeditated, his breathing measured, a glassiness of the corneas, as if his eyes were swelling from an insufficient supply of oxygen, or as if, solely at these moments, all his sangfroid deserted him and he found himself suddenly unable to contain his tears, which meanwhile never quite spilled over.

•

Around this time, as they were waiting, a soldier from Reiter's battalion went mad. He said he could hear radio transmissions from the German side, and also, more curiously, the French. This soldier's name was Gustav and he was twenty, the same age as Reiter, and he had never been assigned to the battalion's communications team. The doctor, a tired-looking man from Munich, examined him and said that Gustav had experienced an episode of auditory schizophrenia, which consisted of hearing voices in the head, and prescribed cold baths and tranquilizers. Gustav's case, however, differed in one critical respect from most cases of auditory schizophrenia: usually the voices the patient hears are directed at him, they talk to him or berate him, whereas in Gustav's case the voices simply issued orders, they belonged to soldiers, scouts, lieutenants giving their daily reports, colonels speaking by phone to generals, quartermasters demanding one hundred pounds of flour, pilots delivering the weather report. The first week of treatment Gustav seemed to improve. He went about in a slight stupor and he resisted the cold baths, but he no longer shouted or claimed his soul was being poisoned. The second week he escaped from the field hospital and hanged himself from a tree.

•

For the 79th Infantry Division there was nothing epic about the war on the western front. In June, after the Somme offensive, they crossed the Maginot Line with few surprises and participated in the siege of a few thousand French soldiers near Nancy. Then the division was quartered in Normandy.

During the train trip Hans heard an odd story about a soldier of the 79th who had gotten lost in the tunnels of the Maginot Line. The section of tunnel he was lost in, as far as the soldier could tell, was called the Charles Sector. The soldier, of course, had nerves of steel, or so it was told, and he kept searching for a way to the surface. After walking some five hundred yards underground he came to the Catherine Sector. The Catherine Sector, it goes without saying, was in no way different from the Charles Sector, except for the signs. After walking half a mile, he got to the Jules Sector. By now the soldier was nervous and his imagination had begun to wander. He imagined himself imprisoned forever in those underground passageways, with no comrade coming to his aid. He wanted to yell, and although at first he restrained himself, for fear of alerting any French soldiers still hiding nearby, at last he gave in to the urge and began to shout at the top of his lungs. But no one answered and he kept walking, in the hope that at some point he'd find the way out. He left behind the Jules Sector and entered the Claudine Sector. Then came the Émile Sector, the Marie Sector, the Jean-Pierre Sector, the Berenice Sector, the André Sector, the Sylvie Sector. When he got to the Sylvie Sector, the soldier made a discovery (which anyone else would've made much sooner). He noticed the curious neatness of the nearly immaculate passageways. Then he began to think about the usefulness of the passageways, that is their military usefulness, and he came to the conclusion that they were of absolutely no use and there had probably never been soldiers here.

At this point the soldier thought he'd gone mad or, even worse, that he'd died and this was his private hell. Tired and hopeless, he lay down on the floor and slept. He dreamed of God in human form. The soldier was asleep under an apple tree, in the Alsatian countryside, and a country squire came up to him and woke him with a gentle knock on the legs with his staff. I'm God, he said, and if you sell me your soul, which already belongs to me anyway, I'll get you out of the tunnels. Let me sleep, said the soldier, and he tried to go back to sleep. I said your soul already belongs to me, he heard the voice of God say, so please don't be a fool, and accept my offer.

Then the soldier awoke and looked at God and asked where he had to sign. Here, said God, pulling a paper out of the air. The soldier tried to read the contract, but it was written in some other language, not German or English or French, of that he was certain. What do I sign with? asked the soldier. With your blood, as is only proper, God answered. Immediately the soldier took out a penknife and made a cut in the palm of his left hand, then he dipped the tip of his index finger in the blood and signed.

"All right, now you can go back to sleep," God said.

"I'd like to get out of the tunnels soon," the soldier pleaded.

"All will proceed as ordained," said God, and he turned and started down a little dirt path toward a valley where there was a village of houses painted green and white and light brown.

The soldier thought it might be wise to say a prayer. He joined his hands and raised his eyes to the heavens. Then he saw that all the apples on the tree had dried up. Now they looked like raisins, or prunes. At the same time he heard a noise that sounded vaguely metallic.

"What is this?" he exclaimed.

From the valley rose long plumes of black smoke that hung in the air when they reached a certain height. A hand grabbed him by the shoulder and shook him. It was soldiers from a company that had come down the tunnel into the Berenice Sector. The soldier began to weep with joy, not much, but enough to find relief.

That night, as he ate, he told his best friend about the dream he'd had in the tunnels. His friend told him it was normal to dream nonsense when one found oneself in such situations.

"It wasn't nonsense," the soldier answered, "I saw God in my dreams, I was rescued, I'm back among friends again, but I can't quite be easy."

Then, in a calmer voice, he corrected himself:

"I can't quite feel safe."

To which his friend responded that in war no one could feel entirely safe. The friend went to sleep. Silence fell over the town. The sentinels lit cigarettes. Four days later, the soldier who had sold his soul to God was walking along the street when he was hit by a German car and killed.

●

During his regiment's stay in Normandy, Reiter often swam, no matter how cold it was, off the rocks of Portbail, near the Ollonde, or off the rocks north of Carteret. His battalion was based in the town of Besneville. In the mornings he went out, with his weapons and a rucksack in which he carried cheese, bread, and half a bottle of wine, and walked to the coast. There he chose a rock well out of sight, and after swimming and diving naked for hours, he would stretch out on his rock and eat and drink and reread his book *Animals and Plants of the European Coastal Region*.

Sometimes he found starfish, which he stared at for as long as his lungs would hold, until finally he made up his mind to touch them just before he returned to the surface. Once he saw a pair of gobies, *Gobius paganellus*, lost in a jungle of seaweed, and he followed them for a while (the seaweed jungle was like the locks of a dead giant), until he was seized by a strange, powerful despair and had to come up quickly, because if he had stayed down any longer the despair would have dragged him to the bottom.

Sometimes he felt so good, drowsing on his damp slab of rock, that he might have chosen never to rejoin the battalion. And more than once he gave serious thought to deserting, living like a tramp in Normandy, finding a cave, feeding himself on the charitable offerings of peasants or small thefts that no one would report. I would learn to see in the dark, he thought. In time my clothes would fall to rags and finally I would live naked. I would never return to Germany. One day I would drown, radiant with joy.

•

Around this time, a medical team came to visit Reiter's company. The doctor who examined him found him as healthy as could be, except for his eyes, which were unnaturally red, for reasons of which Reiter was well aware: the long hours spent diving barefaced in salt water. But he didn't tell the doctor for fear he would be punished or forbidden to return to the sea. In those days, Reiter would have considered it sacrilege to dive with goggles. A helmet yes, goggles categorically no. The doctor prescribed some drops for him and told him to get his superior to issue him an order to be seen by the ophthalmologist. As the doctor left he mused that the lanky boy was probably a drug addict, and he wrote in his diary: how is it that in the ranks of our army we find young men addicted to morphine, heroin, perhaps all sorts of drugs? What do they represent? Are they a symptom or a new social illness? Are they the mirror of our fate or the hammer that will shatter mirror and fate together?

•

One day, without warning, all leaves were canceled and Reiter's battalion, which was in the town of Besneville, joined two other battalions of the 310th Regiment that were stationed in St-Sauveur-le-Vicomte and Bricquebec and they all got on an eastward-bound military train that linked up in Paris with another train carrying the 311th Regiment, and although the division was missing its 3rd Regiment, which apparently it would never regain, they set off across Europe from west to east, and thus passed through Germany and Hungary, finally coming to a halt in Romania, the new posting of the 79th Division.

Some troops set up camp near the Soviet frontier, others near the new border with Hungary. Hans's battalion was stationed in the Carpathians. The headquarters of the division, which was no longer part of the 10th Corps, but of a new corps, the 49th, which had just been formed and for the moment consisted of a single division, was located in Bucharest, although every so often General Kruger, the new commander of the corps, accompanied by General Von Berenberg, formerly Colonel Von Berenberg, the new commander of the 79th, visited the troops and took an interest in their state of preparation.

Now Reiter lived far from the sea, in the mountains, and for the moment he gave up any idea of deserting. For the first few weeks of his stay in Romania all he saw were soldiers from his own battalion. Then he saw peasants, who kept in constant motion, as if they had ants in their pants, going back and forth with bundles of their belongings. They spoke only to their children, who followed them like sheep or little goats. The sunsets in the Carpathians were endless, but the sky seemed too low, just a few yards above the soldiers' heads, which produced a sense of smothering or unease. Daily life, despite everything, was once again peaceful, uneventful.

•

One night some soldiers from Reiter's battalion rose before dawn and left in two trucks for the mountains.

As soon as they had settled themselves on the wooden benches in the back of the truck, the soldiers fell asleep again. Reiter couldn't. Sitting next to the back flap, he pushed aside the canvas that served as roof and watched the scenery. His night-vision eyes, permanently reddened despite the drops he used each morning, glimpsed a series of small, dark valleys between two lines of peaks. Every so often the trucks passed huge stands of pine, which crept threateningly toward the road. In the distance, on a smaller mountain, he made out the silhouette of a castle or fort. When the sun rose he realized it was just a forest. He saw hills or rocky outcroppings that looked like ships about to sink, prows lifted, like enraged horses, nearly vertical. He saw dark mountain paths that led nowhere, but above which, at a great height, soared blackbirds that must be carrion fowl.

At midmorning they came to a castle. The only people there were three Romanians and an SS officer who was acting as butler and who put them right to work, after serving them a breakfast consisting of a glass of cold milk and a scrap of bread, which some soldiers left untouched in disgust. Everyone, except for four soldiers who stood guard, among them Reiter, whom the SS officer judged ill suited for the task of tidying the castle, left their rifles in the kitchen and set to work sweeping, mopping, dusting lamps, putting clean sheets on the beds.

At around three the guests arrived. One was General Von Berenberg, the division commander. With him came Herman Hoensch, a writer of the Reich, and two officers of the 79th's general staff. In the other car came the Romanian general Eugen Entrescu, thirty-five at the time and the rising star of his country's armed forces, accompanied by the young scholar Paul Popescu, twenty-three, and the Baroness Von Zumpe, whom the Romanians had met only the night before at a reception at the German embassy and who by rights should have ridden with General Von Berenberg, but who was finally persuaded by Entrescu's gallant ways and Popescu's amusing and playful manner to give in to their pleas, which were reasonably based on the fact that the baroness would have more room in their car, since they were carrying fewer passengers.

Reiter's surprise when he saw the Baroness Von Zumpe step out of the car couldn't have been greater. But the strangest thing of all was that this time the young baroness stopped in front of him and asked, with real interest, whether he knew her, because his face, she said, looked familiar. Reiter (still standing at attention, staring impassively off at the horizon in martial fashion, or perhaps gazing into nothing) answered that of course he knew her because he had served in the house of her father, the baron, from an early age, as had his mother, Frau Reiter, whom perhaps the baroness might recall.

"That's right," said the baroness, and she began to laugh, "you were the long-legged boy who was always underfoot."

"That was me," said Reiter.

"My cousin's confidant," said the baroness.

"A friend of your cousin," said Reiter, "Mr. Hugo Halder."

"And what are you doing here, at Dracula's castle?" asked the baroness.

"Serving the Reich," said Reiter, and for the first time he looked at her.

He thought she was stunningly beautiful, much more so than when he had known her. A few steps from them, waiting, was General Entrescu, who couldn't stop smiling, and the young scholar Popescu, who

more than once exclaimed: wonderful, wonderful, yet again the sword of
fate severs the head from the hydra of chance.

•

The guests had a light meal and then went out to explore the castle
grounds. General Von Berenberg, initially a proponent of this expedition,
soon felt fatigued and retired, leaving General Entrescu to lead the way,
with the baroness on his arm and the young scholar Popescu to his left,
who made it his business to reel off and elaborate on a host of mostly
contradictory facts. Alongside Popescu was the SS officer, and lagging a
bit behind were Hoensch, the Reich writer, and the two general staff officers. Bringing up the rear was Reiter, whom the baroness had insisted
on keeping with her, arguing that before he served the Reich he had
served her family, a petition Von Berenberg immediately granted.

Soon they came to a crypt dug out of the rock. An iron gate, with a
coat of arms eroded by time, barred the entrance. The SS officer, who
behaved as if he owned the castle, took a key out of his pocket and let
them in. Then he switched on a flashlight and they all ventured into the
crypt, except for Reiter, who remained on guard at the door at the signal
of one of the officers.

So Reiter stood there, watching the stone stairs that led down into
the dark, and the desolate garden through which they had come, and the
towers of the castle like two gray candles on a deserted altar. Then he
felt for a cigarette in his jacket, lit it, and gazed at the gray sky, the distant valleys, and thought about the Baroness Von Zumpe's face as the
cigarette ash dropped to the ground and little by little he fell asleep,
leaning on the stone wall. Then he dreamed about the inside of the
crypt. The stairs led down to an amphitheater only partially illuminated
by the SS officer's flashlight. He dreamed that the visitors were laughing,
all except one of the general staff officers, who wept and searched for a
place to hide. He dreamed that Hoensch recited a poem by Wolfram von
Eschenbach and then spat blood. He dreamed that among them they
had agreed to eat the Baroness Von Zumpe.

He woke with a start and almost bolted down the stairs to confirm
with his own eyes that nothing he had dreamed was real.

When the visitors returned to the surface, anyone, even the least
astute observer, could have seen that they were divided into two groups,
those who were pale when they emerged, as if they had glimpsed some-

thing momentous down below, and those who appeared with a half smile sketched on their faces, as if they had just been reapprised of the naïveté of the human race.

That night, during dinner, they talked about the crypt, but they also talked about other things. They talked about death. Hoensch said that death itself was only an illusion under permanent construction, that in *reality* it didn't exist. The SS officer said death was a necessity: no one in his right mind, he said, would stand for a world full of turtles or giraffes. Death, he concluded, served a regulatory function. The young scholar Popescu said that death, in the Eastern tradition, was only a passage. What wasn't clear, he said, or at least not to him, was toward what *place*, what reality, that passage led.

"The question," he said, "is where. The answer," he answered himself, "is wherever my merits take me."

General Entrescu was of the opinion that this hardly mattered, the important thing was to keep moving, the dynamic of motion, which made men and all living beings, including cockroaches, equal to the great stars. Baroness Von Zumpe said, and perhaps she was the only one to speak frankly, that death was a bore. General Von Berenberg declined to offer an opinion, as did the two general staff officers.

Then they talked about murder. The SS officer said that *murder* was an ambiguous, confusing, imprecise, vague, ill-defined word, easily misused. Hoensch agreed. General Von Berenberg said that he would rather leave the laws to the judges and the criminal courts and if a judge said a certain act was murder, then it was murder, and if the judge and the court ruled it wasn't, then it wasn't, and that was the end of the matter. The two general staff officers agreed.

General Entrescu confessed that his childhood heroes were always murderers and criminals, for whom, he said, he felt a great respect. The young scholar Popescu reminded the guests that murderers and heroes resembled each other in their solitariness, and, at least initially, in the public's lack of understanding of their actions.

Baroness Von Zumpe, meanwhile, said she had never in her life met a murderer, as was only natural, but she had met a criminal, if he could be called that, a despicable being imbued with a mysterious aura that made him attractive to women, in fact, she said, an aunt of hers, her father's only sister, fell in love with him, which almost drove her father mad and led him to challenge the man who had conquered his sister's heart to a duel, and to the surprise of everyone, the challenge was accepted, and the duel took place in the Heart of Autumn forest, outside Potsdam, a place that she, the Baroness Von Zumpe, had visited many years later in order to see with her own eyes the towering gray trees and the clearing, a sloping piece of ground some fifty yards across, where her father had done battle with that unpredictable man, who arrived at seven in the morning with two tramps instead of seconds, two beggars falling down drunk, of course, whereas her father's seconds were the Baron of X and the Count of Y, anyway, such a disgrace that the Baron of X himself, red with fury, was about to raise his own gun and kill the seconds who had come with Conrad Halder, that was the name of my aunt's beloved, as doubtless General Von Berenberg will recall (the general nodded though he had no idea what the Baroness Von Zumpe was talking about), the case was much discussed back then, before I was born, of course, in fact my father, the Baron Von Zumpe, was still a bachelor at the time, anyway, in that little forest with the romantic name the duel was fought, with pistols, of course, and although I don't know what rules were followed I suppose both men aimed and fired at once: my father's bullet passed a fraction of an inch from Halder's left shoulder, and no one heard Halder's shot, though everyone was convinced it hadn't hit its target either, since my father was a much better marksman and if anyone fell it would be Halder, not my father, but then, oh surprise, everyone, including my father, saw that Halder, far from lowering his arm, was still aiming, and then they understood that he hadn't fired yet and the duel, therefore, wasn't over, and then came the most surprising thing of all, especially if we take into account the reputation of the man, the pretender to the hand of my father's sister, who, far from shooting at my father, chose a part of his own anatomy, I think it was his left arm, and shot himself point-blank.

What happened next I don't know. I suppose they took Halder to a doctor. Or perhaps Halder went himself, with his beggar-seconds, to find a doctor to see to the wound, while my father stood motionless in the Heart of Autumn forest, seething with rage or livid at what he had just witnessed, while his seconds gathered around to console him and urge him not to concern himself, one could expect all sorts of buffoonery from these people.

Shortly afterward Halder ran away with my father's sister. For a while they lived in Paris and then in the south of France, where Halder, who was a painter, though I never saw any of his paintings, spent long stretches. Then they got married and settled in Berlin, or so I heard. Life was hard and my father's sister fell gravely ill. The day of her death my father received a telegram and that night he saw Halder for the second time. He found him drunk and half naked, while Halder's son, my cousin, who was three at the time, roamed the house, which was also Halder's studio, completely naked and daubed with paint.

That night they talked for the first time and possibly came to an agreement. My father took charge of his nephew and Conrad Halder left Berlin forever. Occasionally news came of him, always preceded by some small scandal. His Berlin paintings were left in the care of my father, who didn't have the heart to burn them. Once I asked where he kept them. He wouldn't tell me. I asked him what they were like. My father looked at me and said they were just dead women. Portraits of my aunt? No, said my father, other women, all dead.

·

No one at that dinner, of course, had ever seen a painting by Conrad Halder, except for the SS officer, who said the painter was a degenerate artist, clearly a disgrace to the Von Zumpe family. Then they talked about art, about the heroic in art, about still lifes, superstitions, and symbols.

Hoensch said that culture was a chain of links composed of heroic art and superstitious interpretations. The young scholar Popescu said culture was a symbol in the shape of a life buoy. The Baroness Von Zumpe said culture was essentially pleasure, anything that provided or bestowed pleasure, and the rest was just charlatanry. The SS officer said culture was the call of the blood, a call better heard by night than by day, and also, he said, a decoder of fate. General Von Berenberg said culture was Bach and that was enough for him. One of his general staff officers said culture was Wagner and that was enough for him too. The other general staff officer said culture was Goethe, and as the general had said, that was enough for him, sometimes more than enough. The life of a man is comparable only to the life of another man. The life of a man, he said, is only long enough to fully enjoy the works of another man.

General Entrescu, who was highly amused by the general staff officer's claim, said that for him, on the contrary, culture was life, not the life of a single man or the work of a single man, but life in general, any manifestation of it, even the most vulgar, and then he talked about the backdrops of some Renaissance paintings and he said those landscapes could be seen anywhere in Romania, and he talked about Madonnas and said that at that precise instant he was gazing on the face of a Madonna more beautiful than any Italian Renaissance painter's Madonna (Baroness Von Zumpe flushed), and finally he talked about cubism and modern painting and said that any abandoned wall or bombed-out wall was more interesting than the most famous cubist painting, never mind surrealism, he said, which couldn't hold a candle to the dream of a single illiterate Romanian peasant. After which there was a brief silence, brief but expectant, as if General Entrescu had said a bad word or a rude word or a word in poor taste or had insulted his German guests, since it had been his idea (his and Popescu's) to visit that gloomy castle. A silence that was nevertheless broken by the Baroness Von Zumpe when she asked, her tone ranging from innocent to worldly, what it was that the peasants of Romania dreamed and how he knew what those most peculiar peasants dreamed. To which General Entrescu responded with a frank laugh, an open and crystalline laugh, a laugh that in Bucharest's most fashionable circles was described, not without a hint of ambiguity, as the unmistakable laugh of a superman, and then, looking the Baroness Von Zumpe in the eye, he said that nothing about his men (he meant his soldiers, most of whom were peasants) was foreign to him.

"I steal into their dreams," he said. "I steal into their most shameful thoughts, I'm in every shiver, every spasm of their souls, I steal into their hearts, I scrutinize their most fundamental beliefs, I scan their irrational impulses, their unspeakable emotions, I sleep in their lungs during the summer and their muscles during the winter, and all of this I do without the least effort, without intending to, without asking or seeking it out, without constraints, driven only by love and devotion."

•

When it came time to go to sleep or move into another room adorned with suits of armor and swords and hunting trophies, where liquors and little cakes and Turkish cigarettes awaited them, General Von Berenberg excused himself and shortly afterward retired to his chambers. One of his officers, the Wagner enthusiast, followed his lead, whereas the other, the Goethe enthusiast, chose to prolong the evening. The Baroness Von Zumpe said she wasn't tired. Hoensch and the SS officer led the march to the next room. General Entrescu sat beside the baroness. The intellectual Popescu remained standing, next to the fireplace, observing the SS officer with curiosity.

Two soldiers, one of them Reiter, served as footmen. The other was a fat man with red hair, his name Kruse, who seemed on the verge of sleep.

First they praised the assortment of little cakes and then, without pause, they began to talk about Count Dracula, as if they had been waiting all night for this moment. It wasn't long before they broke into two factions, those who believed in the count and those who didn't. Among the latter were the general staff officer, General Entrescu, and the Baroness Von Zumpe. Among the former were Popescu, Hoensch, and the SS officer, though Popescu claimed that Dracula, whose real name was Vlad Tepes, aka Vlad the Impaler, was Romanian, and Hoensch and the SS officer claimed that Dracula was a noble Teuton, who had left Germany accused of an imaginary act of treason or disloyalty and had come to live with some of his loyal retainers in Transylvania a long time before Vlad Tepes was born, and while they didn't deny Tepes a real historical or Transylvanian existence, they believed that his methods, as revealed by his alias or nickname, had little or nothing to do with the methods of Dracula, who was more of a strangler than an impaler, and sometimes a throat slitter, and whose life abroad, so to speak, had been a constant dizzying spin, a constant abysmal penitence.

As far as Popescu was concerned, meanwhile, Dracula was simply a Romanian patriot who had resisted the Turks, a deed for which every European nation should to some degree be grateful. History is cruel, said Popescu, cruel and paradoxical: the man who halts the conquering onslaught of the Turks is transformed, thanks to a second-rate English writer, into a monster, a libertine whose sole interest is human blood, when the truth is that the only blood Tepes cared to spill was Turkish.

At this point, Entrescu, who despite the copious quantities of drink he had downed at dinner and continued to down during the postprandial hour, didn't seem drunk—in fact he gave the impression of being the most sober of the group, along with the fastidious SS officer, who scarcely wet his lips with alcohol—said it wasn't strange, if one cast a dispassionate glance over the great deeds of history (even the blank deeds of history, although this, of course, no one understood), that a hero should be transformed into a monster or the worst sort of villain or that he should unintentionally succumb to invisibility, in the same way that a villain or an ordinary person or a good-hearted mediocrity should become, with the passage of the centuries, a beacon of wisdom, a magnetic beacon capable of casting a spell over millions of human beings, without having done anything to justify such adoration, in fact without even having aspired to it or desired it (although all men, including the worst kind of ruffians, at some moment in their lives dream of reigning over man and time). Did Jesus Christ, he asked, suspect that someday his church would spread to the farthest corners of Earth? Did Jesus Christ, he asked, ever have what we, today, call an idea of the world? Did Jesus Christ, who apparently knew everything, know that the world was round and to the east lived the Chinese (this sentence he spat out, as if it cost him great effort to utter it) and to the west the primitive peoples of America? And he answered himself, no, although of course in a way having an idea of the world is easy, everybody has one, generally an idea restricted to one's village, bound to the land, to the tangible and mediocre things before one's eyes, and this idea of the world, petty, limited, crusted with the grime of the familiar, tends to persist and acquire authority and eloquence with the passage of time.

And then, taking an unexpected detour, General Entrescu began to talk about Flavius Josephus, that intelligent, cowardly, cautious man, a flatterer and odds-on gambler, whose idea of the world was much more complex and subtle than Christ's, if one paid it careful attention, but much less subtle than that of those who, it's said, helped to translate his *History* into Greek, in other words the lesser Greek philosophers, men for hire of the great man for hire, who gave shape to his shapeless writings, elegance to what was vulgar, who converted Flavius Josephus's splutterings of panic and death into something distinguished, gracious, and fine.

And then Entrescu began to envision those philosophers for hire, he saw them wandering the streets of Rome and the roads that lead to the sea, he saw them sitting by the side of those roads, bundled in their cloaks, mentally constructing an idea of the world, he saw them eating in portside taverns, dark places that smelled of seafood and spices, wine and fried food, until at last they faded away, just as Dracula faded away, with his blood-tinted armor and blood-tinted clothing, a stoic Dracula, a Dracula who read Seneca or took pleasure in hearing the German minnesingers and whose feats in Eastern Europe found their match only in the deeds described in the *Chanson de Roland*. Historically, that is, or politically, sighed Entrescu, as well as symbolically or poetically.

And at this point Entrescu apologized for letting himself be carried away by enthusiasm and was silent, and the lull was seized upon by Popescu, who began to talk about a Romanian mathematician who lived from 1865 to 1936, a man who spent the last twenty years of his life devoted to the search for some "mysterious numbers" hidden in a part of the vast landscape visible to man, though the numbers themselves were invisible and could live between rocks or between one room and another or even between one number and another, call it a kind of alternative mathematics camouflaged between seven and eight, just waiting for the man capable of seeing it and deciphering it. The only problem was that to decipher it one had to see it and to see it one had to decipher it.

When the mathematician talked about deciphering, explained Popescu, he really meant understanding, and when he talked about seeing, explained Popescu, he really meant applying, or so Popescu believed. Though perhaps not, he said, hesitating. Perhaps his disciples, among whom I count myself, misinterpreted his words. In any case, as was inevitable, the mathematician went out of his head one night and had to be sent to an asylum. Popescu and two other young men from Bucharest went to visit him. At first he didn't recognize them, but as the days went by and he no longer resembled a raging lunatic but simply a defeated old man, he remembered them or pretended to remember them and smiled. Nevertheless, at his family's request, he remained at the asylum. And anyway, because of his regular relapses, his doctors counseled an indefinite stay. One day Popescu went to see him. The doctors had given the mathematician a little notebook in which he drew the trees that surrounded the hospital, portraits of other patients, and architectural sketches of the houses visible from the grounds. For a long time they were silent, until Popescu decided to speak frankly. With the typical heedlessness of youth, he broached the subject of his teacher's madness or presumed madness. The mathematician laughed. There is no such thing as madness, he said. But you're here, said Popescu, and this is a madhouse. The mathematician didn't seem to be listening: the only real madness, if we can call it that, he said, is a chemical imbalance, which is easily cured by treatment with chemical products.

"But you're here, dear professor, you're here, you're here," shouted Popescu.

"For my own protection," said the mathematician.

Popescu didn't understand him. It occurred to him that he was talking to an utter lunatic, a hopeless lunatic. He covered his face with his hands and didn't move for some time. For a moment he thought he would fall asleep. Then he opened his eyes, rubbed them, and saw the mathematician sitting before him, watching him, his back straight, his legs crossed. Popescu asked whether something had happened. I saw something I shouldn't, said the mathematician. Popescu asked him to explain what he meant. If I explained, answered the mathematician, I would go mad again and possibly die. But for a man of your genius, said Popescu, being here is like being buried alive. The mathematician smiled kindly. You're wrong, he said, in fact I have everything here I need to stave off death: medicine, time, nurses and doctors, a notebook to draw in, a park.

Shortly afterward, however, the mathematician died. Popescu attended the burial. When it was over, he and some other disciples of the dead man went to a restaurant, where they ate and lingered until dusk. They told stories about the mathematician, they talked about posterity, someone compared man's fate to the fate of an old whore, and one boy, scarcely eighteen, who had just returned from a trip to India with his parents, recited a poem.

Two years later, purely by chance, Popescu was at a party with one of the doctors who had treated the mathematician during his stay at the asylum. The doctor was a sincere young man with a Romanian heart, which is to say a heart not deceitful in the slightest. Also, he was a bit drunk, which made confidences easier.

According to this doctor, the mathematician, upon being admitted, showed severe symptoms of schizophrenia, though he made favorable progress after a few days of treatment. One night when the doctor was on duty he went to the mathematician's room to talk a little, because, even with sleeping pills, the mathematician hardly slept and the hospital management allowed him to keep his light on as long as he wanted. The first surprise came when he opened the door. The mathematician wasn't in bed. For an instant the doctor thought he might have escaped but then he discovered him huddled in a dark corner. He crouched down beside him and after verifying that he was in fine physical shape he asked what was wrong. Then the mathematician said: nothing, and met his eyes, and in them the doctor saw a look of absolute fear of a sort he had never seen before, even in his daily dealings with so many madmen of the most varied types.

"What is a look of absolute fear?" Popescu asked.

The doctor belched a few times, shifted in his chair, and answered that it was a kind of look of mercy, but empty, as if all that were left of mercy, after a mysterious voyage, was the skin, as if mercy were a skin of water, say, in the hands of a Tatar horseman who gallops away over the steppe and dwindles until he vanishes, and then the horseman returns, or the ghost of the horseman returns, or his shadow, or the idea of him, and he has the skin, empty of water now, because he drank it all during his trip, or he and his horse drank it, and the skin is empty now, it's a normal skin, an empty skin, because after all the abnormal thing is a skin swollen with water, but this skin swollen with water, this hideous skin swollen with water doesn't arouse fear, doesn't awaken it, much less isolate it, but the empty skin does, and that was what he saw in the mathematician's face, absolute fear.

But the most interesting thing, the doctor said to Popescu, was that after a while the mathematician recovered and his look of alienation vanished without a trace, and as far as he knew, it never came back. That was the story Popescu had to tell, and like Entrescu before him, he expressed regret for going on too long and probably boring them, which the others hastened to deny, although their voices lacked conviction. From that moment on, conversation began to flag and soon afterward they all retired to their rooms.

•

But there were more surprises still in store for Reiter. In the early morning hours he felt someone shaking him. He opened his eyes. It was Kruse. Unable to make out what Kruse was saying, the words whispered in his ear, he grabbed him by the neck and squeezed. Another hand dropped on his shoulder. It was their comrade Neitzke.

"Don't hurt him, idiot," said Neitzke.

Reiter let go of Kruse's neck and listened to the proposal. Then he dressed quickly and followed them. They left the cellar that served as sleeping quarters and turned into a long hallway where Wilke, another comrade, was waiting for them. Wilke was a small man, no more than five foot two, with a wizened face and intelligent eyes. When they reached him they shook hands, because Wilke was a formal man and his comrades knew that with him one had to adhere to protocol. Then they went up a staircase and opened a door. The room they came to was empty and cold, as if Dracula had just stepped out. The only thing there was an old mirror that Wilke lifted off the stone wall, uncovering a secret passageway. Neitzke took out a flashlight and passed it to Wilke.

They walked for more than ten minutes, going up and down stone stairs, not knowing whether they were at the top of the castle or whether they had returned to the cellar by a different path. The passageway split every ten yards, and Wilke, who was in the lead, got lost several times. As they walked, Kruse whispered that there was something strange about the passageways. They asked what was strange and Kruse answered that there weren't any rats. Good, said Wilke, I hate rats. Reiter and Neitzke agreed. I don't like rats either, said Kruse, but there are always rats in the passageways of a castle, especially if it's an old castle, and here we haven't come across a single one. The others meditated in silence on Kruse's remark and after a while they admitted there was something shrewd about it. It really was strange they hadn't seen a single rat. Finally they stopped and shone the flashlight behind them and ahead of them, over the ceiling of the passageway and the floor that snaked away like a shadow. Not a single rat. All for the best. They lit four cigarettes and each man described how he would make love to the Baroness Von Zumpe. Then they moved on in silence until they began to sweat and Neitzke said it was hard to breathe.

Then they turned back, with Kruse leading the way, and they soon reached the mirror room, where Neitzke and Kruse took their leave. After saying goodbye, Wilke and Reiter returned to the labyrinth, but this time they didn't talk, so that the sound of their whispers wouldn't confuse them again. Wilke thought he heard footsteps, footsteps gliding behind him. Reiter walked for a while with his eyes closed. When they were just about to despair, they found what they were looking for: a side passage, very narrow, that ran through the stone walls, walls that looked thick but were apparently hollow, and in which there were peepholes or tiny slits that provided a nearly perfect view of the rooms behind.

And so they were able to look into the room of the SS officer, lit by three candles, and they saw the SS officer up, wrapped in a robe, writing something at a table near the fireplace. The expression on his face was forlorn. And although that was all there was to see, Wilke and Reiter patted each other on the back, because only then were they sure they were on the right path. They moved on.

By touch they discovered other peepholes. Rooms lit by the light of the moon or in shadows, where, if they pressed an ear to the hole bored in the stone, they could hear the snores or sighs of a sleeper. The next lit room belonged to General Von Berenberg. There was a single candle, set in a candlestick on the night table, and its flame wavered as if someone had left the huge window open, making shadows and ghostly shapes that at first disguised the spot where the general knelt at the foot of the big canopied bed, praying. Von Berenberg's face was contorted, Reiter noted, as if he bore a huge weight on his shoulders, not the life of his soldiers, certainly, or his family, or even his own life, but the weight of his conscience, which was something that grew clear to Reiter and Wilke before they moved away from that peephole, struck with astonishment or horror.

Finally, after passing other watch points plunged in darkness and sleep, they arrived at their true destination, the room of the Baroness Von Zumpe, a room lit by nine candles and presided over by the portrait of a soldier or warrior monk with the intent and tortured air of a hermit, in whose face, which hung three feet from the bed, one could observe all the bitterness of abstinence and penitence and self-abnegation.

Beneath a naked man with an abundance of hair on his upper back and legs, they glimpsed the Baroness Von Zumpe, her golden curls and part of her lily-white forehead occasionally emerging from behind the left shoulder of the person thrusting on top of her. The cries of the baroness alarmed Reiter at first, who was slow to understand that they were cries of pleasure, not pain. When the coupling ended, General Entrescu got up from the bed and they watched him walk to a table where a bottle of vodka stood. His penis, from which hung a not negligible quantity of seminal fluid, was still erect or half erect and must have measured nearly a foot long, Wilke reflected afterward, his calculations on the mark.

He looked more like a horse than a man, Wilke told his comrades. And he had the stamina of a horse too, because after swallowing some vodka he returned to the bed where the Baroness Von Zumpe was drowsing and after he had rearranged her he began to fuck her again, at first scarcely moving, but then with such violence that the baroness, on her belly, bit the palm of her hand until she drew blood, so as not to scream. By now Wilke had unbuttoned his fly and was masturbating, leaning against the wall. Reiter heard him moan beside him. First he thought it was a rat that just happened to be breathing its last somewhere nearby. A baby rat. But when he saw Wilke's penis and Wilke's hand moving back and forth, he was disgusted and elbowed him in the chest. Wilke ignored him and continued to masturbate. Reiter glanced at his face: Wilke's profile struck him as very odd. It looked like an engraving of a worker or artisan, an innocent passerby suddenly blinded by a ray of moonlight. He seemed to be dreaming, or, more accurately, momentarily breaking through the massive black walls that separate waking from sleep. So he left him alone and after a while he began to touch himself too, at first discreetly, through his trousers, and then openly, pulling out his penis and adjusting to the rhythm of General Entrescu and the Baroness Von Zumpe, who wasn't biting her hand anymore (a bloodstain had spread on the sheet next to her sweaty cheeks) but crying and speaking words that neither the general nor the two soldiers understood, words that went beyond Romania, beyond even Germany and Europe, beyond a country estate, beyond some hazy friendships, beyond what they, Wilke and Reiter, though perhaps not General Entrescu, understood by love, desire, sexuality.

Then Wilke came on the wall and mumbled something too, a soldier's prayer, and soon afterward Reiter came on the wall and bit his lips without saying a word. And then Entrescu got up and they saw, or thought they saw, drops of blood on his penis shiny with semen and vaginal fluid, and then Baroness Von Zumpe asked for a glass of vodka, and then they watched as Entrescu and the baroness stood entwined, each with a glass in hand and an air of distraction, and then Entrescu recited a poem in his tongue, which the baroness didn't understand but whose musicality she lauded, and then Entrescu closed his eyes and cocked his head as if to listen to something, the music of the spheres, and then he opened his eyes and sat at the table and set the baroness on his cock, erect again (the famous foot-long cock, pride of the Romanian army), and the cries and moans and tears resumed, and as the baroness sank down onto Entrescu's cock or Entrescu's cock rose up into the Baroness Von Zumpe, the Romanian general recited a new poem, a poem that he accompanied by waving both arms (the baroness clinging to his neck), a poem that again neither of them understood, except for the word *Dracula*, which was repeated every four lines, a poem that might have been martial or satirical or metaphysical or marmoreal or even anti-German, but whose rhythm seemed made to order for the occasion, a poem that the young baroness, sitting astride Entrescu's thighs, celebrated by swaying back and forth, like a little shepherdess gone wild in the vastness of Asia, digging her nails into her lover's neck, scrubbing the blood that still flowed from her right hand on her lover's face, smearing the corners of his lips with blood, while Entrescu, undeterred, continued to recite his poem in which the word *Dracula* sounded every four lines, a poem that was surely satirical, decided Reiter (with infinite joy) as Wilke jerked off again.

When it was all over, though for the unflagging Entrescu and the unflagging baroness it was far from over, they filed silently back down the secret passageways, silently replaced the mirror, crept silently down to the improvised underground barracks, and slipped silently into bed next to their respective guns and kits.

•

The next morning the detachment left the castle after the departure of the two carloads of guests. Only the SS officer remained behind while they swept, washed, and tidied everything. Then, when the officer was fully satisfied with their efforts, he ordered them off and the detachment climbed into the truck and headed back down to the plain. Only the SS officer's car—with no driver, which was odd—was left at the castle. As they drove away, Reiter saw the officer: he had climbed up to the battlements and was watching the detachment leave, craning his neck, rising up on tiptoe, until the castle, on the one hand, and the truck, on the other, disappeared from view.

•

While he was posted in Romania, Reiter requested and obtained two leaves that he used to visit his parents. Back in the village, he spent the day lying on the rocky shore watching the sea, but with no urge to swim, much less dive, or he took long walks through the countryside, walks that invariably ended at the ancestral home of the Baron Von Zumpe, empty and diminished, now watched over by the old gamekeeper, with whom he sometimes stopped to talk, although the conversations, if they could be called that, were mostly frustrating. The gamekeeper asked how the war was going and Reiter shrugged. Reiter, in turn, asked about the baroness (actually he asked about the young baroness, which was how the locals referred to her) and the gamekeeper shrugged. The shrugs could mean he didn't know or that reality was increasingly vague, more like a dream, or that everything was going badly and it was best not to ask questions and to gird oneself with patience.

He also spent long periods with his sister, Lotte, who was ten by then and adored her brother. This devotion made Reiter laugh, but it made him sad, too, and he was swamped by grim thoughts in which everything was meaningless, though he was careful not to come to any resolve because he was sure he would end up shot. No one commits suicide in wartime, he thought as he lay in bed listening to his mother and father snore. Why not? Well, for convenience's sake, to postpone the inevitable, because human beings tend to leave their fate in the hands of others. In fact, the suicide rate is highest in wartime, but Reiter was too young then (though he could no longer be called completely untutored) to know that. On both leaves, too, he visited Berlin (on the way to his village) and tried in vain to find Hugo Halder.

He couldn't find him. A family of civil servants with four adolescent daughters lived in Halder's old flat. When he asked whether the previous tenant had left an address where he could be found, the head of the family, a party member, answered curtly that he didn't know, but as Reiter was leaving, one of the daughters, the oldest and prettiest, caught up to him on the stairs and said she knew where Halder was living now. Then she continued down the stairs and Reiter followed her. The girl dragged him to a public park. There, in a corner safe from prying eyes, she turned, as if seeing him for the first time, and hurled herself at him, planting a kiss on his mouth. Reiter pulled away and asked why in heaven she was kissing him. The girl said she was happy to see him. Reiter studied her eyes, a washed-out blue, like the eyes of a blind woman, and realized he was talking to a madwoman.

Even so, he wanted to know what information the girl had about Halder. She said that if he didn't let her kiss him she wouldn't tell him. They kissed again: the girl's tongue was very dry at first and Reiter caressed it with his tongue until it was thoroughly moistened. Where does Hugo Halder live now? he asked. The girl smiled at him as if Reiter were a slow child. Can't you guess? she asked. Reiter shook his head. The girl, who couldn't have been more than sixteen, began to laugh so hard that Reiter was afraid if she didn't stop the police would come, and he could think of no better way of silencing her than kissing her on the mouth again.

"My name is Ingeborg," said the girl when Reiter removed his lips from hers.

"My name is Hans Reiter," he said.

Then she looked at the sandy, pebbly ground and paled visibly, as if she were about to faint.

"My name," she repeated, "is Ingeborg Bauer, I hope you won't forget me."

From this moment on they spoke in fainter and fainter whispers.

"I won't," said Reiter.

"Swear it," said the girl.

"I swear," said Reiter.

"Who do you swear by? Your mother, your father, God?" asked the girl.

"I swear by God," said Reiter.

"I don't believe in God," said the girl.

"Then I swear by my mother and father," said Reiter.

"An oath like that is no good," said the girl, "parents are no good, people are always trying to forget they have parents."

"Not me," said Reiter.

"Yes, you," said the girl, "and me, and everyone."

"Then I swear to you by whatever you want," said Reiter.

"Do you swear by your division?" asked the girl.

"I swear by my division and regiment and battalion," said Reiter, and then he added that he also swore by his corps and his army group.

"Don't tell anyone," said the girl, "but to be honest, I don't believe in the army."

"What do you believe in?" asked Reiter.

"Not much," said the girl after pondering her reply for a second. "Sometimes I even forget what I believe in. There are so few things, and so many things I don't believe in, such a huge number of things, that they hide what I do believe in. Right now, for example, I can't remember anything."

"Do you believe in love?" asked Reiter.

"Frankly, no," said the girl.

"What about honesty?" asked Reiter.

"Ugh, that's worse than love," said the girl.

"Do you believe in sunsets," asked Reiter, "starry nights, bright mornings?"

"No, no, no," said the girl with a gesture of evident distaste, "I don't believe in anything ridiculous."

"You're right," said Reiter. "What about books?"

695

"Even worse," said the girl, "and anyway in my house there are only Nazi books, Nazi politics, Nazi history, Nazi economics, Nazi mythology, Nazi poetry, Nazi novels, Nazi plays."

"I had no idea the Nazis had written so much," said Reiter.

"As far as I can tell, you don't have much idea about anything, Hans," said the girl, "except kissing me."

"True," said Reiter, who was always ready to admit his ignorance.

By then they were strolling through the park holding hands and every so often Ingeborg would stop and kiss Reiter on the mouth and anyone who saw them might have thought they were just a young soldier and his girl, with no money to go anywhere else, very much in love and with many things to tell each other. And yet if this hypothetical observer had approached the couple and looked them in the eyes he would have seen that the young woman was mad and the young soldier knew it and didn't care. Truthfully, by now Reiter didn't care that the girl was crazy, much less about his friend Hugo Halder's address. All he cared about was learning once and for all the few things Ingeborg felt were worthy of swearing by. So he asked and asked and made tentative suggestions: the girl's sisters and the city of Berlin and world peace and the children of the world and the birds of the world and the opera and the rivers of Europe and the faces, dear God, of men she had loved, and her own life (Ingeborg's), and friendship and humor and everything he could think of, and he received one negative response after another, until at last, after they had explored every corner of the park, the girl remembered two things she thought were valid oaths.

"Do you want to know what they are?"

"Of course I do!" said Reiter.

"I hope you won't laugh when I tell you."

"I won't laugh," said Reiter.

"The first is storms," said the girl.

"Storms?" asked Reiter, greatly surprised.

"Only big storms, when the sky turns black and the air turns gray. Thunder, lightning, and peasants killed when they cross fields," said the girl.

"Now I understand," said Reiter, who didn't love storms. "So what's the second thing?"

"The Aztecs," said the girl.

"The Aztecs?" asked Reiter, more perplexed than by the storms.

"That's right, the Aztecs," said the girl, "the people who lived in Mex-ico before Cortés came, the ones who built the pyramids."

"Oh, the Aztecs, those Aztecs," said Reiter.

"They're the only Aztecs," said the girl, "the ones who lived in Tenochtitlán and Tlatelolco and performed human sacrifices and inhab-ited two cities built around lakes."

"Oh, so they lived in two cities built around lakes," said Reiter.

"Yes," said the girl.

For a while they walked in silence. Then the girl said: I imagine those cities to be like Geneva and Montreux. Once I was with my family on holiday in Switzerland. We went by ferry from Geneva to Montreux. Lake Geneva is marvelous in summer, although there are perhaps too many mosquitoes. We spent the night at an inn in Montreux and the next day we returned by ferry again to Geneva. Have you been to Lake Geneva?"

"No," said Reiter.

"It's very beautiful and it isn't just those two cities, there are many towns on the lake, like Lausanne, which is bigger than Montreux, or Vevey, or Evian. In fact there are more than twenty towns, some tiny. Do you see?"

"Vaguely," said Reiter.

"Look, this is the lake"—the girl drew the lake with the tip of her shoe on the ground—"here's Geneva, here, and at the other end, Mon-treux, and these are the other towns. Do you see now?"

"Yes," said Reiter.

"Well, that's how I imagine the lake of the Aztecs," said the girl as she rubbed out the map with her shoe. "Except much prettier. With no mos-quitoes, nice weather all year round, and lots of pyramids, so many and so big it's impossible to count them all, pyramids on top of pyramids, pyramids behind other pyramids, all stained red with the blood of daily sacrifices. And then I imagine the Aztecs, but perhaps that doesn't inter-est you," said the girl.

"It does," said Reiter, who until then had never given the Aztecs any thought.

"They're very strange people," said the girl. "If you look them closely in the face, after a moment you realize they're mad. But they aren't shut up in a madhouse. Or maybe they are. But they don't seem to be. The Aztecs dress with great elegance, they're very careful when they choose what clothes to wear each day, one might think they spent hours in a dressing room, choosing the proper attire, and then they put on very precious plumed hats, and necklaces and rings, as well as gems on their arms and feet, and both the men and the women paint their faces, and then they go out for a walk along the lakeshore, never speaking to one another, absorbed in contemplation of the passing boats, whose crews, if they aren't Aztec, lower their gaze and keep fishing or hurry away, because some Aztecs are seized by cruel whims, and after strolling like philosophers they go into the pyramids, which are completely hollow and look like cathedrals inside, and are illuminated only by a light from above, light filtered through a great obsidian stone, in other words a dark, sparkling light. By the way, have you ever seen a piece of obsidian?" asked the girl.

"No, never," said Reiter, "or maybe I have and I didn't know it."

"You would have known it instantly," said the girl. "Obsidian is a black or very dark green feldspar, a curious thing in itself because feldspar tends to be white or yellowish. The most important kinds of feldspar, for your information, are orthoclase, albite, and labradorite. But the kind I like best is obsidian. Well, back to the pyramids. At the top is the sacrificial stone. Can you guess what it's made of?"

"Obsidian," said Reiter.

"Precisely," said the girl, "a stone like a surgeon's table, where the Aztec priests or doctors lay their victims before tearing out their hearts. But now comes the part that will really surprise you. This stone bed where the victims were laid was transparent! It was a sacrificial stone chosen and polished in such a way that it was transparent. And the Aztecs inside the pyramid watched the sacrifice as if from within, because as you'll have guessed, the light from above that illuminated the bowels of the pyramids came from an opening just beneath the sacrificial stone, so that at first the light was black or gray, a dim light in which only the inscrutable silhouettes of the Aztecs inside the pyramids could be seen, but then, as the blood of the new victim spread across the skylight of transparent obsidian, the light turned red and black, a very bright red and a very bright black, and then not only were the silhouettes of the Aztecs visible but also their features, features transfigured by the red and black light, as if the light had the power to personalize each man or woman, and that is essentially all, but *that* can last a long time, *that* exists outside time, or in some other time, ruled by other laws. When the

Aztecs came out of the pyramids, the sunlight didn't hurt them. They behaved as if there were an eclipse of the sun. And they returned to their daily rounds, which basically consisted of strolling and bathing and then strolling again and spending a long time standing still in contemplation of imperceptible things or studying the patterns insects made in the dirt and eating with friends, but always in silence, which is the same as eating alone, and every so often they made war. And above them in the sky there was always an eclipse," said the girl.

"Well, well, well," said Reiter, impressed by his new friend's knowledge.

For a while, without intending to, the pair walked in silence through the park, as if they were Aztecs, until the girl asked what he would swear by, Aztecs or storms.

"I don't know," said Reiter, who had already forgotten what he had to swear to.

"Choose," said the girl, "and think carefully because it's much more important than you understand."

"What's important?" asked Reiter.

"Your oath," said the girl.

"And why is it important?" asked Reiter.

"For you, I don't know," said the girl, "but for me it's important because it will mark my fate."

At that moment Reiter remembered that he had to swear he would never forget her and he felt great sorrow. For a moment he could scarcely breathe and then he felt as if the words were catching in his throat. He decided he would swear by the Aztecs, since he didn't like storms.

"I swear by the Aztecs," he said, "I'll never forget you."

"Thank you," said the girl, and they kept walking.

After a while, although he no longer cared, Reiter asked for Halder's address.

"He lives in Paris," said the girl with a sigh. "I don't have the address."

"Ah," said Reiter.

"It's only natural that he lives in Paris," said the girl.

Reiter thought that maybe she was right and it was the most natural thing in the world that Halder had moved to Paris. When it began to get dark Reiter walked the girl to her front door and then went running to the station.

•

The attack on the Soviet Union began on June 22, 1941. The 79th Division was attached to the 11th German Army, and a few days later the division's advance troops crossed the Prut and marched shoulder to shoulder into combat, along with the Romanian army corps, who showed much more spirit than the Germans expected. And yet their advance was not as rapid as that of the units of Army Group South, composed of the 6th Army, the 17th Army, and the 1st Panzer Group, as it was called at the time, although during the course of the war it would come to be known—along with the 2nd Panzer Group, the 3rd Panzer Group, and the 4th Panzer Group—as the more intimidating Panzer Army. The human and material resources of the 11th Army were, as might be expected, infinitely smaller, not to mention the matter of the region's terrain and scarcity of roads. Nor could it rely on the surprise factor that had favored Army Groups South, Central, and North. But Reiter's division delivered what its commanders expected of it and they crossed the Prut and fought and then they fought some more on the steppes and hills of Bessarabia and then they crossed the Dniester and came to the outskirts of Odessa and then they advanced, while the Romanians halted, and fought Russian troops in retreat and then they crossed the Bug and kept advancing, leaving a wake of burned Ukrainian villages and granaries and woods that suddenly burst into flames as if by means of a mysterious process of combustion, woods like dark islands in the middle of endless wheat fields.

Who's setting fire to the woods? Reiter asked Wilke sometimes, and Wilke shrugged, and so did Neitzke and Kruse and Sergeant Lemke, exhausted from walking, because the 79th was a light infantry division, in other words a division that moved under its own steam, powered only by mules and soldiers, the function of the mules to pull the heavy equipment and the function of the soldiers to walk and fight, as if lightning warfare hadn't even blinked an eye on the division's organizational charts, like in Napoleonic times, said Wilke, marches and countermarches and forced marches, or rather constant forced marches, said Wilke, and then, without getting up from the ground where he lay like everyone else, he said I don't know who the hell is setting fires, it certainly wasn't us, was it, boys? and Neitzke said no, not us, and Kruse and Barz echoed him and even Sergeant Lemke said no, we burned that village there or we bombed this village to the left or right, but not the woods, and his men nodded and no one said another word, they just watched the blaze, the way the fire turned the dark island into an orangish red island, maybe it was Captain Ladenthin's battalion, someone said, they came this way, they must have encountered resistance in the woods, maybe it was the sapper battalion, said another, but the truth is they hadn't seen anyone in the area, whether German soldiers nearby or Soviet soldiers putting up a fight, only the black woods in the middle of a yellow sea, under a bright blue sky, and suddenly, without warning, as if they were in a great theater of wheat and the wood was the stage and proscenium of that theater in the round, the all-devouring, beautiful fire.

•

After the Bug, the division crossed the Dnieper and forged into the Crimean peninsula. Reiter fought in Perekop and several villages near Perekop whose names he never learned but along whose dirt streets he walked, clearing away corpses and ordering the elderly, women, and children to go inside and not come out. Sometimes he felt dizzy. Sometimes he noticed that when he stood up suddenly, a black fog rose before his eyes, full of granulated dots like a rain of meteors. But the meteors moved in a very odd way. Or they didn't move. They were motionless meteors. Sometimes, along with his companions, he flung himself into the conquest of an enemy position, taking no precautions at all, which gave him a reputation for daring and bravery, though all he sought was a bullet to bring peace to his heart. One night, he got into an unexpected discussion of suicide with Wilke.

"Good Christians masturbate but we don't commit suicide," Wilke said, and before Reiter went to sleep he pondered Wilke's words, because he suspected there might be a hidden truth behind the joke.

And yet his resolve was unshaken. During the battle for Chornomorske, in which the 310th Regiment and especially Reiter's battalion played an important role, Reiter risked his life at least three times, the first during an attack on a brick fortification on the outskirts of Kirovske, at the junction of Chernishove, Kirovske, and Chornomorske, a fort that wouldn't have withstood a single artillery volley, a fort that touched Reiter deeply from the moment he saw it because of the poverty and innocence it radiated, as if it had been built and were manned by children.

The company had no mortar rounds and decided to take it by storm. Volunteers were requested. Reiter was the first to step forward. He was joined almost immediately by Voss, who was also a brave man or a would-be suicide, and three others. The attack was quick: Reiter and Voss advanced along the left flank of the fort, the other three along the right. When they were twenty yards away, rifle fire came from inside. The three who were moving along the right flank dropped to the ground. Voss hesitated. Reiter kept running. He heard the hum of a bullet as it passed an inch from his head but he didn't get down. On the contrary, his body seemed to stretch up in a vain effort to see the faces of the adolescents who would put an end to his life, but he couldn't see anything. Another bullet brushed his right arm. He felt someone push him from behind and knock him down. It was Voss, who might have been rash but still retained some common sense.

For a while he watched as his comrade, after having pulled him to the ground, crawled toward the fort. He saw stones, weeds, wildflowers, and the nails in the soles of Voss's boots as he was left behind, the tiny cloud of dust Voss raised, tiny to us, he mused, but not to the processions of ants marching from north to south as Voss crawls east to west. Then he got up and began to fire at the fort, over Voss's body, and once again he heard the bullets whistle past his body as he fired and walked, like someone strolling and taking photographs, until the fort exploded, hit by a grenade and then another and another, lobbed by the soldiers on the right flank.

The second time he almost died was during the capture of Chornomorske. The two main regiments of the 79th Division led the attack after all the divisional artillery was concentrated near the piers, at the head of the road that linked Chornomorske with Evpatoria, Frunze, Inkerman, and Sevastopol, a road that lacked significant geographic landmarks. The first attack was repulsed. Reiter's battalion, which had been held in reserve, advanced in the second wave. The soldiers rushed over the barbed wire as the artillery adjusted its sights and pulverized the Soviet machine gun nests that had been located. As they ran, Reiter began to sweat, as if suddenly, in a fraction of a second, he had fallen ill. This time, he thought, he would die and the nearness of the sea convinced him even more thoroughly of this idea. First they crossed a field and then they came out into a garden where there was a little house, and from one of the windows, a tiny, asymmetric window, an old man with a white beard watched. It seemed to Reiter that the old man was eating something because his jaws moved.

On the other side of the garden there was a dirt road and a little farther on they saw five Soviet soldiers dragging a field gun behind them. They killed all five and kept running. Some continued along on the road and others turned into a pine grove.

In the grove Reiter spotted a figure in the undergrowth and stopped. It was the statue of a Greek goddess, or so he believed. Her hair was gathered up and she was tall, her expression impassive. Bathed in sweat, Reiter began to shake and stretched out his hand. The marble or stone, he couldn't say which, was cold. There was something absurd about where it stood, because that hidden spot in the trees was hardly the place for a statue. For a brief and painful instant, Reiter thought he should ask it something, but no question occurred to him and his face twisted in a grimace of suffering. Then he ran.

The grove ended at the edge of a ravine from which one could see the sea and the harbor and a kind of seaside drive bordered by trees and benches and white houses and three-story buildings that looked like hotels or spas. The trees were big and dark. In the hills a few houses were in flames and at the harbor a group of miniature people crowded onto a ship. The sky was very blue and the sea looked calm, nearly flat. To the left, along a winding road, the first men of his regiment appeared, as a few Russians fled and others raised their hands over their heads and came out of fish sheds with blackened walls. The men with Reiter went down the hill toward a square on which two new five-story buildings rose, painted white. When they reached the square, they were fired upon from several windows. The soldiers sought cover behind the trees, except for Reiter, who kept walking as if he hadn't heard anything, until he reached the door of one of the buildings. One of the walls was painted with a mural of an old sailor reading a letter. Some of the letter's lines were perfectly legible by the viewer, but they were written in Cyrillic and Reiter didn't understand a thing. The tiles on the floor were big and green. There was no elevator so Reiter began to climb the stairs. When he got to the first landing someone shot at him. He saw a shadow pop up and then he felt a sting in his right arm. He kept climbing. He was shot at again. He stood still. The wound was hardly bleeding and the pain was perfectly bearable. Maybe I'm dead already, he thought. Then he thought he wasn't and he shouldn't faint, not until he took a bullet in the head. He turned toward one of the flats and kicked open the door. He saw a table, four chairs, a glass cabinet full of dishes with a few books on top. In the room he found a woman and two little boys. The woman was very young and gazed at him in terror. I won't hurt you, he said, and tried to smile as he retreated. Then he went into another flat and two militiamen with closely cropped hair raised their hands and surrendered. Reiter didn't even glance at them. People came out of the other flats, looking as if they were starving or like pupils at a reform school. In one room, next to an open window, he found two old rifles that he threw down into the street as he signaled to his comrades to stop shooting.

The third time he almost died was weeks later, during the attack on Sevastopol. This time the advance was driven back. Each time the German troops tried to stake out a line of defense, the city's artillery loosed a rain of projectiles on them. In the area outside the city, near the Russian trenches, there were stacks of the mutilated bodies of German and Romanian soldiers. More than once the struggle was hand to hand. The assault troops reached a trench of Russian sailors and fought for five minutes, after which one side retreated. But then more Russian sailors appeared shouting hurrahs and the battle began again. For Reiter, the presence of the sailors in those dusty trenches was charged with terrible and exhilarating portents. One of them, surely, would kill him and then he would sink down again into the depths of the Baltic or the Atlantic or the Black Sea, because all seas were ultimately the same sea, and at the bottom of the sea a forest of seaweed awaited him. Or he would simply disappear, no more.

To Wilke, the whole business was insane, because where had the Russian sailors come from? what were they doing there, miles from their natural element, the sea and ships? It made no sense unless the Stukas had sunk all the ships in the Russian fleet, Wilke speculated, or the Black Sea had dried up, which naturally he didn't believe. But he said this only to Reiter, because the others never questioned anything they saw or that happened to them. In one attack Neitzke and several others from the company were killed. One night, in the trenches, Reiter rose up to his full height and gazed at the stars, but his attention, inevitably, was diverted toward Sevastopol. The city in the distance was a black mass with red mouths that opened and closed. The soldiers called it the bone crusher, but that night it didn't strike Reiter as a machine but as the reincarnation of a mythological being, a living creature struggling to draw breath. Sergeant Lemke ordered him to get down. Reiter eyed him from above, took off his helmet, scratched his head, and before he could put his helmet back on, he was felled by a bullet. As he dropped he felt another bullet penetrate his chest. He gazed dimly at Sergeant Lemke: he thought the sergeant looked like an ant that gradually grew bigger and bigger. Some five hundred yards away, several artillery rounds fell.

•

Two weeks later Reiter received the Iron Cross. A colonel presented it to him in the field hospital at Novoselivske. The colonel shook Reiter's hand, told him there had been outstanding reports on his actions in Chornomorske and Mykolaivka, and then left. Reiter couldn't talk because a bullet had pierced his throat. The wound in his chest healed well and soon he was transferred from the Crimean peninsula to Krivoy Rog, in Ukraine, where there was a bigger hospital, and his throat was operated on again. After the operation he could eat normally and move his neck as he had before, but he still couldn't talk.

The doctors who treated him didn't know whether to give him leave to return to Germany or send him back to his division, which was still engaged in the siege of Sevastopol and Kerch. The arrival of winter and the Soviet counterattack that overran parts of the German line postponed the decision and finally Reiter was neither sent to Germany nor reinstated in his unit.

But since he couldn't stay at the hospital either, he was sent with three other wounded men from the 79th to the village of Kostekino, on the banks of the Dnieper, which some called Budienny Model Farm and others Sweet Spring, because of a spring, a tributary of the Dnieper, whose waters were of a sweetness and purity unusual in the region. Really, Kostekino was scarcely a village. There were a few houses scattered among the hills, half-collapsed old wooden fences, two rotting granaries, and a dirt road, impassable in winter because of the snow and mud, that connected the village to a town on the rail line. On the outskirts there was an abandoned sovkhoz that five Germans tried to start up again. Most of the houses were abandoned, according to some because the villagers had fled the advance of the German army, according to others because they had been conscripted by the Red Army.

For the first few days Reiter slept in what must have been an agronomy office or possibly the Communist Party headquarters, the only brick and cement building in town, but cohabitation with the few German engineers and convalescents who lived in Kostekino soon grew unbearable. So he decided to take up residence in one of the many empty farmhouses. At first glance, they all looked alike. One night, as he was having coffee at the brick house, Reiter heard a different account of the villagers' disappearance: they had neither been conscripted nor fled. The depopulation was the direct consequence of the passage through Kostekino of a detachment of the Einsatzgruppe C, which proceeded to physically eliminate all the Jews in the village. Since he couldn't speak he didn't ask any questions, but he spent the next day studying the houses more closely.

In none of them did he find any object that might indicate the origin or religion of the former inhabitants. Finally he settled in a house near Sweet Spring. The first night he spent there he was woken several times by nightmares. But he couldn't remember what he had dreamed. The bed he slept in was narrow and very soft, next to the fireplace, on the first floor. The second floor was a kind of attic where there was another bed and a tiny round window, like a porthole. In a big chest he found a number of books, most in Russian, but some, to his surprise, in German. Since he knew that many Eastern European Jews spoke German, he guessed that the house had in fact belonged to a Jew. Sometimes, in the middle of the night, after waking up shouting from a nightmare, he would light the candle he always kept beside the bed and sit still for a long time, with the blankets cast off, contemplating the objects that danced in the candlelight and feeling that there was no hope as he slowly froze in the cold. Sometimes, in the morning, when he awoke, he would lie still again, staring up at the mud and straw ceiling, and it seemed to him there was something indefinably feminine about the house.

Nearby lived some Ukrainians who weren't from Kostekino and had arrived recently to work on the old sovkhoz. When he left the house the Ukrainians lifted their caps and bowed slightly in greeting. The first few days Reiter didn't respond. But then, timidly, he raised his hand and waved as if to say goodbye. Each morning he walked to the stream. With his knife he hacked a hole and then lowered a pot and ladled out some water that he drank where he stood, not minding the cold.

With the arrival of winter all the Germans holed up in the brick building and sometimes they caroused until dawn. Everyone had forgotten them, as if they had disappeared with the collapse of the front. Sometimes they went out in search of women. Other times they made love among themselves and no one said anything. This is a frozen paradise, said one of Reiter's old comrades from the 79th. Reiter stared at him as if he had no idea what he was talking about and the soldier patted him on the back and said poor Reiter, poor Reiter.

At some point, Reiter looked at himself in a mirror he found in a corner of the farmhouse. It had been a long time, and he almost didn't recognize himself. His beard was blond and tangled, his hair long and dirty, his eyes vacant and dry. Shit, he thought. Then he took the bandage off his throat: the wound seemed to have healed without trouble, but the bandage was dirty, and the crusted blood made it stiff, so he decided to throw it in the fire. Then he went looking all over the house for something to use as a bandage and that was how he found the papers of Boris Abramovich Ansky and the hiding place behind the hearth.

•

The hiding place was extremely simple but extremely clever too. The hearth, which also served as cookstove, was wide enough and the flue deep enough so that a person could crouch inside. If the width was apparent at a glance, it was impossible to tell the depth from outside, because the soot-blackened walls afforded subtle camouflage. The eye couldn't discern the gap at the rear, just a crack, but big enough so that one person, sitting with his knees drawn up, could be safe there in the dark. Although for the hiding place to work perfectly, mused Reiter, alone in the solitude of the farmhouse, there had to be two people: one to hide and one to stay in the room and put a pot of soup on to heat and then light the fire and stoke it again and again.

For many days this problem occupied his thoughts, because he believed that if he solved it he would have a better idea of the life or state of mind or the degree of desperation that had once afflicted Boris Ansky or someone Boris Ansky knew very well. On various occasions he tried to light a fire from inside. He managed it only once. Hanging a pot of water or lighting the samovar turned out to be an impossible task, so in the end he decided that whoever built the hiding place had done it thinking that someone, someday, would hide and another person would help him to hide. The rescued, thought Reiter, and the rescuer. The survivor and the victim. The one who flees when night falls and the one who stays and surrenders. Sometimes, in the afternoons, he got into the hiding place, armed only with Boris Ansky's papers and a candle, and he sat there until well into the night, until his joints were stiff and his limbs frozen, reading, reading.

•

Boris Abramovich Ansky was born in 1909, in Kostekino, in the same house that Reiter the soldier now occupied. His parents were Jews, like almost all the villagers, and they made a living selling shirts, which his father bought wholesale in Dnepropetrovsk and sometimes in Odessa and then resold in the neighboring villages. His mother raised chickens and sold eggs and they didn't need to buy vegetables because they kept a garden, small but well tended. They had just one son, Boris, when they were already approaching old age, like the biblical Abraham and Sarah, which filled them with happiness.

Sometimes, when Abraham Ansky saw his friends, he would joke about it, saying his son was so spoiled that every so often he thought the boy should have been sacrificed when he was little. The village's Orthodox Jews were scandalized or pretended to be scandalized and the others laughed openly when Abraham Ansky concluded: but instead of sacrificing him I sacrificed a hen! a hen! a hen! not a sheep or my firstborn but a hen! the hen that lays the golden eggs!

At fourteen Boris Ansky enlisted in the Red Army. His goodbyes were heartbreaking. First his father began to weep inconsolably, then his mother, and finally Boris threw himself into their arms and wept too. The trip to Moscow was unforgettable. Along the way he saw incredible faces, heard incredible conversations or speeches, read incredible proclamations on the walls that announced the paradise at hand, and everything he came upon, whether on foot or on the train, affected him deeply because this was the first time he'd left his village, with the exception of two trips he'd taken with his father to sell shirts in the region. In Moscow he visited a recruitment office and when he tried to enlist to fight Wrangel he was told that Wrangel had already been defeated. Then Ansky said he wanted to enlist to fight the Poles and he was told that the Poles had already been defeated. Then Ansky shouted that he wanted to fight Krasnov or Denikin and he was told that Denikin and Krasnov had already been defeated. Then Ansky said all right, he wanted to fight the

White Cossacks or the Czechs or Koltchak or Yudenitsch or the Allied troops and he was told that all of them had already been defeated. News comes late to your village, they said. And they also asked: where are you from, boy? And Ansky said Kostekino, near the Dnieper. And then an old soldier who was smoking a pipe asked him his name and whether he was Jewish. And Ansky said yes, he was Jewish, and he looked the old soldier in the face and only then did he notice that he was missing an eye, and also an arm.

"I had a Jewish comrade, in the campaign against the Poles," said the old man, exhaling a puff of smoke.

"What's his name?" asked Ansky. "Maybe I know him."

"Do you know all the Jews in the Soviet republic, boy?" the one-eyed, one-armed soldier asked.

"No, of course not," said Ansky, flushing.

"His name was Dmitri Verbitsky," said the one-eyed man from his corner, "and he died fifty miles from Warsaw."

Then the one-eyed man shifted in his chair, pulled a blanket up to his chin, and said: our commander's name was Korolenko and he died the same day. Then, at supersonic speed, Ansky imagined Verbitsky and Korolenko, he saw Korolenko mocking Verbitsky, heard what Korolenko said behind Verbitsky's back, entered into Verbitsky's night thoughts, Korolenko's desires, into each man's vague and shifting dreams, into their convictions and their rides on horseback, the forests they left behind and the flooded lands they crossed, the sounds of night in the open and the unintelligible morning conversations before they mounted again. He saw villages and farmland, he saw churches and hazy clouds of smoke rising on the horizon, until he came to the day when they both died, Verbitsky and Korolenko, a perfectly gray day, utterly gray, as if a thousand-mile-long cloud had passed over the land without stopping, endless.

At that moment, which hardly lasted a second, Ansky decided that he didn't want to be a soldier, but at the very same moment the officer handed him a paper and told him to sign. Now he was a soldier.

•

The next three years he spent traveling. He was in Siberia and at the lead mines of Norilsk and he crossed the Tunguska Basin escorting engineers from Omsk who were looking for coal deposits and he was in Yakutsk and he traveled up the Lena to the Arctic Ocean, beyond the

Arctic Circle, and he accompanied another group of engineers and a neurologist to the New Siberian Islands where two of the engineers went mad, one of them peacefully, but the other dangerously, so that they had to liquidate him immediately on the orders of the neurologist, who explained there was no cure for that kind of madness, especially in the middle of such a blindingly white and mentally unsettling landscape, and then he was at the Okhotsk Sea with a supply detail carrying provisions to a detachment of lost explorers, but after a few days the supply detail got lost too and ended up eating all the provisions for the explorers and then he was in a hospital in Vladivostok and then in Amur and then he saw the shores of Lake Baikal, where thousands of birds flocked, and the city of Irkutsk, and finally he chased bandits in Kazakhstan, before returning to Moscow and attending to other affairs.

And those affairs were reading and visiting museums, reading and walks in the park, reading and the almost obsessive attendance at all kinds of concerts, theatrical evenings, literary and political lectures, from which he drew many valuable lessons that he was able to apply to the freight of lived experience he had accumulated. And it was around this time that he met Efraim Ivanov, the science fiction writer, at a literary café, the best literary café in Moscow, or rather on the terrace of the café, where Ivanov drank vodka at a table off to one side, under the branches of a giant oak that stretched up to the third floor of the building, and they became friends, in part because Ivanov was interested in Ansky's outlandish ideas and in part because Ansky displayed, at least at the time, unqualified and unreserved admiration for Ivanov's science writing, as Ivanov liked to call it, rejecting the official and popular label of fantasy writer. In those days Ansky thought it wouldn't be long before the revolution spread all over the world, because only an idiot or a nihilist could fail to see or sense the potential it held for progress and happiness. Ultimately, thought Ansky, the revolution would abolish death.

When Ivanov told him that this was impossible, that death had been with man from time immemorial, Ansky said that was precisely it, the whole point, maybe the *only* thing that mattered, abolishing death, abolishing it forever, immersing ourselves in the unknown until we found something else. Abolishment, abolishment, abolishment.

•

Ivanov had been a party member since 1902. Back then he had tried to write stories in the manner of Tolstoy, Chekhov, Gorky, or rather he had tried to plagiarize them without much success, which led him, after long reflection (a whole summer night), to the astute decision that he should write in the manner of Odoevsky and Lazhechnikov. Fifty percent Odoevsky and fifty percent Lazhechnikov. This went over well, in part because readers, their memories mostly faulty, had forgotten poor Odoevsky (1803–1869) and poor Lazhechnikov (1792–1869), who died the same year, and in part because literary criticism, as keen as ever, neither extrapolated nor made the connection nor noticed a thing.

In 1910 Ivanov was what is called a promising writer, of whom great things were expected, but Odoevsky and Lazhechnikov had been exhausted as templates, and Ivanov's artistic production came to a dead halt or, depending on one's perspective, a point of collapse, from which he couldn't extricate himself even with the new blend he tried in desperation: a combination of the Hoffmanian Odoevsky and the Walter Scott disciple Lazhechnikov with the rising star Gorky. His stories, he had to acknowledge, were no longer of interest to anyone, and this took its toll on his finances, and above all his self-regard. Until the October Revolution, Ivanov worked sporadically for scientific journals, for agricultural journals, as a proofreader, as a salesman of electric lightbulbs, as a clerk in a lawyer's office, all without neglecting his work for the party, where he did practically everything that needed to be done, from writing and editing pamphlets to procuring paper and serving as a liaison with like-minded writers and some fellow travelers. And he did it all without complaint and without giving up his long-established habits: his daily visit to the watering holes where Moscow's bohemia gathered, and his vodka.

The triumph of the revolution didn't improve his literary or work prospects, rather the reverse. His labors doubled and not infrequently tripled and sometimes even quadrupled, but Ivanov did his duty without complaint. One day he was asked for a story about life in Russia in 1940. In three hours Ivanov wrote his first science fiction tale. It was called "The Train Through the Urals" and it was told from the perspective of a boy traveling in a train the average speed of which was one hundred and twenty-five miles an hour. The boy described everything that passed before his eyes: shining factories, well-tilled fields, new model villages comprising two or three buildings of more than ten stories each, visited by cheerful foreign delegations that took careful note of the advances so as to adopt them in their own countries. The traveling boy in "The Train Through the Urals" was on his way to visit his grandfather, a former Red Army soldier who, after having received a university degree at an age when most students had long finished their studies, headed a laboratory devoted to complicated research shrouded in the deepest secrecy. As they left the station holding hands, the boy's grandfather, an energetic sort who didn't look more than forty although of course he was much older, told the boy about some recent discoveries, but his grandson, a boy after all, made him tell stories about the revolution and the war against the Whites and the foreign intervention, something his grandfather, an old man after all, was happy to do. And that was all. The story's reception was overwhelming.

The first to be surprised, it must be said, was the writer himself. The second was the editor, who had read the story pencil in hand and didn't think much of it. Letters arrived at the magazine's offices asking for more contributions from Ivanov, that "unknown," that "promising voice," "a writer who believes in tomorrow," "a writer who inspires faith in the future we're fighting for," and the letters came from Moscow and Petrograd, but also from combatants and political activists in the farthest corners of the country who identified with the grandfather character, which kept the magazine editor up at night, since he, a dialectical and methodical and materialist and in no way dogmatic Marxist, a Marxist who as a good Marxist hadn't studied only Marx but also Hegel and Feuerbach (and even Kant) and who laughed heartily when he reread Lichtenberg and had read Montaigne and Pascal and was relatively familiar with the writings of Fourier, couldn't believe that of all the good things (or, to be fair, the few good things) the magazine had published, it was this story, cloyingly sentimental and with no scientific basis, that had most moved the citizens of the land of the Soviets.

Something is wrong, he thought. Naturally, the editor's sleepless night was a night of vodka and jubilation for Ivanov, who decided to celebrate his first success in Moscow's worst dives and then at the Writers House, where he dined with four friends who resembled the four horsemen of the Apocalypse. From then on Ivanov was asked only for science fiction stories, and after carefully scrutinizing his first, which he had more or less tossed off, he repeated the formula with variations, drawing on the riches of Russian literature and various chemistry, biology, medical, and astronomy publications that he accumulated in his room just as a moneylender accumulates unpaid promissory notes, letters of credit, canceled checks. In this fashion his name became known in every corner of the Soviet Union and he was soon established as a professional writer, a man who lived solely on the income of his books and who attended meetings and conferences at universities and factories and whose works were fought over by literary magazines and newspapers.

But everything grows old, and the formula of the bright future plus the hero who helps to bring about that bright future plus the boy (or the girl) who in the future (which in Ivanov's stories was the present) enjoys the fruits of the whole cornucopia of Communist inventiveness also grew old. By the time Ansky met Ivanov, the latter was no longer a sales success and his novels and stories, which many considered precious or insufferable, no longer aroused the enthusiasm they had in earlier days. But Ivanov kept writing and he kept being published and he kept bringing in money each month for his arcadian visions. He was still a party member. He belonged to the Association of Revolutionary Writers. His name figured on the official lists of Soviet creators. On the surface he was a happy man, a bachelor with a big, comfortable room in a house in a nice Moscow neighborhood, a man who slept every so often with prostitutes who were no longer young and with whom he ended up singing and weeping, a man who ate at least four times a week at the writers' and poets' restaurant.

Inside, however, Ivanov felt that something was missing. The decisive step, the bold stroke. The moment at which the larva, with a reckless smile, turns into a butterfly. Then came the young Jew Ansky and his peculiar ideas, his Siberian visions, his forays into cursed lands, the plenitude of wild experience that only a young man of eighteen can possess. But Ivanov had been eighteen once, too, and not by a long shot had he experienced anything like what Ansky described. Perhaps, he thought, it's because he's Jewish and I'm not. He soon rejected that idea. Perhaps it's because of his naïveté, he thought. His impulsive character. His scorn for the conventions that govern life, even bourgeois life, he thought. And then he began to think about how repulsive adolescent artists or pseudoartists were when viewed from up close. He thought about Mayakovsky, whom he knew personally, with whom he'd spoken once, perhaps twice, and his enormous vanity, a vanity that likely hid his lack of love for his fellow man, his lack of interest in his fellow man, his outsize craving for fame. And then he thought about Lermontov and Pushkin, as puffed up as movie stars or opera singers. Nijinsky, Gurov. Nadson. Blok (whom he'd met and who was unbearable). Remoras on the flanks of art, he thought. They think they're suns, setting everything ablaze, but they aren't suns, they're just plunging meteors and in the end no one pays them any heed. They spread humiliation, not conflagration. And ultimately it's always they who are humiliated, truly humiliated, bludgeoned and spat upon, execrated and maimed, thoroughly humiliated, taught a lesson, humiliated utterly.

●

For Ivanov, a real writer, a real artist and creator, was basically a responsible person with a certain level of maturity. A real writer had to know when to listen and when to act. He had to be reasonably enterprising and reasonably learned. Excessive learning aroused jealousy and resentment. Excessive enterprise aroused suspicion. A real writer had to be someone relatively cool-headed, a man with common sense. Someone who didn't talk too loud or start polemics. He had to be reasonably pleasant and he had to know how not to make gratuitous enemies. Above all, he had to keep his voice down, unless everyone else was raising his. A real writer had to be aware that behind him he had the Writers Association, the Artists Syndicate, the Confederation of Literary Workers, Poets House. What's the first thing a man does when he comes into a church? Efraim Ivanov asked himself. He takes off his hat. Maybe he doesn't cross himself. All right, that's allowed. We're modern. But the least he can do is bare his head! Adolescent writers, meanwhile, come into a church and don't take off their hats even when they're beaten with sticks, which is, regrettably, what happens in the end. And not only do they not take off their hats: they laugh, yawn, play the fool, pass gas. Some even applaud.

●

And yet what Ansky had to offer was too tempting for Ivanov to pass up, despite his reservations. The pact, it seems, was sealed in the science fiction writer's room.

A month later, Ansky joined the party. His sponsors were Ivanov and one of Ivanov's ex-lovers, Margarita Afanasievna, who worked as a biologist at a Moscow institute. In Ansky's papers, the event is likened to a wedding. It was celebrated at the writers' restaurant and then they made the rounds of several Moscow dives, hauling along Afanasievna, who drank like a condemned woman and who very nearly lapsed into an alcoholic coma that night. In one of the dives, as Ivanov and two writers who had joined them sang songs of lost loves, of glances never to be returned again, of silken words never to be heard, Afanasievna awoke and, with her tiny hand, grabbed Ansky's penis and testicles through his trousers.

"Now that you're a Communist," she said, avoiding his eyes, her gaze fixed on an indeterminate spot between his navel and his neck, "you'll need these to be of steel."

"Really?" asked Ansky.

"Don't play the fool," said Afanasievna's hoarse voice. "I understand you. From the start, I've known who you are."

"And who am I?" asked Ansky.

"A Jewish brat who confuses his desires with reality."

"Reality," murmured Ansky, "can be pure desire."

Afanasievna laughed.

"What should I make of that?" she asked.

"Whatever you like, but take care, comrade," said Ansky. "Consider certain kinds of people, for example."

"Who?" asked Afanasievna.

"The ill," said Ansky. "Tuberculosis patients, say. According to their doctors, they're dying, and there's no arguing with that. But for the patients, especially on some nights, some particularly long evenings, desire is reality and vice versa. Or take people suffering from impotence."

"What kind of impotence?" asked Afanasievna without letting go of Ansky's genitals.

"Sexual impotence," said Ansky. "The impotent are more or less like tuberculosis patients, and they feel desire. A desire that in time not only supplants reality but is imposed on it."

"Do you think," asked Afanasievna, "that the dead feel sexual desire?"

"Not the dead," said Ansky, "but the living dead do. When I was in Siberia I met a hunter whose sexual organs had been torn off."

"Sexual organs!" said Afanasievna mockingly.

"His penis and testicles," said Ansky. "He peed through a little straw, sitting or on his knees, crouching."

"You've made yourself clear," said Afanasievna.

"Well, anyway, once a week, no matter the weather, this man (who wasn't young, either) went into the forest to look for his penis and testicles. Everyone thought he would die someday, caught in the snow, but the man always came back to the village, sometimes after an absence of months, and always with the same news: he hadn't found them. One day he decided to stop looking. Suddenly, he seemed to age: one night he looked fifty and the next morning he looked eighty. My detachment left the village. Four months later we passed through again and asked what had happened to the man without attributes. They told us he had married and was leading a happy life. One of my comrades and I wanted to see him: we found him preparing his gear for another long stay in the forest. He looked fifty again, instead of eighty. Or perhaps even forty in certain parts of his face: around the eyes, the lips, the jaw. Two days later, when we left, I believed the hunter had managed to impose his desires on reality, which, in their fashion, had transformed his surroundings, the village, the villagers, the forest, the snow, his lost penis and testicles. I imagined him on his knees, pissing, his legs well apart, in the middle of the frozen steppe, northward bound, striding toward the white deserts and blizzards with his knapsack full of traps, utterly oblivious of what we call fate."

"That's a pretty story," said Afanasievna as she let go of Ansky's genitals. "A pity I'm too old and have seen too much to believe it."

"It has nothing to do with belief," said Ansky, "it has to do with understanding, and then changing."

•

After this, at least in appearance, Ansky's and Ivanov's lives took different courses.

The young Jew was plunged into frenetic activity. In 1929, for example, at the age of twenty, he participated in the creation of magazines (in which none of his writing ever appeared) in Moscow, Leningrad, Smolensk, Kiev, Rostov. He was a founding member of the Theater of Imaginary Voices. He tried to find a publisher for some of Khlebnikov's posthumous writings. As a reporter for a paper that never saw the light of day, he interviewed General Tukhachevsky and General Blücher. He took a lover, Marya Zamyatina, a doctor ten years older than himself and married to a party boss. He embarked on a friendship with Grigory Yakovin, a great expert in contemporary German history, with whom he went on long walks and carried on conversations about the German language and Yiddish. He met Zinoviev. He wrote a strange poem in German on Trotsky's exile. He also wrote a series of aphorisms in German titled *Reflections on the Death of Evgenia Bosch*, pseudonym of the Bolshevik leader Evgenia Gotlibovna (1879–1924), about whom Pierre

Broué says: "Party member 1900, Bolshevik 1903. Arrested 1913, deported, escaped 1915, took refuge in the United States, pursued revolutionary activities with Pyatakov and Bukharin and opposed Lenin with regard to the national question. Returned after the February Revolution and took a leading role in the Kiev uprising and the civil war. Signatory of the Declaration of 46. Committed suicide in 1924 as a gesture of protest." And he wrote a poem in Yiddish, laudatory, vulgar, full of barbarisms, on Ivan Rajia (1887–1920), one of the founders of the Communist Party of Finland, probably assassinated by his own comrades in a leadership struggle. He read the futurists, the members of the Centrifuge group, the imagists. He read Platonov's first stories and Babel, as well as Boris Pilnyak (whom he didn't like at all) and Andrey Bely, whose novel *Petersburg* kept him up for four days. He wrote an essay on the future of literature, which began and ended with the word *nothing*. Meanwhile, there was trouble in his relationship with Marya Zamyatina, who had another lover besides him, a doctor specializing in lung disease, a man who cured tuberculosis patients! And who lived most of the time in the Crimea and whom Marya Zamyatina described as if he were Jesus Christ reincarnated, minus the beard and plus a white coat, a white coat that cropped up in Ansky's dreams in 1929. And he kept working hard at the Moscow Library. And sometimes, when he remembered, he wrote letters to his parents, to which they responded with love and nostalgia and courage, never mentioning the hunger or scarcity that were rampant in the formerly fertile lands of the Dnieper. And he also had time to write a strange humor piece titled *Landauer*, based on the last days of the German writer Gustav Landauer, who in 1918 wrote his *Address to Writers* and in 1919 was executed for his participation in the Munich Soviet Republic. And in 1929, too, he read a recently published novel, Alfred Döblin's *Berlin Alexanderplatz*, which struck him as notable and memorable and distinguished and drove him to seek out more books by Döblin, finding in the Moscow Library *The Three Leaps of Wang-lun* (1915), *Wadzek's Battle with the Steam Engine* (1918), *Wallenstein* (1920), and *Mountains, Seas, and Giants* (1924).

•

And while Ansky read Döblin or interviewed Tukhachevsky or made love with Marya Zamyatina in his room on Petrov of Moscow Street, Efraim Ivanov published his first great novel, the one that would open the gates of heaven to him, recovering on the one hand the devotion of his readers and on the other winning for the first time the respect of those he considered his equals, those writers, talented writers, who tended the flame of Tolstoy and Chekhov, who tended the flame of Pushkin, of Gogol, who suddenly noticed him, who saw him for the first time, in fact, and accepted him.

Gorky, who at the time had yet to definitively resettle in Moscow, wrote him a letter with an Italian postmark in which one could discern the admonishing finger of the founding father, but in which one could also perceive a wealth of kindness and readerly gratitude.

Your novel, he said, has afforded me some . . . very amusing moments. One detects in it . . . a faith, a hope. Your imagination cannot be called . . . stifled. No, in no way whatsoever . . . can that be said. There are those who speak of . . . the Soviet Jules Verne. After long reflection, however, I think you are . . . better than Jules Verne. A more . . . mature writer. A writer guided by . . . revolutionary instincts. A . . . great writer. As one could only expect of a . . . Communist. But let's speak frankly . . . as Soviets. The literature of the proletariat speaks to . . . today's man. It sets out problems that perhaps will only be solved . . . tomorrow. But it is addressed . . . to today's worker, not the worker . . . of the future. In your next books you must . . . bear that in mind.

If Stendhal, as it is said, danced when he read Balzac's critique of *The Charterhouse of Parma*, Ivanov spilled countless tears of joy upon receiving Gorky's letter.

The novel, so unanimously acclaimed, was called *Twilight* and its plot was very simple: a boy of fourteen abandons his family to join the ranks of the revolution. Soon he's engaged in combat against Wrangel's troops. In the midst of battle he's injured and his comrades leave him for dead. But before the vultures come to feed on the bodies, a spaceship drops onto the battlefield and takes him away, along with some of the other mortally wounded soldiers. Then the spaceship enters the stratosphere and goes into orbit around Earth. All of the men's wounds are rapidly healed. Then a very thin, very tall creature, more like a strand of seaweed than a human being, asks them a series of questions like: how were the stars created? where does the universe end? where does it begin? Of course, no one knows the answers. One man says God created the stars and the universe begins and ends wherever God wants. He's tossed out into space. The others sleep. When the boy awakes he finds himself in a shabby room, with a shabby bed and a shabby wardrobe where his shabby clothes hang. When he goes to the window he gazes out in awe at the urban landscape of New York. But the boy finds only misfortune in the great city. He meets a jazz musician who tells him about chickens that talk and probably think.

"The worst of it," the musician says to him, "is that the governments of the planet know it and that's why so many people raise chickens."

The boy objects that the chickens are raised to be eaten. The musician says that's what the chickens want. And he finishes by saying:

"Fucking masochistic chickens, they have our leaders by the balls."

He also meets a girl who works as a hypnotist at a burlesque club, and he falls in love. The girl is ten years older than the boy, or in other words twenty-four, and although she has a number of lovers, including the boy, she doesn't want to fall in love with anyone because she believes that love will use up her powers as a hypnotist. One day the girl disappears and the boy, after searching for her in vain, decides to hire a Mexican detective who was a soldier under Pancho Villa. The detective has a strange theory: he believes in the existence of numerous Earths in parallel universes. Earths that can be reached through hypnosis. The boy thinks the detective is swindling him and decides to accompany him in his investigations. One night they come upon a Russian beggar shouting in an alley. The beggar shouts in Russian and only the boy can understand him. The beggar says: I fought with Wrangel, show some respect, please, I fought in Crimea and I was evacuated from Sevastopol in an English ship. Then the boy asks whether the beggar was at the battle where he fell badly wounded. The beggar looks at him and says yes. I was too, says the boy. Impossible, replies the beggar, that was twenty years ago and you weren't even born yet.

Then the boy and the Mexican detective set off west in search of the hypnotist. They find her in Kansas City. The boy asks her to hypnotize him and send him back to the battlefield where he should have died, or accept his love and stop fleeing. The hypnotist answers that neither is possible. The Mexican detective shows an interest in the art of hypnosis. As the detective begins to tell the hypnotist a story, the boy leaves the roadside bar and goes walking under the night sky. After a while he stops crying.

He walks for hours. When he's in the middle of nowhere he sees a figure by the side of the road. It's the seaweedlike extraterrestrial. They greet each other. They talk. Often, their conversation is unintelligible. The subjects they address are varied: foreign languages, national monuments, the last days of Karl Marx, worker solidarity, the time of the change measured in Earth years and stellar years, the discovery of America as a stage setting, an unfathomable void—as painted by Doré—of masks. Then the boy follows the extraterrestrial away from the road and they walk through a wheat field, cross a stream, climb a hill, cross another field, until they reach a smoldering pasture.

In the next chapter, the boy is no longer a boy but a young man of twenty-five working at a Moscow newspaper where he has become the star reporter. The young man receives the assignment to interview a Communist leader somewhere in China. The trip, he is warned, is extremely difficult, and once he reaches Peking, the situation may be dangerous, since there are lots of people who don't want any statement by the Chinese leader to get out. Despite these warnings, the young man accepts the job. When, after much hardship, he finally gains access to the cellar where the Chinese leader is hidden, the young man decides that not only will he interview him, he'll also help him escape the country. The Chinese leader's face, in the light of a candle, bears a notable resemblance to that of the Mexican detective and former soldier under Pancho Villa. The Chinese leader and the young Russian, meanwhile, come down with the same illness, brought on by the pestilence of the cellar. They shake with fever, they sweat, they talk, they rave, the Chinese leader says he sees dragons flying low over the streets of Peking, the young man says he sees a battle, perhaps just a skirmish, and he shouts hurrah and urges his comrades onward. Then both lie motionless as the dead for a long time, and suffer in silence until the day set for their flight.

Each with a temperature of 102 degrees, the two men cross Peking and escape. Horses and provisions await them in the countryside. The Chinese leader has never ridden before. The young man teaches him how. During the trip they cross a forest and then some enormous mountains. The blazing of the stars in the sky seems supernatural. The Chinese leader asks himself: how were the stars created? where does the universe end? where does it begin? The young man hears him and vaguely recalls a wound in his side whose scar still aches, darkness, a trip. He also remembers the eyes of a hypnotist, although the woman's features remain hidden, mutable. If I close my eyes, thinks the young man, I'll see her again. But he doesn't close them. They make their way across a vast snow-covered plain. The horses sink in the snow. The Chinese leader sings. How were the stars created? Who are we in the middle of the boundless universe? What trace of us will remain?

Suddenly the Chinese leader falls off his horse. The young Russian examines him. The Chinese leader is like a burning doll. The young Russian touches the Chinese leader's forehead and then his own forehead and understands that the fever is devouring them both. With no little effort he ties the Chinese leader to his mount and sets off again. The silence of the snow-covered plain is absolute. The night and the passage of stars across the vault of the sky show no signs of ever ending. In the distance an enormous black shadow seems to superimpose itself on the darkness. It's a mountain range. In the young Russian's mind the certainty takes shape that in the coming hours he will die on that snow-covered plain or as he crosses the mountains. A voice inside begs him to close his eyes, because if he closes them he'll see the eyes and then the beloved face of the hypnotist. It tells him that if he closes his eyes he'll see the streets of New York again, he'll walk again toward the hypnotist's house, where she sits waiting for him on a chair in the dark. But the Russian doesn't close his eyes. He rides on.

•

It wasn't only Gorky who read *Twilight*. Other famous people did, too, and although none of them wrote to the author to express their admiration, they didn't forget his name, because not only were they famous, their memories were good, too.

Ansky cites four, in a kind of dizzying ascent. Professor Stanislaw Strumilin read it. It struck him as hard to follow. The writer Aleksei Tolstoy read it. It struck him as chaotic. Andrei Zhdanov read it. He left it half finished. And Stalin read it. It struck him as suspect. Of course, none of this reached the ears of our friend Ivanov, who framed Gorky's letter and hung it on the wall, well within eyesight of his increasingly numerous visitors.

Meanwhile, his life changed considerably. He was allotted a dacha outside of Moscow. Sometimes he was asked for his autograph in the metro. There was a table reserved for him each night at the writers' restaurant. He spent his holidays in Yalta, along with other equally famous colleagues. Ah, those evenings at Yalta's Red October hotel (the former English and French hotel), on the huge terrace overlooking the Black Sea, listening to the distant strains of the Blue Volga orchestra, on warm nights with thousands of stars twinkling up above, as the fashionable playwright of the day dropped a clever remark and the metallurgical novelist responded with an unassailable parry, those Yalta nights, with extraordinary women who could drink vodka without swooning until six in the morning and sweaty young people from the Association of Proletarian Writers of Crimea who came to ask for literary advice at four in the afternoon.

Sometimes, when he was alone, and more often when he was alone in front of a mirror, poor Ivanov pinched himself to make sure he wasn't dreaming, that it was all real. And in fact it was all real, at least in appearance. Black thunderclouds hovered over him, but he noticed only the long-yearned-for breeze, the scented breath of wind that wiped his face clean of so much misfortune and fear.

•

What was Ivanov afraid of? Ansky wondered in his notebooks. Not of harm to his person, since as a longtime Bolshevik he'd had many brushes with arrest, prison, and deportation, and although he couldn't be called a brave man, neither could it fairly be said that he was cowardly or spineless. Ivanov's fear was of a literary nature. That is, it was the fear that afflicts most citizens who, one fine (or dark) day, choose to make the practice of writing, and especially the practice of fiction writing, an integral part of their lives. Fear of being no good. Also fear of being overlooked. But above all, fear of being no good. Fear that one's efforts and striving will come to nothing. Fear of the step that leaves no trace. Fear of the forces of chance and nature that wipe away shallow prints. Fear of dining alone and unnoticed. Fear of going unrecognized. Fear of failure and making a spectacle of oneself. But above all, fear of being no good. Fear of forever dwelling in the hell of bad writers. Irrational fears, thought Ansky, especially when the fearful soothed their fears with *semblances*. As if the paradise of good writers, according to bad writers, were inhabited by semblances. As if the worth (or excellence) of a work were based on semblances. Semblances that varied, of course, from one era and country to another, but that always remained just that, semblances, things that only *seem* and never *are*, things all surface and no depth, pure gesture, and even the gesture muddled by an effort of will, the hair and eyes and lips of Tolstoy and the versts traveled on horseback by Tolstoy and the women deflowered by Tolstoy in a tapestry burned by the fire of seeming.

•

In any case, storm clouds hovered over Ivanov, though he never even dreamed they were there, because Ivanov, at this point in his life, saw only Ivanov, attaining the height of ridiculous self-regard during an interview conducted by two young men from the Literary Newspaper of the Komsomols of the Russian Federation, who asked him, among many other questions, the following:

Young Komsomols: Why do you think your first great work, the one that won the acclaim of the worker and peasant masses, was written when you were already nearly sixty? How many years did it take you to come up with the plot of Twilight? *Is it the work of a writer in his prime?*

Efraim Ivanov: I'm only fifty-nine. I won't be sixty for some time. And may I remind you that Cervantes wrote Don Quixote *more or less at the same age I am now.*

Young Komsomols: Do you believe your novel is the Don Quixote *of Soviet science fiction?*

Efraim Ivanov: There's something to that, no doubt.

So Ivanov considered himself the Cervantes of fantastic literature. He saw clouds in the shape of a guillotine, he saw clouds in the shape of a shot in the back of the head, but really he saw only himself riding alongside a mysterious and indispensable Sancho across the steppes of literary glory.

Danger, danger, said the muzhiks, danger, danger, said the kulaks, danger, danger, said the signers of the Declaration of 46, danger, danger, said the dead Orthodox priests, danger, danger, said the ghost of Inessa Armand, but Ivanov was never known for his hearing or his sensitivity to the approach of clouds or the nearness of a storm, and after a more or less mediocre turn as a columnist and lecturer, at which he succeeded brilliantly since he hadn't been asked to be anything more than mediocre, he shut himself up in his Moscow room again and stacked up reams of paper and changed the ribbon on his typewriter, and then he went in search of Ansky, because he wanted to deliver a new novel to his editor in four months, if not sooner.

About this time Ansky was working on a radio project meant to cover all of Europe and extend to the very edge of Siberia. In 1930, said the notebooks, Trotsky was expelled from the Soviet Union (although he was actually expelled in 1929, a mistake attributable to the lack of transparency in the Russian press) and Ansky's spirits began to flag. In 1930, Mayakovsky committed suicide. By 1930, no matter how naïve or foolish one was, it was clear that the October Revolution had failed.

But Ivanov wanted another novel and he went in search of Ansky.

•

In 1932, Ivanov's new novel, titled *Midday*, was published. In 1934, another novel appeared, titled *Dawn*. Both featured an abundance of extraterrestrials, interplanetary travels, fractured time, the existence of two or more advanced civilizations that periodically visited Earth, the struggles (often treacherous and violent) of these civilizations, roving characters.

In 1935, Ivanov's novels were withdrawn from bookstores. A few days later, an official notice informed him of his expulsion from the party. According to Ansky, Ivanov spent three days unable to get out of bed. On the bed were his three novels and he reread them constantly, searching for something that might justify his expulsion. He moaned and whimpered and tried unsuccessfully to take refuge in his earliest childhood memories. He stroked the spines of his books with heartbreaking melancholy. Sometimes he got up and went over to the window and spent hours looking out into the street.

In 1936, at the start of the first great purge, he was arrested. He spent four months in a prison cell and signed all the papers that were put before him. When he got out and his former literary friends treated him as if he had the plague, he wrote to Gorky to ask him to intercede on his behalf, but Gorky, gravely ill, didn't answer his letter. Then Gorky died and Ivanov attended the burial. When he was spotted, two young members of Gorky's circle, a poet and novelist, approached him and asked whether he wasn't ashamed, whether he had gone out of his head, whether he didn't understand that his very presence was an insult to the great man's memory.

"Gorky wrote to me," answered Ivanov. "Gorky liked my novel. This is the least I can do for him."

"The least you can do for him, comrade," said the poet, "is to commit suicide."

"That is a good idea, isn't it?" said the novelist. "Throw yourself out a window, problem solved."

"What are you saying, comrades?" sobbed Ivanov.

A girl in a leather jacket that hung almost to her knees came over to them and asked what was going on.

"It's Efraim Ivanov," answered the poet.

"Oh, never mind, then," said the girl, "make him leave."

"I can't leave," said Ivanov, his face wet with tears.

"Why can't you, comrade?" asked the girl.

"Because my legs refuse to move, I can't take a step."

For a few seconds the girl searched his face. Ivanov, his arms firmly in the grip of the two young writers, couldn't have looked more pathetic, which finally convinced her to help him out of the cemetery. But once they were in the street Ivanov was still unable to get along alone, so the girl walked with him to the tram station and then decided (Ivanov couldn't stop crying and seemed close to fainting) to get on the tram with him, and in this fashion, putting off her departure several times along the way, she helped him up the stairs of his house and helped him unlock the door to his room and lie down in bed, and as Ivanov dissolved in floods of tears and incoherent words, the girl examined his collection of books, which happened to be rather unimpressive, until the door opened and Ansky walked in.

●

Her name was Nadja Yurenieva and she was nineteen. That very night she made love with Ansky, once Ivanov had managed to fall asleep after several glasses of vodka. They did it in Ansky's room and anyone who saw them would have said they fucked as if they had only a few hours left to live. Actually, Nadja Yurenieva fucked like many Muscovites that year of 1936 and Boris Ansky fucked as if when all hope was lost he had suddenly found his one true love. Neither of the two thought (or wanted to think) about death, but both moved, twined their limbs, communed, as if they were on the edge of the abyss.

At dawn they fell asleep, and when Ansky awoke, just after midday, Nadja Yurenieva was gone. What Ansky felt first was despair, and then fear, and after he had dressed he went running to see Ivanov, to get some clue that would lead him to the girl. He found his friend busy writing letters. I have to clear things up, said Ivanov, I have to untangle this mess and only then will I be saved. Ansky asked what mess he was talking about. The damned science fiction novels, shouted Ivanov with all his strength. The shout had a rending violence, like a claw, but not a claw that did any damage to Ansky's or Ivanov's real adversaries. Instead it was like a claw that pounces and floats in the middle of the room, like a helium balloon, a self-conscious claw, a claw-beast that wonders what in God's name it's doing in this rather untidy room, who that old man is sitting at the table, who that young man is standing with tousled hair, then falls to the floor, deflated, returned once more to nothing.

"Good Lord, that was quite a noise I made," said Ivanov.

Then they began to talk about the young Nadja, Nadesha, Nadiushka, Nadiushkina, and Ivanov, before he would say anything, wanted to know whether they had made love. And then he wanted to know how many hours they'd been at it. And then whether Nadiushka was experienced or not. And then the positions. And since Ansky answered all his questions in full and with no hesitation, Ivanov went off on a sentimental tack. Fucking youth, he said. Goddamn fucking youth. Oh, the little slut. What a pair of filthy beasts. Ah, love. And the sentimental side of things, a side he could only imagine and not touch, made him remember that he was naked, not sitting there at the table, where in fact he was wrapped in a red robe, a robe or a dressing gown, to be precise, with the emblem of the Communist Party of the Russian Federation embroidered on the lapel, and a silk handkerchief around his neck, the gift of a faggoty French writer he'd met at a conference and whose work he'd never read, but naked in the figurative sense, naked on every other front, political, literary, economic, and this awareness made him lapse again into melancholy.

"Nadja Yurenieva, I believe, is a student or young poet," he said, "and she hates me with a passion. I met her at Gorky's burial. She and two other thugs slung me out. She isn't a bad person. The others aren't either. I'm sure they're fine Communists, staunch, good-hearted Soviets. Believe me: I understand them."

Then Ivanov motioned Ansky to his side.

"If it had been up to them," he whispered in his ear, "they would've shot me right there, the sons of bitches, and then they would have dragged my body into a mass grave."

Ivanov's breath smelled of vodka and sewers, sour and heavy, like something rotting, reminiscent of empty houses near swamps, nightfall at four in the afternoon, vapors rising from the sickly grass and fogging the dark windows. A horror film, thought Ansky. Where everything has come to a halt, and it comes to a halt because it knows it's lost.

But Ivanov said ah, love, and Ansky, in his fashion, also said ah, love. So over the next few days he set out in tireless search of Nadja Yurenieva, and at last he found her, wearing her long leather jacket, sitting in one of the lecture halls at the University of Moscow, looking like an orphan, a self-designated orphan, listening to the rousing remarks or poems or rhymed nonsense of some pretentious idiot (or whatever he was!) who recited with his gaze fixed on the audience while in his left hand he held the silly manuscript that every so often he glanced at in a theatrical and unnecessary way, since his memory was clearly sharp.

And Nadja Yurenieva saw Ansky and got up discreetly and left the hall where the bad Soviet poet (as oblivious and foolish and prissy and gutless and affected as a Mexican lyrical poet, or actually a Latin American lyrical poet, that poor stunted and bloated phenomenon) reeled off his lines on the steel industry (possessing the same crass, arrogant ignorance as a Latin American poet speaking about his self, his era, his otherness), and she went out into the streets of Moscow, followed by Ansky, who instead of approaching her remained some fifteen feet behind, a distance that shrank as time passed and they walked farther. Never before had Ansky better understood or delighted more in suprematism, Kazimir Malevich's invention, nor the first tenet of Malevich's declaration of independence signed in Vitebsk on November 5, 1920, which proclaims: "The fifth dimension has been established."

•

In 1937 Ivanov was arrested.

Once again he was subjected to a long interrogation and then they left him in a dark cell and forgot about him. His interrogator didn't know a thing about literature. His principal interest was finding out whether Ivanov had met with members of the Trotskyist opposition.

During his time in the cell, Ivanov made friends with a rat he called Nikita. At night, when the rat came out, Ivanov held long conversations with her. As one might imagine, they didn't talk about literature, and certainly not about politics, but about their respective childhoods. Ivanov told the rat about his mother, who was often in his thoughts, and his siblings, but he avoided talking about his father. The rat, whose Russian was scarcely a whisper, talked in turn about the Moscow sewers and the sky in the sewers, where because of the blossoming of certain debris or an inexplicable phosphorescent process, there were always stars. She also talked to him about her mother's warmth and her sisters' foolish capers, how she had laughed at those capers, even now as she remembered them they brought a smile to her narrow rat's face. Sometimes Ivanov let himself succumb to despair and he rested his cheek on his palm and asked Nikita what would become of them.

Then the rat looked at him with sad, perplexed eyes and her look told Ivanov that she was even more innocent than he was. A week after he had been locked in the cell (although for Ivanov it seemed more like a year) he was interrogated again and no one had to hit him to make him sign various papers and documents. He wasn't returned to his cell. They took him straight out to a courtyard where he was shot in the back of the head and his body tossed on the bed of a truck.

●

After Ivanov's death, Ansky's notes grow chaotic, apparently haphazard, although amid the chaos Reiter divined a structure and a kind of order. Ansky talks about writers. He says the only viable writers (though he doesn't explain what he means by viable) are those from the underclass and the aristocracy. Proletarian and bourgeois writers, he says, are merely decorative figures. He talks about sex. He recalls Sade and a mysterious Russian monk, Lapishin, who lived in the seventeenth century and left various writings (complete with the corresponding illustrations) on group sexual practices in the region between two rivers, the Dvina and the Pechora.

Only sex? nothing but sex? Ansky asks himself repeatedly in notes written in the margins. He talks about his parents. He talks about Döblin. He talks about homosexuality and impotence. The American continent of sex, he says. He jokes about Lenin's sexuality. He talks about the drug addicts of Moscow. About the sick. About the killers of children. He talks about Flavius Josephus. His discussion of the historian is tinged with melancholy, though it might be a feigned melancholy. But for whom is he feigning if he knows very well no one will read his notebook? (If it's God he has in mind, then he treats God with a certain condescension, perhaps because God was never lost on the Kamchatka peninsula, cold and hungry, as he was.) He talks about the young Russian Jews who made the revolution and who now (this is probably written in 1939) are dropping like flies. He talks about Yuri Piatakov, assassinated in 1937, after the second Moscow Trial. He mentions names Reiter has never heard before. Then, a few pages on, he mentions them again. As if he were afraid of forgetting them. Names, names, names. Those who made revolution and those who were devoured by that same revolution, though it wasn't the same but another, not the dream but the nightmare that hides behind the eyelids of the dream.

He talks about Lev Kamenev. He mentions his name along with many other names also unknown to Reiter. And he talks about his adventures in different houses in Moscow, with friends who presumably helped him and whom Ansky, to be safe, identifies by numbers, for example: today I was at 5's house, we had tea and talked past midnight, then I walked home, the sidewalks were covered in snow. Or: today I saw 9, he talked to me about 7, and then he began to ramble about illness, whether or not it was a good idea to find a cure for cancer. Or: this afternoon I saw 13 in the metro, though he didn't notice me, I was sitting there half asleep and I let the train go by, and 13 was reading a book on a bench nearby, a book about invisible men, and then his train came and he got up and got on the train without closing his book, even though the train was full. And he also writes: our eyes met. Fucking a snake.

And he doesn't feel sorry for himself.

•

It's in Ansky's notebook, long before he sees a painting by the man, that Reiter first reads about the Italian painter Arcimboldo, Giuseppe or Joseph or Josepho or Josephus Arcimboldo or Arcimboldi or Arcimboldus (1527–1593). When I'm sad or bored, writes Ansky, although it's hard to imagine Ansky bored, busy fleeing twenty-four hours a day, I think about Giuseppe Arcimboldo and the sadness and tedium vanish as if on a spring morning, by a swamp, morning's imperceptible advance clearing away the mists that rise from the shores, the reed beds. There are also notes on Courbet, whom Ansky considers the paradigm of the revolutionary artist. He mocks, for example, the Manichaean conception that some Soviet painters have of Courbet. He tries to imagine the Courbet painting *The Return from the Conference*, which depicts a gathering of drunken priests and ecclesiastical dignitaries and was rejected by the official Salon and the Salon des Refusés, which in Ansky's judgment casts the reject-rejectors into ignominy. The fate of *The Return from the Con-*

ference strikes him as not only inevitable and poetic but also telling: a rich Catholic buys the painting and no sooner does he get home than he proceeds to burn it.

The ashes of *The Return from the Conference* float not only over Paris, reads Reiter with tears in his eyes, tears that sting and *rouse* him, but also over Moscow and Rome and Berlin. Ansky talks about *The Artist's Studio.* He talks about the figure of Baudelaire that appears on the edge of the painting, reading, and stands for Poetry. He talks about Courbet's friendship with Baudelaire, Daumier, Jules Vallès. He talks about the friendship of Courbet (the Artist) with Proudhon (the Politician) and likens the sensible opinions of the latter to those of a pheasant. On the subject of art, a politician with power is like a colossal pheasant, able to crush mountains with little hops, whereas a politician without power is only like a village priest, an ordinary-sized pheasant.

He imagines Courbet in the Revolution of 1848 and then he sees him in the Paris Commune, where the vast majority of artists and men of letters shone (literally) for their absence. Not Courbet. Courbet takes an active role and after the repression he is arrested and locked up in Sainte-Pélagie, where he occupies himself drawing still lifes. One of the charges the state brings against him is that of having incited the multitudes to destroy the column in the Place Vendôme, although Ansky isn't quite clear on this point or his memory fails him or he relies on hearsay. The monument to Napoleon in the Place Vendôme, the monument plain and simple in the Place Vendôme, the Vendôme column in the Place Vendôme.

In any case, the public office that Courbet held after the fall of Napoleon III made him responsible for the protection of the monuments of Paris, which in view of later events must certainly be taken as a monumental joke. France, however, wasn't in the mood for jokes and all the artist's assets were seized. Courbet left for Switzerland, where he died in 1877 at the age of fifty-eight. Then come some lines in Yiddish that Reiter can't quite decipher. He supposes them to be expressions of pain or bitterness. Then Ansky goes off on a tangent about some Courbet paintings. The one called *Bonjour, Monsieur Courbet* suggests to him the beginning of a film, one that gets off to a bucolic start and gradually lapses into horror. *The Young Ladies on the Banks of the Seine* recalls spies or shipwrecked sailors enjoying a brief rest, and Ansky goes on to say: spies from another planet, and also: bodies that wear out more quickly than other bodies, and also: disease, the transmission of disease, and also: the willingness to stand firm, and also: where does one learn to stand firm? in what kind of school or university? And also: factories, desolate streets, brothels, prisons, and also: the Unknown University, and also: meanwhile the Seine flows and flows and flows, and those ghastly faces of whores contain more beauty than the loveliest lady or vision sprung from the brush of Ingres or Delacroix.

Then there are chaotic jottings, the schedules of trains leaving Moscow, the gray noon light falling vertical on the Kremlin, a dead man's last words, the flip side of a trilogy of novels whose titles he notes: *True Dawn, True Dusk, Tremble of Twilight*, whose structure and plots might have lent a bit of order and dignity to the last three novels published under Ivanov's name, the ice-beam of the tapestry, though Ivanov probably wouldn't have agreed to take them under his wing, or maybe I'm mistaken, Ansky thinks and writes, perhaps I judge Ivanov unfairly, since based on all the information I possess he didn't betray me, when it would have been so easy, so easy to say he wasn't the author of those three novels, and yet that was the one thing he didn't do, he betrayed everyone his torturers wanted him to betray, old friends and new, playwrights, poets, and novelists, but he didn't say a word about me. Accomplices in imposture until the end.

What a nice pair we would've made in Borneo, writes Ansky with irony. And then he recalls a joke that Ivanov told him long ago, a joke Ivanov was told at a party at the offices of a magazine where he worked at the time. The occasion was an informal reception for a group of Soviet anthropologists who had just returned to Moscow. The joke, half truth, half legend, was set in Borneo, where a group of French scientists made their way into a region of jungle-covered mountains. After several days of walking, the French reached the source of a river, and on the other side of the river, in the deepest part of the jungle, they found a tribe that lived practically in the Stone Age. The Frenchmen's first guess, explained one of the Soviet anthropologists, a big fat man with the bushy whiskers of a southerner, was that the natives were or might be cannibals, and to be safe and avoid any misunderstanding from the start, they asked them, in the different languages of the coastal natives and accompanying their questions with explicit gestures, whether they ate human flesh or not.

The natives understood and answered emphatically that they did not.

Then the French wondered what they ate, since in their opinion a diet lacking in animal protein was a calamity. When asked, the natives responded that they did hunt, but not much, because in the highland jungle there weren't many animals, and they also ate the pulp of a certain tree, cooked in many different ways, which upon being examined by the skeptical Frenchmen turned out to be an excellent alternative source of protein. The rest of their diet consisted of a wide range of jungle fruits, roots, tubers. The natives didn't plant anything. What the jungle thought fit to give it would give, and what it didn't would be forever taboo to them. They lived in total symbiosis with the ecosystem. When they stripped the bark from certain trees to cover the floors of the little huts they built, they were actually keeping the trees healthy. They lived like garbagemen. They were the garbagemen of the jungle. Their language, however, wasn't crude like that of the garbagemen of Moscow or Paris, nor were they big like them nor did they possess their muscular torsos nor did they have the gaze of those men, the gaze of dealers in shit, but rather they were short and fine boned, and they spoke in soft coos, like birds, and they did their best not to brush against the strangers and their conception of time had nothing to do with the Frenchmen's conception of time. And it was due to this, most likely, said the Soviet anthropologist with bushy whiskers, due to their different conceptions of time, that the catastrophe was hatched, because after spending five days with the natives the French anthropologists thought they had their trust, they were chums now, comrades, good friends, and they decided to delve into their language and customs, and they discovered that when the natives touched someone they didn't look him in the face, whether that someone was a Frenchman or one of their own tribe, for example, if a father embraced his son he tried always to look elsewhere, and if a little girl curled up in her mother's lap, her mother glanced to the side or up at the sky and the little girl, if she was old enough to understand, stared at the ground, and friends who went out together to gather tubers did look each other in the eye, but if after a lucky day one touched another's shoulder, each man averted his gaze, and the anthropologists also noticed and recorded that when the natives shook hands they stood sideways and if they were right-handed they passed the right hand under the left armpit and let it hang limp or gave only a slight squeeze, and if they were left-handed, they passed the left hand under the right armpit, and then one of the Frenchmen, said the Soviet anthropologist, laughing boisterously, decided to demonstrate the greeting of his own people, the handshake of those who hailed from beyond the lowlands, from beyond the sea, from beyond the setting sun, and with gestures or taking another anthropologist as partner he showed them the way men greet each other in Paris, two hands that grasp and pump or shake, faces impassive or friendly or surprised, eyes that frankly meet the other's gaze, while the lips open and say bonjour, Monsieur Jouffroy or bonjour, Monsieur Delhorme, or bonjour, Monsieur Courbet (although it was clear, thought Reiter, reading Ansky's notebook, that there was no Monsieur Courbet present, or if there had been it was a disturbing coincidence), a pantomine that the natives watched with good grace, some with a smile on their lips and others as if sunk in a well of compassion, patient and in their way polite and forbearing, at least until the anthropologist tried to test the handshake on them.

According to the man with the whiskers, this happened in the little village, if one can call a cluster of huts half hidden in the jungle a village. The Frenchman went up to a native and offered his hand. The native looked meekly away and stuck his right hand under his left armpit. But then the Frenchman surprised him and yanked him around by his hand, giving it a good squeeze and pumping it up and down. Feigning surprise and happiness, he said:

"Bonjour, Monsieur l'Indigène."

And he didn't let go of the native's hand and tried to look him in the eye and smiled at him and showed his white teeth and still he didn't let go but instead patted the native's shoulder with his left hand, bonjour, Monsieur l'Indigène, as if he really was very happy, until the native let out a bloodcurdling yell, and then he spoke a word, incomprehensible to the Frenchman and the Frenchmen's guide, and upon hearing this word another native hurled himself at the pedagogic anthropologist, who still hadn't let go of the first native's hand, and with a stone he smashed open the anthropologist's head, and then the anthropologist let go.

The result: the natives rose up and the French had to retreat hurriedly to the other side of the river, leaving behind a dead colleague and in turn inflicting mortal losses on the native side in clashes as they withdrew. For many days, in the mountains and later at the bar in a town on the Bornean coast, the anthropologists racked their brains to explain what could have suddenly plunged a peaceful tribe into violence or terror. After much back-and-forth they thought they'd found the key in the word uttered by the native who had been "assaulted" or "degraded" by the healthy and entirely innocent handshake. The word was *dayiyi*, which translates as cannibal or impossibility, but also has other meanings, including "man who rapes me," which, spoken after a howl, meant or could mean "man who rapes me in the ass," or "cannibal who fucks me in the ass and then eats my body," though it could also mean "man who touches me (or rapes me) and stares me in the eyes (to eat my soul)." In any case, the Frenchmen made their way back up the mountain after a rest on the coast, but they never saw the natives again.

•

When he was near despair, Ansky returned to Arcimboldo. He liked to remember Arcimboldo's paintings, though he knew or pretended to know almost nothing about the painter's life, which wasn't in a state of constant turmoil like Courbet's, true, but in Arcimboldo's canvases Ansky found something that for lack of a better word he called simplicity, a descriptive term that would not have been to the liking of many scholars and exegetes of the Arcimboldian oeuvre.

•

The Milanese painter's technique struck him as happiness personified. The end of semblance. Arcadia before the coming of man. Not all of the paintings, of course, because *The Roast*, for example, was like a horror painting, a reversible canvas that, hung one way, looked like a big metal platter of roast meats, including a suckling pig and a rabbit, with a pair of hands, probably a woman's or an adolescent's, trying to cover the meat so it won't get cold, and, hung the other way, showed the bust of a soldier, in helmet and armor, with a bold, satisfied smile missing some teeth, the terrible smile of an old mercenary who looks at you, writes Ansky, and his gaze is even more terrible than his smile, as if he knew things about you that you never even suspected. *The Lawyer* (a lawyer or high official with his head made of pieces of small game and his body of books) was also like a horror painting. But the paintings of the four seasons were pure bliss. Everything in everything, writes Ansky. As if Arcimboldo had learned a single lesson, but one of vital importance.

•

And here Ansky belies his lack of interest in the painter's life and writes that when Leonardo da Vinci left Milan in 1516 he bequeathed his notebooks and some drawings to his disciple Bernardino Luini, which in time the young Arcimboldo, friend of Luini's son, might possibly have consulted and studied. When I'm sad or in low spirits, writes Ansky, I close my eyes and think of Arcimboldo's paintings and the sadness and gloom evaporate, as if a strong wind, a *mentholated* wind, were suddenly blowing along the streets of Moscow.

•

Then come scattered notes about his flight. Some friends, two men and a woman, spend a whole night talking about the advantages and disadvantages of suicide. In the lapses and lulls in their conversation, they also discuss the sex life of a well-known poet who has recently vanished (in fact he has already been killed). An Acmeist poet and his wife, reduced to destitution and ceaseless indignities. A couple who, amid poverty and isolation, come up with a very simple game. The game of sex. The poet's wife fucks other men. Not other poets, because the poet and therefore his wife are blacklisted and other poets shun them like lepers. The woman is very beautiful. The three friends in Ansky's notebooks who talk all night agree. The three know her or at some point managed to catch glimpses of her. Stunning. An impressive woman. Deeply in love. The poet fucks other women too. Not poetesses or the wives and sisters of other poets, because the Acmeist is walking poison and everyone flees him. Also, it can't be said that he's handsome. Not at all. Closer to ugly. But the poet fucks workers he meets in the metro or waiting in line at some store. Ugly, ugly, but a sweet-tempered man with a velvet tongue.

The friends laugh. Yes, so good is the poet's memory that he's able to recite the saddest poems, and the young and not-so-young workers weep when they hear him. Then they climb into bed. The poet's wife, whose beauty exempts her from having a good memory, but whose memory is even more prodigious than the poet's, infinitely more prodigious, goes to bed with workers or sailors on leave or with gigantic widowed foremen who no longer know what to do with their lives or their strength and to whom the sudden appearance of this incredible woman is like a miracle. They also make love in groups. The poet, his wife, and another woman. The poet, his wife, and another man. Usually it's trios, but occasionally it's quartets and quintets. Sometimes, guided by a presentiment, with great pomp and circumstance they introduce their respective lovers, who, after a week, fall in love with each other and never return, never participate again in these small proletarian orgies, or maybe they do, who can say. In any case, all of this comes to an end when the poet is arrested and never heard from again, because he's been killed.

Then the friends talk more about suicide, its disadvantages and advantages, until the sun comes up and one of them, Ansky, leaves the house and leaves Moscow, without papers, at the mercy of any informer. Then there are landscapes, landscapes seen through glass, shattered landscapes, and dirt roads and nameless country stations where young tramps out of Makarenko gather, and there are hunchbacked adolescents and adolescents with colds, trickles of liquid dribbling from their noses, and streams and hard bread and a thwarted robbery, though Ansky doesn't say how he thwarts it. Finally there's the village of Kostekino. And the night. And the familiar sound of the wind. And Ansky's mother, who opens the door and doesn't recognize him.

•

The last notes are brief. A few months after he returned to the village his father died, as if he had only been waiting for Ansky's arrival to plunge headlong into the next world. His mother arranged the funeral, and at night, while everyone was asleep, Ansky slipped into the cemetery and sat beside his father's grave for a long time, thinking vague thoughts. During the day he slept in the attic, blankets pulled up to his chin, in total darkness. During the night he came down to the first floor and read by the light of the fire, next to the bed where his mother slept. In one of his last notes he mentions the chaos of the universe and says that only in chaos are we conceivable. In another, he wonders what will be left when the universe dies and time and space die with it. Zero, nothing. But the idea makes him laugh. Behind every answer lies a question, Ansky remembers the peasants of Kostekino say. Behind every indisputable answer lies an even more complex question. Complexity, however, makes him laugh, and sometimes his mother hears him laugh in the attic, like the ten-year-old boy he once was. Ansky ponders parallel universes. Around this time Hitler invades Poland and World War II begins. Warsaw falls, Paris falls, the Soviet Union is attacked. Only in chaos are we conceivable. One night Ansky dreams the sky is a great ocean of blood. On the last page of his notebook he sketches a map to join the guerrillas.

•

Yet to be explained was the hiding place for a single person at the back of the fireplace. Who built it? Who hid there?

After much thought, Reiter decided the builder must have been Ansky's father. Probably the hiding place was finished before Ansky returned to the village. The possibility also existed that Ansky's father had built it after his son's return, which was in fact more logical, since only then did his parents learn that Ansky was an enemy of the state. But Reiter sensed that the hiding place, whose creation he imagined to be slow, craftsmanlike, unhurried, had been conceived long before Ansky returned, which gave his father the aura of a seer or a madman. He also came to the conclusion that no one had used the hiding place.

He didn't rule out, of course, the inevitable visit of the party officials, who would've poked around the farmhouse seeking some trace of Ansky. That Ansky would've hidden in the fireplace during these visits was likely, almost certain. But at the crucial moment, when the detachment of the Einsatzgruppe C arrived, no one had hidden there, not even Ansky's mother. He imagined her finding a safe place for her son's notebook and then, in his dreams, he watched her go off with the other Jews of Kostekino toward the waiting German punishment, toward us, toward death.

He saw Ansky in his dreams too. He saw him walking across country, by night, a nameless person heading westward, and he saw him felled in a hail of gunfire.

•

For several days Reiter thought that he had been the one who shot Ansky. At night he had horrible nightmares that woke him up and made him weep. Sometimes he lay still, curled up in bed, listening to the snow fall on the village. He no longer thought about suicide, because he believed he was dead. In the mornings the first thing he did was read Ansky's notebook, opening it at random. At other times during the day he took long walks in the snowy forest, until he reached the old sovkhoz where the Ukrainians worked under the orders of two listless Germans.

When he stopped by the main building in the village to get his food he felt as if he were on another planet. There the fire was always lit and steam from two huge pots of soup filled the ground floor. It smelled of cabbage and tobacco, and his comrades were in shirtsleeves or shirtless. He far preferred the forest, where he sat in the snow until his backside froze. He preferred the farmhouse, where he lit a fire and sat down by the hearth to reread Ansky's notebook. Every so often he lifted his gaze and stared into the fireplace, as if a shadowy figure radiating timidity and goodwill were looking out at him. A shiver of pleasure ran through him then. Sometimes he imagined he lived with the Ansky family. He saw young Ansky and his mother and father traveling the roads of Siberia and he ended up covering his eyes. When the fire in the hearth had burned down to tiny bright embers in the darkness, he climbed carefully into the hiding place, which was warm, and he stayed there a long time, until the morning chill woke him.

One night he dreamed he was back in Crimea. He wasn't sure what part, but it was Crimea. He shot his gun amid the clouds of smoke that erupted here and there like geysers. Then he set off walking and came upon a dead Red Army soldier, facedown, with a rifle still in his hand. When he bent to turn him over and see his face, he feared, as he had so often feared, that the corpse would have Ansky's face. As he grasped the dead soldier by the jacket, he thought: I don't want to bear this weight, I don't, I don't, I want Ansky to live, I don't want him to die, I don't want to be the one who killed him, even unintentionally, accidentally, unawares. Then, with more relief than surprise, he discovered that the corpse had his own face, Reiter's face. When he woke from the dream that morning, his voice had returned. The first thing he said was:

"Thank God, it wasn't me."

•

At the start of the summer of 1942 someone remembered the soldiers in Kostekino and Reiter was returned to his division. He was in Crimea. He was in Kerch. He was on the banks of the Kuban and in the streets of Krasnodar. He traveled through the Caucasus to Budennovsk and he crossed the Kalmuk Steppe with his battalion, always carrying Ansky's notebook under his jacket, between his madman's garb and his soldier's uniform. He swallowed dust and saw no enemy troops, but he saw Wilke and Kruse and Sergeant Lemke, although they were hard to recognize because they had changed, not just their looks but their voices. Now Wilke, for example, spoke only in dialect and almost no one except Reiter understood him, and Kruse's voice had changed, he talked as if his testicles had long since been removed, and Sergeant Lemke no longer shouted, except on rare occasions. Most of the time he addressed his men in a kind of murmur, as if he were tired or he'd been lulled to sleep by the long distances they'd traveled. In any case, Sergeant Lemke was gravely wounded as they tried vainly to fight their way through to Tuapse and he was replaced by Sergeant Bublitz. Then came fall, the mud, the wind, and at the end of the fall the Russians counterattacked.

Reiter's division, which was part of the 17th Army now, not the 11th, retreated from Elista to Proletarskaya and then followed the Manych River up to Rostov. And then it kept retreating west, to the Mius River, where a new front line was established. Summer 1943 came and the Russians attacked again and Reiter's division retreated again. Each time it retreated there were fewer men. Kruse was killed. Sergeant Bublitz was killed. Voss, who was brave, was promoted first to sergeant and then lieutenant, and under Voss the number of casualties doubled in less than a week.

Reiter acquired the habit of inspecting the dead like someone who inspects a lot for sale or a farm or a country house, and then going through the dead man's pockets in case there was any food to be found. Wilke did the same, but rather than doing it in silence he sang to himself: Prussian soldiers may masturbate, but they don't commit suicide. Some of their battalion comrades dubbed them the vampires. Reiter didn't care. In his free time he took a piece of bread and Ansky's notebook from his jacket and began to read. Sometimes Wilke sat down next to him and fell asleep. Once he asked Reiter whether he had written what was in the notebook. Reiter looked at him as if the question was too stupid to merit a reply. Wilke asked again whether he had written it. Reiter thought Wilke must be talking in his sleep. His eyes were half shut and he was unshaven and his cheekbones and jaw seemed to leap from his face.

"A friend wrote it," he said.

"A dead friend," said Wilke's voice in his sleep.

"More or less," said Reiter, and he kept reading.

Reiter liked to fall asleep listening to artillery fire. Wilke couldn't stand a long silence either, and before he closed his eyes he sang to himself. But Lieutenant Voss plugged his ears when he slept and only with difficulty did he awake and readjust to wakefulness and the war. Sometimes he had to be shaken and then he demanded to know what the fuck was going on and struck out in the dark. But he won medals and once Reiter and Wilke accompanied him to division headquarters where

General Von Berenberg in person pinned on his chest the highest honor a soldier of the Wehrmacht could receive. This was a happy day for Voss but not for the 79th Division, which by then had fewer troops than a regiment, since that afternoon, as Reiter and Wilke ate sausages beside a truck, the Russians attacked their position, which meant that Voss and his two companions had to return immediately to the front line. The resistance was brief and they retreated again. In the course of the retreat the division was reduced to the size of a battalion and many of the soldiers looked like madmen escaped from an asylum.

For several days they marched west as best they could, keeping in their companies or in groups that formed and split up at random.

Reiter went off alone. Sometimes he saw squadrons of Soviet planes pass overhead, and sometimes the sky, a blinding blue the minute before, grew overcast and a storm that lasted hours was suddenly unleashed. From a hill he saw a column of German tanks moving east. They looked like the coffins of an extraterrestrial civilization.

He walked at night. During the day he found shelter as best he could and passed the time reading Ansky's notebook and sleeping and watching things grow or burn around him. Sometimes he remembered the seaweed forests of the Baltic and smiled. Sometimes he thought about his little sister and that made him smile too. It had been a long time since he had news of his family. He had never gotten a letter from his father and Reiter suspected it was because his father didn't know how to write very well. His mother had written. What did she say in her letters? Reiter couldn't remember, they weren't very long, but he couldn't remember anything she said, all he remembered was her handwriting, shaky and sprawling, her grammar mistakes, her nakedness. Mothers should never write letters, he thought. His sister's letters, however, he remembered perfectly, and that made him smile, flat on his stomach, hidden in the grass, as sleep overtook him. They were letters in which she talked about the things that had happened to her, about the village, school, the dresses she wore, him.

You're a giant, said little Lotte. At first Reiter was disconcerted by this. But then he thought that for a child, and a child as sweet and impressionable as Lotte, someone of his height was the closest thing to a giant she had ever seen. Your steps echo in the forest, said Lotte in her letters. The birds of the forest hear the sound of your footsteps and stop singing. The workers in the fields hear you. The people hidden in dark

740

rooms hear you. The Hitler Youth hear you and come out to wait for you on the road into town. Everything is happiness. You're alive. Germany is alive. Et cetera.

One day, without knowing how, Reiter found himself back in Kostekino. There were no Germans left in the village. The sovkhoz was deserted and only the heads of a few undernourished and trembling old people looked out of farmhouses to inform him, by signs, that the Germans had evacuated the engineers and all the young Ukrainians who had been working in the village. That day Reiter slept at Ansky's farmhouse and he felt more comfortable than he would have felt at home. He lit a fire in the hearth and lay clothed on the bed. But he couldn't fall asleep right away. He began to think about semblance, as Ansky had discussed it in his notebook, and he began to think about himself. He felt free, as he never had in his life, and although malnourished and weak, he also felt the strength to prolong as far as possible this impulse toward freedom, toward sovereignty. And yet the possibility that it was all nothing but semblance troubled him. Semblance was an occupying force of reality, he said to himself, even the most extreme, borderline reality. It lived in people's souls and their actions, in willpower and in pain, in the way memories and priorities were ordered. Semblance proliferated in the salons of the industrialists and in the underworld. It set the rules, it rebelled against its own rules (in uprisings that could be bloody, but didn't therefore cease to be semblance), it set new rules.

National Socialism was the ultimate realm of semblance. As a general rule, he reflected, love was also semblance. My love for Lotte isn't semblance. Lotte is my sister and she's little and she thinks I'm a giant. But love, ordinary love, the love of a man and a woman, with breakfasts and dinners, with jealousy and money and sadness, is playacting, or semblance. Youth is the semblance of strength, love is the semblance of peace. Neither youth nor strength nor love nor peace can be granted to me, he said to himself with a sigh, nor can I accept such a gift. Only Ansky's wandering isn't semblance, he thought, only Ansky at fourteen isn't semblance. Ansky lived his whole life in rabid immaturity because the revolution, the one true revolution, is also immature. Then he fell asleep and didn't dream and the next day he went into the forest in search of firewood and when he returned to the village, out of curiosity, he went into the building where the Germans had lived during the winter of '42 and found it abandoned and in a shambles, no cooking pots or sacks of rice, no blankets or fires in the grates, the windowpanes broken and the shutters hanging loose, the floor dirty and covered in slicks of mud or shit that clung to the soles of one's boots if one made the mistake of stepping in them. On one wall a soldier had written *Heil Hitler* in charcoal. On another there was a kind of love letter. On the walls—and on the ceiling!—of the floor above someone had amused himself by drawing scenes from the daily life of the Germans who had lived in Kostekino. Thus, in a corner was a sketch of the forest and five Germans, recognizable by their caps, gathering wood or hunting birds. In another corner two Germans made love while a third, with both arms bandaged, watched from behind a tree. In another, four Germans lay asleep after dinner and next to them one could make out the bones of a dog. In the last corner was Reiter himself, with a long blond beard, peering out the window of the Anskys' farmhouse at the passing parade of an elephant, a giraffe, a rhinoceros, and a duck. In the middle of the fresco, if it could be called that, was a paved square, an imaginary square that had never existed in Kostekino, crowded with women or the ghosts of women, their hair standing on end, who ran back and forth wailing as two German soldiers oversaw the work of a squad of young Ukrainians raising a stone statue whose shape couldn't yet be made out.

The drawings were crude and childish and the perspective was pre-Renaissance, but the composition revealed glimpses of irony and thus of a secret mastery much greater than was at first apparent to the eye. As he returned to the farmhouse, Reiter reflected that the painter had talent, but that he had gone mad like the rest of the Germans who spent the winter of '42 in Kostekino. He also pondered his own surprise appearance in the mural. The painter clearly believed that it was he who had gone mad, he concluded. The figure of the duck, bringing up the rear of the procession headed by the elephant, suggested as much. He remembered that in those days he hadn't yet recovered his voice. He also remembered that in those days he had ceaselessly read and reread Ansky's notebook, memorizing each word, and feeling something very strange that sometimes seemed like happiness and other times like a guilt as vast as the sky. And he accepted the guilt and happiness and some nights he even weighed them against each other and the net result of his unorthodox reckoning was happiness, but a different kind of happiness, a heartrending happiness that for Reiter wasn't happiness but simply Reiter.

One night, three days after he had come to Kostekino, he dreamed that the Russians had taken the village and to escape them he had plunged into the stream, Sweet Spring, and swum until he came to the Dnieper, and the Dnieper, the banks of the Dnieper, were swarming with Russians, to the left as well as the right, and they all laughed to see him appear in the middle of the river and fired at him, and he dreamed that to escape the bullets he ducked underwater and let himself be carried along by the current, coming up only to breathe and going under again, and in this way he traveled miles and miles of river, sometimes holding his breath for three minutes or four or five, the world record, until the current had carried him away from the Russians, but even then Reiter kept going under, coming up, taking a breath, and going under again, and the bottom of the river was like a gravel road, every so often he saw schools of little white fish and every so often he bumped into a corpse already picked clean, just the bare bones, and these skeletons that dotted the river could be German or Soviet, it was impossible to say, because their clothes had rotted and the current had swept them downriver, and in Reiter's dream the current swept him downriver, too, and sometimes, especially at night, he came up to the surface and did the dead man's float, to rest or perhaps to sleep for five minutes as the river carried him incessantly southward in its embrace, and when the sun came up Reiter went under again and dove down, returned to the gelatinous bottom of the Dnieper, and so the days went by, sometimes he passed a city and saw its lights, or if there were no lights he heard a vague noise, like the clatter of furniture, as if sick people were moving furniture around, and sometimes he passed under military pontoons and he saw the frozen shadows of the soldiers in the night, shadows cast on the choppy surface of the water, and one morning, at last, the Dnieper flowed into the Black Sea, where it ceased to exist or was transformed, and Reiter approached the shore of the river or the sea with shaky steps, as if he were a student, the student he had never been, who flops down on the sand after swimming to the point of exhaustion, dazed, at the zenith of the holidays, only to discover with horror, as he sat on the beach contemplating the immensity of the Black Sea, that Ansky's notebook, which he was carrying under his jacket, had been reduced to a kind of pulp, the ink blurred forever, half of the notebook stuck to his clothes or his skin and the other half reduced to particles washed away by the gentle waves.

Then Reiter woke and decided he should leave Kostekino as quickly as possible. He dressed in silence and gathered his few belongings. He didn't light a lamp or stir the fire. He thought about how far he would have to walk that day. Before he left the farmhouse he returned Ansky's notebook carefully to the chimney hiding place. Let someone else find it now, he thought. Then he opened the door, closed it with care, and left the village with great strides.

•

Several days later he found a column from his division and returned to the monotony of holding a bit of ground and retreating, until they were destroyed by the Soviets at the Bug, west of Pervomaysk, and the remnants of the 79th were incorporated into the 303rd Division. In 1944, as they headed to Jassy with a Russian motorized brigade on their heels, Reiter and the other soldiers in his battalion saw a blue dust cloud rising toward the midday sky. Then they heard shouts and very faint singing, and shortly afterward, through his binoculars, Reiter saw a group of Romanian soldiers hurtle across a field, as if they were possessed or terrified, and turn onto a dirt track that ran parallel to the road along which his division was retreating.

They didn't have much time, because the Russians would be there from one moment to the next, and yet Reiter and some of his comrades decided to go and see what was happening. They left the hill they were using as a lookout post and crossed the scrubland that separated the two roads, riding in an armored vehicle mounted with a machine gun. They saw a kind of Romanian castle, deserted, the windows closed, with a paved courtyard that stretched to the stables. Then they came out into an open space where there were still some Romanian soldiers, stragglers playing dice or loading paintings and furniture from the castle onto carts they would later pull themselves. At the far end of the space, driven into the yellow earth, there was a great cross built of big pieces of wood varnished in dark shades, probably ripped from the great hall of the estate. On the cross was a naked man. The Romanians who spoke some German asked what they were doing there. The Germans answered that they were fleeing the Russians. They'll be here soon, said the Romanians.

"So what's that?" asked a German, motioning toward the crucified man.

"The general of our corps," said the Romanians as they hurried to pack their plunder onto the carts.

"Are you deserting?" asked one of the Germans.

"That's right," answered a Romanian, "last night the Third Army Corps decided to desert."

The Germans exchanged glances, as if they weren't sure whether to shoot at the Romanians or desert with them.

"Where are you going now?" they asked.

"West, back home," said some of the Romanians.

"Are you sure you're doing the right thing?"

"We'll kill anyone who gets in our way," said the Romanians.

As if to confirm this, most picked up their rifles and there were even a few who took aim openly at the Germans. For an instant it seemed as if the two groups were about to exchange fire. Just at that moment Reiter got out of the vehicle, and paying no heed to the standoff between the Romanians and the Germans, he set out toward the cross and the crucified man. The man had dried blood on his face, as if his nose had been broken with the butt of a rifle the night before, and he had two black eyes and his lips were swollen, but even so Reiter recognized him immediately. It was General Entrescu, the man who had slept with the Baroness Von Zumpe in the castle in the Carpathians and whom he and Wilke had spied on from the secret passageway. His clothes had been torn off, probably while he was still alive, leaving him naked except for his riding boots. Entrescu's penis, a proud cock that measured a foot when erect, according to his and Wilke's reckoning in earlier days, swayed wearily in the evening breeze. At the foot of the cross there was a box of the fireworks with which General Entrescu entertained his guests. The powder must have been wet or the fireworks were old because when they went off all they did was make a little puff of blue smoke that soon rose up to the sky and disappeared. One of the Germans, behind Reiter, made a remark about General Entrescu's member. A few Romanians laughed and all of them, some more quickly than others, approached the cross as if it had suddenly regained its magnetic force.

The rifles were no longer pointed at anyone. The soldiers held them like field tools, as if they were tired peasants marching along the edge of the abyss. They knew the Russians weren't far off and they feared them, but none could resist a last visit to General Entrescu's cross.

"What kind of man was he?" asked a German, knowing it didn't matter.

"He wasn't a bad sort," said a Romanian.

Then they all stood lost in thought, some with their heads bowed and others staring at the general with dazzled eyes. No one thought to ask how they had killed him. Probably they'd beaten him, then knocked him down and kept hitting him. The cross was dark with blood and the stain reached, dark as a spider, to the yellow earth. It didn't occur to anyone to bring him down.

"It'll be a while before you come across another specimen like this," said a German.

The Romanians didn't understand him. Reiter inspected Entrescu's face: his eyes were closed but they might have been wide open. His hands were fixed to the wood with big silver nails. Three to a hand. Heavy blacksmith's nails were driven through his feet. To Reiter's left, a young Romanian, no more than fifteen, his uniform too big on him, prayed. Reiter asked whether there was anyone else left on the estate. They answered that they were the only ones, the 3rd Corps or what was left of the 3rd Corps had arrived at the Litacz station three days ago and the general, instead of seeking a safer place to the west, had decided to pay a visit to his castle, which they found deserted. There were no servants or any animals to be killed and eaten. For two days the general shut himself in his room and wouldn't come out. The soldiers roamed the house until they found the cellar and broke down the door. Despite the qualms of some of the officers, they started to drink. That night half of the 3rd Corps deserted. Those who stayed did so of their own free will, not coerced by anyone. They stayed because they loved General Entrescu. Or something like that. Some went out to loot the neighboring villages and didn't come back. Others shouted up at the general from the courtyard to resume command and decide what to do. But the general remained locked in his room and wouldn't let anyone in. One drunken night the soldiers broke down the door. General Entrescu was sitting in an armchair, surrounded by candelabras and tapers, looking through a photo album. Then what happened, happened. At first Entrescu defended himself, lashing out with his riding crop. But the soldiers were crazed with hunger and fear and they killed him and nailed him to the cross.

"It must have been hard to make such a big cross," said Reiter.

"We made it before we killed the general," said a Romanian. "I don't know why we made it, but we made it even before we got drunk."

Then the Romanians went back to loading their spoils and some Germans helped and others decided to take a look around the house, to see whether there was any liquor remaining in the cellars, and the figure on the cross was left alone again. Before he left, Reiter asked whether they knew a man by the name of Popescu, who was always with the general and was probably employed as his secretary.

"Ah, Captain Popescu," said a Romanian, nodding, in the same tone of voice he might have used to say Captain Duck-Billed Platypus. "He must be in Bucharest by now."

As they headed off toward the scrubland, raising a cloud of dust along the road, Reiter thought he saw some blackbirds flying over the piece of flat ground from where General Entrescu watched the course of the war. One of the Germans riding next to the machine gun wondered, laughing, what the Russians would think when they saw the man on the cross. No one answered.

•

Moving from defeat to defeat, Reiter finally returned to Germany. In May 1945, at the age of twenty-five, after spending two months hidden in a forest, he surrendered to some American soldiers and was interned in a prisoner-of-war camp outside of Ansbach. There he showered for the first time in many days and the food was good.

Half of the prisoners of war slept in barracks that had been built by black American soldiers and the other half slept in big tents. Every other day visitors came to the camp and checked the prisoners' papers, in strict alphabetical order. At first they set up a table outside and the prisoners filed past one by one and answered their questions. Then the black soldiers, with the help of a few Germans, set up a special barracks with three rooms, and the lines now formed in front of this barracks. Reiter didn't know anyone in the camp. His comrades from the 79th and then the 303rd had been killed or taken prisoner by the Russians or had deserted, as he had. What was left of the division had been on its way to Pilsen, in the Protectorate, when Reiter struck off on his own in the midst of the confusion. In the Ansbach camp he tried not to associate with anyone. Some of the German soldiers sang in the afternoons. From their watch posts the black soldiers stared and laughed, but since none of them seemed to understand the words of the songs, they let them sing until lights-out. Others would stroll from one end of the camp to the other, arm in arm, discussing the most peculiar subjects. It was said that hostilities would soon start up between the Soviets and the Allies. There was speculation about the circumstances of Hitler's death. There was talk about hunger and how the potato harvest would once again save Germany from disaster.

Next to Reiter's cot slept a man of about fifty, a Volkssturm soldier. The man had let his beard grow and his German was soft and gentle, as if nothing that happened around him could touch him. During the day he often talked to two other ex–Volkssturm soldiers, who walked and ate with him. Sometimes, however, Reiter saw him alone, writing in lead pencil on various slips of paper that he took out of his pockets and then put away with great care. Once, before he fell sleep, Reiter asked what he was writing, and the man said he was trying to get his thoughts down on paper. Which, he added, wasn't easy. That was all Reiter asked, but after that, every night before they went to sleep, the former Volkssturm soldier found a reason to exchange a few words with him. He said his wife had died when the Russians took Küstrin, where they were from, but he didn't bear anyone a grudge, war was war, he said, and when the war ended it was best for each side to forgive the other and start anew.

Start how? Reiter wanted to know. From zero, and with joy and imagination, whispered the other man in his deliberate German. The man's name was Zeller and he was thin and withdrawn. When Reiter saw him walk through the camp, always with the other two former Volkssturm soldiers, he radiated a great dignity, perhaps in contrast to his two companions. One night Reiter asked whether he had any family.

"My wife," Zeller answered.

"But your wife is dead," said Reiter.

"I had a son and a daughter," Reiter heard him whisper, "but they died too. My son in the battle of Kursk and my daughter during a bombing raid on Hamburg."

"Don't you have any other relatives?" asked Reiter.

"Two little grandchildren, twins, a girl and a boy, but they died in the same raid."

"Good God," said Reiter.

"My son-in-law died too, not in the raid, but days later, from sorrow at the death of his wife and children."

"That's terrible," said Reiter.

"He killed himself by taking rat poison," whispered Zeller in the dark. "He suffered agonies for three days before he died."

Reiter didn't know what to say anymore, partly because he was about to fall asleep, and the last thing he heard was Zeller's voice saying that war was war and it was best to forget everything, everything, everything. The truth is that Zeller possessed an enviable serenity. This serenity was disturbed only when new prisoners appeared or upon the return of the visitors who interrogated them one by one inside the barracks. After three months it was the turn of those whose last names started with Q, R, and S, and Reiter went in to talk to the soldiers and some men in civilian dress, who politely asked him to face forward and sideways and then searched through a couple of files that were probably full of photographs. Then one of the civilians asked what he'd done during the war and Reiter had to tell them that he'd been in Romania with the 79th and then in Russia, where he'd been wounded several times.

The soldiers and civilians wanted to see his wounds and he had to undress and show them. One of the civilians, who spoke German with a Berlin accent, asked him whether he ate well at the camp. Reiter said he ate like a king, and when the one who had asked the question translated for the others, they all laughed.

"Do you like American food?" asked one of the soldiers.

The civilian translated the question and Reiter said:

"American meat is the best in the world."

They all laughed again.

"You're right," said the soldier, "but what you're eating isn't American meat. It's dog food."

This time the translator (who chose not to translate the answer) and some of the soldiers laughed so hard they fell down. A black soldier looked in the door with a worried expression on his face and asked whether they were having trouble with the prisoner. They ordered him to close the door and leave, nothing was wrong, they were telling jokes. Then one man took out a pack of cigarettes and offered one to Reiter. I'll smoke it later, said Reiter, and he stuck it behind his ear. After this the soldiers suddenly turned serious and began to write down the information Reiter gave them: date and place of birth, names of parents, address of parents and of at least two family members or friends, et cetera.

That night Zeller asked what had happened during the interrogation and Reiter told him everything. Did they ask what year and month you joined the army? Yes. Did they ask where your recruitment office was? Yes. Did they ask what division you served in? Yes. Were there photographs? Yes. Did you see them? No. When he had finished his own private interrogation, Zeller pulled his blanket up over his face and seemed to fall asleep but after a while Reiter heard him mutter in the dark.

On the next visit, which took place a week later, only two interrogators came to the camp and there were no lines or interrogations. The prisoners were made to stand in formation and the black soldiers went through the ranks, pulling out approximately ten men, whom they led to two trucks, into which they were loaded after they'd been handcuffed. These prisoners, the camp commander told them, were suspected of being war criminals, and then he ordered them to disband and resume their usual activities. When the visitors returned a week later they moved on to the letters *T*, *U*, and *V* and this time Zeller really got nervous. His voice was as gentle as ever, but his talk and manner of speech changed: words came tumbling from his lips and at night he couldn't stop whispering. He spoke quickly, as if compelled by reasons beyond his control, reasons he scarcely understood. He craned his neck toward Reiter and leaned on one elbow and began to whisper and moan and imagine scenes of splendor that together formed a chaotic assemblage of dark cubes stacked one on top of the other.

During the day things were different. Zeller once again radiated dignity and decorum, and although he didn't associate with anyone except his old comrades from the Volkssturm, almost everyone respected him and believed him to be a decent person. For Reiter, however, who had to endure his nightly disquisitions, Zeller's countenance betrayed a progressive deterioration, as if inside of him a merciless struggle were being waged between diametrically opposed forces. What forces were these? Reiter didn't know, but he sensed that both sprang from a single source, which was madness. One night Zeller said his name wasn't Zeller, it was Sammer, and it therefore stood to reason that he need not appear before the alphabetic interrogators on their next visit.

•

That night Reiter wasn't tired and the full moon filtered through the fabric of the tent like boiling coffee through a sock.

"My name is Leo Sammer and some of the things I've told you are true and some aren't," said the fake Zeller, rolling on his cot as if his whole body itched. "Do you recognize my name?"

"No," said Reiter.

"There's no reason you should, son. I'm not nor have I ever been a famous man, although during the time you've been far from home my name has grown like a malignant tumor and now it turns up on the most unlikely documents," said Sammer in his soft and increasingly rapid German. "Of course, I was never in the Volkssturm. I fought, never let it be said I didn't fight, I did fight, like any wellborn German, but I served in other theaters, not on the military battlefield but on the economic and political battlefield. My wife, thanks be to God, isn't dead," he added after a long silence in which he and Reiter watched the light sweeping the tent like a bird's wing or a claw. "My son died, that much is true. My poor son. An intelligent boy who liked sports and reading. What more can you ask of a son. Serious, an athlete, a good reader. He died in Kursk. At the time, I was the assistant director of an organization responsible for supplying workers to the Reich, whose main offices were located in a Polish town just a few miles outside the territory of the General Government.

When they gave me the news I stopped believing in the war. My wife, to make matters worse, began to lose her grip on her senses. I wouldn't wish my situation on anyone. Not even my worst enemy! A son dead in the prime of life, a wife with constant migraines, and an exhausting job that required maximum effort and concentration from me. But I forged ahead thanks to my methodical nature and tenacity. The truth is, I worked to forget my misfortunes. As a result, I was appointed the head of the government organization to which I lent my services. From one day to the next, our work tripled. Not only did I have to send workers to German factories but now I also had to ensure the proper functioning of the bureaucracy in that rainy part of Poland, a sad backwater we were trying to Germanize, where every day was gray and the earth seemed stained with soot and no one enjoyed himself in civilized fashion, so that even the ten-year-old boys were alcoholics, if you can believe it, poor boys, but they were wild, too, and all they cared about was liquor, as I've said, and soccer.

Sometimes I watched them from the window of my office: they played in the street with a rag ball and their running and jumping were truly pathetic, because the liquor they had drunk was always making them fall or miss easy goals. But I don't mean to go on and on. The point is, these were soccer matches that often ended in blows. Or kicks. Or with empty beer bottles broken over the heads of the rival team. And I watched it all from the window and didn't know what to do. My God, how to end that plague, how to improve the situation of those innocents.

I confess: I was lonely, very lonely. I couldn't rely on my wife. The only time the poor thing left her dark room was to beg me on her knees to let her return to Germany, to Bavaria, to join her sister. My son had died. My daughter lived in Munich, happily married and far removed from my troubles. Work piled up and my fellow workers were losing heart. The war wasn't going well and anyway it no longer interested me. How can someone who's lost a son care about the war? My life, in short, unfolded under permanent black clouds.

Then I received a new order: I was to take charge of a group of Jews from Greece. I think they were from Greece. They might have been Hungarian or Croatian. But probably not, the Croats killed their own Jews. Maybe they were Serbian. Anyway, let's call them Greek. They were sending me a trainload of Greek Jews. Me! And I didn't have anywhere to put them. It was a sudden order, unexpected. I ran a civil operation, not military or SS. I didn't have experts on the subject, I just sent foreign workers to the factories of the Reich, so what would I do with these Jews? Courage, I said to myself, and one morning I went to the station to wait for them. With me I brought the local police chief and all the officers I could muster at the last minute. The train from Greece stopped on a siding. An official made me sign some papers confirming the delivery of five hundred Jews, men, women, and children. I signed. Then I approached the cars and the smell was unbearable. I forbade them all to be opened. This could lead to the spread of disease, I said to myself. Then I phoned a friend, who put me in touch with a man who ran a camp for Jews near Chelmno. I explained my problem, asked what I could do with my Jews. I should say that there were no Jews in the town where I worked, just drunk children and drunk women and old people who spent all day chasing the sun's meager rays. The man from Chelmno said to call back in two days, that believe it or not he had problems of his own.

I thanked him and hung up. I returned to the siding. The official and the engineer were waiting for me. I bought them breakfast. Coffee and sausage and fried eggs and hot bread. They ate like pigs. Not me. I had other things on my mind. They told me I had to unload the train, their orders were to return to southern Europe that very night. I met their gaze and said I would. The official said I could count on him and his guards to empty the cars in exchange for a hand with cleanup from the station crew. I said that was fine.

We set to the task. The smell that came from the cars when they were opened made even the woman who cleaned the station washrooms wrinkle her nose. Eight Jews had died on the trip. The official made the survivors fall into ranks. They didn't look well. I ordered them to be taken to an abandoned tannery. I told one of my employees to go to the bakery and buy all the bread available to distribute to the Jews. Have them charge it to me, I said, but be quick about it. Then I went to my office to take care of other urgent business. At noon I was informed that the train from Greece was leaving the village. From the window of my office I watched those drunken boys play soccer and for an instant I felt as if I'd had too much to drink myself.

I spent the next few hours seeking a more permanent arrangement for the Jews. One of my secretaries suggested I put them to work. In Germany? I asked. Here, he said. It wasn't a bad idea. I ordered that some fifty Jews be given brooms and that they be divided into brigades of ten to sweep my ghost town. Then I returned to the main business of the day. Several factories in the Reich wanted at least two thousand workers and I had missives from the General Government requesting available labor. I made a few phone calls: I said I had five hundred Jews available, but they wanted Poles or Italian prisoners of war.

Italian prisoners of war? I'd never seen an Italian prisoner of war! And I'd already sent all the Polish men I had, keeping only the strictly necessary. So I called Chelmno again and asked once more whether they were interested in my Greek Jews.

"If they were sent to you, it must be for a reason," answered a metallic voice. "You deal with them."

"But I don't run a camp," I said, "I don't have the proper experience."

"You're responsible for them," the voice answered, "if you have any questions ask the people who sent them to you."

"My dear sir," I answered, "whoever sent them to me is probably in Greece."

"Then talk to Greek Affairs, in Berlin," said the voice.

Wise reply. I thanked him and hung up. For a few seconds I wondered whether it was really a good idea to call Berlin. Outside, all of a sudden, a brigade of Jewish sweepers came by. The drunk boys stopped playing soccer and stepped onto the sidewalk, watching the Jews as if they were animals. At first the Jews kept their heads down and swept dutifully, guarded by a village policeman, but then one of them lifted his head, he was no more than a boy, and glanced at the villagers and the ball trapped under the boot of one of those little rogues. For a few seconds I thought they would start to play. Sweepers versus drunkards. But the policeman knew his job and after a while the brigade of Jews had disappeared and the boys went back to playing in the street with their poor excuse for a ball.

Once again, I buried myself in my paperwork. I addressed the matter of a shipment of potatoes that had gotten lost somewhere between the region under my oversight and the city of Leipzig, which was its final destination. I ordered that the matter be investigated. I've never trusted truck drivers. I addressed a matter involving beets. A matter involving carrots. A matter involving ersatz coffee. I put a call through to the mayor. One of my secretaries arrived with a document stating that the potatoes had left my region by rail, not truck. The potatoes had reached the station in carts drawn by mules or horses or donkeys, all of which the peasants still kept, but not by truck. There was a copy of the shipping receipt, but it had been lost. Find that copy, I ordered. Another of my secretaries came in with the news that the mayor was ill in bed.

"Is it serious?" I asked.

"A cold," said my secretary.

"Well, have him get up and come in," I said.

When I was alone I started to think about my poor wife, confined to her bed with the curtains drawn, and the thought made me so upset that I began to pace my office, because if I sat still I ran the risk of suffering a stroke. Then I saw the brigade of sweepers come back along the quite clean street and I was suddenly paralyzed by the sense that time was repeating itself.

But thanks be to God, it wasn't the same sweepers. The problem was that they looked so much alike. The policeman on guard, however, was different. The first officer was tall and thin and very upright in his carriage. The second officer was fat and short and sixty, though he looked ten years older. The Polish boys playing soccer surely felt as I did and they stepped back up on the sidewalk to let the Jews pass. One of the boys said something. From where I stood glued to the window, I imagined he was insulting the Jews. I opened the window and called to the policeman.

"Mr. Mehnert," I called from above, "Mr. Mehnert."

At first the policeman didn't know who was calling him and he looked all around, confused, which made the drunk boys laugh.

"Up here, Mr. Mehnert, up here."

Finally he saw me and stood to attention. The Jews stopped working and waited. All of the drunk boys were staring up at my window.

"If any of those little bastards insults my workers, shoot him, Mr. Mehnert," I said loud enough so that everyone could hear me.

"Everything is fine, excellency," said Mr. Mehnert.

"Did you hear me?" I shouted.

"Perfectly well, excellency."

"Fire at will, at will, is that clear, Mr. Mehnert?"

"Clear as day, excellency."

Then I closed the window and got back to business. I hadn't been studying a circular from the Ministry of Propaganda for five minutes when one of my secretaries interrupted me to say that the bread had been distributed to the Jews, but there hadn't been enough for everyone. Also, as he oversaw the distribution, he had discovered that two more had died. Two dead Jews? I repeated, dazed. But they all got off the train on their own two feet! My secretary shrugged his shoulders. They died, he said.

"My, my, my, these are strange times we live in, aren't they?" I said.

"They were two old people," said my secretary. "An old man and an old woman, to be precise."

"And the bread?" I asked.

"There wasn't enough for everyone," said my secretary.

"That will have to be fixed," I said.

"We'll try," said my secretary, "but it's too late today, it'll have to be tomorrow."

His tone was highly disagreeable. I waved him out. I tried to concentrate on work again, but I couldn't. I went over to the window. The drunk boys were gone. I decided to take a walk, cold air has a calming effect and strengthens the constitution, although I would just as soon have gone home, where a fire in the hearth and a good book awaited me to while away the hours. Before I went out I told my secretary that if anything urgent came up I could be found at the station bar. Out in the street, as I came around a corner, I ran into the mayor, Mr. Tippelkirsch, who was on his way to visit me. He was bundled in a coat and several sweaters that gave him an exceedingly bulky look, with a scarf pulled up to his nose. He explained that he hadn't been able to come before because he was running a temperature of 104 degrees.

Let's not exaggerate, I said without slowing my pace. Ask the doctor, he said behind me. When we got to the station I ran into several peasants waiting for the arrival of a regional train from the east, from General Government territory. The train, they informed me, was an hour late. Nothing but bad news. I had coffee with Mr. Tippelkirsch and we talked about the Jews. I've heard all about it, said Mr. Tippelkirsch, clutching his cup of coffee in both hands. His hands were very white and delicate, crisscrossed with veins.

For a moment I was put in mind of the hands of Christ. Hands worthy of being painted. Then I asked what we should do. Send them back, said Mr. Tippelkirsch. A rivulet ran from his nose. I pointed it out with my finger. He didn't seem to understand. Blow your nose, I said. Oh, pardon me, he said, and after searching his coat pockets he pulled out a white handkerchief, very large and not very clean.

"How do we send them back?" I asked. "By chance do I have a train at my disposal? And if I did, shouldn't I use it for something more productive?"

A kind of spasm shook the mayor and he shrugged.

"Put them to work," he said.

"Then who will feed them? The town? No, Mr. Tippelkirsch, I've considered every possibility and there's only one answer: we must hand them over to another authority."

"And what if, as a temporary measure, we lent a pair of Jews to each peasant in the region, wouldn't that be a good idea?" asked Mr. Tippelkirsch. "At least until we decide what to do with them."

I looked him in the eye and lowered my voice:

"That's against the law and you know it," I said.

"Yes," he said, "I know it, you know it, but our situation is grim and we could use the help. I don't think the peasants will complain."

"No, absolutely unthinkable," I said.

But I thought about it and my thoughts plunged me into a deep, dark pit where all that was visible, lit by sparks from who knows where, was my son's face, flickering between life and death.

I was roused by the chatter of Mr. Tippelkirsch's teeth. Do you feel unwell? I asked. He made as if to reply but couldn't and a few moments later he fainted. From the bar, I called my office and asked them to send a car. One of my secretaries told me he had managed to contact Greek Affairs in Berlin and it accepted no responsibility for the matter. When the car appeared, between the owner of the bar, a peasant, and myself we managed to get Mr. Tippelkirsch into it. I told the driver to leave the mayor at home and then return to the station. In the meantime I played a game of dice by the fire. A peasant who had emigrated from Estonia won every match. His three sons were at the front and each time he won he said something that struck me as very strange, even mysterious. Luck and death go hand in hand, he said. And he gave us a sad-eyed look as if the rest of us should take pity on him.

I think he was a popular man in the village, especially among the Polish women, who had nothing to fear from a widower with three grown and faraway sons, a common old man, as far as I could tell, but not as stingy as most peasants, someone who every so often would make a gift to a woman of a bit of food or an item of clothing in exchange for a night spent at his farm. Quite the lothario. After a while, when the game was over, I bade farewell to those present and returned to my offices.

I called Chelmno again, but this time I couldn't get through. One of my secretaries told me that the official at Greek Affairs in Berlin had suggested I call the General Government SS headquarters. Rather foolish advice, since even though our town and the surrounding region, villages and farms included, were just a few miles outside the boundaries of General Government territory, we actually belonged administratively to a German gau. What to do, then? I decided I'd had enough for the day and turned my attention to other matters.

Before I left for home I got a call from the station. The train still hadn't arrived. Patience, I said. Inside I knew it would never come. On my way home it started to snow.

The next day I got up early and went to the club for breakfast. All the tables were empty. After a while, perfectly dressed, combed, and shaved, two of my secretaries appeared with the news that another pair of Jews had died during the night. Of what? I asked. They didn't know. They were just dead. And this time it wasn't two old people but a young woman and her child, approximately eight months old.

Defeated, I hung my head and stared at myself for a few seconds in the calm, dark surface of my coffee. Maybe they died of cold, I said. It snowed last night. Could be, said my secretaries. I felt as if everything were spinning around me.

"Let's go and see those lodgings," I said.

"What lodgings?" asked my secretaries, startled.

"The place we've put the Jews," I said, already standing and moving toward the door.

Just as I imagined, the old tannery couldn't have been in a worse state. Even the officers on guard complained. One of my secretaries told me the guards were cold at night and shifts weren't scrupulously observed. I told him to fix the matter of shifts with the police chief and to bring them blankets. The Jews, too, of course. The secretary whispered that it would be hard to find blankets for all of them. I told him to try, I wanted to see at least half the Jews with blankets.

"What about the other half?" asked the secretary.

"If they have any fellow feeling, each Jew will share his blanket with another, and if not, that's their business, I've done all I can," I said.

On my way back to my office I noticed that the streets were cleaner than they'd ever been. The rest of the day passed as usual, until that night I received a call from Warsaw, the Office of Jewish Affairs, an organization of whose existence I had previously been unaware. A distinctly adolescent voice asked me whether it was true that I had five hundred Greek Jews. I said yes and added that I didn't know what to do with them, because no one had advised me of their arrival.

"It seems there's been a mistake," said the voice.

"So it seems," I said, and I was silent.

The silence lasted for quite a while.

"That train should have unloaded in Auschwitz," said the adolescent's voice, "or at least I think so, I'm not quite sure. Hold, please."

For ten minutes I stood with the phone to my ear. While I was waiting, one of my secretaries appeared with some papers for me to sign and another came in with a memorandum on low milk production in the region and yet another came to say he had something to tell me, but I shushed him, so he wrote what he had to say on a piece of paper: potatoes stolen in Leipzig by their own growers. Which surprised me greatly because those potatoes had been grown on German farms by people who had just settled in the region and were on their best behavior.

"How?" I wrote on the same paper. I don't know, wrote the secretary under my query, possibly by forging shipping documents.

Yes, it wouldn't be the first time, I thought, but not my peasants. And even if they were guilty, what could I do? Throw them all in prison? And what would I gain by that? Should I let the fields lie fallow? Should I fine them and make them poorer than they already were? I decided I couldn't do that. Investigate further, I wrote under his message. And then I wrote: good work.

The secretary smiled at me, raised his hand, moved his lips as if he were saying *Heil Hitler*, and tiptoed off. At that moment the adolescent voice asked:

"Are you still there?"

"I'm here," I said.

"Look, with the situation as it is we have no transportation available to collect the Jews. Administratively they belong to Upper Silesia. I've talked to my superiors and we're in agreement that the easiest and best thing would be for you to dispose of them."

I didn't answer.

"Do you understand?" asked the voice from Warsaw.

"Yes, I understand," I said.

"Then we have a solution, don't we?"

"That's right," I said. "But I'd like to receive the order in writing," I added. I heard a pealing laugh at the other end of the line. It could be my son's laugh, I thought, a laugh that conjured up country afternoons, blue rivers full of trout, and the scent of fistfuls of flowers and grasses.

"Don't be naïve," said the voice without a hint of arrogance, "these orders are never issued in writing."

That night I couldn't sleep. I understood that what they were asking me to do was to eliminate the Greek Jews myself and at my own risk. From my office the next morning I called the mayor, the fire chief, the police chief, and the president of the War Veterans Association and summoned them to a meeting at the club. The fire chief said he couldn't come because he had a mare about to foal, but I told him this wasn't a game of dice, it was something much more urgent. He wanted to know what the matter was. You'll find out soon enough, I said.

When I got to the club they were all there, around a table, listening to an old waiter tell jokes. On the table was fresh-baked bread and butter and jam. When he saw me, the waiter was quiet. He was an old man, short and very thin. I sat in an empty chair and requested a cup of coffee. When it came I asked the waiter to leave us. Then, briefly, I explained to the others the situation we were in.

The fire chief said a call should be made immediately to the head of some camp that would take the Jews. I said I had already talked to a man at Chelmno, but the fire chief interrupted me and said we should contact a camp in Upper Silesia. The discussion went on like this for a while. They all had friends who knew someone who was friends with someone else, et cetera. I let them talk, calmly drank my coffee, split a roll and spread half with butter and ate it. Then I put jam on the other half and ate it. The coffee was good. It wasn't like the coffee from before the war, but it was good. When I had finished I told them that every possibility had been considered and the order to dispose of the Greek Jews was unequivocal. The problem is how, I said. Do you have any ideas?

The others exchanged glances and no one said a word. To break the uncomfortable silence more than anything else, I asked the mayor how his cold was. I doubt I'll survive the winter, he said. We all laughed, thinking he was joking, but in fact he was serious. Then we talked about country things, some boundary problems caused by a stream that had changed course overnight, shifting an inexplicable and capricious ten yards, a phenomenon for which no one could provide a convincing explanation and that affected the property titles of two neighboring farms whose border was marked by the wretched stream. I was also asked about the investigation of the missing shipment of potatoes. I downplayed the matter. They'll turn up, I said.

At midmorning I returned to my office and the Polish boys were already drunk and playing soccer.

I let two days go by without coming to any decision. No Jews died and one of my secretaries organized three gardening brigades, in addition to the five sweeping brigades. Each brigade was made up of ten Jews and, besides tidying the town squares, they cleared a strip of land along the road, land the Poles had never cultivated and that we, for lack of time and manpower, hadn't either. Little else happened, as I recall.

An enormous sense of boredom overtook me. At night, when I got home, I ate alone in the kitchen, shivering with cold, staring at some vague point on the white walls. I didn't even think anymore about my son killed in Kursk, or put on the radio to listen to the news or light music. In the mornings I played dice at the station bar and I listened to the lewd jokes of the peasants who gathered there to pass the time, without entirely understanding them. Thus two days of inactivity passed, dreamlike, and then two more.

But work was piling up and one morning I knew I could no longer avoid the problem. I called my secretaries. I called the police chief. I asked the chief how many armed men he could spare to deal with the matter. He said it depended, but in a pinch he could call up eight.

"And what do we do with them then?" asked one of my secretaries.

"We're going to solve that right now," I said.

I sent the police chief away but ordered him to keep in close contact with my office. Then, followed by my secretaries, I went out and we all got in my car. The driver drove us to the outskirts of the village. For an hour we meandered along back roads and old cart tracks. In some places there was still snow on the ground. I stopped at a few farms that struck me as ideal and talked to the farmers, but they all came up with excuses and posed objections.

I've been too kind to these people, I said to myself, it's time I got tough. But it isn't in my nature to be tough. There was a hollow that one of my secretaries knew about some ten miles from town. We went to look at it. It wasn't bad. It was in a remote spot, lots of pine trees, dark soil. The bottom of the hollow was covered in masses of fleshy leaves. According to my secretary, people came here in the spring to hunt rabbits. The place wasn't far from the road. When we got back to the city I had decided what had to be done.

The next morning I went in person to fetch the police chief at his house. On the sidewalk in front of my office, eight policemen gathered, joined by four of my men (one of my secretaries, my driver, and two clerks) and two farmers, volunteers who were there simply because they wanted to participate. I told them to act with dispatch and to return to my office to inform me of what had happened. The sun wasn't up yet when they left.

At five in the afternoon the police chief and my secretary returned. They looked tired. They said everything had gone according to plan. They had stopped at the old tannery and left town with two brigades of sweepers. They had walked ten miles. They had turned off the road and headed with weary steps toward the hollow. And there the deed had been done. Was there chaos? Did chaos reign? Did chaos prevail? I asked. A little, they answered sulkily, and I chose not to press them.

The next morning the same operation was repeated, with a few changes: rather than two volunteers we had five, and three policemen were replaced by three others who hadn't taken part in the previous day's labors. Among my men there were changes, too: I sent the other secretary and no clerks, although the driver remained part of the contingent.

Midway through the afternoon another two brigades of sweepers disappeared and that night I sent the secretary who hadn't been at the hollow and the fire chief to organize four new brigades. Before nightfall I set out to visit the scene. We had an accident or a near accident and swerved off the road. My driver, I could see at once, was more agitated than usual. I asked what was wrong. You can speak frankly, I said.

"I don't know, excellency," he answered. "I feel strange, it must be the lack of sleep."

"Aren't you sleeping?" I asked.

"It's hard, excellency, it's hard, God knows I try, but it's hard."

I promised him he had nothing to worry about. Then he got the car back on the road and we drove on. When we arrived I took a flashlight and made my way along a ghostly path. The animals seemed to have suddenly retreated from the area around the hollow. From now on, I thought, this is the realm of insects. My driver followed me a little reluctantly. I heard him whistle and I asked him to stop. At a glance the hollow looked just as it had the first time I saw it.

"And the hole?" I asked.

"Over there," said the driver, pointing toward the far end of the expanse.

I had no desire to undertake a closer inspection and I went home. The next day my troop of volunteers, with the obligatory variations I had imposed for reasons of mental hygiene, returned to work. By the end of the week eight brigades of sweepers had disappeared, which made a total of eighty Greek Jews, but after the Sunday rest a new problem arose. The taxing work had begun to take its toll on the men. The volunteers from the farms, of whom there had been as many as six at a certain point, were reduced to one. The town police complained that their nerves were frayed and when I tried to urge them on I could see they really were at the breaking point. My office staff were either unwilling to continue to take an active part in the operations or they suddenly fell ill. My own health, I discovered one morning as I was shaving, hung by a thread.

I asked them, nevertheless, for a final effort, and that morning, after a notable delay, they escorted two more brigades of sweepers to the hollow. Waiting for them, I was unable to work. I tried, but I couldn't. At six in the evening, after dark, they returned. I heard them singing in the streets, I heard them bid each other farewell. It was clear that most of them were drunk. I didn't blame them.

The police chief, one of my secretaries, and my driver came up to my office, where I awaited them engulfed in the darkest foreboding. I remember that they sat (the driver remained standing by the door) and it wasn't necessary for them to say anything in order for me to understand how much and to what degree the appointed task was wearing them down. Something will have to be done, I said.

That night I didn't sleep at home. I rode around town, in silence, with my driver at the wheel smoking a cigarette I had given him. At some point I fell asleep in the backseat, wrapped in a blanket, and I dreamed that my son was shouting onward! ever onward!

I was stiff all over when I woke up. It was three in the morning when I stopped at the mayor's house. At first no one answered my knock and I almost kicked the door down. Then I heard hesitant footsteps. It was the mayor. Who's there? he asked, in what I imagined was a weasel's voice. That night we talked until dawn. The next Monday, instead of leading more brigades of sweepers out of town, the police waited for the appearance of the young soccer players. In total, they rounded up fifteen boys.

I had them brought into the town hall and I headed there myself with my secretaries and driver. When I saw them, so terribly pale, so terribly thin, so terribly in need of soccer and alcohol, I felt sorry for them. Standing motionless there, they seemed less like children than like the skeletons of children, abandoned sketches, pure will and bone.

I told them there would be wine for all of them and also bread and sausages. No reaction. I repeated what I had said about the wine and food and added that there would probably also be something they could take home to their families. I interpreted their silence as acquiescence and I sent them to the hollow in a truck, accompanied by five policemen and a load of ten rifles and a machine gun that, I had been informed, was always jamming. Then I ordered the rest of the policemen, accompanied by four armed peasants whom I forced to participate under threat of reporting their regular thieving to the state, to escort three full brigades of sweepers to the hollow. I also gave orders that no Jew should leave the old tannery for any reason whatsoever.

At two in the afternoon the policemen who had led the Jews to the hollow returned. They ate at the station bar and by three they were on their way back to the hollow with thirty more Jews. At ten they all returned, the escorts and the drunken boys and the policemen who had led the boys and taught them how to handle guns.

Everything went well, said one of my secretaries, the boys put their hearts into it, and those who wanted to watch watched and those who didn't went away and came back when it was all over. The next day, I caused a rumor to be spread among the Jews that they were all being transported—in small groups because of our lack of resources—to a work camp properly equipped for their stay. Then I talked to a group of Polish mothers, who were easily soothed, and from my office I oversaw two new transfers of Jews to the hollow, in groups of twenty.

But problems resurfaced when it snowed again. According to one of my secretaries, there was no way to dig new graves in the hollow. I told him that must be impossible. In the end, the problem lay in the way the graves had been dug, horizontally rather than vertically, all across the hollow, and not very deep. I organized a group and resolved to fix the problem that same day. The snow had erased any trace of the Jews. We began to dig. After a little while, I heard an old farmer called Barz shout that there was something there. I went to look. Yes, there was something.

"Do I keep digging?" asked Barz.

"Don't be stupid," I answered, "cover it up again, leave it as it was."

Each time someone found something I repeated the same thing. Leave it alone. Cover it up. Go dig somewhere else. Remember the idea isn't to find things, it's to *not* find them. But all my men, one after the other, kept finding something and in fact, as my secretary had said, it seemed there was no room left at the bottom of the hollow.

And yet in the end my tenacity won out. We found an empty space and I put all my men to work there. I told them to dig deep, always down, farther down, as if we were trying to dig all the way to hell, and I also made sure the pit was as wide as a swimming pool. That night, working by flashlight, we managed to finish the job and then we left. The next day the weather was so bad we were able to bring only twenty Jews to the hollow. The boys got drunker than ever. Some couldn't stand up, others vomited on the way back. The truck left them in the main square, not far from my offices, and many stayed there, under the eaves of the gazebo, huddled together as the snow kept falling and they dreamed about liquor-fueled soccer matches.

The next morning five of the boys had come down with pneumonia and the rest, to a greater or lesser degree, were in a pitiable state, unable to work. When I ordered the police chief to replace the boys with our men, at first he was reluctant, but in the end he gave in. That afternoon he disposed of eight Jews. It struck me as a paltry number, and I said as much. There were eight of them, the police chief answered, but it was as if there were eight hundred. I gazed at him in the eyes and understood.

I told him we would wait until the Polish boys recovered. The ill luck that dogged us, however, seemed determined to persist, no matter what we did. Two Polish boys died of pneumonia, in the throes of a fever, with visions of soccer matches in the snow and white holes into which balls and players disappeared, as the town doctor explained. As a token of condolence I sent their mothers a bit of smoked bacon and baskets of potatoes and carrots. Then I waited. I let the snow fall. I let myself freeze. One morning I went to the hollow. The snow there was soft, even excessively soft. For a few seconds I felt as if I were walking across a big dish of cream. When I got to the edge and looked down, I saw that nature had done its work. Magnificent. There was no sign of anything, only snow. Then, when the weather improved, the brigade of drunk boys went back to work.

I gave them a rousing speech. I told them they were doing a good job and now their families had more food, more opportunities. They stared at me and didn't say anything. Still, their indifference and lack of enthusiasm for the task at hand was evident in their bearing. I knew very well they would rather have been in the street drinking and playing soccer. Meanwhile, at the station bar all anyone talked about was how close the Russians were. Some said Warsaw would fall at any moment. They whispered it. But I heard the whispers, and I whispered, too. Ill omens.

One afternoon they told me the boys had drunk so much they had fallen down one after the other in the snow. I scolded them. They didn't seem to understand what I was saying. It didn't matter. One day I asked how many Greek Jews we had left. After half an hour one of my secretaries handed me a detailed account of everything, the five hundred Jews who had arrived by train from the south, those who had died on the trip, those who had died during their stay at the old tannery, those we had dispatched ourselves, those the drunken boys had dispatched, et cetera. I still had more than one hundred Jews and everyone was exhausted, my policemen, my volunteers, and the Polish boys.

What to do? The work was too much for us. Man wasn't made to bear some tasks for very long, I said to myself as I contemplated the horizon from my office window, striped in pink and a cloacal murk. It was too much for me, anyway. I was doing my best, but I couldn't stand it. Nor could my policemen. Fifteen, all right. Thirty, fine. But when one reaches fifty the stomach turns and the head spins and the restless nights and nightmares begin.

I put a halt to the work. The boys went back to playing soccer in the street. The policemen returned to their duties. The peasants returned to their farms. No one from the outside showed any interest in the Jews, so I started up the sweeping brigades again and let some, no more than twenty, do farmwork, making the farmers responsible for their safety.

One night I was gotten out of bed and told I had an urgent call. It was an official from Upper Galicia with whom I had never spoken before. He told me to prepare for the evacuation of Germans from my region.

"There are no trains," I said, "how can I evacuate them all?"

"That's your problem," said the official.

Before he hung up I said I had a group of Jews in my power, what to do with them? He didn't answer. The line had gone dead or he had other people like me to call or the Jews were of no interest to him. It was four in the morning. I couldn't go back to bed. I told my wife we were leaving and then I sent for the mayor and the police chief. When I got to my office they were there, looking as if they had slept little and poorly. They were both afraid.

I reassured them, I told them that if we acted fast no one would be in danger. We put our people to work. Before dawn the first evacuees were already on their way west. I stayed until the end. I spent another day and night in the village. In the distance the sound of artillery could be heard. I went to see the Jews, the police chief is my witness, and I told them to leave. Then I collected the two policemen who were on guard and abandoned the Jews to their fate in the old tannery. That's freedom, I suppose.

My driver told me he had seen some Wehrmacht soldiers passing through without stopping. I went up to my office without knowing very well what I was looking for. The night before I had slept on the sofa for a few hours and I had already burned everything that needed to be burned. The town streets were empty, although women's heads could be glimpsed at some windows. Then I went down the stairs, got in my car, and left, said Sammer to Reiter.

I was a fair administrator. I did good things, guided by my instincts, and bad things, driven by the vicissitudes of war. But now the drunken Polish boys will open their mouths and say I ruined their childhoods, said Sammer to Reiter. Me? I ruined their childhoods? Liquor ruined their childhoods! Soccer ruined their childhoods! Those lazy, shiftless mothers ruined their childhoods! Not me.

·

"Anyone else in my place," said Sammer to Reiter, "would have killed all those Jews with his own hands. I didn't. It isn't in my nature."

One of the men with whom Sammer took long walks around the camp was the police chief. The other was the fire chief. The mayor, Sammer said one night, had died of pneumonia after the war ended. The driver had disappeared at a crossroads, when the car stopped running for good.

Sometimes, in the afternoons, Reiter watched Sammer from the distance and he could see that Sammer, in turn, was watching him out of the corner of his eye, his gaze betraying desperation, unease, and also fear and mistrust.

"We do things, say things, that later we regret with all our souls," Sammer said to him one day, as they were waiting in line for breakfast.

And another day he said:

"When the American police come back and interrogate me, I know they'll arrest me and I'll be subjected to public disgrace."

When Sammer talked to Reiter, the police chief and the fire chief stood to one side, several feet from them, as if they didn't want to meddle in their former boss's affairs. One morning Sammer's body was found halfway between the tent and the latrines. Someone had strangled him. The Americans interrogated perhaps ten prisoners, among them Reiter, who said he hadn't heard anything unusual that night, and then they took away the body and buried it in the common grave of the Ansbach cemetery.

·

When Reiter was allowed to leave the camp, he went to Cologne. There he lived in some barracks near the station and then in a cellar shared with a veteran of one of the armored divisions, a silent man with a burn down one side of his face who could go for whole days without eating, and another man who said he had worked for a newspaper and who, unlike his companion, was friendly and talkative.

The tank veteran must have been about thirty or thirty-five and the former reporter about sixty, though both seemed like children at times. During the war the reporter had written a series of articles in which he described the heroic life in a few Panzer divisions, east and west. He still had the clippings, which the taciturn tank veteran had chance to read with approval. Sometimes he would open his mouth and say:

"Otto, you've captured the essence of the tank man's life."

With a modest shrug, the reporter answered:

"Gustav, my greatest reward is that it should be precisely you, a tank veteran, who assures me I didn't get it all wrong."

"You didn't get anything wrong, Otto," answered the tank man.

"I thank you for your kind words, Gustav," said the reporter.

The two worked occasionally clearing debris for the city or selling the things they found under the rubble. When the weather was nice they went off to the countryside and Reiter had the basement to himself for a week or two. He spent his first few days in Cologne trying to get a train ticket to return to his village. Then he found work as a doorman at a bar that catered to a clientele of American and English soldiers who tipped well and for whom he sometimes did little extra jobs, like finding them flats in certain neighborhoods or introducing them to girls or putting them in contact with black marketeers. So he stayed in Cologne.

During the day he wrote and read. Writing was easy, because all he needed was a notebook and a pencil. Reading was a little harder, because the public libraries were still closed and at the few bookshops one could find (most of them mobile) the prices were exorbitant. Even so, Reiter read and he wasn't the only one: sometimes he looked up from his book and everyone around him was reading too. As if all the Germans cared about was reading and food, which wasn't true but sometimes seemed to be, especially in Cologne.

Meanwhile, Reiter noted, interest in sex had waned considerably, as if the war had used up men's reserves of testosterone, pheromones, desire, and no one wanted to make love anymore. They only fucked whores, as far as Reiter could tell from what he saw on the job. There were some women who dated the occupying forces, but even for them desire was really the mask of something else: a theater of innocence, a frozen slaughterhouse, a lonely street, a movie theater. The women he saw were like girls who've just woken from a terrible nightmare.

•

One night as he stood guard at the door to the bar on the Spengler-strasse, a female voice spoke his name out of the darkness. Reiter looked around and when he didn't see anyone he thought it must be one of the whores, with their strange, sometimes incomprehensible sense of humor. But when his name was called again, he knew the voice didn't belong to any of the women who frequented the bar and he asked what it wanted.

"I just wanted to say hello," said the voice.

Then he saw a flicker of movement and in two strides he was across the street and had grabbed the owner of the voice by the arm and dragged her into the light. The girl who had called him by name was very young. When he asked what she wanted from him, she answered that she was his girlfriend. Frankly, she said, it was sad he didn't recognize her.

"I must look very ugly," she said, "but if you were still a German soldier, you would try to pretend I wasn't."

Reiter examined her carefully but no matter how he tried he couldn't remember who she was.

"War is often linked to amnesia," said the girl.

Then she said:

"Amnesia is when you lose your memory and you don't remember anything, even your name or your girlfriend's name."

And she added:

"There's also such a thing as selective amnesia, which is when you remember everything or think you remember everything and forget only a single thing, the one important thing in your life."

I know this girl, thought Reiter as he listened to her talk, but he couldn't say where or under what circumstances he'd met her. So he decided to proceed calmly and asked if she'd like a drink. The girl glanced at the door of the bar and after considering for a moment, she accepted. They had tea sitting at a table near the entrance. The woman who waited on them asked Reiter who this hatchling was.

"My girlfriend," said Reiter.

The girl smiled at the woman and nodded.

"She's very nice," said the woman.

769

"And hardworking, too," said the girl.

The woman made a face, frowning, as if to say: a girl with initiative. Then she said: we'll see, and she went away. After a while, Reiter turned up the collar of his black leather jacket and went back to the door, because people were beginning to arrive, and the girl remained sitting at the table, every so often reading a few pages from a book and most of the time watching people as the bar filled up. After a while the woman who had served her the cup of tea took her by the arm and led her outside, explaining that the table was needed for customers. The girl said a friendly goodbye to the woman but got no reply. Reiter was talking to two American soldiers and the girl decided not to bother him. Instead she crossed the street, settled into the entranceway of the house opposite, and spent a while watching the constant movement at the bar door.

As he worked, out of the corner of his eye, Reiter watched the doorstep of the house across the street and sometimes he thought he saw a bright pair of cat eyes peering at him from the dark. When there was a lull he ventured into the entranceway and was about to call out to her, but he realized he didn't know her name. With the help of a match he found her asleep in a corner. On his knees, as the match burned down in his fingers, he spent a few seconds gazing at her sleeping face. Then he remembered who she was.

•

When she woke Reiter was still by her side, but the doorway had become a room with a vaguely feminine air, with photographs of performers stuck up on the walls and a collection of dolls and stuffed bears on a chest of drawers. Stacked on the floor, however, were cases of whiskey and wine. A green quilt was pulled up to her neck. Someone had taken off her shoes. She felt so good she closed her eyes again. But then she heard Reiter's voice saying: you're the girl who lived in Hugo Halder's old flat. Without opening her eyes, she nodded.

"I don't remember your name," said Reiter.

She rolled over, turning her back to him, and said:

"You have a terrible memory, my name is Ingeborg Bauer."

"Ingeborg Bauer," repeated Reiter, as if his fate were contained in those two words.

Then she fell asleep again and when she woke up she was alone.

•

That morning, as she walked with Reiter around the destroyed city, Ingeborg Bauer told him that she lived, with some strangers, in a building
near the train station. Her father had died in a bombing raid. Her
mother and sisters fled Berlin before the city was besieged by the Russians. First they were in the country, with one of her mother's brothers,
but despite what they'd imagined, there was nothing to eat in the country and girls were often raped by their uncles and cousins. According to
Ingeborg Bauer the forests were full of graves where the locals buried
city dwellers after they had robbed, raped, and killed them.

"Were you raped, too?" Reiter asked her.

No, she wasn't, but one of her younger sisters had been raped by a
cousin, a boy of thirteen who wanted to join the Hitler Youth and die a
hero's death. So her mother decided they should move on and they left
for a small city in the Westerwald, in Hesse, where her mother was
from. Life there was boring and at the same time very strange, Ingeborg
Bauer told Reiter, because the inhabitants of the city lived as if there
was no war, even though many men had marched to the front with the
army and the city itself had suffered three bombing raids, none of them
devastating, but raids all the same. Her mother got a job at a beer hall
and the girls found occasional work, helping out in offices or filling in at
factories or delivering messages, and sometimes the youngest ones even
had time to go to school.

Despite the constant bustle, life was boring and when peace came
Ingeborg couldn't stand it any longer and one morning, when her mother
and sisters were out, she left for Cologne.

"I was sure," she said to Reiter, "that I would find you here, or someone very like you."

And that was everything that had happened, broadly speaking, since
they kissed in the park, when Reiter was looking for Hugo Halder and
she told him the story of the Aztecs. Of course, Reiter soon understood
that Ingeborg had gone mad, if she wasn't already mad when he met her,
and he also understood that she was sick or maybe just hungry.

He brought her to live with him in the cellar, but since Ingeborg was
always coughing and seemed to have something wrong with her lungs he
looked for new lodgings. He found them in the garret of a half-ruined
building. There was no elevator and some stretches of the stairs were

unsound, with steps that gradually sank under the weight of the climbers, or gaps that yawned over an empty space, so that one could see or guess at the building's innards and the bomb shrapnel. But they had no problem living there: Ingeborg weighed just one hundred and ten pounds and Reiter, although he was very tall, was thin and bony and the steps were perfectly able to support his weight. The same wasn't true for the other tenants. A small, amiable Brandenburger who worked for the occupation troops fell through a gap between the second and third floors and broke his neck. Each time the Brandenburger saw Ingeborg, he greeted her with interest and affection, and each time, without fail, he presented her with the flower he wore in his buttonhole.

At night, before he went to work, Reiter checked to make sure Ingeborg had everything she needed so she wouldn't have to go down the stairs to the street with just a candle to light her way, although in his heart he knew that Ingeborg (and he too) lacked so many things that his precautions were pointless from the outset. At first their relations excluded sex. Ingeborg was very weak and all she wanted to do was talk, or read, when she was alone and there were enough candles. Reiter sometimes fucked the girls who worked at the bar. These were hardly very passionate encounters. On the contrary. They made love as if they were talking soccer, sometimes even with a cigarette still in their mouths or chewing American gum, which had begun to be fashionable, and it was good for the nerves, chewing gum and fucking this way, impersonally, although the act was far from impersonal but rather objective, as if once the nakedness of the slaughterhouse had been achieved everything else was unacceptable theatricality.

Before he began working at the bar Reiter had slept with other girls, at the Cologne or Solingen train stations or in Remscheid or Wuppertal, factory workers and peasants who liked it when men (so long as they looked healthy) came in their mouths. Some afternoons Ingeborg asked Reiter to tell her about his adventures, that was what she called them, and Reiter, lighting a cigarette, would tell her.

"Those Solingen girls thought there were vitamins in semen," said Ingeborg, "just like the Cologne station girls you fucked. I understand them perfectly," said Ingeborg, "I spent a while at the Cologne station too and I talked to them and did what they did."

"You sucked off strangers too, thinking the semen would be good for you?" asked Reiter.

"I did," said Ingeborg. "So long as the men looked healthy, so long as they didn't seem to be rotting away from cancer or syphilis," said Ingeborg. "The peasant women who roamed the station, the factory workers, the madwomen who were lost or had fled their homes, we all believed that semen was a precious nutrient, an extract of all kinds of vitamins, the best remedy for a cold," said Ingeborg. "Some nights, before I went to sleep, huddled in a corner of the station, I would think about the country girl who first came up with the idea, an absurd idea, although certain respected doctors say a daily dose of semen can cure anemia," said Ingeborg. "But I would think about that country girl, that desperate girl who arrived at the same idea by the process of deduction. I imagined her awestruck in the silent city contemplating the ruins of everything and saying to herself that this was how she had always dreamed the city would look. I imagined her as industrious, with a smile on her face, helping anyone who asked, and curious, too, walking the streets and squares and reconstructing the outline of the city where she had secretly always wanted to live. Some nights, too, I imagined her dead, of any disease, a disease that led not to a long, drawn-out death or to a death that was too sudden but to a reasonably prolonged death, one that gave her time to stop sucking dicks and retreat into her own chrysalis, her own sorrows."

"But what makes you think one girl came up with the idea, and not a few at once?" Reiter asked her. "What makes you think a girl came up with it at all, and a country girl at that? Couldn't it have been some fast-talker, wanting to get sucked off for free?"

•

One morning Reiter and Ingeborg made love. The girl was feverish and her legs, under her nightdress, seemed to Reiter the most beautiful legs he had seen in his life. Ingeborg had just turned twenty and Reiter was twenty-six. From then on they began to fuck every day. Reiter liked to do it sitting by the window with Ingeborg straddling him, making love as they looked into each other's eyes or out at the ruins of Cologne. Ingeborg liked to do it in bed, where she cried and writhed and came six or seven times, with her legs on Reiter's bony shoulders, calling him my darling, my love, my prince, my sweetheart, words that embarrassed Reiter, because he found them precious and in those days he had declared war on preciousness and sentimentality and softness and anything overembellished or contrived or saccharine, but he didn't object, since the despair he glimpsed in Ingeborg's eyes, never entirely dispelled even by pleasure, paralyzed him as if he, Reiter, were a mouse caught in a trap.

Of course, they often laughed, though not always at the same things. Reiter, for example, was highly amused when their Brandenburger neighbor fell through the gap in the stairs. Ingeborg said the Brandenburger was a nice person, always with a kind word on his lips, and anyway she couldn't forget the flowers he had given her. Reiter warned her that nice people weren't to be trusted. Most of them, he said, were war criminals who deserved to be strung up in the main square, an image that gave Ingeborg the shivers. How could a person who bought a flower every day to wear in his buttonhole be a war criminal?

Ingeborg, meanwhile, was amused by more abstract things and situations. Sometimes she laughed at the patterns traced by the damp on the garret walls. On the plaster or stucco she saw long lines of trucks emerging from a kind of tunnel, which for no reason she called the time tunnel. Other times she laughed at the cockroaches that occasionally ventured into the attic. Or at the birds that watched Cologne perched in the blackened coffers of the tallest buildings. Sometimes she even laughed at her own disease, a nameless disease (its namelessness gave her real amusement), which had been vaguely diagnosed by the two doctors she'd seen—one of them a patron of the bar where Reiter worked and the other an old man with white hair and a white beard and a booming, theatrical voice whom Reiter paid with bottles of whiskey, one per visit, and who was probably, according to Reiter, a war criminal—as something halfway between a nervous complaint and a pulmonary ailment.

In any case, they spent many hours together, sometimes talking about the most random things, or sometimes with Reiter at the table writing his first novel in a notebook with a cane-colored cover and Ingeborg lying in bed, reading. It was Reiter who usually did the housecleaning and shopping, and Ingeborg cooked, which was something she was quite good at. Their after-supper conversations were strange and on occasion turned into long monologues or soliloquies or confessions.

They talked about books, about poetry (Ingeborg asked Reiter why he didn't write poetry and he answered that all poetry, of any style, was contained or could be contained in fiction), about sex (they had made love in every possible way, or so they believed, and they theorized about new ways but came up only with death), and death. When the old crone made her appearance, they had usually finished eating and the conversation was languishing, as Reiter, drawing himself up like a great Prussian lord, lit a cigarette, and Ingeborg peeled an apple with a short-bladed, wooden-handled knife.

Then, too: their voices dropped nearly to a whisper. Once Ingeborg asked whether he had ever killed anyone. After thinking about it for a moment, Reiter answered that he had. For a few seconds, which stretched on a bit too long, Ingeborg stared at him: his fleshless lips, the smoke that rose along his prominent cheekbones, his blue eyes, his blond, rather dirty hair, perhaps in need of a cut, his country-boy ears, his nose, which, in contrast to his ears, was noble and jutting, his forehead, across which a spider seemed to crawl. A few seconds earlier she might have been able to believe he had killed someone, some nameless person, during the war, but after looking at him she was sure he meant something else. She asked who he had killed.

"A German," said Reiter.

In Ingeborg's restless mind, always prone to wild imaginings, the victim could only be Hugo Halder, the former tenant of her house in Berlin. When she asked Reiter, he laughed. No, no. Hugo Halder was his friend. Then they were quiet for a long time and the remains of their supper seemed to congeal on the table. Finally Ingeborg asked if he was sorry and Reiter made a gesture with his hand that could have meant anything. Then he said:

"No."

And after a long interval he added: sometimes yes, sometimes no.

"Did you know the person?" whispered Ingeborg.

"Who?" asked Reiter as if he were waking up.

"The person you killed."

"Yes," said Reiter, "you could say that. For many nights we slept side by side and there was plenty of talk."

"Was it a woman?" whispered Ingeborg.

"No, it wasn't a woman," said Reiter, and he laughed, "it was a man."

Ingeborg laughed too. Then she began to talk about the way some women were attracted to men who killed women. About the high regard in which woman-killers were held by whores, for example, or by women who chose to love without reservations. In Reiter's opinion these women were hysterics. But Ingeborg, who claimed to know women of the sort, believed they were just gamblers, like cardplayers, more or less, who end up killing themselves late at night, or like the habitués of racetracks who commit suicide in cheap rented rooms or hotels tucked away on back-streets frequented by gangsters or Chinamen.

"Sometimes," said Ingeborg, "when we're making love and you grab me by the neck, I've thought you might be a woman-killer."

"I've never killed a woman," said Reiter. "Such a thing never even oc-curred to me."

•

That was the last they talked about the matter until the following week.

Reiter told her it was possible that the American police and the Ger-man police, too, were looking for him, or that his name was on a list of suspects. The man he had done away with, he said, was called Sammer and he was a killer of Jews. Then you've committed no crime, she tried to say, but Reiter wouldn't let her.

"All of this happened in a prisoner-of-war camp," said Reiter. "I don't know who Sammer thought I was, but he kept telling me things. He was nervous because the American police were going to interrogate him. As a precaution, he had changed his name. He called himself Zeller. But I don't think the American police were looking for Sammer. They weren't looking for Zeller either. As far as the Americans were concerned, Zeller and Sammer were two German citizens above any suspicion. The Amer-icans were looking for war criminals of a certain prestige, people from the death camps, SS officials, party bigwigs. Sammer was just a civil ser-vant of no consequence. They questioned me. They asked what I knew about him, whether he had talked to me about enemies among the other prisoners. I said I didn't know anything, that Sammer had talked only about his son who died in Kursk and his wife's migraines. They looked at my hands. They were young policemen and they didn't have time to waste in a prisoner-of-war camp. But they weren't convinced. They wrote down my name and questioned me again. They asked whether I'd been a member of the National Socialist Party, whether I knew many Nazis, what my family did and where I lived. I tried to be truthful and I gave honest answers. I asked them to help me find my parents. Then the camp began to empty as new groups arrived. But I wasn't released. A comrade told me the guards were only for show. The black soldiers had other things on their minds and they didn't pay us much attention. One morning, during a transfer of prisoners, I slipped out and got away as easy as that.

"I spent a while wandering from city to city. I was in Koblenz. I worked at the mines that were beginning to reopen. There wasn't enough to eat. I felt as if Sammer's ghost was clinging to my heels. I thought about changing my name, too. Finally I got to Cologne and it struck me that everything that could possibly happen to me had already happened and it was pointless to let myself be hunted by Sammer's filthy ghost. Once I was arrested. It was after a scuffle at the bar. The MP came and brought a few of us to the station. They looked for my name in their files, but they didn't find anything and they let me go.

"Around that time I got to know an old woman who sold cigarettes and flowers at the bar. Sometimes I would buy a cigarette or two and I always let her in. The old woman told me that during the war she'd been a fortune-teller. One night she asked me to walk her home. She lived on the Reginastrasse, in a big flat so full of things you could hardly move. One of the rooms looked like the back room of a clothing shop. I'll explain in a minute. When we arrived she poured two glasses of brandy and sat at the table and brought out a pack of cards. I'm going to tell your fortune, she said. There were some boxes full of books. I remember I picked out the complete works of Novalis and Friedrich Hebbel's *Judith* and as I leafed through them the old woman told me that I had killed a man, et cetera. Same story.

"'I was a soldier,' I said.

"'It's written here that during the war you were almost killed many times, but you didn't kill anyone, which is worth something,' said the old woman.

"Is it so obvious? I wondered. Is it just as obvious that I'm a murderer? Of course, I didn't feel like a murderer.

"'I suggest you change your name,' said the old woman, 'and you should listen to me. I was the fortune-teller for many of the big SS bosses and I know what I'm talking about. Don't make the classic English whodunit mistake.'

"'What are you talking about?' I asked.

"'I'm talking about English whodunits,' said the old woman, 'those addictive English whodunits that infected the American whodunits first and then the French and German and Swiss.'

"'And what mistake is that?' I asked.

"'An article of faith,' said the old woman, 'an assumption you can sum up in one word: the killer always returns to the scene of the crime.'

"I laughed.

"'Don't laugh,' said the old woman. 'Listen to me, because I'm one of the few people in Cologne who really care about you.'

"I stopped laughing. I asked her to sell me *Judith* and the works of Novalis.

"'You can keep them,' she said. 'Every time you come to see me you can take two books, but now pay attention to something much more important than literature. You must change your name. You must never return to the scene of the crime. You must break the chain. Do you understand?'

"'A little,' I said, although all I'd really understood, with great pleasure, was the offer of the books.

"Then the old woman told me that my mother was alive and every night she thought about me, and my sister was alive and every morning and afternoon and night she dreamed about me, and that my strides, a giant's strides, echoed in my sister's head. She didn't mention my father.

"And then the sun began to come up and the old woman said:

"'I heard the call of a nightingale.'

"And then she asked me to come with her to a room, the one full of clothes, like a ragpicker's room, and she dug in the mountains of clothes until she reemerged, victorious, with a black leather coat and she said:

"'This coat is for you, it's been waiting for you all this time, since its previous owner died.'

"And I took the coat and tried it on and in fact it fit as if it had been made for me."

•

Later Reiter asked the old woman who the former owner of the coat had been, but on this point the old woman's answers were contradictory and vague.

Once she told him it had belonged to a Gestapo agent and another time she said it had belonged to a lover of hers, a Communist who died in a concentration camp, and once she even told him that the previous owner was an English spy, the first (and only) English spy to parachute down near Cologne in 1941 to reconnoiter for a future uprising of the citizens of Cologne, a prospect greeted with incredulity by the actual citizens of Cologne who happened to talk to him, since in their judgment and that of all Europeans at the time, England was lost, and although this spy, according to the old woman, was Scottish, not English, no one took him seriously, especially when the few who met him saw him drink (he drank like a Cossack although he could hold his liquor admirably: his eyes got misty and he cast sidelong glances at women's legs but he maintained a certain verbal coherence and a kind of chilly elegance that the honorable anti-Fascist citizens of Cologne with whom he had dealings thought were the marks of a bold and dashing character, qualities that only added to his charm), and anyway, in 1941 the time wasn't ripe.

Only twice did the old fortune-teller see this English spy, or so she told Reiter. The first time she put him up at her house and read his fortune. Luck was on his side. The second and last time, she supplied him with clothes and papers, because the Englishman (or Scotsman) was returning to England. It was then that the spy left her his leather coat. Other times, however, the old woman wouldn't hear a word about the spy. Dreams, she said, fantasies, foolish visions, the imaginings of a desperate old woman. And then she repeated that the leather coat had belonged to a Gestapo agent, one of the men who at the end of '44 and the beginning of '45 had tracked down and crushed the deserters who were gathering strength (so to speak) in the noble city of Cologne.

•

Then Ingeborg's health took a turn for the worse and an English doctor told Reiter that the girl, that lovely, delightful girl, probably had no more than two or three months to live and then he just looked at Reiter, who began to weep without a word, but the English doctor wasn't really looking at Reiter, he was staring at his handsome black leather coat, assessing it with the eye of a furrier or a leatherworker, and finally, as Reiter continued to weep, he asked where he'd bought it, where did I buy what? the coat, oh, in Berlin, lied Reiter, before the war, at a shop called Hahn & Förster, he said, and then the doctor said that the furriers Hahn and Förster or their heirs had probably been inspired by the leather coats of Mason & Cooper, the Manchester coat makers, who also had a branch in London, and who in 1938 had made a coat exactly like the one Reiter was wearing, the same sleeves, the same collar, the same number of buttons, to which Reiter responded with a shrug, drying the tears that ran down his cheeks with his coat sleeve, and then the doctor was moved and he stepped forward and put a hand on Reiter's shoulder and said that he too had a leather coat like this, like Reiter's, except that his was from Mason & Cooper and Reiter's was from Hahn & Förster, although by the feel, and Reiter could take his word for it because he was a connoisseur, an aficionado of black leather coats, they were identical, it was as if both had come from the same lot of leather that Mason & Cooper had used in 1938 to make his coat, which was a true work of art, and unreproducible, too, since even though the house of Mason & Cooper was still in business, Mr. Mason, or so he'd heard, had died during the war in a bombing raid, not killed by a bomb, he hastened to explain, but because he had a weak heart, unable to withstand the dash to the shelter or the alarm whistle, the sounds of destruction and the explosions, or perhaps the wail of the sirens, who can say, but whatever the case Mr. Mason was overcome by a heart attack and from that moment on the house of Mason & Cooper experienced a slight drop not just in productivity but in quality too, although perhaps that was an overstatement, since the quality of Mason & Cooper's leather coats was and would continue to be beyond reproach, if not in the detail then in the mood, if one could properly call it that, of the new models, in the intangible something that made a leather coat a work of craftsmanship, a piece of art that kept pace with history but also bucked the tide of history, I don't know whether you follow me, said the doctor, and then Reiter took off the coat and handed it to him, look at it as long as you want, he said as he sat down in one of the two chairs in the office and continued to weep, and the doctor was left with the coat hanging from his hands and only then did he seem to wake from his dream of leather coats and manage to offer a few words of encouragement or words that struggled to form an encouraging sentence, though he knew that nothing could lessen Reiter's pain, and then he draped the coat over Reiter's shoulders and again he thought that this coat, the coat of a doorman at a bar in Cologne's red-light district, was exactly like his, and for a moment he even imagined it *was* his, just a bit more worn, as if his own coat had flown from its wardrobe on a London street and crossed the Channel and the north of France with the sole intent of seeing him again, he, its owner, an English military doctor who led a licentious life, a doctor who treated the destitute for free, so long as the destitute were his friends, or at least the friends of friends, and for a moment he even thought that the weeping young German had lied to him, that he hadn't bought the coat at Hahn & Förster, that it was an authentic Mason & Cooper, acquired in London, at the house of Mason & Cooper, but ultimately, the doctor said to himself as he helped the tearful Reiter back into his coat (so particular to the touch, so pleasing, so familiar), life is a mystery.

•

For the next three months Reiter managed to spend nearly all of his time with Ingeborg. He bought fruit and vegetables on the black market. He found books for her to read. He cooked and cleaned the garret they shared. He read medical books and searched for remedies of every sort. One morning two of Ingeborg's sisters and her mother appeared on the doorstep. Ingeborg's mother spoke little and her manner was formal, but the sisters, one eighteen and the other sixteen, cared only about going out and seeing the interesting parts of the city. One day Reiter told them that the most interesting part of Cologne was the garret where they lived, and Ingeborg's sisters laughed. Reiter, who laughed only when he was with Ingeborg, laughed too. One night he took them to work with him. Hilde, the eighteen-year-old, looked haughtily at the whores who frequented the bar, but that night she went off with two young American lieutenants and didn't come back until late the next day, to the alarm of her mother, who accused Reiter of playing the pimp.

Meanwhile, Ingeborg's illness had sharpened her craving for sex, but the attic was small and they all slept in the same room, which inhibited Reiter when he came home from work at five or six in the morning and Ingeborg demanded that they make love. When he tried to explain that her mother would almost certainly hear them, she wasn't deaf, Ingeborg grew angry and said he didn't want her anymore. One afternoon the younger sister, sixteen-year-old Grete, took a walk with Reiter through the shattered neighborhood and told him that a number of psychiatrists and neurologists had visited her sister in Berlin and the general diagnosis was insanity.

Reiter looked at her: she resembled Ingeborg but she was plumper and taller. In fact, she was so tall and looked so athletic that she might have been a javelin thrower.

"Our father was a Nazi," said Grete, "and Ingeborg was, too, back then, she was a Nazi. Ask her. She belonged to the Hitler Youth."

"So according to you she's crazy?" asked Reiter.

"Completely insane," said the sister.

Soon afterward, Hilde told Reiter that Grete was falling in love with him.

"So she's in love with me, you say?"

"Madly in love," said Hilde, rolling her eyes.

"How interesting," said Reiter.

One morning, after coming in silently, trying not to wake any of the four sleeping women, Reiter got into bed and drew Ingeborg's hot body against him and he knew immediately that Ingeborg had a fever and his eyes filled with tears and he began to feel sick, but so gradually that the feeling wasn't entirely unpleasant.

Then he felt Ingeborg's hand take hold of his cock and begin to stroke it and with his hand he pulled Ingeborg's nightdress up to her waist and found her clitoris and in turn began to stroke her, thinking about other things, about his novel, which was progressing, about the seas of Prussia and the rivers of Russia and the benevolent monsters that dwell in the deep waters off the Crimean coast, until he felt Ingeborg slip two fingers into her vagina and then moisten the entrance to her ass with the same fingers and ask him, no, order him, to penetrate her, sodomize her, right now, immediately, before another moment passed, which Reiter did without thinking twice or weighing the consequences of his actions, though he knew very well how Ingeborg would react, but that night his urges were like the urges of a man in his sleep, unable to foresee anything and attuned only to the moment and so, as they fucked and Ingeborg moaned, from a corner he saw rise not a ghostly figure but a pair of cat eyes, and the eyes floated up and hovered in the dark, and then another pair of eyes rose and settled in the shadows, and he heard Ingeborg order the eyes, in a hoarse voice, to go back to bed, and then Reiter noticed that Ingeborg's body had begun to sweat and he began to sweat too and he thought this was good for the fever, and he closed his eyes and kept caressing Ingeborg's sex with his left hand and when he opened his eyes he saw five pairs of cat eyes floating in the dark, and that did strike him as an unequivocal sign that he was dreaming, because three pairs of eyes, belonging to Ingeborg's sisters and mother, made some sense, but five pairs of eyes lacked spatiotemporal coherence, unless each of the sisters had brought home a lover that night, which was outside the realm of possibility, neither feasible nor credible.

The next day Ingeborg was in a temper and everything her sisters or mother did or said seemed to be done or said to vex her. From then on, the situation grew so tense that she was unable to read and he was unable to write. Sometimes Reiter got the sense that Ingeborg was jealous of Hilde, when the sister she had good reason to be jealous of was Grete. Sometimes, before he left for work, Reiter watched from the attic window as Hilde's two officers shouted her name and whistled from the pavement across the street. More than once he walked her down the stairs and advised her to be careful. Unconcerned, Hilde answered:

"What can they do to me? bomb me?"

And then she laughed and Reiter laughed too.

"The worst thing they can do to me is what you've done to Ingeborg," she said once, and Reiter spent a long time turning her answer over in his head.

What I've done to Ingeborg. But what had he done to Ingeborg but love her?

Finally one day Ingeborg's mother and sisters decided to return to the town in the Westerwald where the family had settled and Reiter and Ingeborg were left alone again. Now we can love each other in peace, said Ingeborg. Reiter looked at her: Ingeborg had gotten up and was tidying the place a little. Her nightdress was ivory and her feet were bony and long and nearly the same color. From that day on her health improved considerably and when the fateful date proclaimed by the English doctor arrived she was better than ever.

Shortly afterward she found work at a seamstress's shop where old dresses were made into new dresses and unfashionable dresses into fashionable dresses. At the shop they had just three sewing machines, but thanks to the resourcefulness of the owner, an enterprising and pessimistic woman who was certain that World War III would begin by 1950 at the latest, the business prospered. At first Ingeborg's work consisted of piecing together patterns created by Mrs. Raab, but soon, due to the small shop's huge volume of work, her task was to visit women's clothing shops and take orders that she later filled herself.

Around this time Reiter finished his first novel. He called it *Lüdicke* and he had to roam the backstreets of Cologne in search of someone who would rent him a typewriter, because he had decided that he wouldn't borrow or rent one from anyone he knew, in other words no one who knew his name was Hans Reiter. Finally he found an old man who owned an old French typewriter and wasn't in the habit of renting it but would sometimes make an exception for writers.

The sum the old man requested was high and at first Reiter thought he had better keep looking, but when he saw the typewriter, in perfect condition, not a speck of dust, every letter ready to leave its impression on the paper, he decided he could permit himself the luxury. The old man asked for the money up front, and that same night, at the bar, Reiter requested and obtained several loans from the girls. The next day he returned and showed the old man the money, but then the man took an accounting book out of his desk and wanted to know his name. Reiter said the first thing that came into his head.

"My name is Benno von Archimboldi."

The old man looked him in the eye and said don't play games with me, what's your real name?

"My name is Benno von Archimboldi, sir," said Reiter, "and if you think I'm joking I'd better go."

For a few seconds both were silent. The old man's eyes were dark brown, although in the dim light of his study they looked black. Archimboldi's eyes were blue and to the old man they looked like the eyes of a young poet, tired, strained, reddened, but young and in a certain sense pure, although it had been a long time since the old man stopped believing in purity.

"This country," he said to Reiter, who that afternoon, perhaps, became Archimboldi, "has tried to topple any number of countries into the abyss in the name of purity and will. As far as I'm concerned, you understand, purity and will are utter tripe. Thanks to purity and will we've all, every one of us, hear me you, become cowards and thugs, which in the end are one and the same. Now we sob and moan and say we didn't know! we had no idea! it was the Nazis! we never would have done such a thing! We know how to whimper. We know how to drum up sympathy. We don't care whether we're mocked so long as they pity us and forgive us. There'll be plenty of time for us to embark on a long holiday of forgetting. Do you understand me?"

"I understand," said Archimboldi.

"I was a writer," said the old man.

•

"But I gave it up. This typewriter was a gift from my father. An affectionate and cultured man who lived to the age of ninety-three. An essentially good man. A man who believed in progress, it goes without saying. My poor father. He believed in progress and of course he believed in the intrinsic goodness of human beings. I too believe in the intrinsic goodness of human beings, but it means nothing. In their hearts, killers are good, as we Germans have reason to know. So what? I might spend a night drinking with a killer, and as the two of us watch the sun come up, perhaps we'll burst into song or hum some Beethoven. So what? The killer might weep on my shoulder. Naturally. Being a killer isn't easy, as you and I well know. It isn't easy at all. It requires purity and will, will and purity. Crystalline purity and steel-hard will. And I myself might even weep on the killer's shoulder and whisper sweet words to him, words like 'brother,' 'friend,' 'comrade in misfortune.' At this moment the killer is good, because he's intrinsically good, and I'm an idiot, because I'm intrinsically an idiot, and we're both sentimental, because our culture tends inexorably toward sentimentality. But when the performance is over and I'm alone, the killer will open the window of my room and come tiptoeing in like a nurse and slit my throat, bleed me dry.

"My poor father. I was a writer, I was a writer, but my indolent, voracious brain gnawed at my own entrails. Vulture of my Prometheus self or Prometheus of my vulture self, one day I understood that I might go so far as to publish excellent articles in magazines and newspapers, and even books that weren't unworthy of the paper on which they were printed. But I also understood that I would never manage to create anything like a masterpiece. You may say that literature doesn't consist solely of masterpieces, but rather is populated by so-called minor works. I believed that, too. Literature is a vast forest and the masterpieces are the lakes, the towering trees or strange trees, the lovely, eloquent flowers, the hidden caves, but a forest is also made up of ordinary trees, patches of grass, puddles, clinging vines, mushrooms, and little wildflowers. I was wrong. There's actually no such thing as a minor work. I mean: the author of the minor work isn't Mr. X or Mr. Y. Mr. X and Mr. Y do exist, there's no question about that, and they struggle and toil and publish in newspapers and magazines and sometimes they even come out with a book that isn't unworthy of the paper it's printed on, but those books or articles, if you pay close attention, *are not written by them*.

"Every minor work has a secret author and every secret author is, by definition, a writer of masterpieces. Who writes the minor work? A minor writer, or so it appears. The poor man's wife can testify to that, she's seen him sitting at the table, bent over the blank pages, restless in his chair, his pen racing over the paper. The evidence would seem to be incontrovertible. But what she's seen is only the outside. The shell of literature. A semblance," said the old man to Archimboldi and Archimboldi thought of Ansky. "The person who really writes the minor work is a secret writer who accepts only the dictates of a masterpiece.

"Our good craftsman writes. He's absorbed in what takes shape well or badly on the page. His wife, though he doesn't know it, is watching him. It really is he who's writing. But if his wife had X-ray vision she would see that instead of being present at an exercise of literary creation, she's witnessing a session of hypnosis. There's *nothing* inside the man who sits there writing. Nothing of himself, I mean. How much better off the poor man would be if he devoted himself to reading. Reading is pleasure and happiness to be alive or sadness to be alive and above all it's knowledge and questions. Writing, meanwhile, is almost always empty. There's *nothing* in the guts of the man who sits there writing. Nothing, I mean to say, that his wife, at a given moment, might recognize. He writes like someone taking dictation. His novel or book of poems, decent, adequate, arises not from an exercise of style or will, as the poor unfortunate believes, but as the result of an exercise of *concealment*. There must be many books, many lovely pines, to shield from hungry eyes the book that really matters, the wretched cave of our misfortune, the magic flower of winter!

"Excuse the metaphors. Sometimes, in my excitement, I wax romantic. But listen. Every work that isn't a masterpiece is, in a sense, a part of a vast camouflage. You've been a soldier, I imagine, and you know what I mean. Every book that isn't a masterpiece is cannon fodder, a slogging foot soldier, a piece to be sacrificed, since in multiple ways it mimics the design of the masterpiece. When I came to this realization, I gave up writing. Still, my mind didn't stop working. In fact, it worked better when I wasn't writing. I asked myself: why does a masterpiece need to be hidden? what strange forces wreath it in secrecy and mystery?

"By now I knew it was pointless to write. Or that it was worth it only if one was prepared to write a masterpiece. Most writers are deluded or playing. Perhaps delusion and play are the same thing, two sides of the same coin. The truth is we never stop being children, terrible children covered in sores and knotty veins and tumors and age spots, but ultimately children, in other words we never stop clinging to life because we *are* life. One might also say: we're theater, we're music. By the same token, few are the writers who give up. We play at believing ourselves immortal. We delude ourselves in the appraisal of our own works and in our perpetual misappraisal of the works of others. See you at the Nobel, writers say, as one might say: see you in hell.

"Once I saw an American gangster movie. In one scene a detective kills a crook and before he fires the fatal shot he says: see you in hell. He's playing. The detective is playing and he's deluded. The crook, who meets his gaze and curses him just before he dies, is also playing and deluded, although his fields of play and delusion have been reduced to almost zero, since in the next shot he's going to die. The director of the film is also playing. So is the scriptwriter. See you at the Nobel. We'll go down in history. We have the gratitude of the German people. A heroic battle remembered for generations to come. An immortal love. A name inscribed in marble. The time of the Muses. Even a phrase as seemingly innocent as *echoes of Greek prose* is all play and delusion.

"Play and delusion are the blindfold and spur of minor writers. Also: the promise of their future happiness. A forest that grows at a vertiginous rate, a forest no one can fence in, not even the academies, in fact, the academies make sure it flourishes unhindered, as do boosters and universities (breeding grounds for the shameless) and government institutions and patrons and cultural associations and declaimers of poetry— all aid the forest to grow and hide what must be hidden, all aid the forest to reproduce what must be reproduced, since the process is inevitable, though no one ever sees what exactly is being reproduced, what is being tamely mirrored back.

"Plagiarism, you say? Yes, plagiarism, in the sense that all minor works, all works from the pen of a minor writer, can be nothing but plagiarism of some masterpiece. The small difference is that here we're talking about *sanctioned* plagiarism. Plagiarism as camouflage as some wood and canvas scenery as a charade that leads us, likely as not, into the void.

"In a word: experience is best. I won't say you can't get experience by hanging around libraries, but libraries are second to experience. Experience is the mother of science, it is often said. When I was young and I still thought I would make a career in the world of letters, I met a great writer. A great writer who had probably written a single masterpiece, although in my judgment everything he had written was a masterpiece.

"I won't tell you his name. It'll do you no good to learn it, nor do you need to know it for the purposes of this story. Suffice it to say that he was German and one day he came to Cologne to give a few lectures. Of course, I didn't miss a single one of the three he gave at the university. At the last lecture I got a seat in the front row, and rather than listen (the truth is he repeated things he'd already said in the first and second lectures), I spent the time observing him in detail, his hands, for example, bony and energetic, his old man's neck, like the neck of a turkey or a plucked rooster, his faintly Slavic cheekbones, his lifeless lips, lips that one could slash with a knife and from which one could be sure not a single drop of blood would fall, his gray temples like a stormy sea, and especially his eyes, deep eyes that at the slightest tilt of his head seemed at times like two endless tunnels, two abandoned tunnels on the verge of collapse.

"Of course, once the lecture was over he was mobbed by local worthies and I wasn't even able to shake his hand and tell him how much I admired him. Time went by. The writer died, and, as one might expect, I continued to read and reread him. The day came when I decided to give up literature. I gave it up. This was in no way traumatic but rather liberating. Between you and me, I'll confess that it was like losing my virginity. What a relief to give up literature, to give up writing and simply read!

"But that's another story. We can discuss it when you return my typewriter. And yet I couldn't forget the great writer and his visit. Meanwhile, I began to work at a factory that made optical instruments. I did well for myself. I was a bachelor, I had money, every week I went to the movies, the theater, exhibitions, and I also studied English and French and visited bookshops where I bought whatever books struck my fancy.

"A comfortable life. But I couldn't shake the memory of the great writer's visit, and what's more, I realized abruptly that I remembered only the third lecture, and my memories were limited to the writer's face, as if it was supposed to tell me something that in the end it didn't. But what? One day, for reasons that are beside the point, I went with a doctor friend of mine to the university morgue. I doubt you've ever been there. The morgue is underground and it's a long room with white-tiled walls and a wooden ceiling. In the middle there's a stage where autopsies, dissections, and other scientific atrocities are performed. Then there are two small offices, one for the dean of forensic studies and the other for another professor. At each end are the refrigerated rooms where the corpses are stored, the bodies of the destitute or people without papers visited by death in cheap hotel rooms.

"In those days I showed a doubtless morbid interest in these facilities and my doctor friend kindly took it upon himself to give me a detailed tour. We even attended the last autopsy of the day. Then my friend went into the dean's office and I was left alone outside in the corridor, waiting for him, as the students left and a kind of crepuscular lethargy crept from under the doors like poison gas. After ten minutes of waiting I was startled by a noise from one of the refrigerated rooms. In those days, I promise you, that was enough to frighten anyone, but I've never been particularly cowardly and I went to see what it was.

"When I opened the door a gust of cold air hit me in the face. At the back of the room, by a stretcher, a man was trying to open one of the lockers to stow away a corpse, but no matter how hard he struggled, the door to the locker or cell wouldn't budge. Without moving from the threshold, I asked whether he needed help. The man straightened up, he was very tall, and gave me what seemed to me a despairing look. Perhaps it was because I sensed despair in his gaze that I was emboldened to approach him. As I did, flanked by corpses, I lit a cigarette to calm my nerves and when I reached him the first thing I did was offer him another cigarette, perhaps forcing a false camaraderie.

"Only then did the morgue worker look at me and it was as if I had gone back in time. His eyes were exactly like the eyes of the great writer whose Cologne lectures I had devoutly attended. I confess that just then, for a few seconds, I even thought I was going mad. It was the morgue worker's voice, nothing like the warm voice of the great writer, that rescued me from my panic. He said: smoking isn't allowed here.

"I didn't know what to answer. He added: smoke is harmful to the dead. I laughed. He supplied an explanatory note: smoke interferes with the process of preservation. I made a noncommittal gesture. He tried a last time: he spoke about filters, he spoke about moisture levels, he uttered the word *purity*. I offered him a cigarette again and he announced with resignation that he didn't smoke. I asked whether he had worked there for a long time. In an impersonal and somewhat shrill voice, he said he had worked at the university since long before the 1914 war.

"'Always at the morgue?' I asked.

"'Here and nowhere else,' he answered.

"'It's funny,' I said, 'but your face, and especially your eyes, remind me of a great German writer.' At this point I mentioned the writer's name.

"'I've never heard of him,' was his response.

"In earlier days this reply would have outraged me, but thanks God I was living a new life. I remarked that working at the morgue must surely prompt wise or at least original reflections on human fate. He looked at me as if I were mocking him or speaking French. I insisted. These surroundings, I said, with a gesture that encompassed the whole morgue, are in a certain way the ideal place to contemplate the brevity of life, the unfathomable fate of mankind, the futility of earthly strife.

"With a shudder of horror, I was suddenly aware that I was talking to him as if he were the great German writer and this was the conversation we'd never had. I don't have much time, he said. I looked him in the eye again. There could be no doubt about it: he had the eyes of my idol. And his reply: *I don't have much time*. How many doors it opened! How many paths were suddenly cleared, revealed to me!

"I don't have much time, I have to haul corpses. I don't have much time, I have to breathe, eat, drink, sleep. I don't have much time, I have to keep the gears meshing. I don't have much time, I'm busy living. I don't have much time, I'm busy dying. As you can imagine, there were no more questions. I helped him open the locker. I wanted to help him slide the corpse in, but my clumsiness was such that the sheet slipped and then I saw the face of the corpse and I closed my eyes and bowed my head and let him work in peace.

"When my friend came out he watched me from the door in silence. Everything all right? he asked. I couldn't answer, or didn't know how to answer. Maybe I said: everything's wrong. But that wasn't what I meant to say."

•

Before Archimboldi left, after they'd had a cup of tea, the man who rented him the typewriter said:

"Jesus is the masterpiece. The thieves are minor works. Why are they there? Not to frame the crucifixion, as some innocent souls believe, but to hide it."

•

On one of Archimboldi's many journeys across the city in search of someone who would rent him a typewriter he once again happened upon the two tramps with whom he had shared a cellar before he moved to the garret.

Little had changed, it seemed, for his old comrades in misfortune. The former reporter had tried to get work at the new paper in Cologne, where they wouldn't take him because of his Nazi past. Little by little his cheerfulness and good nature disappeared as his trials showed no sign of ending and he began to suffer the aches and pains of old age. The tank veteran, meanwhile, now worked at a motorcycle repair shop and had joined the Communist Party.

When the two were together in the cellar, they fought constantly. The tank man took the old reporter to task for his Nazi militancy and cowardice. The old reporter got down on his knees and swore at the top of his lungs that yes, he had been a coward, but never a Nazi, not a real Nazi. We wrote what they told us to write. If we didn't want to be fired, we had to write what we were told, he whined, but the tank man was unmoved, adding to his reproaches the undeniable fact that while he and others like him were fighting in tanks that broke down and caught on fire, the reporter and others like him were content to write propagandistic lies, ignoring the feelings of the tank men and the mothers of the tank men and even the fiancées of the tank men.

"For that," he said, "I will never forgive you, Otto."

"But it isn't my fault," whined the reporter.

"Snivel, snivel," said the tank soldier.

"We tried to make poetry," said the reporter, "we tried to while away the time and stay alive to see what would come next."

"Well, now you've seen what comes next, you filthy swine," answered the tank man.

Sometimes the reporter talked about suicide.

"I don't see any other way out," he said when Archimboldi came to visit them. "As a reporter, I'm finished. As a factory worker, I'm hopeless. As some local government clerk, I'll always be marked by my past. As a free agent, I don't know how to do anything right. So why prolong my suffering?"

"To pay your debt to society, to atone for your lies," shouted the tank man, who sat there at the table pretending to be engrossed in the paper but in fact listening.

"You don't know what you're saying, Gustav," the reporter answered. "My only sin, I've told you a million times, has been cowardice and I'm paying dearly for it."

"You'll have to pay even more dearly, Otto, even more dearly."

During this visit, Archimboldi suggested to the reporter that perhaps his luck would change if he moved to another city, a city less devastated than Cologne, a smaller city where no one knew him. This was a possibility that hadn't occurred to the reporter and from that moment on he gave it serious consideration.

•

It took Archimboldi twenty days to type his novel. He made a carbon copy and then, at the public library, which had just reopened its doors, he searched for the names of two publishing houses where he might send the manuscript. After long scrutiny he realized that the houses that published many of his favorite books had long ago ceased to exist, some because they'd gone bankrupt or because of the apathy or waning interest of their owners, others because the Nazis had shut them down or imprisoned their editors and some because they'd been wiped out in Allied bombing raids.

One of the librarians, who knew him and knew that he wrote, asked whether he needed assistance and Archimboldi told her he was looking for literary publishing houses that were still active. The librarian said she could help. For a while she rummaged through some papers and then she made a phone call. When this was done she handed Archimboldi a list of twenty publishing houses, the same as the number of days he'd spent typing his novel, which was surely a good sign. But the problem was that he had just the original and one copy of the manuscript, which meant he could choose only two places. That night, standing at the door to the bar, he took out the paper every so often and studied it. Never had the names of publishers struck him as so beautiful, so distinguished, so full of promise and hope. Still, he decided to be prudent and not let himself be carried away by enthusiasm. The original he dropped off in person at a publishing house in Cologne. The advantage of this was that if it was rejected Archimboldi could go pick up the manuscript himself and send it out straightaway again. The carbon copy he sent to a house in Hamburg that had published books of the German Left until 1933, when the Nazi government not only shut down the business but also tried to send its editor, Mr. Jacob Bubis, to a prison camp, which it would have done if Mr. Bubis hadn't been a step ahead of them and taken the path of exile.

A month after both were sent, the Cologne publishing house wrote back to say that despite its undeniable merits, his novel *Lüdicke* regrettably wasn't the right fit for their list, but he should be sure to send them his next novel. He chose not to tell Ingeborg what had happened and that same day he went to pick up the manuscript, which took several hours, since no one at the publishing house seemed to know where it was and Archimboldi made it plain he wouldn't leave without it. The next day he took it in person to another Cologne publishing house, which rejected it in a month and a half, using more or less the same words as the first publishing house, perhaps with the addition of a few adjectives, perhaps wishing him better luck the next time around.

Now there was just one publishing house left in Cologne, a house that from time to time published some novel or volume of poetry or history, but whose catalog mainly consisted of practical manuals that might just as easily provide instruction on the proper care of a garden as on the correct administration of first aid or the reconstruction of the shells of destroyed houses. The name of the publishing house was the Adviser, and unlike the first two times, this time the publisher came out in person to receive the manuscript. And it wasn't for lack of employees, as he pointed out to Archimboldi, since he had at least five people working for him, but because he liked to see the faces of the writers who hoped to be published by his company. Their conversation, as Archimboldi remembered it, was odd. The editor had the face of a gangster. He was a young man, just a bit older than Archimboldi, dressed in a well-cut suit that was nevertheless a bit tight on him, as if overnight he had surreptitiously gained twenty pounds.

During the war he had served in a paratrooper unit, although he had never, he hastened to clarify, made a jump, much as he would have liked to. His military record included participation in various battles in different theaters of operations, especially in Italy and Normandy. He said he had been carpet bombed by American planes. And he claimed to know the secret to surviving such an attack. Since Archimboldi had spent the whole war in the east he had no idea what carpet bombing was and he said as much. The editor, whose name was Michael Bittner but who preferred his friends to call him Mickey, like the mouse, explained that carpet bombing was when masses of enemy planes, really huge masses, a vast number, dropped their bombs on a given area, a previously designated piece of countryside, until not a blade of grass was left.

"I don't know whether you get the idea, Benno," he said, fixing his gaze on Archimboldi.

"I get the idea perfectly, Mickey," said Archimboldi, thinking all the while that this man was not only irritating but ridiculous, with the particular ridiculousness of self-dramatizers and poor fools convinced they've been present at a decisive moment in history, when it's common knowledge, thought Archimboldi, that history, which is a simple whore, has no decisive moments but is a proliferation of instants, brief interludes that vie with one another in monstrousness.

•

But what Mickey Bittner wanted, the poor wretch, stuffed into his well-tailored, tight-fitting suit, was to explain the effect of carpet bombing on soldiers and the system he had come up with to combat it. Noise. First of all is noise. The soldier in his trench or his poorly fortified position suddenly hears noise. The noise of planes. But not the noise of fighter planes or fighter-bombers, which is a quick noise, if one can call it that, a low-flying noise. Instead it's a noise that comes from the highest point in the sky, a harsh, roaring noise that heralds nothing good, as if a storm were approaching, as if the clouds were colliding, but the problem is there are no clouds, there is no storm. Of course, the soldier looks up. At first he sees nothing. The artilleryman looks up. He sees nothing. The machine gunner, the mortar operator, the advance scout, look up and see nothing. The driver of an armored vehicle or tank gun looks up. He sees nothing either. As a precaution, however, he turns his vehicle off the road. He parks it under a tree or covers it with a camouflage tarp. Just then the first planes appear.

The soldiers watch them. There are many planes, but the soldiers think they're on their way to bomb some city behind the front lines. A city or bridges or rail lines. There are many, so many they blacken the sky, but their targets are surely in some industrial region of Germany. To general surprise the planes drop their bombs and the bombs fall within specific bounds. After the first wave comes a second wave. The noise grows deafening. The bombs fall and make craters in the earth. The forests are set ablaze. The undergrowth, the main cover in Normandy, begins to disappear. All the hedges are blown to pieces. The terraces collapse. Many soldiers are momentarily deafened. A few can't bear it and go running. By now the third wave of planes is dropping bombs over the chosen swath. Impossible as it seems, the noise grows louder. Call it noise, why not. One might call it a din, a roar, a clamor, a hammering, a great shriek, a bellow of the gods, but *noise* is a simple word that serves just as well to describe what has no name. The machine gunner dies. Another bomb falls directly on his dead body. Bones and shreds of flesh are scattered over spots that thirty seconds later will be pulverized by other bombs. The mortar operator is vaporized. The driver of the armored vehicle starts his engines and goes in search of better shelter, but along the way he is struck by a bomb, and then two more bombs turn the vehicle and the driver into a single formless thing in the middle of the road amid the wreckage and the lava. Then comes the fourth wave and the fifth. Everything is burning. It looks more like the moon than Normandy. When the bombers have finished pounding the designated piece of earth, not a single bird can be heard. In fact, not even in the neighboring areas where no bomb has fallen, to either side of the devastated divisions, does a single bird cry.

Then the enemy troops appear. For them, too, there is horror in forging into that steel-gray territory, smoking and pocked with craters. Every so often there rises up from the fiercely churned earth a German soldier with the eyes of a madman. Some surrender, weeping. Others, the paratroopers, the Wehrmacht veterans, some SS infantry battalions, open fire, try to reestablish lines of command, hold off the enemy advance. A few of these soldiers, the most indomitable, have clearly been drinking. Among them is certainly the paratrooper Mickey Bittner, because his recipe for enduring any kind of bombardment is precisely this: drink schnapps, drink cognac, drink brandy, drink grappa, drink whiskey, drink any kind of strong drink, even wine if that's all there is, to escape the noises, or to confuse the noises with the throbbing and spinning of one's head.

•

Then Mickey Bittner wanted to know what Archimboldi's novel was about and whether it was his first novel or whether he already had a body of work behind him. Archimboldi told him it was his first novel and described the plot in broad strokes. Sounds like it has potential, said Bittner. Immediately he added: but we won't be able to publish it this year. And then he said: of course, there'll be no talk of an advance. And later he clarified: we'll give you five percent of the sales price, which is more than fair. And then he confessed: in Germany people don't read the way they used to, now there are more practical things to think about. And then Archimboldi knew for sure that the man was talking for the sake of talking and that probably all paratrooper bastards, General Student's dogs, talked for the sake of talking, just to hear their own voices and to reassure themselves that no one had strung them up yet.

•

For a few days Archimboldi thought that what Germany really needed was a civil war.

He had no faith that Bittner, who surely knew nothing about literature, would publish his novel. He was nervous and lost his appetite. He hardly read at all and the little he did read disturbed him so much that no sooner did he begin a book than he had to shut it, because he would start to shake and was overcome by an irresistible urge to go outside and walk. He did make love, although sometimes, in the middle of the act, he went off to another planet, a snowy planet where he memorized Ansky's notebook.

"Where are you?" Ingeborg asked when this happened.

Even the voice of the woman he loved reached him as if from a great distance. After two months of receiving no response, negative or positive, Archimboldi visited the publishing house and asked to speak to Mickey Bittner. The secretary told him that Mr. Bittner was now involved in the import and export of essential goods and was rarely to be found at the publishing house, which was still his, of course, although he almost never stopped by. Upon insisting, Archimboldi got the address of Bittner's new office, on the outskirts of Cologne. The office was in a neighborhood of old nineteenth-century factories, above a warehouse stacked with crates, but Bittner wasn't there either.

In his place were three ex-paratroopers and a secretary with silver-colored hair. The paratroopers informed him that Mickey Bittner was in Antwerp just then closing a deal on a shipment of bananas. Then they all started to laugh and it took Archimboldi a moment to understand that they were laughing about the bananas, not at him. Then the paratroopers began to talk about the movies, since they were all avid moviegoers, as was the secretary, and they asked Archimboldi what front he'd been on and in what arm of the service, and Archimboldi said he'd been in the east, always the east, and in the light infantry, although in the last years of the war he hadn't seen a single mule or horse. The paratroopers themselves had always fought in the west, in Italy, France, one of them in Crete, and they had that cosmopolitan air of veterans of the western front, an air of roulette players, late-night revelers, sippers of fine wines, men who visited brothels and greeted the whores by name, an air unlike that of most veterans of the eastern front, who looked more like the living dead, zombies, cemetery dwellers, soldiers without eyes or mouths, but with penises, thought Archimboldi, because the penis, sexual desire, is unfortunately the last thing man loses, when it should be the first, but no, human beings keep fucking, fucking or fucking themselves, which amounts to the same thing, until their last breaths, like the soldier who was trapped under a pile of corpses and there, beneath the corpses and the snow, he dug a little cave with his regulation shovel, and to pass the time he jerked off, more boldly each time, because once the fear and surprise of the first few instants had vanished, all that was left was the fear of death and boredom, and to stave off boredom he began to masturbate, first timidly, as if he were seducing a peasant girl or a little shepherdess, then with increasing determination, until he managed to bring himself off to his full satisfaction, and he went on like that for fifteen days, in his little cave of corpses and snow, rationing his food and indulging his urges, which didn't make him weaker but rather seemed to retronourish him, as if he had drunk his own semen or as if after going mad he had found a forgotten way back to a new sanity, until the German troops counterattacked and discovered him, and here was a curious bit of information, thought Archimboldi, one of the soldiers who freed him from the pile of reeking corpses and the heaps of snow said the man smelled strange somehow, in other words not dirty or like shit or urine, nor like rot or worm meat, in fact, the survivor smelled *good*, the smell was strong, perhaps, but *good*, like cheap perfume, Hungarian perfume or Gypsy perfume, maybe with a faint hint of yogurt, maybe a faint scent of roots, but the predominant smell wasn't of yogurt or roots but of something else, something that surprised all of those present, all the men shoveling out the corpses to send them behind the lines or give them a Christian burial, a smell that *parted the waters*, as Moses parted the waters of the Red Sea, to let the soldier pass, though he could scarcely stand, and where was he going? who could say, surely away from the fighting, surely to a madhouse back home.

•

The paratroopers, who weren't bad people, offered Archimboldi the chance to get in on a job they had to handle that very night. Archimboldi asked what time it would end, because he didn't want to lose his position at the bar, and the paratroopers promised that everything would be over by eleven. They agreed to meet at eight at a bar near the station and when he left the secretary winked at him.

The bar was called the Yellow Nightingale and the first thing that struck Archimboldi when the paratroopers came in was that they were all wearing black leather coats very similar to his. The job consisted of unloading part of a freight car full of U.S. army stoves. Near the freight car, on an isolated bit of track, they met an American who first demanded a certain sum of money, which he counted to the last bill, and then warned them, like someone repeating a familiar order to slow-witted children, that they could take boxes only from that particular freight car, and only the boxes marked PK.

He spoke English and one of the paratroopers answered in English telling him not to worry. Then the American vanished into the darkness and another of the paratroopers appeared with a little truck, its lights off, and after forcing the lock of the freight car they set to work. An hour later they were done and two paratroopers got in the cab of the truck and Archimboldi and the other paratrooper got in the back, in the tiny space left by the boxes. They drove along backstreets, some unlit, to Mickey Bittner's office on the edge of the city. There the secretary was waiting for them with a thermos of hot coffee and a bottle of whiskey. When they had unloaded everything they went up to the office and began to talk about General Udet. As the paratroopers spiked their coffee with whiskey, they slipped into recollections of historic events, which in this case were also manly reminiscences punctuated by disillusioned laughter, as if to say I've seen it all, you can't fool me, I know human nature, the endless clash of wills, my memories are written in letters of fire and they're my only capital, and then they began to recall the figure of Udet, General Udet, the flying ace who killed himself because of slander spread by Göring.

Archimboldi wasn't sure who Udet was, and he didn't ask. The name was familiar, in the way other names were familiar, but that was all. Two of the paratroopers had once managed to catch a glimpse of Udet and they spoke of him in glowing terms.

"One of the best men in the Luftwaffe."

The third paratrooper listened to them and shook his head, not entirely convinced but in no way prepared to argue, and Archimboldi listened in horror, because if there was anything he was sure about it was that the war provided more than sufficient reason to commit suicide, but the tittle-tattle of scum like Göring clearly didn't qualify.

"So this Udet killed himself because of Göring's salon intrigues?" he asked. "So he didn't kill himself because of the death camps or the slaughter on the front lines or the cities in flames, but because Göring called him an incompetent?"

The three paratroopers looked at him as if they were seeing him for the first time, although without much surprise.

"Maybe Göring was right," said Archimboldi, pouring himself a little more whiskey and covering the cup with his hand when the secretary moved to fill it with coffee. "Maybe the man was essentially incompetent," he said. "Maybe he really was a mass of blunted and frayed nerves," he said. "Maybe he was a faggot, like most Germans who let themselves be fucked by Hitler," he said.

"So you're Austrian?" asked one of the paratroopers.

"No, I'm German too," said Archimboldi.

For a while the three paratroopers were silent, as if contemplating whether to kill him or settle for beating him to a pulp. But so assured was Archimboldi, who every so often shot them looks of rage in which many things but fear could be read, that they decided against a violent response.

"Pay him," said one of them to the secretary.

She got up and opened a metal cabinet, in the lower part of which was a little strongbox. The money she handed to Archimboldi represented half his monthly pay at the bar on the Spenglerstrasse. Archimboldi put the money in an inside pocket of his coat as the paratroopers watched nervously (they were sure he had a gun in there, or at least a knife) and then he looked around for the bottle of whiskey and couldn't find it. He asked where it was. I've put it away, said the secretary, you've had enough to drink, kid. Archimboldi liked that she called him kid, but he asked for more anyway.

"Have a last drink and then go because we have things to do," said one of the paratroopers.

Archimboldi nodded. The secretary poured him two fingers of whiskey. Archimboldi drank slowly, savoring the liquor, which he supposed was also contraband. Then he got up and two of the paratroopers escorted him to the door. Outside it was dark and although he knew perfectly well where he was going, he still stumbled into the pits and potholes that dotted the streets in that neighborhood.

•

Two days later Archimboldi paid another visit to Mickey Bittner's publishing house and the same secretary from before recognized him and told him they'd found his manuscript. Mr. Bittner was in his office. The secretary asked whether Archimboldi wanted to see him.

"Does he want to see me?" asked Archimboldi.

"I think so," said the secretary.

It briefly crossed his mind that maybe now Bittner wanted to publish his novel. He might also want to see him so that he could offer him another job on the import-export side of his business. But he thought that if he saw him he would probably break his nose, so he said no.

"Good luck, then," said the secretary.

"Thank you," said Archimboldi.

He sent the recovered manuscript to a publishing house in Munich. After he mailed it, when he got home, he suddenly realized that during all this time he had hardly written anything. He discussed it with Ingeborg while they were making love.

"What a waste of time," she said.

"I don't know how it could've happened," he said.

That night, as he was working the door at the bar, he amused himself by thinking about a time with two speeds, one very slow, in which the movement of people and objects was almost imperceptible, and the other very fast, in which everything, even inert objects, glittered with speed. The first was called Paradise, the second Hell, and Archimboldi's only wish was never to inhabit either.

•

One morning he received a letter from Hamburg. The letter was signed by Mr. Bubis, the great editor, and in it he said flattering things, or at least flattering things could be read between the lines, about *Lüdicke*, a work he would like to publish, that is, of course, if Mr. Benno von Archimboldi didn't already have a publisher, in which case he would be very sorry, because the novel wasn't lacking in merit and was, in a certain sense, rather original, in any case, it was a book that he, Mr. Bubis, had read with great interest, a book he felt he could take a gamble on, although such was the state of publishing in Germany just now that the most he could offer as an advance was such and such, a ridiculous sum, he knew, a sum that fifteen years ago he would never have proposed, but at the same time he guaranteed that the book would receive the finest treatment and be carried in all the best bookshops, not just in Germany but also in Austria and Switzerland, where the Bubis name was remembered and respected by democratic bookshop owners, a symbol of independent and high-quality publishing.

Then Mr. Bubis signed off in a friendly way, begging him to come and visit if someday he should happen to pass through Hamburg, and with the letter he enclosed a leaflet from the publishing house, printed on cheap paper but in a lovely typeface, announcing the impending release of two "magnificent" books, one of Döblin's first works and a volume of essays by Heinrich Mann.

·

When Archimboldi showed Ingeborg the letter she was surprised because she didn't know who Benno von Archimboldi was.

"It's me, of course," said Archimboldi.

"Why did you change your name?" she wanted to know.

After thinking about it for a moment, Archimboldi answered that it was for his safety.

"The Americans might be looking for me," he said. "It's possible the American and German police have put two and two together."

"For the sake of a war criminal?" asked Ingeborg.

"Justice is blind," Archimboldi reminded her.

"Blind when it suits her," said Ingeborg, "and who does it benefit if Sammer's dirty laundry is hung out in public? No one!"

"You never know," said Archimboldi. "In any case it's safest for me if Reiter is forgotten."

Ingeborg looked at him, surprised.

"You're lying," she said.

"No, I'm not lying," said Archimboldi, and Ingeborg believed him, but later, before he left for work, she said with an enormous smile:

"You're sure you'll be famous!"

Until that moment Archimboldi had never thought about fame. Hitler was famous. Göring was famous. The people he loved or remembered fondly weren't famous, they just satisfied certain needs. Döblin was his consolation. Ansky was his strength. Ingeborg was his joy. The disappeared Hugo Halder was lightheartedness and fun. His sister, about whom he had no news, was his own innocence. Of course, they were other things too. Sometimes they were even everything all together, but not fame, which was rooted in delusion and lies, if not ambition. Also, fame was reductive. Everything that ended in fame and everything that issued from fame was inevitably diminished. Fame's message was unadorned. Fame and literature were irreconcilable enemies.

All that day he thought about why he had changed his name. At the bar everyone knew he was Hans Reiter. His acquaintances in Cologne knew he was Hans Reiter. If the police finally did decide to come after him for Sammer's murder, there would be plenty of clues. So why adopt a nom de plume? Maybe Ingeborg is right, thought Archimboldi, maybe deep down I'm sure I'll be famous and with the change of name I'm making the first arrangements for my future protection. But maybe this all means something else. Maybe, maybe, maybe . . .

•

The day after he received the letter from Mr. Bubis, Archimboldi wrote to assure him that his novel wasn't promised to any other publisher and that the advance Mr. Bubis had proposed was satisfactory.

Soon afterward he received a letter in which Mr. Bubis invited him to Hamburg so they could meet in person and proceed to sign the contract. In times like these, said Mr. Bubis, I don't trust the German post or its proverbial punctuality and infallibility. And lately, especially since I returned from England, I've acquired the habit of meeting all my authors in person.

Before '33, he explained, I published many promising young German writers, and in 1940, in the solitude of a London hotel, I set out to pass the time by calculating how many of the first-time writers I published had become members of the Nazi party, how many had joined the SS, how many had written for rabidly anti-Semitic newspapers, how many had made a career in the Nazi bureaucracy. The result almost drove me to suicide, wrote Mr. Bubis.

Instead of committing suicide I simply hit myself. Anyone who saw me would've thought I was mad. Suddenly I felt as if I couldn't breathe and I opened the window. There, unfurled before me, was the great nocturnal theater of war: I watched the bombing of London. The bombs were falling near the river, but in the dark they seemed to drop just a few feet from the hotel. Spotlights crisscrossed the sky. The noise of the bombs grew louder and louder. Every once in a while a small explosion, a flash above the barrage balloons, made one think, even if it wasn't so, that a Luftwaffe plane had been hit. Despite the horror that surrounded me I kept beating myself and cursing. Idiot, ass, cretin, fool, moron, dolt, utterly puerile or senile name-calling, as you see.

Then someone knocked at my door. It was a young Irish bellhop. In a fit of madness I thought I saw James Joyce in his face. Ludicrous.

"Better close the shutters there," he said.

"The what?" I asked, red as a beet.

"The blinds, old man, and downstairs with yer."

I understood that he was ordering me to the cellar.

"Wait a moment, boy," I said, and I handed him a tip.

"Very kind of you, sir," he said before he left, "and now hurry, to the catacombs."

"You go first," I answered, "and I'll catch up."

When he left I opened the window again and stood there watching the blazes on the docks and then I wept for what I thought at the time was a life lost and then saved by a hair.

●

So Archimboldi asked for leave from work and took the train to Hamburg.

Mr. Bubis's publishing house was in the same building it had occupied until 1933. The two neighboring buildings had been flattened by bombs, as had several buildings across the street. Some of the publishing house employees, behind Mr. Bubis's back, of course, said he had personally directed the raids on the city. Or at least on that particular neighborhood. When Archimboldi met Mr. Bubis, the publisher was seventy-four and sometimes he gave the impression of being an ailing man, bad tempered, miserly, mistrustful, a money-grubber who cared little or nothing for literature, though he wasn't really like that at all: Mr. Bubis enjoyed or pretended to enjoy enviable health, never got sick, was always ready with a smile, was as trusting as a child, and wasn't miserly, though at the same time it couldn't be said he paid his employees handsomely.

In addition to Mr. Bubis, who did everything, the publishing house employed a copy editor, a bookkeeper who also handled press relations, a secretary, who often assisted the copy editor and the bookkeeper, and a storeroom attendant, who was hardly ever in the storeroom, which was in the building's cellar and was constantly under repair because it was periodically flooded by rainwater and occasionally even by groundwater, as the attendant explained, which rose and settled in the cellar in big damp patches, very damaging for the books and the health of those who worked there.

As well as these four employees, there was often a respectable-looking woman on the premises, more or less the same age as Mr. Bubis, if not a bit older, who had worked at the house until 1933, Mrs. Marianne Gottlieb, Bubis's most faithful employee, to the extent, or so it was said, that she had driven the car that carried the publisher and his wife to the Dutch border, from where they had continued on to Amsterdam after the car was searched by the border police, who didn't find anything.

How had Bubis and his wife managed to get past the border control? No one knew, but in every version of the story the feat was credited to Mrs. Gottlieb.

When Bubis returned to Hamburg, in September 1945, Mrs. Gottlieb was living in the direst poverty, and Bubis, who by then had lost his wife, brought her to live with him. Little by little Mrs. Gottlieb recovered. First she regained her sanity. One morning she looked at Bubis and recognized him as her old employer, but said nothing. That night, when Bubis got back from city hall, because at the time he was engaged in political matters, he found supper made and Mrs. Gottlieb standing by the table, waiting for him. That was a happy night for Mr. Bubis and Mrs. Gottlieb, although supper ended with the story of Mr. Bubis's exile and Mrs. Bubis's death, and with a flood of tears for Mrs. Bubis's lonely grave in London's Jewish cemetery.

Then Mrs. Gottlieb's health improved somewhat, so that she was able to move into a small flat with a view of a ravaged park that nevertheless came to life in the spring, renewed by the forces of nature, generally indifferent to human deeds, don't you think, said Mr. Bubis, the skeptic, who accepted but didn't share Mrs. Gottlieb's yearning for independence. Soon afterward she asked him for help finding a job, because Mrs. Gottlieb was incapable of being idle. Then Bubis made her his secretary. But Mrs. Gottlieb, who never spoke of these things, had also had her share of nightmarish times, and sometimes, for no apparent reason, her health failed and she fell ill as quickly as she then recovered. Other times it was her mind that faltered. On occasion, Bubis had to meet with the English authorities in a particular place and Mrs. Gottlieb sent him to the other end of the city. Or she scheduled appointments for him with hypocritical and unrepentant Nazis who wanted to offer their services to the city of Hamburg. Or she fell asleep, nodding off in her office with her head resting on the blotter.

Which is why Mr. Bubis found her a new job in the Hamburg archives, where Mrs. Gottlieb would have to handle books and files, all papers, that is, to which she was more accustomed, or so Mr. Bubis supposed. And yet even in the archives, where outrageous behavior was more easily accommodated, Mrs. Gottlieb's bouts of erratic and pragmatic activity persisted in equal measure. And she also continued to visit Mr. Bubis, in hours stolen from sleep, in case her presence might be of any use to him. Until at last Mr. Bubis got bored with politics and city affairs and decided to focus his efforts on what had after all brought him back to Germany: reviving his publishing house.

Often, when he was asked why he had returned, he quoted Tacitus: *Then, besides the dangers of a boisterous and unknown sea, who would relinquish Asia, Africa, or Italy, for Germany, a land rude in its surface, rigorous in its climate, cheerless to every beholder and cultivator, except a native?* Those who heard him nodded and smiled and commented among themselves: Bubis is one of us. Bubis hasn't forgotten us. Bubis bears us no grudge. Some patted him on the back and understood nothing. Others assumed stricken expressions and said what truth there was in the Roman's words. A great man, Tacitus, as is our dear Bubis, on a different level, of course!

The truth is that when Bubis quoted the Latin, he meant it literally. The Channel crossing was something he had always dreaded. Bubis got seasick on boats and vomited and was mostly confined to his stateroom, so that when Tacitus referred to a boisterous and unknown sea, even though what he meant was the Baltic or the North Sea, Bubis always thought of the Channel crossing and how disastrous it proved for his sensitive stomach and his health in general. Similarly, when Tacitus talked about relinquishing Italy, Bubis thought about the United States, New York in particular, where he had received several highly respectable offers of work at publishing houses in the Big Apple, and when Tacitus mentioned Asia and Africa, Bubis was put in mind of the emerging state of Israel, where he was sure there were all sorts of things he could do, in the publishing field, of course, not to mention that it was home to many of his old friends, whom he would have liked to see again.

And yet he had chosen Germany, *cheerless to every beholder and cultivator.* Why? Certainly not out of any loyalty to his homeland, because although Mr. Bubis felt himself to be German, he despised national pride, which to his mind was one of the causes of the death of more than fifty million people, but because Germany was home to his publishing house or to the idea he had of a publishing house, a German publishing house, a publishing house with its headquarters in Hamburg, and its networks, in the form of book orders, linking old bookshops all over Germany, some of whose owners he knew personally and with whom, when he traveled for business, he drank tea or coffee, sitting in a corner of the bookshop, always complaining about hard times, bemoaning the public's indifference, sighing over the middlemen and paper salesmen, grieving for the future of a country that didn't read, in a word, utterly enjoying himself as they nibbled biscuits or little slices of kuchen until at last Mr. Bubis rose and shook hands with the elderly owner of, say, Iserlohn, and then went off to Bochum, to visit the elderly owner of Bochum, who kept certain books with the Bubis logo like relics (relics for sale, of course), books published in 1930 or 1927, that by law, Schwarzwald law, naturally, he should have burned in 1935 at the latest, but that the old bookseller had chosen to hide, out of pure love, which was something Bubis understood (and few others could understand, not excluding the book's author) and for which he showed his gratitude with a gesture of respect that went beyond literature, a gesture, somehow, of honorable tradesmen, of tradesmen in possession of a secret that went back possibly as far as the dawn of Europe, a gesture that was a mythology or else opened the door to a mythology, its two central pillars the bookseller and the editor, not the writer embarked on his unpredictable course or hostage to ghostly imponderables, but the bookseller, the editor, and a long, winding road sketched by a painter of the Flemish school.

•

So it was no real surprise that Mr. Bubis soon tired of politics and decided to reopen his publishing house, because deep down all he really cared about was the adventure of printing books and selling them.

Around this time, however, just before he returned to the building that justice had restored to him, Mr. Bubis was in Mannheim, in the

American zone, when he met a young refugee in her early thirties, of good family and remarkable beauty, and though no one could say how, because Mr. Bubis was hardly a ladies' man, they became lovers. The change this affair wrought in him was plain. His energy, already prodigious considering his age, tripled. His zest for life became overpowering. His faith in the success of his new publishing enterprise (although Bubis would correct anyone who spoke to him of a "new enterprise," since to him it was the same old enterprise, reappearing now after a lengthy and unwelcome hiatus) was contagious.

At the publishing house's opening ceremony, with all of Hamburg's officials and artists and politicians invited, as well as a delegation of book-loving English officers (though regrettably most were enthusiasts of the whodunit or the foxhunting novel in its Georgian incarnation, or the philatelic novel), and not only the German press but also the French, English, Dutch, Swiss, and even American press, his lady friend, as he called her fondly, made her first public appearance, and displays of respect were coupled with perplexity, because everyone expected a woman of forty or fifty, someone more intellectual, and some had thought she would be Jewish, as was the tradition in the Bubis family, while others, judging by experience, imagined that this was just another of Mr. Bubis's pranks, since he was a great one for practical jokes. But the thing was in earnest, as became evident during the party. The woman wasn't Jewish but one hundred percent Aryan, nor was she forty but just over thirty, although she looked twenty-seven at most, and two months later, Bubis's prank or little joke became a fait accompli when he got married, with every honor and flanked by a municipal who's who, at the venerable city hall in the midst of reconstruction, in an unforgettable civil ceremony presided over by the very mayor of Hamburg, who seized the occasion to shower Bubis with flattery, declaring him a prodigal son and model citizen.

•

When Archimboldi arrived in Hamburg, the publishing house hadn't yet attained the high level that Mr. Bubis had set as a second goal (the first was to maintain a constant supply of paper and keep up distribution throughout Germany; the remaining eight were known only to Mr. Bubis), but it was moving ahead at an acceptable pace and its owner and master was satisfied and weary.

Writers had begun to appear in Germany who interested Mr. Bubis, though not much, or at least nowhere near as much as the writers in the Germany of his early days, to whom he remained commendably loyal, but some of the new ones weren't bad, even if among them no glimpse could be seen (or Mr. Bubis was incapable of catching a glimpse, as he himself acknowledged) of a new Döblin, a new Musil, a new Kafka (although if a new Kafka appeared, said Mr. Bubis, laughing, but with a look of profound sadness in his eyes, I would quake in my boots), a new Thomas Mann. The bulk of the catalog was still the house's inexhaustible backlist, but new writers also began to crop up under Bubis's nose from the bottomless quarry of German literature, as well as translations of French and English literature, which in those days, after the long Nazi drought, gained enough loyal readers to guarantee success, or at least prevent losses.

The rate of work, in any case, was steady, if not frenetic, and when Archimboldi arrived at the house his first thought was that Mr. Bubis, busy as he seemed, would have no time for him. But Mr. Bubis, after making him wait ten minutes, ushered him into his office, an office Archimboldi would never forget, because with every shelf crammed full, books and manuscripts collected on the floor in stacks and towers, some so precarious that they in turn spilled over, a chaos that was a reflection of the world, rich and magnificent despite war and injustice, a library of glorious books that Archimboldi would have given anything to read, first editions of the works of great writers with handwritten dedications to Mr. Bubis, books of degenerate art that other publishing houses were once again issuing in Germany, books published in France and England, paperbacks from New York and Boston and San Francisco, as well as American magazines with mythical names that for an impecunious young writer were a treasure trove, the ultimate display of wealth, and turned Bubis's office into something like Ali Baba's cave.

Nor would Archimboldi forget the first question Bubis asked him after the standard introductions:

"What's your real name? Because it can't be the name you've given me, of course."

"That's my name," answered Archimboldi.

"Do you think the years I spent in England or the years in general have made me stupid? No one has a name like that. Benno von Archimboldi. To be called Benno, in the first place, is suspicious."

"Why?" Archimboldi wanted to know.

"You don't know? You really don't?"

"I swear I don't," said Archimboldi.

"Why, because of Benito Mussolini, man! Where's your head?"

At that point Archimboldi thought the money and time he had spent traveling to Hamburg were wasted and he saw himself that very evening on the night train back to Cologne. With luck, he'd be home by the next morning.

"They called me Benno after Benito Juárez," said Archimboldi, "I suppose you know who Benito Juárez was."

Bubis smiled.

"Benito Juárez," he muttered, still smiling. "So it's Benito Juárez, is it?" he asked in a slightly louder voice.

Archimboldi nodded.

"I thought you were going to tell me it was in honor of Saint Benedict."

"I've never heard of a saint by that name," said Archimboldi.

"Well, I know of three," said Bubis. "Saint Benedict of Aniane, who reformed the order of Benedictines in the ninth century. Saint Benedict of Nursia, who in the sixth century founded the order that bears his name and was known as the 'Father of Europe,' a dangerous title, wouldn't you say? And Saint Benedict the Moor, who was black, of the Negro race, I mean, and who lived and died in Sicily in the sixteenth century and was a Franciscan monk. Which of the three do you prefer?"

"Benito Juárez," said Archimboldi.

"And that last name, Archimboldi, you can't expect me to believe everyone in your family is called that?"

"That's what I'm called," said Archimboldi, who was about to abandon this bad-tempered little man midsentence and walk out without saying goodbye.

"No one is called that," Bubis replied gloomily. "I suppose in this case it's after Giuseppe Arcimboldo. And where on Earth does the von come in? Benno isn't satisfied with being Benno Archimboldi? Benno wants to make it plain he's German? What part of Germany are you from?"

"I'm Prussian," said Archimboldi as he stood up, ready to go.

"Wait a moment," protested Bubis, "before you leave for your hotel I want you to see my wife."

"I'm not going to any hotel," said Archimboldi, "I'm going back to Cologne. Please let me have my manuscript."

Bubis smiled again.

"There'll be time for that later," he said.

Then he rang a bell and before the door opened he asked for the last time:

"So you really won't tell me your name?"

"Benno *von* Archimboldi," said Archimboldi, looking him in the eye.

Bubis spread his hands apart and brought them together, as if he were clapping, but without making a sound, and then his secretary poked her head in the door.

"Take the gentleman to Mrs. Bubis's office," he said.

Archimboldi glanced at the secretary, a blond girl with her hair in curls, and when he looked back at Bubis the latter was already immersed in a manuscript. He followed the secretary. Mrs. Bubis's office was at the end of a long hallway. The secretary knocked and then, without waiting for a response, opened the door and said: Anna, Mr. Archimboldi is here. A voice ordered him to come in. The secretary grabbed him by the arm and pushed him in. Then, with a smile, she left. Mrs. Anna Bubis was sitting behind a desk that was nearly empty (especially in contrast to Mr. Bubis's), on which there sat just an ashtray, a pack of English cigarettes, a gold lighter, and a book in French. Archimboldi, despite the years that had gone by, recognized her immediately. It was the Baroness Von Zumpe. And yet he just stood there, determined at least for the moment to say nothing. The baroness took off her glasses, which she hadn't worn before, at least as far as Archimboldi remembered, and contemplated him with a faraway look, as if it were an effort for her to tear herself away from what she was reading or thinking, or perhaps that was her usual expression.

"Benno von Archimboldi?" she asked.

Archimboldi nodded. For a few seconds the baroness said nothing and only studied his face.

"I'm tired," she said. "Would you like to step out for a walk, perhaps for a cup of coffee?"

"All right," said Archimboldi.

As they descended the building's dark stairs, the baroness said that she had recognized him and was sure that he had recognized her too.

"Instantly, Baroness," said Archimboldi.

"But it's been a long time," said the Baroness Von Zumpe, "and I've changed."

"Not physically, Baroness," said Archimboldi behind her.

"And yet your name is unfamiliar," said the baroness. "You were the son of one of our maids, that much I do remember, your mother worked in the house in the woods, but your name is unfamiliar."

Archimboldi thought it was amusing the way the baroness referred to her old country estate. *House in the woods* sounded like a doll's house, a cabin, a hut, a place that existed on the edge of time and remained fixed in a willed and imaginary childhood, comfortable and unspoiled.

"My name is Benno von Archimboldi now, Baroness," said Archimboldi.

"Well," said the baroness, "you've chosen a very elegant name. Rather jarring, but with a certain elegance, I'm sure."

Some of the streets of Hamburg, Archimboldi could see as they walked, were in a worse state than the most devastated streets of Cologne, although in Hamburg he had the impression that the reconstruction efforts were more in earnest. As they walked, the baroness as jauntily as a schoolgirl playing truant, and Archimboldi with his bag over his shoulder, they told each other some of the things that had happened since their last meeting in the Carpathians. Without going into detail, Archimboldi told her about the war, about Crimea, about the Kuban and the great rivers of the Soviet Union, about the winters and the months he spent unable to speak, and somehow, obliquely, he conjured up Ansky, though he never mentioned his name.

The baroness, meanwhile, as if to counterbalance Archimboldi's forced travels, told him about her own journeys, all planned and desired and therefore happy, exotic trips to Bulgaria and Turkey and Montenegro and receptions at the German embassies of Italy, Spain, and Portugal, and she confessed that sometimes she tried to repent of the good times she'd had, but no matter how strongly she rejected her hedonistic behavior on an intellectual or perhaps more accurately a moral level, the truth was that when she thought back on those days she still felt a shiver of pleasure.

"Do you understand? Can you understand me?" she asked as they had cappuccino and cakes at a coffee shop like something out of a fairy tale, next to a big window with views of the river and rolling green hills.

Then Archimboldi, rather than saying whether he understood her or not, asked if she knew what had happened to Entrescu, the Romanian general. I have no idea, said the baroness.

"I do," said Archimboldi, "and if you want, I can tell you."

"My guess is it won't be anything good," said the baroness. "Am I right?"

"I don't know," admitted Archimboldi, "depending on how you look at it, it's either very bad or not so bad."

"So you saw him, did you?" murmured the baroness, gazing out at the river where two ships were passing just then, one on the way to the sea, the other heading inland.

"Yes, I saw him," said Archimboldi.

"Then don't tell me yet," said the baroness, "there'll be time enough later."

One of the waiters at the coffee shop called them a taxi. The baroness gave the driver the name of a hotel. At the front desk there was a reservation in the name of Benno von Archimboldi. The two of them followed the porter to a single room. With surprise, Archimboldi discovered a radio on one of the bureaus.

"Unpack your bag," said the baroness, "and freshen up a little, tonight we dine with my husband."

As Archimboldi put away a pair of socks, a shirt, and a pair of undershorts, the baroness set about finding a jazz station on the radio. Archimboldi went into the bathroom and shaved and splashed water on his hair and then combed it. When he came out the lights were off, except for the lamp on the little night table, and the baroness ordered him to take off his clothes and get in bed. From there, with the covers pulled up to his chin and feeling pleasantly tired, he watched the baroness, standing, dressed only in a pair of black underpants, turn the dial until she found a classical station.

●

In all, he spent three days in Hamburg. Twice he dined with Mr. Bubis. The first time he talked about himself and the second time he met some of the famous editor's friends and hardly opened his mouth, for fear of saying something foolish. In Mr. Bubis's inner circle, at least in Hamburg, there were no writers. A banker, a ruined nobleman, a painter who now only wrote monographs on seventeenth-century painters, and a translator from the French, all well versed in cultural matters, all intelligent, but no writers.

Even so, he hardly opened his mouth.

Mr. Bubis's attitude toward him had changed considerably, which

Archimboldi attributed to the good offices of the baroness, to whom he had finally told his real name. He told it to her in bed, as they made love, and the baroness didn't need to ask him to repeat it. Her attitude, meanwhile, when she demanded he tell her what had happened to General Entrescu, was strange and in a way illuminating. After he told her that the Romanian had died at the hands of his own soldiers in retreat, who beat him and then crucified him, the only thing the baroness chose to ask, as if dying crucified was an everyday occurrence during the war, was whether the body he'd seen on the cross was naked or dressed in uniform. Archimboldi's answer was that to all intents and purposes the body was naked, but scraps of uniform still clung to it, enough so that the Russians who were close on their heels would have known when they reached the spot that the gift the Romanian soldiers had left behind was a general. But he was also naked enough so that the Russians could confirm with their own eyes the colossal size of Romanian members, though General Entrescu's was definitely a misleading specimen, said Archimboldi, because he had seen some Romanian soldiers naked and their attributes were in no way different from, say, the German average, whereas General Entrescu's penis, flaccid and bruised as might be expected of a man who'd been beaten and then crucified, was double or triple the size of a normal cock, whether Romanian or German, or, to give a random example, French.

Having said this, Archimboldi fell silent, and the baroness remarked that such a death would not have displeased the bold general. And she added that Entrescu, despite the successes attributed to him on the battlefield, was always a disaster as a tactician and strategist. As a lover, however, he was the best she'd ever had.

"Not because of the size of his cock," the baroness explained, to clear up any misunderstandings that Archimboldi, next to her in bed, might entertain, "but because of a kind of shape-shifting quality: he was cleverer than a crow when he talked and in bed he turned into a devil ray."

To which Archimboldi replied that from the little he'd been able to observe during Entrescu's short stay with his entourage at the castle in the Carpathians, he believed the crow was actually Entrescu's secretary, Popescu, an opinion that was immediately rejected by the baroness, to whom Popescu was nothing but a cockatoo, a cockatoo flitting after a lion. Except that the lion had no claws or if he did he wasn't prepared to use them, nor did he have the fangs to rip anyone apart, just a somewhat ridiculous sense of his own destiny, a destiny and a notion of destiny that in a way echoed Byron's destiny and notion of destiny, though Archimboldi, who happened to have read Byron by one of those coincidences that arise from the use of public libraries, thought the poet was in no way comparable, even as an echo, to the execrable General Entrescu, adding that incidentally the notion of destiny wasn't something that could be separated from the destiny of an individual (a wretched individual), but that the two things were essentially the same: destiny, ungraspable until it became inevitable, was each person's notion of his own destiny.

To which the baroness responded with a smile, saying it was clear Archimboldi had never fucked Entrescu. Which prompted Archimboldi to confess that it was true, he had never gone to bed with Entrescu, but he had in fact been an eyewitness to one of the general's famous trysts.

"With me, I suppose," said the baroness.

"You suppose right," said Archimboldi.

"And where were you?" asked the baroness.

"In a secret chamber," said Archimboldi.

Then the baroness laughed so hard she couldn't stop and between gasps she said she wasn't surprised he had decided to call himself Benno von Archimboldi. Archimboldi didn't understand what she meant, but he accepted the remark with good grace, laughing with her.

•

So after three very instructive days, Archimboldi returned to Cologne on the night train, with people sleeping even in the corridors, and soon he was back in his attic, relaying to Ingeborg the excellent news from Hamburg, news that upon being shared filled them with such joy that they began to sing and then dance, never fearing that the floor would collapse beneath their feet. Afterward they made love and Archimboldi described the publishing house; Mr. Bubis; Mrs. Bubis; Uta, the copy editor, who could correct the grammar of Lessing, whom she despised with Hanseatic fervor, but not of Lichtenberg, whom she loved; Anita, the bookkeeper or head of publicity, who knew practically every writer in Germany but liked only French literature; Martha, the secretary, who had a literature degree and gave him some books from the publishing house in which he had expressed an interest; Rainer Maria, the storeroom attendant, who, despite his youth, had already been an expressionist poet, a symbolist, and a decadent.

He also told her about Mr. Bubis's friends and Mr. Bubis's list of writers. And each time Archimboldi finished a sentence he and Ingeborg laughed, as if he were telling an irresistibly funny story. Then Archimboldi set to work in earnest on his second book and in less than three months he had finished it.

•

Lüdicke had yet to come off the presses when Mr. Bubis received the manuscript of *The Endless Rose*, which he read in two nights, after which, deeply shaken, he woke his wife and told her they would have to publish this new book by Archimboldi.

"Is it good?" asked the baroness, half asleep and not bothering to sit up.

"It's better than good," said Bubis, pacing the room.

Then he began to talk, still pacing, about Europe, Greek mythology, and something vaguely like a police investigation, but the baroness fell back asleep and didn't hear him.

During the rest of the night, Bubis, who often suffered from fits of insomnia that he knew how to turn to his advantage, tried to read other manuscripts, go over his accounts, write letters to his distributors, all in vain. At the first light of day he woke his wife again and made her promise that when he was no longer head of the publishing house, his euphemism for his own death, she wouldn't abandon Archimboldi.

"Abandon him in what sense?" asked the baroness, still half asleep.

Bubis didn't answer for a moment.

"We have to protect him," he said.

After a few seconds, he added:

"Protect him to the extent possible as his publishers."

These last words the Baroness Von Zumpe didn't hear because she had fallen asleep again. For a while Bubis sat gazing at her face, which was like something out of a Pre-Raphaelite painting. Then he got up from the foot of the bed and went into the kitchen in his bathrobe, where he made himself a cheese sandwich with pickled onions, a recipe he'd been taught in England by an Austrian writer in exile.

"There's something so simple and restorative about a sandwich like this," the Austrian had told him.

Simple, doubtless. And tasty, with an unusual flavor. But not at all restorative, thought Mr. Bubis, one needs an iron stomach to withstand a diet like this. Then he went into the sitting room and opened the curtains to let in the gray morning light. Restorative, restorative, restorative, thought Mr. Bubis as he nibbled distractedly at his sandwich. We need something more restorative than a cheese sandwich with pickled onions. But where to look, where to find it, and what to do with it when we've found it? At that moment he heard the back door open and he listened, with his eyes closed, for the soft step of the maid who came each morning. He could've stood like that for hours. A statue. Instead he left the sandwich on the table and went to his room, where he proceeded to dress for another day of work.

•

Lüdicke garnered two positive notices and one negative notice and three hundred copies in total were sold of the first edition. *The Endless Rose*, which came out five months later, received one positive review and three negative reviews and sold two hundred and five copies. No other editor would have ventured to publish a third book by Archimboldi, but Bubis was ready to take on not only the third but also the fourth, the fifth, and every book that came along. Archimboldi was in good hands.

During this time, Archimboldi's finances improved slightly, but only slightly. The Cologne Cultural Center paid him for two public readings in two different city bookshops, whose owners, it must be said, knew Mr. Bubis personally. Neither reading aroused marked interest. Only fifteen people, counting Ingeborg, came to the first, at which the author read selections from his novel *Lüdicke*, and at the end only three dared to buy the book. At the second reading, of selections from *The Endless Rose*, there were nine, again counting Ingeborg, and at the end only three people were left in the room, the small size of which went some way toward softening the blow. Among them, of course, was Ingeborg, who hours later confessed to Archimboldi that at a certain point she too had considered leaving.

In collaboration with the recently established and somewhat muddled cultural councils of Lower Saxony, the Cologne Cultural Center also organized a series of lectures and readings that began with some pomp and circumstance in Oldenburg and continued on to various towns and villages, each smaller and more godforsaken than the previous one, places no writer had agreed to visit before. The tour ended in the fishing hamlets of Frisia, where Archimboldi unexpectedly found the largest crowds, and where very few people left before an event was over.

Archimboldi's writing, the process of creation or the daily routine in which this process peacefully unfolded, gathered strength and something that for lack of a better word might be called confidence. This "confidence" didn't signify the end of doubt, of course, much less that the writer believed his work had some value, because Archimboldi had a view of literature (though the word *view* is too grand) as something divided into three compartments, each connected only tenuously to the others: in the first were the books he read and reread and considered magnificent and sometimes monstrous, like the fiction of Döblin, who was still one of his favorite authors, or Kafka's complete works. In the second compartment were the books of the epigones and authors he called the Horde, whom he essentially saw as his enemies. In the third compartment were his own books and his plans for future books, which he saw as a game and also a business, a game insofar as he derived pleasure from writing, a pleasure similar to that of the detective on the heels of the killer, and a business insofar as the publication of his books helped to augment, however modestly, his doorman's pay.

The job at the bar he didn't give up, of course, in part because he had grown used to it and in part because the mechanics of it were perfectly adapted to the mechanics of writing. When he finished his third novel, *The Leather Mask*, the old man who rented him the typewriter and to whom Archimboldi had given a copy of *The Endless Rose* offered to sell him the machine at a reasonable price. The price probably *was* reasonable as far as the ex-writer was concerned, especially if one took into account that he hardly ever rented the machine anymore, but for Archimboldi it was still too much, though also a temptation. So, after a few days of thinking about it and doing sums, he wrote to Bubis, for the first time requesting an advance on a book he hadn't yet started. Naturally, he explained in the letter what he needed the money for and solemnly promised to deliver his next book in no more than six months.

Bubis's response was completely unexpected. One morning a couple of deliverymen from the Olivetti branch in Cologne brought Archimboldi a splendid new typewriter and all he had to do was sign some papers acknowledging receipt. Two days later he received a letter from the publisher's secretary in which he was informed that on the boss's instructions a purchase order for a typewriter had been issued in his name. It's a gift from the publishing house, said the secretary. For a few days Archimboldi was nearly dizzy with joy. They *believe* in me, he repeated to himself aloud, as people passed by in silence, or, like him, talking to themselves, a common sight in Cologne that winter.

•

Ninety-six copies of *The Leather Mask* were sold, which wasn't a lot, Bubis said to himself with resignation as he went over his accounts, but the publisher's support for Archimboldi never waned. On the contrary, around this time Bubis had to travel to Frankfurt, and while he was there he made a day trip to Mainz to visit the literary critic Lothar Junge, who lived in a little house on the edge of the city, near a forest and a hill, a little house from which one could hear birdsong, which struck Bubis as incredible, listen, you can even hear the birds singing, he said to the Baroness Von Zumpe, with his eyes wide and a smile from ear to ear, as if the last thing he would've expected to find in that part of Mainz was a forest and a colony of songbirds and a two-story house behind white-washed walls, like something out of a fairy tale, a little house, a little white-chocolate house with beams like slabs of dark chocolate, surrounded by a little garden in which the flowers looked like paper cutouts and a lawn trimmed with mathematical precision, and a little gravel path that crunched underfoot, a noise that set one's nerves or nervelets on edge, all laid out with a ruler, carpenter's square, and compass, as Bubis said under his breath to the baroness just before he let the door knocker (which was in the shape of a pig's head) fall against the heavy wooden door.

Lothar Junge himself came to the door. Of course, they were expected and on the table Mr. Bubis and the baroness found crackers with smoked ham, typical of the region, and two bottles of spirits. The critic was at least six foot three and he moved around the house as if he were afraid of hitting his head. He wasn't fat, but he wasn't thin either, and he dressed in the fashion of the professors of Heidelberg, who never removed their ties except in situations of true intimacy. For a while, as they did justice to the appetizers, they discussed the current German literary scene, a territory through which Lothar Junge moved with the caution of a defuser of unexploded bombs or mines. Then a young writer from Mainz arrived with his wife, followed by another literary critic from the same paper in Frankfurt where Junge's reviews were published. They ate rabbit stew. The wife of the writer from Mainz opened her mouth only once during the meal, to ask the baroness where she'd bought the dress she was wearing. In Paris, answered the baroness, and that was the last time the writer's wife spoke. And yet from then on her face was transformed into a discourse or memorandum on the affronts suffered by the city of Mainz from its founding until the present day. The sum of her pouts or scowls, which flitted at light speed between utter resentment and embryonic hatred of her husband, who in her mind stood for all the unworthy people at the table, didn't pass unnoticed by anyone, except Willy, the other literary critic, whose specialty was philosophy and who therefore reviewed philosophy books and whose hope was someday to publish a book of philosophy, three occupations, if they could be called that, which made him especially insensitive to indications of the state of mind (or soul) of a fellow diner.

The meal finished, they returned to the sitting room for coffee or tea, and Bubis, whose plans did not include spending any longer in that maddening toy house, seized the moment to drag a willing Junge into the back garden, as carefully tended as the front garden, but with the advantage of being bigger, and from which one had an even closer view, if possible, of the surrounding forest. They spoke, first of all, about the critic's writings, which he was dying to see published by Bubis. The latter made vague mention of an idea he'd been toying with for months, which was to create a new imprint, though he took care not to mention what sort of imprint he had in mind. Then they went on to discuss the new authors who were being published by Bubis and Bubis's colleagues in Munich and Cologne and Frankfurt and Berlin, as well as the publishing houses firmly established in Zurich or Bern and those resurfacing in Vienna. At last Bubis asked in a deliberately casual tone what Junge thought, for example, of Archimboldi. Lothar Junge, who walked as cautiously in the garden as he did under his own roof, at first shrugged his shoulders.

"Have you read him?" asked Bubis.

Junge didn't answer. He considered his reply with his head bent, absorbed in contemplation or admiration of the grass, which, as they approached the edge of the woods, became more untidy, less scoured of fallen leaves or twigs or even, as it seemed, of insects.

"If you haven't read him, say so, and I'll send you copies of all his books," said Bubis.

"I've read him," admitted Junge.

"And what did you think?" asked the old editor, stopping by an oak whose very presence seemed to announce in a threatening tone: here ends the realm of Junge and here begins the republic of trees. Junge stopped, too, but a few steps farther on, his head slightly ducked, as if he feared a branch might muss his sparse hair.

"I don't know, I don't know," he murmured.

Then, incomprehensibly, he began to make faces that in some way linked him to the wife of the writer from Mainz, to such a degree that Bubis thought they must be brother and sister and only thus could one fully understand the presence of the writer and his wife at the meal. It was also possible, thought Bubis, that they were lovers, because it was common knowledge that lovers often began to resemble each other, usually in their smiles, their opinions, their points of view, in short, the superficial trappings that all human beings are obliged to bear until their deaths, like the rock of Sisyphus, yes Sisyphus, known as the craftiest of men, son of Aeolus and Enarete, founder of the city of Ephyra, which is the old name for Corinth, a city that the good Sisyphus turned into the staging ground of his happy misdeeds, because with his characteristic nimbleness of body and intellectual inclination to see every turn of fate as a chess problem or a detective story to unravel, and his instinct for laughter and jokes and jests and cracks and quips and gags and pranks and punch lines and spoofs and stories and gibes and taunts and send-ups and satires, he turned to theft, in other words parting all passersby from their belongings, even going so far as to steal from his neighbor Autolycus, also a thief, perhaps with the remote hope that one who steals from a thief is granted one hundred years of forgiveness, and at the same time smitten by his neighbor's daughter, Anticlea, because Anticlea was very beautiful, a treat, but the girl had an official suitor, she was promised to Laertes, of subsequent fame, which didn't daunt Sisyphus, who could count on the complicity of the girl's father, the thief Autolycus, whose admiration for Sisyphus had sprung up like the regard of an objective and honorable artist for another artist of superior gifts, so that even though it could be said that as a man of honor he remained true to his promise to Laertes, he didn't look unkindly upon the romantic attentions Sisyphus lavished on his daughter or treat them as disrespect or mockery of his future son-in-law, and in the end his daughter married Laertes, or so it's said, but only after surrendering to Sisyphus one or two or five or seven times, possibly ten or fifteen times, always with the collusion of Autolycus, who wanted his neighbor to plant the seed of a grandchild as clever as Sisyphus, and on one of these occasions Anticlea was left with child and nine months later, now the wife of Laertes, her son would be born, the son of Sisyphus, called Odysseus or Ulysses, who in fact turned out to be just as clever as his father, though Sisyphus never gave him a thought and continued to live his life, a life of excesses and parties and pleasure, during which he married Merope, the dimmest star in the Pleiades precisely because she married a mortal, a miserable mortal, a miserable thief, a miserable gangster in thrall to his excesses, blinded by his excesses, among which not least was the seduction of Tyro, the daughter of Sisyphus's brother Salmoneus, whom Sisyphus pursued not because he was interested in Tyro, not because Tyro was particularly sexy, but because Sisyphus hated his own brother and wanted to cause him pain, and for this deed, after his death, he was condemned in hell to push a stone to the top of a hill only to watch it roll down to the bottom and then push it back up to the top of the hill and watch it roll again to the bottom, and so on eternally, a bitter punishment out of all proportion to his crimes or sins, the vengeance of Zeus, it's said, because on a certain occasion Zeus passed through Corinth with a nymph he had kidnapped, and Sisyphus, who was smarter than a whip, seized his chance, and when Asopus, the girl's father, came by in desperate search of his daughter, Sisyphus offered to give him the name of his daughter's kidnapper, but only if Asopus made a fountain spring up in the city of Corinth, which shows that Sisyphus wasn't a bad citizen or perhaps he was thirsty, to which Asopus agreed and the fountain of crystalline waters sprang up and Sisyphus betrayed Zeus, who, in a blind rage, sent him ipso facto to Thanatos, or death, but Sisyphus was too much for Thanatos, and in a masterstroke perfectly in keeping with his craftiness and sense of humor he captured Thanatos and threw him in chains, a feat within reach of very few, truly very few, and for a long time he kept Thanatos in chains and during all that time not a single human being died on the face of the earth, a golden age in which men, though still men, lived free of the anxiety of death, in other words, free of the anxiety of time, because now they had more than enough time, which is perhaps what distinguishes a democracy, spare time, surplus time, time to read and time to think, until Zeus had to intervene personally and Thanatos was freed and then Sisyphus died.

But the faces Junge was making didn't have anything to do with Sisyphus, thought Bubis. They resulted instead from an unpleasant facial tic, well, not *highly* unpleasant, but not pleasant either, that he, Bubis, had noted in other German intellectuals, as if after the war some of them had suffered a nervous shock that manifested itself in this fashion, or as if during the war they had been subjected to an unbearable strain that, once the fighting was over, left this odd and harmless aftereffect.

"What do you think of Archimboldi?" repeated Bubis.

Junge's face turned as red as the sunset swelling behind the hill and then as green as the needles of the pines in the forest.

"Hmm," he said, "hmm." And then his eyes drifted toward the little house, as if he expected inspiration or eloquence or some kind of help to come from it. "To be frank," he said. And then: "Honestly, my opinion isn't . . ." And finally: "What can I tell you?"

"Anything," said Bubis, "your opinion as a reader, your opinion as a critic."

"Very well," said Junge. "I have read him, that's a fact."

They both smiled.

"But there's something," he went on, "something about him . . . I mean, he's German, no doubt about that, his prose is German, crude but German, what I mean to say is, he doesn't strike me as a European author."

"American, perhaps?" suggested Bubis, who at the time was nursing the idea of buying the rights to three novels by Faulkner.

"No, not American either, more like African," said Junge, and he made more faces under the tree branches. "Or rather: Asian," murmured the critic.

"From what part of Asia?" Bubis asked.

"Who knows?" said Junge. "Indochina, Malaysia, at his best he seems Persian."

"Ah, the literature of Persia," said Bubis, who in fact knew nothing about Persian literature.

"Malaysian, Malaysian," said Junge.

Then they went on to talk about other Bubis authors whom the critic held in greater esteem or who interested him more, and they returned to the garden with its view of the crimson sky. Soon afterward Bubis and the baroness took their leave with laughter and friendly words, and those present not only accompanied them to their car but stood in the street waving goodbye until Bubis's vehicle disappeared around the first bend.

That night, after remarking with feigned surprise on the mismatch between Junge and his little house, just before they went to bed at their hotel in Frankfurt, Bubis told the baroness that the critic didn't like Archimboldi's books.

"Does it matter?" asked the baroness, who in her own way, independent as she was, loved the publisher and greatly respected his opinion.

"It depends," said Bubis in his drawers by the window as he peered out into the darkness through a tiny parting of the drapes. "To us, it doesn't really matter. But it matters a great deal to Archimboldi."

The baroness said something in reply, something Mr. Bubis didn't hear. Outside everything was dark, he thought, and he parted the drapes a bit more, just a bit. There was nothing to see. Only his own face, Mr. Bubis's increasingly sharp and wrinkled face, and more and more darkness.

●

It wasn't long before Archimboldi's fourth book arrived at the publishing house. It was called *Rivers of Europe*, although it was really about only one river, the Dnieper. One might say the Dnieper was the protagonist and the other rivers were the chorus. Mr. Bubis read the book in one sitting, in his office, and his laughter as he read it could be heard all over the house. This time the advance he sent Archimboldi was bigger than any previous advance, in fact so large that Martha, the secretary, before mailing the check to Cologne, brought it into Mr. Bubis's office and asked (not once but twice) whether the sum was correct, to which Mr. Bubis answered yes, it was, or it wasn't, what did it matter, a sum, he thought when he was alone again, is always approximate, there is no such thing as a correct sum, only the Nazis and teachers of elementary mathematics believed in correct sums, only sectarians, madmen, tax collectors (God rot them), numerologists who read one's fortune for next to nothing believed in correct sums. Scientists, meanwhile, knew that all numbers were only approximate. Great physicists, great mathematicians, great chemists, and publishers knew that one was always feeling one's way in the dark.

●

Around this time, during a routine medical checkup, Ingeborg was diagnosed with a pulmonary condition. At first she didn't say anything to Archimboldi. Instead she just took the pills prescribed for her by a not very bright doctor, though only erratically. When she began to cough up blood, Archimboldi dragged her to the office of an English doctor, who sent her immediately to a German lung specialist. He told her she had tuberculosis, a common illness in postwar Germany.

With the money obtained for *Rivers of Europe*, Archimboldi, on the instructions of the specialist, moved them to Kempten, a town in the Bavarian Alps, where the cold, dry climate would help to cure Ingeborg. Ingeborg got sick leave from work and Archimboldi gave up his job at the bar. Ingeborg's health didn't improve much, but the days they spent together in Kempten were happy.

Ingeborg had no fear of her tuberculosis because she was sure she wouldn't die of it. Archimboldi brought his typewriter, and in a month, writing eight pages a day, he finished his fifth book, which he called *Bifurcaria Bifurcata* and which was about seaweed, as the title clearly indicated. What most surprised Ingeborg about this book, on which Archimboldi spent no more than three hours a day, occasionally four, was the speed with which it was written, or rather how skillfully Archimboldi handled the typewriter, with the familiarity of a veteran typist, as if Archimboldi were the reincarnation of Mrs. Dorothea, a secretary Ingeborg had met as a girl, when she went in with her father one day to the Berlin offices where he worked, for reasons she no longer remembered.

At these offices, Ingeborg said to Archimboldi, there were endless rows of secretaries typing without pause in a very long, narrow room constantly crisscrossed by a brigade of errand boys dressed in green shirts and brown shorts, who ran ceaselessly back and forth delivering papers or retrieving clean copies of documents from the silver trays beside each secretary. And although each secretary was typing a different document, Ingeborg said to Archimboldi, the typewriters seemed to have one voice, as if they were all typing the same thing or all typing at the same speed. Except for one.

Then Ingeborg explained that there were four rows of desks and their respective secretaries. And that presiding over the four rows, facing them, was a single desk, like a manager's desk, although the secretary who sat there wasn't the manager of anything, she was simply the oldest, the one who had worked the longest at that office or government ministry where her father had brought her and where he was probably employed.

And when she and her father stepped into the room, she drawn by the noise and her father wanting to satisfy her curiosity or perhaps surprise her, the main desk, the head desk (although it wasn't a head desk, let me make that clear, said Ingeborg) was empty and all that could be seen in the room were the secretaries typing at a brisk pace and the boys in shorts and kneesocks trotting down the aisles between the rows, and also a big painting that hung from the high ceiling, at the other end of the room, behind the secretaries' backs, a painting of Hitler contemplating a bucolic landscape, a Hitler with something futuristic about him, the chin, the ear, the lock of hair, but above all he was a Pre-Raphaelite Hitler, and the lights that hung from the ceiling and that, according to her father, were left on twenty-four hours a day, and the dirty glass of the skylights that ran the full length of the room, the light from them not only too faint to type by but too faint for anything else, in fact good for *nothing*, except as a reminder that outside that room and that building there was a sky and probably people and houses, and precisely at that moment, just as Ingeborg and her father had walked all the way down one row and had turned around and were on their way back, Mrs. Dorothea came in through the main door, a tiny old woman, dressed in black and wearing slippers hardly suitable for the cold outside, a little old woman with white hair gathered in a bun, a little old woman who sat at her desk and bent her head, as if nothing existed except her and the typists, and just at that moment and in unison, the typists said good morning, Mrs. Dorothea, all at once, but without looking at Mrs. Dorothea and still typing, which struck Ingeborg as incredible, whether incredibly beautiful or incredibly horrible she wasn't sure, but in any case, after this choral greeting she, the girl Ingeborg, stood as still as if she'd been struck by lightning or as if she were finally in a real church where the liturgy and sacraments and pomp were real, where they ached and throbbed like the ripped-out heart of an Aztec victim, so fiercely that she, the girl Ingeborg, not only stood still but also brought one hand to her heart, as if it had been ripped out, and then, just then, Mrs. Dorothea pulled off her cloth gloves, flexed her translucent hands without looking at them, and with her gaze fixed on a document or manuscript to one side, began to type.

At that instant, said Ingeborg to Archimboldi, I understood that there could be music in anything. Mrs. Dorothea's typing was so quick, so particular, there was so much of Mrs. Dorothea in her typing, that despite the noise or the clamor or the rhythmic beat of more than sixty typists working at once, the music that flowed from the oldest secretary's typewriter rose far above the collective composition of her office mates, without imposing itself on them, but rather adjusting to them, shepherding them, frolicking with them. Sometimes it seemed to reach the skylights, other times it wound along at floor level, brushing the ankles of the visitors and the boys in shorts. Sometimes it even allowed itself the luxury of slowing down and then Mrs. Dorothea's typewriter was like a heart, a giant heart beating in the middle of the fog and chaos. But these moments were scarce. Mrs. Dorothea liked speed and her typing was usually ahead of the other typing, as if she were blazing a path in the middle of a dark jungle, said Ingeborg, dark, dark . . .

•

Mr. Bubis didn't like *Bifurcaria Bifurcata*, to the extent that he didn't even finish reading it, although of course he decided to publish it, thinking maybe that idiot Lothar Junge would like this one.

Before he sent it to the printers, though, he passed it to the baroness and asked for her honest opinion. Two days later the baroness said she had fallen asleep and couldn't get past page four, which didn't discourage Mr. Bubis, who anyway didn't put much stock in the literary judgment of his lovely wife. Soon after he sent the contract for *Bifurcaria Bifurcata* to Archimboldi, he received a letter from the writer stating in no uncertain terms his dissatisfaction with the advance Mr. Bubis intended to pay him. For an hour, as Mr. Bubis ate alone in a restaurant with views of the estuary, he thought about how to answer Archimboldi's letter. His first reaction upon reading it was indignation. Then the letter made him laugh. Finally, it saddened him, which was in part due to the river, which at that time of day acquired the hue of old gilt, gold leaf, and everything seemed to crumble, the river, the boats, the hills, the little stands of trees, each thing going its own way, toward different times and different spaces.

Nothing lasts, murmured Bubis. Nothing remains with us for very long. In the letter Archimboldi said he expected to receive an advance *at least* as big as the advance for *Rivers of Europe*. Really, he's right, thought Mr. Bubis: just because a novel bores me doesn't mean it's bad, it just means I won't be able to sell it and it will take up precious space in my warehouse. The next day he sent Archimboldi a slightly larger sum than the latter had received for *Rivers of Europe*.

•

Eight months after their first stay in Kempten, Ingeborg and Archimboldi returned, but this time the town didn't seem as pretty as it had before, so after two days, by which time both were on edge, they left in a cart headed to a village up the mountain.

Fewer than twenty people lived in the village and it was very near the Austrian border. They rented a room from a man who kept a dairy and lived alone, because he had lost his two sons during the war, one in Russia and the other in Hungary, and his wife had died of sorrow, or so he said, although according to the villagers the man had pushed her into a ravine.

The man's name was Fritz Leube and he seemed happy to have guests, although when he saw that Ingeborg was coughing up blood he was upset, because he thought tuberculosis was highly contagious. In any case, they didn't see much of each other. At night, when he came back with the cows, Leube prepared an enormous pot of soup for himself and his two guests, which lasted a few days. If they were hungry, there were all kinds of cheeses and cured meats in the kitchen and cellar, which they could eat whenever they liked. The bread, big round loaves weighing five or six pounds, he bought from one of the village women or picked up if he passed through some other village or went down to Kempten.

Sometimes Leube uncorked a bottle of brandy and stayed up late talking to Ingeborg and Archimboldi, asking them about the big city (for him this meant any city with more than thirty thousand inhabitants) and furrowing his brow at the answers, often ill intentioned, that Ingeborg gave. At the end of these evenings, Leube would recork the bottle and clear the table, and before he went to bed he would say there was nothing like life in the country. In those days Ingeborg and Archimboldi made love constantly, as if they had some foreboding. They did it in the dark room they rented from Leube and they did it in the front room, in front of the hearth, when Leube had gone to work. The few days they were in Kempten they essentially spent fucking. In the village, one night, they did it in the stable, among the cows, while Leube and the villagers slept. In the mornings, when they got up, they looked as if they'd been in a fight. Both had bruises in different places and enormous circles under their eyes that Leube said were typical of city folk who led unhealthy lives.

To recover they ate black bread with butter and drank big bowls of hot milk. One night, after coughing for a long time, Ingeborg asked Leube how his wife had died. Of sorrow, answered Leube, as he always did. "It's strange," said Ingeborg, "in town I've heard it said you killed her."

Leube, aware of the gossip, didn't seem surprised.

"If I had killed her I'd be locked up by now," he said. "All killers, even those who kill for a good reason, go to prison sooner or later."

"I don't think so," said Ingeborg, "there are many people who kill, especially men who kill their wives, who never end up in prison."

Leube laughed.

"That only happens in novels," he said.

"I didn't know you read novels," answered Ingeborg.

"I did when I was younger," said Leube. "I had time to waste then, because my parents were alive. So how am I supposed to have killed my wife?" he asked after a long silence in which the only sound was the crackle of the fire.

"They say you pushed her into a ravine," said Ingeborg.

"Which ravine?" asked Leube, who was finding the conversation more and more amusing.

"I don't know," said Ingeborg.

"There are lots of ravines around here, ma'am," said Leube, "there's the Lost Sheep ravine and the Flower ravine, the Shadow ravine (so-called because it's always deep in shadow) and the Children of Kreuze ravine, there's the Devil's ravine and the Virgin's ravine, Saint Bernard's ravine and the Slabs ravine, from here to the border post there are more than one hundred ravines."

"I don't know," said Ingeborg, "any of them."

"No, not just any of them, it has to be one in particular, because if I killed my wife by pushing her into any old ravine it's as if I didn't kill her. It has to be a specific one, not any of them," repeated Leube. "Especially," he said after another long silence, "because there are ravines that turn into riverbeds during the spring thaw and everything that's been tossed there or has fallen or anything one tries to hide washes down to the valley. Dogs gone over the edge, lost calves, scraps of wood," said Leube almost inaudibly. "What else do my neighbors say?" he asked after a while.

"That's all," said Ingeborg, looking him in the eye.

"They're lying," said Leube, "they're lying and holding their tongues, there are many other things they could say, but they're lying and holding their tongues. They're like animals, don't you think?"

"No, I hadn't got that impression," said Ingeborg, who in fact had hardly spoken to the few villagers, all too busy at their tasks to bother with strangers.

"And yet," said Leube, "they've had time to inform you about my life."

"Very superficially," said Ingeborg, and then she gave a loud and bitter laugh that made her cough once more.

As he listened to her cough Leube closed his eyes.

When she took the handkerchief away from her mouth the stain of blood was like a giant rose in full bloom.

•

That night, after they had made love, Ingeborg left the village and set out along the mountain road. The snow seemed to refract the light of the full moon. There was no wind and the cold was bearable, but Ingeborg wore her heaviest sweater and a jacket and boots and a wool cap. At the first bend the village disappeared from sight and all she could see was a row of pines and the mountains multiplying in the night, all white, like nuns with no worldly ambitions.

Ten minutes later Archimboldi woke with a start and realized that Ingeborg wasn't in bed. He got dressed, looked for her in the bathroom, the kitchen, and the front room, and then went to wake Leube. The man was sleeping like the dead and Archimboldi had to shake him several times, until Leube opened one eye and gave him a terrified look.

"It's me," said Archimboldi, "my wife has disappeared."

"Go find her," said Leube.

The tug Archimboldi gave him almost tore his nightshirt.

"I don't know where to start," said Archimboldi.

Then he went back up to his room and put on his boots and jacket, and when he came downstairs he found Leube, unkempt but dressed to go out. When they reached the center of the village, Leube gave him a flashlight and told him it would be best if they separated. Archimboldi took the mountain road and Leube started down toward the valley.

When he got to the bend in the road Archimboldi thought he heard a shout. He stopped. The shout came again, it seemed to rise from deep in a gorge, but Archimboldi understood that it was Leube, who was shouting Ingeborg's name as he walked toward the valley. I'll never see her again, thought Archimboldi, shivering with cold. In his hurry, he had forgotten to put on gloves and a scarf and as he climbed in the direction of the border post his hands and face froze so stiff he couldn't feel them anymore, and every so often, he stopped and breathed into his hands or rubbed them together, and pinched his face to no avail.

Leube's shouts came at longer and longer intervals until they couldn't be heard anymore. Sometimes Archimboldi got confused and thought he saw Ingeborg sitting by the side of the road, gazing into the chasms that yawned to either side, but when he came closer he discovered that what he had seen was just a rock or a small pine blown down in a gale. Halfway up his flashlight died and he put it in one of his pockets, although he would happily have tossed it onto the snow-covered slopes. Anyway, the road was bathed in moonlight and a flashlight wasn't necessary. Thoughts of suicide and accidents passed through his mind. He stepped off the road and tested the firmness of the snow. In some spots he sank almost up to his knees. In others, closest to the cliffs, he sank nearly to his waist. He imagined Ingeborg walking with a vacant gaze. He imagined her coming close to one of the ravines. Stumbling. Falling. He too went up to the edge of a ravine. But the moonlight illuminated only the road: the bottom of the gorge was still black, a formless black, in which one could glimpse indistinct shapes and outlines.

He returned to the road and kept climbing. At a certain point he realized he was sweating. Perspiration came hot out of his pores and immediately turned into a cold film that in turn was eliminated by more hot perspiration . . . In any case he was no longer cold. When he had almost reached the border post he saw Ingeborg, standing by a tree, looking up at the sky. Ingeborg's neck, her chin, her cheeks, shone as if touched by a white madness. He ran up to her and threw his arms around her.

"What are you doing here?" asked Ingeborg.

"I was afraid," said Archimboldi.

Ingeborg's face was as cold as ice. He kissed her cheeks until she slipped from his embrace.

"Look at the stars, Hans," she said.

Archimboldi obeyed. The sky was full of stars, many more than could be seen at night in Kempten, and many, many more than it was possible to see on the clearest night in Cologne. It's a very pretty sky, darling, said Archimboldi, and then he tried to take her hand and drag her back to the village, but Ingeborg clung to a tree branch, as if they were playing, and wouldn't go.

"Do you realize where we are, Hans?" she asked, laughing with a laugh that sounded to Archimboldi like a cascade of ice.

"On the mountain, darling," he said, still grasping her hand and trying vainly to embrace her again.

"On the mountain," said Ingeborg, "but we're also in a place surrounded by the past. All these stars," she said, "can you possibly not understand, clever as you are?"

"What is there to understand?" asked Archimboldi.

"Look at the stars," said Ingeborg.

He lifted his gaze: it was true, there were many stars, then he turned to look at Ingeborg again and shrugged.

"You know I'm not as clever as all that," he said.

"All this light is dead," said Ingeborg. "All this light was emitted thousands and millions of years ago. It's the past, do you see? When these stars cast their light, we didn't exist, life on Earth didn't exist, even Earth didn't exist. This light was cast a long time ago. It's the past, we're surrounded by the past, everything that no longer exists or exists only in memory or guesswork is there now, above us, shining on the mountains and the snow and we can't do anything to stop it."

"An old book is the past, too," said Archimboldi, "a book written and published in 1789 is the past, its author no longer exists, neither does its printer or the ones who read it first or the time when it was written, but the book, the first edition of that book, is still here. Like the pyramids of the Aztecs," said Archimboldi.

"I hate first editions and pyramids and I hate those bloodthirsty Aztecs," said Ingeborg. "But the light of the stars makes me dizzy. It makes me want to cry," said Ingeborg, her eyes damp with madness.

Then, waving Archimboldi off, she turned toward the border post, which was a small two-story wooden cabin. A slender plume of black smoke rose from the chimney and dissolved in the night sky, and a sign hung from a pole announcing the border.

Next to the cabin there was a shed without walls where a small truck was parked. There was no light, except for the faint shine of a candle coming through a shutter left ajar on the second floor.

"Let's see whether they have anything hot to give us," said Archimboldi, and he knocked at the door.

No one answered. He knocked again, harder this time. The border post seemed deserted. Ingeborg, who was waiting for him a few steps from the porch, had crossed her arms on her chest and her face had grown pale until it was the same shade as the snow. Archimboldi walked around the cabin. In the back, next to the woodpile, he came upon a good-sized doghouse, but he didn't see any dog. When he returned to the front porch Ingeborg was still standing looking up at the stars.

"I think the border guards are gone," said Archimboldi.

"There's a light," answered Ingeborg without looking at him, and Archimboldi didn't know whether she was talking about the starlight or the light visible on the second floor.

"I'm going to break a window," he said.

He looked around on the ground for something solid and couldn't find anything, so after he had pulled away the wooden shutter, he broke one of the panes with his elbow. Then, with his hands, he carefully removed the shards of glass and opened the window.

A thick, heavy smell struck him in the face as he slid inside. In the cabin everything was dark, except for a dim glow from the fireplace. Next to it, in an armchair, he saw a border guard with his jacket undone and his eyes closed, as if he were asleep, but he wasn't asleep, he was dead. In a bedroom on the ground floor, lying on a bunk, he found another person, a man with white hair in a white undershirt and long underwear.

On the second floor, in the room with the candle visible from the road, there was no one. It was just a room, with a bed, a table, a chair, and a small bookshelf holding several books, most of them Westerns. Moving quickly but cautiously, Archimboldi found a broom and newspaper and then swept up the glass he had broken before, tipping it through the hole in the window, as if one of the two dead men—from inside the cabin, not outside—had caused the damage. Then he went out without touching anything and put his arm around Ingeborg, and like that, with their arms around each other, they returned to the village while the whole past of the universe fell on their heads.

•

The next day Ingeborg couldn't get out of bed. She had a temperature of 104 degrees and by evening she was delirious. At midday, while she was asleep, Archimboldi watched from the window of his room as an ambulance drove by toward the border post. Shortly afterward a police car passed and three hours later the ambulance came by on its way down to Kempten with its load of bodies, but the police car didn't return until six, when it was already dark, and when it reached the village it stopped and the police talked to some of the villagers.

Archimboldi and Ingeborg weren't questioned, possibly thanks to Leube's intercession. By evening Ingeborg had begun to hallucinate and that very night she was taken to the Kempten hospital. Leube didn't accompany them, but the next morning, as Archimboldi smoked in the corridor just inside the entrance to the hospital, he saw Leube appear, dressed in a wool jacket, very old and worn, although not without a certain style, with a tie and a pair of crude low boots that looked handmade.

They spoke for a few minutes. Leube said no one in the village knew about Ingeborg's nighttime flight, and if questions were asked, it would be best if Archimboldi said nothing. Then he inquired whether the patient (that was what he said: the patient) was receiving the proper treatment, although by the way he asked it was clear he assumed it couldn't be otherwise, about the hospital food, about the medicine she was being given, and then, abruptly, he left. Before he went, without saying a word, he handed Archimboldi a package wrapped in cheap paper. Inside was a good chunk of cheese, bread, and two kinds of cured meat, the kind they ate every night.

Archimboldi wasn't hungry, and when he saw the cheese and the cured meat he felt an overpowering urge to vomit. But he didn't want to throw the food away and finally he left it in the drawer of Ingeborg's night table. During the night she was delirious again and didn't recognize Archimboldi. At dawn she vomited blood and when they took her for X-rays she shouted at him not to leave her alone, not to let her die at a miserable hospital like this. I won't, promised Archimboldi in the corridor, as the nurses hurried away with the stretcher where Ingeborg fought for her life. Three days later the fever began to subside, although Ingeborg's mood shifts became more pronounced.

She almost didn't speak to Archimboldi and when she did it was to demand that he get her out of there. In the same room were two other women with lung ailments who soon became Ingeborg's mortal enemies. According to her, they envied her for being from Berlin. After four days the nurses were fed up with Ingeborg and at least one doctor saw her— sitting very still in bed, with her smooth hair falling over her shoulders—

as the incarnation of Nemesis. A day before she was released, Leube appeared again at the hospital.

He came into the room, asked Ingeborg a few questions, and then gave her a little package identical to the one he had given Archimboldi several days before. The rest of the time he remained silent, sitting stiffly in a chair, every so often casting curious glances at the other patients and their visitors. When he left he told Archimboldi he wanted to speak to him in private, but Archimboldi didn't feel like talking to Leube, so instead of taking him to the hospital canteen he stood with him in the corridor, which flustered Leube, who had hoped to talk in a quieter spot.

"I just wanted to tell you," he said, "that the young lady was right. I killed my wife. I pushed her into a ravine. The Virgin's ravine. Actually, I don't remember anymore. It might have been the Flower ravine. But I pushed her into a ravine and I watched her body fall, battered against the outcroppings of rock. Then I opened my eyes and searched for her. There she was down below. A spot of color on the stone slabs. For a long time I stared. Then I went down and slung her over my shoulder and climbed up with her, but she didn't weigh a thing anymore, it was like climbing up with a bundle of sticks. I brought her into the house through the back door. No one saw me. I washed her carefully, I dressed her in clean clothes, I laid her out on the bed. How did no one notice all her bones were broken? I said she had died. What did she die of? they asked. Of sorrow, I said. When you die of sorrow it's as if you've broken all the bones in your body, bruised yourself all over, cracked your skull. That's sorrow. I made the coffin myself in a night's work and the next day I buried her. Then I took care of the papers in Kempten. I won't tell you the clerks thought it was normal. Some were suspicious. I saw the looks on their faces. But I didn't say anything and they registered the death. Then I went back to the village and kept living. Alone forever," he whispered after a long pause. "As it should be."

"Why have you told me this?" asked Archimboldi.

"So you can tell the young lady. I want her to know. It's for her sake I'm telling you, so she knows. Agreed?"

"All right," said Archimboldi, "I'll tell her."

When they left the hospital they returned to Cologne by train, but they didn't last three days there. Archimboldi asked Ingeborg if she wanted to visit her mother. Ingeborg answered that one of her plans was never to see her mother or sisters again. I'd like to travel, she said. The next day Ingeborg applied for a passport and Archimboldi took up a collection among their friends. First they were in Austria and then Switzerland and from Switzerland they moved on to Italy. They visited Venice and Milan, like a couple of vagabonds, and between the two cities they stopped in Verona and slept at the boardinghouse where Shakespeare slept and ate at the trattoria where Shakespeare ate, now called Trattoria Shakespeare, and went into the church where Shakespeare once sat and thought or played chess with the parish priest, because Shakespeare, like the two of them, spoke no Italian, but to play chess there was no need to speak Italian or English or German or even Russian.

And since there wasn't much else to see in Verona, they traveled to Brescia and Padua and Vicenza and other cities along the rail line between Milan and Venice, and then they were in Mantua and Bologna and they spent three days in Pisa making love like mad, and they swam in Cecina and Piombino, across from the island of Elba, and then they visited Florence and made their way to Rome.

What did they live on? Probably Archimboldi, who had learned many things working at the bar on the Spenglerstrasse, turned to petty theft. Robbing American tourists was easy. Robbing Italians was only a little more difficult. Archimboldi might have asked for another advance from the publishing house and he might have received it by mail, or perhaps it was the Baroness Von Zumpe herself who delivered it by hand, curious to meet her former servant's companion.

But the meeting was in a public place, and only Archimboldi came. He had a beer, took the money, thanked her, and left. Or that was how the baroness described it to her husband in a long letter written from a castle in Senigallia where she spent fifteen days lying in the sun and going for long swims. Long swims that Ingeborg and Archimboldi couldn't take or that they postponed for another reincarnation, because Ingeborg's health was failing as summer came to an end, and the possibility of returning to the mountains or checking into a hospital was rejected without further discussion. The beginning of September found them in Rome, both dressed in shorts, dune- or desert-yellow colored, as if they were ghosts of the Afrika Korps lost in the catacombs of the early Christians, lonely catacombs where all that could be heard was the erratic drip of some nearby gutter and Ingeborg's cough.

Soon, however, they drifted toward Florence and from there, walking or hitchhiking, they headed to the Adriatic. By then, the Baroness Von Zumpe was in Milan as the guest of some Milanese editors, and from a café bearing an uncanny resemblance to a Romanesque cathedral, she wrote a letter to Bubis in which she gave news of her hosts, who wished Bubis could be there, and of some Turin editors she had just met, one old and very jovial who always referred to Bubis as his brother-in-arms, and one young, Leftist, very handsome, who said that editors, too, why not, should do their part to change the world. On the same trip, at one party or another, the baroness had met a number of Italian writers, some of whom had books that might be interesting to translate. Of course, the baroness could read Italian, although her daily activities somehow left no time for reading.

Every night there was a party. And when there wasn't a party her hosts conjured one up. Sometimes they left Milan in a caravan of four or five cars and drove to a town on the shores of Lake Garda called Bardolino, where someone had a villa, and dawn often found them all, tired and happy, dancing at some trattoria in Desenzano, under the curious gaze of the locals who had been up all night (or had just risen), drawn by the revelry.

One morning, however, she received a telegram from Bubis saying that Archimboldi's wife had died in a remote village on the Adriatic coast. Without knowing quite why, the baroness began to weep as if she had lost a sister and that same day she informed her hosts that she was leaving Milan for the remote village, without knowing very well whether she would have to take a train or a bus or a taxi, since there was no mention of the village in her travel guide. The young Leftist editor from Turin offered to drive her, and the baroness, who'd had a few dalliances with him, was so grateful that the editor was taken aback.

The trip was a threnody or an epicede, depending on the countryside through which they were passing, recited in an increasingly exaggerated and infectious Italian. At last they reached the mysterious village, exhausted after having gone through an interminable list of dead family members (the baroness's as well as the editor's) and lost friends, some of whom were also dead, though they didn't know it. But they still had the strength to inquire after a German man whose wife had died. The villagers, surly and hard at work mending their nets and caulking their boats, told them that a German couple had in fact arrived a few days before and shortly afterward the man had left alone because the woman had drowned.

Where had the man gone? They didn't know. The baroness and the editor asked the village priest, but he didn't know anything either. They also asked the gravedigger and he repeated like a litany what they had already heard: the German had left a little while ago and the German woman wasn't buried in the cemetery, because she had drowned and her body was never found.

That evening, before they left the village, the baroness insisted on driving up a mountain from which there was a view of the whole area. She saw winding paths in shades of yellow that vanished in the middle of little leaden-colored clusters of trees, the clusters like spheres swollen with rain, she saw hills covered in olive trees and specks that moved with a slowness and bewilderment that seemed of this world and yet intolerable.

•

For a long time there was no news of Archimboldi. Despite expectations, *Rivers of Europe* kept selling and a second edition was printed. Soon afterward the same thing happened with *The Leather Mask*. Archimboldi's name appeared in two essays on new German fiction, though he was mentioned in passing each time, as if the authors of the essays were never entirely sure that some joke wasn't being played on them. A few young people read him. His books were cult objects, a caprice of university students.

•

Four years after Archimboldi's disappearance, Bubis received the weighty manuscript of *Inheritance*, a novel more than five hundred pages long, full of crossings out and addenda and lengthy and often illegible footnotes.

The package had been sent from Venice, where Archimboldi, or so he said in a short letter enclosed with the manuscript, had been working as a gardener, something Bubis thought must be a joke, because work as a gardener, he thought, is hard enough to find in any Italian city, let alone Venice. In any case, the publisher's reply was swift. That same day he wrote back, asking what advance Archimboldi wanted and requesting a more or less reliable address at which to send him the money, *his* money, which had gradually been accumulating over the last four years. Archimboldi's response was even briefer. He gave an address in Cannaregio and signed off with the usual pleasantries, wishing Bubis and his wife a happy New Year, because the end of December was approaching.

Over the course of the next few days, very cold days all over Europe, Bubis read the manuscript of *Inheritance* and despite the chaos of the text, in the end he was left with a feeling of great satisfaction, because Archimboldi had lived up to all the hopes he had placed in him. What hopes were these? Bubis didn't know, or care to know. They certainly didn't involve Archimboldi's steady output, which was something any hack could achieve, or his storytelling powers, of which Bubis had been convinced since *The Endless Rose*, or his capacity to inject new blood into the sclerotic German language, a deed accomplished, in Bubis's judgment, by two poets and three or four fiction writers, among whom he counted Archimboldi. But it wasn't that. What, then? Bubis didn't know, although he felt it, and not knowing didn't trouble him in the least, among other reasons perhaps because knowing only led to trouble, and he was a publisher and God's ways truly were mysterious.

•

Since the baroness was in Italy at the time, where she had a lover, Bubis called her and asked her to go and visit Archimboldi.

He would happily have gone himself, but the years hadn't passed for nothing, and Bubis could no longer travel the way he used to do. So it was the baroness who appeared one morning in Venice, accompanied by a rather younger Roman engineer, a thin, bronzed, handsome man who was sometimes addressed by the title of architect and other times doctor, although he was just an engineer, a civil engineer, and a passionate reader of Moravia, to whom he had introduced the baroness, bringing her to one of Moravia's evenings at home in his sprawling apartment, with a view, when night fell and dozens of spotlights came on, of the ruins of a circus, or perhaps it was a temple, of burial mounds and stones that the very light seemed to muddle and obscure and that Moravia's guests watched in laughter or on the verge of tears from the novelist's huge terrace. The novelist didn't impress the baroness or at least didn't impress her as much as her lover had hoped, since in his mind every word Moravia wrote was golden, but for the next few days the baroness couldn't stop thinking about him, especially after she received the letter from her husband and traveled, accompanied by the Moravian engineer, to wintertime Venice, where they got a room at the Danieli, and the baroness, after she showered and changed, but without having breakfast, went out alone with her lovely hair disheveled, seized by an inexplicable haste.

Archimboldi's address was on Calle Turlona in Cannaregio, and the baroness guessed correctly that the street couldn't be too far from the train station, or perhaps from the church of the Madonna dell'Orto, where Tintoretto had worked all his life. So she got on a vaporetto at San Zaccaria and let herself be carried along the Grand Canal, lost in thought, and then she got off in front of the station, asked for directions, and set out on foot, and meanwhile she thought about Moravia's eyes, which were nice, and Archimboldi's eyes, which she suddenly discovered she couldn't remember, and she also thought how different those two men were, Moravia and Archimboldi, the former bourgeois and practical and worldly, though not above paving the way for certain subtle and timeless jokes (not for his own sake but for the sake of his audience), whereas the latter, especially by comparison, was essentially a man of the lower orders, a Germanic barbarian, an artist in a state of permanent incandescence, as Bubis said, someone who would never see the view from Moravia's terrace, the ruins cloaked in light, and would never hear Moravia's records or go for night strolls around Rome with friends, poets and filmmakers, translators and students, aristocrats and Marxists, as Moravia did, always ready with a kind word, a clever remark, a judicious comment, while Archimboldi addressed long soliloquies to himself, thought the baroness as she walked along the Lista di Spagna to the Campo San Geremia and then crossed over the Ponte Guglie and went down some steps to the Fondamenta Pescaria, the unintelligible soliloquies of a maid's son or a barefoot soldier wandering Russian soil, a hell populated with succubi, thought the baroness, and then for no reason she remembered that in the Berlin of her adolescence some people, especially servant girls from the country, called the pederasts succubi, opening their eyes very wide and pretending to look frightened, little maidservants who left their families to come to the big houses in the rich neighborhoods, girls who delivered long soliloquies that made it possible for them to live another day.

But did Archimboldi really soliloquize to himself? the baroness wondered as she turned down Calle Ghetto Vecchio, or was he addressing someone else? And if so, who was that other person? A dead man? A German demon? A monster he had discovered when he worked on her country estate in Prussia? A monster that lived in the cellars of her house when the boy Archimboldi came to work with his mother? A monster hiding in the Von Zumpe forest? The ghost of the peat bogs? The spirit of the rocky beaches along the rough road between the fishing villages?

Pure blather, thought the baroness, who had never believed in ghosts or ideologies, only in her body and the bodies of others, as she walked through the Campo Ghetto Nuovo and then crossed the bridge to the Fondamenta degli Ormesini, and turned left onto Calle Turlona, all old houses, buildings propping each other up like little old Alzheimer's patients, a jumble of houses and mazelike passageways where distant voices could be heard, worried voices asking questions and offering answers with great dignity, until she reached Archimboldi's door, in a house that gave no clear indication, within or without, as to which floor one was on, whether it was the third or the fourth, perhaps the third and a half.

Archimboldi came to the door. His hair was long and tangled and his beard covered his neck. He was dressed in a wool sweater and wide, dirt-stained trousers, an unusual sight in Venice, where there was only water and stones. He recognized her immediately and when the baroness came in she noticed that his nostrils flared, as if he was trying to smell her. The place consisted of two small rooms, separated by a plaster partition, and a bathroom, also tiny and recently installed. The only window was in the room that served as dining room and kitchen, and it looked onto a canal that flowed into the Rio della Sensa. Inside, everything was a dark mauve, shading to black—a provincial black, thought the baroness—in the second room, where Archimboldi's bed and clothes were.

What did they do that day and the next? Probably they talked and fucked, more the latter than the former, because that night the baroness didn't return to the Danieli, to the distress of her engineer, who had read novels about mysterious disappearances in Venice, especially of tourists of the weaker sex, women seduced by the call of the flesh, women hypnotized by the libido of Venetian pimps, slave women who lived between the same walls as the legitimate wives of their masters, fat wives with mustaches who spoke in dialect and left their caves only to buy vegetables and fish, Cro-Magnon women married to Neanderthal men, and serfs educated at Oxford or in Swiss boarding schools tied by one leg to the bed awaiting the Shadow.

In any case, the baroness didn't come back that night and the engineer got quietly drunk at the bar of the Danieli and didn't go to the police, in part because he was afraid of making a fool of himself and in part because he sensed that his German lover was the type of woman who always emerges unscathed without resort to pleas or demands. And that night there was no Shadow, although the baroness asked questions, not many, and showed herself willing to answer those Archimboldi thought fit to ask.

They talked about his job as a gardener, which was real, a job working either for the city of Venice in the few but well-tended public parks or for certain private citizens (or law firms) who kept inner gardens, some splendid, behind the walls of their palazzi. Then they made love again. Then they talked about how cold it was in Venice, a cold Archimboldi warded off by wrapping himself in blankets. Then they kissed for a long time and the baroness chose not to ask how long it had been since he was with a woman. Then they talked about some American writers who were published by Bubis and who visited Venice regularly, although Archimboldi had never heard of them or read anything by them. And then they talked about the baroness's vanished cousin, the ill-fated Hugo Halder, and Archimboldi's family, whom Archimboldi had finally found.

And just as the baroness was about to ask where he had found his family and under what circumstances and how, Archimboldi got out of bed and said: listen. And the baroness tried to listen, but she couldn't hear anything, just silence, utter silence. And then Archimboldi said: this is what it's about, the silence, do you hear it? And the baroness was about to say that one couldn't hear silence, only sound, but the comment struck her as pedantic and she didn't say anything. And Archimboldi, naked, went over to the window and opened it and leaned half his body outside, as if he planned to throw himself into the canal, but that wasn't his intention. And when he pulled his torso back in, he told the baroness to come and look. And the baroness got up, naked too, and came over to the window and watched as the snow fell on Venice.

•

The last visit Archimboldi made to his publisher was to go over the proofs of *Inheritance* with the copy editor and add about one hundred pages to the original manuscript. This was the last time he saw Bubis, who would die a few years later, not without first having published four more novels by Archimboldi, and it was also the last time he saw the baroness, at least in Hamburg.

At the time, Bubis was immersed in the sweeping and often idle debates of the German writers of the Federal Republic and the Democratic Republic, with intellectuals and letters and telegrams streaming through his office during the day, and at night urgent phone calls that generally led nowhere. The atmosphere at the publishing house was one of feverish activity. Sometimes, however, everything halted, and the copy editor made coffee for herself and Archimboldi and tea for a new girl who worked as a designer, because by now the house had grown and the slate of employees had grown and sometimes, at a nearby desk, there was a young copy editor, Swiss, why on earth he lived in Hamburg no one knew, and the baroness came out of her office and so did the head of publicity and sometimes the secretary, and they talked about all sorts of things, about the last movie they'd seen or the actor Dirk Bogarde, and then the bookkeeper and even Marianne Gottlieb would drop by with a smile, and if the laughter was very loud in the big room where the copy editors worked, then Bubis himself would peer in with his teacup in his hand, and they would talk not just about Dirk Bogarde but also about politics and the dirty business that the new Hamburg officials got up to or they talked about some writers who had no ethical sense, self-confessed and happy plagiarists who hid expressions of mingled fear and outrage behind a cheerful mask, writers prepared to cling to *any* reputation, with the certainty that they would thus live on in posterity, *any* posterity, which made the copy editors and the other employees laugh and even prompted a resigned smile from Bubis, since no one knew better that posterity was a vaudeville joke audible only to those with front-row seats, and then they started to talk about *lapsus calami*, many of them collected in a book published long ago in Paris and fittingly titled *Le Musée des erreurs*, as well as others selected by Max Sengen, hunter of errata. And one thing led to another and it wasn't long before the copy editors got out a book (which wasn't the French *Museum of Errors* or Sengen's text), whose title Archimboldi couldn't see, and began to read aloud a selection of cultured pearls:

"Poor Marie! Whenever she hears the sound of an approaching horse, she is certain that it is I." *Vie de Rancé*, Chateaubriand.

"The crew of the ship swallowed up by the waves consisted of twenty-five men, who left hundreds of widows consigned to misery." *Les Cages flottantes*, Gaston Leroux.

"With God's help, the sun will shine again on Poland." *The Deluge*, Sienkiewicz.

" 'Let's go!' said Peter, looking for his hat to dry his tears." *Lourdes*, Zola.

"The duke appeared followed by his entourage, which preceded him." *Letters from My Mill*, Alphonse Daudet.

"With his hands clasped behind his back, Henri strolled about the garden, reading his friend's novel." *Le Cataclysme*, Rosny.

"With one eye he read, with the other he wrote." *On the Banks of the Rhine*, Auback.

"Silently the corpse awaited the autopsy." *Luck's Favorite*, Octave Feuillet.

"William couldn't imagine the heart served for anything other than breathing." *Death*, Argibachev.

"This sword of honor is the most beautiful day of my life." *Honneur d'artiste*, Octave Feuillet.

"I can hardly see anymore, said the poor blind woman." *Beatrix*, Balzac.

"After they cut off his head, they buried him alive." *The Death of Mongomer*, Henri Zvedan.

"His hand was as cold as a snake's." Ponson du Terrail. And here there was no indication of the source of the *lapsus calami*.

The following unattributed quotes from Max Sengen's collection were particularly notable:

"The corpse stared reproachfully at those gathered around him."

"What can a man do who's been killed by a lethal bullet?"

"Near the city there were roaming whole packs of solitary bears."

"Unfortunately, the wedding was delayed fifteen days, during which time the bride fled with the captain and gave birth to eight children."

"Three- or four-day excursions were a daily occurrence."

And then came the commentary. The Swiss boy, for a start, declared that the Chateaubriand quote was entirely *unexpected*, particularly because one sensed it had a sexual subtext.

"Highly sexual," said the baroness.

"Which is hard to believe considering that it's Chateaubriand," said the copy editor.

"Well, the allusion to horses is clear enough," said the Swiss boy.

"Poor Maria!" the head of publicity exclaimed in conclusion.

Then they talked about Henri, about Rosny's *Fateful Day*, a cubist text, according to Bubis. Or the perfect expression of nervous activity and the pursuit of reading, according to the designer, because Henri read not only with his hands clasped behind his back but also as he strolled about the garden. Which could be very pleasant at times, according to the Swiss boy, who turned out to be the only one of those present who occasionally read as he walked.

"The possibility also exists," said the copy editor, "that our Henri has invented a device that allows him to read with his hands free."

"But how," asked the baroness, "does he turn the pages?"

"Very simple," said the Swiss boy, "with a little stick or metal wand that he manipulates with his mouth and that is, of course, part of the reading device, which probably takes the form of a folding tray. One must also keep in mind that Henri is an inventor, which means he belongs to the class of objective men, and he's reading a novel *by a friend*, which is a great responsibility, because his friend will want to know whether he liked the book, and if he liked it he'll want to know whether he liked it a lot, and if he liked it a lot he'll want to know whether Henri considers it a masterpiece, and if Henri admits he thinks it's a masterpiece his friend will want to know whether he's written one of the great works of French letters, and so on until poor Henri's patience is exhausted, since he surely has better things to do than hang that ridiculous device around his neck and pace up and down the garden."

"In any case," said the head of publicity, "by all indications Henri *doesn't* like what he's reading. He's upset, he's afraid his friend's book is no good, he's reluctant to admit the obvious: his friend has written a piece of trash."

"And how do you deduce that?" the copy editor wanted to know.

"By the way Rosny presents him to us. The hands clasped behind the back: disquiet, absorption. He reads on foot and in constant motion: resistance to the facts, agitation."

"But the act of using the reading machine saves him," says the designer.

Then they talked about the Daudet quotation, which, according to Bubis, wasn't an example of *lapsus calami* but of the writer's sense of humor, and about *Luck's Favorite*, by Octave Feuillet (Saint-Lô 1821–Paris

1890), a highly successful writer in his day and a foe of the realist and naturalist novel, whose works had fallen into the most *grievous* oblivion, into the most *deserved* oblivion, and whose *lapsus*, "Silently the corpse awaited the autopsy," in some sense prefigured the fate of his own books, said the Swiss boy.

"Doesn't Feuillet have something to do with the French word *feuilleton?*" asked old Marianne Gottlieb. "I seem to remember it means both the literary supplement of a particular newspaper and the serial novels published in it."

"They're probably the same thing," said the Swiss boy enigmatically.

"The word *feuilleton* certainly does come from Feuillet, the prince of serial novels," said Bubis, feigning confidence, though he wasn't entirely sure.

"But my favorite is Auback's," said the copy editor.

"He must be German," said the secretary.

"That's a good one: 'with one eye he read, with the other he wrote,' it wouldn't be out of place in a biography of Goethe," said the Swiss boy.

"Leave Goethe alone," said the head of publicity.

"Auback might have been French, too," said the proofreader, who had lived in France for many years.

"Or Swiss," said the baroness.

"And what do you think of 'His hand was as cold as a snake's'?" asked the bookkeeper.

"I prefer Henri Zvedan: 'After they cut off his head, they buried him alive,'" said the Swiss boy.

"There's a certain logic to it," said the copy editor. "First they cut off his head. The killers think the victim is dead, but they're in a hurry to get rid of the body. They dig a grave, toss the body in, cover it with dirt. But the victim isn't dead. The victim hasn't been guillotined. They've cut off his head, which in this case might mean they've cut his throat, or tried to cut his throat. There's lots of blood. The victim loses consciousness. His attackers take him for dead. After a while, the victim wakes. The earth has stanched the bleeding. He's buried alive. There you go. End of story," said the copy editor. "Doesn't that make sense?"

"No," said the head of publicity.

"You're right, it doesn't," admitted the copy editor.

"It makes a little bit of sense, dear," said Marianne Gottlieb, "history is full of special cases."

"But this one doesn't make sense," said the copy editor. "Don't try to make me feel better, Mrs. Marianne."

"I think it does make some sense," said Archimboldi, who couldn't stop laughing, "although it isn't my favorite."

"Which one is your favorite?" asked Bubis.

"The Balzac," said Archimboldi.

"Ah, that's a great one," said the copy editor.

And the Swiss boy recited:

"I can hardly see anymore, said the poor blind woman."

•

After *Inheritance*, the next manuscript Archimboldi sent to Bubis was *Saint Thomas*, the apocryphal biography of a biographer whose subject is a great writer of the Nazi regime, in whom some critics wanted to see a likeness of Ernst Jünger, although clearly it isn't Jünger but a fictional character. At the time, Archimboldi still lived in Venice, as far as Bubis knew, and he was probably still working as a gardener, although the advances and checks the publisher sent him periodically would have permitted him to write full-time.

The next manuscript, however, arrived from a Greek island, the island of Icaria, where Archimboldi had rented a little house in the rocky hills with the sea in the distance. Like the final surroundings of Sisyphus, thought Bubis, and he told Archimboldi so in a letter in which he notified him, as usual, that the text had arrived and been read, and in which he suggested three forms of payment, so Archimboldi could choose the one that suited him best.

Archimboldi's response surprised Bubis. In it he said that Sisyphus, once he was dead, had escaped from hell by means of a legal stratagem. Before Zeus freed Thanatos, Sisyphus asked his wife not to perform the usual funeral rites, knowing that the first thing Death would do was come for him. So when he got to hell, Hades scolded him and all the infernal lords naturally clamored to the skies or the vault of hell and tore out their hair and took offense. But Sisyphus said it was his wife's fault, not his, and he requested permission to return to Earth to punish her.

Hades considered it: the proposal Sisyphus made was reasonable and freedom was granted to him on the condition that he stay away for only three or four days, long enough to get his just vengeance and set in motion, however belatedly, the proper funeral rites. Of course, Sisyphus jumped at the chance—not for nothing was he the craftiest man in the world—and he returned to Earth, where he lived happily to a ripe old age, and didn't go back to hell until his body failed him.

According to some, the punishment of the rock had only one purpose: to keep Sisyphus occupied and prevent him from hatching new schemes. But at the least expected moment, Sisyphus will devise something and he'll come back to Earth, Archimboldi ended his letter.

•

The novel he sent to Bubis from Icaria was called *The Blind Woman*. As one might expect, it was about a blind woman who didn't know she was blind and some clairvoyant detectives who didn't know they were clairvoyant. More books soon came to Hamburg from the island. *The Black Sea*, a theater piece or a novel written in dramatic form, in which the Black Sea converses with the Atlantic Ocean an hour before dawn. *Lethaea*, his most explicitly sexual novel, in which he transfers to the Germany of the Third Reich the story of Lethaea, who believes herself more beautiful than any goddess and is finally transformed, along with Olenus, her husband, into a stone statue (this novel was labeled as pornographic and after a successful court case it became Archimboldi's first book to go through five printings). *The Lottery Man*, the life of a crippled German who sells lottery tickets in New York. And *The Father*, in which a son recalls his father's activities as a psychopathic killer, which begin in 1938, when his son is twenty, and come to an enigmatic end in 1948.

•

He lived for a while on Icaria. Then he lived on Amorgos. Then on Santorini. Then on Sifnos, Syros, and Mykonos. Then he lived on a tiny island, which he called Hecatombe or Superego, near the island of Naxos, but he never lived on Naxos. Then he left the islands and returned to the Continent. In those days he ate grapes and olives, big dry olives which in taste and consistency were like clods of dirt. He ate white cheese and cured goat cheese that was sold wrapped in grape leaves and could be smelled from one thousand feet away. He ate very hard black bread that had to be softened with wine. He ate fish and tomatoes. Figs. Water. The water came from a well. He had a bucket and a jerry can like the kind they used in the army that he filled with water. He swam, but the seaweed boy was dead. Still, he was a strong swimmer. Sometimes he dove. Other times he sat alone on the slopes of the hills covered in scrub, until dusk fell or dawn came, thinking, or so he claimed, but really he wasn't thinking anything at all.

•

After he moved back to the Continent, he was reading a German paper on a terrace in Missolonghi when he learned of Bubis's death.

Thanatos had come to Hamburg, a city he knew like the palm of his hand, while Bubis was in his office reading a book by a young writer from Dresden, a viciously funny book that made him laugh until he shook. His laughter, according to the publicity chief, could be heard in the lobby and the bookkeeper's office and also in the copy editors' office and the meeting room and the reading room and the bathroom and the room that served as kitchen and pantry, and it even reached the office of the boss's wife, which was the farthest away of all.

Suddenly, the laughter ceased. Everybody at the publishing house, for one reason or another, remembered the time, eleven twenty-five in the morning. After a while, the secretary knocked at Bubis's door. No one answered. Afraid to disturb him, she decided to wait. Shortly thereafter she tried to transfer a call to him. No one picked up the phone in Bubis's office. This time the call was urgent, and the secretary, after knocking several times, opened the door. Bubis was slumped over, amid his books artfully scattered across the floor, and he was dead, although the expression on his face was happy.

•

His body was burned and his ashes were scattered over the waters of the Alster. His widow, the baroness, took the helm of the publishing house and declared that she had no intention of selling the company. Nothing was said about the manuscript by the young author from Dresden, who had already had problems with censorship in the Democratic Republic.

When he had finished reading, Archimboldi read the whole story again and then a third time and then he got up shaking and went for a walk around Missolonghi, which was full of memorials to Byron, as if Byron had done nothing in Missolonghi but stroll about, from inn to tavern, from backstreet to little square, when it was common knowledge that he had been too ill to move and it was Thanatos who walked and looked and took note, Thanatos who visited not just in search of Byron but also as a tourist, because Thanatos is the biggest tourist on Earth.

And then Archimboldi wondered whether he should send a card to the publishing house with his condolences. And he even imagined the words he would write. But then he decided that none of it made sense, and he didn't write or send anything.

•

More than a year after Bubis's death, when Archimboldi was living in Italy again, the manuscript of his latest novel, titled *The Return*, arrived at the publishing house. The Baroness Von Zumpe had no desire to read it. She gave it to the copy editor and told her to prepare it for publication in three months.

Then she sent a telegram to the return address on the envelope in which the manuscript had arrived and the next day she was on a plane to Milan. From the airport she made it to the station just in time to catch a train to Venice. That evening, in a trattoria in Cannaregio, she saw Archimboldi and gave him a check for the advance on his new novel and the royalties generated by his previous books.

It was a respectable sum, but Archimboldi put the check in his pocket without a word. Then they began to talk. They ate Venetian sardines with slices of semolina and drank a bottle of white wine. They got up and walked around a Venice that was very different from the snowy wintertime Venice they had enjoyed the last time they met. The baroness confessed that she hadn't been back since.

"I've been here only a little while," said Archimboldi.

They were like two old friends who don't need to say much to each other. It was the beginning of fall, the weather mild, and a light sweater was enough to keep warm. The baroness wanted to know whether Archimboldi still lived in Cannaregio. That's right, said Archimboldi, but not on Calle Turlona.

Among his plans was to head south.

•

For many years Archimboldi's home, his only belongings, were his suitcase, which held clothes and a ream of paper and the two or three books he was currently reading, and the typewriter Bubis had given him. He carried the suitcase in his right hand. The typewriter he carried in his left hand. When the clothes got old, he threw them away. When he had finished reading a book, he gave it away or left it on a table. For a long time, he wouldn't buy a computer. Sometimes he went into stores that sold computers and asked the salespeople how they worked. But at the last minute he always balked, like a peasant reluctant to part with his savings. Until laptop computers appeared. Then he did buy one and after a little while he became skilled in its use. When laptops began to come with modems, Archimboldi exchanged his old computer for a new one and sometimes he spent hours on the Internet, searching for odd bits of news, names no one remembered anymore, forgotten occurrences. What did he do with the typewriter Bubis had given him? He flung it off a cliff onto the rocks!

•

One day, as he was exploring the Internet, he found news of a man by the name of Hermes Popescu, whom he was quick to identify as the secretary of General Entrescu, whose crucified body he'd chanced to observe in 1944, as the German army fought in retreat from the Romanian border. On an American search engine he found the man's life story. Popescu had immigrated to France after the war. In Paris he frequented Romanian exile circles, associating especially with those intellectuals who for one reason or another lived on the Left Bank of the Seine. Little by little, however, Popescu realized that this was all, in his own words, a farce. The Romanians were bitterly anticommunist and they wrote in Romanian and their prospects were bleak, their lives barely illuminated by a few faint rays of religious or sexual light.

Popescu soon found a practical solution. In a few deft moves (moves strongly tinged with the absurd), he insinuated himself into murky business deals in which the underworld, espionage, the church, and work permits mingled. Money flowed in. Buckets of money. But he kept working. He managed teams of undocumented Romanians. Then Hungarians and Czechs. Then North Africans. Sometimes, dressed in a fur coat, like a phantom, he went to visit them in their hovels. The smell of the blacks made his head swim, but he liked it. Those bastards are real men, he liked to say. Secretly, he hoped that the smell would cling to his coat, his silk scarf. He smiled like a father. At times he even cried. In his dealings with the gangsters he was different. Sobriety was his distinguishing feature. Not a ring, not a pendant, nothing shiny, not even the slightest glint of gold.

He made money and then he made more money. The Romanian intellectuals came to see him and asked for loans, they needed money, milk for the children, rent, a cataract operation for the wife. Popescu listened to all of them as if he were asleep, in a dream. He gave them everything they asked for, but with one condition, that they stop writing their screeds in Romanian and do it in French. One day he received the visit of a crippled captain formerly of the Romanian Fourth Army Corps, which had been under the command of Entrescu.

When Popescu saw the captain come in, he leaped like a boy from chair to chair. He got up on the desk and danced a Carpathian folk dance. He pretended to urinate in a corner and a few drops trickled out. The only thing he didn't do was frolic on the rug. The crippled captain tried to imitate him, but his handicaps (he was missing a leg and an arm) and his weakness (he was anemic) prevented him.

"Ah, the nights of Bucharest," said Popescu. "Ah, the mornings of Piteşti. Ah, the skies of Cluj rewon. Ah, the vacant offices of Turnu Severin. Ah, the milkmaids of Bacău. Ah, the widows of Constanta."

Then they walked arm in arm to Popescu's flat, on the Rue de Verneuil, very near the École Nationale Supérieure des Beaux-Arts, where they talked more and drank more and the crippled captain had occasion to give Popescu a detailed account of his life, heroic, yes, but full of adversity. Until Popescu, wiping away a tear, interrupted and asked whether he too had been a witness to Entrescu's crucifixion.

"I was there," said the crippled captain, "we were fleeing the Russian tanks, we had lost our artillery, we were running low on ammunition."

"So you were running low on ammunition," said Popescu, "and you were there?"

"I was there," said the crippled captain, "fighting on the sacred soil of my homeland, in command of a few ragged soldiers, the Fourth Army Corps shrunk to the size of a division and no mess officers or scouts or doctors or nurses or anything reminiscent of a civilized war, just tired men and a contingent of madmen that grew by the day."

"So, a contingent of madmen," said Popescu, "and you were there?"

"There I was," said the crippled captain, "and we were all following General Entrescu, we were all waiting for an idea, a sermon, a mountain, a shining grotto, a lightning bolt in the cloudless sky, a sudden flash of lightning, a kind word."

"So, a kind word," said Popescu, "and you were there waiting for this kind word?"

"Like a man waiting for manna from heaven," said the crippled captain, "I was waiting and the colonels were waiting and the generals who were still with us were waiting and the callow lieutenants were waiting and so were the madmen, the sergeants and the madmen, those who would desert in half an hour and those who were already on their way, dragging their rifles over the parched earth, those who left without knowing very well whether they were heading west or east, north or south, and those who stayed behind, writing posthumous poems in good Romanian, letters to their mothers, notes dampened with tears to the girls they would never see again."

"So, letters and notes, notes and letters," said Popescu, "and did you also succumb to lyricism?"

"No, I had no paper or pen," said the crippled captain, "I had obligations, I had men under my command and I had to do something but I didn't know what to do. The Fourth Army Corps had come to a halt at a country house. More than a house, it was a palace. I had to station the healthy soldiers in the stables and the sick soldiers in the stalls. I settled the madmen in the granary and I took the necessary measures to set it on fire if the madness of the madmen went beyond simple madness. I had to speak to my commanding officer and inform him that on that great estate there was no food at all. And my commanding officer had to speak to a general, and the general, who was ill, had to go up the stairs to the second floor of the palace to inform General Entrescu that the situation was untenable, that there was already a smell of rot, that it would be best to strike camp and head west by forced marches. But General Entrescu sometimes came to the door and other times he didn't answer."

"So sometimes he answered and sometimes he didn't," said Popescu, "and you were an eyewitness to all of this?"

"I was a witness, but I heard more than I saw," said the crippled captain, "I and the rest of the officers of what remained of the Fourth Army Corps, dazed, astonished, confused, some weeping and others choking back tears, some lamenting the cruel fate of Romania, a country that for all its sacrifices and virtues should be a beacon of light, and others gnawing their fingernails, all downcast, downcast, downcast, until at last what was fated came to be. I didn't see it. The madmen grew more numerous than the sane. They left the granary. Some noncommissioned officers began to build a cross. General Danilescu had already left, setting out north at dawn without a word to anyone, leaning on his walking stick and accompanied by eight men. I wasn't in the palace when all of this happened. I was nearby with some soldiers preparing defenses that were never used. I remember we dug trenches and found bones. They're sick cows, said one of the soldiers. They're human bodies, said another. They're sacrificial calves, said the first. No, they're human bodies. Keep digging, I said, never mind, keep digging. But more bones turned up. What the fuck is this? I bellowed. What strange land is this? I shouted. The soldiers stopped digging trenches around the palace. We heard a commotion, but we were too exhausted to go and see what was happening. One of the soldiers said that maybe our comrades had found food and were celebrating. Or wine. It was wine. The cellars had been emptied and there was wine enough for all. Then, as I sat by one of the trenches and examined a skull, I saw the cross. A huge cross that a group of madmen was parading around the palace courtyard. When we got back, with the news that the trenches couldn't be dug because the place looked like a graveyard, and perhaps was a graveyard, everything was over."

"So everything was over," said Popescu, "and did you see the general's body on the cross?"

"I saw it," said the crippled captain, "we all saw it and then everyone began to leave, as if General Entrescu might come back to life at any moment and punish us for what we'd done. Before I left, a patrol of Germans arrived who were also fleeing. They told us the Russians were just two villages away and they weren't taking prisoners. Then the Germans left and soon afterward we were on our way, too."

This time Popescu didn't say anything.

They were both silent for a while and then Popescu went into the kitchen and prepared a steak for the crippled captain, asking him, from the kitchen, how he liked his meat, rare or well done?

"Medium rare," said the crippled captain, still sunk in his memories of that terrible day.

Then Popescu served him a big steak, with a pepper sauce, and offered to cut the meat into little pieces for him. The crippled captain thanked him with an absent air. There was no talk while the meal lasted. Popescu stepped away for a few seconds, saying he had to make a phone call, and when he returned the captain was chewing his last piece of steak. Popescu smiled in satisfaction. The captain raised a hand to his forehead, as if he were trying to remember something or his head hurt.

"Burp, burp, if your body demands it, my good friend," said Popescu. The crippled captain burped.

"How long has it been since you ate a steak like that, eh?" asked Popescu.

"Years," said the crippled captain.

"And did it taste divine?"

"It surely did," said the crippled captain, "but talking about General Entrescu has been like opening a door long barred."

"Unburden yourself," said Popescu, "you're among fellow countrymen."

The use of the plural made the crippled captain jump and look toward the door, but it was clear there were only two of them in the room.

"I'm going to put on a record," said Popescu, "would you like to listen to some Gluck?"

"I've never heard of him," said the crippled captain.

"Some Bach?"

"Yes, I like Bach," said the crippled captain, half closing his eyes.

Back at the captain's side, Popescu poured him some Napoleon cognac.

"Is there anything troubling you, Captain, anything on your mind, any story you want to tell me, any way I can help you?"

The captain's lips parted but then they closed and he shook his head.

"I need nothing."

"Nothing, nothing, nothing," repeated Popescu, settling in his armchair.

"The bones, the bones," murmured the crippled captain, "why did General Entrescu bring us to a palace whose grounds were riddled with bones?"

Silence.

"Maybe because he knew he was going to die and he wanted it to be at home," said Popescu.

"Wherever we dug we found bones," said the crippled captain. "The grounds were brimming with human bones. It was impossible to dig a trench without finding little hand bones, an arm, a skull. What was that place? What had happened there? And why did the madmen's cross, seen from the distance, ripple like a flag?"

"An optical illusion, surely," said Popescu.

"I don't know," said the crippled captain. "I'm tired."

"That's right, you're very tired, Captain, close your eyes," said Popescu, but the captain's eyes had been closed for quite a while.

"I'm tired," he repeated.

"You're among friends," said Popescu.

"It's been a long road."

Popescu nodded silently.

The door opened and two Hungarians came in. Popescu didn't even look at them. With his thumb, index finger, and middle finger very near his mouth and nose, he was keeping time to the Bach. The Hungarians stood watching and waiting for a sign. The captain fell asleep. When the music stopped Popescu got up and tiptoed over to the captain.

"Son of a Turk and a whore," he said in Romanian, though his tone was more thoughtful than brutal.

He beckoned for the Hungarians to approach. One on each side, they lifted the crippled captain and dragged him to the door. The captain began to snore more forcefully and his prosthetic leg came off on the rug. The Hungarians dropped him on the floor and tried in vain to screw it back on.

"You clumsy oafs," said Popescu, "leave it to me."

In a minute, as if he'd done nothing else his whole life, Popescu replaced the leg and then, emboldened, he checked the prosthetic arm.

"Try not to lose any parts along the way," he said.

"Not to worry, boss," said one of the Hungarians.

"Do we take him to the usual place?"

"No," said Popescu, "you'd better throw this one in the Seine. And make sure he stays in!"

"Of course, boss," said the Hungarian who had spoken before.

At that moment the crippled captain opened his right eye and said in a hoarse voice:

"The bones, the cross, the bones."

The other Hungarian gently lowered his eyelid.

"Don't worry," said Popescu, laughing, "he's asleep."

•

Many years later, when his fortune was more than considerable, Popescu fell in love with a Central American actress, Asunción Reyes, a woman of extraordinary beauty, whom he married. Asunción Reyes's career in European film (whether French or Italian or Spanish) was brief, but the parties she gave and attended were literally countless. One day Asunción Reyes asked Popescu to do something for a country in need, since he had so much money. At first he thought she meant Romania but then he realized she was talking about Honduras. So that year, at Christmas, he traveled with his wife to Tegucigalpa, a city that to Popescu, an admirer of contrasts and the bizarre, seemed divided into three clearly distinct groups or clans: the Indians and the sick, who made up the majority of the population, and the so-called whites, actually mestizos, who were the minority who wielded power.

All friendly and degenerate people, affected by the heat and diet or lack of diet, people staring nightmare in the face.

Business opportunities existed, that he saw immediately, but the Hondurans, even the Harvard-educated ones, had a natural tendency to theft, violent theft if possible, so he did his best to give up his original idea. But Asunción Reyes was so insistent that on their second Christmas trip he contacted the country's ecclesiastical leaders, the only leaders he trusted. Once contact had been established and after he had talked to several bishops and the archbishop of Tegucigalpa, Popescu contemplated where to invest his capital, in what branch of the economy. The only functioning, profitable sectors were already in the hands of the Americans. One evening, however, at a gathering hosted by the president and the president's wife, Asunción Reyes had a brilliant idea. It simply occurred to her that it would be nice if Tegucigalpa had something like the Paris metro. Popescu, who was daunted by nothing, and was able to see profit in the most outlandish ideas, looked the president of Honduras in the eye and said he could build it. Everyone got excited about the project. Popescu set to work and made money. More money was made by the president and some ministers and secretaries. Nor did the church come out badly. There were opening ceremonies for cement factories and contracts with French and American companies. The preliminaries lasted for more than fifteen years. With Asunción Reyes, Popescu found happiness, but then he lost it and they were divorced. He forgot the Tegucigalpa metro. Death surprised him in a Paris hospital, asleep on a bed of roses.

•

Archimboldi had almost nothing to do with other German writers, in part because the hotels where they stayed when they went abroad weren't the hotels where he stayed. But he did get to know a distinguished French writer, an older writer whose literary essays had brought him fame and recognition, who told him about a house for the vanished writers of Europe, a place of refuge. The Frenchman was a vanished writer himself, so he knew what he was talking about, and Archimboldi agreed to visit the house.

They arrived at night, in a dilapidated taxi driven by a man who talked to himself. The driver repeated himself, swore, repeated himself again, got angry at himself, until Archimboldi lost patience and told him to concentrate on his driving and be quiet. The old essayist, who didn't seem bothered by the driver's monologue, gave Archimboldi a look of mild reproach, as if he were afraid that the driver—the only one in town, after all—might take offense.

The house where the vanished writers lived was surrounded by trees and flowers in a vast garden, with a pool flanked by white-painted wrought-iron tables and umbrellas and lounge chairs. In the back, in the shadow of some hundred-year-old oaks, there was a space to play petanque, and beyond that was the forest. When they arrived, the vanished writers were in the dining room, having supper and watching the news on TV. There were lots of them and almost all of them were French, which surprised Archimboldi, who had never imagined there were so many vanished writers in France. But what struck him most was the great number of women. All were elderly, some dressed with care, even elegantly, and others in an obvious state of neglect, probably poets, thought Archimboldi, wearing dirty robes and slippers, kneesocks, no makeup, their gray hair sometimes piled in wool caps that they must have knitted themselves.

The tables were waited on, at least in theory, by two servers dressed in white, but the dining room actually worked like a buffet with each writer carrying his own tray and helping himself to whatever he liked. What do you think of our little community? asked the essayist, laughing softly, because at that moment, at the other end of the dining room, one of the writers had fallen down in a faint or been struck down by an attack of something and the two servers were trying to revive him. Archimboldi said it was too soon to tell. Then they found an empty table and filled their plates with something that looked like mashed potatoes and spinach, accompanied by a hard-boiled egg and a grilled steak. To drink they poured themselves little glasses of a heavy, earthy-tasting local wine.

At the end of the dining room, next to the fallen writer, there were now a couple of young men, both dressed in white, as well as the two servers and a circle of five vanished writers who watched as their companion was revived. After they ate, the essayist took Archimboldi to the front desk so he could be formally admitted, but since no one was there to help them they went to the TV room, where several vanished writers were drowsing in front of an announcer talking about fashion and the love affairs of French movie and TV celebrities, many of whom Archimboldi had never heard of before. Then the essayist showed him his bedroom, an ascetic room with a single bed, a desk, a chair, a TV, a wardrobe, a small refrigerator, and a bathroom with a shower.

The window looked out over the garden, which was still lit. A scent of flowers and wet grass drifted into the room. In the distance he heard a dog bark. The essayist, who had remained standing in the doorway as Archimboldi examined the room, handed him the keys and assured him that here, though he might not find happiness, which in any case didn't exist, he would find peace and quiet. Then Archimboldi went down to the essayist's room, which was on the first floor and looked like an exact copy of the room he'd been assigned, not so much because of the furnishings and size, but because of the bareness. Anyone would say, thought Archimboldi, that the essayist was another new arrival. There were no books, no clothes strewn about, no wastepaper or personal effects, nothing to differentiate it from his room except for an apple on a white plate on the nightstand.

As if reading his thoughts, the essayist met his eyes. His expression was perplexed. He knows what I'm thinking and now he thinks the same thing and can't understand it, just as I can't understand it, thought Archimboldi. Actually, the look on their faces was more a look of sadness than perplexity. But there's the apple on the white plate, thought Archimboldi.

"That apple has a scent at night," said the essayist. "When I turn out the light. It smells as strongly as Rimbaud's 'Voyelles.' But everything collapses in the end," said the essayist. "Everything collapses in pain. All eloquence springs from pain."

I understand, said Archimboldi, although he didn't understand at all. Then they shook hands and the essayist closed the door. Since he wasn't yet tired (Archimboldi didn't sleep much, although at times he could sleep for sixteen hours straight), he took a walk around the different parts of the house.

In the TV room only three vanished writers were left, all fast asleep, and a man on TV who was apparently about to be murdered. For a while Archimboldi watched the movie, but then he got bored and went into the empty dining room and then walked down several corridors until he came to a kind of gym or massage room, where a young man in a white T-shirt and white pants was lifting weights as he talked to an old man in pajamas, both of whom glanced at him when he came in and then kept talking, as if he wasn't there. The weight lifter seemed to be an employee and the old man in pajamas looked less like a vanished novelist than like a justly forgotten novelist, the typical hard-luck bad French novelist, most likely born at the wrong time.

When he left the house by the back door, he found two old ladies sitting together on a porch swing at one end of a lighted porch. One was talking in a sweet and chirping voice, like the water of a brook that runs over a bed of flat stones, and the other was silent, watching the dark forest that stretched beyond the petanque courts. The one who was talking struck him as a lyric poet, full of things to say that she hadn't been able to say in her poems, and the silent one struck him as a distinguished novelist, tired of pointless sentences and meaningless words. The first was dressed in youthful, even childish clothes. The second was wearing a cheap bathrobe, sneakers, and jeans.

He said good evening in French and the old ladies looked at him and smiled, as if inviting him to sit down with them, and Archimboldi needed no urging.

"Is this your first night at our house?" asked the youthful old lady.

Before he could answer, the silent old lady said the weather was improving and soon everyone would have to go about in shirtsleeves. Archimboldi said she was right. The youthful old lady laughed, perhaps thinking about her wardrobe, and then she asked what he did.

"I'm a novelist," said Archimboldi.

"But you aren't French," said the silent old lady.

"That's right, I'm German."

"From Bavaria?" the youthful old lady wanted to know. "I was in Bavaria once and I loved it. Everything is so romantic," said the youthful old lady.

"No, I'm from the north," said Archimboldi.

The youthful old lady feigned a shudder.

"I've been to Hanover, too," she said, "is that where you're from?"

"More or less," said Archimboldi.

"The food there is impossible," said the youthful old lady.

Later Archimboldi inquired what they did and the youthful old lady told him she had been a hairdresser in Rodez until she got married and then her husband and children wouldn't let her keep working. The other said she had been a seamstress but she hated to talk about her work. What strange women, thought Archimboldi. When he left them he walked into the garden, moving farther and farther from the house, where many of the lights were still on, as if another guest were expected. Walking aimlessly, but enjoying the night and the country smells, he came to the front entrance, a big wooden door that didn't latch tightly and that anyone could force. To one side he discovered a sign he hadn't seen when he arrived with the essayist. In small, dark letters, the sign said MERCIER CLINIC. REST HOME — NEUROLOGICAL CENTER. Without surprise he understood at once that the essayist had brought him to a mental asylum. After a while he returned to the house and went up the stairs to his room, where he retrieved his suitcase and laptop. Before he left he wanted to see the essayist. After he knocked and received no reply, he entered the room.

The essayist was fast asleep, with all the lights off, although light from the front door came in the window, through the parted curtains. The bedclothes were hardly rumpled. The essayist looked like a cigarette covered with a handkerchief. He's so old, thought Archimboldi. Then he left without a sound and as he crossed the garden again he thought he saw a man in white running full speed along one side of the property and ducking behind tree trunks on the edge of the forest.

Only when he was out of the clinic, on the road, did he slow down and try to catch his breath. The road, a dirt road, ran through woods and gentle hills. Every so often a gust of wind made the tree branches sway and ruffled his hair. The wind was warm. At one point he crossed a bridge. When he got to the edge of town the dogs began to bark. Near the square in front of the station he spotted the taxi that had brought him to the clinic. The driver wasn't there, but when Archimboldi passed the car he saw a shape in the backseat that moved and sometimes cried out. The doors of the station were open, but the ticket windows hadn't opened to the public yet. Sitting on a bench he saw three North Africans talking and drinking wine. They exchanged nods and then Archimboldi went out to the tracks. There were two trains stopped by some sheds.

When he went back into the waiting room one of the North Africans was gone. He sat at the opposite end of the room and waited for the ticket windows to open. Then he bought a ticket on the first train out of town.

•

Archimboldi's sex life was limited to his dealings with whores in the different cities where he lived. Some whores didn't charge him. They charged him at first, but later, when Archimboldi began to form part of the landscape, they stopped, or they didn't always charge him, which often led to misunderstandings that were violently resolved.

•

During all those years the only person with whom Archimboldi maintained more or less permanent ties was the Baroness Von Zumpe. Generally their contact was epistolary, although sometimes the baroness made an appearance in the cities and towns where Archimboldi was living and they went for long walks, arm in arm like two ex-lovers who no longer have many secrets to tell. Then Archimboldi accompanied the baroness to her hotel, the best the city or town had to offer, and they parted with a kiss on the cheek, or, if the day had been particularly melancholy, with an embrace. The next morning the baroness would leave first thing, long before Archimboldi got up and came in search of her.

In their letters, things were different. The baroness talked about sex, which she practiced until a very advanced age, about increasingly pathetic or despicable lovers, about parties at which she enjoyed herself as much as she had when she was eighteen, about people Archimboldi had never heard of, although according to the baroness they were household names in Germany and Europe. Of course, Archimboldi didn't watch TV, or listen to the radio, or read the papers. He heard about the fall of the Berlin Wall thanks to a letter from the baroness, who was in Berlin that night. Sometimes, in an access of sentimentalism, the baroness asked him to come back to Germany. I have come back, Archimboldi answered. I'd like you to come back for good, answered the baroness. Stay for longer. Now you're famous. A press conference wouldn't hurt. Though perhaps that might be too much for you. But at least an exclusive interview with some top cultural reporter. Only in my worst nightmares, Archimboldi wrote her.

Occasionally they talked about saints, because the baroness, like some women with intense sex lives, had a mystical streak, although hers was relatively benign and was satisfied aesthetically or through her collector's enthusiasm for medieval altarpieces and carvings. They talked about Edward the Confessor, who died in 1066 and gave his royal ring as alms to Saint John the Evangelist himself, who naturally returned it to him years later by way of a pilgrim from the Holy Land. They talked about Pelagia or Pelaya, an Antiochene actress who, in her apprenticeship to Christ, changed her name several times and passed as a man and assumed countless identities, as if in a fit of lucidity or madness she had decided that her theater was the whole Mediterranean and her single, labyrinthine performance was Christianity.

With the years, the baroness's writing—she always wrote by hand—grew shakier. Sometimes her letters were indecipherable. Archimboldi could make out only a few words. Prizes, honors, awards, candidacies. Prizes for whom, for him, for the baroness? Surely for him, since in her own way the baroness was extremely modest. He could also decipher: work, printings, the lights at the publishing house, which were the lights of Hamburg, when everyone had gone and only she and her secretary were left, and her secretary helped her down the stairs to the street where a car like a hearse awaited her. But the baroness always recovered and after these near-death letters he received postcards from Jamaica or Indonesia, in which the baroness, in a steadier hand, asked whether he'd ever been to America or Asia, knowing very well that Archimboldi had never left the Mediterranean.

Occasionally a long time passed between letters. If Archimboldi moved, as he often did, he sent her his new address. Sometimes, at night, he woke abruptly, thinking about death, but in his letters he avoided mentioning it. The baroness, however, perhaps because she was older, often talked about death, about the dead people she'd known, the dead people she'd loved and who were now just a heap of bones or ashes, about the dead children she'd never known and would so greatly have liked to know and rock in her arms and raise. At moments like these one might have thought she was going mad, but Archimboldi knew that she always maintained her equilibrium and was frank and honest. In fact, the baroness hardly ever told a lie. Everything was an open book from the time she visited her family's country estate, raising a cloud of dust along the dirt road, with her friends, the golden youth of Berlin, ignorant and proud, whom Archimboldi watched from the distance, from a window of the house, as they got out of their cars, laughing.

At some moment, remembering those days, he asked whether she'd ever had news of her cousin Hugo Halder. The baroness said she hadn't, that after the war Hugo Halder was never heard of again, and for a while, maybe just a few hours, Archimboldi toyed with the idea that he himself was really Hugo Halder. Another time, talking about his books, the baroness confessed that she had never bothered to read any of them, because she hardly ever read "difficult" or "dark" novels like the ones he wrote. With the years, too, this habit had grown entrenched, and once she turned seventy the scope of her reading was restricted to fashion or news magazines. When Archimboldi wanted to know why she kept publishing him if she didn't read him, which was really a rhetorical question since he knew the answer, the baroness replied (a) because she knew he was good, (b) because Bubis had told her to, (c) because few publishers actually read the books they published.

At this point it must be said that upon Bubis's death very few believed the baroness would remain at the head of the publishing house. They expected she would sell the business and devote herself to her lovers and her travels, which were her most famous interests. But the baroness took the reins of the publishing house and there wasn't the slightest dip in quality, because she knew how to surround herself with good readers and also because in purely business matters she showed an aptitude that no one had glimpsed before. In a word: Bubis's business continued to grow. Sometimes, half in jest and half seriously, the baroness told Archimboldi that if he were younger she would name him her heir.

When the baroness turned eighty, this very question was asked of her in Hamburg literary circles. Who would take charge of Bubis's publishing house after her death? Who would be named her official heir? Had the baroness made a will? To whom would she leave Bubis's fortune? There were no relatives. The baroness was the last Von Zumpe. On Bubis's side, not counting his first wife, who had died in England, the rest of his family had disappeared in the concentration camps. Neither Bubis nor the baroness had children. There were no siblings or cousins (except Hugo Halder, who was probably dead by now). There were no nieces or nephews (unless Hugo Halder had had a child). It was said that the baroness planned to leave everything, except the publishing house, to

863

charity, and that some picturesque NGO representatives visited her office as one might visit the Vatican or the Deutsche Bank. There were plenty of candidates to succeed the baroness. The most frequently mentioned was a young man of twenty-five who had a face like Mann's Tadzio and the body of a swimmer, a poet and an assistant professor at Göttingen, whom the baroness had assigned to head the house's poetry list. But everything, in the end, remained in the nebulous realm of rumors.

"I'll never die," the baroness said once to Archimboldi. "Or I'll die at ninety-five, which is the same as never dying."

The last time they saw each other was in a ghostly Italian city. The Baroness Von Zumpe wore a white hat and used a cane. She talked about the Nobel Prize and she also complained bitterly about vanished writers, a custom or habit or joke that she believed to be more American than European. Archimboldi was wearing a short-sleeved shirt and he listened to her carefully, because he was going deaf, and he laughed.

•

And at last we come to Archimboldi's sister, Lotte Reiter.

Lotte was born in 1930 and she was blond and had blue eyes, like her brother, but she didn't grow as tall as him. When Archimboldi went away to war, Lotte was nine and what she most wished for was that he would be given leave and come home covered in medals. Sometimes she heard him in her dreams. The footsteps of a giant. Big feet shod in even bigger Wehrmacht boots, so big they had to be made especially for him, striding along with no regard for puddles or brambles, making a beeline for the house where she and her parents slept.

When she woke up she felt so sad she had to do her best not to cry. Other times she dreamed that she too had gone to war, only to find her brother's body riddled with bullets on the battlefield. Sometimes she told her parents her dreams.

"They're just dreams," said her one-eyed mother, "don't dream those dreams, my little kitten."

But her one-legged father asked about certain details, like the faces of the dead soldiers, what were they like? what did they look like? as if they were asleep? to which Lotte answered yes, exactly as if they were asleep, and then her father shook his head and said: then they weren't dead, little Lotte, it's hard to explain, but the faces of dead soldiers are always dirty, as if the soldiers were working hard all day and at the end of the day they didn't have time to wash their faces.

And yet in the dream her brother's face was always perfectly clean, his expression sad but determined, as if despite being dead he was still capable of many things. In her heart, Lotte believed her brother could do *anything*. And she was always alert for the sound of his footsteps, the footsteps of a giant who one day would approach the village, approach the house, approach the garden where she waited for him and tell her that the war was over and he was coming home forever and from that moment on everything would change. But what exactly would change? She didn't know.

The war, in any case, was endless, and her brother's visits grew farther and farther apart until he stopped coming. One night her mother and father began to talk about him, not knowing that she, in bed, the dun-colored blanket pulled up to her chin, was awake and could hear them, and they talked about him as if he were already dead. But Lotte knew her brother hadn't died, because giants never die, she thought, or they die only when they're very old, so old one doesn't even notice they've died, they just sit at the door to their houses or under a tree and fall asleep and then they're dead.

One day they had to leave the village. According to her parents they had no choice because the war was coming. Lotte thought that if the war was coming her brother was coming too, because he lived inside the war the way a fetus lives inside a fat woman, and she hid so they wouldn't take her because she was sure Hans was on his way. For hours they looked for her and at dusk her one-legged father found her hiding in the forest. He gave her a slap and dragged her after him.

As they moved west, along the coast, they passed two columns of soldiers and Lotte called after them, asking whether they knew her brother. The first column was made up of soldiers of all ages, old men like her father and fifteen-year-old boys, some with only half a uniform, and none of them seemed very pleased to be going where they were going, but they all answered Lotte's question politely, saying they didn't know her brother and hadn't seen him.

The second column was made up of ghosts, corpses just risen from a graveyard, specters in gray or verdigris uniforms and steel helmets, invisible to all eyes except Lotte's, and she repeated her question, which a few scarecrows deigned to answer, saying yes, they'd seen him in Soviet country, fleeing like a coward, or they'd seen him swimming in the Dnieper and then drowning, as he well deserved, or they'd seen him on the Kalmuk Steppe, gulping water as if he were dying of thirst, or they'd seen him crouching in a forest in Hungary, wondering how to shoot himself with his own rifle, or they'd seen him on the edge of a cemetery, the stupid bastard, not daring to go in, pacing back and forth until night fell and the cemetery emptied of relatives and only then, the faggot, did he stop pacing and climb the walls, digging his hobnailed boots into the red, crumbling bricks and poking his nose and blue eyes over the edge, peering down at where the dead lay, the Grotes and the Kruses, the Neitzkes and the Kunzes, the Barzes and the Wilkes, the Lemkes and the Noacks, discreet Ladenthin and brave Voss, and then, emboldened, he climbed to the top of the wall and sat there for a while, his long legs dangling, and then he stuck out his tongue at the dead, and then he took off his helmet and pressed both hands to his temples, and then he closed his eyes and howled, that was what the specters told Lotte, as they laughed and marched behind the column of the living.

Then Lotte's parents stopped for a while in Lübeck, along with many others from their village, but her father said the Russians would come and he took his family and kept walking west, and then Lotte lost all sense of time, the days were like nights and the nights like days, and sometimes the days and nights were unlike anything, everything was a continuum of blinding brightness and explosions.

One night Lotte saw shadows listening to the radio. One of the shadows was her father. Another shadow was her mother. Other shadows had eyes and noses and mouths that she didn't recognize. Mouths like carrots, with peeling lips, and noses like wet potatoes. They all had their heads and ears covered with kerchiefs and blankets and on the radio a man's voice said Hitler didn't exist, that he was dead. But not existing and dying were different things, thought Lotte. Until then her first menstrual period had been late in coming. Earlier that day, however, she had begun to bleed and she didn't feel well. Her one-eyed mother told her it was normal, the same thing happened sooner or later to all women. My brother the giant doesn't exist, thought Lotte, but that doesn't mean he's dead. The shadows didn't notice her presence. Some sighed. Others began to weep.

"Mein führer, mein führer," they cried without raising their voices, like women who haven't yet begun to menstruate.

Her father didn't weep. Her mother did weep and the tears flowed only from her good eye.

"He's stopped existing," said the shadows, "he's dead."

"He died like a soldier," said one of the shadows.

"He's stopped existing."

Then they left for Paderborn, where a brother of Lotte's one-eyed mother lived, but when they got there the house was occupied by refugees. They moved in, though there was no sign of the brother. A neighbor told them that unless he was greatly mistaken they would never see him again. For a while they lived on charity, handouts from the English. Then Lotte's one-legged father fell ill and died. His last wish was to be buried in his village with military honors, and his wife and Lotte told him they would make sure it happened, yes, yes, we promise, but his remains were tossed in the common grave in the Paderborn cemetery. There was no time for ceremony, although Lotte suspected that this was *precisely* the time for ceremony, for gallant gestures, for attention to detail.

The refugees left and Lotte's one-eyed mother took possession of her brother's house. Lotte found work. Later she went back to school. Not for long. She returned to work. She quit. She went back to school again for a little while. She found another job, a better one. She left school for the last time. Her one-eyed mother found a boyfriend, an old man who'd been a civil servant in the days of the kaiser and during the Nazi years and had taken up the same job again in postwar Germany.

"A German civil servant," said the old man, "isn't easy to find, even in Germany."

That was the sum total of his shrewdness, his intelligence, his astuteness. And for him it was enough. By then Lotte's one-eyed mother didn't want to return to the village, which had ended up in the Soviet zone. Nor did she want to see the sea again. Nor did she show much interest in learning the fate of her lost son. He must be buried in Russia, she said with a hard, resigned shrug. Lotte began to go out. First she dated an English soldier. Then, when the soldier was transferred, she dated a boy from Paderborn, a boy whose middle-class family wasn't pleased by his romance with the giddy blond girl, because Lotte, in those days, knew every popular dance. What she cared about was being happy, and she cared about the boy, too, not his family, and they were together until he left for university and then their relations ended.

One night her brother appeared. Lotte was in the kitchen, ironing a dress, and she heard his footsteps. It's Hans, she thought. When a knock came on the door she ran to let him in. He didn't recognize her, because she was a woman now, as he told her later, but she had no need to ask him any questions and she clung to him for a long time. That night they talked until dawn and Lotte had time to iron not just her dress but also all her clean clothes. After a few hours Archimboldi fell asleep, with his head resting on the table, and he woke only when his mother touched his shoulder.

Two days later he left and everything returned to normal. By then Lotte's one-eyed mother had replaced the civil servant with a mechanic, a jovial man with his own business, who was doing very well repairing vehicles for the occupation troops and trucks for the farmers and factory owners of Paderborn. As he said himself, he could have found a younger, prettier woman, but he preferred someone decent and hardworking, who wouldn't suck his blood like a vampire. The mechanic's shop was big and at Lotte's mother's request he found a job there for Lotte, but she refused it. Shortly before her mother married the mechanic, Lotte met Werner Haas, a worker at the shop, and since they liked each other and never fought they began to go out together, first to the movies, then to dance halls.

One night Lotte dreamed that her brother appeared outside her bedroom window and asked why their mother was going to marry. I don't know, answered Lotte from her bed. Don't you ever get married, her brother said. Lotte nodded and then her brother's head disappeared and all that was left was the frost-covered window and an echo of the giant's footsteps. But when Archimboldi came to Paderborn, after his mother's marriage, Lotte introduced him to Werner Haas and they seemed to get along.

When her mother got married, the two women went to live at the mechanic's house. The mechanic thought Archimboldi must be a crook, someone who lived off swindles or thieving or black market deals.

"I can smell swindlers at one hundred yards," said the mechanic.

His wife didn't say anything. Lotte and Werner Haas discussed it. According to Werner, the crook was the mechanic, who smuggled parts over the border and often said a car was fixed when it wasn't. Werner, thought Lotte, was a good person, always with a kind word for everyone. Around this time it occurred to Lotte that she and Werner and all the young people born around 1930 or 1931 were fated to be unhappy.

Werner, who was her confidant, listened to her without saying anything, and then they went to the movies, to see American or English films, or they went out dancing. Some weekends they went to the country, especially after Werner bought a broken-down motorcycle that he repaired himself in his free time. For these picnics Lotte prepared sandwiches of black bread and white bread, a bit of kuchen, and never more than three bottles of beer. Werner, meanwhile, filled a canteen with water and sometimes brought sweets and chocolates. On occasion, after walking and eating in the woods, they spread a blanket on the ground and fell asleep holding hands.

The dreams Lotte had in the country were disturbing. She dreamed about dead squirrels and dead deer and dead rabbits, and sometimes she thought she saw a wild boar in the undergrowth and she approached it very slowly, and when she parted the branches she saw an enormous female boar lying on the ground, in its death throes, surrounded by hundreds of little dead boars. When this happened she woke with a start and only the sight of Werner next to her, sleeping placidly, could soothe her. For a while she thought about becoming a vegetarian. Instead, she took up smoking.

Back then, in Paderborn and all over Germany, it was common for women to smoke, but in Paderborn, at least, few did so in public, when they were out for a walk or on their way to work. Lotte was one of the few who smoked openly. She lit her first cigarette early in the morning and as she walked to the bus stop she was already on her second of the day. Werner didn't smoke, and although Lotte insisted he take it up, the most he would do, to make her happy, was to take a few puffs on her cigarette and nearly choke.

When Lotte began to smoke, Werner asked her to marry him.

"I have to think about it," said Lotte, "but for weeks or months, not a day or two."

Werner told her to take all the time she needed, because he wanted their marriage to last a lifetime and he knew it was important not to make a hasty decision. From then on Lotte and Werner saw less of each other. When Werner noticed, he asked her whether she had stopped loving him and when Lotte answered that she was trying to decide whether to marry him or not, he regretted having asked her. They no longer went on excursions as regularly as before, nor did they go to the movies or out to dance. Around the same time, Lotte met a man who worked at a pipe factory that had just been built in the city and she began to see this man, an engineer named Heinrich who lived in a boardinghouse downtown, because his real home was in Duisburg, the site of the factory's main plant.

Shortly after she began to spend time with him, Heinrich confessed that he was married and had a child, but he didn't love his wife and was planning to get a divorce. Lotte didn't care that he was married but she did care that he had a child, because she loved children and the idea of hurting a child, even indirectly, seemed horrible to her. Even so, they saw each other for almost two months, and sometimes Lotte talked to Werner and Werner asked her how things were going with her new boyfriend and Lotte said fine, normal, typical. In the end, however, it became clear that Heinrich would never leave his wife and she broke things off with him, although every so often they went to the movies and then out to dinner.

One day, when she left work, Werner was outside on his motorcycle, waiting for her. This time he didn't talk about marriage or love but just invited her to a café and then took her home. Gradually they began to see each other again, which pleased Lotte's mother and the mechanic, the latter of whom had no children and liked it that Werner was serious and hardworking. The nightmares that had troubled Lotte since childhood came less frequently, until finally they were gone, and she never dreamed at all.

"I'm sure I dream," she said, "like everybody, but I'm lucky enough not to remember anything when I wake up."

When she told Werner that she had thought long enough about his proposal and she would marry him, he began to cry and in a choked voice confessed that he had never been happier than he was at that instant. Two weeks later they were married and during the party, which was held on a restaurant terrace, Lotte remembered her brother, and for a moment she wasn't sure—maybe because she'd had too much to drink—whether she'd invited him to the wedding or not.

They spent their honeymoon in a small spa on the banks of the Rhine and then they each returned to their respective jobs and life went on exactly as it had before. Living with Werner, even in a one-room flat, was easy, because her husband did everything he could to make her happy. On Saturday they went to the movies, on Sundays they often rode into the country on the motorcycle or went dancing. During the week, despite how hard he worked, Werner managed to help her with all the chores. The only thing he couldn't do was cook. At the end of the month, he often bought her a present or took her to the center of Paderborn to choose a pair of shoes or a blouse or a scarf. So that there would be enough money, Werner began to work overtime at the shop or sometimes he did jobs of his own, behind the mechanic's back, fixing tractors or combines for farmers, who didn't pay much but instead gave him sausages and meat and even sacks of flour, which made it look as if Lotte's kitchen was a storeroom or as if the two of them were preparing for the next war.

One day, without having shown any signs of illness, the mechanic died and Werner took over the shop. Some relatives appeared, distant cousins who demanded their share of the inheritance, but Lotte's one-eyed mother and her lawyers fixed everything and in the end the country cousins left with a bit of money and little else. By then Werner had gotten fat and begun to lose his hair, and although there was less physical work, his responsibilities grew, which made him quieter than ever. The two of them moved into the mechanic's flat, which was big but right over the shop, so that the boundary between work and home faded and Werner was always working.

Deep down he would have preferred that the mechanic hadn't died or that Lotte's one-eyed mother had put someone else in charge of the shop. Of course, the new job also had its compensations. That summer Lotte and Werner spent a week in Paris. And for Christmas they went to Lake Constanza with Lotte's mother, because Lotte loved to travel. Back in Paderborn, too, something new happened; for the first time they talked about the possibility of having a baby, something neither of the two was inclined to favor because of the Cold War and the threat of nuclear attack, even though their financial situation had never been better.

For two months they discussed in rather halfhearted fashion the repercussions of taking such a step, until one morning, at breakfast, Lotte told Werner she was pregnant and there was nothing else to discuss. Before the baby was born they bought a car and for more than a week they vacationed in the south of France and in Spain and Portugal. On the way home Lotte asked to drive through Cologne and they went looking for the only address she had for her brother.

In the place where Archimboldi had once lived with Ingeborg, there now rose a new apartment building and no one who lived there remembered a young man matching Archimboldi's description, tall and blond, bony, a former soldier, a giant.

For half the ride home Lotte was quiet, as if in a sulk, but then they stopped to eat at a roadside restaurant and talked about the cities they'd seen and her mood improved considerably. Three months before her son was born, Lotte stopped working. The birth was normal and quick, although the boy weighed more than nine pounds and according to the doctors he was in the wrong position. But at the last minute, it seemed, the baby turned head down and everything was fine.

They called him Klaus, after Lotte's maternal grandfather, although at some point Lotte thought about calling him Hans, after her brother. But the name doesn't really matter, thought Lotte, what matters is the person. From the beginning Klaus was his grandmother's and father's darling, but the boy loved Lotte best. Sometimes she looked at him and saw a resemblance to her brother, as if Klaus were Hans's reincarnation in miniature, which pleased her because until then she had always associated her brother with all things large and outsized.

When Klaus was two, Lotte got pregnant again, but four months later she had a miscarriage, and something must have gone wrong because she couldn't have any more children. Klaus had the childhood of a typical middle-class boy in Paderborn. He liked to play soccer with his friends, but at school he played basketball. Only once did he come home with a black eye. As he explained it, a classmate had made fun of his one-eyed grandmother and they had fought. He wasn't a brilliant student, but he had a great liking for machines of any kind, and he could spend hours in the shop watching his father's mechanics work. He almost never got sick, although the few times he did his temperature soared and he was delirious and saw things no one else could see.

When he was twelve his grandmother died of cancer in the Paderborn hospital. She was on a constant morphine drip and when Klaus went to see her she confused him with Archimboldi and called him my son or talked to him in the dialect of the Prussian village where she was born. Sometimes she told him things about his one-legged grandfather, about the years the old soldier had served faithfully under the kaiser and how much he always regretted not being tall enough to join the elite Prussian regiment that admitted only soldiers over five foot eleven.

"Small in stature, but brave as they come, that was your father," said his grandmother with a morphine-addled smile.

Until then no one had told Klaus anything about his uncle. After his grandmother's death he asked Lotte about him. He wasn't really very interested, but he felt so sad he thought it might take his mind off things. It had been a long time since Lotte thought about her brother and Klaus's question came as something of a surprise. Around this time Lotte and Werner had gotten involved in real estate, which neither of them knew anything about, and they were afraid of losing money. So Lotte's answer was vague: she told him that his uncle was ten years older than she was, more or less, and that the way he made a living wasn't exactly a model for young people, more or less, and that it had been a long time since the family had news of him, because he had disappeared from the face of the earth, more or less.

Later she told Klaus that when she was little she thought her brother was a giant, but that this was the sort of thing little girls often imagined.

Another time Klaus asked Werner about his uncle and Werner said he was a nice man, quiet and very observant, although according to Lotte her brother hadn't always been like that, it was the artillery, the mortars, the bursts of machine gun fire during the war that had made him quiet. When Klaus asked whether he looked like his uncle, Lotte said yes, there was a resemblance, they were both tall and thin, but Klaus's hair was much blonder than her brother's and his eyes might be a brighter blue. Then Klaus stopped asking questions and life went on as it had before his one-eyed grandmother's death.

The new business projects didn't turn out as well as Lotte and Werner had hoped, but they didn't lose money and in fact they made a bit, although they didn't get rich. The shop continued to work at full capacity and no one could have said things were going badly.

At seventeen Klaus got in trouble with the police. He wasn't a good student and his parents had accepted that he wouldn't go to college, but at seventeen he got mixed up, with two friends, in the theft of a car and a later case of sexual assault involving an Italian girl who worked at a small medical supply factory. Klaus's two friends spent a while in prison, because they were legally adults. Klaus was sent to a reformatory for four months and then he came home to his parents. During his time at the reformatory he worked in the repair shop and learned how to fix all kinds of appliances, from refrigerators to blenders. When he got home he was given a job in his father's shop and for a while he stayed out of trouble.

Lotte and Werner tried to convince each other that their son was back on the right track. At eighteen Klaus dated a girl who worked at a bakery, but the relationship lasted scarcely three months, in Lotte's opinion because the girl wasn't exactly a beauty. After that, they didn't meet any other girlfriends and they came to the conclusion that Klaus didn't have any or that for unknown reasons he avoided bringing them home. Around this time, Klaus took up drinking, and at the end of the workday he would go to the beer halls of Paderborn to drink with other young workers from the shop.

More than once, on a Friday or Saturday night, he got into trouble, nothing out of the ordinary, fights with other youths and vandalism, and Werner had to pay the fine and collect him from the police station. One day Klaus decided that Paderborn was too small for him and he left for Munich. Sometimes he called his mother collect and they had forced, trivial conversations that Lotte nevertheless found comforting.

A few months went by before Lotte saw him again. According to Klaus, there was no future in Germany or Europe and the only thing left for him was to try his luck in America, where he planned to go as soon as he could save some money. After he'd worked at the shop for a few months he set sail from Kiel on a German ship whose final destination was New York. When he left Paderborn, Lotte wept: her son was very tall and hardly fragile looking, but still she wept because she had a feeling he wouldn't be happy on the new continent, where the men weren't as tall or as blond as he was, but they were clever and often ill intentioned, the dregs of society, people one couldn't trust.

Werner drove Klaus to Kiel and when he got back to Paderborn he told Lotte the ship was fine, sturdy, it wouldn't sink, and there was nothing dangerous about Klaus's job as a waiter and part-time dishwasher. But his words didn't calm Lotte, who had refused to go to Kiel so as not to "prolong the agony."

When Klaus reached New York he sent his mother a postcard of the Statue of Liberty. This lady is on my side, he wrote. Then months went by and they didn't hear from him. Then more than a year. Until they received another postcard in which he told them he was applying for U.S. citizenship and he had a good job. The return address was Macon, Georgia, and Lotte and Werner each wrote a letter full of questions about his health, his finances, his future plans, which Klaus never answered.

With time, Lotte and Werner got used to the idea that Klaus had left the nest and was fine. Sometimes Lotte imagined him married to an

American, living in a sunny American house, and leading a life similar to the lives one could see in the American movies shown on television. In Lotte's dreams, however, Klaus's American wife had no face. Lotte always saw her from behind, that is, she saw her blond hair, just a shade darker than Klaus's, her tanned shoulders, and her slender, upright figure. She saw Klaus's face, looking serious or expectant, but she never saw his wife's face or the faces of his children, when she imagined him with children. In fact, she never even saw Klaus's children from behind. She *knew* they were there, in some room, but she didn't see them, nor did she hear them, which was the oddest thing, because children are hardly ever quiet for long.

Some nights Lotte spent so long thinking about the life she had imagined for Klaus that she fell asleep and dreamed about her son. Then she saw a house, an American house, but a house she didn't identify as an American house. As she approached the house she could smell something pungent, unpleasant at first, but then she thought: Klaus's wife must be cooking Indian food. And so, in a matter of seconds, the smell became an exotic smell, even pleasant. Then she saw herself sitting at a table. On the table there was a pitcher, an empty plate, a plastic cup, and a fork, nothing else, but all she could think about was who had let her in. No matter how she tried she couldn't remember and that troubled her greatly.

Her suffering was like the screech of chalk on a blackboard. As if a boy were dragging a piece of chalk across a blackboard on purpose to make it screech. Or maybe it wasn't chalk but the boy's fingernails, or maybe it wasn't his fingernails but his teeth. As time went by, this nightmare, the Klaus nightmare, as she called it, became a recurring dream. Sometimes, in the morning, as she helped Werner with breakfast, she would say:

"I had a nightmare."

"The Klaus nightmare?" Werner would ask.

And Lotte, her eyes averted and a distracted expression on her face, would nod. Secretly, both she and Werner hoped that at some point Klaus would come to them asking for money, but the years went by and Klaus seemed lost forever in the United States.

"Knowing Klaus," said Werner, "I wouldn't be surprised if he was living in Alaska by now."

One day Werner got sick and the doctors ordered him to stop working. Since money wasn't a problem he turned the shop over to one of the most experienced mechanics and he and Lotte set out to travel. They took a cruise on the Nile, they visited Jerusalem, they drove a rental car around the south of Spain, they saw Florence and Rome and Venice. The first destination they chose, however, was the United States. They stopped in New York and then they visited Macon, Georgia, and they discovered with sorrow that the house where Klaus had lived was an apartment in an old building near the black ghetto.

On this trip, possibly due to the many American movies they had seen together, it occurred to them that they should hire a detective. They visited one in Atlanta and explained their problem. Werner spoke some English and the detective, a former Atlanta cop, wasn't shy. He left them sitting in his office while he went out to buy an English-German dictionary, then he came running back and picked up the conversation without a break. And he wasn't out to get their money, because from the start he warned them that looking for a naturalized American citizen after so much time was like looking for a needle in a haystack.

"He might even have changed his name," he said.

But they wanted to try and they paid a month's fee and the detective agreed to send the results of his inquiries to Germany. When the month was up a big envelope arrived in Paderborn, in which the detective itemized his expenses and gave an account of the investigation.

Sum total: nothing.

He had managed to find a man who'd known Klaus (the landlord of the building where Klaus lived), which led him to another man, someone Klaus had worked for, but when Klaus left Atlanta he didn't tell either of the two where he planned to go. The detective suggested other lines of inquiry, but to pursue them he needed more money, and Werner and Lotte decided to thank him for his trouble and end the arrangement, at least for now.

A few years later Werner died of heart disease and Lotte was left alone. Any other woman in her situation might well have been devastated, but Lotte didn't let herself be overcome by fate, and instead of sitting idle she doubled and tripled her daily activities. Not only did she keep her investments profitable and the shop in good order but with her remaining capital she got into other businesses and was successful.

Work, a surfeit of work, seemed to rejuvenate her. She was always poking her nose into things, she was never still, some of her employees grew to hate her, but she didn't care. On her vacations, never longer than a week or a week and a half, she sought the warmth of Italy or Spain and sunned herself on the beach or read bestsellers. Sometimes she went on excursions with casual acquaintances, but usually she left the hotel alone and crossed the street to the beach, where she paid a boy to set up a lounge chair and an umbrella. There she took off the top of her bikini or pulled her suit down around her waist, not caring that her breasts weren't what they used to be, and slept in the sun. When she woke she adjusted the umbrella and went back to her book. Sometimes the boy who rented the lounge chairs and umbrellas came by and Lotte gave him money to bring her a rum and Coke or a little pitcher of sangria with lots of ice from the hotel. Sometimes, at night, she sat out on the terrace at the hotel or went to the club, which was on the ground floor and was frequented by German, English, and Dutch men and women more or less her age, and she spent a while watching the couples dance or listening to the orchestra, which occasionally played songs from the early sixties. Seen from the distance, she looked like a lady with a pretty face, someone a little plump, aloof, with a touch of elegance and a certain indefinable sadness. From up close, when a widower or a divorcé asked her to dance or to come for a walk along the beach and Lotte smiled and said no, thank you, she became a country girl again and the refinement vanished and only the sadness was left.

In 1995 she received a telegram from Mexico, from a place called Santa Teresa, in which she was informed that Klaus was in prison. The sender was Isabel Santolaya, Klaus's lawyer. Lotte suffered such a shock that she had to leave her office, go upstairs, and get into bed, although of course she couldn't sleep. Klaus was alive. That was all that mattered to her. She answered the telegram, including her phone number, and four days later, after two operators had asked her whether she would accept the collect call, she heard the voice of a woman speaking to her in English, very slowly, enunciating each syllable, though she still didn't understand anything because she didn't know English. At last the woman's voice said, in a kind of German: "Klaus fine." And: "Translator." And something else that sounded German, or that sounded German to Isabel Santolaya and that Lotte didn't understand. And a phone number, which Isabel Santolaya dictated in English, several times, and which Lotte wrote down on a piece of paper, because everyone knew the numbers in English.

That day Lotte didn't work. She called a secretarial school and said she wanted to hire a girl who spoke perfect English and Spanish, although more than one mechanic at the shop knew English and could have helped her. At the school they told her they had the girl she was looking for and asked when she was needed. Right away, Lotte said. Three hours later a girl of about twenty-five appeared at the shop. She had straight brown hair, was wearing jeans, and joked with the mechanics before she made her way up to Lotte's office.

The girl's name was Ingrid and Lotte explained that her son was in prison in Mexico and she needed to talk to his Mexican lawyer, but the lawyer spoke only English and Spanish. After Lotte finished she thought she would have to explain it all again, but Ingrid was a sharp girl and it wasn't necessary. She picked up the phone and called a public information line to find out the time difference with Mexico. Then she called the lawyer and spent almost fifteen minutes talking to her in Spanish, although occasionally she switched to English to clarify certain terms, and as she was talking she took notes. Finally she said: we'll call you back, and hung up.

Lotte was sitting at her desk and when Ingrid hung up she prepared herself for the worst.

"Klaus is in prison in Santa Teresa, which is a city in the north of Mexico, on the border with the United States," she said, "but he's in good health and he hasn't suffered any physical injuries."

Before Lotte could ask what he was in prison for, Ingrid suggested they have tea or coffee. Lotte made two cups of tea and as she moved about the kitchen she watched Ingrid go over her notes.

"He's accused of killing several women," said the girl after two sips of tea.

"Klaus would never do that," said Lotte.

Ingrid nodded and then said that the lawyer, Isabel Santolaya, needed money.

That night Lotte dreamed for the first time in a long time about her brother. She saw Archimboldi walking in the desert, dressed in shorts and a little straw hat, and everything around him was sand, one dune after another all the way to the horizon. She shouted something to him, she said stop, there's nowhere to go, but Archimboldi kept moving farther away, as if he wanted to lose himself forever in that unfathomable and hostile land.

"It's unfathomable *and* hostile," she told him, and only then did she realize that she was a girl again, a girl who lived in a Prussian village between the forest and the sea.

"No," said Archimboldi, and he seemed to whisper in her ear, "it's just boring, boring, boring . . ."

When she woke she knew she had to go to Mexico without wasting another minute. Ingrid arrived at noon. Lotte watched her through the office window. As was her way, before she came up, Ingrid joked with a few of the mechanics. Her laughter, muffled by the glass, struck Lotte as fresh and carefree. When she was with Lotte, however, Ingrid was much more serious. Before she called the lawyer they had tea with biscuits. For the last twenty-four hours Lotte hadn't had a bite to eat and the biscuits did her good. Ingrid's presence was comforting, too: she was a sensible, unassuming girl, who knew when to joke and when to be serious.

When they called the lawyer, Lotte instructed Ingrid to tell her that she would come in person to Santa Teresa to handle whatever needed to be handled. The lawyer, who seemed sleepy, as if they had got her out of bed, gave Ingrid a few addresses and then they hung up. That afternoon Lotte visited her lawyer and explained the situation. Her lawyer made a few phone calls and then told her to be careful, one couldn't trust Mexican lawyers.

"I know that," Lotte said firmly.

He also advised her on the best way of withdrawing money abroad. That night she called Ingrid at home and asked if she'd like to come with her to Mexico.

"I'll pay you, of course," she said.

"As a translator?" asked Ingrid.

"As a translator, an interpreter, a lady's companion, whatever you want to call it," Lotte said crossly.

"I'll come," said Ingrid.

Four days later they were on a plane to Los Angeles, where they caught a connecting flight to Tucson, and from Tucson they drove to Santa Teresa in a rental car. When Lotte saw Klaus, the first thing he said was that she looked older, which embarrassed her.

It's been a long time, she would have liked to say, but she couldn't speak through her tears. The four of them, she, Klaus, the lawyer, and Ingrid, were in a cement-walled room. The floor was cement too, with damp patches, and there was a plastic table made to look like wood bolted to the floor and two wooden-slat benches also bolted to the floor. She, Ingrid, and the lawyer were sitting on one bench and Klaus on the other. He wasn't handcuffed, nor did he show signs of mistreatment. Lotte noticed that he had gained weight since the last time she saw him, but that was many years ago and Klaus was only a boy then. When the lawyer listed all the murders he was accused of, Lotte thought these people must have gone mad. No one in his right mind could kill so many women, she said.

The lawyer smiled and said that in Santa Teresa there was someone, probably not in his right mind, who had.

The lawyer's office was in the upper part of the city, in the same apartment where she lived. There were two entrances, but it was the same apartment, with three or four extra walls.

"I live in a place like this too," said Lotte, and the lawyer didn't understand, so Ingrid had to explain about the repair shop and the flat above the shop.

In Santa Teresa, on the lawyer's recommendation, they stayed at the best hotel in the city, Las Dunas, although in Santa Teresa there were no dunes of any kind, as Ingrid informed Lotte, whether nearby or fifty miles around. At first Lotte planned to ask for two rooms, but Ingrid convinced her to get just one, which was cheaper. It had been a long time since Lotte shared a room with anyone, and the first few nights she had a hard time falling asleep. To pass the time she turned on the TV, without sound, and watched it from bed: people talking and gesticulating and trying to convince other people of something that was probably important.

At night there were many televangelist shows. The Mexican televangelists were easy to identify: they were dark-skinned and sweated a lot and their suits and ties looked as if they'd been bought secondhand, although they were probably new. Also: their sermons were more dramatic, more showy, with more audience participation, though the audiences seemed drugged and utterly destitute, unlike the audiences of the American televangelists, who were just as poorly dressed but at least seemed to have steady jobs.

Maybe I think that, thought Lotte at night on the Mexican border, just because they're white, some of them perhaps with German or Dutch roots and therefore closer to me.

When she fell asleep at last, with the TV on, she dreamed about

Archimboldi. She saw him sitting on a huge volcanic slab, dressed in rags and with an ax in one hand, looking at her sadly. Maybe my brother is dead, thought Lotte in the dream, but my son is alive.

The second day she saw Klaus she told him, trying to be gentle, that Werner had died some time ago. Klaus listened and nodded with no change of expression. He was a good man, he said, but he said it with the same detachment with which he might speak of a cell mate.

The third day, while Ingrid discreetly read a book in a corner of the room, Klaus asked about his uncle. I don't know what's become of him, said Lotte. But Klaus's question surprised her, and she couldn't help telling him that since she got to Santa Teresa she'd been having dreams about her brother. Klaus asked her to describe a dream. After Lotte did he confessed that for a long time he'd had dreams about his uncle too, and they weren't good dreams.

"What kind of dreams were they?" Lotte asked him.

"Bad dreams," said Klaus.

Then he smiled and they went on to talk about other things.

When visiting hours were over, Lotte and Ingrid would go for drives around the city and once they went to the market and bought Indian crafts. According to Lotte, the crafts had probably been made in China or Thailand, but Ingrid liked them and she bought three little baked clay figures, unvarnished and unpainted, three crude, powerful images of a father, a mother, and a son, and she gave them to Lotte, telling her they would bring her good luck. One morning they went to Tijuana, to the German consulate. They had planned to drive, but the lawyer recommended they take the once-a-day flight between the two cities. In Tijuana they stayed at a hotel in the tourist quarter, noisy and full of people who didn't look like tourists, in Lotte's opinion, and that same morning she managed to speak to the consul and explain her son's case. The consul, to Lotte's surprise, was already aware of everything and, as he explained, a consular officer had gone to visit Klaus, something the lawyer had roundly denied.

Perhaps, said the consul, the lawyer hadn't heard about the visit or she wasn't Klaus's lawyer yet or Klaus had chosen not to tell her about it. Anyway, Klaus was, to all intents and purposes, an American citizen and that posed a series of problems. Under the circumstances, we have to tread carefully, concluded the consul, and it did no good for Lotte to assure him that her son was innocent. In any case the consulate had taken a hand in the matter and Lotte and Ingrid returned to Santa Teresa feeling comforted.

The last two days they weren't able to visit Klaus or call him. The lawyer said prison regulations didn't allow it, although Lotte knew that Klaus had a cell phone and sometimes he spent all day talking to people on the outside. Still, she didn't want to make a scene or challenge the lawyer and she spent those days seeing the city, which struck her as more chaotic than ever and of little interest. Before she left for Tucson she shut herself in the hotel room and wrote a long letter to her son, to be given to him by the lawyer after she'd left. With Ingrid she went to take a look at the outside of the house where Klaus had lived in Santa Teresa, as one might visit a tourist site, and it struck her as acceptable, a California-style house, pleasant to look at. Then they went to the computer and electronics store that Klaus owned downtown and found it closed, as the lawyer had warned, because the property belonged to Klaus and he hadn't wanted to rent it since he was sure he would be released before the trial.

Back in Germany she was suddenly aware that the trip had tired her much more than she'd realized. She spent several days in bed, not setting foot in the office, but each time the phone rang she was quick to answer it, in case the call was from Mexico. In one of her dreams a warm, loving voice whispered in her ear the possibility that her son really was the Santa Teresa killer.

"That's ridiculous," she shouted, and immediately woke up.

Sometimes the person calling was Ingrid. They didn't talk much. The girl asked how she was and inquired whether there had been any new developments in Klaus's case. The language problem had been solved through the exchange of e-mails, which Lotte had translated by one of her mechanics. One afternoon Ingrid stopped by with a present: a German-Spanish dictionary that Lotte thanked her for effusively although secretly she was sure she would never use it. Shortly afterward, however, as she was going through the photographs in the case file the lawyer had given her, she found Ingrid's dictionary and looked up some words. A few days later, and with no little astonishment, she discovered that she had a knack for languages.

In 1996 she returned to Santa Teresa and asked Ingrid to come with her. Ingrid was dating a boy who worked at an architecture studio, though he wasn't an architect, and one night the two of them invited her out to dinner. The boyfriend was very interested in what was going on in Santa Teresa and at first Lotte suspected that Ingrid wanted to travel with him, but Ingrid said he wasn't her boyfriend yet, and she would be happy to come with Lotte.

The trial, which was supposed to take place in 1996, was ultimately postponed and Lotte and Ingrid spent nine days in Santa Teresa, visiting Klaus as often as they could, going for drives around the city, and sitting in their hotel room watching TV. Sometimes, at night, Ingrid would tell Lotte she was going to get a drink at the hotel bar or go dancing at the hotel club and Lotte was left alone and then she changed the channel, because Ingrid always chose shows in English, and she preferred to watch Mexican TV, which was a way, she thought, of being close to her son.

Twice it was after five when Ingrid got back to the room and both times Lotte was awake, sitting at the foot of the bed or in an armchair with the TV on. One night when Ingrid wasn't there Klaus called and the first thing that came to Lotte's mind was that he had escaped that horrible prison on the edge of the desert. Klaus asked how she was, sounding normal and even relaxed, and Lotte answered that she was fine and then she didn't know what to say. When she regained control of herself she asked where he was calling from.

"Prison," said Klaus.

Lotte looked at her watch.

"How is it they let you make calls at this hour?" she asked.

"No one lets me do anything," said Klaus, and he laughed, "I'm calling from my cell phone."

Then Lotte remembered the lawyer had told her that Klaus had a cell phone and after that they talked about other things, until Klaus said he'd had a dream and his voice shifted from casual and cool to a deeper register, which reminded Lotte of the time she'd seen a German actor recite a poem. The poem she didn't remember, it must have been some classic, but the actor's voice was unforgettable.

"What did you dream?" asked Lotte.

"Don't you know?" asked Klaus.

"I don't," said Lotte.

"Then I'd better not tell you," said Klaus, and he hung up.

Lotte's first impulse was to call him right back and keep talking, but it soon occurred to her that she didn't have his number, so after a few minutes' hesitation, she called Isabel Santolaya, the lawyer, know-ing it was rude to call so late, and when the lawyer finally answered Lotte explained, in a mix of German, Spanish, and English, that she needed Klaus's cell phone number. After a long silence the lawyer re-peated the number until she was sure Lotte had gotten it right and then she hung up.

That long silence, meanwhile, seemed to Lotte fraught with ques-tions, because the lawyer didn't put down the phone to go and find the notebook where she had written Klaus's number, but rather remained silent on the other end of the line, perhaps lost in thought, as she de-cided whether to offer it. In any case, Lotte heard her *breathe* in the middle of the silence, almost as if she could hear her *weigh* the two pos-sibilities. Then Lotte called Klaus's cell phone, but the line was busy. She waited ten minutes and called again and it was still busy. Who can Klaus be talking to at this time of night? she wondered.

When she went to visit him the next day she chose not to bring up the matter or ask anything. Klaus, meanwhile, was the same as always, distant, cold, as if he wasn't the one in prison.

Despite it all, on this second visit to Mexico Lotte didn't feel as lost as she had the first time. Sometimes, as she was waiting at the prison, she talked to the women who were on their way to visit the inmates. She learned to say: *bonito niño* or *lindo chamaco*, when the women had chil-dren in tow, or: *buena viejita* or *simpática viejita*, when she saw the in-mates' mothers or grandmothers wrapped in shawls, waiting in line for the start of visiting hours, impassive and resigned. She herself bought a shawl on the third day of her stay, and sometimes, as she walked behind Ingrid and the lawyer, she couldn't help weeping, and then the shawl hid her face and afforded her some privacy.

In 1997 she returned to Mexico, but this time she traveled alone be-cause Ingrid had found a good job and couldn't come with her. Lotte's Spanish, which she had set out to learn, was much better now and she could talk on the phone with the lawyer. The trip went off without inci-dent, although as soon as she got to Santa Teresa, she understood by the expression on Isabel Santolaya's face and then the overly long embrace into which the lawyer folded her that something strange was going on. The trial, which passed as if in a dream, lasted twenty days and at the end Klaus was found guilty of four murders.

That night the lawyer drove her back to the hotel, and since she made no move to leave, Lotte thought she had something to say and didn't know how, so she offered to buy her a drink at the bar, although she was tired and wanted nothing more than to go to bed and sleep. As they drank next to a big window from which one could see the lights of the cars as they passed along a broad avenue lined with trees, the lawyer, who seemed as tired as Lotte, began to curse in Spanish, or so Lotte thought, and then she began openly to cry. This woman is in love with my son, thought Lotte. Before she left Santa Teresa, Isabel Santolaya told her that the trial had been plagued with irregularities and would probably be declared a mistrial. In any case, she promised, I'm going to appeal. During the car trip back, Lotte thought about her son, whom the verdict hadn't affected in the slightest, and the lawyer, and she thought that the two of them, in a strange but also natural way, made a good couple.

In 1998, a mistrial was declared and the date was set for a second trial. One night, as she was talking to Isabel Santolaya on the phone from Paderborn, Lotte asked point-blank whether there was something else between her and Klaus.

"There is," said the lawyer.

"And isn't it too hard for you to bear?" asked Lotte.

"No harder than it is for you," said Isabel Santolaya.

"I don't understand," said Lotte, "I'm his mother but you're free to choose."

"No one's free to choose in love," said Isabel Santolaya.

"And does Klaus feel the same way?" asked Lotte.

"I'm the one who sleeps with him," said Isabel Santolaya curtly.

Lotte didn't understand what she meant. But then she remembered that in Mexico, as in Germany, all prisoners had the right to conjugal visits or visits with their partners. She had seen a TV show about it. The rooms where the prisoners stayed with their wives were unbearably sad, she remembered. The women tried to make them nice but all they managed to do with their flowers and scarves was turn the sad, impersonal rooms into sad, cheap, whorehouse rooms. And that was in nice German prisons, thought Lotte, prisons that weren't overcrowded, that were clean, functional. She didn't want to imagine what a conjugal visit would be like in the Santa Teresa prison.

"I think it's admirable what you're doing for my son," said Lotte.

"It's nothing," said the lawyer, "what Klaus gives me is priceless."

That night, before she fell asleep, she thought about Isabel Santolaya and Klaus and imagined the two of them in Germany or any part of Europe and she saw Isabel Santolaya with a big belly, expecting Klaus's child, and she slept like a baby.

In 1998 Lotte traveled to Mexico twice and spent forty-five days in total in Santa Teresa. The trial was postponed until 1999. When she got to Tucson on the flight from L.A. she had problems with the people at the rental car agency, who refused to rent to her because of her age.

"I'm old but I know how to drive," said Lotte in Spanish, "and I've never had one damn accident."

After wasting half the morning arguing, Lotte hired a taxi to take her to Santa Teresa. The driver's name was Steve Hernández and he spoke Spanish and as they crossed the desert he asked what brought her to Mexico.

"I'm here to see my son," said Lotte.

"The next time you come," said the driver, "tell your son to pick you up in Tucson, because this isn't going to be a cheap ride."

"If only I could," said Lotte.

In 1999 she returned to Mexico and this time the lawyer came to meet her in Tucson. It wasn't a good year for Lotte. Business in Paderborn wasn't going well and she was thinking seriously of selling the shop and the building, including her own flat. Her health wasn't good. The doctors who examined her couldn't find anything wrong, but sometimes Lotte felt incapable of performing the simplest tasks. Whenever the weather was bad she got a cold and had to spend several days in bed, sometimes with a high fever.

In 2000 she couldn't go to Mexico but she talked to the lawyer once a week and got all the latest news. When they didn't talk on the phone they kept in touch by e-mail and she even had a fax installed at home to receive the new documents that kept appearing in the case of the murdered women. Over the course of the year Lotte strove conscientiously to be healthy so she could travel the following year. She took vitamins, hired a physical therapist, visited a Chinese acupuncturist once a week. She followed a special diet with lots of fresh fruit and salads. She stopped eating meat and ate fish instead.

When the year 2001 came she was ready to embark on another trip to Mexico, although her health, despite all her efforts, wasn't what it used to be. Nor were her nerves as steady, as shall be seen.

While she waited at the Frankfurt airport for the flight to L.A., she went into a bookshop and bought a book and a few magazines. Lotte wasn't a good reader, whatever that means, and if every once in a while she bought a book it was usually the kind written by actors when they retire or when it's been a long time since they've made a movie, or biographies of famous people, or those books by TV personalities, supposedly full of interesting stories but in fact with no stories at all.

This time, however, by mistake or because she was in a hurry not to miss her flight, she bought a book called *The King of the Forest*, by someone called Benno von Archimboldi. The book, no more than one hundred and fifty pages long, was about a one-legged father and a one-eyed mother and their two children, a boy who liked to swim and a girl who followed her brother to the cliffs. As the plane crossed the Atlantic, Lotte realized in astonishment that she was reading a part of her childhood.

The style was strange. The writing was clear and sometimes even transparent, but the way the stories followed one after another didn't lead anywhere: all that was left were the children, their parents, the animals, some neighbors, and in the end, all that was really left was nature, a nature that dissolved little by little in a boiling cauldron until it vanished completely.

As the passengers slept, Lotte began to read the novel over again, skipping the parts that weren't about her family or her house or her neighbors or her garden, and when she had finished she had no doubt that the author, this Benno von Archimboldi, was her brother, although there was also the possibility the author had talked to her brother, a possibility Lotte immediately rejected because in her judgment there were things in the book that her brother would never have told to anyone, though she didn't stop to think that by writing them he was telling the whole world.

There was no author photograph on the cover, though there was a birth date, 1920, the year her brother was born, and a long list of titles, all published by the same publishing house. It also said that Benno von Archimboldi had been translated into a dozen languages and that for the past several years he had been mentioned as a possible Nobel recipient. As she waited in L.A. for her connection to Tucson she looked for more books by Archimboldi in the airport bookstores, but there were only books about aliens, people who had been abducted, encounters of the third kind, and sightings of flying saucers.

In Tucson the lawyer was waiting for her and on the way to Santa

Teresa they talked about the case, which according to the lawyer was in a deadlock and had been for a long time, which was good, although Lotte didn't understand this, because to her it sounded like a bad thing. But she didn't want to argue and she turned to admiring the landscape. The car windows were down and the desert air, sweet and warm, was just what Lotte needed after the plane trip.

That same day she visited the prison and felt happy when a little old woman recognized her.

"Bless your eyes, you're back, ma'am," said the old woman.

"Oh, Monchita, how are you?" said Lotte as she gave her a long hug.

"As you can see, dear, still barely holding on," answered the old woman.

"A son's a son," Lotte pronounced, and they hugged again.

Klaus was the same as always, distant, cold, a bit thinner, but as strong as always, with the same nearly imperceptible air of disdain he'd had since he was seventeen. They talked about trivial things, about Germany (although Klaus seemed completely uninterested in anything to do with Germany), about her trip, about the state of the shop, and when the lawyer left to talk to a prison official, Lotte told him about the book by Archimboldi that she'd read during the trip. At first Klaus didn't seem interested, but when Lotte took the book out of her bag and began to read the parts she'd underlined, Klaus's expression changed.

"I'll lend it to you if you want," said Lotte.

Klaus nodded and tried to take it, but Lotte wouldn't let go.

"First let me make a note of something," she said, and she took out her notebook and wrote down the publishing house's contact information. Then she handed him the book.

That night, while Lotte was at the hotel drinking orange juice and eating biscuits and watching late-night Mexican TV, she made a long-distance phone call to the Bubis offices in Hamburg. She asked to speak to the publisher.

"That would be Mrs. Bubis," said the secretary, "but she isn't in yet, call back later, please."

"All right," said Lotte, "I'll call back later." And after a moment she added: "Tell her Lotte Haas, Benno von Archimboldi's sister, called."

Then she hung up and dialed the front desk and asked to be woken in three hours. Without undressing she went to sleep. She heard noises in the corridor. The TV was still on but with the sound muted. She dreamed of a cemetery and the tomb of a giant. The gravestone split and the giant's hand rose up, then his other hand, then his head, a head crowned with long blond hair caked with dirt. She woke before the front desk called. She turned the TV sound back on and spent a while pacing the room and half watching a show about amateur singers.

When the phone rang she thanked the clerk and called Hamburg again. The same secretary answered and said that the publisher was in now. Lotte waited a few seconds until she heard the pleasant voice of a woman she thought sounded highly educated.

"Are you the publisher?" asked Lotte. "I'm Benno von Archimboldi's sister, or Hans Reiter's sister, that is," she said, and then she was quiet because she didn't know what else to say.

"Are you all right? Is there something I can do for you? My secretary said you were calling from Mexico."

"Yes, I'm calling from Mexico," said Lotte, on the verge of tears.

"Do you live in Mexico? What part of Mexico are you calling from?"

"I live in Germany, *meine frau*, in Paderborn, and I own an auto repair shop and a few properties."

"Ah, I see," said the publisher.

Only then did Lotte realize, though she couldn't say why, perhaps it was the way the publisher expressed herself or the way she asked questions, that she was older than Lotte, in other words a very old woman.

Then the sluice gates opened and Lotte said it had been a long time since she saw her brother, that her son was in prison in Mexico, that her husband was dead, that she had never remarried, that necessity and desperation had driven her to learn Spanish, that she still had trouble with the language, that her mother had died and her brother probably didn't even know it, that she planned to sell the shop, that she had read a book by her brother on the plane, that the shock had almost killed her, that as she crossed the desert all she could do was think of him.

Then Lotte apologized and at the same time realized she was crying.

"When do you plan to return to Paderborn?" she heard the publisher ask.

And then:

"Give me your address."

And then:

"You were a very blond, pale child and sometimes your mother brought you with her when she came to work at the house."

Lotte thought: what house is she talking about? and: how would I remember that? But then she thought of the only house where some villagers had worked, the country estate of the Baron Von Zumpe, and she remembered the house and the days she'd gone with her mother and helped her dust, sweep, polish the candlesticks, wax the floors. But before she could say anything, the publisher said:

"I hope you'll hear soon from your brother. It's been a pleasure speaking to you. Goodbye."

And she hung up. In Mexico Lotte sat for a while longer with the phone pressed to her ear. The sounds she heard were like the sounds of the abyss. The sounds a person hears as she plummets into the abyss.

One night, three months after she had returned to Germany, Archimboldi appeared.

Lotte was in her nightdress, about to go to bed, when the doorbell rang. Over the intercom, she asked who it was.

"It's me," said Archimboldi, "your brother."

That night they talked until dawn. Lotte talked about Klaus and the killings of women in Santa Teresa. She also talked about Klaus's dreams, the dreams in which he saw a giant who would rescue him from prison, although you, she said to Archimboldi, don't look like a giant anymore.

"I never was a giant," said Archimboldi as he paced Lotte's living room and dining room and stopped next to a shelf that held more than a dozen of his books.

"I don't know what to do anymore," said Lotte after a long silence. "I don't have the strength. I don't understand anything and the little I do understand frightens me. Nothing makes sense," said Lotte.

"You're just tired," said her brother.

"Old and tired. I need grandchildren," said Lotte. "But you're even older," said Lotte. "How old are you?"

"Over eighty," said Archimboldi.

"I'm afraid of getting sick," said Lotte. "Is it true you might win the Nobel Prize?" asked Lotte. "I'm afraid Klaus will die. He's proud, I don't know who he takes after. Werner wasn't like that," said Lotte. "You and Father weren't either. Why do you call Father one-legged when you talk about him? Why do you call Mother one-eyed?"

"Because they were," said Archimboldi, "have you forgotten?"

"Sometimes I do forget," said Lotte. "The prison is horrible, horrible," said Lotte, "although after a while you get used to it. It's like catching something," said Lotte. "Mrs. Bubis was very nice to me, we didn't talk much but it was very nice," said Lotte. "Do I know her? Have I ever met her?"

"Yes," said Archimboldi, "but you were little and you don't remember anymore."

Then he touched his books with the tips of his fingers. There were all different kinds of editions: hardcover, paperback, pocket-size.

"There are so many things I don't remember anymore," said Lotte. "Good things, bad things, worse things. But I never forget nice people. And that woman was very nice," said Lotte, "even though my son is rotting in a Mexican prison. And who will look after him? Who will remember him when I'm dead?" asked Lotte. "My son has no children, no friends, he doesn't have anyone," said Lotte. "Look, the sun is coming up. Would you like some tea, coffee, a glass of water?"

Archimboldi sat down and stretched his legs. The bones cracked.

"Will you take care of it all?"

"A beer," he said.

"I don't have beer," said Lotte. "Will you take care of it all?"

•

Fürst Pückler.

If you want a good chocolate, vanilla, and strawberry ice cream, you can order a Fürst Pückler. They'll bring you an ice cream in three flavors, but not just any three flavors, only chocolate, vanilla, and strawberry. That's a Fürst Pückler.

When Archimboldi left his sister, he went on to Hamburg, where he planned to catch a direct flight to Mexico. Since the flight didn't leave until the next morning, he went for a walk around a park he didn't know, a big park full of trees and little paved paths along which women strolled with their children and young people skated and every so often students rode on bicycles, and he sat on the terrace of a bar, a terrace quite a distance from the bar itself, almost in the middle of the woods, and he began to read and ordered a sandwich and a beer and paid for them, then he ordered a Fürst Pückler and paid for it because on the terrace one had to pay immediately for anything one had.

The only other person there was three tables away (wrought-iron tables, heavy, elegant, and probably hard to steal), a gentleman of advanced age, though not as old as Archimboldi, reading a magazine and sipping a cappuccino. As Archimboldi was about to finish his ice cream, the gentleman asked whether he'd liked it.

"I did," said Archimboldi, and he smiled.

Drawn or encouraged by this friendly smile, the gentleman got up from his chair and sat down one table away.

"Allow me to introduce myself," he said. "My name is Alexander Fürst Pückler. The, how shall I say, creator of this ice cream," he said, "was a forebear of mine, a very brilliant Fürst Pückler, a great traveler, an enlightened man, whose main interests were botany and gardening. Of course, he thought, if he ever thought about it at all, that he would be remembered for some of the many small works he wrote and published, mostly travel chronicles, though not necessarily travel chronicles in the modern sense, but little books that are still charming today and, how shall I say, highly perceptive, anyway as perceptive as they could be, little books that made it seem as if the ultimate purpose of each of his trips was to examine a particular garden, gardens sometimes forgotten, forsaken, abandoned to their fate, and whose beauty my distinguished forebear knew how to find amid the weeds and neglect. His little books, despite their, how shall I say, botanical trappings, are full of clever observations and from them one gets a rather decent idea of the Europe of his day, a Europe often in turmoil, whose storms on occasion reached the shores of the family castle, located near Görlitz, as you're likely aware. Of course, my forebear wasn't oblivious to the storms, no more than he was oblivious to the vicissitudes of, how shall I say, the human condition. And so he wrote and published, and in his own way, humbly but in fine German prose, he raised his voice against injustice. I think he had little interest in knowing where the soul goes when the body dies, although he wrote about that too. He was interested in dignity and he was interested in plants. About happiness he said not a word, I suppose because he considered it something strictly private and perhaps, how shall I say, treacherous or elusive. He had a great sense of humor, although some passages of his books contradict me there. And since he wasn't a saint or even a brave man, he probably did think about posterity. The bust, the equestrian statue, the folios preserved forever in a library. What he never imagined was that he would be remembered for lending his name to a combination of three flavors of ice cream. That I can assure you. So what do you think?"

"I don't know what to think," said Archimboldi.

"No one remembers the botanist Fürst Pückler now, no one remembers the model gardener, no one has read the writer. But everyone at some moment has tasted a Fürst Pückler, which is best and most pleasing in spring and fall."

"Why not in summer?" asked Archimboldi.

"Because in summer it can be cloying. Ices are best in summer, not ice cream."

Suddenly the park lights came on, although there was a second of total darkness, as if someone had tossed a black blanket over parts of Hamburg.

The gentleman sighed, he must have been about seventy, and then he said:

"A mysterious legacy, don't you think?"

"You're right, I do," said Archimboldi as he got up and took his leave of the descendant of Fürst Pückler.

Soon afterward he left the park and the next morning he was on his way to Mexico.

NOTE TO THE FIRST EDITION

2666 was published posthumously, more than a year after the author's death. It is reasonable, then, to ask how closely the text in the reader's hands corresponds to what Roberto Bolaño would have given us had he lived long enough. The answer is reassuring: the novel as it was left at Bolaño's death is very nearly what he intended it to be. There is no doubt that Bolaño would have worked longer on the book, but only a few months longer; he himself declared that he was near the end, long past the date when he had planned for it to be finished. In any case, not just the foundations but the whole edifice of the novel had already been raised, and its shape, its dimensions, its general content would by no means have been very different from what they are now.

Upon Bolaño's death it was said that the grand project of *2666* had been transformed into a series of five novels corresponding to the five parts into which the work was divided. In fact, in the last months of his life Bolaño insisted on this idea, as he grew less and less certain that he would be able to complete his initial project. It must be said, however, that practical considerations (never Bolaño's strong point, incidentally) figured into this plan: faced with the increasing likelihood of his imminent death, Bolaño thought it would be less of a burden and more profitable, both for his publisher and for his heirs, to deal with five separate novels, short or medium-length, than with a single massive, sprawling work, one not even entirely finished.

After reading the text, however, it seems preferable to keep the novel whole. Although the five parts that make up *2666* can be read independently, they not only share many elements (a subtle web of recurring motifs), they also serve a common end. There is no point attempting to justify the relatively "open" structure that contains them, especially considering the precedent of *The Savage Detectives*. If that novel had been published posthumously, would it not have given rise to all kinds of speculation about its unfinished state?

One other consideration underlies the decision to publish the five parts of *2666* in a single volume, leaving open the possibility that once the essential framework is established, the parts might be published singly, which would allow combinations that the open structure of the novel permits, even suggests. Bolaño, an excellent short story writer and author of several masterly novellas, also boasted, once he had begun *2666*, that he had embarked on a colossal project, far surpassing *The Savage Detectives* in ambition and length. The sheer size of *2666* is inseparable from the original conception of all its parts, as well as from the spirit of risk that drives it and its rash totalizing zeal. On this point, it is worth recalling the passage from *2666* in which, after his conversation with a book-loving pharmacist, Amalfitano, one of the novel's protagonists, reflects with undisguised disappointment on the growing prestige of short, neatly shaped novels (citing titles like *Bartleby the Scrivener* and *The Metamorphosis*) to the exclusion of longer, more ambitious and daring works (like *Moby-Dick* or *The Trial*):

> What a sad paradox, thought Amalfitano. Now even bookish pharmacists are afraid to take on the great, imperfect, torrential works, books that blaze paths into the unknown. They choose the perfect exercises of the great masters. Or what amounts to the same thing: they want to watch the great masters spar, but they have no interest in real combat, when the great masters struggle against that something, that something that terrifies us all, that something that cows us and spurs us on, amid blood and mortal wounds and stench.

And then there is the title. That enigmatic number, *2666*—a date, really—that functions as a vanishing point around which the different parts of the novel fall into place. Without this vanishing point, the perspective of the whole would be lopsided, incomplete, suspended in nothingness.

In one of his many notes for *2666*, Bolaño indicates the existence in the work of a "hidden center," concealed beneath what might be considered the novel's "physical center." There is reason to think that this physical center is the city of Santa Teresa, faithful reflection of Ciudad Juárez, on the Mexican-U.S. border. There the five parts of the novel ultimately converge; there the crimes are committed that comprise its spectacular backdrop (and that are said by one of the novel's characters to contain "the secret of the world"). As for the "hidden center" . . . might it not represent 2666 itself, the date upon which the whole novel rests?

The writing of 2666 occupied Bolaño for the last years of his life. But the conception and design of the novel came much earlier, and its stirrings may retrospectively be detected in various other books by the author, especially those published after *The Savage Detectives* (1998), which not coincidentally ends in the Sonora desert. The time will come to catalog these stirrings thoroughly. For now, it may suffice to note one very eloquent example, from *Amulet* (1999). Rereading that novel offers a single unmistakable clue to the meaning of the date 2666. The protagonist of *Amulet*, Auxilio Lacouture (a character who is herself prefigured in *The Savage Detectives*), tells how one night she follows Arturo Belano and Ernesto San Epifanio on a walk to Colonia Guerrero, in Mexico City, where the two go in search of the so-called King of the Rent Boys. This is what she says:

> I followed them: I saw them go down Bucareli to Reforma with a spring in their step and then cross Reforma without waiting for the lights to change, their long hair blowing in the excess wind that funnels down Reforma at that hour of the night, turning it into a transparent tube or an elongated lung exhaling the city's imaginary breath. Then we walked down the Avenida Guerrero; they weren't stepping so lightly any more, and I wasn't feeling too enthusiastic either. Guerrero, at that time of night, is more like a cemetery than an avenue, not a cemetery in 1974 or in 1968, or 1975, but a cemetery in the year 2666, a forgotten cemetery under the eyelid of a corpse or an unborn child, bathed in the dispassionate fluids of an eye that tried so hard to forget one particular thing that it ended up forgetting everything else.

The text in the reader's possession corresponds to the latest version of the different "parts" of the novel. Bolaño indicated very clearly which of his work files should be considered definitive. Even so, earlier drafts were reviewed with the aim of filling in possible gaps or correcting errors, as well as for anything they might reveal about Bolaño's final intentions. The results of this scrutiny failed to cast much new light on the text and to leave very little room for doubt that it is indeed definitive.

Bolaño was a conscientious writer. He made many drafts of his texts, which he generally wrote quickly but later carefully polished. In all but a few places, the final version of 2666 is clear and clean: deliberately composed, in other words. There has been only the rare need to make minor changes and to correct some obvious errors, with the editors confident in their handling—diligent and expert but above all complicit—of the writer's "weaknesses" and "obsessions."

A final observation is perhaps in order here. Among Bolaño's notes for 2666 there appears the single line: "The narrator of 2666 is Arturo Belano." And elsewhere Bolaño adds, with the indication "for the end of 2666": "And that's it, friends. I've done it all, I've lived it all. If I had the strength, I'd cry. I bid you all goodbye, Arturo Belano."

And so farewell.

IGNACIO ECHEVARRÍA
September 2004